PRAISE FOR WILBUR S

'Wilbur Smith rarely misses a trick'
Sunday Times

'The world's leading adventure writer'
Daily Express

'Action is the name of Wilbur Smith's game
and he is a master'
Washington Post

'The pace would do credit to a Porsche, and the invention
is as bright and explosive as a fireworks display'
Sunday Telegraph

'A bonanza of excitement'
New York Times

'. . . a natural storyteller who moves confidently and
often splendidly in his period and sustains a flow of
convincing incident'
Scotsman

'Raw experience, grim realism, history and romance welded
with mystery and the bewilderment of life itself'
Library Journal

'A thundering good read'
Irish Times

A TIME TO DIE
&
ELEPHANT SONG

Also by Wilbur Smith

THE COURTNEYS

When the Lion Feeds
The Sound of Thunder
A Sparrow Falls
Birds of Prey
Monsoon
Blue Horizon
The Triumph of the Sun

THE COURTNEYS OF AFRICA

The Burning Shore
Power of the Sword
Rage
Golden Fox

THE BALLANTYNE NOVELS

A Falcon Flies
Men of Men
The Angels Weep
The Leopard Hunts in Darkness

THE EGYPTIAN NOVELS

River God
The Seventh Scroll
Warlock
The Quest

Also

The Dark of the Sun
Shout at the Devil
Gold Mine
The Diamond Hunters
The Sunbird
Eagle in the Sky
The Eye of the Tiger
Cry Wolf
Hungry as the Sea
Wild Justice

WILBUR SMITH

A TIME
TO DIE
&
ELEPHANT
SONG

PAN BOOKS

A *Time to Die* first published 1989 by William Heinemann.
First published in paperback 1990 by Pan Books.
Elephant Song first published 1991 by Macmillan.
First published in paperback 1992 by Pan Books.

This omnibus first published 2008 by Pan Books
an imprint of Pan Macmillan Ltd
Pan Macmillan, 20 New Wharf Road, London N1 9RR
Basingstoke and Oxford
Associated companies throughout the world
www.panmacmillan.com

ISBN 978-0-330-45795-8

The author wishes to make grateful acknowledgement to Colin Turnbull's *The Forest People*,
published by Jonathan Cape, which he found invaluable in his research for *Elephant Song*.

1 3 5 7 9 8 6 4 2

A CIP catalogue record for this book is available from
the British Library.

Typeset by SetSystems Ltd, Saffron Walden, Essex
Printed and bound in Great Britain by
Mackays of Chatham plc, Chatham, Kent

A TIME TO DIE

This book is for my wife and the jewel of my life, Mokhiniso, with all my love and gratitude for the enchanted years that I have been married to her

She had sat for well over two hours without moving, and the need to do so was an almost unbearable affliction. Every muscle in her body seemed to quiver with the craving for movement. Her buttocks were numb and despite being advised to do so, she had not emptied her bladder before they had gone into hiding, for she had been embarrassed by the masculine company and still too nervous in the African bush to go off alone to find a private place. She regretted her modesty and her timidity now.

She was staring out through the eye-slit in the rude grass structure of the hide, down a narrow open tunnel that the gunbearers had meticulously cleared through the thick bush, for even a tiny twig might deflect a bullet flying at 3000 feet a second. The tunnel was sixty yards long, paced out so that the telescopic sight of the rifle could be zeroed on precisely.

Without moving her head, Claudia swivelled her eyes towards where her father waited in the hide beside her. His rifle was propped in the vee of a branch in front of him and his right hand rested lightly on the stock. He needed to lift it mere inches to his cheek to be aiming and ready to fire.

Even in her physical discomfort the thought of her father firing that sinister glistening weapon made her angry. Yet he had always filled her with violent and conflicting emotions, nothing he ever did or said seemed to leave her untouched. He dominated her life and she hated him and loved him for it. Always she was trying to break away, and always he drew her effortlessly back. She knew that the main reason that she was still unmarried at twenty-six years of age, despite the way she looked, despite her own singular achievements, despite having had countless proposals, at least two from men with whom she had believed herself in love at the time, the reason for all this was this man who sat beside her. She had never found another to compare with her papa.

7

Colonel Riccardo Monterro, soldier, engineer, scholar, gourmet, multi-millionaire businessman, athlete, *bon-vivant*, ladykiller, sportsman – how many descriptions fitted him perfectly and yet did not describe him as she knew him. They did not describe the kindness and the strength, that made her love him, nor the cruelty and ruthlessness which made her hate him. They did not describe what he had done to her mother that had turned her into a discarded alcoholic shell. Claudia knew he was as capable of destroying her if she let herself be run down by him. He was the bull and she the matador. He was a dangerous man, and therein lay most of his appeal.

Someone had once told her, 'Some women always fall for real bastards.' She had immediately scoffed at the idea, but then thought about it later and came partially to accept it. The Lord knew, Papa was one. A great rumbustious bastard, with all the charm and flashing golden-brown eyes and shining teeth of his Latin origins, he could sing like Caruso and eat all the pasta she could heap on his plate. But although he had been born in Milano, the greater part of him was American for Claudia's grandparents had emigrated to Seattle from Mussolini's Italy when Riccardo was a child.

She had inherited his physical characteristics, the eyes and teeth and glowing olive skin, but she tried to reject every value of his that offended her and to take the opposite path to his. She had chosen to study law as a direct defiance of the lawless streak in him, and because he was a Republican she had decided long before she could understand what politics meant, that she was a Democrat. Because he set so much store by wealth and possessions, Claudia had deliberately turned down the $200,000 job she was offered after graduating fifth in her law class and had taken instead one at $40,000 in the civil rights agency. Because Papa had commanded a battalion of engineers in Vietnam and still talked of 'gooks', her work with the indigenous Inuit people of Alaska gave her satisfaction enhanced by his disapproval. He called the Eskimos 'gooks' as well. Yet here she was in Africa at his request, and the true horror of it was that he was here to kill animals and that she was in collusion with him.

At home what spare time she had was devoted to working without remuneration for the Alaskan Nature and Wildlife Conservation Society. The Society devoted most of its resources and efforts to fighting the oil exploration companies and their

8

depredations on the environment. Her father's company, Anchorage Tool and Engineering, was a major supplier of hardware to the drilling rigs and pipeline contractors. The choices she had made had been calculated and deliberate.

Yet here she was in a foreign land waiting submissively for him to assassinate some beautiful wild animal. Her own duplicity sickened her. They called this expedition a safari. She would never have even contemplated becoming an accomplice in such a heinous enterprise, in fact she had indignantly refused the invitations he had made to her in previous years, but for the secret she had learned a scant few days before her father had invited her. This might be the last time, the very last time, she would be alone with him. That thought appalled her more even than the dirty business in which they were engaged.

'Oh God,' she thought, 'what will I do without him? What will my world be without him?'

As the thought struck her she turned her head, her first movement in two hours, and looked over her shoulder. Another man sat close behind her in the small thatch-walled hide. He was the professional hunter. Although her father had hunted with this man on a dozen other safaris, Claudia had met him for the first time only four days previously when they had disembarked from the South African Airways commercial flight at Harare, the capital city of Zimbabwe. The hunter had flown them out from there in his twin-engined Beechcraft Baron to this vast and remote hunting concession near the Mozambique border which he chartered from the Zimbabwe government.

His name was Sean Courtney. She had known him four days but already she loathed him as if she had known him a lifetime. Not strange that thinking of her father had led her instinctively to look back at him. Here was another dangerous man. Hard, ruthless and so devilishly good looking that her every instinct shrieked a warning at her.

He frowned sharply at her with clear bright green eyes in the darkly tanned face, and the crow's-feet at the corners of his eyes puckered with annoyance at her movement. He touched her on the hip with one finger, cautioning her to stillness again. The touch was light, but she felt the disconcerting male strength in his single finger. She had noticed his hands before, trying not to be impressed by their graceful form. 'The hands of an artist or a surgeon or a killer,' she had thought then, but now that peremp-

9

tory touch offended her. She felt as though she had been sexually violated. She stared fixedly ahead again, through the eye-slit in the grass wall, and she fumed with indignation. How dare he touch her. The spot on her hip burned, as though he had branded her with his finger.

That afternoon before they had left camp, Sean had insisted that each of them shower and bathe with special unscented soap that he provided. He had cautioned Claudia to use no perfume and one of the camp servants had laid out freshly washed and ironed khaki shirt and slacks on her cot in the tent when she returned from the shower.

'Those big cats can smell you from two miles downwind,' Sean had told her. Yet now after two hours in the heat of the Zambezi valley, she could faintly smell him sitting up close behind her, almost but not quite touching her, fresh, male sweat, and she felt an almost irresistible urge to move in the canvas camp chair. He made her feel restless, but she forced herself to sit perfectly still. She found herself breathing deeply, trying to pick up the faint intermittent wafts of his odour, then stopped herself angrily as soon as she realized what she was doing.

Inches in front of her eyes a single green leaf, hanging down into the opening in the grass wall, spiralled slowly on its stalk like a weathercock and almost immediately she felt the shift of the light evening breeze.

Sean had sited the blind below the prevailing wind, and now as the breeze came down to them, it brought a new odour, the stench of the carcass. The bait was an old buffalo cow. Sean had selected her from a herd of two hundred of the huge black animals.

'That old girl is way past breeding,' he had pointed her out. 'Take her low on the shoulder, through the heart,' he had ordered Papa.

It was the first animal Claudia had ever seen killed deliberately. The crash of the heavy rifle had shocked her, but not as deeply as the scarlet gush of blood in the bright African sunlight and the mournful death bellow of the old cow. She had walked back to where they had left the open Toyota hunting car and sat alone in the front seat in a cold sweat of nausea while Sean and his trackers had butchered the carcass.

They had hauled the carcass up into the lower branches of the wild fig tree with the power winch on the front of the Toyota, positioning it with much debate between Sean and his trackers at the exact height which would enable a full grown lion standing on his back legs to reach up and partially satisfy his hunger without enabling a large pride of cats to consume all of it at a sitting and so move on to find other fare.

That had been four days previously, but even then as they worked the metallic-green blow-flies had come swarming to the smell of fresh blood. Now the heat and the flies had done their work, Claudia wrinkled her nose and grimaced at the stench that came down to her on the breeze. The smell seemed to coat her tongue and the back of her throat like slime, and staring at the carcass in the tree, she imagined she could see the black hide undulating softly as the maggots seethed and burrowed into the putrid flesh beneath it.

'Lovely.' Sean had sniffed it before they entered the hide. 'Just like a ripe Camembert. No cat within ten miles will be able to resist it.' While they waited the sun sagged wearily down the sky, and the colours of the bush now glowed with the richer light, in contrast to the washed-out glare of noon.

The faint coolness in the evening breeze seemed to awaken the wild birds from their heat-drugged stupor. In the undergrowth down on the banks of the stream a lourie called 'Kok! Kok! Kok!' as raucously as a parrot, and in the branches directly over their heads a pair of glistening metallic sunbirds flitted busily, with fluttering wings, hanging upside down from the fluffy blooms to suck up the nectar. Claudia lifted her head slowly to watch them with intense pleasure. Though she was so close that she could see their thin tubular tongues thrusting deeply into the yellow flowers, the little creatures ignored her as though she was part of the tree.

She was still watching the birds when she became aware of a sudden tension in the hide. Her father had stiffened, his hand on the buttstock of the rifle clenched slightly. His sense of excitement was almost palpable. He was staring through his peephole, but though she stared as hard she could not see what had excited him. From the corner of her eye, she saw Sean Courtney reach forward between them, his hand moving with infinite stealth, to grasp her father's elbow in a cautionary restraining grip.

Then she heard Sean's whisper, softer than the breeze. 'Wait!' he said.

So they waited, deathly still, as the minutes drew out slowly and became ten and then twenty.

11

'On the left,' Sean said, and it was so unexpected that she started at the barely audible murmur. Her eyes swivelled left. She saw nothing, just grass and bush and shadows. She stared unblinkingly until her eyes smarted and swam with tears and she had to blink rapidly and then look again, and this time she saw something move like mist or smoke, a drift of brown in the long sun-seared grass.

Then abruptly, dramatically, an animal stepped out into the open killing ground below the reeking carcass in the fig tree.

Despite herself, Claudia gasped, and then her breath choked in her throat. It was the most beautiful beast she had ever seen, a great cat, much larger than she had ever expected, sleek and glossy and golden. It turned its head and looked directly at her. She saw that its throat was a soft cream, and sunlight gleamed on the long white whiskers. Its ears were round and tipped with black and held erect, listening. The eyes were yellow, as implacable and glowing as moonstones, the pupils reduced to black arrowheads as it stared up the long clearing at the wall of the hide.

Still Claudia could not breathe. She was frozen with excitement and dread as the cat stared at her. Only when it turned its head away and looked up at the carcass in the tree, could she let out her breath in a soft ragged sigh.

'Don't kill it. Please, don't kill it,' she almost cried aloud. With relief she saw that her father had not moved a muscle and Sean's hand was still on his elbow restraining him.

Only then did she realize that it was a female, there was no mane, a lioness, and she had listened to the camp-fire conversation enough to know that they were hunting only a full-maned lion and that there were heavy penalties, huge fines and even imprisonment for the killing of a female. She relaxed slightly and gave herself over to the full enjoyment of the moment, to the stunning beauty of this beast. Claudia's pleasure had only just begun, for the lioness looked around her once more and then, satisfied that it was safe, she opened her mouth and gave a low mewling call.

Almost immediately, her cubs came tumbling into the clearing. There were three of them, fluffy as children's toys and dappled with their kitten spots. They tripped over paws that were too large for the tiny bodies, and after a few moments of hesitation during which their mother placed no restraint on them, they launched into boisterous mock combat, wrestling and falling over each other with ferocious baby growls.

The lioness ignored them and rose up on her hind legs to the dangling carcass. She thrust her head into the open belly from which the entrails had been plucked, and she began to feed. The row of black nipples down her belly were sucked out prominently and the fur around them matted with the saliva of her offspring. She had not yet weaned them and the cubs took no notice of her feeding and went on with their play.

Then a second lioness stepped into the clearing, followed by two half-grown cubs. This lioness was much darker in colour, almost blue along the spine and her pelt was criss-crossed with old healed scars, the legacy of a lifetime of hard hunting, the marks of hoof and horn and claw. Half of one ear was torn off and her ribs showed through the scarred hide. She was old. The two half-grown cubs that followed her into the clearing would probably be her last litter. Next year, when the cubs had deserted her and she was too weak to keep up with the pride, the hyena would take her, but now she was still living on her store of cunning and experience.

She had let the young lioness go in first to the bait, for she had seen two mates killed in just such a situation, beneath a succulent carcass dangling from a tree, and she mistrusted it. She did not begin to feed, but prowled restlessly around the clearing, her tail flicking with agitation and every so often she stopped and stared intently down the open lane to the grass wall of the hide at the far end.

Her two older cubs gazed up at the carcass, sitting on their haunches and growling with hunger and frustration for the meat was obviously beyond their reach. At last, the bolder of the two backed off then made a running leap at the bait. Hooking on with its front claws, its back legs swinging free, it tried to grab a hasty mouthful, but the young lioness turned on it viciously, snarling and cuffing it heavily until it fell on its back, scrambled to its feet and slunk away.

The older of the two lionesses made no effort to protect her cub. This was the pride law: the full-grown hunters, the most valuable members of the pride, must feed first. The pride survived on their strength. Only after they had gorged could the young ones feed. In the lean times, when game was scarce or when open terrain made hunting difficult, the young might starve to death, and the adult females would not come into season again until game was once more plentiful. In this way, the survival of the pride was ensured.

The chastened cub crept back to join its sibling beneath the carcass and then to compete eagerly with it for the scraps that the lioness ripped out of the buffalo's belly cavity and unintentionally let fall.

Once the young lioness dropped back on all fours in obvious discomfort, and Claudia was horrified to see that her whole head was swarming with white maggots that had crawled out of the meat as she fed. The lioness shook her head, scattering maggots like rice grains. She pawed frantically at her own head to be rid of the fat worms that were trying to crawl into the furry openings of her ears. Then she extended her neck and sneezed violently, blowing live maggots out of her nostrils.

Her young cubs took this as an invitation to play, or to feed. Two of them launched themselves at her head, trying to hang on to her ears, while the third rushed under her belly and attached himself to a nipple like a tubby brown leech. The lioness ignored them and rose once more on her hind legs to continue eating. The cub at her nipple managed to hang on a few seconds longer and then fell under her back paws, and his dignity was trampled as she tugged and heaved at the bait. He crawled out between her legs crestfallen, dusty and dishevelled.

Claudia giggled, she could not help herself, she tried to muffle it with both hands. Immediately Sean dug her hard in the short ribs.

Only the old lioness reacted to her giggle. The rest of the pride were too preoccupied, but the lioness crouched and flattened her ears against her skull, staring fixedly down the opening at the hide. With these eyes on her, Claudia lost any urge to giggle again and she held her breath.

'She can't see me,' she told herself without conviction. 'Surely she can't see me?' But for long seconds, those eyes bored into hers.

Then abruptly, the old lioness rose and slid away into the thick undergrowth beyond the bait tree. She moved like a serpent, a sinuous flowing and gliding of the brown body. Claudia let out her breath slowly, and gulped with relief.

While the rest of the pride romped and tussled and fed beneath

14

the bait tree, the sun slid below the tree-tops and the short African twilight was on them.

'If there is a tom with them, he will come in now,' Sean breathed softly. The night was the time of the cats, the darkness made them bold and fierce. The light was going even as they watched.

Claudia heard something beyond the grass wall beside her, a furtive brush of some creature in long grass, but the bush was full of such small sounds and she did not even turn her head. Then she heard a distinct and unmistakable sound. The footfall of some heavy creature, soft and stealthy, but very close, and she felt her skin crawl with the insects of fear and the prickle of it up the back of her neck. Quickly she turned her head.

Her left shoulder was pressed up against the thatch wall of the hide, and there was a chink in the thatch an inch wide. Her eyes were at the same level as the hole, and through it, she saw movement. For a moment, she did not recognize what she was seeing, and then she knew that it was a tiny expanse of smooth tawny hide, filling the chink, only inches on the far side. As she stared in horror, the tawny pelt slid past her eyes, and now she heard something else, an animal breathing, snuffling at the far side of the thatch wall.

Instinctively, she reached behind her with her free hand, but never taking her eyes from the chink. Her hand was seized in a hard cool grip. The touch that had offended her only minutes before, now gave her more comfort than she had ever believed possible. She did not even marvel that she had reached for Sean's hand, rather than her own papa's.

She stared into the chink, and suddenly, there was another eye beyond, a huge round eye, glistening like yellow agate, a terrible inhuman eye, unblinking, burning into hers with a dead black pupil in its centre, a hand's span from her face.

She wanted to scream, but her throat was closed. She wanted to leap to her feet, but her legs were dead. Her swollen bladder was like a stone in her lower belly, and before she could control it, she felt a few warm drops escape. That checked her, the humiliation was greater than her terror and she tightened her thighs and buttocks and clung to Sean's hand, still staring into that terrible yellow eye.

The lioness sniffed again loudly, and Claudia started silently but held on. 'I won't scream,' she told herself.

Again the lioness snuffled beyond the grass wall, and her nostrils were filled with the man odour and she let out an explosive grunt that seemed to rock the flimsy grass walls. Claudia caught the scream in her throat before it could escape. Then the yellow eye was gone from the chink, and she heard the pad of great paws circling back round the hide.

Claudia swivelled her head to follow the sound, and she looked straight into Sean's face. He was smiling. That was what shocked her after what she had just lived through, there was that devil-may-care grin on his lips and mockery in those green eyes. He was laughing at her. Her terror subsided, and her anger flared.

'The swine.' she thought. 'The arrogant bloody swine.' And she knew that her face was bloodless and that her eyes were dark and wide with terror. She hated herself for it and she hated him for being witness to it.

She wanted to jerk her hand out of his grip. but she could still hear that great cat out there, still very close, circling them and though she loathed him, she knew that without his grip she would not be able to control herself. So she held on. but she turned her face away. following the furtive sounds of the lioness, so that Sean could not see her face.

The lioness passed in front of the blind. Through the peephole she saw the blur of its golden body, quickly gone, and she saw also that the young lioness and the cubs, alerted by the warning grunt, had disappeared into the undergrowth. The killing ground below the bait tree was deserted.

The light was going swiftly now. Within minutes it would be dark, and the thought of that brute in the darkness was almost too much to bear. Sean reached over her shoulder and pressed something small and hard against her lips. For a moment, she resisted and then she opened and let him slide it into her mouth. It was a cube of chewing-gum.

'The man has gone mad.' She was bewildered. 'Chewing-gum at a time like this?'

Then as she crunched down on to the cube she realized that her saliva had dried out and that the inside of her mouth was seared and puckered as though she had bitten into a green persimmon. At the taste of spearmint, her saliva flowed again, but she was so angry with him that she felt no gratitude. He had known that her mouth was dry with terror and she resented that fiercely.

16

The lioness growled in the semi-darkness behind the hide, and Claudia thought longingly of the Toyota that was parked a mile back up the track. Almost echoing her thought, her father asked softly. 'When did you tell the gunbearers to bring the truck?'

'After the last of the shooting light,' Sean answered him quietly. 'Another fifteen or twenty minutes.'

The lioness heard their voices and growled again threateningly.

'Cheeky bitch,' Sean said cheerfully. 'Snarly Sue in person.'

'Shut up!' Claudia hissed at him. 'She'll find us.'

'Oh, she knows we are here now,' Sean replied, and then raised his voice and called. 'Get away with you, you silly old bitch, go on back to your babies.'

Claudia jerked her hand out of his grip. 'Damn you! You'll get us all killed.'

But the loud human voice had alarmed the cat, and for minutes, there was silence beyond the grass wall. Sean took up the short ugly double-barrelled rifle that was propped against the wall beside him and placed it across his lap. He opened the breech of the .577 Nitro Express, and slid the fat brass cartridges out of the chambers, changing them for two others from the loops on the left breast of his jacket. It was a little superstitious ritual of his, that changing of cartridges, he always performed it at the beginning of a hunt.

'Now, listen to me, Capo,' he addressed Riccardo. 'If we kill that old whore without good reason, the game department is going to pull my licence. "Good reason" is when she has already chewed somebody's arm off, not before. Do you hear me?'

'I hear you,' Riccardo nodded.

'All right, don't shoot until I tell you, or by God, I'll shoot you.'

They grinned at each other in the half light, and Claudia realized with disbelief that the two of them were enjoying themselves. These two crazy oafs were actually having fun.

'By the time Job arrives with the truck, it will be pitch dark, and Job can't get the truck up to the hide. We'll have to go down to it in the riverbed. You go first, Capo, and then Claudia between us. Stay close together, and whatever you do, don't run! For the love of God, don't anybody run!'

Then they heard the lioness again, padding softly around them. She growled once more and almost immediately her growl was

17

answered from the far side of the hide. The young lioness was out there now.

'The gang's all here,' Sean commented. The sound of voices and the old lioness's growls had summoned the rest of the pride, and the hunters had become the hunted. They were trapped in the hide. The darkness was almost complete. The sunset was merely a dull red furnace glow on the western horizon.

'Where is the truck?' Claudia whispered.

Sean said, 'It's coming.' Then his voice changed. 'Down!' he said sharply. 'Get down!' And though she had heard nothing, she dropped out of the canvas chair and crouched on the ground.

The lioness had crept up to the front wall again, almost soundlessly, and now she flung herself at it, roaring furiously as she tore at the flimsy structure with her front claws. With horror, Claudia realized that it was coming in on top of her.

'Keep your heads down,' Sean shouted urgently and lifted the double-barrelled rifle just as the wall burst open.

He fired, a stunning burst of sound as the muzzle blast swept through the hide and lit the interior with flame, brilliant as a flashbulb.

'He's killed the brute.' Despite her hatred of blood sport, Claudia felt a guilty relief, but it was short-lived. The shot had merely startled the cat and driven her off for the moment. Claudia heard the lioness gallop away into the undergrowth snarling viciously.

'You missed,' she accused him breathlessly, with the stink of burnt gunpowder in her nostrils.

'Wasn't trying to hurt her.' Sean opened the rifle and reloaded from the cartridge loops on his breast. 'Just a warning shot over her bows.'

'There's the truck coming.' Riccardo's voice was level and unconcerned. Claudia's ears were still singing from the crash of gunfire, but she could make out the distant beat of the Toyota's diesel engine through it.

'Job heard the shot.' Sean stood up. 'He's coming early. All right, let's get ready to move out.'

Claudia scrambled up eagerly, and then looked over the low grass wall of the roofless hide into the dark forbidding forest around her, and remembered the track that led down to the dry riverbed that served as a road. They would have to travel almost

18

a quarter of a mile in the night to reach the safety of the truck. Her spirit quailed at the prospect.

In the trees not fifty yards away, the lioness roared again.

'Noisy blighter,' Sean chuckled, and took her elbow to guide Claudia to the door. This time she did not try to pull away, but instead found herself clinging to his arm.

'Take hold of Capo's belt.' Gently he disengaged her hand and guided it to her father's belt at the small of his back.

'Hold on,' he told her. 'And remember, whatever happens, don't run. It will pull them onto you instantly. Cat with mouse, they can't resist it.'

Sean switched on the flashlight. It was a big black Maglite, but even that powerful beam seemed puny and yellow in the immensity of the forest as he played it in a circle around them. There were eyes reflected in the beam, they glowed like menacing stars, many eyes out there in the dark bush, impossible to tell cubs from full-grown lionesses.

'Let's go,' Sean said quietly, and Riccardo started down the rough narrow track, dragging Claudia with him.

They went slowly, bunched up tightly. Riccardo covering the van with his lighter rifle and Sean in the rearguard, with the heavy rifle and the flashlight.

Each time the torch beam picked up the flash of cat's eyes in the night, they seemed closer, until Claudia could make out the body of the animal behind the glowing eyes. They were pale as moths in the torchlight, nimble and restless, as they circled, both lionesses closing in now, pacing swiftly through the undergrowth, watching them intently, but turning their heads away whenever the powerful light hit their eyes.

The track was steep and rough, and oh, so long. Each step was an agony of impatience for Claudia as she stumbled along behind her father, not watching her footing, but watching instead those pale feline shapes that paraded around them.

'Here comes Snarly Sue!' Sean warned quietly as the old lioness screwed up her courage and came at them out of the night, grunting like a steam locomotive, deafening gusts of sound surging up her throat and out of her open mouth, her long tail lashing from side to side like a hippo-hide whip. They stopped in a tight group, and Sean swung the torch and the rifle on to the charging animal.

'Get out of it!' he yelled at her. 'Go on, scat!' And the lioness came on, her ears flattened against her skull, long yellow fangs and pink tongue curling between her gaping jaws.

'Yah! Snarly Sue!' Sean howled. 'I'll blow your stupid head off!'

She broke her charge at the last possible moment, skidding to a halt on stiff front legs, ten feet from where they were bunched and the dust swirled around her in the torchlight.

'Piss off!' Sean ordered her sternly, and her ears came erect and she turned and trotted obediently back into the forest.

'That was a game of chicken chicken,' Sean chuckled. 'She was just trying it on.'

'How did you know that?' Claudia's voice was cracked and shrill in her own ears.

'Her tail. As long as she keeps waving it, she's only kidding. When she holds it stiff, then look out!'

'Here's the truck,' Riccardo said, and they could see the Toyota's headlights through the trees as it bumped up the dry riverbed below them.

'Praise the Lord,' Claudia whispered.

'It's not over yet,' Sean warned as they moved off down the track once more. 'There is still Growly Gertie to deal with.'

Claudia had forgotten the younger lioness and now she glanced around fearfully, as she stumbled after her father, hanging onto his belt.

Then at last, they were on the bank of the riverbed, fully lit by the headlights of the parked truck which was standing only thirty yards away with its engine running. She could make out the heads of the trackers in the front seat beyond the blaze of headlights. So close, so very close, and she could not help herself. Claudia let go of her father's belt, and ran for the truck, pelting wildly through the thick loose white sand of the riverbed.

She heard Sean shout behind her, 'You bloody idiot!'

And immediately afterwards the fearsome grunting roar of the lioness as she charged. Claudia glanced sideways as she ran, and the great cat was almost on her, coming in at an angle out of the tall reeds that lined the open riverbed. She was huge and pale in the headlights of the Toyota, snake-swift and her roaring cramped Claudia's belly and her feet dragged in the thick white sand.

Claudia saw that the charging lioness carried her tail high and stiff as a steel ramrod, and even in her terror, she remembered

20

what Sean had said and she thought with icy clarity. 'This time she's not going to stop, she's going to kill me.'

For a vital instant, Sean had not realized that the girl had run. He was backing carefully down the steep path into the riverbed, with the flashlight in his left hand and the double rifle in his right. He held the rifle by the grip with the barrels tilted up over his shoulder and his thumb on the slide of the safety-catch and he was watching the old lioness out there on the edge of the reed bed as she crawled on her belly towards them. But he was sure that she was now merely going through the motions of aggression since he had stared down her mock charge. There were two of the cubs well back behind her, sitting up in the grass and watching the performance with huge eyes and candid fascination, but too timid to take part. He had lost sight of the younger lioness, although he was sure that she was now the main threat, but the river reeds were dense and tall.

He had felt Claudia bump against his hip, but he thought she had stumbled, not realizing that she had bumped him as she turned to run. He was still searching for the younger lioness, probing the reed-beds with the torch beam, when he heard the crunch of Claudia's running feet in the sugary river sand, and he whirled and saw her out there in the dry riverbed alone.

'You bloody idiot!' he yelled in fury. The girl had been a constant source of irritation and dissent since she had arrived four days ago. Now she had flagrantly disobeyed his order, and he knew in an instant, even before the lioness launched her charge, that he was going to lose her. Getting a client killed or mauled was the blackest disgrace that could befall a professional hunter. It meant the end of his career, the end of twenty years of work and striving.

'You bloody idiot!' he vented all his bitterness on the running figure. He barged past Riccardo, who was still standing frozen with shock on the path below him, and at that moment, the lioness burst out of the edge of the reed bed where she had been lying.

The riverbed was brilliantly lit by the lights of the truck, so Sean dropped the torch and swung up the rifle with both hands, but he could not fire. The angle was wrong, the girl was between him and the lioness. Claudia ran awkwardly in the clinging sand, her head twisted away from him to watch the charge, her arms pumping frantically out of time with her legs.

'Down!' Sean shouted. 'Fall flat!' But she kept running, blocking his shot and the lioness swept in on her, sand spurting under her paws from which the curved yellow claws were already fully extended. She was grunting and roaring with each stride and her tail was carried stiff and straight.

In the headlights, the shadows of girl and cat on the stark white sand were grotesque and black, coming together swiftly, and Sean saw the lioness gather herself for the leap and he watched helplessly over the open iron sights of the rifle, impossible to separate them, impossible to fire without hitting the girl.

At the last moment Claudia tripped, her legs weak with fear collapsed under her and with a despairing wail, she sprawled face down in the sand.

Instantly, Sean zeroed his aim on the creamy chest of the lioness. With this rifle, he could hit two penny coins flipped simultaneously into the air at a range of thirty paces, left and right, both coins before they fell to earth. With this rifle, he had killed leopard, lion, rhino, buffalo, elephant by the hundred – and men, many men in the days of the Rhodesian bush war. He never needed a second shot. Now the target was open, he could with supreme confidence send a 750-grain soft-nosed mushrooming bullet through the lioness from her chest to the root of her tail. It would be the end of the cat, and of the safari, and probably his licence. At the least, it would mean months of investigation and trial. A dead lioness would bring all the wrath of the government, and the game department, down upon him.

The lioness was almost on top of the fallen girl, only a scant few feet of white sand between them, and Sean dropped his aim. It was a terrible risk, but he thrived on risk. He was gambling with the girl's life, but she had infuriated him, she deserved to take her chance.

He fired into the sand two feet in front of the lioness' open jaws. The huge heavy bullet ploughed in, sending up an eruption of sand, a solid fountain of flying white grains that for a moment, completely enveloped the animal. Sand filled its mouth and was sucked into its lungs as it roared, sand drove into its nostrils clogging them, and sand lashed into its open yellow eyes, tearing, raking, blinding the lioness, disorientating her, breaking the charge instantly.

Sean raced forward, with the second barrel ready to fire, but it wasn't necessary. The lioness had recoiled, rearing back violently, clawing at her sand-clotted eyes, toppling over and then bounding up again, and careering back into the reed-bed, barging blindly into the sheer bank, rolling and falling, and struggling up again. The sound of her wild run and agonized roars dwindled.

Sean reached Claudia and with an arm around her, jerked her to her feet. Her legs were unable to support her, and he had to half carry, half drag her to the Toyota and bundle her into the front seat.

At the same time, Riccardo scrambled into the back seat of the Toyota, and Sean leapt up onto the running board and with his free hand held the rifle like a pistol, pointed out into the darkness, ready for another charge.

'Go!' he shouted at Job, and the Matabele driver let out the clutch and they flew down the riverbed, lurching and jolting over the heavy going.

Nobody spoke for almost a minute, until they had climbed out of the riverbed onto the smoother track and then Claudia said in a small strangled voice, 'If I can't pee right now, I'm going to burst.'

'We could always point you at Snarly Sue like a fire extinguisher and wash her away,' Sean suggested coldly, and in the back seat, Riccardo let out a delighted guffaw. Even though Claudia recognized the nervous relief and tension in her father's laugh, she resented it bitterly. It aggravated the total humiliation she had suffered.

It was an hour's drive back to camp and when they arrived, Moses, Claudia's camp servant, had the shower filled with piping hot water. The shower was a twenty-gallon oil drum suspended in the branches of a mopane tree, a thatched grass screen, open to the stars, and a cement floor.

She stood under the rush of steaming water and as her body turned bright pink, she felt the humiliation and the nausea of the adrenalin over-dose fade away, to be replaced by that buoyant sense of well-being that comes only from having survived extreme danger.

While she soaped herself, working up a rich lather, she listened to Sean. He was fifty yards away at his makeshift gymnasium at the back of his own tent, but his regular hissing breathing carried clearly as he worked with the iron weights. He had not missed a session in the four days she had been in camp, no matter how long and hard the day's hunting had been.

'Rambo!' She smiled contemptuously at his masculine conceit and yet more than once, during the last few days, she had caught herself surreptitiously contemplating his muscled arms, or his flat greyhound belly or even his buttocks, round and hard as a pair of ostrich eggs in his khaki shorts.

Moses carried the lantern ahead of her, escorting her back from the shower in her silk dressing-gown, with a towel tied like a turban around her hair. He had laid out her mess kit for her, khaki slacks and a Gucci tee-shirt, ostrich-skin mosquito boots, exactly what she would have chosen herself. Moses washed her soiled clothes every day, and his ironing was crisp perfection. Her slacks crackled softly as she pulled them on. They added to her sense of well-being.

She took her time drying her hair and brushing it out. She used an artistic trace of make-up and lipstick, and when she looked in the small mirror, she felt even better.

'Who's the vain one now?' she smiled at herself, and went out to where the men were already at the camp-fire, gratified when they stopped talking, and watched her make her entrance. Sean rose from his camp chair to greet her with those silly limey manners that disconcerted her.

'Sit down!' She tried to sound brusque. 'You don't have to keep jumping up and down.'

Sean smiled easily, 'Don't let her see how she is succeeding in getting up your nose,' he warned himself, and he held the canvas camp chair for her while she sat down with the soles of her mosquito boots to the camp-fire.

'Get the Donna a peg,' Sean ordered the mess waiter. 'You know the way she likes it.'

The waiter brought it to her on a silver tray. It was perfect. A dash of Chivas whisky in a crystal glass, barely enough to colour the Perrier water, and filled right up with ice. The waiter was dressed in a snowy white kanza robe, the hem well below his knee, a scarlet sash over his shoulder to denote that he was the head waiter, and a scarlet pillbox fez on his head. His two assistant waiters stood respectfully in the background, also in scarlet fez and flowing white robes. For Claudia it was mildly embarrassing, there were twenty servants to care for three of them, all so sybaritic and colonial and exploitative. This was 1987, for God's sake, and the empire was long gone – but the whisky was delicious.

24

'I suppose you expect me to thank you for saving my life,' she said, as she sipped it.

'Not at all, ducky.' Sean had learned almost immediately that she hated that form of address. 'I wouldn't even expect you to apologize for your crass stupidity. To be quite frank with you, I was worrying more about having to kill the lioness. Now that would have been tragic.'

They fenced lightly, skilfully, and Claudia found herself enjoying it. Every thrust that went through his guard gave her a satisfied glow, better even than a good day in court. She was disappointed when the head waiter announced in sepulchral tones, 'Chef say dinner she is ready, *Mambo*,' and Sean led them into the dining tent that was lit by candles in a many-branched Meissen porcelain candelabra. The cutlery was solid silver, Claudia had furtively checked the hallmarks, and the Waterford crystal wine-glasses sparkled on the table-cloth of Madeira lace-work and a robed waiter stood behind each of their folding canvas safari chairs, ready to serve.

'What do you fancy tonight, Capo?' Sean asked.

'A touch of Wolfgang Amadeus,' Riccardo suggested, and Sean pressed the 'play' button on the tape-deck before going to his seat, and the limpid strains of Mozart's piano concerto number seventeen shimmered in the candlelight.

The soup was made with green peas and pearl barley and buffalo marrow bones, spiced with a fearsome chili sauce that Sean called *Peli Peli Ho Ho*.

Claudia had inherited her father's taste for chili and garlic and red wine, but even she could not face the second course, buffalo tripes in a white sauce. Both men liked their tripes green, which was simply an euphemism for improperly cleaned of the original contents.

'It's only chewed grass,' her father had pointed out, which made her feel squeamish until she turned and caught a whiff of the special dish that chef had prepared for her alone. Beneath a golden pie crust steamed a savoury stew of antelope fillets and kidneys. Chef had shaken his tall white cap when she had suggested the addition of ten cloves of garlic.

'Cook book say no garlic, Donna.'

'My book say plenty garlic, it say very loud ten cloves garlic, okay, chefie?' And the chef had grinned in capitulation. Claudia had almost instantly overwhelmed the entire camp staff with her easy manner and relaxed charm.

The wine was a rich and robust South African Cabernet, every bit as good as her favourite Chianti, and she gave both wine and pie her full attention. The day's rigours and the sun and fresh air had honed her appetite. Like her papa, she could eat and drink freely without adding an ounce of flesh or fat to her waistline. Only the conversation was a disappointment. As on every other evening the men were talking about rifles and hunting and the killing of wild animals. The gun talk was mostly unintelligible gibberish to her.

Her father said things like 'The .300 Weatherby can move a 180-grain bullet at 3200 foot per second, that gives you over 4000 foot/lb of muzzle energy and stupendous hydro-static shock.'

And Sean would respond. 'You Yanks are obsessed with velocity. Roy Weatherby has blown up more bullets on African game than you have eaten spaghetti, Capo. Give me high sectional density, Nosler construction and moderate velocity . . .'

No normally intelligent person could keep that up for hour after hour, she told herself, and yet every night of the safari so far she had gone to bed and left the two of them at the camp-fire still at it over their cognac and cigars.

When they spoke of the animals, however, she could take more interest and even participate, usually to vent her disapproval. They talked mostly of particular individual animals, legendary old males for which Sean had pet names, which annoyed Claudia, just the way it irritated her when he called Papa 'Capo', as though he were a mafia don. One such animal he referred to as 'Frederick the Great', or simply 'Fred'. This was the lion they were hunting now, the lion for which they had hung the buffalo carcass.

'I've seen him twice so far this season, one client even had a shot at him. Mind you, he was shaking so much with nerves he missed him by a football field.'

'Tell me about him.' Riccardo leaned forward eagerly.

'Papa, he told you about him last night,' Claudia reminded him sweetly. 'And the night before, and the night before that. . . .'

'Little girls should be seen and not heard,' Riccardo chuckled. 'Didn't I ever teach you anything? Tell me about Fred, again.'

'He's got to be well over eleven foot, and not just length. He's got a head on him like a hippo, and a mane like a black haystack. When he walks, it ripples and tosses like the wind in a msasa tree,' Sean rhapsodized. 'Cunning? Sly? Fred knows it all,

26

he's been shot at at least three times that I know of. Wounded once by a Spanish hunter over in Ian Piercy's concession three seasons ago, but he recovered. He didn't get that big by being stupid.'

'How are we going to get him?' Riccardo demanded.

'I think the two of you are disgusting,' Claudia cut in before Sean could reply. 'After seeing those glorious creatures today, those beautiful little cubs. How can you bring yourself to kill them?'

'I didn't see any cubs shot today,' Riccardo remarked as he nodded to the waiter offering him another helping of tripe. 'In fact, we went to a great deal of trouble and risk to ensure their survival.'

'You are devoting forty-five days of your life to the sole purpose of killing lions and elephants!' Claudia shot back. 'So don't get all righteous with me, Riccardo Monterro.'

'I am always fascinated by the confused thought processes of your average shrieking liberal,' Sean intervened and Claudia turned on him gleefully, lusting for battle.

'There is no confusion in my mind. You are here to kill animals.'

'The same way that a farmer kills animals,' Sean agreed. 'To ensure a healthy flourishing herd, and a place for that herd to survive.'

'You are not a farmer.'

'Oh yes, I am,' Sean contradicted. 'The only difference is that I slaughter them on the range, not in an abattoir, but like any farmer, my chief concern is the survival of my breeding-stock.'

'They are not domestic animals,' Claudia contested. 'Those are beautiful wild animals.'

'Beautiful? Wild? What the hell has that got to do with it? Like anything else in this modern world, the wild game of Africa has to pay its way if it's going to survive. Capo, here, is paying tens of thousands of dollars to hunt a lion and an elephant. He is giving those animals a monetary value far above goats and cattle, so that the newly independent government of Zimbabwe is willing to set aside concessions of millions of acres in which the game can persist. I hire one of those concessions, and I have the strongest incentive in the world for protecting it from the grazers and poachers and making certain I have plenty of game

27

to offer my hunters. No, ducky, legal safari hunting is one of the most effective arms of conservation in Africa today.'

'So you are going to save the animals by shooting them with high-powered rifles?' Claudia demanded scornfully.

'High-powered rifles?' Sean laughed softly. 'Another emotive liberal parrot cry. Would you prefer us to use low-powered rifles? Won't that be rather like demanding that the butcher uses only blunt knives to cut throats? You are an intelligent woman, think with your head, not your heart. The individual animal is unimportant. His life span is limited to a few short years. In the case of this lion we are hunting, probably twelve years at the very most. What is beyond price is the continued existence of the species as a whole. Not the individual, but his entire kind. Our lion is an old male at the very end of his useful life span during which he has protected his females and his young and already added his genes to the pool of his race. He will die naturally within the next year or two. Much better that his death produce ten thousand dollars in cash which will be spent on providing a safe place for his cubs to live, than having this wilderness encroached upon by swarming black humanity and their scrawny herds of goats.'

'My God, listen to you.' Claudia shook her head sadly. '"Swarming black humanity", those are the words of a racist and a bigot. It's their land, why can't they be free to live where they choose?'

'And that is the logic of woolly-headed liberalism,' Sean laughed. 'Make up your mind whose side you are on, the beautiful wild animals or the beautiful wild blacks. You can't have it both ways; when the two come into competition for living space, the wild animals always come off losers, unless we hunters can pay the bill for them.'

He wasn't an easy man to argue with, she conceded, and she was relieved when her father cut in and gave her a moment to gather her wits.

'There can be no doubt on which side my darling daughter stands. After all, Sean, you are talking to a senior member of the commission for the reinstatement of the Inuit people to their traditional lands.'

She smiled at him sweetly. 'Not Inuit, Papa. People will think you are going soft. Not even Eskimos – your usual description is gooks, isn't it?'

28

Riccardo smoothed back the thick waves of silver at his temples. 'Shall I tell you how my daughter and her commission go about determining how much of Alaska belongs to the Inuits?' he asked.

'He's going to tell you anyway.' Claudia leaned across to stroke her father's hand. 'It's one of his party routines. It's very funny, you'll love it.'

Riccardo went on as though she had not spoken. 'They go down Fourth Street, in Anchorage, that's where all the bars are, and they grab a couple of Eskimos that are still on their feet. They put them in an airplane and fly them down the peninsula, and they say to them: "Now, tell us where your people used to live. Show us your traditional tribal hunting grounds. How about that lake over there, did your people fish there once upon a time?"' Riccardo changed his voice, he was an excellent mimic. '"Sure!!" says the Eskimo in the back seat, squinting out the window, his eyes full of Jack Daniels. "That's where my gran-pappy fished."'

He changed voices, imitating Claudia. '"And what about those mountains over there, the one which we wicked white folk who stole it away from you call Brooks Range, did your gran-pappy ever hunt there?"' He changed to his Eskimo intonation. '"Sure did, man. He shot a whole mess of bears there. I remember my gran-mommy telling me about it."'

'Go on, Papa. You've got a marvellous audience tonight. Mr Courtney is enjoying your wit hugely,' Claudia encouraged him.

'You know something?' Riccardo asked, 'Claudia has never yet had an Eskimo turn down a lake or a mountain she has offered him, isn't that something else? My little girl has got a perfect score, never a single refusal.'

'You are just plain lucky, Capo,' Sean told him. 'At least they might leave you something, here they took the lot.'

* * *

Claudia woke to the clink of crockery outside the flap of her tent and Moses' polite cough. Nobody had ever brought her tea in bed before. It was a luxury that made her feel marvellously decadent. It was still pitch dark and icy cold in the tent. She could hear the crackle of frost on the canvas as Moses opened the flap. She had never expected it to be so cold in Africa.

She sat up in the camp-bed with a quilt over her shoulders, cupping her hands around the tea mug and watched Moses fussing about the tent. He poured a bucket of hot water into her wash basin and set a clean white towel beside it. He filled the tooth mug with boiled drinking water and squeezed toothpaste onto her brush for her. Then he brought a brazier of burning charcoal and placed it in the centre of the tent.

'Too cold today, Donna.'

'And too damned early,' Claudia agreed sleepily.

'Did you hear the lions roaring last night, Donna?'

'I didn't hear a thing.' She yawned. They could have had a brass band playing 'America, the Beautiful' beside her bed without waking her.

Moses finished laying out her clothes on the spare bed. He had polished her boots until they shone.

'You want something, Donna, you call me,' he told her as he backed out of the tent flap.

She shot out of the warm bed and stood over the brazier shivering while she held her panties over the coals to warm them before pulling them on.

The stars were still shining when she left the tent. She paused to look up, still amazed by the jewelled treasure chest of the southern sky. She picked out the great cross with a sense of achievement and then went to the camp-fire where the men were, and held her hands out gratefully to the flames.

'You haven't changed since you were little.' Her father smiled at her. 'Do you remember how I used to battle to get you out of bed to go to school every morning?' And a waiter brought her a second cup of tea.

Sean whistled and she heard Job start the Toyota and drive it around to the front gate of the stockade, and they began pulling on their heavy gear. Jerseys and anoraks, caps and woollen scarves.

When they trooped out to the hunting car, they found the rifles in the racks and Job and Shadrach, the two Matabeles, standing in the back with the little Ndorobo tracker between them. The tracker was a childlike figure who came only to Claudia's armpit, but he had an endearing wrinkled grin and bright mischievous eyes. She had been predisposed to like all the black camp staff, but Matatu was already her favourite. He reminded her of one of the dwarfs from *Snow White*. The three blacks were bundled up

30

against the cold in army-surplus greatcoats and knitted Balaclava caps, and they answered Claudia's greeting with white grins in the darkness. All of them had fallen under her spell.

Sean took the wheel and Claudia sat on the front seat between him and her father. She crouched down behind the windscreen and cuddled against Papa for warmth. In the short time she had been on safari, she had come to love this start to the day's adventure.

They drove slowly over the winding bumpy track and as the night retreated before the advance of dawn, Sean switched off the headlights.

Claudia peered into the combretum forest and down the grassy glades that intersected it that Sean called 'vleis', trying to be the first to spot some elusive and lovely creature, but always Sean or her father murmured first, 'Kudu on the left' or 'That's a reed-buck', or Matatu leaned over from the back to tap her shoulder and point out a rarer sight with his tiny pink-palmed hand.

The dusty track was pocked with the spoor of the animals that had crossed in the night. Once they came across the fresh droppings of an elephant, still steaming in the chill of dawn, a knee-high pile which everybody climbed out of the Toyota to examine closely. At first, Claudia had been disconcerted by this avid interest in dung, but now she was accustomed to it.

'Old beggar,' Sean said. 'On his last set of teeth.'

'How do you know that?' she demanded.

'Can't chew his food,' he replied. 'Look at the twigs and leaves in the dung, almost whole.'

Matatu was crouched by the spoor, examining the great round footprints, the size of dustbin-lids.

'See how smooth the pads of his feet are,' Sean told her. 'Worn down like an old set of car tyres. Old and big.'

'Is it him?' Riccardo asked eagerly, and glanced at the .416 Rigby rifle in the gun-rack behind his seat.

'Matatu will tell us,' Sean shrugged, and the little Ndorobo spat in the dust, and shook his head mournfully as he stood up. Then he spoke to Sean in piping falsetto Swahili.

'It's not the one we want. Matatu knows this bull,' Sean translated. 'We saw this one last year down near the river. He has one tusk broken off at the lip, and the other is worn down

31

to a stump. He might once have had a magnificent pair, but he's far over the other side of the hill now.'

'You mean Matatu can recognize a particular elephant by his footprints?' Claudia looked incredulous.

'Matatu can recognize a particular buffalo out of a herd of five hundred, and he'll know that animal again two years later just by a glance at the spoor.' Sean exaggerated a little for her. 'Matatu isn't a tracker, he's a magician.'

They drove on with small wonders occurring all around them: a kudu bull, grey as a ghost, striped with chalky lines, maned and hump-backed, his long corkscrew horns glinting in the gloom, slipped away into the forest; a genet cat caught out from his nocturnal prowling, spotted and golden as a miniature leopard, peering at them with astonishment from the brown grass of the verge. A kangaroo rat hopped ahead of the Toyota. Troops of chittering guinea fowl with waxen yellow helmets on their heads ran through the grass beside the track and Claudia no longer had to ask, 'What is that bird?' or 'What animal is that?' She was beginning to recognize them and this added to her pleasure.

Just before the sunrise, Sean parked the Toyota at the foot of a rocky hill that rose abruptly out of the forest and they climbed out stiffly and took off their heavy outer clothing. They climbed the side of the kopje, three hundred feet of steep uneven pathway, without a pause, and Claudia tried to disguise her ragged breathing as they came out on the summit. Sean had timed the ascent perfectly, and as they reached the top, the sun burst out of the distant forest and lit it all with dramatic colour and brilliance.

They looked out over a panorama of forest and glade that glowed with golden grass to other high sheer kopjes standing like fairy castles, all turreted and towered in the dawn. Other hills were great dumps of black rock, like the rubble left over from the Creation.

They shed their sweaters, for the climb had warmed them and even the first rays of the sun held the promise of the noonday heat and they sat on the front edge of the hill and played their binoculars over the forest below. Behind them, Job laid out the food box that he had carried up and in minutes, he had a fire going. It had been too early to eat breakfast before they left camp, but now at the odour of frying bacon and eggs, Claudia felt her saliva flooding.

While they waited for their breakfast, Sean pointed out the

terrain. 'That is the Mozambique border over there, just beyond the second kopje, only seven or eight miles from here.'

'Mozambique,' Claudia murmured, peering through her binoculars. 'The name has such a romantic ring to it.'

'Not so romantic. It's just another triumph of African socialism and the carefully thought-out economic policy of chaos and ruination,' Sean grunted.

'I can't take racism before breakfast,' Claudia told him icily.

'All right,' Sean grinned. 'Suffice it to say that just across the border there you have twelve years of Marxism, corruption, greed and incompetence, just beginning to bear fruit. You have a civil war raging out of control, famine that will probably starve a million people, and epidemic disease, including Aids, that will kill another million in the next five years.'

'Sounds like a fun place for a vacation,' Riccardo said. 'How about breakfast, Job?'

Job brought them plates of eggs and bacon and fried French bread followed by mugs of strong aromatic coffee. They ate off their laps, glassing the forest through their binoculars between mouthfuls.

'You are a pretty good cook, Job,' Claudia told him.

'Thank you, ma'am,' Job answered quietly. He spoke English with only a slight accent. He was a man in his late thirties, with a tall and powerful physique and wide-spaced intelligent eyes in the handsome moon face typical of the Matabele and their Zulu origins.

'When did you learn?' Claudia asked, and the Matabele hesitated and glanced at Sean before he said in his deep soft voice, 'In the army, ma'am.'

'Job was a captain in the Ballantyne Scouts with me,' Sean explained.

'A captain!' Claudia exclaimed. 'I didn't realize that . . .' she broke off quickly, looking embarrassed.

'You didn't realize there were black officers in the Rhodesian army,' Sean finished for her. 'There is a lot more to know about Africa than what they show you on CBS television.'

Shadrach, the second gunbearer, was sitting fifty yards farther along the crest, where he had a better view towards the north, and now he whistled softly and pointed up that way. Sean wiped the last of the egg yolk off his plate with the toast and stuffed it in his mouth. He passed the plate to Job. 'Thanks, Job, that was

33

great.' And went to join Shadrach. The two of them peered down into the forest.

'What is it?' Riccardo called impatiently.

'Elephant,' Sean replied, and both Riccardo and Claudia sprang up and hurried to join them.

'Where? Where?' she demanded.

'Big one?' Riccardo asked. 'Can you see his tusks? Is it him?'

'Too far to be sure, a couple of miles.' Sean pointed out the indistinct grey blur amongst the trees and Claudia was amazed that such a huge animal was so difficult to see. It took some minutes before it moved slightly and she was able to pick it out.

'What do you think?' Riccardo asked. 'Could it be Tukutela?'

'It could be,' Sean nodded. 'But it's a thousand to one against it.'

Tukutela. Claudia had listened to them discussing this elephant at the camp-fire. Tukutela, the angry one, was one of those legendary animals of which there were only a handful left in the whole length and breadth of Africa. A bull elephant with tusks that weighed over a hundred pounds each. Tukutela was the main reason that her father had come back to Africa for the last time. For he had once seen Tukutela. Three years before, he had been on safari with Sean Courtney, and the two of them had followed the great elephant for five days. Matatu had led them over a hundred miles on the spoor before they had come up with him. They had stalked to within twenty paces of the enormous and ancient beast as he fed on the fruits of a marula tree. They had studied every wrinkle and crease in his riven grey hide. They were so close that they could have counted the remaining few hairs in his tail, the rest worn away over the years, and they had gazed in silent awe upon his ivory.

Riccardo Monterro would have willingly paid any price to possess those tusks as his own trophy. He had asked Sean in a whisper, 'Isn't there any way I can have him?' And he had seen Sean hesitate before he shook his head.

'No, Capo. We can't touch him. More than my licence and my concession are worth.' For around his neck, Tukutela wore a collar, a sturdy thing of nylon, tough as a heavy-duty truck tyre, and suspended from it was a radio transmitter.

Some years previously, the old bull had been darted from a helicopter by members of the government elephant research

34

project, and while he was unconscious, they had riveted the radio collar around his neck. This made Tukutela a 'designated research animal' and placed him beyond the reach of legal safari hunters. Of course, he was still at risk from ivory poachers, but no licensed hunter could legally hunt him.

While the elephant was under the drug, Dr Glynn Jones, the government veterinarian in charge of the project, had measured his tusks. His report was not for general publication, but his secretary was a nubile blonde who thought that Sean Courtney was the most awe-inspiring thing she had ever seen in her young life. She had duplicated a copy of the report for Sean.

'From Jonesy's measurements, one tusk will weigh 130 pounds and the other a few pounds lighter,' Sean had whispered to Riccardo as they studied the old bull, and they had stared at the tusks hungrily.

At the lip, they were as thick as Sean's thigh and there was no taper to them. They were stained almost black with vegetable juice. The tips were rounded off bluntly, according to Doctor Jones, the left tusk was eight foot four and a half inches, the right tusk eight foot six and a quarter, from lip to tip.

In the end, they had walked away and left the old bull to his solitary wandering, and then only six months ago, the blonde secretary had been making breakfast for Sean in her tiny bachelor flat in the Avenues in Harare, when she mentioned quite casually, 'Did you know that Tukutela has thrown his collar?'

Sean was lying naked on her bed, but he sat up quickly. 'What did you say?'

'Jonesy was in an awful pet. They put the radio direction finder on Tukutela and all they got was his collar. He had managed to tear it off at last and had hurled it into the top of a msasa tree.'

'You clever little beauty,' Sean said happily. 'Come here and get your prize.' And the girl had dropped her dressing-gown on the floor and rushed across the room.

So Tukutela had thrown his collar, and was no longer a 'designated research animal'. Once again, he was legal game. That same day, Sean had sent a cable to Riccardo in Alaska, and received the reply the following afternoon.

'I'M COMING STOP BOOK ME FULL SAFARI 1ST JULY TO AUGUST 15TH STOP I WANT THAT JUMBO STOP CAPO'

And now, as Riccardo stood on the crest of the kopje, studying that far-off smudge of elephant grey in the forest below, he was shaking with excitement.

Claudia studied him with open amazement. This was her father, the coolest cat in the business, the master of *savoir faire*. She had seen him negotiating a ten-million-dollar contract and betting a prince's ransom across the tables at Vegas, without any visible emotion, but here he was shivering with excitement like a schoolboy on his first date, and she felt a rush of affection for him.

'I haven't understood just how much this means to him,' she thought. 'Perhaps I am being too hard. This is the last thing in his life that he truly wants.' And she wanted to put her arms around him and hug him and tell him, 'I'm sorry, Papa. I'm sorry that I have been trying to deprive you of this last pleasure.'

Riccardo was not even aware of her existence. 'It could be Tukutela,' he repeated softly, speaking almost to himself, as though he was trying to will it to be so, but Sean shook his head.

'I've got four good trackers watching the river. Tukutela couldn't cross without them knowing, besides it's still too early. I wouldn't expect him to leave the valley until the last waterholes along the escarpment dry up, another week or ten days at the earliest.'

'He could have slipped through.' Riccardo ignored his explanation. 'It's just possible that it is him down there.'

'We'll go down and take a look, of course,' Sean nodded in agreement. Riccardo's passion did not amaze him as it had his daughter. He understood it totally, had seen it in fifty other men like Riccardo, the powerful, aggressive, successful men, who made up his clientele, men who did not try to conceal or check their instincts. The hunting imperative was part of every man's soul; some denied or suppressed it, others diverted it into less blatantly violent avenues of expression, wielding clubs on the golf course or racquets on the court, substituting a little white ball for the prey of flesh and blood, but men like Riccardo Monterro gave their passions full rein and would settle for nothing less than the ultimate thrill of the chase and the kill.

'Shadrach, bring the *Bwana*'s .416 *banduki*,' Sean called. 'Job, don't forget the water-bottles. Matatu, *akwendi*, let's go!'

They went directly down the steep front slope of the kopje, leaping lightly from boulder to boulder, and at the bottom, they dropped naturally into their running formation with Matatu leading to pick up the spoor, followed by Job and Sean with their almost supernatural eyesight to sweep the forest ahead, the clients in the middle, and Shadrach in the drag to hand Riccardo the Rigby when he needed it. They went swiftly, but it was almost an hour through the forest before Matatu picked up the huge dished spoor in the soft earth, and the litter of stripped twigs and branches that the elephant had strewed behind him as he fed. Matatu stopped on it, turning back to roll his eyes, and give shrill piping cries of disgust.

'It's not Tukutela. It's the old one-tusk bull,' Sean told them. 'The same one whose spoor we saw on the road this morning. He has circled back this way.'

Claudia watched her father's face and saw the intensity of his disappointment, and felt her heart squeeze for him.

Nobody spoke on the march back to the Toyota, but when they reached it, Sean said softly, 'You knew it wasn't going to be that easy, didn't you, Capo.' And they grinned at each other.

'You're right, of course. The chase is everything. Once you kill, it's only dead meat.'

'Tukutela will come,' Sean promised him. 'This is his regular beat. He'll be here before the new moon, that's my promise to you, but in the meantime there is the lion. We will go check bait to see if Frederick the Great is going to oblige us.'

It was only another twenty minutes' driving to the dry riverbed below the hide and the buffalo bait. They left the Toyota parked on the white sand, and Claudia felt a tremor of last night's terror as they climbed the path up the far bank and saw the pad marks of the lioness in the earth behind the hide. Then Sean and his gunbearers were talking excitedly and Matatu was chittering like an agitated guinea fowl.

'What is it?' Claudia demanded, but nobody answered her and she had to trot to keep up with them as they hurried down the open tunnel through the bush to where the remains of the carcass hung in the wild fig.

'Somebody tell me what's happening,' Claudia begged them, but she stayed well back from the bait. The stench was just too much for her to bear. The men showed no distaste at all as they prodded and peered at the reeking remains, and even Claudia could see the difference from the previous evening.

Yesterday, the carcass had been virtually untouched, now more than half of it had been devoured. Only the head and

37

forequarters remained, and Sean had to stretch up above his head to reach it. The bones of spine and ribs had been chewed to splinters, and the thick black skin ripped by claw and fang, so that it hung in tatters like a funeral flag.

While Sean and the gunbearers examined the carcass, Matatu searched the earth around the base of the fig tree, giving excited little yaps like a hound questing for the scent. Sean picked something off the jagged white ribs of the carcass and showed it to Riccardo, and both of them laughed excitedly, passing whatever it was from hand to hand.

'Won't somebody talk to me, please?' Claudia insisted, and Sean called to her.

'Come on then, don't stand so far away.'

Reluctantly, holding her nose theatrically, she approached and Sean held out his right hand to her, palm up. On it lay a single hair, almost as long and black as one from her own head.

'What is it?'

Riccardo took the hair from Sean's hand, holding it between thumb and forefinger, and Claudia saw that the back of her father's arms were goose-bumped with excitement, and his dark Italian eyes glowed as he replied.

'Mane hair.'

Then he seized her hand and pulled her across to the base of the fig tree.

'Take a look at that. Look what Matatu has found for us.'

The little tracker was grinning with proprietorial pride as he indicated the churned earth. Five cubs and two lionesses had trampled the soft footing into talcum dust, but one perfect print stood out in the confusion. It was double the size of the other smudged prints, as big as a soup plate, and, looking at it, Claudia felt again the stirring of terror. Whatever animal had left that pad mark must be monstrous.

'Last night, after the lionesses had seen us off, he came. He waited until the moon had set and he came in the darkest hours of the night,' Sean explained. 'And he left again before dawn. He ate damned nigh half a buffalo, and then he took off again before first light. I told you that he is a cunning old devil.'

'A lion?' Claudia asked.

'Not just any old lion.' Riccardo shook his head. 'Frederick the Great has come at last.'

Sean turned away and beckoned his men to come to him. The

38

three of them, Job and Shadrach and Matatu, squatted around him in a circle and Claudia and Riccardo were forgotten as they planned the hunt, working out their tactics, discussing in detail every aspect, every eventuality. Their concentration was absolute, and it was an hour before Sean stood up and came to where Riccardo and Claudia sat in the shade.

'The trick is going to be getting him to come in before nightfall,' he told them. 'And we all agree that the only way to do that is to set up a fresh bait for him and build a new hide. The lionesses have rumbled this one, and old Fred is going to be as suspicious as all hell. He's going to lurk out there until well after dark or until we can entice him in somehow.'

Sean sat down between them, and was silent for a moment.

'You know, Capo, sometimes for a good friend, someone I can trust, I am prepared to bend the rules a little.' He spoke deliberately, drawing with a twig in the dirt between his feet, and not looking at Riccardo.

'I'm listening,' Riccardo nodded.

'There may be only one way that we will get this lion,' Sean said softly. 'Jack-light him.'

They were silent for a long time, and though Claudia did not know what 'Jack-light' meant, she realized that Sean was suggesting something beyond law or decency, and that her father was tempted. She was angry with Sean for putting temptation in her father's way, but she knew better than to intervene. She kept silent and willed her father to refuse to give in to temptation.

Riccardo shook his head. 'No, let's do it right.'

'We can try,' Sean shrugged. 'But he has been shot at over a bait, and wounded once. It won't be easy.'

They were silent again for almost a full minute, then Sean went on, 'The lion is a nocturnal animal. The night is his time. If you truly want this lion, I think you'll have to take him in darkness.'

Riccardo sighed, and shook his head. 'I want him very badly, but not badly enough to kill him without respect.'

Sean stood up. 'It's your safari, Capo,' he agreed quietly. 'I just want you to know that there are not many men I'd make that offer to. As a matter of fact, offhand I can't think of anyone else I'd do it for.'

'I know,' Capo said. 'Thank you, Sean.' And Sean walked back to the fig tree to help his men to lower the remains of the carcass so the pride could reach it.

39

As soon as he was out of earshot, Claudia asked her father, 'Jack-light? What is that?'

'Putting a spotlight on an animal after dark, and shooting it in the beam. It's illegal, highly illegal.'

'The bastard,' she said bitterly.

Riccardo did not react to her denunciation, but went on softly, 'He was prepared to put his career on the line for me. That's one of the best things anyone has ever done for me.'

'I'm proud that you refused him, Papa, but he is a bastard.'

'You don't understand,' he said, 'You can't possibly understand.' He stood up and walked away, and immediately she felt a throb of guilt. She did understand. She understood that this was his last lion, and that she was spoiling the pleasure of it for him. She was torn between her love for him, and her protective instinct for that marvellous animal and her sense of right and justice.

'It should be easy to do the right thing,' she thought. 'But it so seldom is.'

So over the days that followed, they hunted the old lion with ethical tactics. They had to provide fresh baits for him and the lionesses, and Riccardo shot the buffalo Sean pointed out to him, another barren cow, and then two days later, a decrepit bull with horns worn down to stumps and his ribs showing through his bald mud-caked hide.

Each day Sean moved the bait or repositioned the thatched hide, trying to find a location which the black-maned male would feel sufficiently confident to approach in broad daylight. Evening after evening, they sat in the hide until an hour after darkness had fallen and then drove back to camp dejected and discouraged. When they visited the bait again the following morning they found that the lion had fed, leaving his mane hairs and his huge pad-marks to tantalize them, and had departed again before dawn.

Cursing the beast bitterly, Sean changed tactics. He lowered the remains of the rotten bait on its chain so that lionesses and cubs could reach it readily. By this stage, it was mostly dried skin and gnawed bone. Five hundred metres up the river, he hung a fresh carcass, at a height that only the big lion could reach in a tree that stood alone in a glade of shoulder-high dry winter grass. He hoped that without the harassment of the females and cubs the lion might come earlier to the bait.

To make him feel even more secure, he placed the hide across the dry riverbed in the fork of a teak tree. It was a machan platform fifteen feet above ground level. From the machan, they had a view across the white sand of the dry riverbed.

Sean did not clear all the grass around the bait tree. He wanted the lion to feel protected by good cover. He merely opened a keyhole in the grass, barely as wide as the body of the lion, through which they could see the carcass.

'If he comes, you'll have to wait until he rears up to feed, Capo,' he explained as they went into the machan an hour after noon, to wait out the long drowsy hot afternoon.

Sean allowed Claudia to bring a paperback copy of Karen Blixen's *Out of Africa* to read.

'Just as long as you don't rustle the pages,' he warned her.

The lionesses and their cubs came early. They were so conditioned to feeding from a bait by now, that they showed not the least trepidation at approaching. First they came to the new bait in the grassy glade, and inspected it wistfully. Both lionesses made attempts to feed from it, but it was just out of their reach.

For the last few days, the eyes of the young lioness, Growly Gertie, had been irritated and infected by the river sand that Sean had fired into them. Tears ran down her cheeks and her eyelids were swollen and inflamed, but now they were healing and clearing, the swelling was abating and there were only smears of yellow mucus in the corners of her eyes.

After a while, they gave up trying to reach the carcass, and led their cubs down the riverbank to the old stinking bait.

From the machan, they could hear the pride growling and ripping at the bait five hundred metres downstream, but as the afternoon passed, so the sounds of feeding dwindled into silence as the lionesses satiated themselves and went to lie up in the shade.

Half an hour before sunset, the small hot breeze that had been blowing all afternoon, dropped abruptly and that peculiar hush of an African evening descended on the veld. The sparse winter growth of leaves on the trees was still, not a blade of yellow grass stirred in the glade across the riverbed, and the fluffy papyrus reeds below the bank ceased their perpetual nodding and bowing and stood as though listening intently. It was so quiet that Claudia looked up from her book, and then closed it softly and sat listening to the absolute silence.

Then suddenly a bush-buck barked on the far bank. an alarm call so clear and loud in the hush that Claudia jumped involuntarily. Immediately, she felt Sean's light firm touch on her hip. a warning, and she heard her father's breathing, quick and deep as though he had just finished a hard rally on the court.

The silence had an ominous weight to it now. as though the world held its breath. Then she heard her father exhale softly. and she glanced sideways at him. His expression was rapt as that of a communicant kneeling for the Sacrament. God. he was a handsome man, she thought. Except for the silver wings at his temples, he looked so much younger than his years. so tanned and lean and fit. As yet, there was no external sign of the treachery of his own body that was destroying itself from within.

His excitement was infectious and she felt her own blood course more swiftly, driven by the quickening of her pulse. and she turned her head slowly to follow the direction of her father's gaze, He was looking off to the right, out across the river, to where the trees of the forest met the tall pale grass at the edge of the glade.

The only living creature out there was a grey parrot-like bird perched on the top branch of a bush willow. Sean had told her it was a grey lourie. the notorious 'go away bird' that plagued the hunter with its raucous warning cry. The bird squawked now, 'G'way! G'way!' But as it fluttered on the high branch, it was twisting its neck, craning to peer down into the long grass below the bush willow.

'Here he comes. The bird can see him.' Sean whispered only inches behind her ear, and Claudia strained her eyes looking for she knew not what.

'Watch the grass.' Sean guided her, and she saw the movement. The tips of the grass trembled and pushed, a stealthy furtive movement that passed slowly down the glade towards the riverbank, and then the grass behind it was still again. It was like the movement of a large trout in a still pool, the creature unseen, just the surface bulging and stirring to mark its passing.

All movement ceased for long minutes at a time.

'He's listening and checking the scent.' Sean explained. She had never expected him to show emotion such as excitement, but his whisper was tight and scratchy.

The movement of the grass tips began again, coming on towards the bait tree, and suddenly her father gave a small breathy gasp, and at the same moment, Sean warned her again. Perhaps he had meant to touch her hip once more, but his fingers closed on her upper thigh instead.

His touch was a shock, made more intense by her first sight of the beast. The lion passed through a gap in the grass, which the lionesses had trampled, and she glimpsed the top of his head, the dense bush of his mane, dark and curling, swaying and rippling to his slow imperial stride, and for an instant she caught the flash of yellow eyes below the mane.

She had never seen any creature so menacing, and yet so majestic. It was the briefest glimpse, before the grass covered him again, but it left her shaken and breathless, and Sean's hand was still on her thigh.

Suddenly, she realized that she was sexually aroused, the tension in her lower belly, the hardening thrust of her nipples against the cotton shirt and the warm flooding of her loins surprised her. She felt an almost irresistible urge to let her thighs relax and fall open under Sean's fingers, even though the folly of it would be monumental. If she had been asked to describe a human being who most offended and angered her, the description would have fitted him perfectly. She knew that if she showed the slightest vulnerability, he would exploit it ruthlessly. 'And I don't even like him,' she told herself desperately. Yet her legs were trembling, he must feel it, and she couldn't move.

Then he took his hand off her leg, but the way he did it was offensive. He did not simply lift it away, he turned it into a caress, drawing his fingers lingeringly over her thigh and hip, a disconcerting sensation for which she was unprepared. She felt her cheeks and her throat turn hot with resentment, but she stared out across the riverbed to that stealthy movement that stopped at last below the bait tree.

The silence drew out while Claudia tried to bring her emotions under control.

'It wasn't him,' she told herself. 'I wasn't reacting to him. He has nothing for me. It was the tension and excitement of the moment, nothing to do with him. He's not the least bit attractive to me. I like sensitivity and subtlety, and he is obvious and overpowering and brutal.'

Across the river, there was an abrupt disturbance in the grass and the sound of a heavy body flopping to earth.

Behind her, she felt Sean shake with soft and silent laughter,

43

and for an incredulous moment, she thought he was laughing at her, then he whispered, 'He's lain down. Can you believe it, he's taking a rest right under the bait. The cocky son-of-a-bitch.'

Sean was thinking about the girl as much as about the lion. The unconcealed antipathy she bore him he returned in full measure, which made it more amusing to tease and plague her. Of course, the lion-hide was always a good place to catch a woman off-balance. He had begun many a memorable affair here. When they were in the hide they were psychologically under his control, like children in a classroom. He was the master and they were conditioned to obey his will, and the tension and nervous excitement made them receptive and compliant, the promise of danger and bloodshed heightened awareness, physical and sexual. It had been fun to find out that this bumptious, spoilt, self-righteous American bitch was no different from any of the others.

She was probably hating herself and him at this moment for that momentary lapse. He smiled thinly as he sat up close behind her. He had judged it with the fine instinct of the gifted philanderer, for it was, of course, a gift. He had read with attention Casanova's memoirs and there the old rogue had described it precisely. When she is receptive, every woman gives out subtle little signs, breathing, flush of skin, change of poise, tiny body movements, even odour, that very few men can even recognize, let alone interpret. It was a gift that only the great lovers possessed. Knowing when to act, and how far to push each stage, that was the trick, he told himself.

From where he sat, he could see her right cheek and the long dark lashes of the eye above, even though she was deliberately keeping her head turned away from him now.

She had bound her jet hair into a thick braid that hung down between her shoulder-blades. So her neck was exposed, an elegant column that supported the small neat head. Her neck and cheek were still flushed with angry arousal beneath skin that was already darkened by the African sun to the tone where she could have modelled for an expensive sun cream in one of the glossy women's magazines.

As he studied her, the flush abated and she regained her composure, but under her thin cotton tee-shirt, the nipple on the one pert, almost girlish, breast that he could see, was in silhouette. It was still standing out, the size and colour of a ripe

44

mulberry, a dark wine colour through the thin material, then it began to shrink and subside; the phenomenon intrigued him and he laughed again soundlessly.

'You've given yourself a blinding hard-on,' he chuckled. 'And you can't even stand the little witch.' He switched his attention from her back to the unseen cat in the grass across the river.

It was almost fully dark before they saw the lion again, there was just a fading memory of the sunset on the western horizon but Sean had positioned the bait and blind so that it back-lit the scene for them. They heard the grass rustle and stir as the lion stood up, and they leaned forward eagerly. Riccardo lifted the buttstock of the rifle to his shoulder and peered into the long tube of the telescopic sight.

Abruptly, the lion reared out of the grass, a great dark, shapeless mass, just visible against the pale sky, and they heard the creak of the chain that held the bait as he swung upon it with all his weight, tearing at the carcass as he began to feed.

'Can you see your sights?' Sean asked Riccardo. The lion was making so much noise that he raised his voice to an almost conversational pitch, but Riccardo did not reply. He was moving the long barrel of the rifle in slow circles, trying desperately to pick up the cross hairs of the sight against the last fading glimmer of the sunset.

'No!' he admitted defeat at last. 'It's too dark.'

Claudia felt a lift of relief that she wouldn't have to witness the slaughter, but Sean said quietly, 'All right, we'll just have to sit it out and try and get a crack at him in the dawn.'

'All night!' Despite his injunctions to silence, Claudia was so startled by the prospect of spending the night in the hide that she protested plaintively.

'You signed on to be tough, didn't you?' Sean smiled at her alarm.

'But, but . . . won't Job bring the truck?' She sounded desperate.

'Not unless he hears a shot.' And she subsided miserably in her chair.

The night was interminable and cold, and the mosquitos came from the stagnant green pool in the riverbed and whined around their heads, ignoring the repellent that Claudia smeared on her exposed skin.

Across the river, the lion fed at intervals, and then rested. A

45

little after midnight, he began to roar, crashing bursts of sound that brought Claudia out of an uncomfortable doze, and made her heart jump against her ribs. The terrible sound ended in a diminishing series of throaty grunts.

'Why does he do that?' Claudia asked breathlessly.

'To let the world know who is boss around here.'

Then the hyena came, shrieking and hooting like a pack of ghouls, gibbering with excitement at the smell of the kill, and the lion drove them off, rushing heavily in the grass, snarling and roaring, but they came edging back as soon as he returned to feed, and they tittered and whooped at him, forming a restless circle around the bait tree.

An hour before dawn, Claudia at last fell into a fitful sleep, hunched down in the chair with her neck twisted at an awkward angle, and she awoke with a start, to find it was light enough to make out the links of the chain that held the buffalo carcass.

In the forest close by, a pair of ground hornbills, grotesque black birds as big as a wild turkey with the same bald red heads, were booming their dawn chorus in a ritual duet. Beside her, Riccardo was stretching and yawning and Sean stood up, rocking the machan.

'What's happened?' Claudia mumbled. 'Where's the lion?'

'He took off an hour ago,' her father told her. 'Long before shooting light.'

'Only one way you are going to get this cat, Capo, and that's with a jack-light, or with a hell of a lot of luck.'

'I'm a lucky guy,' Riccardo grinned and they heard the distant beat of the Toyota's engine growing louder as Job came in to pick them up.

They stayed in camp all that day, catching up on sleep lost the previous night, but when they went into the hide again that evening to wait for the lion, he had disappeared. He did not come to the bait the following night either, and the safari came upon a period of hiatus. Sean and his team worked diligently but fruitlessly to find the lion. There was no report from the scouts whom Sean had placed to watch the elephant crossings on the Chiwewe river which was the northern boundary of Sean's concession. Riccardo Monterro was not interested in hunting lesser plains game, such as sable antelope, or kudu, or eland. These activities would have filled the days of another safari.

Only the two lionesses and their cubs stayed on the banks of the riverbed taking up permanent domicile.

'Courtney's five-star hotel.' Sean complained. 'Gourmet meals delivered daily.'

The pride became so accustomed to their visits, that the lionesses retreated only a hundred yards or so into the forest with a few perfunctory low-key growls and watched with interest as a fresh carcass was hauled into the tree. They barely contained their impatience until the Toyota pulled away, and it was still in full view when they came loping back to inspect the latest offering.

However, Frederick the Great did not return. They saw no sign of his huge distinctive pugmarks around the baits or upon the dirt tracks that Sean patrolled each day, searching the area for forty miles around the camp.

'But why would he just vanish like that?' Riccardo protested.

'Because he is a cat – and who knows how a cat thinks!'

*   *   *

Since that brief but torrid episode in the lion hide, the relationship between Sean and Claudia had altered subtly. Their bickering had become more vindictive and bitter, their overt resentment more intense, and their efforts to discomfort each more spirited.

When she called him a racist, he smiled at her. 'In America that word is dreaded as the ultimate insult that can end a man's political career, or ruin his business or ostracize him from society. You are all so terrified of it, and the blacks know it and exploit it to the full. Even the toughest hard-headed businessman or politician rolls over like a puppy dog and whines if you call him that,' Sean told her gleefully. 'This isn't America, ducky, and here we aren't terrified of that word. Here racism is the same as tribalism, and we are all blatant tribalists, especially the blacks. If you want to experience true dedicated tribalism and racism, then come and live in one of the newly independent African states. If you call your average black politician a racist, he would take it as a compliment, it would be the same as calling him a patriot.'

Her wounded protestations were ample reward for his efforts as he looked for new ways to provoke her.

'Did you know I am a South African?' he asked, and she looked appalled.

'I thought you were a Brit.' He shook his head and smiled in that infuriating way of his.

'I imagine you support your government's sanctions against my country.'

'Of course, every decent person does.'

'Even if it means that a million blacks starve as a direct consequence?' He did not wait for her to reply. 'What about disinvestment of American business from my country, you are all for that too?'

'I campaigned for it on campus,' she told him proudly. 'I never missed a rally or a march.'

'So your plan is to convert a country by withdrawing all your missionaries and burning down the cathedral, that's brilliant!'

'You are twisting it.'

'We should be grateful to you for the success of your efforts, you forced your own citizens to sell our assets back to us at five cents in the dollar. Overnight you created two hundred multi-millionaires in South Africa, and every one of them had a white face. Congratulations and our sincere thanks, ducky.'

But while they argued, they were avidly aware of each other, and that physical contact they had shared lay between them like a poisonous serpent, dangerous, but intriguing.

Claudia had been celibate for almost two years now, ever since she had split from the physician whom she had lived with for a short while until his demands for marriage became intolerable. Celibacy did not suit her affectionate Latin nature, but she was fastidious. She found herself lying awake in her tent at night listening to Sean's voice from the camp-fire as he talked to her father, the soft masculine rumble, just low enough for her to be unable to catch the words. Once she thought she heard her name, and she sat up and strained her hearing, disappointed that she could not hear what he said about her.

Then, when at last he called goodnight to Riccardo and went to his own tent, he had to pass close to hers. She lay rigid in bed, listening to his footsteps and watching the beam of his flashlight through the canvas, preparing an icy dismissal in the most insulting terms, and then experiencing the tiniest prick of disappointment as his footsteps passed on without a check.

On the ninth morning of the safari when they drove out to check the bait on the riverbank, the younger lioness, her eyes now completely healed, was once again violently aggressive,

48

snarling at Sean and mock-charging him from a hundred yards with her tail lashing as soon as he dismounted from the Toyota to inspect the bait. When she backed off and turned to retreat, they saw the pink stain of blood on the soft, pale beige fur beneath her tail.

'Growly Gertie has come into season,' Sean exulted. 'Now we have the one bait that Frederick the Great won't be able to resist. You said you were a lucky guy. Capo, now let's find out just how lucky.'

Sean wanted to get this lion before this extraordinary opportunity passed, there was no time to track down one of the huge buffalo herds along the Chiwewe river for a fresh bait, so Riccardo shot a young kudu bull from a herd of bachelors near the camp. They hung the carcass on the bait tree in the glade where they had last seen the big male lion; this time, low enough for the lionesses to reach it easily; and they climbed into the machan in the early afternoon. Within an hour the lionesses had picked up the scent of fresh blood and came trotting down the dry riverbed, followed by the straggling, squabbling bunch of cubs. While the older lioness fed heartily from the fresh kudu carcass, the younger female ate only lightly and sporadically. In between she prowled restlessly around the area of trampled grass beneath the tree, snarling at her cubs, or rolling on her back, or sitting up to lick at the blood smear beneath her own tail. At intervals, she stood staring into the forest and then held her head low to the ground and let out a long, melancholy moan. It was a sound so full of agonized longing that Claudia felt herself empathizing with the sleek and beautiful creature.

'That's right, Gertie.' Sean whispered behind Claudia's shoulder. 'Call to Big Daddy, tell him what sweets you've got for him here.'

'It's not fair,' Claudia thought fiercely. 'It's not fair to use her like this.'

Suddenly both lionesses leapt up to face into the forest, and the older female snarled softly. Alarmed, the cubs ceased their endless play and huddled behind their dams. Then the young lioness went forward through the grass, slinking and undulating her whole body in a blatantly sexual display, and she emitted a series of low welcoming moans.

'Steady, Capo.' Sean's hand was on Riccardo's arm, preventing him from raising the rifle. 'Take your time.'

49

Then out of the forest came the lion. At first they saw only the tip of his mane above the grass, as he came forward at an eager trot to meet the lioness. She rushed forward shamelessly, and in a trampled clearing they came together.

'Wait, Capo,' Sean whispered. He wanted the girl to watch it.

The lioness brushed her body against the male, back and forth she stroked him with the full length of her silken flanks, and the lion fluffed out his mane, so that he seemed to double in size, responding to her advances, licking her face as she cuddled into the dense dark bush of his mane.

Then deliberately she turned and presented him with her hind quarters, cocking her tail high, sending a spurt of pink-stained urine out under his nose. The lion groaned and curled his upper lip, exposing his great, yellow fangs in a rictus of passion; his back arched reflexively and Claudia wriggled in her seat as the lion stretched out his neck and licked the female under the tail with a long, curling, pink tongue.

The lioness submitted to his caress for a minute, then whirled flirtatiously and, from across the river, they heard her low purrs of invitation. Sean placed his hand lightly on Claudia's thigh. The gesture was concealed from her father by the side of the chair. She made no attempt to pull away.

The lioness turned from the male, ran a few light mincing paces and then flattened her body against the earth, looking back over her shoulder. The lion came to where she lay, moving with a stiff-legged gait, and he covered her body with his own, standing astride her, and as he lowered his haunches over hers, his penis unsheathed from its pouch, glistening pinkly, and the lioness laid her tail forward along her back.

Sean ran the tips of his fingers up to the juncture of Claudia's thighs, and he could feel the springing mattress of her pubic hair through the cloth of her breeches. Her thighs opened slightly under his hand.

The lion humped his back over the female in a series of convulsive, regular spasms, and then he threw back his huge, maned head and roared and the lioness roared with him and he reached down and bit her lightly in the back of the neck, a fond possessive gesture.

For long moments, they were frozen together like that and then the lion leaped off her, and at the same moment, Claudia reached down and placed her hand over Sean's. She took his little finger and twisted it back against the joint so viciously that she almost dislocated it, and agony shot up his arm to the shoulder.

He almost cried out in protest, but Riccardo was sitting close and though his view of his daughter's lower body was obscured by the canvas side of the chair, he would certainly guess at Sean's advances. With an effort, Sean kept silent, and drew his hand back, surreptitiously massaging the damaged finger, and he could see the corner of Claudia's mouth was curled in a vindictive little smile.

Across the river the lioness stood up and shook herself. Then she walked out with a slow satisfied air on to the open river-bank. There she paused and looked back at the lion where he was sitting on his haunches still half hidden in the long grass.

'Get ready, Capo.' Sean was still massaging his finger.

It was five o'clock in the afternoon, and the sun was at a perfect angle, lighting the far bank as though it were a stage. The range was a measured ninety-six yards from the machan to the bait tree. Riccardo Monterro was the finest rifleman that Sean had ever guided on safari. At that range, he could place three bullets through the same hole.

The lioness mewled seductively and the lion stood up and followed her out onto the open riverbank. He stood behind her, broadside on to the machan across the river, lit by the golden sunlight.

'He's a gift from heaven, Capo,' Sean whispered, and tapped Riccardo's shoulder. 'Take him!'

Slowly Riccardo lifted the buttstock of the rifle to his shoulder. It was a .300 Weatherby Magnum. The massive cartridge under the firing-pin was loaded with eighty grains of powder and a 180-grain Nosler partitioned bullet. It would cross the open riverbed at over three thousand feet per second. When it entered living flesh, it would drive a shock wave ahead of it that would turn the internal organs, lungs and heart, to jelly and suck that jelly out of a massive exit hole, blowing them in a red spray over the grass beyond where the animal stood.

'Take him!' Sean said, and Riccardo Monterro looked through the telescopic sight; the lion's body filled most of the magnified field of the lens.

He could see the individual hairs in the dense curling bush of mane, and the detail of each sculptured muscle beneath the skin. One inch behind the lion's shoulder, on the lateral centre line of its body, was a tiny scar on the sleek hide. It was shaped like a horseshoe, a lucky horseshoe, and it made a perfect aiming point. He aligned the cross-hairs of the sight on the scar, and they bounced slightly to the elevated beat of his own heart. He took up the slack in the trigger, feeling the final resistance under his finger before the sear released and the rifle fired.

Beside her father, Claudia sat rigid with horror. The lion turned his head and looked across the riverbed at her. The mating had touched and moved her deeply.

'He's too glorious to die,' she thought, and almost without conscious effort, she opened her mouth and screamed with all the strength of her lungs.

'Run, damn you! Run!'

The result stunned even her. She had not believed a living creature could react so swiftly. From lazy immobility, all three animals exploded into flight. They dissolved into golden blurs of movement.

The oldest lioness disappeared almost instantaneously into the long grass, with all the cubs rushing after her. The younger lioness raced along the edge of the bank. So swift was her run that she did not seem to touch the earth; like a swallow drinking in flight she skimmed the surface, and the lion followed her. For all his bulk and the dark mass of his mane, he moved as lightly as she did, reaching out those massively muscled legs in full stride.

Riccardo Monterro swivelled in his chair, the rifle to his shoulder, staring into the brilliant glass lens, swinging with the cat's run. The lioness swerved into the grass and was gone. The lion followed her but the instant before he disappeared, the report of the Weatherby rifle drove in on their eardrums, painful and deafening, and even in full sunlight, a long tongue of flame flashed out across the riverbed.

The lion stumbled in his run and with a single, loud cough vanished into the grass. In the silence, their ears sang with the memory of gunfire, and they stared out at the empty clearing, subdued and appalled.

'Nice work, ducky!' Sean said softly.

'I'm not sorry,' she said defiantly, and her father reloaded the rifle with a savage movement that sent the empty brass case spinning and sparkling away in the sunlight. He stood up, rocking the flimsy machan and without a glance at his daughter, climbed down the makeshift ladder.

Sean picked up his .577 double rifle and followed him down. They stood at the bottom of the tree and Riccardo unbuttoned the flap of his breast pocket and offered Sean a Havana from his pigskin cigar-case. Neither of them usually smoked during the day, but now Sean accepted one and bit off the tip.

They lit their cigars and smoked for a while in silence. Then Sean said quietly. 'Call your shot, Capo.'

Riccardo was a marksman of such expertise that he could tell precisely where his bullet had gone the moment after he fired it. Now he hesitated, and then said grudgingly. 'That cat was motoring. I was too quick. I didn't lead him enough.'

'Gutshot?' Sean asked.

'Yeah,' Riccardo nodded. 'Gutshot.'

'Shit,' said Sean. 'Shit, and shit again.'

They both looked across at the dense stand of long grass and tangled thorny patches of undergrowth on the far bank.

It was ten minutes before the Toyota arrived, summoned by that single gunshot. Job and Shadrach and Matatu were grinning with expectation, they had hunted six safaris with Riccardo Monterro and they had never known him to miss. They jumped out of the Toyota, peered across the river, and their grins faded slowly, and were replaced by expressions of deepest gloom as Sean said, '*Intumbu!* In the guts!'

The three of them went back to the Toyota and began to prepare for the follow-up in silence.

Sean squinted up at the sun. 'Dark in an hour,' he said. 'We haven't got time to let the wound stiffen.'

'We could leave him until the morning,' Riccardo suggested. 'He'll be sick by then.'

Sean shook his head. 'If he dies in there, the hyena will get him. No trophy. Besides which, we can't leave the poor beggar to suffer all night.'

They fell silent as Claudia climbed down the ladder from the machan. When she reached ground level, she would not look at them, but tossed back the plait of dark hair over her shoulder defiantly and marched across to the Toyota. She climbed into the front seat and folded her arms across her small breasts, staring ahead grimly.

'I'm sorry,' Riccardo said. 'I've known her for twenty-six years. I should have guessed she'd pull one like that.'

'You don't have to come, Capo,' Sean did not answer him directly. 'Stay with Claudia. I'll go across and get the job done. That's what you pay me for.'

It was Riccardo's turn to ignore the remark.

'I'll carry the Rigby,' he said.

'Make sure that you are loaded with soft-nosed bullets,' Sean advised.

'Of course.' They walked side by side to the Toyota, and Riccardo changed the lighter Weatherby for the big Rigby. He opened the breech to check that there were soft-nosed mushrooming bullets in the magazine, then filled the loops on his cartridge belt from a fresh packet.

Sean leaned against the side of the Toyota, and changed the cartridges in his big double rifle for others from the loops on the breast of his bush jacket.

'Poor bloody animal,' he said. Although he was looking at Riccardo, he was speaking to Claudia. 'It would have been a good clean kill, but now he's in the grass there, still alive with half his guts shot away. It's the most painful wound there is.' He saw the girl wince and her cheek pale. She would not look at him.

'We'll be lucky if someone doesn't get killed,' Sean went on with ghoulish relish. 'It will probably be Matatu. He has to go ahead on the spoor, and the little beggar always refuses to run. If it's anybody, it will be Matatu that gets it today.'

Despite herself, Claudia glanced piteously at the little Ndorobo.

'Cut it out, Sean,' Riccardo ordered. 'She knows how stupid she has been.'

'Does she?' Sean asked. 'I wonder.' He snapped the rifle closed. 'Okay, Capo, wear your leather jacket. If the lion gets you down, it may protect you a little, not much, but a little.'

The three blacks were waiting on the edge of the bank. Job carried the eight-bore shotgun loaded with buckshot, but the other two were unarmed. It took a peculiar kind of courage to follow a wounded lion into thick cover without carrying a weapon.

Even in her agitation, Claudia noticed the trust with which they looked at Sean Courtney. She sensed that they had shared mortal danger so many times before that a peculiar bond united

54

their small exclusive group. The four of them were closer than brothers, or lovers, and she felt a sting of envy. She had never been that close to another human being in her life.

In turn Sean touched each of them on the shoulder, a light unsentimental gesture of affirmation, and then he spoke softly to Job. A shadow passed over the Matabele's handsome features, and for a moment it seemed that he might protest, but then he nodded acceptance and crossed to the Toyota, standing guard beside Claudia with the shotgun.

Sean held the double-barrelled rifle across the crook of his arm as he combed his thick glossy hair back from his forehead with his fingers and then bound it up out of his eyes with a strip of plaited leather around his forehead.

Even though she loathed him, she found herself admiring the heroic figure he cut as he made these last preparations to face the terrible danger and gruesome death that she had, in a large measure, prepared for him. The sleeves had been cut out of his bush jacket and he wore short, khaki pants, so that his limbs were bare and tanned. He was even taller than her father, but his waist was slimmer and his shoulders wider, and he carried the squat heavy rifle easily in one hand.

He glanced across at her, and his gaze was level and green and contemptuous. She was possessed suddenly, by a premonition of impending disaster, and she wanted to plead with him not to cross the river, but before she could speak he had turned away.

'Ready, Capo?' he asked, and Riccardo nodded, holding the Rigby at high port across his chest. His expression was solemn. 'All right, let's move out.' Sean nodded at Matatu and the little man led them down the bank.

In the riverbed, they fell into hunting formation with the tracker leading. Sean followed close behind him watching the reed bed ahead. Riccardo came next, leaving a gap of ten paces between them to reduce the confusion in a close-quarter *mêlée*, and Shadrach followed him in the drag position.

As they crossed, they filled their pockets with smooth water-worn pebbles from the riverbed. Below the far bank, they paused to listen, then Sean passed Matatu and went up first. He stood alone in the trampled clearing below the bait tree for almost five minutes, listening and staring intently into the tall grass beyond.

Then he began to lob pebbles into the grass, systematically working the area where the lion had disappeared. The pebbles clattered against other stones or bounced off the stems of shrubs, but there was no challenging growl. Sean whistled softly and the others scrambled up the bank and fell into their positions, and Sean nodded at Matatu.

They went forward slowly. There are many grave-stones in Africa marking the resting places of men who hurried after a wounded lion. Matatu concentrated all his attention on the ground at his feet. He never looked up at the wall of grass ahead. He placed his complete trust in Sean. At the edge of the grass, he hissed softly and with his hand behind his back made a secretive gesture.

'Blood,' Sean told Riccardo softly without looking back at him. 'And belly hair. You were right, Capo. It's a gutshot.'

He could see the wet gleam of blood on the stems of the grass.

'*Akwendi!*' he told Matatu, and drew breath like a diver poised on a cliff above a deep and icy pool. He held that breath as he stepped forward and the tall grass closed around him, limiting his vision like the sinister and murky waters of the pool.

*   *   *

The impact of the bullet had been a mighty blow in the lion's flank, that slewed him round and numbed his entire body behind his rib-cage.

Then the grass closed about him as he raced forward, and immediately he felt secure and confident. Within twenty strides he stopped and stood looking back over his shoulder, listening and drawing the scent into his flared nostrils, lashing his tail from side to side.

There was no sensation of pain, just a numbness and weight in his entrails as though he had swallowed an ironstone boulder. He smelled his own blood, and turned to sniff at his side. The exit wound the bullet had left was the size of an egg cup and from it oozed blood that was almost tarry black. Mingled with the blood, were the liquid contents of his own bowels. They made a tiny pattering sound as they dribbled onto the dry earth beneath him. He licked at the wound and blood glutted his jaws.

Then he lifted his head and listened again. He heard human voices in the distance, beyond the river and he growled softly, feeling his anger begin to mount, associating the blood and heaviness in his belly with the presence of man.

Then the lioness called him, a low gasping moan, and he turned and followed her. He did not run now for the weight in his belly hampered him and his back legs felt numb and heavy. The lioness was waiting for him a little farther on. Eagerly she rubbed herself against him, and then tried to lead him away, trotting off ahead of him. He moved heavily after her, stopping to listen and lick the running wound, and she turned back impatiently and moaned at him and nuzzled his face, sniffing and licking at his wound, puzzled and distressed by his behaviour.

His legs were heavy as tree-trunks now, and ahead of him was a thicket of wild ebony. He turned aside and pushed his way into the dense and tangled undergrowth, and he sighed as he lowered his body, curling the black tuft of his tail under him as he lay down.

The lioness fretted and worried at the edge of the thicket, calling to him with small mewling entreaties. Then when he did not respond, she followed him into the thicket and lay down beside him. She licked at his wound and the lion closed his eyes, and began to pant softly as the pain began.

The pain swelled in his body becoming a vast, suffocating weight that grew and grew within him, seeming to distend his belly until it was on the point of bursting. The lion groaned softly and bit at his own flank, trying to kill this thing within him, this living agony that was feeding on his entrails.

The lioness attempted to distract him. She was confused and worried, and she wriggled around and pressed her hindquarters into his face, offering him her swollen and weeping genitalia, but the lion closed his eyes and turned his head away, and each breath rasped like a wood saw in his throat.

Then he heard voices again, the whispered voices of men, and he raised his head and his eyes burned yellow and fierce as he found a focus for his suffering, and hatred grew out of the agony of his belly, and his rage was dark and all-engulfing.

Something crashed into the branches of the wild ebony thicket above his head and he growled, a rattling exhalation of air through his tortured throat.

*   *   *

They went forward slowly into the grass, and it reached above their heads, and enclosed them so closely that they could see no more than two or three paces ahead.

57

The lion's blood was painted on the grass and the stems were pushed over by the passage of his body so the trail was easy to follow. The blood on the grass gave Sean and Matatu the exact height of the wound, and the faeces mixed with the blood told them that the bowels had been penetrated. It was a mortal wound, but death would be slow and agonizing.

Within twenty yards of entering the grass, Matatu paused, and indicated the puddle of dark, tarry blood.

'He stopped here,' he whispered, and Sean nodded.

'He won't have gone far,' Sean guessed. 'He's waiting for us, Matatu, and when he comes, you run back behind me. Do you hear me?'

Matatu grinned at him. They both knew he would not obey. Matatu had never run, he would stand the charge as he always did.

'All right, you stupid little bugger.' Sean was tense. 'Get on with it.'

'Stupid little bugger,' Matatu repeated happily. He knew that Sean only called him that when particularly proud of him, or pleased with him.

They moved along the blood spoor, pausing every three or four paces while Sean lobbed pebbles into the grass ahead of them, and when there was no response, moving forward again cautiously.

Behind him, Sean could hear the click, click of the safety-catch on the Rigby. Riccardo was snapping it on and off as they advanced, a nervous gesture that betrayed his agitation. Although the sound irritated him, Sean felt a stir of admiration for the man. This was probably one of the most dangerous activities in which a man could engage. They don't come much worse than a gut-shot lion in close cover. This was Sean's job, but for Riccardo, it was a once in a lifetime test, and he had not failed it yet.

Sean tossed another pebble into the grass ahead, and listened to it rattle on the branch of a low tree.

As they went on, Sean thought about fear. For some men, fear was a crippling and destroying emotion, but for those like Sean, it was an addiction. He loved the sensation of fear, it was like a drug flowing through his veins, heightening all his senses, so he could feel the chequering on the polished walnut stock of the rifle under his fingers and the brush of each individual blade of grass against his bare legs; his vision was so enhanced that he

58

saw it all through a crystal lens that magnified and dramatized each image, he could taste the very air he breathed and smell the crushed grass under his feet and the blood of the lion they were following. He was vividly, vibrantly alive, and he gave himself up to fear, as an addict would to a syringeful of heroin.

He tossed another pebble into the ebony thicket that stood like an island in the sea of grass just ahead of them, and it fell through the branches, rattling and crackling, and the lion growled from the depths of the thicket.

The fear of death was so pleasurable as to be almost unbearable, an emotional orgasm, stronger than any woman had ever given him, and Sean slid the safety-catch off the rifle and said, 'He's coming, Matatu. Run!' And exultation was in his voice, and time slowed down, another phenomenon produced by fear.

From the corner of his eye, he saw Riccardo Monterro step up beside him, taking his place in the firing line, and he knew what it was costing him.

'Good man!' he said loudly, and at the sound of his voice, the branches of the ebony thicket shook, as a heavy body rushed through them and there was a terrifying, growling, grunting uproar, coming straight at them.

Matatu stood perfectly still, like a guardsman on parade. Matatu had never run. Sean stepped up on one side of him and Riccardo, on the other, and they lifted their rifles and aimed into the wall of grass as that thing rushed in upon them, flattening the tall stems with its charge, roaring now, blasts of sound that were like a physical assault on their senses.

The grass opened in their faces and a huge, tawny body hurled itself upon them.

They fired together and the crash of gunfire drowned the enraged roaring. Sean fired the second barrel, the two shots sounding as one, and the huge 750-grain bullet tore into the charging animal, stopping it as though it had run into a cliff. Riccardo was working the bolt of the Rigby and a rolling echo of gunfire filled all the air about them.

The dead animal fell at their feet, and they stood with rifles raised, staring down at the bleeding carcass, dazed by the swiftness and the savagery and the beat of gunfire in their heads.

In the silence, Shadrach stepped forward. Like Matatu he had

59

stood his ground, and now he stooped to the carcass, and then jerked back and shouted aloud what they had not yet fully realized.

'It's not the lion!'

As he said it, the lion charged. He came straight at them out of the thicket as his mate had done, but even more swiftly, driven by the agony in his belly and the black rage that filled him. He came grunting like a locomotive at full throttle, and they were unprepared, their rifles unloaded, bunched up too closely around the carcass of the lioness, and Shadrach was between them and the lion.

The lion came bursting out of the tall grass in full charge and it seized Shadrach in its jaws, biting into his hip, and the momentum of its charge carried it into the tight knot of men standing close up behind Shadrach.

It knocked them all off their feet, Sean went over backwards, crashing into the earth on his shoulder-blades and the back of his neck with stunning force. He was holding the rifle in front of his chest, instinctively trying to protect it from damage as he went down, and the engraved barrels slammed into his sternum as he hit the earth. Pain shot through his chest but he held on to the weapon and rolled on to his side.

Ten feet away the lion was savaging Shadrach. It had him pinned under its massive paws as it mauled his hip and upper leg.

'Thank God, it's not a leopard,' Sean thought as he broke open the rifle to reload. A leopard will not fix on one man if it attacks a group of hunters. It will bound from one to the other, in rapid succession, maiming and killing all of them with dazzling speed. Furthermore a leopard's main prey is the baboon, so it knows precisely how to despatch a primate. It goes instinctively for the head, taking off the scalp and top of the skull, while its back legs kick down the belly, stripping out the intestines with hooked yellow claws, very quickly, very efficiently.

'Thank God, it's not a leopard.' The great beast was fixed on Shadrach, pinning him with its claws, worrying the leg, and with each growl a scarlet spray of blood puffed out of its jaws. The Matabele gunbearer was screaming and beating ineffectually at the huge maned head with both clenched fists.

Sean saw Riccardo in the grass beyond them scrambling to his knees, crawling towards where the Rigby rifle had been thrown.

60

'Don't shoot, Capo,' Sean yelled at him. In a *mêlée* like this one, an inexperienced man with a loaded rifle was many times more dangerous than the attacking animal. The bullets of the Rigby would crack through the lion's body and smash into anybody beyond.

Sean had two spare cartridges held between the fingers of his left hand. It was the old hunter's trick for the fast reload, and he slid the two cartridges into the empty breeches and snapped the action shut.

The lion was chewing on Shadrach's lower body. Sean could hear the bone crunch and crackle like dry toast under those dreadful fangs. His nostrils were full of the fetid, gamey smell of the lion, of dust and the reek of blood of man and beast.

Beyond them he saw Riccardo had the rifle. He was on his knees, his face ashen with shock, cramming cartridges into the breech of the Rigby.

'Don't shoot!' Sean yelled again. The lion was directly between them. A bullet that hit the animal would come straight on into him.

It takes a special technique to shoot an attacking animal off a prostrate man without killing them both. It was deadly dangerous to run up to them and shoot down into the animal's body with the man lying under it.

Sean made no effort to rise to his feet. He rolled like a log, cushioning the rifle, flipping over three times, the manoeuvre that was second nature from his Scouts' training. Now he was lying alongside the lion, almost touching it, and he thrust the rifle into its lower ribs, aiming upwards, and he fired. It only needed one of those 750-grain bullets.

The shot lifted the lion clear of Shadrach's body, tossing it lightly aside, and the bullet tore out of its back between the shoulders, and went straight on up into the sky.

Sean dropped the rifle and knelt over Shadrach, taking him in his arms, and looked down on the leg. The fangs had inflicted penetrating stiletto wounds. From hip to knee the black flesh was riddled.

'Matatu!' Sean snapped. 'In the Toyota. The medicine box. Get it.' And the tracker vanished into the grass.

Riccardo crawled to Sean's side and looked at the leg.

'Sweet Mother Mary,' he said softly. 'It's the femoral.' Bright arterial blood was pumping up in a regular jet out of the deepest wound, and Sean reached into it, thrusting his fingers into the hot flesh.

He got a grip on the slippery, rubbery, pulsing worm with thumb and forefinger and pinched with all his strength.

'Hurry, Matatu! Run, you little bugger, run!' he bellowed.

It was less than three hundred yards to the Toyota, and Matatu ran like a frightened fawn. He was back within minutes. Job was with him carrying the white chest with the red cross on its lid, and he opened it.

'In the instrument roll,' Sean told Job brusquely. 'Haemostats.'

Job passed him the stainless-steel clamps, and Sean fastened them on the ruptured artery and taped them against the thigh. His hands were wet and bright with blood, but he and Job had done this work fifty times during the bush war, and his movements were swift and confident.

'Rig up a drip set,' he ordered Job. 'We'll give him a bag of Ringers lactate to start with. Rig it.'

As he spoke he was screwing the nozzle on a tube of Betadyne and now he slid the nozzle as deeply as it would go into one of the puncture wounds in Shadrach's thigh and squeezed the thick iodine paste into it until it forced itself out of the mouth of the wound like tobacco-yellow toothpaste. Shadrach lay without protest or any sign of pain, watching them as they worked, replying to Job in monosyllables when he spoke to him in Sindebele.

'Drip set is ready,' Job said.

Without a word, Sean took the canula out of his hands. Shadrach was his man, his responsibility. He would allow no one else to do this, not even Job. He twisted Shadrach's arm, exposing the inside of the elbow and worked up a vein with a skilled milking motion, and he hit it with the needle at the first attempt, and nodded to Job to let the plasma flow.

'Hey, Shadrach!' Sean's grin was remarkably convincing as he laid a blood-smeared palm briefly against the Matabele's cheek. 'I think you poisoned that old lion good. He eats your leg and he's dead – poof! Like that!' Shadrach chuckled. It amazed Riccardo to hear it, even though he had fought and worked with tough men before. 'Give Shadrach one of your cigars, Capo,' Sean suggested, and he began to strap the leg with clean white tape from the chest to stop the residual bleeding.

Once he had strapped the leg, he went over the rest of Shadrach's body quickly. He smeared Betadyne into all the rents and tears left by the lion's claws.

'We can't afford to overlook the merest scratch,' he grunted. 'That old lion has been feeding on putrid carcasses. His teeth and mouth are a reeking pit of infection, and there is rotten meat packed in the grooves of his claws. Gangrene kills most of the victims of a mauling.'

Still not satisfied, Sean injected a full ampoule of penicillin into the transfusion bag. That would swamp the body with antibiotic. Sean nodded and stood up. It had taken him less than thirty minutes, and studying the bandages and the drip set that Job was holding over Shadrach's supine form, Riccardo doubted that a trained doctor could have worked more swiftly or efficiently.

'I'm going to fetch the Toyota,' Sean told them. 'But I'll have to bring it around by way of the ford. That will take a little time, it will be dark by the time I get back.' He could have sent Job to fetch the truck, but he wanted to get the girl to himself. 'There are spare blankets in the chest, keep him wrapped and warm.' He looked down at Shadrach. 'Little scratch like that. I want you back at work pretty damn quick, otherwise I'll dock it off your wages.'

He picked up the .577 and he strode back through the grass to the riverbank. As he trudged through the sandy water-course, his anger at last came upon him, more powerful for being so long delayed.

Claudia was sitting alone in the front of the Toyota as he came up the bank. She looked forlorn and abandoned, but he felt no twinge of pity. She stared aghast at his blood-caked hands.

Sean placed the .577 in the gun-rack without looking at her, and then spilled water from the jerry can over his hands and scrubbed them together, washing off most of the blood. He climbed into the driver's seat and started the Toyota, swung it in a tight circle and sent it back along the track that followed the river downstream.

'Aren't you going to tell me what happened?' Claudia asked at last. She had meant to sound unrepentant and full of bravado, but it came out in a small subdued voice.

'All right,' Sean agreed. 'I'll tell you. Instead of a quick merciful kill there was total chaos and confusion. The lioness charged us first. We shot her by mistake in the long grass. Not that we would have had much option anyway. She was coming all the way.' Sean switched on the headlights, for the sun was gone and the forest darkening. 'Okay, so now the lioness is dead. Her cubs are still unweaned, they are goners, all three of them. They'll starve to death inside a week.'

'Oh no!' Claudia whispered.

'Then the lion charged after his mate. He caught us all ends up. We weren't ready for him, and he got Shadrach down. He almost chewed his leg off. The bone is shattered from hip to knee. He may lose the whole leg, I don't know, perhaps he'll get lucky and just end up with a permanent limp. Anyway you look at it, he's not going to be a tracker any more. I'll find him a job as a skinner or camp servant, but he's a Matabele warrior and menial work is going to break his heart.'

'I'm so sorry.'

'You are sorry?' Sean asked. His voice low and furious. 'Shadrach is my friend and my companion. He has saved my life more times than I can count and I've done the same for him. We have fought a war together, we have slept under the same blanket, eaten from the same plate, trekked ten thousand miles together in the heat and the dust and the rain. He is more than a friend. I have two brothers, same mother and father, but Shadrach means more to me than either of them. Now you tell me you're sorry. Well, thanks a lot, ducky. That's a great comfort.'

'You have every right to be angry. I understand!'

'You understand?' he asked. 'You understand nothing. You are an arrogant ignoramus from a different hemisphere. You are a citizen of the land of the quick fix, and you come and try your simplistic naïve solutions here in Africa. You try to save a single animal from his destiny, and you end up by killing a female and sending her three cubs to lingering death and condemning one of the finest men you'll ever meet to the life of a cripple.'

'What more can I say?' she asked. 'I was wrong.'

'At this late hour your new-found humility is most touching.' His low voice lashed her. 'Sure, you were wrong. Just as you and your people are wrong to try and starve an African nation of thirty million souls into acceptance of another one of your naïve solutions. When the damage you have inflicted is beyond repair, will you again say "I'm sorry, I was wrong," and walk away and leave my land and my people to bleed and suffer?'

'What can I do?'

64

'We have thirty days of safari remaining,' he said bitterly. 'I want you to keep out of my hair for that time. The only reason I don't cancel the show right now, and send you packing back to your Eskimos and your human rights, is that I just happen to think your father is a pretty fine man. From now on, you are under sufferance. Just one more peep out of you and you are on the next plane back to Anchorage. Do I make myself clear?'

'Abundantly.' And there was a trace of spirit in her tone once more. Neither of them spoke again during the rough ride down to the ford and back up the far bank to the glade in which the bait tree stood.

By that time Job and Matatu had a fire going. The glow of the flames guided Sean to where Shadrach lay, and he climbed out of the Toyota and went to him immediately.

'How is the pain?' He squatted beside him.

'It is a little thing,' Shadrach replied, but Sean saw the lie in the grey tone of his skin and the sunken eyeballs, and he filled a disposable syringe from a glass ampoule of morphine. He waited for the drug to take effect before they lifted Shadrach between them and laid him in the back of the truck.

Job and Matatu had skinned out both lions while they waited, and they loaded the bundle of green salted skins onto the bonnet where it would cool in the night wind.

'It's a hell of a lion,' Sean told Riccardo. 'You've got yourself a magnificent trophy!'

Riccardo shook his head and said, 'Let's get Shadrach back to camp.'

Sean drove with care, rolling the truck gently over the rougher spots, trying to protect Shadrach from the worst jolting.

Claudia insisted on sitting in the back with Shadrach, cushioning his head on her lap. Riccardo sat up in front with Sean and he asked quietly, 'What happens now?'

'I'll radio Harare as soon as we get into camp. They will have a private ambulance at the airport to meet him. I'll be gone a couple of days. I'll see Shadrach well taken care of and, of course, I'll have to put in a report to the government game department and try and square it.'

'I hadn't gotten around to thinking about that,' Riccardo said. 'We killed a lioness with cubs and had a man mauled. What will the government do?'

Sean shrugged in the darkness. 'There is a better than even

chance they'll pull my licence and take the concession away from me.'

'Hell, Sean. I didn't realize. Is there anything I can do?'

'Not a thing, Capo, but thanks for the offer. You are out of it. It's between me and the department.'

'I could take full blame for the lioness, say I shot her.'

'No good.' Sean shook his head. 'No blame on the clients. That's departmental doctrine. Whatever you do, I am fully responsible.'

'If they pull your licence . . .' Riccardo hesitated, and Sean shook his head again.

'No, Capo, they won't cancel the safari. That's also departmental doctrine. Finish the safari. Don't offend the paying client. Government needs the hard currency you bring. Only after you have left, they'll bring out the axe for me. You are out of it. I'll be back in two days, and we'll hunt that big elephant together. You don't have to worry.'

'You make me sound like a selfish bastard. I'm worrying about you and your licence, not about enjoying myself.'

'We'll both enjoy ourselves, Capo. After all, if I do lose my licence, it will be the last time that you and I ever hunt together, Capo.'

Claudia could overhear the conversation from where she sat in the back of the truck and she knew why her father did not reply. He knew that it was his last hunt, licence or no licence. Claudia had taken an emotional battering during the last few hours, and thinking about Papa now, she felt the tears well up and scald her eyelids. She fought them back and then it was no longer worth the effort and she wept for all of them, for her father and the lioness and the cubs, for that beautiful male lion, and for Shadrach and his shattered leg.

One of her tears fell on to Shadrach's upturned face, and he stared up at her in perturbation. She wiped the droplet from his cheek with her thumb and her voice was thick and muffled with grief as she whispered to him, 'It's going to be all right, Shadrach.' Even she realized what a crass and fatuous lie that was.

*   *   *

Sean had a scheduled radio contact with his office in Harare at ten o'clock every evening. The journey home was so slow that they reached camp with only minutes to rig the aerial and connect the radio to the Toyota's twelve-volt battery before the schedule.

The contact was good; one of the reasons for the late schedule was the better radio reception in the cool of the evening. Reema's voice with its Gujurati intonation came through clearly. She was a pretty Hindu girl who ran Sean's Harare office with ruthless efficiency.

'We have a casevac.' Sean used the terminology of the bush war for casualty evacuation. 'I want an ambulance standing by to meet me.'

'Okay fine, Sean.'

'Set up a person-to-person telephone call with my brother, Garrick, in Johannesburg for ten a.m. tomorrow.'

'Will do, Sean.'

'Make an appointment for me to see the director of the game department tomorrow afternoon.'

'Director is in New York for the Wildlife Conference, Sean. The deputy director is in charge.'

Sean switched off the hand microphone while he swore bitterly, he had forgotten about the Wildlife Conference. Then he pressed the transmit button again.

'Okay, Reema my love, get me an appointment with Geoffrey Manguza then.'

'Sounds serious, Sean.'

'We just invented the word.'

'What is your ETA? I'll have to file an emergency flight plan for you.'

The security authority was always so jittery about South African hot pursuit of terrorists into Zimbabwe or pre-emptive South African raids on terrorist facilities in Harare itself that they usually required flight plans to be filed forty-eight hours in advance.

'Take off here in fifty minutes. ETA Harare 2300 hours. Pilot and two pax,' Sean told her.

It was half an hour's drive from the camp to the airstrip. Riccardo and Claudia were in the Toyota when they drove out.

Sean took the back seats out of the Beechcraft and placed a mattress on the floor for Shadrach. By this time, Shadrach was feverish and restive. His temperature was 101 and the glands in his groin, hard and lumpy as walnuts. Sean didn't want to look under the dressings on the leg, afraid of what he might find, but one of the minor claw wounds on Shadrach's belly was definitely infected already, weeping watery pus and emitting the first faint odour of putrescence.

Sean administered another dose of penicillin through the canula of the drip set and then he and Job and two of the camp skinners very gently lifted Shadrach into the aircraft and settled him on the mattress.

Shadrach's wife was a sturdy Matabele woman with an infant strapped to her back with a length of trade cloth. They loaded her considerable baggage and then she clambered up and sat beside Shadrach on the mattress, placed the infant on her lap, opened her blouse and gave the child her milk-engorged breast to suckle. The aircraft's empty luggage compartments Job filled with sacks of dried game meat, a valuable commodity in Africa. Then Job drove the Toyota to the far end of the runway to give Sean the headlights for take-off.

'Job will look after you while I am away, Capo. Why don't you take the shotgun and go for dove and sand grouse down at the pools? Best wing shooting you'll ever have, better than white winged dove in Mexico,' Sean suggested.

'Don't worry about us. We'll be just fine.'

'I'll be back as soon as I possibly can. Tukutela won't be crossing before the new moon. I'll be back before then. It's a promise, Capo.'

Sean held out his hand and as Riccardo took it, he said, 'You did good work with the lions, Capo, but then you were never short of bottom.'

'What kind of limey word is that?' Riccardo asked. "Bottom"?'

'How about a good Yankee word then? "Cojones"?'

'That will do,' Riccardo grinned at him.

Claudia was standing beside her father and now she smiled hesitantly, almost shyly, and took a step forward as if to offer her hand.

She had released her hair from its plait and brushed it out into a dense, dark mane around her head. Her expression was soft and her eyes big and dark and lustrous. In the Toyota headlights her classical Latin features went beyond the merely handsome, and Sean realized for the first time that she was truly beautiful. Despite her beauty and her penitent attitude, he kept his own expression cold and forbidding, nodded at her curtly, ignored the tentative offer to shake his hand, climbed up onto the wing of the Beechcraft and ducked into the cockpit.

Sean had cut the airstrip out of the brush himself and levelled it by dragging a bundle of old truck tyres up and down it behind the Toyota. It was narrow, rough and short, with a gradient falling towards the river. He lined up with the Beechcraft's tail-plane backed into the bushes, and stood on the brakes facing down the slope. He aimed at the lights of the Toyota at the far end of the strip while he ran up to full power on both engines and then let the brakes off. Just short of the trees at the end of the strip he pulled on the flaps and bounced the Beechcraft into the air. As always he crossed himself blasphemously with mock relief as he cleared the tree-tops and turned on course for Harare.

During the flight, he tried to plan his strategy. The director of the game department was an old friend, and Sean had successfully dealt with him in equally serious circumstances. However the deputy, Geoffrey Manguza, was a horse of literally another colour. The director was one of the few white civil servants still in charge of a department of government. Manguza would succeed him soon, the first black head of the game department.

He and Sean had fought on opposite sides during the bush war, and Manguza had been an astute guerrilla leader and political commissar. The rumour was that he did not like the safari concession owners, most of whom were white. The concept of private exploitation of State assets offended his Marxist principles, and he had shot too many white men during the war to have any great deal of liking or respect for them.

It was going to be a difficult meeting, Sean sighed.

Reema was waiting for him as he taxied in. As a modern Indian woman, she had abandoned the sari in favour of a neat slacks suit. She was not so modern, however, that she wished to choose her own husband. Her father and her uncles were working on that at the moment, and had already come up with a likely candidate in Canada. A professor of Oriental religions at Toronto University. Sean hated them for it. Reema was an ornament to Courtney Safaris, and he knew that he would never be able to replace her.

She had the ambulance waiting on the tarmac beside the light aircraft hangars. Regularly, Reema bribed the guards on the main gate with dried game meat from the concession. In Africa, meat or the promise of meat opens all gates.

They followed the ambulance to the hospital in the Kombi. While Sean sat in the passenger seat glancing through the most urgent mail she had brought for his attention, Reema recited a list of the important developments during his absence.

'Carter, the surgeon from Atlanta, cancelled . . .' That was a twenty-one-day safari, and Sean glanced up sharply, but Reema soothed him. 'I phoned the German soap manufacturer in Munich, Herr Buchner, the one we turned down in December. He jumped at it. So we are full, back to back, for the rest of the season.'

'How about my brother?' Sean interrupted. He didn't tell her that it was touch and go that there was going to be an end to the season.

'Your brother is expecting your call and as at six o'clock this morning the telephone was still working.' In Zimbabwe that was something that couldn't be taken for granted.

At the hospital, there were at least fifty seriously ill patients awaiting admission ahead of them. The long benches were full of huddled, miserable humanity and the stretchers were blocking the aisles and doorways. The admission clerks were in no great hurry and waved Shadrach's stretcher to a far corner.

'Leave it to me,' said Reema, and she took the senior admissions clerk by the elbow and led him aside with an angelic smile, talking to him sweetly.

Five minutes later, Shadrach's admission papers were processed and he was being examined by an East German doctor.

'How much did that cost?' Sean asked.

'Cheap,' Reema answered. 'A bag of dried meat.'

Sean had picked up sufficient of the German language from his safari clients to be able to discuss Shadrach's case with the doctor. The man was reassuring. Sean said goodbye to Shadrach.

'Reema has your money. She will come to see you each day. If you need anything tell her.'

'I will be with you in spirit when you hunt Tukutela,' Shadrach said softly, and Sean had to clear his throat before he could answer.

'We will hunt many more elephant together, old friend.' And he walked away quickly.

The next morning when at last he got through to Johannesburg, the telephone line was crackling with static.

'Mr Garrick Courtney is in a board meeting,' the girl on the switchboard at Centaine House, the Courtney Group head-quarters, told him. 'But he gave orders to put your call through directly.'

In his mind's eye, Sean saw once again the boardroom, panelled in figured walnut, the huge Pierneef canvases framed by the elaborate panels, and his brother, Garry, sitting at the head of the long table, beneath the crystal chandelier that his grand-mother had imported from Murano in Italy, in the chairman's high-backed throne.

'Sean!' Garry's voice cut through the static, bold and assured. How he had changed from the puny little runt who used to pee his bed.

The job could have been Sean's if he had wanted it and had been prepared to work for it. Sean was the eldest son, but he did not want the job. Still he always experienced a twinge of resentment when he thought of Garry's Rolls and Lear jet and holiday home in the south of France.

'Hello Garry. How's it going?'

'All well here,' Garry told him. 'What's the problem?' It was typical of their relationship that any contact meant there was a problem to solve.

'I might need to put a bit of honey with the cheese,' Sean told him diplomatically. It was their private code for money to Switzerland, and Garry would understand that Sean would be bribing somebody for something. It happened often enough.

'Okay, Sean. Just give me the amount and the account num-ber.' Garry was Sean's partner in the safari company, and held forty per cent of the shares.

'Thanks, Garry, I'll call you some time tomorrow. How's the rest of the family?' They chatted for a few minutes longer, and when he hung up Reema came through from the outer office.

'I managed to get through to the game department at last.' Reema had been trying all morning. 'Comrade Manguza will see you at four-thirty this afternoon.'

Geoffrey Manguza was a tall Shona with a very black com-plexion and close-cropped hair. He wore silver-framed eye glasses, and a dark blue suit. However, his neck-tie was Hermès, Sean recognized the horse carriage logo, and his wristwatch was a Patek Philippe with a black crocodile-skin strap. They were not your run-of-the-mill Marxist accessories and Sean found that encouraging. However, the deputy director did not rise from behind his desk to welcome him.

'Colonel Courtney,' he greeted him unsmilingly, using Sean's previous rank to let him know that he knew that Sean had commanded the Ballantyne Scouts, one of the elite Rhodesian groups, after Ballantyne, the founder of the regiment, had been killed in action. It was also a reminder that they had been enemies, and might still be so.

'I prefer plain mister.' Sean smiled engagingly. 'That other business is behind us now, Comrade Manguza.'

The deputy director inclined his head, neither agreeing nor disagreeing. 'What can I do for you?'

'Unfortunately, I have to report an unintentional transgression of the game regulations . . .' And Geoffrey Manguza's expression hardened, and remained like that while Sean described the accidental shooting of the lioness and Shadrach's subsequent mauling. When Sean finished by submitting the written report that Reema had typed for him, Geoffrey Manguza let the document lie untouched on his desk top while he asked a few pertinent and unsympathetic questions.

'You do realize, Colonel Courtney,' he used the rank again deliberately, 'that I am obliged to take a most serious view of this entire business. It seems to me that there has been negligence and serious disregard for the safety of your clients and your own staff. Zimbabwe is no longer a colony, and you cannot treat our people the way you did before.'

'Before you make your recommendation to the director, I would like to clarify a few points for you,' Sean told him.

'You are free to speak, Colonel.'

'It's almost five o'clock now.' Sean checked his watch. 'Won't you allow me to buy you a drink at the golf club, and we can discuss it in more relaxed surroundings?'

Manguza's expression was inscrutable but after a few moments' thought he nodded. 'As you wish. I have a few small matters to attend to before I leave here, but I will meet you at the club in half an hour.'

He kept Sean sitting on the veranda of the golf club for forty minutes before he put in an appearance. It had once been the Royal Salisbury Golf Club. However, the first two words had been dropped from the title lest they perpetuate the colonial past. Nevertheless, the first remark Geoffrey Manguza made

72

after he had taken the chair opposite Sean and ordered a gin and tonic was, 'Strange isn't it, a few years ago, the only way a black man could have got in here was as a waiter, and now I am on the committee and my handicap is five.' Sean let it pass, and changed the subject to that of rhino poaching across the border with Zambia. Manguza made no effort to pursue that topic. He watched Sean through the silver-rimmed spectacles and as soon as he stopped speaking, cut in immediately.

'You wished to clarify a few points for me,' he said. 'We are both busy men, Colonel.'

This directness was disconcerting. Sean was preparing for a typically round-about African approach, but he adapted his pitch.

'First of all, Mr Manguza, I wanted to tell you what a high price I and my associates place on the Chiwewe concession.' Sean used the word 'price' deliberately. 'I telephoned them this morning and explained this unfortunate incident and they are anxious to have it resolved at any price.' Again he used the word, and paused significantly.

There was a certain etiquette to be observed in negotiations such as these. To the western mind it was bribery, but in Africa it was simply the Dash System, a universal and acceptable means of getting things done. Government might put up posters in all public buildings depicting a booted foot crushing a venomous serpent under the slogan 'Stamp out Corruption' but nobody took that very seriously. In fact, in a bizarre fashion, the posters themselves constituted official recognition of the practice.

At this stage, Geoffrey Manguza should have agreed that recompense was due, or given some other indication of his willingness to listen to reason. He said nothing, merely stared at Sean from behind those glinting lens until Sean was forced to speak again.

'If you've finished your drink, why don't we take a stroll down the eighteenth fairway?' The club veranda was crowded and the happy hour in full swing with too many listening ears. Manguza swallowed the last of his gin and tonic, and without a word led the way down the steps to the lawn.

The last four-ball was coming down the eighteenth, but Sean kept to the edge of the rough, and as the players and their caddies straggled past, Sean said softly, 'I told my associates that you are the most powerful man in the department, and that the white

73

director is merely your rubber stamp. I told them that you had it in your power to sidetrack an official enquiry, and dismiss any charges arising from this most unfortunate incident. I was so certain that I laid a bet of ten thousand US dollars with them. If I win my bet, those winnings are yours, Mr Manguza, paid into any account you nominate anywhere in the world.'

Manguza stopped and turned to face him and Sean was taken aback when he saw his expression. Manguza's voice quivered with fury as he said, 'Your assumption that I am open to a bribe is an insult to me personally. That I could tolerate, but it is also an insult to the revolution and the revolutionary heroes who died in the struggle to free this country of the imperial and colonial yoke, it is an insult to the party and our leaders, to the Marxist spirit and ultimately to the African people as a whole.'

'I only suggested a lousy ten grand, not the return of the monarchy, for the love of Allah.'

'You may smile your supercilious white smile, Colonel Courtney, but we know you well. We know about your South African connections, and about the bunch of Matabele hooligans you have gathered about you. We know that all of them fought with you against the forces of revolutionary democracy. They are counter-revolutionaries and capitalist-roaders and you are their leader.'

'I shot a lioness by mistake, and one of my capitalist-roaders got bitten, that's the full extent of my counter-revolutionary activities.'

'We are watching you, Colonel,' Manguza told him ominously. 'You can be certain that I will make the correct recommendation in your case, and that the insult to me and my people will not be forgotten.'

Manguza turned and strode back towards the club-house and Sean shook his head.

'So we say farewell to the beautiful Chiwewe concession,' he murmured. 'I really blew that one!' Despite his levity, he felt a sliding sensation of disaster in the pit of his stomach.

* * *

The office of Courtney Safaris was in the Avenuès, between Government House and the golf club and Reema was waiting for him in the outer office, its walls decorated with colour posters of

74

wildlife and photographic enlargements of satisfied clients with their trophies.

She jumped up from her desk the moment Sean came in.

'The hospital called an hour ago, Sean. They have amputated Shadrach's leg.'

For long moments, Sean could neither speak nor move, then he crossed slowly to the filing cabinet and took a glass and a half-empty bottle of Chivas from the top drawer. He sagged onto the sofa and poured a three-finger jolt of whisky.

'The ending to a perfect day,' he said, and tossed back the whisky.

Reema left him sitting on the sofa. There were only two more drinks left in the bottle. and when they were gone. Sean went down to the Monomatapa Hotel. The hotel was full of tourists, and amongst them was a blond teutonic Valkyrie in full *Out of Africa* costume. She caught his eye across the lounge the moment that Sean walked in and smiled.

'What the hell!' Sean said to himself. 'It's cheaper than whisky, and no hangover either.'

The German Fräulein laughed delightedly at Sean's rudimentary German, and not long afterwards it transpired that she had the presidential suite on the fourteenth floor all to herself. She ordered a bottle of Mumm from room service and they drank it in bed.

* * *

In the morning, while Reema filed a flight plan for him, taking a bag of dried meat down to air traffic control, Sean returned to the hospital.

They had taken Shadrach's leg off only inches below the hip. The East German doctor showed Sean the X-ray plates. 'Hopeless!' He pointed out the bone fragments. 'Like confetti!'

There was no place to sit in the crowded surgical ward, so Sean stood beside Shadrach's bed for a while and they talked about the battles and the hunts they had shared. They did not mention the leg, and when they had run out of reminiscences, Sean gave the ward sister a hundred dollars to look after him and went out to the airport.

Reema had the flight plan for him and the Beechcraft was

refuelled and loaded with everything from fresh fruit and vegetables to toilet paper for the camp.

'You are a heroine, Reema,' he said, and then standing beside the aircraft, he described the meeting with Geoffrey Manguza.

'It doesn't look very cheerful,' he ended. 'You had better begin looking for another job.'

'I'm sorry for you, Sean,' she said. 'But don't worry about me. I was wondering how to break the news to you. I'm leaving for Canada on September 16th. It's all arranged, I'm going to be the wife of a professor.'

'You be happy,' Sean ordered, and for the first time kissed her, and she blushed under her nut-brown skin which made her prettier than ever.

Sean made three low-level passes over the camp and on the third he saw the Toyota pull out towards the airstrip with Job driving and Matatu standing in the back. He landed and taxied the Beechcraft into its cage of galvanized diamond-mesh wire which was designed to discourage the elephant from pulling the wings off and the lions from chewing the tyres.

When Job and Matatu arrived in the Toyota, they transferred the cargo to it, and then Sean told them about Shadrach's leg.

They had fought all through the bush war together and were hardened to casualties, but Sean saw the pain and grief in his eyes as Job murmured, 'We will need a new number two gunbearer. Pumula, the skinner, is a good man.'

'Yes, we will use him,' Sean agreed.

For a while they stood silently, paying tribute to their maimed companion. Then, still without speaking, they climbed into the Toyota and drove back to camp.

* * *

Rather than slacks, Claudia Monterro wore a dress for dinner that evening, a floating silk chiffon in pure white with silver and turquoise Seminole jewellery. Against her tanned skin and jet black hair the effect was stunning. However, Sean made certain not to show his admiration and he directed all his conversation at her father.

After he had told Riccardo about Shadrach and his meeting with Manguza, the evening was gloomy and cheerless. Claudia left the men at the camp-fire but they did not sit there long before

Riccardo said goodnight and went off to his tent. Sean took a bottle of whisky from the dining tent and went down towards the servants' village.

Job's tent and, those of his two wives were set apart from the others, on the bank of the river overlooking a deep pool where hippo lay like dark rock islands in mid-stream.

When Sean seated himself on the carved native stool across the fire from Job, one of the wives brought two glasses and knelt beside him while he poured a large peg for each of them. The pretty young Matabele girl with Job's infant strapped on her back took the glass to her husband, and Job saluted Sean across the flickering flames.

They drank in silence and Sean watched Job's face in the firelight as he stared out across the river. The silence was companionable and comforting and Sean let his thoughts wander back down the years as he rolled the smoky taste of whisky over his tongue.

He remembered the day he had first met Job Bhekani. It had been on a hill with only a number, Hill 31, a rocky hill, thick with stands of dense wild ebony and Jesse bush where the enemy waited. Job had been on the hill for two days, and his eyes were wild and bloodshot. Sean had parachuted in that morning with five sticks of his own scouts. They fought side by side the rest of that day, and in the dusk when the hill was cleared and those of the enemy still alive had fled down the rocky slopes and disappeared into the forest, Sean and Job had helped each other to where the helicopter waited to take them out. They had gone down the hill slowly, wearily, dragging their weapons, arms around each other's shoulders and their blood mingling when it oozed from under the field dressings.

'Blood brothers whether you like it or not,' Sean had croaked, grinning at Job from under the camouflage cream and soot and dust, and a week later when Job was released from base hospital, Sean had been waiting for him personally with his transfer papers.

'You've been seconded to Ballantyne Scouts, Captain.'

And Job had smiled that rare wide smile and said, 'Let's go, Colonel.'

From his file, Sean knew that Job had been born on the Gwai river and attended the local mission school where he had obtained a bursary to the University College of Rhodesia and Nyasaland from where he had graduated with a first in Politics, History and

77

Social Anthropology. From there he had gone on with another bursary to Brown College in Chicago and got his masters the same year that Ian Smith declared unilateral independence.

Only much later when they had tried and tested their friendship, did Sean learn how Job had herded his father's cattle along the Gwai river and come, even as a child, to know and love the wilds. Job's father was one of the grandsons of King Lobengula, son of great Mzilikazi, so Job was a direct descendant of the royal Zulu line, and this was apparent in his carriage and his features. The powerful jaw and deep forehead, the dark intelligent eyes and domed skull beneath the thick close-cropped curls.

During his studies and his sojourn in America, Job had come to abhor the Communist doctrine and all its works, so it was natural that on his return to Africa, he had enlisted in the Rhodesian African Rifles and within a year had earned his commission.

After the war when the Lancaster House Agreement had given the country over to Robert Mugabe and his people's democracy, Job had sat and passed with honours, the civil service entrance exam, for government and politics was the swift high-road to power and wealth.

However, he was branded a 'sell-out' who had fought the war on the wrong side, the losing side, and he was a Matabele when the power was in the hands of the Shona tribe. Every door to advancement was barred against him. Angry and disillusioned he had come back to Sean.

'Damn it, Job, you are miles too good for any job I could offer you in a safari company.'

'Tracker, skinner, gunbearer, whatever you have, I'll take it,' Job had insisted.

So they had hunted together as they had fought, side by side, and within a year, Sean had made him one of the directors of Courtney Safaris. They always referred to these quiet evenings, drinking whisky around the camp-fire, as directors' meetings.

It amused Job to adopt various roles for different circumstances. In front of safari clients he shifted to what he called, 'Plantation Nigger Mode' when he called Sean *Bwana* and *Nkosi* and acted out the charade of the by-gone colonial era.

'Don't be a prick, Job. You demean yourself,' Sean protested at first.

'It's what the clients expect,' Job had reasoned. 'We are selling them an illusion, man. They are playing eagle scouts and Ernest Hemingway. If they guessed I had a master's in history and politics, it would frighten the hell out of them.' And reluctantly, Sean had gone along with the act.

When they were alone, as they were now, Job changed into what he called his 'Homo Sapiens Mode' and became the thoughtful intelligent educated man he truly was. As they talked, they switched easily from Sindebele to English, each of them as perfectly at ease and comfortable in each other's language as they were in each other's company.

'Look, Sean, don't worry too much about losing this concession. It hasn't happened yet, and even if it does, we'll find a way around it.'

'Give me some comfort. I could do with it.'

'We could apply for another concession, somewhere in Matabeleland where my family still has pull. Down Matetsi way or even on the Gwai river, that's my home turf.'

'No good.' Sean shook his head. 'After this fiasco, I'll have the mark of the beast on me.'

'We'd apply in my name,' Job suggested, and smiled wickedly. 'I'd make you one of my directors and you can call me *Bwana!*'

They laughed together, the mood lightening, and when Sean left Job at his fire and walked back to the main camp in the darkness, he felt cheerful and optimistic for the first time in days. Job had the power to effect that transformation in him.

As he approached his own tent, something pale moved in the moon shadow beneath the trees and he stopped abruptly. Then he heard the tinkle of silver jewellery, and realized that she must have been waiting for him.

'May I speak with you?' Claudia said softly.

'Go ahead,' he invited. Why did that Americanism 'speak with', rather than 'speak to' irritate him so, he wondered.

'I'm not very good at this,' she admitted and he gave her no encouragement. 'I wanted to apologize.'

'You are apologizing to the wrong person, I've still got both my legs.'

She flinched and her voice trembled. 'You are without mercy, aren't you?' Then she lifted her chin. 'All right, I guess I deserved that, I've been an idiot. I thought I knew it all, but it turns out I knew very little, and in my ignorance I've done immense damage. I know it doesn't help much, but I'm desperately sorry.'

'You and I are from different worlds, we have not a single thought or feeling in common. We could never hope to understand each other, let alone be friends, but I do know what it took for you to say that.'

'A truce, then?' she asked.

'All right, a truce.' He held out his hand and she took it. Her skin was smooth as the petal of a rose, her hand slim and cool, but her grip was firm as a man's.

'Good-night,' she said, and released his hand and turned away.

He watched her walk back towards her own tent. The moon was two days from full and the white dress was ethereal and misty. Beneath it her body was slim and her limbs long and elegant.

In that moment, he admired her spirit and liked her more than he had ever done in all the time he had known her.

*   *   *

Sean slept as lightly as a hunter and a soldier. The natural sounds of the bush did not disturb him, not even the shrieks of the hyena pack around the fortified trophy shed, where the lionskins were curing.

However at the light scratch on the canvas of his tent, he was instantly awake and reaching for his flashlight and the .577 propped at the head of his bed.

'Who is it?' he asked quietly.

'It's me, Job.'

Sean glanced at his Rolex wristwatch, the luminous hands pointed to three o'clock.

'Come in, what is it?'

'One of the trackers who we left on the river has come into camp. He has run twenty miles.'

Sean felt the back of his neck prickle and he swung both legs out of bed.

'Yes?' he said eagerly.

'At sunset this evening Tukutela crossed the river out of the National Park.'

'Is it certain?'

'It is certain. They saw him close by. It is Tukutela, the Angry One, and he has no collar around his neck.'

'Where is Matatu?' Sean stood up and reached for his pants,

and the little Ndorobo piped at the entrance. 'I am ready, *Bwana*.'

'Good. We leave in twenty minutes. Marching packs and water-bottles. We'll take Pumula in Shadrach's place. I want to be on Tukutela's spoor before it is light enough to see it.'

Bare-chested, Sean strode across to Riccardo's tent, and heard his even snores as he paused at the flap.

'Capo!' The snores cut off abruptly. 'Are you awake? I've got an elephant for you. Get your arse out of the sack. Tukutela has crossed. We leave in twenty minutes.'

'Hot damn!' He could hear Riccardo was still half asleep. He stumbled about in the dark tent. 'Where the hell are my pants? Hey, Sean, wake Claudia, will you?'

There was a lantern burning in Claudia's tent. She must have heard the excitement.

'Are you awake?' Sean asked at the flap, and she opened it and stood with the lantern light behind her. Her nightdress reached almost to her ankles, there was lace at her throat and cuffs, but the cloth was so fine that the light struck through it, and her naked body was in silhouette.

'I heard you telling Papa,' she said. 'I'll be ready. Will we be walking? Should I wear my hiking boots or moccasins?'

He was certain that she was putting on this show deliberately, and he felt a prudish outrage that was totally alien to his nature. 'Today you'll walk further and faster than you ever have in your life before,' he told her harshly. 'She's showing herself off like a tramp,' he thought, ignoring the proven fact that his taste usually ran strongly towards tramps, 'just when I was starting to respect her,' and a reprimand rose to his lips. He bit it off and tried not to look at the flowing shape of her hips, as graceful as the lines of a celadon porcelain vase thrown by a master craftsman of the T'ang dynasty. He wanted to turn away to show his indifference and his contradictory disapproval, but he was still standing there when she let the tent flap drop.

'Truce, be damned,' he muttered furiously as he strode back to his tent. 'She's still in the ring throwing punches.' But his anger puzzled him. With any other woman, even one half as lovely, he would have been delighted by the exhibition.

'She's got more class than that,' he explained to himself, and then remembered how much he despised and disliked her. 'This bimbo is getting you all up a gum-tree,' he warned himself,

81

and then burst out laughing. The dreadful gloom of Shadrach's amputation and the imminent loss of his licence were dispelled.

He was going to hunt one of Africa's legendary beasts, and the presence of this woman, in some unaccountable manner, added spice to his mood of high anticipation.

* * *

There was frost on the grass in the low vleis they crossed. It sparkled in the headlights, and the game they saw was lethargic with the cold, barely moving out of the road to let the Toyota pass in the night. They reached the ford on the Chiwewe river an hour before dawn. The waters were black and shining as anthracite in the last beams of the moon, and the tall trees along either bank were a silvered host, like two opposing armies of mythical giants.

Sean parked the Toyota well off the track, and left one of the skinners to guard it. They fell naturally into established hunting formation, with the clients in the centre. Pumula took up Shadrach's old position in the drag; a muscular taciturn man with a thick woolly bush of a black beard, he carried Riccardo's Rigby on its sling.

All the men, including Riccardo, were under field packs, even Claudia carried her own water-bottles. Job had Riccardo's second rifle, the Weatherby, over his shoulder, and as always Sean lugged the .577 Nitro Express. Once the hunt had begun he never let it out of his hands. They moved out, heading upstream, and within a mile they had warmed up and were pushing harder. Sean noticed that Claudia moved well on those long legs of hers, and was keeping up without difficulty. She gave him a saucy grin as she noticed his appraisal.

The dawn light was hardening when the tracker who had come in with the news of Tukutela's crossing, exclaimed and pointed ahead. It was light enough to make out a fresh blaze on the trunk of a pod mahogany tree which guarded a low place on the riverbank. 'There!' said the tracker. 'I marked the spoor.'

At a glance, Sean saw that this was a natural crossing place for large animals. Troops of hippo had pioneered a pathway through the reed beds, and down the ten-foot riverbank. Herds of buffalo and elephant passing over it had consolidated it and improved the gradient.

The African veld is criss-crossed with a network of game trails, and a dozen or so of these came in through the forest, like the spokes of a wheel, to concentrate on this river crossing. Everyone in the party quickened step at the tracker's exclamation, but Matatu reached the main pathway ahead of them and darted down it, turning his head to use the light of dawn most effectively, dabbing lightly at the earth with the tip of the peeled wild willow wand he carried.

He had not gone five paces before he straightened and looked back at Sean, his features wreathed in wrinkles of happiness and excitement.

'It is him!' he chirped. 'These are the feet of the father of all elephants. It is Tukutela! It is the Angry One!'

Sean looked down at the great dished spoor in the fine dust of the game path and he felt as though a spring tide had begun to flow in his life.

His excitement was replaced by a sense of destiny, an almost religious gravity.

'Matatu,' he said. 'Take the spoor!' Formally, he announced the start of the hunt.

*   *   *

The spoor was clear as a highway, following the game trail directly into the forest away from the river.

The old bull was striding out briskly as though he knew that the crossing was the danger point. Perhaps that was why he had chosen to cross at sunset, so that darkness would cover him until he was clear.

For five miles he had gone without a check, and then suddenly he had turned aside from the game trail into a thicket of rambling thorn which had come into blossom and new shoot. He had moved back and forth, feeding on the blooms and succulent shoots, and his spoor was confused, the thicket trampled and torn.

Matatu and Job went into the thorn thicket to unravel it, while the rest of the party hung back to let them work unhindered.

'I'm thirsty!' Claudia unhooked one of the water-bottles from her belt.

'No!' Sean stopped her. 'If you drink on your first thirst, you'll want to drink all day, and we have only just begun.'

She hesitated a moment, considering defying him, but then she hooked the bottle back on her belt.

'You are a hard taskmaster,' she said.

Matatu whistled softly on the far side of the thicket.

'He has worked the spoor out,' Sean told them, and let them through the thorn.

'How much have we gained?' he asked Matatu. They had started almost ten hours behind the bull, but every time he had paused to feed, they cut that lead.

'He did not feed long.' Matatu shrugged. 'And now he is going hard again.'

The bull had turned off the game trail and was following a stony ridge, almost as if he was deliberately obscuring his own spoor. He left no indications for the average human eye to follow, but Matatu went after him with complete authority.

'Are you sure he is still on it?' Riccardo asked anxiously.

'Capo, you've hunted with Matatu too often to ask that question,' Sean told him.

'But what can he see?' Claudia wanted to know. 'It's just rocks and gravel.'

'The elephant's pads leave a scuff on the rock, they bruise the lichen, leave smears of dust. There is fine grass growing between the stones, he has disturbed it, bending the stems in the direction of his passing. The disturbed grass catches the light differently.'

'Could you follow it?' Claudia wanted to know, and Sean shook his head.

'No, I'm not a magician.' They had been speaking in barely audible whispers, but Sean said, 'That's enough chatter, let's keep it down to a bellow from now on.'

So they went on in silence, and the forest about them was a perpetually changing show.

There were forty different varieties of the combretum family of trees, and this was not exclusively combretum forest, as many other varieties were mingled with them, each with a distinctive shape of trunk differing in the colour and texture of bark, some with branches denuded by winter, others with dense foliage of a myriad shades of green and gold and orange and cinnabar.

At times, the forest enclosed them like a palisade, then only moments later opened vistas of far hills and weirdly shaped kopjes, of open glades, and vleis from some of which the tall grass had been burned and the tender shoots laid a carpet of green over the black ash.

The new growth of grass had attracted herds of antelope into the vleis. They stood out in the open, sable antelope with long horns curved like scimitars, the proud necks of blood arabs, upper bodies sooty black as the ash of the vlei and their bellies snowy white.

Reed-buck with horns pricked forward inquisitively and tails like white powder puffs, zebra at a distance seeming not striped but a uniform grey colour, and wildebeest with roman noses and scraggly beards chasing each other like clowns in mindless circles, stirring the black ash in a cloud about themselves.

When the lion is not hunting the animals that are his natural prey are amazingly trusting and will stand and stare at him as he slouches past within fifty yards of them. In the same way they seemed to sense that this file of humans was not a threat, and they let them approach closely before moving off at a leisurely trot, and Claudia's delight buoyed her so she felt no fatigue even after four hours of hard walking.

In a gorge between two hills, water had been trapped in a narrow rock-pool. It was stagnant and green and bubbling with the gas of rotting vegetation, but the old bull had drunk from it and left a pile of his spongy yellow dung beside it.

'We'll take ten minutes' rest here,' Sean told them. 'You can have a drink now.' He looked at Claudia. 'But try to limit it to two mouthfuls, unless you'd like to try some of that.' He indicated the foul pool, and she grimaced.

He left her sitting beside her father and went to where Matatu stood alone at the head of the pool.

'What is it?' he asked. After twenty years, he could read the little man's moods. Matatu shook his head and his wrinkles sagged lugubriously.

'Something is not right here,' Matatu told him. 'The bull is unhappy. He goes one way and then the other. He travels swiftly, but without purpose. He does not feed, and he walks as though the ground burns his feet.'

'Why is that, Matatu?'

'I do not know,' he admitted. 'But I do not like it, *Bwana*.'

Sean left him and went back to where Claudia sat. 'Let's take a look at your feet.' He had spotted the slight limp she had developed in the last hour.

'Are you serious?'

She began to smile, but he took one of her feet in his lap, untied the laces, and pulled off her boot and sock. Her feet were long and narrow like her hands, but the skin was delicate and there was a bright pink spot on her heel and another on the ball of her big toe. Sean cleaned the tender spots with cotton wool and surgical spirit. It gave him an intimate and sensuous pleasure to handle those finely formed feet, but he told her severely, 'These must have been hurting you. Don't try and be brave, another few miles and you would have had blisters like a bunch of grapes, and we would have had a cripple on our hands.'

He taped the tender spots. 'Change socks,' he ordered. 'And the next time tell me as soon as it hurts.'

She obeyed him meekly, and they went on.

A little before noon, the spoor changed direction again and ran due east. 'We have gained an hour or two on him,' Sean whispered to Capo. 'But Matatu doesn't like it and neither do I. He's spooky and tense and he's heading straight for the Mozambique border now.'

'Do you think he has sensed us?' Capo was worried, but Sean shook his head.

'Impossible, we are still hours behind him.'

They stopped again briefly at noon to eat and rest, and when they went on again, they had not gone more than a mile before they entered a grove of marula trees. The ripe yellow fruit lay thickly on the ground beneath them and the old bull had not been able to resist that. He had fed heartily, spending at least three hours in the grove, shaking the trees to bring down more fruit, then at last setting off again eastwards as though suddenly remembering a rendezvous.

'At least, we have gained three hours on him,' Sean told them, but he was frowning. 'We are only ten miles from the Mozambique border. If he crosses, we have lost him.'

Sean considered running the spoor. In the old days of the bush war, he and Job and Shadrach never walked in pursuit of the enemy. Running, they had been able to cover sixty or seventy miles in a single day. He glanced back at Claudia; she might surprise him for she moved like an athlete and despite the incipient blisters there was still spring and snap in her step. Then he looked back at Riccardo and abandoned the idea. Capo was wilting in the ninety-five-degree heat of the valley. Sean tended

86

to forget sometimes that Riccardo was only a year or two short of sixty. He had always been so fit, but now he was showing signs of distress, his eyes sunken in plum-coloured hollows and a greyish cast to his skin.

'Old beggar is looking sick,' Sean thought. 'I can't push him harder.'

He had let his attention wander, and now he almost ran into Matatu as the tracker stopped suddenly, still hunched over the spoor.

'What is it?' he demanded. The little man's agitation was obvious. He was shaking his head, and muttering in that obscure Ndorobo dialect that even Sean could not understand.

'What . . .?' Sean broke off as he saw it. 'Oh shit!' he blurted. Two separate pairs of human tracks had come in from the side and now overlaid the elephant bull's pad marks. Here the earth was sandy and friable, the tracks clear.

Two men, wearing rubber-soled shoes. Sean recognized the distinctive pattern of the soles. Those ubiquitous Bata tennis shoes, locally manufactured, and sold for a few dollars in every street market and general dealer's store.

Even Riccardo picked out the alien human prints. 'Who the hell is that?' he demanded, but Sean ignored him and drew aside with Job to watch Matatu work.

Matatu scurried back and forth picking over the spoor like an old hen, and then came back to them. They squatted down, Job on one side of Sean, Matatu on the other – the council of war, from which only Shadrach was missing.

'Two men. One young and tall and thin, he walks on his toes. The other older, shorter, fatter. Both are carrying packs and *banduki*.' Sean knew he had deduced all this from the length of stride, the different way the two men heeled and toed under packs, and the unbalancing of a heavy weapon carried in one hand. 'They are foreigners. The men of the valley do not wear shoes, and these men came in from the north.'

'Zambian poachers,' Job grunted. 'They are after rhino horn, but they stumbled on the elephant and he is too big to let pass.'

'Bastards!' said Sean bitterly. In 1970 there had been an estimated twelve thousand black rhinoceros left in Zambia across the Zambezi river. Now there were none, not a single animal left. A Yemeni nobleman would pay fifty thousand dollars for a dagger with a rhinoceros-horn handle, and the poachers organized themselves like military expeditions. There were still a few hundred rhinoceros left on the southern side of the Zambezi valley, and from the Zambian side the poachers crossed the river in the night, slipping past the game department patrols. Many of the poachers had been bush fighters in the guerrilla war. They were hard men and killers of men as well as of the great animals on which they preyed.

'They will be carrying AKs.' Job looked at him. 'And there are probably more than two men, they will have out-flankers. We are outnumbered and outgunned, Sean. What do you want to do?'

'This is my concession,' Sean said. 'And Tukutela is my elephant.'

'Then you might have to fight them for both.' Job's noble Matabele features were solemn, but his eyes sparkled; he could not conceal the battle lust in them.

Sean stood up. 'Damned right, Job. If we catch them, we are going to fight them.'

'Then we must hurry.' Matatu stood up beside him. 'They are two hours ahead of us, and Tukutela must stop soon to feed. They will have him before we get there.'

Sean strode across to where Riccardo and Claudia were resting in the shade.

'Poachers!' he told them. 'Probably armed with automatic weapons. Two at least, possibly more, all of them ruthless killers.'

They stared at him wordlessly, and Sean went on. 'We will have to move fast to prevent them getting to Tukutela before we do. I'll leave you and Claudia to follow with Pumula at your own speed. Job and Matatu and I are going to run the spoor, and try to drive them off before they get to the elephant. You keep the Rigby, Capo, and Job will take the Weatherby.'

As he began to turn away, Riccardo caught his arm. 'Sean, I want this elephant. More than anything left in my life, I want this elephant.'

'I will try and save him for you,' Sean nodded. He understood entirely. He felt the same way.

'Thank you.' Riccardo let his hand fall to his side and Sean went to where Job and Matatu were waiting. They had handed over their field packs to Pumula and carried only their water-bottles. Sean glanced at his stainless-steel Rolex. Four minutes since they picked up the poachers' spoor, four minutes wasted.

'Hot pursuit!' Sean ordered. 'And expect ambush!'

Job smiled at him. 'Old times,' he said. 'It makes me feel young again.'

Matatu pulled his loin-cloth up between his legs and tucked the skirt under his belt, then whirled and went away on the spoor at a loping trot. Sean had seen him keep up that pace from sun up to sun down. He went out onto the right flank, and Job who was left-handed took his natural side. Sean changed the cartridges in the .577 and began to run. Within seconds, Riccardo's group was out of sight in the forest behind them, and Sean concentrated all his attention ahead.

It required special skills and vast experience to keep the formation intact in this type of broken country. The flankers had to keep slightly ahead of the tracker, anticipating the line of the spoor, sweeping the terrain for ambush, covering and protecting Matatu, and yet keeping fifty paces out on each side, breaking their own trail, and still maintaining contact with the opposite flanker, all this while on the run and mostly out of sight of each other, with Matatu setting a furious pace in the centre.

When the spoor turned, the man on the outer flank had to wheel on the centre, covering twice the distance of his opposite number, and when the spoor crossed open ground, they had to increase the angle on the flank, forming an inverted spearhead formation, always protecting the centre, keeping contact with subtle bird-calls, the flute of a wood dove, the whistle of a bul-bul, the warble of a shrike, the pipe of a black kite, each had meaning, each a command or a warning.

All this and two other essentials, silence and speed. Job and Sean ran like a pair of kudu bulls, lightly and soundlessly, ducking and weaving under branches through thickets and thorns, quick and vigilant.

After the first hour, Matatu flashed a hand signal down a break in forest, and Sean understood it readily. 'Two more,' the signal said.

Another pair of poachers had joined the first two, and they also were closing swiftly with the elephant.

They ran for another hour, never slackening for a moment, and Matatu signalled again from the centre.

'Very close.' An eloquent flash of his pink palm. 'Beware. Danger.' And Sean whistled like a sand grouse, checking the pace, the signal for imminent contact and they came down to a wary trot.

The trail had led them up the side of a low tableland, along an ancient elephant trail that was well trodden into the iron-hard earth. When they came out on top of the flat plateau they felt the stir of the evening breeze, cool and blessed out of the east, and Sean held his sweaty face up to it.

The plateau was less than a mile wide, and they crossed it quickly and reached the far rim, dropping to their bellies and sliding over the sky line without showing a silhouette against the blue and then crouching below the crest and sweeping the ground below them, a shallow valley with another forested tableland beyond. A riverbed meandered down the centre of the valley, its course marked with a narrow ribbon of dark green riverine bush, and the rest of the valley fairly open: pale, winter grass shining in the sunlight, dotted ant-hills, each the size of a cottage, widely separated umbrella acacia with flat tops, and lemon-yellow trunks. Sean surveyed it all swiftly.

Out on the left, Job gave the penny-whistle snort of a reed-buck, one of the most urgent alarm calls in their repertoire. He was pointing down into the valley, half left from their front. Sean followed the gesture. For a moment he saw nothing, and then suddenly Tukutela, the Angry One, stepped into view.

He had been hidden from Sean by one of the huge ant-hills, but now he strode out into the open meadow, and Sean gasped aloud. Even from almost a mile away, Sean realized that he had only poorly remembered the magnificence of this animal.

Tukutela was the dark grey of volcanic rock, tall and gaunt; even at this distance Sean could make out the folds and tucks of his ancient riven hide, and the knotted outline of his spine beneath it. His ears fanned gently with each stride, and their edges were tattered and eroded, like a pair of battle ensigns torn with shot and blackened with the smoke of cannon.

Tukutela's tusks were black also, stained with age and the sap of the tall trees he had destroyed with them. From his gaping lower lip the tusks flared outwards, and then curved in again towards each other so the tips almost met nine feet from his lip. They were without taper, solid columns of ivory, hanging so low that in the centre they drooped below the level of the winter grass, and they seemed to over-burden even that massive frame.

There would probably never be another pair of tusks like that ever again. This elephant was legend and history.

Sean felt a hot flare of guilt. No matter the legality of it, the killing of this beast would be a crime against Africa, an affront to the gods of the wilderness and the very soul of man, yet he knew he would not hesitate to do it, and that knowledge added poignancy to his sense of guilt. As a hunter, the nobler the quarry, the greater the compulsion to take the trophy. Job whistled again, pointing, diverting Sean's attention from the elephant, and only then Sean saw the poachers.

They were already closing in on the bull. He could see all four of them. They had just left the trees at the bottom of the slope, and were moving in single file into the grass meadow. The grass reached to their armpits, and their heads and shoulders bobbed like the cork line of a fishing-net in the pale sea of grass. Each of them carried an AK 47 assault rifle slung over his shoulder.

The light swift bullets those weapons fired were not at all suitable for hunting massive-bodied species, but Sean knew the technique. They would get in close and all four would open fire together, blazing hundreds of rounds into the bull, riddling his lungs with copper-jacketed bullets, bringing him down under the sheer weight of automatic fire power.

The line of poachers was swinging out to flank the elephant, not heading directly towards him, but keeping well below the wind, so that a fluke of the breeze would not carry their scent to him. Despite this detour, they were running hard and gaining on him swiftly. The bull was still totally unaware of their existence, heading with long swaying strides down towards the riverbed, but at this rate, Sean realized that they would intercept him and open fire before he reached it.

The government directive from the game department to the concessionaires was in plain language. Unauthorized armed men in a hunting concession, if apprehended in what was clearly a hunting operation, were presumed to be poachers. Four game department rangers and one concessionaire had been murdered by poachers during the past four years, and the directive was that fire could be opened on poachers without warning. The prime minister, Robert Mugabe, had made it even plainer. 'Shoot to kill,' were his exact words.

The .577 Nitro Express was a devastating weapon at close quarters, but over a hundred yards the heavy bullet dropped away rapidly. The group of poachers was six hundred yards away across the valley floor and Sean jumped up, and crouching low, slipped across the face of the slope to where Job was lying behind a fallen tree-trunk.

He dropped down beside him. 'Give me the Weatherby,' he ordered, and took the lighter weapon from his hands. Job was an excellent shot, but this called for Bisley-standard marksmanship.

Sean jerked the bolt open and checked that there was a cartridge in the chamber. It was a 180-grain Nosler, and Sean tried to estimate how much the bullet would drop over the range of six hundred yards, firing downhill, with a light breeze on his left shoulder. He remembered from the ballistic table that the bullet drop at three hundred and fifty yards would be six inches, at six hundred yards it would probably be four foot or more.

While he worked it out, he stripped off his shirt, rolled it into a bundle and placed it on the fallen tree-trunk behind which he and Job were crouched.

'Back me with the big *banduki*. Shoot very high with it,' he told Job, and settled behind the tree-trunk, resting the fore-end of the Weatherby on the pad of the shirt. He screwed the variable telescopic lens to full power and gazed through it.

He picked up the heads of the file of poachers. With this magnification, he could recognize two of the men as Matatu had described them from their spoor. The tall lean one was leading, and he wore a blue denim jacket, traditional guerrilla uniform from the days of the bush war. Behind him came the shorter heavier man. He had a tiger-striped camouflage cap on his head and wore a plain khaki shirt.

Beyond them Sean could see the elephant. The magnification of the lens foreshortened the range so that the poachers seemed very close to their quarry. Even as he watched them, the leader of the column unslung the automatic rifle from his shoulder and made a gesture with his other hand. Behind him, the other three poachers fanned out into a skirmishing line and slipped their rifles off their shoulders, holding them at high port.

Sean snuggled down behind the Weatherby, digging in his heels, regulating his breathing, his forefinger resting lightly on the trigger. He picked out the tall leader in the denim jacket, and let the cross-hairs of the telescopic sights drift over the man's head.

The image wavered and quivered in the heat, and Sean watched the watery lines of mirage. for they were indicators of the strength and direction of the breeze; when they leaned over, the breeze was gusting, but they rose straight upwards like smoke in the lulls between gusts.

He drew a long breath, let half of it out and held the rest. The mirage steadied in a lull, and he took his aim a full body-length above the poacher's head. The image looked good but he did not pull the trigger. He squeezed the grip of the rifle with his whole hand as though he were modelling clay.

The butt plate slammed back into his shoulder as the barrel jumped high in the typically vicious Weatherby recoil, and he lost sight of the target.

Before he could collect himself, Job exulted, 'Shayile! A hit!' And when Sean brought the lens back there were only three heads showing above the grass.

All three poachers had turned and were firing their weapons back towards the slope where Sean and Job were hidden, blazing wildly on fully automatic, their AKs beating like the rattle of kettledrums.

Beyond them, Sean saw the old bull elephant in full flight. His ears streaming back and his great black tusks lifted high above the grass, he crashed into the narrow ribbon of dark bush and out the other side.

'Run, my beauty,' Sean breathed. 'If I can't have you, nobody else will.' And he turned his full attention back to the band of poachers.

They were a crack unit, that was immediately obvious, two of them were throwing covering fire at the kopje, while the third had run to where the leader had gone down in the grass, and dragged him to his feet. The blue denim-clad leader had lost his rifle, and he was doubled up and clutching his side.

'Nicked him!' Sean muttered, and fired again. He saw dust fly above the grass, as his bullet fell close beside them. The poachers began to pull out, dragging their leader with them, placing an ant-hill between them and the kopje. Both Sean and Job were firing deliberately, but the range was increasing every second, and although Sean saw dust fly very close to the scurrying figures, they could not claim another hit before the band disappeared into the grass and scrub, and the clatter of automatic fire dwindled into silence.

Sean and Job waited fifteen minutes peering down into the

valley, but they did not get another glimpse of them before Sean stood up.

'We'll go and take a look.'

'Careful,' Job warned. 'They could have doubled back to lay an ambush.' That was another old guerrilla trick, and they went down the slope cautiously.

Matatu led them to where the poacher had fallen. It was an area of flattened grass. The man's weapon had disappeared, one of the other poachers must have retrieved it. Matatu picked one of the grass stems and held it out to Sean. The blood on it was almost dry. However, the bleeding had not been profuse and they found less than a dozen droplets on the grass or balled on the dry earth.

'Flesh wound,' Sean grunted. The drift of the breeze must have pushed the bullet off the vital areas of the man's body.

'Who do we follow, Tukutela or the poachers?' Job wanted to know.

'The poachers will be halfway back to Lusaka by now,' Sean grinned. 'Follow the elephant!' he ordered Matatu.

They tracked Tukutela across the riverbed and up the farther side of the valley. After his first panicked rush, the old bull settled down into that swinging stride that ate up the ground at a prodigious rate, and which he could keep up for days. He was boring away towards the east, towards the Mozambique border, only deviating slightly from his course to take a gap in a line of hills, or to climb the easier gradient when there was no pass.

They ran hard on his spoor. Not having to take precaution against ambush, they could push themselves to the limits, but the elephant was pulling away from them, and the day was wasting. The sun was casting their own long shadows ahead of them.

There was no defined border with Mozambique, no fence or cut line through the forest, but a sixth sense warned Sean that they had crossed.

He was about to give orders to halt when Job whistled softly and made a cut-out signal with his left hand. Matatu pulled up and shook his head in agreement, and the three of them bunched up and stood looking along the faint spoor which ran ahead of them into the darkening, eastern forest.

'Mozambique,' Job said. 'He has gone away.' And the others did not deny it.

'He still goes fast.' Matatu spat on the spoor. 'Faster than any man can run. We will not see Tukutela again this year.'

'Yes, but there will be another season,' Sean said. 'Next year, he will range back into the National Park and come again in the new moon across the Chiwewe river. We will be waiting for him.'

'Perhaps.' Matatu took a pinch of snuff from the duiker-horn container that hung around his neck. 'Or perhaps the poachers will find him again, or he will walk onto a land-mine in an old battlefield in Mozambique, or perhaps he will die of his own great age.'

The thought filled Sean with melancholy. Tukutela was a part of the old Africa. Sean had been born too late fully to experience that era. He had only been able to glimpse vestiges of it, yet he had a deep, nostalgic reverence for the history and past of his continent. It was all going so fast, trodden under the greedy rush for power by the thoughtless hordes of the emerging nations, by the unbridled tribal rivalries and the lawlessness of this new age. Once again, Africa was becoming the dark continent, but this time without the glory of its natural treasures, the wild game decimated, the forests hacked down for fuel, the very earth abused by primitive agriculture and animal husbandry, and the Saharan deserts each year marching southwards. Tukutela was one of the very few remaining treasures.

Sean turned back. He had wanted that elephant. He had wanted him with the utmost parts of his being. Now as he turned back into the west, the disappointment weighed down his legs and his heart, and he went heavily.

*　　*　　*

A little before midnight, they found Riccardo and Claudia sleeping on a mattress of cut grass, under a lean-to shelter beside a fire that had burned down to coals, while Pumula sat guard at the second fire close by.

Riccardo came awake the instant Sean touched his shoulder, and he scrambled up eagerly.

'Did you find him? What happened? What about the poachers?'

'He's gone, Capo. Across the border. We chased off the poachers, but Tukutela got clear away,' Sean told him, and Riccardo sagged back on the grass mattress and listened in silence while Sean described the chase and the contact with the poachers.

Claudia sat close to her father, and when Sean told them how Tukutela had crossed into Mozambique, she slipped her arm around his shoulders in a gesture of comfort.

'All right.' Sean stood up. 'There is one of my hunting tracks that cuts through about five miles south of here. Matatu and I will go back to fetch the truck, and Job will lead you to the track. I'll meet you there. Should take us four or five hours.'

By the light of the stars alone, Matatu led Sean for four hours through forest and dense bush, bringing him at last unerringly to where the truck was parked.

It was another hour's drive to the rendezvous where they found Claudia and Riccardo and the others sitting beside a fire on the verge of the rough track. They climbed wearily into the truck and Sean turned back and headed towards camp. It was four o'clock in the morning, over twenty-four hours since they had set out with such high hopes on the hunt.

They drove in silence for a while with Claudia asleep on her father's shoulder. Then Riccardo asked thoughtfully, 'Do you know where Tukutela has gone?'

'Beyond our reach, Capo,' Sean told him grimly.

'Seriously.' Riccardo was impatient. 'Is there one of his regular haunts where he will be headed?'

'That's rough country in there,' Sean murmured. 'Chaos and confusion. Villages burned and deserted, two armies fighting each other, with Mugabe's lads joining in.'

'Where has that elephant gone?' Riccardo insisted. 'He must have an established range.'

Sean nodded. 'We have worked it out, Job, Matatu and I. We reckon that he holes up from July to September in the swamps below the Cabora Bassa dam. Then in late September or the beginning of October, he crosses the Zambezi and heads north into Malawi, into the dense rain forest around Mlanje. He hides there until after the rains break and then comes south again, crosses the Zambezi near Tete and goes back into the Chiwewe National Park again.'

'So he will be heading for the swamps now?' Riccardo asked.

'More than likely,' Sean nodded. 'We'll get another crack at him next season, Capo.'

They reached camp at dawn, and there were steaming hot showers and freshly ironed clothes ready for them, and a huge

96

breakfast spread in the dining tent. Sean loaded crispy bacon and fried eggs onto their plates.

'When we have finished breakfast, we'll catch up on some of the sleep we missed last night, sack out until lunchtime.'

'Suits me,' Claudia agreed readily.

'Then we'll have a conference. We must work out our plans for the rest of the safari, we still have almost three weeks. We can try for another bull elephant, I can't offer you anything like Tukutela, but we might be able to find a sixty-pounder for you, Capo.'

'I don't want a sixty-pounder,' Riccardo said. 'I want Tukutela.'

'Don't we all, but let's drop it now.' Sean's irritation was undisguised. 'We can't do anything about it, let's just drop the subject.'

'What if we crossed the border and followed him into the swamps?' Riccardo did not look up from his eggs and bacon, and Sean studied his face before he laughed mirthlessly.

'For a moment, you had me worried. I thought you meant it. We'll get Tukutela next season.'

'There isn't going to be another season,' Riccardo told him. 'You know damn well that Geoffrey Manguza is going to pull your licence and take Chiwewe away from you.'

'Thanks, Capo, you certainly know how to make me feel good.'

'No sense fooling ourselves. This is our last chance at that elephant.'

'Correction.' Sean shook his head. 'It's over for this season. We had our chance and we blew it.'

'Not if we follow him into Mozambique,' Riccardo said. 'Follow him into the swamps.'

Sean stared at him. 'My God, you are serious!'

'I told you. There is nothing that I want more in this life than that elephant.'

'So you expect Job and Matatu and me to commit suicide for a whim of yours.'

'No, I don't expect it for a whim – let's say for half a million dollars rather.'

Sean shook his head, but no words came out, and Riccardo went on.

'I feel responsible for you losing your licence. With half a million you could buy a good concession in Zambia or Botswana,

97

or fifty thousand acres of game ranch in South Africa. Half a million. Think about it.'

Sean jumped up from the breakfast table so violently that he knocked his plate to the ground. He strode away without looking back.

He stood alone, at the edge of the camp staring down towards the river where a small herd of impala were drinking, and a white-headed fish eagle sat on a dead tree above the green water. He did not see them.

He thought about what it would be like next year without his own concession. He owed his brother, Garry, almost fifty thousand dollars and his overdraft at the bank in Harare was touching ten thousand. Reema had told him that the bank manager was anxious to speak to him. Sean had avoided the appointment on his last visit to Harare.

He was over forty and he had accumulated nothing. His father might be delighted to welcome him back to the family company, but his brother Garry was the chairman now and he would be less enthusiastic.

He thought about air-conditioned offices, neckties and dark business suits, interminable meetings with lawyers and engineers, rush-hour traffic and the smell of the city.

He thought about his father's philosophy, heartily endorsed by his brother, that a man had to start at the bottom of the company and 'work his way up'. Garry had more than twenty years' start on him. Garry loved it and he hated it.

He thought about half a million dollars. With that amount of money in his back pocket, he could thumb his nose at his bank manager, at Geoffrey Manguza, and at Garry Courtney, and at the rest of the world, and tell them all to go and get stuffed.

He turned away from the river, and started down the path to Job's tent. Job was eating alone at his own camp-fire, served by his youngest wife. He gave her a quiet order to leave when he saw Sean coming, then he took the coffee pot off the coals and poured a second mug and dribbled condensed milk from the can into it.

Sean sat on the carved native stool beside him and took the mug from him. He spoke in Sindebele.

'What would you think of a man who followed a great elephant like Tukutela to his secret place in the swamps along the Zambezi?'

98

'A man of such stupidity does not bear thinking of.' Job blew on his coffee to cool it, and they were silent for a long while.

Matatu, who had been sleeping in his hut nearby, sensed the presence of his master, and came out, blinking and yawning in the early sunlight, to squat at Sean's feet. Sean let his hand rest on the little man's shoulder for a moment. He felt him wriggle with pleasure under the touch. He did not even have to ask Matatu. He would go where Sean went, without question, without a moment's hesitation, so Sean spoke directly to Job.

'Job, old friend of many years, I give you something else to think on. Monterro wants to follow the elephant, he is offering half a million dollars. What do you think of half a million dollars?'

Job sighed. 'I do not have to think too long on that. When do we leave?'

Sean squeezed his arm hard, and stood up.

Riccardo was seated at the breakfast table with a cup of coffee and a cigar. Claudia was beside him, and they had been arguing. The girl's face was still flushed and her eyes asparkle, but she lapsed into silence as Sean entered the tent.

'Capo,' Sean said. 'You have no idea what it will be like across there. It will be Vietnam all over again, but this time without the back-up of the US army. Do you understand that?'

'I want to go,' Capo nodded.

'All right. Here are my terms. You will sign an indemnity, for whatever happens to you. I am not responsible.'

'Agreed.'

'Then I want a written acknowledgement of debt for the full amount, binding on your estate in the event of your death.'

'Give me the paper.'

'You are crazy, Capo, do you know that?'

'Sure,' Riccardo grinned. 'But what about you?'

'Oh, I was born crazy,' Sean laughed with him as they shook hands, and then he sobered. 'I want to fly a reconnaissance along the border to make sure there are no surprises waiting for us. If all is clear, we'll cross tonight. It will mean forced marches and travelling light. I want to be in and out in under ten days.'

Riccardo nodded and Sean told him, 'Get some rest now. You are going to need it.'

He was about to turn away when he caught Claudia's furious gaze. 'I'll radio Reema to send down another charter flight to pick you up tomorrow. She'll wangle you on the first commercial flight back to Anchorage.'

Claudia seemed about to reply when Riccardo laid his hand over hers. 'Okay,' he said. 'She'll go. I'll see to it.'

'Damn right, she'll go,' Sean said. 'She certainly isn't coming into Mozambique with us.'

* * *

Sean taped over the identification markings on the Beechcraft's wings and fuselage, obliterating them from the scrutiny of a ground observer. He made certain that the tape was so firmly adhering to the metalwork that the slipstream could not strip it away. While he worked, Job checked the emergency stores aboard the aircraft, in case they were forced down. Rather than the heavy double-barrelled rifle, he loaded Sean's lightweight 30/06 with the black glass-fibre stock.

They took off and Sean banked onto an easterly heading, keeping barely fifty feet above the treetops. He flew with the map on his lap, checking each landmark as it appeared ahead of them. Job sat beside him in the right-hand seat, while Matatu was in the seat behind Job. Even after all these years, Matatu was terrified of flying, and still occasionally suffered from air-sickness. Sean refused to allow him to sit in the seat behind him.

'Silly little bugger will puke down the back of my neck again.' So Job had to run that risk.

They reached the border and turned northwards along it, searching for troop movements or for any evidence of human presence. They found nothing, until thirty minutes later they saw the sheen of water on the horizon, an inland sea formed by the man-made dam on the Zambezi River. 'Cabora Bassa,' Sean grunted. The hydro-electric scheme, one of the biggest and most expensive in Africa, had been built by the Portuguese before they relinquished the colony to self-government.

Although the South Africans would have taken all the power that the project could supply, transporting it southwards across the grids to their great mines at Palabora in the Transvaal, and the revenue would have gone a long way to alleviating Mozambique's desperate economic plight, Cabora Bassa no longer sold a single kilowatt of electricity. The southbound power lines were continually sabotaged by the rebel forces, and the government troops were so demoralized that they made little attempt to protect the repair crews from attack. Thus it was years since a repair had even been attempted.

'By now the turbines are probably just piles of rust. Score another sweeping triumph for African Marxism,' Sean chuckled, and dropped a wing to turn 180 degrees and head back southwards. On this leg he flew deeper into Mozambique, setting a zigzag course to cover more ground, once again searching for occupied villages or mobile military units.

They found only the patterns of old cultivated lands, now gone back to weed and bush, and burned-out deserted villages, with no sign of human life around the shells of roofless huts.

Sean intersected the road running between Vila de Manica and Cabora Bassa, and flew along it for ten miles. He was so low that he could see the ruts and potholes in the surface and weeds growing in the wheel tracks. No vehicle had used it for months, perhaps years. The culverts and bridges had been destroyed by explosives and the bodies of mined vehicles, burned out and rusted, littered the verges.

He turned back towards the west and the border now, searching for a place that all three of them remembered so well. As they came up ahead, Sean recognized the symmetrical hillocks they called Inhlozane, 'The Maiden's Breasts', and south of them the confluence of two minor rivers, now reduced to strings of green pools in wide sand beds.

Job pointed ahead. 'There it is.' And in the back seat, Matatu forgot his fear and discomfort to cackle with laughter and clutch Sean's shoulder.

'Inhlozane. Do you remember, *Bwana*?'

Sean banked steeply over the junction of the two rivers, circling them, all three of them peering down. They could make out no traces of the old guerrilla camp. The last time they had been here was in the spring of 1976 and they had come as the scouts, Ballantyne's Scouts.

Under interrogation, a prisoner had revealed the existence of a major guerrilla training camp in this area, and the Rhodesian high command had sent one of the Vampire jets over on a high photographic run. The camp had been cunningly concealed, and every artifice of camouflage employed. However, the Rhodesian evaluators were highly skilled, most of them ex-RAF personnel. It is possible to camouflage the dugouts and hutments used by hundreds of men and women, but the pathways between them are the tell-tales. Thousands of feet moving daily between barracks and lecture huts, between mess halls and latrines, going out to forage for firewood or carrying water from the river, beat pathways that from the air look like the veins in a dead leaf.

'Between two and two and a half thousand,' the airforce photographic reconnaissance squadron leader had told the briefing. 'They have been there for approximately six months, so training is almost complete. They are probably just waiting for the rains to break before beginning a major offensive.'

A simultaneous incursion by two thousand trained terrorists would have strained the Rhodesian security forces' capabilities to breaking point.

'Preemptive strike,' General Peter Walls, the Rhodesian Commander-in-Chief, had ordered. 'I want a battle plan prepared within twenty-four hours.' The code name chosen for the attack was 'Popeye'.

Rivalry between the Selous Scouts and the Ballantyne Scouts was fierce, and Sean had been jubilant when he had been given the ground attack role of 'Popeye' in preference to the Selous lads.

They had gone in with the slow and ancient Dakotas, crowded on the benches along the fuselage, fifty men and their equipment to an aircraft, sitting on their parachutes. Almost equal numbers of black and white troopers, but homogeneous in their camouflage paint, they had jumped from three hundred feet, just enough height for the parachutes to flare before they hit the ground. From that height they jokingly referred to themselves as 'meat bombs'.

The jump area was twelve miles from the guerrilla training camp, and ninety-six miles inside the Mozambique border. They were on the ground an hour before sunset. All three hundred Scouts were assembled and ready to move out by nightfall.

They had made the approach march by moonlight, each man carrying a pack that weighed almost a hundred pounds, most of that weight made up of ammunition for the RPD machine-guns. They had reached the fork of the river after midnight and prepared their ambush position along the south bank, overlooking the dry riverbed and its shallow green pools, facing the training camp on the far bank.

Sean, with Job beside him, crept along the bank checking every position personally, speaking to his men in whispers, calling them by name. They had lain for the rest of the night behind their machine-guns, and the small sounds and the smells of the wood-smoke and cooking food had drifted across to them on the night breeze.

At dawn, a bugle had sounded reveille in the dark forest that hid the camps, and they had seen the obscure movement of many persons in the gloom beneath the trees.

Twenty minutes later, precisely at the moment of good shooting light, the Vampires had come whistling in from the west and dropped their napalm canisters. Towering balls of orange flame shot through with evil black smoke had erupted into the sky palling the sunrise; the heat and the chemical stink of the napalm came rolling down to where the Scouts lay in ambush. The Vampires had deliberately dropped their loads of napalm along the northern perimeter of the camp, sealing off that escape route with a wall of fire.

The Canberra bombers came in twenty seconds behind the Vampires, and their bomb loads were fragmentation and high-explosive. They fell into the camp with jarring crumping deton-ations, sending up fountains of dirt and debris, and the trainee guerrillas who survived came out of the forest, screaming and howling in a panic-stricken mob.

The napalm had cut them off from the north, and they poured into the riverbed, and came running directly at the waiting machine-guns. Sean let them come, studying them with a de-tached interest. There were almost as many women as men, but it was difficult to differentiate between the sexes. They wore no uniform, some were in khaki shorts and tee-shirts with portraits of guerrilla leaders or political slogans printed on the chests. Others wore blue denim or bush jackets and some were bare-chested and in their underwear. Nearly all of them were young, in their middle or late teens, all of them terrified and running blindly to escape the conflagration of napalm and high-explosive.

They splashed into the pools, and the sand held their feet, slowing them. As they ran, they looked back over their shoulders at the flames and dust of the camp, so none of them saw the gunners that waited for them on the south bank.

The riverbed was filled with struggling humanity, like a pit full of rats, and as the first of them reached the bank on which Sean lay and began to clamber up the steep earthen side, he blew a piercing blast on his whistle. The last note of the whistle was drowned out by gunfire, three hundred automatic weapons opening up together.

Sean had been hardened by years of brutal warfare, but even he found the carnage stunning. At close range, the volleys of machine-gun fire tore a human body to shreds, and went on to destroy the next rank and the next. Shot boiled the white sand of the riverbed, so it rose in a fog waist-high, and turned the running figures to ghostly silhouettes in the dust, and then hid them as they collapsed or were flung carelessly aside by point-blank bursts of fire.

The din lasted for four minutes, and then there were no more targets and the guns fell silent. Between them they had fired fifty thousand bullets into the riverbed and the barrels of the guns were so hot that, like the plate of a stove, they ticked and pinkled as they cooled. Though their ears were dulled and numbed by the roar of gunfire, they could hear the moans and cries of those who still lived in the riverbed.

Sean blew another blast on his whistle and they leaped down the bank, and went forward in a skirmishing line.

Sean's orders were that the only prisoners to be taken were to be officers or political commissars. As they crossed the river, they shot those who showed any signs of life, holding the muzzles against their heads, a single bullet for each, making certain that they would never recover from their wounds to attack another Rhodesian farm house or hack the arms and legs off the black villagers who refused to supply them with food and women. They left nobody alive in the riverbed and then went on to sweep through the camp, tossing grenades into the dugouts, searching the huts for survivors, and more importantly for maps and documents. Like all good Marxists, the guerrillas were obsessed with record-keeping. The capture of the camp archives was one of the major priorities of 'Popeye'.

Racing at the head of his men, Sean was the first to reach the headquarters hut in the centre of the camp. He recognized it by the gaudy flag drooping on its flagpole in front of it.

The doorway was dangerous. He fired a burst through the grass wall and then dived in head first through the window. There was a tall black man in the front office. He was dressed in blue denims, and he was scooping armfuls of documents out of the paraffin boxes that served as filing cabinets and dumping them in the centre of the floor. Clearly he was going to attempt to burn them, but now he dropped his armful of paper and reached for the pistol in the holster on his belt.

Sean kicked his legs out from under him and as he dropped, he slammed the butt of his weapon into the side of his neck just below the ear. As Sean rolled to his feet, Matatu appeared beside him like a grinning gnome and stooped to slit the unconscious guerrilla's throat with his skinning knife.

'No.' Sean stopped him. 'We want that one.' Job was seconds behind him, bursting into the room with the heavy RPD machine-gun held ready across his hip.

'Okay, Captain,' Sean ordered him. 'Get a detail to recover all this bumf.' He glanced at his watch. 'The choppers will be here in twenty minutes.'

The Rhodesian air force was desperately short of helicopters. They were under sanction by every nation in the world except South Africa, and a British warship was blockading the Mozambique channel to deny those ports to them.

They could risk only two helicopters for this operation and one of those was loaded with captured documents, almost five tons of them: lists of the trainees, and their organization, target priorities and supply sheets, equipment dossiers, training manuals, field evaluations of Rhodesian counter measures, communist propaganda, maps of the attack routes and safe corridors, the entire order of battle of the guerrilla army. It was a treasure trove, its acquisition a greater blow to the enemy than the hundreds of bodies lying in the riverbed, but it filled one of the precious helicopters.

The second Alouette helicopter Sean used for 'Casevac' and for ferrying out the prisoners. However, the Scouts had taken more casualties than he had anticipated: three troopers had been injured in the parachute drop, torn cartilages and sprained ligaments, and five others had been wounded by the desultory and quickly suppressed counterfire of the more plucky of the guerrillas. Then one of the guerrillas had feigned dead in the riverbed and thrown a grenade when the Scouts came forward, killing a black trooper and wounding two others. The Scouts always took their dead out for decent burial and the trooper's corpse was already in its green plastic body bag.

In addition to his own casualties, Sean's men had captured eight suspected officers and commissars. The guerrilla leaders wore no insignia of rank but could usually be identified by the superior quality of their clothing, by their sunglasses, wristwatches and by the rows of ballpoint pens in their breast pockets.

They had too many passengers for the helicopters, and Sean was forced to keep five of his prisoners with him for the outward march. He picked those who looked fit enough to survive a forced march with the Scouts, and one of these was the man they had captured in the command hut.

Forty-five minutes after the attack had begun, the last helicopter took off and the Scouts were ready to move out. They could expect the Frelimo counter-attack to be dilatory and unenthusiastic, but Sean was taking no chances. He was on the riverbank surveying the carnage of the killing ground. They couldn't afford the time to make a body count, but the air force would run another reconnaissance later this morning and they would get a fair estimate from the photographs.

'Must be at least fifteen hundred,' Sean decided. They were lying in heaps and windrows like newly cut wheat and already the flies were hanging over them in a grey mist.

Sean turned away from the scene. 'All right,' he called. 'Move them out!'

The first section of fifty men set off at a trot. The troop trucks would race across the border and come in as far as they could to meet them, but the men would still have to run thirty miles or more before they could ride, a full marathon under arms, but most of the ammunition had been shot away and the packs were almost empty.

Job hurried across to where Sean stood on the bank. 'The prisoner you took, Colonel. I have recognized him. It's Comrade China himself.'

'Are you sure?' Sean did not wait for Job to reply. 'Damn, if I had known I would have sent him out on the chopper.'

Comrade China was high on the wanted list of the Rhodesians. He was the area commander of the entire north-eastern sector, the equivalent of a major-general, and one of their most successful commanders, a man with a lot of interesting stories to tell to military intelligence.

'Make sure he gets out safely, Captain,' Sean ordered brusquely. 'Treat him like your new wife.'

'China refuses to march,' Job said. 'We can't shoot him, and we can't carry him. He knows that.'

Sean strode across to where the prisoner was held under guard. He squatted sullenly with his hands behind his head.

'On your feet and march,' Sean ordered, and Comrade China spat on Sean's boots. Sean unbuckled his holster and drew the .357 Magnum revolver. He laid it against the side of the man's head.

'On your feet,' he repeated. 'Your last chance.'

'You won't shoot,' the man sneered. 'You daren't shoot.' And Sean fired. The muzzle was aimed over Comrade China's shoulder, but the barrel was pressed hard against his ear.

Comrade China screamed and clutched at his ear with both hands. A thin trickle of blood from his ruptured eardrum ran out between his fingers. 'On your feet!' Sean said and still holding his damaged ear, Comrade China spat at him again. Sean laid the revolver barrel against his other ear. 'After your ears, we will take out your eyes, with a sharp stick.' Comrade China stood up.

'At the double, move out.' Job took over. He placed his hand between China's shoulder-blades, and sent him tottering down the riverbank.

Sean took one more look around the battlefield. It had been done swiftly and thoroughly, what the Scouts called 'a good kill'.

'All right, Matatu,' Sean said softly. 'Let's go home.' And the little Ndorobo ran ahead of him.

When Comrade China faltered and his knees went rubbery and he collapsed from the agony of his burst eardrum, Sean gave him a subcutaneous shot of morphine from a disposable syringe and a drink from his water-bottle.

'For a soldier of the revolution who shoots babies and chops the feet off old women, this is a stroll in the park,' Sean told him. 'Brace up, China, or I'll blow your other ear out.' And he took one of his elbows and Job the other. Between them, they hoisted him to his feet and half carried him until the morphine had a chance to work, but they kept up the pace of the running column of Scouts through the forest and over the rolling rocky hills.

'You may have killed some of our people today.' After a mile or so the morphine was working and China became loquacious. 'Today you have won a single little battle, Colonel Courtney, but tomorrow we will have won the war.' China's voice was harsh with bitter self-righteousness.

'How do you know my name?' Sean asked with amusement.

'You are famous, Colonel, or should I say infamous. Under you, this pack of killer dogs is even more dangerous than when the murderous Ballantyne himself was leading it.'

'Thank you for the pretty compliment, my old China, but aren't you claiming victory a little prematurely?'

'The side which controls the countryside by night wins the war.'

'Mao Tse-tung,' Sean smiled. 'A most appropriate quotation for one of your name.'

'We control the countryside at last, we have you bottled up in your villages and towns. Your white farmers are losing heart, their women are sick of war. The black peasants are openly sympathetic to our cause. Britain and the world are against you. Even South Africa, your only ally, is growing disenchanted with the struggle. Soon, very soon . . .'

They argued as they ran, and despite himself, Sean could not suppress a grudging admiration for his prisoner. He was quick-witted, his command of English impressive and his grasp of politics and military tactics even more so. He was physically strong and fit. Sean could feel the wiry muscle in his arm as he supported him, and few other men with a burst eardrum could have sustained the pace of the march.

'He would make a superb Scout,' Sean thought. 'If we could turn him . . .' Many of his most valuable men were former guerrillas, captured and skilfully turned by Rhodesian intelligence.

So as they ran on he studied Comrade China with renewed interest. He was probably a few years younger than Sean. He had refined Nilotic features, more Ethiopian than Shona, a narrow high-bridged nose and chiselled lips rather than the broadly negroid. Even the morphine could not dim the intelligence of his large dark eyes. He was a handsome man, and of course, he would be tough and utterly ruthless. He would not have reached his rank were he not.

'I want him,' Sean decided. 'My God, he would be worth another full regiment to us.' And he tightened his grip on the man's arm, a proprietorial gesture. 'This little darling is going to get the full treatment.'

The vanguard ran into a Frelimo patrol in the middle of the morning and brushed them aside, hardly slackening their pace to do so. The corpses in their blotched Frelimo camouflage lay beside the track as they trotted past.

They came up with the troop convoy a little after midday. The trucks were guarded by the Eland armoured cars, and they had cans of ice-cold Castle beer in the cool boxes. The Scouts had covered forty-two miles in just over seven hours, and the beer tasted like nectar.

Sean gave a can to Comrade China. 'Sorry about your ear,' he told him, and saluted him with the beer can.

'I would have done the same to you,' China smiled, but his eyes were inscrutable. 'To our next meeting?' he suggested the toast.

'Until we meet again,' Sean agreed, and handed him over to a guard detail under a white sergeant. Then he climbed into the command armoured car to lead the final stage of withdrawal.

Sean extricated his column and had them back across the border ten and a half hours after the attack began. Ian Smith, the prime minister, came on the radio net in person to congratulate him and inform him of his decoration, a bar to his silver cross.

Sean didn't learn about Comrade China's escape until the column went into laager that evening. Apparently, China had slit the canvas hood of the troop truck and slipped through it while his guard was dozing. Undeterred by his manacles, he had dropped off the speeding truck, screened by the dust boiling out from the back wheels, and rolled into the head-high elephant grass along the verge.

Two months later, Sean had seen an intelligence report that placed China in command of the successful attack that had wiped out a supply convoy on the Mount Darwin road.

'Yes, Matatu, I remember it all very well,' Sean answered his question, and made one more steep turn above the site of the old terrorist base before he returned the Beechcraft to straight and level flight on a southerly heading.

He did not, however, fly as far southwards as the railway line that linked the port of Beira to the land-locked Zimbabwe border. This was a focus for all the military and rebel activity in the area, and the countryside would be swarming with Frelimo and Zimbabwean troops, all armed with RPG rockets and eager to get a shot at an unmarked low-flying aircraft with no flight authorization.

'At least,' Sean told Job, 'it looks like a possibility.'

Job agreed. 'The border opposite our camp seems undefended and deserted.'

'Worth a try for half a million?' Sean asked, and Job just grinned at him.

'One more little chore before we go home,' Sean told them.

It required precise navigation and an eye for the terrain, but Sean crossed back into the Zimbabwean side and flying low they were able to pick out the spot where the previous day they had first come across the poachers' tracks; from that point, with Matatu craning his head to see down and calling directions, they found the tableland and valley where they had come up with the band of poachers and taken them under fire. From the air the distances seemed much shorter than they had on foot.

Matatu directed Sean along the trail the old bull had made towards the border. It seemed that his gift for direction and terrain was not impaired by height above the ground, and Sean was following their course on the map he held in his lap.

'We are crossing back into Mozambique now.' Sean was scribbling notes on the map.

'That way.' Matatu leaned over the back of the seat and pointed out a more northerly track. Sean knew better than to argue with him, and turned a few degrees left.

Minutes later Matatu demanded he turn slightly south again.

'Little bugger is actually sensing the old bull's trail, he is thinking like the elephant,' Sean marvelled and at that moment, Matatu gave a squeak of triumph and pointed urgently out of the side window.

As they flashed across another dry riverbed, Sean glimpsed the tracks trodden in the soft sand. They were so deep that they were filled with shadow, a string of dark beads on the white background. Even Sean, who for twenty years had watched Matatu work, was amazed. On instinct alone, Matatu had followed the bull to this river-crossing. It was a supernatural feat.

Sean circled the tracks, his port wing-tip pointing directly at them, so steep was his turn.

'Which way now?' he called to the back seat, and Matatu tapped his shoulder and pointed downstream. Without demur, Sean followed the gnarled black finger.

'There he is!' Job shouted suddenly, and Matatu shrieked with laughter and clapped his hands, bouncing in his seat like a child at the pantomime.

A mile ahead the river ran into a wide vlei that still held water from the last rains. The elephant's humped back showed above the tops of the tall reeds that surrounded the pool, like a grey whale in a sea of green.

As they raced low towards him, the elephant heard the Beech-craft's engine. He lifted his head and spread his ears wide, turning to face them, and they saw his tusks, those legendary shafts of black ivory raised to the sky. The beauty of their curved symmetry struck Sean all over again.

There was just a glimpse of them as they flashed overhead, but the image was printed vividly on his mind's eye. Half a million dollars and those tusks, he had risked his life a hundred times for much lesser prizes.

'Going back for another look?' Job asked, twisting his head to try and see back over the tail-plane.

'No.' Sean shook his head. 'We don't want to disturb him more than necessary. We know where to find him, let's go home.'

* * *

'It's my half-million dollars that you are so gaily throwing around,' Claudia told her father.

'How do you work that out?' Riccardo asked. He was lying on his camp-bed dressed in a pair of silk pyjama bottoms, his chest and his feet bare. Claudia noticed that most of his body hair was still crisp, curly and black, with only a patch of fuzzy grey in the centre of his chest.

'My inheritance,' she explained sweetly. 'You are blowing my inheritance, Papa.'

Riccardo chuckled. She had the sass of a divorce lawyer, coming bursting into his tent to renew the argument which he thought he had finalized in the mess tent over breakfast.

'If I'm not going to get it in your will, the very least you can do is let me enjoy it with you now.'

'According to the last audit, young lady, you will have a little over thirty-six million coming to you after taxes, and after I have allowed myself this small extravagance. I hasten to add that every cent is tied up in a trust fund that not the most crafty lawyers

111

will ever break. I don't want you handing my hard-earned loot out to one of your bleeding-heart charities.'

'Papa, you know the money has never interested me. What interests me is coming with you on this crazy jaunt after the elephant. I came to Africa with you on the understanding that I was to be included in everything. That was our bargain.'

'I'll say it one more time, *tesoro*, my treasure.' He only called her by that baby name when he was feeling very affectionate or very exasperated. 'You are not coming into Mozambique with us.'

'You'd go back on your solemn promise?' she accused.

'Without a qualm,' he assured her. 'If your safety or happiness was involved.'

She jumped up from the canvas camp-chair and began to prowl around the tent. He watched her with secret pleasure. Her arms were folded over those pert little breasts, and she was frowning heavily, but the frown left no lines on her smooth plastic skin. In looks she reminded him of the young Sophia Loren, his favourite actress. Now she stopped beside the camp-bed and glared down at him.

'You know I always get my way,' she said. 'Why don't you make it easier for both of us, and just say I can come.'

'I'm sorry, *tesoro*. You aren't coming.'

'All right.' She drew a deep breath 'I don't want to do this, Papa, but you leave me no choice. I have begun to understand what this means to you, why you are prepared to pay such a vast sum for a chance to do it, but if I can't go with you, as is my right and my duty, then I will prevent you from going.'

He chuckled again, easily and unconcernedly.

'I am serious, deadly serious, Papa. Please don't make me do it.'

'How can you stop me, little girl?' he asked.

'I can tell Sean Courtney what Doctor Andrews told me.'

Riccardo Monterro came to his feet in one lithe swift movement and seized her arms.

'What did Andrews tell you?' he asked in a voice as thin and cutting as a razor blade.

'He told me that last November you had a little black spot on your right arm,' she said. Instinctively, he put his right arm behind his back, but she went on. 'It had a pretty name, melanoma, like a girl's name, but it wasn't pretty at all, and you left it too late.

112

He cut it out, but the pathologist graded it Clarke 5. That's six months to a year, Papa. That's what he told me.'

Riccardo Monterro sat down on the bed and his voice was suddenly very weary.

'When did he tell you?'

'Six weeks ago.' She sat down beside him. 'That is why I agreed to come to Africa with you. I didn't want to be apart from you for one day of the time we have left. That is why I am coming with you into Mozambique.'

'No.' He shook his head. 'I can't let you.'

'Then I will tell Sean that at any moment it may reach your brain.'

She did not have to elaborate. Andrews had been most graphic as he described the many possible directions the disease could take. If it went to the lungs, it would be death by suffocation, but if it affected the brain or nervous system, it would be either general paralysis or total derangement.

'You wouldn't,' he said, shaking his head. 'The last thing in my life that I really want. You wouldn't deny it to me?'

'Without a qualm,' she repeated his own words. 'If you refuse me my right to be with you for every one of these last days, and to be with you at the end as is the duty of a loving daughter.'

'I can't let you.' He let his face sink into the cup of his hands, a gesture of defeat that hurt her, and it required all her resolve to keep her tone firm.

'And I can't let you die alone,' she replied.

'You don't understand how much I want this thing, it's the last thing in my life. The old bull and I will go together. You don't understand, if you did you wouldn't prevent me.'

'I'm not preventing you,' she said gently. 'I want you to have it, if you will let me come with you.' As she said it, they both became aware of a faint vibration in the air, and they looked up together.

'The Beechcraft,' Riccardo murmured. 'Sean is on his way back to the airstrip.' He glanced at his wristwatch. 'He'll be here within the hour.'

'And what will you tell him?' Claudia asked. 'Will you tell him that I am coming with you?'

*　　*　　*

'No!' Sean let out a bellow. 'No bloody fear! Forget the idea, Capo. She can't come and that's absolutely bloody final!'

'For half a big M. I get to call the shots,' Riccardo told him quietly. 'I say she's coming, so she's coming.'

They were standing beside the Toyota. Riccardo and Claudia had met Sean as he drove into camp. Sean drew a breath and glared at father and daughter as they stood side by side confronting him. He saw that both their expressions were set and determined.

Sean had been on the point of bellowing again, but with an effort he checked himself. 'Be reasonable, Capo.' He moderated his tone. 'You know it's impossible.'

They stared at him grimly, closed against argument or reason. 'It's war out there. I can't take her.'

'Claudia comes with us.'

'The hell she does.'

'What are you making a fuss about, is it because I am a woman?' Claudia spoke for the first time. 'There is nothing a man can do that I can't.'

'Can you pee standing up?' He wanted to disconcert her, make her lose her temper, but she ignored the crude jibe and went on as though he had not spoken.

'You've seen me hike. I can stand the heat and the tsetse fly, I'm as good as my father.'

He turned from her deliberately and spoke to Riccardo.

'As her father you can't allow it. Can you imagine what would happen to her if she were caught by a gang of Renamo cutthroats?'

He saw Riccardo flinch, but Claudia had seen it also and before he could weaken, she took his hand and spoke up firmly.

'Either I go, or nobody goes, and you can kiss your half a million good-bye, Colonel Sean Courtney.'

That was the key, the half-million dollars. She had him, and they both knew it. He couldn't afford to pass it by, but he made one last effort.

'Is she in charge around here, Capo? Do I take my orders from you or from her?'

'That won't work either.' Claudia tried to keep her tone placatory, although she longed to tear into him with tooth and nail. That crude sally of his rankled. 'My father and I are agreed on this. Both of us go, or we call the deal off. Isn't that right, Papa?'

'I'm afraid that's it, Sean.' Riccardo looked tired and discouraged. 'It's not negotiable. If you want your money, you take Claudia along with us.'

Sean turned on his heel and strode away towards his own tent, but after a few paces, he stopped and stood with his hands on his hips.

Sean's shouts had attracted the camp servants, and they hovered around the mess tent and peered out of the doorway and windows of the kitchen hutments, apprehension mingled with curiosity.

'What the hell are you all gawking at?' Sean roared. 'Have you got no work to do around here?' And they disappeared with alacrity.

Sean turned and walked slowly back to where the two of them stood beside the Toyota.

'Okay,' he agreed, staring coldly at Claudia. 'Cut your own throat, but don't come to me for a bandage.'

'I won't, that's a promise.' Her voice was honey dripping, more irksome to him than straightforward gloating would have been, and they both knew that their declared truce was at an end.

'We've got some paperwork to do, Capo.' Sean led the way to the mess tent without looking back at them.

With two fingers, Sean typed out the indemnity statements on his old portable Remington, one for Riccardo and one for his daughter. Each began; 'I acknowledge that I am fully aware of the danger and the illegality . . .' Then he typed an acknowledgement of debt for Riccardo to sign and called Job and the chef to witness the signature. He sealed all the copies in an envelope addressed to Reema at the Harare office and locked it in the small steel safe at the back of the mess tent.

'Let's do it, then,' he said.

*   *   *

The poaching expedition would consist of the three whites, Job, Matatu, Pumula and the stocky, bearded tracker who had picked up Tukutela's spoor at the river-crossing. His name was Dedan.

'It's too many, but each of those tusks weighs 130 pounds,' Sean explained. 'Matatu is too small to act as a porter. We need four big men to bring them back.'

115

Before the equipment was loaded into the Toyota, Sean ordered it laid out, and he opened and checked each pack. Claudia protested when he opened her personal pack. 'That is an invasion of my privacy!'

'So take me to the supreme court, ducky,' he challenged as he went through it remorselessly, throwing out most of the tubes and bottles of cosmetics, allowing her only three tubes of moisturizer and sunscreen.

'One change of underwear,' he ordered, discarding half a dozen pairs of panties. 'But you'll need two more pairs of thick socks. Get them.'

He pulled out her box of Tampax. 'Everything a man can do, and then some,' he remarked coldly. 'You don't need the box, it takes up too much space. Pack them loose.' Her poorly suppressed fury gave him a sour pleasure.

By the time he had finished, they were down to the barest essentials, and the packs were carefully weighed and apportioned depending on the strength and physical condition of each bearer. Sean, Job, Pumula and Dedan carried sixty pounds each, Riccardo and Matatu forty, while Claudia was down to twenty-five pounds.

'I can carry more,' she protested. 'Give me forty, the same as Matatu.' Sean did not bother to answer her.

'And what's more, I eat half as much as any of you!' But he had already turned away to supervise the loading of the Toyota.

*   *   *

There were still four hours of daylight remaining when they left Chiwewe camp, but Sean drove the first section very fast, jouncing them around in their seats. It was partly an expression of his objection to Claudia's presence but mostly an urgent desire to be at the jump-off point before nightfall.

As he drove, he spoke in a tightly controlled voice. 'Before we commence this guided tour of the Mozambiquan paradise of the proletariat, this shining gem of African socialism, will you bear with me while I give you a few facts and figures.' Nobody protested, so he went on. 'Until 1975 Mozambique was a Portuguese colony. For almost five hundred years it had been under Portuguese control and had been a reasonably happy and prosperous community of some fifteen million souls. The Portuguese,

116

unlike the British or German colonists, had a relaxed attitude towards miscegenation and the result was a large mulatto population, and an official policy of "Assimilado" under which any person of colour, if he attained certain civilized standards, was considered to be white and enjoyed Portuguese nationality. It all worked very well, as indeed did most colonial administrations, especially those of the British.'

'Bullshit,' said Claudia demurely. 'That's limey propaganda.'

'Limey?' Sean smiled thinly. 'Careful, your prejudice is showing. nonetheless your average Indian or African living today in a former British colony is a damned sight worse off now than he was then. Certainly that goes one hundred times more for your average black man living in Mozambique.'

'At least they are free,' Claudia cut in, and Sean laughed.

'This is freedom? An economy managed under the well-known socialist principles of chaos and ruination which has resulted in a negative growth rate of up to ten per cent per annum for every year since the Portuguese withdrawal, a foreign debt amounting to double the gross national product, a total breakdown in the educational system, only five per cent of children regularly attending a recognized school, one doctor per forty-five thousand persons, only one person in ten with access to purified drinking water, infant mortality at 340 per 1000 births. The only worse countries in the world are Afghanistan and Angola, but as you say, at least they are free. In America, where everybody eats three huge meals a day, freedom may be a big deal, but in Africa a full belly counts for a hell of a lot more.'

'It can't be as bad as that,' she protested.

'No,' he agreed. 'It's a lot worse. I haven't mentioned two other factors, the civil war and Aids. When the Portuguese were pushed out, they handed over to a dictator named Samora Machel and his Frelimo party. Machel was an avowed Marxist. He didn't believe in the nonsense of elections, and his rule was directly responsible for the present condition of the country, and for the emergence of the National Mozambiquan Resistance or as it is known to its friends and admirers, Renamo. Nobody knows much about it, what its objectives are, who its leaders are, all we know is that it controls most of the country, especially the north, and that it is made up of a pretty ruthless bunch of characters.'

'Renamo is a South African front organization, directed,

supplied and controlled from Pretoria,' Claudia helped him out. 'Committed to the overthrow of sovereign government and the destabilization of the southern continent.'

'Well done, ducky,' Sean nodded approval. 'You've been studying the wisdom and erudition of the Organization of African Unity and the non-aligned nations. You have even mastered their jargon. If only South Africa had the military and technological capability to commit half the skulduggery it is accused of, it would not be simply the most powerful country in Africa, it would be running the entire world.'

'I keep forgetting you are one of them, which is silly of me. You don't attempt to conceal your bigotry. The simple fact is that your government and apartheid are the scourge and the curse of Africa.'

'Of course, we are responsible for everything, the Aids epidemic, the famines of Ethiopia and Angola and Mozambique, the breakdown of government in Uganda and Zambia, the corruption in Nigeria and Zaire, it's all a dirty South African plot. We even killed Samora Machel, we fed vodka to the Russian crew of his Tupolev jet and with our incredibly sophisticated technology, lured them over the border. Machel hit one of our racist mountains with such force that his brains and major organs were instantly expelled from his body, nevertheless our apartheid doctors kept him alive long enough to torture state secrets out of him. That is the truth as determined by UNO and OAU.'

'Shut up,' said Riccardo Monterro. 'I've had enough. Shut up, both of you.'

'Sorry,' Sean grinned at him. 'I get carried away. I just wanted to let you know what to expect when we cross the border. We can just hope that we aren't going to meet any of the lads from either Frelimo or Renamo, there is not a lot to choose between them. They both shoot the same bullets.'

The thought made the back of his own neck prickle, and he felt his mood lighten. He was going into mortal danger again, and the thrill of it began. Somehow having the girl with him no longer irked but rather heightened that anticipation, and he felt his resentment of her begin to fade. He was glad she was here rather than jetting back to Alaska. Sean drove on in a silence that gripped them all, even the men standing braced against the roll-bar in the back of the Toyota. The closer they came to the border, the deeper the silence became.

At last Sean turned and looked over his shoulder, and Job nodded in agreement.

'This is it, ladies and gentlemen,' Sean said quietly. 'All change!' He let the Toyota trundle to a halt where the track crossed a stony ridge.

'Where are we?' Riccardo asked.

'As close as we can safely get to the border, about three miles. From here, it's shanks' pony.'

Riccardo swung one leg out of the truck, but Sean said sharply, 'Hold it, Capo, step onto that slab of rock, leave no tracks.'

One at a time, each carrying their own pack, they alighted from the truck, at Sean's instruction stepping precisely in the footsteps of the person in front. Matatu was the last off, and he came backwards brushing over the sign with a switch of dried grass, wiping out every trace of their departure from the truck.

The chef had come with them to drive the truck back to the camp.

'Go in peace, *Mambo*!' he called to Sean as he pulled away.

'Fat hope,' Sean laughed, and sent him off with a wave. Then to Job, 'Anti-tracking, let's go!'

Neither Riccardo nor Claudia had ever watched anti-tracking procedure, for while hunting they had always run free in pursuit. The formation for anti-tracking was Indian file, Job leading and everyone else stepping in his footprints. Behind them all, Matatu, the old maestro, was covering the sign, replacing a pebble lichenside up, stroking a blade of grass into its original position, flicking at the earth with his grass switch, picking up a leaf dislodged from a low-hanging branch or the bruised blade of grass on which a foot had trodden.

Job avoided the game paths and soft ground, choosing always the line of march which was most obscure and yet moving surprisingly fast, so that within half an hour, Claudia felt the chill of fresh sweat between her shoulder-blades and at the cleavage of her shirt-front.

Job led them to the top of a low kopje, and Sean motioned them to conceal themselves below the skyline with the sunset behind them.

Watching them work, Riccardo remarked softly, 'Pumula and Dedan seem to know what they are doing.' The two of them had moved out to guard the flanks without being ordered to do so.

119

'Yes.' Sean settled down between him and Claudia, using the same low bush for cover. 'They were both non-coms in the Scouts, they've done this before.'

'Why are we stopping here?' Claudia asked.

'We are sitting on the border,' Sean explained, 'and we'll spend the last of the daylight studying the ground ahead. As soon as the moon comes up, we'll move in. You can relax until then.'

He lifted his Zeiss binoculars and stared through them; a few yards away Job lay on his belly and focused his own pair of binoculars in the same direction. They lowered the binoculars from time to time to blink their vision clear or polish an imaginary speck from the lens. Claudia had noticed how they protected and looked after these most essential tools of their craft, but apart from that, their concentration on the terrain ahead was absolute, and ended only when the last gleam of the sunset faded. Then Sean buttoned the binoculars into his top pocket and turned to her.

'Time for your make-up,' he said. For a moment she did not understand and then she felt the greasy touch of camouflage cream on her cheek and instinctively pulled away.

'Hold still,' he snapped. 'Your white face shines like a mirror. It's good for insects and sunburn also.'

He daubed her face and the backs of her hands.

'Here comes the moon.' Sean finished working on his own camouflage and screwed the top back on the tube of cream. 'We can go in now.'

Sean changed the formation once again, putting out flankers, Job and Pumula, while he led the centre and, once again, Matatu brought up the rear, diligently sweeping their tracks.

Once Sean stopped and checked Claudia's equipment. A loose buckle on her pack had been tapping regularly in time with her stride, a noise so small that she had not noticed it.

'You sound like the charge of the Light Brigade,' he breathed in her ear, as he adjusted it.

'Arrogant bastard,' she thought, and they went on in silence, an hour and then another hour without pausing. She never knew the exact moment when she crossed the border. The moonlight through the forest was silvery, and the shadows of the trees flickered over Sean's broad shoulders ahead of her.

Gradually the silence and the moonlight gave the march a

dream-like unreality, and she found herself mesmerized by it, her movements were like those of a sleep-walker, so that when Sean stopped abruptly she bumped into him and might have fallen had he not whipped a hard muscular arm around her and held her.

They stood frozen, listening, staring into the dark forest. After almost five minutes Claudia moved slightly to free herself from his arm, but instantly his grip tightened and she submitted to it. Out on the right flank, Job gave a bird call, and noiselessly Sean sank to the ground drawing her down with him, and her nerves strained tighter as she realized that there must be real danger out there. Now his arm no longer annoyed her. Instinctively she relaxed and pressed a little closer to him. It felt good.

Another soft bird call from the darkness, and Sean put his lips to her ear.

'Stay!' he breathed, and she felt lonely and exposed as he released her, and she watched him disappear like a ghost into the forest.

Sean moved in a low crouch, rifle in one hand, reaching forward to touch the earth with the fingers of his left hand, brushing away the dry twigs and leaves that might crackle under his foot before stepping forward. He sank down ten feet from where Job lay and glanced across at his dark shape. The pale palm of Job's hand flashed a signal, and Sean concentrated on the left front that Job had indicated.

For long minutes, he neither saw nor sensed anything untoward, but he trusted Job completely and he waited with the hunter's patience. Suddenly he caught a taint on the night air and he lifted his nose and sniffed at it. Both his confidence and his patience were repaid. It was the acrid stink of burning tobacco, one of those cheap black Portuguese cigarillos. He remembered them so well, they had been issued to the guerrillas in the days of the bush war, and were probably Frelimo issue still.

He signalled Job and they went forward, leopard-crawling, absolutely silently, forty paces, and Sean picked out the glow of the cigarette as a man drew upon it. Then the man coughed, a soft phlegmy sound, and spat. He was at the base of one of the large trees directly ahead; now Sean could make out his shape. He was sitting with his back to the trunk.

'Who is he? Local tribesman? Poacher? Bee hunter? Refugee?' None of those seemed likely. This one was awake and alert, almost certainly a sentry. As Sean reached that conclusion, he sensed other movement farther out, and he flattened against the earth.

Another man emerged from the forest, and came directly to where the sentry was rising to his feet to meet him. As soon as he stood, Sean could make out the AK 47 rifle slung over his shoulder, muzzle down. The two men talked softly together.

'Changing the guard,' Sean thought as the new sentry leaned against the tree and the other man sauntered back into the forest.

'That is where the camp is,' Sean guessed.

Still on his belly, he leopard-crawled forward, passing well wide of the sentry who would be fresh and vigilant. Once he was within the perimeter, Sean rose into a crouch and went forward swiftly.

He found the camp in a fold of ground up against the hills. It was a fly-camp, no huts nor shelters, only two small fires that had burned down to coals. He counted eleven men lying around the fires, all of them with a blanket pulled completely over their heads in typical African fashion. There might be five or six others on guard duty, but it was a small band.

Even lacking automatic weapons Sean and his men could have dealt with them. All of Sean's men still carried their piano-wire nooses and Matatu his skinning knife with the blade so sharp that it was honed down to half its original width. Nobody in the camp would have even woken up.

Sean shook his head with regret, he was certain now that these were either Frelimo regular troops or Renamo guerrillas. He had no quarrel with them, whoever they were. Just as long as they did not interfere with his elephant hunt. Sean backed away and Job was waiting for him at the perimeter.

'Eleven of them at the fires,' Sean breathed.

'I found two more sentries,' Job agreed.

'Frelimo?'

'Who knows?' Job shrugged, and Sean touched his arm and they crept away, farther out of earshot of the camp so they could speak more freely.

'What do you think, Job?'

'A small group, they mean little. We can go around them.'

'They could be the advance guard for a bigger party,' Sean suggested.

'These are not crack troops,' Job muttered contemptuously.

'Smoking on guard duty, sleeping next to a fire, they aren't soldiers, they are tourists.' Sean smiled at the term of derision. He knew that Job's determination was more Anglo-Saxon than African. Once he had decided, it was difficult to dissuade him.

'You want to go on?' he asked.

'For five hundred thousand dollars,' Job whispered, 'you're damned right I want to go on!'

* * *

Claudia was afraid. The African night was so charged with mystery, with uncertainty and menace. The wait aggravated her feeling of apprehension. Sean had been gone for almost an hour, and though her father was close beside her, she felt alone and very vulnerable.

Then suddenly, Sean was back, and she experienced a rush of relief. She wanted to reach out for him and cling to him, and was ashamed of herself for the weakness. Sean was whispering to her father, and she drew close to listen. Her arm touched Sean's bare arm, but he did not seem to notice, so she left it there for the feeling of security and comfort it gave her.

'Small party of armed men camped up ahead,' Sean was explaining. 'Not more than twenty of them. We don't know who the hell they are, but we can circle around them and keep going, or we can turn back. It's up to you, Capo.'

'I want that elephant!'

'This is probably your last chance to pull out,' Sean warned him.

'You are wasting time,' Riccardo said. Claudia was torn by her father's decision. It would have been such an anti-climax to turn back now, and yet her first taste of the real flavour of Africa had been disconcerting. She realized as the march resumed and she fell in behind Sean, that this was the first time in her life that she had been beyond the trappings and buttresses of civilization, the first time that there was no police force to protect her, no recourse to law or justice or mercy. Here she was as vulnerable as an antelope to the leopard, in a forest full of predators.

She quickened her step, closing up behind Sean and found to her surprise that in some bizarre fashion she was more alive and aware than she had ever been before. For the first time in her life, she was on the bottom rung of existence, the level of survival. It was a novel and quite overwhelming sensation. She was glad that her father had not decided to turn back.

Claudia had long lost all sense of direction for Sean led unpredictably. They turned and twisted through the forest, sometimes moving swiftly and at others, creeping forward a stealthy pace at a time and then freezing into absolute stillness at a signal from the flank which often she had not even heard. She noticed Sean look up at the night sky every few minutes and guessed that he was navigating by the stars, but to her their whorls and blazes and fields were as confused as the lights of a foreign city.

Then after a while, she realized that they had not turned nor paused for a long while, and were once again heading in a straight line. Obviously, they were clear of danger for the moment. With the excitement over, she soon felt the weight of her legs and the weariness in the small of her back. The pack between her shoulders seemed to have quadrupled in weight, and she glanced at her wristwatch. The luminous dial showed her that they had been going for almost five hours since circling around that hidden camp.

'When will we rest?' she wondered, but made it a point of honour to keep close behind Sean, and not to lag by a single pace. Almost as though a refrigerator door had opened, the temperature plunged and when they crossed another open glade, the dew on the long grass soaked the legs of her trousers, and her boots squelched. She shivered, for the first time in real discomfort.

'When will he rest?' She stared at Sean's back, resenting him, willing him to stop. On he went and still on, and she had the feeling that he was deliberately trying to humiliate her, to break her down, to force her to squeal for mercy.

'I'll show you.' She did not slacken her pace as she reached back and unstrapped her Gortex ski jacket from the top of her pack. It was really cold now, the frost crackled underfoot, and her feet were numb but she kept her station in the line and quite suddenly she realized that she could see clearly each thick glossy tress of hair down the back of Sean's neck.

'Dawn. I thought it would never come.' And as she thought it, Sean stopped at last, and she pulled up beside him with the nerves in her legs jumping and trembling with fatigue.

'Sorry, Capo,' Sean spoke softly past her. 'I had to push a

little. We had to get well clear of that bunch before light. How are you making out?'

'No problem,' Riccardo muttered, but in the grey dawn light, his face looked pale and drawn. He was suffering as she was, and she hoped she didn't look as bad. He went to find a place to sit, and lowered himself stiffly.

Sean glanced at Claudia still standing beside him. Neither of them spoke, but he had a faint enigmatic smile on his lips.

'Don't ask me how I feel,' she thought. 'I'd rather drink Drain-o than tell you the truth.'

He inclined his head slightly, condescension or respect, she wasn't sure.

'First day and the third are always the worst,' he said.

'I feel fine,' she said. 'I can go on quite happily.'

'Sure,' he grinned openly. 'But you'd better go and look after Papa rather.'

Sean brought mugs of tea to where she sat beside her father, wrapped in her lightweight down-filled sleeping-bag against the dawn chill. Job had brewed on a tiny smokeless fire which he extinguished immediately the billy boiled. The tea was strong and sweet and scalding, she had never tasted anything more welcome. With it, he handed her a stack of maize cakes and cold cuts of venison. She tried not to wolf them.

'We'll move on in a few minutes,' he warned her, and when he saw the dismay in her eyes, he explained.

'We never sleep next to a cooking-fire, it can attract the uglies.'

They went on five miles and in the middle of the morning, on higher ground in a place secure and easily defended, Sean showed her how to scoop a hollow for her hip and use her pack as a pillow. She fell asleep as though she had been sandbagged.

She could not believe it when he shook her awake only a minute later. 'It's four o'clock.' He handed her a mug and another stack of maize cakes. 'You've slept six hours straight, we are moving out in five minutes.'

Hastily she rolled her sleeping-bag and then peered at herself in the metal hand-mirror which she had surreptitiously retrieved after Sean had thrown it out of her pack.

'Oh God,' she whispered. The camouflage cream had caked and striped with her sweat. 'I look like Al Jolson in drag.' She tidied her hair, dragging her comb through the tangles, and then tied a scarf around it.

125

With short breaks every two hours, they kept going all that night. At first, Claudia's legs felt as though they were in plaster casts, but soon she walked the stiffness out of them and she kept her place in the line without lagging, though the pace Sean set was every bit as hard as the previous night.

In the dawn, they drank tea. Claudia had begun to depend on the brew. She had always been a coffee-drinker, but now on the march, she found herself fantasizing over her next scalding mug of tea.

'It's the only thing keeping me going,' she confided to her father, only half joking.

'They say the limeys conquered their empire on the stuff.' Riccardo nodded agreement, as Sean came across from where he had been in deep discussion with Matatu and Job.

'We are only a few hours' march from the reed-beds where we saw Tukutela from the air.' He looked pointedly at Claudia. 'I'd like to try and get there before we sleep, but, of course, some of us are a little bushed . . .' He let it hang between them, a dare and an accusation.

'I need a little stroll to settle my breakfast,' she said amiably, but she wished her face was not coated with black cream. She hated conceding even the slightest advantage to him.

As Sean walked away, her father swilled the tea leaves in his mug and flicked them out.

'Don't fall for him, *tesoro*. He'd be too big a handful even for you.'

She stared at him, outraged and appalled. 'Fall for him? Are you out of your skull, Papa? I can't stand the sight of him.'

'That's what I mean,' he chuckled.

She jumped up and threw her pack onto her back with unnecessary strength, and then told her father with disdain, 'I could cope with him and five others like him, with my eyes closed and one hand tied behind my back, but I've got better taste than that.'

'Which is fortunate for you,' he murmured just low enough so she was uncertain what he had said.

A little before noon that day, Matatu led them into the papyrus beds which surrounded the green pool which they had seen from the air. He led them directly to the great dished spoor, printed in the mud, and they gathered round to inspect it.

'See!' Matatu told them. 'This is where Tukutela stood when

he heard the *indeki* coming. Here and there he turned to look up in the sky and challenge us.' Matatu imitated the old bull, holding his head at the same angle, humping his back and cupping his hands at each side of his head. It was such a faithful impression, that for a moment, he seemed to become the old bull, and they all laughed. Claudia forgot her fatigue and clapped in applause.

'Then what did the old bull do?' Sean demanded, and Matatu spun and pointed along the run of the spoor.

'He went away with all his speed, he went fast and very far.'

'Well,' Sean said. 'That puts us almost exactly forty-eight hours behind him and we have to sleep now, we'll be fifty-five hours behind him when we march again.'

*   *   *

Tukutela's dam had been the matriarch of a herd of over one hundred beasts. She had come into her last period of oestrus in her fifty-second year, and over the days that it lasted, she had been mounted and serviced by six of the herd bulls, all young animals, vigorous and at the height of their powers.

It was the ideal formula for the conception of an extraordinary calf, old cow and young bull. Although it was uncertain which seed had taken root in her, the old cow had carried the genes of great elephants, big in body and tusk, in natural intelligence and the urge to dominate. These same genes had made her the leader of her herd, and now she transferred them to the foetus she carried in her womb.

She carried him twenty-two months and then in the year when the German askaris under General von Lettow-Vorbeck were ravaging eastern Africa, the year 1915, she had left the herd and accompanied only by another old female past calf-bearing, her companion of forty years, she had gone deep into the fastnesses of the swamps that lie on the south bank of the Zambezi river and there on an islet fringed with ivory nut palms, surrounded by miles of papyrus beds, and with the white-headed fish eagles chanting overhead, she had cleared an area of sandy earth for her couch. When her time came, she had spread her back legs and squatted over the open area, squealing in the agony of her labour, her trunk rolled up on her chest.

Her eyes had no tear ducts to drain them so the tears poured

127

freely down her withered cheeks as though she wept, and the spasms racked her huge gaunt frame.

The other old cow stood close beside her like a midwife, caressing her with her trunk, stroking her back and rumbling with sympathy. She had forced out the calf's head, and then rested for a minute, before the last violent effort expelled the purple-pink foetal sac and the calf had fallen to the earth, rupturing the umbilical cord. Tukutela had begun to struggle immediately, still trapped in the glistening mucus-coated membrane and the old cow, her companion, had stood over him and, with the prehensile tip of her trunk, delicately stripped it away.

Then with her trunk his dam had gently and lovingly lifted him to his feet, and placed him between her front legs, making the deep purring rumble of elephant contentment. Still wet and smooth and shining pinkly from his birthing, covered in copious gingery hair, almost blind, Tukutela had rolled his little trunk back onto his forehead and reached up instinctively to the twin breasts on his mother's chest.

While he tasted for the very first time the rich creamy milk, his dam picked up the foetal sac and afterbirth and stuffed them into her mouth, chewing and swallowing and, at the same time, using her trunk to cover the damp and blood-stained spot upon the earth with sand.

The three of them, his mother, her companion and Tukutela, had remained on the island for almost two weeks while the calf had mastered the use of his legs and trunk, the pigment of his skin had darkened and his eyes adjusted to the harsh African sunlight. Then, when she considered him strong enough, she had taken him to find the herd, pushing him ahead of her and lifting him over the steep and difficult places.

The din of a hundred elephant feeding had carried to them from afar, the crack and crash of breaking branches and the pig-like squeals of the calves at play. Tukutela's dam trumpeted her return and the herd had come rushing up to greet her. Then, discovering the new calf, they had crowded around to touch him with their trunks, puffing his scent into their mouths, so that they would recognize it always thereafter.

Tukutela cowered between his mother's front legs, overwhelmed by the huge bodies that surrounded him, making little baby noises of terror, but his mother draped her trunk over him and rumbled to reassure him. Within hours rather than days, he ventured out from her protection to join the other calves, and to begin carving for himself a niche in the hierarchy of the breeding herd.

The herd was a close-knit-group, almost all its members blood relatives, mutually reliant upon each other so that the education and discipline of the young was a concern of all.

The calves were always kept in the centre of the herd, and their antics were strictly supervised by the old barren cows who were their self-appointed nursemaids. Their care and protection was intense but any infringement of the herd law was punished instantly: a tree branch wielded with gusto across the recalcitrant's back and hind-quarters would ensure terrified squeals and instant obedience.

Tukutela learned his place in every situation; at the centre when the herd was relaxed and feeding; between his mother's front legs when they were on the march, or in flight from danger. He learned to react instantly to the alarm signal, learned to recognize it even when given by an animal on the further outskirts of the group.

At the signal, the instantaneous silence, in contrast to the preceding happy uproar of the herd, was an eerie phenomenon of elephant behaviour.

Tukutela's development was closely parallel to the ages of a human being: his infancy lasted two years during which time he shed the tiny milk tusks with which he had been born and then entered on his juvenile years when his true tusks emerged beyond his lips. At first, these were covered by a cap of smooth enamel, but as soon as he was weaned and began to use his tusks to feed with and in mock combat with his peers, this was worn away and the true ivory beneath exposed.

His tusks would continue to grow in length and girth throughout his entire life even into his extreme old age, but the genes which dictated their extraordinary development came down from his dam along with all her other gifts of strength and bulk and intelligence.

By the age of three, Tukutela had learned the attitudes of threat and submission towards others, and his play was boisterous with much ear-flapping and threatening and barging which further developed his unusually robust frame.

Once his dam weaned him, her care became less intensive and he was allowed more range and freedom, though he still came under her fierce protection at the first threat, and on the march his place was close beside her in the lead, so very early on he learned the herd's territory.

This was a vast area, from the shores of Lake Nyasa in the north to the rain forests of the Chimanimani mountains in the south, west to the deep gorge where the Zambezi river forces itself between narrow rock cliffs with the roar of perpetual thunder and east five hundred miles to where the same mighty river spread out across wide flood plains and swampy littoral before debouching through multiple mouths into the Indian Ocean.

He learned the mountain passes and the ancient elephant roads, he learned the groves where succulent fruits grew and the seasons when they ripened. She led him to burned-out savannahs just as the first tender green shoots pushed through the ashes and to the salt licks where for thousands of years the elephants had come to prise out lumps of mineral-rich earth with their tusks and eat it with all the relish of small boys with sticks of candy, over the centuries quarrying deep excavations in the red African earth.

The herd was on the Mavuradonha mountains in the south when the msasa forests put out new leaf and their sap began to flow; they were in the dense rain forests on Mount Mlanje when the rest of the range baked in the long African droughts. Always the old cow led them to water, for the herd was totally dependent upon that precious fluid. They must drink each day or experience terrible hardship, they needed copious quantities to nurture their great bodies, to cleanse their hides and, more simply, for the luxurious pleasure of the wallow. The watering hole was an important gathering place for the herd, a place where their bonds were reaffirmed and where many of the rituals of their social behaviour were played out. Even the act of procreation usually took place in the water, and when the cows chose the place for their birthing, it was nearly always near water.

Sometimes there was abundant water, the great green African rivers, the mountains upon which the perpetual drizzling rains fell, and the wide swamplands where they waded belly deep through papyrus beds to reach the islands. At other times, they had to dig for it in the dry riverbeds, or patiently wait their turn at the seeps to thrust their trunks into the deep eye of the secret well and suck up a bitter brackish mouthful at a time.

Their range was wide, and their contact with human beings infrequent. There was a great war raging in a far-off land and it had sucked most of the white men to its centre. The men that the herd encountered were usually half-naked and primitive tribesmen who fled before them. Yet Tukutela learned very early that a special aura of dread surrounded these strange hairless baboon-like beings. At five years of age he could identify their peculiar acrid odour on a light breeze from many miles away, and even the faintest taint of it made him and the entire herd uneasy.

Yet Tukutela was eleven years of age before he had his first memorable encounter with human beings. One night while following their time-honoured route along the south bank of the Zambezi, his dam had stopped abruptly at the front of the herd and lifted her trunk at full stretch above her head to scent the air. Tukutela had imitated her and become aware of a tantalizing odour. He had puffed the taste of it into his mouth and his saliva poured down and dribbled from his lower lip. The rest of the herd bunched up behind them and were almost immediately consumed by the same appetite. None of them had ever smelled sugar cane before.

The old matriarch led them up the wind and within a few miles they came out on an area of the riverbank that had been recently cleared and irrigated and planted with cane. The long sword-shaped leaves glistened in the moonlight, and the aroma was rich and sweet and irresistible. The herd rushed into the new fields, pulling up the plants and stuffing them down their throats in a greedy passion.

The destruction was immense, and in the midst of it suddenly the herd was surrounded by lights and the shouts of men's voices and the beating of drums and metal cans. Panic and pandemonium overtook the herd and as they charged out of the field there was a shocking series of loud reports and the bright flash of gunfire in the night. It was the first time Tukutela had ever smelled burned cordite smoke. He would remember it always and associate it with the squeals of those elephants who had been mortally hit.

The herd ran hard at first and then settled into the long stride that covered the ground at the speed of a cantering horse. By morning, one of the young cows, her first calf under her belly, could no longer keep up with the herd and slumped down on her front knees, bright blood trickling from the bullet wound in her flank.

The matriarch turned back to assist her, calling and encouraging her, but the cow could not rise, and the matriarch moved up beside her. Using tusks and trunk, she lifted the fallen animal to her feet and attempted to lead her away. It was in vain, for the dying animal slumped down and lay with her legs folded up under her, and the smell of her blood upset the herd and they milled about her, swinging their trunks and flapping their ears.

One of the herd bulls, in a desperate effort to revive the fallen cow, mounted her in a stylized attempt at copulation, but a gout of arterial blood spurted from her wound and with a groan she toppled over on her side.

Unlike most animals, the elephant recognizes death, especially in one of its own group, and even the immature Tukutela was affected by the strange melancholy that followed the cow's death. Some members of the herd approached the carcass and touched it with their trunks, almost a gesture of farewell, before they wandered away into the grey thorn scrub.

The matriarch stayed on when the others had left, and Tukutela stayed with her. He watched as his dam began to strip the surrounding trees of their branches and pile them over the carcass of the dead cow. Only when it was completely hidden under a great mound of vegetation, was she satisfied.

The dead cow's unweaned calf had stayed beside its mother's corpse, and now the matriarch shooed it ahead of her as she followed the herd. Twice the calf tried to double back to where its mother lay, but the matriarch blocked it, turning it with her trunk and pushed it along.

A mile away, the rest of the herd was waiting in a grove of yellow-stemmed fever trees. Many of the younger calves were suckling, and the matriarch pushed the orphan calf towards where one of the older calves, one almost due to be weaned, was showing only perfunctory interest in his mother's dugs. She shoved the orphan between the cow's front legs and instinctively the little animal rolled its trunk onto its forehead and reached up for the teat. The cow made no objection, accepting the role of foster mother with equanimity. The matriarch stood beside the pair rumbling to them encouragingly, and when she led the herd on, the orphan calf had displaced the older calf between the cow's front legs.

132

It seemed that from then on the herd's contact with men bearing firearms became every season more frequent, especially when the bulls were with the breeding herd.

The mature bulls kept a loose liaison with the breeding herd. They found the noisy and boisterous behaviour of the young animals annoying, and the competition for food demanding. No sooner would one of the bulls shake down a rain of ripe pods from the top branches of a tall thorn tree but a dozen youngsters would rush over to gobble them, or he would push over a msasa tree to get at the new leaf, leaning with his forehead against the trunk, and snapping the three-foot diameter of hard wood with a report like a cannon shot. Immediately four or five greedy young cows would push themselves in front of him before he could sample the juicy pink leaves.

So the bulls would wander away from the herd, singly or in bachelor groups of three or four. Perhaps also they realized instinctively that the herd was likely to attract the hunters, and they would be safer away from it. Sometimes they were only a few miles away, sometimes as far as thirty or forty, but they seemed always to be aware of the herd's location and would return when the cows were in season.

When the bulls were with the herd, was the time that there was most likely to be that sudden crash of gunfire, and the squeal of wounded animals and the headlong rush of huge panic-stricken bodies through the brush.

When Tukutela was a juvenile, under ten years of age, there had been six huge bulls associated with the herd, animals carrying thick shafts of ivory, but over the years that he grew towards maturity these were gradually whittled down. Each dry season one or more of them fell to the sound of riflefire, and only the mediocre bulls, or those with worn or damaged ivory, remained.

By this time, Tukutela had grown into an unusually large young bull, and his tusks were beginning to develop, clean and white and sharp-pointed, already showing promise of what they would one day become. As he grew, so the matriarch, his dam, declined. Slowly the outline of her bones appeared through the folds and hangs of her wrinkled grey hide, so she became a gaunt and skeletal figure. Her sixth and last molar was already chipped and half worn away, she ate with difficulty, and the slow starvation of age had begun. She relinquished her place at the head of the herd to a younger more robust cow, and shambled along behind.

On the steep places where the elephant road climbed the mountain passes Tukutela would wait for her at the crest, rumbling to bring her up over the difficult places, and he stood close to her in the night as he had as a calf.

It had been a dry season and the waterholes were less than half full. The approaches to the water had been churned by the elephant herds and rhinoceros and buffalo to glutinous black mud, in some places deep as an elephant's belly, and it was here that the old matriarch stuck.

Lunging in an attempt to free herself, she fell over sideways and the mud sucked her down until only part of her head was clear.

She struggled for two days. Tukutela tried to help her, but even his enormous strength was of no avail. The mud held her fast, and gave him no footing nor purchase. The old cow's struggles became weaker, her wild screams more feeble, until at last she was still and silent except for the hiss of her breathing.

It took two more days, and Tukutela stood beside her all that time. The herd had long ago departed, but he remained. She gave no outward sign of passing from life to death, other than the cessation of her harsh breathing, but Tukutela knew it instantly and he lifted his trunk high and bugled out his grief in a cry that startled the wild fowl from the waterhole in a cloud of noisy wings.

He went to the edge of the forest and plucked the leafy boughs and he brought them to the waterhole and he covered his dam's muddy carcass with them, building for her a high green funeral bier. Then he left her and went into the veld.

He did not rejoin the herd for almost two years. By that time, he was sexually mature and he could no longer resist the scent of oestrus that the breeze brought down to him.

When he found them, the herd was gathered on the bank of the Kafue river, ten miles upstream from where it makes its confluence with the great Zambezi. Some of the herd members came out to meet him as he approached, and they entwined their trunks with his and pushed their foreheads together in greeting, and then allowed him to join the main body.

There were two cows in season and one of them was an animal of similar age to Tukutela. She was prime, fat with good grazing and browsing that the rains had raised. Her ivory was thin and very white, as straight and sharp as knitting needles, and her ears

134

had not yet been torn or tattered by thorn and sharp twigs. She spread them now as she recognized Tukutela as her peer, and came to twine her trunk with his.

They stood with their heads together rumbling gently at each other, and then disentangled their trunks and began to caress each other lightly with the tips, moving down the length of each other's bodies until they stood head to tail.

The tips of the trunk are as sensitive and dextrous as the fingers of the human hand and Tukutela reached down between her back legs and groped for her vaginal opening. She began to sway from side to side, rocking her whole body, an expression of extreme pleasure. As he manipulated her, so her oestrus discharge flowed down freely drenching his trunk and the aroma of it filled his head. His penis emerged from its fleshy sheath, as long as a man is tall and as thick as one of his legs; the tip of it brushed the earth below his belly. Its length was variegated with blotches of pink and black but the skin was smooth and shining and the head flared like the mouth of a trumpet. Elephants belong to the testiconda group, and his testicles were contained deep in the body cavity so there was no external evidence of them.

When both of them were fully aroused Tukutela nudged her gently down the bank and into the river. The green waters closed over them, intensifying their pleasure in each other, supporting their great bodies, buoying them up so they were light and nimble.

They submerged until only their trunks were above the surface, sporting together, breaking out again like blowing whales, and the water poured off them in sheets, cleansing their grey hides of dust and dirt, darkening them to the colour of coal.

Tukutela reared over her, and placed his forelegs on each side of her back. In the water, she supported him easily. Her vagina was placed far forward between her back legs, and he needed all of his length to reach it. His penis took on a life of its own, pulsing and jerking and twisting as it flared upwards to conform to the angle of her opening. Only the first third of its length was able to bury itself in her. His whole body shuddered and convulsed and both creatures trumpeted together and thrashed the waters to white foam.

He stayed with the herd three days, and then the female's oestrus ended and Tukutela became restless. He had inherited his dam's instinct for survival, and he sensed danger with the herd. On the third day, he ghosted away into the grey thorn scrub. He went alone, with no other bull for company.

Each season, when he returned to the herd he was stronger, his tusks longer and thicker, darkening to the colour of alabaster with vegetable juices. On occasion there were other bulls competing to service the females, and he had to fight for his right.

At first, he was driven off by older more experienced males, but each season his tusks and his cunning grew, until none of the other herd bulls stood up against him, and he had his pick of the cows. However, he never stayed more than a few days with the herd, and always he departed alone and sought out fastnesses which his dam had showed to him, the swamps inaccessible to man, the thickest forests, the tallest beds of elephant grass. It was as though he realized the danger that those tusks would bring upon him.

In his thirty-fifth year, he was a huge animal, weighing seven tons and standing over twelve feet at the shoulder. His tusks, though not anywhere as heavy as they would one day be, were perfectly symmetrical and long and pointed.

For days after leaving the herd that season he had been unaccountably nervous. He moved restlessly, testing the air often, raising his trunk high and then puffing it into his mouth. Once or twice he detected it, but the acrid scent was faint, just a tiny shadow on his consciousness.

However, he could not keep moving endlessly. His huge frame each day required over a ton of grass and leaves and fruit and bark to sustain it. He had to stop to feed. In the early morning, he stood in a dense grove of combretum trees, stripping bark. He used the point of a tusk to prise a gash in the bark, then he gripped the tag end in his trunk and with an upward jerk ripped loose a strip of bark fifteen feet up the bole of the tree. He rolled the bark into a ball and stuffed it into his mouth.

Intent on his task, he relaxed his vigilance. An elephant has poor eyesight, he cannot distinguish stationary objects only a few yards distant, although he can instantly detect movement. Furthermore, his eyes are placed well back in the skull, impeding his forward view and the spread of his ears tends to block his peripheral vision to the rear.

Using the small morning wind to negate the bull's marvellous sense of smell, moving with extreme stealth so that his fine hearing was frustrated, the hunters approached him from behind, staying in his blind spot. There were two of them and they had followed him ever since he had left the herd. Now they crept up very close to him.

The bull turned broadside to the hunters, ready to move on to the next tree and he showed them the long curved gleam of his tusks.

'Take him!' said one man to the other, and the Spanish maker of fine sherries lifted his double-barrelled rifle which was engraved and inlaid with gold and he aimed for Tukutela's brain.

Over his sights, he picked out the dark vertical cleft in the front of the ear and followed it down to its lowest point. That was where the actual opening of the eardrum was situated. Having found it he moved his aim forward three inches along an imaginary line from the aperture of the ear towards the elephant's eye.

The Spanish sherry-maker was on his first African safari. He had shot chamois and moufflon and red deer in the Pyrenees, but a wild African elephant is none of these timid creatures, and the Spaniard's heart was thudding into his ribs and his spectacles were fogged with his sweat and his hands shook. The professional hunter with him had patiently instructed him how and where to place his shot, but now he could not hold his aim upon it, and every second his breathing became more laboured, his aim more erratic. In desperation he jerked the trigger.

The bullet hit Tukutela a foot above his left eye and fifteen inches from the frontal lobe of the brain, but the honeycombed bony sponge of his skull cushioned the shock. He reeled back on his haunches and flung his trunk straight up above his head and gave a deep roaring growl in his throat.

The Spanish hunter turned and ran, and Tukutela whirled to face the movement, launching himself off his haunches. The professional hunter was directly under his outstretched trunk, and he flung up his rifle and aimed into Tukutela's head, into the roof of his open mouth between the bases of the long curved tusks.

The firing-pin fell on a dud primer with a click, the rifle misfired and Tukutela swung his trunk down like the executioner's axe, crushing the man to the earth.

The Spaniard was still running and Tukutela went after him, overhauling him effortlessly. He reached out his trunk and curled

137

it around his waist. The man screamed and Tukutela tossed him thirty feet straight up into the air. He screamed all the way down until he hit the earth and the air was driven from his lungs. Tukutela seized him by one ankle and swung his body against the trunk of the nearest tree with a force that burst the man's internal organs, spleen and liver and lungs.

Tukutela raged through the forest with the corpse held in his trunk, beating it against the trees, lifting it high and slamming it down upon the earth, until it disintegrated and he was left with only the stump of the leg in his grip. He flung that aside and went back to where he had left the professional hunter.

The blow from the trunk had shattered his collar-bone, broken both his arms and crushed in his ribs but the hunter was still alive and conscious. He saw Tukutela coming back for him, the long trunk dangling, the huge ears extended and blood from his wound dribbling down to mingle with the blood of the Spaniard that splattered his chest and front legs.

The hunter tried to drag his mangled body away. Tukutela placed one great foot in the centre of his back, pinning him down, then with his trunk, he plucked off his limbs, one at a time, legs and arms, tearing them away from the joints of hip and shoulder, and throwing them aside. Finally he wrapped his trunk around the man's head and pulled it away from the shoulders. It rolled like a ball bouncing across the ground as Tukutela hurled it from him. His rage abated, overtaken by the pain in his head, and Tukutela stood over the bodies that he had destroyed, rocking from one foot to the other, rumbling in his throat as first the pain and then the melancholy of death came over him.

Despite the pain in his head and the slow drip of blood into his eye from the wound above it, he began the ritual of death that he had learned from his dam so many years previously. He gathered the parts of his victims, the squashed trunks and mutilated limbs and piled them in a heap. He picked their accoutrements out of the grass – rifles, hats, water-bottles – and added them to the bloody pile. Then he began to strip the trees of leafy branches and to cover it all with a mound of green.

The bullet wound healed cleanly, but soon there were other scars to add to the little white star that it left above his eye. A weighted spear from a dead-fall trap opened his thick grey hide from shoulder to knee, and he almost died from the infection that followed. The spread of his ears caught on thorn and hooked twigs, the edges became tattered and eroded. He fought for the cows when he joined the breeding herd, and although none of the other bulls could prevail against him, their tusks slashed and cut and marked him. Then there were other encounters with men.

Despite the dire danger associated with it, that first taste of the sweet juice of the sugar cane so long ago had been addictive. Tukutela became a compulsive garden raider. Sometimes he would lurk for days in the vicinity of a patch of cultivation, getting up his courage. Then when there was no moon, in the deepest hours of the night, he would go in stepping soundlessly as a cat on his big padded feet. Millet, maize, papaya, yams, he loved them all, but sugar cane he could never resist.

At first, he allowed himself to be driven off by the flaming torches and the shouting and the drums, but then he learned to answer the shouts with his own wild screams and to charge at the guardians of the forbidden gardens.

On separate occasions over the next ten years, he killed eight human beings in the course of his raids, pulling their bodies to pieces like a glutton dismembering a chicken carcass. He grew reckless in his greed for the sweet cane. Whereas after previous raids, he would travel a hundred miles in a single non-stop march to distance himself from retribution, this season he began to return to the same field on consecutive nights.

The villagers had sent a message to the *Boma* of the colonial district commissioner, begging for assistance. The D.C. had sent one of his askari armed with a .404 rifle and the askari was waiting for Tukutela. The askari was a policeman and neither a great hunter nor marksman. He hid himself in a pit in the middle of the field, quite happy in his own mind that the elephant would not return to the field that night; for Tukutela had already made a reputation for himself across his vast range and his habits were known: he was notorious as the garden raider who had killed so many villagers, and who never returned to the scene of his crime.

The askari awoke from a deep sleep in the bottom of his pit to find Tukutela blotting out the stars over his head, munching on the standing cane. The askari snatched up his .404 and fired a bullet upwards into Tukutela's belly. It was not a mortal wound and Tukutela hunted the askari remorselessly, quartering downwind until he picked up the scent and following it to the pit where the man crouched paralysed with terror. Tukutela put his trunk down into the pit and plucked him out.

The wound took many weeks to heal. The pain gnawed at his guts and Tukutela's hatred of man grew upon it.

Though Tukutela did not understand the reason for it, his contact with man became ever more frequent. His old range was being whittled down; every season there were more tracks and roads cutting through his secret places. Motor vehicles, noisy and stinking, buzzed through the silent places of the veld. The great forests were being hacked down and the earth turned to the plough. Lights burned in the night, and human voices carried to him wherever he wandered. Tukutela's world was shrinking in upon him.

His tusks were growing all this time, longer and thicker, until in his sixtieth year, they were great dark columns.

He killed another man in 1976, a black man who tried to defend his few wretched acres of millet with a throwing spear, but the head of the spear lodged in Tukutela's neck and formed a chronic source of infection, a constantly suppurating abscess.

Tukutela had long ago ceased to seek out the breeding herd. The scent of oestrus on the wind awakened in him only a sweet fleeting nostalgia, but the driving force of the procreative urge had dulled and he pursued his solitary ways through the shrinking forests.

There were some areas of his old range that remained untouched, and from experience Tukutela came to recognize them and to realize that they formed a sanctuary where he was safe from man's harassment. He did not understand that these were the national parks, where he was protected by law, but he spent more and more of his time in these areas, and over the years learned their precise boundaries, and became reluctant to venture across them into the dangerous world beyond.

Even in these sanctuaries he was wary, driven always by his hatred and fear of them to attack men wherever he found them, or to fly from the first acrid taint of them on the breeze. His faith in the safety of the sanctuary was tested when the hunters found him even there. He heard the report of a firearm and felt the sting of the missile, not differentiating between the sound of a rifle and a dart gun, but when he tried to locate and destroy his attackers, a strange lethargy overtook him, a terrible weakness in his thick columnar legs and he slumped unconscious to the

140

earth. He awoke to the terrifying stench of men all around him, thick and repulsive on the air, even on his own skin where they had touched him. When he lumbered unsteadily to his feet, he found a strange serpentine device suspended around his neck and the chronic abscess on his neck caused by the spear wound was burning with the fires of antiseptics. He tried to wrench off the radio collar, but it defied even his might and so, in frustration, he devastated the forest around him, smashing down the tall trees and ripping out the bushes.

The men who watched his rage from afar laughed and one of them said, 'Tukutela, the Angry One.'

It took Tukutela many long seasons before he at last succeeded in ripping that hateful collar from around his neck, and hurling it into the top branches of a tree.

Although he recognized the sanctuary of the parks in which he now spent most of his days, Tukutela could not deny his deepest instincts and at certain seasons of the year, he became restless. The wanderlust came upon him, the urge to follow once again the long migratory road that his dam had first taken him over as an infant. He would be drawn to the boundary of the park by this irresistible longing and he would feed along it for days gathering his courage until he could no longer contain himself and he would set out fearfully and nervously, but with high anticipation for the far-off fastnesses to the east.

Of these, the vast Zambezi swampland was his favourite. He did not recognize it as his birthplace, he only knew that here the waters seemed cooler and sweeter, the grazing more luxuriant and his sense of peace deeper than any other place in his world. This season as he crossed the Chiwewe river and headed east, the urge to return to that place seemed even greater.

He was old now, long past his seventieth year and he was weary. His joints ached so he walked with a stiff exaggerated gait. His old wounds pained him, especially the bullet which had driven through his bony skull and lodged beneath the skin above his right eye. It had formed a hard encysted lump of gristle which he touched occasionally with the tip of his trunk when the pain was bad.

His craggy old head was weighed down by those huge ivory shafts; each day their burden was less supportable. Those tusks alone were a monument to his former glory. For the old bull was going back rapidly now. The sixth set of molars, the last and largest of his teeth, were all but worn away and the starvation of age was upon him. Every day, he was a little weaker, slowly his food was limited more and more to the softer more readily masticated grasses and shoots, but he could not take enough of them.

His huge frame was gaunt and his skin hung in bags at his knees and around his neck. There was a sense of melancholy in him, such as he had experienced only seldom in his life, the same feeling that had encompassed him as he waited for his dam to die beside the waterhole. He did not recognize that feeling as the premonition of his own impending death.

It seemed to Tukutela that as soon as he crossed out of the park, the pursuit began. He sensed that it was more determined, more persistent than ever before. It seemed to him that the forest was full of the human creatures, following him, waiting for him at each turn, and he could not head directly eastwards but must jink and twist to avoid the imaginary and real dangers that beset him.

However, when the sudden cacophony of gunfire roared out close behind him, Tukutela fled directly eastward at last, instead of doubling back towards the sanctuary of the park. It was a hundred miles and more to where the swamps began and the route was perilous, but he could not deny the deep instinct that drove him on.

Ten hours later, he stopped to bathe and drink and feed in an isolated marshy place, still a great distance from the true swamps. This was one of the way-stations on the old migratory road.

He had not been there for more than a few hours before the aircraft had rushed low overhead, filling the air with its buzzing roar, startling and angering Tukutela. In some vague way, he associated this machine with the deadly danger of the hunters. It left the same foul stench upon the air as the hunting vehicles which he had encountered so often before, and he knew he could rest no longer in this place, the hunters were closing in.

The great swamps were his refuge and he fled towards them.

* * *

'He won't stop now until he is into the swamps.' Sean Courtney was squatting beside the spoor. 'He's thoroughly alarmed, and we can't hope to catch him before he gets into them.'

142

'How far?' Riccardo asked, and Sean stood up and studied him as he replied.

'Eighty or ninety miles, Capo. Just a stroll.' Riccardo wasn't looking well. There were dark sweat patches soaking through his shirt and he seemed to have aged ten years in the last four days.

'What will we do if the old bugger keels over on us?' Sean wondered, and then thrust that thought aside. 'Okay, gang, we'll eat and sleep here. Move on again at four.'

He led them to the edge of the marsh, onto firm dry ground. Fatigue and heat had dulled their appetites. They needed sleep more than food and soon they were sprawled out in the shade like dead men.

Sean woke with the feeling that something was amiss; he sat up quickly, his hand already on the rifle, and swept a glance around him.

'Claudia.' He jumped to his feet. She was gone. Her pack lay ten paces away where she had slept. He wanted to shout for her, flouting his own security rules, and that was a measure of his concern.

He strode out of the perimeter, and whistled for the sentry. Pumula came in immediately.

'The donna,' Sean demanded in Sindebele. 'Where is she?'

'That way.' Pumula pointed towards the river.

'You let her go?' Sean demanded.

'I thought she was going to the bush . . .' Pumula excused himself, '. . . to relieve herself. I could not stop her.'

Sean had already started to run down the hippo path into the reeds that surrounded the largest and deepest of the pools, when he heard the splash of water ahead.

'This dilly bitch is going to drive me crazy,' he told himself as he burst out on the edge of the pool.

The pool was a hundred yards across, deep and green and still. For all its comical appearance the hippopotamus is the most dangerous animal in Africa. It has probably killed more human beings than all the other dangerous species put together. The old bulls are cantankerous and aggressive, a cow with a new calf will attack without provocation and a bite from those gaping jaws whose tusks are adapted to shearing coarse river reeds will cut a man in two. The crocodile is a sly and efficient killer. This pool was the ideal haunt of both hippo and crocodile and Claudia Monterro was in it up to her waist.

Her wet clothing, shirt and panties and socks, all freshly washed, were draped over the reeds at the edge, and Claudia was facing away from him leaning forward and with both hands working up a lather of soap in her hair.

The skin of her back was lightly tanned and flawless except for the paler line left by the strap of a bikini top across her shoulder-blades. Her flanks were lean but elegantly shaped into the waist, and the knuckles of her spine just showed between the ridges of fine athletic muscle on each side of it.

'What the hell do you think you're doing?' Sean snarled, and she turned to face him, hands still in her soapy hair, eyes screwed up against the suds.

'Is this how you get your jollies?' she demanded, but making not the slightest effort to cover her bosom. 'You pervert, creeping and peeping?'

'Get your arse out of there, before you get it bitten off by a croc.' Her jibe had stung him, but even in his anger he saw that her breasts were better than he had guessed. The cold water made the points stick out at him.

'Stop gawking,' she yelled back at him. 'And get lost.' She ducked her head under and then stood erect once again with soap lather streaming down her body, her hair shining and slick as a sheet of black silk over her shoulders.

'Get out of there, damn you, I'm not going to stand here arguing,' he ordered.

'I'll get out when I'm good and ready.'

Sean plunged straight into the pool, and reached her before she could avoid him. He seized her arm, and though it was slippery with soap, he dragged her towards the bank; kicking and lashing at him with her free hand, spitting with fury.

'You bastard, I hate you. Leave me alone.'

He controlled her easily with one hand. In the other, he still held his big double-barrelled rifle. His khaki shorts ran water and his velskoen boots squelched as he dragged her out. He snatched up her wet shirt and threw it at her.

'Get dressed!'

'You've got no right, I'm not going to accept this, you brutal ham-handed . . . you've hurt my arm.' She proffered her upper arm, exhibiting his red fingermarks on the skin, holding the wet shirt loosely at her side, shaking and pale with rage.

Strangely it was her navel that drew his eyes. It stared accusingly at him from the flat plain of her midriff, like a cyclopean eye, a perfect dimple at that moment more erotic than even the dense triangular bush of sodden hair beneath it. He dragged his eyes away, and she was so angry that she seemed totally oblivious of her nudity. He thought she might actually attack him, and he stepped back. As he did so he looked beyond her and saw a tiny arrow-head of ripples slipping silently across the still green surface of the pool towards them. At the apex of the vee-shaped ripple were two black lumps; gnarled and no bigger than a pair of large walnuts, they came at surprising speed.

Sean grabbed her arm, the same arm about whose injuries she was complaining, and jerked her back past him, away from the water's edge so viciously that she sprawled on her hands and knees in the mud.

He swung up the .577 Express rifle and aimed between the black eye lumps of the approaching crocodile. The eyes were at least nine inches apart, he calculated as he rode the pip of the foresight between them, a big old mugger.

The thunder of the rifle was stunning in the silence of the reeds and the bullet flicked an ostrich feather of spray from the surface, dead centre between the eye protuberances. The crocodile rolled sluggishly onto its back, its tiny brain mangled by the shot.

Claudia scrambled to her feet and stared over his shoulder as the reptile flashed its butter-yellow saurian belly. Sixteen feet from chin to the tip of its long crested tail, its jaws clicked as its nerves spasmed from the brain shot. The fangs as long and thick as a human forefinger overlapped the grinning scaly lips. It sank slowly back into the pool, the creamy belly fading into the green depths.

Claudia's fury had evaporated. She was staring into the pool, shivering uncontrollably, shaking her wet hair.

'Oh God, I didn't realize . . . how horrible.' She swayed towards him, shattered and vulnerable. 'I didn't know.' Her body was cold from the pool, long and sleek and wet as she pressed against him.

'What is it?' Riccardo Monterro shouted from the edge of the reed-bed. 'Sean, are you all right? What happened? Where's Claudia?'

At the sound of her father's voice, she jumped back from him guiltily and for the first time tried to cover her breasts and crotch.

'It's all right, Capo,' Sean yelled back. 'She's safe.'

Claudia snatched up her panties and pulled them on hastily, hopping on one foot in the mud, turning her back to him as she picked up her shirt and thrust her arms into the sleeves. When she turned back to him she had recovered her anger.

'I got a fright,' she told him. 'I didn't mean to grab you like that. Don't make any big deal out of it, buster.'

She zipped up the fly of her jeans and lifted her chin. 'I would have grabbed the garbageman if he'd been handy.'

'Okay, ducky, next time I'm going to let them bite you, lion or croc, what the hell.'

'You shouldn't have any complaints,' she said over her shoulder as she marched back up the path. 'You got yourself a big eyeful and I noticed you made a meal of it, Colonel.'

'You're right. You gave me a good peep. Not bad, a bit skinny perhaps – but not bad.'

And his grin expanded as he saw the back of her neck turn angry red.

Riccardo ran down the path to meet them, frantic with worry, and he seized Claudia and hugged her with relief.

'What happened, *tesoro*? Are you all right?'

'She tried to feed the crocs,' Sean told him. 'We are moving out in exactly thirty seconds from now, that shot will have alerted every ugly within ten miles.'

*   *   *

'At least I got that filthy black muck off my face,' Claudia told herself as they struck out away from the marshes. Her damp clothing felt cool and clean on her skin, and she was invigorated by her perilous bathe.

'No harm done,' she thought. 'Except I got ogled.' Even that no longer troubled her. His eyes on her naked body had not been altogether offensive, and in retrospect there was a satisfaction in having tantalized him.

'Eat your heart out, lover boy.' She watched his back as he strode out ahead of her. 'That was the best you are ever likely to lay eyes on.'

Within a mile her clothes had dried and there was no energy for any extraneous activity. The whole of her existence became the act of picking up one foot and swinging it forward after the other.

The heat was fierce and became fiercer still as they reached the rim of the escarpment of the Zambezi valley and started down. The air changed its character. It lay on the earth in silvery streams like water, it quivered and shimmered like curtains of crystal beads and changed the form and shape of things at a distance so that they squirmed and wriggled, doubled in size, assuming monstrous shapes in the mirage, or disappeared from view, swallowed up by the cascades of heated air.

Farther off the air was blue, so when she looked back, the escarpment down which they were climbing was washed with pale blue, misty and ethereal. The sky was a different blue, deep and vigorous, and the clouds stood upon the firmament in towering ranges the colours of lead and silver, their bottoms cut cleanly horizontal to the earth, their heads shaped like full-rigged ships, mainsail and topsail, royal and skysail piled up into the blue heavens. Under the cloud ranges the air was trapped and lay upon the earth so that it felt as heavy as hot syrup. They trudged along beneath its weight.

From the forest around them the minute black mopane flies came swarming and gathered at the corners of their eyes and mouths, crawled up into their nostrils and into their ears to drink the moisture from their bodies. Their insistence was exquisite torture.

As each long mile fell behind them, so vistas of the valley floor opened ahead and on the horizon they could at last make out the dark belt of riverine vegetation which marked the course of the great Zambezi. Always Matatu danced along ahead of them like a wraith, following a trail that no other eye than his could discern, tireless and unaffected by the heat, so that Sean had to call him back for the regular periods of rest with which he interrupted the march.

'There is no sign of game,' Riccardo remarked, peering ahead through his binoculars. 'We haven't seen so much as a rabbit since we crossed into Mozambique.'

It was the first time he had spoken in hours and Sean was encouraged. He had begun seriously worrying about his client. Now he responded quickly.

'This was once a paradise of big game. I hunted here before the Portuguese pulled out and the buffalo were running in herds ten thousand strong.'

'What happened to them?'

'Frelimo fed the army with them. They even offered me the

147

contract for the slaughter, they couldn't understand why I refused. In the end they did it themselves.'

'How did they do it?'

'From helicopters, they flew low over the herds and machine-gunned them. They killed almost fifty thousand buffalo in three months. For all that time the sky was black with vultures and you could smell the killing fields from twenty miles off. When the buffalo were finished they started on the other game, the wildebeest and the zebra.'

'What a cruel and savage land this is,' Claudia said quietly.

'Surely you don't disapprove?' Sean asked. 'It was done by black men, not whites. It couldn't possibly be wrong.' He glanced at his Rolex wristwatch. 'Time to move on.'

He put out his hand to help Riccardo to his feet, but the older man shrugged the hand away. Nevertheless, Sean fell in beside him as the march resumed and let Claudia move up directly behind Matatu, while he chatted quietly to her father, jollying him along, trying to distract him from his weariness.

He recounted anecdotes from the bush war. He pointed out the site of the guerrilla training camp as they passed a few miles north of it and described the raid by the Ballantyne Scouts. Riccardo was interested enough to ask questions.

'This Comrade China sounds like a good field commander,' he commented. 'Did you ever find out what happened to him, after he escaped?'

'He was active right up to the end of the war. A tough cookie, all right. His men had to back-pack all their munitions into Rhodesia and a Russian T.5 anti-tank landmine weighs almost seventy pounds. The story goes that Comrade China brought in one of them at enormous cost in sweat and blood and laid it on the main Mount Darwin road for one of our regular armoured patrols. However, the local blacks had hired a bus that same weekend to go into town to watch the football match and they touched off the landmine. There were sixty-five of them on the bus and twenty-three of them survived the explosion. Comrade China was so incensed by the waste of his precious T.5 that he sent for all the next-of-kin of the victims, and the survivors who were still able to walk, and fined them each ten dollars to cover the cost of another landmine.'

Riccardo had to stop and double over with laughter and Claudia turned on them furiously.

148

'How can you laugh? That is the most outrageous story I have ever heard.'

'Oh, I don't know,' Sean replied evenly. 'I don't think ten dollars was so outrageous. I think old China was being fairly lenient.'

She tossed her head and lengthened her stride to catch up with Matatu, and Riccardo asked still chuckling, 'After the war, what happened to this character?'

Sean shrugged. 'He was in the new government in Harare for a while but then he disappeared in one of the political purges. He might have been liquidated, the old revolutionaries are always looked on with distrust when the regime they fought for comes to power. Nobody likes sharing a bed with a trained killer and toppler of other rulers.'

Sean called a halt an hour before dark for a brew of tea and their frugal evening meal. While Job cooked it over his small smokeless fire, Sean took Matatu aside and talked to him quietly. The tracker watched Sean's face as he spoke, nodding eagerly, and as soon as he finished Matatu slipped away, heading back the way they had come.

Riccardo looked a question as Sean came back to join them and he explained.

'I sent Matatu to back-track us. Make sure we aren't being followed. I'm worried about that shot. It could have called up those uglies we found near the border.'

Riccardo nodded and then asked, 'Have you got a couple of aspirin, Sean?'

Sean opened the side flap of his pack and shook three Anadin tablets from their bottle.

'Headache?' he asked as he passed them to Riccardo, and he nodded as he popped them into his mouth and washed them down with a swallow of hot tea.

'The dust and sun glare,' he explained, but both Sean and Claudia were studying him and Riccardo bridled.

'Damn it, don't look at me like that. I'm fine.'

'Sure,' Sean agreed smoothly. 'Let's eat and move on to find a place to sleep.' He went across to the cooking-fire and squatted beside Job. They talked softly.

'Papa,' Claudia moved a little closer to her father and touched his arm, 'how are you feeling, honestly?'

'Don't worry about me, *tesoro*.'

'It has started, hasn't it?'

'No,' he replied too swiftly.

'Doc Andrews said there might be headaches.'

'It's the sun.'

'I love you, Papa,' she said.

'I know, baby, and I love you too.'

'An ocean and a mountain?' she asked.

'The stars and the moon,' he confirmed, and put his arm round her shoulders. She leaned against him.

As soon as they had eaten, Job doused the fire and Sean got them up and moving again. Tukutela's spoor was easy to follow in the soft earth and he and Job had no need of Matatu for this stage. However, at dark they were forced to stop for the night.

'We'll reach the swamps tomorrow afternoon,' Sean promised Riccardo as they stretched out on top of their sleeping-bags.

Claudia lay awake worrying about her father long after the others were asleep. Riccardo snored softly, lying on his back with arms extended like a crucifix. When she raised herself on one elbow to look at him in the starlight, she heard Sean's light breathing alter subtly and sensed that he was awakened by her movement. He slept as lightly as a cat, sometimes he frightened her.

Even her concern for her father was at last overcome and she fell into that dark drugged sleep of exhaustion. Waking was like coming back from a faraway place.

'Wake up, come on, wake up.' Sean was slapping her face lightly, and she pushed his hand away and sat up groggily.

'What?' she mumbled. 'God, it's still dark.'

He had left her and gone to her father. 'Come on, Capo, wake up, man, wake up.'

'What the hell, what is it?' Riccardo's voice was slurred and grumpy.

'Matatu has just come into camp,' Sean told them quietly. 'We are being followed.'

Claudia felt the icy wind of dread blow across her skin.

'Followed? By whom?'

'We don't know,' Sean said.

'The same bunch that were camped at the border?' Riccardo asked. His voice was still slurred.

'Possibly,' Sean said.

'What are you going to do?' Claudia asked, and was annoyed that her tone sounded afraid and confused.

'We are going to give them the slip,' Sean said. 'Get up on your hind legs.'

They had slept with their boots on. They had simply to roll their sleeping-bags and they were ready to move out.

'Matatu is going to lead you away and cover your spoor,' Sean explained. 'Job and I are going to lay a false trail for them in the original direction. As soon as it's light we'll break away and circle back to join you.'

'You aren't going to leave us alone?' Claudia blurted fearfully, and then bit it off.

'No, you won't be alone. Matatu and Pumula and Dedan will be with you,' Sean told her disdainfully.

'What about the elephant?' Riccardo demanded. His voice had firmed. 'Are you breaking off the hunt? You going to let my elephant get away?'

'For a few lousy gooks armed with a couple of lousy AK 47s?' Sean chuckled. 'Don't be ridiculous, Capo. We will shake them off and be after Tukutela again before you know it.'

*　　*　　*

Sean and Job waited while Matatu assembled his group and then shepherded them away. By now Riccardo and Claudia had learned the basics of anti-tracking and went swiftly under Matatu's direction, while the tracker brushed and covered the sign behind them.

Once they were clear, Sean and Job trampled the area around the camp, back and forth and round in circles until they had confused any remaining spoor and then they fell into single file, Sean leading, and went away at a run. They did not make it too apparent that they were laying a false trail, but adopted all the usual precautions, which would not fool a good tracker.

It was the old Scouts' pursuit pace that Sean set, seven miles an hour, and gradually he began to veer off in a southerly direction. Matatu was heading northwards towards the river and Sean would lead the pursuit directly away from them.

While he ran, Sean puzzled over the identity of his pursuers — government soldiers or rebels, poachers or simply armed bandits looking for plunder – it was impossible to guess. However, Matatu had been worried when he came into camp.

'They are good, *Bwana*,' he had told Sean. 'They have done well to follow the spoor we left, and they were coming on fast. They move in formation like bush fighters, with flankers out.'

'Didn't you get a good look?' Sean had asked, and the little Ndorobo shook his head.

'It was getting dark, and I wanted to get back to warn you. They were closing in swiftly.'

'Even the best tracker won't be able to follow us in darkness, we've got the rest of the night to get clear of them.'

It was a strange reversal of roles, Sean thought grimly, as he and Job trotted through the dark bush. They, the hunters, were now being hunted just as remorselessly.

At first he had considered breaking off the chase after the elephant and doubling back for the border. Riccardo Monterro's condition was causing him real concern, and so was Matatu's warning that their pursuers were skilled and appeared dangerous. However, he had swiftly rejected the idea; they were beyond the point of no return.

'No turning back,' Sean said aloud, and grinned as he admitted to himself the true reasons for his determination, two ivory tusks and half a million dollars in cash. By now he was honestly not certain which of those were the most compelling. Those tusks were beginning to loom large in his imagination. They represented the old Africa, a symbol of a better world that had vanished. He wanted them more than he had ever wanted anything in his life, except perhaps half a million dollars, and he grinned again.

In the first light of dawn, they were running directly southwards and they had covered twenty miles since splitting off from the rest of the party.

'Time to disappear, Job,' he grunted, without breaking stride. There must be no indication to the trackers following them that they were about to split again.

'Good place just ahead,' Job agreed. He was running exactly in Sean's footprints.

'Do it,' Sean said, and as they ran under the low branches of a grevia tree Job reached up and swung himself off the ground. Sean did not look back, did not alter his stride. Job would work

152

himself through the branches of the closely growing grevia until he found a good place to drop off and anti-track away.

Sean ran on for twenty minutes, once again curving away into the south-west, heading for a low ridge that just showed in the dawn ahead of him. He crossed the ridge and as he had anticipated from the lie of the terrain found a small river in the valley beyond. He drank at the edge of the pool, and milled around, splashing water onto the bank as though he were bathing.

A tracker would expect him to choose this as a breakaway point, wading either upstream or downstream before leaving the river again. They would send scouts along both banks to search for sign. Sean waded downstream supporting himself on overhanging branches to give them a trail to confirm their suspicions. Then without leaving the water he returned to the exact spot where he had entered the stream, and on the bank he carefully dried his feet and legs, replaced his dry velskoen shoes that he had hung around his neck on their laces, and back-tracked on his incoming spoor.

He retraced his footsteps to the crest of the ridge, walking backwards, stepping precisely on his original footprints and at the top of the ridge he employed the same trick that Job had. He swung himself into the air from a branch and over-handed himself well clear of the spoor before lowering himself to the edge of a rock slab and anti-tracking away.

'Even Matatu wouldn't be able to unravel that,' he thought with satisfaction, as he struck off back towards the north at a run.

Two hours later he joined up with Job at the rendezvous, and in the early afternoon they came up with the other party waiting for them five miles north of the point where they had split up.

'Good to see you, Sean. We were beginning to worry,' Riccardo told him as they shook hands, and even Claudia smiled as he flopped down beside her and said, 'My kingdom for a cup of tea.'

As he sipped at the mug which Matatu brought him, he listened attentively to the little tracker. Matatu squatted beside Sean and chattered in his excited falsetto.

'Matatu went back and kept an eye on the camp we left,' Sean translated for Riccardo and Claudia's benefit. 'He didn't dare approach too closely but he saw the gang that was following us arrive. This time he counted twelve of them. They searched the area of the camp, and then took the bait and followed the false trail that Job and I had laid for them.'

'So we are clear then?' Riccardo asked.

'Looks like it,' Sean agreed. 'And if we push along we should be able to reach the beginning of the swamps either this evening or early tomorrow.'

'What about Tukutela?' Riccardo asked.

'Well, we know from his track approximately where he would have reached the swamps. We'll just cast along the edge until we find where he went in, but we've lost a lot of ground on him. We'll have to go hard if we don't want him to get away from us. Do you feel up to it, Capo?'

'Never better,' Riccardo said. 'Lead on, man.'

Before they set off again, Sean went quickly over their packs. They had consumed a great deal of the provisions and he redistributed the remainder. By giving both Job and himself an extra ten pounds or so, he was able to reduce Riccardo's pack to twenty pounds and Claudia's to a mere ten pounds, just her sleeping-bag and personal items.

They both responded well to their reduced burdens but Sean once again marched beside Riccardo to encourage him and watch over him. Claudia was still going surprisingly well, he needn't have worried about her at all. Under her light pack she was stepping out lithely. He took pleasure in watching her long legs driving and her hard little buttocks oscillating in those tight blue jeans. They reminded him of the cheeks of a chipmunk chewing a nut.

They were on the valley floor now, and there were open vleis and baobabs, those trees with bloated trunks, bark like a reptile's skin, and crooked bare branches from which a few late cream of tartar pods still hung. It was easy to see why the Zulus said that the gods had accidentally planted the baobab upside down with its roots in the air.

Far ahead of them a slow standing cloud of evaporation marked the position of the swamps, and the alluvial soil was sandy and yielding under foot.

'Just think of this, Capo.' Sean was trying to divert him. 'You are probably one of the last men who will ever hunt a great elephant in the classical tradition of the long chase. This is the way it should be done, man. Not grinding around in a Land-Rover and then leaning out of the window to kill him. This is how

Selous and "Karamojo" Bell and "Samaki" Salmon hunted their elephant.'

He saw Riccardo's expression light up at the idea of being compared to those grand masters of the chase, men from another age when all elephant had been fair game. 'Samaki' Salmon had hunted and killed four thousand elephant in his lifetime. There had been a different morality in those days. Today a man with a bag of those dimensions would be accounted a villain and a criminal but in his day, 'Samaki' Salmon had been respected and honoured. He had even hunted with Edward, Prince of Wales, as his client.

Sean knew that Riccardo had an avid interest in the old-time elephant hunters, so he enlarged on their careers.

'If you want to do it the way "Karamojo" Bell did it, Capo, you have to walk like this. Bell wore out twenty-four pairs of boots a year and had to replace his porters and gunbearers every few weeks. They just couldn't keep up with him.'

'That was the golden age.' Riccardo extended his stride a little as he thought about it. 'You and I should have lived then, Sean. We were born after our time.'

'A true hunter should kill a great elephant with his legs. He should walk him down. That's the respectful and proper way and that is what you are doing now, Capo. Enjoy every step you take, for you are treading in old Bell's footprints.'

Unfortunately the effects of Sean's encouragement were not enduring; within an hour Riccardo was flagging again and Sean noticed a new disconcerting unsteadiness in his gait. He stumbled and would have fallen had not Sean caught his arm.

'We all need a five-minute break and a cup of tea.' Sean led him to the shade.

When Job brought the tea mugs, Riccardo mumbled, 'Have you got a couple more aspirins for me?'

'You all right, Capo?' he asked, as he handed him the tablets.

'Damned headache again, that's all.' But he would not meet Sean's eyes.

Sean looked across at Claudia who was sitting close beside her father, but she also avoided his gaze.

'Do you two know something I don't?' Sean demanded. 'You both look guilty as hell.' He didn't wait for an answer but stood up and went to join Job at the small fire where he was baking a fresh batch of maize cakes for their evening meal.

'The aspirin will make you feel better,' Claudia told her father softly.

'Of course, aspirin is a sure-fire cure for cancer once it reaches the brain,' he agreed, and then as he saw her agonized expression he blurted, 'I'm sorry, I don't know why I said that. Self-pity isn't my usual style.'

'Is it bad, Papa?'

'I can tolerate the headache, but I'm getting a little double vision that worries me,' he admitted. 'Damn it, I was feeling so well a few days ago, it's all happened so quickly.'

'The exertion,' she said, pitying him. 'Perhaps that is what has aggravated it. We should turn back.'

'No,' he said with utter finality. 'Don't even talk about that again.' She inclined her head in aquiescence.

'The swamps are not far ahead. Perhaps we'll have a chance to rest,' she said.

'I don't want to rest,' he said. 'I realize just how little time I have left. I don't want to waste a moment of it.'

Sean came back to them. 'Are you ready to go on?'

Claudia glanced at her wristwatch. They had rested for less than half an hour. It was too short and she would have protested but her father pushed himself to his feet.

'All set,' he said, and she could see that even that short break had refreshed him.

They had been going only a few minutes when Riccardo said quite cheerfully, 'Those hamburgers that Job has cooked smell just great. Makes me feel hungry.'

'Those hamburgers are maize cakes,' Sean chuckled. 'Sorry to disappoint you.'

'You can't bullshit me,' Riccardo chuckled with him. 'I can smell the fried onions and beef.'

'Papa.' Claudia looked back over her shoulder and frowned sharply, and Riccardo stopped chuckling and looked distraught.

'There might be hallucinations,' Doc Andrews had warned Claudia. 'He may begin to see things, or imagine various odours. I can't give you an exact progress of the disease, of course, and there may be periods of swift deterioration followed by longer periods of remission. Just remember, Claudia, that his fantasies will be very real to him, and episodes of hallucination can be followed by periods of complete lucidity.'

That evening Sean would not stop to brew tea. 'We have to

156

try and make up the ground we've lost,' he told them, and they ate the cold maize cakes and biltong – slivers of salted, air-dried venison – on the march.

'One large hamburger with fried onions and all the trimmings coming up, Capo,' Sean teased him. Claudia glared at him, but Riccardo laughed uneasily and munched on the unappetizing fare as he walked.

They no longer had a spoor to follow, so Sean kept going long after night had fallen. The long tortuous miles fell slowly behind them and the brilliant southern stars burned over their heads. It was almost midnight before they stopped and unrolled their sleeping-bags.

Sean let them sleep until the dawn light was strong enough to make out the way ahead. The landscape had changed. During the night they had entered the region that was held in thrall by the great Zambezi. These were ancient flood plains that were inundated when the river broke its banks during the torrential rainy season. They were dry now, although almost devoid of trees; a few long-dead mopane and acacia thorn trees drowned by the floods still held up twisted bare branches to the hazy blue sky, standing out on the empty plains like lonely sentinels.

As they moved out into the open, the dried mud had cracked into bricklets beneath their feet, the edges curling up, and the clumps of swamp grass were brown and matted and dead from drought. When the breeze switched fitfully they could smell the swamps still out of view ahead, the odour of mud and rotting vegetation.

The mirage shimmered across the plains, so there was no clear horizon; land and sky merged into each other like water. When they looked back the tree-line crawled like a long black serpent below the milky sky, undulating and vibrating softly in the mirage, and the dust devils spun upon themselves twisting and swaying like belly-dancers.

Out on the plain Sean felt exposed and vulnerable. There was just the scant chance of a Frelimo patrol plane passing this way searching for Renamo bands and they were as obvious as fleas on a white sheet. He wanted to hurry but then glanced back at Riccardo and knew that they would have to rest again soon.

Ahead of Sean, Matatu gave a cry that made his nerves jump. Sean knew what it meant and he ran forward, passing Claudia, and stopped beside Matatu.

157

'Well, all right!' He clapped Matatu's shoulder and then went down on one knee to examine the earth.

'What is it?' Riccardo sounded alarmed, but Sean lifted his head and grinned at him.

'It's him. Tukutela. We've cut his spoor again just where Matatu predicted that we would.' And he touched the marks of the huge pads whose weight had crushed the bricklets of dried mud to talcum powder. The spoor was so clear that the difference between the bull's rounded front feet and the more oval hind feet was immediately apparent, and the forward edges of each footprint were nicked by his toe-nails.

'Still heading straight for the swamps.' Sean stood and shaded his eyes against the glare as he followed the direction of the spoor. Not far ahead another line of trees was drawn like a pencil along the horizon where a narrow curved finger of higher ground reached out across the plains.

'In a way we are fortunate,' Sean remarked. 'A few years ago there were so many herds of buffalo and game on these flats that Tukutela's spoor would have been wiped out in a few hours by their hooves. Now, since the Frelimo government converted them all to army rations, Tukutela is the only living thing for miles around.'

'How far behind him are we?'

'We've made up a bit of ground.' Sean lowered his hand from his eyes and turned to him. 'But not enough, and if the uglies catch us out here in the open . . . Luckily Tukutela's spoor is headed straight for the line of trees ahead. They will give us some cover.' He gestured to Matatu to take the spoor once again.

Now the expanse of the wide plain was dimpled with old ant-hills, mounds of clay thrown up by colonies of termites, some of them the size of a large cottage. Tukutela's spoor meandered between them. However, the line of growth was by now so close that they could make out the individual trees. The finger of high ground formed a natural causeway from the edge of the forest across the wide plains to the beginning of the true swamps. There were ivory nut palms, bottle-stemmed palms, and the low ilala palms with their fan-shaped leaves, mixed with wild fig and on the highest ridge of the long causeway grew a few massive baobab, with trunks of elephantine grey bark.

With relief Sean followed the spoor of the old bull off the plain and into the trees of the isthmus. Here the elephant had stopped to dig out the juicy roots of an ilala palm, and drop a pile of spongy yellow dung.

'The elephant rested here,' Matatu explained, lowering his voice to a whisper. 'He is an old man now and he tires easily. Here he stood to sleep, see how he shuffled his feet in the dust, and when he awoke he dusted his body. See where he scooped it up with his trunk and threw it over his back.'

'How long did he stay here?' Sean asked, and Matatu put his head on one side as he considered the question.

'He rested here until late yesterday afternoon when the sun was there.' Matatu pointed ten degrees above the western horizon. 'But when he went on he went more slowly. He feels safer now that he is close to the swamps. We have gained on him.'

Sean exaggerated Matatu's estimate as he passed it on to Riccardo and Claudia. He wanted to encourage them. 'We are making really good gains on him now.' He put on a cheerful and confident air. 'We might even catch up with him before he gets into the deep swamps, if we don't waste any time.'

The spoor headed down the isthmus and the old bull had fed quietly as he moved along it, keeping up on top of the low ridge where the bush was thickest. Directly ahead of them stood another gigantic baobab tree. Its bark was grey and folded and riven as the old bull's hide.

For the moment Sean had left Riccardo's side and moved up to his original position behind Matatu. He wanted to caution the tracker not to set too fast a pace, but before he could speak he heard a strange guttural cry behind him and he whirled around.

Riccardo's face was swollen and congested with blood, his eyes blazed and seemed to start from their sockets. Sean thought he was suffering from some kind of seizure, but Riccardo was pointing ahead, his hand shaking with violent emotion.

'There he is,' he croaked, in a thick unnatural voice. 'For God's sake, can't you see him?'

Sean whirled and followed the direction of his outstretched arm.

'What is it, man?'

He was looking ahead, and he did not see Riccardo turn to Pumula and snatch the Rigby rifle off his shoulder, but he heard the metallic clash of the bolt as Riccardo chambered a cartridge.

'Capo, what the hell are you doing?' He reached out to restrain him, but Riccardo shoved him backwards. Sean was unprepared and off balance, and he staggered and almost fell.

Riccardo ran forward to the head of the line and then he stopped and threw up the rifle.

'Capo, don't do it.' Sean was sprinting to catch him, but the Rigby crashed out and the barrel jumped high, driving Capo back a pace with the heavy recoil.

'Have you gone crazy?' Sean could not reach him before he fired again, and the heavy bullet tore a flurry of white wet bark from the trunk of the baobab. The echoes of the shot rolled across the plains.

'Capo.' Sean reached him and seized the rifle, forcing the muzzle up towards the sky just as Capo fired the Rigby for the third time.

Sean wrested the weapon out of his grip.

'In the name of all that's holy, man, what on earth do you think you're doing?'

All their eardrums were numbed by the thunder of gunfire, and Sean's angry outraged voice sounded small and hollow after it.

'Tukutela," Riccardo mouthed. 'Don't you see? Why did you stop me?' His face was still flushed and he was shaking like a man with malarial fever. He reached once more for the Rigby in Sean's grasp, but Sean jerked it away from him.

'Pull yourself together,' he shouted angrily and tossed the empty rifle to Job. 'Don't let him get it again.' And turned back to Riccardo.

'Are you out of your mind?' He seized him by the shoulders. 'The sound of those shots will carry for miles.'

'Leave me!' Riccardo struggled. 'Don't you see him?' And Sean shook him viciously.

'Snap out of it, you're shooting at a tree. You've blown your lid!'

'Give me the rifle.' Riccardo was pleading, and Sean shook him again and roughly turned him to face the baobab.

'Look at it, you bloody madman! There's your elephant!' He shoved him towards it. 'Take a good look!'

Claudia ran forward and tried to restrain Sean. 'Leave him alone, can't you see he's sick?'

'He's gone crazy!' Sean pushed her aside. 'He's calling up

160

every Frelimo and Renamo thug within fifty miles, and he's chased any elephant . . .'

'Leave him,' Claudia came back at him, and Sean let go of her father and stepped back.

'All right, ducky, he's all yours.'

Claudia rushed to her father and embraced him. 'It's all right, Papa! It's going to be all right!'

Riccardo was staring uncomprehendingly at the deep raw wounds in the bark of the baobab from which sap was oozing.

'I thought it was . . .' he shook his head weakly. 'Why did I do that? I don't . . . I thought it looked like an elephant.'

'Yes, Papa, yes.' Claudia was hugging him. 'Don't upset yourself.'

Job and the rest of the hunting team were quiet and unhappy, watching this strange episode that none of them could fathom. Sean turned away in disgust. It took him a few seconds to get full control of himself, then he asked Matatu, 'Do you think we are close enough for Tukutela to have heard the shooting?'

'The swamps are close, and the sound carries over this flat earth as it does over water,' Matatu shrugged. 'Perhaps the elephant heard, who knows?'

Sean looked back the way they had come. From the ridge they could see out across the flood plain into the dusty distances.

'Job, what chance that the terrs heard?'

'We'll find out the hard way, Sean. It depends how close behind us they are.'

Sean shook himself, trying to rid himself of his anger the way a spaniel shakes off water.

'We'll have to rest here. The *mambo* is sick. Brew a billy of tea, and we'll decide what to do,' he ordered.

He walked back to where Claudia was still holding her father. She faced Sean defiantly, turning her body to shield Riccardo from him.

'Sorry I pushed you around, Capo,' Sean said mildly. 'You gave me a hell of a fright.'

'I don't understand,' Riccardo mumbled. 'I could have sworn it was him. I saw him so clearly.'

'We will break for a cup of tea,' Sean told him. 'I think you've got a touch of the sun. It can turn a man's brain to jelly.'

'He'll be fine in a few minutes,' Claudia said confidently, and Sean nodded coldly at her.

161

'Let's get him into the shade.'

Riccardo leaned back against the bole of the baobab and closed his eyes. He looked pale and bewildered, a rash of sweat droplets sparkled on his chin and upper lip. Claudia knelt beside him and dabbed them away with the corner of her scarf, but when she looked up at Sean he jerked his head in a peremptory gesture and she stood up and followed him.

'This doesn't come as any surprise to you, does it?' he accused, as soon as they were beyond earshot. She did not reply and he went on, 'Just what kind of daughter are you anyway? You knew he was sick and you let him come out on this jaunt.'

Her lips were trembling and as he stared into them he saw that her honey-coloured eyes were swimming, he had not expected tears from her. They took him by surprise. He felt his fury slipping away and he had to make an effort to bolster it.

'It's too late to start blubbering now, ducky. We've got to find a way to get him home. He's a sick man.'

'He's not going home,' she murmured, so low that he barely caught the words. Her tears were hanging on thick dark lashes and he stared at her in silence. She swallowed hard and then said, 'He's not a sick man, Sean. He's dying. Cancer. It was diagnosed by a specialist before we left home. He predicted that it could attack the brain like this.'

Sean's fury crumpled.

'No,' he said. 'Not Capo.'

'Why do you think I agreed to let him come and insisted on coming with him? I knew that this was his last hunt – and I wanted to be with him.'

They were silent, staring at each other, then she said, 'You care. I can see that you truly care for him. I didn't expect that.'

'He's my friend,' Sean said, puzzled himself by the depth of his own sadness.

'I didn't think you were capable of gentleness,' she went on softly. 'I may have misjudged you.'

'Perhaps we misjudged each other,' he said, and she nodded.

'Perhaps we did,' she said. 'But thank you anyway. Thank you for caring about my father.'

She began to turn away to go back to Riccardo but Sean stopped her.

'We still haven't settled anything,' he said. 'We haven't decided what we are going to do.'

'We go on, of course,' she answered. 'Right to the bitter end. That's what I promised him.'

'You've got guts,' he told her softly.

'If I have, then I got them from him,' she replied, and went to her father.

The mug of tea and a half dozen Anadin tablets revived Riccardo. He was acting and talking completely rationally again, and none of them made any further reference to his wild behaviour, although quite naturally it had thrown a pall over all of them.

'We must move on, Capo,' Sean told him. 'Tukutela is walking away from us every minute we sit here.'

They followed the ridge of high ground, and now the odour of the swamps was stronger, brought to them by the fitful inconstant wind.

'That's one of the many reasons the elephant like the swamps,' Sean explained to Riccardo. 'There the wind is always shifting, turning and switching. It makes it much more difficult to get close to them.'

There was a gap in the trees ahead, and Sean stopped and they gazed out through it.

'There they are,' he said. 'The Zambezi swamplands.'

The ridge on which they stood was like the back of a sea serpent, swimming across the open flood plains. Now just ahead of them it ducked below the surface and disappeared at the point where the open plains gave way to endless expanses of papyrus and reeds.

Sean raised his binoculars and surveyed the swamps ahead. The reed-beds seemed limitless, but he had flown over them and he knew that they were interspersed with shallow lagoons of open water and narrow winding channels. Farther out, almost on the horizon, he could see the loom of small islets, dark patches of almost impenetrable bush-crowned islands and through the lens of the binoculars he could just make out the curved palm stems with their high fluffy heads.

The past season had been particularly dry and the water level would be low, in most places not more than waist deep, but the mudbanks would be black and glutinous and the channels much deeper. The going would be arduous, and apart from the mud and water, reeds and water plants would impede each step they took, winding themselves around their legs as they tried to move.

For them each mile through the swamps would be the equivalent of five on dry land, while the elephant would be in his element. He loved mud and water. It supported his great bulk and his foot pads were designed by nature to expand as he put his weight upon them, forcing a wide opening, and then they would shrink in diameter as he lifted them, freeing themselves readily from the clinging mud.

Tukutela could gorge on reeds and soft water plants and swamp grass, and the dense bushy islets would afford variety to his diet. The suck of mud and the splash of water would warn him of an approaching enemy and the fitfully turning wind would protect him, bringing the scent of a pursuer down to him from every quarter. In all Tukutela's wide range, this was the most difficult place to hunt him.

'It's going to be a Sunday-school picnic, Capo,' Sean lowered the binoculars. 'Those tusks are as good as hanging over the fireplace in your den already.'

The old bull's spoor went out to the very end of the land bridge, and then down into the papyrus beds, where the undulating sea of green fronds swallowed the trail and left not a sign.

'Nobody can follow a trail in there.' Riccardo stood at the line where dry friable earth ended and damp swamp mud began. 'Nobody can find Tukutela in there,' he repeated, staring at the wall of swamp growth higher than his head. 'Surely they can't?'

'You are right, nobody can find him in there,' Sean agreed. 'That is, nobody except Matatu.'

They were standing in the remains of a village that had been built on the end of the isthmus. Clearly the previous occupants had been fishermen, members of one of the small tribes who live along the banks of the Zambezi and make their livelihood from her abundant green waters. Only the racks on which they had dried their catches of tilapia bream and barbeled catfish still stood, but their huts had been burned to the ground.

Job was searching the outskirts of the village and he whistled for Sean. When Sean went to join him he was standing over an object which lay in the short grass. At first glance Sean thought it was a bundle of rags and then he saw the bones protruding from it. They were still partially covered by shreds of dried skin and flesh.

'When?' Sean asked.

'Six months ago, perhaps.'

164

'How did he die?'

Job squatted beside the human skeleton and when he turned the skull it snapped off the vertebrae of the neck like a ripe fruit. Job cupped it in his hands, and it grinned at him with empty eye-sockets.

'Bullet through the back of the head,' Job said. 'Exit-hole this side.' It was like a third eye in the bone of the forehead.

Job replaced the skull and walked deeper into the grass. 'Here's another,' he called.

'Renamo has been through here,' Sean gave his opinion. 'Either looking for recruits or dried fish or both.'

'Or else it was Frelimo looking for Renamo rebels, and they decided to question them, with an AK.'

'Poor buggers,' Sean said. 'They get it from both sides. There will be plenty more of them lying around, they are the ones who escaped from the huts before they burned.'

They started back towards the village and Sean said, 'They were fishermen, they would have had their canoes here. They will probably be hidden, but we could certainly use one. Go through the edge of the papyrus beds and then search the bush behind the village.'

Sean crossed to where Riccardo and Claudia were sitting together. As he came up, he looked at her enquiringly and she nodded and smiled optimistically.

'Papa's doing fine, what is this place?'

He explained their reasoning as to the fate of the village.

'Why would they kill these innocent people?' Claudia was appalled.

'In Africa these days you don't have to have a reason for killing somebody, other than a loaded gun in your hands, and a fancy to fire it off.'

'But what harm could they have done?' she insisted.

Sean shrugged. 'Harbouring rebels, withholding information, hiding food, refusing the services of their women, any one of those crimes, or none of them.'

The sun was a red ball through the swamp haze, so low above the tops of the papyrus that Sean could look directly at it without screwing up his eyes.

'It'll be dark before we can leave,' he decided. 'We'll have to sleep here tonight and start again at first light tomorrow. One consolation is that now Tukutela has reached the swamps, he will

165

slow down. He's probably not more than a couple of miles ahead of us right now.' But as he said it he thought about those shots that Riccardo had fired. If the bull had heard them, he would still be running. There was, however, no point in telling that to Riccardo. He looked shaken and despondent, and he had been almost silent since the incident.

'He is just a husk of the Capo I knew, poor old devil. The last thing I can do for him is to get him that elephant.' Sean's sympathy was genuine and unaffected and he sat down beside him, and began to draw him out, describing what lay ahead, and how they would hunt for the old bull in the papyrus beds.

The hunt was all that now seemed to interest Riccardo, and for the first time that day he became animated and once he even laughed.

Claudia flashed a grateful smile at Sean, and then stood up and said, 'I've got a little private business to attend to.'

'Where are you off to?' Sean demanded immediately.

'The little girls' room,' she told him. 'And you are definitely not invited.'

'Don't go wandering off too far, and no swimming this time,' he ordered. 'You'll get enough of that tomorrow.'

'I hear and obey, O great white *Bwana*.' She gave him a sarcastic curtsy and set off out of the perimeter of the burned village. Sean watched her go uneasily and was about to call another warning after her when there was a shout from the papyrus bed and his attention was diverted from Claudia.

He jumped up.

'What is it, Job?' he yelled, and went down to the water's edge.

There were more confused shouts and splashing from the depths of the papyrus, and then Job and Matatu emerged, dragging something long and black and waterlogged between them.

'Our first bit of luck.' Sean grinned at Riccardo and slapped him on the shoulder.

It was a traditional *mokorro* dugout canoe, about seventeen foot long, hewn from a single log of the sausage tree, *Kigelia africana*. The body of the dugout was just wide enough for a person to sit in it, but it was usually propelled by a man standing in the stern and wielding a long punt pole.

Job tipped the water out of the craft and they examined it

carefully. The hull had been repaired and caulked in a few places, but seemed reasonably sound.

'Search the village,' Sean ordered. 'They must have had caulking material here. See if you can find it, and then send Dedan and Pumula to cut a couple of punt poles.'

Claudia screamed, and they all spun to face the sound. She screamed again, the sound was strangely muffled and far off, and Sean began to run, snatching up his rifle from where he had left it beside the nearest burnt-out hut.

'Claudia!' he yelled. 'Where are you?' Only his echo mocked him from the forest. 'Where are you? . . . are you?'

* * *

When Claudia stood up and rebuckled her belt, she found that it came in easily a full two notches shorter around her waist. She smiled down at her own belly with approval. Now it was no longer flat but definitely concave. The long march and frugal rations had stripped every last ounce of fat from her frame.

'Strange how in an age of plenty we set out to starve ourselves.' She smiled again. 'I'm going to enjoy putting on those lost pounds, plenty of pasta and red wine when I get home.'

She started back towards the village, and then realized that in her search for privacy she had gone further than she had intended and that a thicket of wiry thorn brush blocked her way back. She turned aside to circumvent it and came upon a broad pathway running directly down through the bush towards the edge of the swamp. She followed it thankfully.

Claudia did not realize that she was following a hippo road, one of the wide thoroughfares that the great amphibians followed on their nightly forays into the forest. However, the road had not been used for many months. The hippopotamus in the area had been decimated along with the other game. She was in a hurry to get back to her father, and she was feeling slightly uneasy at her isolation from the rest of the party. She strode down the pathway, just short of a run.

Ahead of her an old mat of dried papyrus stems was spread across the road from side to side. It had obviously been placed there by the previous occupants of the village, and although it served no purpose that Claudia could imagine, it was no obstacle

167

to her progress and she stepped on to it without slackening her pace.

The pitfall had been dug for the express purpose of trapping a hippopotamus. It was ten feet deep with funnel-shaped sides, that would tumble one of the huge beasts down into its depth and wedge it securely between the earthen walls. The opening was covered by branches strong enough to carry the weight of a man or a lesser animal, but not that of a hippo. Over these branches the builders had spread the papyrus stems.

However, the pitfall had been built a long time previously and both branches and mat had rotted and weakened. They collapsed under Claudia's weight, and she screamed as she dropped through into the pit beneath, and screamed again as she hit the sloping side and bounced off it. The bottom of the pit was covered with a few inches of stagnant water that had seeped into it. Claudia landed awkwardly with one leg twisted up under her and then rolled on to her back in the mud.

The breath had been driven from her lungs and there was a fierce pain in her left knee. For a few minutes she could not respond to the faint shouts she heard from above. She sat up, clutching her injured knee to her chest and gasping wildly to fill her agonized lungs. At last she managed a strangled shout.

'Here! I'm here.'

'Are you all right?' Sean's head appeared above her, peering down anxiously.

'I think so!' she gasped, and tried to stand up, but the pain shot through her knee and she fell back. 'My knee,' she said.

'Hold on. I'm coming down.' Sean's head withdrew. She heard voices. Job and Matatu and her father. Then a coil of nylon rope dropped down towards her, unfurling as it fell. Sean lowered himself swiftly down the rope and dropped the last few feet to land with a splash in the mud beside her.

'I'm sorry,' she said contritely. 'I guess I've done it again.'

'Don't apologize,' he grinned. 'I'm not conditioned to it. For once, it's not your fault. Let's take a look at your leg.'

He squatted beside her. 'Move your foot. Capital! Can you bend your knee? Splendid! At least no bones broken. That's a relief. Let's get you out of this hole.' He tied a loop in the end of the rope and slipped it over her head and shoulders and settled it under her armpits.

'Okay, Job,' he called up. 'Take her up. Gently, man, gently.'

As soon as they reached ground level, Sean made a more thorough examination of her knee.

He rolled up the leg of her jeans and said, 'Shit!'

As a Scout commander he had extensive experience of the type of injury that a paratrooper is prone to, broken bones, torn cartilage, sprained ligaments in ankle and knee. Already Claudia's knee was ballooning and the first tinge of bruising coloured the smooth tanned skin.

'This might hurt a little,' he warned, and manipulated her leg gently.

'Ouch!' she said. 'That's damned sore.'

'Okay,' he nodded. 'It's the medial ligament. I don't think you've torn it, it would be more painful if you had. Probably just sprained it.'

'What does that mean?' she asked.

'Three days,' he replied. 'You won't be walking on it for at least three days.'

He put his arm around her shoulders. 'Can you stand up?' he asked, and when she nodded he helped her to her feet. She leaned against him, standing on her good leg.

'Try putting a little weight on it,' he said, and immediately she exclaimed with pain.

'No, I can't use it.'

He stopped and picked her up in his arms as though she were a child and carried her back to the village. She was surprised by his strength and then, although her knee was beginning to throb, she relaxed in his arms. It was a good feeling. Papa had carried her like this when she was a little girl, and she had to resist the urge to lay her head against Sean's shoulder.

When they reached the village he set her down in the clearing, and Matatu ran to fetch his pack. Her injury had diverted Riccardo's attention from his own troubles, and he came to fuss over his little girl in a way which ordinarily would have annoyed her. Now she submitted to it, thankful for his revived animation and attention.

Sean strapped the knee with an elastic bandage from his first-aid kit and then gave her an anti-inflammatory tablet to swallow with hot tea.

'That's about all we can do for it,' he told her, and sat back. 'Only thing that will fix it is time.'

'Why did you say three days?'

'It takes that long. I've seen a hundred knees just like yours, except that they were usually a lot more hairy and not nearly as pretty.'

'That's a compliment.' She raised an eyebrow. 'You are getting soft, Colonel.'

'Part of the treatment, and of course, totally insincere,' he assured with a grin. 'The only question now, ducky, is what on earth are we going to do with you?'

'Leave me here,' she said promptly.

'Are you out of your mind?' he asked, and Riccardo backed him up immediately.

'That's out of the question.'

'Look at it this way,' she reasoned calmly. 'I cannot move for three days, by which time your elephant will be long gone, Papa.' She held up her hand to forestall his argument. 'We cannot go back. You can't carry me. I can't walk. We would have to sit here anyway.'

'We cannot leave you alone, don't be ridiculous.'

'No,' she agreed. 'But you can leave someone to look after me while you go on after Tukutela.'

'No.' Riccardo shook his head.

'Sean,' she appealed to him. 'Make him see that it is the sensible thing to do.'

He stared at her and the admiration she saw in his gaze gave her a full warm feeling in her chest.

'Damn it,' he said softly. 'You're all right.'

'Tell him it will only be for a few days, Sean. We all know how much that elephant means to Papa. I want to give it to him as my . . .' she almost said 'last gift', but then she changed it, 'as my special gift to him.'

'I can't accept it, *tesoro*.' Riccardo's voice was gruff but blurred and he lowered his head to hide his feelings.

'Make him go, Sean,' Claudia insisted, and gripped his forearm firmly. 'Tell him I'll be as safe here with Job to look after me as I would be in the swamp with the two of you.'

'She just may have a point, Capo,' Sean said. 'But, hell, it's not my business. It's between the two of you.'

'Will you leave us alone, Sean?' Claudia asked, and then without waiting for a reply, she turned to her father. 'Come and sit here next to me, Papa.' She patted the ground beside her.

Sean stood up and walked away, leaving them together in the gathering darkness.

He went to sit beside Job. They sat in the companionable silence of old friends, drinking tea and smoking one of Sean's last cheroots, passing it back and forth between them.

An hour passed. It was entirely dark before Riccardo came to where the two of them sat. He stood over them and his voice was rough and drawn with sadness.

'All right, Sean,' he said. 'She has convinced me to do as she wants. Will you make the arrangements to go on with the hunt first thing tomorrow morning? And, Job, will you stay here and look after my little girl for me?'

'I'll look after her for you, sir,' he agreed. 'You just go kill that elephant. We'll be here when you come back.'

*   *   *

Working in the moonlight they moved out of the burned-out village and built a fly camp a few hundred metres back in the forest.

They made a lean-to shelter for Claudia and under it placed a mattress of cut grass. Sean left the medical kit and most of their remaining provisions in the shelter with her. He detailed both Job and Dedan to remain with Claudia. Job would keep the light 30/06 rifle with the fibreglass stock, and Dedan had his axe and skinning knife.

'Send Dedan back to keep an eye on the isthmus. Any Frelimo or Renamo patrols will come that way. At the first sign of trouble, get the girl into the swamp and hide out on one of the islands.' Sean gave Job his final orders, and then sauntered across to where Riccardo was taking leave of his daughter.

'Are you ready, Capo?'

Riccardo stood up quickly and walked away from Claudia without looking back.

'Don't get into any more trouble,' Sean told her.

'You neither.' She looked up at him. 'And Sean, take care of Papa for me.'

He squatted down in front of her and offered her his hand as he would have if she had been a man, and he tried to think of something witty to say, but he could not.

'Okay, then?' he asked instead.

'Okay, then,' she agreed, and he stood up and walked down to the edge of the swamp where Matatu and Pumula and Riccardo were waiting for him beside the dugout canoe.

Matatu took up his position in the bows of the frail craft, Sean and Riccardo were amidships, sitting on their depleted packs and holding their rifles across their laps. Pumula stood in the stern with one of the freshly cut punt poles and propelled the dugout in response to Matatu's hand signals.

Within seconds of pushing off from the bank, they were surrounded by a high palisade of papyrus, and their view was restricted to the wall of reeds and the small patch of lemon-yellow dawn sky overhead. As they passed, the sharp pointed leaves of the reeds were dashed into their faces, threatening their eyes, and the webs that the tiny swamp spiders had spun between the stems of the reeds wrapped over their faces, sticky and irritating. The night's clammy chill hung over the swamp and when they came out suddenly into an open lagoon, there was a heavy mist lying over the surface and a flock of whistling duck alarmed the dawn with the clatter of their wings.

The dugout was heavily overloaded with the four men aboard. There was only an inch or so of freeboard and if any one of them moved suddenly, water slopped on board and they were forced to use the tea billy to bail almost continually, but Matatu signalled them on.

The sun rose above the papyrus and immediately the mist twisted into rising tendrils and then was gone. The water lilies opened their cerulean blossoms and turned them to face the sunrise. Twice they saw large crocodiles lying with just their eye-knuckles exposed. They sank below the surface as the dugout slid towards them.

The swamps were alive with birds. Bitterns and secretive night herons lurked in the reed-beds, little chocolate-brown jacanas danced over the lily pads on their long legs, while goliath herons as tall as a man fished the back waters of the lagoons. Overhead winged formations of pelicans and white egrets, cormorants and darters with serpentine necks, and huge flocks of wild duck of a dozen different species.

The heat built up swiftly and was reflected from the surface of the water into their faces so that the two white men were soon sweating through their shirts. At places the water was only a few inches deep and they were forced to climb out and drag the dugout through to the next channel or lagoon. Under the matted reeds the mud was black and foul-smelling and reached to their knees.

In the shallower places the elephant's pads had left deep circular water-filled craters in the mudbanks. The spoor of the old bull led them deeper and ever deeper into the swamplands, but there was consolation in the swift progress that the dugout made across the lagoons and channels, thrust on by the long punt pole. For a while, Sean spelled Pumula in the stern but soon Pumula could no longer abide his clumsy strokes and took the pole away from him.

There was only room for one man to stretch out in the bottom of the dugout. Riccardo slept in it that night, while the others sat waist-deep in the mud, leaning against the hull of the canoe and took what rest the clouds of mosquitoes allowed them.

Early the following morning, when Sean stood up out of the mud, he found that his bare legs were swarming with black leeches. The repulsive worms were attached to his skin, bloated with the blood they had sucked from him. Sean used a little of their precious supply of salt to rid himself of them. To pull them loose would leave a wound into which the leech had injected anti-coagulants and which would continue to bleed profusely and probably become infected. However, a dab of salt on each leech made them twist and contort with agony and fall off leaving only a sealed wound on the skin.

When he opened his trousers, Sean found that they had crawled up into the cleft between his buttocks and were hanging like black grapes from his genitalia. He shuddered with horror as he worked on them, while safely in the dugout Riccardo watched with interest and made facetious comment:

'Hey, Sean, this must be the first time you've ever objected to a bit of head!'

*   *   *

Sean set the end of the punt pole in the mud and steadied it while Matatu shinned up it like a monkey and peered ahead. When he came down he told Sean, 'I can see the islands. We are very close. We will be there before noon, and unless Tukutela has heard us, he will be on one of the islands.'

Sean knew from flights over the area and from study of his

173

large-scale map that the islands formed a chain between the swamplands and the main channel of the Zambezi. They dragged the dugout through the shallows, Sean hauling on the nylon rope tied to the bows, and Pumula and Matatu shoving in the stern. When Riccardo offered to assist, Sean told him, 'Take a free ride, Capo. I want you nicely rested so that you don't have any excuses if you mess up your shot at Tukutela.'

At last Sean saw the fronds of the palm trees rising above the screen of papyrus ahead, and abruptly the water deepened, and he went under to his chin. He dragged himself out and they all clambered back on board. Pumula poled them through to the first island. The vegetation was so dense that it overhung the water, and they had to push their way through to reach the shore.

The earth was grey and sandy, leached by a million floods, but it was good to have dry land under foot. Sean spread out their wet clothing and equipment to dry while Matatu slipped away to make a circuit of the island. The water had just boiled in the billy when Matatu was back.

'Yes,' he nodded at Sean. 'He passed here yesterday early, while we were leaving the village, but he has settled down now. The peace of the river is upon him, and he feeds quietly. He left this island at sunrise this morning.'

'Which way did he go?' Sean asked, and Matatu pointed.

'There is another larger island close by.'

'Let's take a look.'

Sean poured a mug of tea for Riccardo and left him with Pumula, while he and Matatu skirted the northern shore, forcing their way through the dense growth until they reached the base of the tallest tree on the island and climbed into its top branches.

Sean settled into a high crotch of the tree, snapped off the few leafy twigs that obscured his view and gazed out on a scene of magnificent desolation.

He was sixty feet above the island and could see to the misty horizon. The Zambezi flowed past the island. Its waters were an opaque glassy green so wide that distance had reduced the great trees that lined the far bank to a dark band that separated green water from the high alps of cumulus cloud that soared anvil-headed into the blue African sky.

The Zambezi flowed so swiftly that its surface was ruffled by eddies and whirlpools and wayward counter currents. Floating carpets of swamp grass had been torn loose by the current and

174

sailed past, seeming as substantial as the island beneath him. Sean thought about crossing that forbidding river in the frail dugout. It would take more than one trip to get them all across and he abandoned the idea. There was only one way out, and that was back the way they had come.

He transferred all his attention to the chain of islands which stood like sentinels between the mother river and her spreading swamps. The nearest island in the chain was three hundred metres away; the channel between was clogged with reeds and water hyacinth and lily pads. The blooms of the water lilies were spots of electric blue against the green water and even in the tree-top Sean could catch wafts of their perfume.

Sean raised his binoculars and meticulously swept the channel and the nearest shore of the island, for even a great elephant could be swallowed up by the sweep and magnitude of this land-and waterscape.

Suddenly his nerves jumped as he saw movement weighty and ponderous in the reeds and the gleam of wet hide in the sunlight. His excitement was stillborn, followed by the pull of disappointment in his guts, as he recognized the broad misshapen head of a hippopotamus emerging from the swamps.

In the lens of his binoculars he could see the pink-shot piggy eyes and the bristles in the disproportionately tiny ears. The hippo fluttered them like the wings of a bird, shaking off the droplets that sparkled like diamond chips, forming a halo above its huge head. It plodded through the mud, crossing from one lagoon to another, pausing only to loose an explosive jet of liquid dung that it splattered with a violent stirring motion of its stubby tail. The force of this discharge flattened the reeds behind the obese animal.

With relief, Sean watched it move on and submerge itself in the further lagoon. The rotten hull of the dugout would have offered no protection from those heavy curved tusks in the gape of huge jaws.

At last Sean glanced across at Matatu in the fork beside him, and the little Ndorobo shook his head.

'He has moved on, so must we.'

They scrambled down to the ground and went back to where they had left Riccardo. The voyage in the *mokorro* and a good night's sleep had invigorated him. He was on his feet, impatient and eager for the hunt, the way Sean had known him before.

'Anything?' he demanded.

'No.' Sean shook his head. 'But Matatu reckons we are close. Absolute silence from now on.'

While they loaded the dugout, Sean gulped a mug of the scalding tea and kicked sand over the fire.

They punted and pushed the canoe across the channel to the next island, and once again Sean climbed into a tree-top while Matatu scurried into the dense undergrowth to pick up the elephant's spoor again. He was back within fifteen minutes and Sean slid out of the tree to meet him.

'He has moved on,' Matatu whispered. 'But the wind is bad.' He looked grave, and took the ash bag from his loin-cloth and shook out a puff of powdery white ash to demonstrate. 'See how it turns and changes like the fancy of a Shangane whore.'

Sean nodded and before they crossed to the next island he stripped off his sleeveless bush shirt. Naked from the waist up he could feel instantly the slightest vagary of the breeze on the sensitive skin of his upper body.

On the next island they found where Tukutela had left the water to go ashore, and the mud he had smeared on the brush as he passed was still slightly damp. Matatu shivered with excitement like a good dog getting his first whiff of the bird.

They left the canoe and crept forward, feeling their way through the heavy bush, thankful for the breeze that clattered the palm fronds overhead to cover the small sounds of their footfalls in the dead leaves and dry twigs. They found where the old elephant had shaken down the nuts from one of the palms and stuffed them down his throat without chewing them with his last worn set of molars, but he had moved on again.

'Run?' Sean whispered, fearful that the bull might have sensed their presence, but Matatu reassured him with a quick shake of his head and pointed to the green twigs that the elephant had stripped of bark and left scattered along his tracks. The raw twigs had not completely dried out, but the spoor led them on a meandering beat across the island and then once more plunged into the channel on the far side. They sent Pumula back to bring the dugout around to where they waited and when he arrived piled Riccardo into it and pushed him across, wading waist-deep beside him, moving stealthily and silently until they reached the next island.

Here they found a pile of dung, spongy and soft with reeds

and hyacinth that the bull had eaten, and beside it the splash mark of his urine as though a garden hose had been played upon the earth. It was still so wet that Sean scooped a handful of the dirt and moulded it into a ball like a child's mud cake. The pile of dung had a dry crust but when Matatu thrust his foot into it, it was moist as porridge and he exclaimed with delight at the body heat still trapped within.

'Close, very close!' he whispered excitedly.

Instinctively Sean reached for the cartridges looped on his belt and he changed them for those in the double-barrelled rifle, careful to mute the click of the rifle's sidelock as he closed it. Riccardo recognized the gesture, he had seen it so often before and he grinned with excitement and clicked the Rigby's safety-catch on and off, on and off. They crept forward in single file, but disappointment dragged them down again as the spoor led them across the island, and then on the far side once more entered the papyrus beds.

They stood facing the wall of reeds, staring at the point where Tukutela had pushed down the stems as he went through. One of the flattened stems quivered and began slowly to rise into its original position. The elephant must have passed only minutes ahead of them. They stood in a frozen group, straining to listen beyond the susurration of the wind in the papyrus.

Then they heard it, the low rumble like summer thunder heard at a great distance, the sound that an elephant makes in his throat when he is content and at peace. It is a sound that carries much farther than its volume would suggest, but nevertheless Sean knew that the bull was not more than a hundred yards ahead of them and he laid his hand on Riccardo's arm and drew him gently up alongside him.

'We have to be careful of the wind,' he began in a whisper, and then they heard the swish and rush of water sucked up in the bull's trunk and squirted back over his own shoulders to cool himself, and they caught a brief glimpse of the black tip of his trunk as he lifted it high above the tops of the papyrus ahead of them.

Their excitement was so intense that Sean felt his throat closed and dry, and his whisper was rough.

'Back off!'

He made a cut-out hand signal which Matatu obeyed instantly, and they backed away, a stealthy pace at a time, Sean leading

Riccardo by the arm. As soon as they were into the undergrowth Riccardo demanded in a furious whisper, 'What the hell, we were so close.'

'Too close,' Sean told him grimly. 'Without any chance of a shot in the papyrus. If the wind had swung just a few degrees it would have been over before it began. We have to let him get across to the next island before we can close in.'

He led Riccardo back faster, and then stopped below the outspread branches of a tall strangler fig.

'Let's take a look,' he ordered. They propped their rifles at the base of the trunk, and Sean helped Riccardo to reach the first branch and then followed him as he climbed upwards from branch to branch.

Near the top of the fig they found a secure stance and Sean steadied Riccardo with a hand on his shoulder, and they stared down into the papyrus beds.

They saw him immediately. Tukutela's back rose above the reeds. It was wet and charcoal-black from the spray of his trunk, the spine was curved and prominent beneath the rough wrinkled hide. He was faced away from them, his huge ears flapping lazily, the edges torn and tattered, the thick veins twisted and knotted like a nest of serpents beneath the smoother skin behind their wide spread.

A row of four egrets rode upon his back, perched along his spine, brilliant white in the sunlight with yellow bills, sitting hunched up but attentive, bright-eyed sentinels who would warn the old bull at the first approach of danger.

While he was in the water, there was no way that they could come at him and he was well over three hundred yards away, far beyond effective rifle shot. So they watched him from the tree-top as he made his slow majestic way across the channel towards the next island.

When Tukutela reached the deepest stretch of open water he submerged completely; only his trunk rose above the surface, waving and coiling in the air like the head of a sea-serpent. He emerged on the far side of the channel with water streaming down his darkly mountainous sides.

Standing together on the branch of the fig, Riccardo and Sean were savouring this high point in both their hunting experience. Never again would there be another elephant like this. No other man would ever gaze upon such a beast. He was theirs. It seemed that they had waited their lifetimes for this moment. The hunter's passion eclipsed all other emotion, at that moment rendering everything else in their lives effete and tasteless. Here was something primeval, sprung from the very wells of the soul and it affected them as great music might affect others.

The old bull lifted his head and turned aside for a moment, affording them just a brief glimpse of his dark-stained ivory, and they stirred unconsciously, affected by the sight of those long perfectly curved shafts as by the creation of a Michelangelo or the body of a beautiful woman. At that moment, there was nothing else in their universe. They were perfectly in tune, a bond of companionship and shared endeavour welded them.

'He's beautiful!' Riccardo whispered.

Sean did not reply, for there was nothing to add.

They watched the old bull reach the far island and heave his body from the water, climb the low bank and stand for a moment, tall and gaunt and shining wet in the sun, before he pushed his way into the undergrowth and it swallowed up even his bulk. The egrets were brushed from his back and rose up like snowy scraps of paper in a whirlwind. Sean tapped Riccardo on the shoulder and he shook himself as though awaking from a dream.

'We'll cross in the canoe,' Sean whispered, and sent Pumula to bring the craft around the islet.

They sat flat in the bottom of the *mokorro* so that their heads would not show above the tops of the reeds and they propelled themselves across the narrow neck of swamp by pulling on the stems of the papyrus. Soundlessly they slid through the reed-beds, and the light breeze held true and steady. Sean felt every light touch of it on his bare shoulders.

They reached the shore and Sean helped Riccardo out of the canoe, and they pulled it up onto the bank, careful not to make the faintest sound.

'Check your load,' Sean whispered, and Riccardo turned the bolt of the Rigby and drew it back just far enough to expose the shining brass cartridge in the chamber. Sean nodded approval and Riccardo closed the bolt silently. They went forward.

They were forced to move in single file, following the path that the bull had opened through the otherwise impenetrable growth. Matatu led them a few paces at a time, and then they all froze to listen.

Suddenly there was a loud crackling uproar in the bushes just

179

ahead of them, and they saw the branches sway and toss and shake. Riccardo swung up the Rigby, but Sean restrained him, grabbing his forearm and pushing the muzzle of the rifle down.

They stood stonily, staring ahead, hearts pounding, and listened to the old bull feeding. Only thirty paces from them he was ripping down branches, swinging his ears back and forth to a leisurely rhythm, rumbling contentedly, and they could not catch even the barest glimpse of grey hide.

Sean still had hold of Riccardo's arm and now he drew him onwards. Step by step they edged through the green press of leaves and vines and drooping branches. Ten paces, and then Sean halted. He eased Riccardo forward, pushing him ahead, and Sean pointed over his shoulder.

For long seconds Riccardo could make out no details in the jumbled growth and confused shadows. Then the bull flapped his ears again, and Riccardo saw his eye through a hole in the vegetation. It was a small rheumy eye, with the slightly opaque blue cast of age, and the tears oozed down the wrinkled cheek below it, giving it a look of great wisdom and infinite sorrow.

That sorrow was contagious, it engulfed Riccardo in a black wave, it weighed down his soul, transforming his ardent predatory passion to a devastating sadness and mourning for this life that was about to end. He did not lift the rifle.

The elephant blinked its eye, the lashes surrounding it were thick and long, and the eye looked deep into Riccardo's own, seemed to pierce his very soul, seemed to mourn for him as he mourned for the old bull. Riccardo did not realize that the evil thing in his brain was once more bending and reshaping reality, he knew only that the sorrow in him was as insupportable as the black oblivion of death.

He felt Sean lightly tap him between the shoulder-blades, screening even that tiny movement from the bull. It was the urgent command to fire, but it was as though Riccardo had left his own body and hovered just above it, looking down upon himself, watching both the man and the beast with death in them and death all about them, and the tragedy engrossed him and robbed him of his will and power of movement.

Once again Sean tapped him. The elephant was fifteen paces away, standing perfectly still, a looming grey shadow in the undergrowth. Sean knew that Tukutela's sudden stillness was the

180

old bull's response to the premonition of danger. He would stand only for a few seconds longer, and then plunge away into the dense undergrowth.

He wanted to seize Riccardo's shoulder and shake him, he wanted to cry out, 'Shoot, man, shoot!' But he was helpless, the slightest movement, the faintest sound would trigger the old bull into flight.

Then it happened as Sean had known and feared it would. It seemed that Tukutela had been snatched away, had disappeared in a puff of grey smoke. It was impossible that such a huge beast could move so quickly and so silently in such dense bush, but he was gone.

Sean seized Riccardo's arm and pulled him along with him, dragging him after the vanished bull. Sean's face was contorted with rage and dark rage filled his chest and made it difficult for him to breathe. He wanted to vent that rage on Riccardo. He had risked his very life to put him in the position to take this animal, and the man had not even raised his rifle.

Sean ran forward, his grip upon Riccardo's arm was savage, and he dragged him through dense scrub and thorn, oblivious to his discomfort. He was certain that Tukutela would try to reach the next island in the chain, and he hoped for another chance at him as he crossed the open channel. He would force Riccardo to take even a long shot, hoping to cripple and slow the bull, so that Sean could follow and finish him off.

Behind him Matatu screamed something that was unintelligible, a warning, a cry for help perhaps, and Sean came up short, and stood listening. Something was happening that was totally unexpected, for which he was unprepared.

He heard the sudden crash and crackle in the undergrowth, and then the wild trumpeting squeal of an enraged elephant, but the sound was from behind him, not the direction in which Tukutela had vanished. For an instant Sean did not understand, and then the reality dawned upon him and he felt the goose bumps rise upon his naked back.

Tukutela had done something that no elephant he knew of had ever done before. The old bull had not fled, but instead had circled downwind of them to get their scent. Even as he stood now, Sean felt the wind touch his naked back, like the caress of a treacherous lover bearing his scent down to where the great bull was rushing through the dense bush, hunting for him.

'Matatu,' Sean yelled. 'Run! Run across the wind!' He shoved Riccardo roughly against the trunk of a towering teak tree.

'Get up there,' he snarled at him. The lower branches were easy to climb, and Sean left him and raced back to protect Matatu.

He charged headlong through the bush, jumping over fallen logs, his rifle held across his chest, and the forest rang to the elephant's wild and angry squeals.

He was closing swiftly, like an avalanche of grey rock. Tukutela rolled through the forest, splitting and dashing the smaller trees that stood in his way, seeking out the evil acrid smell of humanity, following it down so that once again he could wreak upon them the accumulated hatred of his long lifetime.

Suddenly Matatu darted out of the bush just a few paces ahead of Sean. He would stand to meet any odds with Sean beside him, and now instead of running across the wind as Pumula had done, his instinct had led him directly back to his master's side.

As he saw him, Sean changed direction in mid-stride, signalling urgently for Matatu to follow him. He ran a hundred swift paces out to one side, across the wind, trying to deny their scent to Tukutela.

He stopped and crouched with Matatu beside him. His tactic had been successful, Pumula also must have got out of Tukutela's wind. For the moment Tukutela had lost their scent. The forest was absolutely still, the silence so intense that Sean could hear his pulse beating in his own head.

He sensed that the old bull was very close to them, standing as still as they were, listening with ears spread wide, only that long trunk questing for the smell of them. There had never been an elephant like this, he thought, a bull who actively hunted his persecutors. How many times has he been hunted, Sean wondered, how many times has man inflicted hurt upon him that he attacks so fiercely at the first hint of human presence?

'Tukutela, the Angry One, now I know why they named you.'

Then there was a sound in the forest, one that Sean had not expected, a human voice, raised loudly, and it took him a moment to realize that it was Riccardo Monterro.

'Tukutela, we are brothers!' he was calling to the elephant. 'We are all that is left from another age. Our destiny is linked. I cannot kill you!'

The bull heard him and squealed again, a sound so loud and

182

pitched so high that it was like an auger driven into their eardrums. Tukutela charged the sound of the human voice, like a grey battle-tank. He crashed through the undergrowth, going straight for it, and within fifty yards the scent of man, loathsome and infuriating, filled his head once again and he followed it down to its source.

Riccardo Monterro had made no effort to climb the teak tree where Sean had left him, he simply leaned against the trunk and closed his eyes. The pain in his head came upon him as suddenly as the blow of an axe, and it blinded him, filling his vision with bursting stars of light, but through the pain he heard the old bull elephant squeal and the sound filled him with remorse and bitter despair.

He let the Rigby slip from his hands and fall into the leafy trash at his feet and he reached out his empty hands and staggered blindly to meet the elephant, wanting in some desperate way to placate and make recompense to the great beast, calling to it. 'I mean you no harm, we are brothers.' And ahead of him the bush crackled and burst open and Tukutela bore down on him like a collapsing cliff of granite.

Sean raced back to where he had left Riccardo, ducking under branches and bounding over obstacles in his path, and he heard the terrifying rush of the bull and the voice of the man just ahead of him.

'Here!' he screamed. 'Here, Tukutela! Come! Come this way!' trying to pull the elephant off Riccardo and onto himself, but he knew it was of no avail. Tukutela had fixed on his victim, and nothing would deter him. He would carry his charge through to the death.

The centre of Riccardo's vision cleared, and he looked through an aperture in his head that was surrounded by shooting white lights and catherine wheels of spinning fire. He saw Tukutela's vast grey head burst out of the green forest wall above him, and the long stained tusks came over him like the cross-ties of a roof about to fall.

In that moment, the elephant came to embody all the thousands of animals and birds that Riccardo had slaughtered in his lifetime as a hunter. He had a confused notion that the tusks and long trunk poised above him were the symbols of some semi-religious benediction that would absolve him and redeem the blood that he had spilled and all the life he had destroyed. He reached up

183

both hands to them, joyfully and thankfully, and he remembered a phrase from his early religious instruction.

'Forgive me, Father, for I have sinned,' he cried.

Sean saw the bull's head rear out of the thicket ahead of him. It was facing almost directly away from him with ears cocked and rolled along the top edge. He heard Riccardo's voice though he could not understand the words, and he realized that Riccardo must be almost directly beneath the bull's out-thrust tusks and reaching trunk.

Sean plunged from his headlong run to a dead stop in a single pace and threw up the .577 Express rifle. It was the most difficult angle for the brain shot, with the elephant angled away from him, and the bulk of its shoulder covering the spinal column.

The target was no bigger than a ripe apple and there was no indication of where exactly it lay buried in the huge bony casket of the skull. He had to trust his experience and his instinct. For a moment, it seemed as he looked over the open Express sights of the rifle that he could see into the skull, where the brain seemed to glow in the bony depths like a firefly.

Without conscious effort his trigger finger tightened as the pip of the foresight covered that glowing spot. The bullet bored through the sponge of bone as though it were air, it cleaved the old bull's brain, and he felt nothing. His passage from full enraged life to death was a fleeting instant and his legs collapsed and folded under him. He dropped on his chest with an impact that jarred the earth and shook loose the dead leaves from the branches above him. A cloud of pale dust swirled around his massive carcass and his head dropped forward.

His right tusk drove into Riccardo Monterro's body, entering his belly a hand's-breadth below the sternum of his rib cage, and it passed through him at the level of his kidneys and came out through his spine just at the point where it merged with his pelvis.

The shaft of ivory which Riccardo had coveted and risked both fortune and life to obtain, now pinned him to the earth, skewered him as cleanly as a whaler's harpoon. He looked down at the tusk in surprise. There was no pain, no sensation in his lower body which was twisted up under the bull's coiled trunk, no pain even in his head.

For a moment his vision was clear and bright as though every-thing he looked at was lit by brilliant floodlights, and then it

184

began to fade and darkness closed in upon him. Just before the darkness engulfed him completely, he saw Sean Courtney's face floating before him, and heard his voice fading as though he were sinking away into an abyss.

'Capo, Capo,' it echoed in his ears, and Riccardo Monterro made a huge effort and said, 'She loves you. Look after my little girl.' And then the darkness swallowed him and he saw and heard nothing more, ever again.

* * *

Sean's first impulse was to free Riccardo Monterro's body. He tugged at the tusk which impaled him, but it was so thick that he could not get a fair grip upon it, and Riccardo's blood was oozing from the terrible wound. It coated Sean's hands so that he left sticky red prints upon the ivory as he strained at it.

Then he realized the futility of his efforts, and stepped back. The full weight of Tukutela's huge head and body was resting on those tusks. After piercing Riccardo's torso the ivory point had gone on to bury itself deep in the soft sandy earth. It would take half a day's work to free the body.

In death, the man and the beast were locked together, and suddenly Sean realized how appropriate that was. He would leave them like that.

First Matatu and then Pumula appeared from out of the forest and stood beside Sean staring in awe at the grim spectacle.

'Go!' Sean ordered. 'Wait for me at the canoe.'

'The ivory?' Pumula asked diffidently.

'Go!' Sean repeated, and at the tone of his voice, they crept quietly away.

Riccardo's eyes were wide open. Sean closed them with a gentle stroke of his thumb and then unknotted the cotton scarf from around Riccardo's neck and bound up his jaw to prevent it sagging into an expression of idiocy. Even in death, Riccardo Monterro was still a handsome man. Sean leaned against the elephant's head and studied Riccardo's face.

'It happened at just the right time, Capo. Before the disease turned you into a vegetable. While you still had most of your zest and vigour, and it was a fitting end for a man like you. I'm glad you didn't die between soiled sheets. I only pray that I will be as fortunate.'

185

Sean laid his hand upon one of the tusks and stroked it. It had the texture of precious jade beneath his fingertips.

'We'll leave them for you, Capo,' he said. 'These tusks will be your headstone. God knows, you paid for them in full.'

Sean straightened up and followed Riccardo's tracks back into the forest until he found the Rigby lying in the dead leaves. He brought it back and placed it in the crook of Riccardo's right arm.

'A warrior should be buried with his weapons,' he murmured, but there was still something missing. He could not go and leave Riccardo like this. He could not leave him lying exposed to an uncaring sky. He must cover him decently.

Then Sean remembered the legend of this elephant and how he disposed of the dead. He drew the heavy knife from the sheath on his belt and turned to the nearest green bush. He slashed off a leafy branch and covered Riccardo's face with it.

'Yes,' he murmured. 'That's right, that's proper.'

Working swiftly, he hacked down the branches and covered Riccardo's corpse and the head of the old bull under a mound of green leaves.

At last he stood back and picked up the .577. He tucked it under his arm and he was ready to leave.

'No regrets, Capo,' he said. 'For you, it was a good life right up to the very end. Go in peace, old friend.'

He turned away and went down to where the canoe was moored.

* * *

The reeds scraped softly along the hull of the canoe as Pumula poled it along. None of them spoke.

Sean sat amidships, hunched forward with his chin in the cup of one hand. He felt numbed, emptied of all emotion except sadness. It was like coming back from a raid in the days of the bush war with every man silent and sad.

He looked at his right hand in his lap and saw the little half moons of dark red under his fingernails. 'Capo's blood,' he thought, and trailed his hand over the side of the canoe, letting the warm swamp waters wash away the stain.

He let the hunt replay itself through his mind, as though it were a silent recording. He saw it all again very vividly from their first sighting of the old bull to the moment that he rushed forward to find Riccardo Monterro impaled beneath the huge grey head.

Then for the first time, he heard sound. Riccardo's voice echoed in his head, faint and breathless, fading swiftly.

'She loves you,' he had said, and the rest trailed away unintelligibly. 'She loves you.' The meaningless words of a dying man, the wanderings of a diseased brain. Riccardo could have been harking back to any one of the hundreds of women who had filled his life.

Sean lifted his hand out of the water. It was clean, the blood washed away.

'She loves you.' He could have been trying to tell Sean of one particular woman.

Sean looked up from his wet hand and stared ahead. Her memory had been with him these last few days, always there in the recesses of his conscience yet coming to the fore at unexpected moments. Often while thinking of the great elephant, he had suddenly smiled at something she had said. This morning during the final stages of the hunt he had reached outboard from the canoe, and picked the bloom of a water lily. He had held it to his face and smelled the perfume, felt the silky touch of the petals on his lip and thought of Claudia Monterro.

Now he stared ahead and for the first time admitted to himself how much he looked forward to seeing her again. It seemed that she was all that could cancel out his grief for her father. He thought about the sound of her voice and the way she held her head when she was about to challenge him. He smiled at the bright specks of anger he could so readily kindle in her eyes, and the way she pursed her lips when she was trying to prevent herself laughing at one of his own digs.

He thought about the way she walked, and the way she felt when he had carried her in his arms, and he remembered the texture of her skin like the petals of the water lily when he touched her under pretext of helping or guiding her.

'We are absolutely and completely wrong for each other,' he smiled, and the melancholy of a few moments previously loosened its grip. 'If Capo was talking about her, then he had definitely gone completely round the bend.' But his anticipation was honed to a sharper edge.

He looked up at the sky. The sun had set. It would be dark in a short while. Even as he watched, Venus as the evening star appeared with a miraculous suddenness and twinkled low down in the west. One after another, the fixed stars followed her entrance, popping through the darkening canopy of night in strict order of their magnitude.

Sean looked up at the stars and he thought of Claudia, and he wondered why she evoked such contrary feelings in him. He compared her to some of the other women he had known, and realized how shallow and fleeting those experiences had been. Even his marriage had been inconsequential, a wild impulse based on simple-minded lust. It had been swiftly consummated, satiated and terminated, a disastrous mistake which he had never repeated. He could only vaguely remember what the woman who had been his wife looked like now.

He thought about Claudia and realized with a small shock that her image was so clear in his mind that he could almost count the individual lashes around those big honey-brown eyes, and the tiny laughter lines at the corners of her mouth. Suddenly he very much wanted to be with her again, and as he acknowledged that fact he began to worry.

'I must have been crazy to leave her alone,' he thought, and as he stared ahead into the dark swamps a multitude of horrid chances that might have befallen her began to plague him.

'Job is with her,' he tried to console himself. 'But I should have stayed to care for her and sent Job with Capo.' Even though he realized that had been impossible, still he fretted.

He felt the canoe check under him as Pumula rested on his pole, hinting at permission to stop for the night.

'I'll take her for a while,' Sean said. 'We'll keep going until we get back to the village.'

While Pumula and Matatu curled up in the bilges, Sean stood in the stern and swayed to the monotonous thrust and reach of the punt pole. He steered by the cross and the pointers, reckoning true south at the intersection of their extended centre lines.

The papyrus stems hissed softly against the hull in strict rhythm to his thrusts, and soon the work became so repetitive and automatic that he could let his mind wander, and all those wanderings seemed to return in the end to Claudia Monterro at the centre.

He thought about her bereavement, how although she had been expecting it, yet it would still devastate her. He composed the words he would use to tell her and then to comfort her. She knew of his own feelings for her father, and the companionship that they had shared in the hunting veld. She knew of their mutual regard for each other.

'I am the right person to help her through the first sorrow. I knew him so well. I will help her to remember all that was good about him.'

He should have dreaded bearing the sad tidings, but instead he found himself looking forward to taking the role of her comforter and protector.

'Perhaps we will be able to drop the postures of antagonism that we have both forced upon ourselves. Instead of accentuating our differences, perhaps we'll be able to explore what we have in common.' He found himself lengthening and quickening his stroke with the punt pole and he had to force himself to slow down.

'You won't last the night at that pace,' he thought, but his eagerness to be with her kept him going long after fatigue demanded a halt.

Hour after hour he kept it up, until Pumula woke of his own accord and came to spell him, but Sean slept fitfully and was back in the stern as the coming of day turned the eastern sky to a murky ruby and then to pale lemon, and the water fowl flighted overhead, their wings whistling softly as they stabbed at the dawn.

Two hours later, Sean sent Matatu up the punt pole and he had not reached the top before he pointed gleefully ahead. However, it was early afternoon before the prow of the canoe knifed through the last dense stand of papyrus and ran ashore on the sand below the burnt village.

Sean leapt onto dry land and strode through the ruins of the village, trying not to break into a run.

'Job should have kept a better watch,' he thought angrily. 'If we can arrive unseen . . .' he did not finish the thought. Just ahead was the thicket in which they had built Claudia's shelter, and Sean stopped abruptly.

It was too quiet. His sixth sense of danger warned him. Something was wrong. He went down fast and hard, falling flat and rolling quickly into cover with the .577 held in front of him.

He lay and listened. The silence was a physical weight. He wet his lips and imitated the clucking sound of a francolin, one of the Scouts' assembly calls that Job would recognize. There was no reply. He went forward at a leopard crawl, and then stopped again. Something sparkled in the short grass just in front of his face. He picked it up and felt his stomach chill.

It was the empty brass case of a 7.62mm cartridge, and it was head-stamped in Cyrillic script, Soviet military issue for firing in the AK assault rifle. Sean held it to his nose, and smelt the burnt powder. It had been fired very recently. He glanced around him quickly and saw other empty shells lying in the grass, evidence of a fierce fire-fight.

He rolled to his feet and was running, jinking and twisting as he sprinted towards the thicket to throw off the aim of a hidden gunman.

As he reached the edge of the thicket, he dropped to earth again, flicking over as he hit the ground. Immediately, he saw the corpse, it lay face down under a low thorn bush only a few yards ahead. It was a black man. The body had been stripped of clothing and boots.

'Job!' The name ripped from his throat. He crawled forward, until he lay side by side with the body. A single bullet had ploughed out of the man's back, and the flies crawled over the wound. The blood had dried to a black crust and he smelt the whiff of corruption.

'Dead twenty-four hours,' he estimated, and rose to his knees. No further need for caution now. Gently he lifted the dead head. The corpse's neck was stiff with *rigor mortis* and he grunted with vast relief and let the head drop with a thud. The man was a stranger.

'Job!' he called. 'Claudia!' It was a despairing cry, and he ran forward to the lean-to in which he had left her. It was deserted.

'Job!' He looked around him wildly. 'Claudia!'

There was another naked black body lying at the edge of the clearing, and he ran to it. It was another stranger, a skinny little runt of a man with the top shot off his skull. He was also starting to stink, his belly blowing up like a shiny black balloon.

'Two of the bastards,' Sean said bitterly. 'Nice shooting, Job.'

Matatu had followed Sean and was checking the lean-to. He left it and began to work out in circles, darting back and forth like a gun dog quartering for a sitting grouse. Sean and Pumula stood and watched him, not joining his search so that they would not trample the sign.

Within minutes Matatu scurried back.

'They are the same *shifta* who followed us before. There are fifteen of them, they surrounded the hut and came in at a rush. Job shot these two with the 30/06 *banduki*.' He offered Sean the empty cartridge cases. 'There was much struggling, but they took them.'

'The memsahib?' Sean dreaded the reply.

'*Ndio*,' Matatu replied in Swahili. 'Yes, they took her also. She is still limping, but they led her away, one on each side. She was fighting them all the way. Job was hurt, and so was Dedan. Perhaps they were beaten, and I think their arms are bound. They walk unsteadily.' Matatu pointed towards the corpses. 'They stripped their dead of uniforms and boots and *banduki* and then went back.' He pointed along the isthmus.

'When?' Sean asked.

'Yesterday, early. Perhaps they rushed the camp at dawn.'

Sean nodded grimly, but inside he cried, 'Claudia, oh God, if they touch you, I'll rip their guts out.'

'Hot pursuit,' he said aloud. 'Let's go!'

Pumula ran back to grab the equipment and water-bottles from the canoe, and Sean was still shrugging into the shoulder-straps of his pack when he started to run. The near exhaustion of the long night of poling the canoe faded away. He felt strong and angry and indefatigable.

Within the first mile, they settled into the pursuit pace of a Scout raiding party. The spoor was still cold and Sean dispensed with any precautions against ambush. He relied entirely on Matatu to pick up any sign of a booby trap or anti-personnel mine that might have been laid on the tracks to hinder pursuit, but apart from that they went in single file at a speed not much below that of an Olympic marathon.

Claudia's image seemed to dance ahead of Sean and winged his feet.

Fifteen of them, Matatu had said, and they would be tempted by Claudia's sweet white body. There were no signs yet that they had stopped to have sport with her. He accepted without reservation Matatu's interpretation that they had crept up on the camp in the dawn, and taken it at a rush, willing to accept casualties without inflicting them. It seemed that they had wanted prisoners rather than kills. Other than a few blows with a rifle butt, it looked as though both Dedan and Job had come through it unscathed, but it was Claudia who had his full concern.

They were forcing her to march on her injured leg. That would only aggravate the knee, and perhaps cause permanent damage. If she slowed them down too much, they would start to become impatient and threatening. It all depended on just how much they needed a white prisoner as a hostage, probably as a bargaining chip with western governments. It depended on who they were, Frelimo or Renamo or free-lance bandits, it depended on how much control there was over them, on who commanded them, and how strong was his authority, but any way he considered it, Sean knew that Claudia was in terrible danger.

Did they realize that there was a pursuit? They must have read the sign going into the village and known that three men – no, four with Capo – were missing from the original party. The answer was, yes. They probably anticipated a pursuit by this group. That would make them nervous and excitable.

Claudia would be no great advocate for her own safety. He could just imagine her arguing with them, demanding her human and legal rights, refusing to follow their orders. Despite his concern, he grinned without humour, as he thought about it. They probably believed they had caught a pussy-cat, but they would soon realize that they had instead a full-grown female tiger on their hands.

His grin faded. He was certain she would deal with them in precisely the fashion best designed to antagonize them and jeopardize her chances of survival. If the leader of the group was a weak man, she would push him to the point where he had to demonstrate his authority to his own men. African society was patriarchal and he would resent a woman who refused to bow to his will. If they were the same group that had wiped out the village they had amply demonstrated their brutality.

'Just for once, ducky, button those lovely lips of yours,' he pleaded with her silently.

Ahead of him, Matatu checked his run and made a sweeping gesture, and Sean pulled up.

'Here they rested.' Matatu pointed to where the group had sat in the shade of a grove of young mopane.

There were the crushed butts of black cigarettes in the dust, and Matatu pointed to the raw white slashes on the mopane from which branches had been chopped. The smaller twigs had been trimmed from them and discarded. The leaves on these were

192

already wilted, confirming Matatu's estimate of time, yesterday morning.

The cutting of branches puzzled Sean for a moment and then Matatu explained, 'They have built a *mushela* for the mem.' And Sean nodded with relief. Claudia on her injured leg had been holding up the march, but rather than ridding themselves of her through the simple expedient of a bullet in the back of the head, they had built a litter of mopane poles on which to carry her. That was a welcome development, and it changed Sean's estimate of Claudia's chance of survival. They had placed a higher value on her than Sean had dreaded they might.

However, the most crucial period would have come yesterday evening when they decided to camp for the night. Her captors would have had a full day to study her, to ogle her body and puff up their imagination and their courage. Sean found he could not bear to face the possibility of what might have happened to her if the leader had lost control of his men.

'Come on, Matatu,' he growled. 'You are wasting time.' If it had happened at all, it would have happened last night. He was already too late but still every second of delay galled him.

The spoor led them back up the isthmus retracing their own route across the dry flood plains heading towards the south. The trail was broad and easy to follow, fifteen men and their captives making no attempt at anti-tracking. Matatu read the spoor and reported that they were forcing Dedan and Job to carry the litter with Claudia on it, and Sean was happy that the two of them were able to do so. Whatever injuries they had sustained in the attack must have been superficial, and he could be certain that Job would employ every ruse to slow down the march, and allow them to catch up.

Even as he thought it, Matatu exclaimed and pointed to the marks in the soft earth where Job had dropped his end of the litter and sprawled theatrically on his hands and knees, only crawling up after he had been surrounded and hectored by his captors.

'Good man,' Sean grunted without checking his stride. 'But don't push them too far.' It was a delicate game Job was playing.

At pursuit speed they were overhauling the clumsy and slow-moving group so rapidly that Sean was beginning to hope they might catch up with them before nightfall.

'That's going to be interesting,' he decided. 'Three of us with only the .577 against fifteen thugs armed with AKs.'

So far they had found no booby traps set for them. It was usually terr tactics to mine their own spoor and Sean pondered their failure to do so. These could be untrained bandits, or they might lack the light plastic anti-personnel mines, or they could be unaware of the pursuit or, worst thought, they could be planning some surprises later.

'We'll deal with that one also when we come to it.'

Matatu pulled up again. 'They cooked here last night.' He pointed to the remains of a camp-fire, and there were the marks where they had sat while they rested and ate. A few black safari ants were scurrying about the site foraging for the scraps of food that they had spilled and there were more cigarette butts.

'Search,' Sean ordered. 'Job will have tried to get a message to us.' While Matatu and Pumula went over the area carefully but quickly, Sean glanced at his watch: 1600 hours, they had been going just over three hours, they still had plenty of daylight and a good chance to catch them before dark.

'Here is where they put the mem's litter.' Matatu pointed out the marks in the earth. 'Here she stood.'

Sean studied her footprints, smaller, neater and narrower than the boot prints of her captors. When she walked she had favoured her leg, dragging the toe.

'Did you find anything?' he demanded roughly. 'Did Job leave a message?'

'Nothing.' Matatu shook his head.

'All right. We'll drink now,' he ordered, and handed out salt tablets from his pack. He didn't have to caution them to self-control. Three swallows each from the bottles, and then they screwed the stoppers tightly closed. They had paused for less than five minutes.

'Let's go,' said Sean.

An hour later, they found where the raiders had slept that night. The fact that they had moved on after eating and not slept beside their cooking-fire told Sean that they were trained troops.

'Search again,' Sean ordered. Any information that Job could have left for them would be valuable.

'Nothing,' Matatu reported back a few minutes later, and Sean felt a prick of disappointment.

'All right. Keep going,' he ordered, and was about to turn

194

away when something made him pause and he glanced around the camp-site.

'Where did the memsahib sleep?' he demanded.

'There.' Matatu pointed. Somebody, probably Job, had cut an armful of leaves and grass for her mattress. Her body had flattened the pile. Sean squatted beside it, and carefully sifted through it, searching for any clues.

There was nothing. He lifted away the last few leaves and was beginning to rise to his feet. He was disappointed, the feeling that she had left something for him had been very powerful.

'So much for ESP,' he grunted, and then noticed the button, half buried in the dust under the mattress of straw.

He picked it out and stood up. It was a brass button from the waistband of her denim jeans, engraved 'Ralph Hutton'.

'Designer jeans, that's my ducky.' He slipped it into his pocket. 'But it doesn't tell me anything,' he broke off, 'unless . . .' He knelt again and gently brushed aside the dust under where the button had lain. He was right, she had used the button as a marker and beneath it had buried a scrap of cardboard, the flap torn from the lid of a packet of cheap Portuguese cigarillos. It was not more than two inches long and half as wide, very little space for the message she had written with a charcoal stick scavenged from the fire.

'Fifteen Renamo.' That was invaluable intelligence, confirming Matatu's estimate of numbers, and now at least he knew who they were dealing with, Renamo.

'Cave.' The next word puzzled him. 'Cave?' Then suddenly he realized it was the old public schoolboy warning from the Latin 'caveat' – beware.

He smiled despite himself. 'Where did she ever learn a limey expression like that?' Then he remembered she was a lawyer and read on.

'Cave. They expect you.' She and Job would have overheard them discussing the pursuit. That information was just as valuable.

'All OK.' And she had signed it, 'C.'

He stared at the scrap of cardboard, holding it in the palm of his hand as though it were a relic of the true cross.

'You little beauty, you,' he whispered. 'You've got to be the brightest, gutsiest . . .' He shook his head in wonder, a choking sensation in his throat. For the very first time, he admitted his longing for her and then suppressed it firmly as he came to his feet. There was no time nor opportunity for such self-indulgence now.

'Renamo,' he told Matatu and Pumula. 'You were right, there are fifteen of them. They know we are following. We can expect an ambush.'

They both looked grave, and Sean glanced at his wristwatch. 'We can catch them before dark.'

Within an hour they came upon the first ambush that the Renamo had set for them. Four men had lain beside the trail at the point where the causeway across the flood plains joined the main forest on the higher ground. The ambush had been cunningly sited on the far edge of a narrow vlei, across open ground with a good field of fire. It had been abandoned only a short time before they came up to it.

'They are putting down a rolling rearguard.' Sean felt queasy at the risk he had taken with such a reckless pursuit.

In the dust were the distinctive double marks left by the bipod of an RPD light machine-gun, one of the simplest and yet the most deadly effective of all guerrilla weapons. If he had led his men into the vlei while that gun was still in position, it would have all been over in a few hellish seconds. He had been pushing too hard, not taking even elementary precautions. His concern for Claudia had unbalanced his judgement.

Renamo had pulled out just before they reached the vlei, they had judged the time of his arrival with disconcerting accuracy, the margin had been far too narrow. The crew of the RPD would have moved back, and resited the ambush farther along the trail in order not to fall too far behind their main party.

'Flankers out,' Sean ordered reluctantly. 'Ambush precautions.' It would slow them to half their previous speed. Now it would be impossible to catch up with Renamo before nightfall.

Three men were too few. It left only Matatu on the spoor, and Sean and Pumula on the flanks. They had a single weapon between them, the big-bore, slow-firing double. They were going in against trained bush fighters armed with automatic weapons, and they were expected.

'Just another name for suicide,' Sean told himself, but despite the odds he had to restrain himself from quickening the pace.

In the centre, Matatu whistled. At that moment, he was out of Sean's line of sight. Even though it was not a warning signal,

196

Sean fell flat and carefully checked his front and both flanks before he stood up again and went to join him.

Matatu was squatting beside the trail with his loin-cloth drawn up modestly between his legs, but his expression was worried. He stabbed a finger at the spoor without speaking, and Sean saw immediately what was troubling him.

'Where the hell did they come from?' It was a protest more than a question. The odds against them had just been multiplied many times, and for the first time, Sean felt the lead weight of despair on his shoulders.

The original band of Renamo had been reinforced by an even larger group; at a glance it looked like a full company of infantry.

'How many?' he demanded of Matatu, and this time, even he could not give an exact figure. The tracks were overlapped and confused.

Matatu took a little snuff, using the ritual to disguise his uncertainty. He sneezed, and his eyes ran with tears which he wiped away with his thumbs. Then he held up the spread fingers of both hands and shut them four times.

'Forty?'

Matatu grimaced apologetically and showed another set of fingers.

'Between forty and fifty.' Sean unscrewed his water-bottle and took a mouthful. The water was hot as soup, but he gargled with it before he swallowed.

'I will count them later,' Matatu promised, 'when I have learned them all, but now . . .' He spat on the trampled earth, mortified by his failure.

'How far behind are we?' Sean demanded, and Matatu used his forefinger like the hour hand of a clock to indicate a segment of the sky.

'Three hours,' Sean translated. 'We'll never catch them before nightfall.'

When it was dark Sean said, 'We'll eat while we wait for the moon.' But when it rose, it was only a sliver of silver, soon blotted out by cloud, and there was not enough light to follow even that broad clear spoor. Sean thought of keeping going blindly through the night, trying to get ahead of them and then shadowing them hoping for some fortuitous opportunity to reach Claudia and Job and release them.

'That's dreaming in Technicolor,' he told himself.

They had been going hard for days now and were all of them tottering on the edge of exhaustion. Blundering around in the dark, they would either run on top of the Renamo night guards or would miss them completely.

'We'll sleep now.' He was forced to give up at last. As Renamo knew they were being followed they might send a detachment back to try and surprise them.

Sean went into laager for the night well off the trail, in a thicket of thorn that would snag an attacker attempting to sneak up on them. They all desperately needed rest and he would rely on the thorn rather than posting sentries. The night was icy cold and they lay in a huddle sharing each other's body warmth. Sean was already sliding into the black hole of exhaustion when Matatu's whisper called him back.

'There is one of them,' Matatu began, then broke off and Sean opened his eyes with resignation.

'Tell me,' he invited drowsily.

'There is one of these Renamo I have seen before.'

'You know one of them?' Sean came fully awake.

'I think so, but it was long ago, and I cannot remember where.'

Sean was silent as he considered that simple statement, and what it really entailed. Sean would have had difficulty remembering the faces of every person he had met in, say, the last ten years. Here was Matatu bemoaning the fact that he could not instantly recognize a single set of footprints, which he had last seen years previously out of a jumble of other tracks.

Though he had seen Matatu perform similar feats so many times before, yet even he felt a creep of doubt at Matatu's claim.

'Go to sleep, you silly little bugger.' He smiled in the darkness, and took him by the scruff of the neck and shook the little man's woolly head with rough affection. 'Perhaps you'll dream his name in your sleep.'

Sean dreamed of Claudia. She was running naked through a dark forest. The trees were black and leafless with crooked limbs. A pack of wolves pursued her. They also were black as night but with glistening white fangs and red lolling tongues. Claudia called his name as she ran and her skin was pale and luminous as the moon. He tried to go to her but his legs dragged as though he waded through a pool of treacle. He tried to call her name, but his tongue was lead in his mouth and no sound came from his throat.

He awoke with a hand roughly shaking his shoulder, and he tried to shout again but it came out in a garbled slur.

'Wake up!' Matatu shook him. 'You were crying and moaning. Renamo will hear you!'

He sat up quickly. The cold seemed to have frozen the muscles in his legs, and the terror of the dream was still upon him. It took him seconds to focus on reality and remember where he was.

'You're getting past it, boyo.' He was humiliated. A Scout slept soundlessly and awoke to immediate awareness or had his throat cut while he was grunting and snoring.

'It will be light enough soon,' Matatu whispered. Already the dawn chorus of bird calls tinkled and chirruped through the forest and he could make out the lattice-work of thorn branches against the sky.

'Let's go.' Sean stood up.

While the sun was still low and the dew was on the grass, they came up to the dry riverbed in which Renamo had bivouacked for the night. The band had moved on again at first light but could not be far ahead.

Matatu picked Claudia's footprints out of the ruck in the soft sand of the riverbed. 'She moves with less pain,' he told Sean. 'The leg is healing but Job and Dedan are still carrying her. Here she climbed into the litter.'

Matatu left the distinctive feminine prints and hovered over another set of larger male tracks that to Sean were indistinguishable from all the others, except that whoever had made them wore boots with a double herring-bone pattern on the sole.

'I know him,' Matatu whispered. 'I know the way this one walks . . .' He shook his head in frustration and turned away.

They went forward with extreme caution now. The trail led them directly towards the higher ground along the escarpment of the valley, and soon they entered the foothills. Whoever commanded the Renamo column knew exactly where he was headed.

Sean was expecting at any moment to make contact with the rearguard of the column. He dreaded the thought that the first warning they might receive could be the wicked crackle of an RPD light machine-gun, firing at a cyclic rate of six hundred rounds a minute.

Here in the hills every boulder, every fold of ground was a

199

possible enemy redoubt and had to be minutely inspected before they could move on. Sean fretted with impatience but forced himself to gear his advance to the difficult terrain.

They turned the corner of another low hill and through a frieze of graceful msasa trees an open vista stretched ahead to where the massif of the central escarpment rose above its foothills.

'There it is,' Sean murmured. 'That's where they'll be laying for us.'

The spoor was pointed directly at a pass through the escarpment. The entrance was guarded by cliffs of red stone, and the gut of the pass was almost devoid of trees or cover and yet the sides were heavily bushed. It was a natural trap, a perfect killing ground.

Matatu whistled in the centre, and Sean doubled over, keeping off the crest as he ran down to join him. From the centre, there was an unimpeded view up the gut of the valley and Sean saw movement against the scree and yellow grass. He lifted the binoculars to his eyes and the line of dark moving specks resolved through the lens into a column of men.

They were toiling up the incline in single file. Most of them wore tiger-striped camouflage and jungle hats, although a few were dressed in a motley of denim and khaki. The front of the column was already into the bush at the head of the valley at least three miles distant, but through his binoculars, Sean counted twelve men.

The litter was in the centre, four of them were carrying it. Two men on the front poles and two on the back. Sean tried to pick out Claudia's form but before he could refocus his binoculars, the litter and the bearers had reached the tree line and disappeared.

Sean lowered his binoculars and polished the lens with his handkerchief. Pumula had come in from the other flank, and now he and Matatu crouched in the jumble of rock and coarse bush and studied the lie of the land in gloomy silence. Again Sean raised the glasses and studied the steep bushy sides. It was a perfect site for an ambush, they could catch Sean's party in enfilade and crossfire as they tried to climb the valley.

'How many did you see?' Sean asked without lowering his binoculars. 'Have they all gone into the trees at the head of the valley?'

'I saw only a few,' Pumula murmured.

'*Masesh*,' Matatu spat unhappily. He was referring to the lees

200

of the millet beer that after fermentation the Batonka fishermen use as a ground bait to lure the shoals of bream into Lake Kariba's shallows.

He spat again. 'That valley is the mouth of the crocodile. They want us to put our heads into it.'

Sean studied the sides of the valley, taking his time, every few minutes lowering the binoculars to rest his eyes and then lifting them again. He began at the top of the slope and swept gradually downwards. When he reached the bottom, he began at the top again, going over the same ground time and again. He tried not to think of that sighting of the litter, or the tiny figure he thought he had seen upon it. He concentrated entirely on his search and, ten minutes later, he was rewarded.

It was a single flash of sunlight reflected from the lens of a wristwatch or the lens of a pair of field-glasses.

'There they are.' He lowered his own glasses. 'Yes, Matatu, you are right. They have put out the bait, now they are waiting for us.'

He sat down behind the boulder and tried to think it through logically, but Claudia's memory kept intruding and deflecting his reasoning. There was only one certain conclusion, and that was that it was hopeless to continue the pursuit. He looked up. Matatu and Pumula were watching him with expressions of blind faith. In almost twenty years, they had never seen him at a loss. They waited patiently for him to perform the miracle yet again.

Sean found it infuriating. He jumped up and went back down the hill to think without those trusting eyes upon him. He found a spot that was well concealed and yet had a good all-round view so that nobody could sneak up on him and he settled down with the .577 across his lap to consider his options.

The first one he crossed from his mental list was an attack on the Renamo column. Even leaving aside the puny forces he had available, he had to consider the hostages that Renamo had in their hands. Even with a company of fully armed Scouts, he would still have been unable to attack.

'So what can I hope to achieve by following them?' he asked himself. 'Apart from gratifying this new and mawkish desire to be as close as possible to Claudia Monterro.'

Probably the best chance of release of the captives from Renamo clutches was not his own intervention but diplomatic negotiations through Renamo's reputed allies, the South African government in Pretoria. However, even the South Africans would not be able to achieve anything if they were unaware that an American citizen had been captured by Renamo.

'Okay.' Sean made his first firm decision. 'I have to get a message back to the American embassy in Harare.' Immediately he realized that this took care of his other major worry. Matatu and Pumula were his responsibility. Up to now he had been leading them into a suicidal situation. They had been more and more on his conscience the closer they drew to the Renamo column. This was the excuse he had been looking for.

'I'll send both of them back to Chiwewe with a message for Reema.' He opened the flap of his back-pack and found his small leather-covered notepad. He began to compose the message.

Reema had all Riccardo's and Claudia's personal details on the safari files, everything from their physical descriptions to their passport numbers. Riccardo was an important and influential man. Sean would not tell her that he was dead, but implied in his message that both father and daughter were captives of Renamo. The US embassy could be relied on to react swiftly and he would be in contact with Pretoria within hours of receiving the news.

Of course, since the imposition of US sanctions on that country the relations between Washington and Pretoria were at a historically low ebb, and the influence of the US in southern Africa was no longer the overriding factor that it had once been. Nonetheless, the South Africans could be relied on to intercede with Renamo on the simplest humanitarian grounds.

'Okay, that takes care of Matatu and Pumula.' Sean signed the message, tore the pages out of his notepad and folded them. Then as an afterthought he filled another page of instructions for Reema covering the $500,000 that Riccardo's estate owed them. She was to pass these on to Sean's lawyer.

Then, at last, he had to make his own decision. He could run back across the border, carrying the message himself, and within two or three days he could be drinking Castle lager in the Meikles Hotel and working out how to spend Capo's half-million bucks. That was the sensible and logical thing to do but he had already dismissed the idea before he considered it.

'So I'll follow the column and wait for an opportunity.' He grinned at the absurdity of his decision. 'What opportunity?' he wondered at himself. 'A chance to shoot my way into an encampment of fifty-plus terrs with the old .577, free the three prisoners, and with one mighty bound whip them a hundred miles to the border, carrying Claudia with her injured leg on my back!'

He stood up and resettled his pack between his shoulders, and crept back up to the slope where Matatu and Pumula were lying watching the escarpment. He dropped down beside Matatu.

'Anything?' he asked, and Matatu shook his head. They were silent for many minutes while Sean plucked up his courage to tell the little man he was sending him back.

While he did so, he scowled through the binoculars at the spot up the long valley where he knew Renamo had set their ambush. Matatu seemed to sense that something unpleasant was brewing. He kept glancing at Sean with a troubled expression, but when Sean finally turned to him, he burst into a sunny ingratiating grin and wriggled his entire body in his eagerness to please and to stave off whatever was coming.

'I remember,' he said eagerly. 'I remember who he is.'

Side-tracked for the moment, Sean frowned at him in puzzlement. 'Who? Who are you talking about?'

'The leader of the Renamo,' Matatu told him happily. 'I told you yesterday I knew his footprints. Now I remember who he is.'

'Who is he then?' Sean asked suspiciously, ready to reject the information.

'Do you remember when we jumped from the *indeki* to attack the training camp at the fork of the rivers?' Matatu twinkled at him and Sean nodded guardedly. 'Do you remember how we killed them in the riverbed?' Matatu chuckled with the delightful memory of it. 'Do you remember the one we caught while he was trying to burn the books. The one who refused to march, and you blew his ear in?' Now he giggled at that fine joke. 'The blood came out of his earhole and he squeaked like a virgin.'

'Comrade China?'

'China.' Matatu had a little difficulty with the pronunciation. 'Yes, that is the one.'

'No!' Sean shook his head. 'It isn't China. That's not possible!'

Now, Matatu had to cover his mouth to muffle his delighted squeals of laughter. He loved it when he was able to confound and astound his master. There was no better joke than that.

'China!' He spluttered with mirth and stuck his forefinger in his own ear. 'Pow!' he said, and it was so funny he almost choked. 'Comrade China.'

Sean stared at him unseeingly, while he adjusted his mind to this extraordinary intelligence. All his instincts were to reject it out of hand, but Matatu didn't make mistakes of that nature.

'Comrade China!' Sean breathed softly. 'That changes the odds a little.'

He cast his mind back to that distant day. The man had made such an impression upon him that even from the crowded and confused events of that bloody little war, he retrieved a clear image of Comrade China. He remembered his fine Nilotic head and the dark intelligent eyes, but his physical features were hazy compared to Sean's memory of the sense of confidence and purpose that the man exuded. He had been a dangerous man then, and Sean expected that now he would be even more experienced and formidable.

Sean shook his head. At one time his nickname in the Scouts had been 'Lucky Courtney'; it looked as though he had used up his ration of that commodity. He couldn't have chosen anybody he would have wanted less to command the column of Renamo than Comrade China.

Matatu had almost exhausted his mirth, and was now battling with the hiccoughs that followed, clutching at his naked belly and throat to hold them down, while occasional spasms of laughter interspersed the loud hiccoughs.

'I'm sending you back to Chiwewe.' Sean told him harshly, and the laughter and hiccoughs were instantly extinguished. Matatu stared at him in disbelief and utter despair. Sean could not face those eyes, and their tragic accusation.

He turned to Pumula and brusquely called him across to where he lay. 'This note is for the chef at camp. Tell him to radio the message to Miss Reema in Harare. Matatu will guide you back. Don't stop to pick your nose on the way, do you understand me?'

'*Mambo.*' Pumula was an old Scout. He would obey without argument or question.

'All right, go,' Sean ordered. 'Go now.' And Pumula held out his right hand. They shook hands the African way, gripping palms and then thumbs and then palms again. Pumula crawled down off the ridge, and once he was clear, jumped to his feet and trotted away. He did not look back.

At last Sean forced himself to look at Matatu. He crouched

204

low to the ground, trying to make his small frame smaller still to escape Sean's notice.

'Go!' Sean ordered brusquely. 'Show Pumula the way back to Chiwewe.'

Matatu hung his head and shivered like a whipped puppy.

'Get the hell out of here!' Sean growled at him. 'Before I kick your black butt!'

Matatu lifted his head and his eyes were tragic, his expression abject. Sean wanted to pick him up and hug him.

'Get out of here, you stupid little bugger!' Sean made a face of terrifying ferocity, and Matatu crept away a few paces and then paused and looked back imploringly.

'Go!' Sean lifted his right hand threateningly. At last the little man accepted the inevitable and slunk away down the slope. Just before he disappeared into the coarse scrub at the foot of the slope, he paused and looked back one more time, seeking just the faintest sign of encouragement or weakness. He was the epitome of dejection.

Deliberately, Sean turned his back on him and raised the binoculars to study the terrain ahead, but after a few seconds the image blurred and he blinked his eyes to clear them and despite himself, glanced quickly over his shoulder. Matatu had vanished. It was a strange feeling not to have him there. After a few minutes, Sean lifted the binoculars again and resumed his study of the escarpment line, pushing Matatu out of his mind.

On either side of the mouth of the long valley, the red rock cliffs stretched away unbroken for as far as Sean could see. They were not particularly high; at the lowest points they were only a few hundred feet, but they were vertical and some stretches were even overhanging where softer strata of rock had been eroded from under the harder superimposed upper layers, and formed a shallow horizontal cave.

The entrance of the valley was as inviting as the mouth of a carnivorous plant to an insect, and the cliffs were forbidding and inaccessible, but Sean concentrated upon them. He swept them with the binoculars, in both directions as far as he could see. Of course, it might be necessary to move some miles along the cliff to find a route that was scalable, but that would burn up precious time. He kept swinging the binoculars back to the same point.

A quarter of a mile to the right-hand side of the nearest rock portal of the valley, there was a route that looked as though it might just go, but it wouldn't be easy without a companion and lacking even basic rock-climbing equipment. He would be burdened by the rifle and his pack, and he would have to make the attempt in the dark. To go out on that exposed cliff in daylight would be to invite a little AK target practice.

Through the binocular lens, he picked out a rocky buttress which was faulted like a fire escape. It seemed to offer a way round the overhanging section of cliff, and above that it led to a narrow horizontal ledge running several hundred feet in either direction. From that ledge there appeared to be two possible routes to the top of the cliff, one was a narrow crack or chimney and the other an open face down which grew the exposed serpentine roots of a huge ficus tree that stood tall and massive on the skyline. The roots crawled and twined against the sheer red rock, like a nest of mating pythons, that formed a ladder to the top of the cliff.

Sean glanced at his wristwatch. He had three hours to rest before it was dark enough to make the attempt and suddenly, he felt exhausted. He realized that it was not only the physical exertion of the chase, but also the emotional drain of having glimpsed Claudia and Job in the Renamo column, and the parting with Matatu.

He anti-tracked meticulously back off the ridge and searched for a secure place to hole-up during what was left of daylight. When he found a hidy-hole amongst rock and scrub with a safe line of retreat, he loosened his bootlaces to rest his feet, but kept the rifle in his lap and slumped down over it. He munched a maize cake and protein bar from his emergency pack and drank a few careful mouthfuls from his water-bottle.

He knew he would wake when the sun touched the horizon. He closed his eyes and fell almost instantly asleep.

*   *   *

On the journey back to Chiwewe camp, Matatu led Pumula at a steady trot. They kept going through the night and the next afternoon stopped to refill their water-bottles in the marsh where they had spotted Tukutela from the air.

Pumula wanted to rest. Matatu did not bother to argue with him. He faced towards the west and went away at that swaying trot on his skinny knob-kneed legs and Pumula was forced to

206

follow. They crossed the border between Mozambique and Zimbabwe during the dark hours of the night, and ran into the safari camp in the middle of the following afternoon.

The consternation caused by their arrival was tremendous. In his agitation, the chef even forgot to don his tall cap and snowy apron before rushing out of his hut to greet them and demand the news of the *mambo*.

Matatu left Pumula to hand over Sean's written message and answer the barrage of questions. He went to his own hut and curled up like a puppy on his bed, an ancient iron frame with a lumpy coir mattress, a gift from Sean and his most treasured possession. He slept through all the subsequent excitement, even chef bellowing into the microphone of the VHF radio, attempting by volume alone to reach Reema in Harare almost three hundred miles distant.

When Matatu awoke, he had slept five hours. The camp was dark and silent. He repacked the small leather pouch that was his only luggage, retrieved his remaining store of precious snuff from under his mattress and refilled the horn that hung around his neck.

He crept quietly from the sleeping camp. When he was well clear, he straightened up and faced towards the east.

'Silly little bugger,' he said happily, and began to run, going back to his rightful place beside the man he loved more than a father.

*   *   *

Sean woke with the first chill of evening in the air. Ahead the cliffs of the escarpment were fading into the smoky purple dusk. Sean stretched and looked around for Matatu. When he remembered he was gone, it gave him a physical jolt in the pit of his stomach. He tied his bootlaces and drank again. When he stoppered the water-bottle, he held it to his ear and shook it. Still half full.

He opened the breech of the .577, slipped the cartridges out of the twin chambers and exchanged them for two others from the loops on his bush-jacket. He squeezed an inch of black camouflage cream from the crumpled tube and rubbed it over his face and the backs of his hands. That completed his preparation and he stood up and moved quietly up the slope.

He spent the last twenty minutes of daylight glassing the entrance to the valley and the top of the cliffs through his binoculars. As far as he could see, nothing had changed. Then he studied and memorized the route up the cliff face.

As the night spread its cloak over the escarpment, he slipped quietly over the ridge and crept up towards the base of the cliff. The bush grew dense and tangled there and it took him much longer than he had anticipated to reach the rocky wall.

It was almost completely dark by then, but he was able to identify the starting point of the climb by a small bush growing in a crack of the cliff which he had marked through the binoculars.

Sean had never used a carrying sling on his rifle. It could be mortally dangerous in thick bush when the sling caught on a branch just as the buffalo or wounded elephant began its charge. He lashed the short-barrelled weapon under the flap of his back-pack with his sleeping-bag. The butt stuck out on one side of his shoulders and the muzzles on the other, making an awkward unbalanced load. He went to the cliff face and laid his hands on it, getting the feel of it. The stone was still hot from the sun and the texture was smooth, almost soapy under his fingers.

Before the war, rock-climbing had been one of his passions. He loved the risk, the terror of the open face and drop sucking at his heels. He had climbed in South America and Europe, as well as on the Drakensberg and Mount Kenya. He had the requisite sense of balance and the strength in his fingers and arms. He could have been one of the top international climbers but for the intervention of the bush war. However, he had never attempted a climb like this before.

His boots were soft velskoen without reinforced toes. He had no ropes, no anchorman, no pitons nor karabiner, and he would be opening this route in darkness, barely able to see the next hold above, following a pitch which he had studied from a mile distant, going blind on red sandstone, the most treacherous of rock.

He stepped up on the face and began to climb. He used his toes, and his fingers, leaning back from the rock, keeping in fine balance, never stopping, never jerking or fighting the holds, smoothly as molten chocolate, flowing upwards.

At first the holds were solid, the kind he called 'jug handles', then the face leaned out slowly and the holds were mere flakes and indentations. He used them lightly and briefly, a touch of his fingers, a nudge of his toes and he was past, putting the minimum of weight on each but even then feeling the frailer flakes of stone grate and creak threateningly under his fingers – but he was gone before the hold could fail.

In places, he could not see above his head and he climbed by instinct, reaching up in the darkness, his fingertips as sensitive as those of a pianist as they brushed the rock and then locked into it. Without check or pause, he covered the first pitch and reached the ledge a hundred feet up from the base.

The ledge was narrower than it had appeared through the binoculars, no more than nine inches wide. With the pack strapped on his back and the rifle protruding on each side of his shoulders, it was impossible for him to turn his back to the rock and use the ledge as a bench to sit upon.

He was forced to stand facing the cliff, with his heels hanging over the edge, and the weight of pack and rifle pulling on his shoulders, trying to drag him backwards. He was less comfortable on the ledge than he had been on the face. He began to shuffle along it, spreading his arms like a crucifix to steady himself, his fingers groping for irregularities in the rock face, the sandstone an inch from the tip of his nose.

He went left along the ledge, seeking the vertical crack that he had spotted through the binoculars. It had been his first choice of the two possible routes. Sean had the rock-climber's instinctive distrust of roots and branches and tufts of grass. They were always unreliable, too treacherous to risk life upon.

He counted his shuffling crablike paces along the ledge, and by the time he reached a hundred the ledge under his toes had narrowed dangerously and the muscles in his thighs were burning and quivering from the unnatural strain of counter-balancing the rifle and pack.

Twenty paces more and the cliff face was beginning to bulge out towards him, forcing him further backwards and he had to thrust his hips forward to keep himself from toppling out over the sheer drop. It was only a hundred feet to the bottom, but it would crush and kill just as surely as a fall from the top of Eiger north face.

The strain on his legs was intolerable now. He thought of going back and trying the roots of the ficus but he doubted that he still had that choice. He wanted to stop, just to rest his legs a moment

209

and gather himself but he knew that would be the end of it. To stop on a pitch like this was defeat and certain death.

He made himself take another pace and then another, now he was forced backwards so his back was arched and his legs were numb to the ankles; he could feel them juddering under him, he knew they were going. Then suddenly the fingers of his left hand touched the crack, and it was as though a syringeful of adrenalin had been squirted into one of his arteries.

His legs steadied under him, and he managed another pace. His fingers danced over the crack, exploring it swiftly. It was not wide enough to get his shoulder into it, and it narrowed quickly.

Sean thrust his hand into it as deep as it would go and then bunched his fist, jamming it securely into the crack. Now he could hang back on his arm and rest his back and his aching legs. His breathing hissed and sawed in his chest and the sweat was streaming down his body, soaking his shirt. Sweat melted the camouflage cream from his face and burned his eyes, blurring his vision.

He blinked rapidly and lifted his head. He was surprised to see that the cliff face above him was visible against the night sky, and that he could make out the crack running vertically up its side.

He turned his head and saw that while he climbed the moon had cleared the horizon in the east and its beams turned the forest below to a frosty silver.

He could not wait any longer. He had to keep moving. He reached up with his free hand and thrust it into the rock crack above the other and made another jam-hold. Then he twisted his foot and pressed the toe into the crack three feet up from the ledge; he straightened his foot and it wedged securely. He put his weight on it and, with the other foot, stepped up and repeated the action. Hand over hand, foot over foot, he walked up the crack, hanging back from the rock face, once more in balance, the strain removed from his legs and back and his weight evenly distributed.

He could see the top of the cliff now, only a hundred feet above his head, and then he felt the crack begin to open wider; his fists and feet were no longer finding secure jams. One of his feet slipped under him, rasping harshly over the rock until it caught again.

He turned his body, trying to wedge his shoulder into the

crack, but the barrel of the rifle clanged against the face, blocking his turn. He hung there for a few seconds before he could force himself back into balance on his legs and then groped above his head searching the depth of the crack for another secure hold. He found only smooth sandstone, and he knew he was stuck.

He had about fifteen seconds before his legs gave in under him. He understood clearly what he had to do, but it went contrary to all his instincts.

'Do it,' his voice grated in his own ears. 'Do it, or die.'

He reached down and opened the quick release buckle on the waistband of his back-pack. Then he straightened one arm and reached backwards and downwards; the carrying strap slid off his shoulder and down his arm, catching in the crook of his elbow. The altered weight of the pack and the rifle slewed his whole body around and he had to fight to stay on the cliff face.

He thrust his head into the crack, trying to hook onto the rock with his chin and the back of his head, the strap of the back-pack locking his arm behind him. He gathered all his strength, braced his neck muscles, his head jammed in the crack and let go. Now he was held only by his head and feet, he straightened both arms behind him. For an aching moment, the strap caught on a fold of his bush jacket, and then it slipped down over his arm.

The pack dropped off his back and fell away into the darkness. Relieved of the weight, Sean tottered and swayed and then with both arms free, he grabbed wildly at the edges of the rock crack and managed to hold himself from plunging after his pack into the abyss.

He clung to the rock and listened to the pack striking the cliff as it fell, the steel of his rifle barrel ringing like a bronze bell off the rock, waking the echoes and sending them bounding from kopje to cliff, a terrifying sound in the night. Long after the pack and rifle had come to rest at the base of the cliff, the echoes still reverberated against the hills.

Sean swung himself sideways and was able at last to wedge his shoulder into the crack. He rested like that, panting wildly, the terror of death for the moment unnerving him. Then slowly his breathing eased and his terror was replaced by the familiar glow of adrenalin in his blood. Suddenly, it felt very good still to be alive.

'Right to the very edge,' he whispered hoarsely. 'You have been there again, boyo.' The greater the terror, the more intense

211

the thrill. He no longer amazed himself, but here he was again gloating at just how close he could get without going over the edge.

The thrill was too fleeting, within seconds it began to fade, to be replaced by realization of his position. His pack was gone. The rifle, his water-bottles, sleeping-bag, food, all gone. All that remained were the contents of his pockets, and the tiny emergency pack and hunting-knife looped to his belt.

He whispered, 'We'll worry about that when we get to the top.' And he began to climb again. With one shoulder wedged into the crack, he was able to push and drag himself upwards an inch at a time, paying for it with skin from his knuckles and bare knees.

Gradually the crack continued to open wider, until it became a full chimney, and he could get his whole body into it and double one leg under him to propel himself upwards more swiftly. At the top the chimney had eroded and crumbled. One side wall of the chimney had broken away, but it had left a narrow buttress with a flat top. Sean was able to transfer his weight across the chimney until he was standing on this precarious pinnacle.

The top of the cliff was still ten feet above his head. When he reached up to the full stretch of his arms standing on the tips of his toes the ledge was still just out of reach. The chimney wall had broken away clearly leaving a smooth almost polished surface, without even the minutest hold or purchase. A good safe climber moved from hold to hold, with never a single moment when he was totally insecure. In a situation such as this that hypothetical climber would have driven an iron piton into the rock to give him the hold he needed.

'Look Mummy, no pitons,' Sean said grimly. 'We'll have to jump for it.' He would only have one chance at it. If he missed his hold on the ledge once he had launched himself, then the next stop would be the base of the cliff.

He set both feet firmly and sank down at the knees, but he was so cramped on the tip of the buttress that he could not get low enough before his face touched the rock and his backside stuck far out over the drop.

He took a breath and used both arms and legs to propel himself straight upwards. It was an awkward hampered jump but he got high enough to hook both his hands over the edge. For a moment, they began to slide back and then his fingers gripped and held.

212

He kicked both legs and drew himself upwards by the main strength of his arms. His chin came level with the ledge, and in the moonlight he saw in front of him a false crest, simply another ledge below the true top of the cliff.

The ledge was obviously occupied by a colony of rock hyrax. The stink of their droppings, sharp and ammoniacal, filled Sean's lungs as he gasped from the effort of holding himself. The hyrax is a plump fluffy animal. Although it is only the size of a rabbit, it is a remote relative of the elephant, and as endearing in appearance as an infant's soft toy. These hyrax were deep in their rocky burrows now and the ledge seemed deserted. Sean hoisted himself up smoothly and hooked one elbow over the edge; he kicked again, gathering himself for the final effort and then froze.

The silence of the night was cut by a loud high-pitched hiss, like the leaking valve of a truck tyre. In the moonlight what he had taken for a pile of rock lying directly in front of his face, altered shape, seeming to melt and flow.

In an instant, Sean realized that it was a snake. Only one of the adders would hiss as loudly, and only one adder was that large.

It was coiled upon itself, loop after loop of its thick scaly body glistening softly, and as it cocked its neck into the menacing 'S' shape, its eye caught the light of the moon and winked at him sardonically. The huge flat head was the distinctive spade shape of the gaboon adder, the largest of all the adders and one of the deadliest of all Africa's venomous snakes.

Sean could drop back and try to regain his stance on the narrow pinnacle of rock, but that was a slim chance and if he missed it, he would plunge down the cliff face. A much better chance would be to try and brave it out.

He hung with legs free, trying to control his breathing, staring in horror at the loathsome creature. It was cocked to strike, less than two feet from his face, and he knew it could lunge out almost its full body length, seven feet or more. The slightest movement would trigger it.

He hung on his arms, every muscle of his body rigid, staring at the adder, trying to dominate it by the force of his will. The seconds drew out slowly as spilled molasses, and he thought he detected the first relaxation in the taut 'S' of its neck.

At that moment, his left hand slipped, his fingernails rasped on the rock and the adder struck with the force of a blacksmith's hammer.

Sean rolled his head to the side, like a boxer avoiding a punch. The adder's cold scaly nose jarred against his jawbone and there was a fierce tug against his neck and shoulder, so powerful that it jerked one hand loose from its hold on the rock, and spun him half around. He was sideways to the ledge, holding on with only his left arm.

He knew that the adder had hooked its fangs into his shoulder or the side of his throat and he expected the exquisite fire of its venom to kindle in his flesh. The serpent was locked onto him, dangling down the front of his body, thick as a salami sausage; it squirmed and thrashed, hissing explosively in his ear. The cold loathsome touch of its slippery scales brushed against his bare flesh.

Sean almost screamed with the sheer horror of it. The adder's weight threw him about as it lashed from side to side, and its loud hisses deafened him. He felt his single-handed grip on the ledge slipping, but the prospect of the drop below him was suddenly insignificant when compared to this foul creature fastened to his neck.

He felt an icy spray of liquid on the side of his throat and his jaw; it dribbled down the opening of his bush jacket, and with a rush of relief he knew that the adder had missed his throat and had fastened into the collar of his jacket. Its fangs were fully two inches long and viciously recurved, designed to penetrate and hang on to its prey. Hooked into the khaki cotton material of his collar, its violent struggles were forcing the venom out of the hollow bony needles, squirting onto his throat and bare skin.

The realization that the fangs had not penetrated his flesh rallied him, firmed his grip on the ledge and arrested his slow slide into the drop. His right hand was still free. He reached up and seized the adder's neck just at the back of its flat diamond-shaped head. His fingers could barely span the massive body, and he felt the enormous power of its muscles beneath the glassy scales.

He tried to pull it free, but the fangs were like fish hooks in the heavy cloth, and the serpent hissed more viciously and its grotesque body, patterned like a patchwork quilt, coiled around his forearm. He used all his strength, holding onto the ledge with his left arm, heaving at the adder with his right, and he tore the fangs from the roof of its gaping mouth so that its dark blood mingled with the copious flow of its venom, and he flung the twisting coiling body far out over the drop. Then he swung back and grabbed with his right hand at the rock of the ledge.

He was sobbing softly with horror and exertion, and it was fully half a minute before he could gather himself sufficiently to pull himself up and crawl onto the ledge.

He knelt on the rock floor and shrugged out of his bush jacket. The front of it was wet with venom, and one of the adder's fangs was broken off and still buried in the cloth of the collar. He worked it loose and, careful to avoid the needle point, flicked it out over the cliff. Then with his handkerchief he wiped his skin dry.

He considered the danger of wearing the jacket again. The venom might be absorbed through the pores of the sensitive skin under his jaw, it could cause ulcers or worse, but to discard the jacket would expose his body to tomorrow's tropical sun. He hesitated and rolled the jacket and fastened it onto his belt. He would wash it out at the first opportunity.

The thought of water made him aware of his thirst. The climb had dehydrated him, and his water-bottle was with his pack at the bottom of the cliff. He had to find water before tomorrow's noon, but now his first concern must be to get off the exposed face of the cliff and into cover.

He stood up, and felt the night breeze cold on the sweat of his bare upper body. From the ledge on which he stood, it was an easy pitch to the crest, more a scramble than a climb. However, he took it carefully and when he reached the top he lay for a few minutes with just his head peering over the crest.

A haze of light cloud had veiled the moon and Sean could see very little. The bush that grew so densely up the sides of the valley had spread across the tops of the cliff and formed a dark wall just ahead. There were probably forty yards of rocky ground, open except for coarse knee-high grass, and then he would be into the cover of the bush.

He rose to his feet, and ran forward crouching as low as possible as he crossed the skyline, and he was halfway to the edge of the bush when the light hit him.

It stopped him dead as though he had run into the rock cliff, and he flung up his hands instinctively to protect his eyes for his vision had been shattered and starred by the brilliance of the light beamed full into his face. Then he flung himself face forward into the grass and flattened his body against the stony earth.

The beam of light threw long black shadows behind each boulder and cast a bright reflective glow from the pale winter grass. Sean dared not raise his head. He pressed his face to the earth, exposed and vulnerable and helpless in that fierce white beam.

He waited for something to happen but the silence was unbroken. Even the usual night sounds of nocturnal birds and insects were quenched, so that the voice when at last it boomed out of the trees, magnified and distorted by an electronic bullhorn, was as shocking as a blow in the face.

'Good evening, Colonel Courtney.' It was spoken in good English, barely touched by an African accent. 'You made excellent time. Twenty-seven minutes fifteen seconds from the base of the cliff to the top.'

Sean did not move, but he lay and absorbed the bitter humiliation of it. They had been toying with him.

'But I cannot give you high marks for stealth. What was it you threw down the rock? It sounded like a bunch of old tin pots.' The speaker chuckled sardonically and then went on, 'And now, Colonel, if you are sufficiently rested, would you be gracious enough to stand up and raise both hands above your head?'

Sean did not move.

'I beg of you, sir. Don't waste your time and mine.'

Sean lay still, considering wildly the possibility of dashing back over the crest behind him.

'Very well, I see you have to be convinced.' There was a brief pause and Sean heard a soft order given in dialect.

The burst of automatic fire tore into the earth three paces from where he lay. He saw the fiery blur of the muzzle flashes amongst the dark trees and heard the distinctive rush of the RPD light machine-gun, like a strip of heavy-duty canvas being ripped through. The stream of bullets scythed the grass and raised a mist of yellow dust in the bright light.

Sean came slowly to his feet. The beam of light fastened on his face but he refused to turn his head away or shield his eyes.

'Hands at full stretch above the head please, Colonel.'

He obeyed. His naked upper body was very white in the light.

'I am delighted to see you have kept yourself in good shape, Colonel.'

216

Two dark figures detached themselves from the tree line. Keeping well clear of the light beam, they circled out on either side of him and came up in Sean's rear. From the corner of his eyes, Sean saw they wore tiger-striped battle dress and that their AK rifles were aimed at him. He ignored them until suddenly the steel butt plate of one of the rifles crashed into his spine between the shoulder-blades and he fell to his knees.

The voice on the bull-horn gave a sharp order in dialect to prevent them striking him again and they closed on either side of him and forced him to his feet. One of them searched him swiftly, stripping him of knife, belt and emergency pack and patting his pockets. Then they backed off, leaving him naked except for his khaki shorts and velskoen, but they kept their AKs aimed at his belly.

The light bobbed as the man carrying it advanced out of the wall of bush. Sean saw that it was one of those portable battle lights powered by a heavy rechargeable battery pack that the man carried on his back. Slightly behind him, keeping back in the shadow, came the man with the bull-horn.

Even through the dazzling beam of the battle light Sean saw that he was tall and lean, and that he moved with a cat-like grace.

'It's been a long time, Colonel Courtney.' He was close enough not to have to use the bull-horn and Sean recognized his voice.

'Many years,' Sean agreed.

'You'll have to speak up.' The man stopped a few paces in front of Sean and jokingly cupped one hand to the side of his head. 'I am deaf in one ear, you know,' he said, and Sean grinned sardonically at him through his black camouflage cream.

'I should have done a better job, and blown your other ear out while I was about it, Comrade China.'

'Yes,' China agreed. 'We really must discuss old times together.' He smiled and he was even more handsome than Sean remembered, relaxed and charming and debonair. 'However, I'm afraid you have delayed me a little, Colonel. Pleasant though it is to renew acquaintance, I cannot afford more time away from my headquarters. There will be an opportunity to talk later, but now I must leave you. My men will take good care of you.'

He turned and disappeared into the darkness beyond the beam of light. Sean wanted to call after him, 'My men, the girl, are they safe?' but he restrained himself. With a man like this, it was best to show no weakness, to give him nothing he could use to his advantage later. Sean forced himself to remain silent when the guards urged him forward with practised use of their gun butts.

'We'll join the main column soon,' Sean comforted himself. 'And I'll see for myself how Claudia and Job are doing.'

The thought of Claudia was a refreshing draught that he craved even more than sweet cool water.

*   *   *

There were ten men in his guard detail under the command of a sergeant.

Obviously they were picked troops, powerful and lean as the pack of wolves of his nightmare. Soon they intercepted a well-beaten footpath and they closed up around him and urged him to a jog-trot, heading southwards into the night.

None of his captors spoke. It was an eerie experience, just the sound of their light footfalls and quick shallow breathing, the creak of equipment and the hot feral smell of their bodies close around him in the night.

After an hour, the sergeant signalled a pause, and they stopped beside the track. Sean reached across to the nearest guerrilla and tapped the water-bottle on his belt.

The man spoke to the sergeant. The first words since they had started and Sean understood him. He was speaking Shangane. The Shanganes were the remnants of one of the tiny Zulu tribes that had been defeated by King Chaka's impis at the battle of Mhlatuze River in 1818. Unlike so many of the other lesser chieftains, Soshangane had resisted incorporation into Chaka's empire and fled northwards with his shattered impis to found his own kingdom along the borders of present day Zimbabwe and Mozambique.

So the Shangane language was Zulu-based, and over the years many of Sean's camp staff had been Shangane for, like their Zulu ancestors, they were a fine and noble people. Sean spoke their language fluently for it contained many similarities to Sindebele.

He did not, however, make the mistake of letting his captors know this and gave no indication of having understood as the trooper said, 'The *mabunu* wants to drink.'

'Give it to him,' the sergeant replied. 'You know the *inkosi* wants him alive.'

218

The man handed Sean the bottle and though the water was brackish and was tainted by swamp mud, to Sean it tasted like chilled Veuve Clicquot served in a crystal glass.

'The *inkosi* wants him alive,' the sergeant had said. Sean pondered that as he handed the bottle back. The *inkosi*, or chief, was obviously Comrade China, and they had orders to care for him. That gave him a little comfort, but he did not have long to savour it. After only a few minutes, the sergeant gave the order and they resumed that mile-eating jog-trot towards the south.

They ran up the dawn and at any moment Sean expected them to overhaul the main column which was holding Claudia and Job captive, but mile succeeded mile without any sign of them. Now that it was light, Sean could look for the tracks of the column on the footpath ahead but there were none. They must have taken a different route.

The sergeant in charge was a veteran. He had flankers out sweeping the verges of the footpath ahead for an ambush by Frelimo, but what seemed to concern him more than attack from the forest was the menace from the sky. At all times they attempted to keep under the canopy of the forest, and whenever they were forced to cross open ground, they stopped and searched the sky, listened for the sound of engines, before venturing out, and then they crossed to the next line of trees at a full run.

Once during the first morning they heard the sound of a turbo-aircraft engine, faint and very far off, but instantly the sergeant gave an order and they all dived into cover. A trooper lay on each side of Sean and forced him to keep his head down and his face to the ground until the last murmur of the aircraft engine faded.

This preoccupation with aerial attack puzzled Sean; all he had heard and read indicated that Frelimo's air force was so weak and scattered as to be almost non-existent. The types of aircraft they possessed were obsolete and unsuited to ground attack, and a shortage of skilled technicians and spares only compounded their ineffectuality. These men, however, were taking the threat very seriously indeed.

At midday the sergeant ordered a halt. One of the troopers prepared food on a small fire, which he doused as soon as it was cooked. They moved on a few miles before stopping once more to eat the meal. Sean was given an equal share. The maize meal was cooked stiff and fluffy and was well salted, but the meat was rancid and on the point of putrefying. In the average white man it would have caused an immediate attack of enteritis, but Sean's stomach was as conditioned as any African's. He ate it without relish, but without trepidation either.

'The food is good,' the sergeant told Sean in Shangane as he sat beside him. 'Do you want more?' Sean made a pantomine of incomprehension and said in English, 'I'm sorry I don't know what you are saying.' The sergeant shrugged and went on eating. A few minutes later he turned back to Sean and said sharply, 'Look behind you, there's a snake!' Sean resisted the natural impulse to jump to his feet and instead grinned ingratiatingly and repeated, 'I'm sorry I don't understand.'

The sergeant relaxed and one of his men remarked, 'He does not understand Shangane. It is all right to speak in front of him.'

They ignored him for the remainder of the meal and chatted amongst themselves, but as soon as they had finished, the sergeant produced a pair of light manacles from his pack and locked one side on to Sean's wrist and the other onto his own. He delegated sentry duty to two of his men and the rest of them settled down to sleep.

Despite Sean's exhaustion, he had been going for days now on only brief snatches of sleep, he lay awake and pondered all he had learned, and the missing pieces of the puzzle. He was still not certain that he was in Renamo hands, he had only Claudia's brief note to suggest that. On the other hand, Comrade China had been a commissar in Robert Mugabe's Marxist ZANLA army, but Renamo was a rabidly anti-communist organization committed to the overthrow of the Marxist Frelimo government. That didn't add up correctly.

Furthermore, China had fought the Rhodesian army of Ian Smith. What was he doing here across the border, involved in another struggle in a foreign country? Was China a soldier of fortune, a turncoat, or an independent warlord taking advantage of the Mozambiquan chaos for his own private ends? It would be interesting to find out.

With all this to think about, still his last thought before sleep finally overcame him, was of Claudia Monterro. If China wanted him alive, then it was highly probable that he wanted the girl alive as well. With that thought, he fell into a deep, dark sleep with a faint smile on his lips.

He woke to the ache of abused muscles and the bruises left by

220

gun butts, but the sergeant had him up and running immediately southwards again into the cool shades of evening. Within a mile, his muscles warmed and the stiffness evaporated. He settled into the run, matching his escorts easily. Always he looked ahead, hoping at any moment to see the tail of the main column emerge from the darkness ahead, and to see Job and Dedan carrying Claudia's litter.

They ran through the night and when they stopped again to eat, his captors began to discuss him through their mouthfuls of maize and high-smelling meat.

'They say that in the other war, he was a lion, an eater of men,' the sergeant told them. 'It was he that led the attack at Inhlozane, the training camp at the Hills of the Maiden's Breasts.'

The troopers looked at him with interest and dawning respect.

'They say that it was veritably he, in person, who destroyed one ear of General China.'

They chuckled and shook their heads, that was a fine joke.

'He has the body of a warrior,' said one of them, and they considered him frankly, discussing his physique as though he were an inanimate object.

'Why has General China ordered this?' another asked, and the sergeant grinned and picked a shred of meat from his back teeth with a fingernail.

'We must run the pride and the anger out of him,' he grinned. 'General China wants us to change him from a lion into a dog who will wag his tail and do his bidding.'

'He has the body of a warrior,' the first man repeated. 'Now we must discover if he has the heart of a warrior.' And they all laughed again.

'So it's a contest, then.' Sean kept his face impassive. 'All right, you bastards, let's see which dog wags its tail first.'

In a perverse fashion, Sean began to enjoy himself. The challenge was much to his taste. There were ten of them, all in their twenties. He was just over forty years of age, but that handicap made it even sweeter and helped him to endure the monotony and hardship of the days that followed.

He was careful not to let them know that he understood that this was a contest. He knew it was dangerous to antagonize or humiliate them. Their goodwill and respect would be more valuable than their hatred and resentment.

Sean had spent his entire adult life in the close company of black men. He knew them as servants and as equals, as hunters and soldiers, as good and loyal friends and as bitter cruel enemies. He knew their strengths and weaknesses and how to exploit them. He understood their tribal customs, their social etiquette, he knew how to flatter and please and impress them, how to gain their respect and make himself agreeable to them.

He showed them just the right degree of respect, but not enough to make them contemptuous. He took especial care not to challenge the sergeant's authority or force him to lose face in front of his men. He made the most of their sense of humour and of fun. With sign language and a little clowning he made them laugh, and once they had laughed with him their whole relationship altered subtly. He became more a companion than a captive and they no longer used the steel-edged gun butts as instruments of casual persuasion. Most importantly, he was every day picking up little snippets of information.

Twice they passed burned-out villages. The cultivated lands around them had gone back to weeds, the black ashes blowing in the wind.

Sean pointed at the ruins. 'Renamo?' he asked, and his captors were outraged.

'No! No!' the sergeant told him. 'Frelimo! Frelimo!' And then he tapped his own chest.

'Me Renamo,' he boasted, and pointed at his men. 'Renamo! Renamo!'

'Renamo!' they agreed proudly.

'Well, that settles that,' Sean laughed.

'Frelimo. Bang! Bang!' He made the gesture of shooting a Frelimo and they were delighted, joining in the pantomime of slaughter enthusiastically. Their attitude towards him improved even further and at their next meal the sergeant handed him an extra-large cut of rotten meat. While he ate it, openly they discussed his performance to date, agreeing that he was acquitting himself admirably.

'But,' the sergeant asked, 'he can run and we know he can kill men, but can he kill a *henshaw*?'

Henshaw was the Shangane word for a falcon, and Sean had heard them use it many times over the last five days of their trek, and each time as they said the word, they looked up at the sky with a troubled expression. Now, once again at the mention of that bird, they looked unhappy and as a reflex glanced upwards.

222

'General China thinks so,' the sergeant went on. 'But who knows, who knows?'

By now, Sean was confident that his position was fairly secure, his relationship with the band would allow him to take the first liberty, and force a resolution of this trial by attrition.

On the next stage, he began to force the pace. Instead of keeping his station in the file of trotting men two paces behind the Shangane sergeant who led the column, he closed up until he was running on his heels, not quite touching him with each stride, and exaggerating his breathing so that the sergeant could feel it on the back of his thick sweaty back. Instinctively the sergeant lengthened his own stride and Sean matched him, keeping close, too close and pushing him.

The sergeant glanced over his shoulder irritably and Sean grinned at him, breathing into his face. The sergeant's eyes narrowed slightly as he realized what was happening, then he grinned back at Sean and extended his stride into a full run.

'That's it, my friend,' Sean said in English. 'Now let's see whose tail wags.'

The rest of the column had fallen behind. The sergeant called a sharp order to them to close up, and they went away at a killing pace. Within an hour, there were only three of them left, the others were straggled back over a mile of the forest floor and ahead of them the path climbed a steep incline to the crest of another tableland.

Sean moved up slightly until he was running shoulder to shoulder with the tall sergeant, but when he tried to pull ahead the man kept with him. The hillside was so steep that the path went up it in a series of hairpins, and the sergeant forged ahead of Sean at the first bend, but Sean caught him and passed him on the straight.

They ran at the top of their speed now, the lead changing back and forth between them and the third man dropped out before they were halfway up the hillside. They ran grimly, in a wash of sweat, their breathing harsh as the exhaust of a steam engine.

Suddenly Sean darted off the path, scrambling straight upwards, cutting across the bend and coming out fifty feet ahead of the Shangane. The sergeant shouted angrily at this ruse and cut the next bend himself. Now both of them abandoned the pathway and ran straight at the steep slope, jumping over boulders and roots, like a pair of blue kudu bulls in flight.

Sean came out on the crest three feet in front of the sergeant, and threw himself down on the hard earth and rolled onto his back moaning for breath. The sergeant dropped beside him with his breath sobbing in his chest. After a minute, Sean sat up uncertainly and they stared at each other in awe.

Then Sean began to laugh, it was a harsh painful cackle, but after a few seconds the Shangane laughed with him, though clearly each gust of laughter was an agony. Their laughter grew stronger as their lungs regained function, and when the rest of the party struggled to the crest of the hill, they found them still sitting in the grass beside the track, roaring at each other like a pair of lunatics.

When the march resumed an hour later, the sergeant left the endless footpath and struck off across country towards the west and there was at last direction and purpose in the way he led the column.

Sean realized that the trial was over.

*　　*　　*

Before dark they ran into a Renamo line of permanent defences.

They were entrenched along the bank of a wide but sluggish river that flowed green between sand bars and round water-polished boulders. The dugouts and trenches were revetted with logs and sandbags and meticulously camouflaged against aerial discovery. There were mortars and heavy machine-guns dug in, with commanding fields of fire across the river and sweeping the northern bank.

Sean had the impression that these fortifications were extensive and he guessed that this was the perimeter of a large military area, certainly battalion and possibly even division strength. Once they had crossed the river and been passed through the defences, Sean's appearance in the ranks of his escort created a stir of interest. Off-duty troopers turned out of their dugouts and crowded around them and his captors were clearly enjoying the elevated status that a white prisoner bestowed upon them.

The crowd of interested and jocular onlookers abruptly thinned and parted as a tubby bespectacled officer strode through them. His escort saluted him with theatrical flourishes which he returned by touching the rim of his maroon beret with the tip of his swaggerstick.

'Colonel Courtney,' he greeted Sean in passable English. 'We have been warned to expect you.'

For Sean, it was refreshing to notice that Renamo wore conventional badges of rank, based on the Portuguese army conventions. This man had red field officer flashes and the single crowns of a major on his epaulettes. During the bush war the terrs had eschewed the capitalist imperialist traditions, and dispensed with the symbols of an elitist officer class.

'You will spend the night with us,' the major told him. 'And I look forward to having you as our guest in mess tonight.'

This was extraordinary treatment, and even Sean's captors were impressed and in a strange way rather proud of him. The sergeant himself escorted Sean down to the river and even produced a fragment of green soap for him to wash out his bush jacket and shorts.

While they dried on a sun-heated rock, Sean wallowed naked in the pool and then used the last of the soap to wash his hair and rid his face of camouflage cream and ingrained dirt. He had not shaved since he had left Chiwewe camp almost two weeks previously and his beard felt thick and substantial.

He worked up a lather of suds in his armpits and crotch and looked down at his own body. There was not a vestige of fat on him, each individual muscle was outlined clearly beneath the sun-darkened skin. He had not been in this extreme condition since the closing days of the war. He was like a thoroughbred racehorse brought up to its peak by a skilful trainer on the eve of a major race.

The sergeant lent him a steel comb and he brushed his hair out. It fell almost to his shoulders, thick and wavy and sparkling from the wash. He put on his damp clothes and let them dry on his body. He felt good, that charged restless feeling of being at the very pinnacle of physical fitness.

The officers' mess was an underground dugout devoid of ornament or decoration. The furniture was crude and hand-hewn. His hosts were the major, a captain and two young subalterns.

The food made up for its lack of artistic presentation by its abundance. A huge steaming bowl of stew made with sun-dried fish and chillis, the fiery *peri-peri* that was a relic of the Portuguese colonialists, and great mounds of the ubiquitous maize-meal porridge.

It was the best meal Sean had eaten since leaving Chiwewe,

but the highlight of the evening was the drink that the major provided, unlimited quantities of real civilized beer in metal cans. The labels read 'Castle Lager' and in small print at the bottom, 'Verwaardig in Suid Afrika, Made in South Africa'. It was an indication as to which country was Renamo's good friend.

As the guest in mess, Sean proposed the first toast. He stood and raised his beer can.

'Renamo,' he said. 'And the people of Mozambique.'

The major replied, 'President Botha, and the people of South Africa,' which settled it conclusively. They knew Sean was from the south and was, therefore, an honoured guest.

He felt so secure in their company that he could relax and for the first time in months allow himself to get moderately drunk.

The major had fought for the Rhodesians during the bush war. He told Sean that like Job Bhekani he had been a subaltern in the Rhodesian African Rifles, the elite black regiment which had fought so effectively and inflicted such slaughter amongst the ZANLA guerrillas. They soon established the camaraderie of old brothers-in-arms. Without obviously pumping him, Sean was able to nudge the conversation along and pick up the crumbs of information that the major let fall more freely as the cans of beer were consumed.

Sean's estimation had been correct. This was part of the northern perimeter of a Renamo army group. The fortifications were deep and dispersed as a precaution against aerial bombardment. From this base, they marauded southwards, hitting the Frelimo garrisons and strafing and raiding the railway line between Beira on the coast and Harare, the capital of Zimbabwe.

While they were still working on the first case of beer, Sean and the major discussed with seriousness the significance of that rail link. Zimbabwe was a completely land-locked nation. Its only arteries to the outside world were the two railway lines. The major one was southwards, into South Africa, via Johannesburg to the major ports of Durban and Cape Town.

Mugabe's Marxist government bitterly resented being reliant on the nation which, for them, epitomized all that was evil in Africa, the bastion of capitalism and the free-market system, the nation which had for the eleven long years of the bush war propped up the white regime of Ian Smith. Mugabe's hysterical rhetoric against his southern neighbour was incessant and yet the foul hand of apartheid was curled around his jugular vein. His instinct was to look eastward into Mozambique for salvation. During his struggle for independence Mugabe had been nobly assisted by the Frelimo President of Mozambique, Samora Machel, whose own struggle against the Portuguese had only just culminated in freedom from the colonial yoke.

Frelimo, his brother Marxists, had provided Mugabe with recruits and arms and full support for his guerrillas. Without reservation, they had offered him the use of bases within their territory from which to launch his attacks on Rhodesia. It was only natural now that he turned once more to Mozambique to provide an escape from this awful humiliation of being seen by the rest of Africa, by his brothers in the Organization of African Unity, to be dealing with the monster of the south, not only dealing with, but totally dependent upon it for every litre of gasoline, for every ounce of the daily stuff of survival.

The railway line to the port of Beira on the Mozambique channel was the natural solution to his predicament. Of course, the port facilities and the main-line system under the African socialist management had been allowed to fall into almost total disrepair. The solution to that was simple and well-tried: massive aid from the developed nations of the West. As every good African Marxist knew, they were fully entitled to this, and any attempt to withhold it could be countered by the equally simple and well-tried expedient of dubbing it blatant racism. That dread accusation would force immediate compliance. The estimate of the costs of work needed to restore the port and main line to full efficiency was four billion American dollars. However, as actual costs in Africa usually exceeded estimates by a hundred per cent, the sum of eight billion dollars was more realistic. A mere bagatelle, nothing more than their due, a fair price for the West to pay for the pleasure and prestige that Mugabe would derive from being able to thumb his nose at the monster of the south.

There was only one small obstacle in his way, the army of Renamo. It sat astride that vital rail link, attacking it almost daily, blowing up bridges and culverts, ripping out the tracks and shooting up rolling stock.

The actual damage they caused was minor compared to the fact that their depredations gave the Western governments a fine excuse for withholding the funds needed to restore the main line to the condition in which it would be able to carry all of Zimbabwe's imports and exports.

The Frelimo government's efforts to protect the line were so fumbling and inept that the Zimbabweans themselves were forced to assist them. Over ten thousand of Mugabe's own troops were tied up in trying to fend off Renamo attacks on the line. Sean had heard estimates of the cost of these operations to Zimbabwe's economy, already one of the shakiest in sub-Saharan Africa, as high as a million dollars a day.

It was ironic that Mugabe, once the guerrilla, was now forced into the role of passive defender of fixed hardware and permanent positions. He was experiencing the stings of the flea, that he had once so merrily dispensed.

Sean and the Renamo major laughed at the joke, and began on the second case of good apartheid lager. This marked the passing of the time for serious conversation.

Now they reminisced happily about the days of the bush war and they soon discovered that they had both been at the same contact in the Mavuradonhas on the day when they had killed forty-six guerrillas, 'a good kill', as a successful action was always referred to. Sean's Scouts had lain in wait in the gulleys and re-entrances to the hills, acting in the role of stop group, while the RAR had dropped by parachute on the far side and formed the sweep line to drive the terrorists onto the Scouts.

'You drove out as many bush-buck as gooks,' Sean remembered. 'I didn't know which to shoot first.' And they laughed and talked of other dangerous sorties, of crazy ops and of wild chases and 'good kills'.

They drank to Ian Smith, the Ballantyne Scouts and the Rhodesian African Rifles. There was still plenty of beer remaining so they drank to Ronald Reagan and Margaret Thatcher. When they ran out of conservative leaders to toast, Sean suggested, 'Damnation to Gorbachev!'

This was enthusiastically adopted, and the major countered immediately with, 'Damnation to Frelimo and Chissano.' The list of left-wingers was longer than that of conservatives, but they worked their way steadily down it, damning them all from Neil Kinnock to Teddy Kennedy and Jesse Jackson.

When they finally parted, Sean and the major embraced like brothers. Sean had filled all his pockets with cans of beer, so that when he returned to his Shangane guards they too greeted him affectionately as he distributed the cans amongst them.

In the morning, the Shangane sergeant shook him awake while

228

it was still dark. Sean's headache was terrifying and his mouth tasted as though a hyena had slept in it. It was one of the penances of being superbly physically fit. The body's reaction to the abuse of alcohol was proportionately violent, the hangovers more fierce, and he had not a single aspirin for solace.

However, by the middle of the morning Sean had sweated out the last drops of stale beer. Their route was still south and west, and as they ran they saw many more fortifications and strong points. As the major had told him, they were cunningly dispersed and hidden. He saw light field artillery in sandbagged emplacements, together with mortars in their redoubts, and detachments armed with RPG rockets, the mobile hand-held stalwarts of the guerrilla arsenal. All the troops he saw seemed to be cheerful and of high morale, well-fed and equipped. Nearly all of them wore the tiger-striped camouflage and combat boots with rubber soles and canvas uppers.

His escort had replenished their packs from the garrison stores. When they stopped to eat, the maize meal was in two-kilo paper sacks marked 'Premier Mills', and the matches with which they lit the fire were 'Lion Matches' and the new bars of soap 'Sunlight', all with the familiar double legend beneath the name, 'Verwaardig in Suid Afrika, Made in South Africa'.

'It's almost like being home again,' Sean chuckled.

*   *   *

The Renamo defensive lines were in concentric rings like the ripples on a pond, and soon Sean realized they were approaching the centre. They passed what were obviously training areas, where fresh-faced black recruits, both male and female, some of them in their early teens, sat in rows under thatched sun shelters like schoolchildren in a classroom studying the makeshift blackboard so attentively that they barely glanced up as Sean's detachment trotted by.

From the blackboards, Sean saw that the subjects they were being taught ranged from the infantry field manual to political theory.

Beyond the rear training areas they entered what appeared to be a series of low sparsely-manned kopjes. It was only when they were within a few metres of the side of one of these hills, that Sean spotted the entrances to the dugouts.

They were more elaborately constructed and cunningly concealed than the others that they had been passing all day. These would be invisible from the air and impervious to aerial bombardment, and Sean could tell, by the changed deportment of his guards and their more severe posture towards him, that they had reached the headquarters area of the Renamo army group.

Still, he was taken by surprise when without ceremony they turned aside and drew up at the entrance to one of the underground bunkers. There was a brief exchange while the Shangane sergeant handed Sean over to the guards at the entrance, before Sean was hustled down the steps into the subterranean maze of corridors and caverns hacked out of the earth. The bunker was lit by bare electric bulbs and somewhere far-off, he heard the hum of a generator. The side walls were revetted with sandbags that had been dressed neatly and the roof was reinforced with hewn logs.

They entered a communications room. Sean saw at a glance that the radio equipment was sophisticated and well maintained. A large-scale map of the whole northern and central Mozambique provinces of Zambezia and Manica covered one wall.

Sean studied the map surreptitiously. He saw at once that the broken mountainous ground in which this Renamo army group was ensconced was the Serra da Gorongosa, the mountains of Gorongosa, and that the river they had crossed which formed the Renamo defensive line was the Pungwe river. The main railway line ran only thirty or forty miles further south of this position, but before he could glean more information from the map, he was hurried down another short passageway at the end of which there was a curtained-off doorway.

His escort called a respectful request to enter and the reply was sharp and authoritative. One of them prodded Sean and he pushed the curtain aside and stepped into the room beyond.

'Comrade China,' Sean smiled. 'What a pleasant surprise.'

'That form of address is no longer appropriate, Colonel Courtney. In future, please address me as General China, or simply as "Sir".'

He sat at a desk in the centre of the dugout. He was dressed in the ubiquitous tiger-striped battledress, but it was adorned with silver paratrooper wings and four rows of gaudy ribbons across his left breast. A yellow silk scarf was knotted at his throat and his maroon beret and webbing belt hung on a peg behind him. The butt of the automatic pistol in the webbing holster was ivory-handled. General China was obviously taking his conversion from Marxism to capitalism very seriously.

'I understand that you have acquitted yourself well during the last few days and that you are sympathetic towards Renamo, its allies and its objectives.' His attitude towards Sean was benign, and it made him uneasy.

'How do you know that?' he demanded.

'We do have radio, you know, Colonel. We aren't total barbarians.' China indicated the VHF set on the bench along the side wall of the dugout. 'You passed a pleasant evening with Major Takawira, at my suggestion.'

'Now would you like to tell me what the hell this is all about, General. You have abducted the citizens of two friendly and powerful nations, South Africa and America.'

General China held up his hands to stop him. 'Please spare me your outrage, Colonel. Our people in Lisbon and elsewhere have already received complaints from both the Americans and the South Africans. Of course, we have denied abducting anybody, and adopted an attitude of injured innocence.' He paused and studied Sean for a moment. 'Very enterprising of you to have got a message to the American embassy so soon, but then I wouldn't have expected anything less of you.'

Before Sean could reply, he lifted the hand-set of the field telephone on his desk and spoke quietly in a language that Sean recognized as Portuguese but could not understand. He hung up and glanced expectantly towards the screen doorway, and instinctively Sean did the same.

The canvas curtain was drawn aside and three persons ducked through the dugout. There were two uniformed black women carrying sidearms and AK rifles and between them, escorted closely, dressed in sun-bleached but freshly laundered khaki shirt and loose-fitting shorts, the same clothes she had worn when last he saw her, was Claudia Monterro.

She was thin. That was the first thing that struck Sean. Her hair was drawn back and tied in a plait at the back of her head, and she was tanned to the colour of melba toast.

Her eyes were huge in her thin face and he had never before truly noticed the fine structure of her cheek and jaw bones. At the sight of her his heart seemed to stop and swell against his ribs, and then race away again.

'Claudia!' he said, and her head jerked towards him. The blood drained from her face, leaving a *café-au-lait* colour beneath her tan.

'Oh my God,' she whispered. 'I was so afraid . . .' she broke off, and they stared at each other, neither of them moving for a dozen beats of his heart, then she said his name. 'Sean.' And it sounded like a sob. She swayed towards him and lifted her hands, palms upward in a gesture of supplication, and her eyes were filled with all the suffering and hardship and longing of these last days. With two long strides, he reached her and she threw herself against him and closed her eyes and pressed her face against him. She had both arms locked around his chest, the strength of her grip hampered his breathing.

'Darling,' he whispered, and stroked her hair; it felt thick and springing under his fingers. 'My darling, it's all right now.'

She lifted her face to him and her lips quivered and parted. Blood had flowed back under the smooth brown skin. She seemed to glow and the light in her eyes had changed to the sparkle of dark yellow topaz.

'You called me darling,' she whispered.

He lowered his head over her and kissed her. Her lips opened under his and the inside of her mouth was hot and lubricious. He probed it deeply with his tongue and it tasted like the sap of sweet young grass.

From the desk, General China said quietly in Shangane, 'Very well, now take the woman away.'

Her guards seized Claudia and plucked her out of his embrace. She gave a small despairing wail and tried to resist, but they were powerful heavily built women, and between them they lifted her feet off the ground and hustled her back through the screen doorway.

Sean shouted, 'Leave her,' and started after them, but one of the guards drew the pistol from her webbing holster and pointed it at his belly. The canvas screen dropped between them and Claudia's cries of protest dwindled as she was dragged away. In the silence, Sean turned slowly back to the man at the desk.

'You bastard,' he whispered furiously. 'You set that up.'

'It went better than I could possibly have hoped for,' General China agreed, 'although some previous conversation that I had with Miss Monterro concerning you gave me the idea that she

232

was more interested in you as a man than as a professional hunter.'

'I'd like to twist your head off your shoulders. If you hurt her . . .'

'Come, come, Colonel Courtney. I'm not going to hurt her. She is far too valuable. She is a bargaining chip, surely you realize that.'

Slowly Sean's fury abated and he nodded stiffly.

'Okay, China, what do you want?'

'Good.' General China nodded. 'I was waiting for you to ask that question. Sit down.' He indicated one of the stools facing his desk. 'I'll order a pot of tea and we can talk.'

While they waited for the tea, General China busied himself with the papers on his desk, reading and signing a batch of orders. It gave Sean a chance to recover himself. When an orderly brought the tea, General China gestured for him to clear the papers from the desk.

When they were alone again, China sipped at his mug and regarded Sean over the rim. 'You ask what it is that I want. Well, I must confess that at first, it was nothing more complicated than simple retribution. After all, Colonel, it was you that destroyed my command that day at the camp at Inhlozane. You put the only blemish on my professional career, and you inflicted permanent physical damage on my person.' He touched his ear. 'Reason enough for me to want revenge. I'm sure you will agree.'

Sean remained silent. Although he had not tasted tea in days and craved it, he had not touched the mug which stood on the edge of the desk in front of him.

'Of course, I knew that you were operating the Chiwewe hunting concession. In fact, as a junior minister of Mugabe's government, I was one of those who gave approval to the grant. I thought, even then, that it might be useful to have you so close to the border.'

Sean forced himself to relax. He realized that he might learn more, achieve more by a show of co-operation rather than defiance. It was difficult to do, for he could still taste Claudia's mouth. He picked up the tea mug and took a mouthful.

'You certainly get around,' he smiled. 'Comrade one day, general the next. Marxist government minister one day, Renamo warlord the next.'

China waved a hand deprecatingly. 'The dialectics of Marxism

233

'never truly interested me. Looking back now, I realize that I enlisted in the guerrilla army for the very good capitalistic reason. At the time it was the best way to get on in life – does that make any sense to you, Colonel?'

'Perfect sense,' Sean agreed. This time his smile was genuine. 'It's a well-known fact that the only way communism can be made to work is if you have capitalists to pay the bill and manage the show.'

'You phrased that very well.' China nodded his appreciation. 'I only found that out later, once ZANLA had ousted Smith and taken over the government in Harare. I discovered that as a former guerrilla I was feared and mistrusted by the soft fat cats who had avoided the actual fighting but now had taken control of the show. I saw that far from receiving my just rewards, I was more likely to end up in Chikarubi prison so I allowed my capitalistic instinct to guide me. With a few other like-minded citizens, we were arranging another change of government, and we were able to convince some of my old comrades-in-arms, who occupied senior positions in the Zimbabwe army, that I would make a suitable replacement for Robert Mugabe.'

'The good old African game of coup and counter-coup,' Sean suggested.

'It is refreshing to talk to someone who follows the reasoning so readily,' China nodded approval. 'But then you are an African, albeit of the less fashionable hue.'

'I'm flattered to be recognized as one,' Sean told him. 'But to return to your altruistic desire to put the best man in charge . . .'

'Ah, yes . . . well, somebody boasted to a woman, and she told her other lover who just happened to be Mugabe's Chief of Intelligence, and I was forced to cross the border in some haste, and here I fell in with yet others of my former comrades who now had joined Renamo.'

'But why Renamo?' Sean asked.

'It is my natural political home. I am good at what I do and Renamo welcomed me. You see, I am part Shangane. As you know our tribe sprawls over both sides of the artificial line imposed by surveyors of the colonial era, who took no consideration of demographic realities when they agreed on borders.'

'If you are now a capitalist, General China, as you claim to be, then there must be more in it than that. Some future reward in store for you?'

'You do not disappoint me,' China said. 'You are as perceptive and devious as any African. Naturally, there is something in it for me. When I have assisted Renamo to form the new government of Mozambique with South Africa as its ally, between them they will be able to apply irresistible pressure on Zimbabwe. They will be able to force a change of government in Harare . . . a new president to replace Mugabe.'

'From General China to President China in one mighty bound,' Sean cut in. 'I'll give you one thing, General, you don't think small.'

'I'm touched by your appreciation of my aspirations.'

'But where does all this leave me? You talked earlier of revenge for your impaired hearing – what made you so forgiving?'

China frowned and touched his ear. 'To tell the truth I would have enjoyed that. In fact, I had already planned a nocturnal raid on your camp at Chiwewe. I had moved up a unit of my men to the border opposite your concession, and was awaiting only an opportunity to escape from my duties here for a few days personally to pay you a visit, when a change of plan was forced upon me.'

Sean raised an eyebrow to signal his interest and attention.

'Very recently there has been a drastic alteration in the balance of power here in the central province. We of Renamo had fought ourselves into a dominant position. In fact, we control all the country except the major towns, we have reduced food production to the point where Frelimo must rely almost entirely on foreign aid, we have virtually strangled their transport system. We raid the roads and railways at will, and our forces move freely about the countryside recruiting from the villages. We have, in fact, set up our own alternative administration. However, all that changed very recently.'

'What happened?'

China did not answer immediately, but stood up from the desk and went to stand in front of the wall map. 'As a distinguished counter-guerrilla fighter, Colonel Courtney, I do not have to explain our strategy to you nor do I have to lecture you on the weapons that we employ in the "war of the flea". We don't fear nuclear bombs, heavy artillery or modern pursuit planes. We chuckled when Robert Mugabe purchased two squadrons of fighters from his Soviet friends, obsolete MIG 23. Floggers that the Russians were pleased to be rid of and which Mugabe cannot afford to keep in the air. There are few, very few modern weapons that we fear except . . .' China paused and turned to face Sean again, 'but you are the expert, Colonel. You know as much as any man alive about anti-guerrilla operations. What do we fear most?'

Sean did not hesitate. 'Helicopter gunships,' he said.

China sat down heavily in his seat again. 'Three weeks ago the Soviets delivered a full squadron of Hind helicopters to the Frelimo air force.'

Sean whistled softly. 'Hinds!' he said. 'In Afghanistan they call them the Flying Death.'

'Here we call them *henshaw* – the falcons.'

'There is no air force in Africa that could keep a squadron of Hinds in the air for more than a few days, they simply don't have the back-up.' Sean shook his head, but China contradicted him quietly.

'The Russians have supplied technicians and munitions and spares, as well as pilots. They aim to smash Renamo in six months.'

'Will they succeed? Can they succeed?'

'Yes,' China said firmly. 'Already they have severely limited our mobility. Without mobility, a guerrilla army is defeated.' He made a gesture that took in the dugout. 'Here we cower underground like moles, not warriors. Our morale, which was so high just a month ago is crumbling away. Instead of looking proudly ahead, my men cringe and look to the skies.'

'It's not an easy life, General,' Sean commiserated with him. 'I'm sure you'll come up with something.'

'I already have,' China nodded. 'You.'

'Me against a squadron of Hinds?' Sean chuckled. 'I am flattered, but include me out.'

'That is not possible, Colonel. As the Americans say, you owe me one.' He touched his ear. 'And I owe you one, Miss Monterro.'

'All right,' Sean nodded with resignation. 'Spell it out for me.'

'The plan that I have in mind requires a white face and a trained officer who understands black troops and speaks their language.'

'Surely, General China, you don't subscribe to old General von Lettow-Vorbeck's theory that the best bush troops in the

236

world are black soldiers with white officers. Why the hell don't you do whatever this is yourself?'

'I know my own limitations,' China said. 'I am a better administrator than a soldier. Besides, I have explained, I need a white face.' He held up one hand to prevent Sean interrupting again. 'Initially you'll be working with a small group. Ten men.'

'My Shangane escort,' Sean got ahead of him. 'That's the real reason you sent me off on that little jaunt with them.'

'Perceptive, Colonel. Yes, your reputation seems to be well founded. In just a few days you have gained their respect and, dare I say it, loyalty. I think that they'll follow you on the most hazardous assignment.'

'I'll need more than ten Shanganes, there are two others I want with me.'

'Of course, your Matabeles,' China agreed readily. 'They are definitely part of my calculations.'

This was the opportunity to enquire about Job and Dedan for which Sean had been waiting.

'Are they both safe?' he demanded.

'Quite safe and well, I assure you.'

'I won't even discuss anything further until I have seen them and spoken to them,' he said flatly, and China's eyes narrowed.

'I beg you not to adopt that attitude, Colonel. It will only make our future relationship difficult and unpleasant.'

'I mean it,' Sean repeated stubbornly. 'I want to speak to my men.'

General China glanced at his wristwatch and then sighed theatrically.

'Very well.' He lifted the hand-set of the telephone and spoke into it again, then looked up at Sean. 'The two of them will be required to work with you, you can explain that to them. There is an excellent chance that, with all your co-operation, I will be persuaded to give you your freedom. Of course that offer of freedom includes the nubile Miss Monterro.'

'You are very generous,' Sean was ironic.

'Wait until you hear my full terms. You might think I drive a hard bargain.' General China turned to the lieutenant who came through the doorway in response to his summons and said in Shangane, 'Take this man to visit the two Matabele prisoners,' he ordered. 'You may allow them to talk for –' again he glanced at his wristwatch – 'ten minutes. Then bring him back here.'

There were three men in the escort that marched Sean down the underground passages and out into the dazzling sunshine.

The prison barracks consisted of a single hut of mud daub and thatch surrounded by a stockade of poles and barbed wire, the whole covered by a spread of camouflage net. A warder unlocked the gate to the stockade and Sean went in. He walked to the door of the hut.

Over an open fireplace in the centre of the floor stood a black three-legged pot. Two thin mattresses of split reeds on each side of it were the only other furnishings. Dedan was asleep on the one mattress, while on the other Job sat cross-legged and stared into the smouldering coals.

'I see you, old friend,' Sean said softly in Sindebele, and Job came slowly to his feet, and just as slowly began to smile.

'I see you also,' he said, and then they laughed and embraced, clapping each other on the back. Dedan jumped up from the other mattress, grinning with delight, and seized Sean's hand, pumping it brutally.

'What took you so long, Sean?' Job asked. 'Did you find Tukutela? Where is the American? How did they catch you?'

'I'll tell you all that later,' Sean cut him off, 'there are more important things now. Have you spoken to China, did you recognize him as the one we caught at Inhlozane?'

'Yes, the one with the ear. What are our chances with him, Sean?'

'Too early to be sure,' Sean warned. 'But he is talking about some sort of deal.'

'What?' Job broke off, and they both spun to face the door of the hut.

Outside there was the abrupt shrilling of alarm whistles and wild shouts.

'What's going on?' Sean demanded, and strode to the doorway. The gate to the stockade was still wide open, but the guards were scattering, unslinging their weapons and peering up at the sky. The lieutenant was blowing shrill hysterical blasts on his whistle as he ran.

'Air raid,' said Job at Sean's shoulder. 'Frelimo gunships, there was one two days ago.'

Sean heard the engines now, very faint and distant, and the whistling whine of the rotors, growing swiftly shriller and more penetrating.

'Job!' Sean grabbed his arm. 'Do you know where they are holding Claudia?'

'Over there.' Job pointed through the doorway. 'A stockade like this one.'

'How far?'

'Five hundred metres.'

'The gates are open, and the guards are gone. We are going to make a bolt for it.'

'We are in the middle of an army, and what about the gunships?' Job protested. 'Where can we go?'

'Don't argue, let's go.'

Sean raced through the doorway and out of the stockade gates. Job and Dedan were close behind him.

'Which way?' Sean grunted.

'Over there, beyond that clump of trees.'

The three of them ran in a bunch. The camp was almost deserted as Renamo took to their dugouts and bunkers, but Sean saw that there were crews manning the light anti-aircraft guns in the fixed emplacements, and they passed a small detachment armed with the portable RPG rocket-launchers heading for the nearest kopje. Elevation would give them a good field of fire from which to launch. However, the RPG was not an infra-red seeker and had very limited surface-to-air capability.

The Renamo were so preoccupied that not one of them even glanced at Sean's white face as they scurried to take up their positions. Now the whistle of approaching rotors was punctuated by the crackle and rap of ground fire.

Sean did not even look round. Ahead, he saw the glint of barbed wire. The women's stockade was also well camouflaged under brush and netting, and it too seemed deserted by the female wardens.

'Claudia!' he shouted, as he came up to the fence and gripped the wire. 'Where are you?'

'Here, Sean, here!' she yelled back. There were two huts inside the stockade wire. The doors were locked and there were no windows. Claudia's voice came from the nearest building, and was almost drowned out by the thunder of engines, the shriek of rotors, and the roar of ground fire.

'Give me a boost,' Sean ordered, and backed away from the wire. The fence was seven feet high, he judged. Job and Dedan ran forward and crouched below it. Sean sprinted straight at

239

them and as he leapt up, he drove his feet into the cupped hands they had formed for him with interlocking fingers. In unison, they bobbed up and flung their arms high, flipping Sean forward and over. He cleared the wire easily, somersaulted in the air and landed on his feet. He cushioned the shock, tumbling like a paratrooper, and rolled smoothly back onto his feet, using his momentum to hurl himself forward.

'Clear the door!' he yelled at Claudia, as he built up speed and crashed into the crude hand-hewn panel.

It was too solid and heavy to shatter under the drive of his shoulder, but the hinges ripped clean out of the daubed wall, and crashed inwards in a cloud of dust and flying fragments of dried mud.

Claudia was crouched against the far wall, but as he burst into the hut behind the falling door panel, she rushed forward to meet him. He caught her in his arms, but when she tried to kiss him, he whirled her round by one arm, and ran with her to the door.

'What's happening?' she gasped.

'We are making a break.' As they ran out into the sunlight again he saw that Job and Dedan had a hold on the bottom strand of the fence. With all the strength of their arms and legs, they were dragging it upwards, opening a narrow gap between the wire and the sun-baked earth. Sean stooped to the same strand from the inside, settling his grip between the clusters of spikes and he heaved upwards. Under the combined strength of the three of them the ground at the foot of the nearest fence pole cracked and gave, the pole was lifted a few inches out of the hole in which it was planted, and the strand of wire came up in their hands.

'Down on your belly!' Sean grunted at Claudia. 'Get under it!'

She was lean and nimble as a ferret, and the barbs cleared her back with inches to spare as she wriggled through.

'Hold it!' Sean barked at Job, and they strained up, black muscles knotting, faces contorted with the effort.

Sean dropped flat and pushed himself under the wire. Halfway through he felt one of the steel spikes snag in his flesh and stop him dead.

'Pull me through,' he ordered, and while Dedan continued to hold up the wire, Job stooped and they linked hands in a fireman's grip.

'Pull!' Sean ordered, and Job heaved. Sean felt his flesh tear and the blood spurt down his back, then he was free.

As he rolled to his feet Claudia gasped, 'Your back!' But he seized her arm again and demanded of Job, 'Which way?' He knew that Job would have studied the camp during the days he had been imprisoned here. He could rely on his judgement.

'The river,' Job responded immediately. 'If we can float down, clear of the camp.'

'Lead the way,' Sean ordered, and he had to shout to make himself heard. All around them rose the stutter of automatic small arms fire. The deeper clatter of heavy machine-guns, sounding like a stick drawn sharply across a sheet of corrugated iron, and then even that din was drowned out by a thunder like the Victoria Falls in flood. Sean knew exactly what it was, although he had never heard it before. The sound of the Gatling-type, multi-barrelled cannon mounted in the nose of a Hind helicopter, firing 12.7mm bullets like the jet of a fire hose.

He felt Claudia falter beside him at the gut-melting terror of that sound, and he jerked her arm.

'Come on!' he snarled at her. 'Run!' She was still limping slightly from her injured knee ligament, as they followed Job and Dedan down towards the river. Though they were still under the spread branches of the forest, just ahead of them was open ground.

A small party of Renamo were doubling across this opening, coming up the track towards them, eight or nine men in Indian file and each of them carried an RPG mobile rocket-launcher. As they ran, their faces were turned up towards the sky, seeking a target for their rockets.

The detachment of rocketeers was still two hundred metres from them when suddenly the earth around them erupted. Sean had never in all his war experience seen anything like it. The ground dissolved, seemed to turn to a liquid that boiled into a fog of dust under the jet of 12.7mm cannon shells.

Along a wide swathe of cannon fire all was destroyed, even the trees disappeared in a whirlwind of wood fragments and shredded leaves; only the shattered stumps still stood as the storm of fire passed on. The ground was left like the furrows of a freshly ploughed field and on it was scattered the remains of the party of RPG rocket men. They were hacked and minced as

241

though they had been fed through the cogs of some fearsome machinery.

Sean still had a grip on Claudia's arm and he pulled her down into the grass beside the track just as a shadow swept over them. However, the canopy of branches overhead must have screened them from the eyes of the gunner in the helicopter. Job and Dedan had also dived for cover in the grass verge beside the path and avoided detection.

The Hind cruised overhead, barely fifty feet above the tops of the trees, and abruptly they had a full view of the machine as it crossed over the open ground where the torn corpses of the rocket men lay scattered.

Sean felt a physical shock at the sight of it. He had not expected it to be so large and so grotesquely ugly. It was fifty feet long.

The Russians themselves called it 'Sturmovich', the humpback. It was a deformed monster: aberrant and ungainly, the green and brown splotches of tropical camouflage gave it the appearance of disease and leprous decay. The bulging double canopies of armoured glass looked like malevolent eyes and so fierce was their gaze that Sean instinctively flattened himself in the grass and flung a protective arm over Claudia's back.

Below the gross body of the gunship hung an assembly of rocket pods, and as they stared at it in awe the machine hovered and rotated on its own axis, lowered its blunt unlovely nose and fired a spread of rockets.

They launched with fiery sibilance on plumes of white smoke, streaking across the river and bursting on the ant's nests of sandbagged bunkers in fountains of flame and smoke and dust.

The noise was deafening and the shrill whine of the gunship's rotors was like an awl screwing into their eardrums. Claudia covered both her ears and sobbed.

'Oh God! Oh God!'

The Hind revolved slowly, seeking fresh targets, and again they cowered away from it. It moved away from them, hunting along the bank of the river. The Gatling-cannon in its remotely controlled turret in the nose fired blasts of solid metal into the forest, destroying all in its path.

'Let's go!' Sean shouted above the uproar and dragged Claudia to her feet. Job and Dedan ran ahead of them, and the earth ploughed by the gunship's cannons was soft and spongy under their feet.

As they passed the dead men, Job stooped without breaking his run and snatched up one of the undamaged RPG launchers. At the next stride he stooped again and grabbed a fibreglass back-pack that contained three of the finned projectiles for the RPG, and then went bounding away, on towards the riverbank. With her injured knee, Claudia could not match that pace, and even with Sean pulling her along they fell almost a hundred yards behind.

Job and Dedan reached the riverbank. It was steep and rocky, fractured cliffs of water-polished black stone. A gallery of tall riverine trees spread their branches out over the swiftly flowing apple-green waters.

Job looked back at them anxiously, for they were still out in the open. His face contorted as he screamed a warning and dropped the fibreglass pack at his feet and swung the short squat barrel of the RPG up to his shoulder, pointing it at the sky above Sean's head.

Sean did not look up, he knew there was no time for that. He had not isolated the shrieking rotors of the second incoming Hind from the deafening uproar caused by the first machine, but now the din was escalating to the point of pain.

Running beside them was a narrow donga, eroded by the storm waters of the rainy season, but now dry and sheer-sided. Sean swept Claudia off her feet and jumped with her in his arms. The earthen gulley was six feet deep and they hit the bottom with an impact that clashed Sean's teeth together in his jaws just as the lip of the gulley dissolved under a jet of cannon fire.

The earth on which they lay shuddered like a live thing beneath them, as though they were insects being shaken from the flanks of a gigantic horse. Earth, ripped from the lip of the gulley by the sheets of cannon fire, fell on them in clouds, heavy clods raining on their backs, knocking the breath out of them, dust choking them, burying them alive.

Claudia screamed and tried to fight herself out from under the layer of dust and dry earth, but Sean held her down.

'Lie still,' he hissed at her. 'Don't move, you dilly bird.' The Hind swivelled and cruised back, now directly over the gulley, searching for them, the gunner traversing the thick stack of multi-barrels of the Gatling-cannon in its remote turret.

Sean turned his head slightly, looking up from the corner of one eye. His vision was obscured by dust, but as it cleared, he saw the great splotched nose of the Hind hanging in the air only fifty feet directly overhead. The gunner must have picked out their white skins, which made them targets of preference. Only the thin layer of fresh earth protected them from his scrutiny through the gunsight of his cannon.

'Hit him, Job,' Sean pleaded aloud. 'Hit the bastard.'

On the cliff above the river, Job dropped on one knee. The RPG 7 was one of his favourite weapons. The huge gunship was hovering over the gulley only fifty yards away.

He aimed twelve inches below the edge of the pilot's canopy. The RPG was highly inaccurate, and even at point-blank range he gave himself latitude should the missile fly off track. He held the cross-wire steady for a beat of his pumping heart and then pressed the trigger. The exhaust of white smoke blew back over his shoulder and the rocket streaked away, flying fair and true, to strike only inches higher than he had aimed on the rim where the armoured glass canopy joined the camouflaged metal fuselage.

The rocket burst with the force which would blow the engine block out of a Mac truck, or burst the boiler of a railway locomotive. For an instant, the front of the Hind was obliterated by flame and smoke, and Job whooped triumphantly, jumping to his feet, expecting the hideous monster to crash out of the sky in a sheet of its own smoke and fire.

Instead the huge helicopter jumped higher, as though the pilot had flinched at the rocket-burst close beside him, but when the smoke blew away, Job realized with disbelief that the fuselage was unscathed. There was only a sooty black smear on the painted metal to mark the spot where the rocket had struck.

As he stared the ugly nose of the Hind swivelled towards him, and the many-eyed muzzles of the cannon sought him out. Job hurled the RPG launcher away, and jumped out from the cliff top, dropping twenty feet to hit the water, just as the cannon tore the great branches from the tree under which he had stood. Cannon fire chewed through the trunk as cleanly as a lumberjack's cross-saw and the whole tree leaned outwards and then toppled down the cliff and hit the surface of the river in a cloud of spray.

The Hind pulled away, lifting and banking, cruising on down the riverbank. Unharmed by the rocket hit and as deadly as before, it sought its next target.

Sean crawled to his knees, coughing and gasping.

'Are you all right?' he croaked, but for a moment Claudia could not answer him. Her eyes were blinded with sand, and her tears cut wet runnels through the dust that caked her cheeks.

'We've got to get into the water.' Sean pulled her to her feet, and half-pushed half-pulled her up the side of the gully.

They ran together to the top of the cliff and looked down. The felled tree was floating away on the current, a huge raft of leafy branches.

'Jump!' Sean ordered, and Claudia did not hesitate. She threw herself far out, and dropped away to strike the water feet first. Sean followed while she was still in the air.

He surfaced with Claudia's head bobbing beside him. The dust was washed off her face, and her hair was slicked over her eyes, shiny with streaming water.

Together they struck out for the floating mass of branches and leaves. She was a strong swimmer, and even with boots on her feet and fully dressed, she kicked out powerfully and dragged herself through the water with a full over-arm crawl.

As she reached the floating tree trunk, Job stretched out a long arm and drew her in beneath the branches. Dedan was already there and Sean ducked in a second later. They each clung to a branch and the leaves formed a low green bower over their heads.

'I hit him,' Job complained angrily. 'I hit him right on the nose with a rocket. It was like hitting a bull buffalo with a slingshot. He just turned and came straight at me.'

Sean wiped the water from his eyes and face with the palm of his hand. 'Titanium armour plate,' he explained quietly. 'They are almost invulnerable to conventional fire, both pilot's cockpit and the engine compartment are tight and solid. The only thing you can do when one of those bastards comes at you is run and hide.'

He flicked his sodden hair back out of his eyes. 'Anyway, you pulled him off us. He was just about to blast us with that dirty great cannon.' Sean swam across to Claudia.

'You shouted at me,' she accused. 'You were quite rude. You called me a dilly bird.'

'Better abused than dead,' he grinned at her, and she smiled back.

'Is that an invitation, sir? I wouldn't mind a little abuse – from you.' Under water, he slipped an arm around her waist and hugged her.

'My God, how I have missed your cheek and sauce.'

She pressed herself against him. 'I only realized after you were gone . . .' she whispered.

'Me too,' he confessed. 'Up to then, I thought I couldn't stand you. Then I realized I just couldn't do without you.'

'I feel weak when you say that, tell me you really mean it.'

'Later,' he hugged her. 'First let's just try and get out of here alive.' He left her and paddled across to Job's side of the leafy cavern.

'Can you see the bank?'

Job nodded. 'Looks like the raid is over. They are coming out of the bunkers.'

Sean peered out from under the concealing branches. He saw troops moving cautiously about on the near bank.

'They'll be picking up the pieces for a while before they realize that we've scarpered, but keep an eye on them.'

He paddled across to Dedan who was watching the far bank.

'What do you see?'

'They are busy with themselves.' Dedan pointed. A stretcher party was working along the bank, picking up the dead and the wounded, while work details had already begun repairing the damaged fortifications and replacing destroyed camouflage. Nobody looked out across the river.

There was other debris floating downstream with them, severed branches and damaged equipment, empty oil drums, enough to draw attention away from their flimsy refuge.

'If we can avoid discovery until nightfall, we should have floated down beyond the army. Just keep both eyes wide open, Dedan.'

'*Mambo*,' he acknowledged, and concentrated his attention on the bank.

Sean swam quietly back to Claudia and hung on to the branch beside her. She reached out for him immediately.

'I don't like you to be away for even a moment,' she whispered. 'Did you really mean what you said?'

He kissed her and she kissed him back so fiercely that her teeth bruised his lower lip. He enjoyed the mild pain.

She broke the embrace at last and immediately demanded again, 'Did you mean it?'

'I can't do without you,' he answered.

'You can do better than that.'

246

'You are the most magnificent woman I've ever known.'

'That's not bad, but it's still not what I want to hear.'

'I love you,' he admitted.

'That's it, oh Sean, that's it. And I love you too.' She kissed him again, and they were oblivious to all else, their mouths blending and their bodies clinging wetly together below the surface.

Sean did not know how long it was until Job disturbed them. 'We are going ashore,' he called.

The push of the current had forced the floating tree to the outside of the next river bend and it was already dragging on the submerged sand bar. When Sean lowered his feet, he touched bottom.

'Walk it into deeper water,' Sean ordered, and still concealed beneath its leafy bulk, they heaved and pushed it out until they felt it come free of the sand bar and the current picked it up again and drifted it into the next stretch of the river.

Sean was panting from the effort as he hung on to a branch above his head, only his head above the surface. Claudia paddled across to him and hung on to the same branch.

'Sean,' she said, and her mood had changed. 'I haven't been able to ask you, mostly because I don't want to hear the answer.' She broke off and drew a deep breath. 'My father?' she asked.

Sean was silent as he sought the words to tell her, but it was Claudia who spoke again.

'He didn't come back with you, did he?'

Sean shook his head and his sodden locks dangled into his face.

'Did he find his elephant?' she asked softly.

'Yes,' Sean answered simply.

'I'm glad,' she said. 'I wanted that to be my last gift to him.'

Now she let go of the branch and slipped both her arms around Sean's neck, laying her cheek against his so she did not have to watch his face as she asked the next question.

'Is my father dead, Sean? I must hear you say it before I will believe it.'

With his free arm he held her tightly and gathered himself to reply.

'Yes, my darling. Capo is dead, but he died a man's death – the kind he would have wanted, and Tukutela, his elephant, went with him. Do you want to hear the details?'

'No!' She shook her head, holding him tightly. 'Not now, perhaps not ever. He is dead, and a part of me and my life dies with him.'

He could find no word of comfort and he held her as she began to weep for her father. She wept silently, clinging to him, the grief shaking her. Her tears mingled with the droplets of river water on her face, but he tasted their diluted salt on his lips as he kissed her again and his heart went out to her.

So they floated down on the wide green river, with the smoke and the smell of battle drifting over them from the bombarded banks and the faint cries and groans of the wounded carrying to them across the water. Sean let her expend her silent grief, and slowly the sobs that rocked her abated and at last she whispered throatily:

'I don't know how I could have borne it without you to help me. You were so much alike, the two of you. I think that's what attracted me to you in the first place.'

'I take that as a compliment.'

'It was meant as one. He gave me a taste for men of power and strength.'

Floating beside them, almost within touching distance, was a corpse. Trapped air ballooned the tiger-striped camouflage battle jacket and the body floated on its back. The face was very young, a boy of fifteen years perhaps. His wounds were washed almost bloodless, just a faint pinky discharge like smoke in the green water drifted from them, but it was enough.

Sean saw the gnarled saurian heads, scaled like the bark of an ancient oak, coming swiftly down the current following the taint of blood. Ripples spreading front the hideous snouts, long tails fanning, two big crocodiles, racing each other for the prize.

One of the reptiles reached the corpse and reared out of the water; its jaws, lined with uneven rows of yellow fangs gaped wide, then closed over the corpse's arm. The fangs met through dead flesh with a grinding sound that carried clearly to them, and Claudia gasped and turned her head away.

Before the crocodile could pull the body below the surface the second reptile, even larger than the first, fastened its jaws into the dead belly, and began a gruesome tug-of-war.

The fangs of the crocodile are not designed to shear cleanly through meat and bone, so they held on with locked jaws and used their great combed tails to spin in the water, twisting viciously in a lather of white foam, rending the corpse between them, dismembering it, so they could hear the sinews tear and the joints of shoulder and groin separate.

In fascinated horror, Claudia looked back and gagged as one of the giant reptiles rose high out of the water with an arm in its jaws, and gulped at it convulsively. The creamy yellow scales of its throat bulged as the limb slid down and then it lunged back to tear another morsel from the body.

Tugging and fighting over the pathetic human fragments, they worked away from the floating tree and Sean, remembering the long tear in his back from the barbed wire, felt a lift of relief, for his own blood must be scenting the green waters.

'Oh God, it's all so horrible,' Claudia whispered. 'It's becoming a terrible nightmare.'

'This is Africa.' Sean held her, trying to give her courage. 'But I'm here with you now, it's going to be all right.'

'Will it, Sean? Do you think we will get out of this alive?'

'There is no money-back guarantee,' he admitted, 'if that's what you are asking for.'

She gave one last sob, and then leant back in his arms and looked steadily into his eyes.

'I'm sorry,' she said. 'I'm acting like a baby. I nearly let go there, but it won't happen again. I promise you that. At least I've found you, before it's too late.' She smiled at him with forced gaiety, bobbing with water up to her chin. 'We'll live for today, or what is left of it.'

'That's my girl.' He grinned back at her. 'Whatever happens, I'll be able to say I loved Claudia Monterro.'

'And was loved by her in turn,' she assured him, and she kissed him again, a long lingering kiss, warm and spiced with her tears, an expression not of lust but of longing, for both of them a pledge and an assurance, something true and certain in a world of dangerous uncertainty.

Sean was not even aware of his own pervading physical arousal, until she broke the kiss and demanded breathlessly, 'I want you now, this minute. I won't . . . I dare not wait. Oh God, Sean, my darling, now we are alive and in love, but by tonight we could both be dead. Take me now.'

He glanced quickly around their leafy arbour. Through the chinks he could see the banks. They seemed to have drifted below the Renamo fortifications. There was no further sign of life below the galleries of tall riverine trees, and the silence of the African noon was heavy and somnolent. Closer to them, just beyond arm's length, floated Job and Dedan, but only the backs of their bare heads were visible as they surveyed the riverbanks.

Sean looked back at Claudia, looked into her honey-gold eyes, and he wanted her. He knew that he had never wanted anything in his life so desperately.

'Just say it one more time,' she breathed huskily.

'I love you,' he said, and they kissed again, but a different type of kiss, hard where the first had been soft, hot where it had been warm, and savagely urgent where it had been gentle and lingering.

'Quickly,' she said into his mouth. 'Every second is precious.' And her hands below the surface of the water were tearing at their clothing. He had to use one hand to keep them from slipping under the green water, but with the other he helped her as best he could.

She opened the front of his bush jacket and then her own shirt to the waist and pressed herself to him. Her breasts were lubricated by the cool water. Her nipples were hard with wanting him, he could feel them distinctly sliding over his chest, they felt as big as ripe grapes.

He tugged the tongue of the leather belt that held her khaki shorts and she lifted herself to make it easier for him to un-zip the fly, and then kicked to free her legs as he worked the clinging wet cloth down over her buttocks. He slipped the garment over his arm to prevent it floating away and she was naked from the waist down. In frantic haste she opened the front of his trousers and thrust in both hands to scoop him out.

'Oh Sean,' she blurted. 'Oh God, my darling. You are so big, so hard. Oh please, quickly, quickly!'

In the water they were both weightless and as lithe as mating otters. Her long legs closed around his body wrapping him, her knees up under his armpits, her ankles locked across the small of his back as she searched for him blindly. He angled his hips to meet her thrusts and they almost succeeded but it slipped away harmlessly between their tense naked bellies.

She groaned softly with frustration and reached down and seized him again. Then with a lewd and beautiful arching of her back she took in just the tip of him. They strained against each other and suddenly her body went rigid and her golden eyes opened so wide they seemed to fill her face, as he went sliding

250

full length into her. After the cold green water she was so hot that it was almost unbearable and he cried out involuntarily.

Both Job and Dedan glanced around in surprise, then looked away in embarrassment but Sean and Claudia were oblivious to all the world.

It was over very swiftly and she hung around his neck exhausted as a marathon runner at the end of a gruelling race.

Sean recovered his voice first. 'I'm sorry,' he said. 'It was so quick. I couldn't wait. Did you . . . ?'

'I was there long before you.' She grinned up at him, a lopsided and uncertain grin. 'It was like being in an auto accident, quick, but devastating!'

They remained locked together by the embrace of her legs and arms, for a long time, quiet and resting, until she felt him shrivel and slip away and only then she released the grip of her legs and reached up with her mouth to kiss him tenderly.

'Now you belong to me, and I to you. Even if I die today, it won't matter so much. I have had you in me.'

'Let's try for a little more than one day.' He smiled gently down at her. 'Get dressed now, my love.' He handed her back her clothing. 'While I check on what's happening in the real world out there.'

He swam away from her and went to Job. 'What do you see?' he asked.

'I think we are clear of the lines,' Job answered, avoiding Sean's eyes tactfully. Strangely, it did not embarrass Sean that Job knew what had happened between Claudia and himself. He still felt elated and triumphant at the consummation of their love, and nothing could degrade it.

'As soon as it's dark enough, we'll swim the tree in towards the bank and get ashore.' Sean glanced at his Rolex. Not more than two hours to sunset. 'Keep your eyes open,' he said, and swam across to Dedan to repeat the warning.

He tried to estimate the rate of the current by watching the bank, and decided it was not more than two miles an hour. They would still be dangerously close to the Renamo lines when the sun set, and the river was flowing eastwards towards the sea, so they would have to work their way round or through General China's forces to reach the Zimbabwe border in the west. It was a formidable task but Sean still felt optimistic and invulnerable. He left Dedan's side and swam back to Claudia.

251

'You make me feel good,' he said.

'That's going to be my job in future,' she assured him. 'But what do we do now?'

'Nothing until dark, except steer this liner down the river.'

She cuddled against him under the water, and they held each other and watched the riverbanks drift slowly by.

After a while she said, 'I'm getting cold.'

They had been in the water for almost two hours, Sean realized, and though it was only a few degrees below their body temperature it was gradually chilling them through.

She slanted her eyes at him and gave him a naughty grin. 'Can't you think of something to prevent hypothermia?' she asked. 'Or do I have to make a suggestion?'

'Well,' he pretended to reflect, 'we can't light a fire.'

'Can't we?' she asked. 'Do you want a bet?' And she reached down and after a few seconds she whispered, 'See, nothing to it, and I didn't even use matches.'

'It's a miracle!' he agreed, and began to unbuckle her belt again.

'This time let's see if we can make the miracle last longer than ten seconds,' she suggested.

As the sun set, it turned the surface of the river to a luminous serpent with scales of furnace orange and glowing crimson.

'Now we can begin working in towards the bank,' Sean ordered, and they began to swim the floating tree across the current. It was heavy and ungainly, most of its bulk below the surface, and it resisted their efforts to move it closer to the bank. All four of them kept at it, kicking out strongly, and ponderously it began to swing across the wide waters.

The sun slipped below the horizon and the waters turned black as crude oil, the trees along them were dark cut-out silhouettes against the last glow of the sunset, but they were still thirty metres from the southern bank.

'We'll swim from here,' Sean decided. 'Keep close together. Don't get separated in the dark. Is everybody ready?'

They bunched up, clinging to the same branch. Sean reached for Claudia's hand and opened his mouth to give the order, and then closed it again, and cocked his head to listen.

He was surprised that he had not heard it before, perhaps the sound had been muffled by the high banks of the river and the tall trees that lined its winding course. However, it was suddenly loud and unmistakable, the sound of an outboard motor running at high speed.

'Oh shit,' he whispered bitterly, and looked towards the near bank. Only thirty metres away, it could just as well have been thirty miles.

The whine of the motor rose and fell as the acoustics of water and trees played tricks, but it was clearly coming downstream fast, running down from the direction of the Renamo lines. Sean ducked his head to gaze through a chink in the vegetation, and he saw a glow in the darkness, a beam of light that shafted briefly across the night sky and then bounced from the dark trees along the bank, glinted from the water, and swept boldly along the banks.

'Renamo patrol boat,' Sean said. 'And they are looking for us.'

Claudia tightened her grip on his hand, and no one else spoke.

'We'll try to hide in here,' Sean said, 'though I don't see how they can miss us. Get ready to duck under when the light hits us.'

The sound of the motor changed, slowing down, and then the craft swept round the upstream bend of the river a few hundred yards distant but coming down swiftly on the current towards them.

The beam of the spotlight played alternately along each bank, lighting them like day. It was an enormously powerful beam, probably one of the portable battle lights similar to the one which had trapped Sean at the top of the cliffs.

As the beam switched from bank to bank it briefly illuminated the craft and its crew. Sean recognized it as an eighteen-foot inflatable Zodiac driven by a fifty-five-horsepower Yamaha outboard, and though he could not count the occupants, there were at least eight or nine of them and they had a light machine-gun mounted in the bows. The man with the battle light was standing amidships.

The beam of light glanced over their refuge, dazzling them for an instant with its malevolent white eye, passing on and leaving them blinded by its brilliance, then coming back remorselessly and holding them captive. Sean heard someone give an indistinct order in the Shangane language, and the Zodiac altered course towards them, the beam of the battle light still fastened on them.

All four of them sank low in the water, until only their nostrils were exposed and they cowered behind the branch to which they were clinging.

The helmsman of the Zodiac throttled back, and slipped the engine into neutral. The black rubber craft drifted on the current, level with them but twenty feet off; the battle light darted and probed the leafy mass.

'Turn your face away,' Sean told Claudia in a tight whisper, and took her in his arms below the surface. Even their tanned faces would shine in the light and he screened her and turned the back of his head towards the Zodiac.

'There is nobody there,' somebody said in Shangane. Although spoken at conversational level the voice carried clearly across the water to where they were hiding.

'Go around!' another voice ordered in a tone of command, and Sean recognized the Shangane sergeant who had been his escort. A white wake spread out behind the Zodiac as it began to circle the floating tree.

The light beam cast stark black shadows from the tangled branches and struck dazzling reflections when it touched the water. As the Zodiac circled, they paddled quietly to the further side of their leafy refuge, and when the beam fastened on them, they slid softly below the surface, trying not to gasp for breath as they came up again.

The deadly game of hide and seek lasted all of eternity, before the voice in the Zodiac said again, 'There is nobody there. We are wasting time.'

'Keep circling,' the sergeant's voice answered, and then after another minute, 'Gunner, fire a burst into the tree.'

In the bows of the Zodiac, the muzzle flashes of the RPD light machine-gun twinkled like fairy lights, but a storm of shot tore into the floating tree with brutal and stunning savagery. It cracked in their eardrums, and thumped into the branches over their heads cutting loose a shower of leaves and twigs, it ripped away slabs of bark and kicked spray from the surface of the water, odd shots ricocheting into the night, wailing like demented spirits.

Sean pulled Claudia below the surface, but still could hear the bullets plunging into the water above them or striking the trunk of the tree. He kept down until his lungs burned as though they were filled with acid and only then pulled himself to the surface to catch another breath.

The gunner in the Zodiac was firing taps, not a single continu-

254

ous burst. Like a Morse operator on the key, an expert gunner has his own distinctive style that others can recognize. This one fired double taps, five rounds each, it needed a concert pianist's touch on the trigger to achieve such precision.

As Sean and Claudia came back to the surface, straining for the sweet taste of air, Dedan also came up only three feet in front of them. The reflection of the battle light lit his head clearly. His short woolly beard streamed water, his eyes were like balls of ivory in his ebony face and his mouth was open, drinking in air.

A bullet touched his temple, just above the ear. His head flinched to the shot, and it opened his scalp cleanly as a sabre cut. Involuntarily he cried out, a glottal bellow like that of a heart-shot bull buffalo, then his head fell forward and he sank face down into the dark waters.

Sean lunged out and caught his upper arm, pulling him back to the surface before he drifted away, but his head lolled and his eyes had rolled back in their sockets, exposing only the whites.

However, the men in the Zodiac had heard his cry and the Shangane sergeant shouted to one of his men, 'Get ready to throw in a grenade,' then to them, 'Come out of there. I'll give you ten seconds.'

'Job, answer him,' Sean ordered with resignation. 'Tell him we are coming out.'

Matabele and Shangane could understand each other, and Job shouted to them not to fire again.

Claudia helped Sean keep Dedan's head above the surface and between them they pulled him towards the Zodiac. The battle light dazzled them, but hands reached down from out of the glare and one at a time dragged them on board.

Shivering like half-drowned puppies, they huddled in the centre of the boat. They had Dedan's body stretched out between them and Sean lifted his head gently into his lap. He was unconscious, barely breathing, and gently Sean twisted his head to examine the bullet wound across his temple.

For a moment, he did not recognize what he was seeing. From the long shallow wound bulged something white and glistening in the lamp light.

Beside him, Claudia shuddered violently, and whispered, 'Sean, it's his, it's his . . .' She could not bring herself to say it,

255

and only then Sean realized that Dedan's brain, still contained in the tough white membrane of the *dura mater*, was bulging out through the rent in his skull like an inner tube through a hole in an auto tyre.

The Shangane sergeant gave an order and the helmsman gunned the outboard motor and swung the Zodiac upstream. They ran at full throttle back towards the Renamo lines.

Sean sat on the floorboards with Dedan's head in his lap. There was nothing he could do, except clasp his wrist and feel Dedan's pulse grow weaker and more erratic, then finally fade away altogether.

'He's dead,' he said quietly. Job said nothing and Claudia turned her face away.

Sean held the dead head in his lap all the long return. Only when the helmsman cut the engine and coasted in to the bank did he look up. There were lighted lanterns and dark shapes awaiting them at the landing.

The Shangane sergeant gave a brusque order and two of his men lifted Dedan's corpse off Sean's lap and dumped him face down on the muddy bank. Another trooper grabbed Claudia's arm and dragged her to her feet. He shoved her roughly ashore and when she whirled on him furiously to protest, he lifted his AK butt to strike her in the centre of her chest.

Sean was close beside him and he caught the man's arm and stifled the blow.

'Do that again, you son of a syphilitic hyena,' he said softly in Shangane, 'and I'll hack off your *mtondo* with a blunt axe and make you eat it without salt.'

The trooper stared at him, amazed more by his perfect Shangane than the threat itself, and on the bank the Shangane sergeant let out a bellow of delighted laughter.

'Better do what he says,' he warned his trooper, 'unless you are very hungry. This one means what he says.' Then he grinned at Sean. 'So you talk Shangane like one of us, and you understood everything we said!' He shook his head ruefully. 'I won't let you fool me again!'

* * *

Wet, cold and dishevelled they were dragged unceremoniously into General China's bunker and paraded before his desk. One

256

glance at his face and Sean recognized that the man was in a cold fury.

For almost a full minute he stared at Sean without rising from his seat, and then he said, 'The woman is being moved to another camp, well away from here. You will have no further opportunity to see her, until I order it.'

Sean kept his expression neutral but Claudia gave a little cry of protest, and seized Sean's arm as though she could prevent the threatened separation. General China nodded with satisfaction at her distress, and went on quietly, 'She no longer merits the special treatment which she has been given up until now, and I have ordered that she be placed in irons to prevent any further attempts at escape. She will also be kept in solitary confinement.'

The two female gaolers were standing against the wall beside his desk, and he glanced at them and nodded. The taller of the two wore sergeant's stripes on her sleeve. She gave an order to the squat toad-faced trooper beside her, and the woman came forward. The stainless-steel manacles dangled from her hand.

Claudia tightened her grip on Sean's arm and shrank away from her. The woman hesitated, and the tall sergeant gave another sharp command. The gaoler grabbed Claudia's wrist and without apparent effort plucked her away from Sean's side.

With the expertise of long practice, she spun Claudia around and thrust her face hard against the sandbagged wall of the bunker, snapping the manacles on one wrist as she did so, then pulling both Claudia's arms behind her back and locking the second cuff on her other wrist.

She stepped back and the tall female sergeant stepped up and took Claudia's hands and lifted them high between her shoulder-blades. Claudia gasped with pain as she was forced onto her toes. The sergeant inspected the manacles; they were closed snugly around Claudia's wrists, but she was not satisfied. Deliberately the sergeant tightened them two more notches and Claudia gasped again.

'That's too tight, they are cutting into me.'

'Tell that bitch to loosen them,' Sean snapped at General China, and he smiled for the first time that evening and leaned back in his chair.

'Colonel Courtney, I have given orders that the woman is not to be allowed another chance to escape. Sergeant Cara is only doing her duty.'

'She is cutting off the circulation. Miss Monterro could lose her hands to gangrene.'

'That would be unfortunate,' General China agreed. 'However, I will not interfere, unless . . .' he paused.

'Unless?' Sean demanded savagely.

'Unless I am assured of your complete co-operation and unless I have your parole that you will not attempt another escape.'

Sean looked down at Claudia's hands. Already they were beginning to swell and change colour, darkening to a leaden hue, the bright steel bands cutting into her wrists, the veins puffing up into dark blue cords below the manacles.

'Gangrene is a dangerous condition and unfortunately our facilities for amputation of limbs are very primitive,' General China remarked.

'All right,' Sean said heavily. 'I give you my parole.'

'And your co-operation,' he prompted.

'And I promise co-operation,' Sean agreed.

General China gave an order and the sergeant used the key on the manacles, letting them out two notches each and immediately the swelling of Claudia's hands dissipated and her skin colouring began to return to its normal creamy tan as the blood drained away.

'Take her away!' China ordered in English and the sergeant nodded to her assistant gaoler. They each seized one of Claudia's arms and dragged her to the door.

'Wait!' Sean shouted, but they ignored him and when he tried to follow her, the big Shangane sergeant seized his arms from behind in a hammer lock.

'Sean!' Claudia's voice had a note of hysteria. 'Don't let them take me!' But they pushed her out of the bunker and the canvas curtain fell between them.

'Sean!' Her voice came back to him.

'I love you!' he shouted after her, struggling against the sergeant's grip. 'It will be all right, darling. Just remember I love you. I'll do what I have to do to get you out of here.'

The promise rang hollowly in his own ears and her voice was a despairing wail. 'Sean!' And then again very faintly. 'Sean!' Then silence beyond the curtain.

Sean found he was panting with emotion but he forced himself to cease struggling and stand quietly. The sergeant relaxed his grip and Sean shrugged him away and turned to General China.

'You bastard!' he said. 'You rotten bastard!'

'I see that you are in no mood for sensible discussion,' China told him, and glanced at his wristwatch. 'And it's well after midnight. We'll let you cool off.' He looked at the sergeant and changed to Shangane. 'Take them,' he indicated Sean and Job, 'feed them, give them dry clothes and a blanket, let them sleep and bring them to me at dawn tomorrow.' The sergeant saluted and pushed them towards the door.

'I have work for them to do,' China warned him. 'Make sure they are in condition to do it.'

* * *

Sean and Job slept side by side on the floor of a dugout with a guard sitting over them. The floor was of hard-packed damp earth and the blankets were verminous, but neither the discomfort, nor the tickle of insects crawling over his skin, nor even thoughts of Claudia could keep Sean awake.

The sergeant woke him in the dark of pre-dawn from a profound and dreamless sleep by dumping an armful of clothing on his prostrate body.

'Get dressed,' he ordered.

Sean sat up and scratched the bite of a bed bug.

'What's your name?' It was a relief to be able to speak Shangane freely.

'Alphonso Henriques Mabasa,' the Shangane told him proudly, and Sean smiled at the unlikely combination. The name of a Portuguese emperor, and the Shangane name for one who strikes with a club.

'A war club on your enemies and a meat club on their wives?' Sean asked, and Alphonso guffawed.

Job sat up and grimaced at Sean's ribald sally.

'At five in the morning, before breakfast!' he protested, and shook his head sadly, but Sean heard Alphonso delightedly repeating the joke to his men outside the dugout.

'With the Shangane, it doesn't take much to establish the reputation of being a wag,' Job remarked in Sindebele as they sorted through the bundle of clothing Alphonso had brought them. It was all secondhand but reasonably clean. Sean found a military-style cloth cap and a suit of tiger-striped battledress, and

259

discarded his bush jacket and shorts which were by now in rags. He kept on his comfortable old velskoen.

Breakfast was a stew of kapenta, the fingerling dried fish he thought of as African whitebait, and a porridge of maize meal. 'What about tea?' Sean asked, and Alphonso laughed.

'You think this is the Polana Hotel in Maputo?'

Dawn was just breaking when Alfonso escorted them down to the riverbank where they found General China and his staff inspecting the damage done by the Hind gunships.

'We lost twenty-six men killed and wounded yesterday,' China greeted Sean. 'And almost as many deserters during the night. Morale is sinking fast.' He spoke in English and it was clear that none of his staff understood. Despite the circumstances, he looked dapper and competent in his beret and crisply ironed battledress, medal ribbons across his chest and general officer's stars on his epaulettes. The ivory-handled pistol hung on his webbing belt and he wore aviator-style mirrored sunglasses with thin gold frames.

'Unless we can stop those gunships, it will be over in three months, before the rains can save us.'

The rains were the time of the guerrilla when head-high grass, impassable roads and flooded rivers hamstringed the defender and afforded concealment and sanctuary to his tormentor.

'I watched those Hinds in action yesterday,' Sean told him cautiously. 'Captain Job here borrowed one of your RPG 7 rocket-launchers and scored a direct hit with an AP rocket.'

China looked at Job with new interest. 'Good,' he said. 'None of my own men have been able to do that yet. What happened?'

'Nothing,' Job answered simply.

'No damage,' Sean confirmed.

'The entire machine is encased in titanium armour plate,' China nodded, and looked up at the sky, a nervous gesture as though he were expecting one of the humpbacked monsters to appear miraculously. 'Our friends in the south have offered us one of their new Darter missile systems, but there is the difficulty of bringing in the launch vehicles, heavy trucks over these roads and through Frelimo-controlled territory.' He shook his head. 'We need an infantry weapon, one that can be carried and used by foot soldiers.'

'As far as I know there is only one effective weapon of that kind. The Americans developed a technique in Afghanistan.

260

They adapted the original Stinger missile and worked out a way of getting through the armour. I haven't any idea of the details,' Sean added hastily. He knew it was unwise to set himself up as an expert, but the problem was intriguing and he had allowed himself to be carried away.

'You are quite correct, Colonel. The modified Stinger is the only weapon that has proved effective against the Hind. That's your task, the price of your freedom. I want you to procure a shipment of Stingers for me.'

Sean stopped dead on the riverbank and stared at him, and then he began to smile. 'Certainly,' he said. 'A piece of cake. Do you have a preference for colour and flavour, how about baboon-ball blue and kiwi fruit?'

For the first time that morning China smiled back at him. 'The Stingers are here already, it's simply a matter of picking them up.'

Sean's grin faded. 'I hope, most fervently, that this is a joke. I know that Savimbi has been given Stingers by the Yanks, but Angola is on the other side of the continent.'

'Our Stingers are much closer than that,' China assured him. 'Do you remember the old Rhodesian Fire Force base at Grand Reef?'

'I should,' Sean nodded. 'The Scouts operated out of there for almost a year.'

'Of course, I remember.' China touched the lobe of his ear beneath the gaudy beret. 'It was from there you launched the attack on my camp at Inhlozane.' His expression was suddenly bleak.

'That was in another war,' Sean reminded him.

China's expression relaxed. 'As I was saying, the Stingers we want are at Grand Reef.'

'I don't understand.' Sean shook his head. 'The Yanks would never give Stingers to Mugabe. He is a Marxist and there is no deep love between Zimbabwe and the US. It doesn't make sense.'

'Oh yes, it does,' China assured him. 'In a roundabout African way, it makes good sense.' He glanced at his watch. 'Tea time,' he said. 'I believe you were asking for a brew this morning. No matter what side we were on, the war made us all tea addicts.'

China led them back to his command bunker and an orderly brought in the smoke-blackened kettle immediately.

261

'The Americans dislike Mugabe, but they dislike the South Africans more,' China explained. 'Mugabe is harbouring and assisting ANC guerrillas operating across his borders into South Africa.'

Sean nodded grimly. He had seen photographs of the carnage created by a limpet mine detonated in a South African supermarket; it had happened on the last Friday of the month, payday for monthly workers, when the store was crowded with housewives and their offspring both black and white.

'The South Africans have vowed to pursue the guerrillas wherever they run. They have already repeatedly made good that threat, hot pursuit across the borders of all their neighbours. The ANC have announced their intention of stepping up their bombing of soft civilian targets. Mugabe knows what the consequences will be, so he wants a weapon to deal with the South African Puma gunships when they cross his border to cull the ANC.'

'I still don't believe the Yanks would supply him with Stingers,' Sean said flatly.

'Not directly,' China agreed. 'But the British are training Mugabe's army for him. They are the middle men. They have got the Stingers from the Americans and they are training Mugabe's crack Third Brigade to use them at Grand Reef.'

'How the hell do you know all this?'

'You must remember that I was once a minister, albeit a junior one, in Mugabe's cabinet. I still have good friends in high places.'

Sean thought about it. 'You are right,' he nodded. 'It is all typically African. So the Stingers are at Grand Reef.'

'They were delivered by a Royal Air Force Hercules fourteen days ago, and are scheduled to be deployed along the South African and Zimbabwe border by the beginning of next month. They will be aimed at your countrymen, Colonel Courtney.'

Sean felt a stirring of patriotic outrage, but he kept his expression neutral.

'The training is being conducted by Royal Artillery personnel, a captain and two NCOs, so you will begin to understand why I require a white face for my plans.'

'It certainly begins to sound ominous,' Sean muttered. 'Tell me what it is exactly that you require.'

'I want you to go back to Zimbabwe and bring me those Stinger missiles.'

Sean showed no emotion as he asked, 'In exchange?'.

'Once the missiles are delivered to me, I will remove the manacles from Miss Monterro and transfer her to quarters where you will be able to visit her regularly,' he paused and allowed himself a knowing smile, 'and spend some time with her each day or evening in private.'

'What about our release?'

'Yes,' China agreed. 'All three of you will be released after you have performed one additional service for me – after first obtaining the Stingers.'

'And what is that service?'

China held up both hands. 'One thing at a time, Colonel Courtney. The missiles first. Once you have delivered them, we will discuss the final part of our bargain.'

Sean scowled into his tea mug as he turned it over in his mind, trying to find some vantage point to adopt, but China interrupted him.

'Colonel, every minute you waste merely prolongs Miss Monterro's –' he searched for the correct word – 'her discomfort. Until I have those missiles, she will wear her manacles night and day, waking or sleeping, eating or performing all the other essential functions of life. I suggest you begin immediately laying out your plans to procure them for me.'

Sean stood up and went to the large-scale wall map behind China's desk. He didn't really need to study it. He could have closed his eyes and visualized every valley and peak, every wrinkle of land along the border between Mozambique and Zimbabwe. The railway line crossed the border near the little town of Umtali, and twenty kilometres beyond it on the Zimbabwe side a tiny red aircraft symbol marked the position of the Grand Reef airfield and base.

Sean touched the stylized aircraft symbol with his forefinger, and Job came to stand beside him. They both stared at it thoughtfully. How many times had they sortied from that field, shambling out to the rumbling Dakota transports under the burden of parachute and battle packs and weapons. Each of them could picture clearly the position of every building, the hangars and barracks and perimeter defence.

'Twenty Ks from the border post,' Job said softly, 'fifteen minutes by truck, but we'll never get there on foot.'

'You spoke of a plan, General China. What do you have in

263

mind? Can you provide us with vehicles?' Sean asked without looking round.

'Some time ago my men captured three Unimog trucks, with authentic Zimbabwe army paintwork and papers. We have them hidden,' China answered, and Sean breathed a sigh of relief.

'My plan is for you to cross the border disguised as Zimbabwean troops.'

'I'll bet there is a huge volume of military traffic through the border post.'

'There is,' China affirmed.

'We'll need Zimbabwe army uniforms for all the black troops and something for me.' Sean tapped his finger on the map. 'We will have to wheedle our way into the base without firing a shot.'

'I have a British field officer's uniform for you,' China said softly. 'It's genuine and I have the papers to go with it.'

'How the hell did you get that?'

'Three months ago we attacked a Zimbabwe column near Vila de Manica. There was a British observer with the column and he got caught in the crossfire. He was a major in one of the guards regiments, seconded to the high commissioner in Harare as a military attaché, according to his papers.

'The uniform has been cleaned of blood and the tears made by fragmentation grenade have been patched most expertly. The tailor who did the work made my own uniform.' China smoothed the fit of his tunic over his lean flanks and looked pleased with it. 'He will alter the captured uniform to fit you, Colonel. The British major was about your height, but a great deal larger around the waist and backside.'

'A guards regiment,' Sean smiled. 'I don't know about my accent, any Englishman would pick me out as a colonial the instant I open my mouth.'

'You will have to deal only with the Third Brigade guards at the base gates. I assure you they will not have such discerning ears.'

'Okay,' Sean said. 'So we may be able to get in, but how the hell do we get out?' He was beginning to enjoy himself, becoming absorbed with the problem.

'Not so fast, Sean.' Job was studying the map. 'We can't just pitch up at the gates without an invitation and demand entry. With the Stingers there the security will be at a maximum.'

'That is correct,' China concurred. 'However, I have more

good news for you. I actually have a man inside the base. He is a nephew of mine, we are a large family.' He looked complacent as he went on. 'He is in signals, a warrant officer, second in command of the Grand Reef communications centre. He will be able to fake a signal from the Zimbabwe high command authorizing an inspection of the Stinger programme by the military attaché. So the guards at the base will be expecting you. They won't scrutinize your pass too closely.'

'If you have a man inside the base, he'll know exactly where the Stingers are stored,' Job suggested eagerly.

'Right,' China nodded. 'They are in number three hangar. That's second from the left.'

'We know exactly where number three hangar is,' Sean assured him, and frowned as he tried to anticipate the other problems they would encounter.

'I will want to know the packaging of the missiles, sizes and weights.' China scribbled a note on his pad. 'And there must be instruction manuals covering their operation. Those will certainly be in the office of the Royal Artillery captain. I must know exactly where that is.' He ticked off each item on his fingers as it occurred to him, and Job added his own ideas.

'We'll need a diversion,' he suggested. 'A second unit to stage an attack on the base perimeter furthest from the hangar and training centre, plenty of tracer and RPG rocks and white phosphorus grenades – we will need another squad for that.'

It was like old times, how often had they worked together like this, each stimulating the other, their excitement kept under tight rein, but sparkling in their eyes.

Once Job remarked, 'I'm glad it's the Third Brigade we'll be going against, that bunch of nun-killers and child-rapers, they led the purge in Matabeleland.' The slaughter and atrocity that had accompanied the brigade's sweep through the tribal areas from which the Matabele political dissidents had been operating was fresh in both their memories.

'Two of my brothers, my grandfather . . .' Job's voice dropped to a deathly whisper. 'The Third Brigade threw their bodies down the old shaft at Antelope Mine.'

'This isn't personal vengeance,' Sean warned him. 'All we want is those Stingers, Job.' The intertribal hatred of Africa was as fierce as any Corsican vendetta, and Job had physically to shake himself to break the spell of it.

'You're right, but a few Third Brigade scalps would be a nice little fringe benefit.'

Sean grinned. Despite his admonition, the thought of taking on ZANLA again gave him equal satisfaction. How many good men, and women, how many dear friends had he lost to them over the eleven long years of the bush war, and how complex were the lines of hatred and loyalty that held together the very fabric of Africa. Only an African could ever understand it.

'Okay.' Sean brought them back to hard reality. 'We have got in. We have the Stingers, say two loaded Unimogs. I have found the manuals. We are ready to pull out. The diversion has lured most of the guards to the southern perimeter of the base, on the far side of the airfield. Now we have to get out. They aren't going to be so happy about letting us go.'

'We charge the gates,' Job said. 'Use one truck to break down the barricades.'

'Yes,' Sean nodded. 'And then? We aren't going to be able to get out of the country through the border post at Umtali. By that time the whole Zimbabwe army and Frelimo will all be after us.'

They both turned back to the wall map again. Sean reached up and traced the road that branched northwards, just before it reached the town of Umtali, and then ran parallel with the border as it traversed the rugged eastern highlands towards Inyanga National Park, an area of misty peaks and wet densely forested valleys. He touched one of the valleys, a green wedge driven deeply into the barrier of mountains.

'Honde Valley,' he read the legend. The road crossed the head of it and the valley itself was a funnel that led down to the border and the Mozambique uplands. It formed a natural re-entrance to the highlands, a gateway which had been one of the major infiltration routes of the ZANLA guerrillas from their training bases in Mozambique. The hard way, Sean and Job had learned all its secrets, the hidden trails and strong points, the false ports and the concealed passes.

'The track down to St Mary's mission,' Sean said and they stared at it. 'That's as far as we can take the trucks.'

'From there is only six Ks to the border,' Job murmured.

'Six hard Ks,' Sean qualified. 'And we won't be clear just because we have crossed into Mozambique. We will still have them after us until we get into Renamo-held ground.'

Sean turned back to General China. 'I'll want porters waiting for us at St Mary's mission. How far does your control of territory extend?'

'The porters will present no problem.' China came to stand between them and pointed to a speck on the map marked Mavonela. 'And I can have trucks waiting at this village. Once you reach Mavonela, I will consider that you have made good delivery of the missiles.'

'I suggest we don't try and bring out forty Stingers with one column of porters,' Job cut in. 'It will make a perfect target for Mugabe's MIGs. One load of napalm is all it would take.'

'And of course, Frelimo can call in their Hinds,' Sean added. 'You are right, Job. Once it is light enough for air-attack, we will bombshell.' He was referring to the old guerrilla trick of splintering the column and offering numerous small elusive targets, rather than a single large ungainly one. 'Can you arrange for a series of RZs rather than a single RZ at Mavonela village?' He used the old Scouts' abbreviation for a rendezvous.

'Yes,' China nodded. 'We will disperse the transport along the Mavonela road.' He traced it out. 'One truck every kilometre, hidden under camouflage netting, and we'll move the Stingers out on the last stage under cover of darkness.'

'All right, let's draw up a timetable,' Sean said. 'Let's get it all down on paper. I'll need writing material.'

China opened a drawer of his desk and brought out a cheap notebook and ballpoint pen. While they worked, China sent for his quartermaster, a chubby little man who had run a men's outfitters in Beira before economic necessity rather than ideological commitment had forced him to leave the town and seek employment in the deep bush with China's guerrillas.

He arrived carrying the uniform for a staff officer of the Irish Guards in the field, complete with insignia, headgear, webbing and boots in his arms. Sean donned the uniform for a fitting without interrupting their planning session. The tunic and trousers had to be taken in, and the boots were a size too large.

'Better too big than too small,' Sean decided. 'I'll wear a couple of pairs of socks.'

The tailor tucked and pinned and crawled around Sean's feet as he let the trouser bottoms down an inch.

'Fine.' Sean examined the guards major's papers that China

laid out on the desk top. From the photograph, Sean saw that the major had been a fleshy fair-haired individual in his late forties.

'Gavin Duffy,' Sean read the dead man's name aloud. 'You'll have to alter the ID photograph.'

'My propaganda officer will take care of that,' China told him.

The propaganda officer was a mulatto, half Portuguese, half Shangane, and he was armed with a polaroid camera. He took four mug shots of Sean and then spirited away the deceased guards major's ID card to doctor the photograph.

'All right.' Sean turned back to China. 'Now I want to take command of the men who will make up the raiding party and see them properly kitted out. You'll have to explain to them that they are to take their orders from me in future.'

China smiled and stood up. 'Follow me, Colonel. I'll take you to meet your new command.'

He led the way out of the bunker, but once they were on the path through the forest that led down to the river, Sean fell in beside him and they continued to discuss the raid.

'Obviously I am going to need more than the original ten men in Sergeant Alphonso's squad, at least another detachment to make the diversionary attack on the base,' Sean broke off as the mournful wail of the hand-operated sirens rose from the camp around them, and instantly all around them was turmoil and confusion.

'The Hinds!' shouted China. 'Take cover!' And he sprinted for a sandbagged emplacement amongst the trees nearby. There was a twin-barrelled 12.7mm anti-aircraft weapon mounted in the emplacement. It would be a prime target for the Hind gunners and Sean looked around quickly for alternative cover.

In the long grass on the opposite side of the track, he spotted a less conspicuous shell-scrape and ran for it. As he tumbled into it, he heard the oncoming roar of the Hind gunships and the cacophony of ground fire built up swiftly. Job jumped down into the fox-hole and squatted beside him, and then another smaller figure appeared above them and as nimble as a hare leapt into the hole.

For a moment, Sean did not realize who it was, not until the wrinkled face creased like a used napkin into a wide black smile and the man said happily, 'I see you, *Bwana*.'

'You! You silly little bugger!' Sean stared at him in disbelief. 'I sent you back to Chiwewe. What the hell are you doing back here?'

'I went back to Chiwewe, as you commanded,' Matatu said virtuously. 'Then I came back to look for you.'

Sean still stared at Matatu in awe as he considered what that statement entailed. Then he shook his head and began to smile, immediately the little man's answering grin seemed to split his face in two.

'Nobody saw you?' Sean demanded in Swahili. 'You came through the lines into the headquarters of an army, and nobody saw you?'

'Nobody sees Matatu, when Matatu does not want to be seen.'

The earth trembled under them, and the sound of rockets and gunfire forced them to put their heads close together and shout into each other's faces.

'How long have you been here?'

'Since yesterday.' Matatu looked apologetic. He pointed to the sky where the Hinds were circling. 'Since those machines attacked yesterday. I was watching when you jumped into the river. I followed you along the bank when you used the tree as a boat. I wanted to come to you then, but I saw crocodiles. Then in the night the bad men, the *shifta*, came in the boat and brought you back here. I waited and watched.'

'Did you see where they took the white woman?' Sean demanded.

'I saw them take her away last night.' Matatu showed little interest in Claudia. 'But I waited for you.'

'Can you find out where they took her?' Sean asked.

'Of course.' Matatu's grin faded and he looked indignant. 'I can follow them anywhere they took her.'

Sean unbuttoned his tunic pocket and pulled out his new notebook. Crouched in the bottom of the shell-scrape with an air-raid thundering overhead, he composed the first love letter he had written in years. Filling the single tiny sheet of cheap notepaper with all the assurances and comfort and cheer that he could muster, he ended it, 'Be strong, it won't be for much longer and remember I love you. Whatever happens, I love you.'

He ripped the page out of the notebook and folded it carefully.

'Take this to her.' He handed it to Matatu. 'See that she gets it and then come back to me.'

Matatu tucked the scrap of paper into his loin-cloth and waited expectantly.

'Did you see the hole in which I slept last night?' Sean asked.

'I saw you come from there this morning,' Matatu nodded.

'That will be our meeting-place,' Sean told him. 'Come to me there, when the *shifta* are asleep.' Sean looked up at the sky. The raid had been fierce but short-lived. The sound of engines and gunfire was dwindling, but dust and smoke drifted over their shelter.

'Go now,' Sean ordered, and Matatu jumped to his feet eager to obey, but Sean took his arm. It was thin as a child's and Sean shook it affectionately. 'Don't let them catch you, old friend,' he said in Swahili.

Matatu shook his head and twinkled with amusement at the absurdity of that thought and then like a puff of smoke from the genie's lamp, he was gone.

They waited a few minutes to let Matatu get clear and then climbed out of the shelter. The trees around them were torn and shattered with shell and rocket fire; across the river an ammunition store was burning and RPG rockets and phosphorus grenades were exploding, sending dense white smoke towering into the sky.

General China came striding down the path to meet them. There was a sooty stain on the sleeve of his uniform and dust on his knees and elbows. His expression was furious.

'Our position here is totally compromised,' he fumed. 'They raid us at will and we have no response.'

'You'll have to pull your main force back out of range of the Hinds,' Sean shrugged.

'I can't do that.' China shook his head. 'It will mean that we can no longer maintain our stranglehold on the railway. It will mean conceding control of the main road system to Frelimo, and inviting them to come on the offensive.'

'Well then,' Sean shrugged again, 'you are going to take a hammering if you remain here.'

'Get me those Stingers,' China hissed. 'Get them, and get them quickly!' And he strode away down the path.

Sean and Job followed him to the bunker complex on the

riverbank where a company of guerrillas, forty men, obviously forewarned of the general's approach, were drawn up in a makeshift parade ground of beaten earth the size of a tennis court. They seemed oblivious of the air-raid damage, the smoke and debris, and the scurrying first-aid parties and damage control teams around them.

Sean recognized Sergeant Alphonso and his Shanganes in the first rank. He came forward and saluted General China, then wheeled and gave the order for the detachment to stand easy. General China wasted few words and little time. He raised his voice and addressed them brusquely in Shangane.

'You men are being given a special task. You will, in future, take your orders from this white officer.' He indicated Sean beside him. 'You will follow those orders strictly. You all know the consequences of failing to do so.' He turned to Sean. 'Carry on, Colonel Courtney,' he said, then strode away back up the path towards the command bunker. Instinctively Sean almost saluted him and then checked himself.

'Screw you, China,' he muttered under his breath, and then gave his full attention to his new command.

Of course, he already knew Sergeant Alphonso's squad well, but the additional men that China had found for him were as likely a looking bunch as he had seen in the Renamo ranks. China had given him of his very best. Sean moved slowly down the front rank, inspecting each of them. They were all equipped with AKM assault rifles, the more modern version of the venerable AK 47. In places the blueing was worn from the metal with long usage, however the weapons were meticulously clean and well maintained. Their webbing was in first-class order, and their uniforms, although again well worn, were neatly patched and repaired.

'Always judge a workman by the state of his tools,' Sean thought. These were top soldiers, proud and hard. He stared into each of their eyes as he came level with them and saw it there. Of all the people of Africa, Sean felt the greatest rapport with the Zulu-originated tribes, the Angoni and Matabele and Shangane. If he had been given his choice these were exactly the type of men he would have chosen for this assignment.

Once he had finished the inspection, he went back to the front and addressed them for the first time in Shangane. 'You and I together are going to burst the balls of the dung-eating Frelimo.'

he said quietly, and in the front rank Sergeant Alphonso grinned wolfishly.

*   *   *

With her hands still manacled behind her back, the two female wardresses and an escort of five troopers marched Claudia Monterro through the darkness over a rough track. Often she stumbled and when she fell and sprawled full length, she was unable to use her hands to protect herself from the rocky surface. Soon her knees were raw and bleeding, and the march became a torturous nightmare.

It seemed without end, hour after hour it went on and every time she fell the tall sergeant harangued her in a language she could not understand. Each time it required more of an effort to regain her feet, for she was unable to use her hands and arms to balance herself.

She was so thirsty that her saliva had turned to a sticky paste in her mouth, her legs ached and her hands and arms held so long in such an unnatural position were numb and cold. Sometimes, she heard voices in the darkness around her and once or twice smelled smoke and saw the glow of a camp-fire or a feeble paraffin lantern so she knew that she was still within the Renamo lines.

The march ended abruptly. She guessed that they were still near the river, she could feel the chill of its waters in the air and see the taller riverine trees silhouetted against the stars and she could smell humanity around her: stale ash of the cooking-fires and woodsmoke, human sweat in unwashed clothing, and human body wastes and the sour odours of garbage. At last, they led her through a barbed wire gate into another prison compound, and dragged her towards one of a row of dugouts.

The two wardresses took her arms and hustled her down a set of earthen steps and pushed her into the darkness so she tripped and fell once more on her injured knees. Behind her, she heard a door being closed and barred, and the darkness was absolute.

After a short struggle she regained her feet, but when she tried to stand full height, the top of her head bumped on the low roof. It felt like a roof of undressed wooden poles still in their bark. She shuffled backwards, stretching out her fingers behind her until she touched the door. It was of hand-sawn planks, rough

272

and sharp with splinters. She pressed her weight upon it but it was solid and unmoving.

Bent over to protect her head, she shuffled around her prison. The walls were damp earth. Her cell was tiny, about six feet square, and in the far corner she stumbled over the only furnishing it contained. It was metal and she explored it with her foot and found that it was an iron bucket. The ripe stench from it left no doubt of its purpose. She completed the circuit of her cell and came back to the door.

Her thirst was an agony now, and she called through the door. 'Please I need water.' Her voice was a harsh croak and her lips felt tight and dry, ready to split. 'Water!' she called, and then remembered the Spanish word and hoped it was the same in Portuguese. 'Agua!'

It was futile. The earthen walls seemed to swallow and deaden the sound of her voice. She shuffled to the far corner and sank down to the dark floor. Only then she realized just how physically exhausted she was, yet the manacles on her wrists prevented her lying on her back or side. She tried to find a position in which she could rest comfortably and at last by wedging herself upright in a corner of the cell she succeeded.

The cold and something else woke her, and she was confused and disorientated. For a moment she believed she was back in her father's home in Anchorage and she cried out for him.

'Papa! Are you there?'

Then she smelled the damp and the sewage bucket, and felt the cold in her joints and her pinioned arms, and she remembered. Despair swept over her like a black wave and she felt herself drowning in it. Then she heard again the sound that had awakened her, and she went rigid and felt the cold sweat burst out on her neck and forehead.

She knew what it was instantly. Claudia had none of the more usual feminine phobias, she had no terror of spiders or snakes, there was just one unnatural terror which afflicted her. She sat rigid and listened to the scampering sounds of a creature moving about her cell. That sound was the stuff of her nightmares, and she stared into the darkness trying to will it away from herself.

Then suddenly she felt it on her. The sharp little claws pricking her skin, the cold touch of paws on her flesh. It was a rat and by the weight of it on her, it must have been huge, as big as a rabbit, and she screamed wildly and lunged to her feet and kicked out blindly at it. When she stopped screaming at last, she shrank into the corner and found she was trembling in wild spasms.

'Stop it!' she told herself. 'Pull yourself together!' And by an enormous effort of will, she regained control. There was complete silence in the darkness, her screams had frightened the creature away for the time being but she still could not bring herself to sit on the dirt floor again, for she was terrified that it would return.

Despite her exhaustion she stood propped in the corner and waited out the rest of the night. She dozed, almost fell asleep on her feet, then jerked awake again. That sequence happened many times, and then as she came awake for the last time, she realized that the darkness was no longer total and she could see.

Light was filtering into the cell and she blinked and found the source of it. There were slits and gaps between the poles of the low roof. These had been daubed with clay and grass, but in one or two places the dried clay had fallen out of the cracks allowing chinks of light through. Stems of coarse elephant grass hung down untidily from the cracks.

Fearfully she looked around the cell, but the rat had disappeared, it must have squeezed through one of the gaps between the poles.

Claudia stumbled across to the reeking galvanized sewage bucket, and only as she stood over it she realized her predicament. Her hands were locked behind her back and with that realization her need became irresistible.

Her fingers were almost devoid of feeling, but in desperate haste she was able to grip her leather belt and gradually work it through the loops of her trousers until the buckle was in the small of her back. She was whimpering with the effort of self-control needed to delay her bodily functions while she clumsily unclasped the belt.

She had lost so much weight that as soon as her belt was loosened her trousers fell around her ankles and she was able to hook a thumb under the elastic of her panties and drag them down as far as her knees.

Always fastidious, Claudia experienced the worst hardship of her captivity when her efforts to cleanse herself properly failed. She found herself sobbing with humiliation as she finally managed to dress again. Her wrists were rubbed raw and her arms ached from the strenuous efforts needed to perform this simple task.

She huddled in the corner of her cell and the stench of the bucket seemed to permeate the very depth of her soul.

A single ray of sunlight shot through a chink in the roof poles and pinned a brilliant silver coin on the far wall. She watched it move infinitely slowly down the earthen wall, and somehow it seemed to warm and cheer her enough to dull the cutting edge of her despair.

Before the coin of light reached the floor of the cell, she heard a scraping at the door as the bars were drawn and the door forced open against its primitive hinges. The tall sergeant stooped into the cell and Claudia scrambled to her feet.

'Please,' she whispered. 'You must let me wash,' she said in her schoolgirl Spanish, but the wardress showed no sign of having understood. In one hand she carried a metal billy-can of water and in the other a bowl of stiff maize cake. She placed the billy-can on the floor and then tipped the lump of maize cake into the dirt beside it.

Claudia's thirst, which she had managed temporarily to subdue, returned in even greater agony, and she almost whimpered at the sight of the billy. It contained almost two litres of clear water.

She sank down on her knees before it like a worshipper and looked up at the wardress.

'Please,' she said in Spanish. 'I must use my hands, please.' The wardress chuckled, the first animation she had shown, and she nudged the billy dangerously with the toe of her boot; a little water slopped over the rim.

'No,' Claudia croaked. 'Don't spill it.'

On her knees she bent over and tried to reach the water with her tongue, thrusting it out as far as it would reach, and felt the blessed wetness on the very tip, but the rim of the metal billy was cutting into her face.

She looked up again. 'Please, help me.'

The wardress laughed again and leaned against the wall watching her efforts with amusement.

Claudia stooped again and gripped the rim of the billy between her teeth. Carefully she tilted it and a few drops trickled between her lips. The pleasure was so intense that her vision clouded. She drank a sip at a time until the level in the billy had fallen to where the liquid could no longer flow into her mouth. However, the vessel was still more than half full and her thirst seemed only to have been aggravated by what she had managed to drink.

Still holding the rim between her teeth, she carefully raised her head, and tilted it backwards. It was too quick. She choked as the water flooded into her mouth, and the billy slipped from between her teeth, water splashed down her chest and puddled on the floor to be quickly absorbed into the dirt.

The wardress let out a shrill shriek of laughter, and Claudia felt the tears of despair fill her eyes. She only just managed to smother the sob that came up her throat.

The wardress deliberately stepped onto the white maize cake, smearing it into the dirt, then with another snort of laughter snatched up the empty billy and left the cell. Claudia heard her still giggling as she rebarred the door of the cell.

She could judge the passage of time by the angle of the sunlight through the chinks in the roof. The first day seemed interminable. Despite the discomfort of the manacles, she was able to sleep fitfully but while she was awake she occupied herself by planning to increase her chances of survival.

Water was her most pressing need. The little she had drunk might just see her through this day, but she knew that she was already suffering from dehydration.

'I have to find some method of drinking from that billy,' she told herself, and spent most of that afternoon wrestling with the problem. When the solution came to her, she lurched to her feet so hastily that she bumped the back of her head on the log roof. She ignored the hurt and examined the untidy tufts of elephant grass that hung down from between the chinks of the roof. She selected one of the grass stems and took it carefully between her teeth, worried it loose and let it drop to the floor. She knelt over it and by straining backwards managed to get a hand to it. Fortunately it was dry and brittle and snapped readily between her fingers. She broke it into four equal lengths each about nine inches long and, once again by backward contortions, planted them upright in the loose earth of the floor. She turned round, knelt and picked up the first of them between her lips. She tried to blow through it, but it was blocked with pith and dirt. She discarded it and went on to the next.

When she blew through this one, a tiny cork of dirt flew out of the end like a blow-pipe and then it was hollow and clear. She flopped onto her backside and sat in the middle of the dirt floor with the straw still stuck in her mouth, laughing around it with triumph. Her sense of elation and achievement dispelled the

276

corroding sense of despair which had almost destroyed her will to keep on living.

She crawled to the corner and carefully hid the precious straw, and then for the rest of that day planned how she would use it.

The rays of sun no longer penetrated to her cell, and the heavy gloom of evening was on her before she heard the wardress at the door. She huddled in her corner when the sergeant stooped into the cell and carelessly dumped the stodgy lump of boiled maize meal into the dirt and stood the metal billy beside it.

She leaned back expectantly against the door jamb and waited for Claudia to scramble for the food and drink like an animal on all fours. Claudia crouched motionlessly in the furthest corner of the cell and tried to show no expression, but her throat contracted in an involuntary swallowing reflex and her thirst was a raging beast within her.

After she had not moved for a few minutes, the sergeant said something irritable in Portuguese and gestured to the billy. With an immense effort Claudia prevented herself from looking down at it and the woman shrugged and once again stepped onto the maize cake and ground it into the dirt. She gave a snort of unconvincing laughter and backed out through the door, dragging it shut behind her, but the billy-can was left standing at the threshold.

Claudia forced herself to wait until she was certain that the wardress had truly left and was not watching her through a spy hole. Once she was sure she was not observed, Claudia crawled in frantic haste to the corner where she had hidden the straw and picked it up between her lips. Still on her knees she crossed to the billy-can and stooped over it.

She drew the first mouthful through the straw and let it trickle down her throat, closing her eyes with pleasure. It was as though she were drinking down a magic potion. She felt new strength and resolve flow through her veins.

She drank most of the contents of the billy-can, drawing out the pleasure of it until it was almost totally dark in the cell, but she could not bring herself to eat the sticky mess of maize cake smeared into the dirt.

She hoarded the remains of the water, taking the wire handle of the billy-can between her teeth and carefully moving it to the far corner of the cell where she could ration herself to small sips during the long hours ahead. She settled down for the night feeling almost cheerful and a little light-headed as though she had drunk of champagne rather than plain unboiled river water.

'I can endure anything they do to me,' she whispered to herself. 'They aren't going to break me. I won't let them, I won't.'

Her mood did not last. Almost as soon as it was fully dark in the cell, she realized her terrible mistake in leaving the uneaten maize cake on the floor.

Last night there had been only one rat, and it had fled when she screamed at it. This night the odour of food brought them pouring through the gaps in the roof. To her frenzied imagination, it seemed that the floor of the cell was swarming with furry bodies. The smell of them clogged her nostrils, the nauseating ratty smell like boiling horns and hooves in a glue pot. She cowered in her corner, shivering with cold and horror, and they brushed against her legs and scurried over her feet, squeaking and squealing as they fought for the scraps of spilled porridge.

At last, Claudia succumbed to panic. Screaming, on the edge of hysteria, she kicked out at them wildly; one of them whipped round and bit her naked ankle, the sharp little teeth were like a razor cut She screamed again and kicked, trying to dislodge it, but for a few dreadful seconds its curved teeth were buried in her flesh, and then at last she sent it flying into the darkness.

The rat hit the billy-can containing her treasured water and she heard the metal clank against the wall and the liquid splash onto the earthen floor. She crawled to the overturned container and wept with despair.

After long hours of horror and dark terror, the rats consumed the last of the maize and disappeared back through the roof. Claudia sank to her knees, exhausted both physically and emotionally.

'Please God, let it end. I can't go on.

She toppled over on her side and lay in the dirt, shivering and sobbing softly to herself, and at last dropped into the dark void of oblivion.

She woke with something tugging at her hair, and a strange grinding sound very close to her ear. Still groggy with sleep it took her long seconds to realize what was happening to her. She had slumped over sideways and one cheek was pressed to the dirt floor. She lay for a moment, enduring the sharp pulls on her hair and the grinding crunching in her uppermost ear and then the terror came back to her in full force.

278

A rat was chewing off her hair, cutting it with those sharp curved incisors, gathering it for nesting material. So great was her horror that it paralysed her. She could not move. Her whole body tingled, her stomach knotted with cramps and her toes and fingers curled with the strength of revulsion.

Suddenly she was no longer terrified. Her fear changed to anger. In one lithe movement she rolled to her feet and began to hunt the loathsome creature.

Relentlessly she pursued it around the cell, following it only by sound, the tiny scratch and patter of its feet. She no longer kicked out wildly, but deliberately aimed each blow at the sound. Twice the creature tried to climb to safety, but each time Claudia heard it and used her whole body to sweep it from the wall and knock it back to the floor.

This killing anger was an emotion she had never experienced before. It heightened all her senses, it rendered her hearing so acute that she could visualize each movement of her prey; it quickened her physical responses so her kicks were fast and powerful and when one of them landed on the warm furry body, the shrill squeal of pain and fear from the rat inflamed her.

She cornered it against the door of the cell and again stamped on it. She felt the small bones break under her heel, and she stamped again and again, sobbing with the effort, keeping it up until the carcass was soft and mushy under her feet.

When, at last, she backed away and sank down in her corner, she was still trembling, but no longer with terror.

'I've never killed anything before,' she thought, amazed at herself and this secret savage side to her nature which she had never suspected existed.

She waited for the familiar feeling of guilt and disgust to overwhelm her. Instead she felt as strong as though she had come through some ordeal which had armed her and equipped her to overcome whatever dangers and hardships lay ahead.

'I'm not going to give in, not ever again,' she whispered. 'I'm going to fight and to kill if I have to. I shall survive.'

* * *

In the morning when the wardress came for the billy-can, Claudia confronted her resolutely, thrusting her face only inches from the black woman's, and keeping her voice measured but firm.

'Take this out.' She indicated the rat's carcass with her foot. The woman hesitated and Claudia said, 'Do it, now!' And the wardress picked up the mangled carcass by the tip of the tail, and glanced back at Claudia with a measure of respect in her dark eyes.

Carrying the empty billy and the dead rat she left the cell. When she returned a few minutes later with the billy-can refilled and the bowl of maize meal, Claudia subdued her thirst and maintained her new attitude of calm authority as she indicated the sewage bucket.

'That has to be cleaned,' she said, and the woman snapped a retort in Portuguese.

'I'll do it.' Claudia did not waver, holding the woman's gaze until she broke the eye contact. Only then did she turn her back and offer her manacled hands to the wardress.

'Undo these,' she ordered, and obediently the wardress un-clipped the key from her webbing belt.

Claudia almost cried out as the handcuffs came away. The blood rushed back to her hands and Claudia held them to her chest and massaged them tenderly, biting her lips against the pain, horrified by the condition of her swollen hands and torn bruised wrists.

The wardress prodded her in the small of the back and gave an order in Portuguese. Claudia took up the handle of the sewage bucket and, brushing past the woman, climbed the stairs. The sunlight and warmth and clean dry air were like a benediction.

Claudia looked around the stockade quickly. It was obviously a women's prison, for a few dispirited feminine figures lolled in the dust beneath the single ebony tree in the centre. They were in ragged loin-cloths, their naked upper bodies so painfully thin that the ribs stood out clearly beneath the dusty dark skin and their breasts, even those of the younger women, were empty and dangled loosely as the ears of a spaniel. Claudia wondered what their crimes had been, or if their mere existence had caused their captors offence.

She saw that her own bunker was only one of a row of a dozen or so. It was obvious that these were reserved for the more important or dangerous prisoners.

The gates of the stockade were guarded by a pair of burly black females dressed in the usual tiger stripes and toting AK assault rifles. They peered curiously at Claudia and discussed her

280

with animation. Beyond the gates, Claudia had a glimpse of the broad green flow of the Pungwe river, and for a moment entertained fanciful visions of plunging into it to bathe her battered body and wash her filthy clothes, but the wardress prodded her painfully in the back and urged her towards the screened latrines at the rear of the stockade.

When they reached them the wardress made hand signals for Claudia to empty her bucket into the communal pit, and then turned away to chat with one of the other wardresses who had sauntered across to join them with her AK 47 rifle over her shoulder.

The back wall of the latrine was also the rear wall of the stockade. However, it offered no avenue of escape. The poles were as thick as her leg, lashed securely together with bark rope, and their tops were several feet higher than she could reach.

She abandoned the idea of escape before it was fully formed and tipped the contents of the bucket into the deep pit. Immediately a humming cloud of flies rose from the depths and circled her head.

Wrinkling her nose with disgust, Claudia was backing towards the exit when a soft whistle stopped her dead. It was a low-pitched mournful note, so unobtrusive that she would have ignored it completely if she had not heard it so often before. It was one of the clandestine signals that Sean and his trackers used. Sean had told her once that it was the call of a bird called a bou-bou shrike, and because of its associations rather than its pitch, it electrified her.

She glanced quickly towards the screened entrance to the latrine, but it was safe. She heard the voices of the wardress and her colleague still chatting outside, and she pursed her lips and tried a soft unconvincing imitation of the whistle.

Instantly it was repeated from just beyond the back wall of the latrine and Claudia's hopes soared. She dropped the bucket and ran to the wall of poles, putting her eye to one of the larger chinks. She almost screamed when an eye looked back at her from only the thickness of the poles and then a voice, a well-remembered voice, whispered, '*Jambo*, memsahib.'

'Matatu,' she gasped.

'Silly little bugger.' Matatu gave her the only words of English he knew, and she had to fight to prevent herself bursting out with the laughter of relief and hope and amusement at the incongruity of that greeting.

'Oh Matatu, I love you,' she blurted, and a folded scrap of paper was thrust through the chink into her face. The instant her fingers closed on it, Matatu's eye was snatched away from the peep-hole as though on a fishing line.

'Matatu,' she whispered desperately, but he was gone. She had spoken too loudly and she heard the wardress call out, and her footsteps at the entrance.

Claudia spun round and with the same movement crouched over the reeking pit. The wardress looked round the thatched screen and Claudia snapped at her furiously, 'Get out, can't you see I'm busy.'

And the woman involuntarily jerked her head back. Claudia was trembling with excitement as she unfolded the note and recognized the handwriting, and at the same time she was stricken with terror that it would be taken from her before she could read it. She refolded it quickly and slipped it deeply into the back pocket of her trousers, where she would be able to retrieve it even with her hands cuffed behind her.

Now she was eager to return to the privacy of her cell. The wardress pushed her down the stairs, but without the viciousness of before.

Claudia replaced the sewage bucket in the corner and then when the wardress pointed at her wrists, she held them out obediently. The touch of the metal on her abraded and bruised skin seemed even more galling than it had been before. The muscles and tendons of her upper arms and shoulders knotted in protest.

Once Claudia was manacled the wardress seemed to recapture her harsh mood of authority. She tipped the contents of the maize bowl onto the floor and lifted her boot to grind it into the dirt.

Claudia flew at her. 'Don't you dare!' she hissed, thrusting her face close to the woman's, glaring into her eyes so viciously that she recoiled involuntarily.

'Get out!' Claudia told her. '*Allez!* Vamoose!' And the wardress backed out of the cell with a muttered but unconvincing show of defiance, and dragged the door closed behind her.

Claudia was amazed at her own courage. She leaned against the door trembling with the effort that the contest of wills had cost her, only then realizing the risk that she had taken – she could have been brutally beaten or deprived altogether of her precious supply of water.

It was Sean's letter that had given her the strength and bravado to defy the wardress. Leaning against the door, she reached back into her pocket and touched the scrap of folded notepaper, merely to reassure herself that it was safe. She would not read it yet. She wanted to delay and savour that pleasure. Instead, she retrieved her drinking straw from its hiding-place.

After she had drunk from the billy, she ate the maize cake, delicately picking it out of the dirt with her teeth and trying to shake loose the earth and dirt that clung to the sticky lumps of porridge. She was determined not to leave a scrap of it, not only because she was hungry but because she knew she would have need of all her strength in the days ahead, and because she had learned that food scraps attracted the rats. Only when she had eaten and drunk, did she allow herself the luxurious pleasure of reading Sean's note.

She took it out of her pocket and carefully smoothed it between her swollen fingers. Then she squatted and placed it in the beam of sunlight that fell in a corner of the cell, and at last turned and knelt over it.

She read slowly, moving her lips like a semi-literate, forming every word that he had written as though she could taste it on her tongue.

'Be strong, it won't be for much longer and remember, I love you. Whatever happens, I love you.' Her vision swam with tears as she read his last words, and then she sat back and whispered softly, 'I'll be strong. I promise you that I'll be strong for you, and I love you too, with my very existence, I love you.'

*　　*　　*

'They may fight like women,' said Sergeant Alphonso, as he surveyed the piles of captured Zimbabwean army equipment. 'But at least they dress like warriors.'

The uniforms had been supplied by Britain as part of their aid commitment to Mugabe after the capitulation of Ian Smith's white regime. They were the finest quality, and Alphonso and his men stripped off their old faded and patched tiger-striped battledress with alacrity. In particular they were delighted with the gleaming black leather paratrooper boots with which they replaced their eclectic collection of tattered joggers and grubby tennis shoes.

Once they had decked themselves out in this captured finery

and fallen in on the beaten-earth parade ground, Sean and Job went down their ranks checking and instructing them on the correct way to wear each item of uniform. The quartermaster tailor followed behind them, correcting any gross discrepancy in size and fit.

'They don't have to be perfect,' Sean said. 'They won't be on parade, just good enough to pass a casual glance. We haven't got time to waste on the niceties of dress.'

After the men were fully kitted out, Sean and Job worked on their plan of Grand Reef base for the rest of that day and most of the night. First they sat on opposite sides of a desk in the headquarters communications room and brain-stormed for every detail of the base lay-out that they could dredge from their memories. By nightfall, they were satisfied that they had the most accurate picture that they could hope for. However, Sean had learned from experience that it was difficult for an illiterate to visualize physical reality from a two-dimensional drawing, and discreet enquiry had revealed that almost all his new command, although battle-tried warriors, could neither read nor write.

Most of the rest of that night, they worked on building a scale model of the base, setting it out on the beaten surface of the parade ground, working by lantern light. Job had an artistic flair and whittled model buildings from the soft balsa-like wood of the baobab tree, and used water-washed pebbles of various colours from the sandbanks of the river to lay out the airstrip and roads and perimeter fences of the base.

The following morning the raiding party was paraded and inspected by Captain Job and Sergeant Alphonso and then seated around the model in a ring. The model proved to be a major success, provoking lively comment and query.

First Sean described the raid, moving matchboxes down the pebble roadways to represent the column of Unimogs, illustrating the diversionary attack on the perimeter, the withdrawal of the loaded trucks and the rendezvous on the Umtali road. Once he had finished he handed his pointer to Sergeant Alphonso.

'All right, Sergeant, explain it to us again.' The ring of attentive troopers delighted in correcting the occasional mistakes and omissions that Alphonso made. When he was finished he handed the pointer to his senior corporal to repeat the lecture. After five repetitions, they all had it perfectly memorized and even General China was impressed.

'It only remains to see if you can do it as well as you explain it,' he told Sean.

'Just give me the trucks,' Sean promised.

'Sergeant Alphonso was with the unit that originally captured them. He knows where they are hidden. Incidentally the guards major whose uniform you will use was killed in the same action.'

'How long ago was that?' Sean asked.

'About two months ago.'

'Beauty!' said Sean bitterly. 'That means that those trucks have been lying in the bush all that time. What makes you think they are still there, or that they are still in running order?'

'Colonel,' China gave that thin cold smile that Sean was coming to know and loathe so well, 'for Miss Monterro's sake you had better pray they are.' The smile vanished. 'Now, while the men draw their rations and ammunition, you and I will have a final discussion. Come with me, Colonel.'

Once they were in the communications room of the command bunker, China turned to Sean with his expression bleak. 'During the night, I received a radio message from my agent in Grand Reef base. He only transmits in an emergency, otherwise the risk is too high. This is an emergency. Training on the Stinger systems is complete. They have orders to move the missiles out of Grand Reef within the next seventy-two hours, depending on availability of transport aircraft.'

Sean whistled softly. 'Seventy-two hours – in that case we won't make it.'

'Colonel, all I can tell you is that you had better make it. If you don't, you will have no further value to me and I will begin thinking of old times.' He touched his damaged ear significantly. Sean stared him out silently until China went on, 'However, not all the news is bad, Colonel. My agent will meet you in Umtali and give you full intelligence on the buildings where the Stingers are being held, the room used as a lecture theatre, and the training manuals. He will accompany you to the base. He is well-known to the guards at the gates. He will assist your entry and guide you to the training centre.'

'That's something,' Sean growled. 'Where will I meet him?'

'There is a night club in Umtali. The Stardust, a gathering place for pimps and whores. He will be there every evening from eight until midnight. Alphonso knows the Club. He will take you to it.'

'How will I recognize your agent?'

'He will wear a tee-shirt with a large portrait of the comic book hero, Superman, on the chest,' China said, and Sean closed his eyes as though in pain while China went on. 'The man's name is Cuthbert.'

Sean shook his head and whispered, 'I don't believe this is happening to me. Superman and Cuthbert!' He shook his head again as if to clear it. 'What about the RZ with the porters at St Mary's mission?'

'That is arranged,' China assured him. 'The porters will cross the border tomorrow night as soon as it is dark and conceal themselves in the caves in the mountains above the mission station to await your arrival.'

Sean nodded and changed the thread of the discussion.

'If we leave now, how long will it take for us to reach the spot where the Unimogs are hidden?'

'You should be there before noon tomorrow.'

'Is there anything else we should discuss?' Sean asked, and when China shook his head, Sean stood up, slung his AKM assault rifle on one shoulder and with his free hand lifted the small canvas duffel bag that contained the dead guards major's uniform and his personal kit.

'Until we meet again, General China.'

'Until we meet again, I will take good care of Miss Monterro. Never fear, Colonel.'

* * *

The column was heavily laden. Each man carried food and water for two days together with ammunition, the extra belts for the RPD machine-guns, grenades and rockets for the RPG 7 launchers.

Though they could not run under that weight, Sergeant Alphonso in the van set a cracking pace. Before nightfall they passed through the Renamo lines into the 'destruction area', a free-fire zone where there was a possibility of encountering Frelimo patrols, and Sean ordered a change of formation. They opened up to intervals of ten metres between the men in the single file of the main column and he posted flankers at the head and tail to guard against surprise attack.

They kept going hard during the night with ten-minute breaks every two hours, and by dawn they had covered almost forty miles. During the dawn break, Sean moved up to the head of the column and squatted between Alphonso and Job.

'How much further to the trucks?' Sean demanded.

'We have done well,' Alphonso replied, and pointed ahead. 'The trucks are there in that valley.'

They were on the foreslope of another area of hilly forested ground and below them the terrain was broken and bad. Sean appreciated why General China had chosen this area of the Serra da Gorongosa to defend. There were no roads in this wilderness and an attacking army would have to fight its way past an endless series of natural strong points and fortresses.

The valley that Alphonso pointed out was some miles ahead of them and beyond it the country changed from its savage mood and flattened into a broad gentle plain. Down there the dark forest was broken up and blotched with paler grasslands.

Alphonso pointed to the horizon. 'Over there are the railway line and the road to the coast . . .' He was about to speak again when Sean caught his arm to silence him and cocked his head in a listening attitude.

It was some seconds before the sound separated itself from the gentle susurration of the dawn wind in the forest below them and hardened into the whine of turbo engines and spinning rotors.

'There!' Job's eyesight was phenomenal and he picked out the approaching specks even against the dark background of hills and forests.

'Hinds.' Sean spotted them and Alphonso shouted a warning. 'Take cover.' The column scattered into cover and they watched the gunships come on, rising and dropping as they kept low over the hills, sailing northwards towards the Renamo lines in an extended formation.

Sean watched them through the Russian-made binoculars he had acquired from the Renamo stores. It was the first opportunity he had had to study a Hind at leisure. There were four of them and Sean surmised that there would be three flights of four machines to a full squadron of twelve.

'My God, they are grotesque,' he murmured. It seemed impossible that anything so heavy and misshapen could ever break the ties of gravity. The engines were housed in the top of the fuselage below the main rotor and formed the humpback that gave the machine its nickname. The air intakes to the turbos were situated

287

above the cockpit canopy. The belly drooped like that of a pregnant sow. The nose was deformed by the hanging turret which housed the Gatling-cannon and from the stubby wings and bloated belly were suspended an untidy array of rocket systems and ordnance stations and radar aerials.

At the rear of the engine mountings the ungainly lines of the machine were further disturbed by another extraneous structure which seemed to have been tacked onto it as an afterthought.

'Exhaust suppressor boxes.' Sean remembered an article he had read in one of the flying magazines to which he subscribed. These structures masked the exhaust emissions of the twin turbo engines and shielded them from the infra-red sensors of hostile missiles. The author of the article had lauded their efficacy, but although they made the machines almost invulnerable to heat-seekers, the weight of the devices combined with that of the titanium armour to reduce severely the Hind's speed and range. Sean wished he had read the article with more attention, for he could not recall the figures for airspeed and range that the author had quoted.

The flight of gunships passed a mile or so to the east of them boring steadily northwards.

'General China is in for a breakfast show,' Job remarked as he rose from cover to reassemble the column and continue the march.

Although they had been going all night the pace never slackened and even Sean was impressed by the condition and training of Alphonso's company. 'Almost as good as the Scouts,' he decided, and then grinned to himself. 'Nobody could be that good.'

More than once, Sean dropped back to check that the men he had in the drag were anti-tracking and covering spoor. For now there was real danger that a Frelimo patrol might find them. He had fallen only a few hundred metres behind the rear of the column and was down on one knee studying the earth intently, when suddenly he knew that he was not alone, that he was being watched.

Instantly Sean threw himself forward, the rifle coming off his shoulder as he rolled over twice into the cover of a fallen log beside the path and froze, his finger on the trigger, his gaze raking the bush where he thought he had seen the flirt of movement.

It was closer than he had imagined. From the clump of grass

288

right beside him came a mischievous giggle and Sean raised his head and whispered furiously, 'I've warned you not to sneak up on me like that.'

Matatu's head popped out of the grass and he grinned merrily.

'You are getting old, my *Bwana*. I could have stolen your socks and boots without you knowing.'

'And I could have shot your brown backside full of holes. Did you find the mem?'

Matatu nodded and his smile slipped.

'Where is she?'

'Half a day's march upstream, in a stockade with many other women.'

'Is she well?'

Matatu hesitated, torn between telling the truth and telling Sean what would please him. Then he sighed and shook his head.

'They keep her in a hole in the ground, and there are marks on her arms and legs. They force her to work with the shit-buckets . . .' He broke off as he saw Sean's expression and went on hurriedly, 'but she laughed when she saw me.'

'Did you give her the paper?'

'*Ndio*. She hid it in her clothing.'

'Nobody saw you?'

The reply was beneath Matatu's dignity and Sean smiled. 'I know, nobody sees Matatu unless Matatu wants them to . . .' Sean broke off and both of them looked upwards.

Faintly, from far away, came the now familiar whistle of turbo engines and rotors.

'The Hinds, returning from clobbering the Renamo lines,' Sean murmured. The machines were out of sight beyond the canopy of the forest trees, but the sound passed swiftly southwards.

'With their limited range, their base can't be too far,' Sean thought and looked at Matatu thoughtfully. 'Matatu, those *indeki*, could you find the place where they come from, and where they return to?'

Matatu's gaze flickered with a moment's doubt, and then he grinned, once again brimming with bravado.

'Matatu can follow anything, man or animal or *indeki*, anywhere it goes,' he boasted confidently.

'Go!' Sean ordered. 'Find the place. There will be trucks and many white men. It will be well guarded. Don't let them catch you.'

Matatu looked affronted and Sean clasped his shoulder with affection. 'When you have found the place, come back to General China's camp at the Pungwe river. I will meet you there.'

As unquestioningly as a gun dog sent to retrieve a downed pheasant, Matatu bounded to his feet and tucked up the folds of his loin-cloth.

'Until we meet again, go in peace, my *Bwana*.'

'Go in peace, Matatu,' Sean called softly after him as the little man trotted away into the south. Sean watched him out of sight and then hurried to catch up with Alphonso's column.

'They keep her in a hole in the ground, and there are marks on her arms and her legs.' Matatu's words echoed in his head, fuelling his imagination and his anger and his determination.

'Hold on, my love. Stick it out. I'll come to get you . . . soon,' he promised her, and himself.

* * *

They crossed the rim of another line of rocky kopjes, using a screen of jesse bush to conceal their movements against the skyline, and from good cover on the foreslope Alphonso pointed down into the valley below.

'That is how we brought the trucks in,' he explained, and Sean saw that the dry river-course would be the only access for a vehicle into this bad country. Even then it must have been a laborious task negotiating the rocky chutes and barriers that broke up the stretches of smooth river sand in the depths of the gorge.

'Where did you hide the trucks?' Sean asked without lowering his binoculars, and Alphonso chuckled.

'Unless Frelimo is cleverer than I think they are, I will show you.'

They left sentries posted along the ridge, to warn of the approach of an enemy patrol, then Alphonso led the rest of the column down into the gorge. The lower they descended, the steeper became the sides, until there were sheer cliffs on each side and they were forced to traverse along a narrow game trail to reach the river bottom. It was suffocatingly hot in the narrow gorge, no breeze reached down here, and the rock absorbed the sun's heat and threw it back at them.

'The trucks?' Sean demanded impatiently, and Alphonso pointed to the cliffs opposite.

'In there,' he said, and Sean was about to snarl irritably at him when he realized that the cliffs had been carved by wind and flood water over the ages.

'Caves?' he asked, and Alphonso led him through the ankle-deep river sand to the cliff face.

Some of the cave entrances were merely scooped shallowly into the red rock, others had collapsed or were clogged with debris brought down by the summer floods. Alphonso indicated one of these and gave an order to his men. They stacked their weapons and began to clear the debris from the mouth of the cavern.

Within an hour they had opened it sufficiently for Alphonso and Sean to scramble through into the cave. Deep in the gloomy gut, Sean made out the shape of the first truck. His eyes accustomed themselves to the poor light as he moved towards it and he saw others parked beyond it.

'How the hell did you get them in here?' he asked incredulously.

'We pushed and carried them,' Alphonso explained.

'I hope to hell we'll be able to get them out again,' Sean muttered, and climbed onto the running board of the nearest vehicle.

It was coated with a thick layer of red dust. He yanked open the door on the driver's side and sneezed in the dust, but saw with relief that the key was still in the ignition.

He reached in and turned it. Nothing happened. The ignition light stayed dark and the needles on the dashboard instruments never flickered.

'I disconnected the batteries,' Alphonso told him, and Sean grunted.

'Bright lad, but how the hell did you know to do that?'

'Before the war, I was a bus-driver in Vila de Manica,' Alphonso explained. It was odd to think that he had ever had such a prosaic occupation.

'All right,' Sean said. 'Then you can help me get this one started. Is there a tool box?'

Each of the trucks was equipped with two spare tyres, hand

pump, tool box, tarpaulin and long-range fuel tank. Once Sean had reconnected the battery of the first truck, there was sufficient charge to produce a dull red glow in the ignition lamp on the dashboard and to raise the needle of the fuel gauge to the 'half' position but insufficient to kick the engine over.

'Find the crank handle,' Sean ordered. It was secured behind the passenger seat in the cab. Two hefty Shanganes swung the engine over with such gusto that it fired and stuttered and then burst into a steady roar. Thick blue exhaust smoke filled the cavern and Sean lifted his foot off the accelerator pedal. Two of the tyres were flat and had to be pumped by hand. While this was being done, the troopers cleared the last of the rocks and tree trunks from the mouth of the cave and with the transmission in four-wheel drive, Sean reversed sharply down the incline and bounced and jolted over the rough ground.

When the truck hung up on the boulders of the river bank and the wheels spun without purchase, twenty men flung their combined weight on it, and by brute force shoved it through. The Unimog crashed over the lip of the bank and into the riverbed. Sean drove it clear and parked under the opposite cliffs. He left the engine running to charge the depleted battery and they climbed back to the cavern and started work on the second truck.

Apart from flat tyres and batteries, they found no serious defects in any of the vehicles. One after the other, they coaxed the engines to life and then manhandled them down into the riverbed. It was the middle of the afternoon by the time all three trucks were lined up on the white river sand.

'Get the men to change uniforms now,' Sean ordered. 'Leave their other gear in the cave.'

Joking and laughing, they stripped off their Renamo tiger stripes and donned the British-pattern battledress of the Zimbabwean army. While they were busy, Sean went over the vehicles again. He found the army registration papers in a plastic wallet in the cubby-holes of each of the Unimogs.

'Hope we never have to show them,' he grumbled to Job. 'They are probably listed as stolen or destroyed.'

He opened the caps on the fuel tanks and physically checked the contents of each.

'Enough to get us to Grand Reef and back to St Mary's,' he estimated. 'With not much to spare.'

292

He ordered the windscreen and side windows of the cabs to be cleaned, but the bodywork to be left as it was, caked with mud and dust. It gave them the appearance of a patrol returning from a sortie into the deep bush and, more importantly, partially obscured the military markings and registration numbers.

Once the men had changed into their disguise and cached their Renamo uniforms, Sean and Job inspected each man and his equipment minutely, before allowing him to board one of the Unimogs.

It was almost five o'clock before they were ready to leave. Both Job and Alphonso had heavy-vehicle driver's licences and one of the Renamo troopers who gloried in the name of Ferdinand da Costa claimed driving experience. Sean took the passenger seat beside him to check his performance.

Job drove the leading truck, Alphonso in the middle and Sean and the learner driver in the rear. Apart from a heavy foot on the accelerator pedal, Ferdinand da Costa proved himself an adequate driver, but Sean took the wheel from him at the difficult places.

In line astern, they churned through the heavy sand, following in the wheel ruts of Job's Unimog, winding up the river-course for half a mile before they reached the first obstacle.

It required the combined efforts of all forty men to heave and shove the trucks up the first rocky chute in the riverbed, and even then they had to cut twenty-foot-long mopane poles and use them as levers to prise the wheels up over the larger boulders.

The powerful truck motors bellowed in high revolutions, blue diesel smoke billowed from the exhausts and Sean remarked to Job, 'An open invitation to every Frelimo within twenty miles to join the party.' Then he checked his wristwatch. 'We are falling behind our schedule.'

They tried to make up time along the easier stretches of the river-course, but the sunset and darkness caught them still almost twenty kilometres from the main east-to-west road between the sea and the border post at Umtali.

Nightfall made the journey more arduous. Sean dared not use the trucks' headlights, and they had to proceed in darkness alleviated only by starlight and a moon in its last quarter.

It was after midnight before they could at last leave the riverbed by negotiating a low spot in the bank. With four men walking ahead of the lead truck to guide it around ant-bear holes and

293

other concealed obstacles, they struck out directly southwards and within two hours had intersected the overgrown disused track that Alphonso had told Sean about.

Sean called a halt and they spread the field map on the bonnet of the lead truck and by flashlight studied it anxiously.

'We are here,' Alphonso told him. 'This track runs up to an old asbestos mine, it was abandoned by the Portuguese in 1963 at the start of the Frelimo war.'

'We'll rest up here,' Sean decided. 'Get the trucks off the road and covered with branches. We must expect the Hinds to over-fly us sometime tomorrow. No cooking-fires, no smoking.'

At four o'clock that afternoon, they woke those still asleep and ate a hasty meal of cold rations. Sean ordered the journey to be resumed and they stripped the camouflage from the trucks. They boarded the entire raiding party except for the four men who walked ahead of the leading truck, examining the ancient overgrown wheel-ruts of the track for Frelimo anti-vehicle land-mines, probing any suspicious lump or hollow with a bayonet before waving the column forward.

The sun was just setting when they at last came in sight of the main road, its macadamized surface snaking through the open forest and winding around the scattered kopjes. Sean halted the column well back out of sight of the road and went forward with Job, leaving Alphonso in command.

From the top of a commanding hillock they kept the road under observation until it was fully dark. During that time two patrols passed, both heading eastwards, each comprised of three or four battered and dusty Unimogs packed with armed men in Zimbabwean combat gear, and with an RPD light machine-gun mounted above the cab.

They rumbled along with strict intervals of a hundred metres between vehicles and watching them through the binoculars Sean remarked, 'Well, at least we look like the real thing.'

'Except for your pale face,' Job pointed out.

'A birth defect,' Sean apologized. 'But I'll keep it out of sight until it's needed.'

They scrambled down from the hilltop and trudged back along the track to the hidden trucks.

'From here you are on your own,' Sean told Ferdinand, the driver. 'Do try to remember to put the clutch in before you change into bottom gear, you'll find it a great help.'

Dressed in the uniform of the deceased guards major, Sean climbed into the back of the cab, behind Job's driving seat. The space was barely sufficient to contain him; he had to twist his shoulders at an angle from his hips and sit flat on the metal floorboards. It was uncomfortable to begin with, but Sean knew that within a few hours it would become agony. However, he was out of sight and yet able to communicate with Job merely by raising his voice.

Without headlights, the column drove the last mile to the juncture with the main road. The scouts they had sent ahead whistled that the road was clear and they raced forward and swung onto the metalled surface, heading westwards towards the border.

As soon as they were safely onto the highway, they switched on the headlights and dropped their speed to fifty kilometres an hour, and adjusted their spacing to the regulation hundred-metre intervals. To an observer they were just another Zimbabwean mechanized patrol.

'So far, so good,' Job called over the back of the seat to where Sean was hiding.

'What's the time?'

'Seven minutes past eight.'

'Perfect, we'll hit the border post just after ten, when the guards are thinking of going off duty.'

The hundred kilometres to the border seemed much further. The metal floorboards of the cab were corrugated and cut into Sean's buttocks, transferring the impact of every pothole in the neglected highway up his spine into his skull.

'Get under the tarp! Border post ahead!' Job called at last.

'Not too bloody soon,' Sean assured him as the truck slowed and the overhead floodlights flooded the cab. Sean pulled the tarpaulin over his head and sank down as low as he could below the seatback.

He felt the truck brake and trundle to a halt. Job switched off the engine and opened the door of the cab.

'Wish me luck,' he muttered, as he stepped down from the cab.

Neither of them knew what to expect. The border formalities must surely be relaxed to accommodate the interchange of troops guarding the railway line. Job was dressed for the part and in possession of a genuine army pay book and ID. The truck's registration papers were likewise genuine and yet they could be compromised by some small unforeseen detail or by an alert border guard.

If anything went wrong, Job would give a single long blast on his whistle and they would shoot their way out. All the rifles and rocket-launchers were loaded, and the RPD machine-guns on the cabs were manned.

As the minutes drew out so Sean's nerves stretched tighter. He expected at any moment the shrilling of Job's whistle and the shouting and the gunfire.

Then at last there was the crunch of footsteps in gravel and the voices of Job and a stranger approaching the truck. Both doors of the cab opened and Sean tried to shrink himself as the truck tipped slightly under the weight of more than one man climbing aboard.

'Where do you want me to drop you off?' Job asked casually in Shona, and a voice Sean had never heard before replied, 'At the edge of town. I'll tell you where.'

Sean turned his head a stealthy inch and through the gap between the seats saw the blue serge cloth of a customs inspector's uniform. With horror, he realized that Job was giving an off-duty inspector a lift into Umtali.

The truck pulled forward and the inspector lowered the side window and shouted to the guards on the barrier.

'It's all right, open!' And as they accelerated ahead, Sean had a glimpse of the raised barrier through the window. He had to cover his mouth to prevent himself laughing aloud with relief and triumph.

On the back of the Unimog, the troopers seemed infected by the same reckless spirit of abandon. They were singing as the column wound down the hill to the town of Umtali. Job was casually discussing with the customs inspector the merits of the Stardust Night Club, and the price of a short time with one of the bar girls.

'Tell Bodo, the barman at the Stardust, that you are a friend of mine,' the inspector advised Job when they dropped him off on the outskirts of the town. 'He'll get a special price for you, and tell you which of the girls have the clap and which ones are clean.'

As they pulled away, Sean could at last crawl out from behind the seat and slump gratefully into the passenger seat.

'What the hell kind of trick was that?' he complained. 'You damn nearly gave me a hernia.'

'What better way to get VIP treatment,' Job chuckled, 'than to have the head of the customs service as a pal. You should have seen the guards at the border saluting us!'

'Where is this night club?'

'Not far, we'll be there before eleven.'

They drove in silence for a few minutes while Sean rehearsed the next order he had to give. He waited until Job turned the truck into a dimly lit side street and switched off the engine. In the side mirror, Sean watched the other two Unimogs pull in behind them, cut their engines and switch off their headlights.

'Back home again,' Job chuckled. 'Nothing to it.'

'Back home,' Sean agreed. 'And back home is where you are going to stay.'

There was a long silence and then Job turned his head and looked at Sean thoughtfully.

'What do you mean by that?'

'This is the end of the road for us, Job. You aren't coming to Grand Reef, you aren't high-jacking any Stingers, and you sure as hell aren't coming back to Mozambique with me.'

'You're firing me?' Job asked.

'That's it, pal. I've got no more use for you.'

Sean took a small wad of Zimbabwe dollars, part of the expense money General China had provided, and offered it to Job. 'Get rid of that uniform as soon as you can. If they catch you in it, they'll shoot you. Take the next train back to Harare and go see Reema at the office. She's holding about four thousand dollars in back pay and bonus for you. That will be enough to tide you over until Capo Monterro's estate pays out the money it owes us. My lawyers will handle that. You will be entitled to half of that . . .'

Job ignored the proffered money. 'You remember that day on Hill 31?' he asked quietly.

'Shit, Job, don't pull that sob stuff on me.'

'You came back for me,' Job said.

'Because sometimes I'm just a bloody fool.'

'Me too,' Job smiled. 'Sometimes I'm just a bloody fool.'

'Listen, Job, this is not your shauri any more. There is nothing in it for you. Get out. Go back to your village, buy yourself another couple of pretty young wives with Capo's dollars. Sit in the sun and drink a few pots of beer.'

'Nice try, Sean. Pity it didn't work. I'm coming back with you.'

'I'm giving you a direct order.'

'I'm refusing to obey it, so convene a court-martial.'

Sean laughed and shook his head. 'She's my woman, so it's okay for me to risk my life.'

'I've been nursemaiding you for almost twenty years and I'm not giving up now,' Job said, and opened the cab door. 'Let's go and find Cuthbert in his Superman suit.'

Sean left his cap and tunic on the seat, the insignia of a famous regiment would be out of place in a cheap night club. The Stardust was at the end of the lane in a converted furniture factory, a barn-like building with all its windows blacked out. They could hear the music from a hundred paces out, the hypnotic repetitive beat of the new wave African jazz.

Women clustered around the entrance. In the overhead light their dresses were as colourful as butterfly wings. Their hairstyles were flocculent afros, or the intricate beaded dreadlocks of the Rastafarians, their faces painted into death masks of rouge and purple lipsticks with iridescent green eyelids like iguana lizards.

They swarmed around Sean and Job, rubbing themselves against them like cats.

'Hey man, get me in!' they pleaded. 'Give me five dollars to get in, darling, I'll dance with you and jig-jig, man. Everything.'

'Come on, whitey.' A child with a tender immature body in a shiny dress of cheap nylon, the face of a black Madonna and ancient weary eyes, seized Sean's arm. 'Take me with you and I'll give you something you've never had before.' She reached down the front of Sean's body and cupped her hand to fondle him. Sean took her wrist and restrained her.

'What have you got that I've never had before, sweetheart? Aids?'

They pushed their way through the rustling nylon skirts and clouds of cheap perfume and at the door paid their five dollars. The doorman stamped their wrists with an indelible dye in lieu of an entrance ticket and they ducked through the black curtain.

The music was a stunning, painful assault, the lights were revolving strobes and ultra-violet. The dance floor pulsated with humanity transformed into a single primitive organism, like some gigantic amoeba.

'Where is the bar?' Sean bellowed into Job's ear.

'I'm a stranger here myself.' Job seized his arm and they struggled through the engulfing sea of light and sound and gyrating bodies.

The faces around them were transported as in religious fervour, eyeballs rolled glaring white in the rays of the ultra-violet lamps, sweat glistened on upraised arms and streamed in rivulets down jet-black cheeks.

They reached the bar. 'Don't risk the whisky!' Job yelled. 'And make them open the beer in front of you.'

They drank directly from the cans, besieged in a corner of the bar with the ocean of humanity pressing hard against them.

There were a few white faces, all male, tourists and peace corps and military advisors, but most of the clientele were black soldiers still in uniform so that Sean and Job blended into their surroundings.

'Where are you, Cuthbert, in your Superman shirt?' Sean pushed away one of the more persistent bar girls, and peered over the heads of the dancers. 'We'll never find him in here.'

'Ask one of the barmen,' Job suggested.

'Good thinking.' Sean reached across and grabbed the front of the barman's shirt to get his attention, and then stuck a five-dollar bank note into his top pocket and shouted the question in his ear.

The barman grinned and yelled back, 'Wait! I find him.'

Ten minutes later, they saw Cuthbert working his way down the bar towards them, a skinny little man and the Superman tee-shirt was at least two sizes too large for him.

'Hey, Cuthbert, anybody ever tell you that you look like Sammy Davis Junior?' Sean greeted him.

'All the time man, man.' Cuthbert looked pleased, Sean had obviously picked out his pet vanity.

'Your uncle sends his love, can we go somewhere to talk?' Sean suggested as they shook hands.

'Best place to talk is here,' Cuthbert answered. 'Nobody else going to hear a thing you say. Get me a beer, can't talk with a dry throat.'

Cuthbert downed half his beer at a draught and then asked, breathless from the effort, 'You were supposed to be here last night. Where you been, man?'

'We were delayed.'

299

'You should have been here last night. Would have been easy, man. Tonight, well, tonight is different.'

'What has changed?' Sean asked with a sink of dread in his chest.

'Everything changed.' Cuthbert said. 'The Hercules arrived 1700 hours. Come to pick up the goods.'

'Has it left yet?' Sean demanded anxiously.

'Don't know for sure. She was still there when I left the base at 2000 hours. Sitting out there in front of number three hangar. Perhaps she still there now, perhaps she long gone. Who knows?'

'Thanks a lot,' Sean said. 'That's a great help.'

'That's not all, man.' Cuthbert clearly enjoyed being the bearer of evil tidings.

'Hit us with it, Cuthbert.'

He finished the beer in another long swallow and held up the empty can. Sean ordered another and Cuthbert waited for it, drawing out the suspense masterfully.

'Two full para-commandos of the Fifth Brigade came down from Harare in the Hercules. They real cool, those Fifth Brigade cats,' Cuthbert said with relish. 'They real mean dudes, no shit.'

'Cuthbert, you've been watching too much "Miami Vice" on television,' Sean accused, but he was worried. The Fifth Brigade were the elite of the Zimbabwean army, converted by their North Korean instructors into ruthlessly efficient killing machines. Two full para-commandos of a hundred men each, added to the standing garrison of Third Brigade troops, almost a thousand crack veterans on base.

'Your uncle says you are going to take us in, Cuthbert. Pass us through the gates.'

'No way, man!' Cuthbert was vehement. 'Not with those Fifth Brigade cats in there.'

'Your uncle will be pissed off with you, Cuthbert. He's a pretty cool cat himself, man, Uncle China is.' Sean imitated Cuthbert's hip jargon.

Cuthbert looked worried. 'Man, I've fixed your pass,' he explained hurriedly. 'You'll have no trouble getting in. The guards are expecting you. You don't need me, man. No sense I should compromise myself, no sense at all.'

'You've got the pass here?'

'Right on. The password too. You'll have no trouble.'

'Let's go.' Sean took Job's arm and steered him towards the door. 'That Hercules could take off any time.'

Cuthbert hurried between them down the lane to where the three Unimogs were parked.

'Here's the pass.' He handed the plastic-covered card to Sean, it was slashed with a scarlet 'Top Priority' cross.

'The password is a number, "fifty-seven", and your reply is "Samora Machel". Then you show the pass and sign the book. Simple as a pimple, man. You in like Flynn.'

'I'll tell your uncle that you couldn't bring yourself to come with us.'

'Hey, give me a break, will you? No sense me getting culled, man. I'm more use to my uncle alive and kicking than dead meat.'

'Cuthbert, you are wasted in signals, you definitely should be on television.' Sean shook hands with him and watched him scurry back into the Stardust Club.

There were clusters of women around the back of each of the three trucks, giggling and joking with the troopers who hung out over the tail-gates. One of the girls was climbing aboard, boosted by eager hands, her mini-skirt rucked up high on her long thin black legs.

'Get those whores out of there, Sergeant,' Job snapped at Alphonso, and the women around the tail-gates scattered and three or four others descended hastily from the backs of the Unimogs with their skimpy clothing in varying stages of disarray.

Sean and Job climbed into the cab of the lead truck and as they drove off Sean buttoned on his tunic and tipped his cap at a rakish angle over one eye.

'What are we going to do?' Job asked.

'Number three hangar at Grand Reef is in full view of the main road. We will drive up the highway. If the Hercules is still there, we go in. If not, well, we'll go back the way we came.'

'What about the Fifth Brigade?'

'They're just a bunch of ex-gooks,' said Sean. 'You weren't afraid of them before, so what's changed?'

'Just asking to pass the time,' Job grinned at him sideways. 'You want to tell Alphonso about them?'

'What Alphonso doesn't know, won't hurt him,' Sean said. 'Just keep going.'

The column of three trucks drove sedately through the sleeping town of Umtali. The streets were deserted but Job obeyed the traffic lights punctiliously and then they were out on the open highway.

'Twelve minutes past eleven.' Sean checked his watch, and then read the road sign in the beam of the headlights.

'Grand Reef Military Base, fifteen kilometres.'

He felt the familiar tightness in his stomach muscles, the shortness in his breath and consciously slowed and regulated his breathing. It was always like this before a scene.

'There she is,' Job said softly as they topped a rise in the highway.

The airfield was fully lit, the beacon lights glowing orange and the blue and green dotted lines of the taxi-ways and runway beyond them.

In the stark white light of the floods, even at a distance of almost two miles, the Hercules looked gigantic. Its forty-foot-high tail-fin towered above the roof of number three hangar.

Sean recognized immediately that it was one of the Marshall stretched-out conversions of Lockheed's Hercules original C MK3 transports for the Royal Air Force.

The RAF roundels were painted on the monstrous silver fuselage and on the high tail-fin.

'Pull over,' Sean ordered, and Job flicked his tail-light indicators and pulled into the side of the road. He switched off his headlights and one after the other the following Unimogs did the same.

In the silence Sean said softly, 'So the Hercules is still here. We are going in.'

'Let's do it,' Job agreed.

Sean jumped down from the cab and ran back to the second truck just as Alphonso climbed down to the roadside.

'Sergeant, you know what to do. I'll give you forty-five minutes to get into position. Then I want exactly ten minutes of diversionary fire, everything you've got.'

'The first plan was twenty minutes of diversion.'

'That's changed,' Sean told him. 'We expect a much stronger response than we first thought possible. Ten minutes and then pull out fast. Head straight back for St Mary's mission, we are abandoning the RZ on the Umtali pass. Hit them hard and then get out. Understood?'

'Yehbo.'

'Go!' Sean said, and Alphonso jumped up into the cab. Through the open window he saluted Sean and gave him a cheery grin.

'Break a leg,' Sean said softly, and the Unimog pulled out and headed down the highway towards the brightly lit base.

Sean watched the headlights turn off the main highway onto the secondary road that by-passed the perimeter fence of the airfield, then he lost them amongst the trees. Sean marked the time with the bevel ring on his Rolex and walked back to join Job in the leading truck.

He lay back in the passenger seat, pushed his cap to the back of his head and focused his binoculars through the open window at the huge aircraft that squatted on the tarmac under the flood-lights.

The tail ramp at the rear of the fuselage was lowered like a drawbridge. He could see into the cavernous cargo hold.

There were four or five human figures moving about inside the hold and two more at the foot of the ramp. As he watched, a forklift truck trundled out of the open doors of number three hangar. Its fork arms were loaded with a stack of long wooden cases, four of them, one on top of the other. The cases were of raw white wood, and stencilled on them in black paint were letters and numerals which he could not decipher. He did not need to, the shape and size of the crates were unmistakable.

'They are loading the Stingers,' Sean said, and Job sat up straight in the driver's seat.

The forklift truck wheeled around the stern of the Hercules, and then climbed the open ramp and disappeared into the cargo hold. Minutes later it reappeared, drove down the ramp and wheeled into the hangar. Sean glanced at his watch, only five minutes had passed since Alphonso had driven ahead to set up the mock attack.

'Come on,' Sean muttered, and shook the Rolex on his wrist as if to speed up the mechanism.

Twice more, they watched the loaded forklift truck make the journey from out of the hangar, up into the belly of the Hercules and return empty.

Then it turned aside and parked at the far end of the hangar. The driver in blaze orange overalls climbed down from his seat and sauntered back to stand with the two other stevedores at the tail ramp.

'Loading completed,' Sean whispered again, and checked his watch. 'Seven minutes to go.'

Job unbuttoned the flap of his holster and drew the Tokarev 7.62 pistol. He withdrew the magazine and checked the load, then slapped the magazine back into its recess in the pistol grip and returned the pistol to its holster.

Through the binoculars, Sean saw the men who had been working in the cargo hold come down the ramp in a group. Three of them were white men, two of those in flying overalls and the other in British regulation battledress. Two pilots and one of the Royal Artillery instructors, Sean guessed.

'Start up!' he said, and Job kicked the engine to life.

'We should try to knock out those floodlights,' Sean muttered. 'We can't load the truck in the full glare, not with the Fifth Brigade breathing down our necks.'

He was looking at his watch, tilting the dial to catch the glow of the instrument panel.

'Okay, Job. Here we go!' he said, and the Unimog pulled forward. In the rear-view mirror, Sean watched the second truck driven by Ferdinand fall in behind them.

As they drove parallel to the main runway of the airfield Sean was assailed with a thousand memories. It all seemed exactly as it had been ten years before. No hangars nor buildings had been added. He picked out the windows of his old office in the main admin block beyond the control tower, and as Job slowed the truck and turned onto the short driveway that led from the highway to the base gates, Sean almost expected to see the insignia of the Ballantyne Scouts between that of the Rhodesian Light Infantry and the Rhodesian African Rifles on the arch above the gates.

Job halted the truck under the lights facing the wire-mesh gates and two guards came to each of the side windows of the cab. They carried their AK rifles at the trail and peered in at Job and Sean.

Job lowered the side window and exchanged the passwords with the commander of the guard and handed him the plastic-covered pass. The man took it to the guard house and made an entry in the register, then two of his men opened the main gates and he waved the convoy through.

Casually Sean returned the salute that the guards threw him as he passed, and he told Job quietly, 'Just like Cuthbert said, simple as a pimple. Now head straight down towards the admin block, but turn behind the control tower as you reach it.'

Job drove slowly, obeying the on-base fifteen mph speed limit and Sean unbuttoned the flap of his webbing holster and drew his pistol. He withdrew the magazine, pressed two cartridges out into the palm of his hand and then reloaded them in reverse order and slapped the magazine back into its recess in the pistol grip.

'Why do you always do that?' Job asked.

'Just for luck,' he said, as he saw Job watching.

'Does it work?' Job wanted to know.

'Well, I'm still alive, aren't I?' Sean grinned tightly. He pulled back the slide, pumping a round into the chamber of the pistol, engaged the safety and slipped the weapon back into its holster.

'Pull in behind the number three hangar,' he told Job, and he swung the truck across the hard stand in the full glare of the overhead floodlights into the shadowy area at the back of the hangar where they were screened from the control tower and the admin block.

As the truck stopped Sean jumped down and glanced around him quickly. The second Unimog pulled in beside the first, and armed men in battledress swarmed out over the tail-gates of both. With three quick strides Sean reached the back door in the corrugated metal wall of the hangar. It was unlocked and he stepped through. Job followed him immediately.

The hangar was empty except for a single light aircraft parked in the far corner. The bleak concrete floor half the size of a football field was stained with old oil spills, and the steel girders of the roof arched high overhead. It was brightly lit.

The forklift driver and the stevedores in their blaze orange overalls were halfway across the floor, coming directly towards Sean in a group, chatting and smoking cigarettes in direct defiance of the huge prohibition notices in red letters on the hangar walls. They stopped in confusion as they saw Sean come through the door with the armed men behind him.

'Secure them,' Sean ordered. As Job rounded them up swiftly, Sean looked beyond them.

Along the opposite wall of the hangar were a line of office cubicles with side walls of painted chipboard and glass windows. Through a lighted window, Sean saw the head and shoulders of one of the pilots in his blue RAF overalls. He had his back towards Sean, and he was gesticulating as he spoke to somebody out of sight.

By now the stevedores were lying spread-eagled on the concrete floor, each with a man standing over him and the muzzle of an AKM pressed into the back of each of their necks. It had been done swiftly and silently.

With the pistol in his hand, Sean ran to the door of the office cubicle and jerked it open. Two men, one of the pilots and the Royal Artillery captain, were lolling in a pair of dilapidated armchairs under a wall which was covered with a collection of ancient girlie pin-ups which Sean guessed were relics of the bush war. The senior pilot sat on a cluttered desk in front of the lit window. All three of them stared at Sean in amazement.

'This is a commando raid.' Sean told them quietly. 'Stay exactly where you are.'

On the floor between the Royal Artillery captain's feet stood a square black bag with substantial locks and a Royal Artillery decal stuck on the side.

The gunner dropped a hand on it protectively, and Sean knew immediately what the bag contained. The gunner was in his mid-twenties, well built and competent-looking. The name tag on his breast read 'Carlyle'. He had blue eyes and thick sandy-coloured hair.

The senior pilot was a flight lieutenant, but he was middle-aged and over-weight. His flight engineer was balding and nondescript, with real fear in his eyes as he stared at the pistol in Sean's hand. Sean anticipated no trouble from either of them, and transferred his attention back to the gunner. He knew instinctively that this was the main man. He had the shoulders of a boxer, and he hunched them aggressively and scowled at Sean. He was young enough to be foolhardy and Sean held his gaze and warned him.

'Forget it, Carlyle. Heroes are out of fashion.'

'You are a South African,' Carlyle growled as he recognized the accent. 'Whose side are you on?'

'My own,' Sean told him. 'Strictly self-employed.' He glanced down at the black bag and Carlyle pulled it an inch closer to him.

'Captain Carlyle, you are guilty of gross dereliction of duty,' Sean told him coldly, and the gunner reacted to the accusation with the indignation of a professional soldier.

'What do you mean?'

'You should have posted guards while you were loading the

missiles. You let us swan in here . . .' It distracted Carlyle as Sean had intended and gave Job the few seconds he needed to get his men into the office.

'Stand up,' he ordered the airmen, and they obeyed quickly, raising their hands and Job hustled them out of the office.

Carlyle remained in the armchair with the bag between his legs.

'Stand up!' Sean repeated the order.

'Screw you, Boer.'

Sean stepped up to him and seized the handle of the bag. Carlyle grabbed at it to prevent him and Sean brought the barrel of the pistol down across his knuckles. The skin split and Sean heard one of his fingers snap. He had misjudged it, he had not intended to inflict that kind of injury, but he kept his expression fierce.

'You have had your warning,' he said. 'My next offer is a bullet in the head.'

Carlyle was holding his injured hand to his chest, but his face was set and dark with fury as he watched Sean place the bag on the desk.

'Keys!' Sean said.

'Get stuffed,' said Carlyle. His voice was tight and hoarse with pain and Sean saw that his broken finger was standing out at an odd angle and swelling like a purple balloon.

Job reappeared in the door of the office cubicle. 'All secure,' he said, and glanced at his wristwatch. 'Four minutes to diversion.'

'Give me your knife,' Sean told him, and Job slid the trench knife from its sheath and passed it to Sean, hilt first.

Sean slashed the leather along the edge of the bag's steel frame and then pulled open the concertina hinge. There were half a dozen large loose-leaf folders filling the interior of the bag and Sean selected one. The file was covered in War Office red plastic and marked 'Top Secret'; he glanced at the title page:

FIELD MANUAL FOR INFANTRY USE OF THE 'STINGER'
MODEL G4X
SURFACE-TO-AIR MISSILE

'Jackpot.' Sean turned the file so that Job could read it. It was a stupid thing to do. They were both distracted, turned towards the desk, studying the file.

307

Carlyle launched himself out of the chair. He was young and fast. The injury to his hand did not hamper him in the least, and he was across the narrow floor space before either of them could move to stop him and he dived head first into the frosted window in the middle of the far wall. It exploded in a sparkling shower of glass and Carlyle flipped over in mid-air like an acrobat.

Sean leapt to the empty window. Outside on the brightly lit tarmac of the hard stand, Carlyle rolled to his feet and ran. Job pushed Sean aside and stepped up to the window; lifting his AKM and taking deliberate care, he aimed at Carlyle's broad back as he sprinted across open ground towards the base of the control tower.

Sean grabbed the rifle and jerked the barrel down before Job could fire.

'What the hell are you doing?' Job snarled at him.

'You can't shoot him!'

'Why not?'

'He's an Englishman,' Sean explained lamely, and for a moment Job stared at him uncomprehendingly and Carlyle covered the last few yards and dived into the doorway at the base of the control tower.

'Englishman or Eskimo, we are going to have the whole Fifth Brigade down our throats in about ten seconds from now.' Job was obviously trying to control his anger. 'So what do we do now?'

'How long to diversion?' Sean asked to buy time. He had no answer to Job's question.

'Still four minutes,' Job answered. 'And it might as well be four hours.'

As he said it, the sirens began to howl like wolves, bringing the base to full alert. Obviously Carlyle had reached the ops room in the control tower. Sean stuck his head out of the shattered window and saw the guard turning out of the main gate-house on the far side of the runway. They were dragging the spike boards across the approaches to the gates, to cut the tyres of an escaping vehicle to ribbons, and Sean saw the barrels of the 12.7mm heavy machine-guns depressing and traversing to cover the approaches. They were never going to get the trucks out that way.

'You should have let me sort him out,' Job fumed. How could Sean explain it to him? Carlyle had been a brave man doing his

308

duty, and although the lines of loyalty to the old country had become blurred, Sean had the same blood in his veins; it would have been worse than murder to allow Job to shoot him down. It would have been a kind of fratricide.

Outside the hangar, the perimeter lights went on abruptly flooding the high security fence around the runway and taxi-way. The entire base area was lit like daylight.

If the commandos of the Fifth Brigade were in barracks and asleep when the alarm sounded, how long would it take them to come into action? Sean tried to make an estimate and then with self-disgust, realized that he was simply avoiding facing up to his own indecision and lack of any plan. He had lost control, and it was all blowing up in his face.

In a few minutes from now, he and Job and the twenty Shanganes of his commando were going to be overwhelmed. The lucky ones amongst them would be killed outright and so avoid interrogation by the Zimbabwe central intelligence organization.

'Think,' he told himself desperately, and Job was expectantly watching his face, waiting for orders. He had never seen Sean at a loss before. His unquestioning trust irritated Sean and made it even more difficult for him to reach any decision.

'What shall I tell the men?' Job prodded him.

'Get them . . .' Sean broke off as heavy gunfire broke out on the southern perimeter of the base on the opposite side to the hangar and out of their field of vision. Alphonso had been bright enough to realize that the plan had been derailed and he had started his attack a few minutes early.

They heard the whoosh-boom of RPG 7 rockets coming in through the perimeter wire and the duller thud-thud of mortar shells dropping in the base area. The 12.7mm machine-gun at the gates opened up, sluicing green tracer in pretty parabolas high into the darkness.

'How are we going to get out of here?' Job demanded.

Sean stared at him stupidly. He felt confused and uncertain. Panic welled up from deep inside him, he had never suspected such a source existed. He didn't know what order to give next.

'Forget the bloody Stingers, just get us out of here.' Job grabbed his arm and shook it. 'Come on, Sean, snap out of it! Tell me what to do!'

'Forget the Stingers!' The words were like a slap with an open hand across his face. Sean blinked and shook his head. Forget the Stingers and forget Claudia Monterro. Without the missiles, Claudia would stay in the hole in the ground where Matatu had last seen her.

Sean glanced out of the open window again. He could see the gigantic tail-plane of the Hercules and part of the fuselage, the rest of the aircraft was obscured by the angle of the hangar wall. The metallic silver skin of the Hercules glittered in the arc lights.

Sean clamped down hard on the hot effervescence of panic that threatened to swamp him, and felt it subside.

'The lights,' he said, and glanced around him quickly. He spotted the fuse box on the office wall beside the door and he reached it in two strides and jerked open the cover.

The hangar had been built during Hitler's war when the RAF had used Rhodesia as one of its overseas training centres. The electrical wiring dated from that era and utilized the old-fashioned ceramic type fuse-holders.

'Give me an AK round,' Sean snapped at Job. His voice was crisp and decisive and Job obeyed instantly. He flicked one of the brass 7.62mm cartridges from the spare magazine in the pouch on his webbing.

Sean identified the main phase in the fuse box. The in-coming current would be distributed directly from the transformer at the gates, if he could over-load that he would blow the flying fuse on the transformer box.

He pulled out the ceramic fuse-holder and the hangar was plunged into darkness, but the light of the floods through the open window gave him sufficient light to see what he was doing. He jammed the AK cartridge into the lugs of the ceramic fuse-holder and snapped at Job.

'Stand back!'

The last vestiges of his panic were gone. He felt cold and resilient as a knife-blade. His mind was clear and he knew exactly what he was going to do.

He thrust the loaded fuse-holder back into its slot, and a blinding blue explosion of light like a photographer's flash bulb lit the darkened room, and Sean was sent flying backwards. He crashed against the office wall, half stunned, shaking his head, his vision starred with memories of the blue flash.

It took him a few moments to realize that the floodlights

beyond the windows were extinguished and except for fiery bead necklaces of tracer flying across the dark sky and the brief glare of exploding grenades and rockets, the base was in darkness.

'Get the men into the Hercules,' he shouted.

Job was just a dark shadow behind the whirling catherine wheels of fire that still disturbed his vision.

'What? I don't understand?' Job stammered.

'We are getting out in the aircraft.' Sean grabbed his shoulder and thrust him towards the door. 'Get Ferdinand and his boys on board and move your arse.'

Job ran, and Sean blundered blindly after him. His vision was returning swiftly. He turned towards the paler square of light that was the hangar doors.

'What about the prisoners?' Job called from the dark depths of the hangar.

'Turn them loose,' Sean yelled back, and ran for the doors.

Although he did not have the Hercules conversion endorsed on his licence, Sean had flown the type before. In fact, he had accumulated almost 200 hours in the right-hand seat when he had flown with the South African air force in Angola and Namibia on anti-terrorist ops. It all came back to him now. He had enjoyed flying the Hercules and he remembered the remark a Senior pilot had made.

'She's a lamb. I wish my wife was so docile.'

At the hangar door, Sean stopped suddenly.

'Matatu is right, you're getting old, Courtney,' he castigated himself and spun around. He charged back into the dark hangar and almost collided with Job.

'Where you going?'

'I forgot the bag,' Sean yelled. 'Get the men on board.'

He found the gunner's bag on the desk where he had left it and stuffed it under his arm. Job was waiting for him at the foot of the Hercules' loading ramp.

'All the men are on board,' he greeted Sean. 'You should have let me keep the pilot.'

'We didn't have time to convince him to co-operate,' Sean snapped. 'The poor bastard was in a blue funk.'

'Are you going to fly?'

311

'Sure, unless you want a shot at it.'

'Hey, Sean, have you ever flown one of these things?'

'There is a first time for everything.' Sean pointed forward. 'Come on, help me clear the chocks.'

They ran forward and dragged the wheel chocks clear, then Sean led the way up the steep angle of the ramp and stopped at the top.

'Here is the control for the ramp.' He showed Job the rocker switch in the side wall of the fuselage. 'Move it to the "up" position when I have got the first engine started and the red light goes on in that panel. It will switch to green when the ramp is up and locked.'

Sean left him and ran down the length of the Hercules' body. The Shanganes were milling about uncertainly in the darkness.

'Ferdinand!' Sean shouted. 'Get them to sit in the side benches and show them how to strap in.'

Sean groped his way towards the flight deck. He found the wooden missile cases loaded over the Hercules' centre of gravity between the wings. They were piled against the fuselage on wooden pallets and covered with heavy cargo netting. He eased past them and reached the door to the flight deck. It was unlocked and he burst through it and dumped the heavy gunner's bag into the map bin under the flight engineer's steel table. Through the cockpit windows, he saw that the mock attack on the south perimeter was still in full swing, but that the volume of fire from within the base was now much heavier than from the raiders out in the bush beyond the wire.

'The Fifth Brigade has woken up,' Sean muttered, and climbed into the left-hand seat and switched on the lights of the Hercules instrument panel. The vast array of glowing dials and switches was intimidating and confusing, but Sean would not allow himself to be daunted.

It was a lot simpler than starting the old Baron. He merely switched on and ran a finger along the rows of circuit breakers to ensure that they were all in.

'The hell with start-up checks.' He said and hit the start switch for the No. 1 engine. The starter motor whined and he watched the needle creep around the rev counter.

'Come on!' He pleaded. As revolutions touched 10% she automatically primed her combustion chamber with fuel and the

312

engine ignited. He wound her up to 70% of power while he adjusted the earphones of the radio set on his head.

'Job, do you read?'

'Loud and clear, man.'

'Get the ramp up.'

'It's on its way.'

Sean waited impatiently for the ramp warning lamp on the panel to switch from red to green, and the moment it did so, he kicked off the wheel brakes and the Hercules rolled ponderously forward.

He was taxiing on one engine, and had to use gross opposite rudder to meet the asymmetrical thrust. However, as he followed the pale strip of the taxi-way, he worked on the other three engines, and one after the other coaxed them to life, adjusting the controls as the power thrust altered.

'No wind,' he muttered. 'Makes no difference which direction for take-off.'

The main runway had been extended to accommodate the excessive take-off and landing requirements of modern jet fighters. However, the Hercules was STOL – short take-off and landing. It required only a fraction of the available distance and Sean steered her for the main intersection directly in front of the control tower.

So far the Hercules had drawn no fire. The heavy machine-guns at the gates were still firing wildly into the night sky. Poor fire control was always one of the problems with African troops who in all other respects made excellent soldiers.

On the other hand, at the southern perimeter the crack veterans of the Fifth and Third Brigades were showing what well-trained African troops were capable of. Their fire was going in deadly professional sheets, and already they had almost entirely extinguished Alphonso's initial onslaught. Apart from a few desultory mortar shells there was no longer any return fire from the dark sea of bush and forest beyond the base security fence.

It was only a short time before Carlyle managed to alert fully the garrison to the enemy within, and the flight controllers in the blacked-out tower realized that there was an unauthorized take-off in progress.

Sean was taxiing the Hercules at a reckless speed, so fast that she was already developing lift and wanting to fly. He knew that if he came off the concrete taxi-way onto the grass, there was a chance of bellying her or getting her stuck, but not as good a chance as having her shot up by the 12.7mm if he delayed the take-off a moment longer than was necessary.

'Job,' he spoke over the tannoy again, 'I'm going to give you cabin lights so you can make sure the lads are seated and strapped in. Take-off in forty seconds.'

He switched on the cabin lights to prevent chaos in the dark belly of the fuselage and then flicked his headset to the control tower frequency 118.6.

They were calling him stridently. 'Air Force Hercules Victor Sierra Whisky. State your intentions. I say again, Air Force Hercules.'

'This is Air Force Hercules Victor Sierra Whisky,' Sean replied. 'Request taxi clearance to avoid hostile ground fire.'

'Sierra Whisky, say again. What are your intentions?'

'Tower, this is Sierra Whisky. Request . . .' Sean mumbled and slurred his transmission deliberately, forcing the tower to ask for a further repetition. He was watching his engine temperature gauges anxiously as the needles crept up infinitely slowly towards the green.

'Tower, I am having difficulty reading your transmission,' he stalled them. 'Please repeat your clearance.'

Behind him Job barged open the door to the flight deck.

'The men are strapped in ready for take-off,' he called.

'Get into the right-hand seat and strap in,' Sean ordered without looking round. The engine temperature gauge needles were touching the bottom of the green. The main runway was coming up fast. Sean toed the wheel brakes, slowing for the turn and line up.

'Air Force Hercules. You are not cleared to taxi or line up. Repeat you have no clearance from tower. Discontinue immediately and take first left. Return to your holding area. I repeat return to your holding area.'

'Up yours, mate!' Sean muttered, as he pulled on ten degrees of flap and revolved the trim wheel to slightly tail heavy.

'Air Force Hercules. Stop immediately or we will fire upon you.'

Sean switched on the landing lights and swung the monstrous aircraft onto the main runway. She handled as lightly as his little twin Beechcraft.

'You are a pussy cat, darling.' He knew that like a woman an

314

aircraft always responded to loving flattery. He advanced the bank of throttle controls smoothly, and at that moment the heavy machine-gun beyond the tower opened up on them.

However, the Hercules was accelerating strongly and the gunner had not learned the art of forward allowance. He was shooting at the place that the aircraft had been seconds before and perhaps his nerves were still rattling for his fire was high as well as behind. The first long burst of tracer curved away over the high tail-fin.

'That cat needs shooting lessons,' Job remarked calmly. Sean always wondered if Job's cool and phlegmatic behaviour under fire was put on.

The next burst was low and ahead, the tracer splashed across the concrete runway just under the Hercules' nose.

'But he learns fast,' Job grunted a reluctant admission.

Sean was leaning forward slightly in the seat, with his right hand holding the bank of quadruple throttles fully open, with his left feeling the control wheel for signs of life, watching the airspeed needle revolve sedately around the dial.

'Here comes your friend,' Job said, and pointed out of the side panel of the canopy. Sean glanced around swiftly.

An open Land-Rover was tearing wildly across the grass verge alongside the main runway, its headlights cutting crazy patterns in the darkness as it bounced over the uneven ground. It was attempting to cut them off, and Sean could just make out the features of the man who stood in the back of the speeding vehicle.

'He doesn't give up easily, does he?' Sean remarked, and gave his attention back to the Hercules.

Carlyle must have commandeered one of the guard Land-Rovers and its black driver. He was standing in the open back, clinging to the mounting of the RPD machine-gun and his face was pale and contorted in the reflection of the Hercules' landing lights as he egged on the driver to greater speed.

'He's really taking it to heart.' Job leaned forward to watch with interest as Carlyle swung the machine-gun in its mountings, aiming up at the cockpit of the Hercules.

The driver swung the Land-Rover over on two wheels, until it was tearing along beside the huge rolling aircraft, only fifty yards away, almost level with the wing-tip.

'Hey, man,' Job shook his head, 'he's aiming at us personally.'

Carlyle braced himself behind the gun and the muzzle flashes blinked rapidly at them. Bullets raked the perspex canopy starring

315

it with silver dollars, and both of them ducked instinctively as shot flew past their heads.

'He's a better shot than the other cat,' Job murmured and with the tip of his finger touched the drop of blood on his cheek where a splinter had cut him.

Sean felt the controls come to life in his hand as the Hercules approached flying speed and the wings developed lift.

'Come on, pussy cat,' he murmured, and Carlyle fired another burst at the same moment the Land-Rover hit a concrete culvert and bounced wildly, throwing his fire high and wild. He steadied himself and lined up to fire again.

'He's fast becoming my least favourite cartoon character.' Without flinching Job watched him take aim. 'Okay, here it comes!'

From the off-side the heavy machine-gun at the gates fired again and a stream of 12.7mm bullets skimmed the belly of the Hercules and flew on to pour into the racing Land-Rover beyond. They tore the front wheels off her and she somersaulted forward rolling end over end in a cloud of dust. From the corner of his eye, Sean saw Carlyle's body thrown high and clear.

'And so we say farewell to óne of the last authentic heroes,' he intoned gravely, and eased back the control column of the Hercules. The great aircraft responded willingly, pointing her nose upwards.

Sean switched off the landing lights and cabin lights, plunging the machine into darkness so she no longer offered a target to the ground gunners. He hit the toggle to raise the landing gear and dumped flap. Immediately the airspeed mounted and he put down one wing and went into a tight climbing turn.

Another burst of tracer followed them, floating up slowly and then accelerating as it approached until it sped past their wing-tip. Sean met the turn and banked the opposite way, weaving out of range.

'You want to make me sea-sick?' Job asked, and Sean ignored him as he checked the engine dials for possible damage.

It seemed impossible that the enormous target offered by the Hercules had received only a single burst of fire out of all the hundreds of rounds fired at it, but the needles on the dials all registered normal and responded instantly as he eased back on the boost and set revolutions for climb at five hundred feet a minute. However, the slipstream was whistling through the bullet holes in the canopy, ruffling Sean's hair and making conversation difficult, so that he had to raise his voice as he told Job, 'Go back and see if anyone was hit, then do a visual check for damage in the hold.'

The lights of Umtali town were off to the south and beyond them Sean could just make out the loom of mountains. He knew that the highest peak in the chain was 8500 feet above sea level so he allowed a wide separation and levelled out at 10,000, then checked his heading.

Up until now, he had not thought about his navigation and was unsure of the bearings for a return to the Sierra da Gorongosa lines.

'Won't find them marked on any map,' he grinned. 'But we'll try 030 magnetic.' And he banked the Hercules onto that heading.

The adrenalin was still thick in his blood, the rapture of fear swirling him aloft on eagles' wings and he laughed again, just a little shakily and savoured the glorious thrill of it while it lasted.

The dark mountain tops slid away beneath him, just visible in the starlight like the shape of whales deep in an Arctic sea. He picked out the occasional pin-prick of light in the valleys, an isolated farm or mission station or peasant hut, and then as he crossed the frontier into Mozambique, there was nothing but darkness ahead.

'Nothing but darkness,' he repeated, and it seemed symbolic and prophetic. They were going back into the wasteland.

Sean eased back on power and began a gradual descent towards the lowland forests. Now that the mountain peaks were behind them, he didn't want to stay up high offering an easy target for the attack radar of a pursuing MIG fighter or an intercepting Hind gunship.

Job came back and locked the door of the flight deck.

'Any damage?' Sean asked, and Job chuckled.

'The floor of the cargo hold is ankle-deep in puke. Those Shanganes don't fancy your flying, man, they are up-chucking in all directions.'

'Charming.' Sean groped in the side pocket of the pilot's seat and came up with a packet of Dutch cigars, property of the RAF pilot.

'Well, look what we have here.' He tossed one to Job and they lit up and smoked contentedly for a few minutes before Job asked, 'How long before the MIGs catch up with us?'

317

Sean shook his head. 'They are based in Harare, I don't think they can catch us even if they scramble immediately. No. I'm not worried about the MIGs, but the Hinds are another story.'

They were silent again, watching the ripe celestial fruit of the stars that from the dark flightdeck seemed close enough to pluck.

'Are you ready to answer an embarrassing question?' Job broke the silence.

'Fire away.'

'You've got us up here, how the hell are you going to get us down again?'

Sean blew a smoke ring which was instantly obliterated by the slipstream through the bullet holes in the canopy.

'Interesting question,' he conceded. 'I'll let you know when I have an answer myself. In the meantime just worry about finding the Renamo lines in general and China's headquarters in particular.'

Five hundred feet above the tops of the forest trees, Sean levelled the Hercules, and reading the throttle and pitch settings from the instruction engraved on the instrument panel set her up for endurance flying.

'Another two hours before it will be light enough to even start looking for an emergency landing field,' he told Job. 'In the meantime, we can try to find the Pungwe river.'

An hour later, they spotted the gleam of water in the black carpet of forest ahead and seconds later the stars were reflected from a large body of dark water directly below them.

'I'm going back to check it,' Sean warned Job, and put the Hercules into an easy turn, watching the gyro compass on the panel in front of him rotate through 180 degrees before levelling out again.

'Landing lights on,' he murmured and flipped the switch. The tops of the trees below them were lit by the powerful lamps and they saw the river, a dark serpent winding away into the night. Sean threw the Hercules into a hard right-hand turn and then levelled out, flying directly along the course of the river.

'Looks like it,' he grunted, and switched off the landing lights. 'But even if it is the right river, we won't be able to judge whether we are upstream or downstream of the lines until sunrise.'

'So what do we do?'

'We fly a holding pattern,' Sean explained, and banked the Hercules into the first of a monotonous series of figures of eight.

Around and around they cruised, five hundred feet above the tree-tops, crossing and recrossing the dark river at the same point, marking time, waiting for the dawn.

'Sitting duck for a Hind,' Job remarked once.

'Don't wish it on us,' Sean frowned at him. 'If you have nothing else useful to do, get the gunner's bag, it's in the map bin.'

Job lugged the bag to the front of the cabin and set it beside his seat, then settled himself comfortably.

'Read to me,' Sean instructed. 'Find something in there to amuse me and pass the time.'

Job brought out the red plastic-covered 'Top Secret' folders one at a time and thumbed through them, reading out the titles and chapter headings from each index page.

The first three files were all field manuals for the Stinger SAM Systems, covering their deployment in every conceivable situation from the decks of ships at sea to their use by infantry in every climatic zone on the globe, setting out in tables and graphs the missile's performance figures in all conditions from tropical jungle to high Arctic.

'All you ever wanted to know, but were afraid to ask,' Job observed, and picked out the fourth manual from the bag.

STINGER GUIDED MISSILE SYSTEM
Target Selection and Rules of Engagement
Operational Reports

Job read aloud, and then turned to the index and chapter headings.

1. Falklands Islands.
2. Arabian Gulf. 'Sea of Hormuz'
3. Grenada Landings.
4. Angola Unita.
5. Afghanistan.

Job read it out, and Sean exclaimed, 'Afghanistan! See if they give us anything about the Hind.'

Job set the bulky file on his lap and adjusted the beam of the reading lamp from its recess in the cabin roof above his head. He paged through the manual.

'Here we go! Afghanistan,' he read. '"HELICOPTER TYPES."'

'Find the Hind!' Sean ordered impatiently.

'That's it,' Sean encouraged him. 'Look for the Hind.'

'Hare,' said Job. 'Hoplite. Hound. Hook. Hip. Haze. Havoc . . . here it is. Hind.'

'Give me the gen,' Sean ordered, and Job read aloud.

'"This flying piece of artillery ordnance nicknamed by the Soviets, Sturmovich (or hunchback) known to Nato as Hind and to the Afghan rebels and many others who have encountered it in the field as 'The Flying Death', has gained a formidable reputation which is perhaps not fully justified."'

Sean interrupted fervently, 'Brother, I hope you know what you're talking about.'

Job went on,

'"1. Impaired manoeuvrability, hovering and rate of climb characteristics as a consequence of the mass of its armour plating.

"2. A limited range of 240 nautical miles fully loaded, again as a consequence of its armour weight.

"3. A low max. speed of 157 knots and cruise speed of 147 knots.

"4. Very high service and ground maintenance requirements."'

'That's interesting,' Sean cut in. 'Even this big baby,' he patted the Hercules' control column, 'is faster than a Hind. I'll remember that if we meet one.'

'Do you want me to read to you?' Job asked. 'If so, then shut up and listen.'

'My apologies, go ahead.'

'"It is estimated that several hundred machines of this type have been employed in Afghanistan. Generally they have met with great success against the rebels although in excess of 150 have been destroyed by rebel troops armed with the Stinger

SAM. These figures alone prove that the Hind can be effectively engaged by the Stinger SAM System employing the tactics set out in the following chapters.'''

Job read on, giving the engine type and performance, the weapons and other statistics until, at last, Sean stopped him.

'Hold on, Job!' Sean pointed towards the east. 'It is getting light.'

The sky was pale enough to form a distinct horizon where it met the black land mass.

'Put the book away and go call Ferdinand up here. See if he can recognize where we are, and show us the way home.'

A strong odour of vomit surrounded Ferdinand as he stumbled onto the flight deck and the front of his tunic was stained. He leaned for support on the back of the pilot's seat, and Sean moved to put as much distance between them as possible.

'Look out there, Ferdinand.' Sean gesticulated through the bullet-punctured canopy. 'Do you see anything that you recognize?'

The Shangane peered dubiously around him muttering gloomily and then suddenly his expression cleared and lightened.

'Those hills.' He pointed out the side window. 'Yes, I know them. The river comes out between them at a waterfall.'

'Which way is the camp?'

'That way, far that way.'

'How far?'

'Two full days' march.'

'Seventy nautical miles,' Sean translated time into distance. 'We aren't too far out. Thank you, Ferdinand.' Sean broke out of the monotonous figure-of-eight pattern and levelled the Hercules' gigantic wings.

Still low against the forest, he flew westwards, the direction Ferdinand had pointed, while behind them the dawn came on apace turning the eastern sky a hazy carmine. They chased the shades of night as they fled across the dark hills.

Sean aimed the nose of the Hercules at the gap that Ferdinand had pointed out and checked his wristwatch against the panel clock.

'Time for News Desk on the Africa Service of the BBC,' he said, and fiddled with the radio controls. He picked up the familiar signature tune on 15,400 megahertz.

321

'This is the BBC. Here again are the news headlines. In the United States, Governor Michael Dukakis has convincingly carried the State of New York against Senator Jesse Jackson in his bid for the democratic party presidential nomination. Israeli troops have shot dead two more protestors in the occupied Gaza Strip. One hundred and twenty passengers have died in an airline crash in the Philippines. Renamo rebels have highjacked an RAF Hercules transport from a Zimbabwe Air Force base near the town of Umtali. They have flown it into Mozambique where it is being pursued by aircraft of the Zimbabwe and Mozambiquan air forces. A spokesman said that both President Mugabe and President Chissano have given orders that the aircraft, which has no hostages on board but which contains sophisticated modern weapons intended for use against the rebels, is to be destroyed at all costs.'

Sean switched off the set and smiled across at Job.

'You never thought you'd make the news headlines, did you?'

'I can do without the fame,' Job admitted. 'Did you get the bit about being pursued and destroyed at all costs?'

The Hercules was fast approaching the gap in the line of hills. The light had strengthened so that Sean could make out the pearly gleam in the throat of the pass where the river tumbled down over wet black rock.

'Incoming!' Job yelled suddenly. 'One o'clock low!'

With his extraordinary eyesight, he had picked it up an instant before Sean did. The Hind had been lying in ambush, squatting like some monstrous insect in a hidden clearing in the forest, guarding the entrance to the river pass.

As Sean saw it, he understood clearly the tactics Frelimo had used to cut him off from the Renamo lines. They would have sent the full squadron of Hinds in during the night, as soon as they guessed where he was headed.

Operating at the limits of their range, the Hinds would have settled in a defensive line, landing to conserve fuel, hiding in the forest and sweeping with their pulse radars, listening in the silence for the sound of the Hercules' engines.

Almost certainly they had guessed that he would use the river as a navigational landmark. There would probably be other gunships waiting further upstream, forming an intercepting ring around the Renamo lines, but erring too far south, Sean had run headlong into this one.

It leapt out of the forest, rising vertically on the silver blur of its rotor, the deformed nose drooping, like a minotaur lowering its head to charge, blotched with leprous camouflage, obscenely ugly and deadly.

It was still below them but coming up swiftly, swelling in size as they converged. Within moments its Gatling-cannon would bear, already it was training upwards. Sean reacted without thought.

He rammed all four throttle controls fully open and the great turbos screeched as he thrust the nose down, diving straight at the helicopter.

He saw the rockets leaving the weapon pods under the Hind's wings, each one a black dot in the centre of a white wreath of smoke as it dropped clear. He remembered the statistics Job had read him only minutes before. The Hind carried two AT-2 Swatter missiles and four 57mm rocket pods.

He dived the Hercules through the barrage of rockets, they flashed past his head, a storm of smoke and death, and the Hind was only two hundred metres ahead, still rising to meet him, firing rockets at pointblank range but not allowing for his violent manoeuvre.

'Hold on!' Sean shouted at Job. 'I'm going to ram the bastard.'

The killing rage was on him, sweet and hot in his blood, there was no fear at all, just the marvellous urge to destroy.

At the last moment, the pilot of the Hind guessed his intention. They were so close that through the canopy, Sean could clearly make out his features below the helmet. The Russian's face was doughy white and his mouth a shocking red slash like an open wound.

He flicked the gunship over on its side, almost inverting it completely, closing down his collective so the Hind fell like a lead weight, trying to duck under the Hercules' out-spread pinions.

'Got you, you son of a bitch!' Sean exulted, and the Hercules wing hit the tail of the gunship. The shock of impact threw Sean against his shoulder-straps, and the Hercules shuddered and lurched, the airspeed was knocked off her and she quivered on the edge of the stall only two hundred feet above the forest top.

'Come on, pussy cat,' Sean whispered like a lover.

He was babying the controls, coaxing her with gentle fingers.

Her damaged wing was down, tatters of torn metal hanging

323

from it, whipping and banging in the slipstream, and the forest tops reached up like the talons of a predator to claw them out of the sky.

'Fly for me, darling,' Sean whispered, and the four engines, howling with the effort, held her up and then gradually lifted her clear.

The needle of the rate-of-climb indicator rose jerkily, they were climbing at two hundred feet a minute.

'Where's the Hind?' Sean yelled at Job.

'She must be down,' Job called back, both of them screaming at each other with terror and excitement and the triumph of it.

'Nothing could take a hit like that.' Then his voice changed. 'No, there she is, she's still flying. My God, will you look at that mother?'

The Hind was hard hit, skittering out to one side, the tail rotor and the rudder torn, almost completely gone. Obviously her pilot was fighting for her life as she lurched and rolled and wallowed about the sky.

'I don't believe it! She's still shooting at us!' Job cried, and a smoking rocket trail blazed across their nose.

'She's steadying.' Job was watching her through the side window. 'She's coming round, she's after us again.'

Sean met the Hercules' climb, and aimed for the pass through the hills. The rocky cliffs seemed to brush their wing-tips and the foaming white waterfall flashed beneath them.

'He has fired a missile.' As Job called the warning, the pass through the hills opened up ahead of them, and Sean lifted the Hercules' maimed wing high in a maximum-rate turn.

The huge aircraft hugged the cliff face, turning the corner just as the Swatter missile locked onto the infra-red emissions of her exhausts and sped down the gut of the pass. The Hercules cut the turn so finely that Sean had to use full power to hold the nose level, and looking upwards through the skylight of the canopy, he felt as though he could have reached out and touched the rockface as the Hercules stood on one wing-tip. The missile tried to follow her round but at the critical instant the Hercules disappeared from its line of sight, and the rocky corner blocked the infra-red emissions of her exhausts.

The missile crashed into the cliff face, gouging out a great fall of rock and filling the pass behind the Hercules with dust and smoke.

Sean brought the Hercules back on even keel once again, gentling her, favouring her damaged wing.

'Any sign of the Hind?'

'No . . .' Job broke off as he saw the dread shape materialize through the dust and smoke. 'She's there, she's still coming!'

The entire rear section of the Hind's fuselage was twisted askew and half her rudder was missing. She staggered and lurched through the air, only barely under control and falling rapidly behind the fleeing Hercules. The pilot was a brave man, serving her, keeping her in action to the end.

'He's fired again!' Job cried, as he saw the missile drop from under the stubby wing roots and boost towards them on a tail of smoke.

'She's down!' Job watched the tail rotor of the gunship break away and spiral upwards while the body dropped like a spine-shot buffalo bull and hit the trees, breaking up in a tall burst of flame and smoke.

'Break right!' Job called desperately. Although the Hind was dead, her terrible offspring blazed across the sky, bearing down on them mercilessly.

Sean put the Hercules over as hard as she would go. The missile almost missed the turn and went skidding wide in overshoot, but it corrected itself and came around hard, spinning out a long billow of silver smoke behind it, and it fastened on the starboard number two motor.

For a moment, they were blinded as the smoke of the explosion swept over the canopy, and was as suddenly swept away. The Hercules convulsed as though in agony. The missile blast threw her wing up, miraculously knocking her back onto even keel and adroitly Sean held her there.

He looked across in horror at the damage. The number two engine was gone, blown out of its mountings, leaving a terrible gaping wound in the leading edge of the wing. It was a mortal blow. In her death throes, the Hercules careered across the sky, dragged around by the asymmetrical thrust of her live engines, the damaged wing flexing and beginning to fold backwards.

Sean eased back the throttles, trying to relieve the strain and balance the thrust. He looked ahead, and there was the river, wide and shallow and tranquil above the turmoil of the falls. The first rays of the sun were buttering the tops of the trees on either bank and the crocodiles lay black on the white sandbanks.

Sean flipped on the internal tannoy and spoke over the loudspeakers into the cargo hold. 'Hold on! We are going to hit hard!' he said in Shangane, and pulled his own harness adjustment in tighter.

The Hercules lumbered down heavily, both wings so badly damaged that Sean was amazed that she was still airborne.

'Too fast,' Sean muttered. She was dropping like an express elevator. They would hit the trees short of the river. He braced himself to lose a wing with disruption of air flow, and gingerly pulled on full flap to slow her down.

Far from destroying herself, the Hercules responded gratefully to the additional lift, and floated in with a semblance of her old elegance. She skimmed the tree-tops on the riverbank and Sean switched off the fuel pumps, mains and magnetos to prevent fire. He held the nose high, bleeding off speed and the needle on the airspeed indicator wound back sharply. The stall warning buzzer sounded, and then the deafening klaxon of the landing-gear chimed in, trying to warn him that his wheels were still up.

The controls went sloppy as the Hercules approached the stall, but they were out in the centre of the river, twenty feet up, dropping swiftly. The crocodiles slid off the sand-bar directly ahead, churning the green water in panic, and Sean kept feeling the control column back and back, fending her off until the last possible moment.

He felt the tail touch the water and the airspeed indicator was right down to forty knots. The Hercules stalled and belly-flopped into the river. A solid green wave broke over the nose and washed the canopy, spurting in through the bullet-holes.

Both Sean and Job were flung forward violently against their shoulder harnesses, and then the Hercules bobbed up and surfed on her belly, slowing down and turning to stop broadside to the current.

'Are you all right?' Sean barked at Job. For reply, Job unbuckled his harness and leapt out of the co-pilot's seat.

The deck was canted under Sean's feet as he stood up. Through the canopy he saw that the Hercules was floating down aimlessly on the current. Her empty fuel tanks and the air trapped in the fuselage were keeping her afloat.

'Come on!' He led Job back into the main hold and saw at a glance that the cases of missiles were still secured in their heavy cargo nets.

The Shanganes were in a panic, at least two of them injured, writhing and moaning in the puddles of drying vomit on the deck, one with the sharp jagged end of bone protruding through the flesh of his broken arm.

Sean spun the locking wheel on the emergency hatch and kicked it outwards. Immediately the nylon escape chute inflated and popped out like a drunkard's yellow tongue to flop onto the surface of the water below.

Sean leaned out of the open hatch. They were drifting towards another sand-bar and he judged that the water under their keel was only shoulder-deep for he could see bottom clearly.

'Ferdinand.' Sean picked him out of the mob of milling Shanganes. 'This way, get them out!' He saw Ferdinand sober and lash out at the panic-stricken troopers around him, driving them towards the hatch.

'Show them how it's done,' Sean ordered Job. 'And once you are down, get them to haul the hull onto the sand-bar.'

Job folded his arms over his chest and jumped feet first onto the chute. He shot down into the water and then floundered to his feet. The water came up to his armpits and, immediately, he waded to the Hercules' side and threw his whole weight against it.

One at a time, the uninjured Shanganes followed him down the chute, and at the bottom, Job took charge of them. Sean shoved the last trooper through the hatch and then leapt out himself.

The water was just a few degrees below blood warm, and as soon as he surfaced he saw that all the men were straining against the Hercules' floating carcass and slowly moving her across the flow of the river. He added his own weight to theirs, and gradually the bottom shelved beneath their feet, and the water dropped to the level of their waists.

The belly of the Hercules ran aground, and she settled heavily as the fuselage flooded. The men dragged themselves onto the sand-bar and collapsed in sodden heaps, their expressions dull and bovine from the after-effects of terror and exertion.

Sean looked around him, trying to assess their position and plan his priorities. The Hercules was stranded high enough to ensure that only the lower part of the fuselage was flooded and that the missiles would not be submerged and have their delicate electronic circuitry ruined.

The current had swept them in under the sheer riverbank and the summer floods had piled dead trees and driftwood high against it. The sand-bar was merely a narrow strip below the bank.

'We must move fast,' Sean told Job. 'We can expect that the Hind was able to transmit a signal to the rest of the squadron, and they'll come looking for us.'

'What do you want to do first?'

'Unload the Stingers,' Sean answered promptly. 'Get them busy.'

Once Sean climbed aboard again he found that the hydraulic rams on the cargo door were still operating off the batteries and he lowered the ramp.

The weight of each wooden case was stencilled upon it. 152 lb.

'They are light, two men to a case,' Sean ordered, and he and Job lifted them onto the shoulders of each pair as they stepped forward. As soon as they received it, they trotted down the ramp onto the sand-bar, and up the bank into the trees. Ferdinand showed them where to stash them and cover them with driftwood.

It took less than twenty minutes to unload the cargo, and every minute Sean was in a ferment of impatience and anxiety. As the last case was carried ashore, he hurried out onto the ramp and peered up at the sky, expecting to hear the approaching whine of rotors and Isotov turbos.

'Our luck isn't going to last,' he told Job. 'We must get rid of the Hercules.'

'What are you going to do, swallow it or bury it?' Job asked sarcastically.

Against the forward bulkhead of the Hercules' hold was a 120-ton loading winch, used to drag cargo aboard. Under Sean's instruction, four Shanganes ran out the winch cable and used the Hercules' inflatable life raft to take the end of it across the river and shackle it to a tree on the far bank.

While they were doing this, Sean and Job searched the Hercules and stripped it of every item of useful equipment, from the first-aid kit to the stores of coffee and sugar in the tiny forward galley. With satisfaction, Sean saw that the tropical first-aid box was substantial and contained a good supply of malarial prophylactics and antibiotics. He sent it ashore with one of the Shanganes and ran back to the loading ramp.

The dinghy was returning and there was still no sound nor sight of marauding Hind gunships. It was too good to bear thinking about.

'Get everybody ashore,' Sean told Job, and went to the winch controls.

As he engaged the clutch, the steel cable came up taut and the Hercules' hull which was heavily beached on the sand-bar lurched and began to swing. He kept the winch running and the sand gritted and scraped under her belly as she was dragged by her own winch into deeper water.

As soon as she was afloat, Sean half closed the ramp to prevent her flooding too rapidly and winched her into the middle of the river, where the current was swiftest. As soon as she took the current and began to drift downstream, Sean grabbed the bolt cutters from their rack on the bulkhead and sheared the cable. The Hercules floated free.

On an impulse Sean cut a four-foot length from the end of the severed winch cable, and the stainless steel strands immediately began to unravel of their own accord. He rolled three of the separate strands into a tight loop and slipped the roll into his back pocket. Job would fit hardwood buttons to the strands. The garrotting wire was one of the Scouts' favourite clandestine weapons, and Sean had felt half-naked since he had lost his in the pack that he had dropped down the cliff. He transferred his full attention back to the Hercules.

'The fuel tanks are almost empty,' he murmured as he watched her progress downstream. 'She should float until she reaches the falls.' He stayed on board while at least two miles of riverbank went by.

In the meantime, he used the bolt cutters to sever the hydraulic pipes and fuel leads that ran along the roof of the cargo hold. A mixture of hydraulic fluid and Avtur dribbled and spurted and puddled onto the floor of the hold. Satisfied at last that he had done everything possible to throw off the pursuit, he balanced in the open escape hatch and pulled the pin from the phosphorus grenade that he had commandeered from Ferdinand.

'Thanks, old girl,' he spoke aloud to the Hercules. 'You have been a darling. The least I can offer you is a Viking's funeral.' He rolled the grenade down the deck of the hold and then leapt out of the hatch and hit the water. He came up swimming, reaching out in a full over-arm crawl with the image in his mind of those fat black crocodiles he had seen on the sand-bar.

Behind him, he heard the muffled bump of the exploding grenade but he never paused nor looked back until he felt the ground under his feet. By then, the Hercules was a quarter of a mile downstream, burning furiously but still afloat. Black oily smoke boiled up into the clear morning sky.

Sean waded the last few yards to the steep bank and crawled up it on hands and knees. While he sat there panting and gulping for breath, he heard the familiar and by now well-hated sound of rotors and Isotov turbo engines coming in fast. The smoke of the burning Hercules was a beacon that the Hinds would have spotted from fifty miles out.

Sean took a handful of mud from the bank on which he sat and smeared his bare arms and face. He crawled under a dense bush on the bank and watched the Hind come sweeping in over the treetops, banking in a wide circle around the burning hulk of the Hercules and then hovering like an evil vampire two hundred feet above it.

The flames reached one of the fuel tanks and the Hercules exploded in a dragon's breath, scattering pieces of itself across the river, the flames hissing into steam as they hit the water.

The Hind hung over the river for almost five minutes, perhaps searching for survivors, and then abruptly it rose high, turned its nose southwards and dwindled to a speck against the blue.

'Limited range and endurance, like the man said.' Sean stood up from his hiding place. 'Now go home like a good little Ruskie and report the target destroyed. Go tell Bobby Mugabe that he doesn't have to worry about his precious Stingers falling into the wrong hands.'

He reached into his top pocket and brought out the packet of Dutch cigars. The cardboard disintegrated in his hands and the leaf had dissolved into a soggy porridge. He tossed it into the river.

'Time I gave up anyway,' he sighed, and trudged along the bank, heading upstream.

Job was working on the two injured troopers.

'This one has got a nice set of cracked ribs and a broken collarbone.' Job finished the strapping and then indicated the other patient. 'I left this one for you.'

'Appreciate it.' Sean grunted, and examined the broken arm. 'It's a bloody mess.'

'Nice adjective,' Job agreed. Two inches of the shattered humerus protruded from dark bruises and blood clots. A buzzing swarm of metallic-blue flies were circling the clots, and Sean brushed them away.

'What have you done, so far?'

'Given him a handful of painkillers from the med box.'

'That should stun an ox,' Sean nodded. 'Get me a piece of nylon line and two of the strongest Shanganes.'

The arm had shortened dramatically and Sean had to get the ends of the broken bone to meet again. He looped the nylon rope around the trooper's wrist and gave the ends to the Shangane strong men.

'When I say pull, you pull, understand?' he ordered. 'Okay, Job, hold him.'

They had done this before, often. Job took up his position sitting behind the patient and slipped his arms under his armpits and locked them around his chest.

'I'm going to hurt you,' Sean promised the patient, and the man stared back at him impassively.

'Ready?' Job nodded, and Sean glanced up at the rope. 'Pull!' They laid back with a will.

The injured man's eyes snapped wide open, and a rash of sweat droplets like blisters burst out on his skin.

'Pull harder!' Sean snarled at Ferdinand, and the arm began to elongate. The sharp point of protruding bone withdrew slowly into the flesh.

The Shangane ground his teeth together in the effort of re-straining himself from screaming. The sound was like two pieces of glass being rubbed together forcibly, and it grated along Sean's nerve ends.

The point of bone popped back into the swollen purple wound and Sean heard the two ends rasp together deep in the flesh.

'That's it! Hold it!' he told Ferdinand, and deftly placed two splints from the first-aid box along each side of the arm. He strapped them in place with surgical tape, binding it up as firmly as he dared without cutting off the circulation, and then nodded at Ferdinand.

'Slowly. Let it go.' Ferdinand released pressure and the splints held the arm straight.

'Another breakthrough for medical science,' Job murmured. 'An elegant and sophisticated procedure, Doc.'

331

'Can you walk?' Sean asked. 'Or do we have to carry you home?'

'Of course. I can walk.' The trooper was indignant. 'Do you think I am a woman?'

'If you were, we would ask a top bridal price for you,' Sean grinned at him, and stood up.

'Let's inspect the loot,' he suggested to Job. It was their first opportunity to examine the crates from the Hercules.

There were thirty-five of them piled haphazardly under the spreading branches of an African mahogany. With Ferdinand and four of his men assisting, they sorted through them, stacking them neatly after noting the lettering on each.

Thirty-three cases, each weighing 154 pounds were marked:

STINGER GUIDED MISSILE SYSTEM.
1 X GRIP STOCK AND ANTENNA
1 X INTERROGATOR.
5 X LOADED LAUNCH TUBES.

'That gives China 165 shots, and there are eleven Hinds left in the squadron after the one you knocked out of the sky,' Job calculated. 'Sounds good to me.'

'With the way some of these beauties shoot, they are going to need every one of them,' Sean grunted, and then his expression of deliberate pessimism lightened. 'Well, well! Here is one for the book!'

One of the two remaining odd-sized cases was stencilled:

STINGER GUIDED MISSILE SYSTEM.
TRAINING SET M. 134.
TRACKING HEAD TRAINER.

'That will make somebody's life a lot easier,' Job agreed. The captured manuals had discussed this training system which allowed an instructor to monitor a trainee's tracking technique during a simulated missile launch. It would be invaluable equipment for whoever was given the job of teaching the Renamo troops to use the system.

However, it was not until Sean examined the last and smallest case that the full value of the prize dawned on him.

The small wooden crate was stencilled:

'Sweet Trinity,' he whistled. 'It's a post, not a common or garden system, but a ruddy post that we have got ourselves here!'

'Let's take a look!' Job was as excited as he was.

Sean hesitated, like a child tempted to open his gift before the dawn of his birthday. He glanced up at the sky looking for Hinds, strange how he had picked up that nervous habit from his Shanganes.

'We daren't move until dark. Plenty of time to kill,' he capitulated, and leaned over to draw the bayonet from the sheath of Ferdinand's webbing.

Gently he prised open the lid of the crate and lifted away the slabs of white polyurethane packing. The software was contained in a heavy-duty plastic carry pack. He sprang the catches on the lid and opened the case. The dozens of software cassettes were each colour-coded, sealed in transparent glassine envelopes and fitted into tailored slots in the interior. This was what they had read about in the manuals they had borrowed from Carlyle, the British gunnery officer.

'Get the manuals.' Sean told Job. And when he brought them over they squatted beside the open case and pored through the heavy volume which described the post system.

'Here it is! Hind attack system. Colour code red. Numerical code S.42.A.'

Under the post system the Stinger missiles could be programmed to attack various targets by employing tactics and search frequencies specific to that type of aircraft. Simply by inserting one of the micro-cassettes into the console of the launcher, the missile could be instructed to alter its attack technique.

'"System software cassette. S.42.A.."' Job followed the text with his forefinger as he read aloud from the manual, '"is targeted on the Hind helicopter gunship. The system employs a 'two-colour' seeker which registers both infra-red and ultra-violet emissions in two stages. The initial stage will lock to infra-red from the engine exhaust system.

'"The Hind's exhaust suppressors divert and emit those infra-red rays through heavily armoured outlets below the main fuselage. Missile-strikes on this section of the Hind have proved ineffective.

'"The S.42.A. modification automatically switches the guidance system of the Stinger into ultra-violet seeker mode when range-to-target is reduced to a hundred metres. Ultra-violet is emitted principally from the air-intake ports of the Isotov TV3-117 turbo shaft engines. This area is the only section of the fuselage not encased in titanium armour plate and missile-strikes through the engine intake ports have resulted in hundred per cent kills.

'"To achieve effective ultra-violet acquisition, the initial launch of the missile must be made from below and dead ahead of the aircraft, at a range not exceeding 1000 metres nor less than 150 metres."'

Job closed the manual with a snap.

'Big casino!' he said. 'China is getting more than he ever hoped for.'

* * *

There were thirty heavy cases to carry and only twenty uninjured men, including Sean and Job. Sean cached the boxes that they were forced to leave. He would send a detail back to fetch them once they reached the Renamo lines.

Carrying what they could, including the trainer and the post modification equipment, they set out along the bank of the Pungwe river at nightfall, groping for a contact with the Renamo front line. They marched all that night.

The extended column, slowed down by the heavy cases of missiles, covered only twelve miles before sunrise. However, the weather had changed and the wind had backed into the east bringing in low cloud and a cold drizzle of rain that would hide them from the searching Hinds. They kept going all that day.

At dusk Sean let them rest for a few hours, and they huddled miserably in the rain until Sean roused them once again and they stumbled on, slipping and sliding in the mud, and cursing the loads upon their backs. An hour after sunrise the clouds rolled away and their sodden battledress steamed as it dried on their backs.

Two hours later they ran into the ambush.

They were moving through light savannah along the riverbank

334

The flat-topped acacia thorn trees were interspersed with clumps of coarse elephant grass.

Sean heard the metallic snap of the loading handle being jerked back to cock a machine-gun and before the sound had fully registered in his brain, he was diving forward, shouting a warning to his Shanganes. As he hit the sandy earth with his elbows and belly, he saw the muzzle flashes shimmering and dancing like fairy lights in the grass only thirty paces ahead and a blaze of shot passed over his head, making him blink and flinch.

He rolled left to throw the gunner's aim, holding the AKM with one hand as though it were a pistol, firing blindly to further confuse the attackers and groping for the grenade on his belt.

He was on the point of hurling the grenade when behind him Ferdinand shouted a challenge in Portuguese and the firing from the front shrivelled and died away. From the patch of elephant grass just ahead of Sean, a voice replied to the challenge and then Ferdinand was shouting urgently in Shangane, 'Cease fire! Cease fire! Renamo! Renamo!'

There was a long suspicious silence during which Sean kept his right arm cocked back ready to throw the grenade. He had seen too many good men called out to die in a false truce.

'Renamo!' A voice from the front reiterated. 'Friends!'

'All right!' Sean shouted back in Shangane. 'Stand up, Renamo. Let us see your beautiful friendly faces.'

Somebody laughed, and a grinning black face under a tiger-striped camouflage cap popped up out of the grass and ducked back immediately.

After a few seconds, when there was no more firing, another man stood up cautiously, and then another. Sean's Shanganes came to their feet and moved forward, slowly at first and with weapons cocked, and then they were meeting in the open ground, shaking hands and laughing and slapping each other's backs. They had run into the sector held by the battalion under the command of Major Takawira. He recognized Sean immediately and they shook hands with mutual pleasure.

'Colonel Courtney! What a relief to see you alive! We heard on the news from the BBC and Radio Zimbabwe that your aircraft had been shot down in flames with you and all your men wiped out.'

'I need your help, Major,' Sean told him. 'I've left twenty cases of missiles cached out there in the bush. I want you to send a

335

detachment of a hundred men to fetch them in. One of my men will guide them to the cache.'

'I'll send my best men. I'll pick them out personally,' Takawira assured him.

'How far are we from General China's HQ?' Sean asked.

'The Frelimo helicopters have forced him to pull back. His new HQ is only six miles upstream. I have just spoken to him on the radio and the general is most anxious to see you.'

Their progress was a triumphal march, for news of their success flashed through the Renamo lines ahead of them. Men in tiger stripes turned out to cheer them and shake their hands and thump their backs as they passed. The porters bore the cases of missiles aloft as though they were the ark of Jehovah and they, the priests of an arcane religion. They sang the Renamo battle songs as they trotted along proudly under their burdens.

General China was waiting to greet them at the entrance to his newly constructed command bunker, resplendent in crisply laundered battledress and decorations, with the maroon beret cocked jauntily over one eye.

'I knew you would not fail me, Colonel.' For the first time in their acquaintance, Sean had the feeling that his smile was genuine.

'We lost almost thirty men under Sergeant Alphonso,' Sean told him brusquely. 'We were forced to abandon them.'

'No! No, Colonel!' General China clasped his shoulder in an unparalleled display of goodwill. 'Alphonso got out safely. He lost only three men in reaching the mission at St Mary's. I have just had radio contact with them. They will be in our lines by tomorrow evening at the latest. The entire operation was a brilliant success, Colonel.' He dropped his hand from Sean's shoulder. 'Now let us see what you have brought me.'

The porters laid the wooden cases at his feet. A black Caesar receiving the spoils of war, Sean thought ironically.

'Open them!' China beamed. Sean had never expected such childlike excitement from one usually so cold and contained. China was actually performing an ecstatic little jig, and scrubbing his hands together as he watched the junior officers on his staff wielding jemmies and bayonet blades in an attempt to prise up the lid of the first crate. The steel strapping frustrated their efforts.

In the end China could no longer control himself and pushed

his officers away, snatched a jemmy bar out of the hands of one of them and attacked the case himself. He was sweating profusely with excitement and exertion when at last the lid yielded and there were obsequious cries of congratulation from his staff as the contents were revealed.

The Stinger launcher was fully assembled with a missile tube loaded. The IFF interrogator was packed separately in a transparent glassine envelope ready to be plugged into the console head by its short coil of cable. The additional four disposal tubes, each containing a single missile, nestled in the moulded white polyurethane foam packaging. After firing the missile, the empty tube would be discarded and replaced by a fresh tube containing its own sixteen-pound missile.

The laughter and cheering gradually subsided and the general staff crowded forward to examine the contents of the case, albeit with a marked reserve as though they had discovered a nest of poisonous scorpions under a rock and expected that at any second a fanged tail would whip out at them.

General China slowly went down on one knee and reverently lifted the assembled launcher out of its foam nest.

His staff watched in awe as he settled the clumsy weapon on his shoulder. The missile tube extended behind him and the consol with its antenna, looking as mundane as a plastic milk crate almost totally obscured General China's features. He peered studiously into the aiming screen of the console and gripped the triggered pistol stock.

He aimed the Stinger skyward and his staff uttered small sounds of encouragement and admiration.

'Let the Frelimo *henshaw* come now,' China boasted. 'We will see them burn.' And he began to make helicopter and machine-gun noises like a small boy at play, pointing the missile at flocks of imaginary Hind gunships that circled overhead.

'Pow! Pow!' he cried. 'Vroom! Swish! Boom!'

'Ka pow!' With a straight face, Sean joined in and the general's staff howled with delight and tried to out-do each other with the sounds of exploding and crashing helicopters.

Somebody began to sing and they all picked up the refrain, clapping their hands to the rhythm of the Renamo battle anthem, swaying and stamping their feet.

Now there were two hundred men singing, their voices blending and rising into the beautiful melodious sound of Africa that made

337

the goose-pimples rise on Sean's forearms and the hair on the back of his neck prickle. General China stood in the midst of them with the missile on his shoulders and led the chorus. His voice soared above the rest, amazing Sean with its range and clarity, a magnificent tenor which would not have disgraced any of the world's great opera houses.

The song ended with a great shout of defiance, 'Renamo!' and their dark faces were lit by a fierce patriotic ardour.

'In this mood, they'll be hard men to beat,' Sean thought, and General China handed the launcher to one of his men and came to shake Sean's hand.

'Congratulations, Colonel.' He was earnest and happy at the same time. 'I think you have saved the cause. I am grateful.'

'That's fine, China,' Sean was ironical. 'But don't just tell me how grateful, show me.'

'Of course, forgive me.' China put on a little show of repentance. 'In the excitement I almost forgot, there is somebody very anxious to see you.'

Sean felt his breathing shorten and his chest constrict.

'Where is she?'

'In my bunker, Colonel.' General China indicated the carefully concealed entrance to the dugout amongst the trees.

Sean elbowed his way roughly through the ranks of excited soldiers, and as he reached the entrance to the bunker, he could restrain himself no longer and he went down the rough steps three at a time.

Claudia was in the radio dugout, sitting on a bench along the far wall with her two wardresses flanking her. He spoke her name when he saw her and she came to her feet slowly, staring at him, white-faced with disbelief. The bones of her cheeks threatened to burst through the almost translucent skin and her eyes were huge and dark as midnight.

As he crossed to her, Sean saw the marks on her wrists, livid weals crusted with fresh scab and his anger matched his joy. He swept her into his arms and she was as thin and frail as a child. For a moment she stood quiescent in his embrace, and then fiercely she threw her arms around his neck and hugged him. He was surprised by her strength, and she shivered in convulsive spasms as she pressed her face into the hollow of his neck.

They stood locked together, not moving nor speaking for a

338

long time until Sean felt the wetness soaking through his shirt front.

'Please don't cry, my darling.'

Gently he lifted her face between his hands, and with his thumbs wiped the tears away.

'It's just that I'm so happy now,' she smiled through the last of her tears. 'Nothing else matters any more, now that you are back.'

He took her hands and lifted them to his lips, kissing the broken scabbed skin on her wrists.

'They can't hurt me any more, not now,' she said, and Sean turned his head and looked at the two uniformed wardresses who still sat on the bench.

'Your mothers rutted with the stinking dung-eating hyena,' he said softly in Shangane, and they flinched at the insult. 'Get out! Go! Before I rip out your ovaries and feed them to the vultures!'

They glowered and hung their heads until Sean dropped his hand onto the butt of his pistol. Then they moved with alacrity, jumping up from the bench and sidling to the dugout steps.

Sean turned back to Claudia, and for the first time kissed her mouth. That kiss lasted a long time and when they drew unwillingly apart Claudia whispered, 'When they took off the handcuffs and let me wash, I knew you were coming back.'

Her words conjured up a picture of the degradation and brutality she had come through and Sean's reply was bitter.

'The bastard. Somehow I'm going to make him suffer for what he has done to you. I swear that to you.'

'No, Sean. It doesn't matter any more. It's over. We are together again. That is all that matters.'

They had only a few more minutes alone before General China came bustling into the radio dugout at the head of his staff, still smiling and elated.

He ushered Sean and Claudia through into his private office and seemed not to notice that they both treated his affable hospitality with icy reserve. They sat close together in front of his desk, quietly holding hands, not responding to his pleasantries.

'I have prepared quarters for you,' General China told them. 'In fact I have evicted one of my senior commanders and given you his dugout. I hope you will find it adequate for your needs.'

'We aren't planning on a long stay, General,' Sean told him. 'I want to be on my way back to the border, with Miss Monterro, tomorrow morning at the very latest.'

'Ah, Colonel, of course I want to accommodate you. From now on, you are an honoured and privileged guest. You have certainly earned your release. However, for operational reasons that happy moment must be delayed for a few days. Frelimo are moving in large concentrations of troops.'

Reluctantly Sean conceded. 'Fair enough, but in the meantime, we expect five-star treatment. Miss Monterro needs new clothes to replace these rags.'

'I shall have a selection of the best we have sent to your dugout from our stores. However, I cannot promise either Calvin Klein or Gucci.'

'While we are at it, we'll need a team of servants to do our laundry and cleaning and cooking.'

'I haven't forgotten your colonial origins, Colonel,' China answered slyly. 'One of my men was an under-chef at the President Hotel in Johannesburg. He understands European tastes.'

Sean stood up. 'We'll inspect our quarters now.'

'One of my junior officers will escort you,' General China suggested. 'If there is anything further you need, please let him know. He has my personal orders to give you whatever he can to make you comfortable. As I have said before, you are honoured guests.'

'He gives me the creeps,' Claudia whispered, as the subaltern ushered them out of the dugout. 'I don't know when he frightens me more, when he is being charming or menacing.'

'It won't be for much longer.' Sean put his arm round her shoulders and led her into the open air, but somehow the sunlight lacked warmth and despite his assurances to Claudia, the chill of General China's presence persisted.

*　　*　　*

The dugout to which the subaltern led them was in the bush above the riverbank, not more than three hundred yards from the general's HQ. The entrance was screened with a piece of tattered camouflage net and the interior was freshly dug out of the hard red clay of the riverbank.

'It's so new that it probably hasn't yet acquired a permanent

340

population of bed bugs and lice and other wild game,' Sean remarked.

The clay walls were damp and cool and there was ventilation through the spaces between the roof poles.

The only furnishings were a table and two stools of mopane poles against one wall, and opposite that a raised bedstead also of mopane poles and a mattress of combed elephant grass covered with a sheet of faded canvas. There was however, one extraordinary luxury, a mosquito net hung above the bed.

The subaltern who was escorting them summoned the domestic staff and the three of them lined up in front of Sean and Claudia. The two camp boys would take care of their laundry and cleaning under the supervision of the chef.

The chef was an elderly Shangane with a pleasant lined face and silver-frosted hair and beard. He reminded Claudia of a black Santa Claus. They both liked him immediately.

'My name is Joyful, sir.'

'So you speak English, Joyful?'

'And Afrikaans and Portuguese and Shona and . . .'

'Enough already.' Sean held up a hand to stop him. 'Can you cook?

'I'm the best damned cook in Mozambique.'

'Joyful and modest,' Claudia laughed.

'Okay, Joyful, tonight we will have Chateaubriand,' Sean teased him, and Joyful looked doleful.

'Sorry, sir, no fillet steak.'

'All right, Joyful.' Sean relented. 'You just make us the best dinner you can.'

'I'll tell you when it's ready, sir and madam.'

'Don't hurry.' said Claudia, and lowered the netting across the doorway, summarily dismissing all of them.

They stood hand in hand and studied the bed thoughtfully. Claudia broke the silence.

'Are you thinking what I am thinking?'

'Before or after dinner?' Sean asked.

'Both,' she replied, and led him by the hand.

They undressed each other with aching deliberation, drawing out the pleasure of truly discovering each other's bodies.

Though they were already lovers, he had only had one fleeting glimpse of her, and she had never seen him naked. She studied him with big solemn eyes, not smiling, taking her time until he

341

was forced to ask, 'Well, do I get the Monterro seal of approval?'

'Oh, boy!' she breathed, still deadly serious, and he lifted her on to the bed.

It was darkening outside the dugout when Joyful coughed politely beyond the screen doorway.

'Dinner is ready, sir and madam.'

They ate at the table of mopane poles by the light of a paraffin lantern that Joyful had scavenged from somewhere.

'Oh my God!' Claudia cried when she saw what Joyful had provided for them. 'I didn't realize how hungry I was.'

It was a casserole of plump green pigeons and wild mushrooms, with side dishes of steamed yellow yams and cassava cakes and banana fritters.

'General China sent this for you,' Joyful explained, and set cans of South African beer on the crowded table.

'Joyful, you are a paragon.'

They ate in dedicated silence, smiling across the table at each other between mouthfuls. At last Claudia groaned softly.

'I think I can just waddle as far as the bed, but definitely no further.'

'Suits me fine,' he said, and reached across to take her hand.

The mosquito net was a tent over them, creating an intimate and secret temple for their loving. The light from the lantern was soft and golden. It washed subtle tones and shadings across the planes of her face and the rounds and hollows of her body.

The texture of her skin fascinated him. It was so fine-pored as to seem glossed like warm wax. He stroked her shoulders and arms and belly, marvelling at the feel of her.

She rasped her fingernails through his short crisp beard, and pressed her face into the springing curls that covered his chest.

'You are as hairy and hard as a wild animal,' she whispered. 'And as dangerous. I should be terrified of you.'

'Aren't you?'

'A little, yes. That's what makes it such fun.'

She was starved to the point where her ribs showed clearly through her pale skin. Her limbs were slender and childlike, and the marks of her suffering upon them threatened to break his heart. Even her breasts seemed smaller, but it was as though their diminution had merely emphasized the sweet and tender shape. She watched him take the nipple of one between his lips and she stroked the thick curls at the back of his neck.

342

'That feels so good,' she whispered. 'But there are two.' And she took a handful of his hair to direct his mouth across to the other side.

Once while she sat astride him, he looked up at her and reached high to stroke the soft skin of her throat and shoulders and said, 'In this light, you look like a little girl.'

'And me trying so hard to prove to you what a big girl I am,' she pouted down at him, then leaned forward to kiss his mouth.

They slept so intricately entwined that their hearts beat against each other and their breath mingled and they woke to find that they had begun again while they still slept.

'He's so clever,' she murmured drowsily. 'Already he can find his way all on his own.'

'Do you want to go back to sleep?'

'Do I, hell!'

Much later she asked him, 'Do you think we could make this last for ever?'

'We can try.'

But at last through the slats above them, the dawn sent orange-gold fingers of light, and Claudia cried softly, 'No. I don't want it to end. I want to keep you inside me for ever and ever.'

When Joyful brought the tea to the bedside, on the tray with the mugs was an invitation from General China to dine in the mess that evening.

* * *

General China's mess night was for Claudia and Sean less than an unqualified success, despite the general's continued efforts to charm them.

The buffalo meat he served was tough and rank and the beer made the officers of the general's staff loud and argumentative. The weather had changed and was close and sweltering even after dark and the bunker that served as a mess was thick with the smoke of cheap native tobacco and the odour of masculine sweat.

General China drank none of the beer, but sat at the head of the table ignoring the shouted conversation and hearty eating habits of his staff. Instead, he played the gallant to Claudia, engaging her in a discussion which she at first attempted to evade.

Claudia was unaccustomed to the table manners of Africa. She watched with an awful fascination as the stiff maize porridge was scooped from the communal pot in the centre of the table by many hands, moulded into balls between the fingers and then dipped into buffalo-meat gravy. Greasy gravy ran down their chins, and no attempt was made to moderate the conversation during mastication, so that small particles of food were sprayed across the table when one of them laughed or exclaimed loudly.

Despite the fact that she was still half starved Claudia had no appetite for the meal and it took an effort to concentrate on General China's dissertation.

'We have divided the entire country into three war zones,' he explained. 'General Takawira Dos Alves is the commander of the north. He commands the provinces of Niassa and Cabo Delgado. In the south, the commander is General Tippoo Tip, and of course, I command the army of the central provinces of Manica and Sofala. Between us we control almost fifty per cent of the total ground area of Mozambique, and another forty per cent of the country is a destruction zone over which we are forced to maintain a scorched earth policy to prevent Frelimo growing either food for their troops or cash crops to finance their war effort against us.'

'So the reports of atrocities that we have received in the United States are true then.' He had engaged Claudia's interest at last. Her tone was sharp as she accused, 'Your troops are attacking and wiping out the civilian population in those destruction zones.'

'No, Miss Monterro.' China's smile was icy. 'The fact that we have moved the civilian population out of many of those destruction areas, is unavoidably true, but all the atrocities, all the massacres and tortures, have been committed by Frelimo themselves.'

'They are the government of Mozambique, why would they massacre their own people?' Claudia protested.

'I agree with you, Miss Monterro, sometimes it is difficult to follow the devious working of the Marxist mind. The reality is that Frelimo is unable to govern. They are unable to provide even basic protection to the civilian population outside the cities, let alone give them services of health and education and transport and communications. To draw world attention away from the total failure of their economic policies and their lack of popular support, they have provided the international media with a Roman holiday of slaughter and torture which they blame upon

344

Renamo and South Africa. It is easier to kill people than to feed and educate them, and the anti-Renamo propaganda is worth a million lives, to a Marxist that is.'

'You are suggesting that a Khmer Rouge style massacre is being conducted here in Mozambique by the government forces?' Claudia was aghast, pale and perspiring with the noise and fug of the subterranean mess, and with the horror of General China's explanations.

'I am not suggesting, Miss Monterro, I am simply stating the literal truth.'

'But, but, surely the world must do something?'

'The world is uncaring, Miss Monterro. It has been left for us, Renamo, to try to bring down the heinous Marxist regime.'

'Frelimo is the elected government,' Claudia pointed out, but General China shook his head.

'No, Miss Monterro, very few governments in Africa are elected. There has never been an election in Mozambique or Angola or Tanzania or any of the other gems of African Socialism. In Africa the trick is to seize power and hang onto to it at all costs. The typical African government plunges into the void left by the exodus of the colonial power and entrenches itself behind a barricade of AK 47 assault rifles. It then declares a one-party system of government which further precludes any form of opposition and it nominates a presidential dictator for life.'

'Tell me, General China,' Claudia raised her voice above the roar of conversation further down the mess table, 'if one day, your military efforts succeed and you and the other generals of Renamo vanquish Frelimo and become the new government of this country, will you then allow free elections and a truly democratic system to evolve?'

For a moment General China stared at her in astonishment and then he laughed delightedly.

'My very dear Miss Monterro, your childlike belief in the myth of the essential goodness of mankind is really rather touching. I certainly have not fought so hard and so long to gain power, simply to hand it over to a bunch of illiterate peasants. No, Miss Monterro, once we have the power it will remain safely in the right hands.' He extended his own elegantly shaped hands, pink palms uppermost, towards her. 'These,' he said.

'So you are every bit as bad as you say the others are.' There were hot red spots of anger on Claudia's cheeks. This was the man who had put chains on her wrists and incarcerated her in that vile pit. She hated him with all her strength.

'I think you are actually beginning to understand at last, even through the haze of your liberal emotions. In Africa there are no good guys and no bad guys, there are simply winners and losers.' He smiled again. 'And I assure you, Miss Monterro, that I intend to be one of the winners.'

General China turned away from her as one of his signals officers ducked through the low entrance to the bunker and hurried down to the head of the table. With an apologetic salute, he handed the general a yellow message flimsy. China read it without change of expression and then looked up at his guests.

'Please excuse me for a few minutes.' China placed his beret at the correct angle over one eye, then stood and followed the signaller out of the bunker.

The moment he was gone, Claudia leaned across the table to Sean. 'Can't we get out of here now? I don't think I can bear another moment of it. God, how I hate that man.'

'Mess tradition doesn't seem very strict,' Sean murmured. 'If we leave, I don't think anyone is going to take offence.'

As they crossed to the doorway, there was a drunken chorus of suggestive catcalls and whistles, and they went up the steps with relief.

The night air had cooled and Claudia breathed it in deeply and gratefully. 'I don't know which was more suffocating, the fug or the dialectic.' She breathed again. 'I never expected Africa to be like this. It's so confused, so illogical, it turns everything I know to be true upside down.'

'But it's interesting, isn't it?' Sean asked.

'Like a nightmare is interesting. Let's go to bed. At least that's something I can believe in completely.'

They turned towards their dugout shelter, but General China's voice halted them.

'You aren't leaving us so soon?' And his tall lithe form came striding towards them out of the darkness. 'I'm afraid I have disappointing news for both of you.'

'You aren't letting us go. You are reneging on our deal,' Sean said flatly. 'I knew this was coming.'

'Circumstances beyond my control,' China assured him smoothly. 'I have just had a radio report from Sergeant Alphonso. As you know I was expecting his return this evening and he and

346

his men would have escorted you and Miss Monterro safely back to the border, however . . .'

'All right, let's hear it from you, China,' Sean snarled angrily. 'What new scheme have you cooked up?'

General China ignored the accusation and the tone in which it was delivered. 'Sergeant Alphonso reports that there is a massive build-up of enemy to the west of our lines. It seems that, emboldened by their gunships, Frelimo, backed by Zimbabwean contingents, are about to launch a full-scale offensive. We are probably already cut off from the Zimbabwe border. The territory that we once controlled seems certain to have been overrun by the enemy advance. Within hours it will become a battlefield, even now Sergeant Alphonso is fighting his way through and has taken some casualties. I am afraid you would not last long out there, Colonel. It would be suicide for you to try to reach the border now. You must remain under my personal protection.'

'What the hell do you want from us?' Sean demanded. 'You are up to something, I can smell the stink of it from here. What is it?'

'Your lack of confidence in my motives is very distressing,' China smiled coldly. 'However, the sooner the Hind gunships are destroyed, the sooner the Frelimo offensive will collapse and you and Miss Monterro will be returned to the civilized world.'

'I'm listening,' Sean told him.

'You are the only one, you and Captain Job, who understand the Stinger. In this our interests coincide. I want you to train a select contingent of my men to handle the Stingers.'

'That's all you want?' Sean stared into his face. 'We train your men to use the Stinger, then you let us go?'

'Exactly.'

'How do I know you won't move the goal posts again?'

'You pain me, Colonel.'

'Not nearly as much as I'd like to.'

'It's agreed then. You will train my men and in exchange I will have you escorted across the border at the very first opportunity.'

'What option do we have?'

'I'm so pleased that you are being reasonable, Colonel. It makes life much easier for all of us.' His voice became crisp and businesslike. 'We must begin immediately.'

'You'll have to let your staff sober up a little,' Sean told him. 'I'll begin first thing tomorrow, and I'll train the Shanganes under

347

Alphonso and Ferdinand, if Alphonso makes it through the Frelimo offensive intact.'

'How long will it take you?' China wanted to know. 'From now on every hour will be vital to our survival.'

'They are bright lads and willing, I should be able to do something with them in a week.'

'You will not have that long.'

'I'll have the Stingers in action just as soon as I possibly can,' Sean retorted irritably. 'Please believe me, General, I don't want to hang around here a minute longer than I have to. Now we'll bid you good-night.' He took Claudia's arm as he turned away.

'Oh Sean,' she whispered. 'I have the terrible premonition that we are caught up in something from which we are never going to escape.' And Sean squeezed her upper arm to make her stop.

'Look up there,' he ordered softly, and she raised her face.

'The stars?' she asked. 'Is that what you want me to look at?'

'Yes, the stars.' They daubed the night as though a gigantic firefly had been crushed to death and its luminous essence smeared across the vault of heaven.

'They calm the soul,' Sean explained gently.

She breathed softly and deeply. 'Yes, you are right, my darling. Tonight we have our love, let's exploit it to the full and let tomorrow take care of itself.'

She felt safe and invulnerable under the tented mosquito netting. The lumpy grass-filled mattress had taken on the shape of their bodies and she did not notice the harsh touch of the canvas covering against her skin.

'If we made love ten thousand times, it would still not have taken the edge off my need for you,' she whispered, as she slipped over the edge of sleep.

She woke suddenly feeling the tension in his body against hers, and instantly he touched her lips to caution her to silence. She lay frozen in the darkness, not daring to move or breathe, and then she heard it. A soft scraping at the entrance of the dugout as the netting curtain was pushed aside and an animal passed through.

Her heart raced away and she bit her lip to stop herself gasping aloud as she heard the thing crossing the earth floor towards the bed. Its paws were almost soundless, just the faintest tick of grit compressed by the stealthy weight. Then she smelled it, the wild gamey smell of a meat-eating animal and she wanted to cry out.

Beside her, Sean moved suddenly, fast as a striking adder; he lunged through the mosquito net and there was a quick scuffle and squeal and she tried to crawl over Sean's back to escape whatever it was.

'Got you, you little bugger,' Sean said grimly. 'You don't sneak up on me twice and get away with it. Now tell me I'm getting old and I'll wring your neck!'

'You'll be young and beautiful for ever, my *Bwana*,' Matatu giggled, and wriggled like a puppy caught by the scruff of the neck.

'Where have you been, Matatu?' Sean demanded sternly. 'What took you so long, did you meet a pretty girl along the way?'

Matatu giggled again, he loved to be accused by Sean of dalliance and amatory exploits.

'I found the roosting place of the *henshaws*,' he boasted. 'The same way I find where the bees have their hive, I watched their flight against the sun and followed them to their secret place.'

Sean drew him closer to the bed and shook his arm gently. 'Tell me,' he ordered, and in the darkness Matatu squatted down and tucked his loin-cloth between his legs and made little self-important throat-clearing and humming sounds.

'There is a round hill, shaped like the head of a bald man,' Matatu began. 'On one side of the hill passes the *insimbi*, the railway, and on the other side the road.'

Sean propped himself on one elbow to listen and with his other arm, he encircled Claudia's naked waist and held her close. She snuggled against him, listening to Matatu's piping pixie voice in the darkness.

'There are many askari around the hill with big *banduki* hidden in holes in the ground.' Sean formed a vivid mental picture of the heavily garrisoned hilltop as Matatu described it to him. Beyond the outer defensive lines the gunships were laagered in separate sandbagged emplacements. Like battle tanks in hull-down fortifications, they would be impregnable, and yet they had only to rise and hover a few feet above ground level to bring into action their devasting Gatling-cannons and rocket pods.

'Inside the circle of roosting *henshaw*, there are many gharries parked and white men in green clothes who climb on the *henshaw* and look inside them all the time.' Matatu described the mobile workshops and fuel tankers and the squads of Russian mechanics

349

and technicians needed to keep the helicopters flying. The training manuals had pointed up the Hind's excessive requirements of service and maintenance, while those big Isotov turbo engines would guzzle Avgas.

'Matatu, did you see railway gharries on the line near the hill?' Sean asked.

'I saw them,' Matatu confirmed. 'Those big round gharries full of beer – the men who ride in the *henshaw* must be very thirsty.' Once many years ago, on one of his infrequent visits to the city with Sean, Matatu had seen a beer tanker disgorging its load at the main Harare beerhall. He had been so impressed that since that day he was utterly convinced that all tankers of whatever size or type contained only beer. Sean could not change his mind on this, Matatu would never accept that some of them actually carried less noble fluids such as gasoline and he always stared wistfully after any tanker they passed on the road.

Sean smiled now in the darkness at the little man's fixation. Fuel for the gunships was obviously being railed from Harare in bulk tankers, and transshipped into smaller road tankers. It was ironic that the fuel was almost certainly being originally supplied by the South Africans. However, if the helicopter squadron was storing its fuel within the laager itself they were taking a grave risk. It was something to bear in mind.

Matatu remained at the bedside for almost an hour while Sean patiently drew from him every possible detail he could of the gunship laager.

Matatu was certain that there were eleven helicopters in the emplacements, which tallied with his own estimate. Of the original twelve, one had been destroyed in the collision with the Hercules.

Matatu was equally certain that only nine of the gunships were actually flying. Hidden on a nearby kopje, he had watched the helicopters sortie from their laager at dawn, return for refuelling during the day and at nightfall come in to roost. Sean knew that Matatu could count accurately to twenty, but after that, he became vague and any greater number was described progressively as 'many' or 'a great deal' and finally as 'like grass on the Serengeti plains'.

So Sean was now fairly certain that two of the gunships had broken down and were probably awaiting spares, and he accepted Matatu's figure of nine operational gunships, still a formidable force, quite sufficient to turn the tide of the looming battle against Renamo unless they could swiftly be put out of the action.

When at last Matatu had finished his recitation he asked simply, 'Now, my *Bwana*, what do you want me to do?'

Sean considered in silence. There was really no reason why he should not bring Matatu in from wherever he was hiding up in the bush, allowing him openly to join the force of Shangane under his command as a tracker. However, he sensed that there might be some future advantage in keeping Matatu hidden from China's cold reptilian gaze.

'You are my wild card, Matatu,' he said in English and then in Swahili, 'I want you to keep out of sight. Do not let any of the men here see you, except Job and me.'

· 'I heard you, my *Bwana*.'

'Come to me each night as you have tonight. I will have food for you and I will tell you what to do. In the meantime, watch and tell me all you see.'

Matatu went so silently that they heard only the faint rustle of the netting at the entrance as he passed through.

'Will he be all right?' Claudia asked softly. 'I worry about him. He's so cute.'

'Of all of us, he is probably the most likely to survive.' In the dark, Sean smiled fondly after the little man.

'I'm not sleepy any more.' Claudia snuggled against him like a cat, and then much later she whispered, 'I'm so glad Matatu woke us up . . .'

*   *   *

It was still dark when Sean turned Job out of his blanket the next morning. 'We've got work to do,' he told him, and while Job laced on his boots, he described his meeting with General China.

'You mean we are now instructors,' Job laughed softly. 'All we know about those Stingers is what we have read in the manuals.'

'That will have to change,' Sean told him. 'The sooner we get the Shanganes into action, the sooner we are going to get the hell out of here.'

'Is that what China told you?' Job raised an eyebrow at Sean.

'Let's get Ferdinand and his boys cracking,' Sean said brusquely to cover his own misgivings. 'We'll sort them into teams of two

351

men, one to serve the launcher and the other to carry the extra missiles. Of course, the number two must be able to take over if the leader is put down.'

Sean pulled out his notebook and drew the candle stump closer, writing in its guttering yellow light.

'When do you expect Alphonso to get here?' Job stuffed his shirt into the top of his tiger-striped pants.

'Sometime today, if at all,' Sean replied.

'He's the best of the bunch,' Job grunted.

'Ferdinand is not bad,' Sean pointed out, and placed their names at the head of the page as his section leaders. 'Okay, we need thirty names for our number ones, give me some.'

It was like the old days, working together this way and Sean found he was beginning to enjoy himself.

As soon as it was light enough, they paraded the men who had returned in the Hercules from the Grand Reef raid. With the two casualties missing there remained eighteen men under Ferdinand. Sean immediately gave Ferdinand a field promotion to full sergeant, and was rewarded with a huge grin and a flourishing salute that almost swept Ferdinand off his feet with his own vigour.

Sean had to find something to occupy them and keep them out of the way while he and Job gave themselves a crash course on the Stinger missile system.

'Sergeant.' Sean addressed Ferdinand by his rank for the first time. 'Do you see that hill over there?' It was just visible through the trees, shaded blue with distance. 'Take your men for a run around it and get them back here in two hours. Weapons and full field-packs.'

As they watched the column of men doubling away, Sean said, 'If Alphonso and his lads don't arrive by this evening, we'll have to recruit replacements. That's no problem; however, China will be keen to let us have his very best men. At the moment, we are right at the top of his list of favourite flavours.'

'In the meantime, let's hit those manuals,' Job suggested. 'I haven't swotted since varsity days. I'm not looking forward to it.'

Claudia joined them in the dugout, helping them sort through the thick loose-leaf red plastic-covered manuals, picking out the information relevant to their situation and discarding the vast body of technical data that they had no need of, and the operational reports and instructions that did not apply to deployment in this altitude and terrain. After two hours' work they had reduced the mass of information to one manageable slim volume.

'All right.' Sean stood up. 'Let's go find a training ground.'

They picked out a spot a few hundred metres downriver from the dugout where the side of a low kopje formed a natural lecture theatre. The tall riverine mahogany trees spread their branches overhead to provide cover from a surprise raid by the Hind gunships. When Ferdinand and his men returned bathed in sweat from their little outing Sean put them to work clearing the amphitheatre of thorn and scrub and digging shell scrapes conveniently close at hand for use when air raids interrupted classes.

'Right,' Sean told Job and Claudia. 'Now we can uncrate the trainer set and one of the launchers. From now on it's "look and learn", "show and tell" time.'

When they opened the first crate, Sean discovered that the battery power pack was discharged. However, each crate contained a small charger set with appropriate connections and transformers.

Ferdinand and his men under Job's supervision carried the power packs up to the headquarters communications centre and at General China's order, they were given priority use of the portable 220 volt 15 kilowatt generator. Sean connected up the power packs in batches of five, but it would take twenty-four hours before they had power available for all the missile launchers.

With the batteries on charge they laid out the trainer set and one of the launchers on the makeshift table that Ferdinand had built on the floor of the open-air theatre under the trees. While Claudia read aloud from the instruction manual, Sean and Job stripped and reassembled the equipment until they were thoroughly familiar with all of it.

Sean was relieved and pleased to discover that with the exception of the IFF, the operation of the equipment was not a great deal more complicated than the conventional RPG 7 rocket-launchers. The RPG 7 was so much a part of the guerrilla arsenal that, as Job remarked, every single man in China's division could load and lock on a pitch-dark night in a thunderstorm.

'Anyway, we don't need the IFF,' Sean pointed out. 'Everything that flies in these skies, apart from the dicky birds, is a foe.' The IFF, 'Identification Friend or Foe', was a system that interrogated the target, determining from the aircraft's on-board transponder whether it was hostile or friendly, and preventing launch of missile against friendly aircraft.

Claudia found the section on the manual dealing with the IFF and under her tutelage, they disarmed the system, converting the Stinger into a free-fire weapon which would attack any aircraft at which it was aimed.

Without IFF fit, the attack sequence for the missile is straight-forward. The target is picked up in the small screen of the aiming sight, and the safety device above the pistol grip is disengaged with the right thumb. The actuator is engaged by depressing the button built into the reverse of the pistol grip. This starts the run up of the navigational gyro and releases a flow of freon gas to cool the infra-red seekers as they become active. With the sights held on the target, all incoming infra-red radiation is magnified and focused on the detector cell of the missile head. As soon as this radiation is of sufficient concentration to allow the missile to track to its source, the gyro stabilizer uncages, and the missile emits a high-pitched tone.

To fire the missile the operator depresses the trigger in the pistol grip with his forefinger which starts the electric ejector motor. The missile discharges from the launch tube through the frangible front seal and ejects to a safe distance, approximately eight metres from the operator, to protect him from rocket back-blast. At this point the solid fuel rocket motor fires and the blast of exhaust gas flares out the retractable tail-fins and the missile accelerates to four times the speed of sound. When an inertial force of twenty-eight times gravity is attained, the fuse shut-out is thrown open and the missile is armed. It tracks towards the target on a fire-and-forget trajectory, guided not by the operator but by its own proportional navigational system.

With the specialized 'Hind' attack cassette inserted in the launcher's RMP – reprogrammable micro processor – the system switches automatically into 'two colour' mode when it is a hundred metres from the infra-red source. At this point it abandons the infra-red radiations emitted by the engine exhaust suppressors and instead focuses on the much weaker ultra-violet emanations from the engine intakes. On this target the high-explosive war-head hits to kill.

'Even a Shangane could learn how to fire one of these.' Job said, and Sean grinned.

'Tut tut, your Matabele tribal racism is showing again.'

'It's like this, when you are genetically superior, there is simply no point in trying to conceal the fact.'

They both glanced expectantly at Claudia, but she did not even look up from the manual as she drawled, 'You are wasting your time, you two bigots. You aren't going to get a rise out of me this time.'

'Bigot.' Job savoured the word. 'It's the first time anybody has ever called me that. I love it.'

'That's enough fooling around.' Sean broke it up. 'Let's take a look at the trainer.'

After they had connected one of the freshly charged battery packs and assembled the trainer equipment, Sean gave his opinion.

'With this stuff, we can have the lads ready to go into action within days, not weeks.'

Once a micro cassette was inserted in the training monitor, the launcher screen simulated the image of a 'Hind' which the instructor was able to manipulate in various flight patterns, climbing, descending, side-slipping or hovering. While he did so he was able to watch the trainee's reactions as he attempted to acquire the ghost ship on his own screen and attack it with a phantom missile.

Sean and Job played with the trainer like a pair of teenagers, flying the image in complicated manoeuvres. 'It's just like a Pac-man game,' Job enthused. 'But what we need is a dum-dum, a pseudo-Shangane to act as a trainee for us.'

Once more both the men looked at Claudia who was still sitting cross-legged on the table studying the manual.

She looked up as she felt their eyes on her. 'A dum-dum?' she demanded. 'I'll show you dum-dum. Give me the launcher.'

She stood in the centre of the floor of the amphitheatre with the launcher balanced on her shoulder, and stared into the sighting screen. The bulky equipment seemed to dwarf her. She had reversed her camouflage cap so the peak stuck out behind her head, and it gave her the gamine air of a little league baseballer.

'Ready?' Sean asked.

'Pull!' she said, concentrating ferociously on the screen, and Sean and Job exchanged smug supercilious grins.

'Incoming!' Sean called sharply. 'Twelve o'clock high. Lock and load.'

He brought the ghost Hind in on a head-on attack at 150 knots.

'Locked and loaded,' Claudia affirmed, and in their screen, they watched the duplicate sight ring of her missile launcher swing up smoothly and centre on the approaching Hind.

'Actuator on,' she said calmly, and a second later, they heard the launcher sob and growl in her grip, and then settle into a steady insect whine, like an infuriated mosquito.

'Target acquired,' Claudia murmured. The Hind was six hundred metres out but coming in fast, swelling dramatically in the sights.

'Fire!' she said, and they saw the red light blink, and then change to green signalling that the rocket motor of the fictitious missile was running, and almost instantaneously the image of the Hind disappeared from the screen to be replaced by the flashing legend.

'Target destroyed! Target destroyed!'

There followed a profound silence. Job cleared his throat nervously.

'Flukes happen,' said Sean. 'Shall we try it again?'

'Pull!' said Claudia, and concentrated on her aiming screen.

'Incoming,' Sean called. 'Six o'clock high. Lock and load.'

He brought the next Hind in from behind her at tree-top level, attack speed. She had three seconds to react.

'Locked and loaded.' Claudia pirouetted like a ballerina and picked the Hind up in the sight ring. 'Actuator on.' As she said it, Sean flung the Hind into a climbing side-slip, giving her deflection in three planes. It would be like trying to hit a high bird in a gale of crosswind.

In their screen, they watched with disbelief as Claudia swung smoothly, keeping the image in the exact centre of her aiming ring and the missile sobbed and then settled into its high-pitched tone.

'Target acquired. Fire!'

'Target destroyed! Target destroyed!' The screen blinked at them, and they fidgeted uncomfortably.

Job murmured, 'Twice on the trot. That ain't no fluke, man.'

Claudia laid the launcher on the table, readjusted the peak of her cap over her eyes, and then placed her fists on her hips and smiled at them sweetly.

'I thought you said you didn't know how to shoot,' Sean accused her with righteous indignation.

'Would a daughter of Riccardo Enrico Monterro not know how to shoot?'

'But you are stridently opposed to blood sports.'

'Sure,' she agreed. 'I've never shot at a living creature. But I'm death to clay pigeons. Papa taught me.'

'I should have guessed when you said "Pull",' Sean groaned softly.

'As a matter of interest,' Claudia examined the fingernails of her right hand modestly. 'I was Alaska State women's skeet champion three years running, and runner-up at the national championships in '86.'

The two men exchanged embarrassed glances. 'She got you with a sucker punch.' Job shook his head. 'And you walked straight into it with both eyes closed.'

'All right, Miss Alaska,' Sean told her sternly. 'You are so damned clever, you've just landed yourself the job of instructor. From here on you are in charge of this equipment Job and I will split the Shanganes into two classes and give them the basics. Then we'll pass them on to you for simulation. It'll speed up the whole works.'

General China interrupted them as he strode into the amphitheatre, beret cocked jauntily, slapping his swagger-stick against his thigh and taking in their preparations with quick inquisitive eyes.

'How soon can you begin training? I expected to be further along than this.'

Sean recognized the futility of trying to explain to him. 'We'll get along better without interference.'

'I came to warn you that Frelimo have launched their offensive. They are coming at us in force from the south and the west, a two-pronged drive, obviously trying to push us out of these hills, away from the river into more open terrain where they can deploy their armour and their helicopters to better advantage.'

'So they are whipping the hell out of you,' Sean needled him with a thinly concealed sneer.

'We are falling back,' China acknowledged the jibe with just a glitter in his eyes. 'As soon as my men attempt to hold up their advance at a natural strong point, Frelimo simply calls in the

Hinds. The Russian pilots are showing us the close-support skills they learned in the mountains of Afghanistan. They simply obliterate our defences. It is not a pleasant experience to listen helplessly on the radio while my field commanders plead for help. How soon can I send them the Stingers?'

'Two days,' Sean said.

'So long? Is there no way you can hurry it up?' Impatiently, China slapped the swagger-stick into the palm of his hand. 'I want you to let me have at least one trained team immediately. Anything to be able to hit back at them.'

'That, General China, would be crass stupidity,' Sean told him. 'With all due respect,' Sean showed none in the tone of his voice, 'if you deploy the Stingers piecemeal, you'll be tipping your hand to the Hind crews.'

'What do you mean?' China's voice cracked like breaking floe-ice.

'Those Ruskie pilots have met the Stingers before, in Afghanistan, you can be pretty damn sure of that. They'll know every counter-measure in the book and then a few more. Right now they are blissfully convinced that they are the only things in the sky. Their guard is wide open, but you let one Stinger fly and all that will change. Okay, you might put one down, but the rest of the squadron will be ready for you.' China's frozen expression thawed and he looked thoughtful.

'So what do you suggest, Colonel?'

'Hit them all at once with everything you've got.'

'When? Where?'

'When they are least expecting it, a full-scale surprise attack on their laager – at dawn.'

'On their laager?' China shook his head irritably. 'We don't know where they laager at night.'

'Yes, we do,' Sean contradicted. 'I have already pinpointed the laager. I'll train Alphonso and Ferdinand and set up the raid for them. Give me two days, and they'll be ready to go.'

China thought for a moment, hands clasped behind his back, staring up at the blue African sky as though he expected at any moment to see those dread humpbacked shapes appear.

'Two days,' he agreed at last.

'Two days, and when I have your missile crews trained and ready to leave on the raid, you let me and my party go. That is my condition.'

'There is a Frelimo column between here and the Zimbabwe border,' China reminded him.

'We'll take our chances,' Sean snapped. 'That is the bargain, do I have your word on it?'

'Very well, Colonel. I agree.'

'That's fine. Now when do you expect Alphonso and his detachment to arrive?'

'They have already reached our lines. I expect Alphonso and his men will be here in another hour or so, but they will be exhausted, they have been in action almost continuously for twenty-four hours.'

'They aren't on a Sunday school picnic.' Sean was callous. 'Send them to me as soon as they arrive.'

They came in at last, moving with the slack stumbling gait of a heavyweight boxer at the end of ten hard rounds. Their tiger-striped camouflage was encrusted with the filth of the battle-field, and their faces were grey with exhaustion.

While his men collapsed on the floor of the amphitheatre and slept where they fell, Alphonso described to Sean in flat prosaic terms the retreat from Grand Reef base and the flight to the mission station in the gut of the Honde Valley where they had abandoned the Unimog truck and crossed into Mozambique on foot.

'The bush is full of Frelimo, and the air is full of *henshaw*.' He paused and wiped his face wearily on a grubby tattered bandanna. 'It is witchcraft, but the *henshaw* can speak from the sky. They taunt us in the Shangane language. They tell us that they have magic that turns our bullets and rockets to water.'

Sean nodded grimly. The Russians must be using sky-shout amplifiers to demoralize the Renamo defenders. That was another trick they had learned in Afghanistan.

'All along the line our men are being shot to pieces, or are running away. We cannot fight against the *henshaw*.'

'Yes, you bloody well can.' Sean seized the front of his tunic. 'I'll show you how. Get your men up. There'll be plenty of time to sleep later, when we have burned those Russian bastards out of the sky.'

*   *   *

Sean and Job had worked and fought with all these men and had come to know them by name and deed so they had formed a fairly accurate picture of their individual worth and capabilities.

They knew that there were no cowards nor shirkers amongst them. Alphonso had long ago sifted those out. However, there were those whom Job classified as 'oxen', the strong and stupid, the muscle and cannon fodder. The others were of varying degrees of intelligence and adaptability. At the top of the heap were Alphonso and Ferdinand.

Sean and Job sorted them into two groups and concentrated their efforts on the most promising in each group, quickly picking out those who had the image recognition to translate what they saw on the aiming screen of the launchers into finite terms in shape and space.

At the end of almost three hours, they had picked out twenty men who had the potential to assimilate swiftly the necessary training and to act as number ones in the missile teams, and as many again who might be able to fulfil the number two back-up role.

The others who showed no aptitude were allotted to the assault team which would be using conventional weapons in the attack Sean was planning. Of the missile trainees, Sean took one group and Job the other, and they began the monotonous task of familiarizing them with the actual weapons. Once again, they relied on the technique of repetition and reinforcement. Each trainee had his turn at stripping and reassembling, locking and loading, and aiming the launcher. While he did so, he explained to the class exactly what he was doing and Sean and Job corrected their mistakes while the rest of the class taunted them.

It was late afternoon before Sean sent the first group of five men, which included both Alphonso and Ferdinand, to Claudia for simulated attacks with the training equipment.

Alphonso scored three consecutive hits, and was immediately detailed to act as Claudia's assistant and translator. By nightfall, all five members of the first group had scored three consecutive hits which Claudia had arbitrarily decided was her passing standard, and Sean and Job had another ten men ready to begin simulator training as soon as it was sufficiently light the following morning. When it was too dark to continue, Sean dismissed them and Alphonso and his group staggered off wearily into the night, punch-drunk with fatigue and the effort of learning.

Joyful, the chef, had stolen the tripes from the buffalo carcass

360

that had fed the officers' mess the previous evening. After the day's heat, they were a little ripe, but he had disguised that fact with a liberal addition of chopped wild onion tubers and peri-peri sauce. Claudia paled when Joyful proudly placed a steaming bowl of the tripes in front of her. In the end, hunger overcame her fastidiousness.

'Put hair on your chest,' Sean comforted her.

'That, my darling man, isn't high on my list of beauty aids.'

'Okay then,' he smiled at her. 'Put some weight on those skinny little buns of yours.'

'You don't like my buns?'

'I love your buns, that's why I want more of them, as much as I can get.'

When Matatu came creeping in out of the darkness, Sean fed him and he gorged on tripes until his naked belly bulged like a shiny black beach ball.

'All right, you greedy little bugger,' Sean told him. 'Now it's time for you to earn your keep.'

They led him up to the dark amphitheatre where they found that Job was waiting for them. He had already assembled the raw materials for building the scale model of the gunship laager. By the light of two paraffin lanterns, they started to lay it out. Matatu had been a party to these model constructions so many times during the bush war that he understood exactly what was required of him. Like so many who have never acquired the skills of reading and writing, Matatu had a photographic memory.

He strutted about importantly, giving Sean and Job instructions, showing them the topography of the countryside in and surrounding the laager, the shape of the hill on which it had been built, the relationship of it to the main road and the railway line.

Claudia showed a new talent which Sean had not suspected. Using the soft white wood of the baobab tree, she whittled eleven tiny scale models of the Hind gunships. They were fully recognizable as what they represented and when she sat them in their emplacements within the perimeter of the model laager, they added an authentic touch.

It was well after midnight before Claudia and Sean crept naked under the mosquito net in their dugout. They were both weary to their bones but even after they made slow languorous love neither of them could sleep, and they lay close in the darkness and talked. Mention of her father earlier in the day caused

Claudia to hark back to her childhood. Listening to her, Sean was relieved that she was able to speak naturally and easily about her father. She had conquered the initial shock and sorrow and she remembered him now with only a nostalgic melancholy which was almost pleasure in comparison to the pain which had preceded it.

She described to Sean how at the age of fourteen, the very year that her womanhood had first flowered, the wonderfully secure cocoon of her life had burst asunder in the traumatic divorce of her parents. She painted a picture for him of the years that followed. The droughts of loneliness when she was separated from her father followed by the roaring floods of love and conflict when they came together again.

'You can see why I'm such a crazy mixed-up kid,' she told him. 'Why I have to strive to be the best at whatever I do, and why I'm always drawn to try and protect the underdog. Half the time, I'm still trying to win Papa's approval, while the other half of the time, I'm trying to flout and reject his elitist materialistic view of life.' She snuggled against Sean. 'I truly don't know how you are going to handle me.'

'Handling you will always be a pleasure,' he assured her. 'But keeping you in your place looks like a full-time job.'

'That's just the sort of thing that Papa would have said. You and I are in for some rip-roaring fights, mister.'

'Ah, but just think of the reconciliations, what fun they will be.'

In the end, they managed a few hours of sleep, and awoke surprisingly refreshed and clear-headed to take up the training where they had left off at nightfall the previous day.

While Claudia ran the last of the trainees through the attack sequences on the simulator, Sean and Job squatted beside the model of the gunship laager and Sean explained his plans for the attack. Job listened attentively and made the occasional suggestion, until at last they had it all clear in their own minds, the approach march, the attack and the withdrawl with the alternative actions to be taken if there were a hitch anywhere along the line.

'Okay.' Sean stood up. 'Let's give it to the lads.'

The Shangane troopers watched totally absorbed from their perches on the rock slopes of the amphitheatre while Sean and Job described the plans for the raid. They used river pebbles to denote the various units of the raiding party, moving them into place around the laager. When the attack began, Claudia manipulated her model Hinds and there were enthusiastic cheers from the watching Shanganes as one by one they were brought crashing to earth by volleys of Stinger missiles.

'Right, Sergeant Alphonso.' Sean replaced the counters in their original positions. 'Show us the attack again.'

Five times, they went over it. In turn, each of the section leaders described it to them, and the final cheers as the Hinds were destroyed lost none of their gusto for being so often repeated. At the end of the fifth show, Sergeant Alphonso stood up and addressed Sean on behalf of the entire unit.

'*Nkosi Kakulu*,' he began. He had never before used this form of address to Sean. Usually this was reserved for very high-ranking tribal chieftains. Sean was aware of the honour, and this proof that he had at last won the full respect and loyalty of these fiercely proud and hard-bitten warriors.

'Great Chief,' Alphonso said, 'your children are troubled.' There was a murmur of agreement and nodding of heads. 'In all that you have told us of the battle, you have not assured us that you will be there to lead us and to put fire in our bellies as you did at Grand Reef. Tell your children, *Nkosi Kakulu*, that you will be with us in the midst of the fighting and that we will hear you roaring like a lion as the *henshaw* fall burning from the sky, and Frelimo baboons run from us screaming like virgins feeling the prong for the very first time.'

Sean spread his hands. 'You are not my children,' he said. 'You are men of men, just as your fathers were men before you.' There was no higher compliment he could pay them. 'You do not need me to help you to do this thing. I have taught you all I know. The flames in your bellies burn with the same fury as the fire in the tall dry grass of winter. The time has come for me to leave you. This battle is yours alone. I must go, but I will always be proud that we were friends and that we fought side by side as brothers do.'

There was a low chorus of dissent, and they shook their heads and spoke together in low rumbling tones.

Sean turned away, and saw that while he had been speaking General China had come up and now stood quietly amongst the trees at the riverside, watching him. There were a dozen officers and men of his personal bodyguard behind him, all wearing the same maroon berets, but somehow, they seemed insignificant as China stepped forward and instantly commanded the attention of every person in the amphitheatre.

'I see your preparations are complete, Colonel Courtney,' he greeted Sean.

'Yes, they are ready, General.'

'Will you please go over the plans again, for my benefit.'

Sean singled out Sergeant Alphonso. 'Describe the raid for us again,' he ordered, and General China stood in front of the mock-up laager with the swagger-stick clasped behind his back and watched with quick bright eyes, interrupting sharply to ask his questions.

'Why are you using only half the available missiles?'

'The raiding column has to get through the Frelimo lines undetected. The missiles are bulky and heavy, a larger number would be superfluous and make discovery by Frelimo much more likely.'

China nodded, and Sean went on, 'You also have to take into account the possible failure of the raid. If that happens and you have bet all your Stingers on one throw of the dice . . . ' Sean shrugged.

'Yes, of course, it's wise to keep half of the missiles in reserve. Even if the raid fails we will not be left entirely helpless. Carry on.'

Alphonso went through the plan step by step, illustrating with the coloured pebbles how the missile teams would move into position and lie in readiness five hundred metres from the perimeter of the gunship laager, two teams confronting each sandbagged emplacement.

At the signal of a red flare, the assault team would attack in full force from the south, hitting any fuel tankers that might be on the rail spur with RPG 7 rocket fire, sweeping the interior of the laager with mortar fire and then launching a frontal assault on the southern perimeter.

'The *henshaw* will take fright as soon as the shooting begins.' Alphonso explained. 'They will try to escape by flying away, but there will be a moment when they rise from the earth that they will still be low down, standing still in the air, the way a falcon hovers before it stoops. That is the moment we will kill them.'

Sean and China discussed every aspect of the plan until at last, China was satisfied.

'So when will you move out?'

'You keep saying "you".' Sean pulled him up. 'I'm not having anything more to do with it. Sergeant Alphonso will lead the attack. They'll move out this evening two hours before dark to penetrate the Frelimo lines during the night, lay up in cover tomorrow and launch the attack tomorrow night.'

'Very well,' China agreed. 'I'll address the men now.'

He was a compelling orator, Sean admitted, as he listened to China reminding them of the consequences of a Frelimo victory and exhorting them to deeds of valour and self-sacrifice. By the time he ceased speaking their faces were shining and their eyes sparkled with patriotic fervour. General China raised his voice. 'You are warriors so let me hear you sing the Renamo battle anthem.'

The forest echoed and rang to the haunting beauty of their massed voices, and Sean found his vision dissolving into a blur as his eyes filled with emotion. He had not realized how much these men had come to mean to him, until now that he was about to leave them.

'Colonel, I would like to speak to you in private,' General China broke into his sentimental reverie. 'Please come with me.'

With a word to Claudia and Job, Sean excused himself, 'Give them each one more run with the simulator.'

He fell in beside General China and as they set out for the headquarters bunker, Sean took no notice of the fact that China's bodyguard did not accompany them, but remained at the entrance of the amphitheatre in an arrogant manner.

When they reached the command bunker, General China led them through to his underground office. There was tea ready for them and Sean piled brown sugar into his mug and savoured the first steaming mouthful.

'So what did you want to tell me?' he asked.

China was standing with his back to him, studying the wall map of which he had marked the developing Frelimo offensive with coloured pins. He did not answer Sean's question and Sean would not pander to him by asking again. He sipped at the tea and waited.

A signaller came through from the radio room and handed China a message flimsy. As he read it, the General exclaimed with disgust tinged with anxiety and reached up to move a group of coloured pins on the map. Frelimo had broken through in the west and were closing in remorselessly.

'We are not containing them,' China told Sean, without looking around. Another messenger ducked into the bunker. He was one of China's personal bodyguards, wearing the distinctive maroon beret. He whispered something to China and Sean thought he heard the word 'American'. It quickened his interest.

China smiled briefly and dismissed the man with a nod before he turned to Sean.

'It won't work,' he said.

'What won't work?'

'The attack as you have planned it.'

'Nothing is certain in war, as you should know, General. But I disagree. The plan has about a sixty per cent chance of total success. That's pretty good odds.'

'The odds would be considerably higher, perhaps eighty per cent, if you led the attack, Colonel Courtney.'

'I'm flattered by your estimate. However, it's hypothetical. I'm not leading it. I'm going home.'

'No, Colonel. You are leading the attack.'

'We had a bargain.'

'Bargain?' China smiled. 'Don't be naïve. I make bargains and break them as the need arises. The need has arisen I'm afraid.'

Sean sprang to his feet, his face pale as candle wax beneath the deep tan. 'I'm going,' he said. Despite his fury, he managed to keep his voice thin and tight. 'I'm taking my people and I'm leaving now. Right away. You'll have to kill me to stop me.'

China touched his deaf ear, and smiled again. 'That notion is not without its attractions, I assure you, Colonel. However, I don't think it will come to that.'

'We'll see.' Sean kicked back the stool on which he had been sitting and it hit the wall and crashed over on its side. He turned and ducked out of the low doorway.

'You'll be back,' China assured him softly, but Sean gave no sign of having heard him. He came out in the sunlight and strode down towards the river.

He had reached the amphitheatre before he realized that something was desperately amiss.

The Shanganes sat rigid at their places upon the slope, they seemed not to have moved since he had last seen them. Alphonso's features were graven in black ironstone, expressionless and dull, the shield of deliberate stupidity behind which the African distances himself from powers and forces against which he has no other defence.

Job was sprawled across the table in the centre of the amphitheatre. His tunic was floury with dust and his cap still lay in the dirt at his feet. He shook his head in a dazed uncertain fashion and droplets of blood dripped from his nose.

'What happened?' Sean ran to him, and Job stared at him, trying to focus his eyes. He had been brutally beaten. His lips were swollen into purple bruises, his mouth full of blood that stained his teeth like red wine. One eyebrow was cut through, a deep jagged split from which blood trickled down the side of his nose. Blood welled out of both nostrils, swelling into bright pink bubbles as he breathed through it. There were lumps on his forehead like overripe grapes, and the lobe of one ear was torn. Blood dripped onto the front of his dusty tunic.

'Job, what the hell. . .?' Sean caught him by the shoulder. 'Who?'

'I tried to stop them!' Job blurted, his eyes fixed on Sean's face. 'I tried!'

'Take it easy.'

Sean tried to lead him to a seat, but he shook Sean's hands away and said, 'Claudia.'

A flash frost of dread chilled Sean's belly. 'Claudia!' he repeated, and looked around him wildly. 'Where is she, Job? What happened?'

'They took her,' Job repeated. 'China's goons. I tried to stop them.'

Sean reached for the pistol on his webbing belt. 'Where is she, Job?' The pistol grip filled his hand.

'I don't know.' Job wiped the palm of his hand down his face and looked at the blood. 'I was out cold, I don't know for how long.'

'China, you turd-munching bastard, you are going to die.' Sean whirled, ready to go charging back to the headquarters bunker.

'Sean, think first!' Job called urgently, and Sean checked. So often Job had saved him with those two words. 'Think first!'

It required an enormous effort of will, but for seconds, Sean managed to keep his head above the wave of his killing rage.

'The manuals, Job!' he gritted out. 'Burn them!'

Job blinked at him through the blood that spilled from the split eyebrow. 'Burn the manuals!' Sean repeated. 'Insurance, man. We are the only ones who know.'

Job's expression cleared. 'And the cassettes,' he exclaimed.

'Right!' Sean said. 'The cassettes. Give them to me.'

While Job hastily repacked the attack cassettes into their carrying case, Sean walked across to where Alphonso sat at the front of the amphitheatre and unhooked a phosphorus grenade from his belt.

Working swiftly, he used his pistol lanyard and the phosphorus grenade to rig a makeshift self-destruction device in the interior of the case of attack cassettes. He hooked the clip of his pistol lanyard through the pin of the grenade, and laid the grenade itself in the middle of the case. Using the point of a bayonet, he drilled a hole through the lid of the carrying case and threaded the end of the lanyard through it. When he locked the case, he looped the free end of the lanyard securely around his own wrist.

'Let China try and get them away from me now,' he said grimly. If the case were jerked out of his grip, or if he let it fall the lanyard would pull the pin of the grenade, destroying not only the contents but anybody standing nearby. He waited just long enough to watch Job set a match to the pile of instruction manuals.

Once they were fully ablaze he ordered Job, 'Stay here, make certain they are burned to ashes.'

Then lugging the case of cassettes, he started back to the headquarters bunker.

'I said that you would be back,' China greeted him, with that icy sardonic smile which faded swiftly as he saw the case that Sean carried and the lanyard looped around his wrist.

Sean lifted the case in front of him and flaunted it in China's face.

'There is the Hind Squadron, China,' he said, with an effort keeping his voice level. 'Without this your Stingers are useless to you.'

China's eyes flicked towards the entrance of the dugout.

'Don't even think about it,' Sean warned him. 'There is a grenade inside the case, a phosporus grenade. This lanyard is attached to the firing-pin. If I drop it, like if I was to die suddenly or someone were to pull it out of my hand, the whole lot goes up in a nice little bonfire, happy fifth of November.'

They stared at each other across the desk.

'So this is a pretty little stalemate, Colonel,' China's smile was reborn, even colder and more deadly than Sean had seen it before.

'Where is Claudia Monterro?' Sean asked, and China raised his voice, summoning an orderly from the radio room.

'Bring the woman!' he ordered, and they waited, both of them poised and alert, watching each other's eyes.

'I should have thought of the cassettes,' China said in conversational tones. 'That was good, Colonel. Very good. You can see why I want you to lead the attack.'

'While we are on the subject,' Sean replied, 'I have also burned the instruction manuals. There are only the three of us – Job, Claudia and me – who understand the Stingers.'

'What about the Shanganes, Alphonso, Ferdinand?' China challenged, and Sean grinned at him like a death's head.

'Not on, China. They know how to shoot it, but they don't have any idea how to program the micro processors. You need us, China. Without us the Hinds are coming after you, and there's not a damned thing you can do about it. So don't fool with me. I have your survival in my hands.'

There was a scuffle in the outer room, and both of them looked to the entrance as Claudia was pushed through from the radio room.

Her hands were once more manacled behind her back, she had lost her cap and her hair tumbled into her face and down her neck.

'Sean!' she blurted when she saw him, and she pulled against the hands of the two bodyguards who held her, trying to reach him. They jerked her back and threw her against the side wall of the dugout.

'Tell your baboons to knock that off,' Sean snarled, and when they glowered at him, China restrained them with a sharp order.

'Put that woman in the chair!'

They forced her into the solid mahogany seat and at another order from China used the manacles to chain her wrists securely to the heavy arms of the chair.

'I have something of yours, Colonel, and you have something of mine. Shall we work out a deal?' General China suggested.

'Let us go,' Sean said promptly. 'At the border, I'll hand over the cassettes.' And China shook his head regretfully.

'Not acceptable. Here is my counter offer. You lead the attack on the Hind laager. When it is completed successfully, Alphonso will escort you to the border.'

Sean raised the booby-trapped case head high, and China smiled. In retaliation he drew the trench knife from its sheath on his belt. It was ivory-handled with a five-inch blade.

Still smiling he lifted a single hair from Claudia's scalp, and with a sharp jerk pulled it out. He held it up between thumb and forefinger and touched the hair with the blade. Half of the dark strand fell away and floated down to the earthen floor of the dugout.

'That is how sharp it is,' China said softly.

'If you kill her you haven't got anything to bargain with.' Sean's voice was harsh with strain and he was sweating.

'I have this to bargain with,' China replied, and he nodded to his guards at the doorway.

They led in someone whom Sean had never seen before. An apparition with an ancient skull-like head. The hair had fallen out in tufts, leaving shiny black patches on the scalp. The lips had shrunk and peeled back to expose teeth that were too large and white for that ruined head.

At a word from China the guards stripped away the single filthy ragged shift that covered the body, leaving it entirely naked, and for the first time, Sean realized that it was a woman.

Her body reminded him of the horror pictures he had seen of the survivors of Dachau and Belsen. She was a skeleton covered with baggy skin, her empty dugs dangled over the rack of her ribs, her stomach was drawn in so that her pelvic girdle was an empty bony basin. Her arms and legs were fleshless, the bony elbows and knees grotesquely enlarged.

Sean and Claudia stared at her with horror, unable to speak with the shock of it.

'Look at the lesions on her abdomen,' China invited in a pleasant voice, and numbly they obeyed.

They were blind boils, hard and shiny as ripe black grapes beneath the skin, covering her lower belly and disappearing into the wiry mop of her pubic hair.

While all their attention was on this pathetic figure, China reached down quickly with the knife and touched the back of Claudia's hand with the point of the blade. Claudia gasped and tried to jerk her hand away, but it came up short against the manacle chain and she stared down as a thin snake of bright blood trickled down her forefinger and dripped onto the floor.

'What did you do that for, you snot-gobbling bastard?' Sean demanded.

China smiled. 'It's only a scratch.'

Slowly he reached out towards the naked skeletal figure of the black woman, pointing with the knife at her shrunken belly.

'The extreme emaciation, and those characteristic lesions are diagnostic,' he explained. 'The woman is suffering from what we, in Africa, call the "Slim Sickness".'

'Aids,' Claudia whispered, and her voice was filled with the dread that single word conjured up.

Despite himself Sean took a step back from the dreadful figure before him.

''Yes, Miss Monterro,' China agreed. 'Aids in its terminal stage.'

He touched one of the marble-hard chancres on the woman's belly with the point of the blade, and she gave no reaction as it split open and a mixture of pus and dark tarry blood oozed from the wound and trickled down into the matted bush of her pubic hair.

'Blood,' whispered China, and gently scooped it up onto the bright silver blade. 'Warm living blood, swarming with the virus.'

He proffered the blade for Sean's inspection and involuntarily Sean pulled back further as blood dripped from the point.

'Yes,' China nodded. 'Something that even the bravest have reason to fear, the most certain, the most lingering, the most loathsome death of all the ages.'

With his free hand he took hold of Claudia's wrist.

'Consider this other blood. The sweet bright blood of a vibrant, beautiful, young woman.'

The scratch on the back of Claudia's hand was vivid, but the tiny flow of blood from it almost quenched it.

'Blood to blood,' China whispered. 'Sick blood to healthy blood.'

He brought the filthy blade closer to Claudia's hand and she stiffened in the chair, straining silently against the manacle, her face white with horror as she stared at the knife.

'Blood to blood,' China repeated. 'Shall we let them mingle?'

Sean found he could not speak, he shook his head dumbly, staring at the knife.

'Shall we do it, Colonel?' China asked. 'It's all up to you now.' He brought the blade closer to the open wound in Claudia's smooth creamily tanned skin.

'Just another inch, Colonel,' China whispered, and suddenly Claudia screamed; it was a wild ringing release of horror and terror, but China did not flinch. He did not look at her face and his knife hand was steady and tremorless.

'What shall we do, Colonel Courtney?' he asked.

He lowered the knife and touched her wrist with the flat of the blade, leaving a smear of diseased blood on the unblemished skin, only inches from the scratch on Claudia's hand, then slowly he moved the knife downwards.

'Speak quickly, Colonel. In seconds it will be too late.' The knife left a shiny track of blood like the slime trail of some disgusting snail across her skin. Inexorably it moved down towards the open wound.

'Stop it!' Sean screamed. 'Stop it!'

China lifted the blade away, and looked at him enquiringly. 'Does that mean we have reached an agreement?'

'Yes, damn you to hell! I'll do it!'

China tossed the contaminated knife into a corner of the dugout, and then opened one of the drawers in his desk and brought out a bottle of Dettol antiseptic. He soaked his handkerchief in the undiluted fluid, and then carefully wiped the smear of diseased blood from Claudia's skin.

The tension went out of her rigid body and she slumped in the chair. She was panting softly and trembling like a kitten left out in the rain.

'Turn her loose,' Sean croaked, but China shook his head.

'Not until we have made our terms of agreement clear.'

'All right,' Sean snarled. 'And the first of those terms is that my woman comes with me on the mission. No more dugouts filled with rats.'

China pretended to ponder that and then nodded. 'Very well, but the second term is that if you fail me in any way, then Alphonso will kill her immediately.'

'Get Alphonso in here,' Sean demanded. The sweat had not yet dried on his forehead and his voice was still rough and unsteady. 'I want to hear you give him his orders.'

Alphonso stood to attention and listened expressionlessly as China told him, 'However, if the attack fails, if you are intercepted by Frelimo before you reach the laager, or if any of the *henshaw* are allowed to escape . . .'

Sean interrupted. 'No, General, a hundred per cent success is too high to hope for. Let us be reasonable and realistic. If I can destroy all but six of the Hinds, then it must be counted that I have fulfilled my part of the bargain.'

China frowned and shook his head. 'Even six Hinds will be sufficient to ensure our defeat. I'll allow you two If more than two Hinds escape from the laager your mission will be a failure, and you must pay the price.' He turned back to Alphonso and went on with his instructions. 'And so, Sergeant, you will obey all orders from the Colonel, carrying out the attack exactly the way he has planned it, but if the raid fails, if more than two *henshaw* escape, then you are to take full command, and your very first duty will be to shoot the two whites, and their black servant – you will shoot them immediately.'

Alphonso blinked almost sleepily at the order. He did not turn his head to look at Sean, and Sean found himself wondering if, despite their relationship, the friendship that had grown up between them, despite the fact that Alphonso had called him *Nkosi Kakulu* and *Baba*, and had exhorted him to lead the mission, despite all of this, he would carry out the execution order.

Alphonso was an African Shangane and a warrior with a deep sense of tribal loyalty and a tradition of absolute obedience to his chief and tribal elders.

'Yes,' Sean thought. 'He'd probably have a few regrets, but without question or hesitation, he would do it.'

He raised his voice. 'All right, China, we all know exactly where we stand. Let Miss Monterro come to me now.'

The bodyguard removed her handcuffs and politely General China helped her out of the chair. 'I apologize for the unpleasantness, Miss Monterro, but I'm sure you will understand the necessity for it.'

Claudia was unsteady on her feet, and staggered before she reached Sean and clung to him.

'And so I'll wish you farewell and good hunting.' China gave them a small mocking salute. 'One way or the other, we will not meet again, I'm afraid.'

Sean did not deign to reply. With the case of cassettes in one hand and his other arm around Claudia's shoulders, Sean led her to the doorway.

* * *

They moved out two hours before darkness. It was an unwieldy column and the missile-launchers and the back-up missiles made awkward burdens; apart from their weight, the length of the packs made them cumbersome. They hooked up in thick bush when the path narrowed and slowed down the column's ability to react to threat and danger.

At first, Sean kept the column bunched up in a close cohesive whole. They were still some miles from the tenuous front line of the Renamo army, and would not be seriously menaced until much later in the march.

However, taking no chances, Sean kept the assault troops of the vanguard and rear vigilant and at the utmost degree of readiness to repel any attacks and to give the missile-bearers a chance to escape. To ensure this, Sean sent Job to the head of the column while he stayed in the centre where he could reach any trouble spot quickly and where he could be near to Claudia.

'Where is Matatu?' she asked Sean. 'We've just gone off and left him. I'm so worried about him.'

'Don't worry about leaving him behind. He's like one of those puppies which you can't send home. He'll follow me anywhere, in fact the little bugger is probably watching us out of the bush at this very moment.'

And so it proved, for as darkness descended on the column, a small shadow appeared miraculously at Sean's side.

'I see you, my *Bwana*,' Matatu twinkled.

'I see you also, little friend.' Sean touched his woolly head as he would his favourite gun dog. 'I've been waiting for you to find a way for us through the Frelimo lines, and so lead us to the roosting place of the ugly falcons.' And Matatu swelled with self-importance.

'Follow me, my *Bwana*,' he said.

Now with Matatu to guide them, Sean could rearrange the column into a more streamlined formation for passing through the Frelimo advance and getting into their rear.

To his advantage was the size of the battle being fought ahead of him. There were six thousand Frelimo and Zimbabwean troops advancing against less than half that number of Renamo defenders, and the area of the battlefield was tens of thousands of square miles in extent. The fighting ahead of them was taking place in small isolated pockets, while most of the ground was wild and rugged and deserted.

Sean sent Job and Matatu ahead with a small party of assault troops to find the wide gaps in the line and steer them through. The rest of the column followed at a discreet interval, protected by the conventionally armed assault division of Shanganes.

They kept going steadily through the night, runners coming back from Job and Matatu in the vanguard to guide them whenever it was necessary to make a detour or to change direction.

At intervals during the long cold march, they heard distant gunfire and the sound of mortars and heavy machine-guns as elements of the Frelimo advance ran into the Renamo defence. Occasionally they saw the twinkle of signal flares soar above the dark forest, but there was no sound of Isotov turbos and helicopter rotors in the night. It was clear that the Hinds were limiting their depredations to the daylight hours when they could distinguish friend from foe and make their close-support operations more effective.

An hour before dawn Job came back down the column to find Sean.

'We aren't going to reach our first objective until an hour or so after first light,' he reported. 'The pace has been slower than we expected, what do you want us to do? Shall we take a chance on the Hinds finding us?'

Sean looked up at the sky before he replied. The first lemon-coloured flush of dawn was paling out the stars.

'The forest roof isn't dense enough to hide so many men and so much equipment,' he decided. 'We have to keep going and get them into hiding. Tell Matatu to quicken the pace.'

'What about the Hinds?'

'The main fighting is well behind us now, that is where they will be headed, we have to take the chance, but move fast.'

As the light strengthened so the faces of the men in the long column turned more frequently and fretfully to the sky. The pace was fast, almost a run. Although they had been going all night, still the Shanganes bore their heavy burdens with all the hardiness and fortitude of the African, burdens that would have broken the heart and the back of even a strong white man.

It was light enough to define the tree-tops against the orange blossom of dawn when Sean heard the dread whistle of turbos, faint and distant, passing to the east. The Hinds were flying their first sortie of the day, and the alarm was shouted down the length of the column. The porters dived off the path, seeking the nearest cover, and the section leaders crouched ready to wave the captured Frelimo colours that Sean had provided for each of them should the Hinds spot them and come in to strafe them.

The deception was not necessary for the pair of Hinds passed two miles east of their position. Sean saw their silhouettes, like deformed gnats, black against the oncoming dawn, and minutes later heard the thunder of their Gatling-cannons and the boom of their assault rockets as they pounded another Renamo stronghold amongst the ironstone hills far behind them.

Sean got the column moving again and the glimpse that they had been given of 'the flying death' sped their feet. An hour later, the tail end of the column clambered swiftly down the almost sheer side of the gorge at the bottom of which lay the dry riverbed and the caves where the captured Unimogs had been hidden.

It was almost a home-coming and the men crept thankfully into the gloom of the caverns and laid down the heavy packs.

'No fires,' Sean ordered. 'No smoking.'

They ate their rations of cold stodgy maize cakes and dried fish and then curled on the cavern floor and slept like a pack of hounds exhausted at the end of a day's hunting.

Sean found a private place for Claudia at the back of the cavern, behind a natural screen of tumbled sandstone blocks. He spread a blanket on the rocky floor and she sat cross-legged upon it and munched the unappetizing rations; but before she had half finished, she slumped sideways, asleep before her head touched the floor. Sean spread the other blanket over her for it was chilly in the depths of the cavern, and then he went back to the entrance.

Alphonso had rigged the antenna of the small portable two-way VHF radio. He was crouched beside the set with the volume turned low, listening to the situation reports of the Renamo field commanders as they reported in to General China's headquarters.

'It goes very badly,' he told Sean glumly. 'Frelimo will be on the riverbank by noon tomorrow, and unless the general pulls

376

back, he will be overrun.' Alphonso broke off as he recognized their call sign in the jumbled static of the wave band.

'Banana Bush, this is Warthog,' he replied into the hand mike and then gave the 'primary objective established' code, 'Coca-Cola!' Sean smiled at this subtle commentary on modern Africa, and Banana Bush acknowledged and signed off. Their next report was scheduled for dawn tomorrow by which time the fate of the mission would be decided one way or the other.

Sean left Alphonso rolling up the antenna and packing the radio into its carrying case and from the entrance of the cavern watched the party of five men who under Job's supervision were sweeping the sandy riverbed with thorn branches to obliterate the last traces of their passing.

Job climbed back to the mouth of the cave and Sean asked, 'Sentries?'

'On each of the peaks.' Job pointed to the heights above them. 'I have covered every approach.'

'All right.' Sean led him back into the cavern. 'It's time to arm and program the Stingers.'

It took almost a full hour to assemble the launchers, connect the battery-packs and feed the cassettes into the micro computers in the consoles. Finally each of the launchers was fully armed and programmed for 'Two Colour' attack sequence on the Hind gunships, and they handed them back to the Shangane section leaders.

Sean glanced at his wristwatch, mildly surprised that it was still keeping time after all the abuse he had given it recently.

'We can grab a few hours' shut-eye,' he told Job, but neither of them made a move to do so.

Instead, as if by consent, they moved back to the entrance of the cavern, away from the others, and leaned against the rock wall with their shoulders almost touching, staring thoughtfully out into the riverbed where the early sunlight was sparkling the crystalline sand like powder snow.

'If you had taken my advice, you could be living high in the flesh pots of Harare now,' Sean murmured.

'And never have the chance to bag a Hind?' Job smiled carefully, his damaged lip was crusted with a fragile scab and a drop of blood like a tiny ruby appeared as it split open again. He dabbed at it with the corner of his bandanna, as he went on, 'We have hunted all the dangerous game together, Sean, in all the

377

worst places. Buffalo in the jesse bush, elephant in the Kasaga-saga. This will be another trophy, the best and biggest.'

Sean turned to study his face. It was typical of their friendship that their feelings should be so perfectly in tune. During the long night march, Sean's fury and hatred of General China had abated and given way to this emotion which Job had just articulated, the excitement of the hunter. They were both hunters, the chase was a fire and a passion in their blood which they had never attempted to suppress. They understood each other, recognized and accepted this bond between them which had grown stronger over the twenty years of their friendship. Yet they had seldom spoken of their feelings for each other, Sean realized.

'Perhaps now is the time to do so,' he thought, and said aloud, 'We are more than brothers, you and me.'

'Yes,' Job replied simply. 'We are beyond the love of brothers.'

They were silent then, not embarrassed by what had passed between them, but rather fulfilled and fortified by it.

'As a brother,' Sean broke the silence, 'may I ask a favour of you?'

Job nodded, and Sean went on softly, 'There will be hard fighting at the laager. I would not want Claudia to fall into the hands of Frelimo if I were not there to prevent it. That is the favour I ask.'

A shadow passed behind Job's eyes. 'I do not like to think about that possibility.'

'If I am not there, will you do it for me?'

Job nodded. 'I give you my word.'

'If you have to do it, do not warn her, do not speak, do it unexpectedly.'

'She will not know it is coming,' Job promised. 'It will be quick.'

'Thank you,' Sean said, and clasped his shoulder. 'Now we must rest.'

Claudia was still asleep, her breathing was so gentle and silent that, for a moment, Sean was alarmed. He put his face close to hers and felt the warmth of her breath on his cheek. He kissed her and she murmured in her sleep and reached out, fumbling for him and sighing contentedly as he crept into the circle of her arms.

He seemed only to have closed his eyes for a moment, before

378

a light touch on his cheek woke him again, and he looked up to see Job squatting over him.

'It's time,' Job's lips formed the words, and Sean gently disentangled Claudia's arms.

'Sleep sweetly, my love,' he murmured, and left her lying on the blanket.

The others were already waiting for him at the entrance of the cave, Matatu and Alphonso and the section leaders, only lightly armed so that they could move swiftly and steathily.

'Four o'clock,' Job told Sean, and he saw that the light in the riverbed had mellowed, the shadows were lengthening.

There was nothing more to say. They had both done this half a hundred times before.

'See you around,' Job said, and Sean nodded, as he strapped on his pack.

With Matatu dancing ahead of them like a forest sprite, they slipped out of the cavern and into the trees, turning immediately south and settling into their running formation.

Twice they heard the Hind gunships passing at a distance and once they were forced into cover as one of the helicopters came directly overhead.

However, it was high, over four thousand feet Sean estimated, flying at the top of its speed. Studying the aircraft through his binoculars, Sean guessed it had completed a mission and was racing back to the laager to refuel and rearm. To confirm this, he saw that the racks for the Swatter assault missiles below the fuselage were empty, and the nozzles of the rocket pods were scorched with the back blast of discharged rockets.

The Hind was heading on exactly the same bearing as Matatu was leading them, and even as Sean held it in the field of his binoculars, the Hind reduced power on its turbos and commenced its descent, homing in on its laager.

'Not more than five miles ahead,' Sean guessed, and glanced across at Matatu, who was waiting expectantly for Sean's approbation.

'Like a bee to its hive,' Matatu grinned.

'Your eyes are like those of the vulture,' Sean agreed. 'They see all.' And Matatu hugged himself with pleasure and rocked on his haunches. Sean's praise was all the reward he ever asked for.

Half an hour later they leopard-crawled up onto the crest of a low rocky kopje and slid over the skyline into the dead ground below before Sean raised his binoculars. He used his cap to shade the lens; a reflected ray of sunlight would telegraph their position like a heliograph.

He picked up the railway line immediately, less then two miles distant; the ballast was of blue granite and the single set of tracks gleamed dully in the late sunshine, polished by the steel wheels of rolling stock.

He followed the tracks for a mile and found the spur onto which two railway tankers had been shunted. They were partially hidden by scraggly trees and rank bush, but minutes later a feather of dust rose out of the forest and a fuel bowser came down a dirt track and pulled in beside the leading tanker. Sean watched through the binoculars as overall-clad workers connected up the delivery hose and began pumping fuel between the two vehicles.

While this was happening, a Hind gunship rose with dramatic suddenness from the foreslope of the hill just beyond the railway spur, and at last, Sean had a positive fix on the laager.

The Hind rose to three hundred feet above the hill and then turned and bore away, humpbacked and nose-heavy, for one more mission over the battlefield in the north before the light failed, and the fighting was suspended for the night.

Now that he knew exactly where to look, Sean was able to make out other heavily camouflaged emplacements on the slopes of the hill. He counted six of them and said so to Matatu.

'There are two more,' Matatu grinned patronizingly as he pointed out the hidden emplacements that Sean had overlooked. 'And there are three more on the far side of the hill, you cannot see them from here.'

The wisdom of making this reconnaissance in daylight became clearer, as Sean was able to pick out the discrepancies between the model with which they had planned the raid and the actual topography of the laager and its surroundings.

Sean jotted the amendments in his notebook, making new estimates of the ranges and the fields of fire that his missiles could command. One by one, he called over each of the section leaders and pointed out exactly what positions he wanted them to occupy as soon as their teams arrived and darkness had fallen to cover them.

Satisfied that Matatu could supply no further information, Sean despatched him. 'Go back to Job. As soon as it is dark, guide him and all the other soldiers up here.'

When Matatu was gone, Sean devoted the last hour of daylight to watching the gunships return out of the north. There were eleven of them, ample proof of the efficiency of the Russian maintenance crews who must have repaired the two Hinds that Matatu had reported were not flying. The entire squadron, less the single gunship that Sean had knocked out of the sky, was once again operational and doing dreadful execution amongst the Renamo guerrillas.

As each gunship hovered above the hillock and then settled into its emplacement, Sean pointed out the flying characteristics to his section leaders and urged them to mark well the exact position of each emplacement.

'That one is yours, Tendela.' He reinforced the target allocations. 'See how he stands in the sky. You will shoot from that clump of dark trees at the edge of the vlei. Have you marked it well?'

'I have marked it, *Nkosi Kakulu*,' they affirmed. The sky was washed by the blood of the dying day, and as he watched the red orb sink away beneath the trees, Sean wondered how much more blood the dawn would bring.

There was that short period of African twilight during which it was not yet dark enough to move off the ridge. There was nothing further to discuss and Sean and Alphonso sat close together. The feeling was so familiar. No matter how many times Sean waited like this, he would never be able to control or ignore the tension that pulled like rubber bands across his guts. It was the heady anticipation of the draught of terror which soon he would drink to its dregs. He longed for it as the addict does for the needle, and dreaded it to the limits of his soul.

'We will make a good kill,' Alphonso said quietly. 'It will be a fight for men who are truly men.'

Sean nodded. 'Yes, my friend, it will be a good fight, and if we fail, then you must try to kill me. That also will be a good fight.'

'We will see,' Alphonso growled, his eyes reflecting the smoky red glare of the sunset. 'Yes, we will see.'

The crisp silhouette of the hill on which the Hinds were laagered dissolved with the onset of night. Then Venus appeared

381

as the evening star and its cold unwavering light burned directly above the hilltop, seeming to single it out for them.

Within the first hour of darkness, the leading troopers of the raiding column emerged from the trees behind them. Job was at the head of the column with Matatu guiding him and Claudia beside him. Sean met them with a quiet word and immediately began to marshal the troopers into their various units. The section leaders took charge of their missile teams, and the Stinger launchers were unpacked and assembled; the spare missiles in their sealed frangible tubes were checked and readied.

Sean and Job and Claudia went from team to team, running the final checks on the missile launchers, making certain that the battery packs were fully charged and correctly connected, that the cylinders of freon gas were open-valved and that the sighting screens illuminated when the actuator was engaged.

At last, Sean was ready to deploy the missile teams, but before he did so, he called the section leaders together and, for the last time, made each repeat his orders. Satisfied at last, he began to despatch them to their attack positions. He allowed five-minute intervals between each team leaving the ridge.

Alphonso was in charge of the missile teams attacking the eastern perimeter of the laager and because he had farther to go to get into position, he left first.

When it was time for Job, who would lead the missile attack on the western perimeter, to go, he and Sean shook hands briefly. There was no exchange of good wishes, they were both superstitious about that. Instead Job asked facetiously, 'Listen, Sean, about that four thousand dollars in bonus and back-pay, don't you want to pay me out now?'

'Will you take a cheque?' Sean grinned at him through the dark mask of his camouflage cream. Job answered his grin, punched his shoulder and moved away out of earshot so that Sean could speak to Claudia in private.

'I don't want to leave you,' she whispered, and Sean hugged her fiercely.

'Stay close to Job,' he ordered.

'Come back to me safely.'

'Yes.'

'Promise me.'

'I promise,' he said, and she pulled out of his embrace and turned away, disappearing into the darkness after Job.

Sean stared after her, he found that his hands were trembling. He thrust them into his pockets and clenched his fists.

'Love doesn't do much for one's fighting instincts,' he thought, and tried to dismiss her from his mind. 'She'll be all right with Job.'

The assault party was waiting for him patiently, squatting at the edge of the tree-line. Twenty-four men, the cannon fodder, the meat bombs, he thought ruefully, those who had failed the aptitude tests for operating the Stingers. While the missile crews would fire from stand-off positions five hundred metres outside the perimeter of the laager, the assault party would attack it head on and frontal, deliberately drawing fire while trying to flush the Hinds up into the air for the missile gunners to get a fair shot at them. It was this unit who would meet the 12.7mm cannons in their fortified positions, and all the other dangers and obstacles which certainly guarded the laager.

Theirs was the most dangerous task, and for that reason alone, Sean could not delegate the command of them to another. He would lead them in.

'Come on, Matatu,' he said quietly. When there was real danger at hand, wounded game in thick cover or an enemy position to attack, Matatu's self-chosen place was always at Sean's side. Nothing could dislodge him from it.

As a mark of his esteem Alphonso had presented Sean with an AKM assault rifle, the improved and up-dated version of the ubiquitous AK 47 which was much prized and sought after by the Renamo guerrillas. Sean carried this weapon now as he led the assault team down off the ridge, and, with Matatu guiding them through the night, circled out to get in between the main railway line and the laager, as close as was prudent to the spur of line on which the railway fuel tankers stood.

There was no urgency, they had all night in which to get into position, so they went with a stealth which increased the closer they came to the enemy positions.

It was after two o'clock in the morning and the small slice of the moon had set before Sean had them in their jump-off positions, spread out at precise intervals so that at his command, they could sweep forward in skirmishing formation.

He made one final inspection of their dispositions, crawling silently from man to man, personally sighting in the 60mm M4 commando mortars for them, by sense of touch alone checking their equipment, making absolutely certain that each of them clearly understood his objective and then leaving them with a whisper of encouragement and a brief but firm clasp of the shoulder. At last, with everything done that could be done, he settled down to wait.

This was always the worst and the best part of the hunt. As he lay in the silence, he wondered how much of his life he had spent like this, waiting for it to begin, waiting for shooting light, waiting in the blind for that breath-stopping moment when the leopard appeared with magical suddenness in the bait tree, an elegant silhouette against the pale backdrop of the dawn.

His mind went back over the years to those other adventures and wild endeavours, to the terrible risks and almost unbearable thrills, and suddenly it dawned upon him that this was probably the last time it would happen. He was over forty years of age and Claudia Monterro had entered his life, it was time for it to change. There was a sadness and, at the same time, a satisfaction in that thought.

'Let the last be the best of all the game,' he thought, and in the utter darkness of pre-dawn, he heard a sound at once both thrilling and terrifying, the shrill high whine of a mighty turbo engine, howling like a man-eating wolf in the night. It was joined almost at once by another and then another. The Hind squadron was starting engines, warming up for their first sortie in the dawn.

Sean checked his watch and the luminous dial showed eleven minutes before five. It was almost time. Without thinking, he unclipped the curved banana magazine from under the AKM rifle and replaced it with another from the pouch of spare magazines on his webbing. That habitual gesture gave him the comfort of long familiarity, and beside him, Matatu seeing him do it stirred expectantly. The dawn wind came softly as a lover and stroked Sean's cheek.

He turned his head towards the east and held up his hand with fingers spread. He could just make out the silhouette of his fingers against the coming dawn. It was what the Matabele called 'the time of the horns', when a herdsman could first see the horns of his cattle against the sky.

'Shooting light in ten minutes,' Sean reminded himself, and knew how long it would take those minutes to pass.

One after the other, the Hinds shut down their engines to an idle. The ground crews would be completing the refuelling and rearming, the flying crews would be going aboard.

Sean had to judge it exactly, the light must be just right. The Hinds would probably not use landing lights, and missile gunners must be able to see them clearly against the dawn.

The light bloomed swiftly. Sean closed his eyes and counted slowly to ten before he opened them again. Now he could make out the stark outline of the crest of the hill, like a cut-out in black cardboard, the lace-work of the msasa trees stood out against the purple sky, swaying gracefully to the dawn breeze.

'Shoot!' he said, and tapped the shoulder of the mortar man beside him. The trooper leaned forward holding the mortar bomb in both hands and dropped it into the mouth of the mortar tube. The charge in the tail ignited and with a polite pop hurled the signal bomb five hundred feet into the sky above the hilltop. It exploded in a twinkling red flare of lights.

* * *

Claudia Monterro followed Job down off the ridge, keeping so close behind him that she need only reach out her hand to touch him. Job carried one of the missile launchers across his shoulders, and behind Claudia the number two of their team was bowed beneath the weight of the spare rocket tubes.

The footing was loose and dangerous, while quartz pebbles as treacherous as ball-bearings rolled under foot. It pleased her that she was as steady and sure-footed as any of t' m over this difficult ground.

Nevertheless, she was sweating in the night chill as they reached the bottom of the slope and crept forward towards the perimeter of the laager. There was a time, only a few short weeks ago, when she would have felt inept and awkward in these circumstances, but now she orientated herself by the beacon of the evening star above the hilltop and responded instantly to Job's signals, picking her footfalls and anti-tracking almost instinctively.

They reached the dense copse of trees which was their attack position, and crept in amongst them. Claudia helped Job set up the Stinger ready for firing and then found herself a comfortable perch at the base of one of the trees to wait out the night.

Job left her there with just the Shangane number two loader

for company, and he disappeared into the darkness like a hunting leopard. She was unhappy to see him go, but not long ago she would have been panic-stricken. She realized what a measure of self-reliance and fortitude she had been forced to learn in these last few weeks.

'Papa will be proud of me,' she smiled to herself, using the future tense as though her father still existed. 'Of course he does,' she assured herself. 'He's still out there somewhere looking out for me. How else would I have made it this far?' His memory was a comfort, and as she thought about him, he became confused in her mind with Sean, so that they seemed to merge into a single entity as though her father had somehow achieved a new existence in her lover. It was a good feeling that alleviated her loneliness, until suddenly Job returned as silently and abruptly as he had left.

'All the other sections are in position,' he whispered, as he settled down beside her. 'But it's going to be a long night. Try and get some sleep.'

'I'll never be able to sleep,' she answered, keeping her voice so low that he had to lean close to her to catch the words. 'Tell me about Sean Courtney, I want to know everything you know about him.'

'Sometimes he's a hero, and sometimes he's a complete bastard.' Job thought about it. 'But most of the time, he's something in between.'

'Then why have you stayed with him so long?'

'He's my friend,' Job answered simply, and then slowly, haltingly, he began to tell her about Sean, and they talked the night away.

Claudia listened avidly, encouraging him with quiet questions. 'He was married, wasn't he, Job?' Or, 'Why did he leave his home? I have heard that his family is enormously wealthy. Why did he choose this life?'

So the night passed, and in those hours they became friends, the first true friend she had found in Africa, and in the end he said to her in that beautiful deep African voice, 'I shall miss him, more than I can tell.'

'You speak as though the two of you are parting, and that isn't so. It will be the same.'

'No,' Job denied. 'It will never be the same. He will go with you now. Our time together has ended, yours is beginning.'

386

'Don't hate me for it, Job.' She reached out to touch his arm in appeal.

'You two will be good together,' he said. 'I think your journey with him will be as good as mine has been. My thoughts will go with you, and I wish you both great joy in each other.'

'Thank you, Job,' she whispered. 'You will always be our friend.'

Job lifted his arm and with fingers spread held his open hand against the dawn.

'The time of the horns,' he murmured softly. 'Soon now.' And as he said it, a flower of bright crimson fire burst open in the sky above the hill.

*　　*　　*

As the signal flare burst in the dawn sky, the battle was born. Sean always thought of it as the birth of a living thing, a monster which he could only try to direct but which had a life and a will of its own, a terrible thing which swept them all up and carried them along willy nilly.

He had placed the RPG 7 rocket-launchers in the hands of his two best remaining gunners, but the expert marksmen had all gone to man the Stingers. The first rocket flew low, striking the earth twenty feet in front of the nearest fuel tanker; it burst in a vivid yellow flash and Sean saw one of the Frelimo sentries cartwheel bodily into the air. The second rocket was high, missing the tanker by six feet, reaching the top of its trajectory five hundred yards out and then dropping into the forest beyond, its detonation screened by trees and scrub.

'Aim, you Shangane oxen!' Sean bellowed at them, and he was up and running as he realized his mistake in not taking the first crucial shot himself.

The Frelimo sentries were screaming and scattering around the fuel tankers and from the perimeter of the laager a 12.7mm cannon opened up, sluicing gaudy strings of fiery tracer across the sky.

The rocketeer was fumbling to reload the RPG 7, but he was panicky and unsure in the dark. Sean snatched the launcher off his shoulder and with two deft movements had removed the protecting nose cap of the missile and cleared the safety-pin. He

387

swung the launcher over his shoulder and dropped on one knee, aiming at the nearest tanker.

'All the time in the world,' he reminded himself, and waited for the puff of the morning breeze on his cheek to abate. The RPG 7 was wildly inaccurate in a crosswind for the push of the wind on its tail-fins would turn its nose into wind.

The breeze dropped and Sean centred the sights on the fuel tanker. The range was just on three hundred metres, the limit of the rocket's accuracy, and he fired. The missile sped true, and the side of the tanker erupted in a tall sheet of volatile Avgas. The sky filled with flames.

Sean snarled at the rocketeer beside him and the man fumbled another missile out of his pack, the cardboard propellant tube already attached to it.

Burning Avgas illuminated the southern slope of the hill like noonday. Sean was kneeling in the open and the gunner on the 12.7mm swung his aim onto him.

The earth around Sean dissolved into billowing clouds of dust and flying clods, and the rocketeer ducked.

'Come on, you yellow bastard!' Sean completed the loading sequence unaided, making no effort to avoid the aim of the 12.7mm gunner.

He lifted the launcher on to his shoulder, and aimed at the second fuel tanker. It was lit up by the flames as though it were a stage effect, but as he was on the point of firing, the tanker was obscured by a dancing curtain of yellow dust and the volley of cannon fire passed so close to Sean's head that his eardrums creaked and popped as though he were in a decompression chamber.

He held his fire for three seconds and then as the curtains of dust blew open he fired through them, and the second tanker burst, blown clear of the railway lines by the explosion of its lethal cargo.

Burning Avgas flowed down the slope like the lava of a miniature Vesuvius, and Sean threw the launcher at the rocketeer's chest. 'Hit them on the head with the bloody thing!' he yelled at him. 'That's the only damage you are going to do with it!'

The mortar men were making better practice. Sean had sighted their weapons for them and they bobbed and weaved over the short mortar tubes as they dropped the finned projectiles into the open mouths. A steady stream of bombs lobbed high into the dawn sky and then rained down into the hilltop laager.

Sean watched the effect of the bursts with a dispassionate, professional eye.

'Good,' he murmured. 'Good.' But they had only been capable of carrying thirty bombs for each of the mortars; they weighed almost two kilos each and they would be expended in a few short minutes. They must rush the perimeter while the exploding bombs distracted the Frelimo gunners. He hefted the AKM rifle and slipped the safety-catch.

'Go!' Sean yelled, and blew a short series of blasts on his whistle. 'Go!'

The Shanganes came to their feet in a single cohesive movement, and swept down the hill, but there were only twenty of them, a puny line of running men, brightly lit by the flames. The 12.7mm gunners on the hill fastened on them, and the tracer flew in clouds about them, thick as a locust plague.

'Shit!' Sean laughed aloud in terror. 'What a way to go!'

One of the Frelimo guns had picked Sean out of the sweep line and was concentrating his fire on him, but Sean was plunging down hill with long flying strides and the gunner was shooting high and a little behind. Shot flashed past Sean so close he could feel the wind of it tugging at his tunic. Impossibly, he lengthened his stride, and beside him Matatu giggled shrilly, keeping pace with him down the hill.

'What's so goddamned funny, you silly little bugger!' Sean yelled at him furiously, and they hit the level ground beside the burning fuel tankers. The Frelimo gunner's field of fire was blanketed by the rolling screen of black smoke, and in the respite Sean marshalled his sweep line of racing Shanganes, pivoting them on the centre and directing them at the perimeter of the laager, pumping his right fist overhead to urge them on.

They used the smoke to cover themselves for the next two hundred metres of their charge. The dawn breeze was spreading it, sooty black and dense and low along the ground.

A Frelimo sentry staggered out of the smoke ahead of Sean. He wore faded and tattered denim jeans and grubby tennis shoes, he had lost his weapon and a rocket splinter must have hit him in the eye. The eye was dislodged from its socket and hung out on his cheek like a huge wet grape, dangling and bouncing on the thick cord of the optic nerve as the man jerked his head.

Without breaking his stride. Sean hit him in the belly with a tap of three from the AKM. firing from the hip. He jumped over the body as it hit the ground.

They came out of the smoke. still in sweep line. Sean glanced along the line and realized incredulously that they had not yet taken a single casualty. the twenty Shanganes were spread out and going hard. offering only fleeting targets through the smoke and flame to the disorientated Frelimo machine-guns.

At that moment. he saw the single strand of wire and the line of round metal discs on short steel droppers only a dozen paces ahead of him. The discs were each emblazoned with a stylized skull and crossbones in scarlet that caught the ruddy glow of the flames. and almost before he realized it. they were into the minefield that guarded the perimeter of the laager.

Two seconds later. the Shangane running on Sean's right-hand side triggered an anti-personnel mine. From the waist down his body was obscured by the dust and flash of the explosion and he dropped to the earth with both of his legs blown to bloody stumps below the knees.

'Keep going!' Sean screamed. 'We are nearly through!' And now his fear was a grotesque black beast upon his back that weighed him down and choked his breathing. To be maimed was a terror far beyond that of death, and the ground beneath his feet was sown with the steel capsules of terrible mutilation.

Matatu ducked in front of Sean. forcing him to check his stride. 'Follow me. my *Bwana*!' he piped in Swahili. 'Tread where I have trodden.' And Sean obeyed. shortening his stride to that of the little mannikin.

So Matatu ran him through the last fifty paces of the minefield. and Sean knew that he had never witnessed such a display of raw courage and devotion of one human being to another. Two more Shangane went down before they were through, their legs blown away beneath them. They left them lying in puddles of their own blood and minced flesh and jumped over the single strand of wire that marked the far side of the minefield.

Even in the terror and exhilaration of the moment. Sean felt his eyelids scalding with the strength of his gratitude and love for the little Ndorobo. He wanted to pick him up like a child's toy and hug him. Instead he gasped at him. 'You're so damned skinny it wouldn't have gone off even if you had stepped on one.' And Matatu twinkled with delight and ran at Sean's side as he charged the 12.7mm machine-gun in its sandbagged emplacement that lay dead ahead of them.

Sean was firing the AKM from the hip, short raking bursts, and he could see the head of the Frelimo gunner in the embrasure of the parapet of sandbags.

The gunner swivelled the barrel of the heavy machine-gun onto him, aiming for his belly and he was so close that Sean could see his eyes reflecting the red light of the fires as he sighted over it. The instant before he fired, Sean hurled himself forward, dropping under the shot like a runner sliding for the base plate; bullets whipped over his head and the muzzle blast beat in his eardrum, but he rolled forward and came up hard against the parapet, flattening himself against it, so close that he could have reached out and touched the muzzle of the machine-gun.

Sean unhooked the fragmentation grenade from his belt, drew the pin, and popped it into the embrasure beside him as though he were posting a letter.

He smiled as he heard the Frelimo gunner scream something unintelligible in Portuguese.

'Happy birthday!' he said, and the grenade exploded, blowing out through the opening in an exhalation of flame and fumes.

Sean jumped up and rolled over the top of the parapet. There were two men in the emplacement, writhing and wriggling on the floor, and half a dozen others had abandoned the position and were sprinting away up the hill, unarmed and screaming with panic.

Sean left Matatu to finish the two wounded men on the floor with his skinning knife, while he seized the abandoned 12.7mm machine-gun and manhandled it to the rear wall of the emplacement. He aimed it up the hill at the fleeing Frelimo and fired a long traversing burst. Two of the runners dropped in their tracks and grinning happily, crooning to himself with the fun of it, Matatu dragged a steel box of spare ammunition belts across the bloody floor, and helped Sean reload.

With a fresh belt of 250 rounds loaded, Sean traversed the heavy machine-gun and his fire lashed the hillside above him, tracer swirling through the groups of running Frelimo and scattering them.

It seemed to Sean as though more than half the Shangane had survived the minefield and the bloody charge and assault. Roaring wildly with triumph, they were pursuing and harrying the routed defenders.

The barrel of the heavy machine-gun was so hot that it crackled like a horseshoe fresh from the blacksmith's forge.

'Come on!' Sean abandoned it and jumped onto the rear parapet, ready to follow his Shanganes deeper into the laager and to begin wrecking the Russian service installations.

As he stood poised on the parapet, backlit by the burning fuel tankers, a monstrous apparition appeared in the dawn sky ahead of him. Rising on its glittering rotor, turbos shrieking, a Hind gunship lifted out of its sandbagged emplacement not two hundred metres from where Sean stood. It looked like some prehistoric behemoth. Supernatural and other-worldly, it rotated ponderously until the mirrored eyes of the canopy stared at Sean and the multiple cannon barrel in the turret below its nose pointed at him like an accuser's finger.

Sean reached down and seized Matatu by the scruff of his neck and hurled him to the floor of the emplacement, and then threw himself full length on top of him, knocking the breath out of the little man just as a gale of cannon fire dissolved the parapet wall and turned it to clouds of driving dust and gravel.

*   *   *

The suddenness of it all was what shocked Claudia most. One moment the stillness and tranquil darkness of dawn and the next the glare and cacophony of battle, the sky lit by the brilliance of leaping flame and glittering floods of tracers, her ears pounded by bursting mortars, shells and grenades and the blasts of machine-gun fire.

It took long moments for her eyes to adjust to the intensity of light, and to orientate herself to the swift kaleidoscope of the battle. Job had pointed out to her the point on the perimeter of the laager through which Sean would lead the assault and she searched it anxiously. The tiny figures of running men on the exposed slope of the hill were lit by the flames of burning Avgas which cast dark spiderlike shadows that scampered ahead of each man. There were so many of them, little black ants scurrying about, and with a jolt of horror she watched some of them fall and lie very still in the confusion of movement and light and sound.

'Where is Sean?' she whispered anxiously. 'Can you see him?'

'On the left, at the edge of the smoke.' Job told her, and she picked him out by the tiny figure that ran ahead of him like a hunting dog.

'I see him, and Matatu.'

Just in front of the pair the earth seemed suddenly to bloom with dust and flame, and they were gone.

'Oh God. No!' she cried aloud, but as the dust blew aside on the morning breeze, she saw the two of them running on, tracer bullets flickering about them like hellish fireflies.

'Please, please protect him,' she breathed, and lost sight of him as he reached the first emplacement.

'Where is he?' She found that she had seized Job's arm and was shaking it wildly. 'Where is he, can you see him?'

Then suddenly Sean was there again, even at that distance he appeared an heroic figure balancing easily on the sandbagged parapet in the ruddy glow of the flames, and she cried aloud with relief.

Then she saw him cower and from out of the very earth, only a short distance ahead of him, the monstrous shape of a Hind gunship reared into the air and swung its monstrous head towards him, lowering it like a charging bull. She heard the roar of its cannon, and leaping fountains of dust and flying earth obscured Sean's distant figure as cannon shell raked across the hillside.

'Job!' she screamed. 'They have killed him!' She reached out for him again, but Job shook off her hand.

He was down on one knee, the launch tube of the Stinger across his right shoulder, his face in the reflected firelight fixed in a mask of concentration as he stared into the sight screen.

'Quickly!' Claudia whispered. 'Shoot quickly!'

The missile leapt from its long tube, and hot air and stinging particles of dust and dead grass were blown back into Claudia's face as the rocket motor ignited. She slitted her eyes and held her breath as she watched it dart away on its tail of smoke and flame leaving a trail of dazzling smoke behind it as it flew towards the crest of the hill where the Hind hovered against the dark sky.

She saw the slight kick in its trajectory, as the missile changed to the ultra-violet seeker, and lifted its nose fractionally, no longer aiming at the armoured exhaust ports but at the open mouth of the turbo intakes just below the humped gearbox of the rotor.

She thought she saw the missile actually fly squarely into the intake, but the resulting explosion was deceptively mild, contained within the shell of titanium armour plate, so that none of its fury was dissipated. The Hind reeled wildly to the shot, throwing its nose high, falling backwards so that its tail rotor caught the rocky hillside and flipped it over sideways. It tumbled and bounced down the slope, rolling end over end, flames billowing from the throat of the air intake, its huge main rotor thrashing the earth and tearing itself to pieces, fragments hurtling into the night sky.

Claudia sought desperately for Sean, and gasped as she recognized him through the dust and the smoke, leaping back on to the parapet and then plunging on up the hillside with Matatu close behind him.

'Reload!' Job snapped at her, and with a guilty start she reached for the spare missile tube beside her and helped him clip it into the launcher.

The moment the Stinger was reloaded she glanced back at the laager. Sean was gone, but three more of the Hind gunships were airborne, soaring across the dawn, backlit by the flames. They were firing their cannon, some of them seeking targets within the laager where the attackers were in desperate hand-to-hand combat with the Frelimo garrison, others flailing the dark forest beyond the perimeter with their gales of tracer, trying to extinguish the hail of missiles that flew at them from out of the darkness.

Another Hind was hit and fell on its back, bursting into violent flame as it crashed into the rocky crest of the hill, and then another staggered in flight and curved down, mortally wounded, to hit the tree-tops and cartwheel through them to the earth.

As fast as they fell, others rose from their hidden emplacements with cannons blazing, sweeping down upon the attackers. Job leapt to his feet as a gunship tried to break away, climbing steeply up over their heads. He arched his back, pointing the missile almost vertically upwards, like a gun taking on a high-driven pheasant.

The Hind was a thousand feet up, climbing away, seeming to be safely beyond the Stinger's effective range, presenting a difficult angle and impossible trajectory, but the missile darted up, overhauling it effortlessly, and the great machine seemed to wince and tremble to the shot, standing for a moment stationary in the

394

air, before it fell back with its damaged turbos screaming in mortal agony and dived into the valley, striking in a storm of breaking branches and torn tree-trunks.

'Reload.' Job did not even watch the Hind's death agony, and Claudia leaped to help him fit another missile tube to the launcher. She tapped his shoulder as she finished.

'Go!' she said.

Another Hind came out of the forest directly in front of them. The Russian pilot was flying so low that he seemed to be earthbound. He was dodging and ducking the huge machine behind the scattered trees, weaving like a boxer, the down-draught of the rotor flattening the tall elephant grass only a few feet below the Hind's belly.

Job turned to face the oncoming machine, standing out in the open, lit by the flames, and he braced himself. picking up the image of the Hind in the sight screen.

The Hind seemed to steady itself for an instant, and the blast of its Gatling-cannon swept around them like a hurricane wind. Standing beside Job, Claudia was blown off her feet by the force of it, and her ears buzzed with the supersonic shock of passing cannon shells.

Job was thrown on top of her, his weight driving the wind from her lungs, but they had fallen between two round boulders which deflected the rest of the volley of cannon fire, and the Hind passed over them, only feet above where they lay. The blast of its rotors slashed at them, whipping Claudia's hair into her face so that it stung her eyes like a scourge.

Then the Hind slid away like a cruising tiger shark, and Claudia was suffocating by Job's weight on top of her and half-blinded with dust and her own hair. She struggled to free herself and was suddenly aware that her hands were wet, and that hot liquid was spilling over her and soaking her shirt.

'Job!' she blurted. 'Get up! Get off me!' Only when he neither replied nor moved, but lay on her with a heavy loose weight, did she realize that the wetness that was dousing her was Job's blood. That knowledge gave her wild strength and she rolled his body aside, and dragged herself out from under him.

She crawled to her knees and looked down at him. A cannon shell had hit him high in the upper body, and the damage was horrific. It looked as though he had been savaged and mauled by some ferocious beast; his right arm was almost torn from the shoulder and was thrown above his head in a ghastly parody of surrender.

She stared at him numbly and tried to say his name. No sound came from her throat. She reached out and caressed his face, not daring to touch that terribly mutilated body. She felt a terrible sense of loss and opened her mouth again to give vent to her grief with a wail of despair. It came out in a wild shriek of rage. The force of her rage stunned her, and seemed to impel her out of her own body so that she watched herself from afar, amazed by the actions of this savage stranger who had usurped her body and who now lunged for the missile-launcher where it lay beside Job's body.

Then she found herself on her feet with the missile-launcher on her right shoulder, searching the sky for the Hind gunship. It was four hundred metres away, cruising the foot of the hill, sweeping over the forest, picking out its targets from amongst the trees and destroying them with short but terrible blasts of its forward cannon.

As she turned to face it, standing fully upright in the daylight glare of the fires, the pilot must have spotted her, for he swivelled the gunship on its own axis, bringing the cannon in the pod below his cockpit to bear upon her.

'Locked and loaded,' she said, and the voice was strange in her ears as she repeated the litany of death.

'Actuator on.' She saw the image of the Hind appear in the tiny screen before her eyes, and she centred it in the cross hair on the aiming ring and the missile sobbed and then steadied into its high-pitched electronic tone.

'Target acquired,' she whispered, and felt no fear as the silhouette of the Hind altered in her sight screen. Now it was facing her head-on, its cannon almost bearing, the gunner traversing fractionally to pick up her tiny figure in his own sights.

'Fire!' she said quietly, and squeezed the pistol grip. The shoulder pad jolted her as the Stinger launched, and she slitted her eyes against the back blast of the missile as it sped away at four times the speed of sound, running straight and true at the hovering machine.

The cannon in the Hind's nose blazed, but Claudia felt only the disrupted air of shot passing close over her head before the missile jerked almost imperceptibly and arrowed unerringly into the open throat of the machine's turbo intakes. The Hind had

396

only a few feet to drop before it hit the earth and rolled over on to its side. In the moments before it was totally engulfed by burning fuel from the punctured belly tank, Claudia saw the panicky contortions of the pilot trapped under the armoured canopy and then even that was obliterated in a wall of flame.

'That was a human being,' she thought. 'A living and breathing person, and I destroyed him.' She expected a rush of guilt and remorse. How much a part of her was the belief that all life, especially human life, was sacred. The guilt did not come, instead she was borne aloft on a wave of savage triumph, the same berserk fury that had overtaken her so unexpectedly.

She looked around her swiftly, searching the sky for another target, something else to destroy, anything on which to wreak her vengeance. The dawn sky was empty. The burning carcasses of the Hind gunships lay strewn upon the slopes of the hill and amongst the trees of the valley forest.

'They are all down,' she thought. 'We got them all.'

From the forest, the Shanganes of the Stinger sections were swarming up the hill, breaking into the laager to support Sean's assault. She saw the Frelimo defenders throwing down their weapons, and cowering in their dugouts with hands raised pathetically, attempting to surrender, and watched dispassionately as the yelling Shanganes bayoneted and clubbed them like slaughtered chickens.

At her feet Job groaned, and instantly her rage was gone. She flung the empty missile-launcher aside and dropped down on her knees beside him.

'I thought you were dead!' she whispered, as she unwound the scarf from around her own neck with fingers which only now began to tremble. 'Don't die, Job. Please don't die.' The scarf was stained with sweat and dust, and its seams were unravelled and torn but she balled it up and stuffed it into the terrible wound, pressing down on it with her full weight to try and staunch the flood of his life's blood.

'Sean will be here soon,' she told him. 'Don't die, Job. Fight, please fight. I'll help you.'

* * *

Sean and Matatu crouched below the parapet, ducking lower as the storm of cannon fire flew only inches over their heads and filled their eyes and nostrils with dust from the ripped sandbags.

The instant the firing ceased, Sean bobbed up, just in time to see the stricken Hind fall tail-first against the rocky hillside and tear itself to pieces as it rolled down the slope.

'Well, blow me down, those damned Stingers actually work!' he laughed, still flying high on his own fear, and beside him Matatu giggled and clapped his hands.

'Like shooting sand grouse with the .577 *banduki*!' he cried in Swahili, and then leapt to his feet to follow Sean over the parapet.

Three Frelimo troopers bolted out of their dugout as they saw them coming and Sean fired the AKM from the hip, a short tap that caught one of them low in the back and flung him face down. The other two threw down their rifles and fell to their knees, gibbering with terror, hands held high over their heads. Sean ran on past them and they collapsed with relief as he ignored them.

Sean was through the outer defences and into the laager proper with its service areas and hardened helicopter emplacements. The workshops and fuel dumps were heavily sandbagged and covered with camouflage netting. Stray mortar shells were still falling amongst them, kicking up geysers of dust and gusts of whistling shrapnel. One of the Hinds had fallen near the far perimeter of the laager and was burning fiercely, oily black smoke billowing back over the workshops.

In the confusion, human figures scurried about without apparent purpose, unarmed technicians in baggy grey overalls who flung up their arms when they saw Sean, most of them dropping onto their knees to emphasize their surrender. In full camouflage paint and with the blood lust and elation of battle contorting his features, Sean cut a ferocious and terrifying figure.

'Down!' Sean gestured at them with the barrel of the AKM and with transparent relief they fell face down in the dust and clasped their hands behind their heads.

Just ahead he made out the long drooping rotors of a Hind protruding above the sandbagged wall of its emplacement.

'One didn't even get up,' he thought as he raced towards it, and at that moment the rotors began to revolve slowly, building up speed swiftly. Somebody was attempting to start the machine.

Sean darted through the narrow entrance, and into the deep circular emplacement. He checked his charge for a moment to survey the interior.

The Hind in its blotched camouflage towered over him, its

rotors whirling over his head as they built up to start speed on the Isotov turbo engine. Three Russian ground crew were crowded around the front of the machine, and incongruously Sean noticed the crimson arrow emblem painted on the Hind's nose which designated them an 'Excellent Crew'. One of the cherished performance awards of the Soviet air force.

The ground crew turned their white faces towards Sean and gaped at him. He jerked the muzzle of the AKM at them and they fell back.

The canopy of the weapons cockpit of the helicopter was still open, and one of the flight crew was clambering up into it. Only his plump backside in grey flying overalls protruded. Sean reached up between his legs and seized a handful of the man's genitals. The Russian squealed shrilly as Sean used them as a handle to drag him backwards and threw him against the sandbagged side wall of the emplacement.

The spinning rotors whistled shrilly as the turbo engine caught, and Sean jumped up onto the boarding step of the helicopter. The pilot's canopy was also open, and Sean thrust his AKM forward.

The pilot at the controls was young and thin with pale blond hair cut very short. In his haste to get the Hind away he had not even donned his flying helmet. He turned his head to look at Sean. His complexion was marred by angry purple and red acne and his eyes were very pale blue. They widened dramatically as Sean touched the tip of his acne-scarred nose with the muzzle of the AKM and said, 'Party is over, Ivan. Let's go home.'

It was apparent that this helicopter had not been scheduled for the dawn sortie that morning and the pilot and his crew had only begun their attempt to get the machine airborne once the attack had begun. It was less than ten minutes since the first mortar shells had fallen into the laager, not sufficient time, although they had almost made it.

'Kill the engine,' Sean told the pilot, and enforced the order by jamming the muzzle of the AKM into his nose with sufficient force to bring a smear of blood from one nostril and tears from both his pale eyes.

Reluctantly the pilot pushed the fuel mixture control to fully lean and cut both master switches. The whistle of the turbo died away.

'Out!' said Sean, and the pilot understood the gesture and

tone, if not the word. He unclasped his safety-belt and climbed down into the laager.

Sean lined up the pilot, the flight engineer and the three members of the ground crew against the sandbagged wall.

'Welcome to the capitalist world, comrades,' he greeted them, and then looked back at the helicopter.

'Jackpot!' he grinned, still euphoric with the adrenalin in his blood. 'We've got ourselves a real live, working Hind, Matatu!'

Matatu was having a grand time. 'Let's kill them now,' he suggested merrily. 'Give me the *banduki*. Let me shoot them for you.'

Sean had only seen Matatu fire one shot in his entire life, when as a joke Sean had let him fire the double .577. It had lifted Matatu clear off his feet and deposited him ten feet away.

'You couldn't hit one of them, even at this range, you bloodthirsty little bugger.' Sean grinned down at him, and then once more concentrated all his attention on the Hind. The magnitude of the prize he had taken began to dawn upon him.

The Hind would be a magnificent escape vehicle. He and Claudia, Job and Matatu could get out of here with first-class tickets, and then with a drop of spirits, reality overtook him.

Sean had never flown a helicopter, did not even have the vaguest notion of how to do so. All he knew was that it required a delicate and expert touch on the controls and was entirely different from piloting a fixed-wing aircraft.

He looked back at the Russian pilot calculatingly. Despite the acne and his unprepossessing appearance, he thought he detected a stubborn and proud streak in the man's pale eyes and he knew that the air-force officers were amongst the elite of the Soviet armed forces. The Russian was almost certainly a fanatical patriot.

'Not much chance of getting you to act as ferry pilot,' he guessed, and then spoke aloud. 'All right, gentlemen, let's get out of here.' He indicated the exit from the emplacement, and under the barrel of the AKM, they trooped towards it obediently. As the Russian pilot passed, Sean stopped him and lifted the Tokarev pistol from the holster at his hip.

'You won't need that, Ivan,' he said, and tucked the pistol into his own belt.

There was a fortified workshop almost abutting the Hind's emplacement. It had been excavated into the hillside and roofed with poles and sandbags. Sean herded the Russians down into it and then looked around him.

The battle had fizzled out, although there were still a few desultory shots and the pop and bang of burning ammunition. Through the drifts of smoke and dust, he saw the Shanganes of the Renamo force rounding up the prisoners and searching for loot and booty. He recognized some of the missile crews. Once the Hinds had been destroyed, they must have abandoned their Stingers and rushed up the hill to join the sack of the laager.

He saw one of them bayoneting a Frelimo prisoner in the buttocks and legs and roaring with laughter as the man squirmed in the dirt, kicking and contorting his body in an attempt to avoid the point of the blade. Other Renamo were emerging from the dugouts, rifles slung over their shoulders and arms full of booty.

Sean was accustomed to the ethics of irregular troops in Africa, but still this blatant indiscipline annoyed him. He snarled at them, and it was a measure of the force of his personality and the authority that he wielded over them that even in the heady moments of victory, they obeyed him with alacrity. The Renamo who had been torturing his prisoner paused only to dispatch the maimed victim with a bullet in the back of the neck before hurrying to Sean's bidding.

'Guard these white prisoners,' Sean ordered them. 'If harm comes to them, General China will roast your testicles on a slow fire and make you eat them,' he warned.

Without looking back, he strode through the laager, reasserting his command, getting his triumphant howling shrieking Shanganes back to sanity. He saw Sergeant Alphonso ahead of him.

'We can't carry much loot away, let the men take their pick and then I want limpet mines in the store rooms after everything has been drenched with Avgas from the drums,' he ordered Sergeant Alphonso. Sean glanced at his wristwatch. 'We can expect Frelimo to counter-attack the laager within the hour. I want to be gone by then.'

'No!' Alphonso shook his head. 'General China has moved three companies in between us to hold the Frelimo counter-attack. He has ordered you to hold this position until he arrives.'

Sean pulled up short and stared at Alphonso. 'What the hell are you talking about? China is two days' march away on the river!'

Alphonso grinned and shook his head. 'General China will be here in an hour. He followed us with five companies of his best troops. He has never been more than an hour behind us, not since we left the river.'

'How do you know this?' Sean demanded, and Alphonso grinned again and patted the radio on the back of the trooper who stood beside him.

'I spoke to the general ten minutes ago, as soon as we killed the last of the Russian *henshaw*.'

'Why didn't you tell me before this, you bastard?' Sean growled.

'The general ordered me not to. But now he has ordered me to tell you that he is very pleased with the killing of the *henshaw*, and he says that you are like a son to him. When he arrives he will reward you.'

'All right.' Sean changed his orders. 'If we have to hold the laager, get your men into the perimeter defences, we will use the 12.7mm heavy machine-guns.'

Sean broke off as a Shangane trooper came running up the hill towards him.

'*Nkosi!*' The man panted, and as soon as he saw his face, Sean knew it was bad news.

'The woman?' he demanded, seizing the messenger's arm. 'Is the white woman hurt?'

The Shangane shook his head. 'She is safe. She sent me to you. It's the Matabele. Captain Job. He is hit.'

'How bad?' Sean was already starting to run and he shouted the question over his shoulder.

'He's dying,' the Shangane called after him. 'The Matabele is dying.'

Sean knew where to look, he had himself selected the copse of knob-thorn acacia as Job's attack position. The first rays of the morning sun were turning the tops of the knob-thorns to gold as Sean ran down the hill. With the help of two Shanganes, Claudia had moved Job onto level soft ground beneath one of the trees. She had propped his head on one of the back-packs and had a field dressing over the wound.

She looked up and cried, 'Oh, Sean, thank God!' Her shirt was drenched with drying blood and she saw Sean's expression. 'Not my blood,' she assured him. 'I'm all right.'

Sean transferred all his attention to Job. His face was a sickly

402

blue-grey colour and the flesh seemed to have melted like hot tar from his skull.

Sean touched his cheek and his skin was cold as death. Frantically he searched for a pulse in the wrist of Job's good arm and although it was faint and rapid, Sean's relief was intense.

'He's lost huge quantities of blood,' Claudia whispered. 'But, I have contained the bleeding now.'

'He's in shock,' Sean muttered. 'Let me have a look.'

'Don't lift that dressing,' Claudia warned him quickly. 'It's ghastly. He was hit on the point of the shoulder by a cannon shell. It's just mangled flesh and bone chips. His arm is hanging by a shred of muscle and sinew.'

'Take Matatu with you,' Sean cut in brusquely. 'Go up to the laager. Find where they had their first-aid post. The Russians will have a decent stock. Find it. I want plasma and a drip set. Dressings and bandages, those are the most urgent. But if you can find antiseptic and pain-killers . . .'

Claudia scrambled to her feet. 'Sean, I was so worried about you! I saw . . .'

'You don't get rid of me that easy.' He did not look up from Job's face. 'Now, off you go, and get back here as quick as you can. Matatu, go with Donna, look after her.'

The two of them went at a run. Until they returned with medical supplies, Sean was helpless. But for something to keep himself occupied he wet his bandanna from the water-bottle and began to sponge the blood and dirt from Job's face. Job's eyelids fluttered open and Sean saw that he was conscious.

'Okay, Job, I'm here. Don't try and talk.'

Job closed his eyes for a moment and when he opened them again, he swivelled them downwards, too weak to move his head, yet he was trying to look down at his body, trying to check the extent of his injuries. It was always the first reaction.

'Is it lung blood I'm losing? Are both my feet still here, both my hands. . . ?'

'Right arm and shoulder,' Sean told him. '12.7mm cannon nicked you. Just a little bitty scratch. You are going to make it, lad, written guarantee. Would I lie to you?'

A faint smile tugged up the corners of Job's mouth and he lowered one eyelid in a conspiratorial wink. Sean felt his heart begin to break. He knew he had lied. Job wasn't going to make it.

'Relax,' he ordered cheerfully. 'Lie back and enjoy it, as the bishop said to the actress. I'm in charge here now.'

And Job closed his eyes.

*　　*　　*

Claudia picked out the medical dugout by the red cross insignia at the entrance. There were two Shangane Renamo looting the interior, ransacking it for booty, but Claudia shrieked at them so violently that they slunk away guiltily.

The labels on the cartons of medical supplies were all in Russian Cyrillic script. Claudia had to rip the lids open and check the contents of each. She found boxes which contained a dozen plastic bags of clear plasma each, and gave two of them to Matatu. The drip sets were on the shelf below. Field dressings and bandages were easy, but she was flummoxed by the tubes of ointments and pill bottles. However, the contents of one tube were yellow brown and had the characteristic iodine aroma; she selected those and then she found that some of the labels had alternative notations in French and Arabic. She had a smattering of both languages, enough to identify which were antibiotics and pain-killers.

She found two field packs, obviously prepared for use by the Russian first-aid teams and included these in her selection; then she and Matatu, heavily laden, hurried out of the first-aid post.

Before she reached the perimeter of the laager again, a dreadfully familiar figure loomed out of the banks of drifting smoke ahead of her. This was the very last person she had expected to see here.

'Miss Monterro,' General China called. 'What a fortunate encounter. I need your assistance.' China was accompanied by half a dozen officers of his staff.

Claudia recovered swiftly from the shock of the unexpected meeting. 'I'm busy,' she snapped, trying to step around him. 'Job is badly wounded. I have to get back to him.'

'My need is greater than anybody else's, I'm afraid.' China put out an arm.

'Forget it,' Claudia flared at him. 'Job needs this stuff, or he'll die.'

'One of my men will take it to him,' China replied. 'You are coming with me, please. Or I'll have you carried. Not very dignified, Miss Monterro.'

Claudia was still protesting as one of the Renamo officers relieved her of her load of medical supplies, but at last she shrugged with resignation.

'Go with him, Matatu.' She pointed down the hill. The little man nodded brightly and Claudia allowed China to escort her back into the laager.

They picked their way through the shambles of the battle, and Claudia shuddered as she stepped over the charred corpse of one of the Frelimo garrison.

'Colonel Courtney's attack has succeeded beyond even my wildest expectations.' General China was affable and clearly delighted with what he saw around him. 'He even managed to capture a Hind gunship completely intact, together with the Russian air crew and ground crew.'

'I hope you won't keep me long. I have to get back.'

'Captain Job will live or die without you, Miss Monterro. I need your services as a translator in talking to the pilot. '

'I don't speak Russian,' Claudia told him flatly.

'Fortunately the pilot seems to speak Italian, how he learned the language I cannot guess, but he keeps repeating, "*Italiano, Italiano*".' China took her arm and led her down the steps of the sandbagged and camouflaged dugout.

Claudia glanced round the dugout and saw instantly that it was an engineering workshop. A long work-bench ran down each wall. Set up on one of these were a metal lathe and drill press. A wide selection of hand tools was racked in cupboards above the benches and she recognized the electric and gas welding sets at the far end of the workshop. Her father had had his own workshop in the cellar of their home in Anchorage and she had spent so many evenings watching him pottering around down there.

The Russian prisoners, five of them, were at the far end of the underground room.

'Which one of you speaks Italian?' she asked.

A tall thin man stepped forward. He wore grey flying overalls and his face was scarred with acne. His pale blue eyes were shifty and nervous.

'I do, *Signora*.'

'Where did you learn?' Claudia asked.

'My wife is a graduate student from Milano. I met her while she was doing her doctorate at Patrice Lumumba University in Moscow.' His Italian was heavily accented and his grammar uncertain, but she understood him without difficulty.

'I am translating for General China,' she told him, 'but I must warn you that he is a savage and cruel man. I am neither his ally nor his friend. I cannot protect you.'

'Thank you, *Signora*. I understand, but I do not need protection. I am a prisoner-of-war under the Convention of Geneva. I have certain rights. So do my men.'

'What does he say?' China demanded.

'He says he is a prisoner-of-war, and he and his men are protected by the Geneva Convention.'

'Tell him that Geneva is far away. This is Africa and I was no signatory to any agreement in Switzerland. Here he has only such rights as I decide he should have. Tell him he will fly the helicopter under my command and that his ground crew will service and maintain the machine in flying condition.'

As Claudia translated, she watched the pilot's jaw set and his pale blue eyes harden. He turned his head slightly and spoke to his men in Russian. Immediately they began to mutter and shake their heads.

'Tell this black monkey that we insist on our rights,' the pilot spoke scornfully. Claudia had heard that many Russians were racists, and the derogatory term the pilot used suggested that for him at least this was true. 'We refuse to fly or fight for him. That would be a traitorous act.'

His refusal was so obvious, that China did not wait for Claudia's translation.

'Tell him,' he cut in brusquely, 'that I have no time for argument, or for subtle persuasion. I ask once more for his co-operation and if he refuses, I will be forced to demonstrate my serious intentions.'

'*Signore*, this man is very dangerous,' Claudia told the Russian officer. 'I have seen him commit the most unspeakable atrocities. I have suffered torture by him, myself.'

'I am a Russian officer and a prisoner-of-war.' The pilot drew himself to attention, his tone stern. 'I know my duty.'

China was watching his face as the pilot replied. He smiled coldly as Claudia translated. 'Another brave man,' he murmured. 'We must now determine just how brave he is.'

Without looking at his staff officers, he gave them a quiet order in Shangane and while they trundled forward the chariot that held the oxyacetylene gas cylinders, China smiled steadily at the Russian officer. The man returned his regard with a cold pale stare as they matched wills.

China was the one who turned away. He went to the work-bench and swiftly examined the tools and objects scattered upon it. He gave a grunt of approval as he selected a thin steel rod and weighed it in his hand. It was the length and thickness of a rifle ramrod pierced at each end for a connecting screw, probably a control link from the Hind helicopter.

'This will do very nicely,' he spoke aloud, and then picked up a discarded woven asbestos welding glove. He pulled it onto his right hand, and then turned his attention to the gas welding set. Claudia, who had watched her father work, realized that China was well versed in the use of the apparatus. He lit the welding flame on the torch and swiftly adjusted the flow of oxygen and acetylene from their separate cylinders until the flame was a brilliant blue feather, hot and unwavering. Then he took up the metal rod in his gloved hand and began to heat the tip of it in the blue flame.

All the Russians watched him uneasily. Claudia saw the pilot's hard stare flicker uncertainly, as the shine of nervous sweat dewed on his upper lip.

'This man is an animal,' Claudia said softly in Italian. 'You must believe me when I tell you he is capable of the vilest acts. Please, *Signore*, I do not want to watch this.'

The pilot shook his head, dismissing her appeal, but he was staring at the tip of the metal rod as it began to glow cherry red.

'I will not be intimidated by brutish threats,' he said, but she detected the slightest catch and crack in his voice.

In China's gloved hand, the tip of the rod turned slowly to incandescent crimson and then to translucent white heat. China smiled and turned off the flame of the welding torch. He weaved the glowing tip of the rod in a gentle flourish, like a conductor's baton, and smiled at the pilot. It was the humourless reptilian smile of a cobra.

'I repeat my request. Ask him if he will fly for me.'

'*Nyet.*' Even though his voice cracked, the pilot's reply was decisive, and then he added in Russian, '*Obezyana*, black monkey!'

China stood in front of him and made a slow pass with the tip of the rod a few inches in front of the Russian's eyes.

'Tell him, *Signora*,' the pilot whispered, 'that without my eyes, I cannot fly.'

'Very true,' China nodded as Claudia translated, and he left the pilot and walked on down the line of white prisoners, waving the glowing tip of the rod in a slow mesmeric gesture in each of their faces, studying their reactions carefully. The plump mechanic in oil-stained overalls at the end of the line gave China his most satisfying response. He shrank away from the rod until the wall of the dugout stopped him, and sweat ran down his fat rosy cheeks and dripped from the end of his chin. In a squeaky voice, he said something in Russian, and the pilot answered him with a sharp monosyllabic order.

'You don't like it, do you? My fat little white slug.' China smiled thinly at him and let him feel the radiated heat on his cheek. The back of the flight engineer's head was pressed against the wall, and he swivelled his eyes in their sockets to watch the rod.

The metal was cooling and with a small frown of annoyance, China left him and turned back to the work-bench and relit the welding torch. While he carefully reheated the tip of the rod, the mechanic sagged against the sandbags. He was sweating in dark patches through the cotton of his greasy overalls.

The pilot spoke softly to him in an encouraging tone, and the engineer nodded and straightened up. He glanced at his superior with an expression of patent gratitude and watching this brief exchange between the two men, China smiled again, this time with satisfaction.

When Claudia saw that smile, she realized suddenly that China had just run a selection test. He had chosen his victim. The mechanic was the least courageous of the five Russians, and the pilot had inadvertently disclosed his concern and friendship for the man.

'Please,' she whispered in Italian. 'Your friend is in terrible danger. You must do what this man asks if you wish to save him.'

The pilot looked at her, and from his expression Claudia saw he was beginning to waver.

'Please, for my sake. I cannot bear to watch.' But with despair, she saw the Russian's expression change as his resolve firmed once again. He shook his head and China saw that gesture.

He switched off the welding torch and blew softly on the white tip of the metal rod. He let the moment draw out agonizingly; every eye in the bunker was fixed on the point of glowing steel.

Then abruptly he gave an order in Portuguese and two of his men sprang forward and seized the mechanic by his arms. He gave a little squeal of protest, but they hustled him to the work-bench and threw him face down across its top. One of them jumped up and sat between his shoulder-blades pinning him down. He struggled ineffectually, kicking his legs. Swiftly and expertly. they strapped his ankles to the legs of the work-bench, and he lay helplessly sprawled face downwards with his backside sticking up in the air, stretching the cotton seat of his overalls.

The Russian pilot shouted a protest and stepped forward but one of the Renamo officers thrust a pistol into his belly and forced him back against the wall.

'I ask you again,' China told him. 'Will you fly for me?'

The pilot shouted at him in Russian. It was clearly an insult. His face was flushed now, the acne purple and shiny as buttons on his chin and cheeks.

China nodded at his men. One of them drew the trench knife from its sheath on his webbing belt and slit the waistband of the mechanic's overalls. Then he seized the severed edges of cotton and ripped them downwards, tearing the cloth loose so it hung in tatters around the pinioned man's knees. Under the overalls, the engineer wore a pair of elasticized blue underpants. The Renamo pulled these down as far as they would go.

Claudia stared in fascinated horror at the mechanic's exposed buttocks. They were very white and fat and round, covered with a scraggle of dark curly ginger hair. From between his thighs, his wrinkled hairy scrotum protruded backwards like that of a dog.

The pilot was shouting in Russian and Claudia found herself pleading weakly.

'Please, General China, please let me leave, I cannot bear this.' She tried to turn her head away and cover her eyes, but the dreadful fascination of it compelled her to watch through her fingers despite herself.

China ignored both the pilot's and Claudia's pleas, and spoke crisply to the officer who sat between the Russian's shoulder-blades. Still pinning him to the bench, the Renamo reached over and seized one of his buttocks in each of his hands and drew them sharply apart. Claudia's protests dried in her throat and she found herself staring dry-mouthed at the Russian's puckered rosey-brown anus as it nestled like a blind man's eye between his hairy cheeks.

China reached out towards it with the tip of the rod, then stopped three inches short of it. The mechanic felt the heat of it on his most intimate flesh, and began to struggle so violently that two more of the Renamo officers had to throw their combined weight on to his back to keep him pinned down.

'Yes?' China looked across at the Russian pilot. He was raving like a madman, his face contorted with outrage, shouting threats and accusations.

'I regret the necessity,' China said, and thrust the metal rod forward, his wrist cocked like that of a fencing master going on attack, a *flèche*.

As the glowing metal touched the sensitive skin the Russian screamed, a shattering high-pitched shriek that made Claudia cry out pitifully in sympathy.

The metal smoked and sizzled and spluttered, as China rotated his wrist, twisting the rod deeper and deeper into the Russian's body. Now his screams were great explosive gusts of sound, and Claudia clapped her hands over her ears to shut them out and turned away, running into the corner of the dugout and pressing her face against the rough sandbags.

The smoke filled her nostrils, her throat and her lungs, the obscene odour of burning flesh, of charring fat, coated her tongue and her gorge rose. She tried to contain it, but her vomit shot up her throat and in a projectile stream splashed onto the earthen floor between her feet.

Behind her the screams dropped gradually in volume, and became ghastly rattling groans. However, all the Russians were yelling their protest and fury, and the din was confusing.

Another whiff of burned flesh and spilled faeces made her retch again and then she wiped her mouth with the back of her hand and leaned her forehead against the sandbagged wall. She was trembling wildly, and tears and sweat streamed down her cheeks.

Slowly the uproar behind her subsided, and the only sounds in the bunker were the mechanic's groans and gurgles. They were weaker now but nonetheless harrowing. Claudia could tell without looking at him that the Russian was dying.

'Miss Monterro.' China's voice was level and calm. 'Please get a grip on yourself, we still have work to do.'

'You are an animal!' she blurted. 'I hate you! Oh God, how I hate you!'

'Your feelings are not of the slightest interest to me,' China said. 'Now you will tell the pilot that I await his full co-operation.'

The flight engineer's groans distracted her. As she turned to face China, she saw that they had released the stricken man and allowed him to slump to the floor. China had made no effort to withdraw the metal rod from his body, and he was still transfixed. As he rolled weakly about on the earthen floor, he was plucking ineffectually at the protruding end of the rod. The heated metal had adhered to his bowels as it cooled, and was firmly rooted in his flesh. Every time he tugged at it a trickle of liquid faeces bubbled from the terrible wound.

'Speak to the pilot,' China commanded.

Claudia dragged her eyes from the dying man and addressed the pilot. 'Please do what he wants.'

'I cannot, my duty!' the pilot cried.

'The devil with your duty!' Claudia shouted back furiously. 'You and all your men will end up like this!' She gestured to the floor without looking down again. 'That's what will happen to you!' She turned to the other Russians who were shaken and appalled, pale with horror and terror.

'Look at him!' she screamed in English. 'Is that what you want?'

They did not understand the words but her meaning was clear to all of them. They turned their faces towards the pilot.

The pilot resisted their entreaties for a minute, and then at a word from China the Renamo officers seized another one of the ground crew and threw him screaming and kicking face down, across the bench and the Russian pilot threw up both hands in a gesture of resignation.

'Tell him to stop,' he said wearily to Claudia. 'We will do as he orders.'

'Thank you, Miss Monterro.' China smiled at her charmingly. 'You are now free to rejoin Colonel Courtney.'

'How will you communicate with the pilot?' she asked uncertainly.

'Already he understands me.' China transferred the benevolence of his smile to the Russian. 'I assure you that he will learn

411

to speak my language with the utmost fluency in a very short time indeed.' He turned back to Claudia. 'Please convey my respects to Colonel Courtney and ask him to join me at his earliest convenience. I would like to take my leave of him, to thank him and wish him *bon voyage.*' He gave her a mocking bow. 'So God speed, Miss Monterro. I hope that you will remember all of us, your friends in Africa, with affection.'

Claudia could find no words to reply, she turned to the door of the bunker and her legs were shaky and rubbery beneath her.

In a daze of horror, she stumbled down the hill. The sights around her which at another time might have sickened and appalled her, she hardly noticed.

At the foot of the hill, she paused and tried to get a grip on herself. She breathed deeply, trying to quell the intermittent sobs that still caught her unawares and she combed her hair back from her face with her fingers and retied the strip of cloth she was using as a headband. With the tail of her shirt, she wiped the tears and sweat from her face, and was shocked at the grimy smear they left on the cloth.

'I must look like hell,' she whispered, and clenched her hands to hide her broken fingernails, but she braced her shoulders and lifted her chin. 'Sean mustn't see me like this,' she told herself fiercely. 'Pull yourself together, woman.'

Sean looked up as she hurried to where he was still working over Job's blanket-wrapped body.

'What happened?' he demanded. 'What kept you?'

'General China is here. He made me go with him.'

'What did he want? What happened?'

'Nothing, not important. I'll tell you about it later. How is Job?'

'I've got a full litre of plasma into him,' Sean replied. He had suspended the drip set from a branch above them. 'His pulse is better. Job is as tough as an old buffalo bull. Help me dress the wound.'

'Is he conscious?'

'He comes and goes,' Sean warned her.

Beneath the field dressing was such a terrible injury that neither of them could bring themselves to discuss it, especially as Job might be able to hear and understand them.

Sean smothered the entire area with iodine paste, and then bound it up again with pressure pads and clean white bandages

412

from the medical pack. The blood and iodine soaked through the white even as he worked.

Between them they had to roll Job on to his side to pass the bandages over his back. Claudia held the half-severed arm in place, bending the elbow across his chest, and Sean strapped it securely. By the time they finished, Job's entire upper body was swathed in a cocoon of expertly applied bandage from which only his left arm protruded.

'His pulse is going again.' Sean looked up from his wrist. 'I'm going to give him another litre of plasma.'

There was a scattered outbreak of machine-gun and mortar fire from the forest beyond the hill laager, and Claudia looked up apprehensively. 'What's that?'

'Frelimo counter-attack.' Sean was still busy with the drip set. 'But China has three companies in there, and Frelimo are going to be less than enthusiastic now that they have lost their air support. China's lads should be able to hold them off with no trouble.'

'Sean, where did China come from? I thought . . .'

'Yes.' Sean cut in. 'I also thought he was back on the river. The crafty bastard was right on our heels, ready to rush in and grab the spoils.' He finished adjusting the plasma flow in the drip set, and squatted down beside Claudia, studying her face.

'All right,' he said. 'Tell me what happened.'

'Nothing.' She smiled brightly.

'Don't bullshit me, beautiful,' Sean said gently, and put an arm around her. Despite herself she choked on a sob.

'China,' she whispered. 'Right on top of what happened to Job. He made me translate for the Russian pilot. Oh God, I hate him. He's an animal. He made me watch . . .' she broke off.

'Rough stuff?' Sean asked, and she nodded.

'He killed one of the Russians, in the foulest possible way.'

'He's a lovely lad, our China, but try and put it out of your mind, we've got enough troubles of our own. Let the Ruskies worry about theirs.'

'He forced the Russian pilot to agree to fly the helicopter.'

Sean stood up, lifting her to her feet beside him. 'Don't think of China and the Russian any more. All we have to worry about is getting out of here.' He broke off as he saw Sergeant Alphonso and a half dozen of his Shanganes trotting down the hill towards them. All of them were laden with loot.

413

'*Nkosi!*' Alphonso's broad handsome face was wreathed in a beatific grin. 'What a fight, what a victory!'

'You fought like an impi of lions,' Sean agreed. 'The battle is won but now you must help us to get away to the border. Captain Job is badly hurt.'

Alphonso's smile faded; despite their natural tribal enmity, both men had developed a grudging respect for each other.

'How bad?' Alphonso came to stand beside Sean and looked down at Job.

'There was a fibreglass stretcher in the first-aid post,' Claudia said. 'We can carry Job on that.'

'It is two days' march to the border,' Alphonso murmured dubiously. 'Through Frelimo territory.'

'Frelimo are running like dogs with a hot coal under their tails.' Sean's tone was hard. 'Send two of your men to fetch the stretcher.'

'General China calls for you. He is leaving in the Russian *henshaw*. He wants to speak to you before he goes,' Alphonso said.

'All right, but I want that stretcher here when I get back,' Sean warned him, and glanced at his wristwatch. 'We will march for the border in one hour from now.'

'*Nkosi!*' Alphonso agreed cheerfully. 'We will be ready.' Sean turned back to Claudia.

'I'm going to see China. I'm going to try to talk him into flying Job out in the helicopter, but I don't think my chances are particularly rosy. Please stay with Job and keep an eye on his pulse rate. I've found a disposable syringe of adrenalin in the medic pack, use it only as a last resort.'

'Please don't be long,' she whispered. 'I'm only brave when you're here.'

'Matatu will stay with you.'

Sean climbed the hill swiftly, passing the first string of Renamo porters. Obviously China was taking everything he could carry away, including boxes of helicopter spares and hundreds of jerry cans of Avgas. The lines of porters were heading back into the wilderness towards the river, and Sean paid them scant attention. His role was played. He was eager to get out, reach the border, get Job to where he could receive professional medical attention and get Claudia to safety. However, over all his urgency lay the nagging uncertainty, was China really going to stand by his word, and let them go? Was he not being just a trifle optimistic?

'We'll see,' he told himself grimly, and shouted at one of the Renamo officers who was supervising the loading of the porters. 'Where is General China?'

He found him with his staff and the captured Russians in the laager's command bunker, and China looked up from the map he was consulting and smiled affably as Sean entered.

'Colonel Courtney, my felicitations. You were magnificent. A famous victory.'

'And now you owe me a favour.'

'You and your party wish to leave,' China agreed. 'All debts between us have been paid in full. You are free to go.'

'No,' Sean shook his head. 'By my calculation, you still owe me one. Captain Job has been badly wounded. His condition is critical. I want him flown out to Zimbabwe in the captured Hind.'

'You jest, of course,' China laughed lightly. 'I cannot risk sending such a valuable asset on a non-productive mission. No, Colonel, all debts are paid, please don't persist in extravagant demands. With my defective hearing, it only annoys me and I may be tempted to review my generous offer to allow you and, yours to depart unhindered.' He smiled and held out his hand. 'Come now, Colonel. Let us part as friends. You have the services of Sergeant Alphonso and his men. You are a man of infinite resourcefulness. I am sure that you will contrive to get yourself and all your party to safety without any further assistance from me.'

Sean ignored the outstretched hand and China glanced at it and then lowered it to his side. 'So we part, Colonel. Me to my little war and, who knows, perhaps one day, a country of my very own. You to the tender embraces of your very rich, very beautiful young American.' His smile had a sly and foxy slant to it. 'I wish you joy and I am sure you do the same for me.' He turned back to his map, leaving Sean for an instant nonplussed and taken off balance. It was incomplete, it couldn't end like this. Sean knew there was more to come, but General China began dictating orders to one of his officers in Portuguese, leaving Sean standing uncertainly at the door of the bunker.

Sean waited a few moments longer, and then turned abruptly and ducked out through the entrance. Only after he was gone, China lifted his head and smiled after him, a gloating little

415

smile which if Sean had seen it, would have answered his question.

*   *   *

Alphonso's men had worked quickly. The litter was a fibreglass stretcher, one of those lightweight body-moulded types used by mountain rescue teams. Nonetheless it would still require four men to carry it over rough ground, and they had a long hard path to the border.

'Less than a hundred kilometres and not that hard,' Sean reassured himself. 'Two days, if we push it.'

Claudia greeted him with relief. 'Job seems stronger. He was conscious, asking for you, he said something about a hill, Hill 31?'

Sean flickered a smile. 'That's where we met. He's wandering a little, help me to get him onto the stretcher.'

Between them they lifted Job gently and settled him onto the fibreglass stretcher. Sean rigged the drip set on a wire frame above his head, and tucked looted grey woollen blankets around him.

'Matatu,' he said as he stood up. 'Take us home.' And he gestured to the first team of stretcher-bearers to take their positions.

It was less than two hours since sunrise, but they seemed to have lived an entire lifetime in that short period, Sean thought as he glanced back at the hilltop laager. Streamers of smoke drifted from its crest and the last column of General China's porters was disappearing into the forest below it, all heavily laden with booty.

The distant sounds of battle had finally dwindled into silence. The half-hearted Frelimo counter-attack had long ago fizzled out, and China was withdrawing his forces into the bad ground below the Pungwe river.

As Sean watched, the captured Hind helicopter rose slowly out of its emplacement and hung above the hill on its glistening rotor; then abruptly it dipped towards them, the sound of its engine crescendoed and suddenly Sean was staring into the multiple mouths of the Gatling-cannon in its nose.

As it raced towards him, he recognized China's face behind the armoured glass canopy. He was perched in the flight engin-

416

eer's seat, at the controls of the 12.7mm cannon. Sean saw the barrels of the cannon traverse slightly, coming on to aim. The Hind was only fifty feet above them, so close he could see China's teeth flash in his dark face as he smiled.

Their little column had not reached the edge of the forest. There was no cover, no protection from the blast of that terrible weapon, and instinctively Sean reached out and drew Claudia to him, trying to shield her with his own body.

Above them General China lifted his right hand in an ironic salute, and the Hind banked steeply away into the north-west, dwindled swiftly to a speck and was gone. They all stared after it silently, seized by a sense of anti-climax, until Sean broke the spell.

'Let's go, brethren!' And once again the stretcher-bearers started forward at an easy jog-trot, singing very softly one of the ancient marching songs.

Scouting ahead of them, Matatu came across a few scattered parties of Frelimo assault troops, but they were all in headlong retreat from the river wilderness. After the loss of their air support the Frelimo offensive seemed to have collapsed completely and the situation was fluid and confused. Although they were forced to detour further northwards than Sean had planned, Matatu steered them out of contact with any Frelimo and the stretcher-bearers were rotated regularly so they made swift progress.

At nightfall, they stopped to eat and rest. Alphonso made the scheduled radio contact with Renamo headquarters and gave them a position report. He received only a laconic acknowledgement without change of orders.

They feasted on tinned goods looted from the Russian stores, and smoked the perfumed Balkan tobacco in yellow cigarette paper with hollow cardboard filters.

Job was conscious again and complained in a husky whisper, 'There is a lion gnawing on my shoulder.'

Sean injected an ampoule of morphia into his drip set and it eased him, so that he was even able to eat a few mouthfuls of the bland-tasting tinned meat. However, his thirst was far greater than his hunger, and Sean held his head and helped him get down two full mugs of the surprisingly good Russian coffee.

Sean and Claudia sat beside the litter and waited for the moon to rise.

'We are going in through the Honde Valley again.' Sean told

417

Job. 'Once we get you to St Mary's Mission you'll be fine. One of the Catholic fathers is a doctor, and I'll be able to send a message to my brother, Garry, in Johannesburg. I'll ask him to send the company jet to Umtali. We'll fly you into Johannesburg General Hospital before you know what's hit you, mate. There you'll get the best medical attention in the world.'

When the moon rose they went on, and it was almost midnight before Sean called a halt for the night.

He made a mattress of cut grass beside Job's litter, and as Claudia drifted off to sleep in his arms, he whispered to her, 'Tomorrow night, I'll give you a hot bath and put you between clean sheets.'

'Promise?' she sighed.

'Cross my heart.'

From deeply ingrained habit, he woke an hour before first light and went to rouse the sentries for dawn stand-by.

Alphonso threw aside his blanket, stood up and fell in beside him. When they had made the sentry round, they paused on the edge of the camp and Alphonso offered him one of the Russian cigarettes. They smoked from cupped hands, shielding the glow of burning tobacco.

'What you told me about South Africa, is it true?' Alphonso asked unexpectedly.

'What did I tell you?'

'That men, even black men, eat meat every day?'

Sean smiled in the darkness, amused by Alphonso's concept of paradise, a place where a man could eat meat every day.

'Sometimes they get so sick of eating beef,' he teased, 'that they try chicken and lamb just for a change.'

Alphonso shook his head. That was beyond belief, no African could ever tire of beef.

'How much does a black man earn in South Africa?' he demanded.

'About five hundred rand a month if he is an ordinary unskilled labourer, but there are many black millionaires.' Five hundred rand was more than a man earned in Mozambique in a year, even if he were lucky enough to find employment. A million was a figure beyond Alphonso's powers of imagination.

'Five hundred?' He shook his head in wonder. 'And paid in rands, not paper escudos or Zimbabwe dollars?' he demanded earnestly.

'Rands,' Sean confirmed. Compared to other currencies in Africa the rand was as good as a gold sovereign.

'And there are things in the stores, things for a man to buy with his rands?' Alphonso demanded suspiciously. It was difficult for him to visualize shelves laden with goods for sale, other than a few pathetic bottles of locally produced carbonated soft drinks and packets of cheap cigarettes.

'Whatever you want,' Sean assured him. 'Soap and sugar, cooking oil and maize meal.' Half-forgotten luxuries in Alphonso's mind.

'As much as I want?' he asked. 'No rationing?'

'As much as you can pay for,' Sean assured him. 'And when your belly is full, you can buy shoes and suits and ties, transistor radios and dark glasses . . .'

'A bicycle?' Alphonso demanded eagerly.

'Only the very lowest men ride bicycles,' Sean grinned, enjoying himself. 'The others have their own motor cars.'

'Black men own their own motor cars?'

Alphonso thought about that for a long time.

'Would there be work for a man like me?' he asked with a diffidence that was completely out of character.

'You?' Sean pretended to consider it, and Alphonso waited apprehensively for his judgement. 'You?' Sean repeated. 'My brother owns a gold mine. You could be a supervisor on his mine within a year, a shift boss in two years. I could get you a job the same day you arrived at the mine.'

'How much does a supervisor earn?'

'A thousand, two thousand,' Sean assured him, and Alphonso was stunned. His Renamo pay was the equivalent of a rand a day, paid in Mozambique escudos.

'I would like to be a boss supervisor,' he murmured thoughtfully.

'Better than a Renamo sergeant?' Sean teased, and Alphonso chortled derisively.

'Of course, in South Africa you would not have the vote,' Sean ribbed him. 'Only pale faces get to vote.'

'Vote, what is a vote?' Alphonso demanded, and then answered himself. 'I don't have a vote in Mozambique. They don't have the vote in Zambia or Zimbabwe or Angola or Tanzania. Nobody has the vote in Africa, except perhaps once in a man's life to elect a president for life and a one-party government.' He shook his head and snorted. 'Vote? You can't eat a vote. You can't dress in a vote, or ride to work on it. For two thousand rand a month and a full belly you can have my vote.'

'Any time you come to South Africa, you come and see me.' Sean stretched and looked at the sky. He could see the trees against it. Dawn was only a short time away. He crushed out the butt of the cigarette and began to get to his feet.

'There is something I must tell you,' Alphonso whispered, and his altered tone caught Sean's full attention.

'Yes?' He squatted down again and leaned closer to the Shangane. Alphonso cleared his throat in embarrassment.

'We have travelled a long road together,' he murmured.

'A long hard road,' Sean agreed. 'But the end is in sight. This time tomorrow . . .' He did not have to go on and Alphonso did not reply immediately.

'We have fought side by side,' Alphonso said at last.

'Like lions,' Sean confirmed.

'I have called you *Baba* and *Nkosi Kakulu*.'

'You have honoured me thus,' Sean said formally. 'And I have called you friend.'

Alphonso nodded in the darkness. 'I cannot let you cross the Zimbabwe border,' he said with sudden decisiveness and Sean rocked back on his heels.

'Tell me why not.'

'You remember Cuthbert?' Alphonso asked, and it took Sean a moment to place the name.

'Cuthbert, you mean the one from Grand Reef air base. The one who helped us on the raid?' It all seemed so long ago.

'General China's nephew,' Alphonso nodded. 'That is the one I speak of.'

'Sammy Davis Junior.' Sean smiled. 'The cool laid-back cat. I remember him well.'

'General China spoke to him on the radio. This very morning from the laager of the *henshaw*, after our victory. I was in the outer room of the bunker. I heard everything he said.'

Sean felt a cold wind blow down his spine and the hair at the base of his skull prickled.

'What did China tell him?' he asked, dreading the reply.

'He ordered Cuthbert to let the Zimbabwean army know that it was you who led the raid on Grand Reef and stole the *indeki*

420

full of missiles. He told Cuthbert to tell them that you would be crossing back into Zimbabwe through the Honde Valley at St Mary's Mission, and they must wait for you there.'

Sean's gut knotted with shock and for long moments he was stunned by the enormity and cunning of the trap that China had prepared for him. The cruelty of it was diabolical. To allow them to believe that they were being set free, letting them taste the relief of crossing out of harm, when in fact, they were going to a fate even worse than China himself could have meted out to them.

The fury of the Zimbabwe high command would know no bounds. Sean was the holder of a Zimbabwe passport, a document of convenience but one which would make him a traitor and a murderer beyond any help from outside. He would be handed over to the notorious Zimbabwe Central Intelligence Organization and taken to the interrogation cells at Chikarubi prison, and he would never re-emerge from there alive. Job, despite his wounds, would share the same fate.

Even though Claudia was an American citizen, officially she no longer existed. It was weeks since she had been reported missing. By this time, interest in her case even at the United States embassies in Harare and Pretoria would have cooled. Along with her father, she was presumed dead and so she could expect no protection. She was as vulnerable as they were.

The trap was completely closed, there was no way out. The Renamo army behind them, Frelimo on either hand and the Zimbabwean CIO ahead of them. They were marooned in a devastated wasteland, doomed to be hunted down like wild animals or to slow starvation in the wilderness.

'Think!' Sean told himself. 'Find the way out.'

They could attempt to cross the Zimbabwe border at some other point than the Honde Valley, but the CIO would have the entire country alerted for them. There were permanent army blocks on every road. Without papers, they wouldn't get more than a few miles, and then there was Job, what would he do with Job? How could they transport a wounded man when every police and military post would be looking for somebody in a stretcher.

'We must go southwards,' Alphonso said. 'We must go to South Africa.'

'We?' Sean stared at him. 'You want to come with us?'

421

'I can't go back to General China,' he pointed out philosophically. 'Not after I have betrayed him. I will come with you to South Africa.'

'That's a trek of three hundred miles, through two opposed armies, Frelimo and the southern division of Renamo. And what about Job?'

'We will carry him,' Alphonso replied.

'Three hundred miles?'

'Then we will leave him behind.' Alphonso shrugged. 'He is only a Matabele and he is dying anyway, it will be no great loss.'

Sean caught the angry words that rose to his tongue and remained silent while he thought it out. Every way he twisted it and examined it he saw that Alphonso was right. To the north the dubious haven of Malawi was blocked by the waters of Cabora Bassa and by General China's division. To the east lay the Indian Ocean, and to the west the Zimbabwean CIO.

'All right,' Sean admitted reluctantly. 'South is the only way. Perhaps we can squeeze through between Frelimo and the southern division of Renamo. All we have to do is get across a heavily guarded railway line and the Limpopo river, and find enough to eat while we are doing it in a land that has been burned and devastated by ten years of civil war.'

'In South Africa, we will eat meat every day,' Alphonso pointed out cheerfully.

Sean stood up. 'Will your men follow you?'

'I will kill those that don't.' Alphonso was matter-of-fact. 'We can't let them go back to General China.'

'Right,' Sean agreed. 'And you will report on the radio schedule that I have crossed into Zimbabwe. We'll be able to string China along on the radio for four or five days. He won't realize that we have broken away southwards until we are well on our way and beyond his range. You had better talk to your men now. We'll have to turn south right away. Talk to them before they realize for themselves that we are up to something.'

Alphonso called in the sentries, and in the grey light of dawn the faces of the Shanganes were sober and intent as they squatted in a circle around him and listened to Alphonso describe to them the southern paradise to which he would lead them.

'We are all weary of fighting, of living like animals in the bush. It is time we learned to live like men, to find good wives to bear our sons.' He was filled with the fiery eloquence of the recent

422

convert and before he had finished Sean saw the sparkle of anticipation in most of their eyes and he felt a lift of relief. For the first time. he began to believe that the journey ahead might just be possible. with a great deal of endeavour and an even greater deal of luck.

He went to tell Claudia and Job what lay ahead. Claudia was bathing Job's face with a damp rag. 'He's much better. a good night's rest.' Then she broke off as she saw his face. Claudia's spirits visibly plummeted as he explained to them what they had to do.

'It was too good to be true.' she whispered. 'I knew deep down that it wouldn't be that easy. that General China wasn't Santa Claus in disguise.'

Job lay so still on his stretcher that Sean thought he had once again slipped over the edge of consciousness and he reached out to check his pulse. At his touch. Job opened his eyes.

'Can you trust those Shanganes?' he whispered.

'We don't have much choice.' Sean pointed out. and then went on briskly. 'We . . .'

'Leave me here.' Job's whisper was barely audible, but Sean's expression hardened and his voice was brittle with anger.

'Cut out that sort of bullshit.' he warned Job.

'Without me you might have a chance.' Job insisted. 'If you have to drag this stretcher . . .'

'We've got twelve hefty Shanganes,' Sean pointed out.

'Better some of you get through than all of us die. Leave me, Sean. Save Claudia and yourself.'

'I'm getting angry.' Sean stood up and said to Claudia, 'We leave in ten minutes.'

They travelled cautiously southwards all that day. It was an intense relief not to have to watch the sky for the Hind gunships, although out of habit the Shanganes occasionally turned their faces upward. The closer they drew to the railway line, the slower their progress became and they spent much of their time hiding in the dense wild ebony thickets and clumps of jesse until Matatu came ghosting back to assure them that the coast was clear and to lead them onwards.

In the late afternoon, Sean left the main party hiding in a bushy ravine and went forward with Matatu. He was gone for almost two hours and the sun was setting when he reappeared silently and suddenly at Claudia's side.

'You startled me!' she gasped. 'You're like a cat.'

'The railway line is only a mile ahead. The Frelimo guards seem to be in a state of confusion still. There is a lot of military traffic on the line, and a great deal of panicky activity all around. The crossing is going to be a trifle tricky. As soon as the moon comes up, I'll go up and take another look.'

While they waited for the moon, Alphonso rigged the radio aerial and made his scheduled contact with General China's headquarters.

'The dove is in flight.' He gave the prearranged code so that China would believe that Sean and his party had crossed the border. After a brief pause, presumably while he relayed the message, the radio operator came back to Alphonso with the order to return to the main base on the river. Alphonso acknowledged and signed off.

'They won't expect me to arrive back for another two days.' Alphonso grinned as he packed up the radio. 'It will be that long before they start getting suspicious.'

As the moon pushed its bald silver pate above the trees, Sean and Matatu slipped away into the forest to make a final reconnaissance of the railway line.

A mile south of their position they found the place where the line crossed a narrow stream. Although the stream contained only a few shallow puddles, the banks were thick with riverine bush which would afford them good cover. Originally the bush must have been cleared for a hundred yards on each side of the line, but secondary growth had been allowed to spring up to waist height.

'Sloppy Frelimo bastards,' Sean muttered. 'That will give us some cover, and we'll stay in the riverbed.'

The main line crossed the stream over an embankment and culvert. There was a guard post on the approaches, fifty yards uptrack from the culvert. While Sean watched through his binoculars, a Frelimo sentry with his AK rifle slung on his back sauntered down to the bridge over the culvert. He leaned on the guard rail and lit a cigarette. The glow of the cigarette marked his progress as he ambled back to the guard post. He seemed to Sean to be a little unsteady on his feet, and when he reached the guard post, a faint ripple of feminine giggles carried to where Sean and Matatu lay.

'They are having a party,' Sean chuckled.

'Palm wine and jig-jig,' Matatu agreed enviously, and in the moonlight held up his right hand with his thumb trapped between his first two fingers. 'I would like some of that myself.'

'You randy little bugger.' Sean tweaked his ear. 'When we get to Johannesburg, I'll stand you to the biggest, fattest lady we can flush out.' Matatu's taste in amour ran to the mountainous. 'Like Sherpa Tensing on Everest,' Sean often remarked.

The distractions with which the railway guards had provided themselves promised to make their crossing easier. Sean and Matatu withdrew quietly and started back to where they had left the rest of the party.

They had been gone for three hours and it was a few minutes before midnight, as they approached the camp. At the head of the ravine, Sean paused to give the recognition signal, the liquid warble of a fiery-necked nightjar. He didn't want to be shot by one of Alphonso's Shanganes. He waited a full minute for the reply, and when it did not come, he repeated the signal. Still there was silence and he felt the first tickle of alarm.

Instead of going straight in, they circled the ravine cautiously, and in the moonlight Matatu picked up unexpected spoor and squatted over it, frowning with alarm.

Sean whispered. 'Who? Which way?'

'Many men, our own Shanganes!' Matatu lifted his head and pointed to the north. 'They are going out, leaving camp.'

'Outgoing?' Sean was puzzled. 'Doesn't make sense, unless . . . ! Oh God! No!'

Swiftly, quietly, he closed in on the camp. The sentries he had set before he left were gone, their posts deserted. Sean felt panic rise in a wave that threatened to suffocate him.

'Claudia!' he whispered, suppressing the urge to shout her name aloud. He wanted to rush into the camp and find her, but he drew a series of deep breaths and fought back the panic.

He slipped the AKM on to fully automatic and went down on his belly, creeping in. The five Shanganes he had left asleep in the gut of the ravine were gone, all their equipment and their weapons had disappeared. He went on and made out the shape of Job's stretcher in the dappled moonlight; beside it, exactly as he had left her, Claudia's body wrapped in a blanket, but just beyond her another body lay sprawled. In the moonlight, he saw the sheen of wetness on the back of the man's head.

'Blood!'

Sean threw all caution aside and rushed to Claudia's body, dropping to his knees beside her and sweeping her into his arms.

She gasped and cried out, coming out of deep sleep, beginning to struggle in his arms, and then quieting as she realized who he was.

'Sean!' she blurted, still groggy with sleep. 'What is it? What happened?'

'Thank God,' he murmured fervently. 'I thought. . . !' He set her down gently, and reached across to where Job lay in the litter.

'Job, are you all right?' He shook him carefully, and Job stirred and murmured.

Sean jumped to his feet and went to where Alphonso lay. He touched his neck. The skin was warm, his pulse strong and even.

'Claudia!' he called. 'Bring the flashlight.'

In the beam of the flashlight, he examined the laceration in Alphonso's scalp.

'A nice little ding,' he grunted; although the bleeding had staunched spontaneously, he pressed a field dressing over it and bound it in place. 'Good thing they hit him on the head, or they might have done some serious damage.' He grinned wryly at his own joke.

'What happened, Sean?' Claudia demanded anxiously. 'I was fast asleep, I didn't hear a thing.'

'Lucky for you,' Sean tied the tag ends of the bandage, 'or you might have got the same treatment.'

'What happened, where are the others?'

'Gone,' he told her. 'Flown, deserted. They obviously didn't fancy the walk or the destination. They bashed Alphonso on the noggin and took off back to General China.'

She stared at him. 'You mean there are only the four of us now? All the Shanganes except Alphonso have gone?'

'That's right,' Sean agreed and Alphonso groaned and reached up to touch his bandaged head. Sean helped him sit up.

'Sean!' Claudia tugged at his arm and he turned back to her. 'What are we going to do?' Sean glanced across at Job's stretcher. 'What are we going to do with Job? How are we going to carry him? How are we going to get out of here now?'

'That, my love, is an extremely interesting question,' Sean agreed grimly. 'All I can tell you is that by this time tomorrow, our old pal General China is going to know that we are on the

426

run, and he's going to know exactly where we are headed.'

She stared at him aghast. 'What are we going to do?'

'We don't seem to have much choice,' he said. 'There is only one road still open to us – we keep on the way we are going.'

He hauled Alphonso to his feet.

'That's impossible,' Claudia whispered anxiously. 'Two of you cannot carry the stretcher.'

'You're right, of course. We'll have to make some other arrangement.'

Between them, they lifted Job out of the stretcher and laid him on Claudia's blanket, then, while the others watched, Sean began to dismantle the fibreglass stretcher. Before he had finished, Matatu appeared silently out of the darkness and whispered a brief report to Sean.

Sean barely looked up as he told Alphonso, 'You taught them well. Your Shanganes have bomb-shelled, taken off in eleven different directions. If we followed we might catch one or two of them, but some of them are going to get back to China with the good news.'

Alphonso cursed the deserters bitterly, while Sean explained to Claudia and Job.

'I'm going to use the nylon webbing from the stretcher to improvise a sling seat.'

Claudia looked dubious. 'Job isn't strong enough to sit upright. The movement will reopen his wound, the bleeding . . .' She broke off as Sean glared at her.

'Can you think of a better way?' he snarled, and she shook her head.

Sean doubled the length of heavy green canvas and took the rifle slings from his AKM and Alphonso's AK to make carrying loops.

'We'll have to make adjustments as we go along,' he grunted, and then looked at Claudia. 'Instead of finding difficulties, make yourself useful by gathering all the equipment the Shanganes left. We'll have to make a selection.'

He picked out the equipment swiftly, discarding all but the most vital pieces. 'Alphonso and I will be carrying Job between us. On top of that we'll only be able to manage our basic weapons and a blanket each. Claudia and Matatu must lug the medical pack, the water bottles and a blanket each. Everything else will be left behind.'

427

'The canned food?' Claudia asked.

'Forget it,' Sean told her brusquely, and set about apportioning their loads. He cut everything down to the barest minimum, knowing that every pound of weight now would seem like ten after the first few miles. He even made Alphonso abandon his AK rifle and gave him the pistol that he had taken from the Russian pilot to replace it. He restricted himself to two spare clips of ammunition for his own AKM and he and Alphonso retained only a pair of grenades each, one fragmentation and the other phosphorus.

The abandoned equipment they piled in the bottom of the ravine and covered with loose earth and branches to conceal it from casual discovery by a Frelimo patrol.

'Okay, lad,' Sean told Job. 'Time to go.' He glanced at his wristwatch and found it was a little before three o'clock. They were well behind schedule and they only had a few hours of darkness left in which to make the crossing.

He knelt beside Job and eased him up into a sitting position, then restrapped his injured arm firmly against his chest.

'This is the bad part,' he warned him, and between them he and Alphonso lifted Job to his feet. Job endured the movement in stoic silence, and stood supported between them.

Sean and Alphonso adjusted the nylon sling seat over their outer shoulders. They lifted Job into it, and he sat with his feet dangling, his good arm draped around Sean's shoulder while Sean and Alphonso linked their arms behind his back to support him.

'Ready?' Sean asked, and Job grunted softly, trying to conceal the pain that every movement caused him.

'If you think it's bad now . . .' Sean warned him cheerfully, 'just give it a couple of hours!'

They started down the ravine towards the railway line. They moved slowly, accustoming themselves to this awkward form of travel, trying to cushion Job between them, but they stumbled over the broken ground and Job swung on his seat and bumped against them. He made no sound, but Sean heard his ragged breathing close to his ear and when the pain stabbed him especially cruelly, he unconsciously dug his fingers into Sean's shoulder.

Slowly they moved down the shallow stream bed towards the culvert beneath the railway line. Matatu was a hundred yards ahead of them, just visible in the moonlight. Once he signalled them to halt and then after a few minutes beckoned them to come on. Claudia trailed fifty paces behind them so that she would have a start if they were discovered and forced to run back.

Carrying Job between them, it was not possible for Sean and Alphonso to move silently. Once they splashed into one of the muddy pools of the stream and they sounded like a herd of cavorting hippos in the silence.

Matatu had reached the culvert ahead of them and he signalled them frantically to hurry. They staggered forward under Job's weight and were in the open, when on the embankment above them, there was the sudden crunch of footsteps in the gravel ballast and the sound of voices.

Trying to keep low, they kept going at a clumsy run. They reached the culvert and carried Job into the dark concrete tunnel. Claudia was running doubled over only a few yards behind them and Sean reached back with his free hand and dragged her in out of the pale moonlight into the blessed darkness of the culvert.

They leaned against the concrete wall, stooped below the curved roof, trying to quiet their breathing, all of them panting wildly from that charge through the mud and sand of the stream bottom.

The footsteps and the voices above them grew louder and finally stopped almost directly overhead. It sounded like a man and a woman. The Frelimo garrison had either brought their own camp-followers with them, or had found lady friends in the refugee camps that had sprung up along the guarded railway line.

There was a spirited argument going on out there, the man's voice slurred with drink and the woman's shrill and shrewish as she protested and haggled. At last, they heard the man's voice raised in exasperation.

'Dollar *shumi*, ten dollars,' he said, and immediately the woman's voice softened and cooed agreement.

Then there was the sound of feet sliding in gravel and a few pebbles rattled down the embankment in the stream bed.

'They are coming down here!' Claudia breathed in horror, and they instinctively drew back deeper into the dark culvert.

'Quiet!' Sean whispered, and stooped to ease Job out of the canvas sling and prop him against the wall of the culvert.

As he drew the trench knife from the sheath on his webbing two figures appeared in the mouth of the culvert, silhouetted by the moonlight.

They were clinging together and laughing softly, the woman half supporting the man as they staggered forward. Sean gripped the knife underhand, the point of the blade belly high, ready to receive them, but they advanced only a few paces into the intimate darkness of the tunnel and then turned to face each other still giggling and whispering, both of them outlined against the moonlit exterior.

The Frelimo sentry pushed the woman against the wall and propped his rifle beside her while he fumbled to open his own clothing. The woman leaned back against the wall and with a practised gesture lifted the front of her skirt above her waist. Laughing and muttering drunkenly the sentry reeled against her and she used one hand to steady and guide him, the other still holding up her skirt.

If Claudia had reached out a hand she could have touched the couple, but they were locked together oblivious of all around them. The man began to push against her, his voice rising as he exhorted himself to greater effort, his movements becoming more frenzied. The woman clucked like a rider urging a mount forward and the Frelimo went from a canter to full gallop, pounding away with abandon.

Suddenly the man threw his head back, stiffening into rigidity, and crowed like an asthmatic rooster. Slowly he drooped and the woman laughed and pushed him away briskly. Still laughing, she smoothed down her skirt and seized the man's arm. The two of them staggered out into the sandy riverbed and disappeared round the corner of the culvert. The sounds of their scrambled ascent of the embankment dwindled and Sean slid the knife back into its sheath on his belt and said softly, 'That's what we call a tumble in the jungle!'

Claudia giggled with nervous relief. 'Two seconds flat, that just has to be a new world record,' she whispered, and Sean hugged her briefly.

'Shall we also be friends?' he whispered. 'Sorry I snarled at you.'

'I was being a dismal Jane, I deserved it. You won't have any more moaning and whining from me.'

'Stay close.' He turned back to grope for Job and found that he had slid weakly down the wall and was sitting on the sandy floor of the culvert.

As he stooped to help him to his feet, Sean's fingers touched his shoulder. The bandage was damp and his smile faded. The bleeding had started again.

'Nothing we can do about it now,' he thought, and gently eased Job to his feet.

'How are you doing, old son?'

'No worries.' Job's whisper was scratchy and faint.

Sean touched Matatu's shoulder and he obeyed the unspoken command, instantly creeping out the far side of the culvert and disappearing into the scrub on the stream bank.

A few minutes later the soft whistle of a night bird carried to them as Matatu gave the all clear. Sean sent Claudia ahead and gave her a full five minutes to get across the open ground of the cut line.

'Let's go.' Sean looked up from the luminous dial of his Rolex and they lifted Job into the sling seat and started forward into the moonlight.

The next hundred paces seemed like the slowest and longest Sean had ever covered, but at last they were into the forest beyond the cut line, and Claudia was waiting for them there.

'We've made it!' she whispered joyfully.

'We sure have, the first mile was a romp, only three hundred more to go,' he answered grimly, and they kept going.

Counting their paces against the second hand of his wristwatch, Sean estimated that they were averaging two miles an hour. Ahead of them, Matatu selected the easiest going. He was always out of sight in the forest ahead, only his soft bird calls guided them. At intervals Sean checked their heading against the stars, catching glimpses of the Southern Cross and its brilliant pair of pointers through the forest canopy ahead of them.

When the dawn paled out the stars, they stopped once again and Sean allowed them to drink for the first time, two swallows each from one of the water-bottles that Claudia carried. Then he turned his attention to Job's shoulder. The dressing was soaked with fresh blood and Job's face was grey as the ashes of a cold camp-fire. His eyes had sunk into dark sockets and his lips were dry and cracked, his breath whistling softly through them. The pain and loss of blood was taking a dreadful toll.

Gently Sean unwound the bandage and then he and Claudia

exchanged a quick glance. The destruction of tissue was horrifying and the field dressing was caked into the wound cavity. Sean realized that if he tried to remove it, he would tear the flesh to which it had adhered and probably restart the bleeding. He leaned forward and sniffed the wound, while Job grinned at him, a skull-like twitching back of the lips.

'Steak tartare?' he asked weakly.

'All it needs is a little garlic,' Sean grinned back at him, but he had caught the first sickly whiff of corruption. He squeezed another half tube of iodine paste over the original field dressing and then stripped the plastic packaging from a fresh dressing and placed it over the wound.

Claudia held it in place as he rewrapped it with a new bandage from the medical pack. He rolled the blood-soaked bandage and stuffed it into a side pocket. He would wash it out at the first water that they came to.

'We must keep going,' he told Job. 'We've got to get well clear of the railway line. Are you up to it?'

Job nodded, but Sean could see the dread in his eyes. Every step they moved him was an agony.

'I'm going to give you another shot of antibiotic –I can give you a jolt of morphine at the same time?'

Job shook his head. 'Keep it for.when it gets really bad.' He grinned again, a grimace that tugged at Sean's heart. He could not meet Job's eyes. 'Show us your best side,' he said, and made a performance of pulling down the trousers of Job's battledress and darting the hypodermic needle into one of his glossy black buttocks. Claudia averted her gaze modestly and Job whispered, 'It's okay, Claudia, you are allowed to look. Just don't touch, that's all.'

'You're as bad as Sean,' she said primly. 'Downright vulgar, both of you.'

They lifted Job back into the nylon sling seat and went on. By mid-morning the mirage shimmered and rose in glassy whirlpools from the rocky kopjes over which they were trekking, and the tiny mopane flies hovered in a fine mist around their heads, crawling into their nostrils and ears and eyes with infuriating persistence. With the heat came the thirst, and their sweat dried on their shirts and left irregular outlines in white salt on the cloth.

When they stopped at noon in the sparse dappled shade of an African teak, Sean knew they had all had enough and the worst heat of the day was still to come. They laid Job on a hastily cut mattress of dried grass and he lapsed almost immediately into a state that was more coma than sleep, and snored softly through his dry swollen lips.

The carrying sling had rubbed the skin from both Sean's shoulders, for he and Alphonso had changed sides at each of the hourly stops. The harsh nylon straps had galled Alphonso as badly and he muttered sullenly as he examined his injuries.

'Before this, I hated the Matabele simply because they are a flea-infested, thieving bunch of venereal apes. Now I have another reason to hate them.'

Sean tossed him the tube of iodine paste. 'Smear the *muti* on your grievous injuries, then stuff the empty tube in your garrulous mouth,' he advised, and Alphonso went off still muttering to find a place to lie down.

Sean and Claudia found a hollow screened by a low hook-thorn bush a short distance from where Job lay and Sean spread their blankets to make a nest for them.

He settled into it thankfully. 'I'm bushed.'

'How bushed?' Claudia asked, and knelt over him to nibble his ear.

'Not that bushed,' he qualified, and pulled her down beside him.

At sunset, Sean cooked a pot of maize-meal porridge on a tiny smokeless fire while Alphonso rigged the aerial and tuned the radio to the Renamo command frequency. There was a clutter of garbled broken-up traffic on their wavelength, probably Frelimo transmissions, but at last they heard their call sign through the jumble.

'*N'gulube*! Warthog! Come in, *N'gulube*! This is Banana Tree.'

Alphonso acknowledged and then made a fictitious position report that placed them still far north of the railway line, on a march back to the river area. Banana Tree acknowledged and signed off.

'They fell for it,' Sean gave his opinion. 'Looks like the Shangane deserters haven't reached base and blown the whistle on us, not yet anyway.'

In the last of the daylight, they ate the meal of maize porridge and Sean studied his field map and marked in his dead reckoning position. According to the map, the hilly ground seemed to extend for another thirty miles or so, and then descended gently to a more level plain on which a number of small villages and cultivated lands were marked; beyond that was the first natural barrier, another wide river that ran west to east directly across their route.

He called Alphonso across and asked him, 'The southern division of Renamo under General Tippoo Tip, do you know where his area begins, where his main forces are deployed?'

'Like us, they move all the time to confuse Frelimo. Sometimes they are here, other times down here near the Rio Save.' He shrugged. 'Renamo is wherever the fighting is.'

'And Frelimo? Where are they?'

'They chase after Renamo, and then run like frightened rabbits when they catch them,' he guffawed. 'To us now, it doesn't matter who is who and where they are. Everybody we meet down here is going to try and kill us.'

'Great intelligence report,' Sean thanked him, and folded the map into its plastic wallet.

Quickly they finished the frugal meal and Sean stood up.

'All right, Alphonso. Let's get Job up and moving.'

Alphonso belched softly then grinned wickedly. 'He's your Matabele dog. If you want him, you carry him, I've had enough.'

Sean hid his dismay behind a neutral expression.

'You are wasting time,' he said softly. 'Get on your feet!' And Alphonso belched again and held his eyes, still grinning.

Slowly Sean reached down to the trench knife in its sheath and just as deliberately Alphonso reached and touched the Tokarev pistol tucked into his belt. They stared at each other.

'Sean, what is it?' Claudia asked anxiously. 'What is going on?' She had not understood the exchange in Shangane, but the tension was palpable.

'He's refusing to help me carry Job,' he replied.

'You can't carry him alone, can you?' Claudia said anxiously. 'Alphonso *will* help –'

'– or I'll kill him!' Sean replied in Shangane and Alphonso laughed out loud. He stood up and shook himself like a dog, turned his back on Sean, picked up his radio pack, Sean's AKM rifle and most of the water-bottles.

'I'll carry these,' he chuckled, shaking his head at the joke. 'You can carry your Matabele.' He ambled away southwards along the line of march.

Sean dropped his hand from the hilt of the knife and looked

434

across at Job. He was watching quietly from his mattress of grass and Sean snarled at him, 'If you say it, I'll kick your black arse for you.'

'I didn't say nothing.' Job tried to smile, but it was a weak and transient grimace.

'Good,' said Sean grimly, and picked up the nylon sling seat and straps.

'Claudia, give us a hand here.'

Between them, they got Job on his feet and Sean rigged the nylon slings around his waist and under his crotch like a parachute harness, and looped them over his own shoulders. Then he supported Job with an arm around the waist.

'One more river, there's one more river to cross,' he sang hoarsely and untunefully, and grinned at Job. They moved forward. Although Job's feet touched the ground and he tried to take as much of his own weight as possible, he was mainly supported by the straps that crossed over Sean's shoulders and they were locked together like a pair in a harness.

Within the first hundred paces they had established some sort of rhythm, but still their progress was unsteady and painfully slow, set by Job's uncertain footsteps. There could be no attempt at stealth or anti-tracking for Sean had to pick the easiest and most obvious route. They stuck to the open game trails, that complex network that like the veins in a dried leaf meshes the African veld.

Behind them Claudia followed laden with the medical pack and the rest of the water-bottles, but still she carried a leafy branch with which she tried to sweep their tracks. Her efforts might conceal their passing from a casual observer, but a Frelimo tracker would follow them as though he were on the M1 motorway. It was hardly worth the effort, but Sean did not discourage her, he knew how important it was to her to feel that she was pulling her weight and making a useful contribution to their escape.

Sean counted their paces against the second hand of his wristwatch and estimated that they were down to less than a mile an hour, eight miles a day was all the progress they could hope for, and he started to divide that into three hundred but gave up before he reached the depressing answer.

Both Matatu and Alphonso had disappeared into the combretum forest ahead of them and Sean glanced at his watch again.

435

They had only been going a little over thirty minutes, but already their momentum was winding down. Job's weight was heavier, the straps cutting painfully into the flesh of Sean's shoulders, and Job's footsteps were dragging and catching on every irregularity of the game path.

'I'm cutting down to thirty-minute stages,' he told Job. 'We'll take five minutes now.'

When Sean lowered him to a sitting position against the bole of a tree, Job leant his head back against the rough bark and closed his eyes. His breathing sobbed in his chest, and droplets of sweat made slow runnels down his cheeks. Like tiny black pearls, the drops reflected the colour of his skin.

Sean let the five minutes run over to ten and then told Job cheerfully, 'On your feet, soldier, let's eat some ground.'

Getting Job up on his feet again was torture for both of them and Sean realized that trying to be gentle on him, he had allowed Job to rest too long. The wound had begun to stiffen.

The next thirty-minute stage endured so long that Sean was convinced that his watch had stopped. He had to check the sweep of the second hand to reassure himself.

When at last, he lowered him to a sitting position, Job grimaced. 'Sorry, Sean, cramps. Left calf.'

Sean squatted in front of him and felt the knots of tortured muscle in Job's leg. While he massaged it, he spoke quietly to Claudia. 'There are salt tablets in the medic pack, front pocket.'

Job swallowed them and Claudia held the water-bottle to his lips. After two swallows, he pushed it away.

'More,' Claudia urged him, but he shook his head.

'Don't waste it,' he murmured.

'How's that feel?' Sean gave his calf a couple of hard slaps.

'Good for another few miles.'

'Let's go,' Sean said. 'Before it seizes up again.'

It amazed Claudia how the two of them kept going through the night with only those five-minute breaks and the frugal draughts from the water-bottles.

'Three hundred miles of this,' she thought. 'It simply is not possible. Flesh and blood can't take it. It will kill both of them.'

A little before dawn, Matatu popped up like a small black shadow out of the forest and whispered to Sean.

'He has found a waterhole about two or three miles ahead,' Sean told them. 'Can you make it, Job?'

The sun had risen and cleared the tops of the trees and the day's heat was building up like a stoked furnace. When Job collapsed and hung suspended at Sean's side, dangling with his full weight on the cross straps, they were still half a mile from the waterhole.

Sean lowered him to the ground and sat beside him. He was so exhausted himself that, for a few minutes, he could not find the energy to talk or move.

'Well, at least you picked a good place to pass out,' he congratulated Job in a hoarse whisper. They were in a patch of thick thorn bush that would give them shade and cover for the rest of the day.

They made a bed of cut grass for Job in the shade and settled him on it. He was only half conscious, his speech slurred and wandering, and his eyes continually slipping out of focus. Claudia tried to feed him, but he turned his face away. However, he drank thirstily when at last Matatu and Alphonso returned from the waterhole with all the water-bottles refilled. After he had drunk, Job lapsed back into coma and they waited out the heat of the day in the thorn patch.

Sean and Claudia lay in each other's arms, she had become so accustomed to falling asleep in his embrace. She realized that Sean was near the end of his tether. She had never imagined that he could be so finely stretched, that even his strength which she had come to believe was inexhaustible had a limit upon it.

When she woke a little after noon, he lay like a dead man beside her and she studied his face lovingly, almost greedily. His beard was full and beginning to curl and she picked out two curly silver hairs in the dense bush. His features were gaunt, all trace of fat and superfluous flesh burned away and there were lines and weathered creases in his skin that she had never noticed before. She studied them as though his life history were chiselled into them like cuneiform writing on a tablet that she could read. 'God, but I love him,' she thought, amazed at the depth of her own feelings. His skin was burned to the colour of dark mahogany by the sun, and yet it retained a lustre like that of fine leather, well used but polished with care over the years, 'like Papa's polo boots'. She smiled at the simile, but it was somehow apt. She had watched her father in his dressing-room lovingly applying dubbin to the leather with his fingers and polishing it to a dull glow with his own bare palm.

'Boots!' she whispered. 'That's a good name for you,' she told Sean as he slept, and she remembered how her father's boots had flexed and wrinkled at the ankle, almost as supple as silk as he stepped up into the stirrup. 'Wrinkled just like you, my old boot.' She smiled and kissed the lines in his forehead so softly as not to wake him.

She realized then to just what extent the memory of her father had been absorbed in this man who lay for once like a child in her arms. The two men seemed to have merged in one body, and she could concentrate all her love in a single place. Gently she moved Sean's sleeping head until it nestled against her shoulder, and she burrowed her fingers into the dense springing curls at the back of his head and rocked him gently.

Up until this moment, he had succeeded in evoking the full spectrum of her emotions, from anger to sensual passion, everything except tenderness. Now, however, it was complete. 'My baby,' she whispered, as tenderly as a mother. For once she truly felt that he belonged to her completely.

A soft groan shattered her fragile mood, and she raised her head and glanced across at where Job lay beneath the thorn bush nearby, but he relapsed into silence once again.

She thought about the two of them, Job and Sean and their special masculine relationship in which she knew she could never share. She should have been jealous, but instead in some strange way, it made her feel more secure. If Sean could be so constant and self-sacrificing in his love for another man, then she hoped that she could expect the same constancy from him in their own different but even more intense relationship.

Job groaned again and began to thrash about restlessly. She sighed and then gently disentangled herself from Sean's sleeping form, stood up and crossed to where Job lay.

A cloud of metallic-green flies buzzed around the blood-soaked bandage that covered his shoulder. They settled on the soiled dressing and tasted it with their long proboscises, then rubbed their front legs together with delight. Claudia saw that they had laid their rice-grain eggs in thick rafts on the bloody cloth, and with an exclamation of disgust, she fanned them away, and then scraped the loathsome white eggs from the folds of the bandage.

Job opened his eyes and looked up at her. She realized that he was fully conscious once again and she smiled encouragingly at him. 'Would you like another drink?'

'No.' His voice was so low that she had to lean closer to him. 'You have to make him do it,' he said.

'Who? Sean?' she asked, and Job nodded.

'He can't go on like this. He's killing himself. Without him, none of you will survive. You must make him leave me here.' She had begun to shake her head before he stopped speaking.

'No,' she said firmly. 'He would never do it, and I wouldn't let him, even if he wanted to. We are in this together, pardner.' She touched his arm. 'Now, how about that drink?' He subsided, too weak to argue further. Like Sean, Job also seemed to have deteriorated alarmingly in the last few hours. She sat beside him fanning the flies away with an ilala palm frond while the sun slid slowly down the western sky.

In the cool of the afternoon Sean stirred and sat up, instantly wide awake, taking in his surroundings with a quick glance. Sleep revived and fortified him.

'How is he?' he asked, and when she shook her head, he came to squat beside her.

'We'll have to get him up again pretty soon.'

'Give him a few more minutes,' she pleaded, and then went on. 'Do you know what I've been thinking about while I've been sitting here?'

'Tell me,' he invited, and put his arm around her shoulders.

'I've been thinking about that waterhole out there. I've been fantasizing about pouring water over myself, washing my clothes, getting rid of this stink.'

'Have you heard about Napoleon?' he asked.

'Napoleon?' She looked puzzled. 'What does he have to do with bathing?'

'Whenever he returned from a campaign, he would send a galloper ahead of him to Josephine with the message, "*Je rentre, ne te lave pas.*" "I'm coming home, don't bathe." You see he liked his ladies the way he liked his cheese, full bodied. He would have loved you the way you are now! '

'You're disgusting.' She punched his shoulder, and Job groaned.

'Hey, there.' Sean turned his attention to him. 'What's going down, man?'

'I'll take you up on your offer now,' Job whispered.

'Morphine?' Sean asked, and Job nodded.

'Just a little shot, okay?'

439

'You've got it,' Sean agreed, and reached for the medical pack.

After the injection, Job lay with his eyes closed and they watched the taut lines of pain around his mouth slowly relax.

'Better?' Sean asked, and Job smiled softly without opening his eyes. 'We'll give you a few minutes more,' Sean told him. 'While we make the radio sched. with Banana Tree.'

Sean stood up and went across to where Alphonso was already rigging the radio aerial.

'*N'gulube*, this is Banana Tree.' The response to Alphonso's first call was so strong and clear that Sean started.

Alphonso adjusted the gain and then thumbed the microphone and gave another fictitious position report, as though he were still on the return march to the river area.

There was a pause, filled only by the drone and crackle of static, and then another voice equally clear and loud. 'Let me speak to Colonel Courtney!' The intonation was unmistakable and Alphonso looked up at Sean.

'General China,' he whispered, and he offered Sean the microphone but Sean pushed it aside and frowned with concentration as he waited for the next transmission.,

In the silence that followed, Claudia left Job's side and crossed quickly to Sean. She squatted beside him and he placed his arm around her protectively; they both stared at the radio.

'The deserters,' she said softly. 'China knows.'

'Listen!' Sean cautioned. They waited.

'Very well.' China's voice again. 'I can understand that you do not wish to reply. However, I will presume that you are listening, Colonel.'

All their attention was on the radio, and Job opened his eyes. He had heard every word that China spoke quite clearly and rolled his head. Alphonso had left his pack and webbing piled on his blanket not ten paces from where Job lay. The butt of the Tokarev pistol protruded from the side pocket of the pack.

'You have yet to disappoint me, Colonel.' China's voice was mellow and affable. 'It would have been too simple and totally unsatisfying if you had merely blundered into the arms of the reception committee I had arranged for you at the Zimbabwean border.'

Job eased himself up on his good elbow. There was no pain, merely a sensation of weakness and drowsiness. The morphine was working. It was difficult to think clearly. He focused all his attention on the pistol, and he wondered if Alphonso had chambered a round. He began to move towards it extending his legs, digging in his heels, then lifting his buttocks clear and jack-knifing his legs. He made no sound and the others were all concentrating on the voice from the radio.

'So the game is still on, Colonel, or should we rather call it the hunt? You are a great hunter, a great white hunter. You glory in the pursuit of wild animals. You call it sport, and you pride yourself on what you term "fair chase".'

Job was halfway across the clearing. There was still no pain, and he moved a little quicker. At any moment, one of them might turn their head and see him.

'I have never understood your white man's passion for this pursuit. To me it always seemed so pointless. My people have always believed that if you want meat, you should kill it as efficiently and with as little effort as possible.'

Job reached the pile of equipment on Alphonso's blanket and stretched out to touch the hilt of the pistol. However, when he tried to withdraw it from the pocket, his fingertips were numb and it slipped from his hand; but instead of clattering on the hard earth, the pistol dropped soundlessly onto a fold of the blanket and he saw with a rush of relief that the action was cocked and the safety-catch engaged. Alphonso had loaded it, ready for instant use.

Behind him, China's voice still echoed from the radio set, 'Perhaps you have corrupted me, Colonel. Perhaps I am acquiring your decadent European ways, but for the first time, I understand your passion. Perhaps it is simply that at last the game is big enough to excite me. I wonder how you must feel at this change of role, Colonel. You are the game and I am the hunter. I know where you are, but you don't know where I am. Perhaps, I am closer than you believe possible. Where am I, Colonel? You must guess. You must run and hide. When will we meet, and how?'

Job settled his fingers carefully around the butt of the Tokarev. He lifted it and was surprised by the effort it required. He placed his thumb upon the slide of the safety-catch, and it would not budge. He felt panic rising in him. His hand was too weak and numb to move the slide forward into the firing position.

'I do not promise you "fair chase", Colonel. I will hunt you in my own African way, but it will be good sport. I promise you that at least.'

Job exerted all his strength and felt the slide of the safety-catch begin to move under his thumb.

'The time is now 1800 hours Zulu. I will call you on this frequency at the same time tomorrow, Colonel. That is if we have not already met. Until then watch the sky, Colonel Courtney, look behind you. You do not know from which direction I will come. But be sure, I will come!'

There was a faint click as China unkeyed his microphone and Sean reached over and switched off the radio set to conserve the battery. None of them spoke or moved, until another sharper metallic click broke the silence. To Sean the sound was unmistakable, the sound of a safety-catch being disengaged and he reacted instinctively, pushing Claudia flat and whirling round to face it.

For a moment, he was paralysed and then he screamed, 'No! Job, for Christ's sake! No!!' and hurled himself forward, like a sprinter from the blocks.

Job was lying on his side facing Sean, but well beyond his reach. Sean drove himself across the space that separated them, but he seemed to be wading through honey, sticky and slow, it impeded his movements. He watched Job raise the pistol, and he tried to prevent him by the force of his gaze. They were looking into each other's eyes, Sean trying to dominate and command him, but Job's eyes were sad, filled with a deep regret and yet unwavering.

Sean saw him open his lips and heard the muzzle of the pistol click against his teeth as Job thrust it deeply into his own mouth and closed his lips around the muzzle, like a child sucking a frozen lollipop. Sean reached out desperately, straining with all his strength to reach Job's pistol hand and rip the stubby black barrel out of his mouth. His fingertips had only touched Job's wrist when the pistol fired.

The sound was muffled, damped down by the flesh and bone of Job's skull.

In his extremity of effort, Sean's vision was enhanced to unnatural clarity and it seemed that time had been suspended so that everything happened very slowly, like a movie reel run at half speed.

Job's head altered shape, it swelled before Sean's eyes, like a rubber hallowe'en mask filled with high-pressure gas. His eyelids flew wide open and for an instant his eyeballs bulged from their sockets exposing a wide rim of white around their dark iris and then rolling upwards into his skull.

His shattered head changed shape again, elongating backwards, stretching his skin tightly over his cheekbones, and flattening his nostrils as the bullet drew the contents of his skull out through the back of his head, whiplashing his neck to its full stretch so that even in the aftermath of the shot, Sean heard the vertebrae creak and click.

Job was jerked backwards, his arm flung away from his head in a debonair salute with the Tokarev pistol still gripped in his clenched fist, but Sean was quick enough to catch him before his mutilated head hit the hard earth.

He caught Job in his arms and held him to his chest with all his strength. His body was heavy and hot with fever, but slack and plastic as though it contained no bone. It seemed to overflow Sean's enfolding arms, and he held him hard. He felt Job's muscles shiver and shudder, and his legs kicked in a macabre little jigging movement and he tried to hold him still.

'Job,' he whispered, and reached up behind him and cupped his hand over the back of his head, covering the terrible exit wound, as though he were trying to hold it together, to press the spilled contents back into the ruptured skull.

'You fool,' he whispered. 'You shouldn't have done it.' He laid his own cheek against Job's, and held him like a lover.

'We would have made it. I would have got you out.' Still hugging Job's quiescent body, he began to rock him gently, murmuring to him softly, pressing his cheek to Job's, his eyes closed tightly.

'We have come so far together, it wasn't fair to end it here.'

Claudia came to them and went down on one knee beside Sean. She reached out to touch his shoulder and searched desperately for something to say, but there were no words, and she stopped her hand before she touched him. Sean was oblivious of her and everything else around him.

His grief was so terrible to see that she felt she should not watch it. It was too private, too vulnerable, and yet she could not tear her eyes from his face. Her own feelings were overshadowed entirely by the magnitude of Sean's sorrow. She had developed a deep affection for Job, but it was as nothing compared to the love that she now saw laid naked before her.

It was as though that pistol shot had destroyed a part of Sean himself, and she experienced no sense of shock or surprise when he began to weep. Still holding Job in his arms, Sean felt the last involuntary tremors of dying nerves and muscle grow still and the first chill of death sap the heat from this body he hugged so tightly to his chest.

The tears seemed to well up from very deep inside of Sean and they came up painfully, burning all the way, scalding his eyelids when at last they forced their way between them and rolled slowly down his darkly weathered cheeks into his beard.

Even Alphonso could not watch it. He stood up and walked away into the thorn scrub, but Claudia could not move. She went on kneeling beside Sean, and her own tears rose in sympathy with his. Together they wept for Job.

Matatu had heard the shot from a mile out where he was guarding their rear, lying up on their back-spoor to watch for a following patrol.

He came in quickly and from the bush at the perimeter of the camp watched for only a few seconds before he deduced exactly what had happened. Then he crept in quietly and crouched behind Sean. Like Claudia, he respected Sean's mourning, waiting for him to master its first unbearably bitter pangs.

Sean spoke at last, without looking round, without opening his eyes.

'Matatu,' he said.

'*Ndio, Bwana.*'

'Go and find the burial place. We have neither tools nor time to dig a grave, yet he is a Matabele and he must be buried sitting up facing the direction of the rising sun.'

'*Ndio, Bwana.*' Matatu slipped away into the darkling forest and at last Sean opened his eyes and laid Job gently back upon the grey wool blanket. His voice was steady, almost conversational.

'Traditionally we should bury him in the centre of his own cattle kraal.' He wiped the tears from his cheeks with the back of his hand, and went on quietly, 'But we are wanderers, Job and I, he had no kraal nor cattle to call his own.'

She was not certain that Sean was speaking to her, but she replied, 'The wild game were his cattle, and the wilderness his kraal. He will be content here.'

Sean nodded, still without looking at her. 'I am grateful that you understand.'

444

He reached down and closed Job's eyelids. His face was undamaged except for the chips from his front teeth, and with a fold of the blanket, Sean wiped the blood from the corner of his mouth. Now he looked peaceful and at rest. Sean rolled him on his side and began to wrap him in the blanket, using the nylon webbing and the rifle slings to bind his body tightly into a sitting position, with his knees up under his chin.

Matatu returned before he had finished. 'I have found a good place,' he said, and Sean nodded without looking up from his task.

Claudia broke the silence. 'He gave his life for us,' she said quietly. 'Greater love hath no man.' It sounded so trite and unworthy of the moment, that she wished she had not said it, but Sean nodded again.

'I was never able to square the account with him,' he said. 'And now I never will.'

He was finished. Job was trussed securely into the grey blanket, only his head was exposed.

Sean stood up and went to his own small personal pack. He took out the only spare shirt it contained and came back to where Job lay. He knelt beside him again.

'Goodbye, my brother. It was a good road we travelled. I only wish we could have reached the end of it together,' he said softly, and leaned forward and kissed Job's forehead. He did it so unaffectedly that it seemed completely natural and right.

Then with the clean shirt, he wrapped Job's head, hiding the ghastly wound, and he picked him up in his arms and walked with him into the forest, cradling Job's head against his shoulder.

Matatu led him to an abandoned ant-bear hole in the thorn forest nearby. It was the work of a few minutes to enlarge the entrance just enough to slide Job's body down into it. With Matatu assisting him, Sean turned him until he was facing east, with his back to the evening star.

Before they covered the grave, Sean knelt beside it and took the fragmentation grenade from the pocket on his webbing. Matatu and Claudia watched as he cautiously rigged a booby trap with the grenade and a short length of bark twine. As he stood up, Claudia looked at him enquiringly, and he answered her shortly, 'Grave robbers.'

Matatu helped him pack stones around Job's shoulders to hold him in a sitting position. Then with larger boulders, they covered him completely, building a cairn over his grave that would keep the hyena out. When it was done, Sean did not linger. He had said his farewell. He walked away without looking back, and after a few moments Claudia followed him.

Despite her sorrow, in some strange way she felt privileged and sanctified by what she had witnessed. Her respect and love for Sean had been reinforced a hundredfold by the emotions he had displayed at the loss of his friend. She felt that his tears had proved his strength rather than betrayed his weakness, and that rare demonstration of love had only pointed up his manhood. From this terrible tragedy, she had learned more about Sean than she might otherwise have done in a lifetime.

They marched hard that night. Sean forged on as though he were trying to outrun his grief. Claudia did not try to slow him. Although she was now lean and fit as a coursing greyhound, she had to put out all her strength to stay with him, but she did not complain. By sunrise, they had covered almost forty miles from where they had buried Job and ahead of them, lay a wide alluvial plain.

Sean found a grove of tall trees to give them a little shade and while Claudia and Matatu prepared their meal, Sean slung his binoculars across his back and stuffed the field map into his back pocket and went to the base of the tallest tree.

Claudia watched him anxiously as he began to climb, but he was as nimble as a squirrel and as powerful as a bull baboon, using the brute strength of his arms to haul himself up the smooth stretches of the bole where there were no footholds.

When he neared the top of the tree, a white-backed vulture launched herself from her shaggy nest of dried branches and circled anxiously overhead while Sean settled into the fork of a branch only a few feet from the nest.

The vulture's nest contained two large chalky-white eggs and Sean murmured soothingly to the bird still cruising high above. 'Don't worry, old girl. I'm not going to steal them.' Sean did not share the popular distaste for these birds. They performed a vital function in cleansing the veld of carrion and disease, and while grotesque in repose, they were models of elegance and beauty in the air, masters of the sky and of natural flight, revered as gods by the ancient Egyptians and other peoples with a close affinity to nature.

Sean smiled up at the bird. The first smile that had bent his lips since Job had gone, and then he gave his full attention to the terrain spread out below him. The alluvial plain ahead had been intensively cultivated, only scattered groves of trees still stood between the open fields. Sean knew that these would mark the sites of the small family villages shown on his map. He turned his binoculars upon them.

He saw at once that the fields had not been tilled nor planted for many seasons. They were thick with the rank secondary growth that invades abandoned cultivation in Africa. He recognized the tall harsh stems of *Hibiscus irritans* named for the sharp fine hairs that cover the leaves and which brush off on anyone that touches them. He saw castor-oil bush and cotton gone wild, and the orange-coloured blossoms of wild cannabis, whose narcotic properties had first so delighted Jack Kennedy's peace corps boys and girls and which over the years since then, had given solace to the hordes of other European and American youngsters who had followed them out to Africa equipped only with back-packs, dirty blue jeans, good intentions and a hazy belief in beauty, peace and the brotherhood of man. Recently fear of Aids had slowed their arrival to a trickle and Sean was grateful for that. He realized his thoughts were wandering and he pulled himself up and panned his binoculars slowly across the scene of desolation ahead.

He could just make out the roofless ruins of the villages. On some of the huts, the roof timbers were still intact but skeletal and blackened by flames; the thatch burned away. Though he scrutinized the area meticulously, he could make out no sign of recent human presence. The paths between the fields were all overgrown, there was no sign of domestic stock, no chicken nor goat and no tell-tale tendrils of smoke rising from a cooking-fire.

'Somebody, Frelimo or Renamo, has worked this area over pretty thoroughly,' he thought, and then looked away to the east to the distant blue hills of the interior. This early in the morning, the air was still clear and bright and he was able to recognize some of the features and cross-reference them to the topography of his field map. Within fifteen minutes he was able to mark in their position with reasonable accuracy and confidence.

They had made a little better progress than he had estimated. Those mountains out on the right-hand side were the Chimanimani; they formed the border between Mozambique and Zimbabwe but their nearest peaks were almost forty kilometres distant. His map was marked in kilometres, and Sean still liked to work in miles rather than the metric scale.

The larger village of Dombe should be a few kilometres out on his left flank, but he could pick out no indication of its exact whereabouts. He guessed that like the other family villages ahead, it had long ago been abandoned and allowed to return to bush and forest, in which case there would be little prospect of finding food there. With so many feeding from it, the small quantity of maize-meal they had been able to bring with them was almost expended. By tomorrow they would need to begin foraging and that would slow them up. On the other hand, if Dombe was still inhabited, it would certainly be either a Frelimo or a Renamo stronghold. Prudently he resolved to avoid any contact with all other humans. Nobody, not even Alphonso, could say which territory was held by the opposing forces and which was a destruction area devastated equally by both sides. Even those boundaries would be fluid and would alter on a daily, if not an hourly basis, like the amorphous body of an amoeba.

He looked directly southward along their intended route. In that direction, there were no features rising above the plain. This was a part of the littoral that stretched down to the shores of the Indian Ocean, and no mountain nor deep valley ruffled it. The only natural obstacles ahead were the dense hardwood forests, the rivers and the swamps that guarded the approaches to them.

The largest river was the Sabi, or the Rio Save as the Portuguese named it as it flowed in across their border with the land that was to become Zimbabwe and down towards the ocean. It was broad and deep and they would probably need some sort of craft to make the crossing.

The last river, Rudyard Kipling's great grey-green, greasy Limpopo river, all set about with fever-trees, was the final obstacle they would face. It was still three hundred kilometres further south. Three national borders converged and met upon its banks, Zimbabwe, Mozambique, and the Republic of South Africa. If they were able to reach that point then they had reached the northern boundary of the celebrated Kruger National Park, heavily guarded and patrolled by the South African military. Sean studied the map longingly – South Africa and safety, South Africa and home, where the rule of law still held sway and men did not walk each moment in the shadow of death.

A soft whistle brought him out of his reverie, and he looked down. Matatu was at the base of the tree, sixty feet below where he sat. He gesticulated up at Sean.

'Listen!' he signalled. 'Danger!' And Sean felt his pulse trip and accelerate. Matatu did not use the danger signal lightly. He cocked his head and listened, but still it was almost a full minute before he heard it. As a bushman Sean's senses, especially eyesight and hearing, were honed and acute, but compared to Matatu, he was a blind mute.

As he heard and recognized the sound at last, even though it was faint and faraway, Sean's pulse jumped again and he swivelled round in the fork of the branch and looked back northwards, in the direction from which they had come.

Apart from a few high streaks of cirro-stratus cloud, the morning sky was empty blue. Sean put up his binoculars and searched it, looking low along the horizon, close to the tops of the tall hard-wood trees. The distant sound, increasing in volume, gave him a direction in which to search, until suddenly the shape appeared in the field of his binoculars and he felt the slide of dread in his guts.

Like some gigantic and noxious insect, the Hind cruised humpbacked and nose low above the forest tops. It was still some miles distant, but coming on directly towards Sean's tree-top perch.

*   *   *

General China sat in the flight engineer's seat under the forward canopy of the Hind and looked ahead through the armoured windscreen. This early in the morning the air had a crystalline lucidity through which the rays of the low sun lit every detail of the landscape below him with a radiant golden light.

Although he had already flown many hours in the captured machine, he had not yet grown accustomed to the extraordinary sense of power that his seat under the forward canopy aroused in him. The earth and everything in it lay below him, he could look down on mankind and know that he held the power of life and death over them.

He reached out now and gripped the control lever of the Gatling-cannon. The pistol grip fitted neatly into his right hand, and as the heel of his hand depressed the cocking plunger, the remote aiming screen lit on the control panel directly in front of him. As he moved the control lever, traversing, depressing or

449

elevating, so the multiple barrels of the cannon faithfully duplicated each movement and the image of the target was reflected on the screen.

With the slightest pressure of his forefinger, he could send a dense stream of cannon shell hosing down to obliterate any target he chose. Then by simply throwing a switch on the weapons console, he could select any of the Hind's alternative armaments, the rockets in their pods or the banks of missiles.

It had not taken China long to master the complex weapons control system, for the basic training he had received in the Siberian guerrilla training camp so long ago, at the beginning of the Rhodesian war of liberation, had stood him in good stead down the years. However, this was the most awe-inspiring fire power he had ever had at his fingertips and the most exhilarating vantage point from which to deploy it.

At a single word of command, he could soar aloft like an eagle in a thermal, or plunge like a stooping peregrine, he could hover on high or dance lightly on the leafy tops of the forest. The power that this machine had bestowed upon him was truly godlike.

At first there had been serious problems to surmount. He could not work with the captured Russian pilot and crew. They were sullen and unreliable. Despite the threat of horrible death that hung over them he realized that they would seize the first opportunity to escape, or to sabotage his precious new Hind. One of the Russian ground crew need only drain the lubricant from a vital part of the machine, or loosen a bolt, or burn out a section of wiring, and neither China nor any of his Renamo had the technical expertise to recognize the sabotage attempt until it was too late. In addition, the Russian pilot had from the very beginning made communication between them difficult. He had played dumb and deliberately misunderstood China's commands. Trading on the knowledge that China could not do without him, he had become progressively more defiant and recalcitrant.

China had solved that problem swiftly. Within hours of the destruction of the Russian squadron and the capture of the Hind, he had radioed a long coded message to a station two hundred miles further north across the national boundary between Mozambique and Malawi. The message had been received and decoded at the headquarters of a large tea plantation on the slopes of Mlanje mountain, the proprietor of which was a member of the central committee of the Mozambique National Resistance and the deputy director of Renamo intelligence. He had telexed China's report and requests directly to the director general of the central committee at his headquarters in Lisbon, and within six hours a crack Portuguese military helicopter pilot with many thousands of hours flying experience and two skilled aeronautical engineers were aboard a TAP airliner southward bound for Africa. From Nairobi they changed to an Air Malawi commercial flight scheduled directly for Blantyre, the capital of Malawi. There a driver and Land-Rover from the tea plantation were waiting to whisk them out to the private airstrip on the tea estate.

That night the tea company's twin-engined Beechcraft, made a midnight crossing of Lake Cabora Bassa, a perilous journey that the pilot had undertaken many times before, and a single red flare guided him to the secret bush strip that General China's men had hacked out of the wilderness just west of the mountains of Gorongosa.

A double line of Renamo guerrillas, each holding aloft a burning torch of paraffin-soaked rags, provided a flare path and the Beechcraft pilot landed smoothly and without shutting down his engines deposited his passengers, turned and taxied back to the end of the rough airstrip and then roared away, climbed clear and turned northwards again into the night.

There had been a time not long ago when such a complicated route for bringing in men and material would not have been necessary. Only a year previously China's request would have been radioed southwards, rather than north, and the delivery vehicle, instead of a small private aircraft, would have been a Puma helicopter with the South African air-force markings.

In those days when the Marxist President of Frelimo, Samora Machel, had hosted the guerrillas of the African National Congress, and allowed them to use Mozambique as a staging post for their terror attacks with limpet mines and car bombs on the civilian population of South Africa, the South Africans had retaliated by giving their full support to the Renamo forces that were attempting to topple Machel's Frelimo government.

Then to the dismay of the Renamo command, Samora Machel and P. W. Botha, the South African president, had signed an accord at the little town of Nkomati on the border between their two countries, the direct result of which had been a drastic reduction of South African aid to Renamo in exchange for the expulsion of the ANC terror squads from Mozambique.

Both sides had cheated on the agreement, with a wink and a nudge. Machel had closed the ANC offices in Maputo but allowed them to continue their terror campaign without official Frelimo support or approval, and the South Africans had cut back on their support of Renamo, but still the Pumas made their clandestine cross-border flights.

Then the deck had been reshuffled when Samora Machel died in the wreck of his personal aircraft, an antiquated Tupolev which had been retired from airline service in the USSR and magnanimously given to Machel by his Russian allies. The Tupolev's instrumentation was decrepit, and on the night of the crash both the Russian pilots had been so full of vodka that they had neglected to file a flight plan. They were almost two hundred kilometres off-course when they crashed on the South African border, actually striking on the Mozambique side and then by some improbable chance bouncing and sliding across into South Africa.

Despite the evidence of the flight recorder, the Tupolev's black box, which contained a recording of the two Russian pilots' repeated requests for more vodka from the air hostess and an animated and anatomically precise discussion of exactly what they were going to do to her after they had landed, the Russians and the Frelimo government insisted that the South Africans had lured Machel to his death. The Nkomati accord died with Machel on that remote African hillside, and the Pumas resumed their cross-border flights, ferrying supplies to the Renamo guerrillas.

Then gradually news began to filter out of the Mozambiquan wilderness. At first a few dedicated missionaries emerged from the bush to describe the appalling destruction, the misery and the starvation, and the atrocities that were being perpetrated by the ravaging Renamo guerrilla armies over an area the size of France.

A few intrepid journalists managed to get into the battle zone, and one or two of them survived and emerged to relate their accounts of the holocaust that was raging. Some of their reports put the estimate of civilian casualties as high as half a million dead of starvation, disease and genocide.

Refugees, tens of thousands of them, began to stream across the border into South Africa. Terrified, starving, riddled with disease, they told their harrowing stories. The South Africans realized to their horror that they had been nourishing a monster in Renamo.

At the same time, the more moderate Chissano who had replaced Samora Machel as president of the government of Mozambique and Frelimo began making placatory overtures. The two presidents met and the Nkomati accord was hurriedly revived, this time with honest intent. Overnight, the flow of South African aid to Renamo was cut off.

This had all taken place only months before, and General China and his fellow Renamo commanders were angry and desperate men, their stores of food and weapons dwindling rapidly without prospect of resupply. Soon they would be reduced to surviving on plunder and loot, foraging and scavenging from a countryside already ravaged by twelve years of guerrilla warfare. It was inevitable that they would turn their fury on what remained of the civilian population and on any foreigner that they could capture. The world was against them, and they were against the world.

Sitting up in the high seat of the Hind, General China let all this run through his mind. From here he seemed to have an over-view of the chaos and confusion. The entire country was in a state of flux, and always in a situation such as this, there was opportunity for the cunning and the ruthless to seize upon.

Of the Renamo field commanders, General China had proved himself over the years to be the most resourceful. With each victory and success he had established his power more firmly. His army was the most powerful of the three Renamo divisions. The external central committee was nominally the high command of the resistance movement, but paradoxically General China's prestige and influence was becoming progressively greater with each setback that the movement received. More and more the central committee acceded to his wishes. The alacrity with which they had reacted to his request for a Portuguese pilot and engineers demonstrated this most aptly. Of course, the destruction of the Russian squadron and the capture of the Hind had enormously inflated his prestige and importance, while possession of the extraordinary vehicle in which he now soared over the wilderness placed him in a unique position of power.

General China smiled contentedly and spoke into the microphone of his hard helmet. 'Pilot, can you see the village yet?'

'Not yet, General. I estimate four minutes' more flying time.'

The Portuguese pilot was in his early thirties. Young enough still to have dash and fire, but old enough to have accumulated experience and discretion. He was handsome in a swarthy olive-skinned fashion, with a drooping gun-slinger moustache and the dark bright eyes of a predatory bird. From the first he handled the controls of the Hind with precision and confidence, and his skill had increased with each hour flown as he came to terms with every nuance of the Hind's flying characteristics.

The two Portuguese engineers had taken command of the Russian ground crew and supervised every move they made. One of the Hind's principal advantages was that it could be serviced and maintained in all conditions without the need for sophisticated equipment, and the chief engineer assured General China that the spares and tools he had captured at the laager were sufficient to keep the Hind airborne indefinitely. The only shortages were of missiles for the Swatter system and assault rockets, but this was amply compensated for by almost a million rounds of 12.7mm cannon shells they had captured in the laager.

It had taken a hundred and fifty porters to carry the munitions away, while another five hundred porters had each carried a twenty-five-litre drum of Avgas. Renamo used mainly women porters, trained since girlhood to carry weights on their heads. That quantity of Avgas was sufficient to keep the Hind flying for almost two hundred hours, and by then there would be a good chance of capturing a Frelimo fuel tanker, either on the railway line or on one of the roads nearer the coast that were still open to traffic.

However, General China's main concern at that moment was to keep the rendezvous which he had arranged by radio with General Tippoo Tip, the commander of Renamo's southern division.

'General, I have spotted the village,' the pilot spoke in China's headphones.

'Ah, yes, I see it,' China answered. 'Turn towards it, please.'

As the Hind approached Sean shifted his perch, creeping behind a densely leafed bough and flattening himself against the branch. Although he knew it was dangerous to turn his face towards the sky, he relied on the bush of his beard and his deep tan to prevent the sun reflecting off his face and he watched the helicopter avidly.

He realized that their ultimate survival depended on being able

454

to elude this monster, and he studied its shape to estimate the view that the pilot and his gunner commanded from behind their canopies. It might be vital for Sean to know the blind spots of the flight engineer and the field of fire of his weapons.

He saw the cannon in the remote turret below the nose abruptly traverse left and right, almost as though the gunner was demonstrating them for him. Sean could not know that General China was merely gloating on his own power and playing with the weapon controls, but the movement illustrated the Gatling-cannon's restricted field of fire. The barrel could only swing through an arc of thirty degrees from lock to lock, beyond that the pilot was obliged to swivel the entire aircraft on its own axis in order to bring the cannon to bear.

The Hind was very close now. Sean could make out every minute detail of the hull, from the crimson 'Excellent' logo on the nose to the rows of rivet heads that stitched the titanium armour sheets. He looked for some weakness, some flaw in the massive armour, but in the few seconds, before she was overhead, he saw that she was impregnable, except for the air intakes to the turbo engines, like a pair of hooded eyes above the upper pilot's canopy. The intakes were screened by debris suppressors, bossed light metal discs that inhibited the dust and debris thrown up by the down-draught of the rotors when the helicopter hovered close to the ground from being sucked into the turbines. However, the debris suppressors were not so substantial as to prevent the Stinger missiles flying clearly into the intakes, and Sean saw that there was a necessary gap around the edge of the metal boss wide enough for a man to stick his head through. At the correct angle and from very close range an expert marksman might just be able to aim a burst of machine-gun fire through that gap so as to damage the turbine vanes. Sean knew that even a chip from one of those vanes would unbalance the turbine and set up such vibrations in the engine that it would fly to pieces within seconds.

'A hell of a shot, and a hell of a lot of luck,' Sean muttered, staring upwards through slitted eyes. Suddenly the light reflected from the armoured glass canopy altered so that he could see into the interior of the cockpit.

As he recognized General China, despite the hard plastic flying-helmet and the mirrored aviator glasses shielding his eyes, hatred flushed fiercely through Sean's guts. Here was the man on whom he could firmly set the blame for Job's death and all their other woes and hardships.

'I want you,' Sean muttered. 'God, how badly I want you.'

China seemed to sense the force of his hatred for he turned his head slightly and looked down directly at Sean's perch, staring at him evenly through the mirrored lens of his sunglasses, and Sean shrank down upon the branch.

Then abruptly the Hind banked away, exposing its blotched grey belly. The down-draught lashed the tree-top, shaking the branches, and throwing Sean about in the hurricane of disrupted air, and Sean realized that it had been an illusion and that China had not spotted him in his tree-top bower.

He watched the huge machine skitter away on its new heading and then a few miles distant the engine beat changed, the sound of the rotors whined in finer pitch and the Hind hovered briefly above the forest and then sank from view.

Sean clambered down the tree. Matatu had doused the small cooking-fire at the first sound of the Hind's approach, but the canteen of maize porridge had already cooked through.

'We'll eat on the march,' Sean ordered.

Claudia groaned softly, but pulled herself to her feet. Every muscle in her legs and back ached with fatigue.

'Sorry, beautiful.' Sean put an arm around her shoulders and squeezed her. 'China landed only a mile or two east of here. Probably at the village of Dombe, we can be pretty sure he has troops there. We've got to move on.'

They ate the last handfuls of hot sticky salted maize porridge on the march and washed it down with water from the bottles that tasted of mud and algae. 'From now on, we are living off the land,' Sean told her. 'And China is breathing down our necks.'

*   *   *

The Hind hovered a hundred feet above the road that ran through the village of Dombe.

It was the only road, and the village was merely a collection of twenty or so small buildings that had been long abandoned. The glass was broken from the window frames and the white-washed plaster had fallen from the adobe walls in leprous patches. Termites had devoured the roof timbers so that the corroded

456

corrugated sheeting sagged from the roof. Those buildings fronting onto the road had all once been small general dealers' stores, the ubiquitous *dukas* of Africa, owned by Hindu traders. One faded sign hung at a drunken angle. 'Patel & Patel', it proclaimed between the crimson trademarks of the Coca-Cola company.

The road itself was dirt-surfaced and littered with rubbish and debris, weeds growing rankly in the unused ruts.

'Take us down,' China ordered, and the helicopter sank towards the roadway, lifting a whirlwind thick with dead leaves, scraps of paper, discarded plastic bags and other rubbish.

There were men on the verandah of 'Patel & Patel' and armed men amongst the derelict buildings, fifty or more, all heavily armed and dressed in an assortment of camouflage, military and civilian clothing, the eclectic uniform of the African guerrilla.

The Hind settled to the rutted road and the pilot throttled back the turbos; the rotors slowed and the engine noise sank to a low whistle. General China opened the armoured canopy, jumped down lightly to earth and turned to face the group of men on the stoep of the general dealer's store.

'Tippoo Tip,' he said, and opened his arms wide in fraternal greeting. 'How good to see you again.' He raised his voice above the engine whistle.

General Tippoo Tip came down the steps to meet him, his own thick arms held wide as a crucifix. They embraced with the utmost insincerity of two fierce rivals who knew that they might one day have to kill each other.

'My old friend,' said China, and held him at arm's length, smiling warmly and lovingly upon him.

Tippoo Tip was not his real name, he had taken that as his *nom de guerre* from one of the most notorious of the old Arab slave-traders and ivory-runners of the previous century. However, the name and its associations suited him to perfection, China thought as he looked down upon him. Here stood a rogue and brigand cast in the classic mould, a man to admire and to treat with great caution.

He was short, the top of his head on a level with China's chin, but everything else about him was massive. His chest was like that of a bull gorilla, and his thick arms hung in similar fashion, so his knuckles were at the level of his knees. His head was like one of those gigantic Rhodesian granite boulders balanced on the pinnacle of a rocky kopje. He had shaved his pate, but his beard was a thick mattress of woolly black curls, that hung onto his chest. The forehead and nose above it were broad and his lips full and fleshy.

He wore a gaily coloured strip of cotton cloth bound around his forehead, while a gilet of tanned kuku-hide over his naked torso was open down the front to expose his chest. His chest was covered with black peppercorns of wool, and his naked arms protruding from the short sleeves were thick and roped with muscle.

He smiled back at China and his teeth were brilliant as mother-of-pearl, in contrast to the smoky yellow whites of his eyes, laced with a network of veins.

'Your presence has perfumed my day with the scent of mimosa blossom,' he said in Shangane, but his eyes slid past China's face and returned to the huge helicopter from which he had disembarked. Tippoo Tip's envy was so unconcealed that China felt he could smell it and taste it like burning sulphur in the air.

That machine had altered the fine trim and balance of the relationship between these two most powerful of all the Renamo warlords. Tippoo Tip could not keep his eyes off it. It was obvious that he wanted to examine it more closely but China took his arm and led him back towards the shade of the verandah. The pilot had not killed the engines and as China and his host stepped out of the circle of the rotors he gunned the Hind and pulled on his collective. The great machine rose, and turned away.

Tippoo Tip twisted out of China's grip and shaded his eyes to watch it. His smoked yellow eyes were as hungry as though he were watching a beautiful naked woman performing an obscene act. China let him yearn after it until it passed out of sight. He had sent the Hind away purposely because he knew and understood Tippoo Tip. He knew that if the machine had remained, the temptation might have become too strong for him to resist, and treachery was as natural to both of them as breathing was to other men. The Hind was China's joker, his wild card.

Tippoo Tip shook himself and laughed for no apparent reason. 'They told me that you had destroyed the squadron and captured one of those, and I said, "China is a lion among men and he is my brother."'

'Come, my brother,' China agreed. 'It is hot in the sun.'

There were stools ready for them on the verandah in the shade and two of Tippoo Tip's young women brought them clay pots

458

of beer, thick as gruel and refreshingly tart. The girls were both in their teens, pretty little things with eyes like fawns. Tippoo Tip liked women and always surrounded himself with them. It was one of his weaknesses, China thought, and smiled a cold superior smile. He himself could take a boy or a girl with equal enjoyment, but only as a brief diversion and not as a necessity of life, and the women engaged his attention for only a fleeting moment before he turned back to his host.

The bodyguards had retired out of earshot, and Tippoo Tip waved the girls away.

'And you, my brother?' China asked. 'How goes the battle? I hear that you have taken the head of Frelimo and pushed it down between their knees to give them a close-up view of their own fundament. Is that true?'

It was not true, of course. As commander of the southern division of Renamo, Tippoo Tip was closer to the capital and port of Maputo which was the centre of government power. He was, therefore, more prejudiced by the withdrawal of South African military assistance and he stood in the front line of Frelimo counter-attacks and reprisals. China knew that in the last few months Tippoo Tip had experienced heavy reversals and lost many men and much territory in the south, but now Tippoo Tip chuckled and nodded.

'We have eaten everything that Frelimo has sent against us. Swallowed them without a belch or a fart.'

They sparred lightly over the beer pots, smiling and laughing, but watching each other like lions over a kill, on guard and ready at any instant to pounce or defend themselves until, at last, China murmured, 'I am pleased to hear that all goes so well with you. I had come to see if my Hind gunship could assist you against Frelimo.' He spread his hands in a deprecating gesture. 'But I see you have no need of help from me.'

It was a machiavellian ploy, and China watched as the point slid through Tippoo Tip's guard and his expression changed. China knew that it would have been a serious tactical error to ask a man like this for assistance. Tippoo Tip had the nose of a hyena to smell out weakness. Instead China had offered the bait of the Hind, dangled it for an instant before his eyes, and then with a crafty sleight of hand made it disappear again.

Tippoo blinked and behind his grin he searched for a response. He also hated to admit failure or weakness to one who he knew

459

would exploit it ruthlessly, but still he craved and lusted after that fabulous machine.

'The help of a brother is always welcome,' he contradicted pleasantly, 'especially a brother who rides the skies in his own *henshaw*.' And then he went on swiftly, 'And perhaps there is some small service that I can offer in return for your help?'

'Crafty rogue,' China thought, admiring his style. 'He knows I haven't come here out of compassion. He knows I want something.' And both of them retreated, in the African manner, behind another screen of pleasantries and trivialities, coming back only circuitously and almost flirtatiously to the main subject.

'I laid a trap for Frelimo,' Tippoo Tip boasted. 'I pulled back from the Save forests.' In truth he had been driven out of those infinitely valuable indigenous forests only after hard fighting, in the face of the most determined Frelimo attacks since the beginning of the long campaign.

'That was cunning of you,' China agreed, letting the razor edge of sarcasm flash in his tone. 'What a trap to leave the forests to Frelimo and how stupid of them to fall for it.'

The Save forests were a treasure house – seventy-foot-tall leadwoods, which were also called ivory tusk trees for their dense finely grained timber; magnificent Rhodesian mahogany which yielded logs five feet in diameter; and the most rare and valuable of all African trees, the tamboti or African sandalwood with its richly figured and scented timber.

Probably nowhere on the continent was there such a concentration of these precious hardwoods. They constituted the last natural resource of this ravaged land. First the great elephant herds had been wiped out, then the rhinoceros and the buffalo had been machine-gunned from the air. The Soviets and the North Koreans had plundered the vast natural prawn-beds and fisheries of the rich warm Mozambique current along the eastern coast, while foreign adventurers with Frelimo licences and approval had decimated the crocodile population of Lake Cabora Bassa. Only the forests still remained intact.

Even more so than the other newly independent African states, the government of Mozambique was desperately short of foreign exchange. For over a decade they had been fighting a drawn-out guerrilla war that had bled their economy white. Those forests were the last assets they had to sell for hard cash.

'They have moved in with labour battalions, twenty, perhaps thirty thousand slaves,' Tippoo Tip told China.

'So many?' China asked with interest. 'Where did they find them?'

'They have swept the last peasants off the land, they have raided the refugee camps, gathered the vagrants and the unemployed from the slums and streets of Maputo. They call it the "Democratic People's Full Employment Programme", and the men and women work from dawn to sundown for ten Frelimo escudos a day, and the single meal they are fed costs them fifteen Frelimo escudos.' Tippoo Tip threw back his head and laughed, more in admiration than amusement. 'Sometimes Frelimo is not so stupid,' he admitted. 'The labour battalions pay five escudos a day for the privilege of cutting the government timber, a most admirable arrangement.'

'And you have allowed Frelimo to do this?' China asked. It was not the plight of the labour battalions that concerned him. A single sixty-foot log of tamboti was valued at approximately fifty thousand US dollars, and the forests extended for hundreds of thousands of acres.

'Of course I allow them to do this,' Tippoo Tip agreed. 'They cannot move the timber out until the roads and the railway are reconstructed, and until then they are piling the logs in dumps along the old line of rail. My scouts count each log that is added to the stock pile.' Tippoo Tip took a grubby plastic-covered notebook from the pocket of his kudu-skin gilet and showed China the figures that he had neatly noted down in blue ballpoint pen on the back page.

China kept his face impassive as he read the total, but his eyes glittered behind the gold-rimmed sunglasses. That sum of dollars was sufficient to finance the war chest of both armies for a further five years, enough to buy the alliance of nations or to elevate a small warlord to the estate of president over the entire nation for life.

'The time is almost ready for me to return to the forests of Save and collect the harvest that Frelimo has gathered in ready for me.'

'How would you export this harvest? A log of tamboti weighs a hundred tons, who would buy it from you?'

Tippoo Tip clapped his hands and shouted to one of his aides who was squatting in the shade of the building across the street.

461

The guerrilla jumped up and hurried to where the two generals sat. He knelt to unroll a field map on the cracked concrete floor of the verandah between their stools and placed lumps of broken concrete on the corners of the map to hold it flat. Tippoo Tip and China leaned forward to study it.

'Here are the forests.' Tippoo Tip traced out the boundaries of that vast area between the Rio Save and Limpopo rivers, directly south of their own position. 'Frelimo have set up their timberyards, here and here and here.'

'Go on,' China encouraged him.

'The most southerly dump is only thirty miles from the north bank of the Limpopo, thirty miles from the South African border.'

'The South Africans have disavowed us, they have signed an accord with Chissano and Frelimo,' China pointed out.

'Treaty and accords are merely pieces of paper.' Tippoo Tip waved them aside. 'Here, we are discussing half a billion US dollars' worth of timber. I have already received assurances from our erstwhile allies in the south that if I can make good delivery, they will arrange transport to their border and payment in Lisbon or Zurich.' He paused. 'Frelimo has cut and stacked the goods for me, it remains only for me to collect and deliver.'

'And my new helicopter gunship will assist your collection?' China suggested.

'Assist, yes, although I could achieve the same result with my own forces.'

'Perhaps, but a joint operation would be quicker and more certain,' China told him. 'We share the fighting and the spoils. With my *henshaw* and reinforcements from the north it would take a week or less to drive the Frelimo forces out of the forests.'

Tippoo Tip pretended to consider the proposition, and then nodded and asked delicately, 'Of course, I could reward you for your help, with a modest percentage of the value of the timber we capture.'

'Modest is not a word I greatly favour,' China sighed. 'I prefer the good socialist word equal, let us say an equal share?' And Tippoo Tip looked pained and threw up his hands in protest.

'Be reasonable, my brother.' For an hour longer they haggled and argued, slowly drawing closer to striking a bargain over the private distribution of a nation's wealth and the fate of tens of thousands of wretched individuals in the labour battalions.

'My scouts tell me that the people in the logging camps are near the end of their usefulness,' Tippoo Tip remarked at one point. 'Frelimo have fed them on such rations that nearly all of them are sick and starving. They are dying by hundreds each day and they are cutting half the timber that they were two months ago. Frelimo have run out of replacements for the logging gangs and the whole business is running down. There is not much to be gained by waiting any longer, we should attack immediately, before the beginning of the rains.'

China looked at his digital wristwatch, a badge of rank as significant as the star upon his epaulettes. The Hind would be returning to pick him up within half an hour, he must conclude the negotiations and strike the bargain. Within minutes, they had agreed on the last details of the combined operation and then China mentioned casually, 'There is one other matter.' And his tone alerted Tippoo Tip to the importance of the next request. He leaned forward on the stool and placed his hands, as broad and powerful as the paws of a grizzly bear, on his knees. 'I am chasing a small party of white fugitives. It seems that they are attempting to reach the South African border.' Briefly China sketched out a description of Sean's party and ended, 'I want you to alert all your forces between here and the Limpopo to be on the look-out for them.'

'A white man and a white woman, a young white woman. It sounds interesting, my brother,' Tippoo Tip said thoughtfully.

'The man is the most important. The woman is an American and may have some value as a hostage, but otherwise she means little.'

'To me a woman always has value,' Tippoo Tip contradicted him. 'Especially if she is white and young. I like a change of flesh occasionally. Let us make another bargain, my brother, once again equal shares. If I help you to capture these runaway whites, you may have the man, but I will keep the woman. Is it agreed?'

China thought for a moment and then nodded. 'Very well, you may have her, but I want the man alive and uninjured.'

'That is exactly how I want the woman,' Tippoo Tip chuckled. 'So again, we are in accord.' He stretched out his right hand, and China took it. Both of them knew as they stared into each other's eyes that the gesture was meaningless, that their agreement would be honoured only as long as it favoured both of them, and it could be broken without warning by either of them as circumstances altered.

'Now tell me about this young white woman,' Tippoo Tip invited. 'Where was she last seen, and what are you doing to catch her?'

China returned immediately to the map spread between them and Tippoo Tip took note of the new animation in his expression and the eagerness in his voice as he explained how Sean and his party had avoided the trap he had set on the border and how the Shangane deserters had reported their position and their intention of heading southwards.

'We know their last definite position was here.' China touched a spot just north of the railway line. 'But that was three days ago. They could be anywhere along here.' He spread his hand and drew it down across the map. 'One of the party is badly wounded so they have probably not reached this far south. I have patrols, almost three hundred men quartering the ground south of the railway looking for their spoor, but I want you to lay a net, like this, in front of them. How many men can you spare?'

Tippoo Tip shrugged. 'I have already placed three companies here along the Rio Save keeping watch on the logging in the forests. There are five more companies spread across here, further north. If these whites are trying to reach the Limpopo border, they will have to pass right through my lines and the Frelimo guards in the forest. I will radio my company commanders to be fully alert for them.'

General China's tone was sharp and authoritative. 'They must cover every trail, every river crossing. They must stake out a stop line with no gaps in it, and my sweep line coming down from the north will drive them onto it. But warn your section commanders that the white man is a soldier and a good one. He commanded the Ballantyne Scouts at the end of the war.'

'Courtney.' Tippoo Tip broke in. 'I remember him well.' And then he chuckled. 'Of course, it was Courtney who led the raid on your base. No small wonder that you want him so badly. You and Colonel Courtney go back many years. You have a long memory, my brother.'

'Yes,' China nodded, and touched the lobe of his deaf ear. 'Many years and a long memory, but then revenge is a dish that tastes best if it is eaten cold.'

They both looked up as the sound of the Hind's turbos whistled in from the north of the village and China checked his wristwatch. The pilot was precisely on time for the pickup and China felt his confidence in the young Portuguese reinforced. He stood up from the stool.

'We will maintain radio contact on 118.4 MHZ,' he told Tippoo Tip. 'Three schedules daily, six a.m., noon and six in the evening.' But Tippoo Tip was not looking at him, he was looking up longingly at the shape of the Hind as it hovered above the village like some mutated monster from a horror movie.

General China settled himself into the flight engineer's seat and closed the armoured-glass canopy. He raised his right thumb towards where Tippoo Tip stood on the verandah of the derelict *duka* and as he returned the salute, the Hind rose vertically above the village and swung its nose towards the north.

'General, one of the patrols has been calling you urgently on the radio.' The pilot spoke in China's earphones. 'They are using the call sign "Twelve Red".'

'Very well, please switch to the patrol frequency,' China ordered, and watched the digital display on the panel of his radio transmitter.

'"Twelve Red" this is "Banana Tree". Do you read?' he spoke into his helmet microphone. 'Twelve Red' was one of his crack scouting groups sweeping for spoor south of the railway line. Glancing at the map on his knee China tried to guess the scouts' exact position. The section leader answered his call almost immediately.

'"Banana Tree", this is "Twelve Red". We have a confirmed contact.'

China felt the excitement and triumph rise in his chest, but he kept his voice level.

'Report your position,' he ordered, and as the section leader read out the co-ordinates China checked them on his field map, and saw that the patrol was about thirty-five miles due north of the village.

'Have you got that, pilot?' he asked. 'Get there as fast as you can.' And as the engine tone of the Hind rose sharply he called ahead, '"Twelve Red", give us a red flare when you have us in sight.'

Seven minutes later the flare arced up out of the forest almost directly under the Hind's nose, and the pilot slowed the machine and let it drift down towards the tree-tops.

The Renamo patrol had cleared a landing zone with their machetes and the pilot manoeuvred the Hind into it and let her settle in a cloud of dust and debris. He saw with satisfaction that the scouts had thrown out a protective screen around the landing zone. They were crack bush fighters. China leapt eagerly out of the cockpit and the section leader came forward to salute him. He was a lean veteran, festooned with weapons and water-bottles and bandoliers of ammunition.

'They passed this way sometime yesterday,' he reported.

'Are you sure it's them?' China demanded.

'The white man and woman,' the section leader nodded. 'But they buried something over there.' He pointed with his chin. 'We have not touched it, but I think it is a grave.'

'Show me.' China ordered, and followed him into the thorn thicket. The section leader stopped beside a cairn of boulders.

'Yes, a grave,' China said with finality. 'Open it up.'

The section leader snapped an order at two of his men and they laid aside their weapons and went forward. They kicked away the top stones and rolled them down the slope.

'Hurry!' China called. 'Work faster!' And the ironstone boulders rang against each other and struck sparks as they were hurled aside.

'There is the corpse,' the section leader called, as Job's bundled head was exposed. He stepped forward and jerked aside the stained shirt that covered it.

'It's the Matabele.' China recognized Job's features immediately. 'I didn't think he'd get this far. Dig him out and feed him to the hyena,' he ordered.

Two of the scouts reached down and seized Job's blanket-wrapped shoulders and China watched with ghoulish interest. Mutilation of the enemy dead was an ancient Nguni custom, the ritual disembowelment allowed the spirit of the vanquished to escape so that it would not plague the victor. There was, however, a vindictive satisfaction in watching his men exhume the Matabele. He understood what grief this act would cause Sean Courtney, and he relished how he would describe it to him on his next radio transmission.

At that moment, he spotted the short length of bark twine. It was twisted lightly around the blanket-wrapped shoulders of the corpse. For a moment he stared at it with puzzlement and then as he saw it tighten and heard the click of the grenade primer,

466

he realized what it was and he screamed a warning and hurled himself face forward to the earth.

The explosion crushed his eardrums and filled his head with pain. He felt the blast wave hit him and something struck him in the cheek with numbing force. He rolled into a sitting position, and for a moment thought that he had lost his eyesight; then the stars and catherine wheels of light that filled his head dissipated, and with a rush of relief he realized that he could see again.

Blood was streaming down the side of his face, and dribbling from his chin onto the front of his battledress blouse. He whipped the kerchief from around his neck and wadded it into the deep gash that a fragment from the grenade had opened across his cheekbone.

Unsteadily he came to his feet and stared down into the grave. The grenade had gutted one of his men like a fish. He was kneeling and trying to push his own bowels back into the hole, but the wet lining was sticking to his bare hands. The second guerrilla had been killed cleanly. The section leader sprang to China's side and tried to examine the gash in his cheek, but China struck his hands away.

'You white bastard,' his voice was shrill. 'You will pay dearly for that, Colonel Courtney. I swear it to you.'

The wounded guerrilla was still fumbling with his own entrails, but they bulged out between his fingers. He was making a dreadful cawing bubbling sound that only increased General China's fury.

'Get that man out of here!' he screamed. 'Take him away and shut him up!'

They dragged the wounded man away and still China was not satisfied. He was shaking wildly with shock and fury, looking around for something on which to vent his rage.

'You men!' He pointed with a trembling finger. 'Bring your pangas.' Two guerrillas ran forward to obey. 'Pull that Matabele dog out of his hole! That's right. Now use the pangas. Chop him into hyena food. That's it. Small pieces, don't stop! Mincemeat! I want him turned into mincemeat!'

* * *

All that morning Matatu led them southwards through the abandoned fields and past the deserted villages. The weeds and rank secondary growth gave them good cover and they avoided the footpaths and skirted the burnt-out huts.

Claudia was having difficulty keeping up. They had been going with only brief rests since the previous evening and she was reaching the limits of her endurance. There was no sensation of pain. Even the devilish little red-tipped thorns that left red weeping lines across the exposed skin of her arms merely tugged painlessly at her as she passed. Her steps were leaden and mechanical, and though she tried to keep the rhythm of the march, she felt herself running down like a clockwork toy. Slowly Sean drew ahead of her and she could not lengthen her stride to hold him. He glanced over his shoulder and saw how she was lagging and slowed for her to catch up.

'I'm sorry,' she blurted, and he glanced at the sky.

'We have to keep going,' he answered, and she toiled on behind him.

A little after midday they heard the Hind again. The sound of its engines were very faint and grew fainter still, dwindling away into the north.

Sean put out an arm to steady Claudia as she swayed on her feet.

'Well done,' he told her gently. 'I'm sorry I had to do that to you, but we've made good ground. China will never expect us to have got so far south. He has headed back northwards, and we can rest now.'

He led her to a cluster of low thorn acacia which formed a natural shelter. She sobbed with exhaustion as she sank to the hard ground and lay quietly as Sean squatted in front of her to remove her shoes and socks.

'Your feet have hardened up beautifully,' he told her as he massaged them gently. 'Not a sign of a blister. You're as tough as a Scout and twice as gutsy.' She couldn't even raise a smile at the compliment. Sean pulled her sock over his hand, stuck one finger through the hole in the toe and wiggled it like a ventriloquist's dummy.

'Okay. She walks good,' he made the sock speak like Miss Piggie, 'but, buster, you should see her in the sack.'

Claudia giggled weakly and he smiled down at her gently. 'That's better,' he said. 'Now go to sleep.'

For a few minutes longer she watched him working on her sock.

'Which of your trollops taught you to darn?' she murmured drowsily.

'I was a virgin until I met you. Go to sleep.'

'I hate her whoever she was,' Claudia said, and closed her eyes. It seemed to her that she opened them again immediately but the light had changed to soft shades of evening and the midday heat had cooled. She sat up.

Sean was cooking over a small fire of dry sticks, and he looked across at her.

'Hungry?' he asked.

'Starving.'

'Dinner.' He brought the metal billy to her.

'What is it?' she asked suspiciously, and peered down at the heap of scorched black sausages, each the size of her little finger.

'Don't ask,' he said. 'Eat.'

Gingerly she picked one out and sniffed at it. It was still hot from the cooking-fire.

'Eat!' he repeated, and to set an example popped one into his own mouth, chewed and swallowed.

'Damned good,' he gave his opinion. 'Go ahead.'

Carefully she bit into it and it squelched between her teeth and burst, filling her mouth with the consistency of warm custard that tasted like creamed spinach. She forced it down.

'Have another.'

'No thanks.'

'They're full of protein. Eat.'

'I couldn't.'

'You won't last out the next march on an empty stomach. Open your mouth.' He fed her and then himself alternately.

When the billy was empty, she asked again, 'Now tell me, what have I been eating?' But he grinned and shook his head and turned to Alphonso who was squatting across the fire devouring his share of the meal.

'Rig the radio,' Sean ordered. 'Let's hear if China has anything to say.'

While Alphonso was busy stringing the radio aerial, Matatu slipped quietly into camp. He was carrying a cylinder of freshly peeled bark whose ends were stoppered with plugs of dried grass. He and Sean exchanged a few words, and Sean looked serious.

'What is it?' Claudia asked with concern.

'Matatu has seen a lot of sign up ahead. It looks like there is

469

a great deal of patrol activity. Frelimo or Renamo, he can't tell which.'

That made her uneasy and Claudia moved a little closer to where Sean sat and leaned against his shoulder. Together they listened to the radio, and here again there seemed to be a much higher level of traffic, most of it in Shangane or African-accented Portuguese.

'There is something brewing,' Alphonso grunted, as he concentrated on the set. 'They are moving patrols into a stop line.'

'Renamo?' Sean asked, and Alphonso nodded.

'Sounds like General Tippoo Tip's men.'

'What does he say?' Claudia asked, but Sean didn't want to alarm her further.

'Routine traffic,' he lied, and Claudia relaxed and watched Matatu at the cooking-fire as he carefully unstoppered the bark cylinder and shook out its contents onto the coals. As she realized what he was cooking, she stiffened with horror.

'Those are the most disgusting. . . !' She couldn't finish and she stared in awful fascination at the huge hairy caterpillars writhing and wriggling on the coals. Their long ginger hair frizzled off in little puffs of smoke and gradually the worms stopped moving and curled into little crisp black sausages.

Claudia let out a tiny strangled cry and clutched at Sean's arm as she recognized them. 'They aren't. . . !' she gasped. 'I didn't! You didn't make me! Oh! No! I can't believe. . . !'

'Highly nutritious,' Sean assured her, and Matatu seeing the direction of her gaze picked one of the caterpillars out of the coals and passing it quickly from hand to hand to cool it, offered it to her with a magnanimous flourish.

'I think I'm going to throw up,' Claudia said faintly, and turned her face away. 'I can't believe I actually ate one of those.'

At that moment the radio crackled sharply and a voice spoke very faintly in a guttural language that Claudia could not understand. However, Sean's sudden interest in the transmission distracted her from her feelings of nauseous disgust and she asked, 'What language is that?'

'Afrikaans,' he replied shortly. 'Quiet! Listen!' But the transmission faded out abruptly.

'Afrikaans?' she asked. 'South African Dutch?'

'That's right,' Sean nodded. 'We must be getting within extreme range. That was almost certainly a South African military transmission. probably a border patrol on the Limpopo.' Sean spoke briefly to Alphonso and then told Claudia. 'He agrees. South African border patrol. Alphonso says they sometimes pick up skip transmissions like that even further north.' Sean checked his wristwatch. 'Well, it doesn't look as though General China is going to entertain us this evening. We had better pack up and get ready to march.' Sean had half risen when suddenly the radio burst into life again. This time the voice was so clear that they could hear every intake of General China's breath.

'Good evening, Colonel Courtney. Please forgive me for the late schedule. but I have had urgent business to attend to. Come in please. Colonel Courtney.'

In the silence that followed Sean made no move towards the microphone, and General China chuckled softly across the ether.

'Still at a loss for words. Colonel. Never mind. I'm sure you are listening. so I will congratulate you on the ground you have covered to date. Quite remarkable, especially in view of Miss Monterro's brake upon your progress.'

'Arrogant bastard.' Claudia whispered bitterly. 'He is everything and a male chauvinist pig to boot.'

'Quite frankly. Colonel Courtney, you took me by surprise. We have been forced to redeploy our stop lines further south to welcome you.'

Again there was a short silence and then suddenly General China's voice was full of malice.

'You see, Colonel, we have found where you buried your Matabele.' Claudia felt Sean stiffen beside her and the silence drew out until China spoke again. 'We dug up the body and we were able to judge how long it had been in the earth by the extent of putrefaction.' Sean began to tremble and China went on affably. 'A Matabele can stink like a dead hyena and your friend was no exception. Tell me, Colonel, did you put that bullet in his head? Very sensible thing to do. He wasn't going to make it anyway.'

'The swine! The bloody swine!' It was wrung out of Sean.

'Oh and by the way, the booby trap didn't work. Very amateurish effort, I'm afraid.' China laughed easily. 'And don't worry about the Matabele. I made it easier for the hyena. I put two of my men to work on him with pangas. Bite-size chunks, Colonel, Matabele goulash!'

Sean lunged for the microphone and snatched it to his mouth.

471

'You depraved bloody animal!' he yelled into it. 'You filthy ghoul! By Christ, you'd better pray I never get my hands on you!'

Sean broke off, panting with the strength of his outrage.

'Thank you, Colonel.' There was a smile in General China's voice. 'I was getting bored with talking to myself. It's good to be in contact again. I've missed you.'

With a huge effort Sean resisted the temptation to reply and instead switched off the set.

'Pack up.' His voice was still trembling with fury. 'China will have us pretty well pinpointed after that little outburst. We've got to move fast now.'

'Like we were dragging our heels before?' Claudia asked with resignation, but stood up obediently.

Yet their progress was slower this night. Twice before midnight Matatu cautioned them to wait, warned by his animal sixth sense of danger ahead. He went forward to scout the track and found the ambush that had been set for them, and each time they were forced to make a slow and stealthy detour to avoid the trap.

'General Tippoo Tip's men,' Alphonso muttered. 'He must be helping General China. There are men waiting for us on every path.'

However, after midnight their luck changed for the better. Matatu came across a well-used path running almost directly southwards, and discovered that only a short time before a large detachment of men had passed along it in the same direction as they were headed.

'We'll use their spoor to cover our own.' Sean seized the opportunity and put Matatu in the lead, with Claudia following him, while he and Alphonso took the drag, deliberately treading over the small distinctive footmarks of the leading pair, obliterating them and losing them in the heavy sign which the party of Tippoo Tip's men had left behind them.

They hurried along the path until Matatu's sharp ears picked out the tiny sounds that the Renamo patrol was making as it moved forward in the silence of the night. Then they moderated their pace and trailed them at a discreet distance, letting the patrol run interference for them.

Keeping in contact with the enemy, maintaining the strict interval that was the line between discovery and concealment was a delicate and eerie business for which they had to rely completely on Matatu's hearing and night sight, but they were moving at almost double the pace they could have hoped for without this assistance.

A little before dawn the Renamo patrol stopped just ahead of them and they crouched in the darkness and listened to them setting up an ambush on both sides of the pathway. Once the ambush party was settled in, Matatu led them on another detour to meet the path again further on and they struck out southwards once again.

'We have covered twenty-five miles by my reckoning,' Sean murmured with grim satisfaction, as the first delicate light of dawn paled the eastern stars. 'But we cannot risk moving further in daylight, the country is crawling with Renamo. Matatu, find us a place to lie up for the day.'

During that night march, they had moved into an area of wet vlei ground on the approaches to the Save river and now Matatu led them deliberately into the tall swamp grass. They waded knee-deep across the flood plains that guarded the river, picking their way between shallow open lagoons from which the mosquitos rose in grey clouds. The water covered their tracks and Sean brought up the rear of the file, meticulously closing the swamp grass and brushing it upright behind him to disguise their passing.

A few hundred yards off the path Matatu discovered a small dry island only inches above the level of the flood waters and as he stepped onto it there was a violent upheaval in the reeds as a heavy body rushed through it.

Claudia screamed with shock, certain they had blundered into another murderous Renamo ambush. However, Matatu whipped out his skinning knife and with a shrill war-cry dived into the grass; there was a wild commotion as he wrestled with a writhing scaly body twice his own size.

Sean rushed forward to help him and between them they clubbed and stabbed the creature and dragged it out of the grass on to the island. Claudia shuddered with horror as she realized that it was a huge grey lizard, almost seven feet long, with a speckled yellow belly and a long whip of a tail that still twitched and lashed from side to side.

With squeaks of glee, Matatu began immediately to peel off the scaly skin.

'What is it?'

'Matatu's favourite delicacy, leguan.' Sean whetted the blade

473

of his trench knife on the palm of his hand and then helped Matatu butcher the monitor lizard.

The flesh from the tail was white as the fillets of Dover sole, but Claudia grimaced when Sean offered her a strip.

'You and Matatu would eat your own offspring,' she accused.

'That from the girl who dines regularly on mopane caterpillars!'

'Sean, I couldn't. I really couldn't force myself. Not raw.'

'We haven't any dry wood for a fire and you have eaten Japanese sashimi, haven't you? You told me you loved it.'

'That's raw fish, not raw lizard!'

'Same difference, think of it as a kind of African sashimi,' he coaxed her gently. When at last she gave in and tasted it, she found it surprisingly palatable, and her hunger overcame her squeamishness.

For once there was no shortage of water and they filled their bellies with sweet white meat and flood water and then curled up on their blankets. With the tall swamp grass swaying over their heads to protect them from the burning sunlight and the eyes in the sky, Claudia felt secure and gave in to her fatigue.

Once in the middle of the day, she woke and lay in Sean's arms to listen to the sound of the searching Hind.

'China is working the riverbanks ahead of us,' Sean whispered. The sound of the Hind's turbos rose and fell as it turned on each leg of the search pattern, and Claudia felt her stomach muscles knotting and contracting as it grew louder, passing only a short distance south of where they lay, and then finally faded into silence.

'He's gone,' Sean hugged her. 'Get some sleep.'

She woke again with a sense of panic upon her, but when she tried to move she found herself held down firmly and the palm of someone's hand clamped painfully across her mouth. She turned her eyes sideways and Sean's face was close to hers.

'Quiet!' he breathed in her ear. 'Not a peep out of you.'

When she nodded he released her and rolled over to look out through the screen of swamp grass. She did the same and peered out across the shallow waters of the lagoon.

At first she saw nothing and then she heard someone singing. It was a sweet girlish treble softly piping a Shangane love song, and with it came the sound of light footfalls in the shallow lagoon water. The singing came very close, so close that Claudia instinctively shrank nearer to Sean and held her breath.

Then suddenly the singing girl stepped into the line of her vision through the aperture in the grass before Claudia's eyes. She was a slim and graceful lass, just past puberty for though her features were sweet and childlike, her breasts were big and round as tsama melons. She wore only a ragged loin-cloth pulled up between her long coltish legs and her skin glowed in the late afternoon sunlight like burnt molasses. She seemed as wild and fey as a spirit of the forest and Claudia was instantly enchanted by her.

In her right hand the girl carried a light reed fishing spear with multiple barbed grains, and as she waded softly through the lucid warm waters she held the spear poised to strike.

Abruptly the song died on her lips and she froze for an instant and then lunged with the grace of a dancer. The shaft of the spear twitched in her hands and with a happy little cry she lifted a long slimy catfish clear of the water. It wriggled on the end of the spear, its wide whiskered mouth gulping and grunting and the girl clubbed its flattened skull and dropped it into the plaited-reed bag at her waist.

She washed the fish slime from her small pink-palmed hands, picked up the spear and resumed her fishing, coming on directly towards where they lay in the patch of swamp grass. Sean reached out and squeezed Claudia's arm, cautioning her not to move, but the black girl was already so close that with a few more paces, she would stumble over them.

Suddenly she looked up, directly into Claudia's eyes. The two of them stared at each other for only a moment, and then the girl whirled and darted away. In an instant, Sean was up and racing after her, and from the grass on either side both Alphonso and Matatu rushed out to join the chase.

The girl was halfway across the lagoon before they caught up with her; she tried to dodge and double back, but each way she turned there was one of them ready to cut her off and, at last, she stood at bay. Wild-eyed and panting with terror, but holding the fishing spear determinedly in front of her. Her courage and spirit were wasted against the three men facing her; like a cat surrounded by alsatians she had no chance of escape.

Matatu feinted at her flank and the instant she turned the point of the spear towards him, Sean knocked it out of her hands and swept her up under his arm. Kicking and clawing, he carried her back to the island and dumped her on the dry land. She had lost both her straw bag and loin-cloth in the struggle, and she crouched naked and trembling, staring up at the men who surrounded her.

Sean spoke to her in soft soothing tones, but at first she would not reply. Then Alphonso questioned her, and as soon as the girl realized that he was of her own tribe, she seemed to relax slightly, and after another few gentle questions, made a hesitant breathless response.

'What does she say?' Claudia could not restrain her concern for the child.

'She is living here in the swamps to hide from the soldiers,' Sean answered. 'Renamo killed her mother and Frelimo took her father and the rest of her family away to cut trees in the forest. She escaped.'

They questioned the girl for almost an hour. How far ahead was the river? Was there a crossing? How many soldiers were there at the river? Where were the Frelimo cutting trees? And as she replied to each question, the girl's terror abated and she seemed to sense Claudia's sympathy and looked towards her with a pathetic childlike trust.

'I speak English a little, miss,' she whispered at last, and Claudia was startled.

'How did you learn?'

'At the mission, before the soldiers came and burned it and killed the nuns.'

'Your English is good.' Claudia smiled at her. 'What is your name, child?'

'Miriam, miss.'

'Don't get too chummy,' Sean warned Claudia grimly.

'She's a darling little thing.'

Sean seemed about to reply but then thought better of it and looked up at the sunset instead. 'Damn it, we have missed China's radio schedule. Let's get ready to move out. Time to get cracking.'

It took only minutes for them to gird up for the march, and with her pack on her back, Claudia asked, 'What about the girl?'

'We'll leave her here,' Sean said, but something in his voice and the way he looked away worried Claudia. She started to follow Sean as he stepped off the island into the water, and then she stopped and looked back. The black girl still squatted naked, staring after Claudia unhappily, but behind her stood Matatu, and he had the skinning knife in his right hand.

Realization dashed over Claudia like a huge wave of icy anger.

'Sean!' Her voice shook as she called him back. 'What are you going to do to this child?'

'Don't worry about it,' he told her brusquely.

'Matatu!' She began to tremble. 'What are you going to do?' And he grinned at her. 'Are you going to. . . ?' She drew her finger across her own throat, and Matatu nodded merrily and showed her the knife.

'*Ndio*,' he agreed. '*Kufa.*' She knew that Swahili word. Matatu had used it whenever her father had shot down an animal and Matatu had slit its throat. Suddenly she was shaking with anger. She rounded on Sean.

'You're going to murder her!' Her voice was shrill with outrage and horror.

'Wait, Claudia, listen. We can't leave her here. If they catch her . . . It would be suicide.'

'You bastard!' she screamed at him. 'You're as bad as any Renamo thug, as bad as China himself!'

'It's our lives, don't you understand? It's survival.'

'I can't believe what I'm hearing!'

'This is a hard, cruel land. If we are to survive, we have to live by those standards. We can't afford the folly of compassion.'

She wanted to attack him physically, she balled her fists in the effort of self-control, but her voice was still shrill.

'Compassion and conscience are all that separate us from the animals.' She drew a deep breath. 'If you value what there is between us, you won't say anything more, you won't try to rationalize what you almost did to this child.'

'You prefer to be captured by General China?' he demanded. 'This child, as you call her, won't hesitate to give them our exact whereabouts.'

'Don't, Sean! I'm warning you, everything you say is causing damage to our relationship that can never be repaired.'

'All right then.' Sean reached out to take her hands and draw her to him. 'What do you want us to do with her? I'll do whatever you say. You want us to turn her loose to report to the first Renamo patrol that comes along, I'll do it.'

Claudia was standing rigid in the circle of his arms and though the strident edge was gone from her voice, it was cold and determined.

'We'll take her with us.'

Sean dropped his arms. 'With us?'

'That's what I said. If we can't leave her, then that is the only solution.'

Sean stared at her and she went on firmly, 'You said you'd do whatever I say. You gave me a promise.'

He opened his mouth and then closed it and looked at the black girl. She had understood some of the argument, enough to know that her life was at stake and that Claudia was her champion, her saviour. When Sean saw the expression on the child's face, suddenly he was filled with shame and self-disgust. It was an alien sensation. During the bush war the Scouts had left no witnesses. This woman of his was turning him soft, he thought, and then smiled and shook his head – or perhaps she was simply humanizing him.

'All right.' He was still smiling. 'The girl comes with us, on condition that you forgive me.'

The kiss was brief, cool. Claudia's lips were tightly closed. Sean understood it would take time for her to recover from her outrage. She turned from Sean and lifted the black girl to her feet. Miriam clung to her thankfully.

'Fetch her loin-cloth,' Sean ordered Matatu. 'And put your knife away. The girl is coming with us.' Matatu rolled his eyes in disapproval. But he went to find the girl's single item of clothing.

While Miriam rewound the scrap of rag around her waist, Sergeant Alphonso leaned on his rifle and watched her with interest. It was obvious that he was not unhappy with the decision to spare the girl. Claudia did not approve of his appraisal of her protégée and she opened her small personal pack and dug out her one spare shirt, a camouflage Renamo sweat-shirt from General China's stores.

The shirt hung half down Miriam's thighs and satisfied Claudia's sense of decorum. The black girl was delighted, her terror of a few minutes before forgotten as she preened in her new finery.

'Thank you, Donna, thank you very much. You good lady.'

'All right.' Sean intervened. 'The fashion show is over, let's move out.' And Alphonso took Miriam's arm.

Only then the girl realized that she was being abducted, and she pulled away and broke into a passionate protest.

'Damn it!' Sean exploded. 'Now we are really in trouble!'

'What is it?' Claudia demanded.

'She isn't alone. She's got others with her.'

478

'I thought she had lost her parents!'

'That's right, but she's got a brother and sister hidden in the swamps. Two kids so young that they can't fend for themselves. Damn it! Damn it!' Sean repeated bitterly. 'Now what the hell do we do?'

'We fetch the children and take them with us also,' Claudia stated simply.

'Two brats! Are you crazy? We aren't running an orphanage.'

'Do we have to go over this one more time?' Claudia turned her back on him in exasperation and took Miriam's hand. 'It's all right. You can trust me. We'll look after all of you.'

The black girl quietened and stared at Claudia with a puppy's trust and adoration.

'Where are the children? We'll fetch them.'

'Come, Donna. I show you.' Miriam led her by the hand into the swamp.

It was almost dark when they reached the tiny island where Miriam had hidden the children in a clump of papyrus. When she parted the thick green stems, two pairs of huge dark eyes stared out at them like owlets from the nest.

'A boy.' Claudia lifted him out. He was five or six years of age, skinny and shivering with fright. 'And a girl.' She was younger, not more than four years old and Claudia exclaimed as she touched her.

'She's burning up, this child is very sick!' She was too weak to stand and she lay curled like a dying kitten, trembling and mewling softly.

'Malaria,' said Sean, and squatted beside the child. 'She's riddled with it.'

'We've got chloroquine in the medical pack.' Claudia reached for it briskly.

'This is madness!' Sean growled. 'We can't lumber ourselves with this bunch. It's a nightmare!'

'Do shut up!' Claudia snapped. 'How many chloroquine do I give her? The instructions say, "For children under six years, consult a physician." Thanks a lot, we'll try two tablets.'

As they worked over the child, Claudia asked Miriam, 'What are their names? What do you call the children?'

The answer was so long and complicated that even Claudia looked daunted, but she recovered quickly.

'I'll never pronounce that.' she said finally. 'We'll call them Mickey and Minnie.'

'Walt Disney will sue.' Sean warned. but she ignored him and wrapped Minnie in her own blanket.

'You'll have to carry her.' she told Sean matter-of-factly.

'If the little bugger pees on me. I'll wring her neck.' he protested.

'And Alphonso can carry Mickey.'

Sean could see that Claudia's maternal instincts were thoroughly aroused. and his resentment of this additional burden that had been thrust upon them was tempered by the tonic the new responsibilities had been to her. Claudia had sloughed off her exhaustion and lethargy and was more vigorous and incisive than she had been since Job's death.

Sean lifted the child's almost weightless little body on to his back and strapped it there with a strip of the blanket. The heat of the fever soaked through the blanket as though she were a hot-water bottle. However. it was a familiar experience to the child who had been carried since infancy in this fashion. and she was immediately quiet and somnolent. 'I still can't believe what's happening to me.' Sean muttered. 'A goddamned unpaid nursemaid at my age.' But he plunged once more into the swamp.

Before the night had half run. Miriam had proved an asset that far outweighed the additional burden that the two children had placed upon them. She knew the river area with the intimacy of a swamp creature. She went ahead with Matatu and guided him through the labyrinth of islands and lagoons. picking out the secret pathways that saved them hours of wearisome exploration.

A little after midnight. when Orion the great hunter stood directly overhead with his bow at full draw. Miriam led them out onto the bank of the Rio Save and pointed out the ford through which a man could wade to the far bank.

They rested and the women tended the children and fed them morsels of the leguan meat. The chloroquine had taken effect and the little girl was cooler and less fretful. After a hurried meal. the men concealed themselves in the reed-beds and stared out across the black waters in which the stars were reflected like drowning fireflies.

'This is the most dangerous point.' Sean whispered. 'China was patrolling the river all day yesterday in the Hind and he'll be back at first light. We don't dare waste time here. We have to get across and get clear before sunrise.'

'They'll be waiting on the far side,' Alphonso demurred, 'They'll be expecting us.'

'That's right,' Sean agreed. 'They are here, but we know they are here. We'll leave the women on this side and go across to clear the far bank. We can't use firearms, it will have to be knives and wire. It's wet work tonight.' He used the old Scouts' term for it. 'Sebenza enamanzi. In more ways than one, it will be wet work tonight.'

Sean's wire was a four-foot length of stainless steel, the single strand that he had cut from the winch cable of the Hercules aircraft before abandoning it. Job had carved two hardwood buttons and fixed them to either end of the wire to form grips. It rolled into a coil the size of a silver dollar and slipped easily into the grenade pocket of his webbing. Now Sean fished it out and unrolled it. He tested it, settling the wooden buttons between his fingers and jerking it tight, grunting with satisfaction at the familiar tension in the single resilient strand. Then he recoiled the wire and slipped it over his left wrist like a bangle.

The three of them stripped completely naked, wet clothing dripped water to alert an enemy or give him a hold in a hand-to-hand struggle. Each of them wore his knife on a short cord around his bare neck.

Sean went to where Claudia waited with the children in the reeds. When he kissed her, her lips were soft and warm and she clung to him briefly.

'Have you forgiven me?' he asked. For an answer she kissed him again.

'Come back soon,' she whispered.

The three men slid into the water soundlessly, keeping close contact, and dog-paddled quietly out from the bank letting the current carry them well down below the ford.

They landed in a bed of papyrus on the south bank and slid ashore on their bellies. Sean's naked white body gleamed in the starlight. He rolled in the sticky black swamp mud until it coated every inch of his skin, and then he scooped a double handful and rubbed it over his face.

'Ready?' he asked quietly, and freed the trench knife in its sheath at his throat.

'Let's go!'

481

They moved out away from the river and circled back upstream towards the ford. The swamps were confined to the north bank, while this side of the river was drier, and the forests grew almost to the river's edge. They stayed in the shadows beneath the trees for concealment. As they drew closer to the ford they moved more cautiously, spreading out, Sean in the middle and Alphonso and Matatu on the flanks.

Sean smelt Renamo before he saw them. It was the odour of stale native tobacco smoke and dried sweat in unwashed clothing and he froze, listening and staring ahead with all his soul concentrated on it.

A little ahead of him in the darkness, a man coughed softly and cleared his throat, and Sean placed him accurately. He sank down and touched the earth, sweeping a clear spot with his fingertips for his next footstep, so that no twig or dry leaf would betray him. One step at a time, he moved forward until he had the Renamo's head silhouetted against the starry sky. He was sitting behind an RPD machine-gun on its bipod, staring out across the river.

Sean waited and the minutes drew out, five then ten, each one a separate age. Then someone else yawned and stretched out on the left flank and immediately a third voice cautioned him to silence in an angry whisper.

'Three of them.' Sean memorized each position, and then withdrew as quietly and cautiously as he had come in.

On the edge of the forest Alphonso was waiting for him, and minutes later Matatu crept back to join them.

'Three,' Alphonso whispered.

'Yes, three,' Sean agreed.

'Four,' Matatu contradicted them both. 'There is another one just below the bank.' Matatu missed nothing and Sean accepted his estimate without reservation.

Only four Renamo in the ambush, Sean was relieved. He had expected more, but China must be spreading his men thinly to cover every path and every ford of the river.

'No noise,' Sean warned them. 'One shot and we'll have the entire army doing a war dance on our backs. Matatu, you take the one you found below the bank. Alphonso, the one in the reeds who spoke. I'll take the two in the centre.' He slipped the wire bangle off his left wrist and unrolled it, once more stretching and testing it between his hands to get the feel of it.

'Wait until you hear my man blow before you strike yours.' He reached out and lightly touched their shoulders, the ritual benediction, and then they separated and drifted away into the night, back towards the river.

The machine-gunner was exactly where Sean had left him, but as Sean moved in behind him a few scattered clouds obscured the stars, and Sean had to wait for them to clear. Every second's delay increased the chance of discovery and he was tempted to work only by sense of touch, but he restrained himself. As the sky cleared, he was glad he had done so. The sentry had removed his cap and was scratching the back of his head; that raised hand would have blocked the wire and prevented a clean kill. There would have been a scream, gunshots, and every Renamo within miles would have come down upon him.

He waited while the sentry relieved his itch, and readjusted his cap, then as he dropped his hands, Sean reached forward and looped the wire noose around his throat in one swift wrap. In the same movement he hauled back with the full strength of both his arms and shot his right knee between the man's shoulder-blades. The wire sliced through flesh and windpipe as though they were cheddar cheese. Sean felt the momentary check as the wire came up hard against the vertebrae of the neck, but he sawed with both hands, keeping all his weight on the wire, pushing with his knee.

The wire found the gap between the vertebrae and snicked clearly through it. The man's head fell forward, and tumbled into his own lap and the man blew. The air from his lungs rushed out through the open windpipe, in a soft sigh. It was the sound he had told Matatu and Alphonso to wait for. He knew they would be taking their victims at this moment, but there was no sound until the man Sean had killed flopped forward and his carotid artery discharged onto the earth with a regular hiss like milk from the teat jetting into the bucket under the milkmaid's practised fingers.

The sound alerted the fourth Renamo, the only one still alive, and he called out in a puzzled tone.

'What is it, Alves? What are you doing?'

The question guided Sean to him, and he had the knife out of its sheath, holding it under-hand so the point went up at an acute angle under the man's ribs. Sean pinned him down with his left hand, holding his throat closed to prevent him screaming, working the knife with his other hand, opening the wound, twisting and turning the blade with all the strength of his right wrist.

In thirty seconds, it was over. The last tremors shook the body beneath him and Sean released him and stood up. Matatu was already beside him, with his skinning knife ready. The knife and his hands were wet. His own work was done and he had come to help Sean, but it was not necessary.

They waited for a full minute, listening for any alarm, perhaps there was another sentry that even Matatu might have overlooked, but apart from the croaking of the frogs in the reed-beds and the whine of mosquitos there was no sound.

'Search them,' Sean ordered. 'Take whatever we can use.'

One of the rifles, all of the ammunition, half a dozen grenades, spare clothing, all the food. They gathered it up swiftly.

'That's it,' Sean said. 'Dump the rest of it.' They dragged the bodies down the bank and pushed them out into the current, then dropped the heavy machine-gun and the rest of the discarded equipment into the deep water beyond the reeds.

Sean glanced at his watch. 'We are running out of time, we must bring the others across.'

Claudia and Miriam and the children were still in the reed-beds on the south bank where they had left them.

'What happened? We didn't hear anything.' Claudia hugged Sean's naked wet chest with relief.

'Nothing to hear,' Sean told her, and picked up the sleeping children, one on each arm.

Across the current, they formed a human stanchion, locking arms together, bracing each other against the heavy pull of the water that was as deep as Claudia's chin. Without this support the women would have been swept away. Even with it the crossing was arduous and they dragged themselves onto the south bank near exhaustion.

Sean would not let them rest longer than the few minutes it took to dry Minnie and wrap her in a jacket they had looted from one of the dead Renamo; then he had them up again and chivvied them onwards into the forest.

'We have to get clear of the river before sunrise. China will be back as soon as it is light.'

*   *   *

484

General China picked out the group of men on the riverbank at two hundred feet. As the helicopter slanted in towards them, the down-draught of its rotors furred the surface of the Save river with a dark ruffle.

The Portuguese pilot set the machine down at the edge of the forest on the south bank and China clambered out of the weapons cockpit and went striding down towards the river. Although his face was an expressionless mask, his anger boiled behind it and glinted in his eyes. He took the dark glasses from his breast pocket and concealed his eyes behind the lens.

The circle of men opened respectfully and China stepped through and looked down at the disembodied human head that lay on the muddy bank. It had been washed up amongst the reeds, the fresh-water, crabs had nibbled it, and the water had leached the exposed flesh white and clouded the open eyes to opaque marbles, but the clean cut that had severed the neck was still as unmistakable as a hand-written signature.

'That's the white man's work,' China said softly. 'His Scouts called it "wet work", the wire was their trade-mark. When did it happen?'

'Last night.' Tippoo Tip tugged at his own beard with agitation. There had been no survivors of the ambush party, no one of which to make an example.

'You let them get through.' China accused coldly. 'You promised me they would never cross the river.'

'These dogs.' Tippoo Tip snarled. 'Those useless pigs.'

'They are your men,' China pointed out. 'And men take after those who command them. Their failure is your failure, General.'

It was said in front of his own staff, and Tippoo Tip growled with humiliation. He had made the promise and failed, and he shook with anger. He glared round at his men, looking for a victim, but they dropped their eyes and their faces were abject and obsequious. There was no relief there.

Suddenly he drew back his foot and swung a vicious kick at the severed head. The steel toe-cap of his boot crushed in the pulpy waterlogged nose.

'Dog!' he shouted, and booted the head again, sending it rolling down the bank. He followed it shouting with anger, aiming wild kicks at it, until it bounced like a football and plopped over the bank into the river.

He came back to General China, panting with rage.

'Very good, General,' China applauded him ironically. 'Very brave, what a pity you could not do the same to the white man.'

'I had every crossing of the river guarded,' Tippoo Tip started, and then broke off as he noticed the crudely stitched gash on China's cheek for the first time and he grinned viciously. 'You have been wounded. What misfortune. It wasn't the fault of the white man, was it? Surely not. You are too cunning to let him injure you, General China, apart from your ear, of course.'

It was China's turn to bridle with fury. 'If only I had my own men here. These stupid dogs of yours couldn't wipe their own backsides.'

'One of your men is a stooge,' Tippoo Tip roared back at him. 'He's running with the white man, my men are not traitors. I have them in my hands.' He showed those great paws, shaking them in China's face, and General China closed his eyes for a moment and drew a deep breath. He realized that they were on the brink of an irretrievable breach, a few more words like those exchanged and he would have no further co-operation from this great bearded ape. One day he would kill him, but he needed him today.

Today the most important thing in General China's world was getting his hands on the white man, alive if possible, but dead if it had to be. Without Tippoo Tip's help, there was no chance of that. His anger and retribution must wait for another time and opportunity.

'General Tippoo Tip,' his tone was conciliatory, almost humble, 'please forgive me. I let my disappointment run over my good sense. I know you did your best for me. We are, both of us, victims of our own people's incompetence. I ask you to ignore my bad manners.'

Tippoo Tip was taken off-balance as China had intended and the angry words died in his open mouth.

'Even though these fools were unable to stop them, now at last we know exactly where they are. We have their fresh spoor, and a full day in which to follow it. Let us make the most of this opportunity. Let's get this tiresome business over with. Then I, and my helicopter, will be entirely at your disposal for the more important task ahead of us.'

He saw that he had picked the right words. Tippoo Tip's rage gradually gave way to that sly and avaricious expression that China knew so well.

'I have already called up my best trackers,' he agreed. 'I'll have fifty of my men on their spoor within the hour, men who can run an eland off its feet. The white man will be in your hands before the sun sets this evening. This time there will be no mistake.'

'Where are these trackers?' China demanded.

'I have radioed.'

'I will send the helicopter to fetch them.'

'That will save valuable time.'

They watched the Hind rise and bore away northwards, low across the darkly flowing waters of the Save river. As it disappeared they both turned to stare towards the south.

'You no longer control the territory south of the river,' China pointed out. 'These are the forests that you so cunningly relinquished to the Frelimo.' He pointed at the dense stands of hardwoods that stood tall against the southern sky.

'The river is my front line,' Tippoo Tip conceded reluctantly. 'But the nearest Frelimo forces are still many miles further south. My patrols cover this ground without interference from them. The men I am sending after the white man will catch him long before he gets into Frelimo-held territory.' Tippoo Tip broke off and then pointed along the riverbank. 'Ah, here they come.' A long double file of heavily armed guerrillas came trotting down the footpath towards them. 'Fifty of my best men. You will eat white chickens for dinner tonight. Don't worry, my friend. They are as good as on your plate already.'

The two platoons of Renamo halted and fell out on the bank, waiting for their trackers. China was a good judge of troops. He walked amongst them, and he recognized in them that eagerness and enthusiasm tempered by discipline and professionalism that is the peculiar mark of first-class bush fighters. For once he agreed with Tippoo Tip. These were hard men who could be relied upon to get the job done. China beckoned the section leaders across to him.

'You know who you are chasing?' he asked, and they nodded. 'The white man is as dangerous as a wounded leopard, but I want him alive. Do you understand?'

'We understand, General.'

'You have a radio. I want a report of your progress every hour on the command frequency.'

'Yes, General.'

'And when you have the quarry in sight, call me. I will come in the *henshaw*. I want to be there at the death.'

The section leaders looked across the river, their expressions alert, and moments later even with his impaired hearing, China picked up the whistle of the Hind's turbos returning from the north.

'If you do your job, you will be rewarded. But if you fail me, you will regret it. You will regret it deeply.' General China promised them.

As soon as the helicopter landed the two trackers clambered down with alacrity from the small rear cabin and Tippoo Tip shouted at them and pointed to the outgoing spoor that Sean and his party had left.

Watching the trackers begin their task, China was even more confident of the outcome. These two were good. They made a quick cast ahead and then came back to the centre and squatted over the spoor, whispering together softly, touching the faint tracks with the supple wands of wild willow they each carried, intent as a pair of bloodhounds taking the scent of the chase. When they stood up again a change had come over them. They were determined and businesslike. They turned to face the southern forests and went away at a run.

Behind them, the two full platoons of camouflaged Renamo assault troopers fanned out into their running formation and set their pace to match the trackers.

'The white woman can never keep up that speed,' Tippoo Tip exulted. 'We will overtake them before they reach the Frelimo lines, we will have them before the end of this day. This time they'll not escape.' He turned back to China. 'Why don't we follow them in the helicopter?'

China hesitated. He did not want to explain the Hind's short-comings. It was better to let Tippoo Tip go on believing in its infallibility. He would not discuss with him the difficulty of bringing up sufficient fuel, nor the Hind's limited range even with full tanks, nor the fact that his Portuguese engineer had warned him that the turbos were long overdue for service, that the pilot had already reported a malfunction and loss of power in the starboard engine.

'I will wait here,' he said. 'When your men catch up with the white man, they will call on the radio. That is when I will follow them.'

488

China adjusted his dark glasses and sauntered across to the Hind. The pilot was waiting for him, leaning with assumed nonchalance against the camouflaged fuselage below the main cockpit.

'How is the engine behaving?' China asked in Portuguese.

'It is beginning to surge and miss. It needs to be worked on.'

'Fuel?'

'Main tanks are down to quarter. However, I still have the auxiliary.'

'The convoy of porters with the fuel will be at our forward base by tomorrow morning. The engineer can work on her tonight, but I have to have her on standby until dark. I'll need her when they catch up with the runaways.'

The pilot shrugged. 'I'll fly her, if you are willing to take the chance on that engine,' he agreed.

'Keep a listening watch on the radio,' China ordered. 'With luck it will all be over in a few hours.'

* * *

Sean realized that Claudia could not maintain this pace much further. She was running just ahead of him so he could study the changes in her that privation and hard living had brought about. She was so lean and wispy that her scanty threadbare shirt flapped around her flanks, and the legs of her trousers had been reduced by thorns and razor-edged grass to a fringe of tatters that hung halfway down her thighs; below that, the length of her legs was exaggerated by their extreme thinness, yet somehow they had retained their elegant high-bred lines. However, the thorns and sharp grass had wrought havoc on the exposed skin of her arms and legs. It looked as though she had been scourged by a cat-o'-nine-tails, some of the scratches were healed, others scabbed over, but a few still bled.

Her hair had grown into a lank sweat-tangled mop that thumped between her prominent bony shoulder-blades with each pace, and her back was so thin that he could have counted the knobs of her vertebrae beneath her shirt. The perspiration had soaked through in a dark line down her spine, and hard exercise had firmed her buttocks into a pair of Indiarubber balls in the sun-bleached cotton pants; through a tiny three-cornered tear a tender flash of her white bottom winked at him with each pace.

Her legs were floppy with exhaustion, throwing out sideways and her ankles were loose and wobbled under her.

He would have to let her rest very soon and yet she had not complained, not once in all the long tortured hours since they had left the river, and he grinned fondly as he remembered the spoilt arrogant bitch that had stepped off the Boeing at Harare airport so many aeons ago. This was a different woman, tough, determined and with a spirit as resilient as a Damascus steel blade. He knew that she would never give up, she would keep going until she killed herself. He reached forward and tapped her shoulder.

'Ease up, wench. We'll take ten.'

When she pulled up she was unsteady on those long legs and he put an arm around her shoulders to steady her. 'You're a ruddy marvel do you know that?' He eased her down to sit with her back against one of the le 'wood trees and unscrewed the stopper on his water-bottle and passed it to her.

'Give Minnie to me. It's time for her chloroquine.' Claudia's voice was husky with tiredness. Sean swung the little girl off his back and placed her in Claudia's lap.

'Remember, ten minutes, that's all.'

Alphonso had taken the break to rig the radio, Mickey was squatting on one side of him, Miriam on the other. They watched with fascination as he tuned the set and began searching the bands. There was the crackle and buzz of static followed by some faint extraneous snatches of Afrikaans, and then an excited voice speaking in Shangane, very close and loud.

'Very close now,' it said, and the reply came immediately.

'Keep going hard. Push them. Don't let them escape. Call me as soon as you catch them.' That voice was unmistakable and they did not need the acknowledgement to confirm it.

'Very well, General China.'

The transmission ended and Sean and Alphonso exchanged a quick hard frown.

'Very close,' said the Shangane. 'We can't outrun them.'

'You might be able to get away,' Sean said, 'on your own.'

Alphonso hesitated and looked sideways at Miriam. The Shangane maid returned his glance with open trusting eyes and Alphonso coughed and scratched himself with embarrassment.

'I'll stay,' he muttered, and Sean laughed bitterly and said in English, 'Join the club, mate. That little witch didn't take long

490

to hook you. These ruddy sheilas will be the death of all of us yet, you mark my words.'

Alphonso frowned, he did not understand and Sean switched back into Shangane. 'Pack up the radio. If you are going to stand with us, we'd best find a good place to do it. Your dung-eating Renamo brothers are going to be with us very soon.'

Sean turned and looked across at Matatu, and instantly he was on his feet.

'That was China on the radio,' he told him in Swahili.

'He hisses like a cobra,' Matatu nodded.

'His men are on our spoor, they boast to him that they are very close. Are there any more tricks we can use now, old friend?'

'Fire?' Matatu suggested, but without conviction, and Sean shook his head.

'The wind is against us, we'd cook ourselves if we torched the forest.'

Matatu hung his head. 'If we keep the women and children with us, there are no more tricks,' he admitted. 'We are slow, and we leave a spoor that a blind man can follow in a moonless night.' He shook his small grizzled head miserably. 'The only trick we have left is to fight them, and after that we are dead, my *Bwana*.'

'Go back, Matatu. Find how close behind us they really are. We will go ahead and find a good place to fight them.' He touched the little man's shoulder, and then let him go. Sean watched him disappear amongst the tree-trunks and then deliberately altered his expression before he turned to Claudia, striking a lighter more carefree pose and putting a lift in his tone.

'How's our patient?' he asked. 'She looks pretty chirpy to me.'

'The chloroquine has done wonders.' Claudia bounced the child on her lap and as if to confirm her improvement, Minnie stuck her thumb in her mouth and smiled shyly around it at Sean. He felt that smile tug at him with wholly unexpected poignancy.

Claudia laughed. 'No female is immune to your fatal charms. You have collected yourself another fan.'

'Typical woman, all she really wants is a free ride.' But he stroked the child's soft woolly little head. 'All right, sweetness, your horsey is ready to go.'

Trustingly Minnie held out both arms and he swung her up on to his back and strapped her there.

Claudia pulled herself stiffly to her feet and for a moment

leaned against him. 'Do you know something? You are a much nicer person than you pretend to be.'

'Fooled you, didn't I?'

'I'd like to see you with a baby of your own,' she whispered.

'Now you really terrify me. Let's go before you come up with any more crazy ideas like that one.'

But the idea lingered with him as they ran on through the forest, a son of his own from this woman.

He had never even thought about that before, and then, as though to complement the idea, he felt a tiny hand reach across his shoulder from behind and touch his beard, stroking it as lightly as an alighting butterfly. Minnie was reciprocating that caress he had bestowed on her a few minutes earlier and for a moment his throat closed up and made it difficult for him to breathe. He took her tiny hand in his, and it was silken and fragile as the wing of a humming-bird and he was overcome with a feeling of terrible regret. Regret that there would never be a son, he accepted that at last, nor a daughter. It was almost over. The hunting pack was very close behind. They could never outrun them. There was no escape, all they could hope for was a good place in which to make the final stand. After that there was nothing, no escape, no future.

He was so wrapped up in his melancholy that he had run out into the open before he realized it. Claudia pulled up so sharply in front of him that he almost ran into her. He stopped at her side and they looked about them with puzzled uncertainty.

The forest had been laid waste. For as far ahead as they could see the great hardwoods had been swept away as though by a hurricane. Only the stumps remained, raw and bleeding gum as red as heart's blood. The earth was torn and scarred, where the huge trunks had come crashing down. Bright piles of sawdust remained where their branches had been stripped and the logs cut into lengths, and then between the windrows of discarded branches and wilting boughs were the drag roads along which the precious timber had been hauled away.

Miriam stopped beside Sean. 'This is where my people were forced to work,' she said softly. 'Frelimo came and took them to cut the trees. They chained them together and made them work until the meat was torn from the bones of their hands. They beat them like oxen and worked them until they fell and could not rise.'

'How many people?' Sean asked. 'So many trees have been destroyed.'

'Perhaps a man or woman died for every tree,' Miriam whispered. 'They took everybody, thousands upon tens of thousands.' She pointed to the horizon. 'They work far south now and they leave no tree standing.'

Sean felt the anger beginning to rise through his amazement. This was destruction on a scale that affronted the law of nature and the sanctity of life itself. It was not just that those trees had taken three hundred years to reach their full majesty, and had been destroyed with a few hours' callous work with the axe blades. It was more, much more. This forest was the source and fountain of myriad forms of life, insect and bird and mammal and reptile, of man himself. In this vast devastation, all would perish.

It did not end there. With his own fate determined, with a term and a number of the hours that remained of his own life, Sean was overtaken by a prophetic melancholia. He realized that the destruction of this forest was symbolic of the predicament of the entire continent. In a few fleeting decades, Africa had been overtaken by its own inherent savagery. The checks that had been placed upon it by a century of colonialism had been struck off. Chains perhaps those checks had been, but once freed of them, the peoples of Africa were rushing headlong, with almost suicidal abandon, towards their own destruction.

Sean felt himself shaking with impotent rage at the folly of it and at the same time saddened, sickened almost unto death, by the terrible tragedy of it all.

'If I have to die,' he thought, 'then it's best to do so before I see everything I love, the land, the animals, the people, all of it destroyed.'

With his arm round Claudia's thin shoulders and the little black girl strapped on his back, he turned and looked back the way they had come and, at that moment, Matatu came scampering out of the forest behind them.

There was desperate urgency in his gait and the fear of death in his small wizened features.

'They are very close, my *Bwana*. They have two trackers leading them. I watched them work, we will not throw them off. They are good.'

'How many troopers with them?' With an effort Sean cast off the oppressive mantle of dejection.

'As many as the grass on the plains of Serengeti,' Matatu replied. 'They run like a pack of wild dogs on the hunt and they are hard men and fierce. Even the three of us will not stand too long against them.'

Sean roused himself and looked around him. The cut line in which they stood was a natural killing ground, devoid of cover except for the knee-high stumps of hardwood. The open ground stretched two hundred metres wide to where the dead wood was piled in untidy windrows, the leaves long withered and browned, the branches forming a natural barricade.

'We'll make our stand there,' Sean decided swiftly and signalled Alphonso forward. They crossed the open ground at a run, bunched up with the two women in the middle. Miriam was dragging her little brother along by one arm. Alphonso ran protectively beside them. The big Shangane was heavily burdened with the radio and the packs of ammunition and stores they had picked up from the ambush at the Save river, nevertheless he had also carried Mickey whenever the boy tired, only setting him down on his own feet for short intervals. The three Shanganes, man, woman and boy child, had very swiftly formed their own distinct core within the band, drawn together by tribal loyalties and natural physical attraction. Sean knew he could rely on Alphonso to take care of his own, and that allowed him to concentrate on his own particular charges, Claudia and Matatu and now the little girl.

Alphonso needed no orders. Like Sean he had a soldier's eye for terrain and he ran unerringly towards a section of the tumble of discarded branches that formed a natural redoubt, and which commanded the best field of fire across the cut line.

Swiftly they settled in, dragging some of the heavier branches into place to strengthen the position, laying out their weapons and spare ammunition, making their very limited preparations to stand off the first rush of the attackers.

Claudia and Miriam had taken the children a little further back to where a hollow in the earth and two especially large tree-stumps formed some sort of shelter. His own preparations complete, Sean crossed to them quickly, and squatted beside Claudia.

'As soon as the shooting starts, I want you to take Miriam and the children and run for it,' he told her. 'Keep heading south.' He broke off as he realized that she was shaking her head, and her jaw was clenched obstinately.

'I've run far enough,' she told him. 'I'm staying with you.' She laid her hand on his arm. 'No, don't argue. It would be a waste of time.'

'Claudia!'

'Please don't,' she forestalled him. 'There isn't much time left, don't spend it arguing.'

She was right, of course. To try and run further on her own was pointless, not with two children to care for and a team of fifty Renamo on her spoor. He nodded.

'All right,' he agreed, and took the Tokarev pistol from his belt, cocked it and carefully engaged the safety-catch. 'Take this.'

'What's that for?' She stared at the weapon with distaste.

'I think you know what it's for.'

'The same way as Job?'

He nodded. 'It would be easier than going China's way.'   •

She shook her head. 'I couldn't,' she whispered. 'If there is no other way, at the end, won't you do it for me?'

'I'll try,' he said. 'But I don't think I'll have the guts. Here, take it, just in case.' Reluctantly she accepted the pistol and tucked it into her belt.

'Now kiss me,' she said.

Matatu's whistle interrupted their embrace. 'I love you,' Sean murmured in her ear.

'I'll love you . . .' she replied, 'through all eternity.'

He left her and crawled back into the piles of dead wood. At Matatu's side he sank down and peered out through the chink between two branches towards the edge of the forest.

For many minutes he saw nothing, and then there was a shadowy flit of movement amongst the boles of the standing hardwood, and Sean laid his right hand on the pistol grip of the AKM rifle and raised it until the buttstock touched his cheek.

The silence drew out in the languorous sunlit afternoon while they waited. No bird sang, no creature moved, until at last there was a muted bird whistle from the edge of the forest and a man shape detached itself and flitted into the opening, showing for just a small part of a second and then disappearing behind one of the thick tree-stumps. As soon as it was gone another broke from the tree-line a hundred metres further to the left and darted forward. This one also disappeared and almost immediately, out on the right, a third Renamo guerrilla emerged.

'Three only,' Sean murmured, they were not going to expose

more men than that and these were good. They advanced in fleeting rushes. never two together. widely spread out and wary as old tom-leopards coming in to the bait.

'What a pity.' Sean thought. 'We are only going to get one out of this lot. I had hoped for a better killing to get us off the mark.' He concentrated on the advancing scouts. trying to pick the most dangerous of their enemies.

'Probably the one in the centre.' he decided. and almost immediately had his choice confirmed as he saw the flick of the man's hand from behind the stump that hid him. He was signalling one of the others forward. co-ordinating the advance and that marked him as the main man. the one to take out first.

'Let him come in close.' Sean told himself. The AKM was no sniping rifle and he didn't trust its accuracy over a hundred metres. He waited. willing the man in. watching for him over the sights of the rifle.

The Renamo jumped up and kept coming. Sean saw that he was young. mid-twenties. with bandoliers of ammunition over both shoulders. and a Rastafarian hair-style. ribbons of camouflage rag braided into his hair. There was an Arabian cast to his features. and an amber patina to his skin. a good-looking lad except that his left eye was a little askew and it gave his face a sly knowing expression.

Close enough to see the cast in his eye was close enough. Sean lined up carefully on the tree-stump behind which the Renamo had disappeared and drew a breath. exhaled half of it and let the first joint of his right forefinger rest lightly on the trigger.

The Renamo popped up into his sights. Sean took him low. deliberately declining a clean kill. He knew what damage the 7.62 bullet would do as it plunged through his belly at over three thousand feet a second. and he knew from bitter experience just how unnerving it was to have one of your comrades lying in no-man's land with his guts shot out screaming for water and mercy. In the Scouts they called them 'warblers'. and a warbler in good voice could inhibit an attack almost as effectively as a well-placed RPD machine-gun.

Sean heard the bullet hit the Renamo in the stomach. that meaty thump like a water melon dropped on a stone floor. and he went down out of sight in the trash and debris.

Instantly there was a heavy volley of rifle fire from the edge of the forest. but it was obvious from the wild aim that they had not spotted Sean and the firing stuttered swiftly into silence. Renamo was conserving ammunition, a sure sign of their discipline and training. Second-rate African troops started firing at the beginning of a contact and kept shooting until their last round was expended.

'These lads know their business.' Sean confirmed Matatu's estimate. 'We aren't going to hold them long.' The two guerrillas were still pinned down in the middle of the cut line, and there was a low hollow groan from out there as the first pangs of the belly wound hit the downed man.

'Sing to us, Daddy-oh!' Sean encouraged him. 'Let your pals know how it hurts.' But he was studying the forest edge, trying to get some hint of the next play before it developed.

'Now, they'll make a pincer move to try to out-flank us,' he guessed. 'But which flank, left or right?' And as if in answer he saw a tiny blur of movement in the forest. One of them was moving right.

'Alphonso,' Sean called softly. 'They are going to try the right. Stay here. Hold the centre.'

Sean crawled back, until he was hidden by the high windrow of brush. Then he rose to his feet, and ran doubled over, out to the right flank.

Four hundred metres out he dropped to his knees and crawled forward, finding another position facing the forest wall. He wriggled in behind a protective stump and marshalled his breathing, watching the tree-line, the AKM set on automatic fire, and his thumb on the safety-catch.

He had anticipated the next move almost perfectly, the flanking movement came out of the forest only a hundred metres further to his right. A detachment of eight troopers, they came all together, trying to reach the cover of the windrow in a single concerted rush, and Sean let them get half way across the cut line.

'This is better. I should be able to get a brace out of this covey,' he told himself. He had them in enfilade, his fire would be coming in from their flank and sweeping the line. He picked out the section leader who was running slightly ahead of the line. Sean led him by a man's length so that he would run into the stream of fire, taking him at knee height because the AKM rode up brutally in automatic and he held the trigger down.

The section leader dropped as though he had fallen over a trip wire, and the two men following him ran into the same burst. Sean saw the bullets hit them. One of them took it in the shoulder, and a puff of dust flew from his camouflage tunic to mark the strike. The other was a head shot, a clean hit in the temple and as he went down his base-ball cap fluttered from his head like a maimed dove.

'Three.' Sean changed magazines, pleased with the result. He had expected one and hoped for two.

The rest of them had turned and were racing back for the forest, the attack broken completely. Sean got off another quick burst before they reached the trees, and thought he saw one of them hunch his shoulders and lurch to the shot, but he kept going and disappeared.

Almost immediately there was another burst of firing back in the centre, and Sean jumped up from behind his stump and ran back to help Alphonso.

As he ran somebody opened up on him from the forest. Shot passed close to his head with that vicious whiplashing sound that made his adrenalin spurt hotly into his bloodstream. He ducked his head and ran on. He was enjoying himself, riding the curling wave of his terror.

In the centre there was a sharp fire-fight raging. Renamo was trying to rush the open ground, and they were almost across when Sean fell flat in the brush near Alphonso and added the weight of his fire to the defence. The attack wavered and broke, just short of the row of deadwood behind which they lay. The Renamo went ducking and dodging back between the tree-stumps with AK fire kicking up dust around them.

'Two!' Alphonso shouted across at Sean. 'I put two of them down.' But Matatu was tugging at Sean's arm and pointing out to the left flank. Sean was just able to get a glimpse of another group of Renamo cutting across the cut line and reaching cover on this side. The attacks on the right and centre had been diversions. Now there were a dozen or so Renamo coming in behind them, within minutes they would be surrounded, pinned down helplessly.

'Alphonso, they have got in our rear,' Sean called across.

'There was nothing we could do to stop them,' Alphonso answered. 'There are too many, we are too few.'

'I am going back to hold the rear, I'll be with the women.'

'They won't attack again,' Alphonso told him flatly. 'Now that

498

they have us surrounded they will wait for the *henshaw* to come.'

A burst of automatic fire raked the pile of deadwood, and they ducked instinctively.

'They are only shooting to hold us,' Alphonso called. 'They don't have to risk losing more men.'

'How long until the helicopter arrives?' Sean wanted his own estimate confirmed.

'Not more than an hour,' Alphonso told him with finality. 'Then it will all be over very quickly.'

Alphonso was right. Against the Hind, there was no defence, no more tricks to play.

'I'm leaving you here,' Sean repeated, and crawled back to the hollow in which the women were concealed.

Claudia had Minnie on her lap, but she looked up expectantly as Sean slid down the shallow side of the hollow.

'They've got in behind us,' Sean told her shortly. 'We are surrounded.' He dumped the empty AK magazines in front of her. 'There are boxes of spare ammo in Alphonso's pack. You know how to fill these.'

It would keep her busy. The next hour was going to be difficult to live through. Sean crawled to the back lip of the hollow and peered over the edge.

He saw something move in the dried brown leaves fifty paces ahead of him and he fired a quick burst into the brush. His fire was returned from three or four positions in their rear. AK bullets cracked overhead and behind him Minnie wailed with fright. The minutes dragged past slowly, the silence broken every few seconds by sporadic bursts of holding fire from the Renamo positions.

Claudia crawled up beside Sean and stacked the replenished magazines at his right elbow.

'How many boxes left?' he asked.

'Ten,' she told him, and pressed a little closer to him.

It didn't really matter that there were only two hundred rounds remaining in Alphonso's pack. Sean looked up at the sky, any moment now they would hear the whistle of the Hind's turbos.

Claudia read his thoughts, and she groped for his hand. Lying in the hot African sun, they held hands and waited. There was nothing left to say, nothing more that they could do. No defence, however feeble. All that remained was to wait for the inevitable.

Matatu touched Sean's leg. It wasn't necessary to say anything.

Sean cocked his head and picked up the sound. It was higher and steadier than the soughing of the afternoon breeze in the forest-tops.

Claudia squeezed his hand very hard, digging her fingernails into his palm. She had heard it also.

'Kiss me.' she whispered. 'One last time.' And he laid the rifle down and rolled onto his side to take her in his arms. They strained together, holding with all their strength.

'If I have to die,' Claudia whispered, 'I'm glad it will be like this.' And Sean felt her press the loaded Tokarev into his hand.

'Goodbye, my darling,' she said.

He knew that he had to do it, but he did not know where he would find the courage.

The sound of the Hind's engines was rising into a high penetrating shriek.

He slid the safety-catch to the 'off' position and lifted the Tokarev gently. Claudia's eyes were tightly closed and she had turned her head half away. A little sweat-damp tendril of dark hair hung down in front of her ear, and he could see the artery beating under the creamy skin of her temple that the curl had protected from the sun. It was the most difficult task he had ever set himself, but he raised the muzzle of the Tokarev towards her temple.

There was a shattering explosion of a shell-burst on the lip of their shelter. Instinctively Sean pulled Claudia down to protect her. He thought for a moment that the Hind had opened fire, but that was impossible, it was still out of sight and range.

A further series of explosions crashed out in rapid succession, and Sean lowered the pistol and released Claudia. He rolled to the lip of the hollow, and saw that a heavy barrage of fire was sweeping the Renamo positions. Mortar fire, Sean recognized the characteristic bursts of three-inch mortar shells and then the rushing smoke trails of RPG rockets amongst the trees of the forest. The rattling din of small arms drowned out even the sound of the approaching Hind. The entire situation had changed.

Suddenly they were in the midst of a battle, and Sean saw figures running wildly amongst the windrows and stumps, firing as they ran.

'Frelimo!' Matatu was tugging at Sean's arm and screeching with excitement. 'Frelimo!'

Only then Sean understood. Their desultory exchange of fire

with the Renamo pursuers must have called up a large force of Frelimo troops who had been massed in the immediate vicinity, probably preparing to attack the Save river line.

Now the fifty Renamo guerrillas suddenly found themselves attacked by a vastly superior Frelimo force. Judging by the intensity of fire, Sean estimated that there were several hundred Frelimo out there in the forest, front-line regular troops in battalion strength.

He saw the small party of Renamo who had cut them off abandon their positions amongst the dead wood of the cut line, and scuttle away in wild disorder with mortar shells bursting amongst them. Sean snatched up the AKM and helped them on their way with a long burst. One of the running men fell and flopped around into the brush like a beached catfish.

Then he spotted a sweep line of Frelimo infantry coming in from the left at a run. Their camouflage field dress was East German issue, the blotches of green and brown distinctly different from the Renamo tiger-stripes.

Renamo or Frelimo were equally dangerous for them. Sean pulled Claudia down beside him.

'Don't move. The Frelimo probably don't know we are here. They might just chase off the Renamo and overlook us. We've still got a chance.'

Minnie was wailing loudly, terrified by the uproar. Sean called urgently to Miriam, 'Keep her quiet. Stop her screaming.'

The Shangane girl pulled the child down beside her and covered her mouth and nose with her hand, cutting off her wails abruptly.

Sean raised one eye above the lip of the hollow and saw the Frelimo sweep line still bearing down on them, tough-looking troopers, firing from the hip as they came. They would overrun the hollow within seconds. He raised the AKM. Their salvation had been fleeting, the only real change was that now they would be killed by Frelimo rather than by Renamo.

As he raised the AKM and aimed at the belly of the nearest of the oncoming Frelimo troopers, the target was blotted out by a tall curtain of flying dust and from the sky above came the thunderous roll of the heavy 12.7mm cannon. The Frelimo sweep line dissolved before Sean's eyes, blown away by the Hind's concentrated fire, and the dust rolled over the hollow in which

501

they lay, concealing them from the air in those crucial seconds that the Hind hovered above them.

Now all was chaos, two forces inextricably mixed up in the deep forest, mortar and rocket fire crashing through the trees, while over the battlefield the Hind hovered, sending in rockets and bursts of cannonfire to make the confusion complete.

Sean slapped Matatu on the shoulder. 'Fetch Alphonso,' he ordered, and the little Ndorobo disappeared into the dust and gunfire, to emerge only a minute later with the huge Shangane close behind him.

'Alphonso, get ready to make another run for it,' Sean told him tersely. 'Frelimo and Renamo are giving each other a full go out there. We'll try to sneak away before the Hind spots us.' Sean broke off and sniffed the air, and then raised himself quickly on his knees to look back.

Already the air around them was turning a dirty grey, and above the din of battle and the whine of turbos, Sean heard the first faint crackle of burning brush.

'Fire!' he snapped. 'And it's upwind of us!'

One of the exploding rockets had ignited the rows of piled deadwood, and now a dense cloud of smoke rolled down over the hollow where they lay, stinging their eyes and making them cough and choke.

'Now, we have no choice, it's run or cook.' The crackle and roar of the flames was already drowning out the din of battle. Dimly they heard the shrieks of wounded men caught up in the path of the surging fire.

'Let's go!' Sean swept Minnie onto his back and the child locked both arms around his neck and clung to him like a little black flea. Sean pulled Claudia to her feet. Alphonso had Mickey sitting perched on his shoulders, his legs dangling over the bulky radio pack. Miriam was at his side clinging to the arm which held his rifle.

The smoke rolled over them, thick as oil, and they ran with the wind, bunched up to keep contact with each other. The smoke filled their lungs and blotted out the sky, screening them from the fighting men in the forest around them and from the helicopter gunship that hovered above them, and the fire raged close behind them driving them on wildly, but gaining on them with every second.

Sean felt the heat fan the back of his neck, and Minnie

squeaked as a flying spark touched her cheek. Gasping for breath, Claudia stumbled and sank to her knees, but Sean hauled her to her feet and dragged her onwards.

Sean was suffocating, each breath burned all the way down into his lungs. They couldn't go much farther. The heat licked their skin and flying sparks dashed against them and the child on Sean's back screamed in agony and pawed ineffectually at her tortured body as though assailed by a swarm of wasps. She lost her grip and would have fallen, but Sean snatched her off his back and carried her under one arm.

Suddenly, they were into another open cut line. Only dead stumps surrounded them, standing like tombstones in the dense banks of rolling smoke, and the sandy earth beneath their feet had been ploughed up by the teams of loggers.

'Down!' Sean pushed Claudia flat on the ground and placed Minnie in her arms.

The child was struggling wildly. 'Hold her still!' Sean shouted and stripped off his shirt.

'Lie flat, face down!' he ordered and obediently Claudia rolled on her stomach, holding Minnie under her. Sean wrapped the shirt around both their heads to filter out the smoke and sparks and soot. He tore the stopper out of his water-bottle and soaked the shirt, splashing their hair and soaking their clothing.

Minnie was still shrieking and struggling, but Claudia held her down firmly. Sean knelt beside them and scooped loose sand over them, burying them under a mound of earth, like one of those beach games that children play. The smoke was thinner closer to the earth, they could still breathe. Alphonso had seen what he was doing and followed his example, burying Miriam and her little brother in the sand nearby.

Live sparks swirled through the blinding clouds of smoke and settled on Sean's bare skin. They stung like the poisonous bites of safari ants. Sean felt his beard begin to frizzle and his eyeballs drying out in the heat. He emptied his pack on to the ground and pulled the empty canvas bag over his head, poured the contents of the second water-bottle over his torso, and then fell on his back and scooped the loose sand over himself and lay still.

With his head low to the ground the air was breathable, just sufficient oxygen in it to keep him conscious, but his head buzzed and swirled dizzily and the heat came at him in crushing blasts.

He smelled the canvas bag over his head begin to smoulder and the thin layer of sand that covered his body scalded him like a pot fresh from the furnace. He heard the roar of the flames rise to a crescendo, the dry branches crackled like rifle fire in the inferno. The fire was in the windrows all around them, but the wind, generated by its own heat, drove it swiftly onwards.

It swept past them, the roaring subsided, and for an instant the smoke clouds opened allowing them a fleeting gasp of sweet air, but the heat around them was still so fierce that Sean dared not shake off the protective layer of sand that covered his body.

Gradually the heat dissipated, and the gusts of cooler sweeter air became more frequent. Sean sat up and lifted the canvas pack from his head. His skin burned as though acid had been splattered upon it, and the bright red spots where sparks had touched him would soon be blisters.

He crawled to the mound of earth that covered Claudia and the child and scraped it away from their heads. The shirt had kept their mouths and noses clear, and when they sat up and shook off the sand, he saw that they had come off much better than either he or Alphonso had. The fire had run past them, but the air around them was still so thick with smoke that the sky was blotted out.

Sean hauled them to their feet. 'We have to get well away before the smoke clears,' he croaked hoarsely. His throat felt as though he had swallowed a handful of crushed glass, and tears spilled down his sooty scorched cheeks.

Clinging together, picking their way through the blackened, smouldering landscape, like a party of bedraggled soot-covered phantoms, they limped through the swirling fog of smoke. The earth was hot as a flow of volcanic lava, scorching the soles of their boots, but they carried the children, and avoided the piles of glowing ash.

Twice they heard the Hind above them, but although they peered up with red and weeping eyes, they caught not a glimpse of it through the drifting blue clouds and there was no sign of pursuit by either Renamo or Frelimo. The opposing forces had been scattered and swept away by the flames.

'The little bugger has asbestos-lined feet,' Sean muttered, as he watched Matatu dance ahead of them through the thinning smoke. On Sean's back, Minnie whimpered fretfully with the pain of her blisters and at their first rest stop Sean gave her half an aspirin and a swallow from their one remaining bottle of water.

The sunset that evening filled the heavens with flaming crimsons and sombre purples. In the darkness, they lay huddled together, too exhausted and weakened by the smoke to post sentries, and their sleep was interrupted by bouts of painful lung-tearing coughing.

In the dawn, the wind veered into the south but the smoke still hung over the land like a heavy river-mist, reducing visibility to a few hundred feet.

Sean and Claudia treated the children first, smearing their blisters and burns with yellow iodine paste, and though Mickey bore it with the stoicism of a Shangane warrior, the little girl whined with the sting of the iodine and Sean had to take her on his lap and blow on her injuries to cool them.

Once the children were taken care of, the women tended their men. The burns on Sean's chest and back were all superficial, but Claudia treated them with a gentleness that reflected her gratitude and her complete love.

Neither of them spoke of that moment when he had lifted the Tokarev pistol to her temple. They probably never would, but both of them would be conscious of it for ever more. It would always be there between them: for Sean the most horrific moment of his life, worse even than that of Job's death; for Claudia, an affirmation of his devotion to her. She knew that he would have found the strength to do it, but she knew also that it would have cost him dearer than the sacrifice of his own life. She needed no more proof of his love.

The children needed water desperately, they were desiccated by the heat of the flames and the smoke. Sean gave half the remaining water to them, and shared the remainder disproportionately amongst the adults, most of it to the two women and a bare taste to the men.

'Matatu,' he said in a harsh gravelly whisper, 'if you don't find us water before nightfall, then we are as dead as if the *henshaw* had blown us into dust with its cannons.'

They limped on through the blackened and smouldering forest, and in the late afternoon Matatu led them to a shallow clay pan, surrounded by the smoking stumps of burned-out trees. In the centre of the pan, thick with black ash and the charred bodies of small creatures, of snakes and rats and civet cats that had fled there for protection from the flames, was a puddle of filthy water.

Sean strained it through his shirt and they drank it as though it were nectar, groaning with the pleasure through their scorched and smoke-abraded throats. When they had drunk until their bellies ached, they scooped the water over their heads and let it soak their clothing, and they laughed weakly with the joy of it.

A mile beyond the waterhole, they reached the line at which the wind had changed and held the fire, driving it back upon itself. They left behind them the devastation of black ash and smouldering stumps and camped that night amongst the confusion of withered dead branches where the logging gangs had wrought almost as much destruction as the flames had done.

For the first time since the fire, Alphonso rigged the radio aerial, and they gathered round the set and listened for General China's taunts and threats. They all stiffened instinctively as they recognized his voice, but he was talking in Shangane and they could hear the sound of the helicopter's engines in the background. His transmissions were terse and enigmatic, and the replies from his subordinates were equally abrupt and business-like.

'What do you think he is up to?' Sean asked Alphonso, and the Shangane shook his head.

'It sounds like he is moving troops into fresh positions.' But there was no conviction in his tone.

'He hasn't given up?' Sean said. 'He may have lost our spoor in the burn, but I don't think he has given up.'

'No,' Alphonso agreed. 'I know him well. He has not given up. He will follow us all the way. General China is a man who hates very well. He will not let us go.'

'We are in Frelimo-held territory now. Do you think he will follow us in here?'

Alphonso shrugged. 'He has the *henshaw*, he does not have to worry too much about Frelimo. I think he will follow us wherever we go.'

General China made his last transmission and it was obvious he was arranging for refuelling. He had changed to Portuguese and the reply seemed to be from a ground engineer in the same language. Alphonso translated.

'The porters have arrived. We now have reserves of two thousand litres.'

506

China's voice, 'What about the spare booster pump?'

'It's here, my General,' the engineer again. 'I can change it tonight.'

'We must be airworthy again by first light tomorrow.'

'I will have it ready by then. I guarantee it, General.'

'Very well, I'll be landing in a few minutes. Be ready to begin work immediately,' China ordered and then signed off.

They listened for another ten minutes, until it was fully dark, but there were no further transmissions and Alphonso reached across to turn off the radio. On an impulse Sean prevented him doing so and instead switched frequencies. Almost at once, he picked up the South African military traffic. It was much stronger now, they were that much closer to the border on the Limpopo river, and to Sean the sound of Afrikaans was a comfort and a promise.

After a few minutes, Sean sighed and switched off the set. 'Alphonso, you take the first sentry. Go!' he ordered.

*   *   *

With the threat of aerial-surveillance reduced, Sean decided to resume daylight travel, and every mile they covered towards the south the signs left by the logging gangs were fresher and more numerous.

On the third day after the fire, Matatu led them on a wide detour. The hardwood stumps had been cut very recently and they were still weeping sap. The leaves on the discarded branches piled in tall windrows had not dried out and were still green and pliant. Matatu cautioned them to silence and as they trudged on between the piled rows of trash, they heard not far off, the whine of chain saws, and the doleful work chant of the labour gangs.

The forest around them was full of human activity, and the soft soil carried the prints of thousands of bare feet and the skid marks of heavy logs being dragged and manhandled towards the rough logging roads. However, so skilfully did Matatu shepherd them through the torn and despoiled forests that it wasn't until the fourth day of travel that they actually caught sight of any other human beings.

Leaving the others to eat and rest well concealed under a shaggy pile of newly cut branches, Sean and Matatu sneaked forward to the edge of a natural open glade in the forest and through the binoculars Sean lay and watched the Frelimo logging gangs at work on the far side of the opening. Hundreds of black men and women, some of them no more than children, were toiling in teams, supervised by guards in Frelimo camouflage battledress.

The guards all carried AK rifles slung on their shoulders, but they wielded the long hippo-hide whips, the savage African sjambok, which they plied to the naked backs and legs of their charges. The snap of the lash on bare flesh and the agonized yelps carried across five hundred yards of open ground to where Sean and Matatu lay.

The labour gangs were piling the roughly trimmed logs into tall pyramid-shaped stacks, half of them straining and heaving on the heavy ropes while the others pushed against the huge timber baulks from the lower side. The guards urged them to greater effort, calling out the verses of the work-chant to which the gangs responded with a deep melancholy chorus and a concerted heave on the heavy manila ropes.

While Sean watched through his binoculars, one of the huge logs was laboriously hoisted towards the pinnacle of the stack, but before it could be rolled securely into place, one of the ropes parted and the log slewed sideways and went bouncing and rumbling down the side of the pyramid. Wailing with terror the labour gang broke and fled before it, but some of the weaker ones were not fast enough and the log steamrolled over them. Sean heard their shrill shrieks snuffed out and the crackle of their bones like dried twigs being fed through a clothes mangle.

It was too much even for a soldier's hardened stomach, and he touched Matatu's shoulder and they crept away, back to where they had left the others.

That afternoon they passed close to the labour camps, a vast collection of primitive lean-to huts that stank of wood-smoke, open latrines and human misery.

'The cheapest African commodity these days is black flesh,' Sean told Claudia grimly.

'If you told people back home about this, they just simply wouldn't understand what you were talking about. It's just so contrary to our own experience,' said Claudia.

At this time of day, the camps were almost deserted. All the able-bodied were at work in the forest and only the sick and the dying lay under the crude open shelters. Sean sent Matatu into the camp to scavenge, and he must have found one of the field kitchens and eluded the cooks. He returned with a half sack of uncooked maize-meal slung over his shoulder.

They ate handfuls of maize porridge that evening, huddled round the radio, listening to General China's voice on the Renamo command frequency.

Once again after General China had made his last transmission at nightfall, Sean switched to the South African military frequency and listened for almost half an hour, learning the voices and call signs of the various units within range. At last, he felt he had identified the South African border headquarters. It was using the call-sign 'Kudu', that beautiful spiral-horned antelope of the bushveld.

Sean waited patiently for a lull in the military traffic and then he keyed the microphone and spoke in Afrikaans.

'"Kudu", this is "Mossie". This is a storm sending. Do you read me, "Kudu"? This is "Mossie"!'

A storm sending was the call for a top priority message. It was the radio procedure that they had used back in the days of the Rhodesian bush war. He hoped that the South African commander's military experience went back that far. 'Mossie' in Afrikaans was a sparrow and had been Sean's call-sign in those far-off days.

A long silence followed Sean's transmission, in which the static echoed in the void of the stratosphere, and Sean thought that his call had been lost. He lifted the microphone to call again just as the radio came to life.

'Station calling "Kudu",' said a voice, heavy with suspicion. 'Say again your call-sign.'

'"Kudu", this is "Mossie". I repeat "Mossie". Mike Oscar Sierra Sierra India Echo. I request a relay to General De La Rey, the deputy minister of law and order.'

Lothar De La Rey had been Sean's control back in the seventies. Since then he had risen to high political office. 'Kudu' would surely know who he was, and hesitate to refuse a request for relay to such a source.

It was clear that 'Kudu' must be thinking the same thoughts, but taking longer to reach a decision. At last he called again, '"Mossie", standby. We are relaying you to De La Rey.'

Almost an hour later, long after dark, 'Kudu' called again.

'Mossie, this is "Kudu." De La Rey is unobtainable.'

'"Kudu", this is life and death. I will call you on this frequency every six hours until you reach De La Rey.'

'*Dood reg*, "Mossie". We'll keep a six-hour listening watch for you. *Totsiens*.'

*   *   *

They had abandoned their blankets when they fled before the fire, and tonight it was frosty. Sean and Claudia lay in each other's arms and whispered together softly.

'I didn't understand what you were saying on the radio. Who were you speaking with?' Claudia used the Americanism 'with', and Sean corrected it as he replied.

'I was speaking to a South African military base, probably on the border where we are headed.'

'Will they give us assistance?' she asked hopefully.

'I don't know. They might, if I can contact someone I know. I have asked them to try, but they can't get hold of him.'

'Who?'

'During the bush war, although I was in command of the Rhodesian Scouts, I was also reporting to the South African military intelligence,' he explained.

'A spy?' she asked.

'No,' he answered too quickly. 'The South Africans and the Rhodesians were allies, both on the same side. I am a South African, so I was neither a spy nor a traitor.'

'A double agent, then?' she teased him.

'Call it whatever you like, but De La Rey was my South African control. Since the war, I have continued sending him reports from time to time; whenever I have been able to pick up pieces of information about ANC terrorist activity or sanctioneering moves by hostile governments, I pass it on to him.'

'He owes you, does he?' she asked.

'He owes me plenty, besides which we are related. He's a cousin, a first cousin on my grandmother's side.' Sean broke off as a small body insinuated itself between them. 'Well, look who's here! If it isn't Minnie Mouse herself!'

Claudia wriggled around to make room for the child and Minnie settled down happily in the warm cradle formed by their bodies and pillowed her head on Sean's arm. He drew the child's body a little closer.

'She's so cute.' Claudia stroked the child's head. 'I could just eat her up.'

They were silent for so long that Sean thought she had fallen asleep, but Claudia spoke again, softly and thoughtfully.

'If we get out of here, do you think we could adopt Minnie?'

The simple question was fraught with snares and pitfalls. It presupposed a life together thereafter, a settled existence with home and children and responsibilities, all the things that Sean had avoided over a lifetime. It should have startled him, but instead it made him feel warm and comfortable.

* * *

The portable Honda generator clattered noisily and its light bulbs were strung on poles around the grounded helicopter.

The engine hatches were open and the debris suppressors had been removed from over the turbo intakes. The Portuguese engineer in blue overalls supervised and checked every task performed by his Russian prisoners. The Portuguese had very soon come to know and understand General China, and to appreciate just how vulnerable was his own position. During the short time he had been with the Renamo force he had on more than one occasion been a witness to the punishment that General China dealt out to anyone who failed or offended him, and he was conscious now of those dark fanatical eyes upon him as he worked.

It was after midnight, but General China had not yet retired to rest. He had been flying all the previous day, from first light to dusk, only landing to refuel the helicopter. A normal man would have been exhausted by now, certainly the Portuguese pilot had slouched off to his tent many hours before, but General China was indefatigable. He prowled around the helicopter, watching every move, every action, asking questions, demanding haste, as restless as though he were possessed by some dark passion.

'You must have her ready to fly at dawn,' he repeated, it seemed for the hundredth time that night, and then he went striding back to the open canvas-roofed shelter that he was using as his forward headquarters and pored over the large-scale map, studying once more his troop dispositions, brooding over them and muttering to himself.

On the map he had noted the features he had observed from the air, the location of the Frelimo logging camps and the rough roads they had hacked out of the forest. He had very soon realized the scope of the deforestation, and the numbers employed in the forced labour battalions. He had swiftly realized the futility of trying to find such a small party amongst such multitudes. He knew any sign of Sean's progress would have been obliterated by the intense activity in the area. He dared not send trackers or a pursuit into the logging area. He had already lost almost forty men in the Frelimo attack and the subsequent fire.

'No. I must be patient.' he told himself.

He moved his hand down across the map.

The Frelimo logging operation had not yet reached as far south as the hills that guarded the approaches to the Limpopo river-basin; between the hills and the river the forest thinned out and gave way to open mopane veld. It was a strip fifty kilometres wide, good ground for tracking the fugitives, ground that they would be forced to traverse in order to reach the Limpopo and the border.

General China had decided to set his final stop line there. All that day he had ferried in the fresh troops that Tippoo Tip had placed at his disposal. In its rear cabin the Hind was able to carry fourteen men in full field kit, and they had made eleven sorties. They had hopped over the forest, fully laden with assault troops, and landed them along the line of hills with orders to set up observation posts on each hill crest and to patrol the gaps between them. He now had almost a hundred and fifty men in place to cut Sean Courtney off from the Limpopo.

General China stared at the map as though it were a portrait of the white man's face. Once again he experienced the bitter disappointment and frustration. He had almost had the white man in his grasp, pinned down by his pursuit troops, with no possible avenue of escape, and then had come the Frelimo intervention; the forest below him had been obliterated by the roiling clouds of smoke and the screaming of his men on the radio, crying for help as the flames engulfed them.

Tippoo Tip had tried in vain to convince him that Sean Courtney had perished with them in the forest fire, but General China knew better than that. He had dropped his own trackers from

512

the Hind into the blackened ashes as soon as they had cooled sufficiently for men to walk upon them. They had found the spot where the white man had buried his people to evade the heat, the marks of their bodies were still imprinted in the soft earth, and they had found the tracks leading away southwards, ever southwards.

For the rest of that day, China had searched from the low-flying Hind, but the smoke had hampered him, limiting his vision to the small circle directly beneath the Hind's belly.

If anything, this additional failure had intensified his determination. The white man's cunning and his outrageous good fortune in evading all China's best efforts only aggravated his hatred and inflamed his longing for revenge. During those long hours when they had ferried his last line of assault troops into position, China had sustained himself with fantasies of vengeance, dreaming up the most bizarre ordeals for Sean Courtney and his woman once he had them in his power.

There would be no haste then. He would draw out the pleasure, eking out their suffering and pain as jealously as a miser his shekels. He would begin with the woman, of course, and the white man would watch it all. After Tippoo Tip had enjoyed her to the full, they would hand her over to the men. China would personally select the most repulsive, those with hideous features, deformed bodies and elephantine members. Some of his men were truly remarkable in their physical development. He would let them have the woman after Tippoo Tip, and when they were done, he would bring on the sick and diseased, the men with open venereal ulcers and virulent skin disorders, covered with scabs and tropical sores. Then at last he would give her to the men with the slim sickness, the most dreaded of all. Yes, it would be marvellous sport. He wondered how strong the American woman was, how many she could take. Would her mind go before her body? It would be fascinating to find out, and of course, the white man would be forced to watch every second of it.

Only when the woman was finished, would he begin on Colonel Sean Courtney. He had not yet decided what it would be, there were so many possibilities. However, the man was tough, he could be expected to last for days, perhaps even weeks. Planning it, gloating on it, brought a smile to General China's lips and calmed his frustration enough to allow him to drop into his canvas chair, draw the lapels of his greatcoat around him and sink at last into sleep.

He awoke in confusion, unable to orientate himself. Somebody was shaking him urgently, and he threw off the hands and struggled out of his chair, glaring around him wildly. It was morning, the trees around his temporary base were grey skeletons against the paler grey of the dawn sky. The light bulbs still glowed on their poles above the squatting helicopter and the radio on the rough table of hand-planed logs in front of him was squawking urgently.

'Contact! General China, we have a live contact!' It was the commander of the line of men that he had placed upon the hills at the approaches to the Limpopo. He was calling in clear language, proof of his agitation.

Still half asleep, China stumbled to the radio set and seized the microphone. 'This is "Banana Tree", report your position and status correctly,' he snapped, and at the sound of his voice the distant patrol leader steadied himself and corrected his radio procedure.

The fugitives had run into his stop line, at almost precisely the point which China had predicted. There had been a brief fire-fight and then the fugitive band had taken refuge on the crest of a small kopje, almost within sight of the Limpopo river.

'I have called for the mortars to come up,' the patrol leader exulted. 'We'll blow them off the top of that hill.'

'Negative.' China spoke very clearly. 'I say again, negative. Do not open fire on the position with mortars. Do not attack. I want them taken alive. Surround the hill and wait for my arrival.' He glanced across at the helicopter. The titanium engine hatches were back in place, and the Portuguese engineer was overseeing the last of the refuelling. A line of porters, each of them with a twenty-five-litre drum balanced on his head, were queued up, waiting their turns to empty the drums into the helicopter's main tanks.

China shouted to the engineer in Portuguese and he came striding across to the tent.

'We must take off immediately,' he ordered.

'I will complete the refuelling in half an hour.'

'That's too long. How much fuel have you got on board right now?'

'Auxiliary tanks are full, main tank is three quarters.'

514

'That will do, call the pilot. Tell him we must take off right away.'

'I must replace the debris suppressors over the turbo intakes,' the engineer protested.

'How long will that take?'

'Not more than half an hour.'

'Too long!' China shouted with agitation. The pilot was stumbling along the pathway from his tent. Not yet fully awake, he was pulling on his leather flying jacket and the flaps of his helmet dangled loosely around his ears.

'Hurry!' China yelled at him. 'Get her started!'

'What about the suppressors?' the engineer insisted.

'We can fly without them, they are only precautionary.'

'Yes, but. . . !'

'No!' China pushed him away. 'I can't wait! Forget about the suppressors! We fly at once! Get the engines started!'

With the tails of his greatcoat flapping around his legs, General China ran to the helicopter and scrambled up into his seat in the weapons cockpit.

* * *

Sean Courtney lay on his belly between two rocks just below the crest of the kopje and looked out over the tops of the mopane forest. Away towards the south, the dark green belt of trees was just visible in the uncertain light. It marked the position of the Limpopo river.

'So close,' he lamented. 'We so very nearly made it.'

It was against all the odds that they had survived this far, almost three hundred kilometres through a devastated war-torn land and two murderous opposing armies, only to be stopped here in sight of their goal. There was a burst of AK fire from down the slope of the hill, and a ricochet sang away into the dawn sky.

Matatu lay amongst the rocks nearby, and he was still berating himself. 'I am a stupid old man, my *Bwana*. You must send me away and get yourself a clever young one who is not blind and decrepit with age.'

Sean guessed that a Renamo observation post must have spotted them as they crossed one of the open glades between the hills. There had been no warning, no obvious pursuit, no set ambush. Without warning a sweep line of tiger-striped figures had rushed at them from out of the mopane.

They had all been weary after travelling hard all night, perhaps their concentration had been eroded, perhaps they should have stayed in the trees instead of cutting across the open vlei, but it was vain to think about what they might have done.

There had only been sufficient time to snatch up the children and drag the women up the side of the kopje with poorly aimed Renamo fire whining off the rocks around them. Perhaps the Renamo aim had been deliberately wild, Sean pondered. He could guess what General China's orders to his men had been. 'Take them alive!'

'Where is China now?' he wondered. One thing was certain, he was not far away and coming as fast as the Hind would fly. He looked out at the Limpopo river again and there was the foul taste of failure and disappointment on the back of his tongue.

'Alphonso,' he called out. 'Have you got the radio rigged?' It was more for something to occupy his mind than with any real hope of making contact.

Twice during the night he had attempted to make the pre-arranged radio schedule with the South African army. Once he had even heard 'Kudu' calling him very faintly; however, the batteries of their radio had finally begun to fail. The battery test needle had dropped back deeply into the red quadrant of the dial.

'If I try to raise the aerial those baboons down there will shoot my testicles off,' Alphonso growled from amongst the rocks.

'It's almost line of sight to the river,' Sean told him brusquely. 'Give me the aerial.' He raised himself on one elbow and threw the bundle of insulated wire as far out down the slope as he could reach and then stooped to the radio set. When he turned on the power, the control panel glowed feebly.

'"Kudu", this is "Mossie",' he sent out his despairing call, ' "Kudu", do you read me? "Kudu", this is "Mossie"!'

A stray bullet hit the rock above his head, but Sean ignored it.

'"Kudu", this is "Mossie"!'

The two women, white and black, were holding the children and watching him wordlessly.

'"Kudu", this is "Mossie".' He adjusted the gain knob, and

516

then unbelievably, so faintly that he could barely catch the words, a voice answered him.

'"Mossie", this is "Oubaas". I read you strength three.'

'"Oubaas". Oh God,' he breathed. '"Oubaas"!'

Oubaas, the grandfather, was General Lothar De La Rey's code name.

'"Oubaas". We are in deep shit here. Request an immediate hot extraction.' He was asking for a removal while under enemy fire. 'We are seven pax, five adults and two children. Our position is . . .' He read out the map co-ordinates of his dead-reckoning position. 'We are holding a small kopje approximately twenty kilometres north of the Limpopo.' He raised his head and glanced around quickly. 'There are two large kopjes approximately two miles due east of our position. Do you read me, "Oubaas"?'

'I read you "Mossie".' The voice faded and then came back. 'What was your grandmother's maiden name?'

'Oh, sod you!' Sean snarled frustration. Lothar was double-checking his identity at a time like this. 'My grandmother's maiden name was Centaine De Thiry and she is your grandmother also, Lothar, you rotten bastard!'

'Okay, "Mossie". I'm sending a Puma in for a hot extraction. Can you hold out for one hour longer?'

'Pull finger, "Oubaas". We've got gooks all over us.'

'Wilco, "Mossie".' Sean had to put his ear close to the set to catch the last words. 'Give them hell, Sean . . .' And then the signal faded and the last flicker of the battery died.

'They are coming!' Sean looked up from the radio and grinned across at Claudia. 'They are sending a Puma helicopter in to take us out.' Then his grin faded and all their faces turned slowly towards the north. There was a new sound in the dawn, still faint and far off, but they all recognized it. It was the sound of death.

*   *   *

They watched the Hind come down from the north, sweeping in low over the forest, a great hunchbacked monster, blotched with camouflage paint, the first rays of the rising sun reflecting off the cockpit canopy like huge glowing red eyes.

Out of the mopane forest at the foot of the kopje a signal rocket sailed up in a lazy red parabola, calling the Hind in, and it altered course slightly and headed directly towards the crest of the hill on which they lay.

Claudia was at Sean's side and he placed his arm over her shoulders.

'It's so cruel,' she whispered. 'It's like dying twice over.' She pulled the Tokarev pistol from her belt and tried to place it in his hand.

'No!' he rejected. 'I can't do it! I can't screw myself up to that again!' He pushed the pistol away.

'What then?' she asked, and he showed her the fragmentation grenade he held in his right hand.

She glanced at the deeply chequered black metal orb. It looked like some evil poisonous fruit, and she shuddered and averted her eyes.

'It will be as quick and more certain,' he whispered reassuringly. 'And we'll go together, at the very same moment.'

He knew what he had to do. He would hold the grenade between them as they lay chest to chest.

He looked up again at the approaching Hind. It was very close. It was almost time. He would not warn her. He would simply kiss her one last time and then . . .

Suddenly Sean's eyes narrowed. Something about the Hind's silhouette was different. It was coming in swiftly, swelling in size before his eyes and he felt the first stirring of a new excitement as he realized what had been changed on the helicopter.

'There is still a chance,' he whispered to her. 'A small chance, but we are going to take it. Come here, Minnie. Come quickly!' he called in Shangane, and the tiny black girl tottered across to where they lay.

'Hold her,' Sean whispered, and lifted the back of the child's short ragged skirt. Under the skirt, she wore a pair of blue knickers.

Sean pulled open the elastic top of the knickers and pushed something down into them, something as round and black as one of her little buttocks between which it nestled.

'Keep that for me, little one,' he whispered to the child in Shangane as he adjusted the waistband. 'It's a secret. Don't take it out. Just keep it there. Will you do that for me, my little flower?'

Minnie stared at him with dark adoring eyes and nodded solemnly and Sean gave her a hug.

518

The sound of the Hind's turbos was almost unbearably shrill as it came in towards them at the level of the hilltop. When it was two hundred metres out, Alphonso opened fire with his AK rifle, pouring a full magazine into the front canopy. The light bullets left no mark on the armoured glass, and the helicopter slowed and hung motionless on its shining rotor. General China was sitting up in the high-backed seat of the weapons cockpit, so close that they could clearly see the triumphant smirk on his face as he lifted the microphone to his mouth.

His grossly magnified voice boomed out of the speakers of the 'sky shout' system that were slung below the helicopter's stubby wings.

'Good morning, Colonel Courtney. You have led me a merry dance, but the chase is over. Tell your men to lay down their weapons, please.'

'Do it!' Sean shouted at Alphonso, but he snarled a protest and clipped a fresh magazine onto his rifle. 'Do as I tell you!' Sean's voice hardened. 'I have a plan. Trust me.'

Still Alphonso hesitated, and suddenly the Hind's Gatling-cannon thundered, deafening them and kicking a storm of rock chips and dust from the side of the kopje just below where they lay.

'Don't try my patience, Colonel. Tell your men to stand up with their hands high above their heads.'

'Do it!' Sean repeated, and first Matatu and then Alphonso rose slowly to their feet with arms held high.

'Tell them to turn around. I want to make sure they have no surprises for me.'

They shuffled in a circle and China's voice boomed out again.

'Take your clothes off, all of them.'

Slowly they stripped themselves and stood naked before him.

'All right, now move down the hill into the open.'

Still with their hands held high they walked down into the open ground below the crown of rocks.

'Now the two women.'

'Be brave,' Sean whispered to Claudia. 'We've still got a chance, a good chance.'

Claudia stood up slowly.

'Miss Monterro,' China's voice echoed across the forest tops, 'will you be good enough to remove your clothing?'

Briskly, defiantly Claudia unbuttoned her ragged shirt and

pulled it over her tousled head. Her breasts were white in the early sunlight.

'Now your trousers,' China encouraged her. She let them drop around her ankles and kicked them off.

'Very good, and now the rest of it.'

Claudia's lace panties had been washed and worn until they were wispy as spider web, her pubic triangle was a dark shadow under the filmy cloth.

'No.' She shook her head. 'I won't do it.' She crossed her hands in front of her. Her refusal was unmistakable.

'Very well. We'll allow you your modesty for the time being. My men will enjoy it all the more later.' China chuckled. 'Move down into the open, please.'

Claudia walked down the hill, her chin and her small pert breasts held high, and stood between Alphonso and Matatu.

'Now you, woman.' China spoke in Shangane, and Miriam stood up. She did not have a European's shame of nudity and quickly stripped herself naked. Holding her little brother's hand, she went down to join the others.

'And now, Colonel Courtney. The last is the best of all the game.'

Sean rose to his feet and carelessly threw aside his tattered clothing.

'Very impressive, Colonel.' China taunted him. 'For a white man, that is.'

Sean stood and stared up at him impassively, but he was trying to judge the distance to the helicopter. Sixty yards, he estimated, much too far.

'Please come down into the open where I can keep an eye on you, Colonel. We don't want any misunderstanding now, do we?'

Sean took Minnie's hand and led her down the hill. The lump under the little girl's skirt wobbled from side to side like a Victorian bustle, and with her free hand she tugged at the waistband of her knickers to prevent them being pulled down around her knees by the weight.

Ten, fifteen, twenty paces, Sean counted as he moved towards the hovering Hind. He could clearly see the pupils of General China's eyes, forty yards, still too far. He stopped beside Claudia and they stood in a row, naked and vulnerable.

China gave an order in Shangane, and at the foot of the hill his men burst out of the forest and came swarming up the slope.

whooping with triumph. The Portuguese pilot edged the huge machine in closer. and then closer still. showing off his prowess at the controls.

Thirty yards. twenty-five yards. Sean was concentrating on the opening of the air-intakes to the turbo engines. They were the size of garbage bins with the covers missing: he could just make out deep in the circular openings the velvety blur of the rotor blades spinning at incredible speed.

The Hind steadied in the air and hung in front of them. In the cockpit General China twisted his head to peer down the hill at the line of advancing Renamo guerrillas. He was distracted and Sean seized the moment.

He stooped slightly and jerked up the back of Minnie's skirt. In the same movement. he thrust his hand under the waistband of her knickers and closed his hand over the grenade. As it came out. he pulled the pin and let the firing handle fly free. He heard the pin fall on the primer. There was a delay of five seconds. He counted off three under his breath and then reared back like a baseball pitcher just as China looked back at him.

He concentrated on the starboard engine intake. and hurled the grenade. It went up in a flat arc and he willed its flight. trying by sheer force of his mind to steer it into the small circle of the intake.

The grenade struck the bottom of the intake rim. and bounced on the edge. like a million-dollar putt quivering on the lip. Then the tremendous draught of air created by the rotor blades sucked it in. and it popped into the throat of the open duct.

The grenade exploded as it hit the spinning blades. and the great turbo's energy was thrown out of balance. all its mighty power directed upon itself. in an orgy of self-destruction.

As Sean seized Claudia and Minnie under each arm and hurled them face down. the Hind's engine tore itself to pieces in one fatal instant.

The Hind lurched heavily. throwing General China's aim so that the burst he fired from the Gatling-cannon flew almost straight into the sky. and the helicopter rolled on to its back. Smoke and fragments of metal blew in a screaming cloud from its maimed engines.

It struck the side of the hill. and bounced high. fell again. and cart-wheeled down the slope. directly on top of the climbing line of Renamo. They broke and scattered. but most of them could not escape, and the shattered fuselage of the Hind rolled over them and swept them away down the slope.

At last the Hind slithered on its belly like a gigantic toboggan to the bottom of the kopje and came up hard against the tree-line. Avgas, as clear as water, fountained from its ruptured main tanks and sprayed over the hull, sparkling in the sunlight.

Sean and Claudia rose shakily to their knees and watched in awe the magnificent destruction.

Then, incredibly, the canopy of the weapons cockpit opened like the half shell of an enormous oyster and General China crawled out from under it. The Hind's fuel sprayed high in the morning sunlight as innocuous-seeming as a garden sprinkler, and fell upon him in a gentle rain. It soaked his uniform and ran in thin rivulets down his face, but China pushed himself away from the shattered fuselage and set off down the hill at a shambling run.

He had not gone ten shaky paces when the Hind went up in a sheet of flame, and the flames jumped the gap and ignited China's sodden uniform. It turned him into a human torch and he ran on down the slope with the yellow flames streaking out behind him. They could hear his screams even from the top of the hill, it was a high inhuman sound.

China did not reach the trees. He fell at the edge of the forest and his burning flesh touched off the thick brown grass in which he lay. The hillside became his pyre, but still they could hear him screaming in the heart of the flames.

'Back!' Sean shouted, and his voice aroused them from their mesmerized horror. He hauled Claudia to her feet and picked Minnie up in his arms.

In a bunch they fled back into the circle of rocks that crowned the kopje just as a renewed Renamo fusillade whined about them. They lay behind the rocks, not yet bothering to cover their naked bodies and watched the Hind burn, and the flames sweep through the grass at the edge of the forest.

When the flames had passed, a dark charred mound lay on the blackened slope. It might have been merely a pile of discarded sacking, except that when the wind shifted, the odour of burned flesh carried up to them on the crest of the hill.

The shift in the wind carried a new sound to them, and Sean roused himself and looked towards the green Limpopo river on the horizon.

The Puma helicopter was still a dark speck out there, but it was coming on swiftly, the sound of its engines rising on the wind.

'Put your pants on, darling,' Sean hugged Claudia a little closer. 'It looks as though we've got company dropping in on us!'

ELEPHANT SONG

This book is for my wife and the jewel of my life, Mokkiniso, with all my love and gratitude for the enchanted years that I have been married to her

IT WAS A windowless thatched building of dressed sandstone blocks, that Daniel Armstrong had built with his own hands almost ten years ago. At the time he had been a junior game ranger in the National Parks' administration. Since then the building had been converted into a veritable treasure house.

Johnny Nzou slipped his key into the heavy padlock, and swung open the double doors of hewn native teak. Johnny was chief warden of Chiwewe National Park. Back in the old days, he had been Daniel's tracker and gunbearer, a bright young Matabele whom Daniel had taught to read, write and speak fluent English by the light of a thousand campfires.

Daniel had lent Johnny the money to pay for his first correspondence course from the University of South Africa which had led much later to his degree of Bachelor of Science. The two youngsters, one black and one white, had patrolled the vast reaches of the National Park together, often on foot or bicycle. In the wilderness they had forged a friendship which the subsequent years of separation had left undimmed.

Now Daniel peered into the gloomy interior of the godown, and whistled softly.

'Hell, Johnny boy, you have been busy since I've been away.'

The treasure was stacked to the roof beams, hundreds of thousands of dollars' worth of it.

Johnny Nzou glanced at Daniel's face, his eyes narrowed as he looked for criticism in his friend's expression. The reaction was reflex, for he knew Daniel was an ally who understood the problem even better than he did. Nevertheless, the subject was so emotionally charged that it had become second nature to expect revulsion and antagonism.

However, Daniel had turned back to his cameraman. 'Can we get a light in here? I want some good shots of the interior.'

The cameraman trudged forward, weighed down by the

heavy battery packs slung around his waist, and switched on the hand-held arc lamp. The high stacks of treasure were lit with a fierce blue-white light.

'Jock, I want you to follow me and the warden down the length of the warehouse,' Daniel instructed, and the cameraman nodded and moved in closer, the sleek Sony video recorder balanced on his shoulder. Jock was in his middle thirties. He wore only a pair of short khaki pants, and open sandals. In the Zambezi valley heat his tanned bare chest was shiny with sweat and his long hair was tied with a leather thong at the nape of his neck. He looked like a pop star, but was an artist with the big Sony camera.

'Got you, guv,' he agreed, and panned the camera over the untidy stacks of elephant tusks, ending on Daniel's hand as it stroked one elegant curve of glowing ivory. Then he pulled back into a full shot of Daniel.

It was not merely Daniel's doctorate in biology, nor his books and lectures, that had made him an international authority and spokesman on African ecology. He had the healthy outdoors looks and charismatic manner that came over so well on the television screen, and his voice was deep and compelling. His accent had sufficient Sandhurst undertones remaining to soften the flat unmelodious vowel sounds of colonial speech. His father had been a staff officer in a Guards regiment during World War II and had served in North Africa under Wavell and Montgomery. After the war he came out to Rhodesia to grow tobacco. Daniel had been born in Africa but had been sent home to finish his education at Sandhurst, before coming back to Rhodesia to join the National Parks Service.

'Ivory,' he said now, as he looked into the camera. 'Since the time of the pharaohs, one of the most beautiful and treasured natural substances. The glory of the African elephant — and its terrible cross.'

Daniel began to move down between the tiers of stacked tusks, and Johnny Nzou fell in beside him. 'For two thousand years man has hunted the elephant to obtain this living white gold, and yet only a decade ago there still remained over two million elephant on the African continent. The elephant population seemed to be a renewable resource, an asset that was

2

protected and harvested and controlled – and then something went terribly, tragically wrong. In these last ten years, almost a million elephant have been slaughtered. It is barely conceivable that this could have been allowed to happen. We are here to find out what went wrong, and how the perilous existence of the African elephant can be retrieved from the brink of extinction.'

He looked at Johnny. 'With me today is Mr John Nzou, chief warden of Chiwewe National Park, one of the new breed of African conservationists. By coincidence, the name Nzou in the Shona language means elephant. John Nzou is Mr Elephant in more than name alone. As warden of Chiwewe, he is responsible for one of the largest and healthiest elephant herds that still flourish in the African wilderness. Tell us, Warden, how many tusks do you have in this store room here at Chiwewe National Park?'

'There are almost five hundred tusks in store at present – four hundred and eighty-six to be exact – with an average weight of seven kilos.'

'On the international market ivory is worth three hundred dollars a kilo,' Daniel cut in, 'so that is well over a million dollars. Where does it all come from?'

'Well, some of the tusks are pick-ups – ivory from elephant found dead in the Park, and some is illegal ivory that my rangers have confiscated from poachers. But the great majority of tusks are from the culling operations that my department is forced to undertake.'

The two of them paused at the far end of the godown and turned back to face the camera. 'We will discuss the culling programme later, Warden. But first can you tell us a little more about poaching activity in Chiwewe. How bad is it?'

'It is getting worse every day.' Johnny shook his head sadly. 'As the elephant in Kenya and Tanzania and Zambia are wiped out, so the professionals are turning their attention to our healthy elephant herds further south. Zambia is just across the Zambezi river, and the poachers that come across this side are organised and better armed than we are. They shoot to kill – men as well as elephant and rhino. We have been forced to do the same. If we run into a band of poachers, we shoot first.'

'All for these . . .' Daniel laid his hand on the nearest pile of

3

tusks. No two of the ivory shafts were the same; each curve was unique. Some were almost straight, long and thin as knitting-needles; others were bent like a drawn longbow. Some were sharp-tipped as javelins; others were squat and blunt. There were pearly shafts, and others were of buttery alabaster tone; still others were stained dark with vegetable juices, and scarred and worn with age.

Most of the ivory was female or immature; a few tusks were no longer than a man's forearm, taken from small calves. A very few were great curved imperial shafts, the heavy mature ivory of old bulls.

Daniel stroked one of these, and his expression was not simply for the camera. Once again, he felt the full weight of the melancholy that had first caused him to write about the passing and destruction of the old Africa and its enchanted animal kingdom.

'A sage and magnificent beast has been reduced to this,' his voice sank to a whisper. 'Even if it is unavoidable, we cannot escape the inherently tragic nature of the changes that are sweeping through this continent. Is the African elephant symbolic of the land? The elephant is dying. Is Africa dying?'

His sincerity was absolute. The camera recorded it faithfully. It was the most compelling reason for the enormous appeal of his television programmes around the world.

Now Daniel roused himself with an obvious effort, and turned back to Johnny Nzou. 'Tell us, Warden, is the elephant doomed? How many of these marvellous animals do you have in Zimbabwe and how many of those are in Chiwewe National Park?'

'There are an estimated fifty-two thousand elephant in Zimbabwe, and our figures for Chiwewe are even more accurate. Only three months ago, we were able to conduct an aerial survey of the Park sponsored by the International Union for the Conservation of Nature. The entire area of the Park was photographed, and the animals counted from the high-resolution prints.'

'How many?' Daniel asked.

'In Chiwewe alone, eighteen thousand elephant.'

'That's a huge population, something approaching a third of all the remaining animals in the country – all in this area.' Daniel raised an eyebrow. 'In the climate of gloom and pessimism that prevails, this must give you a great deal of encouragement?'

4

Johnny Nzou frowned. 'On the contrary, Doctor Armstrong, we are extremely concerned by these numbers.'

'Can you explain that please, Warden?'

'It's simple, Doctor. We cannot support that many elephant. We estimate that thirty thousand elephant would be an ideal population for Zimbabwe. A single beast requires up to a ton of vegetable matter each day, and he will push over trees that have taken many hundreds of years to grow, even trees with trunks four feet in diameter, to obtain that food.'

'What will happen if you allow that huge herd to flourish and to breed?'

'Quite simply, in a very short period they will reduce this park to a dust bowl, and when that happens the elephant population will collapse. We will be left with nothing – no trees, no park, no elephant.'

Daniel nodded encouragement. When the film was edited he would cut in at this point a series of shots he had taken some years previously in Kenya's Amboseli Park. These were haunting vistas of devastation, of bare red earth and dead black trees stripped of bark and leaves holding up their naked branches in agonised supplication to a hard blue African sky, while the desiccated carcasses of the great animals lay like discarded leather bags where famine and poachers had destroyed them.

'Do you have a solution, Warden?' Daniel asked softly.

'A drastic one, I'm afraid.'

'Will you show us what it is?'

Johnny Nzou shrugged. 'It is not very pretty to watch, but, yes, you may witness what has to be done.'

 Daniel woke twenty minutes before sunrise. Even the intervening years spent in cities out of Africa, and the passage of so many other dawns in northern climes, or in the fluid time zones of jet aircraft travel, had not dulled the habit that he had first acquired in this valley. Of course, the habit had been reinforced during the years of that terrible

Rhodesian bush war, when he had been called up to serve in the security forces.

For Daniel the dawn was the most magical time of each day, and especially so in this valley. He rolled out of his sleeping-bag and reached for his boots. He and his men had slept fully clothed on the sun-baked earth, with the embers of the campfire in the centre of the huddle of their prostrate forms. They had not built a *boma* of thorn branches to protect themselves, although at intervals during the night lions had grunted and roared along the escarpment.

Daniel laced up his boots and slipped quietly out of the circle of sleeping men. The dew that hung like seed pearls upon the grass stems soaked his trouser legs to the knees as he moved out to the promontory of rock at the head of the cliff. He found a seat on the rough grey granite knoll and huddled into his anorak.

The dawn came on with stealthy and deceptive speed and painted the clouds above the great river in subtle talcum shades of pink and grey. Over the Zambezi's dark green waters the river mist undulated and pulsed like ghostly ectoplasm and the dawn flights of duck were very dark and crisp against the pale background, their formations precise and their wing-beats flickering quick as knife-blades in the uncertain light.

A lion roared, near at hand, abrupt gales of sound that died away in a descending series of moaning grunts. Daniel shivered with the thrill of that sound. Though he had heard it countless times, it always had the same effect upon him. There was no other like it in all the world. For him it was the veritable voice of Africa.

Then he picked out the great cat shape below him at the edge of the swamp. Full-bellied, dark-maned, it carried its massive head low and swung it from side to side to the rhythm of its stately arrogant walk. Its mouth was half open and its fangs glinted behind thin black lips. He watched it vanish into the dense riverine bush and sighed with the pleasure it had given him.

There was a small sound close behind him. As he started up, Johnny Nzou touched his shoulder to restrain him and settled down on the granite slab beside him.

Johnny lit a cigarette. Daniel had never been able to talk him out of the habit. They sat in companionable silence as they had so often before and watched the dawn come on more swiftly now, until that religious moment when the sun thrust its burning rim above the dark mass of the forest. The light changed and all their world was bright and glazed as a precious ceramic creation fresh from the firing oven.

'The trackers came into camp ten minutes ago. They have found a herd,' Johnny broke the silence, and the mood.

Daniel stirred and glanced at him. 'How many?' he asked.

'About fifty.' That was a good number. They would not be able to process more, for flesh and hide putrefy swiftly in the heat of the valley, and a lower number would not justify all this use of men and expensive equipment.

'Are you sure you want to film this?' Johnny asked.

Daniel nodded. 'I have considered it carefully. To attempt to conceal it would be dishonest.'

'People eat meat and wear leather, but they don't want to see inside the abattoir,' Johnny pointed out.

'This is a complex and emotional subject we are examining. People have a right to know.'

'In anyone else I would suspect journalistic sensationalism,' Johnny murmured, and Daniel frowned.

'You are probably the only person I would allow to say that – because you know better.'

'Yes, Danny, I know better,' Johnny agreed. 'You hate this as much as I do, and yet you first taught me the necessity of it.'

'Let's go to work,' Daniel suggested gruffly, and they stood up and walked back in silence to where the trucks were parked. The camp was astir, and coffee was brewing on the open fire. The rangers were rolling their blankets and sleeping-bags and checking their rifles.

There were four of them, two black lads and two white, all of them in their twenties. They wore the plain khaki uniform of the Parks Department with green shoulder flashes, and though they handled their weapons with the casual competence of veterans they kept up a cheerful high-spirited banter. Black and white treated each other as comrades, although they were just old enough to have fought in the bush war and had probably been on opposing sides. It always amazed Daniel that so little bitterness remained.

7

Jock, the cameraman, was already filming. It often seemed to Daniel that the Sony camera was a natural excrescence of his body, like a hunchback.

'I'm going to ask you some dumb questions for the camera, and I might needle you a little,' Daniel warned Johnny. 'We both know the answers to the questions, but we have to fake it, okay?'

'Go ahead.'

Johnny looked good on film. Daniel had studied the rushes the previous night. One of the joys of working with modern video equipment was the instant replay of footage. Johnny resembled the younger Cassius Clay before he became Mohammed Ali. However, he was leaner in the face and his bone structure finer and more photogenic. His expression was mobile and expressive and the tones of his skin were not so dark as to make too severe a contrast and render photography difficult.

They huddled over the smoky campfire and Jock brought the camera in close to them.

'We are camped here on the banks of the Zambezi River with the sun just rising, and not far out there in the bush your trackers have come across a herd of fifty elephant, Warden,' Daniel told Johnny, and he nodded. 'You have explained to me that the Chiwewe Park cannot support such numbers of these huge animals, and that this year alone at least a thousand of them must be removed from the Park, not only for the good of the ecology, but for the very survival of the remaining elephant herds. How do you intend removing them?'

'We will have to cull them,' Johnny said curtly.

'Cull them?' Daniel asked. 'That means kill, doesn't it?'

'Yes. My rangers and I will shoot them.'

'All of them, Warden? You are going to kill fifty elephant today?'

'We will cull the entire herd.'

'What about the young calves and the pregnant cows? Won't you spare a single animal?'

'They all have to go,' Johnny insisted.

'But why, Warden? Couldn't you catch them, dart and drug them, and send them elsewhere?'

'The costs of transporting an animal the size of an elephant

8

are staggering. A big bull weighs six tons, an average cow around four. Look at this terrain down here in the valley.' Johnny gestured towards the mountainous heights of the escarpment and the broken rocky kopjes and wild forest. 'We would require special trucks and we would have to build roads to get them in and out. Even if that were possible, where would we take them? I have told you that we have a surplus of almost twenty thousand elephant in Zimbabwe. Where would we take these elephant? There simply isn't space for them.'

'So, Warden, unlike the other countries to the north such as Kenya and Zambia who have allowed their elephant herds to be almost wiped out by poaching and unwise conservation policy, you are in a Catch 22 situation. Your management of your herds of elephant has been too good. Now you have to destroy and waste these marvellous animals.'

'No, Doctor Armstrong, we won't waste them. We will recover a great deal of value from their carcasses, ivory and hides and meat which will be sold. The proceeds will be ploughed back into conservation, to prevent poaching and to protect our National Parks. The death of these animals will not be a complete abomination.'

'But why do you have to kill the mothers and the babies?' Daniel insisted.

'You are cheating, Doctor,' Johnny warned him. 'You are using the emotive, slanted language of the animal rights groups, "mothers and babies". Let's rather call them cows and calves, and admit that a cow eats as much and takes up as much space as a bull, and that calves grow very swiftly into adults.'

'So you feel—' Daniel started, but despite his earlier warning, Johnny was becoming angry.

'Hold on,' he snapped. 'There's more to it than that. We have to take out the entire herd. It is absolutely essential that we leave no survivors. The elephant herd is a complex family group. Nearly all its members are blood relatives, and there is a highly developed social structure within the herd. The elephant is an intelligent animal, probably the most intelligent after the primates, certainly more intelligent than a cat or dog, or even a dolphin. They know – I mean, they really understand . . .' he broke off, and cleared his throat. His feelings had overcome

9

him, and Daniel had never liked nor admired him more than he did at that moment.

'The terrible truth is', Johnny's voice was husky as he went on, 'that if we allowed any of them to escape the cull, they would communicate their terror and panic to the other herds in the Park. There would be a swift breakdown in the elephants' social behaviour.'

'Isn't that a little far-fetched, Warden?' Daniel asked softly.

'No. It has happened before. After the war there were ten thousand surplus elephant in the Wankie National Park. At that time, we knew very little about the techniques or effects of massive culling operations. We soon learned. Those first clumsy efforts of ours almost destroyed the entire social structure of the herds. By shooting the older animals, we wiped out their reservoir of experience and transferable wisdom. We disrupted their migratory patterns, the hierarchy and discipline within the herds, even their breeding habits. Almost as though they understood that the holocaust was upon them, the bulls began to cover the barely mature young cows before they were ready. Like the human female, the elephant cow is ripe for breeding at fifteen or sixteen years of age at the very earliest. Under the terrible stress of the culling the bulls in Wankie went to the cows when they were only ten or eleven years of age, still in puberty, and the calves born of these unions were stunted little runts.' Johnny shook his head. 'No, we have to take out the whole herd at one stroke.'

Almost with relief, he looked up at the sky. They both picked up the distant insect drone of an aircraft engine beyond the towering cumulus clouds.

'Here comes the spotter plane,' he said quietly, and reached for the microphone of the radio.

'Good morning, Sierra Mike. We have you visual due south of our position approximately four miles. I will give you yellow smoke.'

Johnny nodded at one of his rangers, who pulled the tab on a smoke marker. Sulphur-yellow smoke drifted in a heavy cloud across the treetops.

'Roger, Parks. I have your smoke. Give me an indication on the target, please.'

10

Johnny frowned at the word 'target' and laid emphasis on the alternative word as he replied. 'At sunset yesterday evening the *herd* was moving north towards the river five miles south-east of this position. There are fifty-plus animals.'

'Thank you, Parks. I will call again when we locate them.'

They watched the aircraft bank away eastwards. It was an ancient single-engined Cessna that had probably served on fire-force duties as a K-Car, or killer car, during the bush war.

Fifteen minutes later the radio crackled to life again.

'Hello, Parks. I have your herd. Fifty-plus and eight miles from your present position.'

 The herd was spread out down both banks of a dry river-course that was gouged through a low line of flinty hills. The forest was greener and more luxuriant here in the drainage where the deep roots had found subterranean water. The acacia trees were in heavy pod. The pods looked like long brown biscuits, clustered at the tips of the branches sixty feet above ground level.

Two cows moved in on one of the heavily laden trees. They were the herd matriarchs, both of them over seventy years of age, gaunt old dowagers with tattered ears and rheumy eyes. The bond between them was over half a century strong. They were half-sisters, successive calves of the same mother. The elder had been weaned at the birth of her sibling and had helped to nursemaid her as tenderly as would a human elder sister. They had shared a long life, and had drawn from it a wealth of experience and wisdom to add to the deep ancestral instinct with which they had both been endowed at birth.

They had seen each other through drought and famine and sickness. They had shared the joy of good rains and abundant food. They knew all the secret hideaways in the mountains and the water-holes in the desert places. They knew where the hunters lurked, and the boundaries of the sanctuaries within which they and the herd were secure. They had played midwife to each other, leaving the herd together when the time was

11

come upon one of them, and by their presence had fortified each other in the tearing agony of birth. They had stripped the foetal sac from each other's newborn calves, and helped discipline them, instruct them and rear them to maturity.

Their own breeding days were long past, but the herd and its safety were still their duty and their main concern. Their pleasure and their responsibility were the younger cows and the new calves that carried their own blood-lines.

Perhaps it was fanciful to endow brute animals with such human emotions as love and respect, or to believe that they understand blood relationships or the continuity of their line, but no one who had seen the old cows quieten the boisterous youngsters with raised ears and a sharp angry squeal, or watched the herd follow their lead with unquestioning obedience, could doubt their authority. No one who had seen them caress the younger calves with a gentle trunk or lift them over the steep and difficult places on the elephant roads could question their concern. When danger threatened they would push the young ones behind them and rush forward to the defence with ears spread wide and trunks rolled ready to fling out and strike down an enemy.

The great bulls with towering frames and massive girth might overshadow them in size, but not in cunning and ferocity. The bulls' tusks were longer and thicker, sometimes weighing well over one hundred pounds. The two old cows had spindly misshapen ivory, worn and cracked and discoloured with age, and the bones showed through the scarred grey skin, but they were constant in their duty to the herd.

The bulls kept only a loose association with the breeding herd. As they grew older they often preferred to break away and form smaller bachelor groups of two or three males, visiting the cows only when the heady scent of oestrus drew them in. However, the old cows stayed with the herd. They formed the solid foundation on which the social structure of the herd was based. The tight-knit community of breeding cows and their calves relied heavily upon their wisdom and experience for its everyday needs and survival.

Now the two sisters moved in perfect accord to the giant acacia laden with seed pods, and each took up her position on either side of the trunk. They laid their foreheads against the rough bark. The trunk was over four feet in diameter, unyielding as a column of marble. A hundred feet above the ground the high branches formed an intricate tracery and the pods and green leaves a cathedral dome against the sky.

The two old cows began to rock back and forth in unison with the tree-trunk between their foreheads. At first the acacia was rigid, resisting even their great strength. The cows worked on doggedly, pushing and heaving, first one then the other throwing her weight in opposite directions, and a tiny shudder ran up the tree and, high above them, the top branches trembled as though a breeze had passed.

Still they worked rhythmically and the trunk began to move. A single ripe pod came loose from its twig and fell a hundred feet to crack against the skull of one of the cows. She closed her watery old eyes tightly but never broke the rhythm of her heaves. Between them the tree-trunk swayed and shuddered, ponderously at first and then more briskly. Another pod and then another plopped down as heavily as the first drops of a thunderstorm.

The younger animals of the herd realised what they were up to, flapped their ears with excitement and hurried forward. The acacia pods, rich in protein, were a favourite delicacy. They crowded gleefully around the two cows, snatching up the scattering of pods as they fell and stuffing them far down their throats with their trunks. By now the great tree was whipping back and forth, its branches waving wildly and its foliage thrashing. The pods and loose twigs showered down thick as hail, rattling and bouncing from the backs of the elephants crowded beneath.

The two cows, still braced like a pair of book ends, kept doggedly at it until the shower of falling pods began to dry up. Only when the last one was shaken from the branches did they step back from the tree-trunk. Their backs were sprinkled with dead leaves and twigs, bits of dry bark and velvety pods, and they stood ankle-deep in the fallen débris. They reached down and delicately picked out the golden pods with the dextrous fleshy tips of their trunks and curled them up into their gaping mouths, their triangular bottom lips drooping open. The ooze from their facial glands wetting their cheeks like tears of pleasure, they began to feed.

The herd was pressed closely around them at the feast that they had laid. As their long serpentine trunks swung and curled, and the pods were shovelled into their throats, there was a soft sound that seemed to reverberate through each of their great grey frames. It was a gentle rumbling in many different keys, and the sound was interspersed with tiny creaking gurgling squeaks barely audible to the human ear. It was a strangely contented chorus, in which even the youngest beasts joined. It was a sound that seemed to express joy of life and to confirm the deep bond that linked all the members of the herd.

It was the song of the elephant.

One of the old cows was the first to detect a threat to the herd. She transmitted her concern to them with a sound high above the register of the human ear and the entire herd froze into utter stillness. Even the very young calves responded instantly. The silence after the happy uproar of the feast was eerie, and the buzz of the distant spotter plane was loud in contrast.

The old cows recognised the sound of the Cessna engine. They had heard it many times over the last few years and had come to associate it with the periods of increased human activity, of tension and of unexplained terror that they felt transmitted telepathically through the wilderness from the other groups of elephant in the Park.

They knew that the sound in the air was the prelude to a popping chorus of distant gunfire and to the stench of elephant blood on the currents of heated air along the rim of the escarpment. Often after the sounds of aircraft and gunfire had faded, they had come across wide areas of the forest floor caked with dried blood, and they had smelt the odour of fear and pain and death exuded by members of their own race which still mingled with the reek of blood and of rotting entrails.

One of the old cows backed away and shook her head angrily at the sound in the sky. Her tattered ears flapped loudly against her shoulders, a sound like the mainsail of a tall ship filling with wind. Then she wheeled and led the herd away at a run.

14

There were two mature bulls with the herd, but at the first threat they peeled away and disappeared into the forest. Instinctively recognising that the herd was vulnerable, they sought safety in solitary flight. The younger cows and the calves bunched up behind the matriarchs and fled, the little ones racing to keep up with the longer stride of their dams; in different circumstances their haste might have been comical.

'Hello, Parks. The herd is breaking southwards towards the Imbelezi pass.'

'Roger, Sierra Mike. Please head them towards the Mana Pools turn-off.'

The old cow was leading the herd towards the hills. She wanted to get off the valley bottom into the bad ground where pursuit would be impeded by the rock and severe gradients, but the sound of the aircraft hummed across her front, cutting her off from the mouth of the pass.

She pulled up uncertainly and lifted her head to the sky, where tall silvery mountains of cumulus cloud were piled up as high as the heavens. She spread wide her ears, riven and weathered by time and thorn, and turned her ancient head to follow that dreadful sound.

Then she saw the aircraft. The early sunlight flashed from its windshield as it banked steeply across her front, and it dived back towards her, low over the tops of the forest trees, the sound of its engine rising to a roar.

The two old cows spun together and started back towards the river. Behind them the herd wheeled like an untidy mass of cavalry, and as they ran the dust rose in a fine pale cloud even higher than the treetops.

'Parks, the herd is heading your way now. Five miles from the turn-off.'

'Thank you, Sierra Mike; keep them coming nice and easy. Don't push them too hard.'

'Wilco, Parks.'

'All K-Units.' Johnny Nzou changed his call-sign. 'All K-Units, converge on the Mana Pools turn-off.'

The K-Units, or kill teams, were the four Landrovers that were deployed along the main track that ran down from Chiwewe headquarters on the escarpment to the river. Johnny

15

had put them in as a stop line, to head off the herd if it broke awkwardly. It did not look as though that would be necessary now. The spotter plane was working the herd into position with professional expertise.

'Looks as though we'll make it on the first try,' Johnny muttered as he reversed the Landrover and swung it in a full 180-degree turn, then sent it flying down the track. A ridge of grass grew between the sandy wheel-tracks, and the Landrover rocked and rattled over the bumps. The wind whipped around their heads and Daniel pulled his hat from his head and stuffed it into his pocket.

Jock was filming over his shoulder as a herd of buffalo, disturbed by the sound of the Landrover, came pouring out of the forest and crossed the track just ahead of them.

'Damn it!' Johnny hit the brakes and glanced at his wrist-watch. 'Stupid *nyati* are going to screw us up.'

Hundreds of the dark bovine shapes came in a solid phalanx, galloping heavily, raising white dust, grunting and lowing and splattering liquid green dung on the grass as they flattened it.

Within minutes they had passed and Johnny accelerated into the standing dust-cloud and rattled over the loose earth that the herd had ploughed up with their great cloven hoofs. Around a bend in the track they saw the other vehicles parked at the crossroads. The four rangers were standing in a group beside them, rifles in their hands and faces turned back expectantly.

Johnny skidded the Landrover to a halt and snatched up the microphone of his radio. 'Sierra Mike, give me a position report, please.'

'Parks, the herd is two miles from you, just approaching Long Vlei.'

A vlei is a depression of open grassland, and Long Vlei ran for miles parallel to the river. In the rainy season it was a marsh, but now it made an ideal killing ground. They had used it before.

Johnny jumped down from the driver's seat and lifted his rifle from the rack. He and all his rangers were armed with cheap mass-produced .375 magnums loaded with solid ammunition for maximum penetration of bone and tissue. His men were chosen for this work on account of their superior marks-

16

manship. The kill must be as swift and humane as possible. They would shoot for the brain and not take the easier but lingering body shot.

'Let's go!' Johnny snapped. There was no need to give instructions. These were tough young professionals, yet even though they had done this work many times before their expressions were sombre. There was no excitement, no anticipation in their eyes. This was not sport. They clearly did not enjoy the prospect of the bloody work ahead.

They were stripped down to shorts and velskoen without socks, light running gear. The only heavy items they carried were their cheap weapons and the bandoliers of ammunition strapped around their waists. All of them were lean and muscled, and Johnny Nzou was as hard as any of them. They ran to meet the herd.

Daniel fell into position behind Johnny Nzou. He believed that he had kept himself fit with regular running and training, but he had forgotten what it was like to be hunting and fighting fit as were Johnny and his rangers.

They ran like hounds, streaming through the forest effortlessly, their feet seeming to find their own way between scrub and rock and fallen branches and antbear holes. They barely touched the earth in passing. Daniel had run like that once, but now his boots were slamming down heavily and he stumbled once or twice in the rough footing. He and the camera man began to fall behind.

Johnny Nzou gave a hand signal and his rangers fanned out into a long skirmish line, fifty yards separating each of them. Ahead, the forest gave way abruptly to the open glade of Long Vlei. It was three hundred yards wide; the dry beige-coloured grass was waist-high.

The line of killers stopped at the edge of the forest and looked to Johnny at the centre, but his head was thrown back, watching the spotter plane out there above the forest. It was banking steeply, standing vertically on one wing.

Daniel caught up with him, and found that both he and Jock were panting heavily although they had run less than a mile. He envied Johnny.

'There they are,' Johnny called softly. 'You can see the dust.'

17

It lay in a haze on the treetops between them and the circling aircraft. 'Coming on fast.'

Johnny windmilled his right arm and obediently his skirmish line extended and shifted into a concave shape like the horns of a bull buffalo with Johnny at the centre. At the next signal they trotted forward into the glade.

The light breeze was in their faces; the herd would not scent them. Although originally the herd had instinctively fled into the wind so as not to run into danger, the aircraft had turned them back downwind.

The elephant's eyesight is not sharp; they would make nothing of the line of human figures until it was too late. The trap was set and the elephants were coming straight into it, chivvied and sheep-dogged by the low-flying Cessna.

The two old cows burst out of the tree-line at full run, their bony legs flying, ears cocked back, loose grey folds of skin shuddering and wobbling with each jarring footfall. The rest of the herd were strung out behind them. The youngest calves were tiring, and their mothers pushed them along with their trunks.

The line of executioners froze, standing in a half circle like the mouth of a gill net extended to take in a shoal of fish. The elephants would pick up movement more readily than they would recognise the blurred man-shapes that their weak, panic-stricken eyes disclosed to them.

'Get the two old grannies first,' Johnny called softly. He had recognised the matriarchs and he knew that with them gone the herd would be disorganised and indecisive. His order was passed down the line.

The leading cows pounded down directly towards where Johnny stood. He let them come on. He held the rifle at high port across his chest. At a hundred yards' distance the two dowager elephants started to turn away from him, angling off to the left, and Johnny moved for the first time.

He lifted his rifle and waved it over his head and shouted in Sindebele, '*Nanzi Inkosikaze* – here I am, respected old lady.'

For the first time the two elephants recognised that he was not a tree-stump but a deadly enemy. Instantly they swung back towards him, and focusing all their ancestral hatred and

18

terror and concern for the herd upon him, they burst together into full charge.

They squealed their fury at him, extending their stride so that the dust spurted from under their colossal footpads. Their ears were rolled back along the top edge, sure sign of their anger. They towered over the group of tiny human figures. Daniel wished vehemently that he had taken the precaution of arming himself. He had forgotten how terrifying this moment was, with the nearest cow only fifty yards away and coming straight in at forty miles an hour.

Jock was still filming, although the angry shrieks of the two cows had been taken up by the entire herd. They came down upon them like an avalanche of grey granite, as though a cliff had been brought rumbling down with high explosive.

At thirty yards Johnny Nzou mounted the rifle to his shoulder and leaned forward to absorb the recoil. There was no telescopic sight mounted above the blue steel barrel. For close work like this he was using open express sights.

Since its introduction in 1912, thousands of sports and professional hunters had proved the .375 Holland & Holland to be the most versatile and effective rifle ever to have been brought to Africa. It had all the virtues of inherent accuracy and moderate recoil, while the 300-grain solid bullet was a ballistic marvel, with flat trajectory and extraordinary penetration.

Johnny aimed at the head of the leading cow, at the crease of the trunk between her myopic old eyes. The report was sharp as the lash of a bull-whip, and an ostrich feather of dust flew from the surface of her weathered grey skin at the precise point upon her skull at which he had aimed.

The bullet sliced through her head as easily as a steel nail driven through a ripe apple. It obliterated the top of her brain, and the cow's front legs folded under her, and Daniel felt the earth jump under his feet as she crashed down in a cloud of dust.

Johnny swung his aim on to the second cow, just as she came level with the carcass of her sister. He reloaded without taking the butt of the rifle from his shoulder, merely flicking the bolt back and forward. The spent brass case was flung high in a glinting parabola and he fired again. The sound of the two rifle

19

shots blended into each other; they were fired so swiftly as to cheat the ear into hearing a single prolonged detonation.

Once again the bullet struck exactly where it had been aimed and the cow died as the other had done, instantaneously. Her legs collapsed and she dropped and lay on her belly with her shoulder touching that of her sister. In the centre of each of their foreheads a misty pink plume of blood erupted from the tiny bullet-holes.

Behind them the herd was thrown into confusion. The bewildered beasts milled and circled, treading the grass flat and raising a curtain of dust that swirled about them, blanketing the scene so their forms looked ethereal and indistinct in the dust-cloud. The calves huddled for shelter beneath their mothers' bellies, their ears flattened against their skulls with terror, and they were battered and kicked and thrown about by the frantic movements of their dams.

The rangers closed in, firing steadily. The sound of gunfire was a long continuous rattle, like hail on a tin roof. They were shooting for the brain. At each shot one of the animals flinched or flung up its head, as the solid bullets cracked on the bone of the skull with the sound of a well-struck golf ball. At each shot one of the animals went down dead or stunned. Those killed cleanly, and they were the majority, collapsed at the back legs first and dropped with the dead weight of a maize sack. When the bullet missed the brain but passed close to it, the elephant reeled and staggered and went down kicking to roll on its side with a terrible despairing moan and grope helplessly at the sky with lifted trunk.

One of the young calves was trapped and pinned beneath its mother's collapsing carcass, and lay broken-backed and squealing in a mixture of pain and panic. Some of the elephant found themselves hemmed in by a palisade of fallen animals and they reared up and tried to scramble over them. The marksmen shot them down so that they fell upon the bodies of those already dead, while others tried to climb over these and were in their turn shot down.

It was swift. Within minutes all the adult animals were down, lying close together or piled upon each other in bleeding mounds and hillocks. Only the calves were still racing in bewildered circles, stumbling over the bodies of the dead and dying, squealing and tugging at the carcasses of their mothers.

The riflemen walked forward slowly, a tightening ring of gunmetal around the decimated herd. They fired and reloaded and fired again as they closed in. They picked off the calves, and when there remained not a single standing animal, they moved quickly into the herd, scrambling over the gigantic sprawling bodies, pausing only to fire a finishing bullet into each huge bleeding head. Most often there was no response to the second bullet in the brain, but occasionally an elephant not yet dead shuddered and straightened its limbs and blinked its eyes at the shot, then slumped lifelessly.

Within six minutes of Johnny's first shot, a silence fell over the killing ground on Long Vlei. Only their ears still sang to the brutal memory of gunfire. There was no movement; the elephant lay in windrows like wheat behind the blades of the mower, and the dry earth soaked up the blood. The rangers were still standing apart from each other, subdued and awed by the havoc they had wrought, staring with remorse at the mountain of the dead. Fifty elephant, two hundred tons of carnage.

Johnny Nzou broke the tragic spell that held them. He walked slowly to where the two old cows lay at the head of the herd. They lay side by side, shoulders touching, with their legs folded neatly under them, kneeling as though still alive with only the pulsing fountain of life-blood from their foreheads to spoil the illusion.

Johnny set the butt of his rifle on the ground and leaned upon it, studying the two old matriarchs for a long regretful moment. He was unaware that Jock was filming him. His actions and his words were completely unstudied and unrehearsed.

'*Hamba gahle, Amakhulu*,' he whispered. 'Go in peace, old grandmothers. You are together in death as you were in life. Go in peace, and forgive us for what we have done to your tribe.'

He walked away to the edge of the tree-line. Daniel did not follow him. He understood that Johnny wanted to be alone for a while now. The other rangers also avoided each other. There was no banter, nor self-congratulation; two of them wandered amongst the mountainous dead with a strangely disconsolate air; a third squatted where he had fired his last shot, smoking a cigarette and studying the dusty ground between his feet, while the last one had laid aside his rifle and, with hands thrust in his pockets and shoulders hunched, stared at the sky and watched the vultures gather.

At first the carrion birds were tiny specks against the glaring alps of cumulus cloud, like grains of pepper sprinkled on a tablecloth. Then they soared closer overhead, forming circling squadrons, turning on their wide wings in orderly formations, a dark wheel of death high above the killing-ground, and their shadows flitted over the piled carcasses in the centre of Long Vlei.

Forty minutes later Daniel heard the rumble of the approaching trucks, and saw them coming slowly through the forest. A squad of half-naked axemen ran ahead of the convoy, cutting out the brush and making a rough track for them to follow. Johnny stood up with obvious relief from where he had been sitting alone at the edge of the trees, and came to take charge of the butchering.

The piles of dead elephant were pulled apart with winches and chains. Then the wrinkled grey skin was sliced through down the length of the belly and the spine. Again the electric winches were brought into play and the skin was flensed off the carcass with a crackling sound as the subcutaneous tissue released its grip. It came off in long slabs, grey and corrugated on the outside, gleaming white on the inside. The men laid each strip on the dusty earth and heaped coarse salt upon it.

The naked carcasses looked strangely obscene in the bright sunlight, wet and marbled with white fat and exposed scarlet muscle, the swollen bellies bulging as though to invite the stroke of the flensing knives.

A skinner slipped the curved point of the knife into the belly of one of the old cows at the point where it met the sternum. Carefully controlling the depth of the cut so as not to puncture the entrails, he walked the length of the body drawing the blade like a zipper down the belly pouch so that it gaped open and the stomach sac bulged out, glistening like the silk of a parachute. Then the colossal coils of the intestines slithered after it. These seemed to have a separate life. Like the body of an awakening python, they twisted and unfolded under the impetus of their own slippery weight.

The chainsaw men set to work. The intrusive clatter of the two-stroke engines seemed almost sacrilegious in this place of death, and the exhausts blew snorting blue smoke into the bright air. They lopped the limbs off each carcass, and a fine mush of flesh and bone chips flew in a spray from the teeth of the spinning steel chains. Then they buzzed through the spine and ribs, and the carcasses fell into separate parts that were winched into the waiting refrigerator trucks.

A special gang went from carcass to carcass with long boat-hooks, poking in the soft wet mounds of spilled entrails to drag out the wombs of the females. Daniel watched as they split open one of the engorged wombs, dark purple with its covering of enlarged blood vessels. From the foetal sac, in a flood of amniotic fluid the foetus, the size of a large dog, slid out and lay in the trampled grass.

It was only a few weeks from term, a perfect little elephant covered with a coat of reddish hair that it would have lost soon after birth. It was still alive, moving its trunk feebly.

'Kill it,' Daniel ordered harshly in Sindebele. It was improbable that it could feel pain, but he turned away in relief as one of the men struck off the tiny head with a single blow of his panga. Daniel felt nauseated, but he knew that nothing from the cull should be wasted. The skin of the unborn elephant would be fine-grained and valuable, worth a few hundred dollars for a handbag or a briefcase.

To distract himself he walked away across the killing-ground. All that remained now were the heads of the great animals and the glistening piles of their entrails. From the guts nothing of value could be salvaged and they would be left for the vultures and hyena and jackal.

The ivory tusks, still embedded in their castles of bone, were the most precious part of the cull. The poachers and the ivory-hunters of old would not risk damaging them with a careless axe-stroke, and customarily would leave the ivory in the skull until the cartilaginous sheath that held it secure rotted and softened and released its grip. Within four or five days the tusks could usually be drawn by hand, perfect and unmarked. However, there was no time to waste on this procedure. The tusks must be cut out by hand.

The skinners who did this were the most experienced men, usually older, with grey woolly heads and blood-stained loincloths. They squatted beside the heads and tapped patiently with their native axes.

While they were engaged in this painstaking work Daniel stood with Johnny Nzou. Jock held the Sony VTR on them as Daniel commented, 'Gory work.'

'But necessary,' Johnny agreed shortly. 'On an average each adult elephant will yield about three thousand dollars in ivory, skin and meat.'

'To many people that will sound pretty commercial, especially as they have just witnessed the hard reality of the cull.' Daniel shook his head. 'You must know that there is a very strong campaign, led by the animal rights groups, to have the elephant placed on Appendix One of CITES, that is the Convention on International Trade in Endangered Species.'

'Yes, I know.'

'If that happens it would prohibit the trade in any elephant products, skin, ivory or meat. What do you think of that, Warden?'

'It makes me very angry.' Johnny dropped his cigarette and ground it under his heel. His expression was savage.

'It would prevent any further culling operations, wouldn't it?' Daniel persisted.

'Not at all,' Johnny contradicted him. 'We would still be forced to control the size of the herds. We would still be forced to cull. The only difference would be that we could not sell the elephant products. They would be wasted, a tragic criminal waste. We would lose millions of dollars of revenue which at present is being used to protect and enlarge and service the wildlife sanctuaries . . .' Johnny broke off and watched as a tusk was lifted out of the channel in the spongy bone of the skull by two of the skinners and laid carefully on the dry brown grass. Skilfully one of them drew the nerve, a soft grey gelatinous core, from the hollow end of the tusk. Then Johnny went

24

on, 'That tusk makes it easier for us to justify the continued existence of the Parks and the animals they contain to the local tribespeople living in close contact with wild animals on and near the boundaries of the national wilderness areas.'

'I don't understand,' Daniel encouraged him. 'Do you mean the local tribes resent the Parks and the animal population?'

'Not if they can derive some personal benefit from them. If we can prove to them that a cow elephant is worth three thousand dollars and that a foreign safari hunter will spend fifty or even a hundred thousand dollars to hunt a trophy bull, if we can show them that a single elephant is worth a hundred, even a thousand of their goats or scrawny cattle and that they will see some of that money coming to them and their tribe, then they will see the point of conserving the herds.'

'You mean the local peasants do not place a value on wildlife simply for its own sake.'

Johnny laughed bitterly. 'That's a First World luxury and affectation. The tribes here live very close to subsistence level. We are talking about an average family income of a hundred and twenty dollars a year, ten dollars a month. They cannot afford to set aside land and grazing for a beautiful but useless animal to live on. If the wild game is to survive in Africa it has to pay for its supper. There are no free rides in this harsh land.'

'One would think that living so close to nature they would have an instinctive feeling for it,' Daniel persisted.

'Yes, of course, but it is totally pragmatic. For millennia primitive man, living with nature, has treated it as a renewable resource. As the Eskimo lived on the caribou and seal and whale, or the American Indian on buffalo herds, they understood instinctively the type of management that we have never achieved. They were in balance with nature, until the white man came with explosive harpoon and Sharpe's rifle, or, here in Africa, came with his elite game department and game laws that made it a crime for the black tribesman to hunt on his own land, that reserved the wildlife of Africa for a select few to stare at and exclaim over.'

'You are being a racist,' Daniel chided him gently. 'The old colonial system preserved the wild game.'

'So how did it survive for a million years before the white

man arrived in Africa? No, the colonial system of game management was protectionist, not conservationist.'

'Aren't they the same thing, protection and conservation?'

'They are diametrically opposed. The protectionist denies man's right to exploit and harvest nature's bounty. He would deny that man has a right to kill a living animal, even if that threatens the survival of the species as a whole. If he were here today, the protectionist would prohibit us from this cull, and he would not want to look to the final consequence of that prohibition which, as we have seen, would be the eventual extinction of the entire elephant population and the destruction of this forest.

'However, the most damaging mistake that the old colonial protectionists made was to alienate the black tribesman from the benefits of controlled conservation. They denied him his share of the spoils, and built up in him a resentment towards the wild game. They broke down his natural instinct for management of his resources. They took away his control of nature and placed him in competition with the animals. The end result is that the average black peasant is hostile towards the game. The elephants raid his gardens and destroy the trees he uses for firewood. The buffalo and antelope eat the grass on which he feeds his cattle. The crocodile ate his grandmother, and the lion killed his father . . . Of course, he has come to resent the game herds.'

'The solution, Warden? Is there one?'

'Since independence from the colonial system we have been trying to change the attitude of our people,' Johnny told him. 'At first they demanded that they be allowed to enter the National Parks that the white man had proclaimed. They wanted to be allowed to go in and cut the trees and feed their cattle and build their villages. However, we have had a great deal of success in educating them to the value of tourism and safari-hunting and controlled culling. For the first time they are being allowed to participate in the profits, and there is a new understanding of conservation and sensible exploitation, especially amongst the younger generation. However, if the protectionist do-gooders of Europe and America were to force a ban on safari-hunting or the sale of ivory, it would set back all our

26

efforts. It would probably be the death knell of the African elephant and eventually the end of all the game.'

'So in the end it is all a matter of economics?' Daniel asked.

'Like everything else in this world, it is a matter of money,' Johnny agreed. 'If you give us enough money we will stop the poachers. If you make it worth their while, we will keep the peasants and their goats out of the Parks. However, the money must come from somewhere. The newly independent states of Africa with their exploding human populations cannot afford the First World luxury of locking away their natural assets. They must exploit them and conserve them. If you prevent us doing that, then you will be guilty of contributing to the extinction of African wildlife.' Johnny nodded grimly. 'Yes, it's a matter of economics. If the game can pay, then the game can stay.'

It was perfect, Daniel signalled Jock to stop filming and clasped Johnny's shoulder.

'I could make a star out of you. You're a natural.' He was only half joking. 'How about it, Johnny? You could do a hell of a lot more for Africa on the screen than you can here.'

'You want me to live in hotels and jet aircraft instead of sleeping under the stars?' Johnny feigned indignation. 'You want me to build up a nice little roll around my belly.' He prodded Daniel's midriff. 'And puff and pant when I run a hundred yards? No thank you, Danny. I'll stay here where I can drink Zambezi water, not Coca-Cola, and eat buffalo steaks, not Big Macs.'

They loaded the last rolls of salted elephant-hide and immature calf tusks by the glare of truck headlights, and climbed back up the rough winding road to the rim of the escarpment and the headquarters of the Park at Chiwewe in the dark.

Johnny drove the green Landrover at the head of the slow convoy of refrigerator trucks and Daniel sat beside him on the front seat. They talked in the soft desultory manner of old friends in perfect accord.

'Suicide weather,' Daniel wiped his forehead on the sleeve of his bush shirt. Even though it was almost midnight, the heat and the humidity were enervating. 'Rains will break soon.'

'Good thing you're getting out of the valley,' Johnny grunted.

'That road turns into a swamp in the rain and most of the rivers are impassable.'

The tourist camp at Chiwewe had been closed a week previously in anticipation of the onslaught of the rainy season.

'I don't look forward to leaving,' Daniel admitted. 'It's been like old times again.'

'Old times,' Johnny nodded. 'We had some fun. When are you coming back to Chiwewe?'

'I don't know, Johnny, but my offer is genuine. Come with me. We made a good team once; we would be good again. I know it.'

'Thanks, Danny.' Johnny shook his head. 'But I've got work to do here.'

'I won't give up,' Daniel warned him, and Johnny grinned.

'I know. You never do.'

In the morning, when Daniel climbed the small kopje behind the headquarters camp to watch the sunrise, the sky was filled with dark and mountainous cloud and the heat was still oppressive.

Daniel's mood matched that sombre dawn, for although he had captured some wonderful material during his stay, he had also rediscovered his friendship and affection for Johnny Nzou. The knowledge that it might be many years before they met again saddened him.

Johnny had invited him to breakfast on this, his last day. He was waiting for Daniel on the wide mosquito-screened verandah of the thatched bungalow that had once been Daniel's own home.

Daniel paused below the verandah and glanced around the garden. It was still the way that Vicky had planned it and originally laid it out. Vicky had been the twenty-year-old bride that Daniel had brought to Chiwewe all those years ago, a slim cheerful lass with long blonde hair and smiling green eyes, only a few years younger than Daniel at the time.

She had died in the front bedroom overlooking the garden

28

that she had cherished. An ordinary bout of malaria had turned without warning to the pernicious cerebral strain. It had been all over very swiftly, even before the flying doctor could reach the Park.

The eerie sequel to her death was that the elephants, who had never entered the fenced garden before, despite its laden citrus trees and rich vegetable plot, came that very night. They came at the exact hour of Vicky's death and completely laid waste the garden. They even ripped out the ornamental shrubs and rose bushes. Elephant seem to have a psychic sensitivity to death. It was almost as if they had sensed her passing, and Daniel's grief.

Daniel had never married again and had left Chiwewe not long after. The memories of Vicky were too painful to allow him to remain. Now Johnny Nzou lived in the bungalow and his pretty Matabele wife Mavis tended Vicky's garden. If Daniel had been able to choose, he would have had it no other way.

This morning Mavis had prepared a traditional Matabele breakfast of maize porridge and sour milk, thickened in a calabash gourd, the beloved *amasi* of the Nguni pastoral tribes. Afterwards, Johnny and Daniel walked down towards the ivory godown together. Halfway down the hill Daniel checked and shaded his eyes as he stared towards the visitors' camp. This was the game-fenced area on the river bank where the thatched cottages with circular walls stood under the wild fig trees. These structures, peculiar to southern Africa, were known as rondavels.

'I thought you told me that the Park was closed to visitors,' Daniel said. 'One of the rondavels is still occupied, and there's a car parked outside it.'

'That's a special guest, a diplomat, the Ambassador of the Taiwanese Republic of China to Harare,' Johnny explained. 'He is extremely interested in wildlife, particularly elephants, and has contributed a great deal to conservation in this country. We allow him special privileges. He wanted to be here without other tourists, so I kept the camp open for him—' Johnny broke off, then exclaimed, 'There he is now!'

Three men stood in a group at the foot of the hill. It was still too far to make out their features. As they started towards them, Daniel asked, 'What happened to the two white rangers who helped with the cull yesterday?'

'They were on loan from Wankie National Park. They left to go home early this morning.'

Closer to the group of three men Daniel made out the Taiwanese ambassador.

He was younger than he would have expected a man of such rank to be. Although it was often difficult for a Westerner to judge the age of an oriental, Daniel put him at a little over forty. He was tall and lean with straight black hair that was oiled and combed back from a high intelligent forehead. He was good-looking with a clear, almost waxen, complexion. There was something about his features that suggested that his ancestry was not pure Chinese, but mixed with European blood. Though his eyes were liquid jet-black in colour, their shape was rounded and his upper eyelids lacked the characteristic fold of skin at the inner corner.

'Good morning, Your Excellency,' Johnny greeted him with obvious respect. 'Warm enough for you?'

'Good morning, Warden.' The ambassador left the two black rangers and came to meet them. 'I prefer it to the cold.' He was wearing an open-necked short-sleeved blue shirt and slacks, and indeed looked cool and elegant.

'May I present Doctor Daniel Armstrong?' Johnny asked. 'Daniel, His Excellency the Ambassador of Taiwan, Ning Cheng Gong.'

'No introduction is necessary, Doctor Armstrong is a famous man.' Cheng smiled charmingly as he took Daniel's hand. 'I have read your books and watched your television programmes with the greatest of interest and pleasure.' His English was excellent, as though he were born to the language, and Daniel warmed to him.

'Johnny tells me that you are very concerned about the African ecology, and that you have made a great contribution to conservation in this country.'

Cheng made a deprecatory gesture. 'I only wish I could do more.' But he was staring at Daniel thoughtfully. 'Forgive me, Doctor Armstrong, but I did not expect to find other visitors at Chiwewe at this time of year. I was assured that the Park was closed.'

30

Although his tone was friendly, Daniel sensed that the question was not an idle one.

'Don't worry, Your Excellency. My camera man and I are leaving this afternoon. You will soon have the whole of Chiwewe to yourself,' Daniel assured him.

'Oh, please don't misunderstand me. I am not so selfish as to wish you gone. In fact, I am sorry to hear you are leaving so soon. I am sure we would have had a great deal to discuss.' Despite the denial, Daniel sensed that Cheng was relieved that he was leaving. His expression was still warm and his manner friendly, but Daniel was becoming aware of depths and layers below the urbane exterior.

The ambassador fell in between them, as they walked down to the ivory warehouse, and chatted in a relaxed manner, and then stood aside to watch as the rangers and a team of porters began to unload the newly culled ivory from the truck parked at the door to the warehouse. By this time Jock was there with his Sony camera filming the work from every angle.

As each tusk was brought out, still crusted with freshly congealed blood, it was weighed on the old-fashioned platform scale that stood at the entrance to the warehouse. Johnny Nzou sat at a rickety deal table and recorded the weight of each tusk in a thick leather-bound ledger. He then allocated a registration number to it and one of his rangers stamped that number into the ivory with a set of steel dies. Registered and stamped, the tusk was now legal ivory and could be auctioned and exported from the country.

Cheng watched the procedure with a lively interest. One pair of tusks, although not heavy or massive, was of particular beauty. They were delicately proportioned shafts with fine grain and elegant curves, an identical and perfectly matched pair.

Cheng stepped forward and squatted beside them as they lay on the scale. He stroked them with a lover's sensual touch. 'Perfect,' he purred. 'A natural work of art.' He broke off as he noticed Daniel watching him.

Daniel had been vaguely repelled by this display of cupidity, and it showed on his face.

Cheng stood up and explained smoothly. 'I have always been

fascinated by ivory. As you probably know, we Chinese consider it to be a highly propitious substance. Few Chinese households are without any ivory carving; it brings good luck to its owner. However, my family interest goes even deeper than common superstition. My father began his working life as an ivory-carver, and so great was his skill that by the time I was born he owned shops in Taipei and Bangkok, Tokyo and Hong Kong, all of them specialising in ivory artefacts. Some of my earliest memories are of the look and feel of ivory. As a boy, I worked as an apprentice ivory-carver in the store in Taipei, and I came to love and understand ivory as my father does. He has one of the most extensive and valuable collections . . .' he stopped himself. 'Forgive me, please. I sometimes get carried away by my passion, but that is a particularly beautiful set of tusks. It is very rare to find a pair so perfectly matched. My father would be ecstatic over them.'

He watched longingly as the tusks were carried away and packed with the hundreds of others in the warehouse.

'Interesting character,' Daniel remarked, after the last tusk had been registered and locked away, and he and Johnny were making their way up the hill to the bungalow for lunch. 'But how does the son of an ivory-carver get to be an ambassador?'

Johnny chuckled. 'Ning Cheng Gong's father may have come from a humble background, but he didn't remain there. I understand he still has his ivory shops and his collection, but those are merely his hobbies now. He is reputed to be one of the richest men, if not *the* richest man, in Taiwan – and that, as you can imagine, is very rich indeed. From what I hear he has his fingers in all the juiciest pies around the Pacific rim as well as some in Africa. He has a large family of sons and Cheng is the youngest and, they say, the brightest. I like him, don't you?'

'Yes, he seems pleasant enough, but there is just something a little odd. Did you notice his face as he fondled that tusk? It was,' Daniel searched for the word, 'unnatural?'

'You writers!' Johnny shook his head ruefully. 'If you can't find something sensational, you make it up.' And they both laughed.

Ning Cheng Gong stood with one of the black rangers at the foot of the hill and watched Daniel and Johnny disappear amongst the msasa trees.

'I do not like the white man being here,' said Gomo. Under Johnny Nzou, he was Chiwewe's senior ranger. 'Perhaps we should wait until another time.'

'The white man leaves this afternoon,' Cheng told him coldly. 'Besides which you have been well paid. Plans have been made that cannot be altered now. The others are already on their way and cannot be sent back.'

'You have only paid us half of what we agreed,' Gomo protested.

'The other half when your work is done, not before,' Cheng said softly, and Gomo's eyes were like the eyes of a snake. 'You know what you have to do,' Cheng went on.

Gomo was silent for a moment. The foreigner had indeed paid him a thousand US dollars, the equivalent of six months' salary, with the promise of another year's salary to follow after the job was done.

'You will do it?' Cheng insisted.

'Yes,' Gomo agreed. 'I will do it.'

Cheng nodded. 'It will be tonight or tomorrow night, not later. Be ready, both of you.'

'We will be ready,' Gomo promised, and climbed into his Landrover, where the second black ranger waited, and they drove away.

Cheng walked back to his rondavel in the deserted visitors' camp. The cottage was identical to the other thirty which during the dry cool season usually housed a full complement of tourists. He fetched a cool drink from the refrigerator and sat on the screen porch to wait out the hottest hours of the noonday.

He felt nervous and restless. Deep down he shared Gomo's misgivings about the project. Although they had considered every possible eventuality and planned for each of them, there was always the unforeseeable, the unpredictable, such as the presence of Armstrong.

It was the first time he had attempted a *coup* of this magnitude. It was his own initiative. Of course, his father knew about and thoroughly approved of the other lesser shipments, but the risk was far greater this time, in proportion to the rewards. If he succeeded he would earn his father's respect, and that was more important to him even than the material profits. He was the youngest son, and he had to strive that much harder to win his place in his father's affections. For that reason alone he must not fail.

In the years that he had been at the embassy in Harare, he had consolidated his place in the illicit ivory and rhino-horn trade. It had begun with a deceptively casual remark at a dinner-party by a middle-ranking government official about the convenience of diplomatic privilege and access to the diplomatic courier service. With the business training that his father had given him, Cheng recognised the approach immediately for what it was, and made a non-committal but encouraging response.

A week of delicate negotiations followed and then Cheng was invited to play golf with another higher official. His driver parked the ambassadorial Mercedes in the car park at the rear of the Harare golf club and as instructed left it unattended while Cheng was out on the course. Cheng was officially a ten-handicap golfer but could play well below that when he chose. On this occasion he allowed his opponent to win three thousand US dollars and paid him in cash in front of witnesses in the club house. When he returned to his official residence he ordered the driver to park the Mercedes in the garage and then dismissed him. In the boot he found six large rhino horns packed in layers of hessian cloth.

He sent these out in the next diplomatic pouch to Taipei and they were sold through his father's shop in Hong Kong for sixty thousand US dollars. His father was delighted with the transaction and wrote Cheng a long letter of approbation and reminded his son of his deep interest in, and love of, ivory.

Cheng let it be known discreetly that he was a connoisseur of ivory as well as of rhino horn, and he was offered at bargain prices various pieces of unregistered and unstamped ivory. It did not take long for the word to spread in the small closed world of the poachers that there was a new buyer in the field.

Within months he was approached by a Sikh businessman from Malawi who was ostensibly looking for Taiwanese invest-ment in a fishing venture that he was promoting on Lake Malawi. Their first meeting went very well. Cheng found that

Chetti Singh's figures added up attractively, and passed them on to his father in Taipei. His father approved the estimates and agreed a joint venture with Chetti Singh. When the documents were signed at the embassy, Cheng invited him to dinner, and during the meal Chetti Singh remarked, 'I understand that your illustrious father is loving very much the beautiful ivory. As a token of my utmost esteem I could be arranging for a regular supply. I am sure that you would be forwarding the goods to your father without too much scarlet tape. Most miserably the ivory will be unstamped, never mind.'

'I have a deep distaste for red tape,' Cheng assured him.

Within a short time it became obvious to Cheng that Chetti Singh was head of a network that operated in all those African countries that still had healthy populations of elephant and rhino. From Botswana and Angola, Zambia, Tanzania and Mozambique, he gathered in the white gold and the horn. He controlled all aspects of his organisation down to the actual composition of the armed gangs who raided regularly into the National Parks in those countries.

At first Cheng was merely another customer of his, but once the fishing partnership on Lake Malawi began to flourish and they were netting hundreds of tons of tiny kapenta fish each week, drying them and exporting them to the east, their relationship began to change. It became more cordial and trusting. Finally Chetti Singh offered Cheng and his father a proprietary stake in the ivory trade. Naturally he asked for a substantial investment to allow him to expand the scope and range of the partnership's operations, and another larger payment for his share of goodwill in the enterprise. In all, it amounted to almost a million dollars. Cheng, on his father's behalf, was able by astute bargaining to reduce this initial fee by fifty per cent.

Only once he was a full partner could Cheng appreciate the extent and range of the operation. In each of the countries which still harboured elephant herds, Chetti Singh had been able to put in place clandestine circles of accomplices in government. Many of his contacts went as high as ministerial level. Within most of the major National Parks he had informers and officials on his payroll. Some were merely game scouts or rangers, but others were the actual chief wardens in charge of the Parks, those appointed as guardians and protectors of the herds.

The partnership was so lucrative that when Cheng's original term of appointment as ambassador expired, his father arranged through friends high in the Taiwanese government for it to be extended for a further three-year term.

By this time Cheng's father and brothers had become fully aware of the investment opportunities that Africa offered. Beginning with the small but profitable fishing venture and then the ivory partnership, the family had been attracted more and more to the dark continent. Neither Cheng nor his father had any scruples about apartheid and began investing heavily in South Africa. They were well aware that world condemnation and the policy of economic sanctions had depressed the prices of land and other valuable assets in that country to a point where no sensible businessman could resist them.

'Honoured parent,' Cheng had told his father on one of his frequent returns to Taipei, 'within ten years apartheid and white minority rule will have passed from the face of the land. Once that happens, prices in South Africa will rise to find their true levels.'

They purchased great ranches of tens of thousands of acres for the same price as a three-room flat in Taipei. They purchased factories and office blocks and shopping centres from American companies forced by their government to disinvest from South Africa. They paid five and ten cents for a dollar's worth of value.

However, Cheng's father, who had been among other things a steward of the Hong Kong race club, was too astute a gambler to place all his bets on a single horse. They invested in other African countries. An agreement had just been negotiated between South Africa and Cuba and Angola and America for the independence of Namibia. The family invested in property in Windhoek and fishing licences and mineral rights in that country. Through Chetti Singh, Cheng was introduced to ministers of government in Zambia and Zaïre and Kenya and Tanzania who for financial considerations were inclined to look favourably on Taiwanese investment in their countries, at prices which Cheng's father found acceptable.

Nevertheless, despite all these other major investments, Cheng's father, for sentimental reasons, was still drawn to the original ivory venture which had first provoked his interest in the dark continent. At their last meeting he had remarked to Cheng, as his son knelt in front of him to ask his blessing, 'My son, it would please me greatly if, once you return to Africa, you were able to find a large quantity of registered and stamped ivory.'

'Illustrious father, the only sources of legal ivory are the government auctions—' Cheng broke off as he saw his father's expression of scorn.

'Ivory purchased at government auctions leaves very little margin of profit,' the old man hissed. 'I had expected you to show better sense than that, my son.' His father's censure rankled deeply, and Cheng spoke to Chetti Singh at the very next opportunity.

Chetti Singh stroked his rolled beard thoughtfully. He was a handsome man and the immaculate white turban added to his stature. 'I am now thinking of but one single solitary source of registered ivory,' he said. 'And that is being the government warehouse.'

'You are suggesting that the ivory might be taken from the warehouse before the auction?'

'Perhaps . . .' Chetti Singh shrugged, 'but it would be calling for great and meticulous laying of plans. Let me run my mind over and around this vexing problem.'

Three weeks later they met again at Chetti Singh's office in Lilongwe.

'I have occupied my mind greatly, and a solution has occurred to me,' the Sikh told him.

'How much will it cost?' Cheng's first question was instinctive.

'Kilo for kilo, no more than the acquisition of unregistered ivory, but as there will be only opportunity to procure a single and solitary shipment we will be wise to be making it as large as possible. The contents of an entire warehouse, never mind! How would your father be struck by that?'

Cheng knew his father would be delighted. Registered ivory had three or four times the value of illicit ivory in the international market-place.

37

'Let us consider which country will provide us with this merchandise,' Chetti Singh suggested, but it was obvious that he had already decided. 'Not Zaïre or South Africa. Those are two countries where I do not have an effective organisation. Zambia and Tanzania and Kenya have very little ivory remaining. We are left with Botswana, where there is no large-scale culling, or finally Zimbabwe.'

'Good,' Cheng nodded with satisfaction.

'The ivory is accumulated in the game department warehouses at Wankie and Harare and Chiwewe until is being undertaken the bi-annual auction. We would acquire the merchandise from one of those centres.'

'Which one?'

'The warehouse in Harare is too well guarded.' Chetti Singh held up three fingers of his one hand and, having discarded Harare, he folded one down, leaving two fingers raised. 'Wankie is the largest National Park. However, it is far from the Zambian border.' He folded down another finger. 'Which leaves Chiwewe. I have trustworthy agents on the Park's staff there. They tell me that the warehouse is almost full of registered ivory at the present time, and the Park headquarters are less than thirty miles from the Zambezi River and the Zambian border. One of my teams could cross the river and be there in a day's march, never mind!'

'You intend to rob the warehouse?' Cheng leaned forward over his desk.

'Without the shade or fraction of a doubt.' Chetti Singh lowered his raised finger and looked surprised. 'Was that not also your intention all along?'

'Perhaps,' Cheng replied carefully. 'But is it feasible?'

'Chiwewe is in a remote and isolated area of the country but it lies on the river, which is an international boundary. I would send in a raiding party of twenty men armed absolutely with automatic weapons and led by one of my best and most reliable hunters. In darkness they cross the river from Zambia in canoes and in a day's hard marching they reach the Park's headquarters and fall upon it. They dispose of all witnesses . . .'

Cheng coughed nervously and Chetti Singh paused and looked at him questioningly. 'These would not amount to more than four or five persons. The permanent rangers are in my pay. The visitors' camp will be closed against the rainy season and the bulk of the staff will have returned to their villages on leave. The only remaining personnel will be the Park warden and two or three other skeleton staff.'

'Still, is there no way that we can avoid disposing of them?' It was not a matter of scruples that made Cheng hesitate. It was prudent not to take unnecessary risks, if they could be avoided.

'If you can be suggesting alternatives, I would be pleased to cast my mind over them,' Chetti Singh told him, and after a moment's thought Cheng shook his head.

'No, not at the moment, but please go on. Let me hear the rest of your plan.'

'Very well. My men dispose of all witnesses and burn down the ivory warehouse and then immediately retreat across the river.' The Sikh stopped speaking, but he watched Cheng's face with ill-concealed glee, anticipating his next question. It annoyed Cheng that he must ask it, for it sounded naïve even to his own ears.

'But what about the ivory?'

Chetti Singh smirked mysteriously, forcing him to ask again.

'Will your poachers take the ivory? You say they will be a small party. Surely they will not be able to carry that much, will they?'

'That is the absolute beauty of my plan. The raid is a dead herring for the Zimbabwe police.' And this time Cheng smiled at the solecism. 'We want them to believe that the poachers have taken the ivory. Then they will not think to look for it inside their own country, will they?'

Now, as he sat on his verandah in the midday heat, Cheng nodded grudgingly. Chetti Singh's plan was ingenious, except, of course, that it did not take into account the presence of Armstrong and his television crew. In fairness, however, none of them could have foreseen that.

Once again he considered delaying or cancelling the operation entirely, but almost immediately rejected the idea. By this time, Chetti Singh's men would be across the river and marching on the camp. There was no way he could reach them, and warn them to turn back. They were far past the point of no return. If

Armstrong and his camera man were still here when Chetti Singh's men arrived, then they would have to be disposed of along with the warden and his family and staff.

Cheng's train of thought was interrupted by the ringing of the telephone at the far end of the verandah. The VIP cottage was the only one in the visitors' camp equipped with a telephone. He jumped up and went to it quickly. He had been expecting the call. It had been prearranged and was part of Chetti Singh's plan.

'Ambassador Ning,' he said, and Johnny Nzou answered.

'Sorry to trouble you, Your Excellency, but there is a call from your embassy in Harare. A gentleman calling himself Mr Huang. He says he is your *chargé*. Will you take the call?'

'Thank you, Warden. I will speak to Mr Huang.' He knew that it was a party line that crossed a hundred and fifty miles of wild bush from the district telephone exchange at the little village of Karoi, and the voice of his *chargé* relayed from Harare was a whisper that seemed to come from some far corner of the galaxy. The message was the one he had expected, and afterwards Cheng cranked the handle of the antiquated telephone and Johnny Nzou came on the line again.

'Warden, my presence is required in Harare urgently. It is most unfortunate; I was looking forward to a few more days of relaxation.'

'I also regret that you are forced to leave. My wife and I would have liked you to have dinner with us.'

'Perhaps some other time.'

'The refrigerator trucks are taking the elephant meat up to Karoi this evening. It might be best if you travelled in convoy with them. Your Mercedes does not have four-wheel drive, and it looks as though it might rain at any time.'

That also was part of Chetti Singh's plan. The raid had been timed to coincide with the elephant cull and the departure of the refrigerator trucks. However, Cheng hesitated deliberately before he asked, 'When are the trucks leaving?'

'One of them has engine trouble.' Gomo the ranger had sabotaged the alternator. The object was to delay the departure of the convoy until the arrival of the raiding party. 'However, the driver tells me that they should be ready to leave around six o'clock this evening.' Johnny Nzou's voice changed as a thought struck him. 'Of course, Doctor Armstrong is leaving almost immediately, you could drive in convoy with him.'

'No. No!' Cheng cut in quickly. 'I cannot leave that soon. I will wait for the trucks.'

'As you wish.' Johnny sounded puzzled. 'However, I cannot guarantee when the convoy will be ready to leave and I am sure Doctor Armstrong would agree to delay an hour or so.'

'No,' Cheng told him firmly. 'I will not inconvenience or delay Doctor Armstrong. I will travel with your convoy. Thank you, Warden.'

To end the conversation and forestall any further discussion, he hung up the receiver. He frowned. Armstrong's presence was becoming increasingly troublesome. The sooner he disappeared the happier Cheng would be.

However, it was another twenty minutes before he heard the sound of a diesel engine coming from the direction of the warden's bungalow. He stood up and went to the screen door of the verandah and watched the Toyota Landcruiser coming down the hill. On the door of the truck was painted the logo of Armstrong Productions, a disembodied arm with the wrist encircled by a spiked bracelet, and the elbow bent and tensed in a body-builder's stylised pose to raise a heroic bulge of biceps. Doctor Armstrong was at the driver's wheel and his camera man was in the front seat beside him.

They were leaving at last. Cheng nodded with satisfaction and glanced at his wristwatch. It was a few minutes after one o'clock. They would have at least four hours to get well clear before the attack on the headquarters was launched.

Daniel Armstrong saw him and braked the truck. He rolled down the side window and smiled across at Cheng.

'Johnny tells me you are also leaving today, Your Excellency,' he called. 'Are you sure that we can't be of assistance?'

'Not at all, Doctor.' Cheng smiled politely. 'It is all arranged. Please do not worry about me.'

Armstrong made him feel uneasy. He was a big man with thick curly hair that gave him a tousled outdoors appearance. His gaze was direct and his smile was lazy. Cheng thought that to the eyes of a Westerner he might appear extremely attractive, especially if the Westerner were female, but to Cheng's Chinese eye, his nose was grotesquely large and his wide mouth had a mobile childlike expression. He might have dismissed him as offering no serious threat, except for the eyes. Those eyes made Cheng uneasy. They were alert and penetrating.

Armstrong stared at him for a full five seconds before he smiled again and thrust his hand out of the Toyota's rolled-down window.

'Well then, I'll say cheerio, Your Excellency. Let's hope we get an opportunity for that chat one day soon.' He engaged the gear-shift, raised his right hand in salutation and drove down towards the main gates of the camp.

Cheng watched the truck out of sight and then turned and stared down along the crests of the hills. They were jagged and uneven as a crocodile's teeth.

Twenty miles or so to the west, one of the dark cumulus thunder-heads was abruptly shot through by vivid lightning. Even as he watched, rain began to fall from the drooping belly of the cloud mass, first in pale blue streamers and then in a sullen deluge, as impenetrable as a sheet of lead, that obscured the far hills.

Chetti Singh could not have timed it better. Soon the valley and its escarpment would be a morass. A police team sent to investigate any suspicious occurrence at Chiwewe would not only find the road impassable, but if they did succeed in reaching the Park headquarters, the torrential rain would have scoured the hills and washed away all clues and signs of the raiding party's progress.

'Just let them arrive soon,' he hoped fervently. 'Make it today and not tomorrow.' He checked his wristwatch. It was not quite two o'clock. Sunset at seven-thirty, although with the dense cloud cover it would probably be dark before that. 'Let it be today,' he reiterated.

He fetched his binoculars and his battered copy of Roberts' *Birds of South Africa* from the table on the verandah of the cottage. He was at pains to demonstrate to the warden that he was an ardent naturalist. That was his excuse for being here.

He climbed into his Mercedes and drove down to the warden's office behind the ivory godown. Johnny Nzou was at his desk. Like any other civil service employee, half the warden's work was made up of filling in forms and requisitions and registers and reports. Johnny looked up from his piles of paper as Cheng stood in the doorway.

'I thought that while I was waiting for the refrigerator truck to be repaired, I might as well go down to the water-hole at Fig Tree Pan,' he explained, and Johnny smiled sympathetically as he noticed the binoculars and field guide. Both were the paraphernalia of the typical bird-watcher, and he always felt well-disposed towards anybody who shared his love of nature.

'I'll send one of my rangers to call you when the convoy is ready to leave, but I can't promise it will be this evening,' Johnny told him. 'They tell me that the alternator on one truck is burned out. Spare parts are a terrible problem in this country; there just isn't sufficient foreign exchange to pay for everything we need.'

Cheng drove down to the man-made water-hole. Less than a mile from Chiwewe headquarters a borehole had been sunk at the head of a small vlei. From it a windmill pumped a trickle of water into a muddy pond to attract birds and animals to the proximity of the camp.

As Cheng parked the Mercedes in the observation area overlooking the pool, a small herd of kudu that had been drinking from it took fright and scattered into the surrounding bush. They were large beige-coloured antelope, striped with pale chalk lines across their backs, with long legs and necks, and huge trumpet-shaped ears. Only the males carried wide corkscrewed horns.

Cheng was too agitated to use his binoculars, although clouds of birds descended to drink at the water-hole. The fire finches burned like tiny scarlet flames, and the starlings were a shining iridescent green that reflected the sunlight. Cheng was a talented artist not only with ivory carver's knives but also with water colours. One of his favourite subjects had always been wild birds which he depicted in traditional romantic Chinese style.

Today he could not concentrate on them as they settled at the water. Instead he fitted a cigarette into his ivory holder and puffed at it restlessly. This was the spot he had chosen as the rendezvous with the leader of the poachers, and Cheng scanned the encroaching bush anxiously as he fidgeted and smoked.

Still, the first indication he had that someone was there was the sound of a voice through the open window of the Mercedes beside him. Cheng started uncontrollably and turned quickly to the man who stood beside the motor car.

He had a scar that ran down from the corner of his left eye into the line of his top lip. The lip was puckered upwards on that side giving him an uneven sardonic smile. Chetti Singh had warned Cheng about the scar. It was an infallible point of recognition.

'Sali?' Cheng's voice was breathless. The poacher had startled him. 'You are Sali?'

'Yes,' the man agreed, smiling with only half his twisted mouth. 'I am Sali.'

His skin was almost purple black, the scar a livid pink upon it. He was short in stature but with broad shoulders and muscular limbs. He wore a tattered shirt and shorts of faded khaki drill that were crusted and stained with sweat and filth. He had obviously travelled hard, for his bare legs were floured with dust to the knee. In the heat he stank of stale sweat, a goaty and rancid odour that made Cheng draw away fastidiously. The gesture was not wasted on the poacher and his smile broadened into a genuine grin.

'Where are your men?' Cheng demanded, and Sali prodded his thumb towards the dense encircling bush.

'You are armed?' he insisted, and Sali's grin became insolent. He did not deign to reply to such a fatuous question. Cheng realised that relief and nervousness had made him garrulous. He determined to contain himself, but the next question slipped out before he could prevent it.

'You know what has to be done?'

With a fingertip Sali rubbed the glossy streak of scar tissue down his cheek and nodded.

'You are to leave no witnesses.' Cheng saw from his eyes that the poacher had not understood, so he repeated, 'You must kill them all. When the police come there must be no one for them to talk to.'

Sali inclined his head in agreement. Chetti Singh had explained to him in detail. The orders had been agreeable. Sali had a bitter feud against the Zimbabwe Parks Department. Only a year previously Sali's two younger brothers had crossed the Zambezi with a small group of men to hunt rhinoceros. They had run into one of the Parks anti-poaching units who were all ex-guerrilla fighters and armed, like them, with AK 47 assault rifles. In the fierce fire-fight that ensued, one of his brothers had been killed and the other shot through the spine and crippled for life. Despite his wound they had brought him to trial in Harare and he had been sentenced to seven years' imprisonment.

Thus Sali the poacher felt no great affection for the Parks rangers and it showed in his expression as he agreed. 'We will leave nobody.'

'Except the two rangers,' Cheng qualified the threat. 'Gomo and David. You know them.'

'I know them.' Sali had worked with them before.

'They will be at the workshops with the two big trucks. Make sure all your men understand that they are not to touch them or damage the trucks in any way.'

'I will tell them.'

'The warden will be in his office. His wife and their three children are at the bungalow on the hill. There are four camp servants and their families in the domestic compound. Make sure it is surrounded before you open fire. Nobody must get away.'

'You chatter like a monkey in a wild plum tree,' Sali told him scornfully. 'I know all these things. Chetti Singh has told me.'

'Then go and do as you have been told,' Cheng ordered sharply, and Sali leaned in through the Mercedes' window forcing the Chinaman to hold his breath and draw away from him.

Sali rubbed his thumb and forefinger together in the universal sign for money. Cheng reached across and opened the cubbyhole in the Mercedes' dashboard. The ten-dollar bills were in bundles of a hundred, each secured by a rubber band. He counted them into Sali's open hand, three bundles of a thousand dollars each. It would work out to approximately five dollars a kilo for the vast store of ivory in the camp warehouse, ivory that would be worth a thousand dollars a kilo in Taipei.

On the other hand, to Sali the sheaves of green bills represented an enormous fortune. He had never in his entire life held that amount of money in his hand at one time.

His usual reward for poaching a good elephant, for risking his life against the anti-poaching teams by penetrating deep into forbidden territory, for risking his life again by firing at the great beasts with the light bullets of the AK 47, for cutting out the tusks and carrying their galling weight back over heavy broken ground – his usual reward for all that risk and labour amounted to around thirty dollars an elephant killed – say, a dollar a kilo.

The treasury bills that Cheng placed in his hands represented the reward he could expect from five years of hard and dangerous labour. So, compared to that, what was the killing of a few Parks officials and their families? It entailed very little additional effort and minimal risk. For three thousand dollars, it would be a pleasure indeed.

Both men were mightily pleased with their bargain.

'I will wait here until I hear the guns,' Cheng told him delicately, and Sali smiled so broadly that he showed all his large brilliant white teeth right to the wisdoms in the back of his jaw.

'You will not have to wait long,' he promised, and then as silently as he had appeared, he vanished back into the bush.

Daniel Armstrong drove at a sedate pace. The road was fairly good by central African standards; it was graded regularly, for few of the visitors to the park drove four-wheel-drive vehicles. Nevertheless, Daniel was in no hurry and did not push it. His Toyota was equipped with a full range of camping equipment. He never stayed at motels or other formal lodgings if he could avoid them. Not only were they few and far between in this country, but in most cases the food and comforts they offered were much below the standard that Daniel could provide in his own temporary camps.

This evening he would keep going until a little before sunset and then find some inviting stand of forest or pleasant stream at which to pull well off the road and break out the tucker box and Chivas bottle. He doubted that they would get as far as Mana Pools, and certainly they would not reach the main metalled highway that ran from the Chirundu bridge on the Zambezi, south to Karoi and Harare.

Jock was pleasant company. It was one of the reasons that Daniel had hired him. They had worked together on and off over the past five years. Jock was a freelance cameraman and Daniel called him up on contract whenever he had a new project signed up and financed. They had covered huge tracts of Africa together, from the forbidding beaches of the Skeleton Coast in Namibia to the drought and famine-ravaged mountains and ambas of Ethiopia and the depths of the Sahara. Although they had not succeeded in forging a deep or committed friendship, they had spent weeks together in the remote wilderness and there had seldom been any friction between them.

They chatted amicably as Daniel took the heavily laden truck down the twisting escarpment road. Whenever a bird or animal or unusual tree caught their attention Daniel parked the truck and made notes and observations while Jock filmed.

Before they had covered twenty miles they came to a section of the road over which a large herd of elephant had fed during the previous night. They had pulled down branches and pushed over many of the large mopane trees. Some of these had fallen across the roadway, blocking it entirely. From those trees still standing they had stripped the bark, leaving the trunks naked white and weeping with sap.

'Naughty beggars,' Daniel grinned as he contemplated the destruction. 'They seem to delight in blocking the roads.' Yet it was clear demonstration, if any were needed, that regular culling of the herds was absolutely necessary. The mopane forest could survive only a limited amount of this destructive feeding.

They were able to pull off the road and detour around many of the fallen trees, although once or twice they were forced to hitch up a tree-trunk to the Toyota's tow chain and bodily haul it aside before they could pass. Thus it was after four o'clock before they reached the valley bottom and turned eastwards through the mopane forest towards the Mana Pools turn-off, near which they had filmed the elephant cull.

At this stage both of them were engrossed in a discussion of how best Daniel could edit the huge volume of film that they now had on tape. Daniel was experiencing the heightened anticipation he always felt at this stage of a production. It was all in the can. Now he could return to London where, in a hired editing room at Castle Film Studios, he would spend long weeks and months sequestered in a dark room absorbed in the exacting but infinitely rewarding labour of cutting each scene into the next and composing the commentary to support it.

Even though the forefront of his mind was focused on what Jock was saying, he was fully aware of his surroundings. Nevertheless he almost missed it. He drove over it and went on for almost two hundred yards before it fully registered that he had passed something unusual. Perhaps it was a relic of his experiences during the bush war when any extraneous mark on the roadway could give warning of a land mine and violent death buried in the tracks. In those days he would have been much quicker to register and react, but the intervening years had blunted his reflexes.

He braked the truck and Jock broke off what he was saying and glanced at him quizzically.

'What is it?'

'Don't know.' Daniel swivelled in the seat as he reversed the Landcruiser back down the track. 'Probably nothing,' he murmured, but there was a tiny niggling doubt in the back of his mind.

He stopped and pulled on the handbrake and climbed down out of the cab.

'I can't see anything.' Jock hung out of the window on the far side.

'That's just it,' Daniel agreed. 'There is a blank spot here.' He pointed down the dusty roadway whose surface was dimpled and pocked by the marvellous graffiti of the bush. The tiny v-shaped spurs of francolin and other birds, the serpentine tracks of insects and lizards, the larger hoof-prints of various species of antelope and hare, mongoose and jackal were woven into an intricate tapestry of sign except at one point in the roadway where the soft surface was smooth and unblemished. Daniel squatted beside it and studied it for a moment. 'Somebody has swept sign,' he said.

'So what's so bloody extraordinary about that?' Jock climbed down out of the truck and came to join him.

'Nothing, perhaps.' He stood up. 'Or everything. Depends on how you look at it.'

'Shoot?' Jock invited him.

'Only human beings cover their tracks, and only when they're up to no good. Besides that, there aren't supposed to be people wandering around on foot in the middle of a National Park.'

Daniel skirted the area of soft earth that had been carefully swept with a leafy branch and stepped off the track into the stand of tussocked grass on the verge. Immediately he saw other signs of anti-tracking. The grass clumps had been crushed and flattened as a party of men on foot had used them as stepping stones. It seemed to be a large party and Daniel felt the hair on his forearms and at the back of his neck prickle and lift.

Contact! he thought. It was like the old days with the Scouts when they first picked up the sign of a group of guerrilla terrorists. He experienced that same breathless feeling of excitement and the same stone of fear heavy in his bowels.

It took an effort to thrust those feelings aside. Those dangerous days were long past. Still he followed the sign. Although the chase had taken some elementary precautions, they were perfunctory. A cadre of ZANU in the war days would have been more professional. Within fifty yards of the road Daniel found the first clear print of a shod human foot, and a few yards further on the band had joined a narrow game track and formed up in Indian file, abandoning all further attempts at anti-tracking. They had struck out in the direction of the escarpment and Chiwewe base camp with determined stride. Daniel was amazed to find how large the band was. He counted the tracks of between sixteen and twenty individuals in the group.

After following them another two or three hundred yards Daniel stopped and thought about it carefully. Considering the size of the group and the direction from which they had come, the most obvious assumption was that they were a band of Zambian poachers who had crossed the Zambezi River on a raid for ivory and rhino horn. That would also explain the precautions they had taken to cover their tracks.

What he should do now was to warn Johnny Nzou so that he could get an anti-poaching unit in as fast as possible for a follow-up action. Daniel pondered the best way to do this. There was a telephone in the ranger's office at Mana Pools only an hour's drive ahead, or Daniel could turn back to Chiwewe headquarters and take the warning in person.

The decision was made for him as he made out the line of telephone poles in the forest not far ahead. These were cut from native timber and steeped in black creosote to discourage the attack of termites. Between the poles the draped copper telephone wires gleamed in the late sunlight, except between two of the poles directly ahead.

Daniel hurried forward and then stopped abruptly.

The telephone wires had been cut and dangled from the white ceramic insulators at the top of the nearest pole. Daniel reached out for the end of one wire, and peered at it. There was no question about it. It had been deliberately cut. The shear marks made by the cutting edge of a pair of pliers were evident in the malleable red metal of the cable. There were the milling tracks of many men at the base of the pole.

'Why the hell would a poacher want to cut the telephone lines?' Daniel wondered aloud, and his sense of unease turned to alarm. 'This begins to look really ugly. I have to warn Johnny. He has to get on to these gentlemen damned quickly. Only one way to warn him now.'

At a run he started back to where he had left the Land-cruiser.

'What the hell is going on?' Jock wanted to know as he jumped up into the cab and started the motor.

'I don't know, but I don't like it, whatever it is,' Daniel told him as he reversed off the road and then swung back on to it, headed in the opposite direction.

Daniel drove fast now, ripping up a long bank of dust behind the Landcruiser, slowing only for the fords through the steep dry water-courses and then accelerating away again. As he drove, it occurred to him that the gang could reach the head-quarters camp by cutting across the loop that the road made down the pass of the escarpment. It would be a steep climb up on to the plateau, but on foot they could cut almost thirty miles off the longer route that Daniel was forced to follow. He estimated that the telephone lines had been cut about five or six hours earlier. He arrived at that estimate by a process of fieldcraft deduction which included a study of the erosion of the spoor and the recovery time of trodden-down grass and vegetation.

He could not think of any reason why a gang of poachers should want to visit Chiwewe headquarters. On the contrary, he would expect them to give it the widest possible berth. However, their tracks were headed resolutely in that direction, and they had cut the telephone wires. Their conduct was brazen and aggressive. If Chiwewe was indeed their destination then they could be there already. He glanced at his wristwatch. Yes, they could have climbed the escarpment and, by hard marching, have reached the headquarters camp an hour or so ago.

But why? There were no tourists. In Kenya and other countries further north the poachers, having depleted the elephant herds, had taken to attacking and robbing foreign tourists. Perhaps this gang had taken a tip from their northern counterparts. 'But there are no tourists at Chiwewe. There's nothing of value—' he broke off as the fallacy of that assumption occurred to him. 'Shit!' he whispered. 'The ivory.' Suddenly dread chilled the sweat on his cheeks. 'Johnny,' he whispered. 'And Mavis and the kids.'

The Landcruiser was flying down the track now and he slid her into the first hairpin bend that led on to the slope of the escarpment.

As he came through the corner at speed a huge white vehicle filled the road directly ahead of him. Even as Daniel hit the brakes and swung the Toyota hard over he realised that it was one of the refrigerator trucks. He missed its front wing by a foot as he went up on to the verge and tore into a patch of scrub. He came to rest with the nose of the Toyota almost touching the trunk of a big mopane. Jock was thrown up against the dashboard by the deceleration.

Daniel jumped out of the Toyota and ran back to where the refrigerator truck had managed to pull up, blocking his tailgate. He recognised Gomo, the senior ranger, at the wheel and called to him.

'Sorry! My fault. Are you okay?'

Gomo looked shaken by the near collision but he nodded. 'I'm okay, Doctor.'

'When did you leave Chiwewe?' Daniel demanded, and Gomo hesitated. For some reason the question seemed to disconcert him. 'How long ago?' Daniel insisted.

'I don't know for sure . . .' At that moment there was the sound of other vehicles approaching down the escarpment road and Daniel glanced around to see the second truck come grinding through the next bend.

It was running in low gear to combat the gravity of the steep gradient. Fifty yards behind the truck followed Ambassador Ning Cheng Gong's blue Mercedes. The two vehicles slowed and then pulled up behind Gomo's truck and Daniel strode towards the Mercedes.

As he approached, Ambassador Ning opened his door and stepped out into the dusty track.

'Doctor Armstrong, what are you doing here?' He seemed agitated but his voice was soft, barely audible.

'When did you leave Chiwewe?' Daniel ignored the question. He was desperate to know that Johnny and Mavis were safe and the Ambassador's reaction puzzled him.

Cheng's agitation increased. 'Why do you ask that?' he whispered. 'Why are you returning? You were supposed to be on your way to Harare.'

'Look here, Your Excellency. All I want to know is that there has been no trouble at Chiwewe.'

'Trouble? What trouble? Why should there be trouble?' The ambassador reached into his pocket and brought out a hand-kerchief. 'What are you suggesting, Doctor?'

'I'm not suggesting anything.' Daniel found it hard to conceal his exasperation. 'I picked up the tracks of a large party of men crossing the road and heading in the direction of Chiwewe. I am worried that they may be a gang of armed poachers and I am on my way back to warn the warden.'

'There is no trouble,' Cheng assured him. Daniel noticed that a faint sheen of perspiration bloomed on his forehead. 'Everything is well. I left there an hour ago. Warden Nzou is just fine. I spoke to him when we left and there was no sign of any trouble.' He wiped his face with the handkerchief.

'An hour ago?' Daniel asked, and checked his stainless steel Rolex. He felt a vast sense of relief at Ambassador Ning's reassurance. 'So you left there at about five-thirty?'

'Yes, yes.' Cheng's tone sharpened with affront. 'Are you questioning my word? Do you doubt what I am telling you?'

Daniel was surprised by his tone and the strength of his denials.

'You misunderstand me, Your Excellency. Of course I don't doubt what you say.'

Cheng's prestige as an ambassador was the main reason that Chetti Singh had insisted that he be present at Chiwewe. Cheng's natural inclination had been assiduously to avoid the scene of the raid, and even to fly to Taipei while it was in progress to give himself an infallible alibi. However, Chetti Singh had threatened to call off the operation unless Cheng was present to vouch for the fact that the raid had taken place after the convoy of trucks had left Chiwewe. That was the whole crux of the operation. As an accredited ambassador, Cheng's word would carry enormous weight in the subsequent police investigation. The testimony of the two black rangers alone might not have been accepted implicitly. The police might even have decided to give them a little earnest questioning in a back cell at Chikurubi prison and Chetti Singh was not confident that they would have withstood that treatment.

No, the police must be made to believe that when Cheng had left Chiwewe with the convoy all had been well. That way they must assume that the raiders had carried the ivory away with them or that it had been destroyed in the fire that consumed the godown.

'I'm sorry if I gave you the impression that I was doubting your word, Your Excellency,' Daniel placated him. 'It was just that I am worried about Johnny, about the warden.'

'Well, I assure you that you have no reason to worry.' Cheng stuffed the handkerchief in his hip pocket and reached for the packet of cigarettes in the top pocket of his open-neck shirt. He tapped one out of the pack but his fingers were slightly unsteady and he let the cigarette drop into the dust between his feet.

Daniel's eyes were instinctively drawn down as Cheng stooped quickly to retrieve the fallen cigarette. He wore white canvas training shoes and Daniel noticed that the side of one shoe and the cuff of his blue cotton slacks were smeared with a stain that looked at first glance like dried blood.

This puzzled Daniel for a moment, until he remembered that Cheng had been present that morning when the fresh tusks had been unloaded from the truck and stored in the godown. The explanation for the stains on his clothing was obvious; he must have picked them up from a puddle of congealed elephant blood in which the tusks had lain.

Cheng noticed the direction of his gaze and stepped back quickly, almost guiltily, into the driver's seat of the Mercedes and slammed the door. Unthinkingly Daniel noticed the unusual fish-scale pattern that the soles of his training shoes left in the fine dust of the roadway.

'Well, I am happy to have been able to set your fears at rest, Doctor.' Cheng smiled at him through the window of the Mercedes. He had regained his composure and his smile was once again suave and charming. 'I'm glad to have saved you an unnecessary journey all the way back to Chiwewe. I am sure you will want to join the convoy and get out of the Park before the rains break.' He started the Mercedes. 'Why don't you take the lead position ahead of the trucks?'

'Thank you, Your Excellency.' Daniel shook his head and stepped back. 'You go on with the trucks. I won't be joining you. I want to go back anyway. Somebody has to warn Johnny Nzou.'

Cheng's smile evaporated. 'You are giving yourself a great deal of unnecessary trouble, I assure you. I suggest you telephone him from Mana Pools or Karoi.'

'Didn't I tell you? They cut the telephone wires.'

'Doctor Armstrong, that is preposterous. I am sure you are mistaken. I think you are exaggerating the seriousness of this—'

'You think what you like,' said Daniel with finality. 'I'm

going back to Chiwewe.' He stepped back from the window of the Mercedes.

'Doctor Armstrong,' Cheng called after him, 'look at those rain clouds. You could be trapped here for weeks.'

'I'll take the chance,' Daniel told him blithely, but to himself he thought, Just why is he being so insistent? Something is starting to smell distinctly rotten here.

He walked quickly back towards the Landcruiser. As he passed the trucks he noticed that neither of the rangers had dismounted from the driver's cabs. They were both looking sullen and neither of them said anything as he passed close beside them.

'All right, Gomo,' he called, 'pull your truck forward so I can get past you.'

Without a word the ranger obeyed. Then the second truck rumbled past and finally the Ambassador's Mercedes came level. Daniel lifted a hand in farewell. Cheng barely glanced in his direction but gave him a perfunctory salute before following the trucks around the bend and heading on down towards the Mana Pools turn-off.

'What did the Chink have to say?' Jock asked as Daniel reversed back into the roadway and put the Toyota to the steep gradient.

'He says it was all quiet at Chiwewe when he left there an hour ago,' Daniel replied.

'That's a fair do.' Jock reached into the cold box and fished out a can of beer. He offered it to Daniel who shook his head and concentrated on the road ahead. Jock opened the can for himself, took a long slug, and belched happily.

The light began to fade and a few heavy drops of rain splattered against the windscreen but Daniel did not slacken speed. It was completely dark before they reached the crest of the escarpment. The lightning blazed through the darkness, illuminating the forest with a crackling blue radiance and thunder rolled across the sky and cannonaded the ridges of granite which rose on each side of the road.

The rain began to fall like silver arrows in the headlights, each drop exploding in a white blur against the glass then streaming down it so copiously that the wipers could not clear the windshield fast enough. Soon it was oppressively humid in the closed cab and the windscreen began to mist over. Daniel leaned forward to wipe it clear with his hand but when it smeared he gave up the effort and opened his side window a few inches to let in the fresh night air. Almost immediately he wrinkled his nose and sniffed.

Jock smelt it at almost the same moment. 'Smoke,' he exclaimed. 'How far are we from the camp?'

'Almost there,' Daniel replied. 'Just over the next ridge.'

The odour of smoke thinned out. Daniel thought that it might have come from the cooking-fires in the servants' compound.

Ahead of them in the path of the headlights the gates of the main camp sprang out of the darkness. Each whitewashed column was crowned by the bleached skull of an elephant. The sign read:

WELCOME TO CHIWEWE CAMP
THE HOME OF THE ELEPHANTS

and then in smaller letters,

All arriving visitors must report immediately
to the Warden's Office.

The long driveway, lined on each side with dark casia trees, was running ankle deep with storm water and the Toyota's tyres threw up a dense fog of spray as Daniel headed for the main block of buildings. Suddenly the reek of smoke was thick and rank in their nostrils. It was the smell of burning thatch and wood with a foul underlay of something else, flesh or bone or ivory, perhaps, although Daniel had never smelt ivory burning.

'No lights,' Daniel grunted as he saw the loom of dark buildings in the rain ahead. The camp generator was not running; the entire camp was in darkness. Then he became aware of a diffused ruby light that shimmered over the wet casia trees and played gently on the walls of the buildings.

'One of the buildings is on fire.'

Jock sat forward in his seat. 'That's where the smoke is coming from.'

The Toyota's headlights cut a broad swathe through the gloom and then focused on a huge amorphous dark pile ahead of them. The misted windscreen obscured his vision and for some moments Daniel could not decide what it was. The strange glow seemed to emanate from it. Only as they drove closer and the lights lit it more clearly could he recognise it as the blackened, smouldering ruins of the ivory godown. Horrified by what he saw, Daniel let the Toyota roll to a halt and he stepped down into the mud and stared at the ruin.

The heat of the flames had cracked the walls and most of them had collapsed. The fire must have been an inferno to have produced such heat. It still burned and smouldered despite the cascading rain. Oily streamers of smoke drifted across the headlights of the truck and occasionally the flames flared up fiercely until the heavy raindrops beat them down again.

Daniel's sodden shirt clung to his body and the rain soaked his hair, smearing his thick curls over his forehead and into his eyes. He pushed them back and scrambled up on to the tumbled masonry of the wall. The collapsed roof was a thick mattress of black ash and charred beams that clogged the interior of the devastated godown. Despite the rain the smoke was still too dense and the heat too fierce to allow him to approach any closer and discover how much of the ivory still lay under that blackened pile.

Daniel backed away and ran to the truck. He climbed into the cab and wiped the rain out of his eyes with the palm of his hand.

'You were spot-on,' Jock said. 'It looks as if the bastards have hit the camp.'

Daniel did not answer. He started the engine and gunned the Toyota up the hill to the warden's cottage.

'Get the flashlight out of the locker,' he snapped. Obediently Jock knelt on the seat and groped in the heavy tool-locker that was bolted to the truck bed, and came out with the big Maglite.

Like the rest of the camp the warden's cottage was in darkness. The rain streamed down from the eaves in a silver torrent so that the headlights could not illuminate the screened verandah beyond. Daniel snatched the torch from Jock's hand and jumped out into the rain.

'Johnny!' he yelled. 'Mavis!' He ran to the front door of the cottage. The door had been smashed half off its hinges and hung open. He ran through on to the verandah.

The furniture was shattered and thrown about in confusion. He played the torch-beam over the chaos. Johnny's cherished collection of books had been tumbled from their cases along the wall and lay in heaps with their pages fanned and their spines broken.

'Johnny!' Daniel shouted. 'Where are you?'

He ran through the open double doors into the sitting-room. Here the destruction was shocking. They had hurled all Mavis's ornaments and vases at the stone fireplace and the broken shards glittered in the torch beam. They had ripped the stuffing out of the sofa and easy chairs. The room stank like an animal cage and he saw that they had defecated on the carpets and urinated down the walls.

Daniel stepped over the reeking piles of faeces and ran through into the passageway that led to the bedrooms.

'Johnny!' he shouted in anger and despair, as he played the torch-beam down the length of the passage.

On the end wall was a decoration that had not been there before. It was a dark star-shaped splash of paint that covered most of the white-painted surface. For a moment Daniel stared at it uncomprehendingly and then he dropped the beam to the small huddled shape that lay at the foot of the wall.

Johnny and Mavis had named their only son after him, Daniel Robert Nzou. After two daughters, Mavis had finally given birth to a son and both parents had been overjoyed. Daniel Nzou had been four years old. He lay on his back. His eyes were open but sightlessly staring into the beam of the torch.

They had killed him in the old barbaric African way, in the same way that Chaka's and Mzilikazi's impis had dealt with the male children of a vanquished tribe. They had seized little Daniel by the ankles and swung him head-first against the wall, crushing his skull and beating his brains out against the brick-work. His splattering blood had daubed that crude mural on the white surface.

Daniel stooped over the little boy. Despite the deformation

of the crushed skull his resemblance to his father was still marked. Tears prickled the rims of Daniel's eyelids and he stood up slowly and turned to the bedroom door.

It stood half open but Daniel dreaded pushing it all the way. He had to force himself to do it. The hinges of the door whined softly as it swung open.

For a moment Daniel stared down the beam of the Maglite as he let it play around the bedroom and then he reeled back into the passageway and leaned against the wall, gagging and gasping for breath.

He had witnessed scenes such as these during the days of the bush war, but the years had eroded his conditioning and softened the shell that he had built up to protect himself. He was no longer able to look dispassionately on the atrocity that man is able to perpetrate on his fellows.

Johnny's daughters were older than their brother. Miriam was ten and Suzie almost eight. They lay naked and spread-eagled on the floor at the foot of the bed. They had both been raped repeatedly. Their immature genitalia were a torn and bloody mush.

Mavis was on the bed. They had not bothered to strip her entirely, but had merely pushed her skirts up around her waist. Her arms were pulled up above her head and tied by the wrists to the wooden headboard. The two little girls must have died of shock and loss of blood during the prolonged assault upon them. Mavis had probably survived until they were finished with her, then they had put a bullet through her head.

Daniel forced himself to enter the room. He found where Mavis kept her extra bed-linen in one of the built-in cupboards and covered each of the corpses with a sheet. He could not bring himself to touch any of the girls, not even to close their wide staring eyes in which the horror and the terror was still deeply imprinted.

'Sweet Mother of God,' Jock whispered from the doorway. 'Whoever did this isn't human. They must be ravaging bloody beasts.'

Daniel backed out of the bedroom and closed the door. He covered Daniel Nzou's tiny body.

'Have you found Johnny?' he asked Jock. His voice was

hoarse and his throat felt rough and abraded with horror and grief.

'No.' Jock shook his head, then turned and fled down the passage. He blundered out across the verandah and into the rain.

Daniel heard him retching and vomiting in the flowerbed below the stoep. The sound of the other man's distress served to steady Daniel. He fought back his own repugnance and anger and sorrow and brought his emotions back under control.

'Johnny,' he told himself. 'Got to find Johnny.'

He went swiftly through the other two bedrooms and the rest of the house. There was no sign of his friend, and he allowed himself the first faint hope.

'He might have got away,' he told himself. 'He might have made it into the bush.'

It was a relief to get out of that charnel house. Daniel stood in the darkness and lifted his face to the rain. He opened his mouth and let it wash the bitter bile taste from his tongue and the back of his throat. Then he turned the torch-beam on to his feet and saw the clotted blood dissolve from his shoes in a pink stain. He scrubbed the soles in the gravel of the driveway to clean them and then shouted to Jock.

'Come on, we have to find Johnny.'

In the Toyota he drove down the back of the hill to the domestic compound that housed the camp servants. The compound was still enclosed with an earthen embankment and barbed-wire fence from the war days. However the fence was in a ruinous state and the gate was missing. They drove through the gateway and the smell of smoke was strong. As the headlights caught them Daniel saw that the row of servants' cottages was burnt out. The roofs had collapsed and the windows were empty. The rain had quenched the flames, although a few tendrils of smoke still drifted like pale wraiths in the lights.

The ground around the huts was sown with dozens of tiny objects which caught the headlights and sparkled like diamond chips. Daniel knew what they were, but he stepped down from the truck and picked one of them out of the mud. It was a shiny brass cartridge case. He held it to the light and inspected the familiar Cyrillic head stamp in the brass. 7.62 mm, of East European manufacture, it was the calibre of the ubiquitous AK 47 assault rifle, staple of violence and revolution throughout Africa and the entire world.

The gang had shot up the compound, but had left no corpses. Daniel guessed that they had thrown the dead into the cottages before torching them. The breeze shifted towards him so that he caught the full stench of the burned huts and had his suspicions confirmed. Underlying the smell of smoke was the odour of scorched flesh and hair and bone.

He spat out the taste of it and walked down between the huts. 'Johnny!' he shouted into the night. 'Johnny, are you there?' But the only sound was the creak and pop of the doused flames and the sough of the breeze in the mango trees that brought the raindrops pattering down from the branches.

He flicked the torch left and right as he passed between the huts, until he saw the body of a man lying in the open.

'Johnny!' he shouted, and ran to him and fell on his knees beside him.

The body was horribly burned, the khaki Parks uniform burned half away, and the skin and flesh sloughing off the exposed torso and the side of the face. The man had obviously dragged himself out of the burning hut into which they had thrown him, but he was not Johnny Nzou. He was one of the junior rangers.

Daniel jumped up and hurried back to the track.

'Did you find him?' Jock asked, and Daniel shook his head.

'Christ, they've murdered everybody in the camp. Why would they do that?'

'Witnesses!' Daniel started the truck. 'They wiped out all the witnesses.'

'Why? What do they want? It doesn't make sense.'

'The ivory. That's what they were after.'

'But they burned down the warehouse!'

'After they cleaned it out.'

He swung the Toyota back on to the track and raced up the hill.

'Who were they, Danny? Who did this?'

'How the hell do I know? Shifta? Bandits? Poachers? Don't ask stupid questions.'

Daniel's anger was only just beginning. Up until now he had been numbed by the shock and the horror. He drove back past the dark bungalow on the hill and then down again to the main camp.

The warden's office was still standing intact; although when Daniel played the beam of the torch over the thatched roof he saw the blackened area on which someone had thrown a burning torch. Well-laid thatch does not burn readily, however, and the flames had not caught fairly or perhaps had been extinguished by the rain before they could take hold.

The rain stopped with the suddenness which is characteristic of the African elements. One minute it was falling in a furious cascade that limited the range of the headlights to fifty yards, and the next it was over. Only the trees still dripped, but overhead the first stars pricked through the dispersing thunder clouds that were being carried away on the rising breeze. Daniel barely noticed the change. He left the truck and ran up on to the wide verandah.

The exterior wall was decorated with the skulls of the animals of the Park. Their empty eye-sockets and twisted horns in the torch-beam gave a macabre touch to the scene and heightened Daniel's sense of doom as he strode down the long covered verandah. He now realised that he should have searched here first, instead of rushing up to the bungalow.

The door of Johnny's office stood open and Daniel paused on the threshold and steeled himself before he stepped through.

A snowstorm of papers covered the floor and desk. They had ransacked the room, sweeping the stacks of forms off the cupboard shelves and hauling the drawers out of Johnny's desk, then spilling out the contents. They had found Johnny's keys and opened the old green-painted door to the Milner safe that was built into the wall. The keys were still in the lock but the safe was empty.

Daniel's torch-beam darted about the room and then settled on the crumpled form that lay in front of the desk.

'Johnny,' he whispered. 'Oh, Christ, no!'

'I thought that while I was waiting for the refrigerator truck to be repaired, I might as well go down to the water-hole at Fig Tree Pan.' Ambassador Ning's voice interrupted Johnny Nzou's concentration, but he felt no resentment as he looked up from his desk. In Johnny's view one of his major duties was to make the wilderness accessible to anybody who had an interest in nature. Ning Cheng Gong was certainly one of those. Johnny smiled at his accoutrements, the field guide and the binoculars.

He rose from his desk, glad of the excuse to escape from the drudgery of paperwork and went with the Ambassador out on to the verandah and down to his parked Mercedes, where he stood and chatted to him for a few minutes, making suggestions as to where he might get a glimpse of the elusive and aptly named gorgeous bush shrike that Cheng wanted to observe.

When Cheng drove away, Johnny walked down to the vehicle workshops where ranger Gomo was stripping and reassembling the alternator of the unserviceable truck. He was dubious about Gomo's ability to effect the repair. In the morning he would probably have to ring the warden at Mana Pools and ask him to send a mechanic to do the job.

One consolation was that the elephant meat would keep indefinitely in the cold storage of the hull. The truck's refrigerating equipment was plugged in now to the camp generator and the thermometer registered twenty degrees below freezing when Johnny checked it. The meat would be processed and turned into animal feed by a private contractor in Harare.

Johnny left ranger Gomo to his labour over the dismembered alternator and went back to his own office under the casia trees. No sooner had he left the workshop than Gomo looked up and exchanged a significant glance with David, the other black ranger. The alternator he was tinkering with was a worn-out piece of equipment that he had retrieved from the scrap heap in Harare for just this purpose. The truck's original alternator, in perfect working order, was hidden under the driver's seat in the cab. It would take less than ten minutes to bolt it back in place and reconnect the wiring.

Back in his office Johnny settled to the monotony of his

forms and ledgers. Once he glanced at his wristwatch and found that it was a few minutes before one o'clock, but he wanted to finish the week's reports before knocking off for lunch. Of course, it was a temptation to go up to the house early. He liked to be with the children for a while before lunch, especially with his son, but he resisted the impulse and worked on conscientiously. Anyway he knew that Mavis would probably send the children down to fetch him soon. She liked to serve his lunch promptly. He smiled in anticipation of their arrival as he heard a sound at the door and looked up.

The smile faded. A stranger stood in the doorway, a stocky man with bow legs, dressed in filthy rags. Both his hands were behind his back as though he was concealing something.

'Yes?' Johnny asked shortly. 'Who are you? What do you want?'

The man smiled. His skin was very dark with purple black highlights. When he smiled the scar that ran down one cheek pulled his mouth out of shape and the smile was malicious and humourless.

Johnny stood up from the desk and went towards him.

'What do you want?' he repeated, and the man in the doorway said, 'You!' From behind his back he brought out an AK 47 rifle and lifted the barrel towards Johnny's belly.

Johnny was caught totally off guard in the centre of the room. However, his recovery was almost instantaneous. His reflexes were those of a hunter and a soldier. The armoury door was ten paces to his left and he went for it.

The Parks weapons were kept in there. Through the door he could see the rack of firearms on the far wall. With despair turning his legs as heavy as concrete, Johnny realised that none of the weapons in the rack was loaded. That was his own strict safety rule. The ammunition was kept in the locked steel cupboard under the gun-rack.

All this passed through his mind as he leaped for the door. From the corner of his eye he saw the scar-faced brigand swing the AK 47 on to him and halfway across the room Johnny tumbled forward like an acrobat, ducking under the blast of automatic fire that swept across the room.

As he rolled smoothly to his feet he heard the man curse and

Johnny dived forward once more for the doorway. He realised that his assailant was good. He had seen that he was a killer in the practised way he handled the rifle. It was a miracle that he had been able to evade that first close-range volley.

The air was filled with a haze of plaster dust that the bullets had battered from the wall and Johnny dived through it, but he knew he was not going to make it. The man with the AK 47 was too good. He could not be fooled again. The shelter of the doorway was too far for Johnny to reach before the next burst came.

The clock in Johnny's head was running; he anticipated how long it would take for the man to recover his balance. The muzzle of the AK 47 always rode up uncontrollably in automatic fire; it would take him the major part of a second to bring it down, and line up for the second burst. Johnny judged it finely and twisted his body violently aside, but he was a fraction late.

The gunman aimed low to compensate for the rise of the AK. One bullet sliced through the flesh of Johnny's thigh, missing the bone, but the second cut through the lower curve of his buttock and smashed into the joint at the femur, shattering the head and the cup of bone of the pelvis.

The other three bullets of the burst flew wide as Johnny threw himself to one side. However, his left leg was gone and he fell against the door jamb and tried to hold himself from falling. His impetus sent him sliding sideways along the wall, and his fingernails screeched as they gouged the plaster. He ended up facing back into the room standing on one leg. His left leg hung from the shattered joint, and his arms were flung open like a crucifix as he tried to hold his balance.

Still smiling, the gunman clicked the rate-of-fire selector on to single-shot. He wanted to conserve ammunition. A single round cost him ten Zambian kwacha, and had to be carried hundreds of miles in his pack. Each cartridge was precious, and the warden was maimed and completely at his mercy. One more bullet would be enough.

'Now,' he said softly. 'Now you die.' And he shot Johnny Nzou in the stomach.

The bullet drove the breath from Johnny's lungs with an explosive exhalation. He was slammed hard against the wall and doubled over by the brutal force of the impact and then he toppled forward. Johnny had been hit before, during the war, but he had never received a full body strike and the shock of it was beyond his worst expectations. He was numbed from the waist down but his brain stayed clear, crystalline, as though the rush of adrenalin into his bloodstream had sharpened his perception to its limits.

Play dead! he thought, even as he was going down. His lower body was paralysed, but he forced his torso to relax. He hit the floor with the loose unresisting weight of a flour sack and did not move again.

His head was twisted to one side, his cheek pressed to the cold cement floor. He lay still. He heard the gunman cross the floor, the rubber soles of the combat boots squeaking softly. Then his boots entered Johnny's field of vision. They were dusty and worn almost through the uppers. He wore no socks and the stink of his feet was rancid and sour as he stood within inches of Johnny's face.

Johnny heard the metallic snick of the mechanism as the Zambian moved the rate-of-fire selector again, and then felt the cold hard touch of the muzzle against his temple as the man lined up for the *coup de grâce*.

'Don't move,' Johnny steeled himself. It was his last despairing hope. He knew that the slightest movement must trigger the shot. He had to convince the gunman he was dead.

At that moment there was a burst of shouting from outside the room, and then a volley of automatic fire, followed by more shouting. The pressure of the rifle muzzle was lifted from Johnny's temple. The stinking boots turned away and retreated across the floor towards the doorway.

'Come on! Don't waste time!' the scar-faced gunman yelled through the open door. Johnny knew enough of the northern Chinianja dialect to understand. 'Where are the trucks? We must get the ivory loaded!'

The Zambian ran out of the office leaving Johnny lying alone on the cement floor.

Johnny knew that he was mortally hit. He could feel the arterial blood squirting out of the wound in his groin and he rolled on his side and swiftly loosened the top of his trousers.

Immediately he smelled his own faeces and knew that the second bullet had ripped open his intestines. He reached down into his crotch and pressed his fingers into the wound in his groin. Blood spurted hotly over his hand.

He found the open artery and pinched off the end of the severed femoral.

Mavis, and the babies! That was his next thought. What could he do for them? At that moment he heard more firing from up the hill, in the direction of the domestic compound and his own cottage.

It's a gang of them, he realised with despair. They are all over the camp. They are attacking the compound. And then, My babies. Oh, God! My babies!

He thought about the weapons in the room next door, but he knew he could not get that far. Even if he did, how could he handle a rifle with half his guts shot away and his life-blood spreading in a pool under him?

He heard the trucks. He recognised the beat of the big diesels and knew that they were the refrigerator trucks. He felt a surge of hope.

Gomo, he thought. David ... But it was short-lived. Lying on his side, clinging to his severed artery, he looked across the room and realised that he could see through the open door.

One of the white refrigerator trucks pulled into his view. It reversed up against the door of the ivory godown. As soon as it parked, Gomo jumped out of the cab and began a heated, gesticulating discussion with the scar-faced leader of the gang. In his confused and swiftly weakening condition, it took Johnny several seconds to work it out.

Gomo, he thought. Gomo is one of them. He set it up.

It should not have come as such a shock. Johnny knew how pervasive was the corruption in the government, in all departments, not only the Parks Administration. He had given evidence before the official commission of enquiry that was investigating the corruption, and had pledged to help stamp it out. He knew Gomo well. He was arrogant and self-seeking. He was just the type, but Johnny had never expected treachery on this scale.

Suddenly the area around the godown that Johnny could see

was teeming with the other members of the gang. Swiftly Scar-face organised them into a work-party. One of them shot the lock off the door of the warehouse and the bandits laid aside their weapons and swarmed into the building. There were shouts of greedy joy as they saw the piles of ivory and then they formed a human chain and began passing out the tusks, and loading them into the truck.

Johnny's vision began to fade. Clouds of darkness passed across his eyes and there was a soft singing in his ears.

I'm dying, he thought without emotion. He could feel the numbness spreading from his paralysed legs up through his chest.

He forced the darkness back from his eyes and thought that he must be fantasising, for now Ambassador Ning stood in the late sunlight below the verandah. He still had the binoculars slung over his shoulder and his manner was impossibly cool and urbane. Johnny tried to shout a warning to him, but it came out of his throat in a soft croak that did not carry beyond the room in which he lay.

Then to his astonishment he saw the scar-faced leader of the gang come to where the ambassador stood and salute him, if not respectfully, at least with recognition of his authority.

Ning. Johnny forced himself to believe it. It really is Ning. I'm not dreaming it.

Then the voices of the two men carried to where he lay. They were speaking in English.

'You must hurry your men,' Ning Cheng Gong said. 'They must get the ivory loaded – I want to leave here immediately.'

'Money,' answered Sali. 'One thousand dollars . . .' His English was atrocious.

'You have been paid.' Cheng was indignant. 'I have paid you your money.'

'More money. More one thousand dollars.' Sali grinned at him. 'More money or I stop. We go, leave you, leave ivory.'

'You are a scoundrel,' Cheng snarled.

'Not understand "scoundrel", but think you also "scoun-drel", maybe.' Sali's grin widened. 'Give money now.'

'I haven't any more money with me,' Cheng told him flatly.

'Then we go! Now! You load ivory yourself.'

'Wait.' Cheng was obviously thinking quickly. 'I haven't got money. You take the ivory, as much as you want. Take everything you can carry.' Cheng had realised that the poachers would be able to take only a negligible number of tusks from the hoard. They could not possibly manage more than a single tusk each. Twenty men, twenty tusks – it was a small price.

Sali stared at him while he considered the offer. Clearly he had milked every possible advantage from the situation, so at last he nodded.

'Good! We take ivory.' He began to turn away.

Ambassador Ning called after him. 'Wait, Sali! What about the others? Did you take care of them?'

'They all dead.'

'The warden and his woman and children? Them too?'

'All dead,' Sali repeated. 'Woman is dead, and her piccanins. My men make jig-jig with all three women first. Very funny, very nice jig-jig. Then kill.'

'The warden? Where is he?'

Sali the poacher jerked his head towards the door of Johnny's office. 'I shoot him boom, boom. He dead like a *n'gulubi*, dead like a pig.' He laughed. 'Very good job, hey?'

He walked away with the rifle over his shoulder, still chuckling, and Cheng followed him out of Johnny's field of vision. Anger came to arm Johnny and give him just a little more strength. The poacher's words conjured up a dreadful vision of the fate that had overtaken Mavis and the children. He could see it as clearly as if he had been there; he knew about rape and pillage. He had lived through the bush war.

He used the strength of his anger to begin to wriggle across the floor towards his desk. He knew he could not use a weapon. All he could hope for now in the few minutes of life that remained to him was to leave some sort of message. Papers had spilled off his desk and littered the floor. If he could just get to a single sheet, and write on it and hide it, the police would find it later.

He moved like a maimed caterpillar, lying on his back, still clutching the severed artery. He drew up his good knee, dug in his heel and pushed himself painfully across the floor, sliding on his back a few inches at a time, his own blood lubricating his passage. He moved six feet towards the desk and reached out for one of the sheets of paper. He saw then that it was a sheet from the wages register.

He had not touched it when the intensity of the light in the room altered. Somebody was standing in the doorway. He turned his head and Ambassador Ning was staring at him. He had come up on to the verandah. His rubber-soled training shoes made no sound at all. Now he stood petrified with shock in the doorway, and for a moment longer he stared at Johnny. Then he yelled shrilly, 'He is still alive. Sali, come quickly, he is still alive.'

Cheng disappeared from the doorway and ran down the verandah still shouting for the poacher. 'Sali, come quickly.'

It was all over, and Johnny knew it. Only seconds remaining to him. He rolled on his side reached out and snatched up the register sheet. He pressed the sheet flat on the floor with one hand, and then released the severed artery and drew his blood-drenched hand out of the front of his trousers. Immediately he felt the artery begin to pulse and fresh blood jetted from the wound.

With his forefinger he scrawled on the blank sheet of paper, writing in his own blood. He formed the letter N in a large lopsided character, and dizziness made his senses swirl. NI. It was more difficult to concentrate. The down stroke of the I was elongated and curved, too much like a J. Painfully he dotted the letter to make its meaning clearer. For a moment his finger was glued lightly to the paper with his sticky blood. He pulled it free.

He started on the second N. It was crude and childlike. His finger would not follow the dictates of his mind. He heard the ambassador still calling for Sali, and the poacher's answering shout filled with alarm and consternation. NIN — Johnny began the G but his finger wandered off at an angle and the wet red letters wiggled and swam before his eyes like tadpoles.

He heard running feet come pounding down the verandah and Sali's voice. 'I thought he was dead. I finish him good now!' Johnny crumpled the sheet of paper in his left hand, the hand that was clean of blood, and he thrust his closed fist into the front of his tunic and rolled over onto his belly with his arm trapped under him, concealing the balled note.

He did not see Sali come in at the door. His face was pressed to the concrete floor. He heard the poacher's boots squeak and slip on the blood, and then the click of the safety-catch on the rifle as he stood over Johnny's prostrate form.

Johnny felt no fear, only a vast sense of sorrow and resignation. He thought about Mavis and the children as he felt the muzzle of the rifle touch the back of his head. He was relieved that he would not be left alone after they were gone. He was glad that he would never see what had happened to them, would never be forced to witness the signs of their agony and degradation.

He was already dying before the bullet from the AK 47 tore through his skull and buried itself in the concrete under his face.

'Shit,' said Sali. He stepped back and shouldered the rifle, a faint feather of gunsmoke still drifting from the muzzle. 'A hard man to kill. He made me waste *miningi* bullets, each one ten kwacha. Too much!'

Ning Cheng Gong advanced into the room. 'Are you sure that you've finished the job – at last?' he asked.

'His head gone,' Sali grunted as he picked up Johnny's keys from the desk and went to ransack the Milner safe. '*Kufa!* He dead, for sure.'

Cheng moved closer to the corpse, and stared at it with fascination. The killing had excited him. He was sexually aroused, not as much as if it had been a young girl who had died, but aroused, nevertheless. The smell of blood filled the room. He loved that smell.

He was so absorbed that he did not notice that he was standing in a puddle of blood until Gomo called him from below the verandah.

'All the ivory is loaded. We are ready to go.'

Cheng stepped back and exclaimed with disgust as he saw the stain on the cuff of his crisply ironed blue cotton slacks.

'I'm going now,' he told Sali. 'Burn the ivory godown before you leave.'

In the safe Sali had found the canvas bank bag that contained the month's wages for the camp staff, and he grunted without looking up from the contents.

'I burn everything for sure.'

Cheng ran down the verandah steps and climbed into the Mercedes. He signalled to Gomo and the two refrigerator trucks pulled away. The ivory was packed into the holds and then covered with the dismembered carcasses of the culled beasts. A casual inspection would not reveal the hoard, but there was nobody to stop the convoy. They were protected by the badges of the National Parks Board painted on the trucks, and by the khaki uniforms and shoulder flashes of Gomo and David, the two rangers. Not even one of the frequent road-blocks was likely to delay them. The security forces were intent on catching political dissidents, not ivory-runners.

It had all gone as Chetti Singh had planned it. Cheng glanced at the rear-view mirror of the Mercedes. The ivory godown was already ablaze. The poachers were forming up into a column for the return march. Each of them carried a large tusk from the hoard.

Cheng smiled to himself. Perhaps Sali's greed would work to his advantage. If the police ever caught up with the gang, the disappearance of the ivory would be neatly explained by both the fire and the loads the poachers were carrying.

At Cheng's insistence they had left forty tusks in the burning godown, to provide traces of charred ivory for the police forensic laboratory. As Chetti Singh might have said, 'Another dead herring . . .'

This time Cheng laughed aloud. He was elated. The success of the raid and the thrill of violence and death and blood warmed his belly and filled him with a sense of power. He felt masterful and sexually charged, and suddenly he was aware that he had a hard throbbing erection.

He determined that next time he would do the killing himself. It was quite natural to believe that there would be a next time, and many more times after that. Death had made Cheng feel immortal.

'Johnny. Oh, God. Johnny.' Daniel squatted beside him and reached out to touch the side of his throat just below the ear feeling for the pulse of the carotid. It was an instinctive gesture, for the bullet entry wound in the back of Johnny's skull was conclusive.

Johnny's skin was cool and Daniel could not yet bring himself to turn him over and look at the exit wound. He let him lie a little longer and rocked back on his heels, letting his anger flourish to replace the enervating chill of grief. He cherished his rage, as though it were a candle flame on a dark night. It warmed the cold empty place in his soul that Johnny had left.

Daniel stood up at last. He played the torch-beam on the floor ahead of him, and stepped over the pools and smears of Johnny's blood as he went to the armoury.

The remote control for the generator was on the mains panel beside the door. Daniel threw the switch and heard the distant clatter of the diesel engine in the power house down near the main gates to the camp. The diesel engine ran up to speed and settled at a steady beat, then the generator kicked in and the lights flickered and bloomed. Through the window he saw the street lamps lining the driveway light up and in their glow the casia trees were vivid green and shiny with raindrops.

Daniel fetched the bunch of keys that still hung in the lock of the Milner safe and strode through into the armoury. Along with the .375 culling rifles, there were five AK 47 assault rifles on the rack. These were used on anti-poaching patrols when the rangers needed equivalent fire-power to take on the gangs of poachers. Ammunition was stored in the cupboard below the gunrack. He unlocked the steel door. There were four magazines of AK ammunition in each pouched webbing belt hanging on the hooks.

He slung one of these over his shoulder, then lifted an automatic rifle down from the rack and loaded it with deft movements; the old warlike arts once learned were never forgotten. Armed and angry, he ran down the verandah steps.

'Start with the ivory godown,' he decided. 'They'll have been there for sure.'

He circled the burned-out building, searching for sign by the light of the street lamps, flashing his torch at anything that caught his attention. If he had allowed himself to think about it, he would have realised he was wasting his time. The only prints that had withstood the erosion of the rain were those protected by the overhanging verandah roof, a set of heavy tyre tracks in the mud at the front entrance to the ivory godown. Even these were almost erased and only just recognisable.

Daniel ignored them; he was after the gang and they would not be using vehicles. Quickly he widened the circles of his search, trying to pick up an outgoing set of tracks, concentrating on the northern side of the camp's perimeter, for the gang would almost certainly head back to the Zambezi River.

It was useless, as he had known deep down that it would be. After twenty minutes he gave it up. There were no tracks to follow. He stood under the dark trees and raged with frustration and sorrow.

'If only I could get a shot at the bastards,' he lamented. It meant little to him in his present mood that he was one man against twenty or more professional killers. Jock was a camera-man, not a soldier. He would be of no help in a fight. The memory of those mutilated bodies in the bedroom of the bungalow and of Johnny's shattered head overpowered all rational thought. Daniel found that he was physically shaking with the strength of his anger, and that put him on the road to recovering his scattered wits.

'While I'm wasting time here, they're getting clean away,' he told himself. 'The only way is to cut them off on the river. I need help.'

He thought of the Parks camp at Mana Pools. The warden there was a good man. Daniel knew him well from the old days. He had an anti-poaching team and a fast boat. They could get downstream and patrol the river crossing to catch the gang as it attempted to get back on to the Zambian side. Daniel was already starting to think logically as he started back towards the warden's office. From Mana Pools they could ring Harare and get the police to send in a spotter plane.

He knew that speed was vital now. Within the next ten hours the gang would be back across the river. However, he could not leave Johnny like that, lying in his own blood. It meant wasting a few more minutes, but he had to show him some last respect and at the very least cover him decently.

Daniel paused in the doorway to Johnny's office. The overhead lights were brutally explicit; they left nothing of the horror concealed. He set aside the AK 47 and looked around for a covering for his friend's corpse. The curtains over the front windows were green government issue, faded by sunlight, but they would do as a makeshift shroud. He took one of them down, and went with it to where Johnny lay..

Johnny's attitude was tortured. One arm was twisted up under his chest and his face lay in a pool of thick congealing blood. Gently Daniel rolled him over. The body had not yet stiffened in rigor mortis. He winced as he looked at Johnny's face, for the bullet had come out through his right eyebrow. He used a corner of the curtain to wipe his face clean, then arranged him in a comfortable attitude on his back.

Johnny's left hand was thrust into the front of his tunic and his fist was tightly clenched. Daniel's interest quickened as he saw the balled up sheet of paper in his hand. He prised Johnny's fingers open and freed the wad.

He stood up, crossed to the desk and spread the paper on it. He saw at once that Johnny had scrawled on it, using his own blood, and Daniel shivered at the macabre characters.

NJNC. The letters were childlike and crude, smeared and barely legible. They made no sense, although perhaps the J was an I. Daniel studied it. NINC. Still there was nothing obvious in the message. Either it was gibberish or had some obscure meaning that only made sense to a dying man.

Suddenly Daniel felt a stirring in his subconscious, something was trying to surface. He closed his eyes for a minute to give it a chance. Often it helped to let his mind go blank when searching for an elusive idea or memory, rather than to harry the point and drive it further under. It was there, very close now, a shadow just below his conscious mind like the shape of a man-eating shark under the surface of a turgid sea.

NINC.

He opened his eyes again and found himself looking at the floor. There were bloody footprints left by his own boot soles and by those of the killer. He was not thinking about them; he was still grappling with that single cryptic word that Johnny had left for him.

Then he found his eyes had focused on one of the footprints, and his nerves jumped tight and shrieked like the strings of a violin slashed with the bow. The footprint was chequered with a fish-scale pattern.

NINC. It resounded through his mind and then that distinctive footprint turned the sense of it and the echo came back, altered and compelling. NING. Johnny had tried to write NING! Daniel found that he was cold and trembling with the shock of the discovery.

'Ambassador Ning – Ning Cheng Gong.' How was it possible? And yet there were the bloody footprints to confirm the impossible. Ning had been here *after* Johnny was shot. Ning had been lying when he said that he had left ... Daniel broke that train of thought as another memory struck him like a bolt from a cross-bow.

The blood on the cuff of the blue cotton slacks, the tracks of Ning's training shoes and the blood – Johnny's blood. At last his rage had a target on which to focus, but now it was a cold constructive rage. He pressed the bloody note back into Johnny's hand and folded his fingers around it for the police to find. Then he spread the green curtain over Johnny's body, covering the shattered head. He stood over him for a few seconds.

'I'll get the bastard for you, old friend. For you and Mavis and the babies. I promise you, Johnny, on the memory of our friendship. I swear it.' Then he snatched up the rifle and ran from the office, down the steps to where Jock waited beside the parked Landcruiser.

In the few seconds that it took him to reach the truck, the last details fell into place in his mind. He remembered Cheng's perturbation when he thought Daniel might be staying longer at Chiwewe, and his obvious relief when he learned that Daniel was leaving.

He glanced back towards the ruins of the ivory godown and the tyre treads were still just visible in the mud. It was simple and ingenious. Let the gang of poachers draw the pursuit, while

76

they ferried the ivory out in the Parks Board's own trucks. Daniel remembered the surly unnatural behaviour of Gomo and the other driver when he had met them on the road. Now it made good sense. They had been sitting on a load of stolen ivory. No wonder they were acting strangely.

As he slipped behind the wheel of the Landcruiser and ordered Jock to climb aboard, he glanced at his wristwatch. It was almost ten o'clock, nearly four hours since he had passed Cheng and the trucks on the escarpment road. Could he catch them before they reached the main highway and disappeared? He realised that it had been so carefully planned that they must have worked out an escape route and some means of disposing of the ivory. He started the Landcruiser and hit the gear-lever. 'You aren't going to get away with it, you dirty bastard!'

In many places the recent storm waters had scoured the escarpment road, gouging knee-deep gulleys across the tracks and exposing boulders the size of cannonballs. Daniel pushed the Landcruiser over them so violently that Jock seized the grab handle on the dashboard for support.

'Slow down, Danny, damn it. You'll kill us both. Where the hell are we going? What's the rush?'

In as few words as possible Daniel told him the bare outlines.

'You can't touch an ambassador,' Jock grunted as the bouncing truck slammed the words out of him. 'If you're wrong, they'll crucify you, man.'

'I'm not wrong,' Daniel assured him. 'On top of Johnny's note, I feel it in my guts.'

The rain waters had rushed down the slope of the escarpment, but when they reached the floor of the valley they slowed and piled up upon themselves. Only hours before, Daniel had crossed and re-crossed a dry river-bed at the foot of the escarpment. Now he pulled up on the approach to the ford and stared down the beam of the headlights.

'You'll never get through there,' Jock muttered with alarm.

Daniel left the motor running and jumped down into ankle-deep mud. He ran to the edge of the crazy water. It was the colour of creamed coffee, racing past in a muddy blur, carrying small tree-trunks and up-rooted bushes with it. It was almost fifty yards across.

One of the trees growing beside the ford draped its branches out over the torrent, in places just touching the swirling waters with its lowest twigs. Daniel grabbed the main branch for support and let himself down into the river. He edged out across the flood and it took all the strength of his arms to prevent himself from being swept away. The drag of the water was overpowering and his feet were continually lifted clear of the bottom. However, he worked himself out to the deepest section of the river.

It was as deep as his lowest rib. The branch to which he was clinging was creaking and bowing like a fishing-rod to the strain as he began to work his way back to the bank. He emerged from the torrent with water streaming down his lower body, his sodden clothing clinging to his legs and his boots squelching.

'It'll go,' he told Jock, as he clambered back into the cab.

'You're crazy mad,' Jock exploded. 'I'm not going in there.'

'Okay! Fine! You've got just two seconds to get out,' Daniel told him grimly, and changed the gearing of the Toyota into four-wheel drive and low ratio.

'You can't leave me here,' Jock howled. 'The place is lousy with lions. What happens to me?'

'That's your problem, mate. Are you coming or going?'

'Okay, go ahead! Drown us!' Jock capitulated and grabbed the sides of his seat.

Daniel rolled the Landcruiser down the steep approach to the ford, and into the brown waters. He kept her rolling at an even pace and within a few yards the water was above the level of the wheels, but still the nose of the truck was tilted steeply downwards as the bottom fell away.

There was a whoosh of steam as water rushed through the engine compartment and swamped the hot metal of the block. The headlights were obscured as they sank below the surface, becoming two luminous glows in the turgid water. A bow wave rose ahead of the bonnet, as the water came up to the level of the windshield. A petrol engine would have swamped and stalled, but the big diesel pushed them stolidly forward into the flood. Water was pouring in around the door posts. They were calf-deep where they sat.

'You really are crazy,' Jock yelled, and put his feet up on the dashboard. 'I want to go home to mother!'

Now even the Landcruiser was faltering as the air trapped in the body floated her high and her spinning tyres lost traction on the rock-strewn bottom.

'Oh, my God!' Jock cried, as a huge up-rooted tree came hurtling down upon them out of the darkness.

It crashed into the side of the truck, hitting one of the windows, and slewing the whole chassis around. They were hurled downstream, spinning slowly under the weight of the floating tree. As they made one full revolution the mortal embrace of the tree mass was broken.

Released from its grip, they floated free, but they were sinking fast as the trapped air was expelled from the Land-cruiser's body. Water began to seep in, and soon they were sitting waist-deep.

'I'm getting out,' Jock yelled, and threw his weight against the door. 'It won't budge.' He was panicking, as the pressure of water held the door tightly closed.

Then suddenly Daniel felt the wheels touch bottom again. The flood had swept them into a bend of the river and pushed them in against the far bank. The engine was still running. The modified air-intake pipe and filter reached up as high as the cab roof. Daniel had installed it for just such an emergency. In the shallows, the wheels caught at the jagged rock bottom and heaved the Landcruiser's bulk forward.

'Come on, darling,' Daniel pleaded. 'Get us out of here.' And the sturdy truck responded. She shuddered and bounced and tried to drag herself from the waters. The headlights pushed through the surface and blazed out suddenly, lighting the far bank. The flood had cast them up on the shelving mudbank and the truck canted steeply nose-up as her spinning front wheels clawed up the slope.

Ahead of them was a low spot in the riverbank. The Land-cruiser slipped and slewed and crabbed up it, the engine roaring, ferociously tearing out small bushes that had survived the flood and ploughing deep ruts in the soft earth, until suddenly her lugged tyres gained full purchase and hurled her forward up out of the flood. Sheets of water streamed from her bodywork like a surfacing submarine and the big diesel engine bellowed triumphantly as they roared into the mopane forest.

'I'm alive,' Jock whispered. 'Hallelujah!'

Daniel turned parallel with the riverbank, weaving the Landcruiser back and forth between the tree-trunks of the standing mopane until they bumped over the verge on to the roadway. He kicked her out of low ratio and gunned the motor. They sped away towards the Mana Pools turn-off.

'How many more like that?' Jock asked with trepidation. For the first time since Johnny's death Daniel smiled, but it was a grim little smile.

'Only four or five,' he answered. 'A Sunday afternoon stroll. Nothing to it.'

He glanced at his watch. Cheng and the refrigerator trucks had almost four hours' start on them. They must have got through the fords before the drainage of storm waters off the slope of the escarpment had flooded them. The earth beneath the mopane trees was melted like warm chocolate by the rain. This black cotton soil was notorious for bogging down vehicles when it was wet. The Landcruiser slithered and laboured and left deep glutinous ruts behind the churning wheels.

'Here's the next river.' Daniel warned, as the road gradient altered and thick dark riverine bush pressed in close on each side of the narrow track. 'Get your life-jacket on.'

'I can't stand another one like the last.' Jock turned to him, pale-faced in the glow of the instrument panel. 'I promise ten "Hail Mary's" and fifty "Our Father's" . . .'

'The price is right – it'll be a breeze,' Daniel assured him as the headlights lit the ford.

In Africa a flash flood drops almost as abruptly as it rises. The rain had stopped almost two hours earlier, and the slope of the valley was by now almost drained. There was a high-water mark on the far bank of the river almost six feet above the present surface of the shrunken waters, to show how swiftly they had subsided. This time the Landcruiser made light of the crossing. The waters did not even cover the headlights before she triumphantly climbed the far bank.

'The power of prayer,' Daniel grunted. 'Keep it up, Jock. We'll make a believer of you yet.'

The next river had fallen even lower, to the level of the tops of the wheels, and Daniel did not bother to change gear ratios as they splashed through. Forty minutes later, Daniel parked the truck at the front door of the warden's bungalow at Mana Pools Camp. While Jock leaned on the horn button and sounded a long urgent peal, Daniel pounded with both fists on the warden's door.

The warden came stumbling out onto the screened verandah, dressed only in a pair of underpants. 'Who is it?' he called in Shona. 'What the hell is going on?' He was a lean, muscled forty-year-old named Isaac Mtwetwe.

'Isaac? It's me,' Daniel called. 'There's big trouble, man. Get your arse into gear. You've got work to do.'

'Danny?' Isaac shaded his eyes against the glare of the Landcruiser's headlights. 'Is that you, Danny?'

He flashed his torch into Daniel's face. 'What is it? What has happened?'

Daniel answered him in fluent Shona. 'A big gang of armed poachers has hit Chiwewe camp. They wiped out Johnny Nzou and his family, and the entire camp staff.'

'Good God!' Isaac came fully awake.

'My guess is that they're from the Zambian side,' Daniel went on. 'I reckon they're heading back to cross the Zambezi about twenty miles downstream from here. You've got to get your anti-poaching team there to head them off.'

Swiftly Daniel gave him all the other information he had gleaned, the estimated size of the gang, their weapons, the time that they had left Chiwewe and their probable line and speed of march. Then he asked, 'Did the refrigerator trucks come through here from Chiwewe on their return to Harare?'

'At about eight o'clock,' Isaac confirmed. 'They just got through before the rivers flooded. There was a civilian with them, a Chinese in a blue Mercedes. One of the trucks was towing him. The Mercedes was no good in the mud.' Isaac was dressing as he spoke. 'What are you going to do, Danny? I know Johnny Nzou was your friend. If you come with us you might get a shot at these swine.' Although they had fought on opposite sides during the bush war, he knew Daniel's reputation.

However, Daniel shook his head.

'I am going on after the trucks, and that Mercedes.'

'I don't understand.' Isaac looked up from lacing his boots and his tone was puzzled.

'I can't explain now, but it's all part of Johnny's murder. Trust me.' Daniel couldn't tell Isaac about the ivory and Ambassador Ning, not until he had proof. 'Trust me,' he repeated, and Isaac nodded.

'Okay, Danny, I'll get those murdering swine for you before they get away across the river,' he promised. 'You go ahead. Do what you have to do.'

Daniel left Isaac on the Zambezi bank, assembling his strike force of anti-poacher rangers and embarking them into the twenty-foot fast assault craft. There was a big ninety horse-power Yamaha outboard on the stern. Like the rest of them, the boat was a veteran of the bush war.

Daniel drove on westwards into the night, following the track that ran parallel to the Zambezi. Now the tyre tracks of the convoy were even more deeply ploughed into the muddy earth. In the headlights they looked as fresh as if they had been laid only minutes before. Certainly they had been made since the last downpour of rain. The pattern of the treads was clearly moulded in black cotton clay of the roadway.

Obviously one of the trucks was still towing the Mercedes. Daniel could pick out the scuff-marks where the tow rope had touched the earth at intervals. The tow would slow them down considerably, Daniel thought with satisfaction. He must be gaining on them rapidly now. He peered ahead eagerly, half expecting to see the red glow of the Mercedes's tail-lights appear out of the darkness, and he reached out to touch the AK 47 rifle propped between the seats.

Jock noticed the gesture and warned him softly, 'Don't do anything stupid, Danny. You don't have any proof, man. You can't just go blowing the ambassador's head off on suspicion. Cool it, man.'

It seemed that they were further behind the convoy than Daniel had hoped. It was after midnight when they intersected the Great North Road, the metalled highway that crossed the Chirundu bridge over the Zambezi to the north, and to the south climbed the escarpment of the valley on its serpentine route to Harare, the capital of Zimbabwe.

Daniel pulled the Landcruiser into the verge at the road junction. He jumped out with the Maglite in his hand.

In all probability the convoy would have turned south towards Harare. They couldn't have hoped to get two huge government trucks loaded with fresh game meat and ivory through both the Zimbabwean and Zambian customs posts, not even with the dispensation of the most princely bribes.

Daniel found confirmation of his deduction almost immediately. The tyres of the trucks and the Mercedes had been caked with clinging black clay. They left clear tracks on the tarmac of the highway. The tracks gradually faded out as the last vestiges of clay were spun off the tyres, but for almost a mile further the moulded bars of mud from between the treads of the tyres littered the tarmac like squares of chocolate.

'South,' said Daniel, as he climbed back behind the driving-wheel. 'They're heading south, and we're catching up with them every minute.'

He pushed the Landcruiser hard and kicked in the Fairey overdrive. The speedometer needle touched 90 miles per hour and the heavy tyres whined shrilly on the black tarmac surface of the highway.

'They can't be much further ahead,' Daniel muttered. As he said it he saw the glow of headlights in front of them.

He touched the stock of the AK rifle again, and Jock glanced at him nervously.

'For Chrissake, Danny. I don't want to be an accessory to bloody murder. They say Chikurubi prison isn't exactly five-star accommodation.'

The lights were closer now and Daniel switched on the Landcruiser's powerful spotlights, then exclaimed with disappointment. He had expected to see the distinctive hull of the refrigerator truck standing up tall and polar white in the beam of the spotlight. Instead he found a vehicle that he had never seen before. It was a gigantic MAC truck, a twenty-tonner, towing an equally large eight-wheel trailer. Both the hull of the truck and the body of the trailer were covered by heavy-duty green nylon tarpaulin and roped down with a hook-and-eye arrangement that securely protected the cargo. This massive road-rig was pulled off the highway and parked in a lay-by at the roadside facing back northwards towards Chirundu Bridge.

Three men were working around the trailer, adjusting the ropes that held the tarpaulin in place. The beam of the spotlight froze them, and they stared back at the approaching Landcruiser.

Two of the men were black Africans dressed in faded overalls. The third was a dignified figure in a khaki safari suit. He was also dark-complexioned but bearded and wearing some sort of white headgear. It was only when Daniel got closer that he realised that it was a neatly bound white turban and that the man was a Sikh. His beard was carefully curled and rolled up into the folds of the turban.

As Daniel slowed the Landcruiser and pulled in in front of the parked truck, the Sikh spoke sharply to the two Africans. All three of them turned and hurried back to the front of the truck and climbed aboard.

'Hold it a second!' Daniel shouted, and jumped out of the Landcruiser. 'I want to talk to you.' The Sikh was already seated behind the wheel.

'Hold on!' Daniel called urgently, and came level with the cab.

The Sikh was five feet above the level of his head and he leaned out of the window and peered down at Daniel.

'Yes, what is it?'

'Sorry to trouble you,' Daniel told him. 'Have you passed two large white trucks on the road?'

The Sikh stared down at him without answering and Daniel added, 'Very big trucks – you couldn't miss them. Travelling together in convoy. There might have been a blue Mercedes saloon with them.'

The Sikh pulled his head in and spoke to the two Africans in a dialect that Daniel could not understand. While he waited impatiently for a reply, Daniel noticed a company logo painted on the front door-panel of the truck.

CHETTI SINGH LIMITED
IMPORT AND EXPORT

Malawi was the small sovereign state that nestled between the three much larger territories of Zambia, Tanzania and Mozambique. It was a country of mountains and rivers and lakes, whose population was as prosperous and happy under its octogenarian dictator Hastings Banda as any state on the poverty- and tyranny-ridden continent of Africa.

'Mr Singh, I'm in a desperate hurry,' Daniel called. 'Please tell me if you've seen those trucks.'

The Sikh popped his head back out the window in alarm. 'How do you know my name?' he demanded, and Daniel pointed at the logo on the door.

'Ha! You are one very observant and erudite fellow, never mind.' The Sikh looked relieved. 'Yes, my men reminded me that two trucks passed us one hour ago. They were heading south. We did not see a Mercedes with them. I am totally certain of that salient fact. No Mercedes. Absolutely.'

He started the engine of the MAC truck. 'I am happy to have served you. I am also in desperate haste. I must return home to Lilongwe. Farewell, my friend, safe journey and happy landings.' He waved cheerily and let the huge truck roll forward.

Something about his airy manner struck a false note in Daniel's mind. As the heavily loaded trailer rumbled past him, Daniel caught hold of one of the steel slats and swung himself up on to the footplate below the trailer's tailgate. The headlights of the parked Landcruiser gave him enough light to peer between the steel slats of the bodywork and the edge of the tarpaulin cover.

The trailer seemed to be packed with a full load of gunny sacks. Stencilled on one of the sacks that he could see was the legend 'Dried Fish. Product of . . .' The country of origin was obscured. Daniel's nose confirmed the contents of the sacks. The smell of half-rotten fish was powerful and unmistakable.

The truck was gathering speed swiftly and Daniel dropped off and let his own momentum carry him forward as he hit the ground. He ran with it for a dozen paces and then pulled up and stared after the dwindling tail-lights.

His instinct warned him that something was as fishy as the stink from under the tarpaulin of the departing trailer, but what could he do about it? He tried to think. His main concerns were still the convoy of refrigerator trucks and Ning in his Mercedes which were heading southwards, while the Sikh in his MAC truck was rumbling away in the opposite direction. He couldn't follow both of them even if he could prove a connection between them, which he could not.

'Chetti Singh,' he repeated the name and the box number to fix it firmly in his mind. Then ran back to where Jock waited in the Landcruiser.

'Who was that? What did he say?' Jock wanted to know.

'He saw the refrigerator trucks heading south about an hour ago. We're going after them.' He pulled out of the lay-by and they raced on southwards at their top speed.

The road began to climb the hills that led up on to the high central plateau, and the Landcruiser's speed bled off slowly, but still they were doing around 70 miles an hour. Jock had not spoken again since they had met Chetti Singh, but his features were drawn and nervous in the light reflected from the instrument panel. He kept glancing sideways at Daniel as if he were about to protest, but then thought better of it.

The road went into a series of gentle curves as it followed the gradient of the hills. They came through the next curve and without warning one of the white refrigerator trucks blocked the road ahead of them. It was travelling at half the speed of the Landcruiser and diesel smoke belched out of its exhausts as it laboured upwards in low gear. The driver was holding the middle line of the highway, not leaving sufficient space for Daniel to pass him.

Daniel sounded his horn and flicked his spotlights on and off to induce the truck to move over, but it never wavered.

'Move over, you murdering bastard,' Daniel snarled, and hit the horn button with another prolonged blast.

'Take it easy, Daniel,' Jock pleaded. 'You're going over the top. Cool it, man.'

Daniel swung the Landcruiser out on to the far verge of the road, into an overtaking position, and he sounded the horn again. Now he could see the wing mirror on the cab of the truck, and reflected in it the face of the driver.

The driver was Gomo. He was watching Daniel in the mirror but making no effort to give way and let him pass. His expression was a mixture of fear and ferocity, of guilt and bitter resentment. He was deliberately blocking the road, swinging wide on the corners and weaving the truck back and across when Daniel tried to pass him on the wrong side.

'He knows it's us,' Daniel told Jock angrily. 'He knows we've been back to Chiwewe and seen the bloody business there. He knows we suspect him, and he's trying to hold us off.'

'Come on, Danny. That's all in your head, man. There could be a dozen explanations for why he's behaving like this. I don't want any part of this crazy business.'

'Too late, my friend,' Daniel told him. 'Like it or not, you're part of it now.'

Daniel pulled the Landcruiser sharply back in the opposite direction. For once Gomo was slow to react and get across the road to block him. Daniel dropped a gear and thrust the accelerator flat. The Landcruiser jumped forward and got round the truck's tall tail-end. Still holding the accelerator flat to the floorboards, Daniel drew level with the cab, squeezing through the gap between the steel side of the hull and the edge of the road.

Only the nearside wheels of the Landcruiser had purchase on the tarmac surface, the off-side wheels were on the verge of the highway, throwing up a spray of loose gravel, dangerously close to the edge that fell away steeply into the Zambezi valley below them.

'Danny, you mad bastard,' Jock yelled angrily. 'You'll get us both killed. I've had enough of this bullshit, man.'

The Landcruiser hit one of the concrete road-markers with its reflective cat's-eye that warned of the dangerous drop. With a crash they snapped off the road sign, and swayed dangerously, but Daniel held grimly to the outside berth and inched up alongside the cab of the lumbering truck.

Gomo stared down at the Landcruiser from the vantage point of the high cab. Daniel leant forward to see him, lifted one hand from the wheel and made a peremptory hand signal for him to pull over and stop. Gomo nodded and obeyed, swinging the truck back to the left, giving way to the Landcruiser.

'That's more like it,' Daniel grated, and edged back into the space alongside the truck that Gomo had opened for him. He had fallen into the trap and let down his guard. The two vehicles were still grinding along side by side, and Gomo suddenly spun the driving-wheel hard back in the opposite direction. Before Daniel could react, the truck crashed into the side of the Landcruiser and a shower of sparks blazed from the violent contact of steel against steel. The weight and momentum of the huge truck flung the smaller vehicle back over the verge.

Daniel fought the wheel to try and resist the thrust but the struts flew through his fingers and he thought for a moment that his left thumb was dislocated. The pain numbed him to the elbow. He hit the brakes hard and the Landcruiser slowed and allowed the truck to pull ahead, with a shriek of metal between the two vehicles as they disengaged. The Landcruiser came to rest, half over the embankment with one front wheel hanging over the cliff face.

Daniel wrung his injured hand, tears of agony welling into his eyes. Gradually he felt strength return, and with it his anger. By now the truck was five hundred yards ahead and pulling away rapidly.

With the Landcruiser in four-wheel drive, Daniel flung her into reverse. Only three of her wheels had purchase, but she heaved herself gamely back from the drop. Her near side was scraped down to bare gleaming metal where the truck had struck her.

'Okay,' Daniel snarled at Jock. 'Do you want any more proof? That was a deliberate attempt to write us off. That bastard Gomo is guilty as hell.'

The truck had disappeared from view around the next curve of the highway, and Daniel hurled the Landcruiser in pursuit.

'Gomo isn't going to let us get ahead of him,' Daniel told Jock. 'I'm going to get on to that truck and take him out of it.'

'I want no more part of this business,' Jock muttered. 'Leave it to the police now, damn it.'

Daniel ignored his protest and pushed the Landcruiser to its top speed. As they came through the bend the refrigerator truck was only a few hundred yards ahead. The gap between them closed swiftly.

Daniel studied the other vehicle. The scrape marks down its side were not as extensive as the damage to the Landcruiser and Gomo was making better speed now as the slope of the hill eased away towards the crest of the escarpment. The double rear doors into the cargo hold were locked with a heavy vertical bar. The airtight seals were black rubber around the edge of the doors. On the nearside of the hull a steel ladder gave access to the flat roof where the cooling fans of the refrigeration equipment were housed in fibreglass pods.

'I'm going to get on that ladder,' Daniel told Jock. 'As soon as I'm gone, you slide over and grab the wheel.'

'Not me, man. I told you, I've had a gutful. Count me out.'

'Fine.' Daniel did not even glance at him. 'Don't steer! Let her crash and you with her. What's one stupid prick less in this naughty world?'

Daniel was judging the speed and distance between the two converging vehicles. He opened his side door. The retaining catch on the door had been removed to allow unimpeded photography through the opening so the door hinged fully open, to lie flat against the side of the bonnet.

Steering with one hand, Daniel leaned out of the open door. 'Take her, she's yours,' he shouted at Jock. Daniel hauled himself up on to the roof, the pain in his thumb forgotten. At that moment Gomo once again swung across to block the Landcruiser.

As the two vehicles came together Daniel leaped across the narrow gap. He caught the rung of the side ladder and hauled his lower body out from between the steel sides of the vehicles as they clashed together again.

He had a glimpse of Jock at the driver's wheel, pale-faced and sweating in the reflected headlights. Then the Landcruiser swerved away and fell behind the white truck, Jock steering it erratically, letting the slope slow it, finally bringing it to a halt on the side of the road.

Daniel clambered upwards, hand over hand, agile as an ape

on the narrow steel rungs, and reached the flat roof of the truck. The fan housing was in the centre of the roof and a low grab-rail ran the length of the hull, fore and aft. On hands and knees Daniel worked his way forward, falling flat on his belly and clinging grimly to the rail when the centrifugal force of the truck through the bends threatened to throw him from the roof.

It took him fully five minutes to get forward above the articulated driver's cab. He was pretty certain that Gomo had not seen him come aboard. The bulk of the cargo hold would have blocked his rear view. By now he must be fairly confident that he had discouraged the driver of the Landcruiser, for its headlights were no longer visible on the empty road behind the truck.

Daniel worked his way gingerly across to the passenger side of the cab and peered over. There was a running-board below the passenger door, and the sturdy wing mirror standing out from the side of the cab would give him a secure handhold. It only remained to find out if Gomo had taken the precaution of locking the passenger door. There was no reason why he should, Daniel comforted himself, as he looked ahead down the beams of the truck's powerful headlights.

He waited until the road turned left. The pull would hold him against the side of the cab, rather than throwing him clear. He slid over the side and clutched at the wing mirror. For a moment his feet were kicking in air, then they hit the wide steel running-board and found a hold. He was facing inwards, hanging on to the mirror and peering in through the side window of the cab.

Gomo turned a startled face towards him and shouted something. He tried to reach across to the locking handle of the door, but the full width of the passenger seat separated him from it and the truck slewed wildly and nearly left the road, forcing Gomo to grab the wheel again.

Daniel jerked open the side door and threw himself into the cab, sprawling half across the seat. Gomo punched at his face. The fist caught Daniel under the left eye and stunned him for only a moment, then Daniel seized the handle of the vacuum brake control and heaved it full on.

All the gigantic wheels of the truck locked simultaneously and, in a shrieking billow of blue smoke and scorching rubber, the truck skidded and swayed down the highway. Gomo was hurled forward out of his seat. The steering-wheel caught him in the chest and his forehead cracked against the windshield with enough force to star the glass.

Then the next wild swing of the vehicle flung him back, only semi-conscious, into his seat. Daniel reached across him and seized the steering-wheel. He held the truck straight until it came to a halt, half off the highway, with its offside wheels in the drainage ditch.

Daniel switched off the ignition and reached across Gomo to open the driver's door. He grabbed Gomo's shoulder and shoved him roughly out of the cab. Gomo fell the six feet to the ground and ended up on his knees. There was a lump the size and colour of a ripe fig in the centre of his forehead where he had hit the windscreen.

Daniel jumped down and stooped to catch hold of the collar of his uniform tunic.

'All right.' He twisted the collar like a garotte. 'You killed Johnny Nzou and his family.'

Gomo's face was swelling and turning purple black in the vague light reflected from the truck's headlamps.

'Please, Doctor, I don't understand. Why are you doing this?' His voice was a breathless whine as Daniel choked him.

'You lying bastard, you are as guilty—'

Gomo reached under the hem of his tunic. He wore a skinning knife in a leather sheath on his belt. Daniel heard the snap of the buckle as he released the retaining strap and caught the glint of the blade as it came free of the sheath.

Daniel released his collar and jumped back as Gomo slashed upwards. He was only just quick enough, for the blade caught in a loose fold of his shirt and sliced it like a razor. He felt the sting of it as it nicked his skin and left a shallow graze up across his lower ribs.

Gomo came to his feet, holding the knife in a low underhand grip.

'I kill you,' he warned, shaking his head to clear it, weaving the glittering blade in the typical knife-fighter's on-guard stance, aiming the point at Daniel's belly.

'I kill you, you white shit-eater.' He feinted and cut in a side-arm slash and Daniel jumped back as the blade hissed an inch from his stomach.

'Yah!' Gomo chuckled thickly. 'Jump, you white baboon. Run, you little white monkey.' He cut again, forcing Daniel to give ground, and then rushed at him in a furious prolonged attack that forced Daniel to scramble and dance to keep clear of the darting blade.

Gomo changed the angle of his thrusts, going lower, trying to cut Daniel's thighs and cripple him, but always keeping the knife well covered so that Daniel could not grab at his wrist. Moving backwards, Daniel pretended to stumble on the rough footing. He dropped on one knee and put his left hand to the ground to regain his balance.

'Yah!' Gomo thought he saw his opportunity and came in to finish it, but Daniel had snatched up a handful of gravel and now he pushed off and used his momentum to hurl the handful into Gomo's face. It was an old knife-fighter's trick, but Gomo fell for it. The gravel slashed his eyes, and deflected his thrust. Instinctively he threw up his hands to cover his face, and Daniel seized his knife-hand and wrenched it over.

They were chest to chest now, the knife held above their heads at the full stretch of their arms. Daniel snapped his head forward, butting for Gomo's face, and caught him with the top of his forehead across the bridge of his nose. Gomo gasped and reeled backwards, and Daniel brought up his right knee into Gomo's crotch, catching him squarely, crushing his genitals. This time Gomo screamed and his right arm lost its force.

Daniel swung it down and slammed the knuckles of the clenched knife-hand against the steel side of the truck. The knife spun from Gomo's nerveless fingers, and Daniel hooked him behind the heels with one foot, and heaved him backwards so that he tripped and went sprawling into the drainage ditch beside the highway.

Before Gomo could recover his balance and rise, Daniel had snatched up the knife and was standing over him. He placed the point of the blade under Gomo's chin and pricked the soft skin of his throat so that a single droplet of blood welled out on to the silver steel like a bright cabochon ruby.

'Keep still,' he grated, 'or I'll cut your gizzard out, you murdering bastard.' It took a few seconds for him to recover his breath. 'All right. Now get up, slowly.'

Gomo came to his feet, clutching his injured genitals. Daniel forced him back against the side of the truck, the knife still pressed to his throat.

'You've got the ivory in the truck,' he accused. 'Let's have a look at it, my friend.'

'No,' Gomo whispered. 'No ivory. I don't know what you want. You are mad, man.'

'Where are the keys to the hold?' Daniel demanded, and Gomo swivelled his eyes without moving his head.

'In my pocket.'

'Turn around, slowly,' Daniel ordered. 'Face the side of the truck.'

As Gomo obeyed Daniel whipped his arm around his throat in a stranglehold from behind and shoved him forward so that his lumped forehead cracked against the steel hull. Gomo cried out with the pain.

'Give me an excuse to do that again,' Daniel whispered in his ear. 'The sound of your pig squeals is sweet music.'

He pressed the knife into Gomo's back at the level of his kidneys, just hard enough to let him feel the point of it through the cloth of his tunic.

'Get the keys.' He pricked him a little harder and Gomo reached into his pocket. The keys tinkled as he brought them out.

Still holding him in a strangler's grip, Daniel frog-marched him to the rear of the truck.

'Open the lock,' he snapped. Gomo fitted the key and the mechanism turned easily.

'Okay, now get the handcuffs off your belt,' he ordered. The steel manacles were regulation issue for all rangers on anti-poaching duty.

'Snap one link over your right wrist,' Daniel told him. 'And give me the key.'

The cuffs dangling from his wrist, Gomo passed the key over his shoulder. Daniel slipped it into his pocket, then snapped the second link of the handcuffs over the steel bracing of the hull.

Now Gomo was securely chained to the bodywork of the truck and Daniel released his grip on him and turned the locking handle of the rear double doors.

He swung them open. A gust of icy air flowed out of the refrigerated interior and the smell of elephant meat was gamey and rank. The inside of the hold was in darkness, but Daniel jumped up on to the tailgate and groped for the light switch. The striplight on the roof flickered and then lit up the refrigerated compartment with a cold blue glow. Hunks of butchered carcass streaked and marbled with white fat hung from the rows of meat-hooks along the roof rails. There were tons of flesh, packed in so closely that Daniel could see only the first rank of carcasses. He dropped on his knees and peered into the narrow space below them. The steel floor was puddled with dripping blood, but that was all.

Daniel felt a sudden swoop of dismay in his guts. He had expected to see piles of tusks packed beneath the hanging carcasses. He scrambled to his feet and pushed his way into the compartment. The cold took his breath away, and the touch of the raw frozen flesh as he brushed against it was loathsome and disgusting, but he wriggled his way deeper into the hold, determined to find where they had concealed the ivory.

He gave up after ten minutes. There was no place where they could have hidden such a bulky cargo. He jumped down to ground level. His clothing was stained from contact with the raw meat. On hands and knees he crawled under the chassis of the truck, searching for a secret compartment.

When he crawled out again, Gomo crowed at him gleefully, 'No ivory, I tell you, no ivory. You break government truck. You beat me. Plenty trouble for you now, white boy.'

'We haven't finished yet,' Daniel promised him. 'We haven't finished until you sing me a little song, the song about what you and the Chinaman did with the ivory.'

'No ivory,' Gomo repeated, but Daniel grabbed his shoulder and swung him around to face the side of the truck.

With one deft movement he unlocked the link of the cuffs from the bodywork, twisted both Gomo's wrists up behind his back and locked them there.

'Okay, brother,' he muttered grimly. 'Let's go where we have a little light to work in.'

He lifted Gomo's manacled hands up between his shoulder-blades and marched him to the front of the truck. He hand-cuffed him to the front fender between the headlights. Both Gomo's hands were pinned behind his back. He was helpless.

'Johnny Nzou was my friend,' he told Gomo softly. 'You raped his wife and his little daughters. You beat his son's brains out all over the wall. You shot Johnny—'

'No, not me. I know nothing,' Gomo screamed. 'I kill nobody. No ivory, no kill . . .'

Daniel went on quietly, as though Gomo had not interjected.

'You must believe me when I tell you that I'm going to enjoy doing this. Every time you squeal, I will think of Johnny Nzou, and I'll be glad.'

'I know nothing. You mad.'

Daniel slipped the knife-blade under Gomo's belt and sliced through the leather. His khaki uniform trousers sagged down around his hips. Daniel pulled the waistband open and thrust the blade into his trouser top.

'How many wives have you got, Gomo?' he asked. 'Four? Five? How many?' He slit through the waistband and Gomo's trousers slid down around his ankles. 'I think your wives want you to tell me about the ivory, Gomo. They want you to tell me about Johnny Nzou and how he died.'

Daniel pulled the elasticised top of Gomo's underpants down around his knees.

'Let's have a look at what you've got.' He smiled coldly. 'I think your wives are going to be very unhappy, Gomo.'

Daniel took the front tails of Gomo's tunic and ripped them apart so violently that the buttons popped off and flew away into the darkness beyond the headlights. He pulled the separate flaps of the tunic back over Gomo's shoulders, so that he was naked from the throat to the knees. Gomo's body hair covered his chest and paunch with tight black balls of wool. His genitals were massively bunched at the base of his belly, nestled in their own flocculent pelt.

'Sing me a little song about the ivory and Mr Ning,' Daniel invited, and used the flat of the blade to separate Gomo's dangling penis from the bunch.

Gomo gasped and tried to shrink away from the cold metallic

touch, but the radiator grille pressed against his back and he could not move.

'Talk, Gomo, even if it is only to say goodbye to your own *matondo*.'

'You are mad,' Gomo gasped. 'I don't know what you want.'

'What I want,' said Daniel, 'is to cut this off at the root.'

The thick tube of flesh was draped over the flat of the blade. It looked like the trunk of a new-born elephant, long and dark, knotted with veins and with a wrinkled and hooded tip.

'I want to cut this off and force you to kiss it goodbye, Gomo.'

'I didn't kill Johnny Nzou.' Gomo's voice broke. 'It wasn't me.'

'What about his wife and daughters, Gomo? Did you use this big ugly rod of yours on them?'

'No, no! You are mad. I didn't . . .'

'Come on, Gomo. All I have to do is turn the knife a little, like this.' Daniel rolled his wrist slowly, bringing the razor edge uppermost. Gomo's organ was dangling over it, and then the thin skin split. It was just a scratch, but Gomo screamed.

'Stop!' he bleated. 'I will tell you. Yes, all right, I will tell you everything I know. Stop, please stop!'

'That's good.' Daniel encouraged him. 'Tell me about Chetti Singh . . .' He introduced the name with assurance. It was a flier, but Gomo accepted.

'Yes, I tell you about him, if you don't cut me. Please don't cut me.'

'Armstrong.' Another voice startled Daniel. He had not heard the Landcruiser come up. It must have arrived while he was searching the cold compartment of the truck, but now Jock stood in the peripheral shadows of the headlights.

'Leave him, Armstrong.' Jock's voice was rough with determination. 'Get away from that man,' he ordered.

'You keep out of this,' Daniel snapped at him, but Jock stepped closer and with a start Daniel saw that he carried the AK rifle. He handled it with surprising competence and authority.

'Leave him alone,' Jock ordered. 'You've gone too far — much too far.'

'The man is a murderer and a criminal,' Daniel protested, but he was forced to step back before the menace of the AK 47. Jock was pointing it at his belly.

'You haven't any proof. There is no ivory,' Jock told him. 'You don't have anything.'

'He was confessing,' Daniel told him angrily. 'If you just keep out of it—'

'You were torturing him,' Jock answered as angrily. 'You had a knife to his balls. Of course, he was confessing. He has rights; you can't abuse those rights. Unchain him now; let him go!'

'You are a bleeding heart,' Daniel fumed. 'This is an animal—'

'He is a human being,' Jock contradicted. 'And I have to stop you abusing him, or else I'm as guilty as you are. I don't want to spend the next ten years in prison. Turn him loose.'

'He will confess first, or I'll cut his balls out.' Daniel seized a handful of Gomo's genitals and pulled. The loose skin and flesh stretched like shiny black rubber and Daniel held the knife-blade threateningly over it.

Gomo screamed, and Jock lifted the AK 47 and fired. He aimed a foot over Daniel's head. The muzzle blast whipped through Daniel's thick sweat-soaked curls and sent him reeling backwards clutching his ears.

'I warned you, Daniel.' Jock's expression was grim. 'Give me the keys of the handcuffs.'

Daniel was dazed by the blast, and Jock fired again. The bullet ploughed into the gravel between Daniel's boots.

'I mean it, Danny. I swear it. I'll kill you before I let you suck me any further into this business.'

'You saw Johnny . . .' Daniel shook his head and held his ears, but the muzzle blast had temporarily stunned him.

'I also saw you threaten to emasculate this man. That's enough. Give me the keys or the next shot is through one of your knee-caps.' Daniel saw that he meant it and reluctantly tossed him the keys.

'All right, now stand well back,' Jock ordered. He kept the rifle pointed at Daniel's belly as he unlocked one of the cuffs from Gomo's wrist, and handed him the key.

97

'You bloody idiot,' Daniel swore with frustration. 'Another minute, and I would have had him. I would have found out who killed Johnny and what happened to the ivory.'

Gomo unlocked his other wrist and swiftly pulled up his trousers and closed his tunic. Now that he was unchained and dressed, Gomo recovered his bravado. 'He is talking shit!' His voice was loud and defiant. 'I didn't say nothing. I don't know about Nzou. He was alive when we left Chiwewe—'

'All right. You can tell all that to the police,' Jock stopped Gomo. 'I'm taking you to Harare in the truck. Fetch my camera and bag from the Landcruiser. They are on the front seat.'

Gomo hurried back to where the Landcruiser was parked.

'Listen, Jock. Just give me another five minutes,' Daniel pleaded, but Jock waved the rifle at him.

'You and I are finished, Danny. First thing I'm going to do when I reach Harare is make a full report to the police. I'm going to give them chapter and verse.'

Gomo came back, lugging the Sony video recorder and Jock's canvas duffel bag. 'Yes, you tell the police you saw this mad white shit-eater cut my cock,' Gomo shouted. 'You tell them no ivory . . .'

'Get in the truck,' Jock ordered him. 'And start up.' When Gomo obeyed he turned back to Daniel. 'I'm sorry, Danny. You're on your own. You get no more help from me. I'll give evidence against you if they ask me to. I've got to cover my own arse, man.'

'You can't help being a yellow belly,' Daniel nodded. 'But weren't you the one always sounding off about justice – what about Johnny and Mavis?'

'What you were doing didn't have anything to do with justice,' Jock raised his voice above the rumble of the truck's diesel engine. 'You were playing the sheriff and the posse and the hangman, Danny. That wasn't justice; it was vengeance. I want no part of it. You know my address. You can send the money you owe me there. So long, Danny. Sorry it had to end this way.'

He climbed up to the passenger side of the cab. 'Don't try to stop us again.' He brandished the AK 47. 'I know how to use this.'

Jock slammed the door and Gomo swung the truck back on to the highway.

Daniel was left standing in the darkness, staring after the bright red gemstones of the tail-lights until a bend in the road hid them. His ears were still singing from the concussion of the rifle blast. He felt dizzy and nauseous. He staggered slightly as he walked back to where Jock had left the Landcruiser parked, and slumped into the driver's seat.

For a little longer his anger sustained him, anger at Cheng and his accomplices, at Gomo, and most of all at Jock and his interference. Then slowly his anger evaporated and the seriousness of his own predicament began to sink in. He had acted wildly and dangerously. He had made accusations which he could not support; he had damaged property, and he had endangered life and committed aggravated assault on a government official, if not grievous bodily harm. They could get him on half a dozen charges.

Then once again he thought of Johnny and his family, and his personal peril was of no significance.

I was so close to breaking the whole scheme, he thought bitterly. Another few minutes with Gomo and I would have had them. I almost had them for you, Johnny.

He had to decide on his next actions, but his head was aching, and it was hard to think logically. There was no point in chasing after Gomo. He was alerted, and he had somehow managed to get rid of the ivory.

What other courses of action were open to him? Ning Cheng Gong, of course. He was the key to the entire plot. However, the only connection to him, now that the ivory had disappeared, was Johnny's cryptic note and the footprint he had left at the murder scene.

Then there was Chetti Singh. Gomo had tacitly admitted that he knew the Sikh. What had he said when Daniel had tried him with the name? 'Yes, I tell you about him, if you don't cut me . . .'

There was also the band of poachers. He wondered if Isaac Mtwetwe had been able to intercept the gang on the Zambezi crossing, and take prisoners. Isaac would not have the same scruples as Jock. Johnny had also been Isaac's friend. He would know how to get information out of a captured poacher.

'I'll ring Mana Pools from the police post at Chirundu,' he decided, and started the Landcruiser. He U-turned and headed back down the escarpment. The Chirundu bridge police station was closer than Karoi. He had to make a statement to the police and make sure that a police investigation was under way as soon as possible. The police must be warned about Johnny's note and the bloody footprints.

Daniel's head still ached. He stopped the Landcruiser for a few minutes while he found a bottle of Panadol tablets in the first-aid kit and washed down a couple of them with a mug of coffee from the vacuum flask. While he drove on the pain abated and he started to put his thoughts into order.

It was almost four o'clock in the morning when he reached Chirundu bridge. There was a solitary corporal in the police charge office. His arms were folded on the desk in front of him, cradling his head. He was so soundly asleep that Daniel had to shake him vigorously, and his eyes were swollen and bloodshot when at last he raised his head, and blinked uncomprehendingly at Daniel.

'I want to report a murder, a multiple murder.' Daniel began the long laborious process of getting the official machinery in motion.

When the corporal seemed unable to decide upon the correct procedure, Daniel sent him to call the member-in-charge from his rondavel at the back of the station house. When the sergeant came into the charge office at last, he was dressed in full uniform, including Sam Browne belt and cap, but he was still half asleep.

'Ring CID in Harare,' Daniel urged him. 'They must send a unit to Chiwewe.'

'First you must make a statement,' the sergeant insisted.

There was no typewriter in the charge office; this was a remote rural station. The sergeant took down Daniel's statement in halting childlike longhand. His lips moved as he spelled out each separate letter silently. Daniel wanted to take the ballpoint away from him and get it down himself.

'Damn it, sergeant. Those dead people are lying out there. The killers are getting away while we sit here.'

The sergeant went on placidly with his composition, and Daniel corrected his spelling and fumed with exasperation.

However, the pace of the dictation allowed him to phrase his statement carefully. He set down the timetable of the previous day's events: the time that he had left Chiwewe and said goodbye to Johnny Nzou; the time he had found the signs of the raiding party and decided to return to the headquarters camp with a warning; and the time that he had met the refrigerator trucks on the road in company with the ambassador's Mercedes.

He described his conversation with Ambassador Ning and hesitated, wondering whether to mention the bloodstain that he had noticed on his blue slacks. It would sound like an accusation.

'The hell with protocol,' he decided, and described in detail the blue slacks and the training shoes with fish-scale patterned soles. 'They'll have to investigate Ning now.'

He felt a grim satisfaction, as he went on to describe his return to Chiwewe and the carnage he had found there. He made sure to mention the note in Johnny's hand and the fish-scale pattern of the bloody footprint on the office floor without specifically relating either to the Taiwanese ambassador. Let them make their own inferences.

He had a great deal of difficulty when it came to describing his pursuit of the Mercedes and the refrigerator trucks. He had to give his motives without incriminating himself, or pointing too definitely at the suspicions he entertained towards Ning Cheng Gong.

'I followed the convoy to ask them if they had any knowledge of the missing ivory,' he dictated. 'Although I was unable to catch up with Ambassador Ning and the leading truck, I did speak to Ranger Gomo whom I met on the Karoi road and who was driving the second refrigerator truck. He denied any knowledge of these events and allowed me to inspect the contents of the truck. I found no ivory.' It galled him to have to admit this, but he had to cover himself against any charges that Gomo might bring against him later. 'I then determined that my duty was to contact the nearest police station and report the deaths of the Chiwewe warden, his family and staff, and the burning and destruction of buildings and other property.'

It was well after daybreak when Daniel could at last sign the handwritten statement, and only then would the police sergeant respond to his urging to telephone CID headquarters in Harare. This led to a protracted telephone discussion between the sergeant and a series of increasingly senior detectives in Harare as one passed him on to the other. This was the pace of Africa and Daniel gritted his teeth. 'AWA,' he told himself. 'Africa Wins Again.'

At last it was ordered that the sergeant should drive out to Chiwewe camp in the station Landrover while a team of detectives flew down from Harare to land at the Park's airstrip.

'Do you want me to come out with you to Chiwewe?' Daniel asked, when the sergeant finally relinquished the telephone and began preparations for his expedition to the camp.

The sergeant looked nonplussed by the question. He had received no instructions from CID as to what to do with the witness. 'You leave an address and telephone number where we can contact you if we need you,' he decided, after a great deal of frowning thought.

Daniel was relieved to be turned loose. Since arriving at the Chirundu police station, he had had many hours in which to consider the situation, and make his plans to cover every contingency.

If Isaac Mtwetwe had been able to capture any of the poachers, that would still be the swiftest path to Ning Cheng Gong, but he had to talk to Isaac before he handed over his prisoners to the police.

'I want to use your telephone,' he told the police corporal as soon as the station commander and his unit of armed constables had driven away in the green Landrover, heading for Chiwewe.

'Police telephone.' The corporal shook his head. 'Not public telephone.'

Daniel produced a blue ten Zim dollar note and laid it on the desk in front of him. 'It is only a local call,' he explained, and the banknote vanished miraculously. The corporal smiled and waved him towards the telephone. Daniel had made a friend.

Isaac Mtwetwe answered the call almost immediately the Karoi telephone exchange made the connection to Mana Pools.

'Isaac,' Daniel blurted with relief. 'When did you get back?'

'I have just walked into my office this minute,' Isaac told

102

him. 'We got back ten minutes ago. I have one man wounded. I must get him to hospital'

'You made contact, then?'

'Yes, we made contact. Like you said, Danny, a big gang, bad guys.'

'Did you get any prisoners, Isaac?' Daniel demanded eagerly. 'If you managed to grab a couple of them, we're home and dry.'

 Isaac Mtwetwe stood at the wheel of the twenty-foot assault craft and ran downriver in the night.

His rangers squatted on the deck below the gunwale and huddled into their greatcoats, for it was cold out on the water with the wind of their passage accentuating the chill of the river mist.

The outboard motor was running rough and cutting out intermittently. Twice Isaac had to let the boat drift while he went back to work on it. It badly needed a full overhaul, but there was never enough foreign exchange available for spares to be imported. He got her running again and pointed the bows downstream.

A thick slice of moon spiked up above the dark trees that lined the bank of the Zambezi. It gave Isaac just enough light to push the boat up to top speed. Although he knew each curve and stretch of the river intimately for the next fifty miles, right down to Tete and the Mozambique border, the shallows and rocky outcrops were too complex even for him to run in complete darkness.

The glow of moonlight turned the patches of river mist to iridescent pearl dust and gave to the open water a lustre like polished black obsidian. The subdued hum of the motor and the speed of their progress gave no advance warning. They drew level with the hippopotamuses feeding in the reedbanks before the monstrous amphibians were aware of their arrival. In panic they tobogganed down the steep and slippery paths into the river, and went through the surface in a welter of spray. The flocks of wild duck roosting in the lagoons and quiet backwaters were more alert. The assault boat's approach sent them aloft on whistling wings, silhouetted against the rising moon.

Isaac knew exactly where he was heading. He had been a freedom fighter during the bush war and he had crossed this same river to raid the white farms and harass the security forces of Ian Smith's illegal regime. He knew all the techniques and tricks that the poachers employed. Some of them had been his comrades-in-arms in the struggle, but they were the new enemy now. He hated them as much as he had ever hated the Selous Scouts or the Rhodesian Light Infantry.

The Zambezi was almost half a mile wide along this stretch below Chirundu and Mana Pools. The raiders would need craft to cross its mighty green flood. They would get them the same way the guerrillas once had, from the local fisherfolk.

The Zambezi supports an itinerant population of fishermen who build their villages upon her banks. The villages are impermanent, for the tenor of their lives is dictated by the Zambezi's moods. When the river floods her banks and inundates the flood plains, the people must move to higher ground. They must follow the migrations of the shoals of tilapia and tiger fish and barbeled catfish on which they live, so every few months the clusters of rude thatched huts with their fish-smoking racks and smouldering fires are abandoned and allowed to fall into decay as the tribe moves on.

It was part of Isaac's duty to monitor the movements of the fisherfolk, for their exploitation of the river had a profound effect on the river ecology. Now he smelled the smoke and the odour of drying fish on the night air, and throttled back the motor. Softly he crept in towards the northern bank. If the poachers had come from Zambia, that was where they would return.

The odour of fish was stronger and tendrils of smoke drifted out low across the water to mingle with the mist. There were four huts with shaggy thatched roofs in an angle of the bank, and four long dugout canoes drawn up on the narrow beach below them.

Isaac nosed the assault craft on to the beach and jumped

ashore, leaving one of his rangers to hold the bows. An old woman crawled out of the low door of one of the huts. She wore only a skirt of lechwe antelope skins around her waist and her breasts were empty and pendulous.

'I see you, old mother,' Isaac greeted her respectfully. He always took pains to maintain good relations with the river-folk.

'I see you, my son,' the old woman giggled, and Isaac smelled the rank odour of cannabis on her. The Batonka people pound the weed into a paste, then mould it with fresh cow-dung into balls which they dry in the sun and smoke in clay pipes with reed mouthpieces.

The Government had granted them special dispensation to continue the tradition. It was particularly prevalent amongst the old women of the tribe.

'Are all your men in their huts?' Isaac asked quietly. 'Are all the canoes on the beach?'

The old woman blew her nose before she replied. She blocked one nostril with her thumb and from the other shot a shaft of silver mucus into the fire. She wiped the residue from her upper lip with the palm of her hand.

'All my sons and their wives are asleep in the huts, and their children with them,' she cackled.

'You saw no strange men with guns who wished you to ferry them across the river?' Isaac insisted, and the old woman shook her head and scratched herself.

'We saw no strangers.'

'I honour you, old mother,' Isaac told her formally, and pressed a small paper packet of sugar into her withered paw. 'Stay in peace.'

He ran back to the assault craft. The ranger cast off and jumped aboard as soon as Isaac started the motor.

The next village was three miles further downstream. Once again Isaac went ashore. He knew the headman of this village and found him sitting alone in the smoke from the fish-drying fires to keep off the singing clouds of malarial mosquitoes. Twenty years before, the headman had lost one of his feet to a crocodile, but he was still one of the most intrepid boatmen on the river.

Isaac greeted him and gave him a packet of cigarettes and squatted beside him in the smoke.

'You sit alone, Baba. Why can't you sleep? Are there things that trouble you?'

'An old man has many memories to trouble him.' The headman was evasive.

'Like strangers with guns who demand passage in your canoes?' Isaac asked. 'Did you give them what they wanted, Baba?'

The headman shook his head. 'One of the children saw them crossing the flood plains and ran to warn the village. We had time to hide the canoes in the reedbeds and run away into the bush.'

'How many men?' Isaac encouraged him.

The old man showed the fingers of both hands twice. 'They were hard men with guns, and faces like lions,' he whispered. 'We were afraid.'

'When was this, Baba?'

'The night before last,' the headman replied. 'When they found no people in the village and no canoes, they were angry. They shouted at each other and waved their guns, but in the end they went away.' He pointed with his chin, eastwards down the river. 'But now I am afraid they will return. That is why I sit awake while the village sleeps.'

'Are the people of Mbepura still camped at the place of the Red Birds?' Isaac asked, and the headman nodded.

'I think that after these hard men left here, they went down to Mbepura's village.'

'Thank you, old father.'

The place of the Red Birds was named for the flocks of carmine-breasted bee-eaters which burrow their nests into the steep cut-away bank of the river at that point. Mbepura's village was on the north bank, across the river from the clay cliff of the breeding colony. Isaac approached it with the engine idling softly, allowing the flow of the Zambezi to drift him down. All his rangers were alert. They had discarded their greatcoats and now crouched down below the gunwale with their weapons ready.

With a soft burst of the engine, Isaac pushed in closer to the

106

bank. Mbepura's village was another tiny group of shaggy huts near the water's edge. They seemed deserted and the drying fires below the fish-racks had been allowed to burn out. However, he saw in the gleam of the moon that the mooring poles for the canoes were still standing in the shallow muddy landing, but the canoes were missing. The fisherfolk lived by their canoes, their most precious possession.

Isaac let the assault craft drift on downstream well below the village before he gunned the motor and cut back across the flow of the Zambezi, crossing half a mile of open water to the south bank. If the gang had crossed here, then they would be coming back the same way.

Isaac checked the time, turning the luminous dial of his wristwatch to catch the moonlight. He calculated the distance from Chiwewe headquarters and divided it by the probable rate of march of the poachers, and made allowance for the fact that they were probably carrying heavy loads of plundered ivory. He looked up at the moon. Already it was paling at the approach of dawn. He could expect the returning raiders to get back to the Zambezi bank any time within the next two or three hours.

'If I can find where they have cached the canoes,' he muttered. His guess was that they had commandeered Mbepura's entire flotilla of canoes. He recalled that on his last visit to the village there had been seven or eight of these frail craft, each of them hollowed out from a massive log of the kigelia tree. Each of them could accommodate six or seven passengers for the journey across the great river.

The gang would probably have dragooned the men from the village to act as boatmen. The handling of the canoes required skill and experience, for the canoes were cranky and unstable, especially under a heavy load. He guessed that they would probably have left the boatmen under guard on the south bank while they marched on to Chiwewe.

'If I can find the canoes, I've got them cold,' Isaac decided.

He turned the assault boat in towards the south bank a little downstream from where he judged that the canoes would have crossed. When he found the entrance to a lagoon he pressed the sharp bows into the dense stand of papyrus reeds that blocked the mouth. He cut the engine and his rangers used handfuls of the tough papyrus stems to pull themselves deeper into the reedbed while Isaac stood in the bows and sounded for bottom with a paddle.

As soon as it was shallow enough, Isaac and one of his senior rangers waded ashore, leaving the rest of the party to guard the boat. On dry land Isaac gave his ranger whispered orders, sending him down-river to search for the canoes and check the bank for signs of the passage of a large party of marauders. When he had gone, Isaac set off in the opposite direction, upstream. He went alone, swiftly and silently, moving like a wraith in the river mist.

He had judged it accurately. He had not gone more than half a mile upstream when he smelt smoke. It was too strong and fresh to originate from the village on the far side of the broad river, and Isaac knew that there were no habitations on this bank. This was part of the National Park.

He moved in quietly towards the source of the smoke. At this point the bank was a sheer red clay cliff into which the bee-eaters burrowed their subterranean nests. However, there was a break in the cliff directly below where he crouched. It was a narrow gulley, choked with riverine bush that formed a natural landing-place from the river.

The faint glimmer of coming dawn gave Isaac just sufficient light to make out the encampment in the gulley below him. The canoes were drawn up well out of the water so that they would be concealed from anyone searching from a boat. There were seven canoes, the entire flotilla from Mbepura's village across the river.

Nearby, the boatmen were lying around two small smoky fires. They were wrapped in karosses of animal skin and, as protection from mosquitoes, each of them had drawn the covering completely over his head, so they looked like corpses laid out in a morgue. An armed poacher sat at each fire with his AK 47 rifle across his lap, guarding the sleeping boatmen and making certain that none of them sneaked away to the beached canoes nearby.

'Danny figured it exactly right,' Isaac told himself. 'They are waiting for the return of the raiding party.'

He drew back from the cliff edge and silently circled inland. Within two hundred yards he intersected a well-trodden game trail that left the river and headed directly southward in the approximate direction of Chiwewe headquarters camp.

Isaac followed it for a short distance until the game trail dipped through a shallow dry water-course. The bed of the water-course was of sugary white sand and the prints that it held were plain to decipher even in the uncertain pre-dawn light. A large party of men in Indian file had trodden the sand deeply, but their tracks were eroded and overlaid by the tracks of both large and small game.

'Twenty-four hours old,' Isaac estimated. This was the route the raiding party had taken on their outward march. Almost certainly they would use the same trail on their return march to rejoin the waiting canoes.

Isaac found a vantage point from which he was able to overlook a long stretch of the trail while remaining well concealed in a patch of dense Jesse bush. At his back there was a secure escape route for him down a shallow donga, the banks of which were screened with a heavy growth of rank elephant grass. He settled in to wait. The light strengthened swiftly and within minutes he could make out the full length of the game trail winding away into the mopane forest.

The sunrise chorus of birds began with the noisy duet of a pair of Heughlin robins in the donga behind him, and then the first flight of wild duck sped overhead. Their arrowhead formation was crisp and black against the tangerine and heron blue of the dawn sky.

Isaac crouched in his ambush position. There was no way that he could be certain how long the poachers might take on the return march from Chiwewe. Danny had reckoned on ten hours or so. If he were correct they would be arriving any minute now. Isaac checked his wristwatch again. However, Danny's estimate might be wildly inaccurate. Isaac prepared himself for a long wait.

During the war, they had at times lain in ambush position for days on end, once for five days when they had slept and eaten and defecated without rising from where they lay. Patience was the hunter's and the soldier's single most important virtue.

In the distance he heard a baboon bark, that booming alarm call with which the wily ape greets the appearance of a predator. The cry was taken up by other members of the troop, and then gradually silence returned as the danger receded or the baboons retreated deeper into the forest. Now Isaac's nerves were strung out with tension. He knew that the apes might have barked at a leopard, but they would have reacted the same way to the passing of a file of human beings.

Fifteen minutes later and much closer he heard a grey lourie cry 'Go away! Go away!' in a harsh screech. Another one of the sentinels of the bush was reacting to the presence of danger. Isaac never stirred, but he blinked his eyes rapidly to clear his vision.

Minutes later, he picked out another less obtrusive sound from the subtle orchestra of the wilderness. It was the whirring chatter of a honey guide. The sound told him where to look and he spotted the small nondescript brown bird in the top branches of a mopane far ahead.

It flitted above the game trail, flicking its wings, darting from tree to tree and uttering seductive entreaties. If they were prepared to follow the bird, it would lead the honey badger or man to a hive of wild bees. While they robbed the hive the honey guide would hover in close attendance, waiting for its share of the comb and the grubs that it contained. The bird's specially adapted digestive system was capable of breaking down the beeswax and deriving nourishment where no other creature could. Legend maintained that if you failed to leave the bird his portion of the spoils, then the next time he would lead you to a deadly mamba or a man-eating lion.

The honey guide drew closer to where Isaac waited, and suddenly he discerned obscure movement in the forest below the fluttering bird. Swiftly the shadowy shapes resolved into a column of men moving down the game trail. The head of the column drew level with the head of the donga where Isaac lay.

Although they were dressed in tattered and filthy clothing with an eclectic selection of headwear that ranged from baseball caps to faded military floppies, each of them carried an AK 47 rifle and an elephant tusk.

Some of them carried the tusk balanced upon their heads, the natural curve of the ivory drooping down fore and aft. Others carried it over the shoulder, using one hand to balance the burden while the other hand held the assault rifle. Most of them had woven a pad of bark string and soft grass to cushion the galling weight of the ivory on their scalps or collar-bones. The agony that their loads were causing after all these hours and miles of trek was evident on their contorted faces. Yet to each of the raiders the tusk they carried represented an enormous fortune, and they would suffer permanent physical damage rather than abandon it.

The man leading the column was short and squat, with thick bow-legs and a bull neck. The mellow early light caught the glossy scar down the side of his face.

'Sali,' Isaac hissed as he recognised him. He was the most notorious of all the Zambian poachers. Twice before their paths had crossed, and each time it had cost the lives of good men.

He passed close to where Isaac lay at a swinging jog-trot, carrying the thick honey-coloured tusk balanced on his head. He alone of all his men showed no signs of distress from the long march.

Isaac counted the poachers as they passed his position. The slower and weaker ones had fallen far behind the killing pace that Sali set, so the column was strung out. It took almost seven minutes by Isaac's wristwatch for all of them to go by. 'Nineteen.' Isaac counted the last pair as they limped past. Greedily they had selected tusks too heavy for their own strength and they were paying the price now.

Isaac let them go, but the moment they disappeared in the direction of the river, he rose from his ambush position and slipped away into the donga. He moved with extreme caution for he could not be certain that there were not still other members of the gang on the trail behind him.

The assault boat was where he had left it, moored in the reeds at the entrance to the lagoon. Isaac waded out alongside the boat and swung himself in over the gunwale. He noticed that the man he had sent down river had returned.

Quietly he told his men what he had found, and he watched their expressions. They were good men, all three of them, but the odds were formidable even for them, and the enemy were 'hard men with faces like lions', as the headman had described them.

'We will take them on the water,' Isaac told them. 'And we will not wait for them to fire the first shot. They are armed, and they are carrying ivory in the Park. That is enough. We will take them by surprise when they expect us least.'

Robert Mugabe, the president of Zimbabwe, had issued a directive that was unequivocal. They had the right to shoot on sight. Too many Parks men had been killed in these clashes to justify the usual niceties of a formal challenge.

The expressions of the listening rangers hardened and they hefted their weapons with renewed confidence. Isaac ordered them to work the boat out of the reeds and as soon as they reached open water he cranked the starter motor. The engine baulked and fired roughly and cut out. He cranked it again and again until the battery became sluggish. They were drifting away swiftly downstream.

Muttering angrily, Isaac hurried back and pulled the cover off the motor. While he worked on it he was vividly aware that upstream the gang would be loading the plundered ivory into the canoes and preparing to cross back into their own territory and safety.

He left the motor uncovered and ran forward to the controls. This time the motor fired and ran, surged and then faded. He pumped the throttle and she surged again and then settled to a steady beat. The engine whined shrilly as he turned across the current and ran back upstream.

The sound of the unmuted motor carried far ahead, and it must have alerted the gang. As Isaac drove the assault boat around the next bend, all the canoes were strung out across the river racing for the north shore.

The rising sun was behind Isaac's back and the broad stretch of water was lit like a theatre stage. The Zambezi was bright emerald green, the papyrus beds were crowned with gold where the sun's rays struck them. The canoes were starkly lit. Each of the frail craft carried a boatman and three passengers, together with a full load of ivory. Their free-board was only the width of a man's hand, and they lay so low in the water that the men seemed to be crouched on the very surface.

The boatmen were paddling frantically. Their long spear-shaped paddles flashed in the sunlight as they drove for the far bank. The leading canoe was already within a hundred yards of the Zambian papyrus beds.

The propeller of the Yamaha carved a lacy wake from the glossy green surface as Isaac swung the boat in a long curving trajectory to head off the leading canoe from the sanctuary of the reeds.

As the two vessels closed, Isaac made out the scarred visage of Sali. He squatted in the warped bows, turning his head awkwardly to glare back at them, unable to move without upsetting the delicate trim of the canoe.

'This time we've got you,' Isaac whispered, as he pushed the throttle forward to the stop, and the Yamaha shrieked.

Suddenly Sali rose to his feet and the canoe rocked wildly under him. Water slopped in over the wooden sides and the canoe began to flood and settle. Sali shouted a threat at Isaac; his face was contorted into a mask of fury and he lifted the AK and fired a long continuous burst at the boat racing down on him.

Bullets slammed into the fibreglass hull and one of the instrument gauges on the control console in front of Isaac exploded. He ducked, but held her on course to ram the canoe.

Sali flicked the empty magazine out of the rifle, and loaded another from his bandolier. He fired again. The bright brass cases sparkled in the sunlight as they were spewed from the breech. One of the rangers in the front of the assault boat cried out and clutched at his stomach as he tumbled to the deck, and at that moment the bows of the assault boat crashed into the side of the canoe at thirty knots. The brittle kigelia wood shattered, and the men in her were hurled into the river.

At the last moment before the collision, Sali threw the AK 47 aside and dived overboard. He tried to force his body deep beneath the water to escape the speeding hull. He thought he could cover the last few yards to the edge of the reedbed without surfacing and showing himself again. However, his lungs were full of air and the buoyancy prevented him diving deeply enough. Although his head and body were angled down-wards, his feet were only a few inches below the surface.

The propeller of the Yamaha was spinning at peak revolutions as it passed over his left leg. It took his foot off cleanly at the ankle and went over his calf muscles like the blade of a bread-slicing machine, shredding the meat down to the bone.

Then the assault boat was past, turning back steeply with Isaac spinning the wheel. She leaned out into the turn as he lined up the bows for the next canoe in the straggling line. He hit it without a check, steering into the fragile hull and spilling its crew into the river, driving it under and running on, swinging into the next turn like a slalom racer weaving through the poles.

The men in the third canoe saw them coming and threw themselves over the side an instant before the bows struck and then they were splashing and screaming as the swift green current carried them away.

Isaac spun the wheel back the other way, and the next canoe was dead ahead. The crew were shouting and pleading and firing wildly. The volleys of bullets kicked up fountains of spray all around the approaching assault craft in the moments before it struck and trod the shattered canoe under.

The remaining canoes had turned back and were paddling desperately for the south bank. Isaac overtook them effortlessly and smashed in the stern of the nearest vessel. He felt the engine check and shudder as the spinning propeller bit into living human flesh and then it surged forward again.

The last canoes reached the south bank and the poachers spilled out of them and tried to clamber up the sheer cliff. The red clay crumbled under their clawing fingers.

Isaac throttled back and turned the bows upstream holding the assault boat against the current.

'I am a Parks warden,' Isaac yelled across at them. 'You are under arrest. Stand where you are. Do not try to escape or I will fire upon you.'

One of the poachers still clutched his rifle in his hand. He almost reached the top of the bank before the clay broke away under his feet and he slid down to the water's edge. Sitting in the red mud, he threw up the rifle and aimed at the men in the assault boat.

The two unwounded rangers were kneeling at the rail, their rifles cocked and levelled.

'*Bulala!* Kill!' Isaac snapped, and they opened up together, a massed volley of fire that swept the riverbank. They were hand-picked members of the anti-poaching unit, both good marksmen, and they hated the gangs that plundered the elephant herds, savaged their comrades and threatened their own lives.

They laughed as they shot the panic-stricken gang members off the bank. They made a game of allowing them almost to reach the top of the red clay wall before bringing them flopping and kicking back into the river with a short crisp burst of fire.

Isaac made no effort to restrain them. He had a long-outstanding score to settle with these men, and a few years' imprisonment was not enough punishment for their crimes. As the last of them rolled down the bank and sank slowly into the clear green water, he spun the boat and raced back across the river.

Scar-faced Sali was the leader. These others were mere brainless thugs and cannon-fodder. Sali could recruit a new regiment of them for a few dollars a head. Sali was the brains and the guts of the trade, and without him this day's work would count for little. Unless Isaac stopped him now, Sali would be back again next week or next month with another gang of ruffians. He had to crush the head of the mamba or it would strike again.

He raced in close to the edge of the reeds on the north bank, to the spot at which he had rammed the first canoe. Then Isaac turned into the current and throttled back the Yamaha and allowed the current to drift them downstream, using bursts of engine to keep within a few yards of the edge of the reeds.

The two rangers stood at the port rail, and eagerly scrutinised the reedbed as they drifted by.

There was no telling how far the Zambezi current had carried the poacher before he had been able to reach the cover of the papyrus. Isaac would make only one sweep from the boat for a mile downstream. Then he would go ashore with his men and beat back along the north bank on foot to pick up any sign that Sali might have left as he dragged himself from the reeds on to dry land and tried to escape. Then they would follow him, for as far and as long as it took.

Strict interpretation of the law gave Isaac no powers of arrest on the Zambian side of the river, but this was a hot pursuit of a murderer and a notorious bandit. Isaac was prepared to fight if challenged, and put a bullet through his prisoner's head if the Zambian police tried to intervene and take Salí away from him.

At that moment something caught his eye in the reedbed directly opposite the drifting assault boat. Isaac touched the throttle and held the boat stationary against the current.

A small area of reeds had been disturbed, as if something had been dragged through them, a crocodile possibly, or a large leguan lizard, except that clumps of reeds had been twisted and broken as though used as handholds.

'Crocodiles don't have hands,' Isaac grunted, and man-oeuvred the boat in closer. The disturbance must have taken place only minutes before, for under his eyes the flattened reeds were still straightening and rising into their original upright position. Then Isaac smiled thinly.

He reached over the side and snapped one of the reeds and held it to the sunlight. The smear of colour along its fibrous stem came away wet and red on Isaac's fingers and he showed it to the ranger who stood at his shoulder.

'Blood,' the ranger nodded. 'He is hurt. The prop—' before he could finish the sentence somebody screamed in the reeds ahead of them. It was a high ringing cry of utter terror that froze them all for an instant.

Isaac recovered first and nudged the throttle, forcing the bows into the dense stand of reeds. Somewhere ahead of them the human voice screamed and screamed again.

Deep in the river Sali felt the boat run over him. His head was filled with the deafening shriek of the spinning propeller blades. The sound had no direction but assaulted his senses from every angle.

Then something struck his left leg a blow that seemed to dislocate his hip and the force of it spun him end over end in the water and disoriented him. He tried to lunge for the surface but his left leg would not respond. There was no pain, just a great heavy numbness as though the limb was encased in a block of concrete that was drawing him down into the green Zambezi depths.

He kicked out wildly with his good leg and suddenly his head broke the surface. Through streaming eyes he saw the assault boat weaving and zigzagging across the river, smashing up the flotilla of canoes and throwing their crews, splashing and screaming, into the river.

Sali welcomed the respite that this attack on the other canoes had afforded him. He knew that he had a few minutes before the boat came roaring back to find him. He turned his head. The edge of the reedbed was close. With the strength of his fighting anger and outrage still strong upon him, he struck out for it. His leg was a dead weight, a heavy drogue anchor that hampered and slowed him, but he swam with great sweeping overhead strokes of his powerful arms and seconds later grabbed the first handful of papyrus stems. Desperately he dragged himself into the cover of the reeds, sliding his body over the springing mattress of papyrus, the maimed leg slithering after him.

Deep in the reeds, he paused at last and rolled on to his back to look back the way that he had come. His breathing whistled in his throat as he saw the trail of blood that he had laid through the water. He grabbed his own knee, lifted the wounded leg above the surface and stared at it in disbelief.

His foot was gone and white bone protruded from the mangled flesh. His blood spurted and dribbled from the severed vessels so that he floated in a red-brown cloud. Tiny silver fish, excited by the smell of it, darted through the stained water, gobbling the strings and morsels of tattered meat.

Quickly Sali lowered his good leg and tried to touch bottom. The water closed over his head, but his right foot groped unavailingly for the Zambezi's mud bed. He came to the surface again coughing and choking. He was well out of his depth, with only the thick reeds to support him.

Far away across the river he heard the sound of gunfire, and then the high-pitched whine of the returning assault craft. It drew closer and closer, until abruptly it sank to a faint burbling sound and he heard voices. He realised that they were searching the edge of the reedbeds for him, and he shrank down lower in the water.

A cold lethargy was stealing over him as his life-blood leaked away into the river, but he forced himself to rally and began to edge away, deeper into the reeds, towards the Zambian bank of the river. He pushed gently into an opening in the reeds. It was the size of a tennis court enclosed by a palisade of tall swaying papyrus. The surface was paved with the flat circular green leaves of the water-lilies and their blooms raised lovely cerulean heads to the early sunlight. Their perfume was sweet and delicate on the still air.

Suddenly Sali froze with only his head above the surface. Something moved beneath the water-lilies. The water pushed and bulged while the blossoms nodded their heads to the weighty and stealthy movement passing beneath them.

Sali knew what it was. His thick liver-coloured lips split open and he drooled with terror. His blood drifted away on the lily-strewn waters and the thing beneath moved with greater authority and determination, homing in on the tantalising taste of blood.

Sali was a brave man. Very few things in this world could frighten him. However, this was a creature from another world, the secret cold world beneath the waters. His bowels evacuated uncontrollably as terror released his sphincter muscle, and this fresh odour in the water brought the creature to the surface.

A head like a log, black and gnarled and shiny with wetness, pushed through the lilies. Its beady saurian eyes were set on protruding bark-like knobs and it grinned at Sali, with ragged fangs protruding over uneven lips. The wreath of lily blossoms draped across its hideous brow gave the creature a sardonic menace.

Suddenly the great tail broke the surface, double-ridged and crested as it threshed the surface to foam, driving the long scaly body forward with astonishing speed.

Sali screamed.

Isaac stood at the control console and drove the long hull deeper into the papyrus. The tough fibrous stems wrapped around the propeller shaft and slowed the boat, bringing it to a gradual standstill.

They ran to the bows and, grabbing handfuls of papyrus, dragged themselves forward until abruptly they burst into a small patch of open water. Directly in front of the bows there was an enormous disturbance in the water. Sheets of spray were thrown into the sunlight, and splattered over their heads.

In the foam an enormous scaly body rolled and roiled, flashing its butter yellow belly, the long tail cockscombed with sharp scales thrashing the water white.

For an instant a human arm was flung upwards. It was a gesture of entreaty, of terrified supplication. Isaac leaned over the side and seized the wrist. The skin was wet and slippery but Isaac reinforced his grip with both hands and leaned back with all his weight. He could not hold Sali and the weight of the reptile together. The wrist began to slip through his grip until one of the rangers leapt to his side and grabbed Sali's arm at the elbow.

Together, inch by inch, they dragged the man's body from the water. Sali was a man on the torture rack. He was stretched out between the men at one end and the dreadful reptile below the surface.

The other ranger leaned out over the gunwale and fired a burst of automatic fire into the water. The high-velocity bullets exploded on the surface as though they had hit a steel plate and had no effect except to send needles of spray into the eyes of Isaac and the ranger at the rail.

'Stop it!' Isaac panted at him. 'You'll hit one of us!'

The ranger dropped the rifle and seized Sali's free arm.

Now there were three men taking sides in the gruesome tug-of-war. Slowly they dragged Sali's body from the water, until the reptile's huge scaly head was exposed.

Its fangs were buried in the front of Sali's belly. The croco-dile's teeth lack shearing edges. It dismembers its prey by locking on and then rolling its entire body in the water to twist

119

off a limb or a hunk of flesh. As they held Sali stretched over the gunwale, the creature flicked its tail and rolled. Sali's belly was ripped open. The crocodile heaved backwards with its fangs still locked in his flesh and stripped Sali's entrails out of him.

With the release of the strain at one end, the three men were able to heave Sali's body on board. However, the crocodile still held its grip. Although his writhing form lay on the deck, Sali's entrails were stretched over the side, a glistening fleshy tangle of tubes and ribbons like some grotesque umbilical cord that linked him to his fate.

The crocodile jerked again with the full weight and strength of the long tail. The ribbon of guts snapped and Sali screamed for the last time and died on the bloody deck.

For a while there was silence in the boat broken only by the hoarse panting of the three men who had tried to rescue him. They stared in horrified fascination at Sali's mutilated corpse until Isaac Mtwetwe whispered softly, 'I could not have chosen a more fitting death for you.' He spoke in formal ceremonial Shona. 'Go not peacefully, O Sali, evil one, and may all your foul deeds accompany you on your journey.'

'There were no prisoners,' Isaac told Daniel Armstrong.

'Did you say none?' Daniel shouted. The telephone connection was scratchy and faint, with heavy atmospheric interference from the thunderstorm raging further down the valley.

'None, Danny,' Isaac raised his voice. 'Eight dead ones, but the rest of the gang were either eaten by crocs or escaped back into Zambia.'

'What about ivory, Isaac? Did they have tusks with them?'

'Yes, they were all carrying ivory, but it was lost in the river when the canoes went down.'

'Damn it to hell,' Daniel muttered. It would be much more difficult now to convince the authorities that the bulk of the ivory was taken out from Chiwewe in the refrigerator trucks.

The trail to Ning Cheng Gong was growing colder with every hour that passed.

'There is a police unit on its way from here to the headquarters camp at Chiwewe,' he told Isaac.

'Yes, Danny. They are here at the moment. I'm going to join them as soon as I have made arrangements to fly my wounded ranger out to Harare. I want to see what these bastards did to Johnny Nzou.'

'Listen, Isaac, I'm going to follow up the only lead I've got on who was responsible for this business.'

'Be careful, Danny. These people don't mess about. You could get badly hurt. Where are you headed?'

'I'll see you around, Isaac.' Daniel avoided the question. He dropped the telephone back on its cradle and went out to the Landcruiser.

He sat behind the wheel and thought about it. He realised that this was merely a respite. Pretty soon now the Zimbabwean police were going to want to talk to him again, a little more seriously than before. There was only one place to be, and that was outside the country. In any event that was where the trail was leading him.

He drove down to the customs and immigration post and parked in the lot before the barrier. Naturally, he had his passport with him and the papers for the Landcruiser were all in order. The departure formalities took less than half an hour, which by African standards was almost record time.

Daniel drove out across the steel-girdered bridge that spanned the Zambezi and he was aware that he was not entering paradise.

Zambia was, after Uganda and Ethiopia, one of the poorest and sorriest countries on the African continent. Daniel grimaced. A cynic might put that down to the fact that it had been independent from British colonial rule longer than most others. There had been more time for the policies of structured chaos and ruination to take full effect.

Under private ownership the great mines of the Copperbelt had once been amongst the most profitable on the continent, rivalling even the fabulous gold mines further south. After independence, President Kenneth Kaunda had nationalised them and instituted his Africanisation policy. This amounted to firing those skilled and experienced engineers and managers who did not have black faces, a kind of affirmative action. Within a few short years he had miraculously transformed an annual profit of many hundreds of millions into a loss of the same magnitude.

Daniel steeled himself for his encounter with Zambian official-dom.

'Can you tell me if a friend of mine passed through here last night on his way to Malawi,' he asked the uniformed officer who sauntered out of the customs building to search his Land-cruiser for contraband.

The man opened his mouth to protest his outrage at being asked to divulge official information but Daniel forestalled him by producing a five-dollar bill. The Zambian currency, the kwacha, named for 'the dawn of freedom from colonial oppression' had once held value equivalent to the US dollar. Numerous subsequent devaluations had readjusted the official exchange rate to 30:1. The black-market rate was closer to 300:1. The customs officer's scruples evaporated. He was looking at a month's salary.

'What is your friend's name?' he asked eagerly.

'Mr Chetti Singh. He was driving a large truck with a cargo of dried fish.'

'Wait.' The officer disappeared into the station and was back within minutes.

'Yes . . .' he nodded. 'Your friend passed through after midnight.' He showed no further interest in searching the Land-cruiser and stamped Daniel's passport. His step was jaunty as he returned to his post.

Daniel felt a little chill of unease as he left the border post and headed northwards towards Lusaka, the territory's capital. In Zambia, the rule of law ended at the edge of the built-up areas. In the bush the police manned their road-blocks, but were never so foolhardy as to respond to appeals for assistance from travellers on the lonely rutted roads.

During twenty-five years of independence, the roads had fallen into an interesting state of disrepair. In some places the potholes through the eroded tarmac were almost knee deep.

Daniel kept the speed down to twenty-five miles an hour and weaved his way around the worst patches as though he were negotiating a minefield.

The countryside was lovely. He drove through magnificent open forests and glades of golden grass known as 'damboes'. The hills and kopjes seemed to have been built in antiquity by a giant's hand. The walls and turrets of stone were tumbled and eroded into spectacular chaos. The numerous rivers were deep and clear.

Daniel came to the first of the road-blocks.

A hundred yards from the barrier Daniel slowed down to a crawl and kept both hands on the wheel. The police were jumpy and trigger-happy. As he stopped, a uniformed constable wearing mirrored sunglasses thrust the barrel of a sub-machine-gun through the window and greeted him arrogantly.

'Hello, my friend.' His finger was on the trigger and the muzzle was pointed at Daniel's belly. 'Get out!'

'Do you smoke?' Daniel asked. As he stepped down into the road he produced a packet of Chesterfield cigarettes and thrust it into the constable's hand.

The constable withdrew the barrel of the machine pistol while he checked that the packet was unopened. Then he grinned and Daniel relaxed slightly.

At that moment another vehicle drew up behind Daniel's Landcruiser. It was a truck owned by one of the hunting safari companies. The back was piled with camp stores and equipment, and the gunbearers and trackers sat on top of the load.

At the driving-wheel was the professional hunter, bearded, tanned and weatherbeaten. Beside him his client seemed urbane and effete despite his new safari jacket and the zebra skin hatband around his stetson.

'Daniel!' The hunter leaned out of the side window. 'Daniel Armstrong,' he shouted happily.

Then Daniel remembered him. They had met briefly three years previously while Daniel was filming the documentary on hunting safaris in Africa, 'Man is the Hunter'. For a moment he couldn't remember the fellow's name, but they had shared a bottle of Haig at a campfire in the Luangwa valley. Daniel remembered him as a blow-hard, with a reputation more as a hard drinker than a hard hunter. He had consumed more than his fair share of the Haig, Daniel recalled.

'Stoffel.' The name came back to him with relief. He needed an ally and a protector now. The hunters of the safari companies were a class of minor aristocracy in the deep bush. 'Stoffel van der Merwe,' he cried.

Stoffel climbed down from the truck, big and beefy and grinning. Like most professional hunters in Zambia, he was an Afrikaner from South Africa.

'Hell, man, it's good to see you again.' He covered Daniel's hand with a hairy paw. 'They giving you any uphill here?'

'Well . . .' Daniel let it hang there, and Stoffel rounded on the police constable. 'Hey, Juno, this man is my friend. You treat him good, you hear me?'

The constable laughed agreement. It always amazed Daniel to watch how well Afrikaners and blacks got along on a personal level once politics were left out of it; perhaps it was because they were all of them Africans and understood each other. They had been living together for almost three hundred years, Daniel smiled to himself; by this time they damned well should.

'You want your meat, don't you?' Stoffel went on to tease the constable. 'You give Doctor Armstrong here a hard time and no meat for you.'

The hunters had their regular routes to and from the hunting concessions in the remote bush, and they knew the guards manning the road-blocks by name. Between them they had set up a regular tariff of *bonsela*.

'Hey!' Stoffel turned to shout at his trackers on top of the truck. 'Give Juno here a leg of fat buffalo. Look how skinny he's getting. We have to feed him up a bit.'

From under the tarpaulin cover they dragged out a haunch of buffalo, still in its thick black skin, dusty and buzzing with bluebottle flies. The hunters had access to unlimited supplies of game meat, legally hunted and shot by their clients.

'These poor bastards are starved for protein,' Stoffel explained to his client as the American sportsman came to join them. 'For a leg of buffalo he would sell you his wife; for two he would sell you his soul; for three he would probably sell you

124

the whole bloody country. And any one of those would be a bad bargain!' He roared with laughter and introduced his client to Daniel. 'This is Steve Conrack from California.'

'I know you, of course,' the American interjected. 'Great honour to meet you, Doctor Armstrong. I always watch your stuff on TV. Just by chance I've got a copy of your book with me. I'd love an autograph for my kids back home. They're great fans of yours.'

Inwardly Daniel winced at the price of fame but when the client returned from the truck with a copy of one of his earlier books, he signed the flyleaf.

'Where are you headed?' Stoffel asked. 'Lusaka? Let me go ahead and run interference for you, otherwise anything could happen. It could take you a week or all eternity to get there.'

The police guard, still grinning, lifted the barrier and saluted them as they drove through. From there onwards their progress was a royal procession, with lumps of raw meat appearing regularly from under the tarpaulin.

'Roses, roses all the way – and buffalo steaks strewn in our path like mad.' Daniel grinned to himself and put his foot down to keep up with the safari truck.

They were driving through the fertile plains that were irrigated from the Kafue River. This was an area of sugar and maize and tobacco production and the farms were owned almost entirely by white Zambians. Prior to independence, the farmers had vied with each other to beautify their properties. From the main road the white-painted homesteads had glistened, set like pearls in the green and lovingly tended home paddocks. The fences had been meticulously maintained and sleek cattle had grazed within view of the road.

These days the dilapidated appearance of the properties was a deliberate attempt by the owners to divert envious and acquisitive eyes.

'If you look too good,' one of them had explained to Daniel, 'they're going to take it away from you.' He didn't have to explain who 'they' were. 'The golden rule in this country is: if you've got it, for God's sake don't flaunt it.'

The white farmers lived as a tiny separate tribe in their own little enclave. Rather like their pioneering ancestors, they made their own soap and other commodities which were simply unobtainable from the bare shelves of the local trading stores. They lived mostly on the products of their own lands, yet they enjoyed a reasonably good life with their golf clubs and polo clubs and theatrical societies.

They sent their children to school and university in South Africa with the small amounts of fiercely rationed foreign exchange they were granted; they kept their heads down below the parapet and took care not to draw attention to themselves. Even the powers that presided in the government halls in Lusaka realised that without them the precarious economy would collapse completely. The maize and sugar they produced kept the rest of the population from true starvation and their tobacco crops eked out the tiny dribble of foreign exchange brought in by the ruined copper mines.

'Where could we go?' Daniel's informant put the rhetorical question. 'If we leave here, we go in our underclothes. They won't let us take a penny or a stick with us. We've just got to make the best of it.'

As the two-vehicle convoy approached the capital town of Lusaka, Daniel was given a demonstration of one of the many distressing phenomena of the new Africa – the mass movement of rural populations to the urban centres.

Daniel smelt the slum odour as they passed the outskirts of the town. It was a miasma of smoke from the cooking-fires, the stench of pit latrines and festering garbage heaps, of sour illicit beer brewing in open drums, and human bodies without running water or rivers in which to bathe. It was the smell of disease and starvation and poverty and ignorance, the ripe new smell of Africa.

Daniel stood Stoffel and his client a drink in the bar of the Ridgeway Hotel, then excused himself and went to the reception desk to check in.

He was given a room overlooking the swimming-pool, and went to shower away the grime and exhaustion of the past twenty-four hours. Then he reached for the telephone, and called the British High Commission. He caught the telephonist there before the close of the day's business.

'May I speak to Mr Michael Hargreave, please?' He held his

breath. Mike Hargreave had still been in Lusaka two years previously, but he could have been transferred anywhere in the world by now.

'I'm putting you through to Mr Hargreave,' the girl replied after a few moments, and Daniel let his breath out.

'Michael Hargreave speaking.'

'Mike, it's Danny Armstrong.'

'Good Lord, Danny, where are you?'

'Here in Lusaka.'

'Welcome back to fairyland. How are you?'

'Mike, can I see you? I need another favour.'

'Why don't you come to dinner tonight? Wendy will be charmed.'

Michael had one of the diplomatic residences on Nobs Hill, within walking distance of Government House. As with every other house in the street it was fortified like the Maze Prison. The ten-foot perimeter walls were topped with rolled barbed wire and two *malondo*, night watchmen, guarded the gate.

Michael Hargreave quieted his pair of Rottweiler guard dogs, and greeted Daniel enthusiastically.

'You aren't taking chances, Mike.' Daniel gestured towards the security precautions and Michael grimaced.

'On this street alone we average one break-in a night, despite the wire and dogs.'

He led Daniel into the house and Wendy came to kiss him. Wendy was a rosebud, with soft blonde hair and one of those incredible English complexions.

'I had forgotten that you are even more handsome in the flesh than on television.' She smiled at him.

Michael Hargreave resembled an Oxford don more than a spook, but he was indeed an MI6 man. He and Daniel had first met in Rhodesia towards the end of the war. At the time Daniel had been sick and dispirited with what he had come to realise was not only a lost cause, but an unjust one. The breaking point had come when Daniel led a column of the Selous Scouts into the neighbouring state of Mozambique. The target was a guerrilla camp. Rhodesian intelligence had told them it was a training camp for ZANLA recruits, but when they hit the cluster of huts they found mostly old men and women and children. There had been almost five hundred of these unfortunate people. They had left none of them alive.

On the return march Daniel had found himself weeping uncontrollably as he staggered along in the darkness. Years of ever-present danger and endless call-up for active service had worn his nerves thin and brittle. Only much later Daniel realised that he had suffered a breakdown, but at that critical moment he was approached by the clandestine Alpha Group.

The war had dragged on for so many years that a small group of police and army officers had come to realise the futility of it all. Even more they had realised that they were on the side, not of the angels, but of the devil himself.

They decided that they must strive for an end to the bitter civil war, that they must force the white supremacist Smith government to accept a truce negotiated by Great Britain, and thereafter agree to a democratic and free election and the process of national reconciliation between the races. All the members of the Alpha Group were men whom Daniel admired; many were senior officers and most of them had been decorated for their courage and leadership. Daniel was drawn irresistibly to them.

Michael Hargreave had been the head of station for British intelligence in Rhodesia. They had first met once Daniel had committed himself to the Alpha Group. They had worked together closely and Daniel had played a minor role in the process that finally led to the end of those dreadful sufferings and excesses, and that culminated in the Lancaster House Agreement.

Daniel had not been in Zimbabwe when Ian Smith's white regime finally capitulated. His disloyalty had been discovered by Rhodesian intelligence. Warned of his impending arrest by other members of his group, Daniel had fled the country. Had he been captured he would certainly have faced a firing squad. He had only dared return once the country had changed its name to Zimbabwe and the new order, led by Robert Mugabe, had come to power.

When first he had met him, Daniel's relationship with Michael had been detached and professional, but mutual respect and trust had finally transformed it into genuine friendship, which had survived the years.

Michael poured him a whisky and they chatted and reminisced until Wendy called them to the dinner-table. Home cooking was a treat for Daniel, and Wendy glowed with gratification at his performance with knife and fork.

With the brandy Michael asked, 'So what about this favour?'

'Two favours, actually.'

'Runaway inflation – speak up, my lad.'

'Could you possibly arrange to have my film tapes sent back to London in the diplomatic bag? They are more valuable than life itself. I wouldn't trust them to the Zambian post office.'

'That's an easy one,' Michael nodded. 'I'll get them away in tomorrow's bag. What about the other favour?'

'I need some information on a gentleman named Ning Cheng Gong.'

'Are we likely to know him?' Michael asked.

'You should. He's Taiwan's ambassador to Harare.'

'In that case, we will certainly have a file on him. Is he friend or foe, Danny?'

'I'm not sure – not at this stage, anyway.'

'Don't tell me, then.' Michael sighed and pushed the brandy decanter across to Daniel. 'I should have a computer print-out for you before noon tomorrow. Shall I send it around to the Ridgeway?'

'Bless you, old son. I owe you another one.'

'And don't you forget it, Danny boy.'

It was an enormous relief to get rid of the tapes that Jock had shot. They represented a gruelling year's labour and almost Daniel's entire worldly wealth. He believed so strongly in this new project that he had decided that, contrary to his usual practice, he would not seek outside financing. He had put everything he owned at risk, almost half a million dollars that he had painfully accumulated over the last ten years since he had become a full-time author and television producer.

So Daniel's tapes went out the following morning with the diplomatic courier on the British Airways flight and would be in London within twelve hours. Daniel had consigned them to Castle Studios where they would be in safe keeping until he could begin the editorial work to transform it into another one of his productions. He had almost settled on a title for the series, 'Is Africa Dying?'

Rather than entrust it to a messenger, Michael Hargreave personally delivered the computer print-out on Ning Cheng Gong to Daniel at the hotel.

'Nice lad you've picked on,' he commented. 'I haven't read it all, just enough to find out that the Ning family is not one to trifle with. Take it easy, Danny; these are big boys.'

He handed over the sealed envelope. 'Just one condition. As soon as you have read it, I want you to burn it. Do I have your word on that?'

Daniel nodded in agreement and Michael went on, 'I've brought along an askari from the High Commission to guard your Landcruiser for you. You daren't leave a vehicle untended on the street, not in Lusaka.'

Daniel took the envelope up to his hotel room and ordered a pot of tea. When it arrived he locked the door, stripped to his underpants and lay on the bed.

The print-out ran to eleven pages, all of them fascinating. Johnny Nzou had given him only an inkling of the wealth and importance of the Ning family.

Ning Heng H'Sui was the patriarch. His holdings were so diversified and cross-pollinated with international companies and offshore holdings in Luxembourg, Geneva and Jersey that the author of the report admitted laconically at the end of this section, 'List of holdings probably incomplete.'

Going over the data more attentively, Daniel thought he perceived a subtle shift in investment emphasis dating from about the time of Ning Cheng Gong's appointment to his ambassadorial post in Africa. Although the Ning family holdings were still centred on the Pacific rim, the investments in Africa and in Africa-based companies had risen to a significant percentage of the entire portfolio.

Turning the page, he discovered that the computer had analysed this and determined that within six years the African section had increased from zero to just under twelve per cent of the total. There were large holdings in South African mining conglomerates, and in African land and food production companies, and even larger holdings in forestry estates, paper pulp mills and cattle and sheep ranches, all in Africa, south of the Sahara. It didn't take any clairvoyant gift to surmise that Ning Cheng Gong had pointed the family in this direction.

On page four of the computer print-out, Daniel read that Ning Cheng Gong was married to a Chinese girl from another rich Taiwanese family. The marriage had been arranged by the respective families. The couple had two children: a son born in 1982 and a daughter in 1983.

Cheng's interests were listed as oriental music and theatre and collecting oriental art, especially jade and ivory artefacts. He was an acknowledged expert on ivory netsuke. He played golf and tennis and sailed. He was also an expert in the martial arts, having reached the Fourth Dan. He smoked moderately and drank alcohol socially. He did not use any type of narcotic and the only weakness which the report suggested might be used as leverage or influence was that Ning Cheng Gong regularly patronised the high-class brothels of Taipei. His special sexual tastes seemed to lean towards acting out elaborate fantasies of an overtly sadistic nature. In 1987 one of the brothel girls had died during one of these performances. The family had obviously been able to quell any scandal, for no charges were ever brought against Cheng.

'Mike was right,' Daniel conceded as he laid aside the print out. 'He is a big boy and well protected. Best take it one careful step at a time. Chetti Singh first. If I can establish a connection, that might be the key.'

As he dressed for dinner he kept turning the pages of the report on the dressing-table to make certain he had not overlooked any connection with Malawi or with Chetti Singh.

There was none and he went down to dinner feeling depressed and discouraged. The role he had chosen for himself as Johnny Nzou's avenger was daunting.

There were both smoked Scotch salmon and roast sirloin of milk-fed Charollais beef on the five-page menu. However, when he ordered these the waiter shook his head regretfully.

'Sorry, no got.'

It swiftly developed into a guessing game. 'Sorry, no got.'

The waiter looked genuinely distressed as Daniel worked his way unsuccessfully through the menu until Daniel noticed that everyone else in the dining-room was eating stringy roast chicken and rice.

'Yes, got chicken and rice.' The waiter beamed approval. 'What you want for dessert?'

By now Daniel had learned the trick. He checked the other tables. 'How about banana custard?'

The waiter shook his head. 'No got.' But Daniel could tell by his expression that he was getting warm.

Daniel stood up and crossed to a Nigerian businessman at the next table.

'Excuse me, sir, what is that you are eating?'

He returned to his own table. 'I'll have Banana Delight,' he said, and the waiter nodded happily.

'Yes, tonight got Banana Delight.'

This little comedy restored Daniel's good humour and sense of the ridiculous.

'AWA,' Daniel reassured him. 'Africa Wins Again.' And the waiter looked delighted at such obvious praise and encouragement.

 The next morning Daniel headed eastwards towards Chipata and the Malawi border. There was not much point in expecting a sustaining breakfast from the hotel and anyway he was away long before the kitchens opened. He had covered almost a hundred miles before the sun rose, and he kept going most of the day, stopping only to eat beside the road.

He reached the border the following morning and crossed into Malawi with a lightening of his spirits. Not only was this tiny country even more spectacularly beautiful than the one he was leaving, but in comparison the mood of its people was contented and carefree.

Malawi was known as the Switzerland of Africa for its grand mountains and highland plateaux and its lakes and lovely rivers. Its people were famous throughout the southern continent for their intelligence and adaptability. They were sought

132

after at every level of employment from domestic servants to miners and industrial workers. Lacking viable mineral deposits, Malawi's most valuable asset and export were her people.

Under the benevolent despotism of their octogenarian president-for-life, the special talents and strengths of the Malawian people were encouraged and fostered. The rural areas were not neglected and the urban migration was checked. Each family was ordered by the leader to build its own home and make itself self-sufficient in food. As cash crops they grew cotton and ground-nuts. On the large mountainside estates they raised a superior leaf of tea.

As Daniel drove towards the capital, Lilongwe, the contrast with the country he had just left was striking. The villages he passed were clean and orderly and prosperous. The people on the roadside were sleek, well dressed and smiling. Most of the handsome women favoured a full-length skirt printed with the national colours and a portrait of 'Kamuzu' Hastings Banda, the president. Short skirts were forbidden in Malawi by presidential decree, as was long hair on men.

Along the roadside, food and carved wooden curios were offered for sale. It was strange to see a surplus of food in any African country. Daniel stopped to buy eggs and oranges, mandarins, luscious red tomatoes and roasted ground-nuts, and also to exchange cheerful banter with the vendors.

After the misery and deprivation he had witnessed in the country he had so recently left, his mood was uplifted by these delightful people. Given the circumstances to make a good life, there are few peoples on earth so friendly and charming as those of Africa. Daniel found his regard for them strengthened and renewed.

'If you don't like black people, then you shouldn't be living in Africa,' Daniel's father had once said to him. It was a remark that had remained in his memory all these years, the validity of it growing ever more evident.

As he approached Lilongwe Daniel was struck even more forcefully by the contrast with other capitals of the continent. It was a recent capital, planned and built with architectural advice and financial help from South Africa. There was no slum stench here. Instead it was a pretty town, modern and functional.

133

Daniel found it good to be back again.

The Capital Hotel was surrounded by parks and lawns but conveniently situated close to the centre of the town. As soon as he was alone in his room, Daniel checked the local telephone directory which he found in the bedside drawer.

Chetti Singh was a big man in town and obviously enjoyed the sound of his own name. There was a string of numbers listed. He seemed to have his fingers in every honey pot: Chetti Singh Fisheries, Chetti Singh Supermarkets, Chetti Singh Tannery, Chetti Singh Sawmills and Lumber, Chetti Singh Garages and Toyota Agency. The list took up half the page.

Not a difficult bird to point, Daniel admitted to himself. Now let's see if we can get him to flush for a good sporting shot.

While he shaved and showered an attentive room servant carted his travel-stained clothing off to the laundry and ironed a clean but crumpled bush jacket to starchy perfection.

'Good excuse. I need to restock the tucker box,' Daniel told himself as he went downstairs and asked the receptionist directions to Chetti Singh's supermarket.

'Across the park.' The man pointed.

With assumed nonchalance Daniel sauntered across the park. It occurred to him that he was hardly the most inconspicuous visitor in town, with his London tailored bush jacket, silk scarf, and the spectacularly travel-dusted and battered Landcruiser with his strong-arm motif emblazoned all over it.

'Let's pray that Chetti Singh never got a good look at me or the truck that night.'

Chetti Singh's supermarket was on Main Street in a new four-storey building of modern layout, with clean tiled floors and walls. The shelves were piled with abundant wares, all reasonably priced, and the premises were thronged with customers. In Africa this was unusual.

While Daniel joined the relays of housewives wheeling their shopping trolleys down the aisles between the shelves, he was studying the building and its staff.

Four young Asian girls sat at the cash registers guarding the exit. They were quick and efficient. Under their graceful brown fingers the registers tinkled to the sweet music of Mammon.

'Chetti Singh's daughters,' Daniel guessed as he noted the family resemblance. They were pretty as sunbirds in their brightly coloured saris.

In the centre of the floor a middle-aged Asian lady sat at a tall dais from which she could keep a beady eye on every corner of the shop. She wore her hair in an iron-grey plait and though her sari was more subdued in colour, it was edged with gold thread and the diamonds on her fingers ranged from the size of peas to sparrows' eggs.

'Mama Singh,' Daniel decided. When it came to handling the cash, Asian businessmen liked to keep it close to home, which was probably one of the reasons for their universal success. He took his time selecting groceries, hoping for a glimpse of his quarry, but there was no sign of the turbaned Sikh.

At last Mama Singh left her seat on the dais and made an elephantine but dignified progress down the length of the store, until, with her long silken sari sweeping the treads, she mounted a flight of stairs set so discreetly in a corner of the food hall that Daniel had not noticed them before.

She entered a door at a higher level and now Daniel noticed a mirrored window in the wall beside the elevated door. It was obviously a one-way glass. An observer in the room beyond the door would have a clear view over the supermarket floor and Daniel had no doubt that it was Chetti Singh's office.

He turned away from that inscrutable square of glass, aware that he might have been under observation for the past half hour, and that the precaution was probably too late. He made his way to one of the girls at the cash registers and while she totted up his purchases he kept his face averted from the window in the rear wall.

135

Chetti Singh stood at the observation window as his wife came into the office. She saw instantly that he was disturbed. He was plucking thoughtfully at his beard and his eyes were slitted.

'That white man.' He nodded towards the store floor below the window. 'Did you notice him?'

'Yes.' She came to his side. 'I noticed him as he came in. I thought he might be a soldier or a policeman.'

'What made you think that?' Chetti Singh demanded.

She made an eloquent gesture with those lovely hands that were so incongruous on a female of her bulk. They were the hands of the young girl he had married almost thirty years ago, and the pale palms were dyed with henna.

'He stands tall, and walks with pride,' she explained. 'Like a soldier.'

'I think I know him,' Chetti Singh said. 'I saw him very recently, but it was at night and I cannot be absolutely certain.' He picked up the telephone from his desk and dialled two digits.

Standing at the window, he watched his second daughter pick up the telephone from beside her cash register.

'Treasure,' he spoke in Hindi. 'The man at your till. Is he paying with a credit card?'

'Yes, father.' She was the brightest of all his children, as much value to him as a second son, almost.

'Get his name and ask him where he is staying in town.'

Chetti Singh hung up and watched the white man pay for his purchases and leave the store heavily laden. As soon as he had gone, Chetti Singh dialled again.

'His name is Armstrong,' his daughter told him. 'D: A. Armstrong. He says that he is staying at the Capital Hotel.'

'Good. Let me speak to Chawe quickly.'

Below him his daughter swivelled her seat and called one of the uniformed security guards from the main doors. She held out the telephone receiver to him and as he placed it to his ear Chetti Singh asked, 'Chawe, did you recognise the *malungu* who has just left? The tall one with thick curly hair.' Chetti had switched to Angoni.

'I saw him,' the guard replied in the same language. 'But I did not recognise him.'

'Four nights ago,' Chetti Singh prompted him. 'On the road near Chirundu just after we had loaded the truck. The one who stopped and spoke to us.'

There was silence as Chawe considered the question. Chetti Singh saw him begin to pick at a nostril with his forefinger, a sign of uncertainty and embarrassment.

'Perhaps,' Chawe said at last. 'I am not sure.' He removed the thick forefinger from his nose and inspected it minutely. He was a man of the Angoni, a distant relative of the royal line of Zulu. His tribe had migrated this far north two hundred years ago at the time of King Chaka. He was a warrior, not a man given to deep thought.

'Follow him,' Chetti Singh ordered. 'Do not let him see you. Do you understand?'

'I understand, *Nkosi.*' Chawe looked relieved to be ordered into action and he left through the main doors with a spring in his step.

He returned half an hour later, hangdog and crestfallen. As soon as he came in through the main doors Chetti Singh telephoned his daughter again.

'Send Chawe up to my office right away!'

Chawe stood in the doorway at the head of the stairs, as big as a gorilla, and Chetti Singh demanded, 'Well, did you follow him as I ordered?'

'*Nkosi,* it is the same man.' Chawe shuffled his feet. Despite his size and strength, he was terrified of Chetti Singh. He had seen what happened to those who displeased the master. In fact, it was Chawe himself who was usually responsible for enforcing his master's discipline. He did not look directly into his eyes as he went on. 'It is the man who spoke to us on the night,' he said, and Chetti Singh frowned quickly.

'Why are you sure now, when you were uncertain before?' Chetti Singh demanded.

'The truck,' Chawe explained. 'He went to his truck and put the goods he had bought from us into it. It is the same truck, with a man's arm painted on the side, *Mambo.*'

'Good.' Chetti Singh nodded approval. 'You did well. Where is the man now?'

'He drove away in the truck.' Chawe looked apologetic. 'I could not follow him. I am sorry, *Nkosi Kakulu*.'

'Never mind. You did well,' Chetti Singh repeated. 'Who is on duty at the warehouse tonight?'

'I am, *Mambo* . . .' Chawe grinned suddenly, his teeth were large and even and very white, 'and, of course, Nandi.'

'Yes, of course.' Chetti Singh stood up. 'I will come down to the warehouse this evening after business is closed. I want to make sure that Nandi is ready to do her job. I think we may have trouble tonight. I want everything prepared. Have Nandi in the small cage. I don't want any mistakes. Do you understand, Chawe?'

'I understand, *Mambo*.'

'At six o'clock, at the warehouse.' Sometimes it was as well to repeat instructions to Chawe.

'*Nkosi*.' Chawe sidled from the room, still not looking directly at his master.

After he had gone, Chetti Singh sat staring at the closed door for many minutes before he picked up the telephone again.

Direct-dialling to an international exchange was always a lottery in Africa. Zimbabwe was almost a neighbouring state; only the narrow Tete corridor of Mozambique separated them. Nevertheless, it took him a dozen attempts and twenty frustrating minutes before he heard a ringing tone at the other end of the line and was through to the number in Harare.

'Good afternoon. This is the embassy of the Republic of Taiwan. May I help you?'

'I wish speech with the ambassador.'

'I'm sorry. His Excellency is not available at present. May I take a message or put you through to another member of the staff?'

'I am Chetti Singh. We are abundantly acquainted.'

'Please hold on, sir.'

A minute later Cheng came on the line. 'You are not to telephone me at this number. We agreed.'

Chetti Singh told him firmly, 'This is urgent, absolutely.'

'I cannot speak on this line. I will call you back within the hour. Give me your number there and wait for me.'

The private unlisted telephone on Chetti Singh's desk rang forty minutes later.

138

'This line is secure,' Cheng told him as he picked it up. 'But be discreet.'

'Do you know a white chap named Armstrong?'

'Doctor Armstrong? Yes. I know him.'

'This is the one you met at Chiwewe, and who accosted you on the road regarding certain stains on your clothing, is it not?'

'Yes.' Cheng's tone was non-committal. 'It's all right, don't worry. He knows nothing.'

'Then why has he pitched up in Lilongwe?' Chetti Singh demanded. 'You still want me not to worry?'

There was a silence. 'Lilongwe?' Cheng said at last. 'Did he also see you that night on the Chirundu road?'

'Yes.' Chetti Singh tugged at his beard. 'He stopped and spoke to me. He asked if I had seen the Parks trucks.'

'When was that? After we had transferred the ivory to you—?'

'Careful!' Chetti Singh snapped. 'But yes, it was after we had parted our separate ways, never mind. My men and I were tying down the tarpaulins when this white chap in a truck pulled up—'

Cheng cut in, 'How long did you speak to him?'

'A minute, no more than that. Then he went south towards Harare. I think he was following you, without a morsel of doubt.'

'He caught up with Gomo and forced him off the road.' Cheng's voice was sharp and agitated. 'He searched the Parks truck. Of course, he didn't find anything.'

'He is suspicious, indubitably.'

'Indubitably,' Cheng agreed sarcastically. 'But if he spoke to you for only a minute, he cannot connect you. He doesn't even know who you are.'

'My name and address are boldly imprinted upon my truck,' Chetti Singh said.

Cheng was silent again for a slow count of five. 'I did not notice. That was imprudent, my friend. You should have covered it.'

'It is no good closing the stable door after the bird has flown,' Chetti Singh pointed out.

'Where is the—' Cheng broke off. 'Where are the goods? Have you shipped them?'

'Not yet. They will go out tomorrow.'

'Can't you get rid of them sooner?'

'That is beyond the bounds of possibility.'

'You will have to deal with Armstrong then, if he becomes too curious.'

'Yes,' said Chetti Singh. 'I will deal with him most firmly and resolutely. Your side? Is everything taken care of? Your Mercedes?'

'Yes.'

'The two drivers?'

'Yes.'

'Have the authorities visited you?'

'Yes, but it was routine,' Cheng assured him. 'There were no surprises. They have not mentioned your name to me. But you must not telephone me at the embassy again. Use this number only. My security people have cleared this line.' He gave Chetti Singh the number and he wrote it down carefully.

'I will let you know about this chap. He is an absolute nuisance,' Chetti Singh went on.

'I hope not for too much longer.' Cheng cradled the receiver and instinctively reached for one of the assembly of ivory netsuke that were arranged on his desk top.

It was an exquisite miniature carving of a young girl and an old man. The beautiful child sat on the old man's lap staring with a daughter's adoration into his noble, lined and bearded face. Each tiny detail had been executed three hundred years ago by one of the great artists of the Tokugawa dynasty. The ivory had been polished by the touch of human fingers until it glowed like amber. Only when the group was inverted was it disclosed that beneath their flowing robes the couple were naked and that the old man's member was buried almost to the hilt between the girl's thighs.

The humour of it appealed to Cheng. It was one of his favourite pieces from all his vast collection, and he caressed it now between thumb and forefinger like a worry bead. As always, the silken feel of the ivory soothed him and encouraged him to think more clearly.

He had been expecting to hear more of Daniel Armstrong, but this had not lessened the shock of Chetti Singh's message.

The Sikh's questions aroused old doubts and for the thousandth time he went over all the precautions that he had taken.

After leaving the headquarters camp at Chiwewe he had not noticed the blood on his shoes and clothing until Daniel Armstrong had drawn his attention to it. This evidence of his guilt had preyed on his mind for the rest of that arduous journey out of the Zambezi valley. When at last they reached the main highway and found Chetti Singh waiting at the rendezvous, he had confided his worries to the Sikh and showed him the stains on his clothing.

'You were not supposed to go near the scene of the killing. That was foolish, never mind.'

'I had to make sure the job was done, and it was just as well I did. The warden was still alive.'

'You will have to burn that clothing.'

It was unlikely that there would be other traffic this late at night but they took no chances. They reversed the trucks well off the highway and transferred the ivory from the Parks trucks to Chetti Singh's pantechnicon behind a screen of trees. Even with Chetti Singh's gang of men to assist the two drivers, the removal took almost two hours. It was a huge quantity of ivory to move.

In the meantime Chetti Singh watched Cheng build a small fire. When it was burning hotly the ambassador stripped to his underwear. As he dressed again in fresh clothing from his luggage, Chetti Singh squatted beside the fire and burned all the soiled items. The rubber soles of the training shoes flared up fiercely when they caught. He used a stick to poke the charred scraps into the centre of the flames and make certain that they were reduced to fine ash.

'There will still be abundant traces of blood in the Mercedes,' Chetti pointed out as he stood up from the fire. 'On the floor, on the accelerator and brake pedals.' He removed the floor mat and the rubber covers from the control pedals and burned these as well. The stink of the black smoke made his eyes run, but still he was not satisfied.

'We will have to get rid of that car.' He told Cheng what to do. 'I will arrange the rest of it.'

Cheng was the first to leave the rendezvous. Even before the transfer of the ivory to the Sikh's truck was complete, he was on his way back to Harare.

He drove fast, as though trying to escape from his involvement with the raid. The reaction was setting in now. It was the same after one of his sexual pantomimes in the Myrtle Blossom Lady's house in Taipei. Afterwards he felt shaky and nauseated. He always promised himself it would never happen again.

The ambassador's residence was one of many large sprawling colonial buildings in the avenues near the golf club. He reached it well after midnight. He went directly to his own bedroom suite. He had arranged for his wife and the children to fly back to Taiwan the previous week to stay with her family. He was alone in the residence.

He stripped once again and, even though he had not worn it at the scene, placed all his clothing in a plastic bag. He was concerned that the faintest trace of blood might linger upon it. Then he showered. He stood under the steaming spray for almost half an hour, shampooing his hair twice and scrubbing his hands and fingernails with a stiff brush.

When he felt that he had washed away every last trace of blood or gunpowder, he dressed in fresh clothing from his dressing-room and carried the plastic bag containing his clothing back to the Mercedes parked in the residence garage. He placed the plastic bag in the boot beside his canvas grip. He was anxious to get rid of every single item that he had taken to Chiwewe, even his binoculars and his bird-book.

He reversed the Mercedes out of the garage and parked it in the front driveway of the residence. The gates were open and he left the key in the ignition.

Although it was by now after two in the morning and it had been a day and night filled with activity and intense nervous strain Cheng could not sleep. In a brocaded silk robe he paced his bedroom restlessly, until he heard the starter of the Mercedes whirl. He switched off the bedside lamp and darted to the window overlooking the front driveway. He was just in time to see his car, with darkened headlights, pull out of the driveway and turn into the deserted street. He sighed with relief and at last went to bed.

As he composed himself to sleep he thought how swiftly Chetti Singh had arranged it. Chetti Singh's son managed the

Harare branch of the family interests. He was almost as astute and reliable as his father.

In the morning, after breakfast, Cheng telephoned the police and reported the theft of the Mercedes. They found it twenty-four hours later, out near Hatfield on the way to the airport. It had been stripped of tyres and engine and set on fire. The fuel tank had exploded and nothing was left of the vehicle but the soot-blackened carapace. He knew that the insurance company would pay out in full, without too much delay or protest.

The following morning an anonymous caller on Cheng's unlisted line spoke without introduction or explanation.

'Look at page five of today's *Herald*,' he said, then broke the connection, but the accent had been Asian, very similar to Chetti Singh's manner of speech.

Cheng found the article at the foot of the page. It was six lines under an insignificant heading, 'Stabbed in Drunken Brawl'. Gomo Chisonda, a ranger employed by the National Parks Service, had been stabbed to death by an unknown assailant during an argument in a township beerhall.

The next day the same anonymous caller told Cheng, 'Page seven.' This time Cheng was certain that he recognised the voice of Chetti Singh's son.

The heading of the newspaper article was 'Railway Accident', and the squib read, 'The body of David Shiri, an off-duty ranger in the National Parks Service, was found on the railway line near Hartley. The dead man had a high blood alcohol level. A spokesman for Zimbabwe Railways warned the public of the danger of using unguarded crossings. This is the fourth accident of the same kind on the Hartley line since the beginning of the year.' As Chetti Singh had promised, there were no longer any surviving witnesses or accomplices.

Three days later, Cheng received a telephone call from the commissioner of police in person.

'I am very sorry indeed to disturb you, Your Excellency. I presume you have read about the murderous attack on Chiwewe Camp. I believe that you may be able to assist our enquiries into this most unfortunate incident. I understand that you were a visitor at the camp on that day, and that you left only hours before the attack.'

143

'That is correct, Commissioner.'

'Would you have any objection to making a statement to assist us? You know that there is no obligation for you to do so. You are fully protected by diplomatic privilege.'

'I will co-operate in any way possible. I particularly admired and liked the warden who was murdered. I will do all I can to help you apprehend the perpetrators of this foul crime.'

'I am most grateful to you, Your Excellency. May I send one of my senior inspectors to call upon you?'

The inspector was a burly Shona in plain clothes. He was accompanied by a sergeant in the smart uniform of the Zimbabwean police, and both of them were elaborately obsequious.

With profuse apologies the inspector took Cheng through a recital of his visit to Chiwewe, including his departure with the convoy of refrigerator trucks. Cheng had rehearsed all this and he went through it faultlessly. He was careful to mention his meeting with Daniel Armstrong.

When he had finished, the inspector fidgeted uncomfortably before asking, 'Doctor Armstrong has also made a statement, Your Excellency. His account confirms everything you have told me, except that he mentioned that he noticed there were bloodstains on your clothing.'

'When was that?' Cheng looked puzzled.

'When he encountered you and the Parks trucks, as he was returning to Chiwewe, after having seen the tracks of the raiders on the road.'

Cheng's expression cleared. 'Ah yes. I had been an interested spectator of the Parks elephant culling. As you can imagine, there was much blood about during the operation – I could easily have stepped in a puddle.'

The inspector was sweating with embarrassment by this stage. 'Do you remember what you were wearing that evening, Your Excellency?'

Cheng frowned as he tried to remember. 'I was wearing an open-neck shirt, blue cotton slacks, and probably a pair of comfortable running shoes. That is my usual casual attire.'

'Do you still have those items?'

'Yes, of course. The shirt and slacks will have been laundered by now, and the shoes will have been cleaned. My valet is very efficient . . .' He broke off and smiled as though a thought had only just occurred to him. 'Inspector, do you want to see these items? You might even wish to take them away for examination.'

Now the police inspector's embarrassment was painful. He squirmed in his chair. 'We have no right to ask for that kind of co-operation, Your Excellency. However, in view of the statement made by Doctor Armstrong. If you had no objection . . .'

'Of course not.' Cheng smiled reassuringly. 'As I told the commissioner of police, I want to co-operate in every possible way.' He glanced at his wristwatch. 'However, I am due at lunch with the president at State House in an hour. Do you mind if I send the clothing down to your headquarters with a member of my staff?'

Both police officers sprang to their feet. 'I am very sorry to have inconvenienced you, Your Excellency. We appreciate your help. I am sure the commissioner of police will be writing to you to tell you that himself.'

Without rising from his desk, Cheng stopped the inspector at the door. 'There was a report in the *Herald* that the raiders had been apprehended,' he asked. 'Is that correct? Were you able to recover the stolen ivory?'

'The bandits were intercepted at the Zambezi as they tried to cross back into Zambia. Unfortunately all of them were either killed or escaped, and the ivory was destroyed by fire or lost in the river.'

'What a pity . . .' Cheng sighed. 'They should have been made to answer for these brutal killings. However, it has simplified your work, has it not?'

'We are closing the file,' the inspector agreed. 'Now that you have helped us tidy up the loose ends, the commissioner will write to convey his appreciation and that will be the end of the matter.'

The packet of clothing that Cheng selected from his wardrobe and sent to police headquarters, although agreeing with the description he had given the inspector, had never been worn anywhere near Chiwewe or the Zambezi valley. Cheng sighed now as he thought about it. He replaced the ivory netsuke on his desk and stared at it morosely. But it was not the end of the matter, not now that Doctor Daniel Armstrong was nosing around, making trouble.

Could he rely on Chetti Singh once again, he wondered? It was one thing to get rid of two lowly Parks rangers, but Armstrong was game of a larger kind. He had international reputation and fame, there would be questions if he disappeared.

He touched the intercom button and spoke into the microphone on his desk in Cantonese.

'Lee, come in here please.'

He could have asked his question without ordering his secretary through, but he liked to look at her. Although she was of peasant stock from the hills, she was bright and nubile. She had done well at Taiwan University, but Cheng had not chosen her for her academic achievements.

She stood to the side of his desk, close enough for him to touch if he had wished to, in an attitude of servility and submission. Despite her modern accomplishments, she was a traditionally raised girl with the correct attitude to men, and in particular to her master.

'Have you confirmed the reservations with Qantas Airlines?' he asked. With Armstrong sniffing around in Lilongwe, it was as well that the return to Taipei was imminent. He would never have taken the risk of the Chiwewe adventure if he had planned to stay on at the embassy. Already his wife and family had left. He would follow at the end of the month, only eight days from now.

'Yes, the reservations have been confirmed, Your Excellency,' Lee whispered respectfully. To him her voice was as sweet as that of the nightingale in his father's lotus garden in the mountains. It stirred him.

'When are the packers coming in?' he asked, and touched her. She trembled slightly under his hand and that stirred him further.

'They will come in first thing on Monday, my lord.' She used the traditional title of respect. Her straight black hair hung to her shoulders and shimmered with light.

Cheng ran his fingers lightly up the thigh slit of her cheongsam; her skin was as smooth as the ivory netsuke.

146

'You have warned them of the value and fragility of my art collection?' he asked, and pinched her beneath the skirt. He took a nip of that ivory skin between the nails of his thumb and second finger and she winced and bit her lower lip.

'Yes, my lord,' she whispered, with a catch of pain in her voice. He pinched a little harder. It would leave a tiny purple star on the flawless swell of her small firm buttock, a mark that would still be there when she came to him tonight.

The power of pain made him feel elated. He forgot about Doctor Daniel Armstrong and any trouble he might be brewing. For now, the police were off the track, and Lee Wang was lovely and compliant. He had eight days while he was separated from his wife in which to enjoy her to the full. Then he would return home, to his father's approbation.

 Daniel unlocked the rear door of the Landcruiser and packed the groceries and supplies that he had purchased from Chetti Singh's supermarket into his depleted tucker box. Then he went round to the cab and sat at the wheel. While he let the engine warm, he checked his notebook for the list of the Sikh's other business premises.

With help from a few obliging pedestrians he found his way into the light industrial area of the town, down near the railway line and the station. Here it seemed that Chetti Singh owned four or five acres of industrial sites. Some of these were undeveloped and overgrown with rank bush and weed. On one of the vacant lots a large signboard declared:

ANOTHER CHETTI SINGH PROJECT

SITE OF PROPOSED COTTON CARDING FACTORY

Development! Employment! Prosperity! Upliftment!
FOR MALAWI!

On one side of the open plot, behind a barbed-wire security fence, stood the workshops of Chetti Singh's Toyota agency.

At least a hundred new Toyota vehicles were parked in the front lot. They were still coated with the filth of the long rail journey up from the coast on open goods trucks. Clearly they were awaiting delivery service in the main workshop building. Through the open front doors Daniel could see a team of mechanics at work. Though the foremen appeared all to be Asians, some in Sikh turbans, most of the overalled mechanics were black. The enterprise appeared prosperous and well managed.

Daniel drove into the forecourt and left the Landcruiser parked at the reception bay. He spoke to one of the foremen in a blue dust-coat. Under the pretext of arranging a service for the Landcruiser he managed to get a good look around the workshop and administration building. There was no obvious place where a shipment of stolen ivory could be hidden.

While he made a booking to bring the Landcruiser in the following morning at eight o'clock, he chatted casually to the workshop foreman and learned that the sawmill and the Chetti Singh Trading Company warehouse were in the next street, backing on to the vehicle workshop.

He drove away and circled the block. It was easy to pick out the sawmill, even from the far end of the street. A dozen railway trucks stood at the private railway siding, every one of them piled high with heavy logs of indigenous timber cut in the heavily forested mountains. The shrieks of the circular saws carried clearly up the street.

As he drove past the gates he looked into the open sheds where the saws were housed. The spinning discs shone like quicksilver, and spurts of yellow sawdust flew from the rough logs as the blades bit into them. The resinous smell of freshly cut timber was pungent in the hot sunlight and mountains of raw planks were piled in the extensive yards, ready to be loaded on to the waiting railway trucks.

Daniel drove past slowly. Diagonally opposite the sawmill stood the warehouse complex. It was enclosed by a high diamond-mesh fence, green plastic-coated wire on sturdy concrete poles with offset tops angled out towards the street and festooned with barbed wire.

The warehouse was in five semi-detached units; the valleys

and peaks of the common roof formed a saw-tooth pattern of unpainted corrugated asbestos sheeting. The walls were also of the same corrugated asbestos. Each of the five units had separate doors of the roller type usually seen on aircraft hangars.

This time the signboard at the gates read:

CHETTI SINGH TRADING COMPANY
CENTRAL DEPOT AND WAREHOUSE

He was certainly not shy about advertising his name, Daniel thought wryly. There was a swinging boom and a brick-built gatehouse at the entrance and Daniel noticed at least one uniformed guard at the gate. As he drew level with the last building, he saw that the tall asbestos doors had been rolled open and he was able to look down the length of the cavernous warehouse.

Suddenly he leaned forward and his pulse accelerated as he recognised the huge pantechnicon parked in the centre of the warehouse. It was the vehicle that he had last seen on the Chirundu road four nights previously. The ten-wheel trailer with the green tarpaulin cover was still hitched behind it and the red dust that coated it matched that on his own Landcruiser.

The rear doors of the trailer were open and a team of a dozen or so black labourers assisted by a forklift truck were loading a cargo of brown sacks that could have contained maize, sugar or rice.

He could not see any of the distinctive dried fish bags that had been the cargo which he had seen in the Zambezi valley. He lowered the side window, hoping for a whiff of fish, but he smelled only dust and diesel fumes.

Then he was past. He thought about making a U-turn and another passing inspection.

'Hell, I've drawn enough attention already,' he told himself. 'Like the circus coming to town.'

He drove back to the Capital Hotel the way he had come, left the truck in the guests' car park and went up to his room. He ran a bath, as deep and hot as he could stand it, and soaked the dust and grime of the African roads out of his pores, while his skin turned a rich puce.

As the water cooled he twiddled the tap with his toe, adding fresh steaming gouts.

At last he stood to lather his nether regions and regarded himself seriously in the dewy mirror over the washbasin.

'Look here, Armstrong. The sensible thing to do is go to the police with our suspicions. It's their job, let them get on with it.'

'Since when, Armstrong,' he replied, 'did we ever do the sensible thing? Besides, this is Africa. It will take the police three or four days to stir their butts, and Mr Singh has had quite enough time already to get rid of any ivory he may just have lying around. By tomorrow it will probably be too late to catch him at it.'

'You are trying to tell me, Armstrong, that time is of the essence?'

'Precisely, old chap.'

'It couldn't be that you'd enjoy a touch of cloak and dagger, a bit of boy-scouting, a spot of amateur sleuthing?'

'Who me? Don't be silly! You know me.'

'Indeed I do,' he agreed with a wink at his image, and subsided back into the steamy suds, which slopped over the bath rim on to the tiled floor.

The dinner was a vast improvement on his last public meal.

The fillets of bream were fresh from the lake and the wine was a delicious Hamilton-Russell Chardonnay from the Cape of Good Hope. Reluctantly he rationed himself to half the bottle.

'Work to do,' he muttered ruefully, and went up to the room to make his preparations. There was no hurry. He couldn't move until after midnight. When he was ready he lay on the bed and enjoyed the sensation of excitement and anticipation. He kept looking at his wristwatch. It seemed to have stopped and he held it to his ear. The waiting was always the worst part.

Chetti Singh watched the security guards usher the last customer from the supermarket and close the double glass doors. The wall clock pointed to ten minutes past five.

The sweepers were already at work and his daughters were busy at the tills, cashing up the day's receipts. The girls were as devout as virgins ministering at the altar of some arcane religion, and his wife stood over them as dignified as the high priestess. This was the high point of the daily ritual.

At last the procession left the tills and made its way across the shop floor, in strict order of precedence, his wife leading and her daughters following, the eldest first and the youngest last. They entered his office and laid the day's take on his desk, neatly banded bundles of currency notes, and canvas bags of coins, while his wife handed him the print-outs from the tills.

'Oh, good!' Chetti Singh told them in Hindi. 'The best day since Christmas Eve, I am sure.' He could recite the figures over the last six months without consulting his ledgers.

He entered the take in the day-book, and while his family watched respectfully, locked the cash and credit-card vouchers into the big Chubb safe built into the back wall.

'I will be late home for dinner,' he told his wife. 'I must go down to the warehouse to attend to certain matters.'

'Papaji, your meal will be ready when you return.' She clasped her hands to her lips in a graceful gesture of respect, and her daughters imitated her example and then filed from his office.

Chetti Singh sighed with pleasure. They were good girls – but if only they had been boys. It was going to be the devil's own job finding husbands for all of them.

He drove down to the industrial area in the Cadillac. The car was not new. Dearth of foreign exchange would not permit an ordinary citizen to import such a luxurious vehicle. Chetti Singh had, as always, a system. He contacted newly appointed members of the American diplomatic staff before they left Washington. Malawi customs regulations allowed them to import a new car and sell it locally at the end of their term. Chetti Singh paid them twice the US value of the Cadillac in Malawi kwacha on arrival. They could live in princely style on this amount for the full three years of their tour in Malawi while still retaining use of the car and saving their official salaries.

When they left, Chetti Singh took over the vehicle, ran it for a year, until the next arrangement matured at which time he placed the Cadillac on the showroom floor of his Toyota agency with a price tag of three times its original US value. It was usually sold within the week. No profit was too small to despise; no loss was too small to abhor. It was not by accident that over the years Chetti Singh had amassed a fortune the full extent of which not even his wife could guess at.

At the warehouse gates Chawe swung open the boom to allow him to drive the Cadillac through.

'Yes?' Chetti Singh asked the big Angoni.

'He came,' Chawe replied. 'As you said he would. He drove by on this road at ten minutes past four. He was in the truck with the man's arm painted on the door. He drove slowly and he was staring through the fence all the time.'

Chetti Singh frowned with annoyance. 'This chap is becoming an absolute pest. Never mind,' he said aloud, and Chawe looked bemused. His English was rudimentary.

'Come with me,' Chetti Singh ordered, and Chawe climbed into the back seat of the Cadillac. He would never be so presumptuous as to sit beside his master.

Chetti Singh drove slowly along the front of the warehouse complex. All the tall doors were already closed and locked for the night. There were no burglar alarms guarding the area; at night even the perimeter fence was unlit by floodlights.

There had been a period two or three years back during which he had suffered from repeated burglaries and break-ins. Alarms and floodlights had done little to prevent these depredations. In desperation he had consulted the most famous Sangoma in all the territory. This old witch-doctor lived in dread isolation up on the top of the misty Mlanje plateau attended only by his acolytes.

For a fee commensurate with his reputation, the witch-doctor descended from the mountain with his entourage and, with great fanfare and ceremony, he placed the warehouse under the protection of the most powerful and malevolent of the spirits and demons that he controlled.

Chetti Singh invited all the idlers and loafers of the town to witness the ceremony. They watched with interest and trepidation as the witch-doctor decapitated a black cockerel at each of the five doors of the warehouse and sprinkled its blood on the portals. After this, to suitable incantations, he placed the skull of a baboon on each corner-post of the perimeter fence. The spectators had been much impressed and the word spread swiftly through the townships and the beerhalls that Chetti Singh was under magic protection.

For six months thereafter there were no further break-ins. Then one of the township gangs worked up the courage to test the efficacy of the spell, and they got away with a dozen television sets and nearly forty transistor radios.

Chetti Singh sent for the witch-doctor and reminded him that his services carried a guarantee. They haggled until finally Chetti Singh agreed to buy from him at a bargain price the ultimate deterrent. Her name was Nandi.

Since Nandi's arrival there had been only a single break-in. The burglar had died in Lilongwe hospital the following day with his scalp ripped off his skull and his bowels bulging out of the rents in his belly. Nandi had solved the problem, permanently.

Chetti Singh drove the Cadillac around the peripheral pathway inside the fence. The fence was in good order, even the baboon skulls still grinned down from the tops of the corner-posts, but the infra-red alarms were gone. Chetti Singh had sold them at a good price to a Zambian customer. After Nandi's arrival they had become redundant.

Completing the circuit of the fence, Chetti Singh parked the Cadillac at the rear of the warehouse, beside a neat shed of the same corrugated sheeting as the main building. This was obviously a later addition, tacked on as an afterthought to the rear wall of the warehouse.

As Chetti Singh stepped out of the Cadillac, his nostrils flared to the faint but rank odour that wafted from the single small window in the shed. This was set high up and was heavily barred.

He glanced at Chawe. 'Is she safe?'

'She is in the small cage, as you ordered, *Mambo*.'

Despite the assurance, Chetti Singh peered through the peep-hole in the door before he opened it and stepped into the shed. The only light came from the high window and the room was in semi-darkness, made more intense by the contrast of the late sunshine outside.

The smell was stronger now, a pungent wild scent, and

suddenly from the gloom there was a spitting snarl so vicious that Chetti Singh stepped back involuntarily.

'My goodness,' he chuckled to hide his nerves. 'We are in absolutely foul mettle today.'

An animal moved behind the bars of the cage, a dark shape on silent pads and there was a gleam of yellow eyes.

'Nandi.' Chetti Singh smiled. '"The sweet one".' Nandi had been the name of King Chaka's mother.

Chetti Singh reached out to the switch beside the door and the fluorescent tube in the ceiling spluttered and then lit the shed with a cold blue light.

In the cage a female leopard shrank away against the far wall, crouching there, staring at the man with murderous eyes, her upper lip lifting in a creased and silent snarl to reveal her fangs.

She was a huge cat, over seven feet from nose to tail, one of the animals from Mlanje mountain forest, who would turn the scale at 120 pounds. A wild creature captured by the old witch-doctor in her maturity, she had once been a notorious goat-and dog-killer, terrorising the villages on the slopes of the mountain. Shortly before her capture she had savagely mauled a young herdboy who had tried to defend his flock against her.

The forest cats were darker than those of the open savanna, the jet-black rosettes that dappled her skin were close-set, so that she was close in coloration to the melanistic panther. Her tail curled and flicked like a metronome, the gauge of her temper. She watched the man unblinkingly. The force of her hatred was as thick as the wild animal stench in the small hot room.

'Are you angry?' Chetti Singh asked, and her lip lifted higher to the sound of his voice. She knew him well.

'Not angry enough,' Chetti Singh decided, and reached for the cattle prod on the rack beside the light switch.

The cat reacted immediately. She knew the sting of the electric prod. Her next snarl was a crackling rattle and she ran back and forth trying to escape from the torment she had come to expect. At the end nearest the main wall of the warehouse the steel mesh cage narrowed into a bottle-neck just wide enough to admit the leopard's body, a low tunnel that ended against a steel sliding door in the warehouse wall.

The prod was bolted on to a long aluminium pole. Chetti Singh slipped it between the cage bars and reached out to touch the leopard. Her movements became frantic as she tried to avoid the device, and Chetti Singh laughed at her antics as he pursued her around the cage. He was trying to drive her into the bottle-necked tunnel.

At last she flung herself against the bars of the cage, ripping at the steel with her claws as she tried to reach him, coughing and grunting with fury, but the length of the pole kept Chetti Singh out of range.

'Goodness gracious me!' he said, and touched the side of her neck with the points of the prod. Blue electricity flashed and the leopard recoiled from the sting of it and bounded into the tunnel at the end of the cage.

Chawe was ready for this, and he dropped the mesh door behind her. Now she was trapped. Her nose was against the steel hatch in the warehouse wall, while at her heels the mesh door prevented her backing away. The tunnel was so low that it almost touched her back and she could not rear up, it was so narrow that she could not turn her head to protect her heaving flanks. She was helplessly pinioned and Chetti Singh handed the prod to Chawe.

He returned to the table near the door and uncoiled the lead of a small electric soldering iron and plugged it into the wall socket. With the plastic-covered lead trailing behind him he came back to where the leopard crouched in the tunnel. He reached through the bars and stroked her back. Her pelt was thick and silky, and she could not avoid his touch. Her whole body seemed to swell with her fury and she snarled and tried to twist her neck to savage his hand but the bars prevented it.

Chetti Singh lifted the soldering iron and spat on the copper point to test its heat. His spittle sizzled and evaporated in a puff of steam. He grunted with satisfaction and reached through the bars once again. He grasped the leopard's tail and lifted it high, exposing her fluffy genitalia and the tight puckered black collar of her anus.

The leopard hissed with outrage and ripped at the cement floor with her claws fully extended. She knew what was coming and she tried to lower her tail and cover her delicate parts.

155

'Help me,' Chetti Singh grunted, and Chawe seized the tail. It writhed like a serpent in his grip but he forced it upwards, allowing his master free use of both hands.

Chetti Singh inspected the delicate flesh thoughtfully. It was dimpled and cratered with healed scars, some so fresh that the cicatrice was still pink and glossy. He reached out gently with the hot iron, choosing the spot to burn with care, avoiding the freshly healed skin. The cat felt the heat of the approaching iron and her body convulsed in anticipation.

'Just a little one, my beauty,' Chetti Singh assured her. 'Just enough to make you very angry if you should meet Doctor Armstrong tonight.'

Unmolested, leopards are not a serious threat to human beings. Man does not form a part of their natural prey, and their instinctive fear is enough to make them avoid rather than attack him. However, once injured or wounded, or particularly when they are deliberately tormented, they are amongst the most dangerous and vicious of all African animals.

Chetti Singh touched the glowing iron to the soft rim of the leopard's anus. There was a puff of smoke and the stink of burned skin and hair. The leopard shrieked with pain and bit at the steel bars.

Chetti Singh inspected the injury. With practice he could inflict a burn that was exquisitely painful, but which would heal within the week and would not damage the animal's appearance nor hamper her movements when she attacked.

'Good!' he congratulated himself. The iron had only superficially penetrated the outer skin. It was a shallow painful little wound, yet it had infuriated the golden cat.

He laid the soldering iron back on the table and picked up a bottle of disinfectant. It was raw iodine, dark yellow and pungent on the swab that he pressed against the open wound. The sting of it would increase her fury.

The leopard shrieked and hissed and struggled wildly against the restraining bars. Her eyes were huge and yellow and froth lined her open snarling lips.

'That's enough. Open the hatch,' Chetti Singh ordered, and the Angoni released the cat's tail. She whipped it down between her legs to protect herself.

Chawe went to the handle of the steel hatch and raised it. With one last snarl the leopard bounded through the opening and disappeared into the warehouse beyond.

At first it had been difficult to get the cat to leave the warehouse at dawn each morning, but with free use of the electric prod and the lure of the goat's meat on which she was fed, she had at last been trained to return to her cage in the shed on command.

It was the only training she had received. All night she prowled the warehouse, tormented and murderous. At dawn she returned to the shed and crouched there in the gloom, growling softly to herself and licking her deliberately inflicted injuries, awaiting the first opportunity to avenge her humiliation and pain.

Chawe closed the hatch behind the leopard and followed his master out into the last glow of the sunset. Chetti Singh mopped his face with a white handkerchief. It had been hot in the fetid little shed.

'You will remain in your guardhouse at the main gate,' he commanded. 'Do not patrol the fence or attempt to stop the white man from entering the warehouse. If he does get in, Nandi will warn you . . .'

They both smiled at the thought. They remembered the last intruder and his condition as they took him down to the casualty department of the general hospital.

'When you hear Nandi working on him, ring me from the main gate. The telephone is beside my bed. Do not enter the warehouse until I arrive. It will take fifteen or twenty minutes for me to get here. By that time Nandi may have saved us a great deal of trouble.'

His wife had one of her magnificent curries prepared for his dinner. She did not question where he had been. She was a good and dutiful wife.

After dinner he worked on his accounts for two hours. His was a complicated system of accountancy: he kept two separate sets of books, one for the civil tax collector which reflected a fictitious profit figure, and another authentic set which was meticulously correct. From this Chetti Singh calculated the tithe that he paid to the temple. It was one thing to cheat on income tax, but a prudent man did not mess around with the gods.

Before he went to bed he unlocked the steel safe built into the back of his wardrobe and took out the double-barrelled twelve-bore shotgun and a packet of SSG cartridges. He had an official police permit for the firearm, for, whenever possible and convenient, he was a law-abiding man.

His wife gave him a puzzled look, but made no comment. He did not satisfy her curiosity, but propped the weapon in the corner nearest the door, ready to hand. He switched out the lights and under the sheets made love to her with his customary dispatch. Ten minutes later he was snoring sonorously.

The telephone beside his bed rang at seven minutes past two in the morning. On the first peal Chetti Singh was awake, and before it could ring again he had the receiver to his ear.

'In the warehouse, Nandi is singing a pretty song,' said Chawe in Angoni.

'I am coming,' Chetti Singh replied, and swung his legs off the bed.

 There were no street lights, 'which makes the job a little easier,' Daniel murmured as he parked the Landcruiser on one of the open plots three hundred yards from the boundary fence of Chetti Singh's central depot. He had driven the last mile at walking speed without headlights. Now he switched off the engine and stepped out into the darkness. He stood listening for almost ten minutes before he checked his wristwatch. It was a little after one o'clock.

He already wore navy-blue slacks and a black leather jacket. Now he pulled a soft balaclava cap of dark wool over his head. He strapped a small nylon bag around his waist that contained the few items of equipment which he had selected from the tool-box.

Bolted to the Landcruiser's roof were two light aluminium extension ladders that he carried for laying as corduroy when negotiating soft sand or deep mud. They weighed less than seven pounds each. He carried both of them under one arm as he set out across the weed-choked wasteland towards the depot. He kept off the road, well back amongst the scrub.

158

The plot had been used as a rubbish dump. There were piles of garbage. A broken bottle or jagged piece of scrap iron could cut through the canvas and rubber boots he wore. He picked his way with care.

Fifty feet from the fence he laid down the ladders and crouched behind a rusty car body. He studied the depot. There were no lights burning in the warehouse, no floodlights illuminating the fence. That seemed odd.

'Too good? Too easy?' he asked himself, and crept closer. The only light was in the guardhouse at the front gate. It gave just sufficient back lighting with which to examine the fence. He saw at once that it was not electrified, and he could discover no trip-wire for an alarm system.

He moved stealthily to the corner-post at the rear of the property. If there were an infra-red alarm system, the eye would be mounted here. Something white gleamed on top of the post, but on closer inspection he realised that it was the bleached skull of a chacma baboon, and he grimaced. He felt vaguely uneasy as he went back to fetch the ladders from where he had left them beside the wrecked car.

Back at the corner of the fenced area, he settled down to watch for a guard making his rounds. After half an hour he had convinced himself that the fence was unguarded.

He moved in. The quickest and safest method of entry would have been to use the wire-cutters, but if possible he wanted to leave no trace of his visit. He extended both ladders to their full length. Then steeling himself for the squeal of a hidden alarm, he propped one of the ladders against the concrete corner-post. He let out his breath when no alarm sounded.

Carrying the second ladder, he scaled to the top of the fence. Balancing on the top rung, leaning backwards to avoid the offset barbed wire on the summit, he swung the spare ladder over and inwards. He had intended lowering it carefully on the far side, but it slipped from his grip.

Although it fell on grass, which cushioned the impact, the sound was like the report of a .357 magnum in his own ears. He teetered on the top of the ladder, his nerves screwed tight and waited for a shouted challenge or a shot.

Nothing happened, and after a minute he breathed again. He

reached into the front of his clothing under the polo-neck jersey, and brought out the roll of foam rubber which he used as a pillow when sleeping under the stars. It was an inch thick, just enough to pad the top strand of barbed wire. He spread it carefully over the top of the fence.

He took a firm grip between the spikes of the wire with his gloved hands and rolled smoothly over, dropping nine feet to the lawn on the far side. He broke his fall with a forward somersault and crouched low, listening again, peering into the darkness.

Nothing.

Quickly he set up the second ladder against the inside of the fence, ready for a speedy retreat. The unpainted aluminium gleamed like a beacon to catch the eye of a patrolling guard.

'Nothing we can do about that,' he told himself, and crossed to the side wall of the warehouse.

He slipped along the wall, thankful for the darkness, and reached the corner. He crouched there for a minute, listening. Somewhere far away a dog barked, and there was the distant sound of a locomotive shunting in the railway yards. Apart from that, nothing.

He glanced round the corner, and then crept down the long back wall of the warehouse. There was no opening here, except for a single row of the skylight windows very high up under the eaves of the saw-backed roof, at least thirty feet above him.

Ahead he made out a small shed in the gloom. It was attached to the rear wall of the warehouse, but its roof was much lower than that of the main building. As he approached it, he became aware of a faint but foul odour, like guano fertiliser or untanned hides.

The smell was stronger as he circled the shed, but he thought little of it. He was studying the shed. There was a downpipe in the angle where the shed's wall joined that of the main warehouse. He tested the pipe with his weight, and then went up it easily, hand over hand. Within seconds he was lying stretched out on the roof of the shed, looking up at the row of skylights in the main wall now only ten feet above him. Two of the panels stood open.

From the bag in the small of his back he brought out a coil

of nylon rope and quietly tied a Turk's head knot in one end to give it weight.

Balancing on the peak of the shed's roof he flicked the rope out and then got it swinging in an easy circle. With a snap of the wrist he shot the weighted knot upwards. It struck the jamb between the two open panels and then dropped back in a tangle around his shoulders. He tried again with the same result. At the fifth attempt the knot dropped through the open skylight, and immediately he tugged and it whipped back and made three natural turns around the jamb. He pulled back hard and the wraps held. Keeping pressure on the line he began to climb. He used the rubber soles of his canvas boots for purchase against the unpainted asbestos wall, and went up with the agility of a monkey.

He had almost reached the windows when he felt the end of the line start to unravel. With a sickening lurch he dropped back a foot and then it held again. Daniel gathered himself and lunged upwards. A gloved hand over the bottom frame of the open skylight steadied him.

He hung thirty feet above the ground, his feet kicking and slipping against the wall and the steel frame cutting into his fingers, even through the glove. Then with another convulsive effort he flung his right hand up and got a double grip. Now with the strength of both arms he was able to draw himself up smoothly and straddle the frame of the skylight.

He took a few seconds to catch his breath and listen for any sound from the dark interior of the building, then he unzipped the bag and groped for the Maglite flashlight. Before he left the hotel room he had screwed a red plastic shade over the lens. The shaft of light which he shot downwards was a discreet ruby glow that was unlikely to attract attention from outside the building.

Below him the warehouse floor was piled with towers and walls of packing cases in a multitude of sizes and shapes.

'Oh no!' he groaned aloud. He had not expected such abundance. It would take a week to examine all of them, and there were four other bays to the warehouse complex.

He flashed the torch-beam down the wall. The corrugated cladding was fixed to a framework of intricately welded angle iron. The frames formed an easy ladder for him to reach the cement floor thirty feet below. He swarmed down and switched off the flashlight.

Swiftly he changed position in the darkness. If a guard was creeping up on him he wanted to confuse the attack. He crouched between two cases, listening to the silence. He was about to move again, when he froze. There was something, a sound so small that it was just within the range of his comprehension, he felt it with his nerve ends rather than truly heard it. It ceased, if it had ever been.

He waited for a hundred beats of his racing heart but it did not come again. He switched on the torch and the light dispelled his unease.

He moved softly down the aisle between the masses of trade goods and bales and crates. He had seen the pantechnicon parked in the end bay. 'That's the place to start,' he assured himself and he sniffed the dark air for the smell of dried fish.

He stopped abruptly and switched off the torch. Once again he had sensed something, not definite enough to pin-point, not loud enough to be a sound – just a premonition that something was close by in the darkness. He held his breath and there was a whisper of movement, or of his imagination. He could not be certain, but he thought it might be the brush of stealthy footfalls perhaps, or the gentle sough of breathing.

He waited. No. It was nothing but his nerves. He moved on down the dark warehouse. There were no interior walls in the building, only pillars of angle iron supporting the roof, separating the spaces between each of the bays. He stopped again, and sniffed. There it was at last. The smell of dried fish. He went forward more rapidly, and the smell was stronger.

They were stacked against the end wall of the furthest bay, a high pile of sacks, reaching almost to roof level. The smell was strong. Printed on each sack were the words: 'Dried fish. Product of Malawi.' together with a stylised rising sun emblem with a crowing cockerel surmounting it.

Daniel groped in his bag and brought out a twelve-inch screwdriver. He squatted before the pile of fish sacks and began to probe them, stabbing the point of the screwdriver through the weave of the jute sacks, and then working it around to feel for any hard object packed beneath a layer of dried fish. He worked quickly, five or six quick stabs to each sack as he passed, reaching up to the sacks above his head, and then scrambling up the pyramid to reach the summit.

At last he stopped and thought about it. He had presumed that the ivory would be packed inside the fish sacks, but now he reconsidered and discovered the fallacy of his original theory. If Ning Cheng Gong had indeed transferred the ivory from the refrigerator trucks to Chetti Singh's pantechnicon, then there certainly would not have been the opportunity to repack it in the sacks and seal them during the few hours before Daniel had intercepted Chetti Singh on the Chirundu road. The very best they could have done was to lay the ivory on the floor of the cargo bed and pile the fish sacks over it.

Daniel clucked his tongue with annoyance at his own impetuosity. Of course, the fish sacks were too small to contain the larger tusks of the hoard, and they would make an impossibly flimsy packing in which to smuggle the ivory out of Africa to its final destination, wherever that might be. The heavy pointed tusks would surely work their way through the outer layer of fish and rupture the woven jute sacks.

'Damn fool.' Daniel shook his head. 'I had a fixed idea ...' He flashed the shaded ruby beam of the torch about, and his nerves jumped tight. He thought he saw something big and dark move in the shadows at the extreme range of the beam, the glint of animal eyes, but when he steadied the torch and stared hard, he realised that it was his imagination again.

'Getting old and windy,' he rebuked himself.

He slid down the pyramid of fish sacks to the floor, then he hurried along the aisle between the mountains of goods. He examined the labelling on the packing cases as he passed. 'Defy Refrigerators', 'Koo Canned Peaches', 'Sunlight Soap Powder'. Each case consigned to 'Chetti Singh Trading Company'. It was all incoming cargo. He was looking for an outgoing cargo.

Ahead of him he made out the shape of a fork-lift truck standing high on the loading ramp near the main doors. As he moved towards it he saw a large case balanced on the fork arms of the truck. Beyond it, almost blocking the ramp, was a high pile of identical cases. They were ready for loading on to the empty railway truck that stood waiting in the bay below the ramp.

Obviously, this was an outgoing cargo and he almost ran down the length of the bay. As he approached he realised that they were traditional tea-chests, with sturdy plywood sides and solid frames, bound with flexible steel straps.

Then he felt an electric tickle of excitement lift the hair on his arms as he read the address stencilled on the side of the nearest chest:

LUCKY DRAGON INVESTMENTS
1555 CHUNGCHING S ROAD
TAIPEI

TAIWAN

'Son of a gun!' Daniel grinned happily. 'The Chinese connection! Lucky Dragon. Lucky for some!'

He crossed to the fork-lift truck and reached across to the controls. He clicked on the master switch and operated the controls. The electric motor purred and the chest rose silently. At head-height Daniel stopped it. He slipped beneath the suspended case. He did not want to leave any trace of his visit by interfering with the lid or sides of the case.

Working between the forked arms of the trunk, he thrust upwards into the bottom of the tea-chest with the screwdriver. The plywood crackled as he punched out a circular opening just large enough to admit his hand. He found that the interior of the case was lined with a heavy-duty yellow plastic sheet that resisted his efforts to tear through. He paused to find the clasp-knife in his bag, and then slit out a flap of the sheeting.

There was the familiar smell of dried tea leaves, and he began to dig into the compressed black vegetable mass, spilling the tea out on to the concrete floor. Soon he had dug into the full length of the screwdriver without encountering any alien object hidden in the case. He felt the first prickle of doubt. There were hundreds of tea-chests piled on the ramp; any of them could contain the tusks, or none of them.

He widened the hole with a few more blows of the screwdriver, then he drove the steel point up into the mass of tea with all the strength of his doubt and frustration.

It hit something solid with a force that jarred his wrist, and he almost shouted aloud with triumph. He ripped at the edges of the hole until he could get both hands into the chest, and he dug out lumps of tea that fell on to the ramp around his feet.

Now at last he could touch the hard object buried in the tea. It was round and smooth. Crouching under the chest he twisted his neck to look up into the aperture, slitting his eyes against the soft rain of dried tea leaves that trickled from the hole. In the beam of the torch he made out the soft creamy alabaster gleam.

With the point of the screwdriver he attacked the exposed surface of the object, stabbing and prising it, until at last a splinter lifted and he pulled it loose. It was the size of his thumb.

'No more doubts,' he whispered, as he examined the sample and picked out the distinctive chicken-wire pattern of the ivory grain. 'Now I've got you, you murdering bastards.'

Quickly he stuffed the torn flap of plastic back into the hole to prevent any more tea spilling out on to the ramp. Then he swept up the fallen leaves and scooped them into his pockets. It wasn't a very effectual job of tidying up, but he hoped that the loaders would be careless enough not to notice anything amiss when they started work again in the morning.

He went to the controls of the fork-lift and lowered the tea chest to its original place on the ramp. He flashed the beam of the torch around to make certain he had left no other evidence of his visit – and this time he saw it clearly.

A great dark shape crouched at the edge of the ramp, watching him with eyes that glowed like opals even in the muted beam of the torch. As the light struck it the creature seemed to dissolve like a puff of smoke, almost supernatural in its uncanny stealth. Daniel recoiled instinctively against the side of the fork-lift, trying to probe the darkness with the torch.

Then suddenly there was a sound that ripped across his nerve ends like an emery wheel. It echoed through the dark cavern of the warehouse and rang against the high roof. It was a hacking cadence, like a wood-saw cutting metal, and it set his teeth on edge. He knew what it was instantly, but he found it difficult to believe what he was hearing.

'Leopard!' he breathed, and with a chill in his guts he realised his danger.

All the advantage was with the beast. The night was its natural environment. Darkness made it bold; darkness made it aggressive.

He pulled the red filter off the lens of the torch and now the bright white shaft of light sprang out across the warehouse. He swept it back and around, and he glimpsed the cat again. It had moved in behind him, circling in. That was the most hostile manoeuvre. The predator circles its prey before rushing in for the kill.

As the light hit it, the leopard flashed away. With one lithe bound, it disappeared behind the wall of tea-chests, and its fierce chorus of hatred echoed through the darkness once again.

'It's hunting me!'

Whilst he was warden of Chiwewe one of his rangers had been mauled by a leopard, and Daniel had been first on the scene to rescue him. Now he recalled vividly the terrible injuries the beast had inflicted.

The other dangerous cat of Africa, the lion, does not have the instinctive knowledge of how best to attack the upright two-legged figure of a man. He will charge in and knock a victim down and then will bite and claw indiscriminately at whatever part of the man's body he can reach, often gnawing and crunching a single limb until the victim is rescued.

The leopard, on the other hand, understands the human anatomy. Baboons form a large part of the leopard's prey, and it knows how to go directly for the head and the vulnerable guts of the primate. Its usual attack is to leap on to its victim and hook into his shoulders with the front claws, while its back legs kick like those of a domestic cat playing with a ball of wool.

The long talons, unsheathed, will disembowel a man with half a dozen swift kicks, stripping his guts out. At the same time the leopard sinks his teeth into the face or throat and with one front claw reaches over to hook the back of its victim's scalp and tear it off the skull. Often the dome of the skull comes away with the scalp, like the top sheared off a soft-boiled egg, leaving the brain exposed. All this flashed through

Daniel's mind as the leopard circled him, its wild savage call echoing through the open bays of the warehouse.

Still crouched beside the fork-lift, Daniel zipped his leather jacket tightly up under the chin to protect his throat and slid the nylon bag around from the small of his back to cover his stomach. Then he shifted the screwdriver to his right hand, and with his left swung the torch to cover the leopard's menacing circles.

'My God, he's a huge brute!' Daniel realised, as he saw the true size of the cat. In the torchlight it was panther black. Bush-lore has it that the dark-coloured cats are the most ferocious of the breed.

It was impossible to hold the leopard in the beam of light. It was as elusive as a shadow. Daniel knew he would never make it back to where he had broken into the warehouse. It was too far to go with his back unprotected. The cat would be on him before he had covered half the distance. He flicked the torch-beam away for a second, seeking another avenue of escape.

The fish sacks. He saw the pyramid piled against the near wall, reaching as high as the windows, thirty feet above the warehouse floor.

'If I can just reach the skylight,' he whispered. There was a long drop down the outside wall, but he had the nylon rope to lower himself at least part of the way. 'Move!' he told himself. 'You're running out of time. It's going to rush you any moment now.'

He screwed up his nerve to leave the haven of the fork-lift. The machine covering his back was a solid comfort – while in the open he was vulnerable and puny against the speed and strength of the leopard. The moment he left the shelter of the fork-lift, the leopard sawed again, its savage cry more vicious and eager.

'Get out of it!' Daniel yelled at it, hoping to disconcert it with the sound of a human voice. The cat ducked sideways and disappeared behind a pile of packing cases – and Daniel made his mistake.

It was a stupid, unforgivable mistake. He, of all people, knew that you must never run from a wild beast. In particular you must never turn your back on one of the cats. Their instinct is to pursue. If you run, they must charge, just as a domestic cat cannot resist the flight of the mouse.

Daniel thought that he might just be able to reach the pyramid of fish sacks. He turned and ran, and the leopard exploded in a silent rush out of the darkness behind him. He never even heard it come. It landed with all its weight and the full momentum of its charge in the middle of his back, between his shoulder-blades.

Daniel was hurled forward. He felt its claws bite in and hold, and for a moment he thought they were hooked into his own flesh. Instead of bearing him down to the concrete floor the leopard slammed him into the pile of sacks. They cushioned the impact, but still it drove half the air from Daniel's lungs and he felt as though his ribs had collapsed.

The leopard was still mounted high on his shoulders, but as Daniel staggered under its weight he realised that its claws were hooked into the leather of his jacket and the thick woollen sweater beneath it.

Somehow Daniel managed to keep on his feet, supporting himself against the sloping wall of sacks. He could feel the cat on his back gather itself, bringing up its back legs, coiling its body like a spring, ready to lash downwards across his buttocks and the back of his thighs. It would open his flesh to the bone, slicing through blood vessels and arteries, a crippling injury from which he would probably bleed to death within minutes.

Daniel pushed off from the sacks with both arms, flipping backwards, rolling his body into a ball with his knees up under his chin. The leopard's claws tugged at the nylon belt of the bag and then kicked on downwards, but Daniel had drawn his legs up and clear. The cat's back paws with the curved claws outspread, struck at air, missing his flesh.

Now man and beast with their combined weight crashed to the concrete floor. Daniel was a big man and the leopard was underneath him. A single hissing snarl was forced from its lungs by the impact and Daniel felt its claws release their hold in the leather of his jacket. He twisted violently and reached over his shoulder with one hand, the screwdriver still clutched in the other. As he came to his knees, he seized a thick fold of skin at the scruff of the leopard's neck and, with the strength of his terror, tore the creature from his back and hurled it against the pile of packing-cases.

It rebounded at him like a rubber ball.

The torch had been knocked from his grip by the leopard's first charge. It rolled across the concrete floor until it came up against one of the packing-cases. Its beam was angled upwards now and reflected from the pale plywood case. The reflection gave Daniel just enough light to anticipate the leopard's charge.

Its jaws were open to their full gape, and its extended front paws reached for his shoulders. As it smashed into him, chest to chest, its back legs cocked up in the instinctive disembowelling movement and its head shot forward to sink its fangs into his face and throat. This was the classic leopard attack and Daniel countered with the screwdriver held sideways between both his hands, thrusting it like a curb bit into the leopard's open mouth.

One of the beast's front fangs broke off cleanly at the gum as it struck steel, and then Daniel was on his back holding the leopard off his face with the screwdriver. It snarled again and a hot mist of spittle blew into his face, the stink of carrion and death filled his nostrils.

He felt one forepaw stretch out over his shoulder, reaching out to the back of his scalp to rip it off his skull. At the same time the back legs jack-knifed up, claws fully extended to tear out the front of his belly. However, the back of Daniel's head was pressed up hard against one of the fish sacks and the leopard hooked its claws, not into the thin flesh of his scalp, but into the coarse jute of the sack only an inch from his ear. Then the cat slashed down with both back legs together, but instead of unzipping his belly, the claws bit into the tough nylon belt of the bag at his stomach.

For a moment the animal's attack was stalled. It ripped at the jute sack, seeming not to realise its error, and the back legs kicked downward spasmodically, tearing the nylon with a sharp rending sound.

As it struggled, the leopard pulled back its head, trying to avoid the steel shaft that Daniel was still forcing deeply between its open jaws. Instantly Daniel whipped the screwdriver back, releasing his grip on the sharpened end and then drove it forward again, aiming the point at one of the leopard's eyes.

His aim was wild, the point of the screwdriver shot into the cat's flaring nostril, but instead of finding the nasal channel into the brain, it deflected slightly, penetrated the gristle of the nose, and ran along the outside of the cheekbone below the dappled skin. The point emerged from beneath the leopard's ear, and the cat screamed with the shock and agony. For a moment it relaxed its attack. Daniel rolled over, and threw the leopard off him.

It seemed a miracle that up to now the leopard had not drawn blood, but as Daniel threw it backwards, the cat held on instinctively with one paw. The claws raked down Daniel's arm, slicing through the leather and wool and reaching the muscle of his forearm. It felt like a sword cut, and the pain goaded Daniel to throw in his last desperate reserve of strength.

He kicked out with both feet together, and his heels crashed into the feline body just as it gathered itself for the next charge. The kick drove it backwards in a snarling, snapping ball of dark fur that gleamed and rippled in the torchlight.

There was a space between the fish sacks at Daniel's back, it was just wide enough to admit his body. He flung himself backwards into the narrow cave. Now his back and flanks were protected, and the leopard could only attack from directly in front.

It thrust its head, growling and gaping into the narrow space, trying to reach him. Daniel stabbed for its eyes with the screwdriver. Again he missed, but the steel point lacerated the leopard's curling pink tongue, and it leaped backwards, hissing and spitting with pain.

'Go on! Get out of it!' he howled, more to bolster his own courage than with any hope of driving off the infuriated beast. He drew his legs up under him and worked his way as far as he could into the narrow gap between the fish sacks.

The leopard paced back and forth across the entrance, blotting out the feeble torchlight with each pass. Once it stopped and sat on its haunches, wiping its wounded nose with one paw, like a domestic cat, and then licking its own blood from the fur.

Then it bounded forward, blocking the entrance to the narrow cave, and stretched in one forepaw to try and reach

Daniel again. He stabbed at the groping limb and felt it hit and penetrate. The leopard spat explosively and pulled back. It began to patrol the entrance to his cave, pausing every few minutes to lower its head and let out one of those terrible sawing roars.

Daniel felt the blood sliming down his forearm under the sleeve and dripping from his fingers. He held the screwdriver between his knees, ready to fend off the next attack, and then, one-handed, bound his handkerchief around the torn arm to stem the bleeding. He pulled the knot tight with his teeth. The wound seemed superficial. The leather sleeve had saved him from serious injury, but the arm was already beginning to throb. Daniel knew how truly dangerous even the lightest scratch from a carnivore's teeth or claws could be, if untreated.

That was only one of his worries. The leopard had him trapped and soon it would be morning. It was a wonder that the roars of the animal had not yet attracted attention. He could expect a guard to arrive at any moment.

As he thought it, the warehouse was suddenly flooded with light. It was so brilliant that the leopard recoiled on to its haunches and blinked in confusion. Daniel heard the faint rumble as the main doors rolled open, driven by their electric motor. It was followed immediately by the sound of a motor car coming in through the opening.

The leopard snarled and slunk back towards the rear of the warehouse, carrying its head low and looking back over its shoulder.

Then somebody shouted, 'Hey, Nandi! Back to your cage! Back! Back!' Daniel recognised Chetti Singh's voice.

The leopard broke into a crouching run, and disappeared from Daniel's sight.

Chetti Singh spoke again. 'Lock the leopard in the cage quickly!' and there was the metallic clang of a cage door being slammed. 'Can you see the white man? Be careful, he may still be alive.'

Daniel shrank back as far as he could into the narrow opening between the sacks. He had no real hope of avoiding detection, and the screwdriver was not much of a weapon.

'There is a torch lying over there, still burning.'

'And over there, by the fish sacks. That looks like blood.'
Cautious footsteps approached.

'Nandi has done her work.'

'Give me the torch.'

The voices were closer.

Suddenly a pair of legs came into Daniel's view and then the man stooped and flashed the torch into the dark crack where Daniel squatted.

'My goodness!' the same voice said in English. 'Here the fellow is, and he is still in excellent fettle. How do you do, Doctor Armstrong? I am delighted to make your formal acquaintance at last.'

Daniel glared silently into the dazzling torch-beam and Chetti Singh went on in a jocular tone. 'You won't be needing that weapon, never mind. Please be good enough to hand it over.'

Daniel made no move to obey and Chetti Singh chuckled. 'This is a shotgun of fine English construction, dear sir, made by Mr Purdey, no less. It is loaded with bullshot cartridges. The Malawi police are very understanding on the little matter of defending self. I beg you most humbly to entertain my request for co-operation.'

With resignation Daniel tossed the screwdriver at his feet, and Chetti Singh kicked it away.

'You may now emerge from your kennel, Doctor.'

Daniel crawled out, and holding his injured arm to his chest, rose to his feet.

Chetti Singh pointed the shotgun at his belly and spoke to the uniformed guard in Angoni. 'Chawe, check the cases. See if the *malungu* has opened any of them.'

Daniel recognised the black guard from the supermarket. He was a big dangerous-looking brute. I prefer the leopard for a sparring partner, Daniel thought wryly as he watched the Angoni stride away down the ramp towards the fork-lift.

Before he reached the machine Chawe exclaimed and went down on one knee to scoop up a handful of spilled tea that Daniel had overlooked. Quickly he followed the trail of tea to the broached case on the fork-lift.

'Lift the case, Chawe!' Chetti Singh ordered and Chawe climbed behind the controls of the fork-lift and raised the case high.

172

A trickle of black tea leaves dribbled from under it. Chawe jumped down and thrust his arm into the hole that Daniel had gouged out of the plywood.

'You are a jolly clever fellow.' Chetti Singh shook his head at Daniel in mock admiration. 'Just like Sherlock Holmes, no less. But sometimes it is not wise to be too clever, my dear sir.'

Looking into the Sikh's eyes, Daniel discounted the man's stilted clownish speech. Those eyes were deadly. This was no clown.

'Chawe, where did the white man leave his truck?' he asked without moving the aim of the shotgun from the pit of Daniel's belly.

'He came without lights, but I heard the truck on the south side. I think he parked in the open land there.' They were speaking in Angoni believing that Daniel could not understand it, but his knowledge of Zulu and Ndebele allowed him to make sense of it.

'Go! Fetch the truck,' Chetti Singh ordered.

After Chawe had gone, Daniel and Chetti Singh confronted each other in silence. Daniel was looking for some sign of weakness or indecision. The Sikh was calm and contained, the shotgun steady in his hands.

'My arm is badly hurt,' Daniel said at last.

'My sincere commiseration, my dear Doctor.'

'There is danger of infection.'

'No.' Chetti Singh smiled. 'You will be dead before infection can manifest itself.'

'You intend killing me?'

'That is an amazingly facetious question, Doctor. What alternative do I have? You have been clever enough to discover my little secret. As I have often concluded, too much knowledge is a terminal disease. Ha, ha!'

'If I'm going to die, why don't you satisfy my curiosity and tell me about Chiwewe? Who proposed the raid, you or Ning Cheng Gong?'

'Alas, dear sir. I know nothing of Chiwewe or this other fellow. Besides I do not feel in a talkative frame of mind.'

'You have nothing to lose by telling me. Who owns the Lucky Dragon Investment Company?'

'I am afraid, Doctor, that you will have to take your curiosity to the grave with you.'

They heard the Landcruiser coming and Chetti Singh stirred. 'That did not take Chawe long. You could not have been at many pains to conceal your vehicle. Let us go to the main door to greet him. Will you lead the way, please, Doctor, and bear in mind that Mr Purdey's excellent firearm is only a foot from your spinal column.'

Still nursing his injured arm Daniel set off towards the warehouse doors. As they emerged from the aisle between the rows of packing-cases he saw a green Cadillac parked beside the empty railway truck.

Probably Chetti Singh had remained safely in the Cadillac until the leopard had returned to its cage. Daniel remembered the shed at the back of the building, and the foul animal smell that he had noticed earlier. He was piecing it all together, working out where the leopard was kept and how it was controlled. Even so, it was clear that neither Chetti Singh nor his henchman trusted the animal. On the contrary they had been extremely nervous when the leopard was loose.

When they reached the main doors, Chetti Singh motioned Daniel to a standstill. Then abruptly the heavy door began to roll aside, revealing Daniel's Toyota parked facing the entrance with its headlights burning. Chawe was standing at the external control box of the electrically operated door. When the door was fully opened, he withdrew his key-card from the lock of the control box. It was on a short key-chain and he dropped it into his hip pocket.

'Everything is ready,' he told Chetti Singh.

'You know what to do,' Chetti Singh replied. 'I don't want any birds to fly back to settle on my roof. Make sure you leave no sign. It must be an accident, a nice simple accident on the mountain road. You understand that?' They were speaking Angoni again, secure in the belief that Daniel could not understand.

'There will be an accident,' Chawe agreed. 'And perhaps a little fire.'

Chetti Singh turned his attention back to Daniel. 'Now, dear sir. Kindly mount to the controls of your automobile. Chawe will tell you where to go. Please obey him most faithfully. He shoots very well with the shotgun.'

Obediently Daniel climbed up into the cab of the Landcruiser and, at a word from Chetti Singh, Chawe took the seat directly behind him. Once they were settled, Chetti Singh passed the shotgun to the big Angoni. It was done as quickly and as neatly as an expert loader serving his gun in a Scottish grouse butt. Before Daniel could take any advantage, the double barrel was pressed firmly into the back of his neck, held there by Chawe.

Chetti Singh stepped back to the open window beside Daniel.

'Chawe's English is absolutely atrocious, never mind,' he said jovially, and then switched to the *lingua franca* of Africa. '*Wena kuluma Fanika-lo* – you speak like this?'

'Yes,' Daniel agreed in the same language.

'Good, then you and Chawe will have no difficulty understanding each other. Just do as he orders, Doctor. At that range the shotgun will make a most unsightly mess of your coiffure, no doubt.'

Chetti Singh stepped back, and at Chawe's command Daniel reversed the Landcruiser, swung it in a U-turn and drove out through the main gates into the public road.

In the rear-view mirror he saw Chetti Singh walk back to the green Cadillac and open the driver's door. Then the angle changed and Daniel could no longer see into the warehouse.

From the back seat Chawe gave curt directions, emphasising each with a jab of the shotgun muzzle into the back of Daniel's neck. They drove through the silent and deserted streets of the sleeping town, heading east towards the lake and the mountains.

Once they were out into the country Chawe urged him to increase speed. The road was good, and the Landcruiser buzzed along merrily. By now Daniel's wounded arm was stiff and painful. He nursed it on his lap, driving with one hand and trying to ignore the pain.

Within an hour the gradient changed and the road began a series of hairpins as it climbed the first slopes of the mountain. On each side the forest was denser and darker, pressing in upon the highway and the Landcruiser's speed bled off as she climbed.

The dawn came on stealthily, and beyond the shafts of the headlights Daniel saw the shapes of the forest trees emerging from the gloom. Soon he could see their high tops defined against the dawn sky. He turned his wrist and glanced at his watch. His sleeve was stiff with dried blood, but it was light enough now to read the dial clearly. Seven minutes past six.

He had had plenty of time to consider his predicament and to assess the man who held the gun to his head. He judged him to be a tough opponent. There was not the least doubt that he would kill without hesitation or compunction, and he handled the shotgun with a disheartening competence. On the other hand it was an awkward weapon to use in the confines of the Landcruiser's cab.

Daniel considered his alternatives. He quickly discarded the idea of attacking Chawe in the truck. He would have his head blown off before he could turn to face him.

He might kick open the side door and throw himself out of the cab, but that meant that he would have to reduce the Landcruiser's speed below fifty to avoid serious injury when he hit the ground. Gradually he lifted his foot from the accelerator. Almost immediately Chawe sensed the change in the engine beat and thrust the shotgun into the nape of his neck.

'*Kawaleza!* Go faster!'

That horse wouldn't run. Daniel grimaced and obeyed. On the other hand Chawe wasn't likely to shoot him at this speed and risk the sudden loss of control and the inevitable pile-up.

He expected an order to stop or pull off the road when they reached their destination, wherever that might be. That would be the time to make his play. Daniel settled down to wait until then.

Suddenly the road was steeper, and the bends sharper. The dawn was grey. As they came through each turn in the road, Daniel had glimpses of the valley below. It was filled with silver mist banks, through which he made out the white cascades of a mountain river, running deep in its gloomy gorge.

Another bend loomed ahead and as he braced himself to negotiate it, Chawe spoke sharply, 'Stop! Pull in to the edge. Over there.'

Daniel braked and pulled over, on to the verge.

They were at the top of a cliff. The edge of the road was guarded by a line of white-painted rocks. Beyond that the chasm gaped. It was a drop of two or three hundred feet to the rocky riverbed below.

Daniel pulled on the handbrake and felt his heart bounding against his rib cage. Would the shot come now? he wondered. It would be a stupid thing to do if they wanted to make it look like an accident, but then the big Angoni did not seem to be labouring under a heavy burden of brains. 'Switch off the engine,' he ordered.

Daniel did as he was told.

'Put your hands on your head,' Chawe ordered, and Daniel felt a small lift of relief. He had a few seconds longer. He obeyed and waited.

He heard the click of the door latch, but the pressure of the steel muzzle against his spine never slackened. He felt the cool draught of air as Chawe swung the back door open.

'Do not move,' he warned Daniel, and slid sideways from his seat still aiming the shotgun in through the open door. Now he was standing alongside the car.

'Open your door slowly.' The shotgun was aimed through the side window into Daniel's face. He opened the door. 'Now come out.' Daniel stepped down.

Still covering him with the shotgun, holding it in one hand like a horse pistol, Chawe reached out with his left hand through the open door. Daniel saw that he had the steel jack-handle lying on the rear seat. During the journey he must have taken it from under the front seat. In that instant Daniel understood how Chawe planned to get rid of him.

Chawe would prod him to the edge of the precipice with the shotgun, and then a single blow to the back of the skull with the jack-handle would tumble him two hundred feet into the rocky gorge. After that the Landcruiser, with the driver's door open and probably with a burning rag stuffed into the filler of the fuel tank, would be pushed over the cliff on top of him.

It would look like another tourist killed by negligent driving on a notorious stretch of mountain road. Nothing to excite police suspicion, or to tie the incident to Chetti Singh and a cargo of contraband ivory in Lilongwe a hundred miles from the scene.

At that moment Daniel saw his opportunity.

Chawe was reaching in through the open door, and he was just marginally off balance. Although the shotgun was still pointed at Daniel's guts, he would be slow to adjust his aim if Daniel moved quickly.

Daniel hurled himself forward, not at the man or the gun but at the door. He crashed into it with his full weight, and it slammed shut with Chawe's arm trapped between steel edge and jamb.

Chawe screamed in agony. The sound of it did not cover the crack of breaking bone, sharp as a stick of dry kindling snapped across the knee. His forefinger, thick as a blood sausage, slipped across the trigger, firing one of the barrels. The blast of shot missed Daniel's head by a foot, though the detonation fluttered his hair and made him wince. The recoil threw the barrel high.

Using his momentum Daniel charged him head on, seizing the shotgun with both hands, at buttstock and hot barrel. Chawe's grip on the weapon was single-handed and weakened by the agony of broken bone trapped in the door. He fired the second barrel, but the shot flew harmlessly into the sky.

Daniel slammed the side of the breech into his face, catching him across the upper lip, crushing his nose and shearing off all his upper teeth at the gum. Chawe bellowed through a mouthful of blood and broken teeth, as he tried to pull his arm from the steel trap of the door.

Daniel had the advantage of a double-handed grip on the shotgun and used it to tear the weapon from Chawe's right hand. He lifted the shotgun high, reversed it and drove the steel butt-plate into Chawe's face, catching him in the side of the jaw with the full force of the blow.

Chawe's jawbone shattered at the hinge and his face changed shape, sagging at one side as the bone collapsed. Stunned and uncoordinated he fell backwards, held only by his trapped arm. Daniel yanked the door handle and it flew open, releasing Chawe's arm when he was not expecting it.

Chawe reeled backwards, not in control of his legs, windmilling his arms to try and retain his balance, the shattered arm flapping uselessly below the joint of the elbow. One of the white-washed boulders at the edge of the cliff caught his heels and he jerked backwards, as though plucked on a wire, and disappeared over the precipice.

Daniel heard him scream. The sound receded swiftly as he fell and was cut off abruptly on the rocks at the bottom. The silence afterwards was profound.

Daniel found himself leaning against the Landcruiser with the shotgun still clutched to his chest, panting from those few seconds of wild exertion. It took a moment to gather himself and then he went to the edge of the cliff and looked over.

Chawe lay on his face on the rocks at the edge of the waterfall directly below, his limbs spread like a crucifix. There was no scuff mark at the brink of the precipice to mark his fall.

Daniel thought swiftly. Report the attack? Tell the police about the ivory? Hell, no! A white man had better not kill a black man in Africa, even in self-defence, even in a civilised state like Malawi. They would crucify him.

His mind was made up by the sound of a heavy vehicle descending the mountain road in low gear. Swiftly he slipped the shotgun on to the floorboards of the Landcruiser and pulled a light tarpaulin over it. Then he crossed to the edge of the cliff, unzipped the fly of his trousers and forced himself to urinate over the drop.

The descending truck appeared around the bend of the road above him. It was a timber lorry piled with cut logs that were chained to the cargo bed. There were two black men in the cab, the driver and his assistant.

Daniel made a show of shaking off the drops and zipping his fly closed. The black driver grinned and waved at him as the lorry rumbled past and Daniel waved back.

As soon as it was out of sight he ran to the Landcruiser and drove on up the mountain. Within two hundred yards he found a disused logging track that branched off the main road. He drove through the dense secondary growth that clogged the track until he was out of sight of the road. He left the Landcruiser there and went back on foot, ready to duck into cover at the sound of another vehicle.

At the top of the cliff he checked that Chawe's body still lay on the rocks below. His instinct was to leave him there and get far away from the scene as quickly as possible. He suspected that a Malawian prison was no great improvement on any other in Africa. His arm was very painful now. He could feel the first fires of infection kindling, but he didn't want even to look at it until he had cleaned up the evidence against himself.

He skirted the top of the cliff until he found a way down. It was a game path used by hyrax and klipspringer, steep and precarious. It took him twenty minutes to reach Chawe's body. The skin was cold as a reptile's when Daniel touched Chawe's throat. There was no need to check for a pulse. He was dead meat. Swiftly Daniel turned out his pockets. He found that a greasy well-thumbed pass-book was the only piece of identification. He wanted to get rid of that. Apart from a filthy tattered handkerchief and some loose coins, the only other items were four SSG shotgun cartridges and the key-card for the control box of the electric door on the warehouse that Daniel had seen him operate. That might come in useful.

Satisfied that he had made it as difficult as he could for the police to identify the corpse, if they ever found it, Daniel rolled Chawe to the river edge, his broken arm flopping and catching under him, and shoved him into the racing water.

He watched the body splash as it struck, then swirl and roll as it was carried swiftly downstream and disappeared around the next bend. He hoped that it would hang up on a snag somewhere in the inaccessible depths of the gorge long enough for the crocodiles to get a decent meal and further complicate the process of identification.

By the time he had climbed back up the cliff and reached the Landcruiser again, his arm felt as though it were on fire. Sitting at the driver's wheel, with his medical box on the passenger seat beside him, he stripped back the torn blood-caked sleeve and pulled a face at what he found beneath it. The claw wounds were not deep but already they were weeping yellow watery fluid and the flesh around them was swollen a hot crimson.

He packed the lacerations with thick yellow Betadine paste and bandaged it, then he filled a disposable syringe with a broad-spectrum antibiotic and shot it into the biceps of his own left arm.

All this took time. It was almost eight o'clock when he checked his wristwatch again. He reversed back down the logging trail and on to the main mountain road. He drove slowly past the top of the cliff, and the tracks of his tyres and the imprint of his feet showed clearly in the soft earth of the verge. He considered trying to obliterate them, and thought about the driver of the timber lorry who had seen him there.

'I've hung around here long enough,' he decided. 'If I'm going to stop Chetti Singh, I've got to get back to Lilongwe.' And he set off back towards the capital.

As he drew closer to the urban areas, the traffic on the road was heavier. He drove sedately, avoiding drawing attention to himself. Many of the vehicles he passed were Landrovers or Toyotas, so his truck was not remarkable. However, he regretted the touch of vanity that had led him to display his personal logo so prominently.

'Never thought I'd make a fugitive from justice,' he muttered, but still he knew that he could no longer parade around Lilongwe in the Landcruiser.

He drove to the airport and left the truck in the public carpark. He took his spare toilet-kit and a clean shirt from his sports grip and went to the men's washrooms in the airport building to clean up. He bundled his torn and blood-stained shirt and jersey and stuffed them into the refuse bin. Although it was still stiff and sore, he did not want to disturb the wound. After he had shaved, he dressed in a clean shirt whose long sleeves covered his bandaged arm.

When he checked his image in the washroom mirror he was reasonably respectable-looking and he headed for the public telephone booths in the main concourse.

A South African Airways flight from Johannesburg had just landed and the concourse was crowded with tourists and their luggage. No one paid him any attention. The police emergency number was prominently displayed on the wall above the payphone. He disguised his voice by muffling it with a folded handkerchief over the mouthpiece and by speaking in Swahili.

'I want to report a robbery and a murder,' he told the female police operator. 'Give me a senior officer urgently.'

'This is Inspector Mopola.' The voice was deep and authoritative. 'You have information of a murder?'

'Listen carefully,' Daniel told him, still in Swahili. 'I'm only going to say this once. The ivory stolen from Chiwewe National Park is here in Lilongwe. At least eight people were murdered during the robbery. The stolen goods are hidden in tea-chests which are being stored at the warehouses of the Chetti Singh Trading Company in the light industrial area. You had better hurry. They will be moved soon.'

'Who is this speaking, please?' the inspector asked.

'That isn't important. Just get down there fast and get that ivory,' Daniel told him, and hung up.

He went to the Avis car rental counter in the airport concourse. The Avis girl gave him a sweet smile and allotted him a blue Volkswagen Golf. 'I'm sorry. Without a reservation that is all we have available.'

Before he left the carpark, he stopped beside his dusty old Landcruiser and surreptitiously transferred the shotgun wrapped in tarpaulin to the boot of the Volkswagen. Then he retrieved his Zeiss binoculars and slipped them into the cubbyhole. As he drove away, he checked that the Landcruiser was tucked away at the furthest end of the crowded lot where it would escape casual observation.

He kept to the south side of the railway tracks, and found his way through the streets of the business area to the open-air market that he had noticed during his earlier explorations of the town.

At ten-thirty in the morning the market was crowded with vendors displaying their wares and shoppers haggling over them. Dozens of trucks and mini-buses thronged the area around it. They gave him cover. He parked the little blue Volkswagen amongst them, positioning her carefully. The market was on rising ground that overlooked the railway tracks and the light industrial area beyond.

He found himself less than half a mile from the Chetti Singh warehouse and the Toyota workshops, so close that he could read the huge lettering of the company signboard on the buildings with the naked eye. Through the nine-power lens of the Zeiss binoculars he had a fine view of the front of the warehouse and the main doors. He could almost make out the expressions on the faces of the men working on the loading ramps.

A regular stream of trucks passed in and out of the main warehouse gates, amongst them he recognised the big pantechnicon and trailer. However, there was no sign yet of any police activity and it was almost forty minutes since he had made his phone call to them.

'Come on, people! Get the lead out,' he muttered impatiently. As he said it he saw a shunting locomotive come puffing up the main line to the rail spur that entered the warehouse complex. It was running in reverse, the engine-driver leaning out of his side window.

As it approached, one of the warehouse guards swung open the mesh gate on the boundary fence and the loco rolled through, slowing as it entered the open doors of the warehouse. It passed out of Daniel's sight, but seconds later he heard the faint but characteristic clash of steel as the coupling engaged. There was another delay and then the loco re-emerged from the warehouse, drawing three trucks behind it. It gathered speed gradually as the heavily laden trucks gained momentum.

The goods trucks were each covered by heavy-duty canvas covers. Daniel stared at them through the Zeiss binoculars but could make out no definite indication that the tea-chests were under those covers.

He lowered the binoculars and hammered his clenched fist against the steering-wheel of the Volkswagen and groaned aloud with frustration. Where the hell were the police? It was at least an hour and a half since he had phoned them. Even in his agitation, he realised that it would certainly take them longer than that to obtain a search warrant.

'It just has to be the ivory,' he muttered to himself. 'There was no other outbound cargo stacked on that ramp. It's the ivory, I'd take any odds, and it's on its way to Taiwan.'

The loco was drawing the three trucks sedately down the curving rail spur towards the main line and the goods yards, but it had to pass very close to where Daniel was parked on the outskirts of the market-place.

Daniel started the Volkswagen and pulled out into the main road. He accelerated, passing a heavily laden lorry, and sped down to the level-crossing which the loco must cross to reach the main goods yard. The red warning lights were flashing, the warning bell trilling, and the swinging barrier came down in front of him to guard the crossing, forcing him to brake to a halt. The loco rumbled slowly over the crossing directly in front of the stationary Volkswagen, moving not much above walking speed.

Daniel pulled on the handbrake, and, leaving the engine running, jumped down into the road and slipped under the barrier. The first truck rolled past close enough to touch.

The railways consignment card was clipped into the holder on the side of the truck, and he read it easily as it came level and passed slowly in front of him.

CONSIGNEE: LUCKY DRAGON INVESTMENT CO
Destination: Taiwan via Beira
Cargo: 250 cases Tea

The last lingering doubt was dispelled. Daniel stared angrily after the departing train. They were going to get away with it, right under his nose.

The warning lights switched off, the bell fell silent and the barrier began to rise as the loco and its rolling stock pulled away. Immediately the drivers of the traffic backed up behind the Volkswagen began to sound their horns and flash their lights impatiently.

Daniel strode back to the hire car and drove on. He took the first road to the left, running parallel to the railway tracks and found another place to park from where he had a view into the railway goods yard.

He watched through the binoculars as the three trucks were shunted and coupled on to the end of a long goods train. The caboose was locked on behind them and, finally, the whole assembly of coaches and goods trucks pulled out of the yard. With a green mainline loco pulling them, it set off for Mozambique and the port of Beira five hundred miles away on the seaboard of the Indian Ocean.

There was nothing he could do to stop it happening. Wild fantasies flashed through his mind, of trying to hijack the loco, of rushing down to police headquarters and demanding that they take immediate action before it was too late and the train crossed the border. Instead, he drove back to his original vantage point beside the open-air market and resumed his vigil through the binoculars.

He felt tired and dispirited, and remembered that he had not slept at all the previous night. His arm was stiff and sore. He unwrapped the bandage and was relieved to see that there were no further obvious signs of infection. On the contrary the rips in his forearm were beginning to scab over as well as he could have hoped for. He replaced the bandage.

While he watched the warehouse, he tried to work out some means of stopping the ivory shipment, but he knew that his hands were tied. In the end it all came down to the death of Chawe. Chetti Singh had only to point at him, and he stood accused of murder. He dared not draw official attention to himself.

While he waited and watched, he thought about Johnny Nzou and Mavis and their children, mourning them and nursing his hatred for their murderers.

Almost two hours after the goods train had left, he noticed sudden activity around the warehouse. Chetti Singh's green Cadillac drew up at the main gates, followed by two grey-painted police Landrovers, each filled with uniformed constables.

There was a short discussion with the guards at the gates, then the three vehicles drove into the property and parked beside the open warehouse doors. Eleven police constables led by an officer climbed out of the Landrovers. The officer spoke briefly to Chetti Singh beside the Cadillac. Through the binoculars Daniel saw that the Sikh appeared dapper and unconcerned; his turban was crisp and white above his darkly handsome face.

The police officer led his men into the warehouse, only to emerge again an hour later, strolling along at Chetti Singh's side. The officer was gesticulating and talking persuasively, very obviously apologising to Chetti Singh, who smiled and waved away his protestations and finally shook his hand magnanimously.

The contingent of police constables reboarded their Landrovers and drove away. Standing beside the green Cadillac, Chetti Singh watched them go, and it seemed to Daniel through the binocular lens that he was no longer smiling.

'Bastard!' Daniel whispered. 'You haven't got away with it yet.' He finally got control of his anger and started to think rationally once again.

Could he stop the shipment before it left the country? he wondered. And almost immediately he abandoned the idea. He knew that the goods train was on a non-stop run and would reach the border within hours.

What about intercepting it at the port of Beira, before it was loaded on a tramp steamer bound for the Far East? This was a better bet, but still long odds. From what little he had learned about Chetti Singh so far, it was clear that he had a network of influence and bribery that extended over many countries in central Africa, certainly over Zimbabwe and Zambia, and why not over Mozambique, one of the most corrupt and chaotic states on the continent?

He was certain that a great deal of contraband passed through that warehouse over there, and Chetti Singh would have secured his pipeline to the outside world. As Malawi was a land-locked state, that pipeline must include the port captain and the Mozambiquan army, police force and customs service. They would be paid off by Chetti Singh and would protect him. Still, he decided, it was worth a try.

Daniel drove down to the main post office in the town centre. It was highly unlikely that the Malawi Police had the sophisticated equipment to trace a telephone call swiftly, but once again, he took the precaution of making his message short and of muffling his voice with a handkerchief and speaking in Swahili.

'Tell Inspector Mopola that the stolen ivory was shipped out of the warehouse at eleven thirty-five a.m. by goods train to Beira. It is hidden in a shipment of tea-chests consigned to Lucky Dragon Investment Company in Taipei.'

Before the operator on the police exchange could ask for his name he cradled the receiver, and crossed to a small general dealer's store on the opposite side of the street. If the police weren't going to do anything, it was all up to him.

He purchased a packet of safety-matches, a roll of Sellotape, a box of mosquito coils and two kilos of frozen minced meat, then drove back to the Capital Hotel.

As soon as he entered his hotel room he was aware that somebody had searched it. When he opened his canvas valise he saw that the contents had been disarranged.

'Nothing for Chetti Singh there,' he muttered with grim satisfaction. He had deposited his passport and traveller's cheques in the hotel safe at the cashier's desk downstairs, but the search of his possessions confirmed his estimate of Chetti Singh. 'He's not only a tough bastard, but a cunning one. He's organised and he hasn't missed a trick so far. Let's see if we can spoil his record, but first I need some shut-eye.'

He changed the dressing on his arm, and gave himself another shot of antibiotic and then fell on the bed.

He slept until dinner-time, then showered and changed. He felt refreshed and more cheerful. His arm was less painful and the stiffness had eased. It seemed that his mind had been busy even while he slept, for the details of his plan were clear as he sat down at the writing-desk and laid his small purchases out in front of him. He lit one end of a mosquito coil and left it smouldering as he worked, timing the rate at which it burned.

Using his clasp-knife he snipped the heads off the safety-matches. He used up the entire package of matches and discarded the decapitated sticks in the waste-paper bin. He stuffed the match heads back into the paper wrapping, and taped it all up.

It made a neat package the size of his fist, a very functional little incendiary bomb. He checked the burning rate of the mosquito coil. It was approximately two inches per half hour. The acrid insecticidal smoke made him sneeze, so he took the coil to the bathroom and flushed it down the toilet.

He returned to the desk and cut two fresh coils five inches long, to give a delay of a little over one hour. They were the time-fuses of his make-shift bomb, one as a back-up should the other fail. He pierced the paper packet of match heads, inserted the ends of the coils in the punctures and taped them carefully in place.

Then he went downstairs and stood himself a good dinner and half a bottle of Chardonnay.

After dinner he checked Chetti Singh's residential address in the telephone directory, and found the street in the town map provided so thoughtfully by the Lilongwe Chamber of Commerce.

Then he went down to the Volkswagen in the hotel parking lot and drove through the almost deserted streets. He passed the lighted shop-front of Chetti Singh's supermarket, then circled the block. In the alley behind the building he noted the bags of garbage and empty cardboard boxes piled against the rear wall of the supermarket, awaiting collection. He smiled with satisfaction as he noticed the smoke-detector of the fire-warning system high on the wall above the piles of garbage.

From there he drove out to the airport. The Landcruiser was now conspicuous in the almost deserted airport carpark. He gave the attendant a ten kwacha note and asked him to keep an eye on it. Then he opened the back doors of the truck and rummaged around in his medical box until he found the plastic canister of sleeping capsules.

Parked under a street light he opened the plastic bag of minced meat in his lap. By this time it had defrosted. With his thumbnail he split open the sleeping capsules and poured the white powder over the meat. He used fifty capsules.

That should be enough to stun a bull elephant, he decided with satisfaction, and thoroughly mixed the drug into the chopped meat.

Then he drove out to Chetti Singh's home in the elite suburb behind State House and the main government buildings. The house was the grandest on the street, set in two or three acres of lawns and flowering shrubs. He parked the Volkswagen further down the street in an unlit section and walked back along the sidewalk.

As he came level with the fence surrounding Chetti Singh's property, two dark shapes detached themselves from the shadows and hurled themselves against the wire mesh. German Rottweilers, Daniel noted, as the two guard dogs clamoured for his blood. My least favourite animals, after the hyena. On the other side of the fence, they kept pace with him as he followed the sidewalk to the end of the property.

As he passed the gates at the entrance to the driveway he noted that the padlock on the chain was of simple construction. Two minutes' work with a paper-clip.

He left the two Rottweilers staring after him hungrily and turned the corner into an unlit side street. From his pocket he brought out the packet of doped minced meat and divided it into two equal portions. Then he walked back the way he had come. The dogs were waiting for him. He tossed a portion of the meat over the fence and one of the dogs sniffed it and then gulped it down. Then he threw the second portion to the other dog and watched while it was devoured.

He returned to the Volkswagen and drove back into town. He parked a block away from the supermarket. Still sitting in the front seat, he lit the ends of the mosquito coils protruding from the packet of match heads. He blew on them gently to make sure they were burning evenly, then left the Volkswagen and sauntered down the alley behind the supermarket.

It was dark and deserted. With barely a check in his stride, he dropped the incendiary bomb into one of the cardboard cartons that made up the pile of rubbish and sauntered out of the alley.

Back in the Volkswagen he checked the time; it was a few minutes before ten o'clock. He drove back and parked three blocks away from Chetti Singh's home. He pulled on the black leather gloves. From under the driver's seat he brought out the twelve-gauge shotgun still wrapped in its sheet of light tarpaulin. He broke down the weapon into its three component parts and wiped them down meticulously, made certain there were no fingerprints. Then he refitted the forestock to the double barrels. When he stepped out of the Volkswagen he slipped the barrels down one leg of his trousers, while the breech and buttstock section he tucked under his leather jacket.

The barrels in his pants hampered his gait, but it was better to limp a little than parade fully armed through the streets. He had no idea how often the police patrolled this area. He checked his pockets to make sure that he had the spare cartridges and Chawe's warehouse keys. Then he limped on one stiff leg towards the Sikh's home.

There were no guard dogs to greet him when he reached the corner fence of the property, and neither of them appeared even when he whistled softly for them. The dosage of the drug he had given them might have put them out for good and all. At the gates to the driveway it took him even less than the two minutes he had estimated to deal with the padlock. He left the gates wide open and moved quietly across the lawns, avoiding the crunching gravel of the driveway.

Daniel was prepared for a challenge from a night-watchman; even though Malawi was not as lawless and uncontrolled as Zambia, there might have been a guard. However, Chetti Singh seemed to place more faith in animals than in humans.

No challenge came, and from the shelter of a spreading bougainvillaea arbour he surveyed the main house. It was in low ranch-house style with large picture windows, most of which were curtained and lit. Occasionally he saw the shadows of the occupants flit across the curtains and he could distinguish between the silhouettes of Mama Singh and her more sylphlike daughters.

The double garage was attached to the main house. One of the doors stood open and through it he made out the gleaming chrome work of the Cadillac. Chetti Singh was at home.

Still standing in shadow, Daniel reassembled the shotgun and slipped two SSG cartridges into the breeches. At close range they would almost cut a man in half. He closed the action, and set the safety-catch. Turning the dial of his wristwatch to catch the light from the windows he read the luminous numerals. In something under twenty minutes, depending on the burning rate of the mosquito coils, the packet of match heads would explode into bright phosphorous flame. The garbage pile should burn with a heavy outpouring of smoke and within seconds the fire alarms would detect it.

Daniel moved quickly across the open lawn, watching the windows of the house. The gravel crunched lightly under his feet and then he was into the garage. He tensed for any outcry, and when none came he checked the doors of the Cadillac. They were all locked.

In the garage wall nearest the driver's side of the Cadillac there was a door that obviously connected with the main house. Chetti Singh would have to come through that.

He probably had another fifteen minutes before the fire alarm was reported and Chetti Singh came rushing into the garage to drive to the scene of the fire. It was a long time for

Daniel to wait, and he tried to put from his mind any consideration of the morality of what he was about to do.

Killing Chawe had been an act of self-defence, but Daniel had killed deliberately before, during the bush war. However, he had never derived any pleasure or satisfaction from it, as some of the others had done. Even though it had been his duty as a soldier, the sickening guilt and remorse after each episode had built up slowly within him. That guilt had contributed overwhelmingly to the final revulsion and rejection of the whole ethic of the war which had led him to join the Alpha group.

Yet here he was preparing to kill again, in a much more cold-blooded and calculating manner. Those other nameless victims that he had left as blood-soaked bundles lying in the battle-scorched veld had been patriots too, in their own light, brave black men, almost certainly braver than he, who had been prepared to die for their own vision of freedom and justice. In the end they had succeeded where he had failed. Even though long dead, their vision still burned brightly where his had dimmed and faded away. The Rhodesia he had fought for no longer existed. For him those long-ago killings had been an obscene ritual, without passion and, he now realised, without morality.

On the other hand, could he justify what he was about to do by the memory of Johnny Nzou? Could he convince himself of the justice of it, become executioner when no judge had passed sentence? Was there enough angry fire in his belly to carry it through?

Then he remembered Mavis Nzou and her children, and the fire burned up brightly. He knew he could not turn away from it. He had to do it. He knew he would be sick with guilt after the fire of his anger had turned to cold grey ash, but he had to do it.

Somewhere in the house beyond the door he heard a telephone ring. Daniel stirred, shaking himself like a spaniel coming from the water on to the bank, throwing off the doubts and uncertainty. He tightened his grip on the stock of the shotgun and lifted it to high port.

There were hurried footsteps beyond the door, the lock

191

turned and then it was thrown open. A man came through. The light was behind him and for a moment Daniel did not recognise Chetti Singh without his turban. He stooped beside the Cadillac. His keys tinkled as he searched for the lock, and cursed softly when he could not find it and turned back to the light switch on the wall.

Light flooded the garage.

Chetti Singh was bare-headed. His long, never-trimmed hair and beard twisted up into a top-knot on his head were lightly streaked with grey. His back was still half-turned to Daniel as he fingered the bunch of keys, and then thrust one of them into the Cadillac's door lock.

Daniel stepped up behind him and poked the muzzle of the shotgun into his back. 'Don't do anything heroic, Mr Singh. Mr Purdey is looking down your spine.'

Chetti Singh's body froze, but his head swivelled slowly until he was gawking at Daniel over one shoulder.

'I thought . . .' he said, and then caught himself.

Daniel shook his head. 'It didn't work out that way. Chawe wasn't very bright, I'm afraid. You should have fired him long ago, Mr Singh. Now move around to the other side of the car, but move slowly. Please let us keep our dignity.'

He jabbed the gun into the Sikh's back, hard enough to bruise him through the thin cotton shirt which was all he wore above a pair of khaki slacks and sandals. Chetti Singh had obviously dressed in great haste.

They moved in close file around the front of the Cadillac's fancy radiator grille to the passenger door.

'Open the door. Get in,' Daniel instructed.

Chetti Singh settled himself on the gleaming leather uphol-stery, and looked up into the barrel of the shotgun only inches from his face. He was sweating more heavily than the warm night air warranted. Beads of sweat twinkled on his beaky nose and slid down his cheeks into the plaited beard. He smelt of curry spices and fear, but there was a tiny spark of hope in his eyes as he offered the keys of the Cadillac to Daniel through the open door.

'Are you going to drive? Here are the keys; take them. I place myself in your hands, absolutely.'

'Nice try, Mr Singh,' Daniel smiled coldly. 'But you and Mr Purdey are not going to be separated for a moment. Just slide across to the driver's seat, nice and slowly.'

Awkwardly Chetti Singh moved his big frame across the console between the seats, grunting with the effort, and Daniel prodded him with the shotgun.

'That's it. You are doing very well, Mr Singh.' He slid into the passenger seat as Chetti Singh settled at the wheel. He held the shotgun across his lap, out of sight of any casual observer, but with the muzzle still pushed hard into the Sikh's lower ribs. With his free hand he closed the door.

'All right. Start up. Drive out.'

As the headlights swept across the lawns, they lit the body of one of the Rottweilers lying on the grass.

'My dogs — my daughter is very fond of them.'

'She has my commiserations.' Daniel gave the taunt back to him. 'But the animal is doped, not dead.'

They drove out into the street. 'My shop — my supermarket in town is on fire. I think this is your doing, Doctor. It is an investment of several millions.'

'Again, you have my commiserations,' Daniel nodded. 'It's a tough life, Mr Singh, but worse for the insurance company than for you, I imagine. Now drive to the warehouse please.'

'The warehouse? Which warehouse?'

'Where you and Chawe and I met earlier today, Mr Singh. That warehouse.'

Chetti Singh turned in the correct direction, but he was still sweating. The smell of curry and garlic was very strong in the confined interior of the Cadillac. With his free hand Daniel adjusted the air-conditioning.

Neither of them spoke but Chetti Singh kept glancing in the rear-view mirror, obviously hoping for assistance. However, the streets were deserted until they stopped at a traffic light at the entrance to the industrial area. Then headlights flooded the interior from the rear, and a Landrover pulled up alongside them. It was painted grey and when Daniel glanced sideways at it, he made out the peaked cap brims of the two police constables in the front seat.

Beside him he felt Chetti Singh stiffen and gather himself. Stealthily the Sikh reached out for the door handle at his side.

'Please, Mr Singh,' Daniel said pleasantly. 'Don't do it. Blood and guts all over the upholstery will ruin your Caddie's resale value.'

Chetti Singh deflated slowly. One of the police constables was now staring across at them. 'Smile at him,' Daniel instructed.

Chetti Singh turned his head and snarled like a rabid dog. The constable looked away hurriedly. The lights changed and the Landrover pulled forward.

'Let them get ahead,' Daniel instructed.

At the next intersection the police vehicle turned left.

'You did that well,' Daniel congratulated him. 'I am pleased with you.'

'Why are you victimising me in such a barbarous fashion, please, Doctor?'

'Don't spoil your record by asking facetious questions,' Daniel advised him. 'You know why I'm doing this.'

'The ivory was no concern of yours, surely, Doctor?'

'The theft of the ivory is the concern of any decent man, but you are correct. That is not the main reason.'

'The business with Chawe. That was not personal. You brought that upon yourself. You should not blame me for trying to protect myself. I am a very wealthy man, Doctor. I would be glad to make up to you any injury to your dignity or person you might have suffered. Let us discuss a figure. Ten thousand dollars, US, of course,' Chetti Singh babbled.

'Is that your final offer? I find it miserly, Mr Singh.'

'Yes, you are right. Let's say twenty-five – no, make that fifty. Fifty thousand US.'

'Johnny Nzou was one of the best friends I ever had,' Daniel said softly. 'His wife was a lovely lady, they had three children, two girls and a little boy. They named the boy after me.'

'Now you have me at a loss, never mind. Who is Johnny Nzou?' Chetti Singh asked. 'Let's say fifty thousand for him, as well. One hundred thousand US dollars. I give it to you, and you walk away. We forget this foolishness. It never happened. Am I correct, Doctor?'

'A little late for that, Mr Singh. Johnny Nzou was the warden at Chiwewe National Park.'

194

Chetti Singh let out his breath softly. 'I am terribly sorry about that, Doctor. Those were not my orders . . .' There was the brittle edge of panic in his voice. 'I had nothing to do with that. It was – it was the Chinaman.'

'Tell me about the Chinaman.'

'If I tell you, will you swear not to harm me?'

Daniel seemed to consider this at length. 'Very well,' he nodded at last. 'We will go to your warehouse where we can have a private uninterrupted chat. You will tell me all you know about Ning Cheng Gong, and afterwards I will release you, immediately, unharmed.'

Chetti Singh turned to stare at him in the reflected light from the instrument panel. 'I trust you, Doctor Armstrong. I think you are a man of integrity. I believe you will keep your word.'

'To the letter, Mr Singh,' Daniel assured him. 'Now just keep heading for the warehouse.'

They passed the sawmills. The lumber-yard was brightly lit and the teams of sawyers were at work in the long sheds. The squeal of the saw-blades slicing into timber carried clearly even into the air-conditioned interior of the Cadillac.

'Business must be good, Mr Singh. You are working night-shift.'

'I have a large consignment going to Australia at the end of the week.'

'You will want to survive long enough to enjoy those profits. Just keep co-operating.'

At the end of the street the warehouse stood in darkness. Chetti Singh stopped at the main gates. The gatehouse was deserted and unlit.

'Left-hand drive,' Chetti Singh remarked, indicating the controls of the Cadillac with an apologetic shrug. 'You must operate the gate from your side.' He handed Daniel a plastic-coated electronic key-card similar to the one retrieved from Chawe's corpse, and lowered the electric window.

Daniel leaned out and pressed the card into the slot of the control-box. The gate boom rose and Chetti Singh drove through. Behind them the boom dropped again automatically.

'Your guard leopard must save you a great deal in the way of wages.' Daniel's tone was mild and conversational but he kept a firm pressure of the shotgun into Chetti Singh's ribs. 'But I don't understand how you have made the animal so vicious. In my experience, leopards will not attack a man unless provoked.'

'That is true.' Chetti Singh was more relaxed since they had struck their bargain. He had stopped sweating and now he chuckled for the first time. 'I was advised by the man who sold it to me. Every once in a while it is necessary to give the brute a little gingering up, never mind. I use a hot iron under its tail . . .' He chuckled again, this time with genuine amusement. 'My goodness, it makes the animal very angry indeed. You never heard such a racket.'

'You deliberately torment it to make it vicious?' Daniel asked, shocked despite himself. His tone made evident his disgust and contempt, and Chetti Singh bridled.

'You English and your love of animals. It is merely a form of training to make it more efficient. The injuries are superficial and heal readily.'

They drew up outside the warehouse and once again Daniel used the electronic key-card to open the roller door. As they drove through, the door rumbled closed behind them.

'Park over there on the loading ramp,' Daniel ordered. The headlights swept powerfully down to the girders and corrugated sheeting of the wall at the far end of the cavernous building. The floor was as cluttered as before with a vast array of trade goods.

For an instant the leopard was caught in the full beam as the Cadillac drove on to the ramp and the headlights were deflected upwards. The great cat was crouched on the summit of a neatly squared pile of packing-cases. As the light struck it, the leopard crouched, yellow-eyed, and puckered its lips into a snarl. The light glinted on its exposed canine fangs. Then it dropped out of sight behind the pile of cases.

'Did you notice the injury to its face?' Chetti Singh asked virtuously. 'You did that, and yet you accuse me of cruelty, Doctor Armstrong. The brute is extremely aggressive and impossible to control at the moment. I may have to destroy it. It is too dangerous, even to me and my men.'

'This will do.' Daniel ignored the rebuke. 'We can talk here.

Switch off the engine and the headlights.' Daniel reached up to the cabin light in the centre of the roof and a soft glow replaced the harsh white glare as the headlights faded.

They sat in silence for a while longer, and then Daniel asked quietly, 'So, Mr Singh, how and when did you first meet Ning Cheng Gong?'

'It was about three years ago. A mutual friend told me he was interested in ivory and other commodities which I could supply,' Chetti Singh answered.

'What were they, these other commodities?'

When Chetti Singh hesitated, Daniel jabbed him sharply with the shotgun barrels.

'Let us both keep to our side of the bargain,' he suggested mildly.

'Diamonds . . .' Chetti Singh wriggled away from the shotgun. 'From Namibia and Angola. Emeralds from Sandwana. Rare Tanzanite gemstones from the mines at Arusha in Tanzania, some dagga from Zululand . . .'

'You seem to have access to many sources of supply, Mr Singh.'

'I am a businessman, Doctor. I think I am good, probably the best. That is why Mr Ning dealt with me.'

'It was mutually beneficial, then?'

Chetti Singh shrugged. 'He was able to use the diplomatic bag. Absolutely secure shipment . . .'

'Except when the products were too bulky,' Daniel pointed out. 'As was this last consignment of ivory.'

'As you say,' Chetti Singh agreed. 'But even then his family connections were abundantly useful. Taiwan is a convenient *entrepôt.*'

'Give me the details of your transactions. Dates, commodities, values . . .'

'There were many,' Chetti Singh protested, 'I cannot remember them all.'

'You have just told me that you are a good businessman.' Daniel prodded him again, and Chetti Singh tried to avoid the shotgun barrel but he was already hard up against the door and could move no further. 'I'm sure you remember every single transaction.'

'All right,' he capitulated. 'The first was in early February three years ago. Ivory, value five thousand dollars. It was a trial shipment. It went well. At the end of that month there was a second transaction, rhino horn and ivory, sixty-two thousand dollars. In May of the same year, emeralds, four hundred thousand . . .'

Daniel had trained his memory over the years as an interviewer. He knew he could retain the details until he had a chance to write them down. The recital went on for almost twenty minutes. Chetti Singh was quick and incisive until suddenly he ended on a home note.

'Then this last shipment, the one you know about.'

'Good.' Daniel nodded. 'We come to the Chiwewe raid, at last. Whose idea was that, Mr Singh?'

'The ambassador. It was his idea,' Chetti Singh blurted.

'I think you are lying. It is highly unlikely that he could have known about the ivory godown. Its whereabouts are not public knowledge. I think that it was more likely your area of expertise . . .'

'All right,' Chetti Singh agreed. 'I have known about it for some years. I was awaiting an opportunity. However, Ning told me he wanted a large *coup*. His term of office was almost expired. He was returning home and he wanted to impress his family, his father.'

'But you recruited the raiders, didn't you? Ning could not have done that. He did not have your contacts.'

'I didn't give the orders to kill your friend,' Chetti Singh's voice trembled. 'I didn't want that to happen.'

'You were just going to leave them alive to tell their story, to explain to the police about Ning?'

'Yes – no, no! It was Ning's idea. I do not believe in killing, Doctor.'

'Is that why you sent Chawe and me into the mountains together?'

'No! You gave me no choice, Doctor Armstrong. Please, you must understand. I am a businessman, not a brigand.'

'All right, let's leave that for the moment. Now tell me, what was your further arrangement with Ning? Surely you were going to continue such a lucrative partnership, even after he returned to Taiwan?'

'No!'

'Please don't lie to me. That is breaking our agreement.' Daniel jammed the steel muzzles into him so hard that he squealed.

'Yes, all right, please you are hurting me. I can't speak if you do that.'

Daniel relaxed the pressure a little.

'I must warn you, Mr Singh, that I would be delighted if you gave me an opportunity to break our contract. Johnny Nzou's two daughters were about ten and eight years old. Your men raped them. His son Daniel, my godson, was just four. They beat his brains out against the wall. It was not a pretty sight. Yes, I would enjoy it if you reneged on our bargain.'

'I don't want to hear these things, please, Doctor. I am a family man, myself. You must believe that I didn't want—'

'Let's talk about Ning rather than your delicate sensibilities, Mr Singh. You and Ning have plans for the future, don't you?'

'We have discussed certain possibilities,' Chetti Singh admitted. 'The Ning family have vast holdings in Africa. After this last shipment of ivory, Cheng's status in the family will be absolutely enhanced. Cheng has expectations that his father will place him in charge of the African division of Lucky Dragon, that is the family holding company.'

'You have a niche in these plans, don't you? Your expert services will be in demand. Surely you have discussed it with Ning?'

'No—' Chetti Singh squealed again as the steel eyes of the shotgun barrels burrowed into his flesh. 'Please don't do that, Doctor. I suffer from high blood pressure; this uncivilised behaviour is absolutely prejudicial to my health.'

'What are your arrangements with Cheng?' Daniel insisted. 'Where will you operate next?'

'Ubomo,' Chetti Singh squeaked. 'Lucky Dragon plans to move into Ubomo.'

'Ubomo?' There was surprise in Daniel's tone. 'President Omeru?'

The sovereign state of Ubomo was one of the few success stories of the continent. Like Malawi, it nestled on the escarpment of the Great Rift Valley, a country of lakes and mountains, on the eastern flank of Africa, where open savannah and primeval equatorial forest met. Like Hastings Banda, President Omeru was another benevolent despot, ruling in the age-old African fashion. Thanks to him his country was free of debt, and not as yet divided or ravaged by tribal warfare.

Daniel knew that Omeru lived in a small brick cottage with a corrugated-iron roof and drove his own Landrover. No marble palaces, no stretched black Mercedes, no executive jet for him. He flew to the meetings of the Organization of African Unity in the tourist class cabin of a commercial airline as a deliberate example to his people. He was a beacon of hope, not the type to deal with Lucky Dragon.

'Omeru? I don't believe it,' Daniel said emphatically.

'Omeru is yesterday's man. He is old, redundant. He resists change and development. Soon he will go. It is being arranged. Soon there will be a new man in Ubomo, young, dynamic . . .'

'And greedy,' Daniel suggested. 'What will Cheng and Lucky Dragon have to do with all this?'

'I do not know the details. Cheng does not trust me that far. All I know is that he has asked me to deploy my people in Ubomo, to make my dispositions. Ready for the day.'

'When will it be?'

'I do not know. I told you. But I think soon.'

'This year? Next year?'

'I do not know, you must believe me, Doctor. I have held nothing back from you. I have fulfilled my part of the bargain. Now you must keep yours. I think you are a man of honour, an Englishman, a gentleman. Am I correct, Doctor?'

'What was our bargain, Mr Singh? Refresh my memory,' Daniel asked, never relaxing the pressure of the shotgun for a moment.

'After I told you all I know about Cheng, you promised to release me immediately, unharmed.'

'Have I harmed you, Mr Singh?'

'No, not yet.' But Chetti Singh was sweating again now, more copiously than before. The expression on the white man's face was murderous.

Daniel reached across him, and seized the door handle. It was so unexpected, so quick that Chetti Singh had no chance to react. He was hunched against the door, trying to get away from the shotgun.

'You are free to go, Mr Singh,' Daniel said softly. With one hand he wrenched open the driver's door of the Cadillac and placed his other hand in the centre of Chetti Singh's chest. With all the strength of his anger and disgust, he shoved.

The door flew open. Chetti Singh was leaning his full weight against it. The thrust of Daniel's arm hurled him outwards. He fell on his back on to the cement floor of the warehouse, and rolled over twice. He lay there stunned and paralysed with shock.

Daniel slammed the door of the Cadillac shut and locked it. He switched on the headlights. For a moment nothing changed. Chetti Singh lay on the floor outside the vehicle and Daniel stared down at him mercilessly through the shatterproof glass. Somewhere in the dim depths of the warehouse the leopard sawed hoarsely.

Chetti Singh bounded to his feet and threw himself against the side of the Cadillac, scrabbling at the window with his bare hands. His face contorted.

'You cannot do this to me. The leopard ... Please, Doctor.' His voice was muted by the intervening glass, but still the raw panic was shrill in his voice and a dribble of saliva broke from the corner of his mouth.

Daniel regarded him dispassionately, his arms folded and his jaw clenched.

'Anything,' screamed Chetti Singh. 'I'll give you anything ...' He glanced over his shoulder, and his expression was wild with terror as he turned back to Daniel. He had glimpsed that deadly shadow, circling silently in the gloom.

'Money,' he mouthed imploringly, slapping his pink palms on the glass. 'Please, I'll give you as much – a million dollars. I will give you anything. Just let me in. Please, please, I beg you, Doctor. Don't leave me out here.'

The leopard coughed, an abrupt explosion of sound filled with infinite menace. Chetti Singh spun round to face the darkness, cowering against the side of the vehicle.

'Get back, Nandi!' His voice was a high-pitched shriek. 'Back! Back to your cage!'

They both saw the leopard then, crouched in the alley between two walls of packing-cases. Its eyes reflected the head-lights, yellow and glittering. Its tail flicked back and forth with a mesmeric rhythm. It was watching Chetti Singh.

'No!' screamed Chetti Singh. 'No, you can't leave me to that brute. Please, Doctor. Please I implore you.'

The leopard raised its lip in a silent snarl of hatred and Chetti Singh urinated in a steady stream down the front of his khaki slacks. It puddled on the cement floor around his sandalled feet.

'It's going to kill me! This is inhuman. Please ... You can't allow this – please let me in.'

Suddenly Chetti Singh's nerve snapped. He pushed himself off the side of the Cadillac and ran for the closed main doors of the warehouse, a hundred feet away in the looming darkness. He had not covered half that distance before the cat was on him. It came from behind, snaking low across the bare cement floor, and rose to settle upon Chetti Singh's shoulders.

They looked like some grotesque hunchbacked creature with two heads, and then Chetti Singh was thrown forward by the leopard's weight and borne to the floor. In a kicking clawing tangle they rolled together, Chetti Singh's screams blending with the rattling growls of the leopard.

For a moment the man came to his knees, but instantly the leopard was on him again, going for his face. Chetti Singh tried to hold it off with his bare hands, thrusting them into its open jaws and the leopard clamped down on his wrist.

Even in the closed sedan Daniel heard the bones of the wrist go, crunching like dry toast, and Chetti Singh screamed on a shriller note. Goaded to superhuman effort by the pain he came to his feet with the leopard hanging on his arm.

He staggered in an erratic circle, beating at the cat with his fist, trying to break its grip on his other wrist. The leopard's back legs were slashing down the front of his thighs, ripping the khaki slacks, blood and urine mingling as the hooked yellow claws opened his flesh from groin to knee.

Chetti Singh blundered into a high pile of cardboard cartons, bringing them tumbling down around himself, and then his strength could no longer sustain the weight of the animal upon him. He collapsed again with the leopard still on top of him. The leopard ripped and bit and worried, and Chetti Singh's movements were becoming uncoordinated. Like an electric toy with a weakening battery he was slowing down. His screams were becoming feebler.

Daniel slid across to the controls of the Cadillac. As he started the engine, the leopard sprang back from its victim and stared at the vehicle uncertainly. Its tail lashed from side to side.

Daniel reversed slowly down off the loading ramp, and then manoeuvred the Cadillac so that its bulk would be between him and the leopard when he left the car and went to the door. He left the engine running and the headlights on and stepped out of the Cadillac. He watched the leopard steadfastly as he backed the few paces to the control-box. The leopard was almost thirty yards from him but he never took his eyes off it as he inserted the key into its slot and the heavy door rumbled open. He left the key in the slot, and then dropped the shotgun and backed out through the door.

He was careful not to run or to make any other hurried movement that might provoke the leopard, even though the body of the Cadillac should inhibit a charge, and the animal already had its victim. Daniel was now well out of the cat's attack circle.

Daniel turned at last and strode away into the night. He used Chawe's key-card to let himself out into the street, closed the main gates behind him and then broke into a jog-trot.

When they found Chetti Singh in the morning it would be apparent that for some unexplained reason he had gone to the wrong premises in response to the fire alarm call, and he had been attacked by his own animal while he was in the process of opening the warehouse door. The police would reason that left-hand drive controls of the Cadillac had made it necessary for him to leave the vehicle in order to operate the door controls. Daniel had left no fingerprints or other incriminating evidence behind him.

When he reached the furthest corner of the perimeter fence, Daniel paused and looked back. The glow of the Cadillac's headlights still lit the open warehouse door. He saw a dark feline shape, low and slinky, slip out through the door and streak to the high mesh of the perimeter fence. The leopard went over the fence with the ease of a bird taking flight.

Daniel smiled. He knew that the poor tormented brute would head unerringly for its home in the misty forested mountains. After what it had suffered, it deserved that freedom at least, he thought.

Thirty minutes later he reached the hired Volkswagen. He drove to the airport and parked it in one of the Avis bays. He dropped the keys in the return box of the locked and deserted Avis office and then went to his Landcruiser in the public car-park.

At the Capital Hotel he packed quickly, stuffing his few possessions into the canvas valise. He used one of his neckties as a sling for his arm. All that exertion had aggravated the injury. The sleepy night clerk at the hotel cashier's desk printed his credit card and he carried his own bag out to the Land-cruiser.

Unable to restrain his curiosity he drove past the Chetti Singh supermarket. There was no damage to the main building, although in the back alley a couple of firemen were still hosing down the pile of scorched garbage and the smoke-stained rear wall, watched by a dozen or so local residents in their night-clothes.

He turned westwards and left Lilongwe, heading back towards the Zambian border post. It was a three-hour drive. He turned on the radio and tuned to the early-morning service of Radio Malawi, listening to the music and news reports.

He was approaching the border post when it came on the six o'clock news. It was the second item after a report on the breaching of the Berlin Wall and the flood of East Germans to the West.

'Meanwhile, here in Lilongwe we have just received a report that a prominent Malawi businessman and entrepreneur has been savagely mauled by his own pet leopard. Mr Chetti Singh was rushed to the Lilongwe General Hospital where he is now in the intensive-care unit. A hospital spokesman said that Mr Singh was suffering from extensive injuries and his condition is described as critical. The circumstances of the attack are unknown, but the police are seeking an employee of Mr Singh's, a certain Mr Chawe Gundwana, who they hope will be able to assist them with their enquiries. Any person knowing the whereabouts of Mr Gundwana is asked to report to the nearest police station.'

Daniel switched off the radio and parked outside the Malawi customs and immigration post. He was expecting trouble. There might be an APB out on him already, especially if Chetti Singh was in a condition to speak and had given Daniel's name to the police. Chetti Singh's survival had not been part of Daniel's calculations. He had expected the leopard to do a more thorough job. His mistake had been in moving the Cadillac too soon. It had distracted the leopard from its victim.

One thing was certain: Chetti Singh was going to need a few gallons of blood transfusion. In Africa that involved an additional hazard.

He hummed his own version of the old song:

> Ashes to ashes
> and dust to dust.
> If the leopard don't get him,
> then HIV must.

Then with some trepidation, he took his passport into the border post. He need not have worried. The law was all smiles and courtesy.

'Did you enjoy your holiday in Malawi? We are always pleased to see you, sir. Come again soon, sir.'

Old Hastings Banda had them well trained. They all appreciated the vital role that tourism played in their lives. There was none of the have-not resentment that was so evident in other parts of the continent.

He folded a five-dollar bill into his passport as he approached the post on the Zambian side, a hundred yards in distance but, it seemed to him, a mighty leap back into the dark ages as he passed between the two countries.

He telephoned Michael Hargreave within an hour of arriving in Lusaka, and Michael invited him to dinner that evening.

'Where are you heading next, you roving bedouin you?' Wendy demanded as she served him a second helping of her famous Yorkshire pudding. 'God, what a lovely adventurous, romantic life you lead. I really must find you a wife; you make all our husbands restless. How long will you be with us?'

'That depends on what Michael can tell me about a mutual acquaintance called Ning Cheng Gong. If he's still in Harare, that's where I will be heading. If not, well, it's back to London, or possibly Taiwan.'

'You're still chasing after the Chink?' Michael asked, as he pulled the cork from a bottle of reasonable *deuxième cru* claret that had come out in the diplomatic bag. 'Are we allowed to know what it's all about yet?'

Daniel glanced at Wendy, and she pulled a face. 'Do you want me to go to the kitchen?'

'Don't be an ass, Wendy. I've never had any secrets from you,' Daniel soothed her, and then turned back to her husband. 'I have proved to my own satisfaction that Ning Cheng Gong arranged the attack on the Chiwewe ivory godown.'

Michael arrested the claret glass on the way to his lips. 'Oh dear. Now I see what it's all about. Johnny Nzou was your pal, I remember. But Ning! Are you sure? He's an ambassador, not a gangster.'

'He's both,' Daniel disagreed. 'His hatchet man was a Sikh from Lilongwe, name of Chetti Singh. They have quite a few secrets between them. Not only ivory, but everything else from drugs to diamonds.'

'Chetti Singh. I've heard that name recently.' Mike thought for only a second. 'Yes, on the news this morning. He was mauled by his own pet leopard, wasn't he?' His expression changed again. 'Just about the time you were in Lilongwe. What a coincidence, Danny. Has it got anything to do with your arm being in a sling, and your smug expression?'

'I'm a reformed character, you know me,' Daniel assured him. 'Would never dream of any rough stuff, but I did find out something from Chetti Singh during my brief chat to him before the unfortunate incident with the leopard. It's something that might interest you spooks at MI6.'

. Michael looked pained. 'Ladies present, old boy. We don't mention the firm like that. Never bruit it about. Bad form.'

Wendy stood up. 'On second thoughts, I *will* go and keep an eye on Cheffie. I'll be ten minutes, enough time for boy talk, I hope.' She took her wine-glass with her.

'Coast clear,' Michael murmured. 'Fire away, Danny.'

'Chetti Singh tells me that there is a *coup* being set up in Ubomo. Omeru is going to get the chop.'

'Oh, dear me; not Omeru. He wears a white hat. One of the good guys. That will never do. Have you any details?'

'Not many, I'm afraid. Ning Cheng Gong is in it, and his family, but not as principals, I suspect. I think they are merely eager sponsors of the proposed revolution, with expectations of rights and privileges later on.'

Michael nodded. 'Usual set-up. They get a slice of the pie when the new ruler of Ubomo divides it up. No idea who he will be?'

'None, I'm afraid, but it will be soon. My bet is within the next few months.'

'We'll have to get a warning to Omeru. The PM might want to fly in an SAS battalion to guard him. I know she's particularly pro the old boy and Ubomo is, after all, a member of the Commonwealth.'

'I'd be obliged if you could check up on Ning Cheng Gong while you're at it, Mike.'

'He's gone, Danny. Flown the coop. Spoke to my opposite number in Harare only this morning. Of course, I knew of your interest in him, so I dropped the question into the conversation. Ning held a farewell party at the Chinese embassy on Friday evening and flew home on Saturday.'

'Damn it,' Daniel exclaimed. 'That shoots down all my plans. I was going to go down to Harare—'

'Wouldn't have been a good idea,' Michael broke in. 'It's one thing feeding an ordinary law-abiding citizen to his own leopard, but one can't go around beating up ambassadors. It's considered very poor form indeed.'

'He's no longer ambassador,' Daniel pointed out. 'I could follow him to Taiwan.'

'Another very mediocre idea, if you don't mind my saying so. Taiwan is Ning's home wicket. From what I hear, his family all but owns the island. Whole place is sure to be bristling with Ning's uglies. If you're determined to play the avenging angel, best bide your time. If what you tell me is correct, Ning will be back in Africa soon. Ubomo is a nice neutral turf, better than Taiwan. At least I could back you up there. We've got an office in Kahali, the capital – in fact there is a chance that—' Michael broke off. 'Bit premature, but there is talk that I may be sent to Kahali on my next posting.'

Daniel stared into his glass, swilling the contents slowly as though admiring the ruby lights in the wine. At last he sighed and nodded.

'You're right, as always.' He grinned at Michael ruefully. 'I was getting carried away, besides which I'm terrifyingly short of cash. Doubt I could raise the airfare to Taipei.'

'Never have believed it of you, old boy. Thought you were rolling in the filthy stuff. Always been green with envy. All those million-dollar TV contracts.'

'Everything I have is wrapped up in those video cassettes you sent to London for me. Not worth a damn until I cut and dub them. That's what I'll have to do right now.'

'Before you go, you'd better give me a briefing on all you know about this pair, Singh and Ning. I'll follow up on my side, in case . . .'

'In case anything happens to me,' Daniel finished for him.

'Never said that, old boy. Perish the thought. Although this time you do seem to have picked on a pair of heavyweights.'

'I'd like to leave my Landcruiser and all my gear here in Lusaka with you in the usual way, if that isn't inconvenient?'

'Pleasure, dear boy. My home is your home. My garage is your garage. Feel free.'

The next morning Daniel returned to the Hargreaves' home. Michael was at work, but Wendy and her domestic staff helped him unpack the Landcruiser. His equipment was stiff with dust and the accumulated filth of six months' bush living. Between them they cleaned it all and repacked it into the vehicle. They threw away the perishables and Daniel made a list of replacements. Then he parked the Landcruiser in the spare garage, and put the battery on charge, ready for his next expedition, whenever that might be.

When Michael came home for lunch from the High Commission, he and Daniel spent an hour sequestered in his study. After that the three of them split a bottle of wine, sitting under the marula trees beside the swimming-pool.

'I passed on your message to London,' Michael told him. 'Apparently Omeru is in London at the moment. The Foreign Office had an urgent word with him, but it didn't do much good, by all accounts. Without chapter and verse – and your intelligence was rather vague – the old boy pooh-poohed the idea of a *coup*. "My people love me," he said, or words to that effect. "I am their father." Turned down the PM's offer of support. Nevertheless Omeru is cutting short his visit, and going back to Ubomo, so we might have done some good.'

'Probably sent him straight into the jaws of the lion,' Daniel said morosely, and watched Wendy heaping his plate with fresh salad grown in her own vegetable garden.

'Probably,' Michael agreed cheerfully. 'Poor old blighter. Speaking of lion's jaws, and that sort of thing, I have more news for you. I buzzed our man in Lilongwe. Your friend Chetti Singh is off the danger list. Hospital describes his condition as "serious but stable", although they did have to amputate one arm. Seems as though the leopard chewed it up rather thoroughly.'

'Wish it had been his head.'

'Can't have everything, can we? Must be thankful for small mercies. Anyway, I'll keep you posted while you are in London. Have you still got that flat in Chelsea, near Sloane Square?'

'It's not a flat,' said Wendy. 'Bachelor house of ill-repute, more like it.'

'Nonsense, old girl,' Michael twitted her. 'Danny is a monk; never touches the stuff – do you? Is the telephone number the same, 730-something? I've got it written down somewhere.'

'Yes, same address. Same number.'

'I'll ring you if anything comes up.'

'What can I bring you from London when I come back, Wendy?'

'You can bring me the entire stock of Fortnum's,' she sighed. 'No, I'm joking. Just some of those special biscuits in the yellow tin; I hallucinate about them. And some Floris soap, and perfume, Fracas. Oh! And undies from Janet Reger the same as you brought last time, and while you're about it, some real English tea, Earl Grey.'

'Easy, old girl,' Michael chided her. 'Lad's not a camel, you know. Keep it down to a ton.'

Later that afternoon, they drove Daniel out to the airport and put him on the British Airways flight. It landed at Heathrow at seven the next morning.

 That same evening the telephone in Daniel's Chelsea flat rang. Nobody knew he was back in town. He debated with himself whether to make the effort to answer it, and gave in after the tenth peal. He couldn't ignore such persistence.

'Danny, is it really you, or that cursed answering machine? I refuse to talk to a robot, matter of principle.'

He recognised Michael Hargreave's voice immediately.

'What is it, Mike? Is Wendy okay? Where are you?'

'Still in Lusaka. Both of us fine, old boy. More than I can say for your pal, Omeru. You were right, Danny. News has just broken. He's got the axe. Military *coup*. We've just had a signal from our office in Kahali.'

'What's happened to Omeru? Who's the new man in power?'

'Don't know to both questions. Sorry, Danny. It's all a bit confused still. Should be on the BBC news your end, but I'll ring again tomorrow as soon as I have any more details.'

That evening it was tucked in at the end of the news on BBC 1 over a file photograph of President Victor Omeru. Just a bare statement of the *coup d'état* in Ubomo, and the takeover by a military junta. On the TV screen Omeru was a craggily handsome man in his late sixties. His hair was a silver fleece and he was light-skinned, the colour of old amber. His gaze from the television screen was calm and direct. Then the weather forecast came on and Daniel was left with a sense of melancholy.

He had met Victor Omeru only once, five years ago, when the President had granted him an interview covering the dispute with Zaïre and Uganda over the fishing rights in Lake Albert. They had spent only an hour together, but Daniel had been impressed by the old man's eloquence and presence, and even more so by his obvious commitment to his people, to all the various tribal groupings that made up his little state, and to the preservation of the forest, savannah and lakes that were their national heritage.

'We see the riches of our lakes and forests as an asset that must be managed for posterity, not something that is to be devoured at a single sitting. We look upon nature's bounty as a renewable resource which all the people of Ubomo have the right to share, even those generations as yet unborn. That is why we resist the plunder of the lakes by our neighbours,' Victor Omeru had told him, and it was wisdom of a kind that Daniel had seldom heard from any other statesman. His heart had gone out to someone who shared his own love and concern for the land that had given them birth. Now Victor Omeru was gone and Africa would be a poorer, sadder place for his passing.

Daniel spent the whole of Monday in the City talking to his bank-manager and his agent. It went well and Daniel was in a far better mood when he returned to the flat at nine-thirty that evening.

There was another message from Michael on the answering machine. 'God, I hate this contraption. Call me when you come in, Danny.'

It would be two hours later in Lusaka, but he took Michael at his word.

'Did I get you out of bed, Mike?'

'No matter, Danny. Hadn't turned the light off yet. Just one bit of news for you. The new man in Ubomo is Colonel Ephrem Taffari. Forty-two years old. Apparently educated at London School of Economics and University of Budapest. Other than that, nobody knows much about him except that he has already changed the country's name to the People's Democratic Republic of Ubomo. Bad sign. In African Socialist-speak "democratic" means "tyrannical". There have been reports of executions of members of the former government, but one expects that.'

'What about Omeru?' Daniel demanded. It was strange how strongly his sympathies inclined towards someone he had known for such a short time so long ago.

'Not specifically mentioned on the butcher's bill, but presumed to be amongst those put to the wall.'

'Let me know if you pick up anything about my friends Chetti Singh or Ning Cheng Gong.'

'Will do, Danny.'

 Now Daniel put the events in Ubomo out of his mind and his world shrank down to the space enclosed by the four walls of the cutting-room at the studio in Shepherd's Bush. Day after day, he sat in the semi-darkness, concentrating his entire being on the small glowing screen of the editing console.

In the evenings, dizzy with mental exhaustion and red-eyed with strain, he staggered out into the street and caught a taxi back to the flat, stopping only at Partridge's in Sloane Street to pick up the makings of a sandwich supper. Each morning he awoke in darkness before dawn and was back at the studio long before the daily commuter invasion of the city was under way.

He was caught up in an ecstasy of creative endeavour. It heightened his emotional awareness to the point where all of his existence was in those lambent images that flashed before his eyes. The words to describe them bloomed in his mind so that he spoke into the microphone of the recorder with only occasional references to his notes.

He relived every moment of the scenes that unfolded before him to the point where he could smell the hot dusty musky perfume of Africa and hear the voices of her people and the cries of her animals ringing in his ears as he worked.

So great was Daniel's absorption in the creative process of dubbing and fine cutting his series that over the weeks that

212

followed the recent events in Africa retreated into the mists of distance. It was only when, with a shock that started his adrenalin flowing, he saw Johnny Nzou's face looking at him out of the small screen and heard his voice speak from beyond the grave, that it all rushed back upon him and he felt his determination grow stronger.

Alone in the darkened cutting-room he replied to Johnny's image, 'I'm coming back. I haven't forgotten you. They haven't got away with what they did to you. I promise you that, old friend.'

By the end of February, three months after he had started the editing, he had a rough cut of the first four episodes of the series ready to show his agent. Elna Markham had sold his very first production and they had been together ever since. He trusted her judgement, and stood in awe of her business acumen.

She had an uncanny ability to judge to within a dollar just how much the trade would bear, and then to squeeze that very last dollar out of the deal. She wrote a formidable contract which covered every conceivable contingency, and several that fell outside that definition. She had once written a spin-off clause into one of his contracts. He had smiled at it when he read it, but two years later it had yielded a wholly unexpected royalty of fifty thousand dollars from Japan, a country that hadn't even entered into Daniel's original calculations.

At forty years of age, Elna was tall and willowy with dark Jewish eyes and a figure like a *Vogue* model. Once or twice over the years, they had almost become lovers. The closest they had come to it was three years previously, when they had shared a bottle of Dom Perignon in his flat to celebrate a particularly lucrative sale of subsidiary rights. She had drawn back from the very brink.

'You are one of the most attractive men I have ever met, Danny, and I'm sure we'd make tremendous music together, but still you're more valuable to me as a client than as just another good romp.' She had buttoned up her blouse and left him to the agonies of sexual frustration.

Now they spent the morning in the preview theatre at the studios watching the first four episodes straight through, back

213

to back. Elna made no comment until the last tape was played out, then she stood up.

'I'll take you to lunch,' she said.

In the taxi she talked of everything but the production. She took him to Mosimann's in West Halkin Street. The club that Anton Mosimann had fashioned out of an old church was now a high cathedral of gastronomy. Anton himself, resplendent in his whites and his tall chef's hat, rosy-complexioned as a cherub, came out of his kitchens to chat to them at their table, an honour afforded only to his more favoured members.

Daniel was in a fever of anxiety to learn Elna's opinion of his work, but this was an old trick of hers to build up tension and expectation. He played along with her, discussing the menu and chatting unconcernedly about irrelevancies. Only when she ordered a bottle of Corton-Charlemagne did he know for certain that she liked it.

Then she flashed dark Jewish eyes at him over the rim of the glass and said in that husky sexy voice, 'Marvellous, Armstrong, bloody marvellous. Your best yet, I kid you not. I want four copies immediately.'

He laughed with relief. 'You can't sell it yet – it's not finished.'

'Can't I? You just watch my dust.'

She showed it to the Italians first. They always favoured his work. The Italians had an historical and emotional interest in Africa, and over the years Italy had proved to be one of Daniel's best markets. He loved the Italians and they loved him.

A week later Elna brought the draft Italian contract around to his flat. Daniel contributed a plateful of smoked salmon sandwiches and a bottle to the proceedings and they sat on the floor, put Beethoven on the CD player and ate the sandwiches while Elna went over the contract with him.

'They liked it as much as I did,' she told him. 'I've jacked them up twenty-five per cent on the last advance they gave us.'

'You're a witch,' Daniel told her. 'It's black magic.' The Italian advance almost covered the entire cost of production of the series. The rest of it would all be profit. The big gamble had paid off handsomely, and he had no backers to share it with. After Elna had taken her commission, it was all his. He tried to estimate what his ultimate pay-off would be. Half a million certainly; probably a lot more, depending on the Americans. When all the world rights had been sold, it might be as much as three million dollars. He had impressed even himself.

After ten years of hard work, he had broken clear. No more overdrafts; no more taking his begging bowl from one arrogant sponsor to another. From now on he had charge of his own destiny; he had creative and artistic control over his work, and the rights to the final cut. In future it would be the way he wanted it, not the view imposed upon him by his backers.

It was a good feeling, a bloody wonderful feeling.

'What have you got lined up for the future?' Elna asked as she helped herself to the last of the smoked salmon.

'I haven't thought about it yet,' he lied. He always had two or three projects in the warming oven of his mind. 'I still have to finish the last two episodes.'

'I've had a few approaches from interested parties with money to invest. One of the big oil companies wants you to do a series on the South African apartheid society and the effect of sanctions on—'

'Hell, no!' It was marvellous to be able to turn down an offer of work in such a peremptory fashion. 'That's all cold porridge and last night's leftovers. The world is changing. Just look at Eastern Europe. Apartheid and sanctions are yesterday's news. They won't even exist by this time next year. I want something fresh and exciting. I've been thinking about the rain forests – not the Brazilian forests, that's been done and overdone, but the African equatorial region. It's one of the very few unknown parts left on this planet, yet ecologically it's of vast importance.'

'Sounds good. When will you start?'

'My God, you are a hard taskmistress. I haven't even finished the last one and you're on to me about the next.'

'Since Aaron divorced me, somebody has to keep me in the style to which I've grown accustomed.'

215

'All the duties of matrimony with none of the privileges and pleasures.' He sighed dramatically.

'You still on about that, silly boy. You could talk me into it yet, and you might not like it. Aaron didn't.'

'Aaron was a big prick,' Daniel said.

'That was part of the trouble,' she chuckled, huskily sexy. 'He wasn't.' Then she changed the subject. 'By the way, what happened between you and Jock? I had a very strange phone call from him. He said you'd had a major punch-up. He implied that you had blown your mind and gone over the top, nearly got him into all sorts of trouble. He said that you and he would not be working together again. Is that right?'

'Not to put too fine a point on it, yes, that's right. We have come to a parting of the ways.'

'Pity. He has done some fantastic work on this "Africa Dying" series. Do you have a replacement cameraman in mind?'

'I don't. Do you?'

She thought about it for a while. 'Would you have any objection to working with a female?'

'I can't think why I should, as long as she can stand the pace. Africa is a raw, rough country. It takes a certain resilience and toughness to cope with the physical conditions.'

Elna smiled. 'The lady I have in mind is tough enough and talented enough. You have my word on it. She's just done a piece for the BBC on the Arctic and the Inuit Indians, Eskimos to you. It's good, very good.'

'I'd like to see it.'

'I'll get you a print.'

Elna sent the tape round to the studio the next day but Daniel was so totally involved in his own work that he dropped it into a drawer of his desk. He meant to view it that evening, but instead he let it slide.

Three days after he had finished the series, the tape was still in his desk, forgotten in the excitement of all the other things which were happening around him.

Then Michael Hargreave called from Lusaka again. 'Danny, I'm going to send you a bill for these calls. Costing HM Government a ruddy fortune.'

'I'll buy you a case of bubbly next time I see you.'

'You must be in the chips, dear boy, but I'll accept the offer. The good news is that your friend, Chetti Singh, is out of hospital.'

'Are you sure, Mike?'

'Good as new. Remarkable recovery, so they tell me. I had our man in Lilongwe check it for me. Only one arm, but apart from that Chetti Singh is back in business. You'll have to send him another leopard for Christmas, the last one didn't work.'

Daniel chuckled ruefully. 'Did you hear anything of my other pal?'

'The Chink? Sorry, not a dickie bird. Gone home to Daddy and the Lucky Dragon.'

'Let me know if he pitches up. I won't be able to leave London for a couple of months at least. It's all happening here.'

Daniel was not exaggerating. Elna had just sold the 'Africa Dying' series to Channel 4 for the highest price ever paid for an independent production. They were also breaking their advance planning and screening the first episode at prime time on Sunday evening six weeks from now.

'I'm going to throw a viewing party for you on the big night,' Elna told him. 'Oh God, Danny, I always knew you were the tops. It's so good to be able to prove it. I've invited people from all the Continental and North American stations to watch it. This is going to take them by storm, believe me.'

The Saturday before the party she rang Daniel at his flat. 'Have you had a chance to look at that tape I sent you?'

'Which one?'

'Which means you haven't,' she groaned. 'The tape about the Arctic, "Arctic Dream", the one shot by that camerawoman, Bonny Mahon. Don't be obtuse, Danny.'

'Damn! I'm sorry, Elna, I just haven't had a chance to get around to it.'

'I've invited her to the party,' she warned him.

'I'll look at it now, right away,' he promised, and went to rescue the tape from his desk drawer.

He had been intending to skip-view the tape, but found that he was not able to give it such a cavalier treatment. From the opening sequence he found himself captivated.

It opened with an aerial sequence of the eternal ice of the far north, and the images which followed were striking and unforgettable. There was a particular sequence of a vast herd of barren ground caribou swimming across one of the open leads in the ice. The low yellow sun was behind them so that when the herd bull rose from the dark water and shook himself, he filled the air around him with a cloud of golden droplets which framed him in a precious nimbus like an animal deity from some pagan religion.

Daniel found himself enthralled to the point where his professional judgement was suspended. Only after the tape had run to its conclusion did he attempt to analyse how the camerawoman had achieved her effects. Bonny Mahon had understood how to use the extraordinary light to endow it with a texture and mood that reminded him overpoweringly of the luminous and ethereal masterpieces of Turner.

If he were ever to work in the gloomy depths of the equatorial forests, that use of available light would be critical. There was no doubt that she had the gift of exploiting it. He looked forward to meeting her.

For the viewing party Elna Markham had hired half a dozen extra television sets, and placed them in strategic positions in her flat, including the guest toilet. She was determined that no one should have an excuse for missing the event that they had all assembled to celebrate.

As befitted the guest of honour, Daniel arrived half an hour late and had to fight his way in through the front door. Elna's parties were extremely popular, and the large drawing-room was bulging at the seams. Fortunately it was a balmy May evening, and the guests had overflowed on to the terrace overlooking the river.

For six months Daniel had lived like a recluse. It was good to have human contact again. Of course, he knew most of those present and his reputation was such that they sought him out eagerly. He was the centre of an ever-changing circle of admirers, most of them old friends, and he was vain enough to enjoy the attention, although he knew just how ephemeral it could be. In this business, you were only as good as your last production.

Despite the gay and amusing company, Daniel felt his nerves screwing up tight as the hour approached, and he found it harder to concentrate on the clever conversation and repartee that flitted and sparkled in the air around his head like a flock of humming-birds. Not even the prettiest of the many lovely ladies present could hold his attention for long.

Finally Elna clapped her hands and called them to order. 'People! People! This is it!' And she went from room to room, switching on the television sets, tuning them to Channel 4. There was a noisy chatter of expectation as the opening credits began to roll and the theme music swelled and then the first sequence of Daniel's production opened with a view that was the spirit of Africa distilled to its essence.

There was a scorched sepia plain on which the scattered acacia trees stood dark green with twisted stems and flat anvil heads. A single elephant strode across the plain, an old bull, grey and wrinkled, his tusks stained with vegetable juices, thick and curved and massive. He moved with ponderous majesty, while around him fluttered a shining cloud of white egrets, their wings pearly and translucent. On the far horizon, against the aching African blue of the sky, floated the snowy pyramid of Kilimanjaro, detached from the burned ochre earth by the heat mirage. It had the same ethereal delicacy as the egrets' wings.

The tipsy laughter and chatter quietened and the crowded rooms fell silent, captivated by the timeless and eternal majesty of the vision that Daniel evoked for them.

Then they gasped with shock as the two old matriarchs of the Zambezi herd charged together headlong from the screen, tattered ears flapping, red earth dashed from under their great pads, until their wild infuriated squeals were cut off abruptly by the crash of gunfire. The bullet-strikes were an ostrich feather of dust dancing for an instant on the seared grey skin of each of their foreheads, and then the mountainous carcasses fell

219

to earth, twitching and shuddering in the dreadful palsy of the brain shot.

For forty-five minutes Daniel led his audience captive in golden chains of imagination through the majestic and ravaged continent. He showed them unearthly beauty and cruelty and ugliness, by contrast all the more shocking.

As the last image faded, the silence persisted for several seconds. Then they began to stir and come back to reality across six thousand miles. Someone clapped softly and the applause swelled and went on and on. Elna came to stand beside Daniel. She said nothing but took his hand and squeezed it.

After a while Daniel felt that he had to escape the crush of human bodies, and the boisterous congratulations. He needed space to breathe. He slipped out on to the terrace.

He stood alone at the railing and looked down, but did not see the boat lights on the dark Thames. Already he was experiencing the first reaction to the heady elation that had buoyed him up through the first part of the evening. His own images of Africa had moved him and saddened him. He should have been inured to them by now, but it was not so. Particularly disturbing had been the sequence with Johnny Nzou and the elephants. Johnny had been there all the time, at the periphery of his conscious mind all these months, but now his full-blown memory emerged again.

Suddenly, overpoweringly, the urge to return to Africa came upon Daniel with all its old force. He felt restless and discontented. Others might applaud what he had done, but for him it was over. His nomadic soul urged him onwards. Already it was time to move, to make for the next horizon, the next tantalising adventure.

Somebody touched his arm. For a moment he did not respond. Then he turned his head to find a girl beside him. She had red hair. That was the first impression he had of her, thick bushy, flaring red hair. The hand on his arm had a disconcerting, almost masculine, strength. She was tall, almost as tall as he was, and her features were generous – a wide mouth and full lips, a large nose saved from masculinity by the upturned tip and delicately sculpted nostrils.

'I've been trying to get to you all evening,' she said. Her voice was deep with a self-assured timbre. 'But you're the man of the moment.'

She was not pretty. Her skin was heavily freckled from sun and wind, but she had a clean outdoors glow. In the terrace lights her eyes were bright and green, fringed with lashes as dense and thick as bronze wire filaments. They gave her a candid and quizzical air.

'Elna promised to introduce us, but I've given up waiting for it to happen. I'm Bonny Mahon.' She grinned like a tomboy and he liked her.

'Elna gave me a tape of yours.' He offered his hand and she took it in a firm strong grip. All right, he thought, she's tough, as Elna said she was. Africa won't daunt her. 'You're good. You have an eye and an instinct for the light. You're very good.'

'So are you.' Her grin widened. 'I'd like to work with you some time.' She was direct, unaffected. He liked her even more.

Then he smelt her. She wore no perfume. It was the true undisguised smell of her skin, warm, strong and aphrodisiac.

'It could happen,' he told her. 'It could happen sooner than either of us suspects.' He was still holding her hand and she made no effort to withdraw it. They were both aware of the sexual ambiguity in his last remark. He thought that it would be exciting to take this woman to Africa with him.

Some miles north of where Daniel and Bonny stood on the terrace and appraised each other both professionally and physically, another person had watched the first episode of 'Africa Dying'.

Sir Peter 'Tug' Harrison was the major shareholder and CEO of British Overseas Steam Ship Co. Ltd. Although BOSS was still listed under 'Shipping' on the London Stock Exchange it had changed its nature entirely in the fifty years since Tug Harrison had acquired a controlling interest in it.

It had started out in the late Victorian era running a small fleet of tramp steamers to Africa and the Orient, but it had never prospered greatly and Tug had taken it over at the outbreak of the Second World War for a fraction of its value. With the profits of its wartime operation Tug had branched out in many directions and BOSS was now one of the most powerful conglomerates listed on the London Stock Exchange.

Tug had always been sensitive to the vagaries of public opinion and to the image that his company projected. He had as strong an instinct for these subtleties as he had for the commodity index and the fluctuations on the world stock markets. It was one of the reasons for his huge success.

'The mood is green,' he had told his board only a month ago. 'Bright green. Whether or not we agree with this new passion for nature and the environment, we have to take cognisance of it. We have to ride the green wave.'

Now he sat in his study on the third floor of his home in Holland Park. The house stood in the centre of a row of magnificent townhouses. It was one of the most prestigious addresses in London. The study was panelled in African hardwood from BOSS's concessions in Nigeria. The panels were selected and matched and polished so that they glowed like precious marble. There were only two paintings hanging on the panels, for the wood grain itself was a natural work of art. The painting facing the desk was a Madonna and Child from Paul Gauguin's first sojourn in the South Pacific islands, and the other painting, which hung behind him, was a Picasso, a great barbaric and erotic image of a bull and a nude woman. The pagan and profane set off the lyrical and luminous quality of the Mother and God-child.

Guarding the doorway was a set of rhinoceros horns. There was a burnished spot on one of the horns, polished by Tug Harrison's right hand over the decades. He stroked it each time he entered or left the room. It was a superstitious ritual. The horns were his good-luck charms.

As an eighteen-year-old lad, penniless and hungry, owning nothing but an old rifle and a handful of cartridges, he had followed that rhino bull into the shimmering deserts of the Sudan. Thirty miles from the banks of the Nile, he had killed the bull with a single bullet to the brain. Blood from a severed artery in its head had washed a little runnel in the desert earth, and from the bottom of the shallow excavation Tug Harrison had picked out a glassy stone with a waxy sheen that had almost filled the palm of his hand.

That diamond was the beginning. His luck had changed from the day of the rhino. He had kept the horns, and still he reached out to them every time he was within arm's length of them. To him they were more valuable than either of the fabulous paintings that flanked them.

He had been born in Liverpool's slums during the First World War, son of a drunken market porter, and had run away to sea at the age of sixteen. He had jumped ship at Dar es Salaam to escape the sexual attentions of a brutal first mate, and had discovered the mystery and the beauty and promise that was Africa. For Tug Harrison that promise had been fulfilled. The riches that he had wrested from the harsh African soil had made him one of the hundred richest men in the entire world.

The television set was artistically concealed behind the hardwood panelling. The controls were set into the intercom panel on his desk-top. Like most intelligent and busy men, he shunned the mindless outpourings of the television programmes, limiting his viewing to selected programmes, mostly the news and current affairs items.

However, anything African was his vital interest and he had noted the title 'Africa Dying' and punched the programme time into his desk-top alarm.

The discreet electronic chimes aroused him from his study of the financial statements which lay on the pigskin blotter in front of him. He touched the controls, and the panel in the wall directly across the figured-silk Qum carpet from his desk slid open.

He adjusted the volume of sound as the theme music floated into the room. Then the image of a great elephant and a snowy peak filled the screen, and instantly he was transported back fifty years and thousands of miles in time and space. He watched without moving until the final frame faded. Then he reached out to touch the controls. The screen went black and the silent panel closed like a sleepy eyelid.

Tug Harrison sat for a long time in silence. At last he picked up the eighteen-carat gold pen from the desk set and scribbled a name on his note-pad. 'Daniel Armstrong.' Then he swivelled his chair and took down his copy of *Who's Who* from the bookshelf.

Daniel walked from Shepherd's Bush to Holland Park. Just because he was a potential millionaire didn't mean he should toss away a fiver on a few minutes' taxi ride. The weather was bright and warm and the trees in the squares and parks were decked in early summer greenery. As he strode along, glancing with abstract appreciation at the girls in their thin dresses and short skirts, he was thinking about Tug Harrison.

Ever since Elna Markham had phoned him to pass on Harrison's invitation, he had been intrigued. Of course, he knew of the man. Harrison's tentacles reached into every corner of the African continent, from Egypt to the banks of the Limpopo river.

Daniel knew the power and wealth of BOSS and its influence in Africa but little about the man behind it. Tug Harrison was a man who seemed to have a knack for steering well clear of public controversy and the attentions of the tabloid press.

Wherever Daniel travelled in Africa these days he could discern Tug Harrison's influence, like the spoor of a cunning old man-eating lion. He left his tracks, but like the beast he was seldom seen in the flesh.

Daniel pondered the reasons for Harrison's peculiar success on the African continent.

He understood the African mind as few white men could. He had learned as a lad in the lonely hunting and prospecting camps in the remote wilderness, when his only companions for months on end had been black men. He spoke a dozen African languages but, more important, he understood the oblique and lateral reasoning of the African. He liked Africans, felt comfortable in their company, and knew how to inspire their trust. On

224

his African travels Daniel had met men and women of mixed blood whose mothers were Turkana or Shona or Kikuyu, and who boasted that Tug Harrison was their true father. There was never any proof of their claims, of course, but often these people were in positions of influence and affluence.

There were very seldom news reports or photographs of Harrison's visits to the African continent, but his Gulfstream executive jet was often parked discreetly at the furthest end of the airport tarmac in Lusaka or Kinshasa or Nairobi.

Rumour placed him as an honoured guest and confidant in Mobutu's marble palaces or at Kenneth Kaunda's presidential residence in Lusaka. They said that he was one of the very few who had access to the shadowy Renamo guerrillas in Mozambique as well as to the guerrilla bush camps of Savimbi in Angola. He was also welcomed by the legitimate regimes that they opposed. They said that he could pick up the telephone at any hour of the day or night and within minutes be speaking to de Klerk or Mugabe or Daniel Arap Moi.

He was the broker, the courier, the adviser, the banker, the go-between, and the negotiator for the continent.

Daniel was looking forward to meeting him. He had tried many times before, without success. Now as an invited guest he stood outside the imposing front door and felt a little tickle of nerves. That premonition had served him well in the African bush; it had warned him so often of dangerous beasts and even more dangerous men.

A black servant in flowing white kanza and red fez opened the front door. When Daniel spoke to him in fluent Swahili, the wooden mask of his face cracked into a huge white smile.

He led Daniel up the wide marble staircase. There were fresh flowers in the niches of the landings, and Daniel recognised some of the paintings from Harrison's fabled art collection gracing the walls – Sisley, Dufy and Matisse.

Before the tall double doors of red Rhodesian teak, the servant stood aside and bowed. Daniel strode into the room and paused in the centre of the silk Qum carpet.

Tug Harrison rose from behind his desk. It was at once obvious how he had earned his nickname. He was big-boned but compact, although the exquisitely tailored pin-stripe suit smoothed the raw powerful angles of his frame and the heavy jut of his belly.

He was bald, except for a fringe of silver hair like that of a tonsured monk. His pate was pale and smooth while the skin of his face was thickened and creased and tanned where it had been unprotected by a hat from the tropical sun. His jaw was determined and his eyes were sharp and piercing, giving warning of the ruthless intelligence behind them.

'Armstrong,' he said. 'Good of you to come.' His voice was warm as molasses, too soft for the rest of him. He held out his hand across the desk, forcing Daniel to come to him, a subtle little dominance ploy.

'Good of you to ask me, Harrison.' Daniel took his cue and eschewed the use of his title, setting equal terms. The older man's eyes crinkled in acknowledgement.

They shook hands, examining each other, feeling the physical power of each other's grip without letting it develop into a boyish contest of strength. Harrison waved him to the buttoned leather chair beneath the Gauguin and spoke to the servant.

'*Letta chai*, Selibi. You will take tea, won't you, Armstrong?'

While the servant poured the tea, Daniel glanced at the rhino horns on the entrance wall.

'You don't see trophies like that often,' he said, and Harrison left his desk and crossed to the doorway.

He stroked one of the horns, caressing it as though it were the limb of a beautiful and beloved woman. 'No, you don't,' he agreed. 'I was a boy when I shot them. Followed the old bull for fifteen days. It was November and the temperature at midday was 120 degrees in the shade. Fifteen days, two hundred miles through the desert.' He shook his head. 'The crazy things we do when we are young.'

'The crazy things we do when we are older,' Daniel said, and Harrison chuckled.

'You are right. Life is no fun unless you are at least a touch crazy.'

He took the cup that the servant offered him. 'Thank you, Selibi. Close the doors when you leave.'

The servant drew the double doors closed and Harrison went back to his desk.

226

'I watched your production on Channel 4 the other night,' he said, and Daniel inclined his head and waited.

Harrison sipped his tea. The delicate porcelain cup looked fragile in his hands. They were battler's hands, scarred and ravaged by tropical sun and hard physical labour and ancient conflicts. The knuckles were enlarged but the nails were carefully manicured.

Harrison put the cup and saucer down on the desk in front of him and looked up at Daniel again.

'You got it right,' he said. 'You got it exactly right.'

Daniel made no comment. He sensed that any modest or deprecating comment would only irritate this man.

'You got your facts straight, and you drew the right conclusions. It was a refreshing change after all the sentimental and ill-informed crap that we hear every day. You put your finger on the roots of Africa's problems, tribalism and overpopulation and ignorance and corruption. The solutions you suggested made sense.' Harrison nodded. 'Yes, you got it right.'

He stared at Daniel thoughtfully. Harrison's faded blue eyes gave him a strangely enigmatic expression, like a blind man.

Don't relax, Daniel warned himself. Not for a moment. Don't let the flattery soften you up. This is what it's all about. He's stalking you like an old lion.

'Someone in your position is able to influence public opinion as others are never able to do,' Harrison murmured. 'You have a reputation, an international audience. People trust your vision. They base their view on what you tell them. That's good.' He nodded even more emphatically. 'That's very good. I would like to help and encourage you.'

'Thank you.' Daniel let a small ironical smile lift one side of his mouth. One thing he was certain of: Tug Harrison did nothing without good reason. He made no free gifts of his help and encouragement.

'What do they call you, your friends? Daniel, Dan, Danny?'

'Danny.'

'My friends call me Tug.'

'I know,' Daniel said.

'Our thinking is so much in accord. We share the same commitment to Africa. I think we should be friends, Danny.'

227

'All right, Tug.'

Harrison smiled. 'You have every reason to be suspicious I understand. I have a certain reputation. One should not always judge a man on his reputation, however.'

'That is true.' Daniel smiled back at him. 'Now tell me what you want from me.'

'Damn it!' Harrison chuckled. 'I like you. I think we understand each other. We both believe that man has a right to exist upon this planet, and that, as the dominant animal species, he has the right to exploit the earth for his own benefit, just as long as he does so on a basis of sustained and renewable yield.'

'Yes,' Daniel agreed. 'I believe that.'

'It is the balanced, pragmatic view. I would expect no less of a man of your intelligence. In Europe man has been farming the earth, felling the forests and killing the animals for centuries, and yet the earth is more fertile, the forests denser, the animals more numerous than they were a thousand years ago.'

'Except downwind of Chernobyl, or where the acid rain falls,' Daniel pointed out. 'But yes, I agree; Europe isn't in bad shape. Africa is another story.'

Harrison cut in, 'You and I love Africa. I feel that it is our duty to combat its evils. I can do something to alleviate the grinding poverty in some parts of the continent, and by investment and guidance offer some of the African people a better way of life. You, with your special gifts, are in a position to counter much of the ignorance that exists about Africa. You can clear the woolly-headed confusion of the armchair-conservationists and urban animal rights fanatics, those who are so cut off from the earth and the forests and the animals that they are actually menacing the elements of nature which they believe they are protecting.'

Daniel nodded thoughtfully and non-committally. It was weak tactics to disagree with the man until he had listened to everything he had to say, and heard the full proposal that Harrison was obviously working towards. 'In principle all you say makes excellent sense. However, if you could be a little more specific, Tug.'

'Right,' Harrison agreed. 'Of course you know the state of Ubomo, don't you?'

Daniel felt a little electric shock tickle the hair at the back of his neck. It was so unexpected and yet, in some bizarre manner, he felt that it was predestined. Something had been leading him inexorably in that direction. It took him a moment to recover himself, then he said, 'Ubomo, the land of the red earth. Yes, I have been there, though I can't claim to be an expert on the country.'

'Since independence from Britain in the sixties, it has been a little backwater.' Harrison shrugged. 'There wasn't much to know about it. It was the fief of an arrogant old dictator who resisted all change and progress.'

'Victor Omeru,' Daniel said. 'I met him once, but it was years ago, when he was bickering with his neighbours about the fishing rights in the lake.'

'That was typical of the man. He resisted all change on principle. He wanted to keep to the traditional ways and customs. He wanted to keep his people docile and compliant.' Harrison shook his head. 'Anyway, that is all history. Omeru has gone and there is a dynamic young man at the head of government. President Ephrem Taffari is there to open up the country and bring his people into the twentieth century. Apart from the fishing rights, Ubomo has considerable natural assets. Timber and minerals. For twenty years I have tried to convince Omeru that these should be developed for the benefit of his people. He has resisted with a blind intransigence.'

'Yes. He was stubborn,' Daniel agreed. 'But I liked him.'

'Oh, yes, he was a lovable old codger,' Harrison agreed. 'But that is no longer relevant. The country is ripe and ready for development and, on behalf of an international consortium of which BOSS is the leading member, I have negotiated the concession to undertake a major part of this development.'

'Doesn't sound as though you need me, then.'

'I wish it were as easy as that.' Harrison shook his head. 'We are being overtaken by the wave of hysteria that is sweeping the world. It is a psychological law that every mass popular movement is hi-jacked by fanatics and pushed beyond the dictates of reason and common sense. The pendulum of public feeling always swings too far in each direction.'

'You are running into opposition to your plans to develop

the natural resources of Ubomo. Is that what you are trying to tell me, Tug?'

Harrison cocked his head on one side. He looked like an eagle when he did that, a great bald-headed bird of prey. 'You are direct, young man, but I should have expected that.' He sat down behind his desk and picked up an ivory-handled duelling pistol which he used as a paper weight. He spun it on his forefinger and the gold inlay on the barrel sparkled like a Catherine-wheel.

'There was a female scientist working in Ubomo during Omeru's presidency,' he went on at last. 'She and the old man had a close relationship and he gave her all sorts of special privileges that he denied other journalists and researchers. She published a book on the forest-dwellers of Ubomo. You and I would call them pygmies, although that term is unfashionable in today's climate. The title was . . .' Harrison paused to think, and Daniel intervened.

'The title was *The People of the Tall Trees*. Yes, I have read the book. The author's name is Kelly Kinnear.'

'Have you met her?' Harrison demanded.

'No.' Daniel shook his head. 'But I would like to. She writes well. Her style reminds me of Rachel Carson. She is a—'

'She is a trouble-maker,' Harrison cut in bluntly. 'She is a shit-stirrer.' The coarse term seemed uncharacteristic of him.

'You'll have to explain that to me.' Daniel kept his voice even and his expression neutral. He didn't want to declare his sentiments until he had heard Harrison out.

'When he came to power, President Taffari sent for this woman. She was working in the forest at the time. He explained to her his plans for the advancement and development of the country, and asked for her support and her assistance. The meeting was not a success. Kelly Kinnear had some misguided sense of loyalty to old President Omeru and she resisted President Taffari's overtures of friendship. She is entitled to her views, of course, but then she began a campaign of agitation within Ubomo's borders. She accused Taffari of violations of human rights. She also accused him of planning to rape the country's natural resources by uncontrolled exploitation.' Harrison threw up those powerful scarred hands. 'In fact she went into female hysterics and attacked the new government in every way she was able. There was no logic nor reason nor even factual basis for these attacks. Taffari had no alternative but to send her packing. He chucked her out of Ubomo. She is, as you probably know, a British subject, and she ended up back here in the UK. However, she had not learned her lesson and she continues her campaign against the government of Ubomo.'

'BOSS has nothing to fear from someone like that, surely?' Daniel probed gently, and Harrison looked across at him sharply, searching for traces of irony in the question. Then he transferred his attention back to the duelling pistol in his right hand.

'Unfortunately, the woman has built up a foundation of influence on the strength of her writings. She is articulate and,' he hesitated, 'and personable. She manages to hide her fanaticism under a cloak of reasoned logic which is, needless to say, based on false assumptions and distorted facts. She has managed to recruit the support of the Green Party in this country and on the Continent. You are right, BOSS has nothing to fear from such an obvious charlatan, but she is a nuisance. She looks good on television. Now she has come to know of our interest in Ubomo and the plans that our consortium has to develop the area. She and her supporters are making a great deal of noise. You might have seen that piece in the *Guardian* recently?'

'No.' Daniel shook his head. 'I don't read the *Guardian*, and I've been pretty busy recently. I'm a little out of touch.'

'Well, take my word for it then, it is making life just a trifle uncomfortable for me. I have shareholders to answer to and an annual general meeting coming up. Now, I've just learned that this woman has acquired a small block of shares in BOSS, which gives her the right to attend the AGM and to speak. You can be certain she will have the radical press and a bunch of those lunatics from "Friends of the Earth" there with her, and she will make a circus of the occasion.'

'Awkward, Tug.' Daniel nodded, stifling his smile. 'How can I help you?'

'Your influence in public and scientific circles is far greater than Kelly Kinnear's. I have spoken to many people in various disciplines and diverse walks of life about you. You are well

231

respected; your views on Africa are taken seriously. What I propose is that you go to Ubomo and make a documentary that sets out the true facts and examines the issues that this Kinnear woman has raised. It would blow her away like a puff of smoke. Television is a much more powerful medium than the printed word, and I could guarantee you maximum exposure. BOSS owns extensive media interests . . .'

Daniel listened to him with rising incredulity. It was like listening to a client propositioning a prostitute for the performance of a particularly lurid perversion. He felt the urge to laugh with outrage, to reject violently this insult to his integrity. This man truly believed that he was for sale. It took an effort for him to sit still and listen expressionlessly.

'Of course, I could also guarantee that you would receive the whole-hearted co-operation of President Taffari and his government. They would provide everything that you require. You need only ask and there would be military transport – helicopters, lake patrol boats – at your disposal. You could go anywhere, even into the closed area of the forest reservations. You could speak to anybody . . .'

'To political prisoners?' Daniel could not help himself. It slipped out.

'Political prisoners?' Harrison repeated. 'What the hell would you want to speak to politicals for? This will be a documentary on the environment and the development of a backward society.'

'Just suppose I did want to talk to political detainees,' Daniel insisted.

'Look here, young man. Taffari is a progressive leader, one of the few honest and committed leaders on the continent. I don't think he is holding any political prisoners. It isn't his style.'

'What happened to Omeru?' Daniel asked, leaning forward intently, and Harrison laid the duelling pistol on the blotter in front of him. Its barrels were pointing at Daniel's chest.

'Do I detect hostility towards the Ubomo government?' he asked softly. 'Towards my proposition?'

'No,' Daniel denied it. 'I just have to know what I'm getting myself into. I'm a businessman, like you, Tug. I want the hard facts, not the hard sell. You understand that. I'm sure you'd want the same, if you were in my position. If I'm going to put my name to something, I must know what it is.'

'All right.' Harrison relaxed. He understood that explanation. 'Omeru was an obstinate old man. Taffari had no option but to hold him incommunicado during the transition period. He was under house-arrest, being treated well. He had access to his lawyers and his doctor when he died of a heart attack. Taffari has not announced his death yet. It would seem to point in undesirable directions.'

'Like summary execution without trial,' Daniel suggested. He felt a pang of mourning for the old president.

'It might look like that,' Harrison agreed, 'although I am assured by Taffari – and I have every reason to believe him – that it was not the case.'

'All right, I accept your assurance on that point,' Daniel said. 'Now what about the costs of this production? It wouldn't be cheap. Off the top of my head, I would estimate the cost at a couple of million. I take it that you would want a first-rate job. Who pays for that? BOSS?'

'That would be a little obvious,' Harrison demurred. 'It would reduce the stature of your production to a simple piece of company propaganda. No, I would arrange outside finance. The money would come through a far eastern company. Although it is a member of the consortium, it is not openly associated with BOSS at this stage. They own a film company in Hong Kong which we would use as a front.'

'What is the name of the parent company? And where is it based?' Daniel asked. He felt the first tiny premonition, that sense of predestination that had disturbed him before.

'The parent company is Taiwanese, not well known but very rich, very powerful. First-class people to deal with, I assure you, but of course, I would personally underwrite any contract that you have with them.'

'What is the company's name?'

'It's a rather flamboyant name, but typically Chinese. The Lucky Dragon Company.'

Daniel stared at him, unable to speak for a moment. In some strange fashion Ning Cheng Gong's destiny had been linked

233

with his by the murder of Johnny Nzou. He knew that it had to be played out to the very end.

'Is something worrying you, Danny?' Harrison looked concerned and Daniel realised that he had allowed his agitation to show.

'No. I was just considering your proposal. On principle I accept the assignment.' He took a grip on himself. 'Subject to contract, of course. There would be many items to negotiate. I would want a percentage of the total gross, an agreed advertising budget, choice of my own crew, especially the cameraman, and I'd want final cut.'

'I am sure we'll be able to come together on the details.' Harrison smiled, and with one finger rotated the duelling pistol until the barrels were no longer pointed at Daniel's chest. 'Ask your agent to call me as soon as she can. And now I think the sun is definitely over the yard-arm. We can drink to our arrangement in something a little more substantial than Darjeeling.'

'Look here, Bonny, it would be much easier if you had an agent,' Daniel told her seriously. 'I don't enjoy haggling with you. I believe an artist's job is to be creative, not to waste talent examining the fine print in a contract.'

'You've been honest with me. I'll be frank with you, Danny. I don't like shelling out twenty per cent of my hard-earned gelt to a middleman. Besides which, I don't agree with you. Writing a contract of employment can be as creatively satisfying as painting a picture or setting up a camera angle.' She kicked off her shoes. Her bare feet were strong and shapely as her hands. She twisted her long denim-clad legs under her and settled back on his buttoned leather sofa. 'Let's talk business.'

'Okay, let's do it,' he capitulated. 'On principle I won't pay a crew by the hour, and I don't recognise overtime. We work whenever there is work to do, and for as long as it takes. We go wherever I say, and we live off the land. No five-star accommodation.'

'That sounds to me like two thousand a week,' she said sweetly.

'Dollars?'

'This isn't New York, brother Dan. It's London. Pounds.'

'That's stiff. I don't get anywhere near that myself,' he protested.

'No, but you probably get twenty per cent of the gross, whereas I will have to be content with a lousy five per cent.'

'Five per cent of the gross on top of two thousand a week.' Daniel looked horrified. 'You have to be joking.'

'If I were joking, I'd be smiling, wouldn't I?'

'I've never given a cut to a cameraman — forgive me, a camera person before.'

'Once you get used to the idea, you won't find it unbearably painful.'

'I tell you what, let's call it twelve hundred a week, and forget about any percentage.'

'The acoustics are terrible in here. I can't believe what I thought I just heard. I mean, you wouldn't want to insult me, would you, Danny boy?'

'Would you do me a favour, Miss Mahon? Would you do up the top button of your shirt while we talk?'

The upper part of her chest was freckled like her face. It showed in the deep V of her open neck, but below a clear line where the sun had not stained it, her skin was as white as buttermilk. Under the thin cotton shirt her breasts, unfettered by any brassière, were tight and firm.

She glanced down into her deep cleavage. 'Is there something wrong with them?' She grinned slyly.

'No. Nothing at all. That's what I'm complaining about.'

She closed the button. 'Did I hear you say seventeen-fifty and four per cent?' she asked.

'You are right. There is something wrong with the acoustics,' he agreed. 'I said fifteen hundred and one and a half per cent.'

'Two per cent,' she wheedled him, and when he sighed and agreed, she added craftily, 'And a hundred a day location allowance.'

It took them almost three hours to hammer out the terms of her employment and at the end he found his liking for her tempered by respect. She was a hard lassie.

'Do we need a letter of intent?' he asked. 'Or will a handshake do?'

'A handshake will do fine,' she answered. 'As long as I have a letter of intent to back it up.'

He went through to his office and tapped out a draft of their agreement on his word-processor, and called her through to check the text on the screen. She stood behind him and leaned over his shoulder to read it. One of her breasts pressed taut and weightily on his shoulder. It was warm as a tsama melon that had lain in the desert under the Kalahari sun.

'You didn't put in the bit about first-class air tickets,' she pointed out. 'And the salary to commence from date of signature.'

The smell of her skin that he had noticed on their first meeting was more pronounced. He inhaled it with pleasure. It reminded him forcefully that he had been celibate for almost a year.

'Good boy,' she complimented him as he made the alterations she requested. 'That will do very nicely indeed.' The timbre of her voice had altered, it was softer and more resonant. There was also a subtle change in the odour of her body as well. He recognised the heady musk of female arousal; she was pumping the air full of pheromones which put his own hormones on red alert.

He was having difficulty concentrating as he ran off four copies of the agreement, one for each of them and another each for Elna and BOSS's legal department.

Bonny reached over him to sign all four copies, and now she pressed herself against his back and her breath was hot on his cheek. She handed the pen to him and he signed below her.

'Handshake?' he asked, and offered his open right hand. She ignored it, and instead reached over his shoulder and unbuttoned his shirt. She ran her hand down inside it.

'I can think of something more binding than a plain little old handshake,' she whispered, and pinched his nipple between her fingernails. He gasped; it was more pleasure than pain.

'Danny boy, you and I are going to be alone in the jungle for six months or so. I'm a girl of healthy appetites. It's going to happen sooner or later. It might as well be sooner. It would be

236

hell if we waited until we got out there and then found that we didn't like it. Don't you agree?'

'Your logic is irrefutable,' he laughed, but it was shaky and rough. She took a pinch of his chest curls and used it as a goad to force him to his feet.

'Where's the bedroom? We might as well be comfortable.'

'Follow me.' He took her by the hand and led her to the door.

Standing in the centre of the bedroom floor she stepped back when he tried to embrace her. 'No,' she said. 'Don't touch me. Not yet. I want to draw it out until it's unbearable.'

She stood facing him, an arm's length between them. 'Do what I do,' she ordered, and began to unbutton her shirt.

Her nipples were tiny, like miniature rosebuds, carved from pale pink coral.

'You're as hairy and muscular as a grizzly bear. It gives me goose bumps,' she said, and he saw her nipples rise into rosy points. The colour darkened and the skin surrounding them puckered. His own flesh responded even more dramatically, and she stared at him shamelessly and chuckled as she unbuckled her own belt.

Her jeans were tight and she wriggled and squirmed to get them down.

'Exodus,' he said, 'chapter three.'

'That's not original.' She glanced down at herself complacently. 'I've had the quotation applied to myself before, the burning bush.' She combed her fingernails lingeringly through the thick mop of flaming curls at the base of her flat white belly. It was so crisp and dense that it rustled. It was one of the most excruciatingly erotic gestures he had ever watched.

'Come on,' she encouraged him. 'You're falling behind.'

He dropped his own trousers around his ankles.

'Who have we here?' She studied him frankly. 'Standing to attention and positively aching to sacrifice himself in the burning bush?' And she reached out to capture him expertly. 'Come along, my little mannikin,' she murmured throatily, grinning that sly tomboy grin and led him to bed.

BOSS's head office was at Blackfriars in the City, just opposite the pub that stood on the site of the old monastery that gave the area its name.

Daniel and Bonny came out of the main entrance of the tube station and paused to stare at the building.

'Shit!' said Bonny sweetly. 'It's imperial Roman rococo, with just a touch of Barnum and Bailey.'

BOSS House made the Unilever building down the street look insubstantial. For each of Unilever's Greek columns it had four, for each of Unilever's statues of the Olympian gods, it had a dozen. Where Unilever had used granite, BOSS had built in marble.

'If I'd seen this first I'd have held out for five thousand a week.' Bonny squeezed his arm. 'I think I've been done in more ways than one.'

They climbed the steps to the main entrance, while the statues of the gods frowned down at them from the pediment, and went in through the revolving glass doors. The floor of the entrance lobby was in a chessboard pattern of black and white marble. The roof was vaulted and gilded, with panels in the rococo style depicting either the Last Judgement or the Ten Commandments. It wasn't easy to tell which, but there was a great deal of action in progress between the nymphs and cherubs and seraphim.

'Bless us, Father, for we have sinned.' Bonny rolled her eyes at the ceiling cheerfully.

'Yes, but wasn't it fun!' Daniel murmured.

The senior public relations officer was waiting for them at the reception counter. He wore a dark three-piece suit and projected the BOSS image of the young executive.

'Hello, I'm Pickering,' he greeted them. 'You must be Doctor Armstrong and Miss Mahon.' He took Bonny's hand and eyed her quickly from the top of her flaming coiffure to her cowboy boots, clearly torn between disapproval of her denims and beaded leather waistcoat and hearty approval of her bosom. 'I'm supposed to set up a Ubomo briefing for you.'

'Fine. Let's get on with it then.' Daniel managed to divert his attention from Bonny's cleavage, and Pickering led them up the sweeping opera house staircase, giving them his tourist-guide patter as they went.

He pointed out the mirrored panels. 'French, of course, from Versailles after the Revolution. And those two are Gainsboroughs; the tapestry is Aubusson; that's a Constable . . .'

They left behind them the splendours of the public rooms and plunged into labyrinthine corridors in the upper rear of the building, passing scores of tiny offices divided by prefabricated partitions in which the BOSS battalions laboured under the humming air-conditioning units. Very few people raised their heads as the three of them passed.

'Cattle.' Bonny nudged Daniel. 'How can they stand life in this abattoir of the spirit?'

Eventually Pickering ushered them into a conference room. Clearly it was the venue of the lower and middle-ranking executives. The floors were covered with industrial stud-rubber tiles and the partition walls displayed charts of the company's administrative organisation and departmental structures. The furniture was laminate and chrome, with plastic upholstery.

Daniel smiled as he imagined how this room would probably contrast with the magnificence of the main boardroom that must be situated somewhere in the front of the building, close to Tug Harrison's personal office.

There were four men waiting for them, clustered around the table of snacks and refreshments in the corner. Pickering introduced them.

'This is George Anderson, one of our senior geologists; he is in charge of the Ubomo mineral developments. This is his assistant Jeff Aitkens. And this is Sidney Green who co-ordinates the timber and fishing concessions in Ubomo, and this is Neville Lawrence from our legal section. He will also be able to answer any questions you may have on the financial projections. Now, may I offer you a sherry?'

Bonny Mahon's presence did more than the cheap sherry to relax the atmosphere.

Pickering allowed them ten minutes, then he shepherded them to their plastic-covered chairs at the imitation-walnut-veneered conference table.

'Well, now. I'm not going to stand too much on ceremony here. This is *en famille*. My instructions are that this is to be a totally frank and open briefing. You must feel free, Doctor Armstrong, to ask whatever questions occur to you, and we will try our best to answer them. First of all just let me say how delighted and excited we are that BOSS is to be associated with this enormous project to uplift the Ubomo economy and to develop the rich natural resources of that beautiful little country for the good of all its citizens.' He allowed himself a sanctimonious smirk and then adopted a more businesslike tone. 'BOSS's concessions fall into four categories. Firstly, there are the mining and mineral deposits. Secondly, the timber and agricultural developments. Thirdly, the fishing and aquaculture projects, and lastly, the hotel, casino and tourist industry. We hope that the development of all these resources will eventually lead to Ubomo becoming one of the most prosperous little countries on the African continent. Before I ask our experts to discuss the economic potential of Ubomo in detail, I'm going to give you some background figures and facts. Let's put the map of Ubomo up on the screen.'

Pickering turned to the console of the audio-visual equipment and adjusted the overhead lighting.

'All right. Here we go.' The map of Ubomo appeared on the screen on the end wall. 'The People's Democratic Republic of Ubomo,' he intoned, 'is situated between Lakes Albert and Edward on the escarpment of the Great Rift Valley in eastern central Africa. It is bounded on the west by Zaïre, the former Belgian Congo, and on the east by Uganda . . .' Pickering pointed out the boundaries and the main features. 'The capital, Kahali, lies on the lakeshore below the foothills of the Ruwenzori range or, as they are more romantically known, the Mountains of the Moon. The first European explorer to chronicle the existence of these mountains was Captain John Hanning Speke who travelled in this area in 1862.'

Pickering changed the display on the screen. 'The total population of Ubomo is estimated at four million, although there has never been a census. You can see the breakdown into tribes. The largest tribe is the Uhali. However, the new President Taffari and most of his military council are Hita. In all a total of eleven tribal groups are represented in Ubomo, the smallest of which is the Bambuti, commonly known as the pygmies. About twenty-five thousand of these diminutive people live in the northern equatorial rain forests of the country. This is where BOSS's major mineral concessions are situated.'

Pickering was good at his job. He had assembled his information carefully and presented it in a lively and interesting fashion. However, there was very little he had to tell them that Daniel did not already know.

Bonny asked a few questions and Pickering addressed his replies to her bosom. Daniel found that Pickering's inability to take his eyes off those protuberances was beginning to irritate him. Daniel had conceived a proprietary interest of his own in this area.

After Pickering, the other company experts rose in succession to elaborate on BOSS's plans. Sidney Green showed them architect's impressions of the resorts and casinos that they would build upon the lakeshore. 'We anticipate the main tourist trade would come from southern Europe, particularly Italy and France. Flying time from Rome under eight hours. We are looking at an eventual half-million visitors a year. Apart from tourism we are planning a major aquaculture industry . . .'

He went on to explain how the lake waters would be pumped into shallow dams in which freshwater shrimp and other exotic aquatic life would be cultured.

'We are aiming for an eventual annual harvest of a million tons of dried protein from aquaculture, together with another million tons of dried and frozen fish from the lakes themselves. We are considering the possibility of introducing high-yield fish populations to the lakes to augment the indigenous species.'

'What about the effect of these enterprises on the ecology of the lake itself?' Daniel asked diffidently. 'Particularly the construction of the marinas and yacht harbours and the introduction of exotic species such as carp and Asian shrimp to the lake waters.'

Green smiled like a second-hand car salesman. 'These are at present being fully investigated by a team of experts. We expect their report to be ready by the middle of the year. However, we do not anticipate any problems in that area.'

Quite right, Daniel thought. They aren't going to make waves if my new and good friend Tug is hiring and firing.

Sidney Green swept forward, still smiling, to discuss the agricultural potential.

'In the low-lying wooded savannah that covers the eastern half of the country the tsetse fly, *glossina morsitans*, closes a great deal of prime country to cattle-ranching. At the earliest opportunity we, in co-operation with the Ubomo government, will undertake a programme of aerial spraying to eradicate this insect menace. Once this is done, beef production will be of great importance to the economy.'

'Aerial spraying?' Daniel asked. 'What chemicals will be used?'

'I am pleased to say that BOSS has acquired several thousand tons of Selfrin at most favourable prices.'

'Would the favourable price have anything to do with the fact that Selfrin has been banned in the continental United States and in the European Common Market countries?'

'I assure you, Doctor Armstrong,' Green smiled blandly, 'that the use of Selfrin has not been banned in Ubomo.'

'Oh, that's good.' Daniel nodded, and returned his smile. He had smelled Selfrin in the Okavango swamps and the Zambezi valley. He had seen the devastation of entire insect species and the birds and small mammals that fed upon them. 'As long as it's legal, nobody can have any objection, can they?'

'Quite so, Doctor Armstrong.' Sidney Green changed the display on the lecture screen. 'Those areas of the savannah that are unsuitable for cattle-breeding will be planted with cotton and sugar cane. Irrigation water will be pumped from the lakes. The swamps and wetlands in the north will be drained — but these, of course, are long-term projects. Our immediate cash flow will be assured by logging operations in the timber-rich forests of the western mountain range.'

'The "Tall Trees",' Daniel murmured.

'I beg your pardon?'

'No, nothing of importance. Please continue. I'm finding this fascinating.'

'Of course, the logging operation will be carried out in concert with the mining operations. Neither project on its own

242

would be profitable, but carried out in unison each becomes highly lucrative. In fact the timber will cover the direct cost of the development and the mineral recovery will be almost entirely profit. However, I will leave George Anderson, our senior geologist, to explain all this to you.'

Anderson's expression was as stony as one of his geological samples. His style was terse and dry.

'The only viable mineral deposits so far discovered in Ubomo lie in the north-western quadrant, below the forests that cover the lower northern slopes of the mountain range and lie within the basin of the Ubomo River.' He moved the cursor on the map display in a slow northern sweep. 'This forest cover consists of almost fifty varieties of economically significant trees, amongst which are the African oak, the African mahogany, the African walnut, the red cedar and the silk-cotton tree. I will not weary you with their botanical names, but suffice it to say that their existence holds out major economic advantages, as my colleague has pointed out.' He nodded wearily at Green, who flashed his bright salesman smile in return.

'The forest soils are for the most part leached laterites, the colour of which gives the Ubomo River its name, the Red River, and indeed the country itself, the Land of Red Earth. Fortunately, these soils are very thin, generally less than fifty feet in depth, and below them lies a folded pre-Cambrian formation.' He gave a dry and weary little smile. 'Again, I will not tax you with the technicalities, but these soils contain significant quantities of the rare earth, monazite, together with viable deposits of platinum almost evenly distributed in the upper levels. This series is unique. There is no other known formation that comprises this particular spectrum of minerals. Each of these individual minerals occurs in low concentrates, in some cases they are mere traces. Separately none of these would be workable, but taken together they will be highly lucrative, and their profitability will be enhanced by the valuable stands of timber harvested in the process of exposing the ore body.'

'Excuse me, Mr Anderson,' Daniel interrupted. 'Are you considering strip-mining the Ubomo river basin?'

George Anderson looked as though he had experienced a sudden stomach cramp.

'Doctor Armstrong, the term "strip-mining" is an emotionally charged one, filled with negative undertones. BOSS has never undertaken strip-mining operations anywhere in the world. I must be very firm on that issue.'

'I beg your pardon, I thought that the company's copper mines at Quantra in Chile were strip-mines.'

Anderson looked affronted. 'Open-cast mines, Doctor Armstrong, not strip-mines.'

'Is there a difference?'

'Of course there is. However, I think that this is neither the time nor the place to examine those differences. Just let me say that the open-cast mines that we intend developing in Ubomo will take full account of the sensitive environment of the area. We will operate on a refill-and-renew policy. BOSS has a green approach to nature. In fact, Doctor Armstrong, we are convinced that in the long term the environment will be significantly improved by what we are going to do for the country.'

He looked at Daniel challengingly, and Daniel almost rose to accept it. Then with an effort he forced himself to smile and nod. 'You must excuse me playing the devil's advocate, Mr Anderson. These are the kind of questions people will ask, and I must be able to answer them. That's what BOSS is paying me for.'

Anderson looked mollified. 'Yes, of course. However, I must reiterate. BOSS is a green company. It's Sir Peter's firm policy. I know he is even considering altering the company logo. As you know the present design is a miner's pickaxe and a ploughshare. Well, he intends adding a green tree, to show our concern for nature.'

'I think that's very tasteful.' Daniel smiled placatingly. He knew that this discussion would be reported to Tug Harrison – there was even a likelihood that at this moment it was being recorded. If he displayed open hostility and opposition to the company, his free ticket to Ubomo and his contact with the Lucky Dragon and Ning Cheng Gong would evaporate. 'With the assurances that you gentlemen have given me, I will be able to go to Ubomo with a clear conscience and I will endeavour to show the world the enormous benefits that will accrue to the country from the intensive development that the BOSS consortium is undertaking.'

He spoke for the benefit of the hidden microphones, and then paused for emphasis. 'Now, what I want from you is an architectural mock-up of the hotel and casino development on the lakeshore. I'd like to film the area as it is today, and then superimpose the concept over it, to bring out the best features of the design and how it blends into the natural background.'

'Sidney Green will take care of that, I'm sure.' Pickering nodded.

'Right, then I want details of the present per capita income of the average Ubomo citizen, and an estimate of what that income will be in, say, five or ten years' time, after the full benefits of the development programme begin to make themselves felt.'

'You'll see to that, won't you, Neville?'

The meeting ran on for another half hour before Daniel summed up with a note of finality. 'As a film-maker, I have to have a theme for this production. The general concept of Africa these days is one of a continent in trauma, plagued by seemingly insurmountable problems, demographic, economic and political. I want to strike a different note here. I want to show the world how it could be, how it should be. I see the theme of my production as . . .' He paused for dramatic effect, and then held up his hand to frame an imaginary screen. '"Ubomo, High Road to the African Future".'

The men at the table burst into spontaneous applause, and Pickering refilled the sherry-glasses.

As he escorted Daniel and Bonny back to the front of the building Pickering told them jovially, 'I say, that went rather well. I think you both made a very good impression.' He beamed like an approving schoolmaster. 'And now a little treat in store for you. Sir Peter Harrison, himself . . .' his voice took on a reverential tone, as though he had mentioned the name of a deity, 'Sir Peter in person has expressed the wish to have a word with you and Miss Mahon.'

He did not wait for their agreement but led them to the elevators.

They waited a mere five minutes in the antechamber to Tug Harrison's office, barely long enough to appreciate the priceless works of art displayed on the walls and in the glass-fronted cabinets. Then one of three comely secretaries looked up and smiled.

'Please follow me. Sir Peter is expecting you.'

As she led them towards the door at the far end of the antechamber, Pickering dropped away. 'I'll be waiting for you outside. Don't stay more than three minutes. Sir Peter is a busy man.'

The tall windows of Harrison's office looked out across the Thames to the National Theatre. As he turned from the window, the sunlight flashed off his bald head like a heliograph.

'Danny,' he said, offering his gnarled right hand. 'Have they looked after you?'

'Couldn't be better,' Daniel assured him. 'On the strength of what they've told me, I have come up with a theme for the production, "Ubomo, High Road to the African Future".'

'I like it!' said Tug Harrison without hesitation, but he was studying Bonny Mahon as he said it. The approbation could have been as much for her as for Daniel's title.

Exactly three minutes after they had entered the inner sanctum of BOSS, Tug Harrison drew back the cuff of his Turnbull and Asser shirt. Both his cuff-links and his wristwatch were of gold and diamonds.

'It was good to see you, Danny. Very pleasant meeting you, Miss Mahon, and now, if you'll excuse me . . .'

At the front doors of the BOSS building, Pickering had a taxi waiting for them.

'It's on the company account,' he said, shaking hands and giving Bonny's bosom a wistful farewell appraisal. 'It will take you wherever you want to go.'

'Caviar Kaspia,' Daniel told the driver recklessly, and when they were seated at a window table in the discreetly panelled front room of the lovely little restaurant, Bonny whispered, 'Who is paying?'

'BOSS,' he assured her.

'In that case I'll have 250 grams of the Beluga, with hot blinis and cream.'

'Spot on,' Daniel agreed. 'I'll join you and we'll split a bottle of bubbly. What do you fancy, Pol Roger, or the Widow?'

'What I truly fancy can wait until after lunch when we get

246

back to your flat, but in the meantime a glass of the Widow will help to pass the time – and build up your strength.' She slanted her eyes lewdly. 'You are going to need it. That's a direct threat.'

Bonny tucked into the caviar with the relish and appetite of a schoolboy at half-term.

'So what did you think of BOSS?' Daniel asked.

'I think Tug Harrison is one very sexy man. The smell of serious money and power is a stronger aphrodisiac than caviar and champagne.' She grinned at him with sour cream rimming the fine coppery down on her upper lip. 'Does that make you jealous? If it doesn't, it was meant to.'

'I am devastated. But apart from Harrison's sex appeal, what did you think of BOSS's plans for Ubomo?'

'Mind-boggling!' she enthused through a half-chewed blini. It was an expression that particularly irritated Daniel. 'Awesome!' That was even worse. 'If only you paid me enough to enable me to buy a block of BOSS shares! Someone is going to make a bagful of tom in Ubomo.'

'That's all there is to it?' Daniel smiled to make a joke of it. Yet was this the girl who had conjured up that hauntingly evocative sequence of caribou in the Arctic sunlight? 'A bagful of tom? Is that it?'

For a moment she looked mystified by the question, and then she dismissed it light-heartedly. 'Of course. What else is there, lover?' She mopped up the last grains of the Beluga with a scrap of blini pancake. 'Do you think that your newly acquired expense account could run to another pot of fish eggs? Not often a poor working girl gets a shot at them.'

 Bonny Mahon was nervous. It was an unfamiliar sensation. The skirt and stockings felt just as unfamiliar. She was accustomed to the firmer embrace of denim. However, the occasion was sufficiently unusual to call for a change of her customary attire. She had even gone to the extraordinary lengths of visiting a hairdressing salon. Usually she managed or, she grinned at the thought, mismanaged her own hairstyle. She had to admit that the girl at Michaeljohn had done a better job.

She considered her reflection in one of the gilt-framed antique mirrors opposite where she sat in the lobby of the Ritz Hotel in Piccadilly.

'Not bad,' she admitted. 'I could pass for a lady at a hundred paces.' She preened her new curls which were fashionably anointed with gel. It was an uncharacteristic gesture, a symptom of the nervous anticipation with which she regarded the coming meeting.

The female secretary who had arranged the meeting over the telephone had suggested that the car pick her up at her lodgings. Bonny had shied away from the idea. She didn't want anybody to see her digs; she was economising and the area of south London where she presently resided was hardly salubrious.

The Ritz was the first alternative rendezvous that came to mind. It was more the image that she wished to project. Even though his secretary had arranged the date she had high hopes for what would come out of it.

'I mean, it just has to be a proposition, doesn't it?' she reassured herself. 'There was no doubt about the way he looked at me. I've never been wrong about that before. He's got a head of steam for me.'

She glanced at her wristwatch. It was exactly seven-thirty. He was the type who would make a point of being punctual, she thought, and when she looked expectantly towards the main doors a page was already coming towards her. She had taken the precaution of tipping the doorman and telling him where to find her.

'Your car has arrived, madam,' the page informed her.

A Rolls-Royce stood at the kerb. It was an iridescent pearly grey and the windows were smoked and opaque, giving the magnificent vehicle a surrealistic appearance.

The handsome young chauffeur, who wore a dove-grey uniform and cap with a patent-leather brim, greeted her as she came down the steps.

'Miss Mahon? Good evening.'

He opened the rear passenger door and stood aside for her.

Bonny settled into the sensual embrace of the soft grey Connolly leather.

'Good evening, my dear,' Tug Harrison greeted her in that dark-molasses voice that sent a shiver of unease and anticipation up her spine.

The chauffeur closed the door behind her, and sealed her in a cocoon of wealth and privilege. She inhaled the rich expensive smell of leather and cigar-smoke and some marvellous after-shave, the aroma of power.

'Good evening, Sir Peter. It was so good of you to invite me,' she said, and bit her own lip in anger. It sounded wrong, too gushing and subservient. She had planned to be cool and unimpressed by his condescension.

'Chez Nico,' Tug Harrison told the chauffeur, and then touched the button on the arm-rest that operated the sound-proof glass division between the driver and passenger seats.

'You don't mind my cigar, I hope?' he asked Bonny.

'No. I enjoy the smell of a good cigar. It's a Davidoff, isn't it?' It wasn't a guess. She had noticed the discarded band tucked into the ashtray. She had an eye for detail; it was the secret of her success as a photographer.

'Ah!' Tug Harrison acknowledged. 'A connoisseur.' He seemed amused. She hoped he had not noticed her little cheat, and she changed the subject quickly.

'I've never been to Chez Nico. Mind you, that's not surpris-ing. Even if I could get a reservation, I'd never be able to meet the bill. They say you have to book weeks in advance. Is that true?'

'Some people might have to.' Tug Harrison smiled again. 'I really don't know. I'll ask my secretary; she makes my arrange-ments.'

God, it was all going wrong. Every time she said anything, it came out sounding callow and gave him reason to despise her. For the remainder of the short journey she let him do the talking, yet despite her poor start to the evening, Bonny's imagination was running riot. If only she played her cards correctly from now on, this could be her future – Rolls-Royce and dinner at Nico's, a charge account at Harrods and Harvey Nichols and a flat in Mayfair or Kensington, holidays in

Acapulco and Sydney and Cannes and a sable coat. Pleasures and riches without end. 'This could be the big casino. Just cool it, girl.'

She had spent most of the afternoon tucked up in bed with Danny, but that seemed like a hundred years ago in another half-forgotten land. Now there was Sir Peter Harrison and a new world of promise.

The restaurant surprised her. She had expected a pompous dimly lit atmosphere, and instead it was gay and the lighting was cheerful. The lovely stained-glass ceiling was in green garden colours and captured a mood of *art nouveau*. Her own mood expanded and lightened in sympathy.

As they were ushered to the special table in the elbow of the L-shaped room, the conversation at the other tables faltered and all heads revolved to follow them and then came back close together to whisper his name and barter the latest gossip about him. Tug Harrison was the stuff of legend. It felt good to be at his side and savour the envious glances of other women.

Bonny knew just how striking were her tall athletic body and her flaming hair. She knew everyone would be jumping to conclusions about her status in Sir Peter's life.

'Please God, just let it come true. I'd better remember to take it easy on the wine. Perrier and a quick wit, those are the watch-words for this evening.'

It was easier than she expected. Tug Harrison was urbane and attentive. He made her feel pampered and very special by directing all his attention and charm upon her.

Nico Ladenis came up from his kitchen, especially to speak to Tug Harrison. With his dark satanic good looks Nico had a fearsome reputation. If he served the best food in England, he expected it to be treated with respect. If you ordered a gin and tonic to ruin your palate at the beginning of one of his celestial repasts you had to expect his wrath and contempt. Tug Harrison ordered a chilled La Ina for himself and a Dubonnet for Bonny. Then he and Nico discussed the menu with the same serious attention that Tug would give to BOSS's quarterly report.

When Nico left, sending one of his underlings to take their order, Tug turned to Bonny to ask what she had chosen, but she feigned a girlish confusion. 'Oh, it all sounds so gorgeous that I can't possibly make up my mind. Won't you order for me, Sir Peter?'

He smiled and she sensed that she was on the right track at last. She was getting the feel of the relationship, her intuition working up to cruise speed. Clearly, he liked to be in charge of any situation, even to choosing the meal.

She went very gently on the Chevalier-Montrachet that he ordered to complement her salmon. She encouraged him to relate the adventures of his young days in Africa. It was not difficult to show intense interest in his conversation, for he was a fine raconteur. His voice was like the caress of velvet gloves, and it didn't matter that he was old and that his skin was wrinkled and bagged and foxed by the tropical sun. Recently she had read somewhere, perhaps in the *Sunday Times Magazine*, that his personal fortune was over three hundred million pounds. At that price, what were a few wrinkles and scars?

'Well, my dear.' At last Tug dabbed his leathery lips with the folded table-napkin. 'May I suggest that we take coffee at Holland Park. There are a few small matters that I would like to discuss with you.'

Modestly she hesitated a moment. Could she afford to make herself too readily available? Shouldn't she play just a little hard to get? Should she hold out until the second time of asking? But what if there were no second time? She quailed at the thought.

Go for it now, honeychild, she counselled herself, and smiled at him. 'Thank you, Sir Peter. I'd love that.'

She was awed by the splendour of the Holland Park house. It was hard not to rubberneck like a tourist as he led her up to his study and settled her into a deep leather armchair. It was a masculine room with a set of rhinoceros horns on the panelled wall. She noticed the two paintings and shivered as she recognised their value.

'Are you cold, my dear?' He was solicitous and motioned the black servant in flowing white kanza to close the window. Sir Peter brought the coffee cup to her with his own hands.

'Kenya Blue,' he told her. 'Specially picked from my private plantation on the slopes of Mount Kenya.'

251

He dismissed the servant and lit a cigar.

'And now, my dear . . .' He blew a streamer of cigar smoke towards the ceiling. 'Tell me, are you sleeping with Daniel Armstrong?'

It was so unexpected, so brusque and alarming that she lost her equilibrium. Before she could prevent herself she flared at him, 'Just who the hell do you think you're talking to?'

He raised a beetling silver eyebrow at her. 'Ah, a temper to match the colour of your hair, I see. However, that's a fair question, and I'll answer straight. I think I am talking to Thelma Smith. That's the name on your birth certificate, isn't it? Father unknown. My information is that your mother died in 1975 of an overdose. Heroin, I believe. That was the period when a shipment of bad stuff got loose in the city.'

Bonny felt a cold nauseous sweat break out on her forehead. She stared at him.

'Like your mother's, your own career has been, shall we say, chequered. At the age of fourteen, a juvenile school of correction for shop-lifting and possession of marijuana. Then at eighteen, a nine-months' sentence for theft and prostitution. It seems you robbed one of your clients. While in women's gaol you developed your interest in photography. You served only three months of your sentence. Time off for good behaviour.' He smiled at her. 'Please correct me if I have got any of these facts wrong.'

Bonny felt herself shrinking down into the huge chair. She still felt sick and cold. She kept silent.

'You changed your name to the more glamorous version and got your first job in photography with Peterson Television in Canada. Dismissed in May 1981 for stealing and selling video equipment belonging to the company. They declined to press charges. Since then a clean record. Reformed, perhaps, or just getting a little more clever? Whichever is the case, it seems you are not burdened by too many moral qualms and that you'll do almost anything for money.'

'You bastard,' she hissed at him. 'You've been leading me on. I thought . . .'

'Yes, you thought that I was lusting after all that decidedly palatable flesh.' He shook his head with regret. 'I am an old

252

man, my dear. As the flames burn lower, I find my appetite becomes more refined. With due respect for your obvious charms, I would class you as Beaujolais nouveau, a hearty young wine, tasty but lacking integrity or distinction. The wine for a younger palate, like Danny Armstrong's perhaps. At my age I prefer something like a Latour or a Margaux – older, smoother and with more class to it.'

'You old bastard! Now you insult me.'

'That was not my intention I merely wanted us to understand each other. I want something other than your body. You want money. We can do a deal. It's a purely commercial arrangement. Now to return to my original question. Are you sleeping with Daniel Armstrong?'

'Yes,' she snarled at him. 'I'm screwing his arse off.'

'An expressive turn of phrase. I take it that no mawkish sentiments complicate this relationship? That is, not on your side at least?'

'There is only one person I love, and she's sitting right here in this room.'

'Total honesty,' he smiled. 'Better and better, especially as Danny Armstrong is not the type to treat it so lightly. You have a certain influence and leverage over him, so you and I can do business now. What would you say to twenty-five thousand pounds?'

The sum startled Bonny, but she screwed up her courage and followed her intuition. She dismissed the offer scornfully, 'I'd say "Up yours, mate!" I read somewhere that you paid ten times more than that for a horse.'

'Ah, but she was a thoroughbred filly of impeccable blood-lines. You wouldn't set yourself in that class, surely?' He held up his hands to forestall her furious response. 'Enough my dear; it was just a little joke, a poor one, I agree. Please forgive me. I want us to be business associates, not lovers, nor even friends.'

'Then before we talk about a price, you'd better explain what I have to do.' Her expression was bright and foxy. He felt the first vestiges of respect for her.

'It's very simple really . . .' And he told her what he wanted.

Daniel had spent every day that week at the Reading Room of the British Museum. This was invariably his practice before leaving on an assignment. In addition to books specifically on Ubomo, he asked the librarian for every publication that she could find on the Congo, the Rift Valley and its lakes, and the African equatorial forest.

He started with the books of Speke and Burton, Mungo Park and Alan Moorehead, re-reading them for the first time in years. He skipped through them rapidly, merely refreshing his mind on the half-forgotten descriptions of the nineteenth-century explorations of the region. He moved on to the more recent publications.

Amongst these he found Kelly Kinnear's book, *The People of the Tall Trees*, listed in the bibliography.

He called for a copy of her book and studied the author's photograph on the inside of the dust-jacket. She was rather pretty, with a strong and interesting face. The blurb did not give her birth date but it listed her honours and degrees. She was primarily a medical doctor, although she also had a Ph.D. in Anthropology from Bristol University. 'When not conducting research in the field, Doctor Kinnear shares a cottage in Cornwall with two dogs and a cat.' That was the only personal information that the blurb contained and Daniel returned to the photograph.

In the background of the photograph was a palisade formed by the trunks of large tropical trees. It seemed as though she stood in a forest clearing. She was bare-headed, dark hair pulled back from her face and twisted into a thick plait that had fallen forward over one shoulder and hung down her chest. She wore a man's shirt. It was difficult to tell what her figure was like, but she seemed slim and small-breasted. Her neck was long, with clean graceful lines, and her collar-bones formed a sculptured cup at the base of her throat.

Her head sat well on the column of her neck, strong square jaw and high cheekbones like an American Indian. Her nose was thin and rather bony and her mouth was determined, perhaps obstinate. Her eyes were probably her best feature, wide-set and almond-shaped, and she stared coolly at the camera. He judged that she had been in her early thirties when the photograph was taken, but there was no indication as to how old she was now.

'A handful,' Daniel decided. 'No wonder she has my friend Tug running scared. This is a lady who gets her own way.'

He flicked through to the first dozen pages of *People of the Tall Trees*, and read the introduction in which Kelly Kinnear explored the first references to the pygmies in the writings of antiquity.

This began with the report of the Egyptian leader Harkhuf to his child-Pharaoh Neferkare. Two thousand five hundred years before the birth of Christ, Harkhuf had led an expedition southwards to discover the source of the Nile river. In his field report, discovered four and a half thousand years later in Pharaoh's tomb, Harkhuf described how he had come to a mighty forest to the west of the Mountains of the Moon, and how in that dark and mysterious place he had encountered a tiny people who danced and sang to their god. Their god was the very forest itself and the description of their dancing and worship was so tantalising that Pharaoh despatched a messenger ordering Harkhuf to capture some of these tiny god dancers and bring them back to Memphis.

Thus the pygmies became familiar figures in ancient Egypt. Over the ages since then, many strange legends have grown up around these tiny forest people, and much that is fanciful and apocryphal has been written about them. Even their name was based on a misconception. 'Pugme' was a Greek unit of measurement, from elbow to knuckle, an imaginative estimate of their height by people who had never seen them.

Daniel had read all this before and he passed quickly to the more enjoyable portion of the book, the author's description of three years spent living with a pygmy clan in the depths of the equatorial forests of Ubomo.

Kinnear was a trained and professional anthropologist with a keenly observant eye for detail and the ability to marshal her meticulously garnered facts and extract from them reasoned conclusions, and yet she possessed the ear and heart of a story-teller. These were not dry scientific subjects she was describing but human beings, each with his own character and idiosyncra-

255

sies; here was a warm, loving and lovable people pictured against the awe-inspiring grandeur of the great forest, a merry people, wonderfully in tune with nature, expressing themselves with songs and dances and impish humour. At the end the reader was forced to share with the writer her obvious affection for and understanding of her subject, but even more, her deep concern for the forest in which they lived.

Daniel closed the book and sat for a while in the pleasant glow of well-being that it had inspired. Not for the first time he felt a desire to meet and talk to the woman who had created this small magic, but now at last he knew how and when to do so.

The annual general meeting of the shareholders of BOSS was set for a week before his departure for Ubomo, and Pickering in public relations arranged an invitation for Daniel and Bonny to attend.

The AGM was always held in the ballroom of BOSS's own magnificent headquarters in Blackfriars.

The AGM was always held on the last Friday of July and began at seven-thirty in the evening. It ran for an hour and twenty-five minutes: ten minutes to read the previous minutes, an hour of sonorous prose from Sir Peter as he made his chairman's report and, finally, fifteen minutes of appreciation by the members of his board, capped by a vote of thanks and approbation, proposed by an individual planted in the body of the shareholders. The vote was always passed unanimously by a show of hands. That's the way it always went. It was company tradition.

Security at the door was very strict. The name of every person entering was checked against the current register of shareholders and special invitations were scrutinised by uniformed members of BOSS's security staff.

Sir Peter didn't want wild Irishmen or anti-Rushdie fundamentalists letting off bombs in the middle of his carefully rehearsed speech, nor did he want freelance journalists or trade unionists, or other free-loading riff-raff making pigs of themselves at the heavily laden buffet table and complimentary bar.

Daniel had mistimed their departure from the flat in Chelsea. They would have been at Blackfriars thirty minutes earlier but Bonny had, at the last minute, begun feeling very healthy. She had made a suggestion which Daniel, always the perfect gentleman, had been unable to refuse. Afterwards it had been necessary to take a shower together during which Bonny had started a water fight which had reduced the bathroom to a sodden shambles with water running out under the door into the passageway.

All this took time, and then they had battled to find a taxi. When they finally flagged one down in the King's Road they ran into traffic along the Embankment and only arrived at the BOSS building after Sir Peter was in full stride, mesmerising his audience with an account of BOSS's performance over the previous twelve months.

All seats were taken and the overflow crowded the back of the hall. They sneaked in, and Daniel shepherded Bonny into a corner near the bar, and pressed a large whisky and soda into her hand.

'That should hold you for half an hour,' he whispered. 'Just please don't start feeling healthy again until we get home.'

'Chicken.' She grinned at him. 'You can't take it, Armstrong.'

The shareholders around them frowned and shushed disapproval and they settled down contritely to an appreciation of Sir Peter 'Tug' Harrison's wit and erudition.

On the dais Sir Peter faced them from the centre of the long table with a microphone in front of him and the members of his board spread out on each side of him. Amongst them there was an Indian maharajah, an earl, an East European pretender and a number of run-of-the-mill baronets. All were names and titles that looked good on the company letter-head, but not a person in the room that evening had any illusion as to where the true power and might of BOSS lay.

Sir Peter stood with his left hand thrust into his jacket pocket, occasionally extending the forefinger of his right hand and pointing at his audience. As he made each point, he stabbed his forefinger like a pistol barrel at them, and even Daniel found himself flinching and blinking as though a shot had been fired at his head.

Everything Sir Peter had to tell them was good news, from the results of offshore oil drilling in the Pemba channel, to the cotton harvests and ground-nut crop of Zambia, and the increase in both pre-tax profits and declared dividends. The audience hummed with delight at each fresh revelation.

Sir Peter glanced at his watch. He had been running for fifty minutes – ten to go. It was time to move on to future plans and projections. He took a sip of water, and when he resumed, his voice was velvety and seductive.

'My lords, ladies and gentlemen, I have given you the bad news . . .' He paused for laughter and a volley of applause. 'Now let me move on to the good news. The good news is Ubomo, the People's Democratic Republic of Ubomo and your company's participation in a new era for that beautiful little country – the opportunity that we have, not only to provide employment but also prosperity for a sadly disadvantaged population of four million souls.' For nine minutes more he enthralled them with the promise of bright new profits and sky-rocketing dividends and then he ended, 'And so, ladies and gentlemen, what we see before us is Ubomo, the high road to the future of the African continent.'

'Hell!' Daniel whispered, his voice blanketed by the applause. 'That's a blatant case of plagiarism. The old bastard lifted it straight from me.'

When Sir Peter sat down the company secretary gave them two minutes to express their approval fully before he leaned over his microphone.

'My lords, ladies and gentlemen, I am now opening the meeting to the floor. Are there any shareholders' questions, please? Your chairman and board will endeavour to answer them to the best of their ability.'

His magnified voice was still reverberating through the hall when another voice cut in.

'I have a question for the chairman.' It was a feminine voice, clear, self-assured, and surprisingly loud – so loud that on the dais Sir Peter winced.

Up until then Daniel had been trying to identify Doctor Kinnear in the body of the crowded hall, but without success. She was either not present or she was obscured by the crush of other shareholders. He had given up the search.

Now there was no mistaking her. She was very much present, standing on her chair, three rows from the front. Daniel grinned with delight. The echoing volume of Kelly Kinnear's voice was explained. She had armed herself with an electronic bull-horn. How she had smuggled the device past the hawk-eyed security guards was a mystery, but now she was wielding it with telling effect.

So often at other meetings that Daniel had attended, the questions from the floor, no matter how pertinent or penetrating, had lost all their force simply because they were not audible to the bulk of the audience. 'What did he say?' and 'Speak up!' were the cries that greeted them, and the game was lost with the first delivery.

This was not happening to Kelly Kinnear. Perched high on her chair, in full view of the entire audience, she was lashing Sir Peter Harrison at a range of thirty paces in a ringing young voice.

She was smaller than Daniel had expected, but her neat little body was poised and graceful, almost birdlike, and there was a force and presence about her that transcended her physical size.

'Mr Chairman, BOSS has very recently included the image of a green tree in the company emblem. What I want to know is whether this is to enable you to cut it down?'

There was a stunned silence. Her sudden appearance had been greeted with amused and admiring smiles from most of the audience, the natural masculine reaction to a pretty girl, but now the smiles were replaced by puzzled expressions.

'For thirty years, Sir Peter,' Kelly Kinnear went on, 'ever since you have been chairman of BOSS, the slogan of the company has been "Dig it up!" "Chop it down!" or "Shoot it!"'

The puzzled expressions turned to frowns, shareholders exchanged worried glances.

'For many years BOSS employed professional hunters to massacre wild animals. The meat was used to feed the company's thousands of employees. The policy of cheap food was only discontinued relatively recently. That was the "shoot it" philosophy.'

The back of Kelly Kinnear's slim sun-tanned neck was flushing with her mounting anger. The thick dark braid of hair hanging down between her shoulder-blades twitched like the tail of a lioness.

'For thirty years, BOSS has been ripping the mineral riches from Africa's soil and leaving gaping craters and devastation in its wake. That's the "dig it up" mentality. For thirty years, BOSS has been slashing down the natural forests and putting the land to cotton and ground-nuts and other cash crops that drain the soil, that poison it with nitrate fertilisers, that contaminate the streams and rivers. That's the "chop it down" philosophy.'

Her whole body quivered with indignation, a phenomenon that intrigued Daniel.

'Those cash crops produce no food for the people who once lived upon the land. They are forced to trek away from the devastation that BOSS has created to live in the odious slums of Africa's sprawling new towns. These people are turned into outcasts by BOSS's greed.'

Sir Peter turned his head and raised an eyebrow at the company secretary. Obediently the secretary leapt to his feet.

'Will you please state your name, and put your question briefly and clearly?'

'My name is Doctor Kelly Kinnear, and I am putting my question. Will you just give me a chance?'

'That is not a question. You are haranguing . . .'

'Listen to me,' she ordered, and hopped around on the chair to face the ballroom filled with shareholders. 'For most of us, our personal welfare ranks far ahead of tropical forests and lakes in a faraway land. The princely dividends paid by BOSS are more important to us than exotic birds and unfamiliar animals and tribes of indigenous people. It's so easy to pay lip service to the environment as long as it doesn't affect our own pockets—'

'Order! Order, please!' bawled the company secretary. 'You are out of order, Doctor Kinnear. You are not asking a question.'

'All right,' Kelly rounded on him. 'I'll ask a question. Is the chairman of BOSS aware that while we sit here, the tropical rain forests of Ubomo are being destroyed?' She glared at him. 'Does the chairman realise that over fifty species of wildlife have become extinct in Ubomo as a direct result of the activities of BOSS?'

'Shame! Sit down!'

'The death of a species affects us directly. It will lead in the end to our own extinction, the death of man on earth.'

There was a hum of indignation and outrage from the shareholders. Sir Peter Harrison smiled and shook his head pityingly, making no attempt to respond to her attack. He knew where the loyalty of his shareholders lay.

'Sit down!' somebody shouted again. 'You silly bitch!'

'Doctor Kinnear,' the company secretary called, 'I must ask you to resume your seat at once. This is a deliberate attempt to disrupt our proceedings.'

'I accuse you, Mr Chairman,' Kelly pointed a quivering finger at Sir Peter, 'I accuse you of rape.'

There were shouts of protest, some of the other shareholders were on their feet.

'Shame!'

'The woman's a lunatic!'

One of them attempted to pull Kelly down off her chair, but it was obvious that she had surrounded herself with a small group of supporters of her own, half a dozen young men and women in casual dress, but with determined expressions. They closed up around her. One of the young men pushed her attackers away.

'Let her speak!'

'I accuse you of the rape of Ubomo. Already your bulldozers are ripping into the forests—'

'Get her out of here!'

'Doctor Kinnear, if you don't heed the chair I will have no alternative but to have you forcibly removed.'

'I'm a shareholder. I have every right—'

'Throw her out!'

There was confusion and uproar in the front of the hall, while on the dais Sir Peter Harrison looked bored and detached.

'Answer me!' Kelly yelled at him, surrounded by her struggling cohorts. 'Fifty species doomed to extinction so that you can drive around in your Rolls—'

'Ushers! Ushers!' yelped the company secretary, and from every corner of the room the uniformed security men leapt into the fray.

As one of them elbowed Daniel aside and charged forward, Daniel could not help himself. He thrust out his right foot, a cunning little ankle-tap that knocked one of the usher's large black boots across his own ankle. The man tripped himself and was hurled forward by his own momentum. He flew headlong into a row of chairs and, amidst loud cries of protest and outrage, knocked the occupants into a heap. Chairs crashed, and women screamed.

The press photographers loved it, and their flashes bloomed and lit the hall with a flickering like summer lightning.

'While you mouth your sanctimonious platitudes and put a little green tree on the BOSS emblem, your bulldozers are tearing the guts out of one of the most vulnerable and precious forests in the world.' Kelly Kinnear's amplified voice rose above the uproar. She was still on her chair, but swaying precariously in the storm that raged around her, a small heroic figure in the confusion.

'Those forests do not belong to you. They do not belong to the cruel military tyrant who has seized power in Ubomo and who is your accomplice in this atrocity. Those forests belong to the Bambuti pygmies, a tribe of gentle inoffensive people who have lived there since time immemorial. We, the friends of the earth, and all decent people everywhere say "keep your greedy hands off the—"'

Three of the BOSS ushers formed a scrimmage line; in their black uniforms they resembled a New Zealand front rank. They broke through her ring of defenders and reached up to drag Kelly Kinnear down from her perch.

'Leave me alone,' she yelled at them, and turned her bull-horn into an offensive weapon, raining blows upon them until the trumpet cracked and shattered and she was defenceless.

Between them they dragged her down off her perch and bore her, kicking and clawing and biting, from the hall. A kind of

262

awed calm returned. Like the survivors of a bomb blast, the shareholders picked up the chairs and straightened their clothing and examined themselves for injuries.

On the dais Sir Peter rose unhurriedly to his feet and resumed his place at the microphone. 'Ladies and gentlemen, the floor show was unscheduled, I assure you. On behalf of BOSS and my board, I sincerely apologise for this outburst. If it served any useful purpose at all, it was as a graphic illustration of the difficulties we face when we try to improve the lot of our fellow men.'

Those who had been distracted gathered themselves and turned to listen to his rich dark seductive tones. After the shrill denunciations and accusations, it was a soothing balm.

'Doctor Kelly Kinnear is notorious for her intemperate views. She has declared a one-woman war on the government of President Taffari of Ubomo. She has, in fact, made as much of a nuisance of herself in that country as she did here tonight. You have seen her in action, ladies and gentlemen, so you will not be particularly surprised to hear that she was deported from Ubomo and formally declared an undesirable. The vendetta that she is waging is personal and spiteful. She sees herself as an injured party, and she is taking her revenge.'

He paused again, and shook his head.

'However, we must not make the mistake of believing that what we have witnessed tonight was the isolated act of some poor misguided soul. Unfortunately, ladies and gentlemen, in this crazy new world of ours we are surrounded by the loonies of the left. This lady, who has just left us . . .' They laughed uncertainly, beginning to recover from the effects of Kelly Kinnear's attempt at persuasion, 'this lady is one of those who prefers that tens of thousands of her fellow human beings suffer starvation and misery, rather than that a single tree be cut down, rather than that a single plough should run a furrow, rather than that a single animal should die.' He paused and scowled at them sternly, exerting the full force of his personality, reasserting his control that for a minute had been shaken by the small determined woman with the loud-hailer. 'This is a nonsense. Man has as much right to life as any other species on this planet. However, BOSS recognises its responsibility to the environment. We are a green company committed to the well-being of all creatures on this earth, men and animals and plants. Last year we spent over a hundred thousand pounds on environmental studies prior to proceeding with some of our enterprises. One hundred thousand pounds, ladies and gentlemen, is a great deal of money.' He paused for the applause from his audience. Daniel noted that he was careful not to compare this great deal of money to BOSS's taxable profits for the same period, profits of almost one billion pounds.

As the applause died away he continued. 'We spent that money, not to impress anybody, not as some grand public relations gesture, but in a genuine and sincere attempt to do the right thing by all the world. We know in our hearts that what we are doing is right and proper. So do you, who are the most important members of BOSS, the shareholders. Our conscience is clear, ladies and gentlemen! We can go forward with confidence and enthusiasm to keep our company what it has always been, one of the great forces for good in an otherwise sad and naughty world.'

The meeting overran its usual duration by almost twenty minutes, a great deal of extra time being devoted to a standing ovation for the chairman's impromptu speech.

For once the traditional vote of thanks was passed not by a show of hands, but by thunderous acclaim.

'Tug hammers loony Greens' was the headline in the tabloid press the following morning and the general consensus in the media was that it had been not so much a confrontation, as a massacre of the innocents.

There was no direct flight from Heathrow to Kahali in Ubomo. Although the airport had been renamed the Ephrem Taffari airport, and twenty-five million dollars had been loaned by the World Bank to extend the main runway to accommodate intercontinental jet aircraft and to refurbish the airport buildings, there had been a series of delays in the construction work due to the fact that much of the original loan capital seemed to have evaporated. Rumour in the streets of Kahali suggested that the missing funds had found a happy home in a numbered Swiss bank account. Another twenty-five million was needed to complete the project and the World Bank was demanding unreasonable assurances and guarantees before supplying it. In the meantime travellers were forced to travel to Ubomo via Nairobi.

Daniel and Bonny took the British Airways flight to Nairobi, and Daniel paid almost five hundred pounds in excess baggage charges for Bonny's video equipment. In Nairobi they were obliged to overnight at the Norfolk Hotel before they could catch the scheduled flight to Kahali on Air Ubomo which operated between the two capitals.

With a day to spare, Danny asked Bonny to shoot some background and filler footage. What he really wanted was the opportunity to watch her in action and to get used to working with her in the field. This was to be a dress rehearsal. He hired a combi with a cut-out roof and a Kikuyu driver. They drove out to the Nairobi National Park on the outskirts of the city.

The Park was another of Africa's surprises. Within a few miles of the Lord Delamere bar in the Norfolk Hotel, it was possible to witness wild lions making their kills. The boundary of the Park ran hard up against the Jomo Kenyatta Airport and the grazing herds of antelope did not even raise their heads as the great jet aircraft on final approach howled only a few hundred feet above them.

Daniel had filmed in the Park many times over the past few years. The Park warden was an old friend. They greeted each other in Swahili and shook hands with the double grip, palm then thumb, of brothers.

The warden delegated one of his senior rangers to escort and guide them, and gave Daniel *carte blanche* to go anywhere, even to disregard one of the strictest Park rules and leave the vehicle to film on foot.

The ranger led them to a stand of flat-topped acacia forest beside the river where a huge bull rhino was in ponderous courtship with a female in full oestrus. So absorbed were these antediluvian monsters with each other that Daniel and Bonny were able to leave the combi and creep up close.

Without making it obvious, Daniel was watching Bonny narrowly. The Sony video camera was a top-of-the-range model, sleek in design but heavy even for a man to carry. Daniel wanted to see how she handled it, and he made no offer to assist her. With a sharp warning in Swahili, he prevented the black ranger when he made an attempt to do so.

He had come to know Bonny's body in the most intimate way over the past weeks. He knew that there was no fat on her and that her limbs were clad in sleek hard muscle. She was in the prime physical condition of a trained athlete. In their playful wrestling contests he had been forced to extend his full strength to subdue her and get her to the bed when she challenged him outrageously to do so. She enjoyed her love-making with plenty of rough and tumble.

Still, he was surprised at the ease with which she lifted the camera and her lightness and agility on her feet even in the heat of the acacia forest and over the broken ground. The earth was studded with the spoor of rhino and buffalo that had been deeply trodden into the wet clay of the rainy season and was now baked hard as terracotta. It could turn an unwary ankle and the wait-a-bit thorns were viciously hooked to catch in flesh or cloth. Bonny avoided these snares with ease.

The bull rhino was displaying aggressively for the benefit of the female who had wandered into his territory and who he was now holding captive to his lust. Every time she attempted to reach the boundary of his territory he headed her off, snorting and blowing like a steam engine, raising gales of dust from under his high stamping feet.

The female swished her great grey backside from side to side in flirtatious refusal of his advances, affording him fleeting whiffs of her heady oestrus odours which drove him into further ecstasies of excitement. Every few minutes he rushed away to scent mark the borders of his territory and warn off any possible rivals who might be tempted to trespass on this ardent courtship.

As soon as he reached the boundary, he pointed his rump at one of the trees or shrubs which were his signposts, curled his tail up on to his back, unsheathed his massive pink penis from its scabbard of grey wrinkled skin and, aiming backwards between his rear legs, released a cloud of urine with the force of a fire hose that almost flattened the target. Honour satisfied, he rushed back, grunting with passion to the bashful female, who immediately fled towards the furthest boundary of his domain with him in full pursuit.

At the best of times the rhino is afflicted with poor eyesight, but now these two were almost completely blinded by single-minded passion. Daniel and Bonny had to be alert and ready to run or dodge at any instant, for the rushes of the two inflamed creatures were wild and erratic. Unless they were quick on their feet, they could be trampled by those horny pads or gutted by a random thrust of one of the long polished nose horns.

It was hard dangerous work with death only an instant or a foot away, but Bonny showed no fear at all. Rather she seemed elated and excited by the danger. Her eyes shone and the sweat soaked her flaming hair and darkened the back of her shirt as they ran side by side through the forest or ducked behind one of the acacia trunks to avoid a sudden random rush by one of the animals.

Apart from her lack of fear, Bonny showed a physical stamina that impressed Daniel. He was unburdened by the equipment which she carried, and yet he was tiring in the heat and the dust while she seemed quite unaffected.

Suddenly the bull swirled without warning. Perhaps he had detected a breath of their body smell through the clouds of love perfume with which the female was filling his wide flaring nostrils. He charged straight at them and Daniel grabbed her arm.

'Freeze!' he whispered urgently, and they sank to their knees and froze into utter stillness.

From a distance of twenty feet the huge creature confronted them, blowing and huffing and snorting. His piggy eyes blood-shot with passion and fury, he peered myopically at them, waiting for some small movement that would convince him that they were neither a rock nor a bush, and thus worthy of the full weight of his jealous wrath.

Daniel tried to hold his breath, but his lungs were scalding from his exertions and he choked to breathe. Suddenly he was aware of a faint electric whirring sound close to his left ear, and he swivelled his eyes in their sockets without moving his head.

To his astonishment and incredulity, Bonny was still filming. The lens of the Sony was only feet from the rhino's nose. They could see right up his wide nostrils to the shiny wet pinkness of his nasal mucosa, and she was filming it. That impressed Daniel as nothing before had done.

I've got myself one hell of a camera jockey, he thought. Jock would have been on the next plane home by now.

Suddenly the rhino switched around, a movement so quick and agile that it seemed impossible in such a massive creature. Love had triumphed over aggression. He rushed back to his paramour, huffing and puffing with eagerness.

Bonny was laughing. Daniel could not believe what he was hearing. 'Come on!' She was on her feet again with a lithe bound.

By the time they caught up with the couple in a glade of pale grass beside the rocky watercourse, the cow had at last succumbed to the bull's persistent courtship. She allowed him to place his chin on her rump, and she stood quiescent and submissive under this significant caress.

'Get ready,' Daniel warned Bonny. 'It's going to happen at any moment.'

Suddenly the bull reared up over the female.

Bonny captured every titanic convulsion, every straining, thrusting drive of the enormous bodies. And then very swiftly it was over, and the bull dropped off the cow and stood heaving and blowing from the effort.

'You got it, and we've taken too many risks already,' Daniel whispered. 'Let's get out of here.'

He took her arm and drew her away. They retreated carefully, a pace at a time, watching the bull all the way.

A hundred yards from the two rhino, Daniel deemed them well out of harm's way and they set off towards the combi, still elated by the thrill and the danger, laughing and chatting, not bothering to look backwards, until Daniel snapped abruptly, 'Look out! He's coming again.'

The bull was charging straight at them, an ungainly gallop that did not swerve or deviate, glaring malevolently at them over the wickedly curved horn.

'I think he's got our wind.' Daniel grabbed Bonny's arm. He looked about them quickly. The nearest cover was a small thorn bush twenty paces ahead. 'Come on.' They ran for it together and crawled under the outstretched branches. The hooked thorns raked their shirts and exposed skin.

'He's still coming.' Bonny's voice was hoarse with dust and exertion.

'Get down. Keep still.' They crouched on the stony ground and watched in helpless horror as the rhino rushed straight at their hiding-place.

'This time, he's not going to stop.' For the first time Bonny showed signs of fear.

Four tons of prehistoric monster, horned and menacing, towered over them. It sniffed the thorn leaves that gave them such flimsy shelter and its breath rattled the branches and blew into their faces.

Then abruptly and unexpectedly, the bull switched around and presented them, at a range of only a few feet, with its fat rounded hindquarters. They stared in horror as its penis unsheathed from between its back legs.

'We are on his boundary,' Daniel breathed.

'He's going to mark this bush! Us!'

It pointed at them like a pink fire-hose.

'We're trapped,' Bonny wailed. The thorns hemmed them in. 'What can we do?'

'Just close your eyes, and think of England.'

A steaming cloud engulfed them, blowing over them with the force of a tropical hurricane, not a simple jet but a storm of scalding liquid that sent Daniel's bush hat flying from his head and soaked them both to the skin. The bull wriggled his tail with satisfaction, stamped his back feet and then charged away with the same impetuosity with which he had arrived.

Daniel and Bonny sat under the dripping thorn bush and stared at each other in horror. Their faces were running wet as though they had stood out in the monsoon rain and the odour was overpowering.

Daniel moved first. He wiped his face with the palm of his hand, a slow theatrical gesture beginning at the top of his forehead and ending at his chin. Then he inspected his hand.

'Now that . . .' he said in a sepulchral tone, 'really pisses me off!'

For a moment Bonny continued to stare at him, and then she let out a shriek of wild mirth and they fell against each other and laughed. Clinging together, sodden and stinking, they laughed until they couldn't stand up, and then they laughed some more. Rhino urine had lacquered their hair into sticky dreadlocks, and stained their clothing with interesting patterns.

They sneaked into the Norfolk Hotel through the rear entrance behind the kitchens and fled across the lawns to their cottage suite, where they stood under the shower for twenty minutes and, still giggling, shampooed and soaped each other until their bodies glowed.

Later, in a towelling bathrobe, Daniel sat in front of the television set while Bonny connected up her equipment.

He gave all his attention to the screen and, from the first minute, knew that he had made the right choice in hiring Bonny Mahon. Her technique was of superbly professional quality, and she had a fine eye and sense of timing. She knew when she needed to be close in and when to pull back, but more important, and infinitely rarer, she had a distinctive style, the style that he had first recognised in her Arctic film.

'You're good,' he told her when the screen went blank. 'You're damn good.'

'You don't know how good,' she grinned at him. 'I'm only just starting to get the feel of the light here. It's different, you know. Each place is different. Give me another week and I'll show you just how good I am.'

An hour later, dressed in clean clothing, they sauntered across the courtyard in the cool Kenyan dusk and stopped for a minute beside the aviary of wild birds in the centre of the lawn to admire the brilliant colours of the turacos and the gold-breasted starlings behind the wire. Other guests were also drifting in the direction of the grill room.

Daniel had paid no attention to the small figure standing near them, until she turned towards him and greeted him by name. 'Please forgive the intrusion. You are Daniel Armstrong, aren't you?'

Daniel started as he recognised her. 'Doctor Kinnear! The last time I saw you was at BOSS's annual general meeting.'

'Oh, were you there?' She laughed. 'I didn't notice you.'

'No, you did seem to have other things on your mind at the time.' Daniel smiled back at her. 'What happened to your bullhorn? Were you ever able to get it repaired?'

'Japanese rubbish,' Kelly Kinnear said. 'A couple of good shots to the head and it falls to pieces.'

She had a sense of humour of course – he knew that from her writing – but her eyes were even lovelier than the photograph on the dust-jacket had suggested. He liked her instantly. It must have been obvious, for Bonny pulled her hand out of his, and he felt a twinge of guilt.

'May I introduce you to my assistant, Bonny Mahon?'

'Actually, I'm a lighting cameraman, not an assistant,' Bonny corrected him tartly.

'Yes,' Kelly agreed. 'I know your work. You filmed "Arctic Dream". It was very good.' She had a disarmingly direct gaze and Bonny looked slightly abashed by the praise.

'Thank you. But I must warn you, I haven't read your book, Doctor Kinnear.'

'That puts you in a majority of several hundred million, Miss Mahon.' Kelly sensed the antagonism in the other woman but showed no sign of offence, and turned back to Daniel. 'I think I have seen every one of your productions over the years. In fact, you are responsible for me being in Africa at all. When I graduated I was going to Borneo to work with the Penan tribe. Then I saw one of your earlier series on the lakes of the Rift Valley. That changed my mind. After that I just had to come to Africa.' Kelly broke off and laughed softly with embarrassment. 'I know that this will sound terribly jejune, but I am a fan of yours. The truth is I've been hanging around here, just hoping to bump into you ever since I heard that you were in Nairobi. I just had to talk to you.'

'You aren't staying here at the Norfolk, then?' Daniel was feeling better disposed to her every minute. It is difficult to dislike someone who admits to being your fan.

'Good Lord, no.' Kelly laughed again with surprising gusto. She had perfect teeth, even her molars were free of fillings. 'I'm not a successful TV producer. I'm just a poor disadvantaged field researcher without a sponsor. The Smithsonian pulled my grant after I was slung out of Ubomo by Taffari.'

'Let me stand you a steak then,' Daniel offered.

'A steak! I salivate at the thought. I've been living on groundnuts and dried lake-fish since I got back.'

'Yes, why don't you join us, Doctor Kinnear?' said Bonny in a voice of poisoned honey, placing emphasis on the plural pronoun.

'How sweet of you, Miss Mahon.' Kelly glanced at her coolly, and hostility flashed between them like a discharge of static electricity. Their method of communication was too esoteric for Daniel to appreciate, and he smiled amiably.

'Let's go and find some food,' he said, and led them towards the doors of the Ibis grill room that opened on to the courtyard.

'Are you going to film in Kenya?' Kelly asked. 'What are you doing in Nairobi, Doctor Armstrong?'

'Danny,' he invited her to drop the formalities. 'We are on our way to Ubomo, as a matter of fact.'

'Ubomo!' Kelly stopped dead and looked up at him. 'That's marvellous. It's a perfect subject for you, a microcosm of emerging Africa. You are one of the few people who could do it properly.'

'Your trust is flattering, but daunting.' Daniel smiled down at her. For a moment he had forgotten Bonny, until she squeezed his arm to remind him that she was there.

'I'll pay for my supper by telling you all I know about the country,' Kelly offered.

'Deal,' Daniel agreed, and they went into the mellow lighting and flowers and tinkling piano of the Ibis room.

As the two women studied the menu, Daniel surreptitiously compared one with the other.

The obvious difference between them was size. Bonny was almost six feet tall. Kelly was six inches shorter, and they were different in many other ways, from the colour of their hair and eyes to their skin tones. However, Daniel sensed that the differences extended far beyond physical characteristics.

Bonny was bold, direct and almost mannish in her attitude to life. Even from the earliest days of their relationship, Daniel had detected depths in her which he would rather leave unexplored. On the other hand Kelly Kinnear's manner seemed totally feminine, although he knew from her book that she was determined and fearless. It took a special kind of courage to live alone in the great forests with only the Bambuti for companions. He also knew from the book that she was intelligent and gentle, that her concern was for the spiritual rather than the material values of life, but in the ballroom at BOSS House he had witnessed a graphic demonstration of her contradictory, aggressive and warlike spirit.

Both women were attractive in totally different ways. Bonny was brazen, she hit you in the eye at fifty paces, a copper-headed Valkyrie. Kelly was shaded with delicate nuances. She was softer and more discreet, with facets that changed when viewed from different angles. In repose her face was almost plain, her nose and mouth austere, but when she smiled her entire face softened. As he had first noted from the photograph on the dust-jacket of her book, her eyes were her best feature. They were large and dark and expressive. They could glow with a merry impish light, or burn with a passionate sincerity and intelligence. And something else that the photograph didn't show, Daniel grinned to himself. Her boobs were miniature works of art.

Kelly looked up from the menu and caught the direction of his eyes. With a moue of disappointment, as though she had expected better of him, she moved the menu slightly to screen her bosom from his appraisal.

'When are you leaving for Ubomo?'

'We are flying in tomorrow,' Bonny answered for him, but Kelly did not acknowledge the interruption. She directed the next question at Daniel.

'Have you been in since the *coup*?'

'No, I was last there four years ago.'

'That was when Victor Omeru was president,' Kelly stated.

'Yes, I met Omeru. I liked him. What happened to him? I heard that it was a heart attack?'

Kelly shrugged non-committally, then changed the subject as the head-waiter came to take their orders. 'May I really order a steak, or were you just being cruel?'

'Have the porterhouse,' Daniel invited magnanimously.

When the food was in front of them Daniel returned to the subject. 'I heard that you and Omeru got on particularly well together.'

'Who told you that?' Kelly looked up sharply, and Daniel caught himself just in time. Tug Harrison was not a name to bandy about in front of this lady.

'I think I read it in an article somewhere ,' he hedged. 'It was some time ago.'

'Oh yes.' Kelly gave him release. 'Probably the *Sunday Telegraph*. They did a profile on Victor – on President Omeru – and they gave me an honourable mention.'

'That was it. What is happening in Ubomo? You promised to brief me. You said it was a microcosm of emerging Africa. Explain that.'

'Ubomo has got all the major problems common to every other African state: tribalism, population explosion, poverty, illiteracy. And now that President Omeru has gone and that swine Taffari has taken over, it's got itself another set of problems, such as one-party tyranny, a president for life, foreign exploitation and corruption and incipient civil war.'

'Sounds like the perfect society. Let's start with tribalism in Ubomo. Tell me about it.'

'Tribalism, the single greatest curse of Africa!' Kelly took a bite of underdone porterhouse and for a moment closed her eyes in ecstasy. 'Heaven,' she whispered. 'Bliss! All right, tribalism in Ubomo. There are six tribes but only two really count for anything. The Uhali are the most numerous, almost three out of four million. Traditionally they are an agrarian and lakeside people, tillers of the soil and fishermen. They are gentle, industrious people. Yet for centuries they have been enslaved and in the thrall of the much smaller tribe, the Hita. The Hita are fierce, aristocratic people closely related to the Masai and Samburu of Kenya and Tanzania. They are pastoralists and warriors. They live with and for their cattle, and despise the rest of humanity, including us Europeans, I may add, as inferior animals. They are beautiful people, tall and willowy. Any Hita *morani* under six foot three is considered a midget. Their women are magnificent with regal Nilotic faces;

274

they would grace the catwalk at any Paris fashion show. Yet they are a cruel, arrogant and brutal people.'

'You are taking sides. You are as much a tribalist as any of them, Kelly,' Daniel accused.

'Live long enough in Africa, as you know, Danny, and you come to be like them, a tribalist.' Kelly shook her head ruefully. 'But in this case, it's justified. Before the British pulled out of Ubomo back in 1969, they held a Westminster-style election and, of course, the Uhali by weight of numbers, took power and Victor Omeru became president. He was a good president. I'm not suggesting he was a saint, but he was as good as any other ruler in Africa, and a damned sight better than most. He tried to accommodate all his people, all the tribes, but the Hita were too proud and bloody-minded. As natural warriors and killers they gradually took over the army and, of course, the outcome was inevitable. Ephrem Taffari is now despot, tyrant and president for life. A million Hita totally dominate a majority of three million other tribes including the Uhali and my beloved little Bambuti.'

'Tell me about your Bambuti, the "people of the tall trees",' Daniel invited, and she smiled with pleasure.

'Oh, Danny, you know the title of my book!'

'Not only do I know it, but I've actually read it. More than once. Three times in fact, the last time a week ago.' He grinned at her. 'At the risk of sounding jejune,' he teased her with her own phrase, 'I'm a fan.'

'Yech!' Bonny spoke for the first time in fifteen minutes. 'Excuse me while I throw up.'

Daniel had almost forgotten her existence, and now he reached out to take her freckled hand that lay on the table cloth beside him. Bonny pulled it away before he could touch it and placed it in her lap.

'I'd like some more wine, if anybody is interested,' she pouted.

Daniel dutifully refilled her glass while Kelly concentrated tactfully on the last morsels of her steak.

At last Daniel broke the awkward silence. 'We were talking about the Bambuti. Tell me about them.'

Kelly looked up at him again, but did not answer immediately. She seemed to be struggling with a difficult decision. Daniel waited.

'Look here,' Kelly said at last. 'You want to know about the Bambuti. All right, what would you say if instead of talking about them I actually took you into the forest and showed you? How would you like to film them in their natural surroundings? I could show you things that nobody else has ever filmed, sights that very few Westerners have ever seen.'

'I'd jump at the chance, Kelly. Hell, I can't think of anything I'd like more, but isn't there just one little problem? President Taffari hates your guts and will hang you from the highest tree the moment you put one foot across the border.'

Kelly laughed. He was beginning really to enjoy the sound of her laughter. It had a delicious purring quality that made him feel good and want to laugh in sympathy. 'He's not much into hanging, is our boy Ephrem. He has other little tricks he prefers.'

'So, how would you manage the guided tour of Ubomo without Taffari's blessing?'

She was still smiling. 'I've lived in the forest for almost five years. Taffari's authority ends where the tall trees begin. I have many friends. Taffari has many enemies.'

'How will I contact you?' Daniel insisted.

'You won't have to. I'll contact you.'

'Tell me, Kelly, why are you risking your life to be back? What work is so important that you must do it without a field grant, without any kind of support, and under the threat of arrest, and possible death?'

She stared at him. 'That's an amazingly stupid question. There is enough work in the forests to keep me going for a lifetime. Amongst other things, I'm doing work on the physiology of the Bambuti. I have been studying the dwarfism of the pygmies, attempting to determine the cause of their stunted growth. Of course, I'm not the first to do this type of research, but I think I've come up with a new angle. Up until now everybody has concentrated on the growth hormone . . .' She broke off and smiled. 'I won't bore you with the details, but I believe it's the hormone receptors that are lacking.'

'Oh, we aren't bored.' Bonny made no effort to veil her

sarcasm. 'We're fascinated. Do you plan to give the pygmies an injection and turn them all into giants like the Hita?'

Kelly refused to be annoyed. 'The small stature of the Bambuti is a benevolent mutation. It makes them ideally suited for life in the rain forests.'

'I don't understand,' Daniel encouraged her. 'Explain how being small is a benefit.'

'Okay, you asked for it. Firstly, there is heat dissipation. Being so tiny they can shed the heat that builds up in the humid windless atmosphere beneath the forest canopy. Then again, their size makes them agile and nimble in the dense tropical growth. You will be astonished to see how the Bambuti move through the forest. The Egyptians and the early explorers truly believed that they had the power of invisibility. They can simply vanish before your eyes.'

Her own lovely eyes shone with enthusiasm and affection as she talked about these people whom she had made her own.

Daniel ordered dessert and coffee, and Kelly had still not exhausted the subject.

'The other area of my research is even more important than growth hormones and receptors. The Bambuti have a marvellous knowledge of plants and their properties, particularly medicinal properties. I estimate that there are well over half a million different species of plants growing in the rain forests, hundreds of them with already proven properties beneficial to man. I believe that the cure for most of our ills and diseases might be locked up in those plants, a cure for cancer, and for AIDS. I've had promising indications in all those directions.'

'Science fiction,' Bonny scoffed, and filled her mouth with chocolate ice cream.

'Do shut up, Bonny,' Daniel snapped at her. 'This is fascinating. How advanced is your research?'

Kelly pulled a face. 'Not as far as I'd like. I have the old women of the Bambuti helping me gather the leaves and barks and roots. They describe their properties and I try to catalogue and test them and isolate the active ingredient, but my laboratory is a thatched hut, and I am fresh out of money and friends . . .'

'Still I'd like to see it.'

'You will,' she promised, and she was so carried away by Daniel's interest in her work that she laid her hand on his arm. 'You'll come to Gondala where I live?'

Bonny was watching the other girl's hand on Daniel's tanned and muscular forearm. It was a small hand, like the rest of her body, neat and graceful.

'Sir Peter would be interested in the formula for curing AIDS,' Bonny said, still staring at the hand. 'BOSS could market it through their pharmaceutical company. It would be worth a billion—'

'BOSS? Sir Peter?' Kelly jerked her hand off Daniel's arm and stared at Bonny. 'Sir Peter who? Which Sir Peter?'

'Tug Harrison, ducky,' Bonny told her with relish. 'Tug is bank-rolling the production that Daniel is going to shoot in Ubomo. The idea is that Danny and I are going to show the world what a hell of a job BOSS are doing. They are going to call it "Ubomo, High Road to the African Future". Isn't that a cute title? It's going to be Danny's masterpiece—'

Kelly didn't wait for her to finish. She leapt to her feet and knocked over her cup. Spilled coffee spread across the table-cloth and cascaded into Daniel's lap.

'You!' Kelly stared down at him. 'You and that monster Harrison! How could you?'

She whirled and ran from the restaurant, shoving her way through a pack of American tourists who were blocking the aisle.

Daniel was on his feet mopping the coffee that had soaked his trousers. 'What the hell did you do that for?' he snarled at Bonny.

'You and the tree doctor were getting just a mite too chummy for my taste.'

'Damn you,' Daniel flared. 'You've screwed up a chance to film something unique. I'll talk to you later.'

He strode angrily after Kelly Kinnear. She was not in the hotel lobby. Daniel headed for the front entrance and called the doorman.

'Did you see a woman—' He broke off as he spotted Kelly on the far side of the road. She was astride a dusty 250 cc Honda motor cycle, and at that moment she jumped on the kick-starter and the engine shrilled to life. She swung the handlebars hard over, banking the cycle into a tight turn, the engine whining and popping jets of oily blue exhaust smoke.

'Kelly!' Daniel shouted. 'Wait! Give me a chance. I can explain.'

She wrenched the throttle grip fully open and the cycle reared up on its back wheel as it accelerated. She turned her face to him as she flew past where he stood. Her expression was at once angry and stricken and he could have sworn that there were tears on her cheeks.

'Hired gun!' she cried at him. 'Judas!' And then the motor cycle howled away. She banked it sharply, the steel foot-rest raised a shower of sparks as it grazed the tarmac, and she weaved into the traffic in Kimathi Avenue.

Daniel ran down to the corner. He caught one more glimpse of her two hundred yards down the avenue, leaning over the handlebars like a jockey, her braid standing out stiffly from the back of her head in the wind.

He looked around for a taxi to follow her, and then realised the futility of even trying. With the lead she had, and the Honda's manoeuvrability no car could hope to catch her.

He turned on his heel and marched back towards the hotel, intent on finding Bonny Mahon. Before he reached the entrance he realised the danger of confronting her in his present mood. It could only lead to bloody battle, and probably the break-up of their relationship. That did not worry him too much, but what restrained him was the danger of losing a cameraman. It might take weeks to find a replacement, and that could lead to a cancellation of his contract with BOSS, the end of his quest to follow the Lucky Dragon, and Ning Cheng Gong, into Ubomo.

He checked his stride and thought about it. It wasn't worth the pleasure of pinning back Bonny Mahon's ears.

'I'd better go and cool off somewhere.' He chose the Jambo Bar, one of the notorious bars down near the station.

It was full of black soldiers in camouflage, and male tourists and bar girls. Some of the girls were spectacular, Samburu and Kikuyu and Masai, in tight shiny skirts with beads and bright ribbons braided into their hair.

Daniel found a bar stool in the corner, and the antics of the middle-aged European tourists on the dance floor helped to alleviate his foul mood. A recent survey of the Nairobi bar girls had determined that ninety-eight per cent of them were HIV positive. You had to have a death wish to enjoy fully all that these ladies had to offer.

An hour and two double whiskies later, Daniel's anger had cooled sufficiently, and he headed back to the Norfolk Hotel. He let himself into the cottage suite and saw Bonny's khaki slacks and panties in the centre of the sitting-room floor where she had dropped them. This evening her untidiness irritated him even more than usual.

The bedroom was in darkness, but the lights in the courtyard shone through the curtains sufficiently for him to make out Bonny's form under the sheet on her side of the bed. He knew she was feigning sleep. He undressed in the darkness, slipped naked into his side of the bed, and lay still.

Neither of them moved or spoke for fully five minutes and then Bonny whispered, 'Is Daddy cross with his little girl?' She used her simpering childish voice. 'His little girl was very naughty . . .' She touched him. Her fingers were warm and silky down his flank. 'She wants to show him how sorry she is.'

He caught her wrist, but it was too late. She was cunning and quick and soon he didn't want her to stop.

'Damn it, Bonny,' he protested. 'You screwed up a chance . . .'

'Shh! Don't talk,' Bonny whispered. 'Little girl will make it better for Daddy.'

'Bonny . . .' His voice trailed away, and he released her wrist.

In the morning when Daniel checked the hotel bill before paying it, he noticed an item for 120 Kenya shillings. 'International telephone calls'. He taxed Bonny with it.

'Did you make an overseas call last night?'

'I called my old mum to let her know I'm all right. I know how stingy you are, but you don't grudge me that, do you?'

Something in her defiant manner troubled him. When she went ahead to see her video equipment safely packed into the taxi, Daniel lingered in the suite. As soon as she was gone he called the telephone exchange and asked the operator for the overseas number that was on his bill.

'London 727 6464, sir.'

'Please get it for me again now.'

'It's ringing, sir.'

A voice answered on the third ring.

'Good morning, may I help you?'

'What number is that?' Daniel asked, but the speaker was guarded.

'Who did you want, please?'

Daniel thought he recognised the voice, the strong African accent. He took a chance.

'Is that you, Selibi?' he asked in Swahili.

'Yes, this is Selibi. Do you want to speak to the *Bwana Mkubwa*? Who shall I say is calling?'

Daniel hung up the receiver and stared at it.

Selibi was Tug Harrison's manservant. So Bonny had telephoned Tug's flat the previous evening while he had been at the Jambo Bar.

'Curiouser and curiouser,' Daniel muttered. 'Miss Bonny isn't all she pretends to be – unless her old mum lives in Holland Park.'

 Every seat on the Air Ubomo flight to Kahali was taken. Most of the other passengers seemed to be businessmen or minor civil servants or politicians. There were half a dozen black soldiers in camouflage and decoration ribbons, berets and dark glasses. There were, however, no tourists – not yet, not before BOSS opened the new casino on the lakeshore.

The hostess was a tall Hita girl in flamboyant national dress. She handed out packets of sweet biscuits and plastic mugs of luke-warm tea with the haughty air of a queen distributing alms to her poor subjects. Halfway through the four-hour flight she disappeared into the toilet with one of the soldiers and all cabin service came to a halt.

They hit heavy clear-air turbulence over the eastern rim of

the Great Rift Valley and a corpulent black businessman in one of the front seats entertained them all with a noisy regurgitation of his breakfast. The air hostess remained ensconced in the rear toilet.

At last they were over the lake. Although like most names with colonial overtones, its name had been changed, Daniel still preferred Lake Albert to Lake Mobutu. The waters were pure azure, flecked with white horses and the sails of fishing dhows, and so wide that for a while there was no shore in sight. Then slowly the western shoreline emerged from the haze.

'Ubomo,' Daniel whispered, more to himself than to Bonny. The name had a romance and mystery that made the skin on his forearms tingle.

He would be following in the footsteps of the great African explorers. Speke had passed this way, and Stanley and ten thousand other hunters and slavers, soldiers and adventurers. He must try to instil some of that feeling of romance and history into his production. Across these waters had plied the ancient Arab dhows laden with ivory and slaves, the black and white gold that had once been the continent's major exports.

Some estimates were that five million souls had been captured like animals in the interior and herded down to the coast. To cross this lake they had been packed like sardines into the dhows, the first layer forced to lie on the bilge deck curled against each other, belly to back, like spoons. Then the removable deck planks were laid over them giving them eighteen inches of space, and another layer of human beings and another deck, until four decks were in place, crammed with howling, whining slaves.

With fair winds the crossing took two days and three nights. The Arab slave-masters were satisfied with a fifty per cent survival rate. It was a process of natural selection. Only the strong came through. On the eastern shore of the lake the living were lifted out of the holds coated with faeces and vomit. The dead were tossed overboard to the waiting crocodiles. The survivors were allowed to rest and gather strength for the last stage of the journey. When their masters deemed them fit, they were chained and yoked in long lines, each slave carrying a tusk of ivory, and they were marched down to the coast.

Daniel wondered if he could simulate some of the horrors of the trade with actors and a hired dhow. He anticipated the outcry that this would raise. So often he had been accused by reviewers and critics of depicting gratuitous violence and savagery in his productions. There was only one reply: 'Africa is a savage and violent continent. Anybody who tries to hide that from you is no true story-teller.' Blood was the fertiliser that made the African soil bloom.

He looked northwards across the shining waters. Up there where the Nile debouched from the lake there was a triangular wedge of land that fronted on to the river called the Lado Enclave. It had once been the private estate of the King of Belgium. The herds of elephant that inhabited those lands were more prolific and prodigiously tusked than anywhere else on the continent, and the Belgians had guarded and cherished them.

By international treaty the ownership of the Lado Enclave passed to the Sudan at the death of the Belgian king. When this happened the Belgian colonial service withdrew precipitately from the Lado, leaving a power vacuum. The European ivory-poachers swarmed in to take advantage. They fell upon the elephant herds and slaughtered them. Karamojo Bell describes in his autobiography how he followed a Lado herd from dawn until dusk, running to keep pace with them, shooting and running on again. In that single bloody day he killed twenty-three elephant.

Little had changed in the years since then, Daniel thought sadly. The slaughter and the rapine continued. And Africa bled. Africa cried to the civilised world for help, but what help was there to give? All the fifty member states of the Organization of African Unity combined were capable of generating only the same gross domestic product as little Belgium in the northern hemisphere.

How could the First World help Africa now? Daniel wondered. Aid poured into this vast continent was soaked up like a few raindrops upon the Saharan sands. A cynic had defined aid as simply the system by which poor white people in rich countries gave money to rich black people in poor countries to put into Swiss bank accounts. The sad truth was that Africa no longer mattered, particularly since the Berlin Wall had come down and Eastern Europe had started to emerge from the dark age of Communism. Africa was redundant. The rest of the world might give it passing sympathy, but Africa was beyond help. Europe would turn its attention to a more promising subject closer to home.

Daniel sighed and glanced at Bonny in the seat beside him. He wanted to discuss his thoughts, but she had kicked off her sandals and had her bare knees up against the back of the seat in front of her. She was chewing gum and reading a trashy science fiction paperback.

Instead Daniel looked out of the window again. The coast of Ubomo came up to meet them as the pilot began his descent. The savannah was red-brown as the hide of an impala antelope and studded with acacia trees. Upon the lakeshore the fishing villages were strung like beads, bound together by the narrow strip of green gardens and shambas that the lake waters nurtured. The village children waved as the aircraft passed overhead, and when the pilot turned on to final approach Daniel had a distant view of blue mountains clad with dark forest.

The air hostess re-emerged from the toilet, looking smug and adjusting her long green skirt, and ordered them in English and Swahili to fasten their seat-belts.

The unpainted galvanised roofs of the town flashed beneath them and they touched down heavily on the dusty strip. They taxied past the skeleton of steel and concrete beams that would have been the grand new Ephrem Taffari airport building if only the money had not run out, and came to a halt in front of the humbler edifice of unburnt brick that was a relic of Victor Omeru's reign.

As the door of the aircraft opened, the heat pressed in upon them and they were sweating before they reached the airport building.

A Hita officer in camouflage battledress and maroon beret singled Daniel out of the straggling group of passengers and came out on the field to meet him.

'Doctor Armstrong? I recognised you from the photograph on the dust-jacket of your book.' He held out his hand. 'I'm Captain Kajo. I will be your guide during your stay. The president, in person, has asked me to welcome you and assure you of our whole-hearted co-operation. Sir Peter Harrison is a personal friend of his, and President Taffari has expressed the wish to meet you as soon as you have recovered from the ill-effects of your journey. In fact he has arranged a cocktail party to welcome you to Ubomo.'

Captain Kajo spoke excellent English. He was a striking young man, slim and tall in the classical Hita mould. He towered over Daniel by a couple of inches. His jet eyes began to sparkle as he studied Bonny Mahon.

'This is my camera operator, Miss Mahon,' Daniel introduced them, and Bonny looked back at Captain Kajo with equal interest.

In the army Landrover, piled with their luggage and video equipment, Bonny leaned close to Daniel and asked, 'Is it true what they say about Africans being . . .' she sought the adjective, 'about them being large?'

'I've never made a study of it,' Daniel told her. 'But I could find out for you, if you'd like.'

'Don't put yourself out,' she grinned. 'If necessary, I can do my own research.'

Since he had learned about her secret phone call to Tug Harrison, Daniel's misgivings about her had increased. Now he didn't trust her at all, and he didn't even like her as much as he had only as recently as the previous day.

It was new moon, but the stars were clear and bright. Their reflections danced on the ruffled lake waters. Kelly Kinnear sat in the bows of the small dhow. The rigging creaked to the gentle push of the night breeze as they tacked across the lake.

The stars were magnificent. She turned her face up to them and whispered the lyrical names of the constellations as she recognised each of them. The stars were one of the few things she missed in the forest, for they were for ever hidden by the high unbroken canopy of the tree-tops. She savoured them now, for soon she would be without them.

285

The helmsman was singing a soft repetitive refrain, an invocation to the spirits of the lake depths, the *djinni* who controlled the fickle winds that pushed the dhow across the dark waters.

Kelly's mood was changeable as the breeze, dropping and shifting and then rising again. She was elated at the prospect of going once more into the forest, and the reunion with dear friends she loved so well. She was fearful of the journey and the dangers that still lay ahead before she could reach the safety of the tall trees. She was anxious that the political changes since the *coup d'état* would have destroyed and damaged much in her absence. She was saddened by the memory of damage already done, destruction already wrought upon the forest in the few short years since she had first entered their hushed cathedral depths.

At the same time, she was gladdened by the promises of support she had received and the interest she had been able to stir up during her visit to England and Europe, but disappointed that the support had been mainly moral and vocal rather than financial or constructive. She mustered all her enthusiasm and determination and forced herself to look ahead optimistically. We'll win through. We must win through.

Then suddenly and irrelevantly she thought of Daniel Armstrong, and she felt angry and unhappy again. Somehow his treachery was all the more heinous by reason of the blind faith and trust that she had placed in him before she had actually met him.

She had pre-judged him from what she had seen on the television screen and read in a few newspaper and magazine articles about him. From these she had formed a highly favourable opinion, not simply because he was handsome and articulate and his screen presence impressive, but because of the apparent depth of his understanding and his compassion for this poor wrecked continent which she had made her own.

She had written to him twice, addressing her letters to the television studio. Those letters could never have reached him or, if they did, they must have been overlooked in the huge volume of mail she was sure was addressed to him. In any event she had received no reply.

Then when the unexpected opportunity had presented itself

in Nairobi, Daniel Armstrong had, at first meeting, borne out all the high hopes she had placed in him. He was warm and compassionate and approachable. She had been aware of the instant *rapport* between them. They were people from the same world, with similar interests and concerns and, more than that, she knew that an essential spark had been struck between them. The attraction had been mutual; they had both recognised it. There had been a meeting and a docking of their minds as well as an undeniable physical attraction.

Kelly did not consider herself to be a sensual person. The only lovers she had ever taken were men whose intellects she admired. The first had been one of her professors at medical school, a fine man twenty-five years her senior. They were still friends. Two others were fellow students, and the fourth the man she eventually married. Paul had been a medical doctor like herself. The two of them had qualified in the same year and had come out to Africa as a team. He had died from the bite of one of the deadly forest mambas within the first six months and at every opportunity she still visited his grave at the foot of a gigantic silk-cotton tree on the banks of the Ubomo River deep in the forest.

Four lovers in all her thirty-two years. No, she was not a sensual person, but she had been intensely aware of the strong pull that Daniel Armstrong had exerted upon her, and she had experienced no great urge to resist it. He was the kind of man for her.

Then suddenly it was all a lie and a delusion, and he was just like the rest of them. A hired gun, she thought angrily, for BOSS and that monster Harrison. She tried to use her anger to shield herself against the sense of loss she felt at the destruction of an ideal. She had believed in Daniel Armstrong. She had given him her trust and he had betrayed it.

Put him out of your mind, she determined. Don't think about him again. He's not worth it. But she was honest enough to realise that it was not going to be that easy.

From the stern the helmsman of the dhow called softly to her in Swahili and she roused herself and looked forward. The shoreline was half a mile ahead, the low line of beach surf creaming softly in the starlight.

Ubomo. She was coming home. Her mood soared.

Suddenly there was a cry from the helm and she spun about. The two crew men, naked except for their loin-cloths, ran forward. In haste they seized the main sheet and brought the boom of the sail crashing down upon the deck. The lateen sail billowed and folded and they sprang upon it and furled it swiftly. Within seconds the stubby mast was bare and the dhow was wallowing low on the dark waters.

'What is it?' Kelly called softly in Swahili, and the helmsman answered quietly, 'Patrol boat.'

She heard it then, the throb of the diesel engine above the wind and her nerves sprang tight. The crew of the dhow were all Uhali tribesmen, loyal to old President Omeru. They were risking their lives, just as she was, by defying the curfew and crossing the lake in darkness.

They crouched on the open deck and stared out into the darkness, listening to the beat of the engine swelling louder. The gunboat was the gift of an Arab oil sheikh to the new regime, a fast forty-foot assault craft with twin cannon in armoured turrets fore and aft. It had seen thirty years' service in the Red Sea. It spent most of its time tied-up in the port of Kahali, with engines broken down, awaiting spare parts. However, they had picked a bad night for the crossing; the gunboat was for once seaworthy and dangerous.

Kelly saw the flash of foam at the bows of the oncoming patrol boat. It was heading up from the south. Instinctively she crouched lower, trying to shield herself behind the bulwark as she considered her position. On its present course the patrol boat must surely spot them. If Kelly were found on board the dhow, the crew would be shot without trial, one of those public executions on the beach of Kahali which were part of Ephrem Taffari's new style of government. Of course she would be shot alongside them, but that did not concern Kelly at that moment. These were good men who had risked their lives for her. She had to do all in her power to protect them.

If she were not found on board, and there were no other contraband, the crew might have a chance of talking themselves out of trouble. They would almost certainly be beaten and fined, and the dhow might be confiscated, but they might escape execution.

She reached for her backpack that lay in the bows. Quickly she undid the straps that held the inflatable mattress strapped to the underside of the pack. She unrolled the nylon-covered mattress and frantically blew into the valve, filling her lungs and then exhaling long and hard, all the time watching the dark shape of the patrol boat loom out of the night. It was coming up fast. There was no time to inflate the mattress fully. It was still soft and floppy as she closed the valve.

She stood up and slung the pack on her back and called back to the helmsman, 'Thank you, my friend. Peace be with you, and may Allah preserve you.' The lake people were nearly all Muslim.

'And with you be peace,' he called back. She could hear the relief and gratitude in his tone. He knew she was doing this for him and his crew.

Kelly sat on the bulwark and swung her legs overboard. She clutched the semi-inflated mattress to her chest and drew a deep breath before she dropped into the lake. The water closed over her head. It was surprisingly cold and the heavy pack on her back carried her deep before the buoyancy of the mattress asserted itself and lifted her back to the surface.

She broke through, gasping and with water streaming into her eyes. It took her a few minutes to master the trim of the bobbing mattress, but at last she lay half across it, her legs dangling, the strap of the backpack hooked over her arm. It held her head clear, but she was low down in the water. The waves dashed into her face and threatened to overturn her precarious craft.

She looked for the dhow and was surprised to see how far she had drifted from it. As she watched, the boom was hoisted and the sail filled. The ungainly little boat turned to run free before the breeze, trying to get clear of the forbidden coast before the patrol boat spotted her.

'Good luck,' she whispered, and a wave broke into her face. She choked and coughed, and when she looked again both the dhow and the patrol boat had disappeared into the night.

She kicked out gently, careful not to upset her balance, conserving her strength for the long night ahead. She knew that some monstrous crocodiles inhabited the lake; she had seen a photograph of one that measured eighteen feet from the tip of its hideous snout to the end of its thick crested tail. She put the picture out of her mind and kept kicking, lining herself up by the stars, swimming towards where Orion stood on his head upon the western horizon.

A few minutes later she glimpsed a flash of light far upwind. It may have been the searchlight of the patrol boat as it picked up the shape of the dhow. She forced herself not to look back. She didn't want to know the worst, for there was nothing more she could do to save the men who had helped her.

She kept swimming, kicking to a steady rhythm. After an hour she wondered if she had moved at all. The backpack was like a drogue anchor hanging below the half-inflated mattress. However, she dared not jettison it. Without the basic equipment it contained, she was doomed.

She kept on swimming. Another hour and she was almost exhausted. She was forced to rest. One calf was cramping badly. The breeze had dropped and in the silence she heard a soft regular rumbling, like an old man snoring in his sleep. It took her a moment to place the sound.

'The beach surf,' she whispered, and kicked out again with renewed strength.

She felt the water lift and surge under her as it met the shelving bottom. She swam on, torturously slowly, dragging herself and the sodden pack through the water.

Now she saw the ivory-nut palms above the beach silhouetted against the stars. She held her breath and reached down with both feet. Again the water closed over her head, but with her toes she felt the sandy bottom, six feet below the surface, and found enough strength for one last effort.

Minutes later she could stand. The surf knocked her sprawling, but she dragged herself up again and staggered up the narrow beach to find shelter in a patch of papyrus reeds. Her watch was a waterproof Rolex, a wedding gift from Paul. The time was a few minutes after four. It would be light soon. She must get in before a Hita patrol picked her up, but she was too cold and stiff and exhausted to move just yet.

While she rested she forced herself to open the pack with numb fingers and to empty out the water that almost doubled its weight. She wrung out her few spare items of clothing and wiped down the other equipment as best she could. While she worked she chewed a high-energy sugar bar and almost immediately felt better.

She repacked the bag, slung it, and started back northwards, keeping parallel to the lake, but well back from the soft beach sand which would record her footprints for a Hita patrol to follow.

Every few hundred yards there were the gardens and thatched buildings of the small shambas. Dogs barked and she was forced to detour round the huts to avoid detection. She hoped that she was heading in the right direction. She reasoned that the captain of the dhow would have come in upwind of his destination to give himself leeway in which to make his landfall so she must keep northwards.

She had been going for almost an hour, but reckoned that she had covered only a couple of miles when, with a surge of relief, she saw ahead of her the pale round dome of the little mosque shining like a bald man's head in the first pearly radiance of the dawn.

She broke into a weary trot, weighed down by the pack and her fatigue. She smelt woodsmoke, and saw the faint glow of the fire under the dark tamarind tree, just where it should have been. Closer, she made out the figures of two men squatting close beside the fire.

'Patrick!' she called hoarsely, and one of the figures jumped up and ran towards her.

'Patrick,' she repeated, and stumbled and would have fallen if he had not caught her.

'Kelly! Allah be praised. We had given you up.'

'The patrol boat . . .' she gasped.

'Yes. We heard firing and saw the light. We thought they had caught you.'

Patrick Omeru was one of old President Omeru's nephews. So far he had escaped the purges by Taffari's soldiers. He was one of the first friends that Kelly had made after her arrival in Ubomo. He lifted the pack from her shoulders, and she groaned with relief. The wet straps had abraded her delicate skin.

'Kill the fire,' Patrick called to his brother, and he kicked sand over the coals. Between them they led Kelly to where the truck was parked in a grove of mango trees behind the derelict mosque. They helped her into the back and spread a tarpaulin over her as she lay on the dirty floorboards. The truck stank of dried fish.

Even though the truck jolted and crashed through the potholes, she was at last warm, and soon she slept. It was a trick she had learned in the forest, to be able to sleep in any circumstances of discomfort.

The sudden cessation of engine noise and movement woke her again. She did not know how long she had slept, but it was light now and a glance at her watch showed her it was after nine in the morning. She lay quietly under her tarpaulin and listened to the sound of men's voices close alongside the truck. She knew better than to disclose her presence.

Minutes later, Patrick pulled back the tarpaulin and smiled at her.

'Where are we, Patrick?'

'Kahali, in the old town. A safe place.'

The truck was parked in the small yard of one of the old Arab houses. The building was dilapidated, the yard filthy with chicken droppings and rubbish. Chickens roosted under the eaves or scratched in the dirt. There was a strong smell of drains and sewage. The Omeru family had fallen on hard times since the old president's downfall.

In the sparsely furnished front room, with its stained walls on which old yellowed newspaper cuttings had been pasted, Patrick's wife had a meal ready for her. It was a stew of chicken spiced with chilli and served with a bowl of manioc and stewed plantains. She was hungry, and it was good.

While she ate, other men came to speak to her. They slipped in quietly and squatted beside her in the bare room. They told her what had happened in Ubomo during her absence, and she frowned while she listened. Very little of it was good tidings. They knew where she was going and they gave her messages to take with her. Then they slipped away again as quietly and furtively as they had arrived.

It was long after dark when Patrick stood up and told her quietly, 'It is time to go on.'

The truck was now loaded with dried fish in woven baskets. They had built a small hiding-place for her under the load. She crawled into it and Patrick passed her pack in to her, then sealed the opening behind her with another basket of fish.

The truck started and rumbled out of the yard. This part of the journey was only three hundred miles. She settled down and slept again.

She woke every time the truck stopped. Whenever she heard voices, the loud arrogant voices of Hita speaking Swahili with the distinctive cutting accent, she knew they had halted at another military road-block.

Once Patrick stopped the truck along a deserted stretch of road and let her out of her hiding-place and she went a short distance into the veld to relieve herself. They were still in the open grassland savannah below the rim of the Great Rift. She heard cattle lowing somewhere close and knew that there was a Hita *manyatta* nearby.

When she woke again it was to a peculiar new motion and to the chant of the ferrymen. It was a nostalgic sound and she knew she was nearly home.

During the night she had opened a small peephole from her little cave under the baskets of dried fish into the outside world. Through it she caught glimpses of the expanses of the Ubomo River touched with the hot orange and violet of the breaking dawn.

The silhouettes of the ferrymen passed back and forth in front of her peephole as they handled the lines that linked the ferry-boat from one bank of the river to the other. The ferry across the Ubomo River was almost at the edge of the great forest. She could imagine it as clearly as if she were actually looking at it.

The wide sweep of the river was the natural boundary between savannah and forest. The first time she had stood upon its bank she had been amazed by the abruptness with which the forest began. On the east bank the open grass and acacia dropped away towards the lake, while on the far bank stood a gigantic palisade of dark trees, a solid unbroken wall a hundred feet high, with some of the real giants towering another fifty feet above those. It had seemed to her at once both forbidding and frightening. On the far bank the road tunnelled into the forest like a rabbit hole.

In the few short years since then, the forest had been hacked back as the land-hungry peasantry nibbled at its edges. They had toppled the great trees that had taken hundreds of years to grow and burned them where they fell for charcoal and fertiliser. The forest retreated before this onslaught. It was now almost five miles from the ferry to the edge of the tree-line.

In between lay sprawling shambas with fields of plantains and manioc. The worked-out ground was being abandoned to weeds and secondary growth. The fragile forest soils could bear only two or three years of cultivation before they were exhausted and the peasant farmers moved on to clear more forest.

Even when it reached the retreating forest edge, the road was no longer a tunnel through the trees, roofed over with a high canopy of vegetation as it once had been. The verges of the road had been cut back half a mile on each side. The peasants had used the road as an access to the interior of the forest. They had built their villages alongside the road and hacked out their gardens and plantations from the living forest that bordered it. This was the terribly destructive 'slash and burn' cultivation method by which they felled the trees and burned them where they fell. Those true giants of the forest, whose girth defied the puny axes, they destroyed by building a slow fire around the base of the trunk. They kept it burning week after week until it ate through the hardwood core and toppled two hundred feet of massive trunk.

The road itself was like a deadly blade, a spear into the guts of the forest, steeped in the poison of civilisation. Kelly hated the road. It was a channel of infection and corruption into the virginal womb of the forest.

Looking out of her peephole she saw that the road was wider now than she remembered it. The deep rutted tracks were churned by the wheels of logging and mining trucks and the other heavy traffic that had begun using it since President Omeru had been overthrown and the forest concession given to the powerful foreign syndicate to develop.

She knew from her studies and the meticulous records that she kept that already the road had altered the local rainfall patterns. The mile-wide cutline was unprotected by the umbrella of the forest canopy. The tropical sun struck down on this open swathe and heated the unshielded earth, causing a vast updraught of air above the road. This dispersed the rain clouds that daily gathered over the green forest. Nowadays little rain fell along the roadway, although it still teemed down at the rate of three hundred inches a year upon the pristine forests only a few miles away.

The roadside was dry and dusty and hot. The mango trees wilted in the noonday heat and the people living beside the road built themselves *barazas*, thatched roofs supported by poles without walls, to shield them from the cloudless sky above the roadway. Without the forest canopy the whole Ubomo basin would soon become a little Sahara.

To Kelly the road was the Sodom and Gomorrah of the forest. It was temptation to her Bambuti friends. The truck-drivers had money and they wanted meat and honey and women. The Bambuti were skilled hunters who could provide both meat and honey, and their young girls, tiny and graceful, laughing and big-breasted, were peculiarly attractive to the tall bantu men.

The roadway seduced the Bambuti and lured them out of the fastness of the deep forest. It was destroying their traditional way of life. It encouraged the pygmies to over-hunt their forest preserves. Where once they had hunted only to feed themselves and their tribe, now they hunted to sell the meat at the roadside *dukas*, the little trading stores set up at each new village.

Game was each day scarcer in the forest and soon, Kelly knew, the Bambuti would be tempted to hunt in the heartland, that special remote centre of the forest where by tradition and religious restraint no Bambuti had ever hunted before.

At the roadside the Bambuti discovered palm wine and bottled beer and spirits. Like most stone-age people, from the Australian Aboriginals to the Inuit Eskimos of the Arctic, they had little resistance to alcohol. A drunken pygmy was a pitiful sight.

In the deep forest, there was no tribal tradition that restrained the Bambuti girls from sexual intercourse before marriage. They were allowed all the experimentation and indulgence they wanted with the boys of the tribe, except only that intercourse must not be with a full embrace. The unmarried couple must hold each other's elbows only, not clasp each other chest to chest. To them the sexual act was a natural and pleasant expression of affection, and they were by nature friendly and full of fun. They were easy game for the sophisticated truck-drivers from the towns. Eager to please, they sold their favours for a trinket or a bottle of beer or a few shillings, and from the lopsided bargain they were left with syphilis or gonorrhoea or, most deadly of all, AIDS.

In her hatred of the road, Kelly wished there was some way to halt this intrusion, this accelerating process of degradation and destruction, but she knew that there was none. BOSS and the syndicate were behemoths on the march. The forest, its soil, its trees, its animals, birds and its people were all too fragile. All she could hope for was to help retard the process and in the end to save some precious fragment from the melting-pot of progress and development, and exploitation.

Abruptly the truck swung off the road and in a cloud of red talcum dust drew up at the rear of one of the roadside *dukas*. Peering from her peephole, Kelly saw that it was a typical roadside store with mud walls and roof, thatched with ilala palm fronds. There was a logging truck parked in front of it and the driver and his mate were haggling with the store-keeper for the purchase of sweet yams and strips of dried game meat blackened with smoke.

Patrick Omeru and his brother began to unload some of the baskets of dried fish to sell to the store-keeper and as they worked he spoke without looking at Kelly's hiding-place.

'Are you all right, Kelly?'

'I'm fine, Patrick. I'm ready to move,' she called back softly.

'Wait, Doctor. I must make certain that it is safe. The army patrols the road regularly. I'll speak to the store-keeper; he knows when the soldiers will come.'

Patrick went on unloading the fish. In front of the *duka* the truck-driver completed his transaction and carried his purchases to the logging truck. He climbed on board and started up with a roar and cloud of diesel smoke, then pulled out into the rutted roadway towing two huge trailers behind the truck. The trailers were laden with forty-foot lengths of African mahogany logs, each five feet in diameter, the whole cargo comprising hundreds of tons of valuable hardwood.

As soon as the truck had gone, Patrick called to the Uhali store-keeper and they spoke together quietly. The store-keeper shook his head and pointed back along the road. Patrick hurried back to the side of the fish truck.

'Quickly, Kelly. The patrol will be coming any minute now, but we should hear the army vehicle long before it arrives. The store-keeper says that the soldiers never go into the forest. They are afraid of the forest spirits.'

He pulled away the fish baskets that covered the entrance to Kelly's hiding-place, and she scrambled out and jumped down to the sun-baked earth. She felt stiff and cramped, and she stretched her body to its full extent, lifting her hands over her head and twisting from the waist to get the kinks out of her spine.

'You must go quickly, Kelly,' Patrick urged her. 'The patrol! I wish I had someone to go with you, to protect you.'

Kelly laughed and shook her head. 'Once I'm in the forest, I will be safe.' She felt gay and happy at the prospect, but Patrick looked worried.

'The forest is an evil place.'

'You are also afraid of the *djinni*, aren't you, Patrick?' she teased him as she shrugged her pack on to her shoulders. She knew that, like most Uhali or Hita, Patrick had never entered the deep forest. They were all terrified of the forest spirits. Whenever possible the Bambuti were at pains to describe these malignant spirits and to invent horror stories of their own dreadful encounters with them. It was one of the Bambuti devices for keeping the big black men out of their secret preserves.

'Of course not, Kelly.' Patrick denied the charge a little too hotly. 'I am an educated man; I do not believe in *djinni* or evil spirits.' But even as he spoke his eyes strayed towards the impenetrable wall of high trees that stood just beyond the half-mile wide strip of gardens and plantations. He shuddered and changed the subject.

'You will get a message to me in the usual way?' he asked anxiously. 'We must know how he is.'

297

'Don't worry.' She smiled at him and took his hand. 'Thank you, Patrick. Thank you for everything.'

'It is we who should thank you, Kelly. May Allah give you peace.'

'*Salaam aleikum*,' she replied. 'To you peace also, Patrick.' And she turned and slipped away under the wide green fronds of the banana trees. Within a dozen paces she was hidden from the road.

As she went through the gardens she picked the fruits from the trees, filling the pockets of her backpack with ripe mangoes and plantains. It was a Bambuti trick. The village gardens and the villages themselves were considered fair hunting grounds. The pygmies borrowed anything that was left untended, but stealing was not as much fun as gulling the villagers into parting with food and valuables by elaborate confidence tricks. Kelly smiled as she recalled the glee with which old Sepoo related his successful scams to the rest of the tribe whenever he returned from the villages to the hunting camps in the deep forest.

Now she helped herself to the garden produce with as little conscience as old Sepoo would have evinced. In London she would have been appalled by the notion of shoplifting in Selfridges, but as she approached the edge of the forest she was already beginning to think like a Bambuti again. It was the way of survival.

At the end of the last garden there was a fence of thorn branches to keep out the forest creatures that raided the crops at night, and at intervals along this fence, set on poles were grubby spirit flags and juju charms to discourage the forest demons and *djinni* from approaching the villages. The Bambuti always howled with mirth when they passed this evidence of the villagers' superstition. It was proof of the success of their own subtle propaganda.

Kelly found a narrow gap in the fence, just big enough to accommodate the pygmy who had made it and she slipped through.

The forest lay ahead of her. She lifted up her eyes and watched a flock of grey parrots flying shrieking along the tree-tops a hundred feet above her.

The entrance to the forest was thick and entangled. Where the sunlight had penetrated to the ground it had raised a thicket of secondary growth. There was a pygmy track through this undergrowth, but even Kelly was forced to stoop to enter it. The average Bambuti was at least a foot shorter than she was, and with their machetes they cut the undergrowth just above their own head-height. When fresh, the raw shoots were easy to spot, but once they dried, they were sharp as daggers and on the level of Kelly's face and eyes. She moved with dainty care. She did not realise it herself, but in the forest she had learned by example to carry herself with the same agile grace as a pygmy.

It was one of the Bambuti's derisive taunts that somebody walked like a *wazungu* in the forest. *Wazungu* was the derogatory term for any outsider, any foreigner. Even old Sepoo admitted that Kelly walked like one of the real people and not like a white *wazungu*.

The peripheral screen of dense undergrowth was several hundred feet wide. It ended abruptly and Kelly stepped out on to the true forest floor.

It was like entering a submarine cavern, a dim and secret place. The sunlight was reflected down through successive layers of leaves, so that the entire forest world was washed with green, and the air was warm and moist and redolent of leaf mould and fungus, a relief from the heat and dust and merciless sunlight of the outside world. Kelly filled her lungs with the smell and looked around her, blinking as her eyes adjusted to this strange and lovely light. There was no dense undergrowth here, the great tree-trunks reached up to the high green roof and shaded away into the green depths ahead, reminding her of the hall of pillars in the mighty temple of Karnak on the banks of the Nile.

Under her feet the dead leaves were thick and luxuriant as a precious oriental carpet. They gave a spring to her step and rustled under her feet to give warning to the forest creatures of her approach. It was unwise to come unannounced upon one of the wicked red buffalo or to step upon one of the deadly adders that lay curled upon the forest floor.

Kelly moved swiftly, lightly, with the susurration of dead

leaves under her feet, stopping once to cut herself a digging-stick and to sharpen the point with her clasp-knife as she went on.

She sang as she went, one of the praise songs to the forest that Sepoo's wife, Pamba, had taught her. It was a Bambuti hymn, for the forest itself is their god. They worship it as both Mother and Father. They do not believe a jot in the hobgoblins and evil spirits whose existence they so solemnly endorse and whose depredations they recount with so much glee to the black villagers. For the Bambuti the forest is a living entity, a deity which can give up or withhold its bounty, which can give favours or wreak retribution on those who flout its laws and do it injury. Over the years she had lived under the forest roof Kelly had come more than halfway to accepting the Bambuti philosophy, and now she sang to the forest as she travelled swiftly across its floor.

In the middle of the afternoon it began to rain, one of those solid downpours that were a daily occurrence. The heavy drops falling thick and heavy as stones upon the upper galleries of the forest roared like a distant river in spate. Had it fallen on bare earth with such force, it would have ripped away the topsoil and raked deep scars, washed out plains and scoured the hillsides, flooding the rivers and wreaking untold harm.

In the forest the top galleries of the trees broke the force of the storm, cushioning the gouts of water, gathering them up and redirecting them down the trunks of the great trees, scattering them benevolently across the thick carpet of dead leaves and mould, so that the earth was able to absorb and restrain the rain's malevolent power. The rivers and streams, instead of becoming muddied by the torn earth and choked by uprooted trees, still ran sweet and crystal clear.

As the rain sifted down softly upon her, Kelly slipped off her cotton shirt and placed it in one of the waterproof pockets of her pack. The straps would cut into her bare shoulders so she rigged the headband around her forehead and kept her arms clear as the pygmy women do. She went on, not bothering to take shelter from the blood-warm rain.

Now she was bare-chested, wearing only a brief pair of cotton shorts and her canvas running shoes. Minimal dress was

300

the natural forest way. The Bambuti wore only a loincloth of beaten bark.

When the first Belgian missionaries had discovered the Bambuti, they had been outraged by their nakedness and sent to Brussels for dresses and jackets and calico breeches, all in children's sizes, which they forced them to wear. In the humidity of the forest these clothes were always damp and unhealthy and the pygmies for the first time had suffered from pneumonia and other respiratory complaints.

After the constraints of city life, it felt good to be half-naked and free. Kelly delighted in the rain upon her body. Her skin was clear and creamy pale, almost luminous in the soft green light and her small taut breasts joggled elastically to her stride.

She moved swiftly, foraging as she went, hardly pausing as she gathered up a scattering of mushrooms with glossy domed heads and brilliant orange gills. These were the most delicious of the thirty-odd edible varieties. On the other hand there were fifty or more inedible varieties, a few of which were virulently toxic, dealing certain death within hours of a single mouthful. The rain ceased but the trees still dripped.

Once she stopped and traced a slim vine down the trunk of a mahogany tree. She dug its pure white roots out of the rain-soaked leaf mould with a few strokes of her digging-stick. The roots were sweet as sugar cane and crunched scrumptiously as she chewed them. They were nutritious and filled her with energy.

The green shadows crowded closer as the day died away and the light faded. She looked for a place to camp. She did not want to be bothered with having to build a waterproof hut for herself, the hollow at the base of one of the giant tree-trunks would do admirably as a hearth for a single night.

Her feet still rustled through the dead leaves, even though they were now dampened. Suddenly there was an explosive sound, a rush of air under pressure like a burst motor-car tyre, only ten feet or so ahead of her. It was one of the most terrifying sounds in the forest, worse than the bellow of an angry buffalo or the roaring grunt of one of the huge black boars. Kelly leaped involuntarily backwards, from a steady run she rose two feet in the air and landed as far as that back in her own tracks.

Her hand was shaking as she flicked the headband off her forehead and dropped the backpack to the leafy floor. In the same movement she dipped into one of the pockets and brought out her slingshot.

Because of her slingshot the Bambuti had given her the name 'Baby Archer'. Though they mocked her merrily, they were really impressed by her skill with the weapon. Even old Sepoo had never been able to master it, though Kelly had tutored him patiently. In the end he had abandoned the effort with a haughty declaration that the bow and arrow were the only real weapons for a hunter, and that this silly little thing was only suitable for children and babies. So she had become 'Baby Archer', Kara-Ki.

With one quick motion she slipped the brace over her wrist and drew the heavy surgical elastic bands to her right ear. The missile was a steel ball-bearing.

On the forest floor ahead of her something moved. It looked like a pile of dead leaves or an Afghan rug patterned in the colours of the forest, golds and ochres and soft mauves, striped and starred with diamonds and arrowheads of black that tricked the eye. Kelly knew that what seemed to be an amorphous mass was in reality a serpentine body, coiled upon itself, each coil as thick as her calf, but laced and camouflaged with cunning and seductive colour. The gaboon adder is, except for the mamba, Africa's most venomous snake.

In the centre of this coiled pyramid of body, the head was drawn back like a nocked arrow upon the S-bend of the neck. The head was pig-snouted, flattened and scaled, the eyes were raised on horny protuberances, the colour and lucidity of precious topaz. The pupils were bright as jet and focused upon her. The whole head was bigger than both her fists held together. The feathery black tongue flicked from between the thin grinning lips.

Kelly held her aim for only a fraction of a second and then let fly. The silver ball-bearing hummed as it flew, glinting like a drop of mercury in the soft green light. It struck the gaboon adder on the point of its snout and split its skull with such force that jets of blood spurted from the nostrils and the grotesque head was whipped over backwards. With one last

302

explosive hiss the adder writhed into its death throes, the great coils of its body sliding and twisting over themselves, convulsing and contorting, exposing the pale belly latticed with diagonal scales.

Kelly circled the adder cautiously, holding the pointed digging-stick at the ready. As the shattered head flopped clear she darted forward and pinned it to the earth. Holding it down with all her weight while the adder wound itself around the shaft, Kelly opened the blade of her clasp-knife with her small white teeth and with a single slash lopped off the snake's head.

She left the headless body to finish its last reflexive throes and looked around her for a campsite. There was a natural cave in the base of one of the tree-trunks nearby, a perfect night shelter.

The Bambuti had never fathomed the art of making fire and the women carried a live coal with them when they moved from hunting-camp to hunting-camp, but Kelly flicked her plastic Bic lighter and within minutes she had a cheerful little fire burning at the base of the tree. She opened her pack and set up her camp. Then, armed with the digging-stick and clasp-knife, she returned to the carcass of the gaboon adder. It weighed almost ten kilos, far too much for her own needs. Already the red serowe ants had found it. Nothing lay long on the forest floor before the scavengers arrived.

Kelly cut a thick section from the centre of the carcass, scraped the ants away, and skinned the portion with a few expert strokes. The meat was clean and white. She lifted two thick fillets from the bone and placed them over the coals of her fire on a skillet of green twigs. She scattered a few leaves from one of the herby bushes over the fire and the smoke flavoured and perfumed the flesh. While it grilled, she strung the orange-gilled mushrooms on another green twig. Like a kebab she placed it on the fire, turning it regularly.

The mushrooms had a richer fungus flavour than black truffles and the flesh of the adder tasted like a mixture of lobster and milk-fed chicken. The exertions of the day had sharpened her appetite and Kelly could not remember a more delicious meal. She washed it down with sweet water from the stream nearby.

During the night she was awakened by a loud snuffling and gulping close to where she lay in her tree-trunk shelter. She did not need to see to know what had disturbed her. The giant forest hog can weigh as much as 650 pounds and stand three feet high at the shoulder. These pigs, the largest and rarest in the world, are as dangerous as a lion when aroused. But Kelly felt no fear as she listened to it gobbling the remains of the adder's carcass. When it was finished the pig came snuffling around her camp, but she tossed a few twigs on the coals and when they flared up the pig grunted hoarsely and shambled away into the forest.

In the morning she bathed in the stream and combed out her hair and replaited it while it was still wet into a thick dark glistening braid that hung down her naked back.

She ate the rest of last night's adder steak and mushrooms cold and was on her way again as soon as it was light enough. Although she had a compass in her pack, she navigated chiefly by the fungus plates and the serowe ant nests, which were attached only to the southern side of the tree-trunks, and by the flow and direction of the streams she crossed.

In the middle of the afternoon she cut the well-defined trail she was searching for, and turned to follow it in a south-westerly direction. Within the hour she recognised a landmark, a natural bridge across one of the streams formed by the massive trunk of an ancient tree that had fallen across the water-course.

Sepoo had told her once that the tree bridge had been there 'since the beginning of time', which meant in his living memory. Time and numbers were not concrete concepts in the pygmy mind. They counted 'one, two, three, many'. In the forest where the seasons made no difference to the rainfall or temperature, they regulated their lives on the phases of the moon, and moved from one camp to the next every full moon. Thus they never stayed long enough at one site to deplete the game or the fruits in the area, or to pollute the streams and sour the earth with their wastes.

The tree bridge was polished by generations of their tiny feet and Kelly inspected it minutely for fresh muddy tracks to judge how recently it had been used. She was disappointed and hurried on to the campsite nearby where she had hoped to find them. They were gone, but judging by the sign, this had been their last camp, they would have moved weeks previously at the full moon.

There were three or four other localities where they might be at this moment, the furthest almost a hundred miles away towards the heartland of the vast area which Sepoo's tribe looked upon as their own.

However, there was no telling which direction they had chosen. Like all tribal decisions, it would have been made at the last moment by a heated and lively debate in which all joined with equal voice. Kelly smiled as she guessed how the argument had probably been resolved. She had seen it so often. One of the women, not necessarily the eldest or most senior, fed up with the silliness and obstinacy of the men, not least that of her own husband, would suddenly have picked up her bundle, adjusted her headband, bowed forward to balance the weight, and trotted off down the trail. The others, many of them still grumbling, would have followed her in a straggling line.

In the Bambuti community there were no chiefs or leaders. Every adult male or female of whatever age had equal voice and weight. Only in a few matters such as when and where to spread the hunting-nets, the younger members would probably defer to the experience of one of the famous older hunters, but only after suitable face-saving argument and discussion.

Kelly looked around the deserted campsite and was amused to see what the tribe had abandoned. There were a wooden pestle and mortar used for pounding manioc, a fine steel mattock, a disembowelled transistor radio and various other items obviously purloined from the villages along the road. She was certain that the Bambuti were the least material people on earth. Possessions meant almost nothing to them, and after the fun of stealing them faded, they swiftly lost interest in them.

'Too heavy to carry,' they explained to Kelly when she asked. 'We can always borrow another one from the *wazungu*, if we need one.' Their eyes danced at the prospect, and they screamed with laughter and slapped each other on the back.

The only possessions they treasured enough to keep and

hand down to their children were the hunting-nets of woven bark. Each family had a hundred-foot length which they strung together with all the others to make the long communal net. The game was shared, with all the usual vehement debate, according to a time-honoured system amongst all those who had participated in the hunt.

Living within the bounty of the forest they had no need to accumulate wealth. Their clothing of bark-cloth could be renewed with a few hours' work, stripping and beating out the pith with a wooden mallet. Their weapons were disposable and renewable. The spear and the bow were whittled from hardwood and strung with bark fibre. The arrow and the spear were not even tipped with iron, but the points were simply hardened in the fire. The broad mongongo leaves roofed over their huts of arched saplings, and a small fire gave them warmth and comfort in the night.

The forest god gave them food in abundance, what need had they of other possessions? They were the only people Kelly had ever known who were completely satisfied with their lot, and this accounted for a great deal of their appeal.

Kelly had been looking forward to being reunited with them and she was downcast at having missed them. Sitting on a log in the deserted camp that was so swiftly reverting to jungle, she considered her next move. It would be futile to try and guess in which direction they had gone, and foolhardy to try and follow them. Their tracks would long ago have been obliterated by rain and the passage of other forest creatures, and she knew only this relatively small area of the forest with any certainty. There were twenty thousand square miles out there that she had never seen and where she might lose herself for ever.

She must give up trying to find them, and go on to her own base camp at Gondala, the 'place of the happy elephant'. In time the Bambuti would find her there and she must be patient.

She sat a little longer and listened to the forest. It seemed at first to be a silent lonely place. Only when the ear had learned to hear beyond the quiet did one realise that the forest was always filled with living sound. The orchestra of the insects played an eternal background music, the hum and reverberation like softly stroked violins, the click and clatter like tiny castanets, the wails and whine and buzz like the wind instruments. From the high upper galleries the birds called and sang and the monkeys crashed from branch to branch or lowed mournfully to the open sky, while on the leaf-strewn floor the dwarf antelope scuttled and scampered furtively.

Now when Kelly listened more intently still, she thought she heard far away and very faintly the clear whistle from high in the trees that old Sepoo solemnly swore was the crested chameleon announcing that the hives were overflowing and the honey season had begun.

Kelly smiled and stood up. She knew as a biologist that chameleons could not whistle. And yet . . . She smiled again, settled her pack and stepped back on to the dim trail and went on towards Gondala. More and more frequently there were landmarks and signposts she recognised along the trail, the shape of certain tree-trunks and the juncture of trails, a sandbank at a river crossing and blazes on the tree-trunks which she had cut long ago with her machete. She was getting closer and closer to home.

At a turning in the trail she came suddenly upon a steaming pile of yellow dung, as high as her knee. She looked about eagerly for the elephant that had dropped it, but already it had disappeared like a grey shadow into the trees. She wondered if it might be the Old Man with One Ear, a heavily tusked bull elephant that was often in the forest around Gondala.

Once the elephant herds had roamed the open savannah, along the shores of the lake and in the Lado Enclave to the north of the forest. However, a century of ruthless persecution, first by the old Arab slavers and their minions armed with muzzle-loading black powder guns and then by the European sportsmen and ivory-hunters with their deadly rifled weapons had decimated the herds and driven the survivors into the fastness of the forest.

It gave Kelly a deep sense of satisfaction to know that, although she seldom saw them, she shared the forest with those great sagacious beasts, and that her home was named after one of them.

At the next stream she paused to bathe and comb her hair and don her T-shirt. She would be home in a few hours. She had just tied the thong in her braid and put away her comb when she chilled to a new sound, fierce and menacing. She came to her feet and seized her digging-stick. The sound came again, the hoarse sawing that roughened her nerves like sandpaper, and she felt her pulse accelerate and her breath come short.

It was unusual to hear a leopard call in daylight. The spotted cat was a creature of the night, but anything unusual in the forest was to be treated with caution. The leopard called again, a little closer, almost directly upstream on the bank of the river, and Kelly cocked her head to listen. There was something odd about this leopard.

A suspicion flitted across her mind, and she waited, crouching, holding the sharpened digging-stick ready. There was a long silence. All the forest was listening to the leopard, and then it called again, that terrible ripping sound. It was on the riverbank above her, not more than fifty feet from where she crouched.

This time, listening to the call, Kelly's suspicion became certainty. With a blood-curdling scream of her own, she launched herself at the creature's hiding-place brandishing her pointed stick. There was a sudden commotion amongst the lotus leaves on the bank and a small figure darted out and scampered away. Kelly took a full round-armed swing with her stick and caught it a resounding crack on bare brown buttocks. There was an anguished howl.

'You wicked old man!' Kelly yelled, and swung again. 'You tried to frighten me.' She missed as the pixie figure leaped over a bush ahead of her and took refuge behind it.

'You cruel little devil.' She hounded him out of the bush, and he darted around the side, shrieking with mock terror and laughter.

'I'll beat your backside blue as a baboon's,' Kelly threatened, her stick swishing, and they went twice round the bush, the small figure dancing and ducking just out of range. They were both laughing now. 'Sepoo, you little monster, I shall never forgive you!' Kelly choked on her laughter.

'I am not Sepoo. I am a leopard.' He staggered with mirth and she nearly caught him. He made a spurt to keep just out of range and squealed merrily.

In the end she had to give up and lean, exhausted with laughter, on her stick. Sepoo fell down in the leaves and beat his own belly and hiccuped and rolled over and hugged his knees and laughed until the tears poured down his cheeks and ran into the wrinkles and were channelled back behind his ears.

'Kara-Ki.' He belched and hiccuped and laughed some more. 'Kara-Ki, the fearless one, is frightened by old Sepoo!' It was a joke that he would tell at every campfire for the next dozen moons.

It took some time for Sepoo to become rational again. He had to laugh himself out. Kelly stood by and watched him affectionately, joining in some of his wilder outbursts of hilarity. Gradually these became less frequent, until at last they could converse normally.

They squatted side by side and talked. The Bambuti had long ago lost their own language, and had adopted those of the *wazungu* with whom they came in contact. They spoke a curious mixture of Swahili and Uhali and Hita with an accent and colourful idiom of their own.

With his bow and arrow Sepoo had shot a colobus monkey that morning. He had salted the beautiful black and white pelt to trade at the roadside. Now he built a fire and cooked the flesh for their lunch.

As they chatted and ate, she became aware of a strange mood in her companion. It was difficult for a pygmy to remain serious for long. His irrepressible sense of fun and his merry laughter could not be suppressed. They kept bubbling to the surface, and yet beneath it there was something new that had not been there when last Kelly had been with him. She could not define exactly what had changed. There was an air of preoccupation in Sepoo's mien, a worry, a sadness that dimmed the twinkle of his gaze and in repose made his mouth droop at the corners.

Kelly asked about the other members of the tribe, about Pamba, his wife.

'She scolds like a monkey from the treetops, and she mutters like the thunder of the skies.' Sepoo grinned with love un-dimmed after forty years of marriage. 'She is a cantankerous old woman, but when I tell her that I will get a pretty young wife she replies that any girl stupid enough to take me, can have me.' And he chortled at the joke and slapped his thigh, leaving monkey grease on the wrinkled skin.

'What of the others?' Kelly pressed him, seeking the cause of Sepoo's unhappiness. Was there dissension in the tribe? 'How is your brother Pirri?'

That was always a possible cause of strife in the tribe. There was a sibling rivalry between the half-brothers. Sepoo and Pirri were the master hunters, the oldest male members of the small tribal unit. They should have been friends as well as brothers, but Pirri was not a typical Bambuti. His father had been a Hita. Long ago, further back than any of the tribe could remember, their mother while still a virgin had wandered to the edge of the forest where a Hita hunting-party had caught her. She had been young and pretty as a pixie and the Hita had held her in their camp for two nights and taken it in turns to have sport with her. Perhaps they might have killed her carelessly when they tired of her, but before that happened she escaped.

Pirri was born from this experience and he was taller than any other men of the tribe and lighter in colour and finer-featured, with the mouth and thin nose of the Hita. He was different in character also, more aggressive and acquisitive than any Bambuti Kelly had ever met.

'Pirri is Pirri,' Sepoo replied evasively, but although the old antagonism was still evident, Kelly sensed that it was something other than his elder brother that worried him.

Although it was only a few hours' journey to Gondala, the two of them talked the daylight away and evening found them still squatting at the cooking-fire with the threat of rain heavy in the air. Kelly used the last of the light to cut the thin supple wands of the selepe tree and, as Pamba had taught her, to plant them in a circle in the soft earth and bend them inwards and plait them into the framework of a traditional Bambuti hut. Meanwhile old Sepoo went off on his own. He returned just as she was completing the framework, and he was bowed under a burden of mongongo leaves with which to thatch the hut. The structure was complete within an hour of the work commencing. When the thunderstorm broke, they were huddled warm and dry in the tiny structure with a cheerful fire flickering, eating the last of the monkey steaks.

At last Kelly settled down on her inflated mattress in the darkness and Sepoo curled on the soft leaf mould close beside her, but neither of them slept immediately. Kelly was aware of the old man lying awake and she waited. With darkness as a cover for his unhappiness Sepoo whispered at last, 'Are you awake, Kara-Ki?'

'I am listening, old father,' she whispered back, and he sighed. It was a sound so different from his usual merry chuckles.

'Kara-Ki, the Mother and Father are angry. I have never known them so angry,' Sepoo said, and she knew that he meant the god of the Bambuti, the twin godhead of the living forest, male and female in one. Kelly was silent for a while in deference to the seriousness of this statement.

'That is a grave matter,' she replied at last. 'What has made them angry?'

'They have been wounded,' Sepoo said softly. 'The rivers flow red with their blood.'

This was a startling concept, and Kelly was silent again as she tried to visualise what Sepoo meant. How could the rivers run with the blood of the forest? she wondered. She was finally forced to ask, 'I do not understand, old father. What are you telling me?'

'It is beyond my humble words to describe,' Sepoo whispered. 'There has been a terrible sacrilege and the Mother and Father are in pain. Perhaps the Molimo will come.'

Kelly had been in camp with the Bambuti only once during the Molimo visitation. The women were excluded, and Kelly had remained in the huts with Pamba and the other women when the Molimo came, but she had heard its voice roaring like a bull buffalo and trumpeting like an enraged elephant as it rampaged through the forest in the night.

In the morning Kelly had asked Sepoo, 'What creature is the Molimo?'

'The Molimo is the Molimo,' he had replied enigmatically. 'It is the creature of the forest. It is the voice of the Mother and the Father.'

Now Sepoo suggested that the Molimo might come again, and Kelly shivered with a little superstitious thrill. This time

311

she would not remain in the huts with the women, she promised herself. This time she would find out more about this fabulous creature. For the moment, however, she put it out of her mind and, instead, concerned herself with the sacrilege that had been committed somewhere deep in the forest.

'Sepoo,' she whispered. 'If you cannot tell me about this terrible thing, will you show me? Will you take me and show me the rivers that run with the blood of the gods?'

Sepoo snuffled in the darkness and hawked to clear his throat and spat into the coals of the fire. Then he grunted, 'Very well, Kara-Ki. I will show you. In the morning, before we reach Gondala we will go out of our way and I will show you the rivers that bleed.'

In the morning Sepoo was full of high spirits again, almost as though their conversation in the night had never taken place. Kelly gave him the present which she had brought for him, a Swiss army knife. Sepoo was enchanted with all the blades and implements and tools that folded out of the red plastic handle, and promptly cut himself on one of them. He cackled with laughter and sucked his thumb, then held it out to Kelly as proof of the marvellous sharpness of the little blade.

Kelly knew he would probably lose the knife within a week, or give it away to someone else in the tribe on an impulse, as he had done with all the other gifts she had given him. But for the moment his joy was childlike and complete.

'Now you must show me the bleeding rivers,' she reminded him as she adjusted the headband of her pack, and for a moment his eyes were sad again. Then he grinned and pirouetted.

'Come along, Kara-Ki. Let us see if you still move in the forest like one of the real people.'

Soon they left the broad trail, and Sepoo led her swiftly through the secret unmarked ways. He danced ahead of her like a sprite and the foliage closed behind him, leaving no trace of his passing. Where Sepoo moved upright, Kelly was forced to stoop beneath the branches, and at times she lost sight of him.

No wonder the old Egyptians believed the Bambuti had the power of invisibility, Kelly thought, as she extended herself to keep up with him.

If Sepoo had moved silently she might have lost him, but like all the pygmies he sang and laughed and chattered to her and the forest as he went. His voice ahead guided her, and warned the dangerous forest creatures of his approach so that there would be no confrontation.

She knew that he was moving at his best pace, to test and tease her, and she was determined not to fall too far behind. She called replies back to him and joined in the chorus of the praise songs and when he stepped out on the bank of the river many hours later she was only seconds behind him.

He grinned at her until his eyes disappeared in the web of wrinkles and shook his head in reluctant approval, but Kelly was not interested in his approbation. She was gazing at the river.

This was one of the tributaries of the Ubomo that had its source high up in the Mountains of the Moon, at the foot of one of the glaciers above fifteen thousand feet, the altitude where the permanent snowline stood. This river found its way down through lakes and waterfalls, fed by the mighty rains that lashed this wettest of all mountain ranges, down through the treeless moors and heather, down through the forest of giant prehistoric ferns, until at last it entered the dense bamboo thickets which were the domain of gorilla and spiral-horned bongo antelope. From there it fell again another three thousand feet through rugged foothills until it reached these true rain forests with their galleried canopies of gigantic hardwoods.

The Bambuti called this river Tetwa, after the silver catfish that abounded in its sweet clear waters and shoaled on the yellow sandbanks. The Bambuti women shed even their tiny loin-cloths when they went into the waters of the Tetwa to catch the barbeled catfish. Each of them armed with a fish basket of woven reeds and bark, they surrounded the shoal and splashed and shrieked with excitement as they flipped the struggling slippery silver fish from the sparkling water.

That had been before the river began to bleed. Now Kelly stared at it in horror.

The river was fifty yards wide and the forest grew right to the edge and formed a canopy that almost, but not quite, met overhead. There was a narrow irregular gleam of sky high above the middle of the river-course.

From bank to bank the river ran red, not the bright red of heart blood, but a darker browner hue. The sullied waters seemed almost viscous. They had lost their sparkle and were heavy and dull, running thick and slow as used engine oil.

The sand spits were red also, coated with a deep layer of thick mud. The carcasses of the catfish were strewn on the red banks, thick as autumn leaves, piled upon each other in their multitudes. Their skulls were eyeless and the stench of their putrefying flesh was oppressive in the humid air below the forest canopy.

'What has done this, Sepoo?' Kelly whispered, but he shrugged and busied himself rolling a pinch of coarse black native tobacco in a leaf. While Kelly went down the bank, he lit his primitive cheroot from the live coal he carried wrapped in a pouch of green leaves around his neck. He puffed great clouds of blue smoke, squeezing his eyes tightly shut with pleasure.

As Kelly stepped out on to the sand spit, she sank almost knee-deep into the mud. She scooped up a handful of it and rubbed it between her fingers. It was slick as grease, fine as potter's clay, and it stained her skin a dark *sang de boeuf*. She tried to wash it off, but the colour was fast and her fingers were red as those of an assassin. She lifted a handful of mud to her nose and sniffed it. It had no alien smell.

She waded back to the bank and confronted Sepoo. 'What has done this, old father? What has happened?'

He sucked on his cheroot, then coughed and giggled nervously, avoiding her gaze.

'Come on, Sepoo, tell me.'

'I do not know, Kara-Ki.'

'Why not? Did you not go upstream to find out?'

Sepoo examined the burning end of his green-leaf cheroot with great interest.

'Why not?' Kelly insisted.

'I was afraid, Kara-Ki,' he mumbled, and Kelly suddenly realised that for the Bambuti this was some supernatural occurrence. They would not follow the choked rivers upstream for fear of what they might find.

'How many rivers are like this?' Kelly demanded.

'Many, many,' Sepoo muttered, meaning more than four.

'Name them for me,' she insisted, and he reeled off the names of all the rivers she had ever visited in the region and some that she had only heard of. It seemed then that almost the entire drainage area of the Ubomo was affected. This was not some isolated local disturbance, but a large-scale disaster that threatened not only the Bambuti hunting areas but the sacred heartland of the forest as well.

'We must travel upstream,' Kelly said with finality, and Sepoo looked as though he might burst into tears.

'They are waiting for you at Gondala,' he squeaked, but Kelly did not make the mistake of beginning an argument. She had learned from the women of the tribe, from old Pamba in particular. She lifted her pack on to her back, adjusted the headband and started up the bank. For two hundred yards she was alone, and her spirits started to sink. The forest area ahead was completely unknown to her, and it would be folly to continue on her own if Sepoo could not be induced to accompany her.

Then she heard Sepoo's voice close behind her, protesting loudly that he would not take another step further. Kelly grinned with relief and quickened her pace.

For another twenty minutes Sepoo trailed along behind her, swearing that he was on the point of turning back and abandoning her, his tone becoming more and more plaintive as he realised that Kelly was not going to give in. Then quite suddenly he chuckled and began to sing. The effort of remaining miserable was too much for him to sustain. Kelly shouted a jibe over her shoulder and joined in the next refrain of the song. Soon Sepoo slipped past her and took the lead.

For the next two days they followed the Tetwa River and with every mile its plight was more pitiful. The red clay clogged it more deeply. The waters were almost pure mud, thick as oatmeal porridge and there were dead roots and loose vegetation mixed into it already beginning to bubble with the gas of decay; the stink of it mingled with that of dead birds and small animals and rotting fish that had been trapped and suffocated by the mud. The carcasses were strewn upon the red banks or floated with balloon bellies upon the sullied waters.

Late in the afternoon of the second day they reached the far

315

boundary of Sepoo's tribal hunting-grounds. There was no signpost or other indication to mark the line but Sepoo paused on the bank of the Tetwa, unstrung his bow and reversed his arrows in the rolled bark quiver on his shoulder, as a sign to the Mother and the Father of the forest that he would respect the sacred place and kill no creature, cut no branch nor light a fire within these deep forest preserves.

Then he sang a pygmy song to placate the forest, and to ask permission to enter its deep and secret place.

> Oh, beloved mother of all the tribe,
> You gave us first suck at your breast
> And cradled us in the darkness.
> Oh respected father, of our fathers
> You made us strong
> You taught us the ways of the forest
> And gave us your creatures as food.
> We honour you, we praise you . . .

Kelly stood a little aside and watched him. It seemed presumptuous for her to join in the words, so she was silent.

In her book, *The People of the Tall Trees*, she had examined in detail the tradition of the forest heartland and discussed the wisdom of the Bambuti law. The heartland was the reservoir of forest life which spilled over into the hunting preserves, renewing and sustaining them.

It was also the buffer zone which separated each of the tribes from its neighbours, and obviated friction and territorial dispute between them. This was only another example of the wisdom of the system that the Bambuti had evolved to regulate and manage their existence.

So, Kelly and Sepoo camped that night on the threshold of the sacred heartland. During the night it rained, which Sepoo proclaimed was a definite sign from the forest deities that they were amenable to the two of them continuing their journey upstream.

Kelly smiled in the darkness. It rained, on average, three hundred nights a year in the Ubomo basin, and if it had not done so tonight Sepoo would probably have taken that as even more eloquent assent from the Mother and Father.

They resumed the journey at dawn. When one of the striped forest duiker trotted out of the undergrowth ahead of them and stood to regard them trustingly from a distance of five paces, Sepoo reached instinctively for his bow and then controlled himself with such an effort that he shook as though he were in malarial ague. The flesh of this little antelope was tender and succulent and sweet.

'Go!' Sepoo yelled at it angrily. 'Away with you! Do not mock me! Do not tempt me! I am firm against your wiles . . .'

The duiker slipped off the path and Sepoo turned to Kelly. 'Bear witness for me, Kara-Ki. I did not trespass. That creature was sent by the Mother and Father to test me. No natural duiker would be so stupid as to stand so close. I was strong, was I not, Kara-Ki?' he demanded piteously, and Kelly squeezed his muscular shoulder.

'I am proud of you, old father. The gods love you.'

They went on.

In the middle of that third afternoon Kelly paused suddenly in mid-stride and cocked her head to a sound she had never heard in the forest before. It was still faint and intermittent, blanketed by the trees, but as she went on it became clearer and stronger with each mile until it resembled in Kelly's imagination the growling of lions on the kill, a terrible savage and feral sound that filled her with despair.

Now the River Tetwa no longer flowed, it was dammed with branches and debris, so that in places it had broken its banks and flooded the forest floor and they were forced to wade waist-deep through the stinking swamp. Then abruptly, with a shock of disclosure, the forest ended and they were standing in sunlight where sunlight had not penetrated for a million years.

Ahead of them was such a sight as Kelly could not have conceived in her most hideous nightmares. She gazed upon it until night fell and mercifully hid it from her and then she turned away and went back.

In the night she came awake to find herself weeping aloud and Sepoo's hand stroking her arm to comfort her.

The return journey down the dying river was slower, as though she were burdened by her sadness and Sepoo shortened his stride to match her.

Five days later, Kelly and Sepoo reached Gondala.

 Gondala was a site unique in this part of the forest. It was a glade of yellow elephant grass less than a hundred acres in extent. At the south end it rose to meet a line of forest-clad hills. For part of the day the tall trees threw a shadow across the clearing, keeping it cooler than if it had been exposed to the full glare of the tropical sun. Two small streams bounded this wedge of open ground, while the slope and elevation disclosed a sweeping vista over the treetops towards the north-west. It was one of the few vantage points in the Ubomo basin from which the view was not obscured by the great forest trees. The cool air in the open glade was less humid than that of the deep forest.

Kelly paused at the edge of the forest, as she always did, and looked out at the mountain peaks a hundred miles away. Usually the Mountains of the Moon were hidden in their own perpetual clouds. This morning, as if to welcome her home, they had drawn aside the veil and stood clear in all their glistening splendour. The glaciated massif of Mount Stanley was forced upwards between the faults of the Great Rift Valley to a height of almost seventeen thousand feet. It was pure ice-white and achingly beautiful.

She turned away from it reluctantly and looked across the clearing. There was her homestead and laboratory, an ambitious building of log, clay plaster and thatch which had taken her almost three years to build, with a little help from her friends.

The gardens on the lower slopes were irrigated from the streams and fenced in to protect them from the forest creatures. There were no flowerbeds. The garden was not ornamental but provided the small community of Gondala with a large part of its sustenance.

As they left the forest, some of the women working in the garden spotted them and ran to greet Kelly, shrieking and laughing with delight. Some were Bambuti, but most were Uhali women in their traditional colourful long skirts. They surrounded her and escorted her up to the homestead.

The commotion brought a solitary figure out of the laboratory on to the wide verandah. He was an old man with hair as silver as the snows on Mount Stanley that faced him from a hundred miles away. He was dressed in a crisp blue safari suit and sandals. He shaded his eyes and recognised her and smiled. His teeth were still white and perfect in his dark intelligent face.

'Kelly.' He held out both hands to her as she came up on to the verandah, and she ran to meet him. 'Kelly,' he repeated, as he took her hands. 'I was beginning to worry about you. I expected you days ago. It's good to see you.'

'It's good to see you also, Mr President.'

'Come now, my child. I am no longer that, at least not in Ephrem Taffari's view, and when did we last stand on ceremony, you and I?'

'Victor,' she corrected herself. 'I have missed you so, and I have so much to tell you. I don't know where to begin.'

'Later.' He shook his handsome grizzled head and embraced her. She knew that he was over seventy years old but she could feel that his body had the strength and vigour of a man half that age. 'First let me show you how well I have taken care of your work during your absence. I should have remained a scientist rather than becoming a politician,' he said. He took her hand and drew her into the laboratory, and immediately they were engrossed in technical discussion.

President Victor Omeru had studied in London as a young man. He had returned to Ubomo with a Master's degree in electrical engineering and for a short time had been employed in the colonial administration until he had resigned to lead the movement towards independence. Yet he had always retained his interest in the sciences and his learning and skills had always impressed Kelly.

When he had been overthrown in Ephrem Taffari's bloody *coup*, he had fled into the forest with a handful of loyal followers and sought sanctuary with Kelly Kinnear at Gondala. In the ten or so months since then, the settlement in the glade had become the headquarters of the Uhali resistance movement against Taffari's tyranny, and Kelly had become one of his most trusted agents. When he was not receiving visitors from outside the forest and planning the counter-revolution, he made himself Kelly's assistant and in a very short time had become invaluable to her.

For an hour the two of them were happily engrossed with slides and retorts and cages of laboratory rats. It was almost as though they were deliberately putting off the moment when they must discuss urgent and ugly reality.

Kelly's research was handicapped by inadequate equipment and shortage of expendable supplies. All of this had to be portered into Gondala, and since Kelly's field grant had been rescinded and Victor Omeru deposed, she had been even more restricted. Nevertheless, they had made some exciting discoveries. In particular they had been able to isolate an anti-malarial substance in the sap of the selepe tree. The selepe was a common plant of the forest that the pygmies used for the dual purposes of building their huts and treating fever.

Malaria was a resurgent menace in Africa where more and more frequently there appeared strains resistant to the synthetic prophylactics. Soon malaria might rank, once again, as the greatest killer on the continent, apart from AIDS. It seemed ironic that both these scourges should have their origin in the cradle of man himself, in the Great Rift Valley of East Africa, where man had stood upright and taken his first uncertain footsteps into glory and infamy. Was it not possible that the ultimate cure for both these diseases might yet come from this same area of the globe? They both reasserted that hope, as they had done a thousand times before.

In addition to the malarial cure, there were the other possibilities that Kelly and Victor Omeru were considering. The one disease to which the Bambuti were susceptible was cancer of the pancreas. This was caused by some factor of their diet or environment in the forest. The women of the tribe used an infusion of the root of a vine that contained a bitter milky sap to treat the disease, and Kelly had witnessed some seemingly miraculous cures. She and Victor Omeru had isolated an alkaloid from the sap which they hoped was the active agent in the cure, and they were testing it with encouraging results.

They were using the same alkaloid to treat three of the Uhali men in camp who were suffering from AIDS. It was too soon to be certain, but once again the results were most encouraging and exciting. Now they discussed them avidly. This excitement and the pleasure of reunion lasted them through the frugal lunch of salads that they shared on the verandah of the thatched bungalow.

Kelly revelled in the joy of conversing with such a cultured and erudite man. Victor Omeru's presence had transformed her lonely isolated life at Gondala. She loved her Bambuti friends, but they came and went without warning, and though their simple happy ways were always a joy, they were no substitute for the stimulation of a superior educated mind.

Victor Omeru was a man she could respect and admire and love without reservation. As far as Kelly was concerned, he was without vice, overflowing with humanity and compassion for his fellow men, and at the same time with a deep and abiding respect and concern for the world in which they lived and the other creatures that shared it with them.

She saw in him the true patriot, completely devoted to his little nation. He was, in addition, the only African Kelly had ever met who was above tribalism. He had spent his entire political life trying to appease and ameliorate the terrible curse that was, in both their views, the single most tragic fact of the African reality. He should have been an example to the rest of the continent, and to his peers in the high councils of the Organisation of African Unity.

When, almost single-handed, he had obtained independence from the colonial administration, the preponderance of his fellow Uhali tribesmen had swept him into the presidential office and overturned at a single stroke the centuries of brutal domination by the proud Hita aristocracy.

The greatest crisis of his presidency had come within the very first days of independence. The Uhali tribe had turned upon the Hita in a savage orgy of retribution. In five terrible days, over twenty thousand Hita had perished. The mob had torched their *manyattas*. Those Hita who survived the flames were hacked to death with hoes and machetes. The tools with which the enslaved Uhali had tilled the fields and hewn the firewood for their masters were turned upon them.

The proud Hita women, tall and stately and beautiful, were

stripped of their traditional ankle-length robes, and the elaborately plaited locks in which they gloried were hacked roughly from their heads. They were herded naked before the jeering Uhali mob, and pelted with excrement. Some of the women were lifted struggling and naked and impaled upon the poles of the *manyattas'* outer stockade.

The younger women and girls had been yoked between two of their own oxen, secured with rawhide thongs by each ankle. Then the mob had urged the oxen forward and the girls had been torn apart.

Kelly had not been there to witness these atrocities. She had been a schoolgirl in England at the time, but the legend had become history of how Victor Omeru had gone out to plead with the mob and physically to interpose himself between them and their Hita victims. With the sheer force of his personality he had brought the slaughter to an end, and virtually saved the Hita tribe from genocide and extinction. Nevertheless, thousands of Hita perished and fifty thousand fled for sanctuary into the neighbouring countries of Uganda and Zaïre.

It had taken a major exercise of statesmanship over decades of wise government for Victor Omeru to cool the terrible tribal animosities of his people, to persuade the exiled Hita to return to Ubomo, to restore their herds and their grazing lands to them, and to bring their young men in from the traditional pastoral ways to education and advancement in the modern Ubomo nation he was trying to build.

In recompense for those terrible first days of independence Victor had always thereafter erred on the side of leniency towards the Hita tribe. To demonstrate his trust and faith in them he allowed them gradually to take control of Ubomo's little army and police force. Ephrem Taffari himself had travelled abroad to complete his education on a special scholarship provided by Victor Omeru out of his own meagre presidential salary.

Victor Omeru was paying for that generosity now. Once again the Uhali tribe groaned beneath the Hita tyranny.

As so often happens in Africa, the cycle of oppression and brutality had run its full course, but even now as they sat on the wide verandah of the bungalow, immersed in discussion,

Kelly could still detect the suffering and concern for his nation and all his people in Victor Omeru's dark eyes.

It seemed cruel to add to his misery but she could no longer keep it from him.

'Victor, there is something awful happening up there, in the rivers of the forest, in the sacred Bambuti heartland. Something so terrible that I hardly know how to describe it to you.'

He listened without interruption, but when she had finished he said quietly, 'Taffari is killing our people and our land. The vultures smell death in the air and they are gathering, but we will stop them.'

Kelly had never seen him so angry before. His face was hard and his eyes were dark and terrible.

'They are powerful, Victor. Rich and powerful.'

'There is no power to match that of honest men and a just cause,' he replied, and his strength and determination were contagious. Kelly felt her despair slough away, leaving her feeling renewed and confident.

'Yes,' she whispered. 'We will find a way to stop them. For the sake of this land we must find a way.'

 'Formosa' meant beautiful. The name was appropriate, Tug Harrison conceded, as the Rolls-Royce Silver Spirit left the littoral plain and climbed up into the green mountains. The road swept around a shoulder of one of the peaks and for a moment Tug gazed out across the broad Formosa Straits and fancied he saw the loom of mainland China lurking like a dragon a hundred and more miles out there in the blue distance. Then the road turned again and they were back into the forests of cypress and cedar.

They were four thousand feet above the humid tropical plain and the bustle of Taipei, one of the busiest and most affluent cities in Asia. The air up here was sweet and cool; there was no need of the Rolls's superb air-conditioning system.

Tug felt relaxed and clear-headed. It was one of the joys of having your own jet aircraft, he smiled. The Gulfstream flew when he was ready, wherever he wanted to go. There was none of the aggravation of large airports and throngs of the great unwashed multitude. No miles of corridors to traverse nor luggage carousels at which to play the guessing game of 'will it come or won't it', no surly customs officials and porters and taxi-drivers.

Tug had taken it in easy stages from London. Abu Dhabi, Bahrain, Brunei, Hong Kong – he had spent a day or two in each of those centres in all of which he had major games in play.

The stop-over in Hong Kong had been particularly worthwhile. The richest and more prudent of the Hong Kong businessmen were intent on moving out their assets and relocating ahead of the termination of the treaty and the reversion of the territory to mainland China. In the permanent suite which he kept at the Peninsula Hotel, Tug had signed two agreements which should net him ten million pounds over the next few years.

When his chief pilot touched down at Taipei airport, ground control directed Tug's Gulfstream to taxi to a discreet parking billet behind the Cathay Pacific hangars and the Rolls-Royce was waiting on the tarmac, with the youngest son of the Ning family to meet him.

Customs and Immigration, in the shape of two uniformed officials, were ushered aboard, bobbing and smiling, by his host. They stamped Tug's red diplomatic passport and placed the 'in bond' seals on his private bar and departed, all within five minutes.

In the meantime Tug's matched set of Louis Vuitton luggage was being transferred to the boot of the Rolls by a team of white-jacketed and -gloved servants. Within fifteen minutes of touch-down, the Rolls whisked him out of the airport gates.

Tug felt so good that he was inclined to philosophise. He compared other journeys he had made when he was young and poor and struggling. On foot and bicycle and native bus he had crossed and recrossed the African continent. He remembered his first motor vehicle, a Ford V-8 truck with front mudguards like elephant ears, smooth tyres that never ran fifty miles without puncturing, and an engine held together with baling-wire and hope. He had been immensely proud of it at the time.

Even his first air flight on one of the old Sunderland flying boats that once plied the African continent, landing to refuel on the Zambezi, the great lakes, and finally the Nile itself, had taken ten days to reach London.

Truly to appreciate luxury it was necessary to have withstood severe hardship, Tug believed. The early days had been tough. He had revelled in each one of them but, hell, the touch of silk against his skin and the Rolls upholstery under his backside felt wonderful and he was looking forward to the negotiations that lay ahead. They would be hard and without quarter, but that was the way he liked it.

He loved the cut and thrust of the bargaining table. He enjoyed changing his style to match each adversary he faced. He could flash the cutlass or palm the stiletto as the occasion warranted. When called for he could shout and bang the table and curse with the same vigour as an Australian opal miner or a Texan rough-neck on an oil rig, or he could smile and whisper honeyed hemlock as skilfully as could the man he was now going to meet. Yes, he loved every moment of it. It was what kept him young.

He smiled genially and turned to discuss oriental netsukes and ceramics with the young man who sat beside him on the pale green leather back seat of the Rolls.

'Generalissimo Chiang Kai-shek brought the cream of China's art treasures with him from the mainland in 1949,' Ning Cheng Gong was saying, and Tug nodded.

'All civilised men must be thankful for that,' he agreed. 'If he had not done so, they would have been destroyed in Mao's cultural revolution.'

As they chatted, Tug was studying his host's youngest son. Even though he had not yet shown himself to be a force in the Ning financial dynasty, and up until now had been overshadowed by his elder half-brothers, Tug had a full dossier on Cheng.

There was some indication that Cheng, even as the youngest son, was his father's favourite, the child of his old age, by his third wife, a beautiful English girl. As often happens, the admixture of oriental and occidental blood seemed to have brought out the good traits of both parents. It seemed that

325

Ning Cheng Gong had bred true, for he was clever, devious, ruthless, and lucky. Tug Harrison never discounted the element of luck. Some men had it and others, no matter how clever, did not.

It seemed that old Ning Heng H'Sui was bringing him on carefully, like a fine thoroughbred colt, preparing him for his first major race with patience and diligence. He had given Cheng all the advantages, without allowing him to grow up soft.

After his master's degree at Chiang Kai-shek University, Ning Cheng Gong had gone straight into the Taiwanese army for national service. His father had made no effort to beat the draft on his behalf. Tug supposed that it was part of the toughening process.

Tug Harrison had a copy of the young man's military service record. He had done well, very well, and had ended his call-up with the rank of captain and a job on the general staff. Of course, the commander of the Taiwanese army was a personal friend of Ning Heng H'Sui, but his selection would not have been entirely based on preferment rather than ability. There had been only one small shadow on Cheng's service record. A civilian complaint had been brought against Captain Ning, and investigated by the military police. It involved the death of a young girl in a Taipei brothel. The full report of the investigating officer had been carefully removed from Ning's service record and only the recommendation that there was no substance in the accusation remained, together with an endorsement by the Attorney-General that no charges be pursued. Once again Tug Harrison scented the intervention of the Ning patriarch in this dossier. It increased Tug's respect for the power and influence of the family.

At the end of his national service, Ning Cheng Gong had gone into the Taiwanese diplomatic corps. Perhaps old Heng had not yet considered him ready to join the Lucky Dragon. Once again young Cheng's progress had been meteoric, and he had been given an ambassadorship within four years, admittedly it was to a small and insignificant little African country, but by all accounts he had done well. Once again Tug had been able to obtain a copy of his service record from the Taiwanese foreign office. It had cost him ten thousand pounds sterling in bribes, but Tug considered it a bargain. In this dossier he had again found some evidence of Cheng's unusual erotic tastes.

The body of a young black girl had been fished out of the Zambezi river only partially devoured by crocodiles. There was certain mutilation of the corpse's genital and mammary areas which had led the police to pursue further enquiries. They found that at the time the Chinese ambassador had been staying at a game lodge on the Zambezi south bank, near the girl's village. The missing girl had been seen entering Cheng's bungalow late on the evening before she disappeared. She had not been seen again alive. This was as far as the enquiry had been allowed to run, before being quashed by a directive from the president's office. Now the ambassador's term of office had run its course. He had resigned from the diplomatic service and returned to Taiwan to take up a position with the Lucky Dragon company, at last.

His father had given him the equivalent rank of vice-president, and Tug Harrison found him interesting. Not only was he clever but he was good-looking to the Western eye. His mother's influence was discernible in his features; although his hair was jet black there were no epicanthic folds in his upper eyelids. His English was perfect. If Tug closed his eyes he could imagine he was conversing with a young upper-class Englishman. He was suave and urbane, with just the slightest perceptible streak of ruthlessness and cruelty in him. Yes, Tug decided, he was a young man with prospects. His father could be proud of him.

Tug felt the familiar stab of regret as he thought of his own feckless offspring, weaklings and wastrels all three. He could only console himself by believing that the fault must lie in their maternal line. They were the sons of three different women all of whom he had chosen for their physical attractiveness. When you are young there is no reasoning with an erect penis, he shook his head regretfully, it seemed to inhibit the flow of the blood to the brain. He had married four women whom he would not have employed as secretaries, and three of them had given him sons in their mirror image, beautiful and lazy and irresponsible.

Tug frowned at this shadow across his sunny mood. Most

327

men give more thought and care to the breeding of their dogs and horses than they do to selecting a dam for their own children. Fatherhood was the only endeavour in his entire life in which Tug Harrison had failed dismally.

'I am looking forward to viewing your father's collection of ivory,' Tug told Cheng, putting unprofitable regret out of his mind.

'My father will be pleased to show it to you,' Cheng smiled. 'It is his chief delight, after the Lucky Dragon, of course.'

As he said it, the Rolls sailed around another hairpin and directly ahead stood the gates to the Ning estate. Tug had seen a photograph of them, but still he was not prepared for the actuality. They reminded him instantly of those gigantic garish sculptures in the Tiger Balm Gardens in Hong Kong.

The Lucky Dragon entwined itself around the gateway like a prehistoric monster, glittering with emerald-green ceramic tiles and gold leaf. Its talons were hooked and raised, its wings were spread fifty feet wide, its eyes glowed like live coals and its crocodile jaws were agape and lined with jagged fangs.

'My goodness!' said Tug mildly, and Cheng laughed lightly and deprecatingly.

'My father's little whimsy,' he explained. 'The teeth are real ivory and the eyes are a pair of cabochon spinel-rubies from Sri Lanka. They weigh together a little over five kilos. They are unique and are valued at over a million dollars, hence the armed guards.'

The two guards came to attention as the Rolls slid through the gateway. They were dressed in paramilitary uniform with blancoed webbing and burnished stainless helmets similar to those worn by the honour guard at Chiang Kai-shek's tomb in Taipei. They carried automatic weapons and Tug Harrison guessed that they had other duties apart from guarding the Lucky Dragon's jewelled eyes. Tug had heard that young Cheng, using his military experience, had personally recruited these guards from the ranks of the Taiwanese marines, one of the elite regiments of the world, to protect his father.

Old Ning Heng H'Sui had left more than a few widows and orphans behind him as he hacked his way to power. Rumour had it that he had once been head of one of Hong Kong's powerful secret societies, and that he still maintained close ties with the Tongs. He might now be an art collector and artist and poet, but there were many who remembered the old days and would dearly love to pay off a few ancient scores.

Tug felt no repugnance at all for the old man's personal history, just as he felt none for the youngest son's sexual foibles. Tug had a few secrets of his own, and knew the whereabouts of more than one unmarked grave in the African wilderness. He had lived his whole life in the company of, and in competition with, ruthless predatory men. He made no moral judgements. He accepted mankind as he found it, and looked instead for the profit to be made from its strengths or weaknesses.

Cheng returned the salute of the silver-helmeted guards with a nod and the Rolls passed beneath the Lucky Dragon's arched belly and entered a fantasy land of gardens and lakes, pagodas and arched Chinese bridges. Shoals of jewel-coloured khoi glided beneath the lake waters, and flocks of snow-white pigeons swirled about the eaves of the pagodas. The lawns were green and smooth as a silk kimono stretched over a pretty girl's thigh. The rhododendrons were in full bloom. It was peaceful and lovely, in contrast to the tasteless dragon sculpture at the main gateway.

The Rolls drew up at the entrance to a building that reminded Tug of a miniature of the Winter Palace in Peking. The fountains that surrounded it shot a sparkling lacework of foam high into the cool mountain air. A cortège of white-jacketed servants waited on each side of the entrance to welcome Tug, and they bowed deeply as Cheng led him into the vaulted interior.

The panelled walls had been slid aside so that the gardens seemed part of the décor. The furnishings were simple and exquisite. The floors of red cedar glowed and the cigar-box smell of the woodwork perfumed the air. A few ceramic treasures which would have graced any museum collection were arranged to full effect, and a single flower arrangement of cherry blossom was the centre-piece of the room.

'One of the maids will make tea for you, Sir Peter,' Cheng told him, 'while the other draws your bath and unpacks your suitcases. Then you will want to rest for an hour. My father

329

invites you to take lunch with him at twelve-thirty. I will return a few minutes before that time to take you up to the main house.'

Tug realised that this was simply one of the guest houses, but he showed no sign of being impressed and Cheng went on, 'Of course, all the servants are at your command. If there is anything you should want,' Cheng placed a slight emphasis on the sentence, that turned it into a leer, 'you need only ask one of the servants. You are my father's honoured guest. He would be deeply humiliated if you were to lack anything at all.'

'You and your father are too kind.' Tug returned the young man's bow. There would have been a time, not too many years ago when Tug would have availed himself of the discreet invitation, but now he was thankful that the irrational and uncontrollable element of sexuality had faded from his existence. So much of his youthful time and energy had been spent in sexual pursuit. At the end he had very little to show for all the effort, apart from three useless sons and a couple of million a year in alimony payments. No, he was glad it was over. His existence now was calmer and saner. Youth was an over-rated period in a man's life, filled with so much confusion and anxiety and unhappiness.

The two Chinese girls who helped him down the tiled steps into the steaming perfumed bath wore only brief white kilts and he could look upon their pale creamy skins and cherry-blossom nipples with a connoisseur's appreciation and only a brief sweet nostalgic stirring of the loins.

'No,' he reiterated as he sank into the water, 'I'm glad I'm not young any more.'

Tug spurned the embroidered robes that the girls had laid out for him and chose instead one of his dark Savile Row suits with a Turnbull and Asser shirt and MCC tie that the valet had steamed.

'Damned fancy dress will make me feel like a clown. Old Heng knows it; that's why he tried to get me into it.'

Young Cheng was waiting for him at the appointed time. His eyes flicked over Tug's suit but his expression never changed. Didn't fall for it, did I? Tug thought smugly. I wasn't born yesterday, was I?

330

They strolled up the covered pathway, pausing to admire the lotus flowers and water-lilies and the rhododendrons until they turned through an arched gateway festooned with drapes of blue wistaria and abruptly the main house was disclosed.

It was stunning, a creation of unblemished white marble and ceramic roof-tiles in peaks and gables, modern and yet time-lessly classical.

Tug did not miss a stride, and sensed the young man's disappointment beside him. He had expected Tug, like all other visitors, to gawk.

The patriarch, Ning Heng H'Sui, was very old, older than Tug by ten years or more. His skin was dried and folded like that of the unwrapped mummy of Rameses II in Cairo Museum, and spotted with the foxing of age. On his left cheek grew a mole the size and colour of a ripe mulberry. It is a common Chinese superstition that the hairs growing from a facial mole bring good luck, and Heng H'Sui had never shaved his. A bunch of hair sprouted from the little purple cauliflower and hung down in a silver tassel below his chin above the simple tunic of cream-coloured raw silk he wore.

So much for the dragon embroidery he tried to rig me with, Tug thought, as he took his hand. It was dry and cool and the bones were light as a bird's.

Heng was desiccated with age; only his eyes were bright and fierce. Tug imagined that the giant man-eating dragons of Komodo might have eyes like that.

'I trust you have rested after your journey, Sir Peter, and that you are comfortable in my poor house.' His voice was thin and dry as the sound of the wind rustling the autumn leaves and his English was excellent.

They exchanged pleasantries while they measured and sized each other. It was their first meeting. All Tug's negotiations up until this point had been with the elder sons.

All the sons were here now, waiting behind their father, the three elder brothers and Cheng.

One at a time Heng H'Sui waved them forward with a bird-like flutter of his pale dry hand, and they greeted Tug cour-teously in strict order of seniority.

Then Cheng helped his father back to his cushioned seat

overlooking the garden. It was not lost on Tug that the youngest, rather than the eldest, was so honoured. Though there was no exchange of glances between the other brothers and no change of expression, Tug felt the sibling rivalry and jealousy so strong in the sweet mountain air that he could almost taste it. All this was good intelligence he was gathering about the family.

Servants brought them pale jasmine tea in bowls so fine that Tug could see the outline of his own fingers through the china. He recognised the cream on white leaf design, so subtle and understated as almost to elude casual examination. The bowl was a masterpiece of a fifteenth-century potter of the Ching Ti emperor of the Ming dynasty.

Tug drained the bowl and then, as he was about to set it down on the lacquered tray, he let it slip from his fingers. It struck the cedarwood floor and shattered into a hundred precious fragments.

'I am so sorry,' he apologised. 'How clumsy of me.'

'It is nothing.' Heng H'Sui inclined his head graciously, and gestured for a servant to sweep away the broken shards. The servant was trembling as he knelt to the task. He sensed his master's wrath.

'I do hope it was not valuable?' Tug asked, testing him, trying to unsettle him, paying him back for the trick with the dragon robe. An angry man, one with hatred in his heart, has his judgement impaired. Tug studied Heng H'Sui for a reaction. They both knew that Tug was fully aware that the bowl was priceless.

'It was of no value, I assure you, Sir Peter. A mere trifle. Think no more of it,' the old man insisted, but Tug saw that he had got to him. There was a man of passion lurking behind that dried-out mask with the tasselled cheek piece. However, the old man was exhibiting class and style and control. A worthy adversary, Tug decided, for he had no illusion as to any fiduciary relationship between them merely on account of the mutually convenient and probably transient partnership of BOSS and the Lucky Dragon.

With the breaking of the bowl he had achieved a momentary advantage over the patriarch. He had thrown him off balance.

The old man sipped the last of the pale tea from his own bowl which was identical to the one which Tug had broken, and then held out his hand with a quiet word of command. One of the servants knelt and placed a square of silk in his wrinkled paw. Heng H'Sui wiped out the bowl carefully and then wrapped it in the silk and handed it to Tug.

'A gift for you, Sir Peter. I hope that our friendship will not be as frail as this little bauble.'

Tug conceded that Heng had snatched back the advantage. Tug was left with no option but to accept the extravagant gift and the loss of face that the subtle rebuke entailed.

'I will treasure it for the generosity of the giver,' he said.

'My son,' Heng indicated him with a flick of his blue-veined hand, 'tells me that you have expressed a desire to see my collection of ivory. Do you also collect ivory, Sir Peter?'

'I don't, but I'm interested in all things African. I flatter myself that I know more than the average man about the African elephant. I know how much value your people place on ivory.'

'Indeed, Sir Peter, never dispute the efficacy of charms with a Chinese, especially those of ivory. Our entire existence is ruled by astrology and the courting of fortune.'

'The Lucky Dragon?' Tug suggested.

'The Lucky Dragon, certainly.' Heng's parchment dry cheeks seemed about to tear as he smiled. 'And the Dragon at my gate has fangs of pure ivory. I have been caught up in the spell of ivory all my life. I started my career as an ivory-carver in my father's shop.'

'Yes, I know that the netsuke that bears your personal chop fetches prices equivalent to those of the great master carvers of antiquity,' Tug told him.

'Ah, those were made when my eye was sharp and my hand steady.' Heng shook his head modestly, but did not deny the value of his own creations.

'I would dearly love to see some examples of your work,' Tug suggested, and Heng gestured to his youngest son to help him rise.

'So you shall, Sir Peter. So you shall.'

The ivory museum was at a distance from the main house.

They went slowly along the covered walkway through the gardens, holding back for Heng H'Sui's short laboured pace.

He stopped to feed the khoi in one of the ornamental pools, and as the fish roiled the water in a feeding frenzy, the old man smiled at their antics.

'Greed, Sir Peter; without greed where would you and I be?'

'Healthy greed is the fuel of the capitalist system,' Tug agreed.

'And the stupid unthinking greed of other men makes you and me rich, does it not?'

Tug inclined his head in agreement and they went on.

There were more paramilitary guards in silver helmets at the door of the museum. Tug knew without being told that their vigil was perpetual.

'Picked men.' Heng noticed his glance. 'I trust them more than all these modern electronic devices.'

Cheng relinquished his father's arm for a moment to punch the entry code into the control box of the alarm system and the massive carved doors swung open automatically. He ushered them through.

The museum was without windows. There was no natural light, and the artificial lighting had been skilfully arranged. The air-conditioning was set to the correct humidity to preserve and protect the ivory. The carved doors closed with a pneumatic hiss behind them.

Tug took three paces into the spacious antechamber and then halted abruptly. He stared at the display in the centre of the marble floor.

'You recognise them?' Heng H'Sui asked.

'Yes, of course.' Tug nodded. 'I saw them once, long ago, at the Sultan of Zanzibar's palace before the revolution. There has been speculation ever since as to what happened to them.'

'Yes. I acquired them after the revolution in 1964 when the Sultan was exiled,' Heng H'Sui agreed. 'Very few people know that I own them.'

The walls of the room were painted blue, that particular milky blue of an African noon sky. The colour was chosen to show off the exhibits to best effect and the dimensions of the antechamber had obviously been designed for the same purpose, to complement the pair of ivory tusks.

Each tusk was over ten feet long, and its diameter at the lip was larger than a virgin's waist. The legend inked on each tusk was in Arabic script written a hundred years ago by a clerk of the Sultan Barghash recording the weight when it arrived in Zanzibar. Tug deciphered the writing: the heaviest tusk had weighed 235 pounds, the other only a few pounds less.

'They are lighter now,' Heng H'Sui anticipated his question. 'Between them they have dried out by twenty-two pounds, but still it takes four men to carry one of them. Think of the mighty animal who originally bore them.'

They were the most famous tusks in existence. As a student of African history, Tug knew the story of these extraordinary objects. They had been taken a hundred years ago on the southern slopes of Kilimanjaro, by a slave named Senoussi. The slave's master was a villain named Shundi. He was one of the cruellest and most unscrupulous slavers and ivory-traders on the African east coast, an area notorious for the depredations of the slave-masters. When he had first come upon it, Senoussi had in awe delayed killing the old bull. He had crouched over his flintlock musket and studied this extraordinary creature with respect for several hours before he had summoned the courage to creep forward and send a lead ball through its heart.

According to Senoussi's later account to his master, the bull ran off only a hundred yards before collapsing. He was an extremely old elephant with his fourth and last molars almost worn away, on the verge of the slow starvation of great age. Although not particularly big-bodied, his neck and forequarters were overdeveloped to carry that great weight of ivory. Senoussi observed the bull had been forced to raise his head and lift the tips of his tusks free of the earth before he could move.

When Shundi displayed the tusks in the ivory market in Zanzibar they caused a sensation amongst traders accustomed to dealing with massive tusks. The Sultan had purchased the pair from Shundi for a thousand pounds sterling, which was a huge sum of money in those days. Tug had first seen them in the palace of the Sultan's successors overlooking the Zanzibar waterfront.

Now he approached them with awe and stroked one of them, staring up at the massive ivory arches that almost met

335

high above his head. This was legendary treasure. To Tug, somehow, these tusks seemed to embody the history and the soul of the entire African continent.

'Now let me show you the rest of my poor little collection,' Ning Heng H'Sui suggested at last, and led the way past the towering ivory columns to the archway artfully concealed in the rear wall of the antechamber.

The interior of the building was a labyrinth of dimly lit passages. The floor was carpeted with midnight-blue Wilton, soft and soundless to the tread. The walls were the same colour, but set flush into them on each side of the passage were the showcases.

The proportions of each case were designed to the shape and size of the single exhibit it contained. The lighting of the cases was dramatically arranged so that each treasure was revealed in crisp detail and seemed to float airily and independently of the dim surroundings.

Firstly, there were religious and sacred objects, a Bible with covers of carved ivory and precious stones bearing the double-headed eagle of Imperial Russia.

'Peter the Great,' Heng murmured. 'His personal Bible.'

There was a copy of the Torah, the yellow parchment rolled on to an ivory distaff, and contained in an ivory case with the Star of David carved upon it.

'Salvaged from the great synagogue at Constantinople when it was destroyed by the Byzantine emperor Theodosius,' Heng explained.

Amongst other treasures there were icons of ivory set with diamonds and Hindu statuettes of Vishnu, a copy of the Koran covered with beaten gold and ivory, and ancient Christian statues of the Virgin and the saints, all carved from ivory.

Then, as they moved along the dim passageway, the nature of the exhibits became more profane, and secular. There were women's fans and combs and necklaces from ancient Rome and Greece, then an extraordinary object shaped like a two-foot rolling pin with a rooster head carved at one end. Tug did not recognise it and Heng explained expressionlessly.

'It belonged to Catherine the Great of Russia. Her physicians convinced her that ivory was a sovereign specific against syphilis. It is an ivory dildo, made to her own design.'

Occasionally Heng instructed his son to open one or two of the cases so that Tug could handle the exhibits and examine them more closely.

'The true joy of ivory lies in the feel of it in the hand,' Heng suggested. 'It is as sensuous as the skin of a lovely woman. See the grain, Sir Peter, that lovely subtle cross-hatching that no synthetic substance can duplicate.'

There was one object the size and shape of a football, carved like lacework. Within it were eight more balls, free and complete, one within the other like the layers of an onion. The artist had carved the inner balls through the minute apertures in the outer layers. In the centre of the ball was a carving of a rose bud, perfect in every detail.

'Three thousand hours of work. Five years from the life of a master craftsman. How can you place a value on that?' Heng asked.

Two hours after entering the museum they came at last to the room that contained the netsukes.

During the Tokugawa Shogunate in Japan, only the aristocracy were allowed to wear personal adornment. Amongst the newly emerging and affluent middle class the netsuke button, worn on the sash and used to secure a pill box or tobacco pouch, was an essential article of dress. The beauty and intricacy of the carving enhanced the owner's prestige.

Heng had assembled a collection of over ten thousand pieces. However, as he explained to Tug, he could only display a few of his favourites, and amongst them were his own creations. These were cased separately, and once again Tug was invited to take them in his hand and to admire the craftsmanship.

'Of course, I was obliged to seek out and buy back my own work.' Heng smiled and tugged at the tassel of hair that hung from his cheek. 'I have agents around the world still searching for my creations. I estimate there are at least a hundred that have so far eluded me. Ten thousand dollars if you find one, Sir Peter,' he promised.

'And worth every cent,' Tug agreed as he examined one of the tiny ivory buds. The detail and rendition was extraordinary and the subject matter covered a wide range of humanity and the animal world, from birds and mammals to men and beautiful women and children in every possible pose and indulging in every activity, from war to love, from death to childbirth.

Somehow, Heng the artist had managed to transform even the mundane into something remarkable and exciting. Subjects that might have been merely pornographic and coarse were instead spiritual, ethereal and moving.

'You have a rare gift,' Tug acknowledged. 'The heart and eye of a great artist.'

For a short while the two men were in accord, and then they left the treasure house and returned to the main house where servants had set out writing materials and light refreshments at a long lacquer-work table. They removed their footwear and settled themselves on cushions about the table and, at last, the real work began.

In London, Tug had negotiated and signed a document of intent with the elder Ning sons. This was subject to ratification by the patriarch. Tug had never expected this to be a simple procedure and he was not to be disappointed.

A little after midnight they adjourned and Tug was escorted back to the guesthouse by Cheng. The two female servants were waiting for him with tea and refreshments. They helped him change into his night clothes, then drew back the quilts on the low wide bed and waited expectantly.

Tug dismissed them and they left at once. He had not been able to discover where the video camera and microphone were concealed, but he was certain they were there. He switched off the light and lay for a while, well pleased with the progress he had made. Then he slept soundly and awoke eager for the fray.

In the middle of the following afternoon, Tug and Heng H'Sui shook hands. From all that Tug had learned about the old man, he believed that like himself Heng was a man of peculiar integrity. Between them that handshake was as good as any formal document. Of course, the lawyers on both sides would now come in and complicate and muddy the issues, but even they could never weaken the central pillars of the agreement. Between Tug and Heng it was sacrosanct, the honour of buccaneers.

'There is one other matter I would like to discuss with you,' Heng murmured, and Tug frowned.

'No, no, Sir Peter. It is a personal matter, not part of our agreement.' And Tug relaxed.

'I will do what I can to help you. What is it about?'

'Elephant,' Heng said. 'Ivory.'

'Ah.' Tug smiled and nodded. 'Why didn't I guess?'

'At the time that bloodthirsty madman Idi Amin took over Uganda, the largest elephant still alive on the African continent were in the Uganda National Park near the Murchison Falls at the headwaters of the Nile,' Heng explained.

'Yes,' Tug agreed. 'I saw a dozen animals in that Park that had tusks over a hundred pounds a side. They were wiped out by Idi Amin's henchmen and the ivory stolen by him.'

'Not all of them, Sir Peter. I have it on good authority that some of those animals, the largest of them, escaped annihilation. They crossed the border into Ubomo and reached the rain forests on the slopes of the Mountains of the Moon, that area which now forms part of our syndicate's concession.'

'It is possible,' Tug conceded.

'It is more than that. It is fact,' Heng contradicted him. 'My son Cheng', he indicated the man at his side, 'has a reliable agent in Ubomo. An Indian who has co-operated with us on many occasions. His name is Chetti Singh. Do you know him?'

'I have heard of him, vaguely.' Tug frowned again. 'Let me think ... Yes, he is connected with the illegal export of ivory and rhino horn. I have heard he is the mastermind behind all African poaching.'

'Chetti Singh has been in the forests of the Ubomo basin within the last ten days,' Heng went on. 'He has seen with his own eyes an elephant bull with tusks almost as large as those I showed you today.'

'How can I help you?' Tug insisted.

'I want those tusks,' Heng murmured, the passion of the collector barely concealed behind the time-eroded mask of his face. 'More than the ore and the hardwoods of the forest, I want that ivory.'

'President Taffari can sign a special Protected Game licence. I believe there is provision for that in the constitution. If there isn't, it can be changed. I presume that your man Chetti Singh will be able to arrange for the ivory to be harvested. He is the master poacher. If that is the case, I will send my Gulfstream to Ubomo to pick up the tusks and ferry them to you here. I can foresee no problems, Mr Ning.'

'Thank you, Sir Peter,' Heng smiled. 'Is there anything I can do for you in exchange?'

'Yes.' Tug leaned forward. 'As a matter of fact there is.'

'You only have to ask,' Heng invited.

'Before I do that, I must explain something of the new hysteria that is sweeping the Western world. Fortunately for you, you are not subject to the same pressures. There is a new thinking, especially amongst the young but also, regrettably, amongst those who should know better. This philosophy is that we have no right to utilise the natural assets of our planet. We cannot be allowed to mine the earth of its bounty, because our excavations will disfigure the beauty of nature. We cannot be allowed to cut the trees for timber, because they belong not to us but to posterity. We cannot be allowed to kill a living creature for its meat or fur or ivory, because all life is somehow sacred.'

'This is a nonsense.' Heng dismissed it with a brusque gesture, his dark eyes sparkling. 'Man is what he is today because he has always done these things.' He touched the cedar panels of the wall beside him, the hem of his silk tunic, the gold and ivory ring on his finger, the precious ceramic bowl on the table before him. 'All these were mined or felled or killed, as is the very food we eat.'

'You and I, we know that,' Tug agreed. 'But this new madness is a force to be reckoned with, almost an unreasoning religious fanaticism. A jihad, if you like, a holy war.'

'I mean no disrespect, Sir Peter, but the occidental is emotionally immature. I like to think that we of the east have more sophistication. We are not so readily caught up by such exaggerated behaviour.'

'That is why I appeal to you, sir. My company, BOSS, has recently become a victim of this campaign. The attention of the British public has been drawn to our operations in Ubomo by groups of these people who call themselves childish names such as "Greenpeace" or "The Friends of the Earth".'

Heng grimaced at the title, and Tug nodded. 'I know it

sounds silly and harmless, but one such organisation is led by a fanatical young woman. She has chosen my company as her target. She has already managed to do us some damage. There is a small but noticeable decline in sales and income that is directly attributable to her campaign. Some of our major markets in the United Kingdom and the United States are getting nervous, and asking us to back off from Ubomo, or at least to play down our involvement, and I personally have received hate mail and death threats.'

'You do not take those seriously?'

'No, Mr Ning, I do not, although these are from people who blow up animal experimentation laboratories and set fire to furrier's shops. However, I think it might be prudent to play down BOSS's role in Ubomo, or at least to give it better public relations.'

'What do you propose, Sir Peter?'

'Firstly, I have already hired an independent film-producer, quite well-known in Europe and America, to film a television feature on Ubomo with particular emphasis on the benefits to the country of our involvement.'

'You do not plan to expose all the syndicate's operations to the camera, Sir Peter?' There was a tone of alarm in Heng's question.

'Of course not, Mr Ning. The film-producer will be carefully guided to show our syndicate in the best possible light. It may even be necessary to prepare some exhibits for him to film.'

'To put on a little show for his benefit?' Heng suggested.

'Exactly, Mr Ning. We will keep him away from the sensitive areas of our operations.'

Heng nodded. 'That is wise. You seem to have arranged matters without my help.'

'You are in a better position than I am, Mr Ning. These so-called green people cannot reach you here in Taiwan. Your own Chinese people are too pragmatic to take up such an immature attitude to mining and forestry, especially as nearly all the products that we reap will be shipped here. You are invulnerable to this childish but dangerous influence.'

'Yes.' Heng nodded. 'I see that all you have said makes good sense, but where does it lead us?'

'I want Lucky Dragon to become the figurehead of the

syndicate. I want one of your best men, rather than one of mine, to go to Ubomo and take charge of the operations there. I will pull out my geologists and forestry experts and architects; you will put in Chinese experts. I will gradually sell off my share of the syndicate to Hong Kong front companies and other oriental nominees. Although you and I will meet regularly and discreetly direct the syndicate operations, BOSS will gradually withdraw from the scene.'

'You will become the invisible man, Sir Peter.' Heng chuckled with genuine amusement.

'The invisible man, I like that.' Tug laughed with him. 'May I know who it is that you would send to Ubomo to take charge there?'

Ning Heng H'Sui stopped laughing and tugged thoughtfully at the silver tuft that hung from his cheek.

His sons, sitting below him at the long lacquer table, leaned forward, trying not to display their eagerness, watching their father's face with impassive expressions that were betrayed by their eyes.

'Ha!' Heng coughed and wet his lips from the tea bowl. 'That will require some consideration, Sir Peter. Will you give me a week or so to decide?'

'Of course, Mr Ning. It is not a decision to be taken lightly. We will need somebody clever and dedicated and ...' he hesitated as he weighed the adjective, discarding 'ruthless' as too explicit, 'and strong, yet diplomatic.'

'I will telephone you with my decision. Where will you be, Sir Peter?'

'Well, I am flying to Sydney tomorrow morning, and from there I will go on directly to Nairobi and Kahali in Ubomo to meet President Taffari. However, my aircraft has direct satellite communication. You can contact me in flight as easily as if I were in the next room.'

'These modern miracles.' Heng shook his head. 'Sometimes it is difficult for an old man to adjust.'

'It seems to me that you are old only in experience and sagacity, Mr Ning. In courage and dash you are young, sir,' Tug said, not entirely in flattery, and Ning Heng H'Sui inclined his head graciously.

Cheng had waited patiently for exactly the right moment to present his father with the gift that he had brought for him from Africa. It was almost two weeks since Sir Peter Harrison had visited Taiwan and still his father had made no announcement within the family as to which of his sons he was sending to run the syndicate's operation in Ubomo.

All the brothers knew it must be one of them. They had known it the moment that the Englishman had made the request. Cheng had noticed the others lean forward at the words, and he had seen his own excitement and expectation mirrored in their eyes. Ever since then, the brothers had been walking around each other like dogs with stiff legs. The extent of Lucky Dragon's investment in the Ubomo syndicate was unprecedented. When the project was fully financed and developed, the family would be committed to raising almost a thousand million dollars, much of it borrowed from banks in Hong Kong and Japan.

It must be one of the sons. Ning Heng H'Sui would never put so much trust in an outsider. Only his age forced him to delegate the task to one of them. Not long ago he would have taken command in Ubomo into his own hands, but now his sons knew he had to give it to one of them, and each of them would kill for the honour. That command would be the ultimate accolade which would show clearly whom Heng had chosen as his heir.

Cheng longed for the honour with a passion so intense that it denied him sleep and spoiled his appetite. In the two weeks since Sir Peter's visit, Cheng had lost weight and become pale and hollow-cheeked. Now, when he exercised in the gymnasium with his hired sparring partners, his body was lean to the point of emaciation. Every rib showed through the hard rubbery casing of muscle. However, his blows and kicks had lost none of their fury. As he fought, his dark eyes, sunken into bruised-looking cavities, glittered with a feverish intensity.

He found every excuse to be in his father's company. Even when the old man was painting, or meditating with the Confucian priests at the shrine in the gardens of the estate, or cataloguing his ivory collection, Cheng tried to be with him, keeping himself close. Yet he sensed that the moment was not exactly right to make the gift. He believed that his father's choice must in the end come down to that between his second brother, Wu, and Cheng himself.

The eldest brother, Fang, was tough and ruthless, but lacking in guile and cunning, a good hatchet man but not a leader. The third son, Ling, possessed an unreliable temperament. He was clever, as clever as either Wu or Cheng, but he was easily panicked and inclined to fly into a rage when things went against him. Ling would never head Lucky Dragon. He might become Number Two perhaps, but never Number One. No, Cheng reasoned, the choice must be between himself and Wu. As a child he had recognised Wu as his main rival and in consequence he hated him with a single-minded malevolence.

While she had been alive, Cheng's English mother had protected him from his half-brothers. But after she died he had been at their mercy. It had taken all these years to learn to hold his own and insinuate himself ever deeper into his father's favour.

Cheng recognised that this would be his chance, his only chance for supremacy. His father was old, more than old, he was ancient. Despite his seemingly boundless strength and energy, Cheng sensed that his father was near death. It might come at any moment of any day, and he went cold at the thought.

He knew that unless he consolidated his accession while his father still lived, Wu would wrest it from him with the help of his two full brothers, the moment his father died. He sensed also that his father was on the point of deciding on the Ubomo project. He knew that this was his moment. This was the slack water of the tide of his fortunes, and now they must turn and begin to flood, or he would be for ever stranded on the mudbanks.

'Honourable Father, I have something for you. A small and humble token of the respect and gratitude I feel for you. May I present it?'

Fortune seemed to conspire with Cheng to provide an appropriate opportunity. The old man was spry today, his mind quick and his waning bodily strength in some measure restored. He had eaten a ripe fig and an apple for breakfast, and had composed a classical stanza while Cheng walked him down to the shrine. It was an ode to the mountain peak that stood above the estate. The poem began:

> *Beloved of clouds*
> *who caress her face . . .*

It was good, although not as good as his father's paintings and ivory carvings, Cheng thought. However, when the old man recited it, Cheng clasped his hands.

'I am awed that so much genius resides in one person. I wish only that I had inherited a few grains of it for myself.'

He thought he might have overdone it a little, but the old man accepted the praise and for a moment tightened his grip on Cheng's arm.

'You are a good son,' he said. 'And your mother . . .' his voice trailed off mournfully, 'your mother was a woman . . .' He shook his head and Cheng thought incredulously that the old man's eyes had moistened. It must have been his imagination. His father was not prey to weakness and sentimentality. When he looked again his father's eyes were clear and bright, and the old man was smiling.

That morning Heng stayed on at the shrine much longer than he usually did. He wanted to inspect the work on his own tomb. One of the most famous geomancers on the island had come to position the tomb precisely and to orientate it so that it stood neither on an earth dragon's head nor on his tail. That would have disturbed the old man's death sleep. The geomancer had worked with a compass and a magic bag for almost an hour, directing the efforts of the priests and the servants to get the marble sarcophagus laid properly.

All this preparation for his own funeral put Heng into a pleasant relaxed mood, and when they were finished Cheng seized the moment and asked to be allowed to present his gift.

Heng smiled and nodded. 'You may bring it to me, my son.'

'Alas, father, the nature of the gift makes that impossible. I must take you to it.'

Heng's expression changed. These days he seldom left the

estate. He seemed about to refuse. However, Cheng had anticipated his reaction. All he needed to do was lift one hand and the Rolls that was parked behind the clipped privet hedges beyond the lotus pools slid silently forward.

Before the old man could protest, Cheng had helped him into the back seat and settled him comfortably with a cashmere rug over his knees. The chauffeur knew where to take them. As the Rolls came down the mountain road on to the littoral plain, Heng and Cheng were isolated and protected from the heat and humidity, and from the teeming humanity that clogged the road with Vespa motorcycles and buses, wild chicken taxis and heavily laden trucks.

When they entered Chung Ching South Road in the Hsimending area of the city the chauffeur slowed and turned in through the gates of the Lucky Dragon company's main city warehouse. The guards jumped to attention as they recognised the couple in the back seat.

One of the warehouse doors stood open and after the car drove through, the steel shutter doors rolled closed behind it. The Rolls parked on one of the loading ramps and Cheng helped his father out of the back door and took his elbow to lead him to a carved teak chair that stood like a throne, covered with embroidered silk cushions, overlooking the floor below the ramp.

As soon as his father was comfortable, Cheng signalled one of the servants to bring freshly made tea. He sat on one of the cushions lower than Heng and they drank tea and talked quietly of unrelated subjects. Cheng was drawing out the moment, trying to spice his father's anticipation. If he succeeded, the old man did not show it. He barely glanced towards the floor below.

Ten brawny workmen knelt in a row facing the throne. Cheng had dressed them in black tunics, with red headbands, and the emblem of the Lucky Dragon embroidered on their backs also in red. He had rehearsed them carefully and they were motionless, heads bowed respectfully.

Finally, after ten minutes of talk and tea, Cheng told his father, 'This is the present I have brought you from Africa.' He indicated the rows of chests, arranged behind the workmen. 'It is such a poor little present that now I am ashamed to offer it to you.'

'Tea?' Heng smiled. 'Cases of tea? Enough tea to last me the rest of my lifetime. It is a fine gift, my son.'

'It is a poor gift, but may I open the cases for you?' Cheng asked, and the old man nodded his permission.

Cheng clapped his hands and the ten workmen sprang to their feet and ran to seize one of the tea-chests and bring it forward. They worked swiftly, efficiently. With half a dozen blows of a slap-hammer and a twist of a jemmy bar, they lifted the lid off the first case.

Heng showed the first sign of animation and leaned forward in the high chair. Two of the workmen lifted out the first tusk from its bed of caked black tea.

Cheng had long ago arranged that it should be one of the largest and most finely shaped tusks in the entire shipment of stolen ivory. He had asked Chetti Singh to mark the case that contained it before the shipment left the Indian's warehouse in Malawi.

The tusk was long, over seven feet long, but not as thick and blunt as one of the typical massively heavy tusks from further north than Zimbabwe. Yet from an entirely aesthetic point of view this one was more pleasing, its girth more in proportion to its length and the curve and taper were elegant. It was neither cracked nor damaged and the patina above the lip was creamy yellow.

Involuntarily Heng clapped his hands with pleasure and exclaimed aloud.

'Bring it to me!' Two of the workmen, struggling under the burden, climbed the concrete steps and knelt before him offering the lovely tusk. Heng stroked the ivory and his eyes sparkled in the cobweb of wrinkles that surrounded them.

'Beautiful!' he murmured. 'The most beautiful of all nature's creations, more beautiful than pearls or the feathers of the brightest tropical birds.' He broke off abruptly as his fingers detected the rough patch on the tusk. He leaned closer and peered at it and exclaimed again. 'But this tusk bears a government stamp. "ZW". That is a Zimbabwe government number. This is legal ivory, Cheng.' He clapped his hands again. 'Legal ivory, my son, many more times more valuable for those numbers. How did you do it? How many more tusks are there?' His father's unrestrained pleasure was giving Cheng huge face. He must be careful to remain humble and dutiful.

'Every one of those cases is filled with ivory, honoured Father. Every tusk is stamped.'

'Where did you get them?' Heng insisted, and then raised his hand to prevent Cheng replying.

'Wait!' he ordered. 'Wait. Do not tell me!' He was silent, staring at his son for a while, and then he said, 'Yes. That is it. I know where this ivory comes from.' With a wave of his hand he sent the black-clad workmen out of earshot and leaned closer to Cheng, dropping his voice to a whisper. 'I read some time ago that there was a raid by a gang of poachers on a government ivory store in Zimbabwe. A place called Chiwewe? The gangsters were wiped out, but the ivory was not recovered, is that not so, my son?'

'I read the same newspaper article, honoured Father.' Cheng dropped his eyes and waited while the silence drew out.

Then Heng spoke again. 'The man who planned that raid was clever and bold. He was not afraid to kill for what he wanted,' he whispered. 'The kind of man that I admire. The kind of man that I was once, when I was young.'

'The kind of man that you still are, Father,' Cheng said, but Heng shook his head.

'The kind of man that I would be proud to have as my son,' Heng went on. 'You may present the rest of your gift to me now.'

Now Cheng's standing, in his father's eyes, was so enormous that he wriggled in his seat with pleasure and shouted for the workmen to open the other cases.

For the next two hours Heng examined the shipment of tusks. He gloated over every single piece, picking out a dozen or so of the loveliest or most unusual for his special collection. He was particularly interested in deformed ivory. The nerve of one of the tusks had been damaged, while it was still immature, by a hand-hammered lead ball from a native poacher's musket. The result was that the tusk had split into four separate shafts and these had twisted around each other in the same way as the

348

strands of a hemp rope. The original lead musket-bullet, heavily
corroded, was still embedded in the root of the tusk, and the
entwined spirals of ivory resembled the horns of the legendary
unicorn. Heng was delighted with it.

Cheng had seldom seen him so animated and voluble, but at
the end of the two hours he was obviously fatigued, and Cheng
helped him back into the Rolls and ordered the chauffeur to
return to the estate.

Heng laid his head back on the soft Connolly leather and
closed his eyes. When Cheng was sure the old man was asleep,
he gently adjusted the cashmere rug over him. One of Heng's
hands had dropped on to the seat beside him. Cheng lifted it
into his lap and before he covered it with the cashmere he
caressed it so gently as not to wake his father. The hand was
thin and bony and the skin was cool as that of a corpse.
Suddenly the long thin fingers tightened on Cheng's wrist and
the old man spoke without opening his eyes.

'I am not afraid of death, my son,' he whispered. 'But I am
terrified that all that I have achieved will be destroyed by
careless hands. Your brother Wu is strong and clever, but he
does not have my spirit. He does not care for fine and beautiful
things. He does not love poetry or painting or ivory.'

Heng opened his eyes and turned his head to stare at his son
with those bright implacable lizard's eyes.

'I knew that you had inherited my spirit, Cheng, but until
today I doubted that you had the warrior's steel. That is the
reason why I hesitated to choose between you and Wu. However, this gift that you have given to me today has changed that
thinking. I know how you obtained that ivory. I know that it
was necessary to squeeze the juice from the ripe cherry.' This
was Heng's euphemism for drawing blood. 'And I know that
you did not shrink from it. I know also that you succeeded in a
difficult enterprise, whether by luck or cunning I do not really
care. I prize both luck and cunning equally.'

He tightened his grip until it was painful but Cheng did not
wince or pull away.

'I am sending you to Ubomo, my son, as the representative of
the Lucky Dragon.'

Cheng bowed his head over his father's hand and kissed it. 'I will not fail you,' he promised, and a single tear of joy and of pride fell from the corner of his eye and sparkled like a jewel on the pale dry skin of his father's hand.

Ning Heng H'Sui made the formal announcement of his selection the following morning. He made it while seated at the head of the lacquer table overlooking the garden.

Cheng watched the faces of his brothers while the old man spoke. Wu remained as impassive as the ivory carving his father had made of him years ago. His face was bland, smooth and creamy yellow, but his eyes were terrible as he returned Cheng's stare across the table. When the old man finished speaking there was a moment's silence which seemed to last an eternity as the three elder brothers contemplated the world that had changed for them.

Then Wu spoke. 'Honourable Father, you are wise in all things. We, your sons, bow to your will as the rice stalks bow to the north wind.'

All four of them bowed so low that their foreheads almost touched the table-top, but when they straightened the other three were looking at Cheng. Cheng realised at that moment that it might be possible to attain too much face. His face was greater than that of all his half-brothers combined and he felt an icicle of fear slide down his spine, for his brothers were watching him with the eyes of crocodiles. He knew that he dare not fail in Ubomo. They would be waiting to rend him if he did.

Once Cheng was back in his own apartment, the fear fell away to be replaced by the elation of success. There was so much work to do before he returned to Africa, but for the moment he could not concentrate his mind upon it. Tomorrow certainly, but not now. He was too charged with excitement, his mind restless and unfocused. He needed to steady himself, to burn off the excess energy that made him both physically and mentally overwrought.

He knew exactly how to achieve this. He had his own special

ritual for purging his soul. Of course, it was dangerous, terribly dangerous. On more than one occasion before it had brought him to the very brink of disaster. However, the danger was part of the efficacy of the ritual. He knew that if anything went wrong he would have lost all. The monumental successes of these last few days, his father's selection and the ascendancy over his brothers would all be wiped away.

The risk was enormous, completely out of proportion to the fleeting gratification that he would achieve. Perhaps it was the gambler's urge to flirt with self-destruction. After each episode he always promised himself that he would never indulge in the madness again, but always the temptation proved too strong, particularly at a time such as this.

As soon as he entered his apartment his wife made tea for him, and then called the children to pay him their respects. He spoke to them for a few minutes and took his infant son on his lap, but he was distracted and soon dismissed them. They left with obvious relief. These formal interviews were a strain for all of them. He was not good with children, even his own.

'My father has chosen me to go to Ubomo,' he told his wife.

'It is a great honour,' she said. 'I offer you my felicitations. When will we leave?'

'I shall go alone,' he told her, and saw the relief in her eyes. It annoyed him that she made it so obvious. 'Of course, I will send for you as soon as I have made the arrangements.'

She dropped her eyes. 'I will await your summons.' But he could not concentrate on her. The excitement was fizzing in his head.

'I will rest for an hour. See that I am not disturbed. Then I have to go down to the city. There is much work to do before I leave. I will not return tonight, and I shall probably stay at the apartment in Tunhua Road. I shall send you a message before I return.'

Alone in his own room he teased himself with the telephone. He placed the cordless instrument on the table and stared at it, rehearsing every word he would say and his breathing was short and quick as though he had run up a flight of stairs. His fingers trembled slightly when at last he reached out for it. The telephone was fitted with a special coding scrambler. It could not be tapped and it was impossible for any other person, civil or military or police, to trace the special number that he punched into the key panel.

Very few people had this number. She had told him once that she had given it to only six of her most valued clients. She answered it on the second ring and she recognised his voice instantly. She greeted him with the special code name she had assigned him.

'You have not been to see me for almost two years, Green Mountain Man.'

'I have been away.'

'Yes, I know, but still I missed you.'

'I want to come tonight.'

'Will you want the special thing?'

'Yes.' Cheng felt his stomach clench at the thought of it. He thought he might be sick with fear and loathing and excitement.

'It is very short notice,' she said. 'And the price has risen since your last visit.'

'The price does not matter. Can you do it?' He heard the high strained tones of his own voice. She was silent, and he knew she was baiting him. He wanted to scream at her and then she said, 'You are fortunate.' Her voice changed. It became obscenely soft and slimy. 'I have received new merchandise; I can offer you a choice of two.'

Cheng gulped and cleared his throat of a plug of phlegm before he could ask. 'Young?'

'Very young. Very tender. Untouched.'

'When will you be ready?'

'Ten o'clock tonight,' she said. 'Not before.'

'At the sea pavilion?' he asked.

'Yes,' she replied. 'They will expect you at the gate. Ten o'clock,' she repeated. 'Not earlier, not later.'

Cheng drove to the apartment building in Tunhua Road. It was in the most prestigious part of the city and the accommodation was expensive, but it was paid for by Lucky Dragon.

He left his Porsche in the underground garage and rode up to the top floor apartment in the elevator. By the time he had showered and changed it was still only six o'clock and he had plenty of time in which to prepare himself.

He left the apartment building on foot and set off down Tunhua Road. He loved the *renao* of Taipei. It was one of the things that he missed most while he was away. *Renao* was a concept that was almost impossible to translate from the Chinese to any other language. It meant festive, lively, joyous and noisy all at the same time.

It was now the ghost month, the seventh lunar month when the ghosts return from hell to haunt the earth and have to be placated with gifts of ghost money and food. It was also necessary to keep them at a distance with fireworks and dragon processions.

Cheng paused to laugh and applaud one of the processions led by a monstrous dragon with a huge papier-mâché head and fifty pairs of human legs beneath its serpentine body. The jumping-jack fireworks popped with spurts of blue smoke about the ankles of the spectators and the band beat drums and gongs and the children shrieked. It was good *renao* and it heightened Cheng's excitement.

He threaded his way through the crowds and the bustle until he reached the East Garden area of the city and left the main thoroughfare to enter a back alley.

The fortune-teller was one Cheng had used for ten years. He was an old man with thin wispy grey hair and a facial mole like Cheng's father had. He wore traditional robes and a mandarin cap and sat cross-legged in his curtained cubicle with his paraphernalia around him.

Cheng greeted him respectfully and at his invitation squatted facing him.

'I have not seen you for a long time,' the old man accused him, and Cheng apologised.

'I have been away from Taiwan.'

They discussed the fee and the divination that Cheng required.

'I am about to undertake a task,' Cheng explained. 'I wish to have spirit guidance.'

The old man nodded and consulted his almanacs and star guides, nodding and mumbling to himself. Finally he handed Cheng a ceramic cup filled with bamboo rods.

Cheng shook this vigorously and then spilled the rods on to the mat between them. Each rod was painted with characters

353

and emblems and the old man studied the pattern in which they had fallen.

'This task will not be undertaken here in Taiwan, but in a land across the ocean,' he said, and Cheng relaxed a little. The old man had not lost his touch. He nodded encouragement.

'It is a task of great complexity and there are many people involved. Foreigners, foreign devils.'

Again Cheng nodded.

'I see powerful allies, but also powerful enemies who will oppose you.'

'I know my allies, but I do not know who will be my enemies,' Cheng interjected.

'You already know your enemy. He has opposed you before. On that occasion you overcame him.'

'Can you describe him?'

The fortune-teller shook his head. 'You will know him when you see him again.'

'When will that be?'

'You should not travel during the ghost month. You must prepare yourself here in Taiwan. Leave only on the first day of the eighth lunar month.'

'Very well.' That suited Cheng's plans. 'Will I overcome this enemy once again?'

'To answer that question it will be necessary to make a further divination,' the old man whispered, and Cheng grimaced at this device for doubling the fee.

'Very well,' he agreed, and the fortune-teller replaced the bamboo sticks in the bowl and Cheng shook them out on to the mat.

'There are two enemies now.' The fortune-teller picked two rods out of the pile. 'One is the man that you know, the other is a woman whom you have not yet met. Together they will oppose your endeavours.'

'Will I overcome them?' Cheng asked anxiously, and the old man examined the fall of the bamboo rods minutely.

'I see a snow-capped mountain and a great forest. These will be the battleground. There will be evil spirits and demons . . .' The old man's voice trailed away, and he lifted one of the bamboo sticks from the pile.

'What else do you see?' Cheng insisted, but the old man coughed and spat and would not look up at him. The bamboo sliver was painted white, the colour of death and disaster.

'That is all. I can see no more,' he mumbled.

Cheng took a new thousand Taiwan dollar note from his top pocket and laid it beside the pile of bamboo rods.

'Will I overcome my enemies?' Cheng asked, and the note disappeared like a conjuring trick under the old man's bony fingers.

'You will have great face,' he promised, but still he would not look directly at his client, and Cheng left the cubicle with some of his good feelings dissipated by the ambiguous reply. More than ever now he needed solace, but it was still only a little after eight o'clock. She had told him not to come before ten.

It was only a short walk to Snake Alley, but on his way Cheng paused in the forecourt of the Dragon Mountain Temple and burned a pile of ghost money in one of the gaudy pyramid furnaces to placate the ancestral ghosts who would be prowling the night around him.

He left the temple and cut through the night market where the stall-holders offered a bewildering array of wares and the prostitutes plied their trade in flimsy wooden sheds in the back areas of the market. Both storekeepers and painted ladies haggled loudly with their potential customers, and the spectators joined in with comment and suggestion and laughter. It was good *renao*, and Cheng's spirits revived.

He entered Snake Alley down which the shê-shops were crowded closely together. Outside each stall were piled snake baskets of steel mesh and the front windows were filled with the largest and most spectacularly coloured of the serpents which gave the alley its name.

Many of the shops had a live mongoose tethered outside the front door. Cheng stopped to watch an arranged contest between one of these sleek little predators and a four-foot cobra. The cobra reared up as it confronted the mongoose, and the crowd gathered quickly and shrieked with delight. With its striped hood fully extended, the cobra revolved and swayed like a flower on its stalk to watch the circling mongoose with unblinking bright eyes while its feathery black tongue tasted the scent of its adversary on the air. The mongoose danced in and then leapt back as the cobra struck. For an instant the snake was off balance and fully extended and the mongoose darted in for the kill. It seized the back of the glistening scaled head and its needle teeth crunched into bone. The snake's body whipped and coiled in its death throes and the proprietor of the shê-shop separated the mongoose from its victim and carried the writhing reptile into his shop, followed by two or three eager male customers.

Cheng did not join them. He had his own special shê-shop, and he wanted a particular type of snake, the rarest, the most expensive, the most effective.

The snake-doctor recognised Cheng over the heads of the crowd that thronged the alley. His shop was famous. He did not have to stage mongoose fights to attract his customers. He beamed and bowed, and ushered Cheng through to the back room which was curtained off from the public gaze.

It was not necessary for Cheng to state his requirements. The shê-shop owner knew him well, over many years. It was Cheng who had arranged his supply of the most virulently poisonous reptiles from Africa. It was Cheng who had introduced him to Chetti Singh, and made the first consignments of snakes through the diplomatic bag. Of course, Cheng took a commission on each shipment.

Cheng had also persuaded him to deal in rare African birds. Once again these had been supplied by Chetti Singh and the trade was now worth over a quarter of a million US dollars a year. There were collectors in Europe and America who would pay huge sums for a pair of saddle-billed storks or bald ibis. The African parrots, although not as colourful as the South American varieties, were also much sought after. Chetti Singh could supply all these, and once again Cheng took his commission.

However, the main source of the snake-doctor's income was still the supply of venomous snakes. The more venomous, the more valuable they were to Chinese gentlemen with faltering potency. The African mamba had been entirely unknown in Taiwan or mainland China until Chetti Singh had made the first shipment. Now they were the most prized of all snakes on the island, and commanded a price of two thousand US dollars apiece.

The snake-doctor had a particularly beautiful specimen ready in a mesh cage on his stainless-steel-topped table. Now he drew on a pair of elbow-length gloves, a precaution that he would have scorned had he been dealing with a cobra.

He opened the sliding lid of the cage a crack and slipped in a long steel forked rod. Deftly he pinned the mamba's head and the snake hissed sharply and twined itself around the steel rod. Now the snake-doctor opened the lid fully and seized the mamba behind the head, careful to get thumb and forefinger aligned behind the protuberances of the skull so the snake could not pull free of his grip.

The instant he released the pressure of the forked rod, the snake wrapped itself in tight coils around his forearm. It was six feet long and angry. It exerted all its rippling scaled strength to pull its head free, but the snake-doctor prevented the points of the skull from being drawn through his fingers.

The mamba's jaws gaped wide open and its short fangs were erect in the pale soft mucous lining of its mouth. The clear venom oozed down the open channel in the fangs and dripped from the points like dew from a rose-thorn.

The snake-doctor held the reptile's head on a small anvil and with a sharp blow of a wooden mallet crushed the skull. The snake's body whipped around wildly in the death frenzy.

Cheng watched impassively as the snake-doctor hung the writhing body on a meat hook and then used a razor to slit open the belly cavity and drain the blood into a cheap glass tumbler. With a surgeon's skill he removed the venom sacs from the mamba's neck and placed them in a glass bowl. After that he lifted out the liver and gall bladder and placed them in a separate bowl.

Next he peeled off the snake's skin, ringing the neck with the razor and stripping the skin like a nylon stocking from a girl's leg. The naked body was pink and glistening. The snake doctor took it down from the meat hook and laid it on the steel table-top. With half a dozen blows of a cleaver he chopped it into pieces, and dropped them into a soup kettle that was already boiling on the burner of a gas stove at the rear of the shop. As he added herbs and spices to the kettle he intoned a magical incantation that had remained unchanged since the Han dynasty of 200 BC when the first snake-doctors had developed their art.

Once the soup was cooking, the snake-doctor turned back to his table. He spilled the gall bladder and liver into a small mortar and pounded them to pulp with a ceramic pestle. Then he looked up at Cheng enquiringly.

'Do you wish to take the tiger juice?' he asked. It was a rhetorical question. Cheng always drank the venom.

Again it was part of the gambler's thrill to flirt with death, for if he had a tiny gum boil or a scratch on his tongue, a bleeding rash in his throat or a raw spot in his guts, even a duodenal or gastric ulcer, the mamba venom would find it and kill him within minutes, and it would be an excruciating death.

The snake-doctor added the translucent sacs of venom to the mortar and pounded them in with the liver. Then he scraped the pulp into the glass tumbler of dark blood and while he stirred it he added a dash of medicine from each of three other bottles.

The concoction was black, and thick as honey. He handed the tumbler to Cheng.

Cheng drew a deep breath and then tossed back the liquid at a single gulp. It was bitter with gall. He placed the empty glass on the metal table-top, and folded his hands in his lap. He sat without showing any emotion, while the snake-doctor recited spells from his magic book over him.

If the venom did not kill him, Cheng knew that the potion would arm his manhood. It would transform his flaccid penis into a steel lance. It would turn his testicles into cannonballs of iron. He waited quietly for the first symptoms of poisoning. After ten minutes he felt no ill-effects, but his penis stirred and swelled into a semi-erection. He moved a little to give it space in his trousers and the snake-doctor smiled and nodded happily at the success of his treatment.

He went to fetch the soup kettle from the gas burner and poured some of the liquid into a rice bowl and then added a piece of mamba flesh, cooked white and flaking. He offered the bowl and a pair of ivory chopsticks to Cheng.

Cheng ate the meat and drank the soup and when he had finished he accepted a second bowl. At the end of the meal he belched loudly to show his appreciation, and again the snake-doctor nodded and smiled.

Cheng consulted his wristwatch. It was nine o'clock. He rose to his feet and bowed. 'Thank you for your assistance,' he said formally.

'I am honoured that my humble efforts have pleased you. I wish you a sword of steel and many happy hours in the velvet scabbard.'

There was no question of payment. The snake-doctor would make a deduction from Cheng's commission on the supply of African snakes and wild birds.

Cheng walked back quickly to the apartment building in Tunhua Road. He sat in the black leather driving seat of the Porsche and for a few minutes enjoyed the tight full sensation of his erection before he started the engine and drove out of the garage.

It took him forty minutes to reach the sea pavilion. The grounds were surrounded by a high wall topped with a ridge of ceramic tiles, except on the open sea side. Coloured paper lanterns hung from the traditionally-shaped pediment of the gate. It looked like the entrance to a pleasure garden or fairground. Cheng knew that the lanterns had been lit especially to welcome him.

The guards had been warned to expect him and they made no effort to detain him. Cheng drove through and parked above the rocky headland. He locked the Porsche and stood for a moment inhaling the kelp odour of the sea. There was a fast motor launch moored at the private jetty. It would be needed later. Cheng knew that in less than two hours the speed boat could be over the thousand-yard sounding, over the oceanic depths of the East China Sea. A weighted object, such as a human body, dropped overboard from there would fall into the primeval ooze of the seabed, never to be recovered. He smiled. His erection had abated only slightly.

He went up to the pavilion. It was also of traditional architecture. It reminded Cheng of the house in the willow-tree pattern on the blue porcelain plates. A servant met him at the door, led him into an inner room and brought him tea.

359

It was exactly ten o'clock when she entered the room from behind the bead curtain.

She was slim as a boy in her tight brocaded tunic and silk pantaloons. He had never been able to guess her age for she wore a mask of make-up like a player in a Peking opera. Her almond eyes were starkly outlined in jet black, while her lids and cheeks were hectically rouged to the carmine colour that the Chinese find so attractive. Her forehead and the bridge of her nose were ash white and her lips a deep startling scarlet.

'Welcome to my house, Green Mountain Man,' she lisped, and Cheng bowed.

'I am honoured, Myrtle Blossom Lady.'

She sat on the sofa beside Cheng and they exchanged formal and polite conversation, until Cheng indicated the cheap imitation leather briefcase he had placed on the table in front of him.

She appeared to notice it for the first time, but did not deign to touch it herself. She inclined her head and her assistant glided into the room on slippered feet. She must have been watching them from behind the beaded curtain. She left again as silently as she had entered, taking the briefcase with her.

It took her a few minutes to count the money in the back room and to put it in a safe place. Then she returned and knelt beside her mistress. They exchanged a glance. The money was all there.

'You say that there is a choice of two?' Cheng asked.

'Yes,' she agreed. 'But would you like to make sure the room is to your taste, and that the equipment is in order?'

She led Cheng through to the special room at the back of the pavilion.

The central piece of furniture was a gynaecologist's couch, complete with stirrups. It was fitted with a plastic cover that could be removed and destroyed after use, and there was also a plastic sheet laid over the floor. The walls and ceiling were tiled and washable. Like an operating theatre, it could be scrubbed down to its present sterile condition.

Cheng moved to the table on which the instruments were laid out. There was a selection of silk cords of various lengths and thicknesses arranged in neat coils on the tray. He picked up one of these and ran it through his fingers. His erection, which had softened, revived strongly. Then he turned his attention to the other items on the table, a full set of stainless steel gynaecological instruments.

'Very good,' he told her.

'Come,' she said, and took his hand. 'You may choose now.'

She led him to a small window in the near wall. They stood hand-in-hand in front of it and looked through the one-way glass into the room beyond.

After a few moments the female assistant led two children into the room. They were both dressed in white. In the Chinese tradition, white was the colour of death. Both the little girls had long dark hair and pretty little nut-brown pug faces. Cambodian or Vietnamese, Cheng guessed.

'Who are they?' he asked.

'Boat people,' she said. 'Their boat was captured by pirates in the South China Sea. All the adults were killed. They are orphans, nameless and stateless. Nobody knows they exist; nobody will miss them.'

The female assistant began to undress the two little girls. She did it skilfully, titillating the hidden audience like a strip-tease artiste.

One girl was at least fourteen. Once she was naked Cheng saw that she had full breasts and a dark tussock of pubic hair, but the other girl was barely pubescent. Her breasts were flower buds, and the fine haze of pubic down did not conceal the plump cleft of her pudenda.

'The young one!' Cheng whispered hoarsely. 'I want the young one.'

'Yes,' she said. 'I thought that would be your choice. She will be brought to you in a few minutes. You may take as long as you wish. There is no hurry.'

She left the room, and suddenly the music swelled from hidden speakers – loud Chinese music with gongs and drums that would cover any other sound, such as a little girl's screams.

The colonials of Victorian times had sited Ubomo's Government House with care on high ground above the lake, with a view out across the waters, and they had surrounded it with lawns and exotic trees brought out from Europe to remind them of home. In the evenings the breeze came down from the Mountains of the Moon in the west, with the memory of glaciers and eternal snows, to take the edge off the heat.

Government House was still as it had been in the colonial era, no more pretentious than a comfortable redbrick ranch house with high ceilings, enclosed on all sides by a wide fly-screened verandah. Victor Omeru had kept it that way. He would not spend money on grand public buildings while his people were in want. The aid that he received from America and Europe had all gone into agriculture, health and education, not personal aggrandisement.

Tonight the verandahs and lawns were crowded as Daniel Armstrong and Bonny drove up in the army Landrover that had been placed at their disposal. A Hita corporal in camouflage overalls, with a sub-machine-gun slung over one shoulder, waved them into a parking slot between two other vehicles with diplomatic licence plates.

'How do I look?' Bonny asked anxiously as she checked her lipstick in the rear-view mirror.

'Sexy,' Daniel told her truthfully. She had teased her hair out into a great tawny red mane and she wore a green mini-skirt tight around her buttocks and high on her thighs. For such a big girl she had shapely legs.

'Give me a hand. Damned skirts!' The Landrover stood high and her skirt rode up as she slid down. She showed a flash of lace pantie that rocked the Hita corporal on to his heels.

There were floodlights in the jacaranda trees and an army band belted out popular jazz with a distinctive African beat that lifted Daniel's spirits and put a spring in his step.

'All this in your honour,' Bonny chuckled.

'I bet Taffari tells that to all his guests.' Daniel smiled.

Captain Kajo, who had met them at the airport, hurried towards them as soon as they stepped on to the lawn. He was looking at Bonny's legs from twenty paces away, but he addressed Daniel.

'Ah, Doctor Armstrong, the president has been asking for you. You are the guest of honour tonight.'

He led them up the front steps on to the verandah. Daniel picked out President Taffari instantly, even though he had his back turned to them. He was the tallest in a room full of tall Hita officers. He wore a maroon mess jacket of his own design, although his head was bare.

'Mr President.' Captain Kajo addressed his back deferentially, and Taffari turned and smiled and displayed the medals on his chest. 'May I present Doctor Daniel Armstrong and his assistant Miss Mahon?'

'Doctor!' Taffari greeted Daniel. 'I am a great admirer of your work. I could not have chosen anybody more qualified to show my country to the world. Up until now we have been kept in obscurity and medieval isolation by the reactionary old tyrant we overthrew. It is time that Ubomo came into its own. You will help us, Doctor. You will help us bring my beloved country into the twentieth century by focusing world attention upon us.'

'I'll do all in my power,' Daniel assured him cautiously. Although he had seen photographs of him, Daniel was unprepared for Taffari's eloquence and presence. He was a striking-looking man, exuding power and confidence. He stood a full head taller than Daniel's six feet and had the features of an Egyptian pharaoh carved in amber.

His eyes slid past Daniel and settled on Bonny Mahon. She stared back at him boldly and wet her bottom lip with the tip of her tongue.

'You are the photographer. Sir Peter Harrison sent me a videotape of "Arctic Dream". If you can photograph Ubomo with the same understanding and craft, I will be well pleased, Miss Mahon.'

He looked down at her bosom, at the big golden freckles on her upper chest that gave way to a narrow strip of unblemished creamy skin above the top of her green dress. The exposed cleavage between her breasts was deep and tightly compressed.

'You are very kind, Mr President,' she said, and Taffari laughed softly.

'Nobody has ever called me that before,' he admitted, and then changed the subject. 'What do you think of my country so far?'

'We only arrived today,' Bonny pointed out. 'But the lake is lovely and the people are so tall, the men so handsome.' She made it a personal compliment.

'The Hita are tall and handsome,' Taffari agreed. 'But the Uhali are small and ugly as monkeys, even their women.' The Hita officers of his staff laughed delightedly and Bonny gulped with shock.

'Where I come from we don't talk disparagingly of other ethnic groups. It's called racism, and it's unfashionable,' she said.

He stared at her for a moment. Clearly he was unaccustomed to being corrected. Then he smiled, a thin, cool little smile. 'Well, Miss Mahon, in Africa we tell the truth. If people are ugly or stupid we say so. It's called tribalism, and I assure you it's extremely fashionable.'

His staff roared with laughter, and Taffari turned back to Daniel.

'Your assistant is a woman of strong views, Doctor, but I believe you were born in Africa. You have a keener understanding. It shows in your work. You have put your finger on the problems that face this continent, and poverty is the most crippling of those. Africa is poor, Doctor, and Africa is passive and supine. I intend to change that. I intend to endow my country with the spirit and confidence to exploit our natural wealth and to develop the strength and native genius of our people. I want you to record our endeavours.'

His staff officers, all in the same maroon-coloured mess jackets, applauded this statement.

'I'll do my best,' Daniel promised.

'I'm sure you will, Doctor Armstrong.' He was looking at Bonny again, but he went on speaking to Daniel. 'The British ambassador is here tonight. I'm sure you will want to pay your respects.' He summoned Kajo to him. 'Captain, please take Doctor Armstrong to meet Sir Michael.'

Bonny began to follow Daniel, but Taffari stopped her with a touch on the arm. 'Don't go yet, Miss Mahon. There are a few things I would like to explain to you, such as the differences between the Uhali and the tall handsome Hita whom you so admire.'

Bonny turned back to him, thrust out one hip in a provocative stance and crossed her arms beneath her breasts, pushing them up so that they threatened to pop out of the green dress into his face. 'You should not judge Africa by the standards of Europe,' he told her. 'We do things differently here.'

From the corner of her eye Bonny saw that Daniel had left the verandah and followed Kajo down on to the floodlit lawn. She leaned close to Taffari, her eyes not much below the level of his.

'Goody!' she said. 'I'm always looking for new and different ways.'

Daniel paused at the bottom of the steps and began to grin as he picked out the familiar figure on the crowded lawn. Then he hurried forward and seized his hand.

'*Sir* Michael, forsooth! British ambassador no less, you sly dog. When did all this happen?'

Michael Hargreave gripped his elbow in a momentary display of un-British and undiplomatic affection. 'Didn't you get my letter? All very sudden. Hauled me out of Lusaka before you could say "Bob's your uncle". Sword on both shoulders from H.M. "Arise, Sir Michael", and all that. Shot me down here. But you *did* get my letter?'

Daniel shook his head. 'Congratulations, Sir Michael. Long overdue. You deserve it.'

Hargreave looked embarrassed and dropped Daniel's hand. 'Where's your drink, dear boy? Don't touch the whisky. Locally made. Convinced it's actually bottled crocodile piss. Try the gin.' He summoned a waiter. 'Can't think why you didn't get my letter. Tried to ring you at the flat in London. No reply.'

'Where's Wendy?'

'Sent her back to Lusaka to pack up. New chap there has agreed to look after your Landcruiser and gear. Wendy will be here in a couple of weeks. Sends her love, by the way.'

'Did she know you'd see me here?' Daniel was puzzled.

'Tug Harrison gave us the word that you'd be in Ubomo.'

'You know Harrison?'

'Everybody in Africa knows Tug. Finger in most pies. Asked me to keep an eye on you. Told me about your assignment here. You're going to film Taffari and make him and BOSS look good; that's what he told me. Right?'

'A little bit more complicated than that, Mike.'

'Don't I know it! Complications you haven't dreamed of yet ...' He drew Daniel away to a deserted corner of the lawn, out of earshot of the other guests. 'But first of all, what do you think of Taffari?'

'I wouldn't buy a second-hand country from him without checking the tyres.'

'Check the engine as well, while you're about it,' Michael smiled. 'The indications are that he's going to make Idi Amin look like Mother Theresa. I saw him giving you fifty lyrical words on his plan for peace and prosperity in the land.'

'Rather more than fifty,' Daniel corrected him.

'What it actually amounts to is peace for the Hita, prosperity for Ephrem Taffari, and screw the Uhali. My pals at MI6 tell me that he already has his numbered bank accounts in Switzerland and the Channel Islands all set up, and nice little sums tucked away in them. American foreign aid.'

'That shouldn't surprise you. Everybody's doing it, aren't they?'

'Par for the course; got to admit it. But he is being rather naughty to the Uhali. Chopped old Victor Omeru, who was rather a decent sort, and now he's kicking the manure out of the rest of the Uhali tribe. Some nasty rumours flying about, dark deeds. We don't really approve. Even the PM is a bit browned off with him already, which reminds me – got some news of a pal of yours.'

'A pal of mine?'

'The Lucky Dragon. Rings a bell, doesn't it? And you'll never guess who they're sending out to run the operation here.'

'Ning Cheng Gong,' Daniel said quietly.

It had to be. That was the reason he was here in Ubomo. He had sensed it all along. This was where he would meet Cheng again.

'You've been reading my mail,' Michael accused. 'Ning Cheng Gong is right. He arrives next week. Taffari is giving

366

another party to welcome him. Any excuse for a party with our Ephrem, even you.' He broke off and stared at Daniel. 'You all right, dear boy? Taking your anti-malarial, are you? Gone as white as a sheet.'

'I'm fine.' But Daniel's voice was hoarse and scratchy. He had a terrible mental image of the bedroom of the cottage at Chiwewe, and of the desecrated bodies of Mavis Nzou and her daughters. It left him feeling sick and shaken. He wanted to think of something else, anything but Ning Cheng Gong.

'Tell me everything about Taffari and Ubomo that I need to know,' he demanded of Michael Hargreave.

'Tall order, dear boy. Can only give you the headlines now, but if you drop in at the embassy, I'll give you a full briefing, and a peep at some of the files. Your eyes only, of course. Even got a couple of bottles of genuine Chivas tucked away.'

Daniel shook his head. 'We're going up the lakeshore tomorrow to start filming. Taffari has put the entire navy at our disposal. One clapped-out World War Two gunboat. But I could drop in at the embassy tomorrow evening.'

When it was time to go, Daniel looked around for Bonny Mahon but could not find her. He saw Captain Kajo with a group of other officers at the bar and went across to him.

'I'm leaving now, Captain Kajo.'

'That's all right, Doctor. President Taffari has left already. You are free to go.' You could only tell that Kajo was drunk by his eyes. They had that coffee-coloured haze over the whites. In a white man they would have been bloodshot.

'We will meet tomorrow morning, Captain? What time?'

'Six o'clock at the guest house, Doctor. I will pick you up. We must not be late. The navy will be waiting for us.'

'Have you seen Miss Mahon?' Daniel asked. One of the other Hita officers sniggered drunkenly and Kajo grinned.

'No, Doctor. She was here earlier on. But I haven't seen her in the last hour. She must have left. Yes, come to think of it now, I did see her leave.' He turned away, and Daniel tried not to scowl and look abandoned as he went out to the Landrover in the carpark.

The government guest house was in darkness when he drove up and parked under the verandah. She might be in bed, already asleep with the light out. Despite his altered opinion of her, he felt a stab of disappointment when he switched on the bedroom light and saw that the servants had turned down the beds and rigged the mosquito nets. She had given him the excuse to end it – why was he not more pleased that it was over?

He had drunk just enough of the local gin to have a headache. He picked up Bonny's bag from the foot of the bed and carried it through to the second bedroom. Then he went into the bathroom and swept her toiletries and cosmetics into her sponge bag and dumped them in the washbasin of the second bathroom down the passage. Then he held his head under the cold tap and took three Anadin tablets. He dropped his clothes on the floor and climbed naked under the mosquito net.

He woke with headlights sweeping the front of the guest house and shining through the curtains on to the wall above his bed. Tyres crunched on the gravel drive. There were voices, and then a car door slammed and the vehicle pulled away. He heard her come up the verandah steps and open the front door. A minute later the bedroom door opened stealthily and she crept into the room.

He switched on the bedside light and she froze in the middle of the floor. She carried her shoes in one hand and her bag in the other. Her hair was in a wild tangle, sparkling like copper wire in the light, and her lipstick was smeared over her chin.

She giggled and he realised she was drunk.

'Have you any idea of the risk you're taking, you silly bitch?' he asked bitterly. 'This is Africa. What you'll get is a four-letter word and it's not the one you're thinking of, sweetheart. It's spelt A I D S.'

'Tut! Tut! Jealous, are we? How do you know what I've been doing, darling?'

'It's no big secret. Everybody at the party knew. You've been doing what any good little whore does.'

She took a wild round-arm swing at his head. He ducked under the blow, and the momentum carried her on to the bed. She pulled the mosquito net down on top of herself and fell in a tangle of long legs. The mini-skirt pulled up almost as high as her waist, her buttocks were bare and white as ostrich eggs.

'By the way,' he said, 'you've left your knickers with Ephrem.'

She crawled up on to her knees and pulled down the green skirt.

'They are in my handbag, ducky.' She got unsteadily to her feet. 'Where the hell are my things?'

'In your room, your new room across the passage.'

She flashed at him. 'So that's the way you want it?'

'You didn't really think I'd want to pick up Ephrem's leftovers, did you?' Daniel tried to keep his tone reasonable. 'Off you go, there's a good little harlot.'

She picked up her handbag and shoes and marched to the door. There she turned back to him, swaying with a drunkard's dignity.

'It's all true, what they say,' she told him with vindictive relish. 'They *are* big. Bigger and better than you'll ever be!' She slammed the door behind her.

Daniel was on his second cup of breakfast tea when Bonny came out on to the verandah and, without greeting him, took her place at the breakfast table opposite him.

She wore her usual working uniform of faded blue jeans and denim top, but her eyes were puffy and her expression disgruntled with hangover. The guest house chef was an anachronism from the colonial era and he served a traditional English breakfast. Neither of them spoke while Bonny demolished her plateful of eggs and bacon. Then she looked up at him.

'So what happens now?'

'You make a film,' he said. 'Just the way it's written in your contract.'

'You still want me around?'

'As a cameraman, yes. But from now on it's a business relationship.'

'That suits me just fine,' she agreed. 'It was getting to be a bit of a strain; I'm not good at faking it.'

Daniel stood up abruptly, and went to fetch his gear from the bedroom. He was still too angry to risk getting into an argument with her.

Before he was ready, Captain Kajo arrived with three soldiers in the back of his Landrover. They helped carry out the heavy video equipment and load it into the back of the truck. Daniel let Bonny sit up in the cab beside Captain Kajo, while he rode in the back with the heavily armed Hita soldiers.

The town of Kahali was very much as he remembered it from his last visit. The streets were wide and dusty where the potholes had eaten, cancer-like, through the tarmac. The buildings looked like those from the movie set of an old-fashioned Western.

The main difference that Daniel noticed was the mood of the people. The Uhali women still wore their colourful ankle-length robes and turbans, the Moslem influence apparent in their demeanour, but the expressions on their faces were guarded and neutral. There were few smiles and no laughter in the open-air market where the women squatted in lines with their wares spread out on sheets of cloth in front of them. There were army patrols in the market-place and on the street corners. The populace averted their eyes as the Landrover passed.

There were very few tourists, and these were dusty, unshaven and rumpled, probably members of an overland safari making their way down the length of the African continent in a huge communal truck. They were haggling for tomatoes and eggs in the market. Daniel grinned. They were paying for a glimpse of purgatory. The overland safari meant amoebic dysentery and punctures, five thousand miles of potholes and army road-blocks, probably the only package holiday on the globe with no repeat customers. Once was enough to last a lifetime.

The gunboat was waiting for them at the wharf. Seamen in navy blue uniforms and bare feet carried the video equipment up the gangplank and the captain shook hands with Daniel as he came aboard.

'Peace be with you,' he greeted him in Swahili. 'I have orders to take you where you want to go.'

They left the harbour and turned northwards, parallel to the lakeshore. Daniel stood out on the foredeck and his good spirits returned swiftly. The water was a dark and lovely blue, sparkling in the sunlight. There was a single cloud on the northern horizon, as white as a seagull and not much larger. It was the spray column where the lake spilled over its rocky rim into a deep gorge and became the infant Nile.

The ultimate source of the White Nile had been debated for two thousand years and had still not been entirely agreed upon. Was it those falls where the Victoria Nile out of Lake Victoria joined the Albert Nile in Lake Albert and spilled over at the beginning of the incredible journey down to Cairo and the Mediterranean Sea? Or was it higher still, as Herodotus had written long before the birth of Christ? Did it spring from a bottomless lake lying between the two mountains Crophi and Mophi and fed by their eternal snows?

With the lake-spray in his face, Daniel turned to look westward, trying to make out the loom of the romantic mountain peaks in the distance, but today, as on most days, it was a diffuse blue cloud mass, blending with the blue of the African sky.

Many of the earlier explorers had passed close by the Mountains of the Moon without ever dreaming of their existence. Even Henry Morton Stanley, that ruthless, driven, Americanised Welsh bastard, had lived for months in their shadow before the perpetual clouds had opened and astonished him with a vista of snowy peaks and shining glaciers. It gave Daniel a mystic feeling to sail upon these waters that were the life-blood pumped from the heart mountains of this savage continent.

He turned and glanced up at the open bridge of the gunboat. Bonny Mahon was filming. She had the Sony camera balanced on her shoulder and pointed towards the shore. He grimaced with reluctant approval. Whatever their personal problems, she was a true professional. At the end she'd probably get a good shot of the devil on her way through hell, and the thought made him grin and took the edge off his antagonism towards her.

He went back to the chartroom below the bridge and spread the survey maps and architect's drawings that BOSS had provided for him on the table.

The site that had been chosen for the hotel and casino was seven miles up the coast from the port of Kahali. Daniel saw that it was a natural bay with an island guarding the entrance. The Ubomo River, pouring down the escarpment of the Rift Valley from the great forests and snowy mountain ranges, debouched into the bay.

On the map it looked an ideal site for the holiday complex that Tug Harrison hoped would make Ubomo one of the more desirable holiday destinations for tourists from southern Europe.

To Daniel there seemed to be only one drawback. There was already a large fishing village sited on the bay. He wondered what Tug Harrison and Ning Cheng Gong planned to do about that. European sunbathers would not want to share the beach with native fishermen and their nets, while the odour of sun-dried fish on the racks would not encourage the appetite or add much to the romantic attractions of Fish Eagle Bay Lodge, as the project had already been named.

The captain hailed Daniel from above. He left the chart-table and went out to the open deck, just as the gunboat rounded the headland and Fish Eagle Bay opened ahead of them.

Daniel saw at once why the name had been chosen. The island at the mouth of the bay was heavily forested. Nourished by the lake's sweet clear waters, the ficus and wild mahogany trees had grown into giants with branches spreading out high over the rocky shore and the surrounding lake waters. Hundreds of mating pairs of fish eagles had built their nests in the high branches. With russet and chestnut plumage and glistening white heads, these were the most spectacular of all the African raptors. The great birds sat on every prominent perch, while still others sailed overhead on wide pinions, throwing back their heads in flight to utter the wild yelping chant that is so much a part of the African pageant.

The gunboat anchored and launched an inflatable Zodiac to take Daniel and Bonny to the island. For an hour they filmed the eagle colony. Captain Kajo threw dead fish off the rocky cliff and Bonny captured exciting sequences of rival eagles contending for the offerings and engaging in ritual aerial combat by hooking each other's talons and spinning and swirling in flight.

Daniel helped her lug the Sony camera up the smooth, massive trunk of a wild fig tree to film the eagle chicks in the nest. The parent birds attacked them both on the exposed branch, coming in on screaming power-dives with talons extended and curved yellow beaks agape, pulling away at the last possible moment so that the draught of the great wings buffeted them on their exposed perch. By the time Bonny and Daniel reached the ground, their personal antagonism had·been shelved and they were operating as a professional film crew again.

They returned to the Zodiac and ran out to the gunboat. As they came aboard, the captain weighed anchor and pushed on slowly into·the bay. It was a spectacular site with volcanic rock cliffs climbing sheer out of the blue water and bright orange sand beaches in between the black rock.

Once again they climbed into the Zodiac and landed on one of the beaches near the mouth of the Ubomo River. Leaving Captain Kajo and the two seamen on the beach with the boat, Daniel and Bonny climbed to the highest point on the cliffs and were rewarded with a panoramic view over the bay and the lake.

They could look down on the large fishing village at the mouth of the Ubomo River. Twenty or so dhow-rigged boats were drawn up on the beach while as many more were dotted out upon the lake waters. On gull-winged sails the fleet was bearing in towards the bay, the night's fishing over, coming in to land the catch.

Along the head of the beach the fishing-nets were spread out in the sunlight to dry and the smell of fish carried up to them, even on the top of the cliff. Naked black children played upon the beach and splashed in the lake. Men worked on the dhows or sat cross-legged with needle and palm to repair the festooned nets. In the village the women moved gracefully in their long skirts as they pounded grain in the tall wooden mortars, swinging rhythmically to the rise and fall of the pestles in their hands, or squatted over the cooking-fires on which stood the black three-legged pots.

Daniel pointed out the various features which he wanted filmed and Bonny followed his instructions and turned the camera lens to record it all.

'What will happen to the villagers?' she asked, still peering into the viewfinder of the Sony. 'They're scheduled to start digging the foundations of the casino in three weeks . . .'

'I expect they'll move them to another site,' Daniel told her. 'In the new Africa people are moved about by their rulers like chess pieces . . .' He broke off and shaded his eyes, peering out along the road that led back along the lakeshore towards the capital.

Red dust blew in a slow sullen cloud out across the blue lake waters, carried on the mountain breeze from up-country.

'Let me have a look through your telephoto lens,' he asked Bonny, and she handed him the camera. Swiftly Daniel zoomed the lens to full power and picked up the approaching column of vehicles.

'Army trucks,' he told her. 'And transporters . . . I'd say those were bulldozers on the transporters.' He handed her back the camera, and Bonny studied the approaching column.

'Some kind of army exercise?' she guessed. 'Are we allowed to film it?'

'Anywhere else in Africa I wouldn't take the chance of pointing a camera at anything military, but here we've got President Taffari's personal *firman*. Shoot away!'

Quickly Bonny set up the light tripod she used only for long-range telephoto shots and zoomed in on the approaching military convoy. Meanwhile, Daniel moved to the edge of the cliff and looked down on the beach. Captain Kajo and the sailors from the gunboat were stretched out on the sand. Kajo was probably sleeping off the previous evening's debauch. Where he lay he was out of sight of the village. Daniel strolled back to watch Bonny at work.

The convoy was already approaching the outskirts of the village. A mob of children and stray dogs ran out to greet it. The children skipped along beside the trucks, laughing and waving, while the dogs yapped hysterically. The vehicles drew up in the open ground in the centre of the village which was both soccer pitch and village square. Soldiers in camouflage uniform, armed with AK 47 rifles, jumped down and formed up into their platoons on the soccer ground.

A Hita officer climbed on to the cab of the leading truck and began to harangue the villagers through a bull-horn. The sound of his electronically distorted voice carried intermittently to the crest of the cliff on which Daniel was standing. He lost the sense of some of the Swahili as the breeze rose and fell, but the gist of it was clear.

The officer was accusing the villagers of harbouring political dissidents, obstructing the economic and agricultural reforms of the new government, and engaging in counter-revolutionary activities. While he was speaking, a squad of soldiers trotted down to the beach and rounded up the children and fishermen there. They herded them back to the village square.

The villagers were becoming agitated. The children hid amongst the skirts of the women and the men were protesting and gesticulating at the officer on the cab of the truck. Now soldiers began moving through the village, ordering people out of the thatched huts. One old man tried to resist being dragged from his home, and a soldier clubbed him with the butt of an AK 47. He fell in a huddle on the dusty earth and they left him there and moved on, kicking open the doors of the huts and shouting at the occupants. On the beach another group of soldiers was meeting the incoming fishing fleet and prodding the fishermen ashore at bayonet point.

Bonny never looked up from the viewfinder of her camera. 'This is great stuff! God, this is the real thing. This is Emmy Award territory, I kid you not!'

Daniel did not reply. Her gloating excitement should not have offended him as much as it did. He was a journalist himself. He understood the need to find fresh and provocative material to stir the jaded emotions of a television audience reared on a diet of turmoil and violence, but what they were witnessing here was as obscene as scenes of SS troopers clearing out the ghettoes of Europe.

The soldiers were beginning to load the fisherfolk on to the waiting trucks, women were screaming and trying to find their own children in the throng. Some villagers had managed to collect a pathetic bundle of possessions, but most of them were empty-handed.

The two yellow bulldozers rolled down off their low trailer beds with engines pulsing and blue diesel smoke blowing from the exhaust stacks. One of them swung in a tight circle with a track locked, and lowered the massive frontal blade. Gleaming in the afternoon sunlight the blade sliced into the wall of the nearest hut and the thatched roof collapsed.

'Beauty!' Bonny murmured. 'I couldn't have staged it better. That was an incredible shot!'

The women were wailing and ululating, that peculiar chilling sound of African grief. One of the men broke away and ran towards the cover of the nearest field of sorghum. A soldier shouted a warning at him, but he put his head down and ran faster. A short burst of automatic rifle-fire popped like a string of fire-crackers and the man collapsed and rolled in the dust and lay still. A woman screamed and ran towards the fallen body carrying an infant strapped in a shawl on her back and an older child in her arms. A soldier barred her path with a bayoneted rifle and turned her back towards the truck.

'I got it!' Bonny exulted. 'The whole thing. The shooting and all. It's in the can. Shit, this is great!'

The soldiers were drilled and ruthless. It all went very quickly. Within half an hour the entire populace of the village had been rounded up, except for the fishermen still out on the lake. The first truck, fully loaded, pulled away, heading back the way it had come.

The huts were collapsing one after the other as the two bulldozers moved down the rows.

'God, I hope I don't run out of film,' Bonny muttered anxiously. 'This is a once-in-a-lifetime chance.'

Daniel had not spoken since the operation had begun. He was part of Africa. He had seen other villages wiped out. He remembered the guerrilla camp in Mozambique. Since then he had seen Renamo rebels work over a village, and he had witnessed forced removals by the minions of apartheid in South Africa, but he had never grown hardened to the suffering of the African people. He was sick to his guts as he watched the rest of the little drama unfold.

The remaining fishing-boats ran in unsuspectingly to the beach, where the soldiers were waiting to drag the crews ashore. The last truckload of villagers rolled away in a column of red dust, and as soon as it was out of sight, one of the yellow bulldozers waddled down on to the beach and swept the abandoned fishing-boats into a pile, like firewood kindling.

Four soldiers brought the body of the old man and the one who had tried to escape, carrying them by ankles and wrists, dead heads lolling backwards. They tossed them on to the funeral pyre of shattered hulls and torn sails. One of the soldiers hurled a lighted torch of thatch on to the top of the pile. The flames took hold and burned so fiercely that the soldiers were driven backwards, holding up their hands to protect their faces.

The bulldozers crawled back and forth over the remains of the huts, flattening them under the steel tracks. A whistle shrilled and the soldiers formed up quickly and re-embarked into the waiting troop-carriers. The yellow bulldozers crawled back on to their transporters, and the entire column wound away.

After they had gone, the only sound was the hushed whisper of the evening breeze along the cliff face and the distant crackle of the flames.

'Well,' Daniel tried to keep his tone neutral, 'the site is clear for the new casino. Taffari's investment in happiness for his people is secure . . .' his voice broke. He could not go on. 'The bastard!' he whispered. 'The murderous bloody bastard.'

He found that he was shaking with anger and outrage. It required an immense effort of will to bring his emotions under control. He strode to the edge of the cliff overlooking the beach. The gunboat was still anchored out in the deeper water in the middle of the bay and the Zodiac was drawn up on the beach with one of the soldiers guarding it, but Captain Kajo and the other sailor were no longer asleep on the sand. It was obvious that they had been awakened by the sound of gunfire and activity in the destroyed village.

Daniel looked around for Kajo and picked him out at last. He was climbing the cliff face half a mile away, and it was clear from his manner that he was agitated. He was searching for them, stopping every few minutes to shout through cupped hands and peer about him anxiously.

Daniel ducked back out of sight and snapped at Bonny. 'Nobody must know that we shot that footage. It's dynamite.'

'Gotcha!' she agreed.

'Give me the tape. I'll take care of it, in case they want to check what you've filmed.'

Bonny ejected the tape from the camera and handed it over. He wrapped it in a jersey and stuffed it into the bottom of his rucksack. 'All right, let's get out of here before Kajo finds us. He must never guess that we saw what we saw.'

Bonny gathered up her equipment swiftly and followed Daniel as he cut inland away from the remains of the village and the lakeshore. Within minutes they were into the tall grass and scrub of the savannah.

Daniel circled back through the elephant grass and scrub until he reached the lakeshore again near the mouth of the bay, opposite Fish Eagle Island. They scrambled down the cliff to the beach and Daniel paused to let Bonny catch her breath.

'I don't understand how they let a film crew loose in the area on the very day they were going to wipe out the village,' she gasped.

'Typical African screw-up,' Daniel told her. 'Somebody forgot to tell somebody else. The last *coup* attempt they made in Zambia, one of the conspirators broke into the radio station and announced the revolution while all his co-conspirators were still in barracks eating breakfast. He had the wrong day. It was supposed to be the following Sunday. AWA. Are you ready to go on?'

Bonny stood up. 'AWA?' she asked.

'Africa Wins Again,' Daniel smiled grimly. 'Let's go!'

Assuming a casual manner they set off side by side along the firm damp sand at the edge of the water.

They could see the beached Zodiac in the distance, but the demolished village was still hidden by the bulge of the cliff face.

They had not covered more than two hundred yards before Kajo hailed them from the cliff top. They stopped and looked up at him, waving as though they had only just noticed him for the first time.

'He's peeing in his pants,' Bonny murmured. 'He doesn't know if we witnessed the raid or not.'

Kajo came pelting down the cliff path, slipping and sliding on the steep places. He was out of breath when he reached the beach and confronted them.

'Where have you been?' he demanded.

'Out at the point,' Daniel told him. 'We filmed the casino site. Now we are going down to film the hotel site at the river mouth, where the fishing village is—'

'No! No!' Kajo grabbed Daniel's arm. 'That is enough. No more filming. We must go back to the boat. It is finished for

378

today.' Daniel shrugged off his hand and argued with him for a while. Then finally, with a show of reluctance, he allowed himself to be led towards the Zodiac and ferried aboard the gunboat.

As soon as he reached the bridge, Kajo held a whispered discussion with the ship's captain and they both looked to the head of the bay. There were still streamers of smoke from the burning fishing boats drifting out over the water. The ship's captain looked worried and gave orders to get under way in unnecessarily loud and agitated tones.

Before Daniel could prevent her, Bonny walked to the stern rail and aimed the Sony camera back towards the shore. Captain Kajo scrambled down the bridge ladder and ran down the deck shouting.

'No! Wait! You must not film that!'

'Why not? It's only a bush fire, isn't it?'

'No! Yes! It's a bush fire, but it's classified material.'

'A top secret bush fire?' Bonny teased him, but she obediently lowered the camera.

As soon as they were alone Daniel scolded her. 'Don't get too damned clever. That little joke could have backfired on us.'

'On the contrary, I convinced Kajo that we are innocent,' she argued. 'When are you going to let me have my tape back?'

'I'll keep it,' he answered. 'Kajo's still suspicious. My bet is that when we reach Kahali, he'll check your equipment.'

It was after dark when the gunboat tied up at its berth. During the transfer of Bonny's video equipment from the vessel to the army Landrover on the wharf, the aluminium case that contained her tapes disappeared. Although she screamed at Kajo, and shook her finger in his face and threatened to report his inefficiency to President Taffari, Kajo just kept on smiling blandly. 'Don't worry, Miss Mahon. It will turn up. I give you my personal guarantee.'

Kajo arrived at the guest house the following morning, all smiles and apologies, carrying the missing case. 'All present and correct, Miss Mahon. One of those stupid Uhali porters mislaid it. Please accept my heartfelt apologies.'

'You can be damned certain they scanned every tape in the box,' Daniel assured her when Kajo had gone. He tapped the buttoned pocket of his bush jacket. 'I'm going to get this tape of the raid down to Mike at the British embassy. It's the only safe place for it. Are you coming?'

'I have an engagement.' She looked defiant.

'If you're going to visit your new boy friend, just be careful. That's my advice to you. You've seen his style.'

'Ephrem is an honourable man,' she flared. 'I can't believe he knew anything about that raid.'

'Believe what you want, but don't tell anybody about this tape. Not even Tug Harrison.'

Bonny froze and stared at him. She had gone very pale.

'What are you talking about?' she demanded.

'Come on, Bonny, give me some credit. I checked that phone call you made from the Norfolk Hotel in Nairobi. Of course you're reporting to Tug Harrison. How much is he paying you to spy on me?'

'You're crazy.' She tried to brazen her way out of it.

'Yes, I probably am. I fell for you, didn't I? But you'll be crazy if you tell Tug about this tape.'

He left her staring after him and he drove down the hill towards the British embassy. The grounds of the embassy were walled and the gates were guarded by soldiers of President Taffari's personal bodyguard in camouflage uniforms and maroon berets. Michael Hargreave came out of his office to greet Daniel.

'Morning, Sir Mickey.'

'Danny boy! I spoke to Wendy last night. She sends you her love.'

'When is she arriving?'

'Not for another few weeks, more's the pity. Her mother is unwell, so Wendy has to go home first instead of coming directly from Lusaka . . .'

Still chatting, he led Daniel into his office, but as soon as he closed the door his manner changed.

'News for you, Danny. The Chinaman has arrived. Landed this morning in BOSS's executive jet. My information is he came from Taiwan via Nairobi. Moved into BOSS headquarters in Lake House immediately to take over as head of the syndicate, and Taffari is throwing one of his bashes for him on

Friday evening. Expect you'll get an invitation from Government House.'

'That should be interesting.' Daniel smiled grimly. 'I'm looking forward to seeing that gentleman again.'

'That may be sooner than you think.' Michael Hargreave glanced at his wristwatch. 'Have to leave you, dear boy. Making a luncheon speech to the assembled Rotarians of Ubomo, would you believe? Those files I promised you are all with my secretary. She'll give you a room to work in. Have a peep at them, then give them back to her. No notes nor photostats, please, Danny. Eyes only.'

'Thanks, Mike; you're a hero. But one other favour, please?'

'Fire away. Anything to please. Hargreave family motto, don't you know?'

'Will you keep an envelope in your personal safe for me, Mike?'

Michael locked the sealed envelope containing the Fish Eagle Bay tape into his strong room, then shook hands and excused himself.

Daniel watched him from the verandah as he was driven away by his uniformed chauffeur in the ambassadorial car. Despite the Union Jack pennant on the bonnet, it was a ten-year-old Rover in need of a paint job. The ambassador to Ubomo did not rate a Rolls-Royce.

Daniel went back to the files that Michael's secretary had laid out for him in a back room. When he left the embassy three hours later, his original impression of Ephrem Taffari had been reinforced a hundredfold.

'He's a tough and wily bird,' Daniel muttered as he started the Landrover. 'He and Bonny Mahon should have fun together.'

 The motorcycle escort, sirens wailing, was forced to moderate its speed by the condition of the road through the new area of squatters' slums that had grown up around the capital. The tarmac was pitted with sharp-edged craters, while chickens and pigs scattered, cackling and grunting, ahead of the outriders.

The presidential car, another recent gift from the same middle eastern oil potentate, was a black Mercedes. It was a mark of his high regard that President Taffari had sent it down to Lake House on the waterfront to fetch his guest to the audience. Ning Cheng Gong sat behind the chauffeur and studied these first glimpses of Ubomo with interest.

After what he had observed in Asia and the other parts of Africa in which he had served, the poverty and degradation of the slums through which they drove neither repelled nor shocked him. From his father he had learned to look upon swarming humanity as either a source of cheap labour, or a market for the goods and services he had to sell.

'Without human beings there is no profit,' his father had pointed out on numerous occasions. 'The more people the better. Always when human lives are cheap, there are great fortunes to be made. We, the Lucky Dragon, must resist any effort to limit population growth in the Third World. People are our basic stock-in-trade.'

Cheng smiled at his father's wisdom, derived from a study of history. His father's view was that only when human populations had been checked and limited by extraneous factors had the common man regained dignity and a measure of control over his own destiny. The terrible depredations of the great plagues of medieval times had broken the slavery of the feudal system of Europe. They had reduced human populations to the point where men had scarcity value and could bargain for their labour once again.

The great wars of this century had smashed the class system of inherited privilege and fortune, and ushered in this aberrant age of human rights, in which the common men of inferior races were taught that they were the equal of their betters. In Cheng's view, and that of his father, common men had no such divine rights, any more than the antelope in the wild deserved special protection from the lion.

When the mass of humanity reached such proportions that human life was cheap, that was the age of opportunity for the great predators to emerge. Predators like Lucky Dragon. In Africa that time was fast approaching as populations swarmed like hiving bees.

He thought about the little Cambodian boat girl, whose

corpse now lay in the dark depths of the China Sea. There were millions and tens of millions more like her, in India and China and Africa and South America, for men like him.

Cheng had recognised in the burgeoning populations of Africa a unique opportunity. That was the main reason that Lucky Dragon was drawn so irresistibly to this continent. That was why he was going now to a meeting with the president of this country which would soon be made to render up its wealth to him. He would suck the juice from it, throw away the empty skin, and pluck another from the tree. He smiled at the metaphor and raised his eyes to the green hill above the town on which Government House stood.

President Ephrem Taffari had an honour guard in maroon uniforms and white sun-helmets drawn up to welcome him and a red carpet laid across the green lawn. He came down the carpet to meet Ning Cheng Gong personally and to shake his hand. He led him up on to the wide verandah and seated him in one of the carved armchairs under the revolving fan that hung from the ceiling.

An Uhali servant in ankle-length white robes, scarlet sash and tasselled fez offered him a silver tray of frosted glasses. Cheng refused the champagne and chose a glass of freshly squeezed orange juice.

Ephrem Taffari took the armchair opposite him and crossed one long leg clad in crisp white cotton trousers over the other. He smiled at Cheng with all his charm.

'I wanted our first meeting to be informal and relaxed,' he explained, and made a deprecatory gesture towards his own open-neck sports shirt and sandals. 'So you will excuse my casual attire and the fact that I have none of my ministers with me.'

'Of course, Your Excellency.' Cheng sipped the orange juice. 'I am also delighted by this opportunity to get to know you and to be able to speak freely without the inhibition of having other people present.'

'Sir Peter Harrison speaks very highly of you, Mr Ning. He is a man whose opinion I value. I am sure that our relationship will be mutually rewarding.'

For another ten minutes they traded compliments and protestations of friendship and goodwill. Both of them were at ease with this flowery circumlocution; it was part of their separate cultures and they understood instinctively the moves and countermoves as they circled and closed in on the real business of their meeting.

Finally Cheng took a sealed envelope from the inside pocket of his white silk tropical suit. It was a piece of expensive stationery, glossy and cream-coloured with a dragon motif embossed on the back flap.

'My father and I want you to believe, Mr President, that our commitment to your country is unswerving. We would like you to accept this as an earnest token of our friendship and concern.'

Cheng made his offering seem like a free and unsolicited gift, whereas both of them were aware that it had been the subject of intense and protracted bargaining. There had been other bidders in the market, not least of them the Arab oil sheikh who had provided the gunboat and the presidential Mercedes. It had taken all Sir Peter Harrison's influence to secure the deal for the BOSS and Lucky Dragon syndicate.

The envelope contained the second instalment due to Ephrem Taffari in his personal capacity. The first instalment had been paid over ten months previously, on signature of the original agreement.

President Taffari picked up the envelope and turned it over to examine the seal. His fingers were long and elegantly shaped, and very dark against the stiff creamy paper.

He split the corner of the envelope with his thumbnail and unfolded the two documents it contained. One was a deposit receipt to a numbered bank account in Switzerland. The amount of the deposit was ten million US dollars. The other was a share transfer document, notarised in Luxembourg. A total of thirty per cent of the syndicate's share equity was now registered in the name of Ephrem Taffari. The syndicate's formally registered name was 'The Ubomo Development Corporation'.

The president returned the documents to the open envelope and slipped it into the pocket of his flowered sports shirt.

'Progress has not been as rapid as I had hoped,' he said, his tone still courteous but underlaid with steel. 'I hope that will change with your arrival, Mr Ning.'

'I am aware of the delays. As you know, my field-manager has been in Kahali for the last week or so. He has given me a full report of the situation. I believe that some of the blame must attach to the previous management, put in place by BOSS. There has been some reluctance to exploit all the available assets.' Cheng made a delicately pejorative gesture. 'Mr Purvis of BOSS, who is now safely on his way back to London, was a sensitive man. You know how squeamish these Englishmen can be. My field-manager informs me that we are short of labour.'

'I assure you, Mr Ning, that you will have all the labour you require.' Taffari's smile became strained at the thinly veiled complaint.

'Thirty thousand,' Cheng said softly. 'That was the original estimate approved by you, Your Excellency. So far we have been given fewer than ten thousand.'

'You will have the rest before the beginning of next month.' Taffari was no longer smiling. 'I have given orders to the army. All political detainees and dissidents are to be rounded up and sent to the labour camps in the forest.'

'These will be members of the Uhali tribe?' Cheng asked.

'Of course,' Taffari snapped. 'You didn't think for a moment that I would send you Hita, did you?'

Cheng smiled at the absurdity of that notion. 'My field-manager tells me that the Uhali are good workers, hardy and intelligent and compliant. We will need most of them in the forest to begin with. It seems that we are experiencing problems there caused by the terrain and the climate. The roads are bad and machinery is bogging down. We will be forced to use more men.'

'Yes, I warned the BOSS people of that,' Taffari agreed. 'They were reluctant to use what they considered to be . . .' He hesitated. 'That man Purvis referred to our convict labour as slave labour.' He looked mildly amused by such pedantic definitions.

'These Westerners,' Cheng sympathised. 'The English are bad enough, but the Americans are even worse. They do not understand Africa or the orient. Their minds stop at Suez . . .' he broke off. 'I assure you, Mr President, that an easterner is now in control of the syndicate's operation. You will find that I do not suffer from these Western scruples.'

'It is a relief to be able to work with somebody who understands the necessities of life,' Taffari agreed.

'Which brings me to the hotel and casino project at Fish Eagle Bay. I understand from my field-manager that nothing has been done there, apart from the original survey of the area. He tells me that there is still a fishing village on the hotel site.'

'Not any longer,' Taffari smiled. 'The area was cleared two days ago, soon after Purvis left for London. The village was a hotbed of counter-revolutionary activity. My soldiers rounded up all the dissidents. Two hundred able-bodied prisoners are already on their way to the concession area in the forest to join your labour force. The hotel site is ready for construction to begin.'

'Your Excellency, I can see that you and I are going to work well together. May I show you the modifications that I have made to the schedule of works drawn up by Purvis?' He opened his briefcase and unfolded a large computer spreadsheet that covered the entire table between them.

Taffari leaned forward and listened with interest as Cheng pointed out the way in which he had restructured almost the entire syndicate operation.

At the end of the lecture Taffari's admiration was unconcealed. 'You have accomplished all this in the short time since you arrived in Ubomo?' he asked, but Cheng shook his head.

'Not all of it, Your Excellency. Some of the replanning was done before I left Taipei. I had the benefits of my father's advice and the assistance of his headquarters staff at Lucky Dragon. Only part of the planning was necessitated after my arrival in Kahali, on the advice of my field-manager, and his report on the conditions and problems we have encountered in the forest.'

'Remarkable!' Taffari shook his head. 'Sir Peter Harrison's opinion of you seems to be well founded.'

'Planning is one thing,' Cheng pointed out modestly. 'Execution is another thing entirely.'

'I am sure that you will bring the same energy and drive to that part of the operation.' Taffari looked at his wristwatch. 'I am expecting a guest for lunch . . .'

'I am sorry, Your Excellency. I have overstayed my welcome.' Cheng made as if to rise.

'Not at all, Mr Ning. I absolutely insist that you join us for lunch. It may amuse you to meet my other guest, a member of the film team which Sir Peter Harrison has hired.'

'Ah, yes.' Cheng looked dubious. 'Sir Peter explained to my father and myself why he had invited a film company to Ubomo. I am not certain that I agree with him, however. The English have a saying about sleeping dogs. In my view, it may be better not to draw world attention to our operations. I would like to cancel the project and send the film team out of Ubomo.'

'I am afraid it is too late for that.' Taffari shook his head. 'We have already received a great deal of adverse publicity. There is a woman, a protégée of the previous president, Omeru . . .'

For another ten minutes they discussed Sir Peter's plan to defuse Kelly Kinnear's propaganda campaign by a counter-campaign of their own.

'In any event,' Taffari pointed out, 'we can always suppress anything we don't like about this film production. Sir Peter Harrison has an approval clause written into the contract. We can even suppress the final product completely, and destroy all copies of the film, if we feel that is advisable.'

'Of course, you are taking precautions to make certain that these people do not get to see any of our sensitive areas? The convict labour camps, the main logging operations, and the re-fill mining?'

'Trust me, Mr Ning. They will see the pilot scheme only. I have a reliable military officer accompanying them at all times.' He broke off at the sound of an approaching vehicle. 'Ah! That would be the person we are discussing, the cameraman and Captain Kajo.'

'Cameraman?' Cheng asked, as they watched Bonny Mahon and Captain Kajo cross the lawn towards them.

'Inaccurate, I agree,' Taffari chuckled. 'But is there such a term as camerawoman, I wonder?' He stood up and went to meet his guest.

Captain Kajo came to attention and saluted. Taffari ignored him. Kajo's job was done. He had delivered Bonny. He turned on his heel and returned to wait in the army Landrover. He knew it might be a long wait.

Cheng studied the woman as Taffari led her down the verandah. She was too big and bosomy. She had no delicacy of bone structure nor refinement of feature. Both her nose and mouth were too large for his taste. Her freckled skin and coppery hair repelled him. Her voice and laughter, as she joked with Taffari, were loud and vulgar. Her confident attitude and powerful limbs made Cheng feel threatened as though she were challenging his masculinity. He did not like a woman to be as strong and assertive as a man. He compared her unfavourably with the dainty ivory-skinned women of his own race, with their straight black hair and submissive self-effacing manner.

However, he rose politely and smiled and shook her hand, and saw that Taffari was quite smitten by the woman.

He knew that Taffari had a dozen Hita wives who were amongst the most beautiful of the tribe, but he supposed that the president was attracted by the novelty of this gross creature. Perhaps he felt that it would add to his status to have a white woman as a plaything. However, Cheng guessed shrewdly that he would tire of her soon enough and discard her as casually as he had taken her up.

'Mr Ning is the chief executive officer of the Ubomo Development Corporation,' Taffari told Bonny. 'Technically he is your boss.'

Bonny chuckled. 'Well, I can report that we are doing a hell of a job, boss.'

'I am delighted to hear that, Miss Mahon.' Cheng was unsmiling. 'It is an important task that you are undertaking. What have you accomplished so far?'

'We've been working here in Kahali and on the lake. We've already filmed the site of the new hotel and casino.'

Both Cheng and Taffari listened seriously to her report.

'Where are you moving to after this?' Cheng wanted to know.

'After we finish here we are driving up-country to the forest area. A place called Sengi-Sengi. Have I got that right, Your Excellency?' She looked at Taffari.

'Quite right, my dear Miss Mahon,' Taffari assured her. 'Sengi-Sengi is the corporation's pilot scheme for utilising the forest assets.'

Cheng nodded. 'I will be visiting the project myself at the very first opportunity.'

'Why don't you come up to Sengi-Sengi while we are filming?' Bonny suggested. 'It would give much more weight to the production to have you in it, Mr Ning.' She paused as another thought struck her, and then with a boyish grin she turned to Ephrem Taffari. 'But it would really be terrific to have you in the production, Mr President. We could interview you on the site of the project at Sengi-Sengi. You could explain to us your hopes and dreams for your country. Just think of that, Your Excellency.'

Ephrem Taffari smiled and shook his head. 'I'm a busy man. I don't think I could spare the time.'

But she could see he was tempted. He was enough of a politician to relish the prospect of favourable exposure to a wide audience.

'It would be very valuable,' she urged him. 'For both Ubomo and your personal image. People out there in the big world have heard about you only vaguely. If they could see you, it would change their whole perception. I assure you from a professional point of view that you would look plain bloody marvellous on the screen. You are tall and handsome and your voice is sensational. I swear I'd make you look like a film star.'

He liked the idea. He liked the flattery. 'Well, perhaps . . .'

They both realised that he wanted to be persuaded just a little longer.

'You could fly up to Sengi-Sengi by helicopter,' Bonny pointed out. 'It would take half a day, no more . . .' She paused and pouted suggestively and touched his arm. 'Unless, of course, you decided to stay over for a day or two. That would be okay by me, also.'

 Daniel and Bonny, accompanied as always by Captain Kajo, drove up from Kahali. Although it was only a little over two hundred miles it took them two full days, for much of that time was spent not in travelling but in filming the changing countryside and the rural tribes in their traditional *manyattas* that they found along the way.

Captain Kajo was able to smooth the way and negotiate with

the tribal elders. For a few Ubomo shillings he arranged that they had the run of any of the Hita villages that they passed. They filmed the young girls at the water-holes, clad only in tiny beaded skirts as they bathed and plaited each other's hair. The unmarried girls dressed their coiffures with a mixture of cow dung and red clay until it was an intricate sculpture on top of their heads, adding inches to their already impressive height.

They filmed the married women as they returned to the village in long files clad in flowing red matronly togas, swaying gracefully under brimming calabashes of water drawn from the spring.

They filmed the herds of dappled, multi-coloured cattle with their wide horns and humped backs against a background of flat-topped acacia and golden savanna grasslands.

They filmed the herdboys bleeding a great black bull, twisting a leather thong around its neck to raise the congested vein beneath the skin, then piercing it with the point of an arrow and capturing the scarlet stream of blood in a bottle-shaped calabash. When the gourd was half filled they sealed the wound in the bull's neck with a handful of clay, and topped up the calabash with milk stripped directly from the udder. Then they added a dash of cow's urine to curdle the mixture into thick cheesy curds.

'Low cholesterol,' Daniel pointed out when Bonny gagged theatrically. 'And look at those Hita figures.'

'I'm looking,' Bonny assured him. 'Oh, hallelujah, I'm looking.'

The men wore only a red blanket over one shoulder, held with a belt at the waist. They allowed the skirts to flap open casually in the breeze, especially when Bonny was nearby. They let her film as much as she wished of everything they possessed, staring into the lens with masculine arrogance, the elongated loops of their earlobes stopped with bone and ivory earrings.

On the main road their Landrover passed ore trucks and logging trailers coming in the opposite direction. The weight of these massive vehicles, even though spread over a dozen axles and banks of massive tyres, rutted the road deeply and raised a fog of dust that covered the trees for a mile on both sides of the roadway with a thick coating of dark red talcum. Bonny gloried in the effect of the sunlight through the dust cloud and the shapes of the trucks lumbering out of it like prehistoric monsters.

When at last, on the second day, they crossed the river on the ferry and reached the edge of the great forests, even Bonny was awed by the height and girth of the trees.

'They're like pillars holding up the sky,' she breathed as she turned her camera upon them. The quality of the air and light changed as they left the dry savannah behind them and entered this humid and lush forest world.

At first they followed the main highway with its mile-wide open verges. Then, after fifty miles, they turned off on to one of the new development roads, freshly cut into the virgin forest. The deeper they journeyed into the forest, the closer the trees crowded the roadway, until at last their high branches met overhead and they were in a tunnel filled with dappled and greenish light.

Even the bellow of the truck engines that passed them seemed muted, as though the trees were blanketing and absorbing the alien and offensive sound. The surface of the road had been corduroyed with logs laid side by side, and over this was spread a layer of flinty gravel to give the great trucks footing.

'The returning ore trucks bring the gravel back from the quarries near the lakeshore,' Captain Kajo explained. 'If they did not, the road would become a bottomless swamp of mud. It rains almost every day here.'

Every mile or so there were gangs of hundreds of men and women working on the road, spreading gravel and laying new logs to hold the surface together.

'Who are they?' Daniel asked.

'Convicts,' Kajo dismissed them lightly. 'Instead of spending money keeping them locked up and fed, we let them work off their debt to society.'

'A lot of convicts for such a small country,' Daniel pointed out. 'You must have a lot of crime in Ubomo.'

'The Uhali are a bunch of rogues, thieves and trouble-makers,' Kajo explained and then shuddered as he looked beyond the toiling lines of prisoners to the impenetrable forest behind them.

'I hate this place,' he said with abrupt and unusual vehemence. 'It is a dark and evil place, fit only for monkeys and their close relatives, the Bambuti pygmies.'

'Shall we see any pygmies?' Bonny demanded eagerly.

'Some of the tame ones trade along the road,' Kajo muttered. 'And their women whore with the truck-drivers. But the wild ones are forest animals. You won't see them; nobody does.' He shuddered again. 'I hate this place. We should cut down all these trees and sell them, and plant grass pasture in their place so that our cattle can multiply.' It was spoken with the fierce Hita love of cattle, the tribe's greatest treasure.

'If the trees were gone, the rains would cease. Then the rivers that flow down to the lake and water your herds would dry up. All things in nature depend upon each other. If you destroy one, you damage all,' Daniel began to explain, but Kajo snarled at him as he wrestled with the wheel of the Landrover as it bounced over the corduroy of logs.

'It is not necessary to patronise me, Doctor Armstrong. I have a university degree and, strange as it may seem, I can actually read. I know all these white elitist theories that you and people like you propound. It is all very well for you, rich white people, to tell us to starve ourselves and our cattle herds so that you can come here as tourists to stare for a few days at the beautiful view and admire the wild animals, then go home to your penthouses in New York and your mansions in England . . .' He broke off and drew a deep breath. 'Forgive me, Doctor. I did not mean to give offence but we Africans have to live here. We also have a right to a good life. These trees that you admire so much belong to us. We·have a rapidly expanding population to care for, Ubomo's population is growing by six per cent every year. We need food and shelter and education, and we need land. Our people are crying out for land. These forests are useless to us unless we utilise them. We should cut them down and burn them and use the earth for gardens and pastures . . .'

Daniel was saddened as he listened. Kajo was an educated and intelligent young man. If he still clung to the traditional view, what hope was there of convincing the unsophisticated country people like those that they had filmed in the *manyattas*?

'Your white elitist theories,' Kajo had said. That was the viewpoint that could turn a continent into a desert. One day the Sahara might stretch from Cairo to the flat-topped mountain that guarded the Cape of Good Hope.

So they came eventually to Sengi-Sengi. The road ended at a considerable settlement in the midst of the forest. The larger trees had been left standing, but beneath them the undergrowth and lesser trees had been cleared to make way for the compounds that housed the labour force, for machine workshops and administrative buildings.

The huts in the compound that housed the labour force were made from materials gathered on the site. The walls were of raw timber, plastered with red clay and the roofs were of thatch. The workshops and offices were prefabricated structures, constructed in sections so that they could be taken down and moved to a new site with little effort or expense.

Kajo parked the Landrover in front of the main office building, another temporary structure set on brick piers to allow air to circulate below the floorboards and in that way to cool the interior and keep it dry during the daily rainstorms. He led them up the steps. 'I must introduce you to the field-manager of UDC.'

'What does UDC stand for?' Bonny wanted to know.

'Ubomo Development Corporation,' Kajo replied, and would have gone on to explain further, but the manager's secretary looked up from her typewriter as they entered the reception area of the building.

She was a Hita girl in her mid-twenties, probably a graduate of the new technical college in Kahali, dressed in Western-style clothing and wearing lipstick and eye shadow. Her apparel seemed incongruous after the natural beauties they had so recently filmed in the *manyattas*.

'You must be the film people,' she greeted them brightly in Swahili. 'We have been expecting you.'

'We were delayed—' Kajo started to explain, but broke off as the door to the inner office opened and the field-manager came out, smiling brightly.

'Welcome to Sengi-Sengi,' he said, as he came towards them. 'You should have been here yesterday, but better late than never!'

Kajo was standing in front of Daniel, obscuring him for the moment with his six foot six height. Now he moved aside, and Daniel and the field-manager confronted each other.

'Mr Chetti Singh,' Daniel said softly. 'I never expected to see you again. What a great pleasure this is.'

The bearded Sikh stopped as though he had walked into a glass wall and stared at Daniel.

'You know each other?' Captain Kajo asked. 'What a happy coincidence.'

'We are old friends,' Daniel replied. 'We share a common interest in wildlife, especially elephants and leopards.' He was smiling as he extended his hand to Chetti Singh. 'How are you, Mr Singh? Last time we met you had suffered a little accident, hadn't you?'

Chetti Singh had turned a ghastly ashen colour beneath his dark complexion, but with an obvious effort he rallied from the shock. For a moment his eyes blazed and Daniel thought he might attack him. Then he accepted Daniel's pretence of friendliness, and tried to smile, but it was like an animal baring its teeth.

He reached out to accept Daniel's proffered handshake, but he used his left hand. His right sleeve was empty, folded back and pinned upon itself. The blunt outline of the stump showed through the striped cotton. Daniel saw that the amputation was below the elbow. It was a typical mauling injury. The leopard would have chewed the bone into fragments that no surgeon could knit together again. Although there were no scars or other injuries apparent at a glance, Chetti Singh's once portly body had been stripped of every ounce of superfluous fat and flesh. He was thin as an AIDS victim, and the white of his eyes had an unhealthy yellowish tinge. It was obvious that he had been through a bad time, and that he was not yet fully recovered.

His beard was still thick and glossy, curled up under his chin, the ends tucked into his spotless white turban.

'Indeed, what an absolute pleasure to see you again, Doctor.' His eyes gave the lie to the words. 'Thank you for your kind sympathy, but happily I am fully recovered, except for my missing appendage.' He wiggled the stump. 'It's a nuisance, but

I expect to receive full compensation for my loss from those responsible, never mind.'

His touch was cool as a lizard's skin, but he withdrew his hand from Daniel's and turned to Bonny and Kajo. His smile became more natural and he greeted them cordially. When he turned back to Daniel he was no longer smiling.

'And so, Doctor, you have come to make us all famous with your television show. We shall all be film stars . . .' He was watching Daniel's face with a strange greedy expression, like a python looking at a hare.

The shock of the meeting had been almost as great to Daniel as it had obviously been to the Sikh. Of course, Mike Hargreave had told him that Chetti Singh had survived the leopard attack, but that had been months ago and he had never expected Chetti Singh to turn up here in Ubomo, thousands of miles from where he had last seen him. Then, when he thought about it, he realised that he should really have been prepared for this. There was a strong link between Ning Cheng Gong and the Sikh. If Ning were placed in charge in Ubomo, he would naturally appoint as his assistant somebody who knew every wrinkle of the local terrain, and who had his networks securely in place.

In retrospect, it was obvious that Chetti Singh had been the perfect choice for Ning. The Sikh's organisation had infiltrated every country in central Africa. He had agents in the field. He knew whom to bribe and whom to intimidate. But most of all, he was totally unscrupulous and bound to Ning Cheng Gong in loyalty and fear and greed.

Daniel should have expected Chetti Singh to be lurking in Ning's shadow, should have been prepared to face his vengeance. It did not need the expression in Chetti Singh's eyes to warn him that he was in mortal danger.

The only escape from Sengi-Sengi was along the single roadway through the forest, every mile of which was controlled by company guards and numerous military road-blocks.

Chetti Singh was going to try to kill him. There could not be a single doubt of that. He had no weapon nor any other form of defence. Chetti Singh commanded the ground and could choose the time and the place to do it.

Chetti Singh had turned back and was chatting to Captain Kajo and Bonny. 'It is too late already for me to offer to show you around. It will be dark in a short while. You will want to move into the quarters we have prepared for you ...' He paused and beamed at them genially. 'Besides which, I have exciting news for you. I have just this minute received a fax from Government House in Kahali. President Taffari, in the very flesh, is coming to Sengi-Sengi by helicopter. He will arrive tomorrow morning and he has most graciously consented to a film interview on the site of our operation here. It is a great honour, I assure you. President Taffari is not a man to be taken lightly, and he will be accompanied by the chief executive officer of UDC, none other than our own Mr Ning Cheng Gong. He is another eminently important personage. Perhaps he will also consent to play a part in your production ...'

 It was raining again as Chetti Singh's secretary showed them to the quarters that had been set aside for them. The rain rattled like birdshot on the roofs of the buildings and the already saturated earth steamed with a mist that was blue as smoke in the twilight beneath the forest canopy.

Wooden catwalks had been laid between the buildings and the secretary provided them with cheap plastic umbrellas gaudily emblazoned with the slogan: 'UDC means a better life for all'.

The guest quarters were a row of small rooms like stables in a long Nissen hut. Each room contained rudimentary furniture – bed, chair, cupboard and desk. There was a communal washroom and lavatory in the centre of the long hut.

Daniel checked his own room carefully. The door had a lock that was so flimsy that it would yield to any determined pressure, besides which Chetti Singh certainly had a duplicate key. The window was covered by a mosquito screen and there was a mosquito net hanging above the bed, none of which was any protection. The walls were so thin that he could hear Kajo moving around in the room beside his.

It was going to be a pleasant stay.

Okay, folks, we'll have a competition, he grinned ruefully to himself. Guess when Chetti Singh will make his first attempt to bump us off. First prize is a week's holiday at Sengi-Sengi. Second prize is two weeks' holiday at Sengi-Sengi.

Dinner was served in the mess for senior staff. It was another Nissen hut comfortably furnished as a bar and canteen. When Daniel and Bonny entered there was a mixed bag of Taiwanese and British engineers and technicians filling the mess with cigarette smoke and noisy chatter. Nobody took much notice of him, but Bonny caused a mild sensation, as usual, especially with the group of Brits playing darts and drinking lager at the bar.

The Taiwanese seemed to be keeping to themselves and Daniel sensed a tension between the two groups. This was confirmed when one of the British engineers told Daniel that since Ning had taken over UDC, he had been ousting the British engineers and managers and replacing them with his own Taiwanese.

Bonny was instantly adopted by the British contingent and after dinner Daniel left her playing darts with a couple of beefy mining engineers. She intercepted Daniel heading for the door and she grinned at him maliciously as she whispered, 'Enjoy your lonely bed, lover.'

He grinned back at her as icily. 'I never did like a crowd.'

As he made his way through the darkness along the slippery mud-caked catwalk, a spot in the centre of his back itched. It was the spot into which somebody sneaking up behind him might stick a knife. He quickened his pace.

When he reached the door of his room in the Nissen hut, he pushed it open but hung back for a minute. There could be somebody waiting for him in the darkened room. He gave them a chance to move before he slipped his arm around the door frame and switched on the overhead light. Only then did he venture in cautiously. He locked the flimsy door and drew the curtains and sat on the bed to unlace his boots.

There were just too many ways that Chetti Singh could choose to do it. He knew he couldn't guard against them all. At that moment he felt something move under the bedclothes on which he was sitting. It was a slow, stealthy, reptilian sliding movement beneath the thin sheet and it touched his thigh. An icy dart of fear shot up his spine, stiffening every muscle in his body.

He had always had an unreasoning fear of snakes. One of his earliest memories was of a cobra in his nursery. It had only been a few months after his fourth birthday, but he vividly remembered the grotesque shadow that the reptile's extended hood had thrown upon the nursery wall as it reared in the diffuse beam of the nightlight that his mother had placed beside his bed. He remembered the explosive hisses with which the snake had challenged his own wild and terrified screams, before his father had burst into the nursery in his pyjamas.

Now he knew with the utmost certainty that the thing beneath the sheet was a snake. He knew that Chetti Singh or one of his men had placed it there. It must be one of the more deadly species, one of the mambas, slim and glittering with their thin grinning lips, or a forest cobra, black as death, or one of the thick repulsive gaboon adders.

Daniel sprang from the bed and spun around to face it. His heart hammered wildly as he looked around for a weapon. He snatched up the flimsy chair, and with the strength of his fear tore off one of the legs. With this weapon in his hand he regained control of himself. He was still breathing rapidly and he experienced a quick rush of shame. As a game ranger he had stood down the determined charges of buffalo and elephant and the great killer cats. As a soldier he had parachuted into enemy territory and fought it out in hand-to-hand combat, but now he was panting and shaking at a phantom of his imagination.

He steeled himself to go back to the bed. With his left hand he took the corner of the sheet, raised the chair leg with the other hand and flung back the bedclothes.

A striped forest mouse sat in the centre of the white sheet. It had long white whiskers and its bright inquisitive button eyes blinked rapidly in the sudden light.

Daniel was barely able to arrest the blow that he had already launched at it, and he and the tiny creature stared at each other in astonishment. Then his shoulders sagged and shook with nervous laughter. The mouse squeaked and leapt off the bed. It darted across the floor and vanished into a hole in the wainscoting and Daniel collapsed on to the bed and doubled up with laughter.

'My God, Chetti Singh,' he gasped. 'You won't stop at anything, will you? What other nefarious tricks have you got up your sleeve?'

 The helicopter came in from the east. They heard the *whoppity-wop* of its rotors long before it appeared in the hole in the forest canopy high above. It descended into the clearing with all the grace of a fat lady lowering herself on to a lavatory seat.

The helicopter was a French-built Puma and it was obvious that it had seen many years of hard service, probably with a few other airforces, before it had reached Ubomo.

The pilot cut the motors and the rotors slowed and stopped. President Taffari vaulted down from the main hatch. He was lithe and vitally handsome in combat fatigues and parachutist's boots. Bonny moved in with the camera and he flashed a smile as bright and almost as wide as the medal ribbons on his chest, and stepped forward to greet the reception committee headed by Chetti Singh.

Behind him Ning Cheng Gong used the boarding ladder to descend from the Puma. He was dressed in a cream-coloured tropical suit. His skin was almost a matching creamy yellow that contrasted strongly with his eyes, dark and bright as polished onyx.

He looked around quickly, searching for somebody or something, and he saw Daniel standing back, out of camera shot. Ning Cheng Gong's eyes licked Daniel's face for only an instant, like the black tongue of an adder, and then were past. His expression did not change. There was not the least sign of recognition, but Daniel knew with certainty that Chetti Singh had managed to get a message to his master, to warn him of Daniel's presence in Ubomo. Daniel was startled by his own reaction. He had known that Cheng would be on the helicopter. He had steeled himself for the first sight of him, but still it was as much of a physical shock as a punch under the ribs. It required an effort to respond normally to President Taffari's handshake and greeting.

'Ah, Doctor; as you see, Mohammed has come to the mountain. I have set aside the afternoon to co-operate with your filming. What do you want me to do? I am yours to command.'

'I am very grateful, Mr President. I have drawn up a shooting schedule. In all, I will need about five hours of your time, that includes make-up and rehearsal . . .' Daniel resisted the temptation to glance in Cheng's direction, until Chetti Singh intervened.

'Doctor Armstrong, I'd like you to meet the managing director, head of UDC, Mr Ning.'

Daniel was almost overcome by a strange sense of unreality as he shook Ning's hand and smiled and said. 'We know each other. We met briefly in Zimbabwe, when you were ambassador there. I don't suppose you recall?'

'Forgive me.' Cheng shook his head. 'I met so many people in the course of my official duties.' He pretended not to remember and Daniel forced himself to keep smiling. It seemed incredible that the last time he had seen this man was on the escarpment of the Zambezi valley, only hours before he discovered the mutilated and abused corpses of Johnny and his family. It was as though all the sorrow and anger in him had grown stronger and more bitter for being bottled up all this time. He wanted to shout out his rage, 'You filthy, greedy butcher!'

He wanted to clench his fists and attack that smooth bland face, to batter it into pulp and feel the bones break under his knuckles. He wanted to gouge out those implacable shark's eyes and pop them between his fingers. He wanted to wash his hands in Ning Cheng Gong's blood.

He turned away as soon as he could. He could trust himself no longer. For the first time, he faced what he had to do. He had to kill Ning Cheng Gong, or be killed in the attempt.

He expected no personal gratification from it. It was the fulfilment of the oath he had sworn over the body of his friend.

It was a simple duty and a debt to the memory of Johnny Nzou.

'You may think that I am standing on the bridge of a battleship . . .' Ephrem Taffari smiled into the lens of Bonny's camera, 'but I assure you that I am not. This is in fact the command platform of Mobile Mining Unit Number One, known here by the affectionate acronym MOMU.'

Although Taffari was the only person in camera-shot, the rest of the platform was crowded with company personnel. The chief engineer and the geologist had briefed the president on his spiel, making certain that he had a grasp of all the technical details. The crew of the unit were still at the command console of MOMU. The operation of the complex machine could not be interrupted even for such an important visitor as the state president.

Daniel was directing the sequence, and both Chetti Singh and Cheng were spectators, although they kept in the background. Bonny had seen to Taffari's make-up herself. She was as good as any specialist make-up artist that Daniel had worked with.

'I am standing seventy feet above the ground,' Taffari went on. 'And I am racing forward at the breathless speed of a hundred yards an hour.' He smiled at his own humour.

Daniel had to admit that he was a natural actor, completely at ease in front of the camera. With those looks and with that voice he could grab the complete attention of any female audience anywhere in the world.

'The vehicle on which I am riding weighs one thousand tons . . .'

Daniel was making editing notes on his schedule as Taffari spoke. At this point he would cut away to a full shot of the gigantic MOMU vehicle riding on its banks of tracks. There were twelve separate sets of steel tracks each of them ten feet wide to give it stability over the most uneven terrain. Steel hydraulic rams automatically adjusted the trim of the main platform keeping it on an even keel, tilting and dipping to counterbalance the ponderous wallowing, pitching movements of the tracks as they climbed and fell over the contours of the forest floor.

The size of the machine was not much less than the battleship that Taffari had suggested in his opening remarks. It was over one hundred and fifty yards long and forty wide.

Taffari turned and pointed forward over the railing.

'Down there,' he said, 'are the jaws and fangs of the monster. Let's go down and take a look.'

It was easily said on camera, but it meant moving down to a new vantage point and setting up the angles, then rehearsing the new shot. However, Taffari was a joy to work with, Daniel admitted. He needed only one walk-through and he knew his lines. He delivered them with natural timing and without fluffing once, even though he was forced to raise his voice to a shout to compete with the noise of the machinery.

This shot was good cinema. The excavators were on long gantries. Like the necks of a herd of steel giraffe drinking at a water-hole, they moved independently, rising and falling. The excavator blades rotated ferociously, slicing out the earth and throwing it back on to the conveyor belts.

'These excavators can reach down thirty yards below the surface. They are cutting a trench sixty yards wide and digging out over ten thousand tons of ore an hour. They never stop. Day and night they keep on burrowing away.'

Daniel looked down into the cavernous trench that the MOMU was opening into the red earth. It would be a good place to dispose of a corpse, his corpse. He glanced up without warning; both Ning Cheng Gong and Chetti Singh were watching him intently. They were still standing on the command platform seventy feet above him. Their heads were close together, almost touching, and they were talking, their voices wiped out by the roar of the great spinning excavator heads and the thunder of the conveyor belts. From their expressions Daniel was left with no doubt about the subject of their discussion. For an instant he caught their eyes and then they both looked away and moved back from the rail. After that it was difficult for Daniel to concentrate on the work in hand, yet he had to take advantage of every minute that Ephrem Taffari was available to him.

Once again the camera crew climbed the steel ladder up to the central platform of the MOMU. Chetti Singh and Ning Cheng Gong had disappeared, and that made Daniel even more uneasy.

From the height of the platform they could look down on to the tube mills. These were four massive steel drums, lying horizontally on the deck of the MOMU, and revolving like the spin-dryer in a domestic washing-machine. However, these drums were forty yards long, and each one was loaded with one hundred tons of cast-iron cannonballs. The red earth coming up from the excavated trench on the conveyor belts was continually being dumped into the open mouths of the drums. As the earth passed down the length of the drum, the clods and rocks were pounded to fine talcum by the tumbling iron balls. The red powder that poured from the far end of the tube mills went directly into the separator tanks.

The film team moved down the steel catwalks until they were above the separators, and here Taffari continued his explanation for the benefit of Bonny's camera.

'The two valuable minerals that we are after are either very heavy or magnetic. The rare earth monazite is collected by powerful electromagnets.' His voice was almost drowned by the roar of the machinery. That didn't worry Daniel. Later he would have Taffari make another clear recording of his speech and in the studio he would dub the tape to give it good sound.

'Once we have taken out the monazite, the remainder goes into the separator tanks in which we float out the light material and capture the heavy ore of platinum.' Taffari went on, 'This is a very sensitive part of the operation. If we were to use chemical catalysts and reagents in the separator tanks we would be able to recover over ninety per cent of the platinum. However, the chemical effluent from the tanks would be poisonous. It would be absorbed into the earth and washed by rain into the rivers to kill everything that came in contact with it – animals, birds, insects, fish and plant life. As president of the Democratic People's Republic of Ubomo, I have given an inviolable instruction that no chemical reagents of any kind are to be used during platinum mining operations in this country.' Taffari paused and stared into the camera levelly. 'You have my absolute assurance on that point. Without using reagents, our recovery of ore drops to sixty-five per cent. That means tens of millions of dollars are lost from the process. However, my government and I are determined to accept that loss, rather than to run any risk of chemical pollution of our environment. We are determined to do all in our power to make this a safe and happy world for our children, and your children, to enjoy.'

He was utterly convincing. When you listened to that deep reassuring voice and looked at that noble face, you could not possibly doubt his sincerity. Even Daniel was moved, and his critical faculties were suspended for the moment. 'This bastard could sell pork pies in a synagogue.' He tried to get his cynical professional judgement functioning again.

'Cut,' he snapped. 'That's a wrap. That was marvellous, Mr President. Thank you very much. If you'd like to go back to the mess for lunch, we'll finish up here. Then this afternoon we'll film the final sequences with the maps and models.'

Chetti Singh reappeared, like a turbaned genie from a lamp, to usher Taffari down from the MOMU and to drive him back to the base camp where Daniel knew a sumptuous buffet lunch was awaiting him. The food and liquor had been flown up from Kahali in the Puma helicopter.

Once the others had left, Daniel and Bonny captured the last sequences on the MOMU which didn't require Taffari to be present. They filmed the heavy platinum concentrates pouring into the ore bins in a fine dark stream. Each bin had a capacity of a hundred tons and when it was full it dropped automatically on to the bed of a waiting trailer and was towed away.

It was three o'clock before they had wrapped up all the shots that Daniel wanted on the MOMU and by the time they got back to the base camp at Sengi-Sengi, the presidential lunch was just ending.

In the centre of the conference room of the headquarters hut was an elaborate scale model of a typical mining scenario, employing the MOMU unit. It was designed to illustrate the entire procedure. The model had been built by BOSS technicians in London. It was an impressive piece of work, complete in detail, authentic in scale.

Daniel planned to alternate between shots of the model and

helicopter shots from the Puma of the actual forest terrain with the real MOMU in action. He believed that on the screen it would be difficult to tell the difference between them.

The scale model showed the mining track, sixty yards wide, cut and cleared through the forest by the team of loggers and bulldozers working ahead of the MOMU. Daniel planned to devote a few days' filming to the logging operation itself. The felling of the tall trees would yield riveting footage. The ponderous arabesques of the yellow bulldozers dragging the logs out of the jungle, the gangs loading them on to the logging trucks, would all be good cinema.

In the meantime Daniel must take full advantage of the day's filming in which Taffari had agreed to participate. He watched Bonny fussing over him, whispering and giggling as she powdered his face. She was making it very obvious to anyone watching that they were lovers. Taffari had drunk enough to lower his inhibitions and he caressed her openly, staring at the big breasts that she thrust only inches from his nose.

She really sees herself as First Lady of Ubomo, Daniel marvelled. She hasn't the least idea how the Hita treat their wives. I'd love it to happen. She deserves anything that comes her way.

He stood up and interrupted the flagrant display. 'If you're ready, Mr President, I'd like you standing here, beside the table. Bonny, I want the shot from this side. Try to get both General Taffari and the model in focus . . .'

Taffari moved to his mark and they rehearsed the shot. He got it right at the first attempt.

'Very good, sir. We'll go for it now. Are you ready, Bonny?'

Taffari's military swagger-stick was of polished ivory and rhino horn, the shaft topped by a miniature carving of an elephant. It looked more like a field marshal's baton than that of a general officer. Perhaps he was anticipating the day when he would promote himself, Daniel thought wryly.

Now Taffari used the baton to point out the features of the model on the table in front of him. 'As you can see, the mining track is a narrow pathway through the forest, only sixty yards wide. It is true that along that track we are felling all the trees and removing the undergrowth for the MOMU to follow.'

He paused seriously, and looked up at the camera. 'This is not wanton destruction but a prudent harvest, like that of a farmer husbanding his fields. Less than one per cent of the forest is affected by this narrow strip of activity, and behind the MOMU comes a span of bulldozers to refill the mining trench and to compact and consolidate the soil. The trench itself is painstakingly following the land contours to avoid soil erosion. As soon as the trench is refilled, a team of botanists follows up to replant the open ground with seeds and saplings. These plants have been carefully selected. Some of them are quick-growing to act as a ground cover; others are slower growing, but in fifty years from now will be fully mature and ready to be harvested. I will not be there when this happens, but my grandchildren will. The way that this operation has been planned, we will never harvest more than one single per cent of the forest each year. You don't have to be a mathematician to realise that it will be the year AD 2090 before we have worked it all, and by that time the trees that we plant now, in 1990, will be a hundred years old and we can safely begin the whole cycle over again.' He smiled reassuringly into the lens, handsome and debonair. 'A thousand years from now the forests of Ubomo will still be yielding up their largesse to generations yet unborn, and offering a haven for the same living creatures that they do now.'

It all made sense, Daniel decided. He had seen the proof of it in operation. That narrow track through the forest could not seriously threaten any species with extinction. Taffari was proposing exactly the same philosophy in which Daniel himself believed so implicitly, the philosophy of sustained yield, the disciplined and planned utilisation of the earth's resources, so that they were always renewing themselves.

For the moment, his animosity towards Ephrem Taffari was forgotten. He felt like applauding him.

Instead he cleared his throat and said, 'Mr President, that was an extraordinary performance. It was inspirational. Thank you, sir.'

Sitting on the tailboard of the Landrover, Chetti Singh smoothed the document over his own thigh. He had developed a remarkable dexterity with his left hand.

'This scrap of paper takes all the fun out of it,' he remarked.

'It is not meant to be fun,' Ning Cheng Gong said flatly. 'It is meant to be a present for my honourable father. It is meant to be work.'

Chetti Singh glanced up at him and smiled blandly and insincerely. He did not like the change that was so apparent since Ning had returned from Taipei. There was a new force and strength in him now, a new confidence and determination. For the first time Chetti Singh found that he was afraid of him. He did not enjoy the sensation.

'Still, work goes better when it is fun,' Chetti Singh argued to bolster himself, but found he could not meet Ning's dark implacable stare. He dropped his eyes to the document and read,

PEOPLE'S DEMOCRATIC REPUBLIC OF UBOMO
Special Presidential Game Licence

The bearer, Mr Ning Cheng Gong, or his authorised agent, is hereby empowered by special presidential decree to hunt, trap or kill the following protected species of wild game anywhere in the Republic of Ubomo. To wit, five specimens of Elephant (Loxodonta Africana).

He is further empowered for reasons of scientific research to collect and have in his possession, to export or sell, any part of the aforesaid specimens including the skins, bones, meat and/or ivory tusks thereof.

Signed, Ephrem Taffari
President of the Republic.

The licence was a rush job. There was no precedent for the form or wording of it and at Cheng's request the president had scribbled it out on a scrap of notepaper and the government printer had set it up under the coat of arms of the Republic of Ubomo, and delivered it within twelve hours for President Taffari to sign.

'I am a poacher,' Chetti Singh explained, 'the best in Africa. This piece of paper turns me into a mere agent, an underling, a butcher's apprentice . . .'

Cheng turned away impatiently. The Sikh was annoying him. There were things other than this petty carping to occupy him. He paced the forest clearing, lost in thought. The ground was muddy and rutted underfoot and the humidity steamed up the lenses of his sunglasses. He removed them and slipped them into the breast-pocket of his open-neck shirt. He glanced around him at the solid green wall of jungle that hemmed in the clearing. It was dark and menacing and he suppressed the sense of unease that it evoked and instead glanced at his wristwatch.

'He is late,' he said sharply. 'When will he come?'

Chetti Singh shrugged and folded the game licence with one hand. 'He does not have the same sense of time that we do. He is a pygmy. He will come when it suits him. Perhaps he is already here, watching us. Perhaps he will come tomorrow or next week.'

'I cannot waste any more time,' Cheng snapped. 'There is other important work to do.'

'More important than your honourable father's gift?' Chetti Singh asked, and his smile was ironical.

'Damn these black people.' Cheng turned away again. 'They are so unreliable.'

'They are monkeys,' Chetti Singh agreed, 'but useful little monkeys.'

Cheng made another turn around the clearing, his feet squelching in the red mud, and then stopped in front of Chetti Singh again.

'What about Armstrong?' he asked. 'We have to deal with him.'

'Ah, yes!' Chetti Singh grinned. 'That will be fun, indeed.' He massaged the stump of his missing arm. 'I have dreamed about Doctor Armstrong every night for nearly a year. And yet I never thought to have him delivered so neatly to Sengi-Sengi. Like a trussed chicken, never mind.'

'You will have to deal with him while he is still here,' Cheng insisted. 'You can't allow him to leave here alive.'

'Perish the thought,' Chetti Singh agreed. 'I have been devot-

408

ing much contemplation to the problem. I wish the good doctor's demise to be suitably symbolic and painful, and yet to be adequately explainable as a most unfortunate accident of fate.'

'Don't wait too long,' Cheng warned.

'I have five more days,' Chetti Singh pointed out complacently. 'I have seen the filming schedule. He cannot finish his work at Sengi-Sengi before that—'

Cheng cut in impatiently, 'What about the red-haired woman, his assistant?'

'At the moment President Taffari is having some bonking fun with her, but nevertheless I think it might be prudent to arrange for her to accompany Doctor Armstrong on the long journey—' Chetti Singh broke off abruptly and stood up. He peered into the forest and when Cheng opened his mouth to speak he silenced him with an imperative gesture. For another minute he stood listening with his head cocked before he spoke again. 'I think he is here.'

'How do you know?' Despite himself Cheng's voice was a cautious whisper and he cleared his throat nervously as he peered into the jungle.

'Listen,' said Chetti Singh. 'The birds.'

'I hear nothing.'

'Precisely.' Chetti Singh nodded. 'They have fallen silent.' He stepped towards the green wall and raised his voice, calling in Swahili. 'Peace be with you, son of the forest. Come forward, so that we may greet each other as friends.'

The pygmy appeared like a trick of the light in a hole in the wall of vegetation. He was framed in a wreath of shining green leaves, and a ray of sunshine through the top branches that surrounded the clearing danced upon his glossy skin and threw each muscle of his powerful little body into high relief. His head was small and neat. His nose was broad and flat and he wore a goatee beard of soft curling black wool, laced with silvery grey.

'I see you, Pirri, the great hunter,' Chetti Singh greeted him with flattery and the little man came into the clearing with a lithe and graceful step.

'Did you bring tobacco?' he asked in Swahili, with a childlike

409

directness, and Chetti Singh chuckled and handed him a tin of Uphill Rhodesian.

Pirri unscrewed the lid. He scooped out a loose ball of yellow tobacco and wadded it under his top lip and hummed with pleasure.

'He is not as small as I thought he would be,' Cheng remarked as he studied him. 'Or as dark.'

'He is not a full-blooded Bambuti,' Chetti Singh explained. 'His father was a Hita, or so it is said.'

'Can he hunt?' Cheng asked dubiously. 'Can he kill an elephant?'

Chetti Singh laughed. 'He is the greatest hunter of all his tribe, but that is not all. He has other virtues, not possessed by his brethren, by reason of his mixed blood.'

'What are they?' Cheng wanted to know.

'He understands the value of money,' Chetti Singh explained. 'Wealth and property mean nothing to the other Bambuti, but Pirri is different. He is civilised enough to know the meaning of greed.'

Pirri was listening to them. Not understanding the English words, his head turned to each of them as they spoke, and he sucked his wad of tobacco. He was dressed only in a brief loin-cloth of bark cloth, his bow standing up behind his shoulder and his machete in a wooden scabbard at his waist. Abruptly he interrupted their discussion of him.

'Who is this *wazungu*?' he asked in Swahili, indicating Cheng with his woolly bearded chin.

'He is a famous chief, and rich,' Chetti Singh assured him, and Pirri strode across the clearing on muscular legs with bulging calves and looked up at Cheng curiously.

'His skin has the malaria colour and his eyes are the eyes of the mamba,' he announced without guile. Cheng understood just enough Swahili to bristle.

'He may know greed, but he does not know respect.'

'It is the Bambuti way,' Chetti Singh tried to placate him. 'They are like children; they say whatever comes into their heads.'

'Ask him about the elephant,' Cheng instructed, and Chetti Singh changed his tone of voice and smiled ingratiatingly at Pirri.

'I have come to ask you about elephant,' he said, and Pirri scratched his crotch, taking a large handful of the contents of his loin-cloth and joggling it thoughtfully.

'Ah, elephant!' he said vaguely. 'What do I know about elephant?'

'You are the greatest hunter of all the Bambuti,' Chetti Singh pointed out. 'Nothing moves in the forest but Pirri knows of it.'

'That is true,' Pirri agreed, and studied Cheng reflectively. 'I like the bracelet on this rich *wazungu*'s wrist,' he said. 'Before we talk of elephant he should give me a gift.'

'He wants your watch,' Chetti Singh told Cheng.

'I understood!' Cheng snapped. 'He is impertinent. What would a savage do with a gold Rolex?'

'He would probably sell it to one of the truck-drivers for one hundredth of its value,' Chetti Singh replied, enjoying Cheng's anger and frustration.

'Tell him I will not be blackmailed. I will not give him my watch,' Cheng stated flatly, and Chetti Singh shrugged.

'I will tell him,' he agreed, 'but that will mean no gift for your honourable father.'

Cheng hesitated and then unclipped the gold bracelet from his wrist and handed it to the pygmy. Pirri cooed with pleasure and held the wristwatch in both hands, turning it so that the small diamonds around the dial sparkled.

'It is pretty,' he giggled. 'So pretty that suddenly I remember about the elephant in the forest.'

'Tell me about the elephant,' Chetti Singh invited.

'There were thirty elephant cows and calves in the forest near Gondala,' Pirri said. 'And two large bulls with long white teeth.'

'How long?' Chetti Singh demanded, and Cheng who had followed the conversation thus far leaned forward eagerly.

'One elephant is larger than the other. His teeth are this long,' said Pirri, and unslung his bow from his shoulder and held it above his head and stood on tiptoe. 'This long,' he repeated. 'As high as I can reach with my bow, from the tip of the tooth to the lip, but not counting the part concealed in the skull.'

'How thick?' Cheng asked in atrocious Swahili, his voice

411

coarse with lust, and Pirri turned to him and half-circled his own waist with his dainty childlike hands.

'This thick,' he said. 'As thick as I am.'

'That is a great elephant,' Chetti Singh murmured with disbelief, and Pirri bridled.

'He is the greatest of all elephants and I have seen him with my own eyes. I, Pirri, say this thing and it is true.'

'I want you to kill this elephant and bring me his tusks,' Chetti Singh said softly, and Pirri shook his head.

'This elephant is no longer at Gondala. When the machines of yellow iron came into the forest, he ran from their smoke and noise. He has gone into the sacred heartland where no man may hunt. It is decreed by the Mother and the Father. I cannot kill this elephant in the heartland.'

'I will pay you a great deal for the teeth of this elephant,' Chetti Singh whispered seductively, but Pirri shook his head firmly.

'Offer him a thousand dollars,' Cheng said in English, but Chetti Singh frowned at him.

'Leave this to me,' he cautioned. 'We don't want to ruin the trade with impatience.' He turned back to Pirri and said in Swahili, 'I will give you ten bolts of pretty cloth which the women love, and fifty handfuls of glass beads – enough to make a thousand virgins spread their thighs for you.'

Pirri shook his head. 'It is the sacred heartland,' he said. 'The Mother and the Father will be angry if I hunt there.'

'In addition to the cloth and beads, I will give you twenty iron axe-heads and ten fine knives with blades as long as your hand.'

Pirri wriggled his whole body like a puppy. 'It is against law and custom. My tribe will hate me and drive me out.'

'I will give you twenty bottles of gin,' Chetti Singh said. 'And as much tobacco as you can lift from the ground.'

Pirri massaged his crotch frantically and rolled his eyes. 'As much tobacco as I can carry!' His voice was hoarse. 'I cannot do it. They will call out the Molimo. They will bring down the curse of the Mother and Father.'

'And I will give you a hundred silver Maria Theresa dollars.' Chetti Singh reached into the pocket of his bush jacket and

412

brought out a handful of silver coins. He juggled them in one hand, jingling them together and making them sparkle in the sunlight.

For a long moment Pirri stared at them hungrily. Then he let out a shrill yelp and sprang in the air and drew his machete. Chetti Singh and Cheng stepped back nervously, expecting him to attack them, but instead, Pirri whirled and, with the blade held high above his head, rushed at the wall of the forest and swung a hissing stroke at the first bush. Shouting with anger and temptation, he hacked and slashed at the forest growth. Leaves and twigs flew, and branches were sliced through. Slabs of bark and white wood rained down from the bleeding trunks under his onslaught.

At last Pirri stopped and rested on his blade, his muscular chest heaving, sweat pouring down his face and dripping into his beard, sobbing with exertion and self-loathing. Then he straightened up and came back to where Chetti Singh stood and said, 'I will kill this elephant for you, and bring you his teeth. Then you will give me all those things you promised me, not forgetting the tobacco.'

Chetti Singh drove the Landrover back along the rudimentary forest track. It took almost an hour for them to reach the main corduroy roadway on which the convict gangs were working, and over which the great ore-carriers and the logging trucks rumbled and roared.

As they left the overgrown logging track and joined the heavy flow of traffic towards Sengi-Sengi, Chetti Singh turned to grin at the man beside him.

'That takes care of the gift for your father. Now we must apply all our ingenuity and brains to a little gift for me – the head of Doctor Daniel Armstrong on a silver platter, with an apple in his mouth.'

Daniel had been waiting for this moment, praying for it.

He was high on the command deck of the MOMU and it was raining. The air was blue and thick with falling rain, and visibility was down to fifty feet or less. Bonny was sheltering in the command cabin at the end of the platform, keeping her precious video equipment out of the rain. The two Hita guards had gone down to the lower deck and for a moment Daniel was alone on the upper deck.

Daniel had become hardened to the rain. Since arriving at Sengi-Sengi he seemed always to be wearing wet clothing. He was standing now in the angle of the steel wall of the command cabin and the flying bridge, only partially shielded from the driving rain. Every now and then a harder gust would throw heavy drops into his face and force him to slit his eyes.

Suddenly the door to the command cabin opened and Ning Cheng Gong came out on to the flying bridge. He had not seen Daniel and he crossed to the forward rail under cover of the canvas sun awning and leaned on the rail, peering down at the great shining excavator blades that were tearing into the earth seventy feet below his perch.

It was Daniel's moment. For the first time they were alone and Cheng was vulnerable.

'This one is for Johnny,' he whispered, and crossed the steel plates of the bridge on silent rubber soles. He came up behind Cheng.

All he had to do was stoop and seize his ankles. A quick lift and shove, and Cheng would be hurled over the rail and dropped into the deadly blades. It would be instantaneous and the chopped and dismembered corpse would be fed into the tube mills and pounded to paste and mixed with hundreds of tons of powdered earth.

Daniel reached out to do it, but before he could touch him he hesitated involuntarily, suddenly appalled at what he was about to do. It was cold-blooded, calculated murder. He had killed before as a soldier, but never like this, and for a moment he was sick with self-loathing.

'For Johnny,' he tried to convince himself, but it was too late. Cheng whirled to face him.

414

He was quick as a mongoose confronted by a cobra. His hands came up, the stiff-fingered blades of the martial arts exponent, and his eyes were dark and ferocious as he stared into Daniel's face.

For a moment they were poised on the edge of violence, then Cheng whispered, 'You missed your chance, Doctor. There will not be another.'

Daniel backed away. He had let Johnny down with such weakness. In the old days it would not have happened. He would have taken Cheng out swiftly and competently and rejoiced at the kill. Now the Taiwanese was alerted and even more dangerous.

Daniel turned away, sickened by his failure, and then he started. One of the Hita guards had come up the steel ladder silently as a leopard. He was leaning against the rear rail of the bridge with his maroon beret cocked over one eye and the Uzi sub-machine-gun on his hip pointed at Daniel's belly. He had been watching it all.

That night Daniel lay awake until after midnight, unnerved by the narrowness of his escape and sickened by the savage streak in himself that allowed him to pursue such a brutal vengeance. Yet even this attack of conscience did not shake his determination to act as the vehicle of justice and in the morning he awoke to find his lust for revenge undiminished, and only his temper and his nerves shaky and uncertain.

This led directly to his final bust-up with Bonny Mahon. It began when she was late to start the day's assignment, and kept him waiting in the teeming rain for almost forty minutes before she finally sauntered out to meet him.

'When I said five o'clock, I didn't mean in the afternoon,' he snarled at her, and she grinned at him, all rosy and smug.

'What do you want me to do, commit hara-kiri, O Master?' she asked. He was about to let fly a verbal broadside, when he realised that she must have come directly from Taffari's bed without bathing, for he caught a whiff of the musky odour of their lovemaking on her, and had to turn away. He felt so furious that he could not trust himself not to strike her.

For Chrissake, Armstrong, get a hold on yourself, he cautioned himself silently, you're going to pieces.

They worked in brittle antagonism for the rest of the morning, filming the bulldozers and chainsaws as they cleared the mining track for the monstrous MOMU to waddle down.

It was heavy going in the mud and rain, and dangerous with falling tree trunks and powerful machinery working all around them. This did nothing to improve his mood but Daniel managed to keep a check on his tongue until just before noon when Bonny announced that she had run out of tape and had to break off to return to the main camp to fetch new stock from the cold rooms.

'What kind of half-baked cameraman runs out of stock in the middle of a shoot?' Daniel wanted to know, and she rounded on him.

'I know what's eating you up, lover boy. It's not shortage of film, it's shortage of good rich fruitcake. You hate me for what Ephrem is getting and you're not. It's the old green-eyed monster.'

'You've got an inflated idea of the value of what you sit on,' Daniel came back as angrily.

It escalated rapidly from there until Bonny yelled into his face, 'Nobody talks to me like that, Buster. You can stick your job and your insults up your left earhole, or in any other convenient orifice.' And she sloshed and slipped in the red mud back to where the Landrover was parked.

'Leave the camera in the Landrover,' Daniel shouted after her. It was all hired video equipment. 'You've got your return ticket to London and I'll send you a cheque for what I owe you. You're fired.'

'No, I'm not, lover boy. You're way too late. I resigned! And don't you forget it.' She slammed the door of the Landrover and raced the engine. All four wheels spinning wildly and throwing up sheets and clods of red mud, Bonny tore up the track and left him glaring after her. His bad temper increased as he belatedly thought of a dozen other clever retorts that he should have thrown at her while he had the chance.

Bonny was as angry, but her mood was longer-lasting and more vindictive. She racked her imagination for the cruellest revenge she could conjure up, and just before she reached the main camp at Sengi-Sengi it came to her in a creative flash.

'You are going to rue every single lousy thing you said to me, Danny boy,' she promised aloud, grinning mercilessly. 'You ain't going to shoot another tape in Ubomo, not you, nor any other cameraman that you hire to replace me. I'm going to make damned double sure of that.'

 His body was long and supple. In the dim light beneath the mosquito-net his skin shone like washed coal, still damp with the sweat of love. Ephrem Taffari lay on his back on the rumpled white sheet and she thought he was probably the most beautiful man she had ever seen.

Slowly she lowered her head and laid her cheek against his naked chest. It was smooth and hairless, and his dark skin felt cool. She blew softly on his nipple and watched it pucker and harden in response. She smiled. She felt aglow with well-being. He was a wonderful lover, better than any white man she had ever had. There had never been anyone else like him. She wanted to do something for him.

'There is something I must tell you,' she whispered against his chest, and with one lazy hand he stroked the thick glistening coppery bush of hair back off her face.

'What is it?' he asked, his voice soft and deep and replete, almost uninterested.

She knew she would have his complete attention again with her next statement, and she delayed the moment. It was too sweet to waste. She wanted to draw every last possible enjoyment from it. It was double pleasure – her revenge on Daniel Armstrong and her offering to Ephrem Taffari which would prove to him her loyalty and her worth.

'What is it?' he repeated. He took a handful of her hair and twisted it just hard enough to hurt. He was a master in inflicting pain, and her breath caught with masochistic pleasure.

'I'm telling you this to show you how completely I am yours, how much I love you,' she whispered. 'After tonight you'll never be able to doubt where my loyalties lie.'

417

He chuckled and shook her head gently from side to side, his fingers still locked in her hair, still hurting exquisitely.

'Let me judge that, my little red lily. Tell me this terrible thing.'

'It is a terrible thing, Ephrem. On the instructions of Daniel Armstrong I filmed the forced removal of the villagers from Fish Eagle Bay to make way for the new casino.'

Ephrem Taffari stopped breathing. For twenty beats of his heart under her ear he held his breath. Then he let it out softly, and his pulse rate was slightly elevated as he said quietly, 'I don't know what you are talking about. Explain this to me.'

'Daniel and I were on top of the cliff when the soldiers came to the village. Daniel ordered me to film them.'

'What did you see?'

'We saw them bulldoze the village and burn the boats. We saw them load the people into the trucks and take them away . . .' She hesitated.

'Go on,' he ordered. 'What else did you see?'

'We saw them kill two people. They clubbed an old man to death and they shot another when he tried to escape. They threw their bodies on the fire.'

'You filmed all that?' Ephrem asked, and there was something in his tone that made her suddenly uncertain and afraid.

'Daniel forced me to film it.'

'I do not know anything about these events, this atrocity. I gave no orders,' he said, and with a surge of relief she believed him.

'I was sure you didn't know about it.'

'I must see this film. It is evidence against those who perpetrated this atrocity. Where is the film?'

'I gave it to Daniel.'

'What did he do with it?' Ephrem demanded, and now his voice was terrible.

'He said that he had lodged it with the British Embassy in Kahali. The ambassador, Sir Michael Hargreave, is an old friend of his.'

'Did he show the film to the ambassador?' Ephrem wanted to know.

'I don't think so. He said that it was dynamite, that he wouldn't use it until the time was ripe.'

'So you and Armstrong are the only ones who know about it, who know that the film exists?'

She hadn't thought of it that way, and now it gave her an uneasy feeling.

'Yes, I suppose so. Unless Daniel has told anybody. I haven't.'

'Good.' Ephrem released her hair and stroked her cheek. 'You are a good girl. I am grateful to you. You have proved your friendship to me.'

'It is more than friendship, Ephrem. I have never felt about another man the way I feel for you.'

'I know,' he whispered, and lifted her head and kissed her on the lips. 'You are a wonderful woman. My own feelings for you grow stronger all the time.' Gratefully she pressed her own full body to his sleek feline length.

'We must get that film back from Sir Michael. It could do untold damage to this country and to me as the president.'

'I should have told you sooner,' she said. 'But only now I realise how much I love you.'

'It is still not too late,' he assured her. 'I will speak to Armstrong in the morning. I will give him my word that the guilty persons will be brought to justice. He must give me the film to be used in evidence.'

'I don't think he will do that,' she said. 'That tape is too sensational. It is worth a million to him. He won't want to give it up.'

'Then you will have to help me get it back. After all, it is your film. Will you help me, my beautiful red and white lily?'

'You know I will, Ephrem. I'll do anything for you,' she murmured, and without another word he made love to her, that beautiful devastating love of which only he was capable.

Afterwards she slept.

When she awoke it was raining again. It always seemed to be raining in this terrible green hell of jungle. The rain clattered and drummed on the roof of the VIP guest bungalow, and the darkness was complete.

She groped instinctively for Ephrem but the bed beside her was empty. The sheets on which he had lain were already cool. He must have left her some time ago. She thought he might have gone to the bathroom, and felt the pressure in her own bladder which had woken her.

She lay and listened for him to return, but after five minutes when he had not come, she crept out from under the mosquito-net and groped her way through the darkness to the bathroom door. She bumped into a chair and stubbed her bare toe before she reached it. She found the light switch and blinked in the sudden glare of white tiles.

The bathroom was empty, but the toilet seat was raised to prove he had been there before her. She flapped it down and perched naked upon it, still groggy with sleep, her red hair tangled over her eyes.

Outside the rain battered down and a sudden flare of light-ning lit the window. Bonny reached across to the side wall for the roll of toilet paper in its holder and her ear was inches from the thin prefabricated partition wall of the bungalow. She heard voices, indistinct but masculine, from the room beyond.

She was slowly coming fully awake, and her interest was aroused. She pressed her ear to the wall and she recognised Ephrem's voice. It was crisp and commanding. Somebody an-swered him but the sound of the rain intruded and she could not recognise the speaker.

'No,' Ephrem replied. 'Tonight. I want it done immediately.' Bonny was fully alert now, and at that moment the rain stopped with dramatic suddenness. In the silence she heard the reply and recognised the speaker.

'Will you sign a warrant, Mr President?' It was Chetti Singh. His accent was unmistakable. 'Your soldiers could carry out the execution.'

'Don't be a fool, man. I want it done quietly. Get rid of him. You can get Kajo to help you, but do it. No questions, no written records. Just get rid of him.'

'Ah, yes. I understand. We will say that he went to film in the jungle. Later we can send a search party to find no trace of him. A great pity. But what about the woman? She is also a witness to our arrangements at Fish Eagle Bay. Do you want me to take care of her at the same time?'

'No, don't be an idiot! I will need her to recover the tape from the embassy. Afterwards, when the tape is safely in my

420

hands, I will reconsider the problem of the woman. In the meantime just take Armstrong out into the jungle and get rid of him.'

'I assure you, Mr President, that nothing would give me more pleasure. It will take me an hour or so to make the arrangements with Kajo, but it will be all over before daylight. I give you my solemn promise.'

There was the sound of a chair being pushed back and heavy footsteps, then a door slammed and there was silence from the sitting-room of the bungalow.

Bonny sat frozen for a moment, chilled by what she had heard. Then she sprang to her feet and darted across the floor to the light switch and plunged the bathroom into darkness. Swiftly she groped her way to the bed and crept under the mosquito net. She lay rigid under the sheet, expecting Ephrem Taffari to return at any moment.

Her mind was racing. She was frightened and confused. She had not expected any of this.

She had thought that Ephrem might seize the videotape and arrest Daniel, then deport him immediately and declare him an undesirable alien, or something like that. She hadn't been too clear as to what Ephrem would do to Daniel, but she had never dreamed for a moment that he would have him killed, squashed like an insect without pity or remorse. With a jolt she realised just how naïve she had been.

The shock was almost too much to bear. She had never hated Daniel. Far from it, she had been as fond of him as she was capable of, until he had begun to bore and irritate her. Of course, after Ephrem had taken over Daniel had insulted and fired her, but she had given him some reason for that and she didn't hate him — not to the point of wanting him killed.

'Keep out of it,' she warned herself. 'It's too late now. Danny has to take his own chances.'

She lay waiting for Ephrem to come back to bed, but he did not come and she thought of Daniel again. He was one of the few men she had ever genuinely admired and liked. He was decent and good and funny and handsome . . . She broke that chain of thought.

Don't be a bleeding heart, she thought. It didn't turn out the way you expected but that's tough on Danny. And yet there had been a veiled threat to her in what Ephrem had said. 'When the tape is safely in my hands I will reconsider the problem of the woman.'

Ephrem still hadn't come. She sat up in bed and listened. The rain had stopped completely. Reluctantly she slipped out from under the mosquito-net and picked her robe from the foot of the bed. She crossed to the door that opened on to the verandah of the bungalow and opened it quietly.

She crept down the verandah. The light from the sitting-room windows beamed out on to the verandah floor. She moved into a position from where she could see into the sitting-room while remaining in shadow. Ephrem Taffari sat at the desk against the far wall. His back was to her. He was dressed in a khaki T-shirt and camouflage trousers. He was smoking a cigarette and studying the papers that were strewn across the desk-top. He seemed to be settled to his work.

It would take her less than ten minutes to reach the row of guest bungalows at the east side of the compound and get back to the bedroom.

The wooden catwalks were wet and red with mud. She was barefoot. Daniel might not be in his room. She thought of every excuse for not going to warn him.

I owe him nothing, she thought, and heard Ephrem's voice again in her imagination: 'Just take Armstrong out into the jungle and get rid of him.'

She backed away from the lighted window, not yet certain what she would do until she found herself running along the catwalk beneath the dark trees that dripped with rain. She slipped and fell on her knees but jumped up and kept running. There was red mud on the front of her robe.

She saw through the trees that there was one light on in the row of guest rooms. The rest of them were in darkness. As she came closer she saw with relief that the light was in Daniel's room.

She did not go up on to the verandah of the guest house, but jumped down off the catwalk and made her way around the back of the building. Daniel's window was curtained. She scratched softly on the mosquito-mesh screen that covered it, and at once heard a chair scrape back on the wooden floor.

She scratched again and Daniel's voice asked softly, 'Who is it?'

'For God's sake, Danny, it's me. I have to talk to you.'

'Come inside. I'll open the door.'

'No, no. Come out here. It's desperate. They mustn't see me. Hurry, man, hurry.'

Half a minute later his broad-shouldered form loomed out of the darkness, backlit by the lighted bungalow window.

'Danny, Ephrem knows about the Fish Eagle Bay tape.'

'How did he find out?'

'That doesn't matter.'

'You told him, didn't you?'

'Damn you to hell – I have come to warn you. He's issued orders for your immediate execution. Chetti Singh and Kajo are coming for you. They're going to take you into the jungle. They don't want any evidence.'

'How do you know this?'

'Don't ask bloody fool questions. Believe me, I know. I can't waste another minute. I've got to get back. He'll find I'm gone.' She turned away, but he seized her arm.

'Thanks, Bonny,' he said. 'You're a better person than you think you are. Do you want to make a break for it with me?'

She shook her head. 'I'll be all right,' she said. 'Just get out of here. You've got an hour, tops. Get going!'

She pulled out of his grip and hurried away through the trees. He caught one last glimpse of her: the lights from the bungalow transformed her tumbled hair into a roseate halo and the long white robe made her look like an angel.

'Some angel,' Daniel muttered, and stood for a full minute in the darkness deciding what he could do.

While there had been only Chetti Singh and Ning Cheng Gong to deal with he had stood a chance. Like him, they had been constrained by the necessity of working in secrecy. None of them had been able to attack the other openly, but now Chetti Singh had open sanction to kill him, a special presidential licence. Daniel grinned as mirthlessly as a wolf. He could expect the Sikh to act swiftly and ruthlessly. Bonny was right. He had to get out of Sengi-Sengi within the next few minutes, before the executioners arrived.

From the angle of the building he threw a quick glance down the verandah and around the compound. All was quiet and dark. He slipped back into his room, and lifted his small travel bag down from the cupboard. It contained all his personal documents, passport, airline tickets, credit cards and travellers' cheques. Apart from his clothing and toilet bag there was nothing else of value in the room.

He pulled on a light wind-cheater and checked that the key of the Landrover was in his pocket. He extinguished the lights and went out. The Landrover was parked at the far end of the verandah. He opened the door quietly and threw his bag on to the passenger seat. All the hired VTR equipment was packed into the rear compartment and there was a selection of basic camping and first-aid equipment in the lockers, but there was no weapon of any kind, apart from his old hunting-knife.

He started the Landrover. The engine noise seemed excessively loud in the darkness. He did not switch on the headlights and he let in the clutch gently, keeping the engine revs down. He drove slowly through the darkened compound towards the main gates. He knew that the gates were never closed at night, and that a single guard was on duty there.

Daniel was under no illusion as to just how far he was going to get in the Landrover. There was only one road from Sengi-Sengi to the Ubomo river ferry, and there was a road-block every five miles.

A radio call from Sengi-Sengi would alert every one of them. The guards would be waiting for him with their fingers on the triggers of their AK 47s. No, he would be lucky to make it through the first block, and then he would have to take to the jungle. He didn't relish that prospect. He had been trained for survival and warfare in the drier bushveld of Rhodesia, a long way further south. He would not be nearly as adept in the rain forest, but there was no other way open to him.

The first thing was to get clear of Sengi-Sengi. After that he would face each problem as it arose.

And this is number one, he thought grimly as suddenly the floodlights at the main gates switched on in a bright halogen dawn. The entire compound was brightly lit.

There were half a dozen figures running from the barrack

area where guards were quartered. It was obvious they had dressed hastily; some were in undervests and shorts. Daniel recognised both Captain Kajo and Chetti Singh.

Kajo was brandishing an automatic pistol and Chetti Singh was trotting along behind him, shouting and waving at the approaching Landrover, his white turban very visible in the glare of the floodlights. One of the guards was trying to shut the gates. He already had one wing of the steel-framed mesh gate half across the roadway.

Daniel switched on his headlights, put his hand flat on the horn and drove hard at him, the hooter blaring. The guard dived nimbly aside, and the Landrover slammed into the un-locked leaf of the gate and whipped it aside. He roared through.

Behind him he heard the rattling clamour of automatic rifle-fire. He felt half a dozen bullets slam into the aluminium bodywork of the Landrover, but he crouched low over the wheel and kept his foot hard down on the accelerator.

The first bend in the roadway rushed towards him in the headlights. Another burst of automatic fire splattered against the rear of the vehicle. The rear window exploded in a storm of glass splinters and something struck him high in the back within an inch of his spine. He had been hit by a bullet before, in that long-ago war, and he recognised the sensation. From the position of the wound, high and close to the spine, it had to be a lung shot, a mortal wound. He expected to feel the choking flood of arterial blood into his lungs.

Keep going as long as you can, he thought, and swung the Landrover into the bend at full throttle. She went up on two wheels but didn't roll.

When he glanced in the rear-view mirror the camp lights were obscured by forest trees, a dwindling glow in the darkness behind.

He could feel hot blood running down his back, but there was no choking, no weakness, not yet anyway. The wound was numb. He could think clearly. He could keep going.

He knew exactly where the first road-block was situated. 'Approximately five miles ahead,' he reminded himself. 'On the first river crossing.'

He tried to remember how the road ran to reach it. He had driven over it half a dozen times during the last three days' filming. He could remember almost every twist, every track that led off it.

He made his decision. He leaned back against the seat. The wound stabbed him like a knife in the back, but he wasn't losing much blood.

Internal bleeding, he thought. You aren't going to walk away from this one, Danny boy. But he kept going, waiting for the weakness to overcome him.

There were five logging roads branching off from the main highway before it reached the first road-block. Some of them were disused and overgrown, but at least two were still being subjected to heavy daily traffic. He chose the first of these, two miles from Sengi-Sengi and turned on to it, heading westwards. The Zaïre border was ninety miles in that direction, but the logging track only ran five miles through the forest before it intersected the MOMU excavation.

He would have to dump the Landrover and try to make the remaining eighty miles on foot through uncharted forest. The last part of the journey would be over high mountains, glaciers and alpine snowfields. Then he thought about the bullet wound in his back and knew he was dreaming. He wasn't going to get that far.

The logging track he was on had been deeply rutted and chopped up by the gigantic treaded tyres of the trucks and heavy trailers. It was a morass of mud the consistency and colour of faeces, and the Landrover churned through it in four-wheel drive, pounding through the knee-deep ruts. Flying mud stuck to the glass of the headlights and dimmed the beams to a murky glow that barely lit the roadway twenty paces ahead.

The wound in his back was beginning to ache, but his head was still clear. He touched the end of his own nose with his forefinger to check his co-ordination. No sign of losing it yet.

Suddenly he was aware of lights far ahead of him on the track. One of the logging trucks was coming towards him, and instantly he realised the possibility it offered. He slowed the Landrover and searched the verge of unbroken jungle that pressed in upon the track. He sensed rather than saw a break in the foliage and swung the Landrover boldly into it.

For fifty paces or so he forced his way through almost impenetrable undergrowth. It scraped along both sides of the bodywork, and small trees and branches thumped along beneath the chassis. The soft forest floor sucked at the wheels and the Landrover's speed bled off until at last she was high-centred and stranded.

Daniel cut the engine and switched off the headlights. He sat in the darkness and listened to the logging truck rumble past, headed eastwards towards Sengi-Sengi along the road he had come. When the sound of the huge diesel engine had dwindled into silence, he leaned forward in the seat and steeled himself to examine the bullet wound in his back. Reluctantly he twisted one arm up behind him and groped towards the centre of pain.

Suddenly he exclaimed and jerked his hand away. He switched on the interior lights and examined the razor scratch on his forefinger. Then quickly he reached behind himself again, and cautiously fingered the wound. He laughed aloud with relief. A shard of flying glass from the rear window had sliced open his back, and lodged against his ribs. It was a long superficial wound with the sharp glass still buried in it.

He worked it loose and examined it in the overhead light. It was bloody and jagged, and the bleeding had started again. But you aren't going to die from it, he reassured himself, and tossed the splinter out of the side window and reached for the first-aid kit which was under the VTR equipment in the back of the vehicle.

It was difficult to treat the wound in his own back, but he managed to smear it liberally with Betadine ointment and strap an untidy dressing over it and knot the ends of the bandage in front of his chest. All the time he was listening for other vehicles on the logging road, but he heard only the small jungle sounds of bird and insect and beast.

He found the Maglite in his kit and went back on foot to the road. From the verge he examined the muddy rutted tracks. As he had hoped, the logging truck had completely obliterated the Landrover's tracks with its own massive multiple wheels. Only the spot where he had driven over the verge still carried the Landrover's prints. He picked up a dead branch and swept them away carefully. Then he turned his attention to the

427

foliage that the Landrover had damaged as it crashed into the forest.

He rearranged it as naturally as possible and smeared mud on the raw broken ends of branches and twigs so they would not catch the eye. After half an hour's work he was certain that nobody would suspect that a vehicle had left the road here and was hidden only fifty feet away in the dense undergrowth.

Almost immediately his work was put to the test. He saw headlights approaching from the direction of Sengi-Sengi. He drew back a little way into the forest and dropped flat. He smeared his face with a handful of mud and then covered the backs of his hands. His wind-cheater was dark forest green in colour; it would not show up in the lights.

He watched the vehicle approaching along the logging track. It was moving slowly and as it drew level with his hiding-place he saw that it was an army transport painted in brown and green camouflage. The rear was crowded with Hita soldiers and he thought he glimpsed Chetti Singh's white turban in the driver's cab, but he couldn't be certain. One of the soldiers in the rear was flashing a spotlight along the verges of the road. They were obviously searching for him.

Daniel dropped his face into the crook of his arm as the beam of the spotlight played over where he lay. The truck passed on without slowing and was soon out of sight.

Daniel stood up and hurried back to the stranded Landrover. Swiftly he made a selection of items from the lockers, most importantly the hand-bearing compass. He packed them into the small day pack. From the first-aid kit he took field dressings and antiseptic and anti-malarial tablets. There was no food in the truck. He'd have to live off the forest. He could not carry the pack the normal way without restarting the bleeding so he slung it over the other shoulder. He guessed that the wound really required stitching, but there was no way in which he could even attempt that.

I have to get across the MOMU track before first light, he thought. That's the one place I'll be in the open and vulnerable.

He left the Landrover and struck out westwards. It was difficult to orientate in darkness and the dense forest. He was forced to flash the torch and study the compass every few hundred yards. The going was soft and uneven and his progress was slow as he found his way between the trees. When he reached the MOMU excavation the open sky above it was flushing with dawn's first light.

He could make out the trees on the far side of the clearing, but the MOMU itself had passed on weeks before and was already working six or seven miles further north. This part of the forest should be deserted, unless Kajo and Chetti Singh had sent a patrol down the strip to cut him off.

It was a chance he had to take. He left the shelter of the forest and started across. He sank to his ankles in the red mud and it sucked at his boots. Every second he expected to hear a shout or a shot, and he was panting with exertion when at last he reached the far tree-line.

He kept going for another hour before he took his first rest. Already it was hot and the humidity was like a Turkish bath. He stripped off all his clothing, except for shorts and boots, rolled it into a ball and buried it in the thick soft loam of the forest floor. His skin was toughened by sun and weather and he had a natural resistance to insect stings. In the Zambezi valley he had been able to tolerate even the bite of the swarming tsetse fly. As long as he kept the wound on his back covered he should be all right, he decided.

He stood up and went on. He navigated by compass and wristwatch, timing his average stride to give him an estimate of distance covered. Every two hours he rested for ten minutes. By nightfall he calculated he had covered ten miles. At that rate it would take eight days to reach the Zaïre border but, of course, he wouldn't be able to keep it up. There were mountains ahead, and glaciers and snowfields, and he had abandoned most of his clothing. It was going to be interesting out on the glaciers in his present attire, he decided, as he made a nest in the moist leaf mould and composed himself for sleep.

When he woke it was just light enough to see his hand in front of his face. He was hungry and the wound in his back was stiff and painful. When he reached to touch it he found it was swollen and the flesh hot. All we need is a nice little infection, he thought, and renewed the dressing as best he could.

By noon he was ravenously hungry. He found a nest of fat white grubs under the bark of a dead tree. They tasted like raw egg yolks.

'What doesn't kill you, makes you fat,' he assured himself, and kept on towards the west, the compass in his hand. In the early afternoon he thought he recognised a type of edible fungus and nibbled a small piece as a trial. In the late afternoon he reached the bank of a small clear stream, and as he was drinking he noticed a dark cigar shape lying at the bottom of the pool. He cut a stake and sharpened one end, carving a crude set of barbs above the point. Then he cut down one of the hanging ant's nests from the branches of a silk-cotton tree and sprinkled the big red ants on the surface of the pool, taking care to stand well back from the edge with the crude spear in his right hand.

Almost immediately the fish rose from the bottom and began to gulp down the struggling insects trapped in the surface film. Daniel drove the point of his fish spear into its gills and brought it out flapping and kicking on to the bank. It was a barbeled catfish, as long as his arm. He ate his fill of the fatty yellow flesh and the rest of the carcass he smoked over a fire of green leaves. It should keep him going for a couple more days, he decided. He wrapped it in a package of leaves and put it in his pack.

However, when he woke the next morning his back was excruciatingly painful, and his stomach was swollen with gas and dysentery. He couldn't tell whether it was the insect grubs, the fungus or the stream water that had caused it, but by noon he was very weak. His diarrhoea was almost unremitting, and the wound felt like a red-hot coal between his shoulder-blades.

It was about that time that Daniel had the first sensation that he was being followed. It was an instinct that he had realised he possessed when he was a patrol leader with the Scouts in the valley. Johnny Nzou had trusted this sixth sense of his implicitly and it had never let them down. It was almost as though Daniel was able to pick up the malevolent concentration of the hunter following on his tracks.

Even in his pain and weakness Daniel looked back and felt a presence. He knew that he was out there, the hunter.

Anti-tracking, he told himself, knowing that it would slow his progress, but it would almost certainly throw off his real or imaginary pursuer, unless he was very good indeed, or unless Daniel's anti-tracking skills had atrophied.

At the next river-crossing he took to the water, and from then on he used every ruse and subterfuge to cover his tracks and throw off the pursuit. Every mile he grew slower and weaker. The diarrhoea never let up, his wound was beginning to stink, and he knew with clairvoyant certainty that the unseen hunter was still after him – and drawing closer every hour.

 Over the years Chetti Singh, the master poacher, had developed various systems of contacting his hunters. In some areas it was easier than others. In Zambia or Mozambique he had only to drive out to a remote village and talk to a wife or brother, and rely on them to pass the message. In Botswana or Zimbabwe he could even rely on the local postal authority to deliver a letter or telegram, but contacting a wild pygmy in the Ubomo rain forest was the most uncertain and time-consuming of all.

The only way to do it was to drive down the main highway and stop at every *duka* or trading-store, to accost every half-tame Bambuti that he met upon the roadside and bribe them to get a message to Pirri in the forest. It was amazing how the wild pygmies maintained a network of communication over those vast and secret areas of the rain forest, but then they were garrulous and sociable people.

A honey-seeker from one tribe would meet a woman from another tribe who was gathering medicine plants far from her camp, and the word would be passed on, shouted from a forested hilltop in a high penetrating sing-song to another wanderer across the valley, or carried by canoe, along the big rivers, until at last it reached the man for whom it was intended. Sometimes it took weeks, sometimes, if the sender was fortunate, it might take only a few days.

This time Chetti Singh was extremely lucky. Two days after

he had given the message to a straggling group of pygmy women at one of the river crossings, Pirri came to the rendezvous in the forest. As always he appeared with the dramatic suddenness of a forest sprite and asked for tobacco and gifts.

'Have you killed my elephant?' Chetti Singh asked pointedly, and Pirri picked his nose and scratched himself between the legs with embarrassment.

'If you had not sent for me, the elephant would by now be dead.'

'But he is not dead,' Chetti Singh pointed out. 'And thus you have not earned those marvellous gifts I promised you.'

'Just a little tobacco?' Pirri pleaded. 'For I am your faithful slave, and my heart is full of love for you. Just a small handful of tobacco?'

Chetti Singh gave him half what he asked for and while Pirri squatted down to suck and enjoy it, he went on, 'All I have promised you — I will give you that much again if you kill another creature for me, and bring me its head.'

'What creature is this?' Pirri asked guardedly, narrowing his eyes suspiciously. 'Is it another elephant?'

'No,' said Chetti Singh. 'It is a man.'

'You want me to kill a man!' Pirri stood up with alarm. 'If I do that the *wazungu* will come and take me and put a rope around my neck.'

'No,' said Chetti Singh. 'The *wazungu* will reward you as richly as I will.' And he turned to Captain Kajo. 'Is that not so?'

'It is so,' Kajo confirmed. 'The man we wish you to kill is a white man. He is an evil man who has escaped into the forest. We, the men of the government, will reward you for hunting him.'

Pirri looked at Kajo, at his uniform and gun and dark glasses and knew he was a powerful government *wazungu*, so he thought about it carefully. He had killed white *wazungu* before in the Zaïre war when he was a young man. The government had paid him for it then and it had been easy. The white *wazungu* were stupid and clumsy in the forest. They were easy to follow and easy to kill. They never even knew he was there until they were dead.

'How much tobacco?' he asked.

'From me, as much tobacco as you can carry,' said Chetti Singh.

'From me also, as much tobacco as you can carry,' said Captain Kajo.

'Where will I find him?' asked Pirri, and Chetti Singh told him where to begin his search, and where he thought the man was heading.

'You want only his head?' Pirri asked. 'To eat?'

'No.' Chetti Singh was not offended. 'So that I know you have killed the right man.'

'First I will bring you this man's head,' said Pirri happily. 'Then I will bring you the teeth of the elephant, and I will have more tobacco than any man in the world.' And like a little brown ghost he disappeared into the forest.

 In the early morning, before the heat built up, Kelly Kinnear was working in the Gondala clinic. She had more patients than usual, most of them suffering from infectious tropical yaws, those great suppurating ulcers that would eat down to the bone unless they were treated. Others were malarial or had swollen eyes running with fly-borne ophthalmia. There were also two new cases of AIDS. She didn't need blood slides to recognise the symptoms, the swelling of the lymph glands and the thick white thrush that coated their tongues and throats like cream cheese.

She consulted Victor Omeru and he agreed that they should try the new treatment on them, the herbal extract of the selepi tree bark that was looking so promising. He helped her prepare the dose. The amount was necessarily an arbitrary decision, and they were discussing it when there was a sudden commotion outside the clinic front door.

Victor glanced out of the window and smiled. 'Your little friends have arrived,' he told Kelly, and she laughed with pleasure and went out into the sunshine.

Sepoo and his wife Pamba were squatting below the verandah, chatting and laughing with the other waiting patients. When they saw her they both squealed with delight and came running, competing with each other to take her hands and tell her all the news since their last meeting, trying to shout each other down to be the first to impart the choicest morsels of scandal and sensation from the tribe. One on each hand they led her to her usual seat on the top step of the verandah and sat beside her, still chattering in unison.

'Swilli has had a baby. It is a boy and she says she will bring it to show you at the next full moon,' said Pamba.

'There will be a great net hunt soon, and all the tribes will join . . .' said Sepoo.

'I have brought you a bundle of the special roots I told you about last time we met,' shrilled Pamba, not to be outdone by her husband. Her bright eyes were almost hidden in a cobweb of wrinkles and half her teeth were missing.

'I shot two colobus monkeys,' boasted Sepoo. 'And I have brought you one of the skins to make a beautiful hat, Kara-Ki.'

'You are kind, Sepoo,' Kelly thanked him. 'But what news from Sengi-Sengi? What about the yellow machines that eat the earth and gobble up the forest? What news of the big white man with curly hair and the woman with hair like fire who looks into the little black box all the time?'

'Strange,' said Sepoo importantly. 'There is strange news. The big man with curly hair has run away from Sengi-Sengi. He has run into the forest to hide.' Sepoo was gabbling it out to prevent Pamba from getting in before him. 'And the government *wazungu* at Sengi-Sengi have offered Pirri, my brother, vast treasure and reward to hunt the man and kill him.'

Kelly stared at him in horror.

'Kill him?' she blurted. 'They want Pirri to kill him?'

'And cut off his head,' Sepoo confirmed with relish. 'Is it not strange and exciting?'

'You have to stop him!' Kelly sprang to her feet, dragging Sepoo up with her. 'You must not let Pirri kill him. You must rescue the white man and bring him here to Gondala. Do you hear me, Sepoo? Go, now! Go swiftly! You must stop Pirri.'

'I will go with him to see that he does what you tell him, Kara-Ki,' Pamba announced. 'For he is a stupid old man, and if he hears the honey chameleon whistle or meets one of his cronies in the forest, he will forget everything you have told him.' She turned to her husband. 'Come on, old man.' She prodded him with her thumb. 'Let us go and find this white *wazungu* and bring him back to Kára-Ki. Let us go before Pirri kills him and takes his head to Sengi-Sengi.'

Pirri the hunter went down on one knee in the forest and examined the tracks. He adjusted the hang of the bow on his shoulder and shook his head with reluctant admiration.

'He knows that I am here, close behind him,' he whispered. 'How does he know that? Unless of course he is one of the *fundis*.'

He touched the spoor where the *wazungu* had left the water. He had done it with great skill, leaving only traces that someone as good as Pirri could detect.

'Yes, you know I am following you,' Pirri nodded. 'But where did you learn to move and cover your tracks almost as well as a Bambuti?' he muttered.

He had picked up the *wazungu*'s tracks where he had crossed the broad road that the big yellow earth-eating tree-gobbling machine had left through the forest. The earth there was soft and the *wazungu* had left tracks that a blind man could follow on a dark night. He was heading westwards towards the mountains, as Chetti Singh had said he would.

Pirri thought immediately that it would be an easy hunt and a quick kill, especially when he had found where the *wazungu* had broken off a piece of poisonous fungus from a dead tree and eaten a little of it. He found the man's teeth marks in the piece of fungus that he had discarded, and Pirri laughed. 'Your bowels will turn to water and run like the great river, O stupid *wazungu*. And I will kill you while you squat to shit.'

Sure enough, he had found the place where the *wazungu* had slept the previous night and close by where he had voided his bowels for the first time. 'You will not go far now,' he chuckled, 'before I catch you and kill you.'

Pirri glided onwards, softly as a wisp of dark smoke blending with the gloom and shadows and sombre colours of the deep forest, following the easy trail at twice the speed of the man who had laid it. At intervals he found dribbles of his poisoned yellow dung, and then the trail reached the bank of a small stream and went into the water and vanished.

Pirri worked for almost half a day, casting both banks for a mile both upstream and down before he found where the *wazungu* had left the water again.

'You are clever,' he conceded. 'But not as clever as Pirri.' And he took the spoor again, going slowly now, for the man he was following was good. He laid back trails and false sign and used the water, and Pirri had to unravel each of his tricks, frowning while he worked it out and then grinning with approbation. 'Ah yes, you will be a worthy one to kill. You would long ago have got clean away from a lesser hunter. But I am Pirri.'

In the late afternoon of the second day he had reached a clearing and he caught his first glimpse of the *wazungu*. At first he thought it was one of the rare forest antelope on the opposite hillside. He caught just a tiny flicker of movement in one of the forest glades, almost a mile distant across the valley. For an instant even Pirri's phenomenal eyesight was cheated. It did not seem to be a man, certainly not a white man, and then as he disappeared into the tall trees at the edge of the forest he realised that the man had covered himself with mud from head to foot and wore a hat of bark and leaves which distorted the outline of his head and made it difficult to make out his human shape.

'Ha!' Pirri rubbed his belly with delight and granted himself another small pinch of tobacco under his upper lip to reward himself for the sighting. 'Yes, you are good, my *wazungu*. Even I will not be able to catch you before darkness falls, but in the morning your head will be mine.'

That night Pirri slept without a fire at the edge of the clearing where last he had seen the white man, and was moving again just as soon as it was light enough to make out the sign.

In the middle of the morning he found the *wazungu*. He was lying at the foot of one of the towering African mahogany trees and at first Pirri thought he was already dead. He had tried to cover himself with dead leaves, a pathetic last effort to thwart the remorseless little hunter.

Pirri moved in very slowly, taking every precaution, trusting nothing. He carried his broad-bladed machete ready in his right hand, and the weapon was honed to a razor edge.

When at last he stood over Daniel Armstrong he realised that although he was sick and wasted, he was not yet dead. He was unconscious, breathing with a soft bubbling sound in the back of his throat, curled like a sick dog under the blanket of leaf trash. His head was tilted at an angle, and the sweat had washed away the mud camouflage below his jaw line, leaving a white line. A perfect aiming mark for the decapitating stroke.

Pirri tested the edge of the blade of the machete with his thumb. It was sharp enough to shave his beard. He lifted it high above his head with both hands. The man's neck was no thicker than that of one of the forest duikers which were Pirri's usual prey. The machete would hack through meat and bone just as readily, and the head would spring away from the trunk with the same startling alacrity. He would hang it by its thick curly hair from a branch for an hour or so, to allow the blood to drain from the severed neck, then he would smoke it over a slow fire of green leaves and herbs to preserve it, before slinging it in a small carrying net of bark string and bearing it back to his poaching master, Chetti Singh, to collect his reward.

Pirri felt a little cold gust of regret as he paused at the top of his stroke before sending the blade hissing down. Because he was a true hunter he always experienced this sadness for his quarry at the moment of the kill, the creed of his tribe was to respect and honour the animals he killed, especially when the quarry had been cunning and brave and worthy.

Die swiftly, he made his silent entreaty.

He was on the point of slashing downwards when a voice said quietly behind him, 'Hold your blade, my brother, or I will put this poison arrow through your liver.'

Pirri was so startled that he leapt in the air and whirled to face about.

Sepoo was five paces behind him. His bow was arched and

the arrow was drawn to his cheek, the poison on the tip of the arrow was black and sticky as toffee and it was pointed unwaveringly at Pirri's chest.

'You are my own brother!' Pirri gasped with the shock. 'You are the fruit of my own mother's womb. You would not let your arrow fly?'

'If you believe that, Pirri, my brother, you are even more stupid than I believe you to be. Kara-Ki wants this white *wazungu* alive. If you tap a single drop of his blood, I will put this arrow through you, from brisket to backbone.'

'And I,' said Pamba his wife from the forest shadows behind him, 'I will sing and dance around you as you lie writhing on the ground.'

Pirri backed away sharply. He knew he could talk Sepoo into or out of almost anything, but not Pamba. He had a vast respect for and healthy fear of his sister-in-law.

'They have offered me great treasure to kill this *wazungu*.' His voice was shrill. 'I will share it equally with you. As much tobacco as you can carry! I will give it to you.'

'Shoot him in the belly,' ordered Pamba cheerfully, and Sepoo's arm trembled with the strain of his draw as he closed one eye to correct his aim.

'Wait,' shrieked Pirri. 'I love you, my dear sister; you would not allow this old idiot to kill me.'

'I am going to take a little snuff,' said Pamba coldly. 'If you are still here when I finish sneezing . . .'

'I am going,' howled Pirri, and took another dozen paces backwards. 'I am going.' He ducked into the undergrowth and the instant he was out of the line of fire he screamed, 'You foul old monkey woman . . .'

They could hear him slashing out with his machete at the bushes around him in fury and frustration. 'Only a decrepit venereal baboon like Sepoo would marry a drooling old hag . . .'

The sounds of his ranting fury gradually diminished as he retreated into the forest and Sepoo lowered his bow and turned to his wife.

'I haven't enjoyed myself so much since the day Pirri fell into his own trap on top of the buffalo that was already in the pit!' he guffawed. 'But he described you well, my lovely wife.'

Pamba ignored him and went to where Daniel Armstrong lay unconscious, half buried in dirt and dead leaves. She knelt beside him and examined him quickly but thoroughly, plucking the ants from the corners of his eyes and his nostrils.

'I will have to work hard to save him for Kari-Ki,' she said as she reached into her medicine bag. 'If I lose this one, I don't know where I will find another one for her.'

While Pamba ministered to Daniel, Sepoo built a hut over him where he lay and then lit a little fire to disperse the mosquitoes and the humidity. He squatted in the doorway and watched his wife work.

She was the most skilled medicine woman of all the Bambuti, and her fingers were swift and dextrous as she cleaned the wound in the *wazungu*'s back and applied a poultice of mashed and boiled roots and leaves. Then she forced him to drink copious quantities of a hot infusion of herbs that would bind his bowels and replace the fluid that his body had shed.

She crooned and muttered encouragement to the unconscious man as she worked, her bare dugs swinging wrinkled and empty as a pair of leather tobacco pouches from her bony chest and her necklace of ivory and beads clicking each time she moved.

Within three hours Daniel had regained consciousness. He looked up dazedly at the two little old people crouched over him in the smoky hut and asked in Swahili, 'Who are you?'

'I am Sepoo,' said the man. 'A famous hunter and a renowned sage of the Bambuti.'

'And I am Pamba, the wife of the greatest liar in all the forest of Ubomo,' said the woman, and cackled with laughter.

By the next morning Daniel's diarrhoea had dried up and he could eat a little of the stew of monkey meat and herbs that Pamba had prepared for him. By the following morning the infection of the wound in his back had abated and he was strong enough to begin the journey to Gondala.

Daniel went slowly at first, using a staff to steady himself, for his legs were still wobbly and his head seemed to be filled with wool and floating clear of his shoulders. Pamba kept him company, leading him at a gentle pace through the forest and keeping up a constant chattering punctuated with shrieks of merry laughter, Sepoo ranged afar hunting and scavenging in the usual Bambuti manner.

Daniel had already guessed the identity of the mysterious Kara-Ki who had sent the pygmies to rescue him, but as soon as Pamba gave him an opportunity he questioned her further, trying to get her to describe her patron in detail.

'Kara-Ki is very tall,' Pamba told him, and Daniel realised that to a Bambuti everybody else in the world is very tall. 'And she has a long pointed nose.'

All Bambuti noses were flat and broad. Pamba's description could apply to any *wazungu*, so Daniel gave up and hobbled on after the little woman.

Towards dusk Sepoo suddenly appeared again from the forest with the carcass of a duiker he had killed hanging over his shoulder. That night they feasted on grilled liver and fillets. The next morning Daniel was strong enough to discard his staff and Pamba increased the pace of the march.

They reached Gondala the following afternoon. The pygmies had given Daniel no warning that they had arrived, and as he stepped out of the forest he was presented with the dramatic view of the little community. Its open gardens and streams, and the high snow-capped mountains forming a grand backdrop to the scene.

'Daniel,' Kelly Kinnear greeted him as he climbed the verandah steps, and even though he had half expected it, Daniel was unprepared for his own pleasure at meeting her again. She looked fresh and vital and attractive, but he sensed a reserve in her as she came to him and shook his hand. 'I was so worried that Sepoo might not get to you in time . . .' Then she broke off and stood back. 'God, you look awful. What on earth happened to you?'

'Thanks for the compliment,' he grinned ruefully. 'But to answer your question – a great deal has happened to me since we last met.'

'Come into the surgery. Let's have a look at you, before we do anything else.'

'Couldn't I have a bath first? I find it difficult even being near myself.'

She laughed. 'You are rather strong on the nose, but so are most of my patients. I'm used to it.'

She took him into the surgery and laid him on the examination table. After she had gone over him thoroughly and inspected the wound on his back, she remarked, 'Pamba has done a pretty good job. I'll give you a shot of antibiotic and I'll put a fresh dressing on your back after your bath. It should have had stitches but it's too late for that now. You'll have a new interesting scar to add to all the others.'

As she washed her hands in the basin, she smiled at him over her shoulder. 'You look as though you've been in a fight or two.'

'Always the other guy's fault,' he assured her. 'Talking about fights, you never let me explain myself at our last meeting. You jumped on your motorbike before I had a chance.'

'I know. It's my Irish blood.'

'Can I explain now?'

'How about a bath first?'

The bathroom was a thatched hut, and the bath was a galvanised iron tub just large enough to contain him if he kept his knees up under his chin. The camp servants filled it with buckets of steaming water heated on the fire outside. There was clothing laid out for him: khaki shorts and shirt, faded and worn but clean and crisply ironed, together with a pair of rawhide sandals. One of the servants took away his stinking blood-stained shorts and muddy boots.

Kelly was waiting for him in her surgery when he had dressed.

'What a transformation,' she greeted him. 'Let's fix that back.'

He sat on the single chair and she stood behind him. Her fingers were cool and light and quick on his skin. When she spoke he could feel her breath on the back of his neck and smell her. He liked the feel of her hands and the sweet clean smell of her breath.

'I didn't thank you for sending your pygmies to save my life,' he said.

'All in the day's work. Think nothing of it.'

'I owe you one.'

'I'll call on you.'

'You were the very last person I'd have expected to find here,' Daniel told her. 'But when Pamba described you I began to suspect who you were. How did you get into the country? And what the hell are you doing here? If Taffari gets hold of you it will be a shooting party on the beach or a head-dress of hornets.'

'Oh, so you're beginning to find out the truth about Ephrem Taffari, that he's not the saint and saviour you thought he was?'

'Don't let's fight again,' he pleaded. 'I'm still too weak to defend myself.'

'You're as weak as a bull. Look at all that muscle. Okay, now it's time for your shot. Lie on the bed and drop your shorts.'

'Hey! Can't I have it in the arm?'

'You haven't got anything I haven't seen before. Get on the table.'

Grumbling he lay face down, and lowered his shorts halfway.

'Nothing to be ashamed of, in fact, not bad at all,' she assured him, and slid the needle home. 'Okay, that does it. Get dressed and come to dinner. I've got another surprise for you. A dinner guest, somebody you haven't seen for years.'

In the sunset they crossed from the clinic to Kelly's living quarters at the end of the clearing. On the way they stopped for a minute to watch the sunset turn the Mountains of the Moon to a splendour of gold and flames.

'I carry the memory of this beauty wherever I travel in the world,' Kelly whispered. 'It's one of the things that draws me back.'

And Daniel was moved as much by her reaction to it as by the grandeur of the scene itself. To express his accord with her he wanted to take her arm and squeeze it, but he kept his distance and after a while they moved on.

There was a dinner-table laid on the verandah of Kelly's bungalow and a solitary figure seated at it, who rose as they approached.

'Doctor Armstrong. How good to see you again.'

Daniel stared at him in astonishment and then hurried forward. 'I heard that you were dead, Mr President, that you had died of a heart-attack or been shot by Taffari.'

'The news of my death was slightly exaggerated.' Victor Omeru chuckled and took Daniel's hand.

'I found a flask of whisky in my medical chest,' Kelly said. 'Tonight seems like an auspicious occasion to administer it.' She poured a little of the golden liquid into each of their glasses and offered them the toast. 'To Ubomo! May it soon be released from the tyrant.'

Dinner was a simple meal of fish from the river and vegetables from the gardens of Gondala, but there was plenty of it and the conversation at the table never slackened or palled.

Victor Omeru explained to Daniel all the circumstances of the revolution and his overthrow, his escape into the forest and his activities since then.

'With Kelly's help, I have been able to turn Gondala into the headquarters of the resistance to Taffari's brutal dictatorship,' he ended, but Kelly pressed him eagerly.

'Victor, tell Daniel what Taffari has done to the country and its people since he seized power. Daniel has been duped into believing that Taffari is a black Christ figure. In fact, Daniel is here to shoot a production that was to extol Taffari's virtues . . .'

'No, Kelly,' Daniel interrupted her. 'That's not the way it was. It's far more complicated than that. Originally I accepted the commission to make the film for personal and private reasons.' He went on to explain the murder of Johnny Nzou and his family. He told them of Ning Cheng Gong's involvement and how he had traced the Lucky Dragon to Ubomo. He told them about Chetti Singh.

'I'll be frank with you both,' he said at last. 'I wasn't concerned with Taffari and Ubomo's real problems when I came here. I wanted my revenge and the film contract was only a means to that end. Then, after my arrival, I began to find out more about what was really going on in the country . . .'

He told them about the atrocity at Fish Eagle Bay and the forced labour he had witnessed and filmed. Victor Omeru and

Kelly exchanged glances, and then Victor nodded and turned back to Daniel.

'Taffari has seized at least thirty thousand of the Uhali people to work in the mines and the logging camps. They are slaves, kept in the most appalling conditions. They are dying like flies in the camps, starved, beaten, shot. I cannot begin to describe to you the horror of it.'

'And he is devastating the forest,' Kelly cut in. 'He is destroying millions of acres of the rain forest.'

'I saw the mining unit at work,' Daniel said. 'Actually, what he is doing there at least is in line with my own convictions on controlled use of a country's natural assets on a renewable and sustainable yield basis.'

Both Kelly and Victor stared at him in disbelief, and then Kelly blurted out angrily, 'You approve of what he is doing to the forest? Are you out of your mind? It's rape and pillage. I was right about you the first time! You *are* one of the plunderers!'

'Hold it, Kelly.' Victor held up his hands. 'Don't use inflammatory language. Let Daniel tell us what he saw and what he filmed.'

With an obvious effort Kelly brought herself under control, but she was still pale with anger and her eyes blazed.

'All right, Daniel Armstrong, tell us what Taffari showed you and let you film.'

'He showed me the MOMU unit at work . . .'

'*The* MOMU,' Kelly interjected. 'MOMU *singular*—'

'Kelly, please.' Victor stopped her again. 'Let Daniel finish before you interrupt.' She was breathing heavily, but she nodded and sat back as Daniel went on.

'Bonny and I filmed the MOMU and Taffari explained how the track of the vehicle would be replanted after it had passed.'

'Replanted!' Kelly snapped, and Victor shrugged helplessly and let her continue. 'My God! Did he tell you about the chemical reagents they've started using in the past few weeks to refine the platinum as it passes through the tube mills of the MOMU?'

'No.' Daniel shook his head. 'He told us of his determination that no reagents nor catalysts were to be used during the

444

mining process. Even though it meant a forty per cent drop in the production of platinum and monazite.'

'And you believed him?' Kelly demanded.

'I saw it with my own eyes,' Daniel told her. He was starting to get angry. 'I filmed it. Of course I believed him.'

Kelly jumped up from the table and fetched a map of Ubomo from the next room. She spread it in front of Daniel.

'Show me where you saw the MOMU in action,' she ordered. Daniel considered the map and then placed his finger on a spot just north of Sengi-Sengi.

'Hereabouts,' he said. 'A few miles north of the camp.'

'Sucker!' Kelly blazed at him. 'Taffari set you up. He showed you the pilot scheme. It was a little show for your benefit. The main mining operation is here.' She placed her fist over an area fifty miles further north. 'Here at Wengu. And it's a damned sight different from what Taffari showed you.'

'How is it different?' Daniel demanded. 'And by the way, I don't like being called a sucker.'

'You let yourself be conned.' Kelly moderated her tone. 'But I'll tell you how the main operation is different from the pilot. First of all, it is—'

'Hold on, Kelly,' Victor Omeru intervened gently. 'Don't tell him about it. It would be much more impressive, and he'd be more likely to believe you if you showed him.'

For a moment Kelly stared at Victor and then she nodded. 'You're right, Victor. I'll take him up to Wengu and show him. And while we are there, you can film just what that bastard is doing to the forest, and show it to your great pal Sir Tug Bloody Harrison, if he doesn't know already.'

'I'm not a cameraman,' Daniel objected.

'If you don't know how to use a VTR after being around them for so many years, then you aren't very bright, Doctor Daniel.'

'All right, I could use a camera. Not very artistically but adequately, if only I had one. Where do you suggest I find a VTR in the middle of the forest?'

'What happened to the one your red-haired girlfriend had?' Kelly demanded.

'Bonny isn't my girlfriend. You're a great one for hurling

445

accusations,' he began, and then broke off and stared at Kelly. 'Damn it!' he said. 'You're right. I left the VTR in the Land-rover. If Taffari's lads haven't found it yet, then it's still there.'

'Why don't you go back and fetch it?' Kelly enquired sweetly. 'I'll send Sepoo with you.'

'I have brought you the head of the white *wazungu*,' Pirri, the hunter, announced dramatically and unslung the net bag of plaited bark fibre from his shoulder and dropped it in front of Chetti Singh.

The head rolled out of the bag and Chetti Singh jumped back and exclaimed with revulsion. There was no skin left on the head. The raw meat was putrefying and the stench was fierce enough to make him gag.

'How do I know that this is the head of the white *wazungu*?' Chetti Singh demanded.

'Because I, Pirri the hunter, say it is so.'

'That's not the highest recommendation, never mind,' Chetti Singh said in English, and then reverted to Swahili. 'This man has been dead a long time; the ants and the worms have half eaten him. You did not kill him, Pirri.'

'No,' Pirri admitted. 'This stupid *wazungu* had eaten a poison mushroom and died in the forest before I could find him and kill him. The ants had eaten him, as you say, but I have brought you his head, and that was our bargain.' Pirri mustered all his dignity and drew himself up to his full four foot six inches. 'Now you must give me what you promised me, especially the tobacco.'

It was a long and forlorn hope. Even Pirri realised that. To obtain this head Pirri had exhumed one of the mass graves that the Hita guards had dug in the forest for the corpses of the slave labourers who died in the camps.

'You are certain that this is the head of the white *wazungu*?' Chetti Singh demanded. He did not believe the pygmy, but on the other hand he had to placate both Ning Cheng Gong and

President Taffari. He dared not admit to them that there was a possibility that Armstrong had escaped. Pirri was offering him an easy exit from his dilemma.

'It is the *wazungu*,' Pirri affirmed, and Chetti Singh thought about it for a while.

'Take this ...' he touched the reeking head with his toe, 'take it back into the forest and bury it.'

'What about my reward? Especially the tobacco?' Pirri's tone became an ingratiating whine.

'You did not bring me the whole head. The skin and hair were missing. Therefore I cannot give you the whole reward. And I will give it to you only when you bring me the teeth of the elephant, as we agreed.'

Pirri let out a shout of anger and drew his machete.

'Put that knife away,' said Chetti Singh reasonably. 'Or I will shoot your head off with this.' He showed the pygmy the Tokarev pistol concealed in the pocket of his bush jacket.

Pirri's scowl became a beatific smile. 'It was only a little joke, O master. I am your slave.' And he sheathed the machete. 'I will go and fetch the teeth of the elephant as you command.' He picked up the severed head. But as he skipped away into the forest Pirri's guts and chest were filled with so much anger that he thought they might burst.

'Nobody cheats Pirri,' he whispered, and slashed at a tree-trunk with the machete as he ran. 'Pirri will kill the man who cheats him,' he promised. 'You want a head, O one-armed and greasy man. I will give you a head. Your own.'

'Daniel Armstrong is dead,' Chetti Singh told them. 'The Bambuti brought me his head. He died in the forest.'

'There can be no doubt?' President Taffari demanded.

'None at all,' Chetti Singh affirmed. 'I saw the head with my personal eyes.'

'That means the woman is the only living witness.' Ning Cheng Gong looked relieved. 'You should get rid of her immediately, Your Excellency. She should disappear in the forest, just the way that Armstrong did.'

Ephrem Taffari picked up his empty glass and rattled the ice cubes. Captain Kajo hurried across the room and took the glass from his hand. At the small bar in the corner of the president's office he poured gin and tonic.

'Aren't you forgetting the videotape?' Taffari asked, as Kajo respectfully handed him the drink.

'Of course not,' Cheng said. 'But once she has recovered the tape from the embassy we must get rid of her.' He hesitated. 'I could arrange that personally.'

Ephrem Taffari smiled at him over the rim of the glass. 'Ah, yes.' He nodded. 'I have heard that you have a rather unusual hobby, Mr Ning.'

'I am not quite sure what you are implying, Mr President,' he answered stiffly. 'I was merely offering to make certain that the job was done properly. We don't want any more loose ends.'

'Quite right, Mr Ning,' Taffari agreed. 'The woman is becoming a bore. I have lost interest in her. Once we have recovered the tape, she is yours. Just make certain that there are no mistakes.'

'Trust me, Mr President.'

'Oh yes, Mr Ning, I trust you just as completely as you trust me. After all, we are partners, are we not?'

 'My arrangement with Danny was that he would pick it up personally.' Sir Michael Hargreave inspected his fingernails with some interest and then placed his hand in his pocket and went to the window of his office in the British embassy. He looked out over the lake. 'Daniel didn't say anything about handing it over to a third party. You must understand my position, Miss – ah – Miss Mahon.'

The punkah fan on the ceiling squeaked and whirled and Bonny thought quickly. She knew that she must not appear too eager, even though she was acutely aware of what the consequences might be if she returned to Ephrem empty-handed.

'I didn't realise it would be a problem.' She stood up. 'Danny asked me to pick it up. He'll probably be bitter with me for not bringing it back, but I don't imagine the tape is of any real importance. I'm sorry I didn't think to ask Danny for a note. Anyway, thank you for your time and I'll explain to Danny that you couldn't see your way clear to handing the tape to me.'

She held out her hand and gave him her sexiest smile, thrusting out her bosom. Sir Michael's gaze wavered from her eyes, and then he seemed to make up his mind.

'Look here, I suppose it will be all right. I mean, you are Danny's assistant. Not as though you were a total stranger . . .' He hesitated.

'I don't want you to do anything you feel is not right,' Bonny told him. 'I'm sure Danny will understand that you didn't trust me.'

'Good Lord, my dear young lady, it isn't a case of not trusting you.'

'Oh, that's what I thought it was.' She fluttered her eyelids at him.

'Would you mind signing a receipt? Sorry to be so awkward, but I must cover myself with Danny.'

'I understand, Sir Michael.'

He scribbled out a receipt on a sheet of the embassy stationery and she signed it and wrote out her full name and passport number at the foot of the page.

Sir Michael went into the adjoining room and she heard him put a key into a lock and then the metallic sound of the door lugs of a steel safe opening and closing. A few minutes later he returned and handed her a bulky manila envelope with Daniel's name printed on it. She tried not to make her relief apparent, but her hand shook as he handed it to her.

'Please give Danny my best salaams.' Sir Michael walked her to the front door of the embassy. 'When is he coming back from Sengi-Sengi?'

'I'm flying up to join him this afternoon . . .'

Bonny had her nerves under control and chatted easily. They shook hands at the door.

'Having one of our regular cocktail parties next Saturday,'

Sir Michael said. 'If you and Danny are back in town by then, you must come along. I'll have Miss Rogers send you an invitation to the guest house.'

The news of Daniel Armstrong's disappearance had not yet been reported to the embassy. Ephrem Taffari wanted all the loose ends tidied up before the alarm was raised.

Bonny went out to where Captain Kajo was waiting at the wheel of an army Landrover. She clutched the envelope in her lap, but managed another smile and wave for Sir Michael as they pulled out of the embassy gates.

Then she let out a deep breath and fell back against the seat.

'President Taffari is waiting for you on his yacht, Miss Mahon,' Captain Kajo told her, and took the lakeside road down to the harbour.

The yacht was moored at the naval jetty beyond the fish factory. The vessel had been the toy of a wealthy Asian business-man, one of those whom Taffari had deported and sent back to the United Kingdom when he came to power. Of course, he had confiscated all the Asian's property, and this vessel was now the presidential yacht.

It was a forty-five-foot Camper and Nicholson with lovely lines, equipped with every luxury, although most of the electronic equipment had long ago failed and had not been replaced, and the paintwork and sails were no longer pristine. However, the bar was well stocked and since the yacht very seldom left its berth, the lack of navigational and sailing gear was not critical.

There were two men in the main cabin, seated at the red teak saloon table facing each other.

President Taffari was perusing the monthly operating report and profit-and-loss accounts of UDC, smiling and nodding as he did so. Ning Cheng Gong was watching him expectantly. When Taffari lowered the document and looked up, Cheng answered his smile.

'I am impressed, Mr Ning. It is only a very short time since you arrived in Ubomo to take control of the company, but the results are really quite spectacular.'

'You are very gracious, Your Excellency.' Cheng bowed slightly. 'But I can truthfully say that I expect an even greater improvement in the months ahead. There were many problems that my English predecessor left for me, but these are being resolved.'

'What about the vehicle maintenance depot? This is one of my major areas of concern.' Taffari's smile faded.

'And rightly so, Mr President. We have over a thousand heavy vehicles in service, not counting the actual MOMU installations. Our maintenance costs were running at over three million dollars a month when I took over. As you can see, I have managed to reduce these by almost forty per cent . . .'

Their discussion lasted another hour before there were footsteps on the deck outside and a polite knock on the cabin door.

'Who is it?' Taffari called.

'Captain Kajo, Mr President, and Miss Mahon.'

Taffari glanced at Cheng significantly and the Chinaman nodded. This was the reason that the meeting was being held on board the yacht, rather than in the boardroom at Lake House.

'Come in!' Taffari ordered, and the door slid aside. Kajo stooped his long frame into the cabin and saluted awkwardly.

'I have Miss Mahon waiting in the Landrover on the dock,' he reported.

'Did she pick up the packet?' Taffari asked anxiously.

'Yes, sir. She has it with her.'

Again Taffari and Cheng exchanged glances, but now both of them were smiling again.

'All right, Captain.' Taffari nodded. 'You have your orders.'

'Yes, Mr President. I am to accompany Mr Ning and Miss Mahon on the expedition to Lamu Island and I am to—'

'No need to repeat them, Captain,' Taffari interrupted. 'Just carry them out to the letter. Now you may bring Miss Mahon aboard.'

She burst into the cabin and went directly to Ephrem Taffari, ignoring the other man at the table.

'I've got it, Ephrem,' she gloated. 'Here it is.' She laid the envelope in front of him and he picked it up, tore it open and shook out the video cassette.

'Are you sure this is the one?'

'Yes, that's my notation on the label. My handwriting. It's the one, all right.'

'Well done. I am extremely pleased with you,' Taffari told her. 'Come and sit beside me, my dear.'

She accepted the offer with alacrity and Taffari laid his hand on her thigh below the table-top.

'Captain Kajo,' Taffari ordered. 'There is a bottle of champagne in the refrigerator. This calls for a celebration.'

Kajo went to the bar and busied himself with the bottle. The cork popped and a little froth gushed on to the carpet. It was Australian rather than French, but none of them complained. Kajo turned back to the bar, screening the row of glasses on the bar top while he poured the wine. He gave Bonny her glass first, and then served the others in order of their seniority.

Taffari lifted his glass towards Bonny. 'To you, my dear. You have saved me and my country from a potentially damaging situation.'

'Thank you, Mr President.' Bonny took a mouthful of the champagne. She noticed but did not remark on the slightly bitter aftertaste, for she had learned not to give him the least pretext for offence. And when Kajo refilled her glass, she drank it without question. The unpleasant taste was less noticeable now.

'I thought we might go for a sunset cruise on the lake,' Taffari told her, and Bonny smiled at him but her cheeks felt strangely numb.

'That would be fun,' she tried to say, but it came out slurred and jumbled. Bonny broke off and stared at them. Their faces were receding and there was a ringing sound in her head. It became louder and her vision was darkening. There was only a tiny hole in the centre of the blackness in which she could see Ephrem's face, as though through the reverse end of a telescope, small and remote.

His voice boomed and echoed in her drugged brain. 'Goodbye, my dear,' he said, and her head dropped forward on to the table-top.

There was silence in the cabin for a full minute after Bonny Mahon had collapsed. Then President Taffari gathered his papers and placed them in his briefcase. He stood up and Kajo hurried to open the door for him. Taffari paused in the doorway and looked back. Ning Cheng Gong was still seated opposite the unconscious girl. He was watching her with a strange pale intensity.

At the head of the gangplank Taffari paused to talk to Captain Kajo. 'Make sure the yacht is washed down thoroughly before you bring her back to port. You know how to use the pressure hose?'

'I do, Your Excellency.'

Taffari went down the gangplank to his Mercedes and Kajo stood to attention and saluted as he drove away.

The yacht's diesel engine was already running, the exhausts bubbling softly under the stern. Kajo cast off the lines and went to the wheel. He eased the yacht away from the jetty and turned her bows towards the harbour entrance.

It was a two-hour run out to Lamu Island, and the sun had already set when he dropped anchor in the lee of the uninhabited horseshoe-shaped rock.

'We have arrived, Mr Ning,' he said into the voice tube.

'Help me, please, Captain.'

Kajo went down into the cabin. Bonny Mahon was lying, still unconscious, on the carpeted deck. Between them they carried her up into the open cockpit and while Kajo held her upright Ning strapped her wrists and ankles to the stainless steel railings. He spread a nylon sheet under her with the end hanging over the stern, to make it easier to hose down the deck later.

'I don't need any further assistance,' he told Kajo. 'Take the rubber dinghy and go ashore on the island. Stay there until I call you. No matter what you may hear you will remain ashore. Do you understand?'

'Yes, Mr Ning.'

Cheng stood by the stern rail and watched Kajo in the stern of the dinghy disappear into the darkness. The little three hp outboard puttered softly, and the beam of Kajo's flashlight threw an erratic beam in the darkness. At last he reached the island and the outboard motor cut out into silence. The flashlight was extinguished.

Cheng turned back to the girl. She sagged against her bonds. She looked very pale in the cockpit lights and her hair was an untidy copper bush.

Cheng took a few moments longer to savour the moment. Physically the woman was unattractive to him, and she was much older than he liked, but none the less he felt his excitement mounting. Soon he would be so absorbed and transported that such small adverse considerations would be of no account.

He looked around him carefully, taking his time, considering the circumstances. Lamu Island was twelve miles from the mainland and the lake crocodiles infested the waters around it. They would immediately devour any offal that was dropped overboard. On top of which he was under the protection of President Taffari.

He went back to the girl and adjusted the tourniquet around her upper arm, massaging the veins in the inside of her elbow until they stood out thick and blue in the cockpit lights. He had used the drug on many previous occasions, and he kept the antidote and disposable syringe available at all times.

Only seconds after he injected the antidote, Bonny Mahon opened her eyes and peered at him groggily.

'Good evening, Miss Mahon.' Cheng's voice was throaty with excitement. 'You and I are going to have a little fun together.'

There had been an almost immediate *rapport* between Daniel and Sepoo. It was strange for in every way they were completely different: in size and colour and shape and mentality there was no similarity whatsoever.

It had to be a thing of the spirit, Daniel decided as he followed Sepoo through the forest. They were children of Africa, its pulse beat in both of them, its soul was their soul. They understood and loved this land's beauty and savagery and treasured its bounty. They understood and loved its creatures and counted themselves merely one amongst this multitude of species.

When they camped that night they sat close to each other beside the fire and talked quietly. Sepoo spoke to him of the secrets and the mystery of the forest and the deeply felt beliefs of his people, and Daniel understood. In some measure they were his beliefs too and he accepted the reasons for the customs of these people as Sepoo explained them, and admired the wisdom and virtue of their lore. Sepoo called him 'Kuokoa', which meant 'The one I rescued'. Daniel accepted the name, even though he knew it was meant as a monument to Sepoo's deed and a reminder of his debt to the old man.

They came to the MOMU track through the forest near Sengi-Sengi in the late afternoon and lay up at the forest edge until it was dark. Then they crossed the open ground in the night.

Sepoo led Daniel to the logging road where he had abandoned the Landrover almost ten days previously but even Sepoo could not lead him directly to the stranded vehicle. It was only the following day that they at last found the Landrover exactly as Daniel had left it behind its screen of dense undergrowth, sunk to its axles in the soft forest floor.

There were no fresh human tracks around it and the video equipment was still in its aluminium carrying cases. Daniel laid it out on the tailboard of the vehicle and checked it quickly. The camera was not working. Either the batteries were flat after standing so long, or else the moisture had penetrated the mechanism. Daniel noticed droplets behind the glass of the lens and condensation beaded the casing.

It was a bitter disappointment, but Daniel could only hope that the batteries could still be recharged or that a rudimentary cleaning and drying, once he reached Gondala, would get the camera serviceable again. He gave Sepoo the case of cassettes to carry while he took for himself the camera, the lens and the spare battery packs, a burden of almost seventy pounds to lug through the steaming forest.

Heavily laden as he was, the return took almost twice as long as the outward march and it rained most of the time. As soon as he reached Gondala, Daniel recruited Victor Omeru's assistance. He knew that Victor was a qualified electrical engineer.

Victor had built and installed a turbine generator beneath the waterfall at the head of the Gondala glade. It generated 220 volts and almost ten kilowatts of power, sufficient to supply the community with lighting and to operate Kelly's laboratory equipment.

So Victor was able to place the battery packs for the video on charge and found only one of them was defective. The camera and the lens were a different problem altogether. Daniel would not have known where to begin to look for the fault, but Victor stripped the camera and cleaned the condensed moisture. He checked the circuits and found one of the transistors was blown. He replaced it with one that he cannibalised from Kelly's gas spectroscope. Within twenty-four hours he had the VTR functioning again, then he took down the lenses and cleaned and dried them out and reassembled them.

Daniel realised just what a difficult task the old man had undertaken in such primitive conditions.

'If you never get your country back, I've always got a job for you, sir,' he told Victor.

'That's not such a good idea,' Kelly warned him. 'You'd probably end up working for him.'

'All right,' Daniel said. 'I've got a camera. Now what do you want me to film?'

'We leave tomorrow morning at first light,' Kelly told him.

'I'm coming along, Kelly,' Victor Omeru told her.

'I don't think that is very wise, Victor.' She looked dubious. 'You're much too valuable.'

'After all my hard work, I deserve a little reward, don't you think?' He turned to Daniel. 'Besides which, you might have another breakdown in the equipment. Come on, Doctor Armstrong, put in a good word for me.'

'Chauvinists, both of you,' Kelly protested. 'You're ganging up on me just because I am a female. I'll have to call Pamba to my aid.'

'Hell no!' Daniel shook his head. 'That is using too much gun!' But he shared Kelly's misgivings. Victor Omeru was over seventy years of age and the going would be tough. It was almost fifty miles to Wengu. He was about to say so when Victor intervened quietly.

'Seriously, Ubomo is my country. I cannot rely on second-hand reports. I have to see for myself what Taffari is doing to my people and my land.'

Neither of them could argue with that, and when the safari started out from Gondala the following morning, Victor Omeru was with them.

Sepoo had recruited eight men from his clan to act as porters and Pamba appointed herself as caravan manager to make certain that they applied themselves and did not lose interest in the typical Bambuti fashion, dropping their bundles to wander off fishing or honey hunting. Every man in the clan stood in awe of Pamba's tongue.

On the third day they reached the first of the bleeding rivers and the Bambuti men lowered their loads to the ground and huddled on the bank. There was no laughter nor banter. Even Pamba was silent and subdued.

Daniel climbed down into the stinking morass of red mud, dead animals and poisoned vegetation, and scooped a handful of it. He sniffed it and then threw it from him and tried to wipe the filth from his hands.

'What is it, Kelly?' He looked up at her on the bank above him. 'What caused this?'

'It's the reagent that Taffari swore to you that he would never use.' She was dressed only in a cotton T-shirt and shorts with a coloured headband around her brow, and her small neat body seemed to quiver with outrage.

'Victor and I have been monitoring the effluent from the mining operation. At first it was pure mud. That was bad enough. Then recently, in the last few weeks, there's been a change. They have begun using a reagent. You see, the platinum molecules are coated with sulphides. The sulphides reduce the efficiency of the recovery process by forty per cent. They are using a reagent to dissolve the sulphide coating and to free the platinum.'

'What does the reagent consist of?' Daniel demanded.

'Arsenic.' She spat the word like an angry cat. 'They are using a two per cent solution of white arsenic to break down the sulphide coating.'

He stared at her in disbelief. 'But that's crazy.'

'You said it,' Kelly agreed. 'These aren't sane or responsible people. They are poisoning the forest in a murderous orgy of greed.'

457

He climbed up out of the dead river and stood beside her. Slowly he felt her outrage seep into his own conscience.

'The bastards,' he whispered. It was as though she realised the moment of his total commitment to her cause, for she reached out and took his hand. It was not a gentle or an affectionate gesture. Her grip was fierce and compelling.

'You haven't seen it all yet. This is just the beginning. The real horror lies ahead at Wengu.' She shook his arm demandingly. 'Come!' she ordered. 'Come and look at it. I challenge you to remain on the sidelines after you have seen it.'

The little column moved on, but after another five hours' march the Bambuti porters abruptly halted and dropped their packs and whispered together.

'Now what is the trouble?' Victor wanted to know, and Kelly explained.

'We have reached the boundary of the clan hunting area.' She pointed ahead. 'From here onwards we will be entering the sacred heartland of the Bambuti. They are deeply troubled and perplexed. So far only Sepoo has seen what is happening at Wengu. The others are reluctant to go on. They are afraid of the wrath of the forest god, the Mother and Father of the forest. They understand that a terrible sacrilege has been committed and they are terrified.'

'What can we do to persuade them?' Daniel asked, but Kelly shook her head.

'We must keep out of it. It is clan business. We must leave it to Pamba to convince them.'

The old lady was at her best now. She spoke to them, sometimes haranguing them shrilly, at others dropping her voice to a dovelike cooing and taking one of their faces in her cupped hands to whisper into an ear. She sang a little hymn to the forest and smeared ointment on each of their bare chests to absolve them. Then she performed a solitary dance, shuffling and leaping as she circled. Her withered breasts bounced against her belly and her skirt of bark cloth flipped up at the back to expose her surprisingly neat and glossy little buttocks as she cavorted.

After an hour one of the porters suddenly picked up his load and started along the path. The others, grinning sheepishly, followed his example and the safari went forward into the sacred heartland.

They heard the machines at dawn the next morning and as they went on the sound became louder. The rivers they crossed were waist-deep and thick as honey with the fearful red-poisoned mud. Apart from the distant growl and roar of the machines, the forest was silent. They saw no birds or monkeys or antelope, and the Bambuti were silent also. They kept close together and they were afraid, darting anxious glances into the forest around them as they scurried forward.

At noon Sepoo halted the column and conferred with Kelly in a whisper. He pointed towards the east and Kelly nodded and beckoned Daniel and Victor to her.

'Sepoo says we are very close now. Sounds in the forest are very deceptive. The machines are working not more than a few miles ahead. We dare not approach closer for there are company guards at the forest edge.'

'What are you going to do?' Victor asked.

'Sepoo says there's a line of hills to the east. From there we'll be able to overlook the mining and logging area. Pamba will stay here with the porters. Just the four of us, Sepoo and I, you, Daniel, and Victor, will go up on to the hills.'

Daniel unpacked the VTR and he and Victor checked it.

'Come on,' Kelly ordered, 'before the light goes or it begins to rain again.'

They climbed the hills in Indian file with Sepoo leading. However, even when they came out on the top they were still hemmed in by the forest. The great trees soared high overhead and the undergrowth pressed in closely about them, limiting visibility to twenty or thirty feet. They could hear the bellow of diesels below them, closer and clearer than before.

'What now?' Daniel wanted to know. 'Can't see a damned thing from here.'

'Sepoo will give us a grandstand view,' Kelly promised, and almost as she said it, they reached the base of a tree that was a giant amongst a forest of great trees.

'Twenty pygmies holding hands can't encircle this tree,' Kelly murmured. 'We've tried it. It's the sacred honey tree of the tribe.' She pointed at the primitive ladder that scaled the massive trunk.

The pygmies had driven wooden pegs into the smooth bark to reach the lowest branches and from there they had strung liana ropes and lashed wooden steps that ascended until they passed out of sight into the forest galleries a hundred feet above where they stood.

'This is a Bambuti temple,' Kelly explained. 'Up there in the high branches they pray and leave offerings to the forest god.'

Sepoo went first for he was the lightest and some of the pegs and steps were rotten. He cut new ones and hammered them into place with the hilt of his machete, and then signalled the others to follow him.

Kelly went next and reached down to give Victor a hand when he faltered. Daniel came last, carrying the VTR slung over his shoulder and reaching up to place Victor's feet on the ladder rungs when he could not find them for himself.

It was slow progress, but they helped the old man up and reached the upper gallery of the forest safely.

This was like the land at the top of Jack's beanstalk, an aerial platform formed by interlinked branches and fallen debris. New plants had taken root in the suspended leaf mould and trash and formed a marvellous hanging garden where strange and beautiful flowers bloomed and a whole new spectrum of life flourished closer to the sun. Daniel saw butterflies with wings spread as wide as his hands, and flying insects that sparkled like emeralds and princely rubies. There were even lilies and wild gardenias growing in this fairyland. Daniel caught the flash of a bird so jewelled and splendid that he doubted his own eyes as it vanished like a puff of brilliant smoke amongst the foliage.

Sepoo barely allowed them to rest before he began to climb again. The trunk of the tree was half as thick at this level, but still as huge as its neighbours had been at their bases. As they went higher so the light changed. It was like coming up from the depths of the ocean. The green submarine glow brightened until abruptly they burst out into the sunlight and exclaimed with wonder.

They were on the top branches of the sacred honey tree. They looked down upon the carpet of the forest roof. It spread away, undulating like the billows of the ocean, green and unbroken on every side, except in the north. All their eyes turned in that direction and their cries of wonder faded and they stared in horror and disbelief.

In the north the forest was gone. From the base of the green hill below them, as far as they could see to the north, to the very foothills of the snowclad mountains the forest had been erased. A red plain of desolation lay where once the tall trees had stood.

None of them could speak or move. They clung to their lofty perch and stared speechlessly, turning their heads slowly from side to side to encompass the enormity of the bare devastated expanse.

The earth seemed to have been raked by the claws of some rapacious beast, for it had been scoured by the torrential rain waters. The topsoils had been torn away, leaving stark canyons of erosion; the fine red mud had been washed down to clog and choke the rivers through the forest. It was a desolate lunar landscape.

'Merciful God!' Victor Omeru was the first to speak. 'It is an abomination. How much land has he defiled? What is the full extent of this destruction?'

'It's impossible to calculate,' Kelly whispered. Even though she had seen it before, she was still stunned by the horror of it. 'Half a million – a million acres, I don't know. But remember, they've been at work here for less than a year. Think of the destruction in another year from now. If those monsters . . .' she pointed at the line of MOMU vehicles that were strung along the edge of the forest at the foot of the hill, 'if those monsters are allowed to continue.'

It was an effort for Daniel to drag his eyes from the wide vista of destruction and to concentrate on the line of yellow machines. From their high vantage point they seemed as tiny and innocuous as a small boy's toys left in the sandbox. The MOMU were in a staggered formation, like a line of combine-harvesters reaping one of those endless wheat fields on the Canadian prairie. They were moving so slowly that they appeared to be standing still.

'How many?' Daniel asked, and counted them aloud. 'Eight, nine, ten!' he exclaimed. 'Running side by side that gives them a cutline almost four hundred yards wide.'

'It doesn't seem possible that just ten machines have been able to inflict such terrible damage.' Victor's voice shook uncertainly. 'They are like giant locusts – remorseless, insensate, terrible.'

The caterpillar tractors were working ahead of the line of MOMUs, scything the forest to make way for the monstrous earth-eating machines to follow.

Even as they watched, one of the tall trees quivered and swayed. Then it began to move, swinging ponderously as the steel blades ate through the base of its trunk. Even at this distance they heard the scream of living timber rending. It sounded like the death throes of a wounded animal. The falling tree gathered momentum, its death cry rose higher and shriller, until the trunk thudded into the red earth and the mass of foliage shivered, then lay still.

Daniel had to look away. Sepoo was perched beside him on a high branch, and he was weeping. The tears ran very slowly down his wrinkled old cheeks and dripped unheeded on to his naked chest. It was a terrible intimate grief, too painful for Daniel to watch.

He looked back just in time to see another tree fall and die, and then another. He unslung the VTR from his shoulder and lifted it to his eyes, focused the telephoto lens, and began to film.

He filmed the devastated bare red plain on which not a living thing remained, not an animal, or bird, or a green leaf.

He filmed the line of yellow machines grinding inexorably forward, keeping their formation rigidly, attended by an endless horde of container trucks, like worker ants behind the queen ant, carrying away the succession of eggs she laid.

He filmed the red poison spewing from the dump chutes at the rear of the MOMU, falling carelessly upon the savaged earth where the next rainstorm would carry it away and spread it into every stream and creek for a hundred miles down the contour.

He filmed the fall of the trees ahead of the line of yellow machines and the giant mechanical saws mounted on specially modified caterpillar tractors. Fountains of wet white sawdust flew high into the air as the spinning silver blades bit in and the tree-trunks fell into separate logs.

He filmed the mobile cranes lifting the logs on to the trailer beds of the logging vehicles.

He filmed the hordes of naked Uhali slaves working in the red mud to keep the roads open for the massive trucks and trailers to pass over, as they bore away the looted treasures of the forest.

He had hoped that the act of manipulating the camera and viewing the scene through the intervening lens might somehow isolate him from reality, might allow him to remain aloof and objective. It was a vain hope. The longer he watched the destruction, the more angry he became until his rage matched that of the woman who sat on the branch beside him.

Kelly did not have to give voice to her outrage. He could feel it like static electricity in the air around her. It did not surprise him that he was so in tune with her feelings. It seemed only right and natural. They were very close now. A new bond had been forged between them, to reinforce the attraction and sympathy that they had already conceived for each other.

They stayed in the treetop until nightfall, and then they remained another hour, sitting in darkness as though they could not tear themselves away from the terrible fascination of it. They listened to the growl of engines in the night and watched the floodlights and the swinging headlights turn the forest and the devastated red plain to daylight. It never stopped, but went on and on, cutting, digging, roaring, spilling out poison and death.

When at last it began to rain again and the lightning and the thunder crashed overhead, they crept down from the treetop and made their way slowly and sadly back to where Pamba waited in the forest with the porters.

In the morning they started back through the steaming silent forest towards Gondala, stopping only for Daniel to film the polluted, bleeding rivers. Victor Omeru went down into the muck and stood knee-deep in it and spoke into the camera, giving articulate voice to all their sorrow and rage.

His voice was deep and compelling and filled with concern and compassion for his land and its people. His silver hair and dark noble features would hold the attention of any audience, and his credentials were impeccable. His international reputation was such that nobody could seriously doubt that what he described to them was the truth. If Daniel could show this to the outside world, he knew that he would be able to communicate his own sense of outrage.

They moved on slowly. The Bambuti porters were still subdued and dismayed. Although they had not witnessed the mining, Sepoo had described it to them and they had seen the bleeding rivers. Yet even before they reached the boundary between the heartland and their traditional hunting grounds they were given even greater cause for sorrow.

They cut the tracks of an elephant. They all recognised the spoor of the beast, and Sepoo called him by name. 'The Old Man with One Ear,' he said, and they all agreed. It was the bull with half his left ear missing. They laughed for the first time in days as though they had met an old friend in the forest, but the laughter was short-lived as they studied the spoor.

Then they cried out and wrung their hands and whimpered with fear and horror.

Kelly called urgently to Sepoo. 'What is it, old friend?'

'Blood,' Sepoo answered her. 'Blood and urine from the elephant. He is wounded; he is dying.'

'How has this happened?' Kelly cried. She also knew the elephant like an old friend. She had come across him often in the forest when he had frequented the area round Gondala.

'A man has struck and wounded him. Somebody is hunting the bull in the sacred heartland. It is against all law and custom. Look! Here are the tracks of the man's feet lying over the spoor of the bull.' He pointed out the clear imprints of small bare feet in the mud. 'The hunter is a Bambuti. He must be a man of our clan. It is a terrible sacrilege. It is an offence against the god of the forest.'

The little group of pygmies were shaken and horrified. They clustered together like lost children, holding each other's hands for comfort in these dreadful days when all they believed in was being turned upside down – first the machines in the forest and the bleeding rivers, and now this sacrilege committed by one of their own people.

'I know this man,' Pamba shrieked. 'I recognise the mark of his feet. This man is Pirri.'

They wailed then and covered their faces, for Pirri had made his kill in the sacred places and the shame and the retribution of the forest god must come down upon all of them.

 Pirri the hunter moved like a shadow. He laid his tiny feet down gently upon the great pad marks of the elephant, where the bull's weight had compacted the earth and no twig would snap and no dead leaf would rustle to betray him.

Pirri had been following the elephant for three days. During all that time Pirri's entire being had been concentrated upon the elephant, so that in some mystic way he had become part of the beast he was hunting.

Where the bull had stopped to feast on the little red berries of the selepe tree, Pirri read the sign and could taste the tart acidic juice in his own throat. Where the elephant had drunk at one of the streams, Pirri stood upon the bank as he had done and felt in his imagination the sweet clear water squirt and gurgle into his own belly. Where the elephant had dropped a pile of yellow fibrous dung on the forest floor, Pirri felt his own bowels contract and his sphincter relax in sympathy. Pirri had become the elephant, and the elephant had become Pirri.

When he came up with him at last, the bull was asleep on his feet in a matted thicket. The branches were interwoven and covered with thorns that were hooked and tipped with red; they could flay a man's skin from his limbs. As softly and slowly as Pirri moved, yet the elephant sensed his presence and came awake. He spread his ears, one wide and full as a mainsail, the other torn and deformed, and he listened. However, he heard nothing, for Pirri was a master hunter.

The elephant stretched out his trunk, sucked up the air and blew it softly into his mouth. The olfactory glands in his top lip opened like pink rosebuds and he tasted the air, but he tasted nothing, for Pirri had come in below the tiny forest breeze and he had smeared himself from the top of his curly head to the pink soles of his feet with the elephant's own dung. There was no man-smell upon him.

465

Then the elephant made a sound, a gentle rumbling sound in his belly and a fluttering sound in his throat. It was the elephant song. The bull sang in the forest to learn if it was another elephant or a deadly enemy whose presence he sensed.

Pirri crouched at the edge of the thicket and listened to the elephant sing. Then he cupped his hand over his mouth and his nose and he gulped air into his throat and his belly and he let it out with a soft rumbling and fluttering sound.

Pirri sang the song of the elephant.

The bull sighed in his throat and changed his song, testing the unseen presence. Faithfully Pirri replied to him, following the cadence and the timbre of the song, and the elephant bull believed him.

The elephant flapped his ears, a gesture of contentment and trust. He accepted that another elephant had found him and come to join him. He moved carelessly and the thicket crackled before his bulk. He came ambling forward to meet Pirri, pushing the thorny branches aside.

Pirri saw the curved shafts of ivory appear high above his head. They were thicker than his waist and longer than he could reach with his elephant spear.

The elephant spear was a weapon that Pirri had forged himself from the blade of a truck spring that he had stolen from one of the *dukas* at the roadside. He had heated and beaten it until the steel had lost its temper and he was able to work it more easily. Then Pirri had shaped and sharpened it, and fitted it to a shaft of hard resilient wood and bound the blade in place with rawhide. When the rawhide dried it was hard and tight as the steel it held.

As the elephant's head loomed above him, Pirri sank down and lay like a log or a pile of dead leaves on the forest floor. The elephant was so close that he could make out clearly every furrow and wrinkle in the thick grey hide. Looking up he could see the discharge from the glands in the elephant's head running like tears down his cheeks, and Pirri gathered himself.

Even with the spear he had made, which was sharp and heavy and almost twice as long as Pirri was tall, he could never drive the point through the hide and meat and the cage of ribs to pierce the bull's heart or his lungs. The brain in its bony casket was far beyond his reach. There was only one way that a man of Pirri's size could kill an enormous beast like this with a spear.

Pirri rolled to his feet and bounded up under the elephant's belly. He stood between the bull's back legs and he braced himself and drove the point of the spear upwards into the angle of his groin.

The elephant squealed as the blade sliced through the baggy skin that hung around his crotch and lanced up into the sac of his bladder. The razor steel split his bladder open and the hot urine sprayed out in a yellow jet. He convulsed with agony, hunching his back, before he began to run.

The elephant ran screaming through the forest, and the foliage crashed and broke before him.

Pirri leaned on his bloody spear and listened to the elephant run out of earshot. He waited until the silence was complete and then he girded up his loincloth and began to follow the dribbled trail of blood and urine that steamed and reeked on the forest floor.

It might take many hours to die, but the elephant was doomed. Pirri, the hunter, had struck a mortal blow and he knew that before tomorrow's sunset the elephant would be dead.

Pirri followed him slowly, but he did not feel the fierce hunter's joy in his heart. There was only a sense of emptiness and the terrible guilt of sacrilege.

He had offended his god, and he knew that now his god must reject and punish him.

 Pirri the hunter found the carcass of the elephant bull the next morning. The elephant was kneeling, with his legs folded up neatly beneath him. His head was supported by the massive curves of ivory that were half buried in the soft earth. The last rainstorm had washed his hide so that it was black and shiny and his eyes were open.

He appeared so lifelike that Pirri approached him with great caution and at last reached out with a long thin twig to touch the open staring eye fringed with thick lashes. The eyelid did not blink to the touch and Pirri noticed the opaque jelly-like sheen of death over the pupil. He straightened up and laid aside his spear. The hunt was over.

By custom he should now sing a prayer of thanks to the forest god for such largesse. He actually uttered the first words of the prayer before he broke off guiltily. He knew that he could never sing the hunter's prayer again, and a profound sadness filled his being.

He made a small fire and cut the rich fatty meat out of the elephant's cheek and cooked it on a skewer over the coals. For once this choice morsel was tough and tasteless in his mouth. He spat it into the fire and sat for a long time beside the carcass before he could rouse himself and shrug off the sense of sorrow that weighed him down.

He drew his machete from its sheath and began to chop one of the thick yellow tusks from its bony canal in the elephant's skull. The steel rang on the skull and the bone chips flew and fell about his feet as he worked.

That was how the men of his clan found him. They were drawn to Pirri by the sound of his machete hacking through bone. They came out of the forest silently, led by Sepoo and Pamba, and they formed a circle around Pirri and the elephant.

He looked up and saw them, and he let the machete fall to his side, and he stood with blood on his hands, not daring to meet their eyes.

'I will share the reward with you, my brothers,' he whispered, but nobody answered him.

One at a time the Bambuti turned from him and disappeared back into the forest as silently as they had come, until only Sepoo remained.

'Because of what you have done the forest god will send the Molimo to us,' said Sepoo, and Pirri stood with despair in his heart and could not raise his head to meet his brother's eyes.

Daniel began a review of the videotapes as soon as they reached Gondala.

Kelly set aside a corner of her laboratory for him to work in and Victor Omeru hovered over him, making comments and suggestions as he compiled his editing notes.

The quality of the material he had gathered was good. As a cameraman he rated himself as competent but lacking the artistry and brilliance of somebody like Bonny Mahon. What he compiled was an honest sober record of the mining and logging operation in the Wengu forest reserve, and of some of the consequences.

'It has no human warmth to it,' he told Victor and Kelly at dinner that evening. 'It appeals to reason, not to the heart. I need something more.'

'What is it you want?' Kelly asked. 'Tell me what it is and I'll get it for you.'

'I want more of President Omeru,' Daniel said. 'You have presence and style, sir. I want much more of you.'

'You shall have me.' Victor Omeru nodded. 'But don't you think it is time we dispensed with the formalities, Daniel? After all, we have climbed the sacred honey tree together. Surely that entitles us to use each other's Christian names?'

'I'm sure it does, Victor,' Daniel agreed. 'But even you won't be enough to convince the world. I have to show them what is happening to human beings. I have to show them the camps where the Uhali forced labour units are housed. Can we arrange that?'

Victor leaned forward. 'Yes,' he said. 'You know that I am the leader of the resistance movement to Taffari's tyranny. We are growing stronger every day. At present it is all very much underground, but we are organising ourselves and recruiting all the most important and influential people who reject Taffari. Of course, we are mostly Uhali, but even some of Taffari's own Hita people are becoming disenchanted with his regime. We will be able to get you to see the labour camps. Of course, you won't be able to get into the camps, but we should be able to get you close enough to film some of the daily atrocities which are being perpetrated.'

469

'Yes,' Kelly asserted. 'Patrick and the other young resistance leaders will be arriving here within the next few days for a conference with Victor. He will be able to arrange it.' She broke off and thought for a moment. 'Then there are the Bambuti. You can show your audience how the destruction of the forest will affect the pygmies and destroy their traditional way of life.'

'That's exactly the type of material I still need,' Daniel replied. 'What do you suggest?'

'The Molimo ceremony,' Kelly said. 'Sepoo tells me that the Molimo is coming and he has agreed that you may witness it.'

Patrick, Victor Omeru's nephew, arrived at Gondala a day earlier than was expected. He was accompanied by a retinue of a dozen or so Uhali tribesmen. The pygmies had guided them through the forest. Many of the delegation were also relatives of Victor Omeru, all of them educated and committed young men.

When Daniel showed them the tapes he had already filmed and described the material he still required, Patrick Omeru and his men were enthusiastic.

'Leave it to me, Doctor Armstrong,' Patrick told him. 'I'll arrange it for you. Of course, there will be some danger involved. The camps are well protected by the Hita, but we'll get you as close as is humanly possible.'

When Patrick and his men left Gondala, Daniel and Sepoo went with them.

The two of them returned to Gondala nine days later. Daniel was thin and gaunt. It was obvious that they had travelled hard and unremittingly. His clothing was mud-stained and tattered and Kelly saw at once that he was near the point of exhaustion as he stumbled up on the verandah of the bungalow.

Without thinking she ran to greet him and the next moment they were in each other's arms. It startled both of them. They clung to each other for a moment, but when Daniel turned his mouth down towards hers, Kelly broke away and shook his hand instead.

'Victor and I were so worried,' she blurted, but she was blushing a deep rose colour that Daniel found enchanting, and she released his hand quickly.

That afternoon, after Daniel had bathed and eaten and slept for two hours, he showed them the new material. There were sequences of the forced labour gangs working along the logging roads. They had obviously been filmed from a distance with a telephoto lens.

The Hita guards stood over the gangs with clubs in their hands, and they struck out seemingly at random at the half-naked men and women toiling in the mud and slush below them.

'I've got much too much of this,' Daniel explained, 'but I'll edit it down, and keep only the most striking sequences.'

There were sequences of the gangs being marched in slow exhausted columns back to the camps at the end of the day's work, and other shots, taken through wire, of their primitive living conditions.

Then there were a series of interviews, shot in the forest, with prisoners who had escaped from the camps. One of the men stripped naked in front of the camera and displayed the injuries that the guards had inflicted upon him. His back was cut to ribbons by the lash, and his skull was criss-crossed with scars and half-healed cuts where the clubs had fallen.

A young woman showed her feet. The flesh was rotting and falling away from the bone. She spoke in soft Swahili, describing the conditions in the camp. 'We work all day in the mud – our feet are never dry. The cuts and scratches on them fester like this, until we cannot walk. We cannot work.' She began to weep softly.

Daniel was sitting beside her on the log. He looked up at the camera which he had previously set up on a tripod. 'This is what the soldiers in the trenches of France during World War One called "trench foot". It's a contagious fungoidal infection that will cripple the sufferer, will literally rot his feet off if it is not treated.' Daniel turned back to the weeping woman and asked gently in Swahili, 'What happens when you can no longer work?'

'The Hita say that they will not feed us, that we eat too

much food and are no longer of any use. They take the sick people into the forest . . .'

Daniel switched off the VTR and turned to Kelly and Victor. 'What you are about to see are the most shocking sequences I have ever filmed. They're similar to the scenes of the Nazi death squads in Poland and Russia. Some of the quality might be rather poor. We were filming from hiding. It's horrible stuff. You might prefer not to watch it, Kelly?'

Kelly shook her head. 'I'll watch it,' she said firmly.

'Okay, but I warned you.' Daniel switched on the VTR and they leaned forward towards the tiny screen as it flickered and came alive again.

They were looking into a clearing in the forest. One of the UDC bulldozers was gouging a trench in the soft earth. The trench was forty or fifty yards long and at least ten feet deep, judging by the way the bulldozer almost disappeared into it.

'Patrick was able to find out from his spies where they were doing this,' Daniel explained. 'So we could get into position the night before.'

The bulldozer completed the excavation and trundled up out of the trench. It parked nearby. The shot was cut off.

'This next sequence is about three hours later,' Daniel told them.

The head of a column of prisoners appeared out of the forest, chivvied on by the Hita guards on the flanks. It was apparent that all the prisoners were sick or crippled. They staggered or limped slowly into sight. Some were supporting each other with arms around the shoulders, others were using crude crutches. A few were carried on litters by their companions. One or two of the women had infants strapped on their backs. The guards marched them down into the trench and they disappeared from sight.

The guards formed up in a line on top of the excavation. There were at least fifty of them in paratrooper overalls with sub-machine-guns carried on the hip. Quite casually they began firing down into the trench. The fusillade went on for a long time. As each paratrooper emptied his Uzi machine-gun, he reloaded it with a fresh magazine and recommenced firing. Some of the men were laughing.

Suddenly one of the prisoners crawled up over the bank of the pit. It was almost unthinkable that he could have survived this long. One of his legs was half shot away. He dragged himself along on his elbows. A Hita officer unholstered his pistol and stood over him and shot him in the back of his head. The man collapsed on his face and the officer put his boot against his ribs and shoved him over the lip of the trench.

One at a time the soldiers stopped shooting. Some of them lit cigarettes and stood in groups along the edge of the grave, smoking and laughing and chatting.

The driver of the bulldozer climbed back on to his machine and eased it forward. He lowered the blade and pushed the piles of loose earth back into the trench. When the excavation was refilled he drove the bulldozer back and forth over it to compact the earth.

The soldiers formed up into a column and marched away along the track they had come. They were out of step and slovenly, chatting and smoking as they went.

Daniel switched off the VTR and the screen went blank. Kelly stood up without a word and went out on to the verandah of the bungalow. The two men sat in silence until Victor Omeru said quietly, 'Help us please, Daniel. Help my poor people.'

The word went through the forest that the Molimo was coming, and the clans began to gather at the tribal meeting place below the waterfall at Gondala.

Some of the clans came from two hundred miles away, across the Zaïre border, for the Bambuti recognised no territorial boundaries but their own. From every clan area and from every remote corner of the forest they came, until there were over a thousand of the little people gathered together for the terrible Molimo visitation.

Each woman built her leafy hut with the doorway facing the doorway of a particular friend or a close and beloved relative, and they gathered in laughing groups throughout the encampment, for not even the threat of the Molimo could quench their high spirits or dull their cheerful nature.

The men met old cronies and hunting companions that they had not seen since the last communal net hunt, and they shared tobacco and tall stories, and gossiped with as much relish as the women at the cooking-fires. The children squealed and ran unchecked amongst the huts, tumbling over each other like puppies, and they swam in the pool below the waterfall like sleek otter cubs.

One of the last to arrive at the meeting place was Pirri the hunter. His three wives staggered under the heavy sacks of tobacco they carried.

Pirri ordered his wives to build his hut with the doorway facing the doorway of his brother Sepoo. However, when the hut was finished, Pamba closed in the doorway of Sepoo's hut and built another opening facing in the opposite direction. In Bambuti custom this was a terrible snub, and it set the women at the cooking-fires chattering like parrots at roosting time.

Pirri called to old friends, 'See how much tobacco I have. It is yours to share. Come, fill your pouches. Pirri invites you, take as much as you wish. See here! Pirri has bottles of gin. Come drink with Pirri.' But not a man of all the Bambuti took advantage of the offer.

In the evening, when a group of the most famous hunters and story-tellers of the tribe were gathered around a single fire with Sepoo in their midst, Pirri came swaggering out of the darkness with a bottle of gin in each hand and elbowed a place for himself at the fire. He drank from the open gin bottle and then passed it to the man on his left. 'Drink!' he ordered. 'Pass it on, so that all may share Pirri's good fortune.'

The man placed the untouched bottle on one side and stood up and walked away from the fire. One after the other, the men stood up and followed him into the darkness until only Sepoo and Pirri were left.

'Tomorrow the Molimo comes,' Sepoo warned his brother softly, and then he also stood up and walked away.

Pirri the hunter was left with his gin and his bulging tobacco pouch, sitting alone in the night.

Sepoo came to the laboratory to call Daniel the following morning, and Daniel followed him into the forest, carrying the camera on his shoulder. They went swiftly, for Daniel had by now learned all the tricks of forest travel, and even his superior height and size were no great handicap. He could keep up with Sepoo.

They started off alone, but as they went others joined them, slipping silently out of the forest, or appearing like dark sprites ahead or behind them, until at last there was a multitude of Bambuti hurrying towards the place of the Molimo.

When they arrived there were already many others before them, squatting silently around the base of a huge silk-cotton tree in the depths of the forest. For once there was no laughter nor skylarking. The men were all grave and silent.

Daniel squatted with them and filmed their sombre faces. All of them were looking up into the silk-cotton tree.

'This is the home of the Molimo,' Sepoo whispered softly. 'We have come to fetch him.'

Somebody in the ranks called out a name. 'Grivi!' And a man stood up and moved to the base of the tree.

From another direction another name was called. 'Sepoo!' And Sepoo went to stand with the first man chosen.

Soon there were fifteen men at the base of the tree. Some were old and famous, some were mere striplings. Young or old, callow or proven, all men had equal right to take part in the ceremony of the Molimo.

Suddenly Sepoo let out a shout and the chosen band swarmed excitedly up into the tree. They disappeared into the high foliage and for a time there was only the sound of their singing and shouting. Then down they came again, bearing a length of bamboo.

They laid it on the ground at the foot of the tree and Daniel went forward to examine it. The bamboo was not more than fifteen feet long. It was cured and dried out, and must have been cut many years before. There were stylised symbols and crude animal caricatures scratched on it, but otherwise it was simply a length of bamboo.

'Is this the Molimo?' Daniel whispered to Sepoo while the men of the tribe gathered around it reverently.

'Yes, Kuokoa, this is the Molimo,' Sepoo affirmed.

'What is the Molimo?' Daniel persisted.

'The Molimo is the voice of the forest,' Sepoo tried to explain. 'It is the voice of the Mother and the Father. But before it can speak, it must be taken to drink.'

The chosen band took up the Molimo and carried it to the stream and submerged it in a cool dark pool. The banks of the pool were lined with ranks of little men, solemn and attentive, naked and bright-eyed. They waited for an hour and then another while the Molimo drank the sweet water of the forest stream, and then they brought the Molimo to the bank.

It was shining and dripping with water. Sepoo went to the bamboo tube and placed his lips over the open end. His chest inflated as he drew breath and the Molimo spoke from the tube. It was the startlingly clear sweet voice of a young girl singing in the forest, and all the men of the Bambuti shuddered and swayed like the top leaves of a tall tree hit by a sudden wind.

Then the Molimo changed its voice, and cried like a duiker caught in the hunter's net. It chattered like the grey parrot in flight and whistled like the honey chameleon. It was all the voices and sounds of the forest. Another man replaced Sepoo at the tube, and then another. There were voices of men and ghosts and other creatures that all men had heard of but none had ever seen.

Then suddenly the Molimo screamed like an elephant. It was a terrible angry sound and the men of the Bambuti swarmed forward, clustering around the Molimo in a struggling heaving horde. The simple bamboo tube disappeared in their midst, but still it squealed and roared, cooed and whistled and cackled with a hundred different voices.

Now a strange and magical thing took place. As Daniel watched, the struggling knot of men changed. They were no longer individuals, for they were pressed too closely together. In the same way that a shoal of fish or a flock of birds is one beast, so the men of the Bambuti blended into an entity. They became one creature. They became the Molimo. They became the godhead of the forest.

The Molimo was angry. It roared and squealed with the

voice of the buffalo and the giant forest hog. It raged through the forest on a hundred legs that were no longer human. It revolved on its axis like a jellyfish in the current. It pulsed and changed shape, and dashed one way and then the other, flattening the undergrowth in its fury.

It crossed the river, kicking up a white foam of spray, and then slowly but with awakening purpose began to move towards the gathering place of the tribe below the waterfall at Gondala.

The women heard the Molimo coming from a long way off. They left the cooking-fires and seized the children and ran to their huts, dragging the little ones with them. Wailing with terror, they closed the doors of the huts and crouched in the darkness with the children clutched to their breasts.

The Molimo rampaged through the forest, its terrible voice rising and falling, crashing through the undergrowth, charging one way and then the other, until at last it broke into the encampment. It trampled the cooking-fires and the children screamed as some of the flimsy huts were knocked askew by its ungoverned anger.

The great beast raged back and forth through the camp, seeming to quest for the source of its outrage. Suddenly it revolved and moved purposefully towards the far corner of the camp where Pirri had built his hut.

Pirri's wives heard it coming and they burst from the hut and fled into the jungle, but Pirri did not run. He had not gone to the silk-cotton tree with the other men to fetch the Molimo down from its home. Now he crouched in his hut, with his hands over his head and waited. He knew there was no escape in flight, he had to wait for the retribution of the forest god.

The Molimo circled Pirri's hut like one of the giant forest millipedes, its feet stamping and kicking up the earth, screaming like a bull elephant in the agony of a ruptured bladder.

Then abruptly it charged at the hut in which Pirri was hiding. It flattened the hut, and trampled all Pirri's possessions. It stamped his tobacco to dust. It shattered his bottles of gin and the pungent liquor soaked into the earth. It kicked the gold wristwatch into the fire and scattered all his treasures. Pirri made no attempt to fly its wrath or to protect himself.

The Molimo trampled him; squealing with rage it kicked and

pummelled him. It crushed his nose and broke his teeth; it cracked his ribs and bruised his limbs.

Then suddenly, it left him and rushed back into the forest from whence it had come. Its voice had changed, the rage was gone out of it. It wailed and lamented as though it mourned the death and the poisoning of the forest and the sins of the tribe that had brought disaster upon them all. Slowly it retreated and its voice became fainter, until at last it faded into the distance.

Pirri picked himself up slowly. He made no effort to gather up his scattered treasures. He took only his bow and his quiver of arrows. He left his elephant spear and his machete. He limped away into the forest.

He went alone. His wives did not go with him, for they were widows now. They would find new husbands in the tribe. Pirri was dead. The Molimo had killed him. No man would ever see him again. Even when they met his ghost wandering amongst the tall trees, no man or woman would acknowledge it.

Pirri was dead to his tribe for ever.

'Will you help us, Daniel?' Victor Omeru asked.

'Yes,' Daniel agreed. 'I will help you. I will take the tapes to London. I will arrange to have them shown on public television in London and Paris and New York.'

'What else will you do to help us?' Victor asked.

'What else do you want of me?' Daniel countered. 'What else is there I can do?'

'You are a soldier, and a good one, from what I have heard. Will you join us in our fight to regain our freedom?'

'I was a soldier, long ago,' Daniel corrected him, 'in a cruel unjust war. I learned to hate war in a way that no one can until they have experienced it.'

'Daniel, I am asking you to take part in a just war. This time I am asking you to make a stand against tyranny.'

'I am no longer a soldier. I am a journalist, Victor. It is not my war.'

478

'You are a soldier still,' Victor contradicted him. 'And it is your war. It is the war of any decent man.'

Daniel did not reply immediately. He glanced sideways at Kelly, on the point of asking for her support. Then he saw her expression. There was no comfort for him there. He looked back at Victor, and the old man leaned closer to him.

'We Uhali are a peaceful people. For that reason we, alone, do not have the skill necessary to overthrow the tyrant. We need weapons. We need people to teach us how to use them. Help me, please, Daniel. I will find all the young brave men you need, if only you will promise to train and command them.'

'I don't want—' Daniel began, but Victor forestalled him.

'Don't refuse me outright. Don't say anything more tonight. Sleep on it. Give me your answer in the morning. Think about it, Daniel. Dream of the men and women you saw in the camps. Dream of the people you saw killed or deported at Fish Eagle Bay, and the mass grave in the forest. Give me your answer in the morning.'

Victor Omeru stood up. He paused beside Daniel's chair and placed his hand on his shoulder.

'Good night, Daniel,' he said, and went down the steps and crossed in the moonlight to his own small bungalow beyond the gardens.

'What are you going to do?' Kelly asked softly.

'I don't know. I really don't know.' Daniel stood up. 'I'll tell you tomorrow. But right now, I'll do what Victor suggested, I'm going to bed.'

'Yes.' Kelly stood up beside him.

'Good night,' he said.

She was standing very close to him, her face tilted up towards him.

He kissed her. The kiss held for a long time.

She drew back only a few inches from his mouth and said, 'Come.' And led him down the verandah to her bedroom.

It was still dark when he woke the next morning under the mosquito net with her.

Her arm was thrown over his chest. Her breath was warm on his neck. He felt her come softly awake.

'I'm going to do what Victor wants,' he said.

She stopped breathing for a few moments then she said, 'It wasn't meant as a bribe.'

'I know,' he said.

'What happened between us last night is a thing apart,' she said. 'I wanted it to happen from the first day I met you – no, from before that. From the first time I saw your images on the screen, I was half in love with you.'

'I've also been waiting for you a long time, Kelly. I knew you were out there somewhere. At last I've found you.'

'I hate to lose you so soon,' she said, and kissed him. 'Please come back to me.'

Daniel left Gondala two days later. Sepoo and four Bambuti porters accompanied him.

He paused at the edge of the forest and looked back. Kelly was on the verandah of the bungalow. She waved. She looked very young and girlish, and he felt his heart squeezed. He did not want to go – not yet, not so soon after he had found her. He waved and forced himself to turn from her.

As they climbed the lower slopes of the mountain the forest gave way to bamboo, which was so dense that in places they were forced to their hands and knees to crawl through the tunnels which the giant hog had burrowed. The bamboo was solid overhead.

They climbed higher and came out at last on to the bleak heath slopes of the high mountains, twelve thousand feet above sea level, where the giant groundsel stood like battalions of armoured warriors, their heads spiked with red flowers.

The Bambuti huddled in the blankets that Kelly had provided, but they were miserable and sickening, totally out of their element. Before they reached the highest pass, Daniel sent them back.

Sepoo wanted to argue. 'Kuokoa, you will lose your way on the mountains without Sepoo to guide you and Kara-Ki will be angry. You have never seen her truly angry. It is not a sight for any but the brave.'

'Look up there.' Daniel pointed ahead to where the peaks showed through the cloud. 'There is cold up there that no Bambuti has ever experienced. That shining white is ice and snow so cold that it will burn you like fire.'

So Daniel went on alone, carrying the precious tapes inside his jacket close to his skin, and he crossed below the moraine of the Ruwatamagufa glacier and came down into Zaïre two days after leaving Sepoo. He had frostbite on three of his fingers and one of his toes.

The Zaïrean district commissioner at Mutsora was accustomed to refugees coming across the mountains, but seldom with white faces and British passports and fifty-dollar bills to dispense. He did not turn this one back.

Two days later, Daniel was on the steamer going down the Zaïre River and ten days after that he landed at Heathrow. The tapes were still in his pocket.

 From his Chelsea flat Daniel telephoned Michael Hargreave at the embassy in Kahali.

'Good Lord, Danny. We were told that you and Bonny Mahon disappeared in the forest near Sengi-Sengi. The army has had patrols out searching for you.'

'How secure is this line, Mike?'

'I wouldn't stake my reputation on it.'

'Then I'll give you the full story when next we meet. In the meantime, will you send me that packet I gave you for safe-keeping? Get it to me in the next diplomatic bag?'

'Hold on, Danny. I gave the package to Bonny Mahon. She told me that she was collecting it on your behalf.'

Daniel was silent for a beat as he worked it out. 'The little idiot. She played right into their hands. Well, that settles it. She's dead, Mike, as sure as fate. She handed over the package and they killed her. They thought I was dead, so they killed her. Nice and neat.'

'Who are "they"?' Michael demanded.

'Not now, Mike. I can't tell you now.'

'Sorry about the package, Danny. She was very convincing. But I shouldn't have fallen for it. Must be getting senile.'

'No great harm done. I have some stronger medicine to replace it.'

481

'When will I see you?'

'Soon, I hope. I'll let you know.'

Despite the short notice, the studio gave him a cutting-room to work in. He worked without a break – it helped to allay his sadness and guilt at what had happened to Bonny Mahon. He felt responsible. The final cut of the videotape did not have to be perfect, and it was not necessary to dub the Swahili dialogue into English. He had a copy ready to show within forty-eight hours.

It was impossible to get through to Tug Harrison. All Daniel's calls were intercepted on the BOSS switchboard and were not returned. Of course, the number of the Holland Park address was not listed, and he could not remember the number that he had telephoned from Nairobi to check on Bonny Mahon. So he staked out the house, leaning against a car with a newspaper as though he were waiting for someone, and watching the front of the building.

He was fortunate. Tug's Rolls-Royce pulled up at the front door that same day a little after noon, and Daniel intercepted him as he climbed the front steps.

'Armstrong – Danny!' Tug's surprise was genuine. 'I heard that you had disappeared in Ubomo.'

'Not true, Tug. Didn't you get my messages? I telephoned your office half a dozen times.'

'They don't pass them on to me. Too many freaks and funny bunnies in this world.'

'I must show you some of the material I have been able to shoot in Ubomo,' Daniel told him.

Tug hesitated and consulted his wristwatch dubiously.

'Don't mess me around, Tug. This stuff could sink you. And BOSS.'

Tug's eyes narrowed. 'That sounds like a threat.'

'Just a friendly piece of advice.'

'All right, come in,' Tug invited, and opened the front door. 'Let's have a look at what you have for me.'

Tug Harrison sat behind his desk and watched the tape run through from beginning to end without moving, without uttering a word. When the tape was finished and the screen filled with an electronic snowstorm, he pressed the remote control button, ran the tape back and then played it a second time, still without comment.

Then he switched off the tape and spoke without looking at Daniel. 'It's genuine,' he said. 'You couldn't have faked it.'

'You know it's genuine,' Daniel told him. 'You knew about the mining and logging. It's your bloody syndicate. You gave the orders.'

'I meant the labour camps, and the use of arsenic. I knew nothing about that.'

'Who is going to believe that, Tug?'

Tug shrugged and said, 'So Omeru is still alive.'

'Yes. He is alive and ready to give evidence against you.'

Tug changed the subject again. 'Of course, there are other copies of this tape?' he said.

'Silly question,' Daniel agreed.

'So this is a direct threat?'

'Another silly question,' Daniel said again.

'You are going to go public with this?'

'That's three in a row,' Daniel said grimly. 'Of course, I'm going public. Only one thing will stop me. That is if you and I can make a deal.'

'What deal are you offering?' Tug asked softly.

'I will give you time to get out. I will give you time to sell out your interest in Ubomo to Lucky Dragon or anyone else who will buy.'

Tug did not answer immediately but Daniel saw the faintest gleam of relief in his gaze.

Tug drew a breath. 'In return?'

'You will finance Victor Omeru's counter-revolution against Taffari's regime. After all, it won't be the first *coup* in Africa that you have orchestrated, Tug, will it?'

'How much will this cost me?' Tug asked.

'Only a small fraction of what you would lose if I were to release the tape before you have a chance to pull out. I could get a copy around to the Foreign Office and another to the American ambassador within thirty minutes. It could be on BBC 1 at six o'clock . . .'

'How much?' Tug insisted.

'Five million in cash, paid into a Swiss account immediately.'

'With you as the signatory?'

'And Omeru as a counter-signatory.'

'What else?'

'You will intercede with the president of Zaïre. He is a friend of yours, but no friend of Taffari's. We want him to allow clandestine passage of arms and munitions across his border with Ubomo. All he has to do is turn a blind eye.'

'Is that all?'

'That's the lot.' Daniel nodded.

'All right. I agree,' Tug said. 'Give me the account number and I'll deposit the money before noon tomorrow.'

Daniel stood up. 'Cheer up. All is not lost, Tug,' he advised. 'Victor Omeru will be very kindly disposed towards you once he is reinstated in his rightful position. I am sure he will be prepared to renegotiate the contract with you – with the proper safeguards in place this time.'

After Daniel had left, Tug Harrison sat staring at his Picasso for fully five minutes.

Then he glanced at his watch. There was a nine-hour time difference in Taipei. He picked up the telephone and dialled the international code, followed by Ning Heng H'Sui's private number. The old man's eldest son, Fang, screened the call, and then passed him on to his father.

'I have a very interesting proposition for you,' Tug told the old man. 'I want to fly out to speak to you face to face. I can be in Taipei within twenty-four hours – will you be there?'

He made two other phone calls. One to his chief pilot's home number to warn him to get the Gulfstream ready, and the second to the Crédit Suisse Bank in Zurich.

'Mr Mulder, I will be making a large transfer from the number two account within the next twenty-four hours. Five million sterling. Make certain there is no delay once you receive the code card instruction.'

Then he hung up the telephone and stared at the painting again without seeing it. He had to decide what reason he would give Ning for wanting to sell his share in UDC. Should he say that he was in a cash bind? Or that he needed to be liquid for a new acquisition? Which would Ning fall for more readily?

What was his price? He mustn't set it too low, for that

484

would arouse the cunning old oriental's suspicions immediately. Not too high either. Low enough to excite his greed, high enough not to alarm him. It was a nice calculation. He would have the duration of the flight to Taipei to consider it.

'That young fool Cheng has dropped me in it. It's only right that his father be made to pay.'

He thought about Ning Cheng Gong. He has been too good a choice, Tug smiled bitterly. He had asked for a ruthless one, and got more than he bid for.

Of course, Tug had known about the forced labour, but not the details of their treatment. He had not wanted to know. Neither had he known for certain about the use of the arsenic reagents, though he had suspected that Cheng was using them. The platinum recovery figures had been too high, the profits too good, for it not to be so. He had not wanted to know any of the unpleasant details. But, he thought philosophically, the enhanced profitability of the mining venture would make it easier to sell out his interests to Lucky Dragon.

Ning Heng H'Sui would think he was getting the bargain of his life.

'Good luck, Lucky Dragon,' Tug grunted. 'You're going to need all of it.'

Three months to the day since his last crossing Daniel stood on the moraine below the Ruwatamagufa glacier. This time he was properly equipped for the alpine conditions; there would be no more frostbite. And this time he was not alone.

The line of porters, each man bowed forward against the headband of his pack, stretched back as far as Daniel could see, into the mountain mist. They were all men of the Konjo tribe, dour mountaineers who could carry heavy loads at these high altitudes. There were six hundred and fifty porters, and each man carried an eighty-pound pack.

In all, that made twenty-six tons of arms and ammunition. There were no sophisticated weapons in the loads, only the tried and true tools of the guerrilla and the terrorist, the ubiquitous AK 47 and the Uzi, the RPD light machine-gun and the RPG rocket-launcher, Tokarev automatic pistols and American M26 fragmentation grenades, or at least convincing copies of them made in Yugoslavia or Romania.

All of these were readily obtainable at short notice in any quantity required, as long as the buyer had cash. Daniel was amazed how easy it had been. Tug Harrison had supplied him with the names and telephone numbers of five dealers, one in Florida, two in Europe and two in the Middle East.

'Take your pick,' Tug had invited. 'But check what you're getting before you pay. Some of that stuff has been floating around for forty years.' Daniel and his instructors had personally opened every case and laboriously checked each piece.

Daniel had calculated that the very minimum number of instructors he needed was four. He went back to Zimbabwe to find them. They were all men he had fought with or against during the bush war. They were all Swahili speakers and they were all black. A white face attracted a lot of attention in Ubomo.

The leader of the group of four was an ex-sergeant-major in the Ballantyne Scouts, a man who had fought with men like Roland Ballantyne and Sean Courtney. He was a magnificent figure of a Matabele warrior called Morgan Tembi.

There was another recruit in the party, a cameraman to replace Bonny Mahon. Shadrach Mbeki was a black South African exile who had done good work for the BBC, the best man that Daniel could find at such short notice.

To the north Mount Stanley was hidden in clouds, and the cloud dropped down to form a grey cold ceiling only a hundred feet above their heads, but to the east below the cloud it was open. Daniel gazed down upon the forest almost ten thousand feet below. It looked like the ocean, green and endless, except to the north where a dark cancer had bitten into the green. The open mined area was deeper and wider than when Daniel had last seen it from this vantage point only a few short months ago.

The cloud and the mist dropped over them abruptly, blotting out the distant carnage, and Daniel roused himself and started down, the long column of porters unwinding behind him. Sepoo was waiting for him where the bamboo forest began at the ten thousand foot level.

'It is good to see you again, Kuokoa, my brother. Kara-Ki sends you her heart,' he told Daniel. 'She asks that you come to her swiftly. She says she can wait no longer.'

The men of Sepoo's clan had cut out the trail through the bamboo, widening it so that the porters could pass through without having to stoop.

Below the bamboo where the true rain forest began at the six thousand foot level, Patrick Omeru was waiting with his teams of Uhali recruits to take over from the Konjo mountaineers. Daniel paid off the Konjo and watched them climb back through the bamboo into their misty highlands. Then the Bambuti guided them on to the newly opened trail, back towards Gondala.

After Kelly's message Daniel could not restrain himself to the pace of the heavily laden convoy, and he and Sepoo hurried ahead. Kelly was on the trail coming to meet them, and they came upon each other suddenly around a bend in the forest path.

Kelly and Daniel came up short and stared at each other, neither of them seemed able to move or even to speak until Kelly said huskily, without taking her eyes from Daniel's face, 'Go on ahead, Sepoo. Far, far ahead!'

Sepoo giggled happily and went without looking back.

 During Daniel's absence, Victor Omeru had built his new headquarters in the edge of the forest beyond the waterfall at Gondala where it would be hidden from any possible aerial surveillance. It was a simple *baraza* with half walls and a thatched roof. He sat with Daniel on the raised dais at one end of the hut.

Daniel was meeting the resistance leaders, many of them for the first time. They were seated facing the dais on long split-pole benches, like students in a lecture theatre. There were thirty-eight of them, mostly Uhali tribesmen, but six were influential Hita who were disenchanted with Taffari and had thrown in their lot with Victor Omeru as soon as they heard that he was still alive. These Hita were vital to the plan of action that Daniel had devised and discussed with Victor.

Two of them were highly placed in the army and one was a senior police officer. The other three were government officials who would be able to arrange permits and licences for travel and transport. All of them would be able to supply vital intelligence.

At first there had been some natural objection to Daniel's new cameraman filming the proceedings, but Victor had interceded and now Shadrach Mbeki was working so unobtrusively that they soon forgot his presence. As a reward for his assistance Victor Omeru had agreed that Daniel could make a film record of the entire campaign.

Daniel opened the meeting by introducing his four Matabele military instructors. As each man rose and faced the audience, Daniel recited his curriculum vitae. They were all impressive men, but Morgan Tembi in particular they regarded with awe.

'Between them they have trained thousands of fighting men,' Daniel told them. 'They won't be interested in parade-ground drills or spit and polish. They will simply teach you to use the weapons we have brought over the mountains and to use them to the best possible effect.' He looked at Patrick Omeru in the front row. 'Patrick, can you come up here and tell us how many men you have at your disposal, and where they are at the present time?'

Patrick had been busy during Daniel's absence. He had recruited almost fifteen hundred young men.

'Well done, Patrick, that's more than we need,' Daniel told him. 'I was planning on a core of a thousand men – four units of two hundred and fifty, each under the command of one of the instructors. More than that will be difficult to conceal and deploy. However, we will be able to use the others in non-combatant roles.'

The staff conference went on for three days. At the last session Daniel addressed them again.

'Our plans are simple. That makes them good – there is less

to go wrong. Our whole strategy is based on two principles. Number one is that we have to move fast. We have to be in a position to strike within weeks rather than months. Number two is total surprise. Our security must be iron-clad. If Taffari gets even a whiff of our plans he'll crack down so hard that we'll have no chance of success whatsoever. There it is, gentlemen, speed and stealth. We will meet again here on the first of next month. By then President Omeru and I will have a detailed plan of action drawn up. Until then you will be taking orders from your instructors in the training-camps. Good luck to all of us.'

Pirri was confused and angry and filled with formless despair and hatred.

For months now he had lived alone in the forest with not another man to talk to, or woman to laugh with. At night he lay alone in his carelessly built leaf hut far from the huts of other men and he thought of his youngest wife. She was sixteen years of age, with plump little breasts. He remembered the wetness and lubricious warmth of her body, and he moaned aloud in the darkness as he thought that he would never again know the comfort of a woman's body.

During the day he was lethargic and without care. He no longer hunted with his old intensity. Sometimes he sat for hours gazing into one of the dark forest pools. Twice he heard the honey chameleon call and he did not follow. He grew thin and his beard began turning white. Once he heard a party of Bambuti women in the forest, laughing and chattering as they gathered mushrooms and roots. He crept close and spied upon them, and his heart felt as though it would break. He longed to join them, but knew he could not.

Then one day while wandering alone, Pirri cut the trail of a party of *wazungu*. He studied their tracks and read that there were twenty of them, and that they moved with purpose and determination as though on a journey. It was exceedingly strange to find other men in the forest, for the Hita and Uhali

489

were afraid of hobgoblins and monsters, and never entered the tall trees if they could avoid doing so. Pirri recovered a little of his old curiosity, and he followed the tracks of the *wazungu*. They were moving well, and it took him many hours to catch up with them. Then he discovered a most remarkable thing.

Deep in the forest he found a camp where many men were assembled. They were all armed with the *banduki* that had a strange banana-shaped appendage hanging from beneath – either a tail or a penis, Pirri was not certain. And while Pirri watched in astonishment from his hiding-place, these men fired their *banduki* and made a terrible clattering clamour that frightened the birds into flight and sent the monkeys scampering away across the forest galleries.

All this was extraordinary, but most marvellous of all was that these men were not Hita. These days only Hita soldiers in uniform carried *banduki*. These men were Uhali.

Pirri thought about what he had seen for many days, and then the acquisitive instinct, which had been dormant in him since the coming of the Molimo, began to stir. He thought about Chetti Singh, and wondered if Chetti Singh would give him tobacco if he told him about the armed men in the forest. He hated Chetti Singh who had cheated and lied to him but as he thought about the tobacco, the saliva jetted from under his tongue. He could almost taste it in his mouth. The old tobacco hunger was like a pain in his chest and his belly.

The next day he went to find Chetti Singh and he whistled and sang as he went. He was coming alive again after the Molimo death. He stopped only once, to hunt a colobus monkey that he spied in the treetops eating the yellow fruit of the mongongo tree. His old skills came back to him and he crept to within twenty paces of the monkey without it suspecting his presence, and he shot a poisoned arrow that struck one of its legs.

The monkey fled shrieking through the branches, but it did not go far before it fell to earth, paralysed by the poison, its lips curled up in the dreadful rictus of agony as it frothed and trembled and shook before it died. The poison on Pirri's arrow was fresh and strong. He had found the nest of the little beetles only days before and had dug them up and crushed them to paste in a bark crucible and smeared his arrow-tips with the juices.

With his belly full of monkey meat and the wet skin folded into his bark-fibre bag, he went on towards the rendezvous with the one-armed Sikh.

Pirri waited two days at the rendezvous, the clearing in the forest that had once been a logging camp but was now overgrown and reverting to jungle. He wondered if the Uhali storekeeper who kept the little *duka* on the side of the main highway had passed on his message to Chetti Singh.

Then he began to believe that Chetti Singh had received the message but would not come to him. Perhaps Chetti Singh had learned of the Molimo death and was also ostracising him. Perhaps nobody would ever speak to Pirri again. His recent high spirits faded as he sat alone in the forest waiting for Chetti Singh to come, and the sense of despair and confusion overwhelmed him all over again.

Chetti Singh came on the afternoon of the second day. Pirri heard his Landrover long before it arrived and suddenly his anger and hatred had something on which to focus.

He thought how Chetti Singh had cheated and tricked him so many times before. He thought how he had never given him everything he had promised; always there was short-weight of tobacco, and water in the gin.

Then he thought how Chetti Singh had made him kill the elephant. Pirri had never been as angry as he was now. He was too angry even to lash out at the trees around him, too angry to shout aloud. His throat was tight and closed, and his hands shook. Chetti Singh was the one who had brought the curse of the Molimo down upon him. Chetti Singh had killed his soul.

Now he forgot about the armed *wazungu* in the forest. He even forgot about the tobacco hunger, as he waited for Chetti Singh to come.

The mud-streaked Landrover butted its way into the clearing, pushing down the thick secondary growth of vegetation ahead of it. It stopped and the door opened and Chetti Singh stepped down.

He looked around him at the forest and wiped his face with a white cloth. He had put on much weight recently. He was plumper now than he had been before he had lost the arm. His shirt was stained dark with sweat between his shoulder-blades where he had sat against the leather seat.

He mopped his face and adjusted his turban before he shouted into the forest, 'Pirri! Come out!'

Pirri sniggered with laughter and whispered aloud, mimicking the Sikh. 'Pirri! Come out!' And then his voice was bitter, 'See how he oozes grease like a joint of pork on the coals. Pirri, come out!'

Chetti Singh strutted around the clearing impatiently. After a while he opened his fly and urinated, then he zipped his trousers and looked at his wristwatch.

'Pirri, are you there?'

Pirri did not answer him, and Chetti Singh said something angrily in a language that Pirri did not understand, but he knew that it was an insult.

'I am going now,' Chetti Singh shouted, and marched back to the Landrover.

'O master,' Pirri called to him. 'I see you! Do not go!'

Chetti Singh spun around to face the forest. 'Where are you?' he shouted.

'I am here, O master. I have something for you that will make you very happy. Something of great value.'

'What is it?' Chetti Singh asked. 'Where are you?'

'Here I am.' Pirri stepped out of the shadows with the bow slung over his shoulder.

'What stupidity is this?' Chetti Singh demanded. 'Why do you hide from me?'

'I am your slave.' Pirri grinned ingratiatingly. 'And I have a gift for you.'

'What is it? Elephant teeth?' Chetti Singh asked, and there was greed in his voice.

'Better than that. Something of greater value.'

'Show me,' Chetti Singh demanded.

'Will you give me tobacco?'

'I will give you as much tobacco as the gift is worth.'

'I will show you,' Pirri agreed. 'Follow me, O master.'

'Where is it? How far is it?'

'Only a short distance, only that far.' Pirri indicated a small arc of the sky with two fingers, less than an hour's travel.

Chetti Singh looked dubious.

'It is a thing of great beauty and value,' Pirri wheedled. 'You will be very pleased.'

'All right,' the Sikh agreed. 'Lead me to this treasure.'

Pirri went slowly, allowing Chetti Singh to keep close behind him. He went in a wide circle through the densest part of the forest, crossing the same stream twice. There was no sun in the forest; a man steered by the fall of the land and the run of the rivers.

Pirri showed Chetti Singh the same river twice from different directions. By now, the Sikh was totally lost, blundering blindly after the little pygmy with no sense of distance or direction.

After the second hour Chetti Singh was sweating very heavily and his voice was rough. 'How much further is it?' he asked.

'Very close,' Pirri assured him.

'I will rest for a while,' Chetti Singh said and sat down on a log. When he looked up again, Pirri had vanished.

Chetti Singh was not alarmed. He was accustomed to the elusive comings and goings of the Bambuti. 'Come back here!' he ordered, but there was no reply.

Chetti Singh sat alone for a long time. Once or twice he called out to the pygmy. Each time his voice was shriller. The panic was building up in him.

After another hour he was pleading. 'Please, Pirri, I will give you anything you ask. Please show yourself.'

Pirri laughed. His laughter floated through the trees and Chetti Singh sprang to his feet and plunged off the faint track. He stumbled towards where he thought he had heard the laughter.

'Pirri!' he begged. 'Please come to me.' But the laughter came from a new direction. Chetti Singh ran towards it.

After a while he stopped, and looked about him wildly. He was streaming sweat and panting. Laughter, mocking and faint, trembled in the humid air. Chetti Singh turned around and staggered after it. It was like chasing a butterfly or a puff of smoke. The sound flitted and flirted through the trees, first from one direction, then the other.

Chetti Singh was weeping now. His turban had come loose and hooked on a branch and he did not stop to retrieve it. His hair and beard tumbled down, streaming down his chest and flying out behind him. His hair was soaked with sweat.

He fell and dragged himself up and ran on, his clothing stained with mud and leaf mould. He screamed his terror to the trees, and the laughter became fainter and fainter, until at last he heard it no more.

Chetti Singh fell on his knees and held up his hand in supplication. 'Please,' he whispered, with tears streaming down his face. 'Please don't leave me alone here.'

And the forest was silent with dark menace.

Pirri followed him for two days, watching him stagger haphazardly, ranting and pleading, through the forest, watching him grow weaker and more desperate, stumbling over dead branches, falling into streams, crawling on his belly, shaking with terror and loneliness. His clothing was ripped off him by branch and thorn. Only a few rags still hung on his body. His skin was scratched and lacerated, and the flies and the stinging insects buzzed around the wounds. His beard and long hair were tangled and matted, and his eyes were wild and mad.

On the second day, Pirri stepped out of the forest ahead of him and Chetti Singh screamed like a woman with the shock and tried to drag himself to his feet again.

'Don't leave me alone again,' he screamed. 'Please, anything you ask, but not again.'

'Like you, I am alone,' Pirri said with hatred in his heart. 'I am dead. The Molimo has killed me. You are talking to a dead man, to a ghost. You cannot ask mercy from the ghost of a man you murdered.'

Deliberately Pirri fitted an arrow to his little bow. The poison was black and sticky on the point.

Chetti Singh gaped stupidly. 'What are you doing?' he blurted. He knew about the poison, he had seen animals die from Bambuti arrows.

Pirri lifted his bow and drew the arrow to his chin.

'No!' Chetti Singh held up his hand to ward off the arrow just as Pirri released it.

The arrow, aimed at his chest, hit Chetti Singh in the palm of his open hand and stuck firmly, its point buried between the bones of the first and second fingers.

Chetti Singh stared at it.

'Now we are both dead,' said Pirri softly, and vanished into the forest.

Chetti Singh stared in horror at the arrow in his palm. The flesh around it was already stained purple by the poison. Then the pain began. It was stronger than anything that Chetti Singh had ever imagined. It was fire in his blood, he could feel it running up his arm into his chest. The pain was so terrible that for a long anguished moment it took his breath away and he could not scream.

Then he found his voice and the sound of his agony rang through the trees. Pirri paused for a while to listen to it. Only when the forest was silent again did he move on.

 'We are ready,' Daniel said quietly, but his voice carried to every man seated in the headquarters hut at Gondala.

They were the same men who had gathered here a month ago, and yet they were different. There was an air of confidence and determination about them that had not been there before.

Daniel had spoken to his Matabele instructors before the meeting. They were pleased. No man had been dropped from the training camps for any reason except sickness or injury.

'They are *amabutho* now,' Morgan Tembi had told Daniel. 'They are warriors now.'

'You have done well,' Daniel told them. 'You can be proud of what you have achieved in so short a time.'

He turned to the blackboard on the thatched wall behind him and pulled aside the cloth that had covered it. The board was covered with diagrams and schedules.

'This, gentlemen, is our order of battle,' Daniel said. 'We will go over it, not once but until every one of you can recite it in your sleep,' he warned them. 'Here are your four cadres, each of two hundred and fifty men. Each cadre is assigned different targets and objectives – the main army barracks, the airfield, the harbour, the labour camps . . .' Daniel worked down the list. 'Now, most important of all, the radio and television studio in Kahali. Taffari's security forces are good. Even with initial surprise we cannot hope to hold all our objectives longer than the first few hours, not without popular support. We have to secure the studio. President Omeru will be moved to the capital well ahead of time and will be in hiding in the old quarter, ready to come out and broadcast an appeal to the people. As soon as the populace sees him on television and realises that he is alive and leading the rising, we can expect every man and woman to join us. They will come out on to the streets and join the battle. Taffari's storm-troopers may be better armed than we are, but we will crush them by sheer weight of numbers.

'However, there is one other condition that we have to fulfil in order to ensure success. We have to take out Taffari himself within the first hour. We have to crush the head of the snake. Without Taffari they will collapse. There is nobody to replace him. Taffari himself has seen to that. He has murdered all possible rivals. He is a one-man band, but we have to get him with the first surprise stroke.'

'That won't be so easy.' Patrick Omeru came to his feet. 'He seems to have a kind of sixth sense. He has already survived two assassination attempts in the short time he has been in power. They are beginning to say he is using witchcraft, like Idi Amin—'

'Sit down, Patrick,' Daniel interrupted him sharply.

'Witchcraft' was a dangerous word to use, even to a group of educated and intelligent men such as this. They were still African, and witchcraft was rooted in the African soil.

'Taffari is a cunning swine. We all know that. He seldom sticks to any routine. He changes plans at the very last moment. He cancels appointments without reason and he sleeps at the home of a different wife each night, in random order. He's cunning, but he is no wizard. He'll bleed good red blood, I promise you that.'

They cheered him for that and the mood of the gathering improved. They were confident and eager again.

'However, there is one routine that Taffari has established. He visits the mining operation of Wengu at least once a month.

He likes to see his treasure coming out of the earth. At Wengu he is isolated. It is the one place in the entire country where he is most vulnerable.' Daniel paused and looked down at them. 'We are fortunate to have some good intelligence from Major Fashoda.' He indicated the Hita officer on the dais beside him. 'As you all know, Major Fashoda is the transport officer on Taffari's staff. He is the man responsible for arranging Taffari's personal transport. Taffari always uses a Puma helicopter to visit Wengu. He has ordered a Puma to stand by for Monday the 14th. This indicates a high probability that his next inspection tour to Wengu will be on that date. It gives us five days to make our final preparations.'

 Ning Cheng Gong sat beside President Taffari on the padded bench in the fuselage of the airforce Puma helicopter. Through the open hatch he could see the green blur of the treetops as the Puma sped low across the forest. The wind buffeted them and it was noisy in the cabin. They had to raise their voices and shout to be heard.

'What news of Chetti Singh?' Ephrem Taffari shouted, his mouth close to Cheng's ear.

'Nothing,' Cheng shouted back. 'We found his Landrover, but no sign of him. It has been two weeks now. He must have died in the forest, as Armstrong did.'

'He was a good man,' Taffari said. 'He knew how to get work out of the convict labour. He was good at keeping costs down.'

'Yes,' Cheng agreed. 'He will be very hard to replace. He spoke the language. He understood Africa. He understood . . .' Cheng bit his lip. He had been on the point of using a derogatory term for black people. 'He understood the system,' he ended lamely.

'Even in the short time since his disappearance there has been a marked drop in production and profits.'

'I'm working on it,' Cheng assured him. 'I have some good men coming to replace him. Mining men from South Africa, as good as Chetti Singh. They also know how to get the most work out of these people.'

Taffari nodded and stood up. He made his way down the length of the cabin to speak to his companion.

As usual, Taffari was travelling with a woman. His latest flame was a tall Hita girl, a blues singer in a night club in Kahali. She had a face like a black Nefertiti. Taffari was also accompanied by a detachment of his presidential guard. Twenty crack paratroopers under the command of Major Kajo. Kajo had received promotion after the disappearance of Bonny Mahon. Taffari appreciated loyalty and tact, and Kajo was a man on the way up.

Cheng had come to detest these presidential inspection tours of the mining and logging concessions. He hated low-flying in one of the ancient Pumas of the Ubomo airforce. The helicopter pilots were notorious daredevils. There had been two fatal crashes in the squadron since his arrival in Ubomo.

More even than the physical danger, Cheng was uncomfortable with Taffari's searching questions and penetrating eye for figures and production details. Under his dashing martial exterior he had an accountant's mind. He understood finance. He could form a shrewd judgement as to when profits were falling below estimate; he had an instinct for money, and he could sense when he was being cheated.

Of course, Cheng was milking the syndicate, but not excessively, not blatantly. He was merely showing a benign bias towards the Lucky Dragon. He had done it skilfully. Not even a trained auditor would have picked it up, but President Taffari was already suspicious.

Cheng used this respite, sitting between two heavily armed paratroopers, feeling slightly queasy with air sickness, to go over all his financial dispositions and to search for any weak spots in his system that Taffari might be able to pin-point.

At last he decided that, at least temporarily, it might be prudent to reduce the amount he was skimming. He knew that if Taffari's suspicions ever became certainty he would not hesitate to terminate his contract, permanently, with the seal of a Kalashnikov No. 47. There would be another unmarked grave in the forest along with those of Chetti Singh and Daniel Armstrong.

At that moment the Puma banked sharply and Cheng clutched at his seat. Through the open fuselage hatch he had a glimpse of the bare red earth of the mining cut and the line of yellow MOMUs strung out along the edge of the forest. They had arrived at Wengu.

Daniel watched the Puma circle the landing-pad, slow down in flight and at last hover, nose-heavy, against a backdrop of purple cumulus cloud. There were puddles of rainwater on the concrete pad and the windsock flapped, sodden on its pole.

A small delegation of Taiwanese and black managers and officials were gathered in front of the main administrative building, confirming that Daniel's intelligence had been correct. Ephrem Taffari was on board the hovering helicopter.

Daniel's perch in the middle branches of the mahogany tree was three hundred and twenty yards from the landing pad. He had climbed to his perch during the night. Sepoo had waited at the base of the tree and when Daniel lowered the light nylon rope, he had hooked on the bundle of sniper's equipment.

By dawn Daniel was settled close in against the main trunk of the tree, beneath a tangle of vines and leafy climbing plants. He had cut a narrow window in the foliage which gave him a clear view of the helicopter pad. He wore a full camouflage sniper's coverall and mesh face-mask. His hands were covered with gloves.

His rifle was a 7mm Remington Magnum and he had chosen a 160 grain soft-point bullet, a compromise between velocity and high ballistic coefficient that would not be too severely affected by a cross-wind. He had tested the rifle extensively and it was shooting consistent four-inch groups at 350 yards. That wasn't good enough for any fancy head shots. He would aim for the centre of the chest. The expanding bullet could be expected to rip out Taffari's lungs.

It felt vaguely obscene to be thinking like this again. The last time had been ten years previously when the Scouts had staked out a ZANU cadre leader's kraal in Matabeleland. The man had been too wily and elusive for them to attempt an arrest. They had culled him without warning. Daniel had fired the shot and had felt sick for days afterwards.

Daniel thrust the memory aside. It might dilute his determination. Thinking like that might make his trigger finger just that crucial thousandth of a second slow when the image in the Zeiss lens was right.

If Taffari was on board the Puma, then Cheng must be with him. Cheng was the chief executive officer of UDC and he had accompanied every other presidential tour of the workings. If he could take Taffari with the first shot, then he could rely on a moment of utter astonishment and paralysis amongst his retinue. There would be a chance to get Cheng with the second shot, if he were quick enough.

There would be no hesitation about that kill. Deliberately he conjured up the memory of Johnny Nzou and his family to steel himself. He recalled every dreadful detail of the murder scene at Chiwewe and felt the sour hatred and rage swell in his chest. Ning Cheng Gong was his real reason for being in Ubomo at all. The second bullet was for him.

Then there was Chetti Singh. Daniel doubted that even if the Sikh were a member of the presidential party he would get the opportunity of a third shot. The paratrooper guards were trained soldiers. He might get a second shot, but not a third before they reacted.

Chetti Singh would be taken care of later, once the rising succeeded. He was in charge of the labour camps. Daniel's film of the executions in the forest would be damning evidence at his trial. He could afford to wait for Chetti Singh.

In the short time that it took the Puma to sink down towards the landing-pad, Daniel reviewed his dispositions, even though it was too late to change them now.

Victor Omeru was in Kahali. He had travelled down to the lakeside in one of the logging trucks, disguised as the mate of the Uhali driver. The arms and ammunition had been distributed in the same manner, transported in the UDC trucks. It was a nice irony, using the tyrant's own system to defeat him.

At this moment there were two revolutionary commandos in the capital, waiting for the word to strike. As soon as it was received, a detachment would storm the TV and radio studios. Victor Omeru would broadcast to the nation, calling upon them to rise. He would tell them that Taffari was dead and promise them an end to their suffering.

Meanwhile the other two commandos were deployed here at Wengu and Sengi-Sengi. Their first objectives would be to wipe out Taffari's Hita escort and to release the thirty thousand captives.

The signal for the rising to begin would be the shot that Daniel fired through Ephrem Taffari's lungs. Victor and Patrick Omeru would be informed by radio the moment that happened. There was a powerful radio in the UDC administrative building beside the landing-pad, but they would probably not be able to reach that immediately. As a back-up Daniel had a portable VHF transmitter, with which they could contact the headquarters at Gondala. Kelly was the radio operator who would transmit the signal that the rising had begun.

Daniel had drawn up four fall-backs and alternative plans to deal with every foreseeable contingency, but everything hinged on getting Taffari with the first shot. If Daniel failed there, he could expect Taffari to react with the speed and fury of a wounded lion. He would rally his men – it didn't bear thinking about. Daniel put the possibility out of his mind. He had to get Taffari.

The Puma was only fifty feet above the concrete landing-pad, sinking towards it slowly.

Daniel laid his cheek against the buttstock of his rifle and stared into the brilliant field of the telescopic sight. It was set to nine magnifications. He could see the expressions on the faces of the little reception committee at the landing-pad.

He lifted his aim, and captured the image of the helicopter. The lens was too high-powered to show him more than the hatchway in the Puma's fuselage. The flight engineer stood in the opening, directing the aircraft's descent. Daniel focused his attention on him, keeping the cross-hair of the telescope on his chest, using the buckle of his safety strap as an aiming point.

Suddenly another head appeared over the engineer's shoulder. Beneath the maroon beret with its glittering brass cap-badge were Ephrem Taffari's noble aquiline features.

'He's come,' Daniel exulted. 'It's him.'

He lifted the cross-hairs of the sight and tried to hold between Taffari's dark eyes. The movement of the helicopter, his own heart beat and hand shake, the inherent inaccuracy of the rifle all made it an impossible shot, but he concentrated all his mind and his will on Taffari. He purged himself of any last vestige of conscience and of mercy. Once again he forced upon himself the cold hard determination of the assassin.

At that moment the first raindrop struck the back of his neck. It startled him, his aim trembled, then another raindrop splashed against the lens of the Zeiss scope, and a soft wavering line of rain water ran down across the glass and dimmed the brilliance of the telescopic image.

Then it started to rain in real earnest, that sudden tropical deluge that seemed to turn the air to mist and blue water. It was like standing beneath a torrent in a mountain stream.

Daniel's vision dissolved. The crisply detailed human shapes he had been watching an instant before became dim blurs of movement. The men waiting on the landing-pad raised coloured umbrellas, and swarmed forward to meet the president, to offer him protection from the roaring rain.

There was misty movement and confusion. The colours of the umbrellas ran and starred and confused his eye. He saw a distorted image of Ephrem Taffari vault down lightly from the hatchway. Daniel had expected him to pose theatrically above the heads of the crowd and perhaps make a brief speech, but he vanished instantly. Though Daniel tried desperately to keep the cross-hairs on him, somebody raised a wet umbrella and held it over him.

Ning Cheng Gong's misty figure appeared in the hatchway, distracting Daniel's concentration. He swung the sights back towards Cheng, and then stopped himself. It had to be Taffari first. Desperately he swung the telescope back and forth, questing for a view of his target. The welcoming delegation had crowded around Taffari, umbrellas raised, obscuring him completely. The rain struck the concrete pad with such force that each drop exploded in a burst of spray.

Rain was splattering against the lens of the telescopic sight and streaming down Daniel's face beneath the mask.

Hita paratroopers were jumping down from the helicopter and clustering around their president. No sign of Taffari now, and everybody was running towards the waiting Landrovers, crouched down under the lofted umbrellas, splashing through the pools of rain water.

Taffari appeared again, stepping out fast in the slanting rain, heading for the leading vehicle. Even at a walking pace and taking into account the velocity of the 7mm bullet, Daniel would have to lead him by two feet or more. He could barely distinguish him through the clouded lens. It was an almost impossible shot, but he tightened up on the trigger, just as one of the Hita bodyguards ran forward to assist his master.

The shot went off before Daniel could stop himself. He saw the Hita paratrooper spin round and go down, shot through the chest. It would have killed Taffari as cleanly, if the man had not covered him.

The whole pattern of moving men in the rain exploded. Taffari threw down the umbrella he carried and darted forward. All around him men were running in confusion.

Daniel jacked another round into the chamber of the rifle and fired again, a snap shot at Taffari. It had no effect, a clean miss. Taffari kept running. He reached the Landrover and before Daniel could reload, he had jerked open the door and thrown himself into the front seat of the vehicle.

Daniel glimpsed Ning Cheng Gong in the thick of it, and fired again. He saw another paratrooper go down on his knees, hit low in the body, and then the other soldiers were blazing away wildly towards the edges of the forest, uncertain from which direction Daniel's shots were coming.

Daniel was still trying desperately to get another shot at Taffari, but the Landrover was pulling away. He fired at the head he could see behind the windscreen, not certain whether it was Taffari or a driver. The windscreen shattered, but the vehicle did not check or swerve.

He emptied the magazine at the accelerating vehicle. Then as he tried to reload from the bandolier at his waist, he saw three or four of the Hita guards and the civilian officials take hits and go down sprawling in the rain. There was the swelling clatter of small-arms fire.

The men of his own commando had opened fire from their positions in the forest outside the perimeter.

The uprising had begun, but Taffari was still alive.

Daniel saw the Landrover make a wide circle, swinging past the office building and come back round under the hovering helicopter. The Puma was hanging twenty feet above the ground, almost hidden by the falling curtains of rain. Taffari was leaning out of the driver's window, signalling frantically for the pilot to pick him up again.

At that moment a man appeared out of the jungle on the far side of the clearing. Even at that distance Daniel recognised Morgan Tembi, the Matabele instructor. He carried the tube of an RPG rocket-launcher on his shoulder as he raced forward.

None of the Hita bodyguard seemed to have spotted him. A hundred paces from the hovering Puma, Morgan dropped on one knee, steadied himself and fired a rocket.

It rode on a tail of white smoke, whooshing in to hit the Puma well forward, almost in line with the perspex pilot's canopy.

The cockpit and the pilot in it were obliterated by the burst of smoke and flame. The Puma performed a lazy cartwheel in the air and fell to earth on its back. The spinning rotors smashed themselves into tiny fragments on the concrete landing-pad. An instant later a ball of fire and black smoke devoured the machine.

Morgan Tembi jumped to his feet and ran back towards the edge of the forest. He never made it. The Hita bodyguards shot him down long before he could reach cover, but he had cut off Taffari's escape.

It had taken less than a minute but already the Hita were recovering from the shock of the surprise attack. They were piling into Landrovers and following Taffari as he drove for the roadway beyond the office building. Taffari must have realised the strength and numbers of the attackers and decided that his best bet would be to try and break out and reach the nearest road-block on the Sengi-Sengi road which was manned by his own men.

Three Landrovers filled with his own guards were flying after him. Most of the civilian officials were lying flat on the ground, trying to keep below the wild cross-fire, although some of them were running for the shelter of the office buildings. Daniel saw Cheng amongst them. His blue safari suit was distinctive, even in the rain mist. Before he could get a shot at him Cheng reached the building and ducked through the front door.

Daniel turned his attention back to the four escaping Landrovers. They had almost reached the main road into the forest and the fire that the Uhali commando was turning upon them was furious but inaccurate. It seemed to be totally ineffectual. With Morgan Tembi dead they were blazing away without aiming, like the raw untried recruits they truly were.

Taffari was already out of range from where Daniel was perched in the mahogany tree. He was going to get clear away. The whole attack was becoming a fiasco. The Uhali were forgetting all their training. The plan was falling to pieces. The rising was doomed within minutes of beginning.

At that moment a huge yellow D10 caterpillar lumbered out of the forest.

'At least somebody has remembered his orders,' Daniel snarled to himself. He was angry at his failure, taking the full blame on himself.

The caterpillar tractor waddled forward, straddling the roadway, cutting off the flying convoy of Landrovers.

A small band of Uhali emerged from the forest and ran behind it, dressed in blue denim and other civilian clothing. They used the tractor as a barricade and opened fire on the leading Landrover as it raced towards them.

At close range their concentrated fire was at last effective. Taffari, in the leading Landrover, saw his escape cut off and spun the truck in a hard 180-degree turn. The other trucks followed him round.

They came back across the open ground in a line, and they were within range again. Daniel fired at Taffari's head, but the Landrover was doing sixty miles an hour and bouncing over the rough track. Daniel never saw the strike of his bullets, and the line of the Landrovers tore away down the track that led to where the MOMU units were working. That direction was a dead end. The road ended at the mining excavation. The situation had been retrieved from total disaster by the driver of the caterpillar tractor.

By now the column of Landrovers was out of sight from where Daniel was perched in the mahogany tree.

He left the rifle hanging on its strap and swung out of the branch. He used the nylon rope to abseil down the trunk of the tree, kicking himself outwards with both feet, dropping so swiftly that the rope scorched the palms of his hands. As he hit the ground Sepoo ran forward and handed him his AK 47 assault rifle and the haversack that contained the spare magazines and four M26 grenades.

'Where is Kara-Ki?' he demanded, and Sepoo pointed back into the forest. They ran together.

Two hundred yards further into the forest Kelly was crouched over the VHF radio transmitter. She jumped up when she saw Daniel.

'What happened?' she shouted. 'Did you get him?'

'It's a total balls-up,' Daniel told her grimly. 'Taffari's still out there. We haven't got control of the radio station at Wengu.'

'Oh God, what happens now?'

'Transmit!' He made the decision. 'Give Victor the go-ahead. We are committed now. We can't turn back.'

'But if Taffari—'

'Damn it, Kelly, just do it! I'm going to try and retrieve the ball. At least Taffari didn't get clear away. We are still in with a chance. For the present we've got him bottled up here at Wengu.'

Kelly did not argue again, she knelt beside the radio set and lifted the microphone to her lips.

'Forest Base, this is Mushroom. Do you read me?'

The portable transmitter did not have the range to reach Kahali on the lakeshore direct. They must relay through the more powerful set at Gondala.

'Mushroom, this is Forest Base,' the voice of Kelly's male nurse from the Gondala clinic came back immediately. He was a trusted Uhali retainer of many years' standing.

'This is a relay for Silver Head in Kahali. Message reads, "The Sun has Risen". I say again, "The Sun has Risen".'

'Stand by, Mushroom.'

There was a few minutes' silence, then Gondala came back on the air. 'Mushroom, Silver Head acknowledges "The Sun has Risen".'

The revolution was launched. Within the hour Victor Omeru would be on television announcing it to his nation. But Taffari was still alive.

'Kelly, listen to me.' Daniel took her arm and dragged her up to face him, making sure he had her full attention. 'Stay here. Try and keep in contact with Gondala. Don't go wandering off. Taffari's storm-troopers will be scattered everywhere. Stay here until I come back for you.'

She nodded. 'Be careful, darling.'

'Sepoo.' Daniel looked down at the little man. 'Stay here. Look after Kara-Ki.'

'With my life!' Sepoo told him.

'Kiss me!' Kelly demanded of Daniel.

'Just a quick one. More to follow,' Daniel promised.

He left her and ran back towards the UDC buildings.

Before he had gone a hundred yards he heard men in the forest ahead. 'Omeru!' he shouted. It was the password.

'Omeru!' they shouted back. 'The Sun has Risen!'

'Not yet, it bloody hasn't,' Daniel muttered, and went forward.

There were a dozen men of the commando, the blue denim jackets were almost a uniform.

'Come on!' He gathered them up.

Before they reached the road that ran down to the mining cut he had thirty men with him. The rain had stopped by now, and Daniel paused on the edge of the forest. Before them stretched the endless plain of churned earth that the MOMU units had devoured. The line of machines was ahead of them, ranged along the boundary where forest and red mud met. They looked like a line of battleships in a storm.

Closer still were the four Landrovers, scattered at abandoned angles on the muddy plain. As Daniel watched, the Hita guards were straggling across the open ground towards the nearest MOMU.

Daniel recognised Ephrem Taffari's tall uniformed figure leading them. It was clear that he had selected the nearest MOMU as the most readily defensible strong-point available to him, and Daniel conceded grimly that it was a good choice.

The steel sides of the gigantic machine would offer almost complete protection from small-arms fire. Even the RPG rockets would make no impression on its massive construction.

To reach it an attacker would have to cross soft open ground that could be covered by fire from the upper platforms of the MOMU. Just as important, the steel fortress was manoeuvrable. Once he was in control of it, Taffari could drive it anywhere.

Daniel looked about him quickly, by now there were fifty or so Uhali guerrillas congregated around him. They were noisy and over-excited, behaving like green troops after their first taste of fire. Some of them were cheering and firing at the distant figures of Taffari and his guards. They were well out of range, and it was a dangerous waste of their precious stocks of ammunition.

There was no point in trying to get them under control. He had to attack before they lost their wild spirits, and before Taffari reached the MOMU and organised its defence.

'Come on!' Daniel shouted. 'Omeru! "The Sun has Risen"!'

He led them out on to the open ground, and they followed him in a rabble, cheering wildly.

'Omeru!' they yelled. Daniel had to keep the momentum going.

The mud was ankle-deep in places, knee-deep in others. They passed the abandoned Landrovers. Ahead of them Daniel saw Taffari reach the MOMU and haul himself up one of the steel boarding ladders. As they ploughed on through the mud, their progress slowed to a plodding walk.

Taffari was organising his men as they came aboard the MOMU. They were taking cover behind the massive steel machinery. Bullets started slashing amongst the attackers, plugging into the mud, cracking around their heads. The man beside Daniel was hit. He went down face first in the mud.

The attack slowed, bogging down in the mud. The Hita on the MOMU were lodging in, hidden behind steel bulkheads. They were shooting accurately, and more of Daniel's men were falling.

The attack stalled, some of the Uhali broke and started to stumble back towards the forest. Others crouched behind the stranded Landrovers. They were not soldiers. They were clerks and truck-drivers and university students faced by crack paratroopers in an impregnable steel fortress. Daniel could not blame them for breaking, even though the revolution was dying in the mud with them.

He could not go on alone. Already the Hita had singled him out. Their fire was concentrating on him. He stumbled back to the nearest Landrover and crouched behind its chassis.

He saw the crew of the MOMU desert their stations and huddle helplessly on the lower platform. One of the Hita paratroopers gestured to them imperiously and with obvious relief they swarmed down the steel ladder and dropped into the mud like sailors abandoning a sinking ocean liner.

The engine of the MOMU was still running. The excavators were chewing into the earth, but now with no direction the gigantic rig was wandering out of its formation. The crews of the other rigs in the line saw what was happening and they too abandoned their posts and streamed overboard, trying to escape the bursts of gunfire that rattled and clanged against the steel plating.

It was a stand-off. Taffari's men had command of the MOMU and Daniel's commando were stalled in the mud unable to advance or retreat.

He tried to think of some way to break the *impasse*. He could not expect his shattered and demoralised survivors to mount another charge. Taffari had fifteen or twenty men up there, more than enough to hold them off.

At that moment he became aware of another eerie sound, like the mewling of seagulls or the cry of lost souls. He looked back and at first saw nothing. Then something moved at the edge of the forest. At first he could not make it out. It was not human, surely?

Then he saw other movement. The forest was coming alive. Thousands of strange creatures, as numerous as insects, like a column of safari ants on the march. They were red in their myriads, and the wild plaintive cry rose louder and more urgently from them as they swarmed out of the forest into the open.

Suddenly he realised what he was seeing. The gates of the labour camps were open. The guards had been overwhelmed and the Uhali slaves had risen out of the mud. They were red with it, coated with it, naked as corpses exhumed from the grave, starved to stick-like emaciation.

They swarmed forward in their legions, in their thousands,

women and men and children, sexless in their coating of mud, only their white and angry eyes glaring in the muddy red masks of their faces.

'Omeru!' they cried, and the sound was like a stormy sea on a rocky headland.

The fire of the Hita paratroopers was blanketed by the roar of their voices. The bullets of the AK 47 assault rifles made no impression on the densely packed ranks, where one man fell a dozen more swarmed forward to replace him. On the MOMU fortress the Hita guards were running out of ammunition. Even at this distance Daniel could sense their panic. They threw aside their empty rifles, the barrels hot as though from the furnace.

Unarmed they climbed the steel ladders to the highest platform of the ungainly yellow rig. Helplessly they stood at the railing and watched the naked red horde reach the machine and climb up towards them.

Daniel recognised Ephrem Taffari amongst the Hita on the upper deck. He was trying to speak to the slaves, spreading his arms in an oratorial gesture, trying to reason with them. In the end, when the front rank was almost upon him Taffari drew his pistol and fired down into them. He kept firing as they engulfed him.

For a time Daniel lost him in the struggling red mass of naked humanity. He was like a fry absorbed by a gigantic jelly fish. Then he saw Taffari again, lifted high above the heads of the mob by hundreds of upraised arms. They passed him forward struggling wildly.

Then they hurled him from the top of the MOMU.

Ephrem Taffari turned in the air, ungainly as a bird trying to fly with a broken wing. He dropped seventy feet, into the spinning silver blades of the excavator head. The blades sucked him in and in a single instant chopped him to a paste so fine that his blood did not leave so much as a stain on the wet earth.

Daniel stood up slowly.

On the MOMU they were killing the Hita paratroopers, tearing them to pieces with their bare hands, swarming over them screaming and exulting.

Daniel turned away. He started back towards where he had left Kelly. His progress was slow. Men of the commando clustered around him, shaking his hand, thumping him on the back, laughing and shouting and singing.

There was still some desultory small-arms fire in the forest. The administrative offices were on fire. Flames leapt high, crackling and pouring out black smoke. A roof collapsed. People were trapped in there, burning to death. The mob raged everywhere, chasing the guards and officials and engineers and clerks of the company, black and Taiwanese, anybody connected with the hated oppressor. They caught them and killed them, kicking and beating them as they writhed on the earth, hacking at them with spades or machetes, throwing their dismembered bodies into the flames. It was savage. It was Africa.

Daniel turned away from the horror. One man could not stop the orgy. They had suffered too long; their hatred was too fierce. He left the track and went into the forest to find Kelly.

He had not gone a hundred yards before he saw a small figure running towards him through the trees.

'Sepoo!' he called, and the pygmy darted to his side and seized his arm and shook it.

'Kara-Ki!' he screeched incoherently, there was a gash in his scalp and he was bleeding heavily.

'Where is she?' Daniel demanded. 'What has happened to her?'

'Kara-Ki! He has taken her. He has taken her into the forest.'

Kelly knelt in front of the radio set, gently manipulating the fine-tuning knob of the receiver. Although her transmitter did not have the range to reach the capital of Kahali on the lakeshore, Sepoo had climbed into the silk-cotton tree above her and strung the aerial wire from the top branches. She was picking up the transmission of Radio Ubomo on the twenty-five metre band with very little atmospheric disturbance.

'This next request is for Miriam Seboki of Kabute who is

eighteen years old today, from your boy friend, Abdullah, who wishes you many happy returns and says he loves you very much. He has requested, "Like a Virgin" by Madonna, so here it is just for you, Miriam . . .' The harsh cacophony of the music was aberrant in the forest silences and Kelly turned down the volume. Immediately she was aware of other sounds even more obscene, the distant fusillade of gunfire and the wild screams of fighting and dying men.

She tried to blot the sounds from her mind, tried to calm her anxiety and fear for the progress of the rising. She waited, powerless and afraid, for something to happen.

Suddenly the music was cut off, and the only sound from the speaker was the whistle and crackle of static. Then abruptly a new voice came on the air.

'People of Ubomo. This station is now under the control of the Freedom Army of Ubomo. We bring you the President of Ubomo, Victor Omeru, speaking to you in person from the radio studio in Kahali.'

There was a burst of martial music, the old national anthem, that Ephrem Taffari had banned when he seized power. Then the music ended. There was a pause and at last the thrilling voice that Kelly loved so well reverberated from the speaker.

'My beloved people of Ubomo, you who have suffered so much beneath the yoke of the oppressor, this is Victor Omeru. I know that most of you believed that I was dead. But this is not a voice from the grave. It is indeed I, Victor Omeru, who call upon you now.' Victor was speaking in Swahili, and he went on, 'I bring you tidings of hope and of great joy. Ephrem Taffari, the bloody tyrant, is dead. A loyal and true band of patriots has overthrown his cruel and brutal regime and given him the punishment he so justly deserves. Come forth, my people, a new sun rises over Ubomo . . .' His voice was so compelling, so sincere, that for a moment Kelly almost believed what he was saying – that Taffari was already dead and the revolution was secure. Then she heard the sound of gunfire and she glanced over her shoulder.

There was a man standing close to her. He had come up soundlessly behind her. He was an Asian, almost certainly Chinese. He wore a blue safari suit damp with rain or sweat and stained with mud and blood. His long straight black hair hung down over his forehead. There was a shallow cut in his cheek from which the blood had dripped to stain the front of his jacket.

He carried a Tokarev pistol in one hand, and there was a wild and hunted look in his eyes – eyes so dark that there was no division between iris and pupil, black eyes like a mako shark. His mouth was contorted with fear or anger, and the hand that held the pistol twitched and trembled.

Although she had never seen him before, Kelly knew who he was. She had heard Daniel speak of him so often. She had seen his photograph in the out-of-date copies of the Ubomo *Herald* newspaper that occasionally reached Gondala. She knew that he was the Taiwanese managing-director of UDC, the man who had murdered Daniel's friend, Johnny Nzou.

'Ning,' she said, and scrambled to her feet trying to back away from him, but he sprang forward and seized her wrist.

She was shocked by his strength. He twisted her arm up behind her back.

'A white woman,' he said in English. 'A hostage . . .'

Sepoo rushed at him, trying to help her, but Cheng swung the pistol in a short vicious arc and the barrel struck the little man above the ear, splitting open his scalp. He dropped at Cheng's feet. Still holding Kelly with the other hand, Cheng stretched down and aimed the pistol at Sepoo's temple.

'No,' screamed Kelly, and threw herself back against Cheng's chest. It spoiled his aim, and the bullet ploughed into the earth six inches from Sepoo's face. The shot roused him, and Sepoo rolled to his feet and darted away. Cheng fired another shot at him as he ran, but Sepoo vanished into the undergrowth.

Cheng twisted her arm savagely, pulling her up on to her toes with the agony in her shoulder-blade.

'You're hurting me,' she cried.

'Yes,' Cheng agreed. 'And I will kill you if you resist me again. Walk!' he ordered. 'Yes, like that. Keep going if you don't want me to hurt you again.'

'Where are we going?' Kelly asked, trying to keep the pain out of her voice, trying to be calm and persuasive. 'There is no escape into the forest.'

'With you there is,' Cheng said. 'Don't talk. Be quiet! Keep going.'

He pushed and dragged her onwards, and she dared not resist. She sensed that he was desperate enough to do anything. She remembered what Daniel had told her about him, about the murdered Matabele family in Zimbabwe, about the rumours of children and young girls tortured for his perverted pleasure. She realised that her best chance, perhaps her only chance, was to comply with anything he ordered her to do.

They covered half a mile, staggering and stumbling, made clumsy by the wrist-lock that Cheng had on her, and by his wild haste. When they came out suddenly on to the bank of a narrow stream she realised that it was the Wengu, the small river that gave the area its name. It was one of the tributaries of the main Ubomo River.

It was also one of the bleeding rivers, clogged with the poison effluent from the MOMU vehicles. It was stinking and treacherous. Even Cheng seemed to realise the danger of trying to wade across it.

He forced Kelly to her knees, and stood over her, panting and looking about him uncertainly.

'Please . . .' she whispered.

'Be silent!' he ranted at her. 'I told you not to speak!' He screwed her wrist to enforce the order, and despite herself she whimpered aloud.

After another few moments, he asked suddenly, 'Is this the Wengu River? Which direction does it run? Does it go southwards towards the main road?'

Instantly she realised which way his mind was working. Of course, he would have an intimate knowledge of the area. It was his concession. He would have studied the maps. He would certainly know that the Wengu made a circle to the south, an ox-bow that intersected the main road. He would know that there was a Hita military post at the bridge.

'Is it the Wengu?' he repeated, twisting her wrist until she screamed, and she almost answered truthfully before she caught herself.

'I don't know.' She shook her head. 'I don't know anything about the forest.'

514

'You lie,' he accused, but he was obviously uncertain. 'Who are you?' he demanded.

'I'm just a nurse with the World Health Organization. I don't know about the forest.'

'All right.' He hauled her to her feet. 'Get going!'

He shoved her forward, but now they turned southwards following the bank of the Wengu River. Cheng had made up his mind.

Kelly deliberately kicked and scuffed the soft earth as he pushed her along. She put all her weight on her heels, trying to lay as good a spoor as possible for Sepoo to follow. She knew Sepoo would be coming, and with him must come Daniel.

She tried to snap any green twig that came within reach as Cheng forced her through the undergrowth. She managed to tear a button off her shirt and drop it, an identification for Sepoo to pick up. At every opportunity she tripped over a dead branch or fell into a hole and dropped to her knees, holding him up as much as possible, slowing down their progress, giving Sepoo and Daniel a chance to catch up.

She began whining and whimpering loudly and when Cheng raised the pistol threateningly, she screamed, 'No, please! Please don't hit me!'

She knew her cries would carry, that Sepoo with his sensitive, forest-trained ears would hear her at a distance of quarter of a mile and pin-point her position.

Sepoo picked the shirt button out of the leaf trash of the forest floor, and showed it to Daniel.

'See, Kuokoa, Kara-Ki is laying sign for us to follow,' he whispered. 'She is clever as the colobus, and brave as the forest buffalo.'

'Keep going.' Daniel prodded him impatiently. 'Make your speeches later, old man.'

They went on along the spoor, quick, silent and alert. Sepoo pointed out the sign that Kelly had left, the broken twigs, the heel marks and the places where she had deliberately fallen to her knees.

'We are close now.' He touched Daniel's arm. 'Very close . . .'

'Be careful not to run into him. He might lay an ambush . . .'

Kelly screamed in the forest ahead of them. 'No, please! Please don't hit me!' And for an instant Daniel lost control. He lunged forward, rushing to her defence, but Sepoo seized his wrist and hung on doggedly.

'No! No! Kara-Ki is not hurt. She is warning us. Don't rush in like a stupid *wazungu*. Use your head now.'

Daniel pulled himself together, but he was still trembling with rage.

'All right,' he whispered. 'He doesn't know I am here but he has seen you. I'm going to circle round them and lie-up downstream. You must drive him on to me, just as you drive the duiker in the net hunt. Do you understand, Sepoo?'

'I understand. Give the call of a grey parrot when you are ready.'

Daniel screwed the folding bayonet off the muzzle of his AK 47 and propped the rifle against the tree beside him. Cheng was using Kelly as a shield. The rifle was useless. He abandoned it.

Armed only with the bayonet, he circled out swiftly away from the river-bank. Twice more he heard Kelly's voice, pleading and whining, giving him a pin-point on her position.

It took him less than five minutes to get downstream of Cheng and Kelly and to flatten himself against the bole of one of the trees growing on the bank. He cupped his hands over his mouth and gave an imitation of the squawk of a roosting parrot. Then he crouched down with the bayonet at the ready.

Sepoo's voice shrilled through the trees. He was using the high ventriloquist's tone that would deceive the listener as to direction and distance. 'Hey, *wazungu*. Let Kara-Ki go. I am watching you from the trees. Let her go, or I will put a poison arrow into you.'

Daniel doubted that Cheng could understand the Swahili words, but the effect would be the same, to concentrate Cheng's attention upstream while driving him down to where Daniel was waiting.

He crouched and listened. A few minutes later, Sepoo called again, 'Hey, *wazungu*, do you hear me?'

516

Silence fell again and Daniel strained his eyes and his hearing.

Then a branch rustled just ahead of him, and he heard Kelly's voice, muffled and terrified.

'Please don't . . .' she began, but was cut off by Cheng's brusque whisper.

'Shut your mouth, woman, or I will break your arm.'

They were very close to where Daniel waited. He tightened his grip on the hilt of the bayonet. Then he saw movement in the undergrowth, and a moment later made out the blue of Cheng's jacket.

Cheng was moving backwards, holding Kelly against his chest, facing the direction of Sepoo's voice, aiming the Tokarev pistol over Kelly's shoulder, ready to fire the moment Sepoo showed himself. He was backing directly towards the tree where Daniel waited.

Daniel knew that Cheng was an exponent of the martial arts. In any hand-to-hand combat, Daniel would be at a terrible disadvantage. There was one sure way. That was to drive the point of the bayonet into his kidneys from behind. It would cripple him instantly.

He stepped out from behind the tree with the bayonet held low and underhand. He launched the stroke, but at the same instant Cheng twisted violently sideways. Daniel never knew what had alerted him, for he had made no sound. It could only have been the almost supernatural instinct of the Kung Fu fighter.

The bayonet caught Cheng in the flank, an inch above the hip bone. It went in to the hilt, but Cheng's turn tore the weapon from Daniel's grip.

Cheng released Kelly, shoving her away from him and brought the Tokarev round to fire into Daniel's face. Daniel grabbed the wrist of his pistol hand and forced it upwards. The first shot went into the branches above their heads.

Cheng twisted in Daniel's grip, and as Daniel tried to hold him, he whipped his body back again and his knee came up, aimed for Daniel's crotch. Daniel caught the kick on his thigh, but the force of it paralysed his leg.

From the corner of his eye he saw Cheng's left hand, stiff as an axe-blade, flick towards his head, aimed at his neck below the ear. He hunched his shoulders and caught it on the thick muscle of his upper biceps. The strength and power of it sickened him. His grip on Cheng's pistol hand slackened.

The hand flicked at him again, and this time Daniel knew it would snap his neck like a dry twig. Kelly had not fallen, despite the vicious shove Cheng had given her between the shoulder-blades. She gathered herself and hurled herself back at him, shoulder first into Cheng's side, into the flank that the bayonet had laid open. The force of it turned the blow aside from Daniel's exposed neck and Cheng stumbled against him and dropped the pistol with a shout of pain.

Desperately Daniel locked his free arm around the back of Cheng's head and threw himself backwards, in the direction in which Cheng had been thrown by Kelly's charge. Cheng could not resist and they fell, locked together, down the sheer bank of the river, dropping six feet into the thick red ooze, going under completely.

Almost immediately their heads broke out through the surface. Both of them were gasping for breath, still locked together.

Daniel's leg was still paralysed. Cheng was wiry and quick. Daniel realised that he could not hold him. Kelly saw he was in distress and stooped. She picked up the bayonet, and in the same movement threw herself feet first down the bank, sliding on her backside, the bayonet poised.

Cheng squirmed over the top of Daniel, whipping one arm around his neck from behind. His back was turned to Kelly, the jacket of his safari suit shining wetly with red mud.

Kelly stabbed from as high as she could reach. Her first blow struck one of Cheng's ribs and was deflected. Cheng grunted and convulsed. She lifted the bayonet and stabbed again and this time the point found a gap between his ribs.

Cheng released the armlock from Daniel's neck and wriggled around to face Kelly in the mud. The bayonet was still lodged high in his back, the blade half buried.

Cheng reached out for Kelly with both hands, his mud-daubed features contorted with an animal ferocity. Daniel recovered and threw himself forward on to Cheng's back, locking both arms around his throat, bearing him down with all his weight. The hilt of the bayonet was trapped between them and the blade was forced all the way home. A mouthful of blood burst over Cheng's lips and poured down his chin.

Daniel heaved and shoved his head below the surface, and held it there. As Cheng was struggling in the red mud, one of his arms broke out and groped blindly for Daniel's face, trying to reach his eyes with hooked fingers. Daniel held on grimly, and the hand fell away. Cheng's movements in the mud became feebler and more erratic.

Kelly waded to the bank and crouched there, watching in fascinated horror.

Suddenly a rush of slow fat bubbles rose out of the red ooze and burst upon the surface as Cheng's lungs emptied. Only Daniel's head was clear of the mud. He lay there for a long time, never relaxing his grip on Cheng's submerged throat.

'He's dead,' Kelly whispered at last. 'He must be dead by now.'

Slowly Daniel released his grip. There was no movement below the surface. Daniel dragged himself to the bank, like an insect moving through treacle.

Kelly helped him up the bank. His injured leg trailed behind him. On the top the two of them knelt together clinging to each other. They stared down into the riverbed.

Slowly something rose to the surface like a dead log. The mud coated Cheng's corpse so thickly that it almost obscured the human shape. They stared at it for fully five minutes before either of them spoke.

'He drowned in his own cesspool,' Daniel whispered. 'I couldn't have chosen a better way.'